背單字 × 學文法 × 用句型 × 通片語

想要創造奇蹟，就靠這本搞定！

“

User's Guide 使用說明

滿分奇蹟密技 1. 把握時間快速投入學習

面對滿滿的 7000 單字直撲而來、心無頭緒茫茫然的你請別擔心，本書特別依照難易度將所有單字劃分成六個 Level，學習者只要稍微翻翻書頁，就能立刻找出適合自己的程度，迅速埋首書堆、潛心學習！

滿分奇蹟密技 2. 一字多用就可事半功倍

看到密密麻麻的文字就會胃絞痛、慌張害怕的你請別擔心，本書按照字母排序，詳細列出每個單字的常用詞義與詞性，而且每個詞性都有它的專屬例句示範。此外，本書甚至補充了同反義字，運用聯想法就能一次打包、通通學會，是不是非常方便！

滿分奇蹟密技 3. 釐清盲點才能戰勝考題

有能力大聲背誦單字，卻始終弄不清主詞受詞的你請別擔心，「文法字詞解析」就是要給學習者更清楚的說明。從時態、動詞變化、到易混淆的觀念用法全都有，對照著例句看，就能從中領悟英文的嚴謹結構。單字跟文法，從來就不是不同的兩回事！

滿分奇蹟密技 4. 抓住重點不怕用不出來

閱讀文章總是很順利，但碰到寫作就鬼打牆的你請別擔心，本書根據例句，適時地挑選出眾多萬用句型，只要將它們通通筆記下來，勤加練習，在考場上即使腦袋一片空白都能下筆如有神！

Level 1 基礎英文能力——邁向1000單字

Aa

a/an [ə/æn] Track 0001
冠 一、一個
▸There is a box of green apples on the floor for you to eat.
地板上有一箱青蘋果是要給你吃的。

文法字詞解析
a box of 意思是「一箱」，可以做為單位量詞用在可數或不可數名詞之前。

萬用延伸句型
There is / are... 可放在句首，指出「某地點有某物」。

a·ble [ˈebl] Track 0002
形 能幹的、有能力的 同 capable 有能力的
▸She is able to speak English fluently（流利地）.
她能夠很流利地講英文。

文法字詞解析
副詞「fluently（流利地）」由形容詞 fluent 加上副詞字尾 ly 組成，用來修飾動詞 speak。

a·bout [əˈbaut] Track 0003
副 大約 介 關於 同 concerning 關於
▸副 Would you like to come to our party at about six p.m. tomorrow? 你明天下午大約六點的時候願意來參加我們的派對嗎？
▸介 I talked to him about the weather.
我和他談論關於天氣的事情。

a·bove [əˈbʌv] Track 0004
形 上面的 副 在上面 介 在……上面 名 上面
▸形 You can write to us at the above address.
你可以寫信到上面的地址給我們。
▸副 There are several bags of biscuits（餅乾）on the shelf（架子）above. 上面的架子有幾袋餅乾。
▸介 There are many white birds flying above the blue sea.
藍色海面上有許多白色的鳥兒飛翔著。
▸名 In addition（附加）to all of the above, there is something else I want to talk about.
除了上述事情之外，我還想說點別的事情。

文法字詞解析
above、on、over 都可用來表示「某物在某物上面」，但 above 通常是指兩物沒有接觸，而 on 則是兩物有接觸，例如「在桌上 on the table」，over 則可以用在某物越過或覆蓋在另一物上。

ac·cord·ing [əˈkɔrdɪŋ] Track 0005
介 根據……
▸According to the weather report it will rain today, so let's bring the raincoats with us. 天氣預報說今天會下雨，所以我們還是隨身帶著雨衣吧！

文法字詞解析
will 加上原形動詞用來表示未來發生的事件、動作。

實用片語用語
according to 根據……的說法。可用在句首或句中，後面加上名詞或代名詞。

a·cross [əˈkrɔs] Track 0006
副 橫過 介 穿過、橫過 同 cross 越過
▸副 It is too difficult for a child to swim across the river.
要一個孩子游過這條河太困難了。
▸介 It is too dangerous（危險的）for a kid to cross the street by himself. 要一個小孩獨自過馬路太危險了。

實用片語用語
too...to... 太……以至於不能……

010

基礎英文能力——邁向1000單字 Level 1

act [ækt] Track 0007
名 行為、行動、法案 動 行動、扮演、下判斷
▸名 An act asks us to not kill the animals in danger.
有一項法令要求人們不要殘殺瀕臨絕種的動物。
▸動 He is very good at acting. 他很擅長演戲。

實用片語用語
ask sb. to do sth. 要求某人做某事

ac·tion [ˈækʃən] Track 0008
名 行動、活動 同 behavior 行為、舉止
▸Many young people enjoy watching action films very much.
很多年輕人非常喜歡看動作片。

文法字詞解析
enjoy 後面若要接動詞，形式必須是動名詞（V-ing）。

ac·tor [ˈæktə] Track 0009
名 男演員 同 performer 演出者
▸He has become an excellent（優秀的）actor.
他成為了一名優秀的演員。

文法字詞解析
此處使用現在完成式 has become，說明從過去就已經開始的動作，持續到現在才完成。現在完成式的形式是助動詞 have / has + 過去分詞 p.p.。

ac·tress [ˈæktrɪs] Track 0010
名 女演員 同 performer 演出者
▸What do you think about the actress in that movie?
你覺得那部電影裡的那個女演員怎麼樣？

萬用延伸句型
What do you think about / of...? 此句型為固定用法，用於徵詢他人的意見。

add [æd] Track 0011
動 增加 反 subtract 減去
▸Would you like to add some pepper in the soup?
你要不要在湯裡加些胡椒呢？

萬用延伸句型
Would you like to... 的句型用於有禮貌的請示他人意見。

add·ress [əˈdrɛs] Track 0012
名 住址、致詞、講話 動 發表演說、對……說話
同 speech 演說
▸名 It will be too difficult for me to find you if you do not tell me your address.
如果你不告訴我你的地址，那麼我就很難找到你了。
▸動 It is too early for the president（總統）to address his people now. 總統現在對民眾發表演說還為時過早。

萬用延伸句型
用現在代替未來的條件句型：S. + V.（未來式）If + S. + V.

a·dult [əˈdʌlt] Track 0013
形 成年的、成熟的 名 成年人 反 child 小孩
▸形 Don't let him watch that adult movie! He's only six!
別讓他看那部成人片，他才六歲耶！
▸名 We're all adults here; there's nothing to be shy about.
我們都是成年人了，沒什麼好害羞的。

萬用延伸句型
There's nothing to... 沒有什麼好……的

a·fraid [əˈfred] Track 0014
形 害怕的、擔心的 反 brave 勇敢的
▸Let's get on the bus right away. I am so afraid of being late.
我們快上公車吧，我很怕會遲到。

實用片語用語
be afraid of sth. 害怕某物

af·ter [ˈæftə] Track 0015
形 以後的 副 以後、後來 連 在……以後 介 在……之後
反 before 在……之前
▸形 I never saw him again in the years after.
在之後的幾年我再也沒見過他了。

實用片語用語
show up 出席、露面

A B C D E F G H I J K L M N O P Q R S T U V W X Y Z

011

滿分奇蹟密技 5. 延伸說法擴充實用知識

「怎麼單字加個介係詞就看不懂了」、「要怎樣才能學到日常生活用語」，總是充滿好奇的你請別擔心，「實用片語用語」就是要彌補只學單字仍不夠用的缺憾，除了列出大考常出現的必備片語外，還補充了許多生活和網路用語，讓你可以跳脫課本的桎梏，隨時隨地看懂英文、運用英文！

滿分奇蹟密技 6. 多聽多說克服心理障礙

發現外國人迎面而來就想避開、學了英文卻不敢開口的你請別擔心，本書不只在單字上標出了自然發音的音節點、KK 音標的發音標示，還收錄了外師親錄的單字 MP3，只要將音軌放到手機裡，就能無時無刻置身在英語環境中！

“

Preface 作者序

各位讀者大家好！

不論是英語初學者，或是接觸英語已有一段時間的人，相信大家都知道單字的重要性，一個單字可以有很多意思、很多詞性，也可以組成各式各樣的片語，或是用單字書寫千變萬化的句型。但是，正因為單字無所不在、範圍又多又廣，所以難以統整、歸納出一套清楚、有效的學習方法。

由教育部公布的升大學必備七千單字，替國、高中生訂定了一個範圍，因此學習英文單字不再是無邊無際、難以掌握的。然而，「七千」如此龐大的數字，反而讓孩子們聽了十分卻步，為了應付大考，許多人只好開始拿著單字本硬記死背，好不容易記全了單字的所有意思，卻被它的詞性弄得頭昏腦脹；學會了字義跟詞性，卻因為不懂文法、句型結構，所以還是寫不出完整的句子；或者是在閱讀測驗中，看到似曾相識的單字，組成片語、慣用語後卻猜不透意思，因此備感挫折。

因此，為了讓眾多找不到方法來有效學習的人，能在背單字時，也能同時將文法和句型融會貫通，我編寫了這一本《100% 滿分命中奇蹟：7000 英文單字 X 文法＋句型＋片語》。透過有條理的例句示範和重點提示，幫助學習者更清楚每個單字的用法。

本書將 7000 單字依難易度分為六個 level，讀者可以依照自己的程度選擇 level，快速進入學習。內容方面，每個單字不只標上音節點、音標輔助發音，還有外籍人士親錄的 MP3 音軌，發音正確且道地，讀者可以隨時聽、隨時培養語感。並且，所有的單字都按照詞性，羅列出最常使用的字義，還搭配上同、反義字，兩相比較，更能清楚用法，更能利用連想來充實字彙量。

如果一個單字只有一個例句，那有三種詞性的話，又要從何得知另外兩種詞性的用法呢？所以，本書逐條撰寫所有詞性的例句，學習者可以一目瞭然每個單字在不同詞性時所擺放的位置、搭配何種介係詞、辨別它們的使用時機。

除此之外，只背單字是萬萬不夠的，懂得如何在句子中、文章裡、對話時靈活運用，才是真正的學會一個單字。因此，絕不能把文法、句型、片語和單字拆開來、當作四個不同的領域看，必須同時並進、同步學習，才能完整理解整個英語的語言結構。因此，本書將例句中的文法和句型特別抓出，補充相關的解說，無論是時態、動詞變化、字詞解析、特殊句型、延伸的片語用語，都在這個部分有精細的說明，並且透過適時地重複提點同樣的觀念，讓學習者可以一再複習、掌握技巧、並運用自如。

最後，仍要提醒各位讀者，學習語言若只是坐在桌前苦讀，那一定十分枯燥乏味，如果可以多方蒐集資訊，多看報章雜誌、書籍電影、多聽廣播或音樂，想必能替艱苦的學習之路增添不少趣味，這也是為什麼本書補充許多現代社會常會用到的生活片語、用語的原因，畢竟，語言絕不只是考試的內容，更是人與人之間溝通的媒介。我期許這本書能讓覺得「學英文很挫折」的讀者們，產生不一樣的看法，也祝福各位讀者，都能找到樂在其中的英語學習法，並收穫滿滿。

Content 目錄

002 使用說明
004 作者序

Level 1 基礎英文能力——邁向1000單字

010 Aa
017 Bb
026 Cc
034 Dd
039 Ee
043 Ff
050 Gg
054 Hh
059 Ii
060 Jj
062 Kk
064 Ll
069 Mm
075 Nn
078 Oo
082 Pp
088 Qq
089 Rr
094 Ss
110 Tt
118 Uu
119 Vv
120 Ww
127 Yy
128 Zz

Level 2 基礎英文能力——邁向2200單字

132 Aa
137 Bb
145 Cc
158 Dd
166 Ee
171 Ff
177 Gg
181 Hh
185 Ii
188 Jj
189 Kk
190 Ll
194 Mm
200 Nn
204 Oo
206 Pp
218 Qq
219 Rr
223 Ss
236 Tt
244 Uu
245 Vv
247 Ww
251 Yy
251 Zz

Level 3 進階英文能力——邁向3200單字

254 Aa
261 Bb
268 Cc
279 Dd
286 Ee
292 Ff
297 Gg
300 Hh
304 Ii
308 Jj
309 Kk
311 Ll
315 Mm
322 Nn
324 Oo
326 Pp
336 Qq
337 Rr
345 Ss
360 Tt
367 Uu
368 Vv
370 Ww
373 Yy
373 Zz

Level 4 進階英文能力——邁向4200單字

376 Aa
386 Bb
389 Cc
406 Dd
415 Ee
423 Ff
429 Gg
433 Hh
437 Ii
445 Jj
446 Kk
446 Ll
450 Mm
456 Nn
458 Oo
461 Pp
472 Qq
472 Rr
480 Ss
489 Tt
493 Uu
494 Vv
497 Ww
498 Yy

挑戰英文能力——邁向5400單字

502 Aa
509 Bb
517 Cc
533 Dd
538 Ee
542 Ff
547 Gg
551 Hh
556 Ii
560 Jj
562 Kk
562 Ll
566 Mm
573 Nn
575 Oo
580 Pp
589 Qq
590 Rr
597 Ss
615 Tt
622 Uu
623 Vv
626 Ww
630 Yy
631 Zz

Level 6

挑戰英文能力——邁向7000單字

634 Aa
644 Bb
648 Cc
663 Dd
674 Ee
681 Ff
685 Gg
687 Hh
690 Ii
696 Jj
696 Kk
697 Ll
700 Mm
705 Nn
708 Oo
712 Pp
720 Qq
721 Rr
730 Ss
744 Tt
751 Uu
754 Vv
757 Ww
759 Xx
759 Yy
759 Zz

基礎英文能力——
邁向 1000 單字

學英文從單字開始，
許自己一個不可思議的滿分奇蹟！

Level 1 基礎英文能力——邁向1000單字

a/an [ə/æn]

Track 0001

冠 一、一個

▶There is a box of green apples on the floor for you to eat.
地板上有一箱青蘋果是要給你吃的。

文法字詞解析
a box of 意思是「一箱」，可以做為單位量詞用在可數或不可數名詞之前。

萬用延伸句型
There is / are... 可放在句首，指出「某地點有某物」。

a·ble [ˋebḷ]

Track 0002

形 能幹的、有能力的 同 capable 有能力的

▶She is able to speak English fluently（流利地）.
她能夠很流利地講英文。

文法字詞解析
副詞「fluently（流利地）」由形容詞 fluent 加上副詞字尾 ly 組成，用來修飾動詞 speak。

a·bout [əˋbaʊt]

Track 0003

副 大約 介 關於 同 concerning 關於

▶副 Would you like to come to our party at about six p.m. tomorrow? 你明天下午大約六點的時候願意來參加我們的派對嗎？

▶介 I talked to him about the weather.
我和他談論關於天氣的事情。

a·bove [əˋbʌv]

Track 0004

形 上面的 副 在上面 介 在……上面 名 上面

▶形 You can write to us at the above address.
你可以寫信到上面的地址給我們。

▶副 There are several bags of biscuits（餅乾）on the shelf（架子）above. 上面的架子有幾袋餅乾。

▶介 There are many white birds flying above the blue sea.
藍色海面上有許多白色的鳥兒飛翔著。

▶名 In addition（附加）to all of the above, there is something else I want to talk about.
除了上述事情之外，我還想說點別的事情。

文法字詞解析
above、on、over 都可用來表示「某物在某物上面」，但 above 通常是指兩物沒有接觸，而 on 則是兩物有接觸，例如「在桌上 on the table」，over 則可以用在某物越過或覆蓋在另一物上。

ac·cord·ing [əˋkɔrdɪŋ]

Track 0005

介 根據……

▶According to the weather report it will rain today, so let's bring the raincoats with us. 天氣預報說今天會下雨，所以我們還是隨身帶著雨衣吧！

文法字詞解析
will 加上原形動詞用來表示未來發生的事件、動作。

實用片語用語
according to 根據……的說法。可用在句首或句中，後面加上名詞或代名詞。

a·cross [əˋkrɔs]

Track 0006

副 橫過 介 穿過、橫過 同 cross 越過

▶副 It is too difficult for a child to swim across the river.
要一個孩子游過這條河太困難了。

▶介 It is too dangerous（危險的）for a kid to walk across the street by himself. 要一個小孩獨自過馬路太危險了。

實用片語用語
too...to... 太……以至於不能……

act [ækt]
Track 0007

名 行為、行動、法案 動 行動、扮演、下判決

▶名 An act asks us to not kill the animals in danger.
有一項法令要求人們不要殘殺瀕臨絕種的動物。

▶動 He is very good at acting. 他很擅長演戲。

實用片語用語
ask sb. to do sth. 要求某人做某事

ac·tion [ˋækʃən]
Track 0008

名 行動、活動 同 behavior 行為、舉止

▶Many young people enjoy watching action films very much.
很多年輕人非常喜歡看動作片。

文法字詞解析
enjoy 後面若要接動詞，形式必須是動名詞（V-ing）。

ac·tor [ˋæktɚ]
Track 0009

名 男演員 同 performer 演出者

▶He has become an excellent（優秀的）actor.
他成為了一名優秀的演員。

文法字詞解析
此處使用現在完成式 has become，說明從過去就已經開始的動作，持續到現在才完成。現在完成式的形式是助動詞 have / has + 過去分詞 p.p.。

ac·tress [ˋæktrɪs]
Track 0010

名 女演員 同 performer 演出者

▶What do you think about the actress in that movie?
你覺得那部電影裡的那個女演員怎麼樣？

萬用延伸句型
What do you think about / of...? 此句型為固定用法，用於徵詢他人的意見。

add [æd]
Track 0011

動 增加 反 subtract 減去

▶Would you like to add some pepper in the soup?
你要不要在湯裡加些胡椒呢？

萬用延伸句型
Would you like to... 的句型用於有禮貌的請示他人意見。

add·ress [əˋdrɛs]
Track 0012

名 住址、致詞、講話 動 發表演說、對……說話
同 speech 演說

▶名 It will be too difficult for me to find you if you do not tell me your address.
如果你不告訴我你的地址，那麼我就很難找到你了。

▶動 It is too early for the president（總統）to address his people now. 總統現在對民眾發表演說還為時過早。

萬用延伸句型
用現在代替未來的條件句型：S. + V.（未來式） If + S. + V.

a·dult [əˋdʌlt]
Track 0013

形 成年的、成熟的 名 成年人 反 child 小孩

▶形 Don't let him watch that adult movie! He's only six!
別讓他看那部成人片，他才六歲耶！

▶名 We're all adults here; there's nothing to be shy about.
我們都是成年人了，沒什麼好害羞的。

萬用延伸句型
There's nothing to... 沒有什麼好……的

a·fraid [əˋfred]
Track 0014

形 害怕的、擔心的 反 brave 勇敢的

▶Let's get on the bus right away. I am so afraid of being late.
我們快上公車吧，我很怕會遲到。

實用片語用語
be afraid of sth. 害怕某物

af·ter [ˋæftɚ]
Track 0015

形 以後的 副 以後、後來 連 在……以後 介 在……之後
反 before 在……之前

▶形 I never saw him again in the years after.
在之後的幾年我再也沒見過他了。

實用片語用語
show up 出席、露面

▶副 He arrived shortly（不久）after.
不久後他就抵達了。

▶連 I'll call you after I get home.
我到家以後會打給你。

▶介 He showed up after dinner.
他在晚餐後出現了。

af·ter·noon [ˋæftɚˋnun] Track 0016

名 下午 反 morning 上午

▶He won't be here in the afternoon. 他下午不會在這裡。

文法字詞解析
若要說精確的「某一天的下午」，介係詞要用 on，例如：on the afternoon of 12th June（六月十二日的下午），若沒有精確的時間，則介係詞用 in。

a·gain [əˋgɛn] Track 0017

副 又、再

▶Could you call me again at night and tell me about this matter?
晚上你能再打個電話給我，和我說說這件事嗎？

a·gainst [əˋgɛnst] Track 0018

介 反對、不同意 同 versus 對抗

▶Many people are against his plan.
很多人都反對他的計畫。

age [edʒ] Track 0019

名 年齡 動 使變老 同 mature 使成熟

▶名 Can you tell me your age? 你可以告訴我你的年齡嗎？

▶動 How she's aged these years! 她這幾年變老了不少啊！

萬用延伸句型
「How + adj. / adv. S. + V.！」為感嘆句句型，用來表示說話者驚訝、驚嘆。

a·go [əˋgo] Track 0020

副 以前 同 since 以前

▶How did she look when you met her in the store a week ago?
一星期前你在商店裡遇見她的時候，她看起來怎麼樣啊？

a·gree [əˋgri] Track 0021

動 同意、贊成 反 disagree 不同意

▶The boss agreed to let him go home early.
老闆同意讓他早點回家。

文法字詞解析
let 所引導的祈使語氣，有「讓某人做某事」的意思。後面需要接受格，再接原形動詞，並且動詞前不加不定詞 to。

a·gree·ment [əˋgrimənt] Track 0022

名 同意、一致、協議 反 disagreement 意見不一

▶We all nodded in agreement at his suggestion.
對於他的提議，我們都很同意地點頭。

實用片語用語
nod in agreement 同意地點頭

a·head [əˋhɛd] Track 0023

副 向前的、在……前面 反 behind 在……後面

▶My dad is the man walking up ahead.
我爸就是那個走在前面的男人。

air [ɛr] Track 0024

名 空氣、氣氛 同 atmosphere 氣氛

▶The air smells terrible in this room.
這房間裡面的空氣聞起來很糟。

文法字詞解析
例句中有連綴動詞 smell，這類感官動詞後面可以接形容詞來修飾句子裡的主詞。

air·mail [ˋɛr͵mel] Track 0025

名 航空郵件

▶How long will it take if you send it by airmail?
如果你用航空郵寄它的話，要花費多久時間呢？

萬用延伸句型
How long will / does it take... ……要多久？

air·plane/plane [ˋɛr͵plen]/[plen] Track 0026

名 飛機

▶We don't have enough money to go there by plane.
我們沒有足夠的錢搭飛機去那裡。

文法字詞解析
搭乘交通工具的介係詞要用 by。若要表示「用走的」的話，可以說 on foot 或 by walking。

air·port [ˋɛr͵port] Track 0027

名 機場

▶There is a large airport in the area where I live.
在我住的地區有一個很大的機場。

all [ɔl] Track 0028

形 所有的、全部的 副 全部、全然 名 全部 同 whole 全部

▶形 All my relatives came to visit me in the hospital.
我所有的親戚都來醫院探望我。

▶副 I've been waiting all day for your call.
我等你打來等了一整天。

▶名 All agree that he's probably lying.
全部人都同意他大概在說謊。

文法字詞解析
have / has been V-ing 是現在完成進行式的用法，說明過去開始的某一個動作，一直持續到現在，而且還在進行中。

al·low [əˋlaʊ] Track 0029

動 允許、准許 同 permit 允許

▶Her mom won't allow her to keep a cat.
她媽媽不准她養貓。

實用片語用語
allow sb. to do sth. 允許某人做某事；如果 allow 後面沒有受詞的話，則使用 S. allow + V-ing 的形式。

al·most [ˋɔl͵most] Track 0030

副 幾乎、差不多 同 nearly 幾乎、差不多

▶It's almost dark now. 天幾乎要黑了。

a·lone [əˋlon] Track 0031

形 單獨的 副 單獨地

▶形 He is always alone. 他總是一個人。

▶副 I don't mind going to a movie alone.
我不介意單獨一人去看電影。

a·long [əˋlɔŋ] Track 0032

副 向前 介 沿著 同 forward 向前

▶副 Can you please move along?
可不可以拜託你們往前移動？

▶介 Do you like to walk along the river in summer?
你喜歡在夏天沿著河岸散步嗎？

實用片語用語
along with 和……在一起
例如：My girlfriend came along with me last night. 昨晚我女友跟我一起來。

al·ready [ɔlˋrɛdɪ] Track 0033

副 已經 反 yet 還（沒）

▶Everyone has already left the office at seven.
七點時大家都已經離開辦公室了。

文法字詞解析
at 若要作為時間介係詞，後面必須要加精確的時刻。

al·so [ˋɔlso] *Track 0034*

副 也 同 too 也

▶You can also just buy the book from the store.
你也可以就在商店買這本書。

萬用延伸句型
Not only...but also... 不但……還……
例如：She is not only beautiful but also elegant. 她不只很美而且還很優雅。

al·ways [ˋɔlwez] *Track 0035*

副 總是 反 seldom 不常、很少

▶He is always hungry.
他總是很餓。

文法字詞解析
always, seldom 都是頻率副詞，頻率副詞還有以下幾個（依頻繁程度由高至低）：usually（常常），often（通常），sometimes（有時），never（從不）。須注意，seldom, never 都有否定的意思存在，因此使用附加問句時要用肯定疑問。例如：You seldom go out, do you?

am [æm] *Track 0036*

動 是

▶I am so tired after a long day of work.
工作這麼長的一天，我已經很累了。

a·mong [əˋmʌŋ] *Track 0037*

介 在……之中 同 amid 在……之間

▶She's my favorite among all my cousins.
在我的表兄弟姊妹中，她是我最喜歡的一個。

文法字詞解析
among 和 between 同樣都有「在……之間」的意思，among 用在三個以上的選項中，而 between 則用在兩者之間。

and [ænd] *Track 0038*

連 和

▶Both the English teacher and the Chinese teacher agree to this plan. 英文和國文老師都同意這個計畫。

萬用延伸句型
Both A and B... A 和 B 都……

an·ger [ˋæŋgɚ] *Track 0039*

名 憤怒 動 激怒 同 irritation 激怒

▶名 She could barely control（控制）her anger when she heard the news.
她聽到消息時，幾乎控制不了憤怒。

▶動 Don't try to anger the cows. They'll kick you.
別惹那些牛，牠們會踢你。

an·gry [ˋæŋgrɪ] *Track 0040*

形 生氣的 同 furious 狂怒的

▶I think he will be very angry with you.
我想他會對你很生氣。

實用片語用語
be angry with / at / about... 對……感到生氣

an·i·mal [ˋænəml̩] *Track 0041*

形 動物的 名 動物 同 beast 動物、野獸

▶形 It's not healthy to cook with animal fats every day. 每天都用動物脂肪來烹調並不健康。

▶名 What's your favorite animal in the zoo?
你最喜歡動物園的哪一種動物？

文法字詞解析
every day 是時間副詞，表示每一天；everyday 是形容詞，意為「每天的、日常的」。

萬用延伸句型
What's you favorite...？你最喜歡的……是什麼？

an·oth·er [əˋnʌðɚ] *Track 0042*

形 另一的、再一的 代 另一、再一

▶形 Let's take another way to the airport, shall we?
我們從另外一條路去機場，好嗎？

▶代 I don't like this one. Let's choose（選擇）another one.
我不是很喜歡這一個，我們選擇另外一個吧。

萬用延伸句型
Shall we...? 我們……好嗎？ 用於提出建議、徵求他人同意時。

an·swer [ˋænsɚ]

Track 0043

名 答案、回答 動 回答、回報 同 response 回答

▶名 Would you like to know the answer to this question?
你想不想知道這個問題的答案呢？

▶動 Would you like me to answer the telephone for you?
你要我幫你接電話嗎？

萬用延伸句型
answer the phone call 接電話；make a phone call 打電話

ant [ænt]

Track 0044

名 螞蟻

▶Killing ants is his favorite hobby. 殺螞蟻是他最喜歡的嗜好。

an·y [ˋɛnɪ]

Track 0045

形 任何的 代 任何一個

▶形 Do you have any pets? 你有任何寵物嗎？

▶代 I looked for apples in the fridge, but didn't find any.
我在冰箱裡找蘋果，但一個都沒找到。

an·y·thing [ˋɛnɪˏθɪŋ]

Track 0046

代 任何事物

▶Is there anything important you want to tell me?
你是不是有什麼重要的事要告訴我？

ape [ep]

Track 0047

名 猿

▶How often do you go to the zoo to see the cute apes?
你多久去動物園看一次可愛的猿猴呢？

萬用延伸句型
How often do you...? 你有多常／多久一次……？

ap·pear [əˋpɪr]

Track 0048

動 出現、顯得 反 disappear 消失

▶My friend has not appeared at the party yet.
我的朋友還沒有出現在派對上。

文法字詞解析
not...yet 還沒，通常與完成式連用。

ap·ple [ˋæpḷ]

Track 0049

名 蘋果

▶There are many apples on the big trees in our garden.
我家花園裡的大樹上長滿了蘋果。

A·pril/Apr. [ˋeprəl]

Track 0050

名 四月

▶My birthday is in April. 我的生日在四月。

文法字詞解析
年份、季節、月份前面要加介係詞 in。

are [ɑr]

Track 0051

動 是

▶There are a lot of good teachers in our school.
我們學校有很多優秀的老師。

文法字詞解析
a lot of + 可數／不可數名詞，表示「很多」。

ar·e·a [ˋɛrɪə]

Track 0052

名 地區、領域、面積、方面 同 region 地區

▶How long will it take for us to plant trees all around this area?
我們在這個地方栽滿樹木要花費多久時間？

arm [ɑrm]

Track 0053

名 手臂 動 武裝、裝備

▶名 His arms are much longer than mine.
他的手臂比我的長多了。

▶動 You need to arm yourself before heading out into battle（戰鬥）. 你出發去戰鬥前得先把自己武裝好。

實用片語用語
head out 前往

ar·my [`ɑrmɪ]

Track 0054

名 軍隊、陸軍 同 military 軍隊

▶Would you like to join the army? 你要不要加入軍隊啊？

實用片語用語
join the army 從軍

a·round [ə`raʊnd]

Track 0055

副 大約、在周圍 介 在……周圍

▶副 I'm just looking around the area.
我只是在這一區到處看看而已。

▶介 We have to take the road around the building.
我們得走繞過這棟大樓的那條路。

實用片語用語
have / has to... 必須……

art [ɑrt]

Track 0056

名 藝術

▶My sister takes art classes here. 我姐姐在這裡上美術課。

實用片語用語
take a class（學生）上課，give a class（老師）授課

as [æz]

Track 0057

副 像……一樣、如同 連 當……時候 介 作為
代 與……相同的人事物

▶副 Let's finish this job as soon as possible!
我們儘快完成這項工作吧！

▶連 The phone rang just as I was leaving.
當我正要離開時電話正好響了。

▶介 He works here as a clerk. 他作為職員在這裡工作。

▶代 My son did as I said. 我兒子照著我說的去做了。

文法字詞解析
1. as soon as possible 越快越好，儘快
2. as...as 用來比較兩個事物，表示同等、一樣。使用在句中的形式是：S1. V. as adj. / adv. as S2.

ask [æsk]

Track 0058

動 問、要求 同 question 問

▶There are many kinds of questions for the students to ask.
學生們有各式各樣的問題要問。

實用片語用語
ask sb. (not) to do sth. 請求某人（不要）做某事。
例如：Mom asks me not to play computer games too long.
媽媽叫我不要玩太久的電腦遊戲。

at [æt]

Track 0059

介 在

▶Would you like to see her at the end of the meeting?
你想在會議結束時見見她嗎？

Au·gust/Aug. [ɔ`gʌst]

Track 0060

名 八月

▶An important leader will take part in the meeting in August.
將有一名重要元首參加八月份的會議。

aunt/aunt·ie/aunt·y

Track 0061

[ænt]/[`ænti]/[`æntɪ]

名 伯母、姑、嬸、姨

▶How long will you stay at your aunt's home in the country?
你會在你鄉下姑媽的家住多久？

au·tumn [ˋɔtəm]

Track 0062

名 秋季、秋天

▶There are four seasons in a year and autumn is the most beautiful one. 一年有四季，而唯獨秋季最為美麗。

文法字詞解析
「最……的」可用「the most...」來表示。

a·way [əˋwe]

Track 0063

副 遠離、離開

▶She comes from a land far, far away.
她來自一個很遠很遠的國度。

ba·by [ˋbebɪ]

Track 0064

形 嬰兒的 名 嬰兒 同 infant 嬰兒

▶形 What does the baby carriage（嬰兒車）you bought yesterday look like? 你昨天買的那輛嬰兒車長什麼樣子？

萬用延伸句型
What does sth. / sb. look like? 某物／某人長什麼樣子？

▶名 Have you ever seen her new baby girl?
你有見過她剛出生的小女兒嗎？

back [bæk]

Track 0065

形 後面的 副 向後地 名 後背、背脊 動 後退
反 front 前面、正面

▶形 There is a map of the world on the back wall.
後面的牆上有一幅世界地圖。

▶副 Let's walk back home together after school!
放學後我們一起走路回家吧！

▶名 We wrote our names on the back of the tickets so that we can distinguish（區分）them. 我們在票的背後寫上名字，這樣我們才能把它們區分開來。

▶動 He backed away when he saw the giant dog.
他看到那隻巨大的狗時便後退離開了。

實用片語用語
back away 退開

萬用延伸句型
...so that... ……以便……

bad [bæd]

Track 0066

形 壞的 反 good 好的

▶The apples have gone bad. Please throw them away.
蘋果都壞掉了，請把它們丟掉吧。

實用片語用語
throw away 丟掉

bag [bæg]

Track 0067

名 袋子 動 把……裝入袋中 同 pocket 口袋

▶名 Could you help me carry this bag? It's too heavy for me!
你能幫我拿這個袋子嗎？對我來說太重了。

萬用延伸句型
Could you help me...? 可以請你幫我……嗎？ 此句型可用在有禮貌的請求他人協助。

▶動 She bagged all the leftovers（剩菜）to bring home to her dog. 她把剩菜都裝進袋子裡，以帶回家給她的狗。

ball [bɔl]

Track 0068

名 舞會、球 同 sphere 球

▶He threw the ball at his dog. 他把球丟向他的狗。

bal·loon [bəˋlun]

Track 0069

名 氣球 動 如氣球般膨脹

▶名 There is a man selling colorful（多彩的）balloons at the south gate of the park.
公園的南門有個賣彩色氣球的人。

▶動 Trade deficits（赤字）have ballooned in recent years.
貿易逆差在近年來已經急速增大。

文法字詞解析
in recent years 近年（習慣與現在完成式連用）

ba·nan·a [bəˋnænə]

Track 0070

名 香蕉

▶Would you like to buy bananas, pears（梨）or apples?
你想買香蕉、梨子、還是蘋果呢？

band [bænd]

Track 0071

名 帶子、隊、樂隊 動 聯合、結合 同 tie 帶子

▶名 There's a poster of my favorite band on the wall.
牆上有張我最喜歡的樂團的海報。

▶動 The settlers（移民者）banded together for protection（保護）.
移民者們聯合起來保護自己。

實用片語用語
band together 聯合起來

bank [bæŋk]

Track 0072

名 銀行、堤、岸

▶Could you walk me to the nearest bank?
您可以陪我走到最近的銀行嗎？

萬用延伸句型
Could you walk me to...? 你可以陪我走去……嗎？
等同於 Could you walk with me to...?

bar [bɑr]

Track 0073

名 條、棒、橫木、酒吧 動 禁止、阻撓 同 block 阻擋、限制

▶名 Let's go to that little bar after work.
下班後我們去那個小酒吧吧。

▶動 The large group of cows are barring the road.
那一大群牛擋在路上。

文法字詞解析
bar 的動詞變化 bar, barred, barred

bar·ber [ˋbɑrbɚ]

Track 0074

名 理髮師 同 hairdresser 美髮師

▶Not everyone can be a good barber.
並不是每個人都能成為一位優秀的理髮師。

base [bes]

Track 0075

名 基底、壘 動 以……作基礎 同 bottom 底部

▶名 Welcome to our secret base.
歡迎來到我們的秘密基地。

▶動 The movie was based on a true story.
那部電影是根據真實故事改編的。

base·ball [ˋbes͵bɔl]

Track 0076

名 棒球

▶We play baseball only on weekends.
我們只在週末打棒球。

文法字詞解析
on 後面加上時間詞的複數（例如：weekends、Thursdays）就有「每逢……」的意思，等同於 every + 時間。

bas·ic [ˋbesɪk]
Track 0077

名 基本、要素 形 基本的 同 essential 基本的

▶名 There are some basics that you should know before you sign up.
在你報名之前，你應該瞭解一些基本事項。

▶形 These novels all follow a basic plot（情節）.
這些小說的情節都很基本。

實用片語用語
sign up 報名、註冊

bas·ket [ˋbæskɪt]
Track 0078

名 籃子、籃網、得分

▶I took some eggs out of the basket.
我從籃子裡拿出一些蛋。

bas·ket·ball [ˋbæskɪt͵bɔl]
Track 0079

名 籃球

▶How about playing basketball with us after school?
放學之後跟我們一起去打籃球怎麼樣？

萬用延伸句型
How about...? ……如何？

bat [bæt]
Track 0080

名 蝙蝠、球棒

▶He smashed（打碎）the window with a bat.
他用球棒打碎了那扇窗戶。

bath [bæθ]
Track 0081

名 洗澡 動 給……洗澡

▶名 Taking a warm bath before going to bed at night feels great.
晚上睡覺前洗個熱水澡感覺太棒了。

▶動 She bathed in the tub（澡盆）every night.
她每天都在澡盆裡泡澡。

實用片語用語
take a bath 泡澡；take a shower 淋浴

bathe [beð]
Track 0082

動 沐浴、用水洗 同 wash 洗

▶The lady doesn't know how to bathe her baby.
那位太太不知道如何替寶寶沐浴。

bath·room [ˋbæθ͵rum]
Track 0083

名 浴室

▶How long does it take for you to clean the bathroom?
你打掃一次浴室要花多久時間？

be [bi]
Track 0084

動 是、存在

▶I am only too pleased to be able to help you.
我非常高興能夠幫助你。

文法字詞解析
be 的動詞變化：
am, was, been（搭配第一人稱名詞）；
are, were, been（搭配第二人稱或複數名詞）；
is, was, been（搭配第三人稱名詞）

beach [bitʃ]
Track 0085

名 海灘 動 拖（船）上岸 同 strand 海濱

▶名 There are a great number of people lying on the beach.
有很多人躺在海灘上。

▶動 They beached the ship on the island.
他們將船拖到島上。

bear [bɛr]

Track 0086

名 熊 動 忍受、負荷、結果實、生子女 同 withstand 禁得起

▶名 Would you like a teddy bear or a toy dog as a birthday gift?
你想要一隻玩具熊還是玩具狗作為生日禮物？

▶動 I can't bear to watch this terrible scene.
我忍受不了看這糟糕的畫面。

文法字詞解析
bear 的動詞變化： bear, bore, born

實用片語用語
bear to v. / n. / that 忍受……

beat [bit]

Track 0087

名 打、敲打聲、拍子 動 打敗、連續打擊、跳動 同 hit 打

▶名 Can you hear the beat of the drum（鼓）？
你有聽到擊鼓聲嗎？

▶動 It's too hard for us to beat that strong team.
要打敗那麼強的隊伍對我們來說太難了。

實用片語用語
beat 的動詞變化： beat, beat, beaten

beau·ti·ful [ˋbjutəfəl]

Track 0088

形 美麗的、漂亮的 反 ugly 醜陋的

▶There are always lots of beautiful girls and handsome（英俊的） boys in art school.
藝術學院裡通常都有好多帥哥美女。

beau·ty [ˋbjutɪ]

Track 0089

名 美、美人、美的東西

▶My mother is a natural beauty.
我媽是個天生的美人。

be·cause [bɪˋkɔz]

Track 0090

連 因為 同 for 為了

▶I cannot go to work because I have a cold.
因為感冒了，所以我不能去上班。

文法字詞解析
because 是連接詞，後面可以直接加子句，because of 是介係詞片語，後面必須接名詞或動名詞。

be·come [bɪˋkʌm]

Track 0091

動 變得、變成

▶When you become a parent in the future, you will understand how your parents feel.
一旦你以後為人父母，就會理解你爸媽的感覺了。

文法字詞解析
become 的動詞變化：become, became, become

bed [bɛd]

Track 0092

名 床 動 睡、臥

▶名 My bed is my favorite thing in the room.
我的床是我在房間裡最喜歡的東西。

▶動 I usually bed down at around eleven p.m.
我通常都會在晚上十一點去睡覺。

文法字詞解析
bed 的動詞變化：bed, bedded, bedded

bee [bi]

Track 0093

名 蜜蜂

▶My grandmother is always as busy as a bee.
我奶奶和總是和蜜蜂一樣忙碌。

實用片語用語
as busy as a bee 是固定用法，形容非常忙碌。

be·fore [bɪˋfor]

Track 0094

副 以前 介 早於、在……以前 連 在……以前
反 after 在……之後

▶副 I've never been here before. 我從來沒來過這裡。

▶介 I started studying three days before the exam.
我在考前開始唸書。

▶連 We ate dinner before going to the movie.
我們在去看電影前先吃了晚餐。

be·gin [bɪˋgɪn]

Track 0095

動 開始、著手 反 finish 結束、完成

▶It's never too late for you to begin learning.
無論何時開始學習都為時不晚。

文法字詞解析
begin 的動詞變化： begin, began, begun

萬用延伸句型
it's never too late to... ……永遠不嫌晚。

be·hind [bɪˋhaɪnd]

Track 0096

副 在後、在原處 介 在……之後 反 ahead 在前

▶副 The stronger men went out with the guns and the weaker ones stayed behind.
較強壯的男人們帶著槍出去了，而較弱的則留在原地。

▶介 She's the one in red sitting behind Joey.
她是坐在喬伊後面，穿紅色的那個。

文法字詞解析
第二句的原句是：「She is the one who is in red sitting behind Joey.」；此為分詞片語。

be·lieve [bɪˋliv]

Track 0097

動 認為、相信 同 trust 信賴

▶You shouldn't believe others so easily.
你不該這麼輕易相信他人。

bell [bɛl]

Track 0098

名 鐘、鈴 同 ring 鈴聲、鐘聲

▶Did the bell ring yet? 鐘響了沒？

文法字詞解析
ring 可作為名詞「鈴聲」，亦可做動詞「響（鈴）」。

be·long [bəˋlɔŋ]

Track 0099

動 屬於

▶Put the bowl back where it belongs. 請把碗放回該放的地方。

實用片語用語
belong to 屬於
例如：The doll belongs to my sister. 那個洋娃娃是屬於我妹妹的。

be·low [bəˋlo]

Track 0100

介 在……下面、比……低 副 在下方、往下
同 under 在……下面

▶介 I live on the floor below his. 我住在他樓下那一層。

▶副 The lady who works below is our boss's daughter.
在樓下工作的那個小姐是我們老闆的女兒。

be·side [bɪˋsaɪd]

Track 0101

介 在……旁邊
同 by 在……旁邊

▶Would you like to sit beside me while watching the match?
看比賽的時候你願意坐在我旁邊嗎？

best [bɛst]

Track 0102

形 最好的 副 最好地 反 worst 最壞的

▶形 Not everyone can buy the best goods at the best price.
不是每個人都能以最優惠的價格買到最好的東西。

▶副 Listen to your mom; she knows best.
聽媽媽的話，她最懂。

bet·ter [ˋbɛtɚ]

Track 0103

形 較好的、更好的 副 更好地 反 worse 更壞的

▶形 This pen is hard to use. I need a better one.
這筆真難用，我需要一支更好的。

▶副 Are you feeling better now? 你感覺有好一點嗎？

文法字詞解析
better 是 good 的比較級；best 是 good 的最高級

be·tween [bɪˋtwin]

Track 0104

副 在中間 介 在……之間

▶副 We have a meeting and a lecture（講座）today. Would you like to have a cup of coffee between? 我們今天要參加會議和講座，在這中間你想不想去喝杯咖啡？

▶介 Would you like to tell me what came between them?
你願意告訴我他們為什麼分開嗎？

實用片語用語
come between 使……分開

bi·cy·cle/bike [ˋbaɪsɪkl]/[baɪk]

Track 0105

名 自行車 同 cycle 腳踏車

▶How long does it take for you to go to work by bike?
你騎自行車上班要多久時間？

big [bɪg]

Track 0106

形 大的 反 little 小的

▶The room isn't big enough to fit us all.
這房間不夠大，裝不下我們全部人。

bird [bɝd]

Track 0107

名 鳥 同 fowl 禽

▶Some birds flew over our heads just now.
剛才有些鳥飛過我們的頭頂上。

實用片語用語
just now 剛才，不久的片刻前

birth [bɝθ]

Track 0108

名 出生、血統 反 death 死亡

▶She has been sick since birth. 她從出生以來就有疾病。

bit [bɪt]

Track 0109

名 一點

▶The soup is a bit too hot. 這個湯有點太燙了。

實用片語用語
a bit too... 有點太……

bite [baɪt]

Track 0110

名 咬、一口 動 咬 同 chew 咬

▶名 This chocolate tastes great. Want a bite?
這巧克力好好吃。要來一口嗎？

▶動 A snake bit him yesterday. 昨天一隻蛇咬了他。

文法字詞解析
bite 的動詞變化：bite, bit, bitten

black [blæk]

Track 0111

形 黑色的 名 黑人、黑色 動（使）變黑 反 white 白色

▶形 Her black dress is the loveliest thing I've ever seen.
她的黑洋裝是我見過最美的東西。

▶名 My favorite color to wear is black.
我最喜歡穿的顏色是黑色。

▶動 The gentleman blacks his shoes every day.
那名紳士每天都把鞋子擦黑。

block [blɑk] Track 0112

名 街區、木塊、石塊 動 阻塞 反 advance 前進

▶名 How long will it take me to get to that block by bus?
我坐公車到那個街區要多久？

▶動 The truck is blocking the road. 那台卡車阻擋在路上。

blood [blʌd] Track 0113

名 血液、血統

▶Some people like the taste of blood. 有些人喜歡血的味道。

blow [blo] Track 0114

名 吹、打擊 動 吹、風吹 同 breeze 吹著微風

▶名 His leaving was a terrible（可怕的）blow to her.
他的離去對她是個可怕的打擊。

▶動 He blew the horn to warn（警告）the people in the neighboring（鄰近的）town. 他吹號角警告鄰近小城的居民。

實用片語用語
blow up 爆炸

blue [blu] Track 0115

形 藍色的、憂鬱的 名 藍色

▶形 Would you like to buy this blue shirt or that red one?
你想買這件藍襯衫，還是那件紅襯衫？

▶名 Her favorite color used to be blue.
她以前最喜歡的顏色是藍色。

文法字詞解析
used to +v. 用來表示以前的習慣。

boat [bot] Track 0116

名 船 動 划船 同 ship 船

▶名 How long does it take for us to get there by boat?
我們坐船去那裡要多久？

▶動 Can you tell me how often you go boating on the lake?
能不能告訴我你們多久去湖上划一次船？

bo·dy [ˋbɑdɪ] Track 0117

名 身體 反 soul 靈魂

▶Not everyone is as good at using body language as you are.
不是每個人都像你一樣擅長使用肢體語言。

實用片語用語
body language 肢體語言

bone [bon] Track 0118

名 骨 同 skeleton 骨骼

▶The dog was excited when I gave it a bone.
當我給那隻狗一根骨頭時，牠很興奮。

文法字詞解析
情緒動詞轉成形容詞時，如果是以過去分詞的形式表現，就是「感到……的」的意思，例如 excite（使……興奮）就可以變成 excited（感到興奮的）。

book [bʊk] Track 0119

名 書 動 登記、預訂 同 reserve 預訂

▶名 I'm afraid it's too difficult for me to finish writing that book alone. 恐怕我獨自一個人來寫完這本書太難了。

▶動 I booked a train ticket for my mom.
我替我媽預訂了一張火車票。

文法字詞解析
finish + N. / V-ing 完成

born [bɔrn] Track 0120

形 天生的 同 natural 天生的

▶She was born in Germany（德國）. 她是在德國出生的。

實用片語用語
born with silver spoon in one's mouth 含著銀湯匙出生，比喻生在富裕人家。

both [boθ]
Track 0121

形 兩、雙 代 兩者、雙方 反 neither 兩者都不

▶形 Both sides were wounded（傷害）during the war.
戰爭過程中雙方都受傷了。

▶代 The two hats look so beautiful; why not buy both?
這兩頂帽子都很漂亮，為什麼不把它們都買下呢？

bot·tom [ˋbɑtəm]
Track 0122

名 底部、臀部 形 底部的 反 top 頂部

▶名 If you help me, I will thank you from the bottom of my heart.
如果你幫助我，我會打從心底感謝你的。

▶形 If you dig deeper, you will find that the bottom layer（層）is all sand.
如果你再挖深一點，你就會發現最下面的一層全是沙子。

實用片語用語
from the bottom of sb's heart 衷心地

bowl [bol]
Track 0123

名 碗 動 滾動

▶名 Let's go buy some more bowls because there are not enough for so many guests. 我們再去買幾個碗吧，因為我們有這麼多客人，碗不夠用了。

▶動 He bowled the ball into the gutter（溝）.
他把球滾進了溝裡。

實用片語用語
a bowl of 一碗
例如：Would you like to have a bowl of rice?
你想不想來碗白飯？

box [bɑks]
Track 0124

名 盒子、箱 動 把……裝入盒中、裝箱 同 container 容器

▶名 I brought home a box of chocolates.
我帶了一盒巧克力回家。

▶動 They boxed the apples before shipping them to market.
他們把蘋果裝箱後再運往市場出售。

實用片語用語
box office 票房
以前看戲時，要將入場費是要放在位於入口的一個小箱子中。箱子裝滿時就會有工作人員將箱子帶進辦公室中結算，那個辦公室就被稱為「盒子辦公室」（Box Office），也就成了中文的「票房」。
例如：That movie is a box office hit in Korea. 那部片在韓國很賣座。

boy [bɔɪ]
Track 0125

名 男孩 反 girl 女孩

▶Would you like to have a boy or a girl in the future?
將來你是想要生個男孩還是女孩呢？

brave [brev]
Track 0126

形 勇敢的 同 valiant 勇敢的

▶He is a brave man, but he still screams when seeing a spider.
他是個勇敢的男人，但看到蜘蛛時一樣會慘叫。

bread [brɛd]
Track 0127

名 麵包

▶How about some bread and a cup of coffee for you?
給你拿點麵包和一杯咖啡怎麼樣？

break [brek]
Track 0128

名 休息、中斷、破裂 動 打破、弄破、弄壞 反 repair 修補

▶名 Let's have a break; I'm too tired.
我們休息一下吧，我太累了。

▶動 I broke my mother's favorite vase.
我打破了我媽媽最喜歡的花瓶。

文法字詞解析
break 的動詞變化：break, broke, broken

實用片語用語
break up 分手
例如：We broke up last week.
我們上禮拜分手了。

break·fast [ˋbrɛkfəst]

Track 0129

名 早餐 反 dinner 晚餐

▶Have you had breakfast yet? 你吃早餐了嗎？

文法字詞解析
yet 用在疑問句時，放在句尾，是「已經」的意思。

bridge [brɪdʒ]

Track 0130

名 橋

▶I have to cross a bridge to get to school every day.
我每天都要過一條橋去上課。

文法字詞解析
cross 是動詞，意思是「渡過」；across 是介係詞，有「橫越」的意思。
例如：They walked across the street without looking at the traffic light.
他們不看紅綠燈就過馬路。

bright [braɪt]

Track 0131

形 明亮的、開朗的 同 light 明亮的

▶The lamp is not bright enough. 這燈不夠亮。

bring [brɪŋ]

Track 0132

動 帶來 同 carry 攜帶

▶Can you bring me a sandwich?
你可以幫我帶個三明治嗎？

文法字詞解析
bring 的動詞變化：bring, brought, brought

實用片語用語
bring sb. sth. 替某人帶某物

broth·er [ˋbrʌðɚ]

Track 0133

名 兄弟 反 sister 姊妹

▶My brother and I look the same.
我和我哥哥長得一模一樣。

brown [braʊn]

Track 0134

形 褐色的、棕色的 名 褐色、棕色

▶形 I left my brown jacket on the bus.
我把棕色的夾克丟在公車上了。

▶名 Some people can't wear brown because it makes them look old. 有些人不能穿棕色，因為會讓他們看起來很老。

bug [bʌg]

Track 0135

名 小蟲、毛病 同 insect 昆蟲

▶Those bugs are actually quite cute if you look closely（近的）.
靠近看的話，那些小蟲其實還蠻可愛的。

實用片語用語
如果電腦的軟體、應用程式、網頁出現問題，我們也可以說這些是「computer bug」。
例如：Can you help me fix computer bugs? 你可以幫我解決電腦問題嗎？

build [bɪld]

Track 0136

動 建立、建築 同 construct 建造

▶I can't imagine（想像）how they built such a long bridge.
我無法想像他們是怎麼蓋出這麼長的一座橋的。

文法字詞解析
build 的動詞變化：build, built, built

build·ing [ˋbɪldɪŋ]

Track 0137

名 建築物

▶I don't think the building is big enough to hold so many people.
我覺得這個建築物不足以容納那麼多的人。

實用片語用語
enough to + V. 足以

bus [bʌs]

Track 0138

名 公車

▶Can you tell me how long it will take for me to get to your company（公司）by bus?
你能告訴我坐公車到你們公司要多久嗎？

A B C D E F G H I J K L M N O P Q R S T U V W X Y Z

bus·y [ˋbɪzɪ]

Track 0139

形 忙的、繁忙的 反 free 空閒的

▶Not all people are as busy as you always are.
不是所有人都像你一樣總是忙個不停。

but [bʌt]

Track 0140

副 僅僅、只 連 但是 介 除了……以外 同 however 可是、然而

▶副 It took her but a few days to learn to play the song.
她只不過幾天的時間就學會彈那首歌了。

▶連 He was sick, but he still went to work.
他生病了，但他還是去上班了。

▶介 No one saw it happen but me.
除了我以外沒有人看到那件事發生。

but·ter [ˋbʌtɚ]

Track 0141

名 奶油

▶The cake will taste better if you put some more butter and sugar into it. 如果你加一些奶油和白糖，蛋糕會嚐起來更好。

文法字詞解析
由 if 所引導的副詞子句必須接現在式代替未來式。

but·ter·fly [ˋbʌtɚ͵flaɪ]

Track 0142

名 蝴蝶

▶I found a butterfly that got hurt when I was walking in the park.
我在公園散步的時候，發現一隻受傷的蝴蝶。

實用片語用語
have butterflies in one's stomach 「肚子裡有蝴蝶飛來飛去」，意指某人非常緊張

buy [baɪ]

Track 0143

名 購買、買 動 買 同 purchase 買

▶名 That pot was a really good buy. 買那個鍋子很划算。

▶動 Would you like to go buy some decorations（裝飾）with me this weekend?
這個週末你跟我去買些裝飾用品好嗎？

文法字詞解析
buy 的動詞變化：buy, bought, bought

實用片語用語
buy one get one free 買一送一

by [baɪ]

Track 0144

介 被、藉由、在……之前、在……旁邊

▶I want to know how long it will take for us to get to Tokyo by air.
我想知道我們搭飛機飛往東京要多久。

cage [kedʒ]

Track 0145

名 籠子、獸籠、鳥籠 動 關入籠中

▶名 Let's put the bird in the cage so that it won't fly away.
讓我們把鳥兒關在鳥籠裡吧，以防止牠飛走。

▶動 They caged the rabbit so that it wouldn't run around the house. 他們把兔子關在籠子裡，以免牠在房子裡亂跑。

cake [kek]

Track 0146

名 蛋糕

▶I'm really terrible at cutting cakes. 我超不會切蛋糕。

實用片語用語
a piece of cake 小事一樁
例如：Don't worry, I can handle it. It's just a piece of cake. 別擔心，我可以處理好這件事的，這只不過是小事一樁。

call [kɔl]

Track 0147

名 呼叫、打電話 動 呼叫、打電話

▶名 I was woken up by a strange call last night.
我昨晚被一通奇怪的電話吵醒。

▶動 Can you call Jenny for me? 你可以幫我打電話給珍妮嗎？

cam·el [ˋkæmḷ]

Track 0148

名 駱駝

▶Camels can live a month without water.
駱駝可以不喝水活一個月。

文法字詞解析
介係詞 with out 的意思是「沒有……」，後面要接名詞或動名詞。

ca·me·ra [ˋkæmərə]

Track 0149

名 照相機

▶My camera broke for the third time this month.
我的相機光是這個月就已經壞掉三次了。

camp [kæmp]

Track 0150

名 露營 動 露營、紮營

▶名 They made camp after a long day of hiking.
爬了漫長一天的山，他們停下來紮營。

▶動 Should we invite him to go camping with us?
我們應該邀他跟我們一起去露營嗎？

文法字詞解析
should 在這裡表示「應該、應當」。

can [kæn]

Track 0151

動 裝罐 助動 能、可以 名 罐頭

▶動 I like eating canned food for dinner.
我喜歡吃罐裝食品當晚餐。

▶助動 Can you speak English? 你會講英語嗎？

▶名 My cat enjoys hearing the sound of me opening a can.
我的貓最喜歡聽我開罐頭的聲音。

文法字詞解析
can 的動詞變化：can, canned, canned

can·dy/sweet [ˋkændɪ]/[swit]

Track 0152

名 糖果 同 sugar 糖

▶I brought some candy for the little girl next door.
我帶了一些糖果給住隔壁的小女孩。

cap [kæp]

Track 0153

名 帽子、蓋子 動 給……戴帽、覆蓋於……的頂端 同 hat 帽子

▶名 My cap was blown away when I was on the boat.
我在搭船的時候，帽子被吹走了。

▶動 Remember to cap the pen or the ink（墨水）will dry up.
記得把筆蓋蓋上，不然墨水會乾掉。

文法字詞解析
cap 的動詞變化 cap, capped, capped

實用片語用語
remember to V. 記得去做……；
remember V-ing 記得做過……

car [kɑr]

Track 0154

名 汽車

▶There is a big white car in front of Jack's home.
有一輛白色的大車停在傑克家門前。

實用片語用語
in front of 在……前面

card [kɑrd]

Track 0155

名 卡片

▶How long will it take for the card to reach his mother?
這張卡片寄達他母親那裡要花多久時間？

care [kɛr] Track 0156

名 小心、照料、憂慮 動 關心、照顧、喜愛、介意
同 concern 使關心

▶名 Please handle this box with care. 請小心搬運這個箱子。

▶動 I don't care what he says; I'm still angry.
我不管他說什麼，我還是很生氣。

實用片語用語
care for sb. / take care of sb. 照顧某人

care·ful [ˋkɛrfəl] Track 0157

形 小心的、仔細的 同 cautious 十分小心的

▶He is not careful enough to find all the mistakes in the papers.
他不夠仔細，沒能找出文件裡的所有錯誤。

實用片語用語
be careful to V. 小心地做……

car·ry [ˋkærɪ] Track 0158

動 攜帶、搬運、拿 同 take 拿、取

▶Let's carry this big table to our room.
我們把這張大桌子搬到我們房間去吧。

實用片語用語
carry-on 隨身行李
我們在國外的機場報到、準備搭飛機前，服務人員都會問：「Do you have any carry-on with you?」這裡的carry-on就是「隨身行李」的意思。

case [kes] Track 0159

名 情形、情況、箱、案例 同 condition 情況

▶There is a case full of clothes in my mother's bedroom, but the case is not ours. 在我媽媽的臥室裡有個箱子裡滿是衣服，但這箱子卻不是我們的。

實用片語用語
In case of... 如果發生……
例如：Please call me in case of emergency.
萬一發生緊急事件就打電話給我。

cat [kæt] Track 0160

名 貓、貓科動物 同 kitten 小貓

▶My cat thinks she is the most beautiful animal in the world.
我的貓覺得自己是全世界最美的動物。

catch [kætʃ] Track 0161

名 捕捉、捕獲物 動 抓住、趕上 同 capture 捕獲

▶名 What a good catch! You could sell it for a lot of money.
這捕獲物真棒！你可以賣很多錢。

▶動 My cat is not interested in catching mice.
我的貓對抓老鼠沒有興趣。

文法字詞解析
catch 的動詞變化：catch, caught, caught

cause [kɔz] Track 0162

動 引起 名 原因 同 make 引起、產生

▶動 What caused her to be so angry?
是什麼造成她那麼生氣？

▶名 They're holding the concert for a good cause.
他們為了慈善的原因辦這場音樂會。

cent [sɛnt] Track 0163

名 分（貨幣單位）

▶These cents are not enough for us to buy even a piece of cake.
這幾分錢還不夠我們買塊蛋糕呢！

cen·ter [ˋsɛntɚ] Track 0164

名 中心、中央 反 edge 邊緣

▶Have you been to the new shopping center yet?
你去過那家新的購物中心了沒？

萬用延伸句型
Have you been to... yet? 你去過……了沒？

cer·tain [ˋsɝtən] Track 0165

形 一定的 代 某幾個、某些 反 doubtful 不明確的

▶形 For a certain reason, no one likes going to that market. 因為某種特定原因，沒人喜歡去那家市場。

▶代 Certain of the people are new. 這之中的某些人是新來的。

實用片語用語

be certain of... 確信……

例如：I am certain of my answer to this question.
我很確定我對這個問題的回答。

chair [tʃɛr] Track 0166

名 椅子、主席席位 同 seat 座位

▶He's so fat he broke the chair he sat on. 他胖到連他坐的椅子都壞了。

萬用延伸句型

so… that… 如此……以致於……

chance [tʃæns] Track 0167

名 機會、意外 同 opportunity 機會

▶There's a high chance he will be late. 他有很高的機率會遲到。

chart [tʃɑrt] Track 0168

名 圖表 動 製成圖表 同 diagram 圖表

▶名 The chart he drew is hard to understand. 他畫的那張圖表很難懂。

▶動 Do you know how to chart the course of the ship? 你知道怎麼把船的航線標出來嗎？

chase [tʃes] Track 0169

名 追求、追逐 動 追捕、追逐 同 follow 追逐

▶名 The car chasing scene was my favorite. 我最喜歡飛車追逐那段劇情。

▶動 A kitten is chasing after a mouse on the street. 有隻小貓正在大街上追趕一隻老鼠。

實用片語用語

chase after 追趕、追逐

check [tʃɛk] Track 0170

名 檢查、支票 動 檢查、核對

▶名 I usually pay my rent by check. 我通常用支票付房租。

▶動 Can you check the numbers for me? 你可以幫我檢查一下這些數字嗎？

chick [tʃɪk] Track 0171

名 小雞

▶The chick is so tiny I can hold it in my hand. 這隻小雞小到我可以拿在手中。

chick·en [ˋtʃɪkɪn] Track 0172

名 雞、雞肉

▶Would you like a bit more salt in your chicken soup? 你要不要在雞湯裡多加些鹽呢？

chief [tʃif] Track 0173

形 主要的、首席的 名 首領 同 leader 首領

▶形 My brother is the chief engineer（工程師）in his company. 我哥哥是他們公司的首席工程師。

▶名 The police chief is a tall, unhappy man. 這位警察局長是個高而憂鬱的男人。

child [tʃaɪld] Track 0174

名 小孩 同 kid 小孩

▶Why won't my child play with other kids?
為什麼我的孩子都不跟其他小孩玩？

文法字詞解析
1. 要注意 child 的複數是 children。
2. play 是「玩耍」的意思，因為我們是「跟某個人玩」，不是「玩」某人，所以要 play 後面要接介係詞 with。

Christ·mas/Xmas [ˋkrɪsməs] Track 0175

名 聖誕節

▶A big party will be held in the company on Christmas this year.
今年公司將在聖誕節那天舉行一個盛大的派對。

實用片語用語
Hold + (event) 舉辦（活動）

church [tʃɝtʃ] Track 0176

名 教堂

▶I go to church with my parents sometimes.
我有時候會和父母一起去教堂。

ci·ty [ˋsɪtɪ] Track 0177

名 城市

▶Not all the people like to live in a big city.
並不是所有的人都喜歡居住在大城市。

class [klæs] Track 0178

名 班級、階級、種類 同 grade 階級

▶There are very few boys in my class.
我們班上沒幾個男生。

實用片語用語
very few 幾乎沒有

clean [klin] Track 0179

形 乾淨的 動 打掃 反 dirty 髒的

▶形 That restaurant isn't clean; I don't want to eat there.
那家餐廳不乾淨，我不想在那裡吃。

▶動 We do not have enough people to clean all the rooms in this building. 我們的人手不夠清理大樓裡的所有房間。

clear [klɪr] Track 0180

形 清楚的、明確的、澄清的 動 澄清、清除障礙、放晴
反 ambiguous 含糊不清的

▶形 I just love the clear weather today.
我真愛今天晴朗的天氣。

▶動 He spent a whole day clearing the snow from the road.
他花了一整天清除路上的雪。

climb [klaɪm] Track 0181

動 攀登、上升、爬

▶The boy is not old enough to climb up this mountain with his parents.
這個男孩還不夠大，不能跟著他的爸爸媽媽一起爬山。

實用片語用語
climb up 爬上去；climb down 爬下來

clock [klɑk] Track 0182

名 時鐘、計時器

▶It's not polite to give a clock to another as a present here.
在這裡送別人鐘當禮物是不禮貌的。

文法字詞解析
這裡的 as 有「作為」之意。

close [klos]/[kloz]

Track 0183

形 靠近的、親近的 動 關、結束、靠近 反 open （打）開

▶形 All his close friends are girls. 他所有要好的朋友都是女生。

▶動 How about closing the window for a while?
把窗戶關起來一會兒怎麼樣？

實用片語用語
close down 永久關閉、停業，也可以説 shut down。
例如：The restaurant in my neighborhood closed down due to lack of customers.
我家社區裡的餐廳因為門可羅雀所以關門大吉了。

cloud [klaʊd]

Track 0184

名 雲 動 （以雲）遮蔽

▶名 The shape of the clouds today is pretty strange.
今天雲的形狀超奇怪的。

▶動 The fog clouds the road ahead. 大霧籠罩著前面的路。

coast [kost]

Track 0185

名 海岸、沿岸

▶I'm visiting the west coast this summer vacation.
這個暑假我要去西岸玩。

coat [kot]

Track 0186

名 外套 同 jacket 外套

▶There are lots of holes in the coat. 這外套有很多洞。

實用片語用語
coat with / in 覆蓋……的表面。
例如：The gingerbread is coated with sugar. 薑餅上包了一層糖。

co·coa [ˋkoko]

Track 0187

名 可可粉、可可飲料、可可色

▶Would you like to have a cup of cocoa in our store when you come by next time?
下次你路過的時候，要不要到我們店裡來喝杯可可呢？

cof·fee [ˋkɔfɪ]

Track 0188

名 咖啡

▶Sir, would you like black coffee today?
先生，請問您今天想要黑咖啡嗎？

co·la/Coke [ˋkolə]/[kok]

Track 0189

名 可樂

▶I can't tell between Coke and Pepsi.
我分不清楚可口可樂和百事可樂。

實用片語用語
can't tell between A and B
分不清楚 A 跟 B

cold [kold]

Track 0190

形 冷的 名 感冒 反 warm 暖的

▶形 It is so cold outside; let's just stay at home and watch TV（電視）. 外頭很冷，我們就待在家裡看電視吧。

▶名 He caught a cold after playing basketball in the rain.
他在雨中打籃球後就感冒了。

實用片語用語
catch a cold 感冒

co·lor [ˋkʌlɚ]

Track 0191

名 顏色 動 把……塗上顏色

▶名 My daughter's favorite color is pink.
我女兒最喜歡的顏色是粉紅色。

▶動 There are many crayons（蠟筆）in the box for the children to color their pictures with.
盒子裡有很多蠟筆供孩子們為他們的畫塗上顏色。

come [kʌm]

Track 0192

動 來 反 leave 離開

▶Can you come over after you finish your homework?
你功課做完後可以過來我這裡嗎？

實用片語用語
come over 過來（某人身邊）

com·mon [ˋkɑmən]

Track 0193

形 共同的、平常的、普通的 名 平民、普通 反 special 特別的

▶形 Pandas are not a very common animal.
熊貓不是常見的動物。

▶名 Many commons died in this attack（襲擊）while some were injured（受傷的）.
在這次襲擊中有很多平民死亡和一些平民受傷。

實用片語用語
have sth. in common with sb. 和某人有共同點。
例如：She has nothing in common with her sister. 她和她姊姊完全不一樣。

con·tin·ue [kənˋtɪnjʊ]

Track 0194

動 繼續、連續 同 persist 持續

▶Let's continue to work and try to finish before sunset.
我們繼續工作吧，努力在太陽下山前完成。

cook [kʊk]

Track 0195

動 烹調、煮、燒 名 廚師

▶動 I can't cook at all. 我完全不會煮菜。

▶名 I'm the most horrible cook on earth. 我是全球最糟糕的廚師。

實用片語用語
can't do sth. at all 完全不會做……

cook·ie/cook·y [ˋkʊkɪ]

Track 0196

名 餅乾

▶The little boys are fighting over a cookie.
那些小男孩為了一塊餅乾在打架。

cool [kul]

Track 0197

形 涼的、涼快的、酷的 動 使變涼 反 hot 熱的

▶形 Don't you just love the cool weather?
你不覺得很喜歡這涼快的天氣嗎？

▶動 Cool down, there isn't anything to go mad about.
冷靜下來，沒什麼好生氣的。

實用片語用語
cool down / calm down 冷靜下來

corn [kɔrn]

Track 0198

名 玉米

▶We feed corn to our chickens. 我們都用玉米來餵小雞。

cor·rect [kəˋrɛkt]

Track 0199

形 正確的 動 改正、糾正 同 right 正確的

▶形 I don't know the correct answer,either.
我也不知道正確答案。

▶動 I had to correct all his mistakes. 我得改正他所有的錯誤。

文法字詞解析
either 用在否定句句尾，表示「也」；如果是肯定句的「也」則是 too。

萬用延伸句型
All present and correct. 全員到齊。

cost [kɔst]

Track 0200

名 代價、價值、費用 動 花費、值 反 income 收入、收益

▶名 I bought this necklace（項鏈）at one thousand dollars; the cost sounds reasonable（合理的）.
我用一千美元買下了這條項鏈，這個價錢聽起來很合理。

▶動 This house cost me a lot. 這房子花了我很多錢。

文法字詞解析
cost 的動詞變化： cost, cost, cost

實用片語用語
at all cost 無論如何
例如：The law has to be adopted at all cost. 這條法規無論如何都要通過。

count [kaʊnt]
Track 0201

動 計數 名 計數

▶動 She is seventeen yet still can't count.
她都十七歲了還是不會算數。

▶名 Would you like another piece of cake? By my count you've had only two.
你要再來一塊蛋糕嗎？按我的計算，你只吃了兩塊。

萬用延伸句型
Count me in. 算我一份。

coun·try [ˋkʌntrɪ]
Track 0202

形 國家的、鄉村的 名 國家、鄉村 同 nation 國家

▶形 My aunt lives in a country house.
我阿姨住在鄉下的房子裡。

▶名 Some people love their country way too much.
有些人實在太過愛國了。

course [kors]
Track 0203

名 課程、講座、過程、路線 同 process 過程

▶What will we be learning in this course?
我們在這個課程中會學到什麼？

文法字詞解析
will be + v-ing 是未來進行式，用來表示未來某一個時間點正在進行的事情。

cov·er [ˋkʌvɚ]
Track 0204

名 封面、表面 動 覆蓋、掩飾、包含 反 uncover 揭露、發現

▶名 A good cover is important for a book.
一個好的封面對一本書來說很重要。

▶動 The table is covered with dust（灰塵）.
這張桌子覆蓋滿了灰塵。

文法字詞解析
cover A with B 用 B 蓋住 A

實用片語用語
cover all the bases 面面俱到。
例如：It's difficult to cover all the bases.
想要面面俱到是很困難的。

cow [kaʊ]
Track 0205

名 母牛、乳牛

▶How often do you feed these cows per（每）day?
你一天餵這些牛幾次？

cow·boy [ˋkaʊ͵bɔɪ]
Track 0206

名 牛仔

▶The cowboy walks into the bar（酒吧）and orders（點餐）a beer. 那名牛仔走進酒吧，點了一杯啤酒。

crow [kro]
Track 0207

名 啼叫、烏鴉 動 啼叫、報曉

▶名 The little girl is talking to the crow outside the window.
那個小女孩在和窗外的烏鴉對話。

▶動 Our rooster crows at nine a.m. Isn't that a bit late?
我們的公雞都早上九點報曉，這不會有點太晚了嗎？

文法字詞解析
crow的動詞變化：crow, crowed, crowed或crow, crew, crowed

cry [kraɪ]
Track 0208

名 叫聲、哭聲、大叫 動 哭、叫、喊 同 wail 慟哭

▶名 She felt much better after a good cry.
好好哭一場後，她感覺好多了。

▶動 "Are you crazy?" he cries.
「你瘋了喔？」他大叫。

實用片語用語
cry out for help 大聲求救
例如：The wowan in danger is crying out for help.
那位遇到危險的女子正在大聲呼救。

cub [kʌb]

Track 0209

名 幼獸、年輕人

▶The cute little bear cubs are sleeping on their mother.
那些可愛的小熊睡在牠們的媽媽身上。

cup [kʌp]

Track 0210

名 杯子 同 glass 玻璃杯

▶Would you like a cup of milk and a piece of bread for your breakfast this morning?
今天的早餐你要不要一杯牛奶加片麵包呢？

實用片語用語
someone's cup of tea 某人的喜歡的事物。
例如：The girl with long hair is my cup of tea. 那位長髮女孩是我的菜。

cut [kʌt]

Track 0211

動 切、割、剪、砍、削、刪 名 切口、傷口 同 split 切開

▶動 He cut the rope with a knife.
他用刀子切斷了繩子。

▶名 Let me look at the cut on your finger.
讓我看看你手指上的傷口。

文法字詞解析
cut 的動詞變化：cut, cut, cut

實用片語用語
cut off 切除、切斷
例如：Our electricity is cut off because of the earthquake. 因為地震的關係，我們的電源全都被切斷了。

cute [kjut]

Track 0212

形 可愛的、聰明伶俐的 同 pretty 可愛的

▶They start arguing（爭吵）over whose baby is the cutest.
他們為了誰的寶寶最可愛而爭吵。

dad·dy/dad/pa·pa/pa/pop

Track 0213

[ˋdædɪ]/[dæd]/[ˋpɑpə]/[pɑ]/[pɑp]

名 爸爸

▶Have you ever seen her daddy? What does he look like?
你見過她爸爸嗎？他長什麼樣子？

萬用延伸句型
Have you ever... 你是否曾經……？

dance [dæns]

Track 0214

名 舞蹈 動 跳舞

▶名 My friend in the dance department is always practicing.
我舞蹈系的朋友總是在練舞。

▶動 Would you like to dance with me?
你願意跟我跳支舞嗎？

實用片語用語
dance to sb's tune 聽從某人的指揮
例如：He is so selfish that he makes everyone dance to his tune. 他太自私了，他要求所有人都聽他的指揮。

danc·er [ˋdænsɚ]

Track 0215

名 舞者

▶Most of the dancers I know are very pretty.
我認識的舞者幾乎都長得很漂亮。

dan·ger [ˋdendʒɚ]

Track 0216

名 危險 反 safety 安全

▶The kidnapped（被綁架的）students are in danger.
那些被綁架的學生遇到危險。

實用片語用語
in danger 處於危險中；out of danger 脫離險境

dark [dɑrk]
Track 0217

名 黑暗、暗處 形 黑暗的 反 light 明亮的

▶名 We can't see a thing in the dark.
我們在黑暗中什麼也看不見。

▶形 The streets here are too dark. 這裡的街道太黑了。

實用片語用語
in the dark 除了有「在黑暗中」的意思外，也可以衍生為「蒙在鼓裡、一無所知」。例如：Her husband cheated on her but she was totally in the dark.
她丈夫偷吃但她卻一無所知。

date [det]
Track 0218

名 日期、約會 動 約會、定日期 同 appointment 約會

▶名 Have you set the date for the wedding?
你們已經確定婚期了嗎？

▶動 They've been dating for two years.
他們已經在一起兩年了。

文法字詞解析
1. 在第二個例句中，因為是從兩年前一直到現在都在交往，而且現在還持續在交往中，所以是用現在完成進行式。

萬用延伸句型
第二個例句也可以寫成：They've been dating since two years ago.

daugh·ter [ˋdɔtɚ]
Track 0219

名 女兒 反 son 兒子

▶Every mother thinks her own daughter is the prettiest.
每個媽媽都覺得自己的女兒最漂亮。

day [de]
Track 0220

名 白天、日 反 night 晚上

▶This is my first day at work. 這是我第一天工作。

實用片語用語
day by day 一天天
例如：After a serious accident, his legs got worse day by day. 經過一場嚴重的車禍後，他的雙腿情況一天比一天糟。

dead [dɛd]
Track 0221

名 死者 形 死的 反 live 活的

▶名 There are twenty dead in the big fire last night.
昨夜發生的這場大火中有二十名死者。

▶形 There were tens of thousands of dead bodies left on the battlefield（戰場）after war.
戰爭過後，成千上萬的屍體被遺留在戰場上。

實用片語用語
tens of thousands of 成千上萬的
ten thousands 是「一萬」，tens of thousands of 就是「好幾萬」。

deal [dil]
Track 0222

動 處理、應付、做買賣、經營 名 買賣、交易 同 trade 交易

▶動 I can't deal with this alone. 這我沒辦法一個人應付。

▶名 It's a deal! I'll do your homework for you, and you'll cook me lunch. 交易成立！我幫你寫功課，你煮午餐給我吃。

文法字詞解析
deal 的動詞變化：deal, dealt, dealt

實用片語用語
deal with 應付

dear [dɪr]
Track 0223

形 昂貴的、親愛的 副 昂貴地
感 呵！唉呀！（表示傷心、焦慮、驚奇等）
同 expensive 昂貴的

▶形 Dear John, I'm breaking up with you.
親愛的約翰，我要和你分手。

▶副 The jewels（珠寶）cost us too dear.
這些珠寶花費我們太高價了。

▶感 Oh dear, I've forgotten to put on pants.
哎呀，我忘記穿褲子了。

death [dɛθ]
Track 0224

名 死、死亡 反 life 生命、活的東西

▶Everyone is afraid of death in one way or another.
大家或多或少都有點怕死。

De·cem·ber/Dec. [dɪ`sɛmbɚ]

Track 0225

名 十二月

▶Do you want to go skiing（滑雪）with us in December?
你十二月份想跟我們出去滑雪嗎？

de·cide [dɪ`saɪd]

Track 0226

動 決定 同 determine 決定

▶Once she decides to do something, no one can stop her.
一旦她決定要做一件事，就沒有人能夠阻止得了她。

文法字詞解析

decide 後面如果要接動詞，一定要用 to V. 的形式。

deep [dip]

Track 0227

形 深的 副 深深地 反 shallow 淺的

▶形 I don't like swimming in deep pools.
我不喜歡在太深的游泳池游泳。

▶副 Her emotions（情緒）run deep, it's hard to tell what she's thinking. 她的情緒總是藏得很深，很難知道她在想什麼。

deer [dɪr]

Track 0228

名 鹿

▶She is a sweet girl that looks like a baby deer.
她是個甜美的女孩，看起來像隻小鹿似的。

desk [dɛsk]

Track 0229

名 書桌

▶I left my homework on the desk.
我把功課放在書桌上了。

die [daɪ]

Track 0230

動 死 同 perish 死去

▶My uncle died last week. 我叔叔上禮拜過世了。

文法字詞解析

die 的動詞變化： die, died, died

萬用延伸句型

Never say die. 永不放棄。

dif·fer·ent [`dɪfərənt]

Track 0231

形 不同的 反 identical 同一的

▶How about we go to a different restaurant for our dinner? I want to try something new.
換到另外一家餐廳吃晚餐好嗎？我想嚐嚐新的菜色。

difficult [`dɪfə͵kʌlt]

Track 0232

形 困難的 反 easy 簡單的

▶The test was too difficult for me.
這考試對我來說太難了。

dig [dɪg]

Track 0233

動 挖、挖掘 反 bury 埋

▶I am so embarrassed I want to dig a hole and jump into it.
我丟臉到真想挖個洞跳下去。

文法字詞解析

dig 的動詞變化： dig, dug, dug

實用片語用語

dig one's own grave 自掘墳墓
例如：Those who eat a lot and don't do exercise are digging their own grave.
那些光吃不動的人是在自掘墳墓。

din·ner [`dɪnɚ]

Track 0234

名 晚餐、晚宴 同 supper 晚餐

▶Would you like to have dinner with me?
你想跟我一起吃晚餐嗎？

dir·ect [də`rɛkt]

Track 0235

形 筆直的、直接的 動 指示、命令 同 order 命令、指示

▶形 She has a very direct way of speaking.她說話非常直爽。

▶動 The nice lady directs us to the department store.
那個好心的太太指示我們去百貨公司的路。

實用片語用語
direct 也有不停歇的意思。
例如：We will fly direct from Taipei to Tokyo.
我們將從台北直飛東京。

dirt·y [`dɝtɪ]

Track 0236

形 髒的 動 弄髒 反 clean 清潔的

▶形 I can't stand living in a dirty room.
我受不了住在髒的房間裡。

▶動 The children dirtied the floor. Let's clean it up.
孩子們把地板弄髒了，我們打掃一下吧。

實用片語用語
1. can't stand + N. 無法忍受
2. 除了 stand 之外，片語「do with」也有忍受的意思。
例如：I can't do with her behavior.
我無法忍受她的行為。

dis·cov·er [dɪ`skʌvɚ]

Track 0237

動 發現 同 find 發現

▶He discovered a new insect. 他發現了一種新的昆蟲。

dish [dɪʃ]

Track 0238

名 （盛食物的）盤、碟 同 plate 盤、碟

▶Can you wash the dishes tonight?
你今天晚上可以洗盤子嗎？

do [du]

Track 0239

助動 （無詞意） 動 做 同 perform 做

助動 Do you want some coffee? 你想來點咖啡嗎？

▶動 Could you help me get it done before this Friday? It's urgent（緊急的）.
你能在本週五前幫我把它做完嗎？這件事很緊急。

文法字詞解析
do 的動詞變化：do, did, done

實用片語用語
get sth. done 完成某事

doc·tor/doc [`daktɚ]

Track 0240

名 醫生、博士 同 physician 醫師

▶The doctor is so handsome I can't look at him directly.
那個醫生太帥了，我不敢直視。

實用片語用語
look at sth. / sb. 看某物／某人

dog [dɔg]

Track 0241

動 尾隨、跟蹤 名 狗

▶動 He likes her so much he dogs her everywhere.
他太喜歡她了，以致她去哪他都跟蹤她。

▶名 There are three dogs and five cats in their house.
他們家有三條狗和五隻貓。

文法字詞解析
dog 的動詞變化：dog, dogged, dogged

doll [dɑl]

Track 0242

名 玩具娃娃 同 toy 玩具

▶Would you like a beautiful doll as your seventh birthday（生日）gift?
你想不想要一個漂亮的玩具娃娃作為七歲生日的禮物？

實用片語用語
英文的序數寫法是在基數後面加 th，例如 seven（七）加 th 就變成第七個。例外：一（one → first）、二（two → second）、三（three → third）、五（five → fifth）、九（nine → ninth）、十二（twelve → twelfth）、二十以上的十位數（twenty → twentieth, thirty → thirtieth, etc.）。

dol·lar/buck [`dalɚ]/[bʌk]

Track 0243

名 美元、錢

▶I spent two dollars on this cheap dress.
我花了兩美元買這件便宜的洋裝。

實用片語用語
spend on 花費（金錢、時間、精力）

萬用延伸句型
sb. spend + (time) + V-ing / N.

door [dor]

Track 0244

名 門 同 gate 大門

▶Would you close the door? I feel a little cold.
你願不願意關上門？我覺得有點冷。

dove [dʌv]

Track 0245

名 鴿子

▶Do you know how many doves there are on the center square（廣場）？你知道中央廣場上有多少隻鴿子嗎？

文法字詞解析
這個例句是由一個問句併入另一個問句所構成，可以拆成主要子句「Do you know?」和附屬子句「How many doves are there on the center square?」當附屬子句併入主要子句時，要將動詞放回主詞後面，不可倒裝。

down [daʊn]

Track 0246

形 向下的 副 向下 介 沿著……而下 反 up 在上面

▶形 Dick is feeling a bit down today. Let's go comfort（安慰）him. 迪克今天情緒有點低落，我們去安慰他一下吧。

▶副 The boy climbed down the tree. 男孩爬下了樹。

▶介 Their house is halfway down the hill.
他們的房子坐落在半山腰。

實用片語用語
pace up and down 來回走
例如：Laura paced up and down the room. 蘿拉在房間裡來回踱步。

down·stairs [ˌdaʊn`stɛrz]

Track 0247

形 樓下的 副 在樓下 名 樓下 反 upstairs 在樓上

▶形 The children are downstairs. Would you like me to go get them? 孩子們在樓下，你要我去叫他們嗎？

▶副 Could you go downstairs to get some bread for me in the kitchen? 你可以下樓到廚房幫我拿點麵包嗎？

▶名 The downstairs consisted of（包含）three large rooms.
樓下有三個大房間。

doz·en [`dʌzn̩]

Track 0248

名（一）打、十二個

▶It is reported that dozens of people died in the big fire.
據報導，有很多人在那場大火中喪命。

實用片語用語
a dozen of 一打；dozens of 許多

draw [drɔ]

Track 0249

動 拉、拖、提取、畫、繪製 同 drag 拉、拖

▶The little girl drew a picture of a horse.
小女孩畫了一幅馬的圖。

文法字詞解析
draw 的動詞變化 draw, drew, drawn

實用片語用語
draw + 錢／金額 領錢
例如：Could you please give me a second? I have to draw some money. 麻煩稍等一下，我得領個錢。

dream [drim]

Track 0250

名 夢 動 做夢 反 reality 現實

▶名 I had such a strange dream last night.
我昨晚做了一個好奇怪的夢。

▶動 He dreamed about making lots of money.
他的夢想是賺很多錢。

文法字詞解析
dream 的動詞變化 dream, dreamed, dreamed 或是 dream, dreamt, dreamt

實用片語用語
dream about 夢想

drink [drɪŋk]

Track 0251

名 飲料 動 喝、喝酒

▶名 How about getting some drinks? I am a little thirsty（口渴的）. 我們去弄點飲料怎麼樣？我有點渴了。

▶動 She likes to drink wine when having dinner.
她吃晚餐的時候喜歡喝酒。

文法字詞解析
drink 的動詞變化：drank, drank, drunk

實用片語用語
a drunk 喝醉的人
例如：There was a drunk in front of your house last night. 昨晚你家門口有個醉漢。

drive [draɪv] Track 0252

名 駕車、車道 動 開車、驅使、操縱（機器等）
同 move 推動、促使

▶名 It's too cold for us to go for a drive.
現在開車出去兜風實在太冷了。

▶動 He drove the truck into a ditch（水溝）.
他把卡車開進水溝去了。

文法字詞解析
drive 的動詞變化：drive, drove, driven

實用片語用語
drive A into B 把 A 嵌進 B
例如：Dad used a hammer to drive a nail into the wall.
爸爸用槌子把螺絲釘嵌進牆壁裡。

driv·er [ˋdraɪvɚ] Track 0253

名 駕駛員、司機

▶Not every person can be a skilled driver without professional（專業的）training.
不是每個人都能不通過專業訓練就成為一名熟練的駕駛員。

dry [draɪ] Track 0254

形 乾的、枯燥無味的 動 把……弄乾、乾掉
同 thirsty 乾的、口渴的

▶形 The paint on the chair is not yet dry.
椅子上的油漆還沒乾呢。

▶動 The clothes are taking forever to dry.
衣服一直乾不了。

文法字詞解析
dry 的動詞變化：dry, dried, dried

duck [dʌk] Track 0255

名 鴨子

▶Could you help me count how many ducks there are in the river?
你能幫我數數看河裡一共有多少隻鴨子嗎？

duck·ling [ˋdʌklɪŋ] Track 0256

名 小鴨子

▶The ugly duckling grew up to be a beautiful swan（天鵝）.
那隻醜小鴨長大變成了美麗的天鵝。

dur·ing [ˋdjʊrɪŋ] Track 0257

介 在……期間

▶Could you help me look after my baby during my business（商業）trip?
我出差的期間你可以幫我照顧我的寶寶嗎？

實用片語用語
look after 照顧，和「take care of」的意思一樣。

each [itʃ] Track 0258

形 各、每 代 每個、各自 副 各、每個

▶形 There are new houses on each side of the street.
街道兩邊都有新房子。

▶代 How long will it take for each of them to finish our job?
要多久他們各人才能做完自己的那份工作？

▶副 They said the oranges there are forty cents each.
他們說那裡的橘子每個售價四十分錢。

ea·gle [ˋigḷ] Track 0259

名 鷹

▶We sat there all afternoon watching the eagles.
我們在那裡坐了一整個下午觀賞老鷹。

實用片語用語
eagle eye 形容如老鷹搜尋獵物時一樣銳利的眼睛
例如：The teacher watched his students with eagle eyes during the exam. 考試期間，那位老師用銳利的目光仔細巡視他的學生。

ear [ɪr] Track 0260

名 耳朵

▶His ears turn red when he is angry.
他生氣的時候耳朵會變紅。

實用片語用語
in one ear and out another 左耳進右耳出
例如：What her mothers says to her goes in one ear and out another.
她媽媽跟她說的話她都左耳進右耳出。

ear·ly [ˋɝlɪ] Track 0261

形 早的、早期的、及早的 副 早、在初期 反 late 晚的

▶形 There are many people standing outside the supermarket（超市）in the early morning.
一大早就有很多人站在超市的外面。

▶副 You'll have to get up early tomorrow.
你明天得早起。

實用片語用語
The early bird catches the worm. 早起的鳥兒有蟲吃。

earth [ɝθ] Track 0262

名 地球、陸地、地面 同 globe 地球

▶We have only one earth and we should protect it.
我們只有一個地球，應該要保護它。

實用片語用語
on earth 到底
這個片語要放在疑問詞後面，有強調、加強語氣的感覺。
例如：What on earth are you talking about? 你到底在說什麼？

ease [iz] Track 0263

動 緩和、減輕、使舒適 名 容易、舒適、悠閒
同 relieve 緩和、減輕

▶動 Give me some medicine to ease the pain（疼痛）.
給我一點藥減輕疼痛吧。

▶名 He can always solve（解決）math problems with ease.
他總是能很輕鬆地解決數學難題。

實用片語用語
at ease 安心、自在
例如：I felt at ease when I was with my old friends. 當我和老朋友在一起時，我感到很自在。

east [ist] Track 0264

形 東方的 副 向東方 名 東、東方 反 west 西方

▶形 Have you listened to the weather report? How long will the east wind last?
你聽了天氣預報嗎？這陣東風會持續多久呢？

▶副 The place I want to go to is ten miles east of the town.
我要去的那個地方在城鎮的東邊十英里處。

▶名 Some of my classmates come from the east.
我有些同學是從東方來的。

eas·y [ˋizɪ] Track 0265

形 容易的、不費力的 反 difficult 困難的

▶Playing the violin is easy for him. 拉小提琴對他來說很容易。

eat [it] Track 0266

動 吃 同 dine 用餐

▶There was no time for me to eat my breakfast because I got up too late this morning.
我今天早上沒有時間吃早餐，因為起得太晚了。

文法字詞解析
eat 的動詞變化：eat, ate, eaten

edge [ɛdʒ]
Track 0267

名 邊、邊緣 同 border 邊緣

▶I'm going camping with my friends at the edge of the forest.
我要和朋友們一起到森林的邊緣露營。

egg [ɛg]
Track 0268

名 蛋

▶They threw eggs at the man's house.
他們拿蛋砸那個男人的家。

實用片語用語
put all your eggs in one basket 將所有雞蛋放在同一個籃子裡，意指不懂得分散風險。

eight [et]
Track 0269

名 八

▶He was eight years old when the accident happened.
意外發生時，他八歲。

eigh·teen [ˋeˋtin]
Track 0270

名 十八

▶You are eighteen, old enough to take care of yourself.
你十八歲了，可以自己照顧自己了。

eight·y [ˋeti]
Track 0271

名 八十

▶The old man is eighty years old. 這個老人八十歲了。

ei·ther [ˋiðɚ]
Track 0272

形（兩者之中）任一的 代（兩者之中）任一 副 也（不）

▶形 I'm okay with either of these two restaurants.
去這兩家餐廳之中任一家我都沒問題。

▶代 Which of the two movies do you want to see? I'm fine with either. 你想看這兩部電影中的哪一部？我任一部都好。

▶副 If you're not going, I'm not either. 你不去的話我也不去。

實用片語用語
either A or B 不是 A 就是 B、A 或 B 都可以
例如：I would be fine with either herbal tea or coffee.
給我花草茶或是咖啡都可以。

e·le·phant [ˋɛləfənt]
Track 0273

名 大象

▶There are two elephants in our zoo. 我們動物園裡有兩頭大象。

e·le·ven [ɪˋlɛvn̩]
Track 0274

名 十一

▶There are eleven players in a football team.
一個足球隊裡有十一個球員。

else [ɛls]
Track 0275

副 其他、另外

▶We must hurry, or else we'll be late.
我們得快點，不然就要遲到了。

實用片語用語
or else 否則，和 otherwise 同義。

end [ɛnd]
Track 0276

名 結束、終點 動 結束、終止 反 origin 起源

▶名 The end of the movie is very sad. 這部電影的結局很悲傷。

▶動 I think it's time to end our relationship（關係）.
我想該是結束我們之間關係的時候了。

實用片語用語
end up... 以……告終
例如：Her crush on him ended up in a broken heart.
她對他的迷戀最後以心碎收場。

Eng·lish [ˋɪŋglɪʃ]

Track 0277

形 英國的、英國人的 名 英語

▶形 Could you introduce（介紹）me to your English friend?
你願意把我介紹給你的英國朋友嗎？

▶名 The little boy speaks English, Chinese and Japanese.
那個小男孩會說英文、中文和日文。

e·nough [əˋnʌf]

Track 0278

形 充足的、足夠的 名 足夠 副 夠、充足 同 sufficient 足夠的

▶形 I don't think a hundred dollars is enough.
我覺得一百美元不夠。

▶名 He said he had enough money to buy a new house.
他說他的錢足夠買一幢新房子。

▶副 This house is cheap enough for us.
這房子對我們來說夠便宜了。

萬用延伸句型
adj/adv enough to + V. 足夠做…… 或者也可以用：so adj/adv as to V.

en·ter [ˋɛntɚ]

Track 0279

動 加入、參加 反 exit 退出

▶Everyone shut up when the boss entered the room.
老闆一走進房間，大家都閉嘴了。

實用片語用語
enter for 參加、加入
例如：Even though she is under 13, she still enters for the speech contest for teenagers.
雖然她未滿十三歲，她還是參加了青少年演講比賽。

e·qual [ˋikwəl]

Track 0280

名 對手 形 相等的、平等的 動 等於、比得上 同 parallel 相同的

▶名 Don't even try; you are not his equal in strength（力氣）.
還是別嘗試吧，力氣上你不是他的對手。

▶形 Women and men should have equal rights.
女人與男人應該要有平等的權利。

▶動 Ten plus（加上）five equals fifteen.
十加五等於十五。

文法字詞解析
equal 的動詞變化：equal, equaled, equaled 或 equal, equaled, equalled

實用片語用語
be equal to / in 相等於

e·ven [ˋivən]

Track 0281

形 平坦的、偶數的、相等的 副 甚至 同 smooth 平坦的

▶形 I can't ride a bike if not on even ground.
如果不是平地，我就不會騎腳踏車。

▶副 Even John, who is always happy, cried at the news.
就連總是很開心的約翰聽到這個消息也哭了。

eve·ning [ˋivnɪŋ]

Track 0282

名 傍晚、晚上

▶I'll visit him tomorrow evening. 我明天傍晚會去拜訪他。

ev·er [ˋɛvɚ]

Track 0283

副 曾經、永遠 反 never 不曾

▶Have you ever seen a double rainbow?
你看過雙層彩虹嗎？

文法字詞解析
ever since 自從過去以來，必須搭配現在完成式使用。

ev·er·y [ˋɛvrɪ]

Track 0284

形 每、每個 反 none 一個也沒

▶How often do you and your family go back to your hometown（家鄉）every year? 你和你的家人每年回老家幾次啊？

實用片語用語
every other... 每隔……
例如：Mom does the laundry every other day. 媽媽每兩天洗一次衣服。

ex·am·i·na·tion/ex·am [ɪg͵zæməˋneʃən]/[ɪgˋzæm]

Track 0285

名 考試

▶There are plenty（大量）of students taking this exam.
有很多學生參加這場考試。

ex·am·ine [ɪgˋzæmɪn]

Track 0286

動 檢查、考試 同 test 考試

▶How long will it take for the customs（海關）officer to examine your luggage（行李）?
海關人員檢查你的行李要多久時間？

ex·am·ple [ɪgˋzæmp!]

Track 0287

名 榜樣、例子 同 instance 例子

▶For example, a dog is a kind of animal.
舉例來說，狗是一種動物。

實用片語用語

For example 例如、舉例來說，等同於「For instance」。

ex·cept/ex·cept·ing [ɪkˋsɛpt]/[ɪkˋsɛptɪŋ]

Track 0288

介 除了……之外 同 besides 除……之外

▶The whole class is going on the trip except for him.
除了他，全班都要參加這場旅行。

文法字詞解析

1.except for 是為介係詞片語，後面只能加名詞。
2. 不只是 except for，「excepting」、「other than」、「but」也是「除了……之外」的意思。

eye [aɪ]

Track 0289

名 眼睛

▶My eyes are tired after studying.
唸完書後我的眼睛很累。

實用片語用語

catch sb.'s eye 吸引某人的目光
例如：She dressed so beautifully that she she caught every man's eye.
她穿的那麼美，吸引了所有男人的目光。

Ff

face [fes]

Track 0290

名 臉、臉部 動 面對 同 look 外表

▶名 There's something strange on your face.
你臉上有怪怪的東西。

▶動 Can you turn around and face me? It's too hard to talk like this.
你可以轉過來面對我嗎？不然這樣超難講話的。

實用片語用語

1. turn around 轉過身
2. be faced with 面臨……
例如：The town is faced with the menace of the typhoon.
這個小鎮面臨颱風的威脅。

fact [fækt]

Track 0291

名 事實 反 fiction 虛構

▶He's really stupid. That's a fact.
他真的很笨，這是事實。

萬用延伸句型

In fact, S. + V. 事實上，……
例如：In fact, I'm not allowed to go out at night.
事實上，我不被允許在晚上出門。

fac·to·ry [ˋfæktərɪ]

Track 0292

名 工廠 同 plant 工廠

▶My parents work in the factory over there.
我父母在那邊的工廠工作。

fall [fɔl]

Track 0293

名 秋天、落下 動 倒下、落下 同 drop 落下、降下

▶名 During the afternoon, there was a sudden heavy fall of snow.
下午突然下起了大雪。

▶動 Many trees and houses fell down in that big rainstorm（暴風雨）.
在那場暴風雨中有許多樹和房子都倒了。

文法字詞解析
fall 的動詞變化：fall, fell, fallen

實用片語用語
fall down 落下、倒下、失敗

false [fɔls]

Track 0294

形 錯誤的、假的、虛偽的 反 correct 正確的

▶True or false questions are my favorite.
我最喜歡是非題了。

fa·mi·ly [ˋfæməlɪ]

Track 0295

名 家庭 同 relative 親戚、親屬

▶Her family is poor but happy.
她的家庭很窮，但很快樂。

fan [fæn]

Track 0296

名 風扇、狂熱者 動 搧、搧動

▶名 Would you like me to turn on the fan? It's so hot in the room.
你要我把風扇打開嗎？房間裡太熱了。

▶動 Grandma is always sitting there fanning herself.
奶奶總是坐在那裡幫自己搧風。

文法字詞解析
fan 的動詞變化：fan, fanned, fanned

實用片語用語
turn on / off 開啟／關閉
要注意 turn on / off 和 open / close 之間的差異。舉例來說，「trun on the computer」是「開啟電腦的電源」，「open the computer case」則是「把主機拆開」。

fa·nat·ic [fəˋnætɪk]

Track 0297

名 狂熱者 形 狂熱的

▶名 He's the only religious（宗教的） fanatic I know.
他是我認識的唯一一個宗教狂熱分子。

▶形 She's fanatic over pop idols.
她對流行偶像非常狂熱。

far [fɑr]

Track 0298

形 遙遠的、遠（方）的 副 遠方、朝遠處 同 distant 遠的

▶形 The store is too far away to reach by walking.
那家店用走的去太遠了。

▶副 Don't go far; you might get lost.
不要走遠，你可能會迷路。

實用片語用語
1. far away 遠處、很遠
2. far from 一點也不
例如：Those who eat fast food every day are definitely far from healthy. 那些每天吃速食的人一定一點也不健康。

farm [fɑrm]

Track 0299

名 農場、農田 動 耕種 同 ranch 大農場

▶名 Would you like to work on a farm?
你願意在農場工作嗎？

▶動 My grandparents used to farm.
我祖父母以前是種田的。

實用片語用語
work on a farm 在農場工作，作農活

farm·er [ˋfɑrmɚ]

Track 0300

名 農夫

▶There are still a great many poor（貧窮的）farmers in China at present.
目前，在中國仍然有許多貧困的農民。

實用片語用語
a great many 很多

fast [fæst]

Track 0301

形 快速的 副 很快地 反 slow 緩慢的

▶形 I took a fast train to Taipei.
我搭很快的火車去台北。

▶副 He can run faster than I can. 他能跑得比我快。

文法字詞解析

比較級的用法：比較級形容詞／副詞 + than + 比較的對象

fat [fæt]

Track 0302

形 肥胖的 名 脂肪 反 thin 瘦的

▶形 The dog is fatter than his owner（主人）.
那隻狗比牠的主人還胖。

▶名 If you eat too much food cooked in deep fat, you will put on weight soon.
如果你吃太多油炸食品，你就會很快增肥的。

fa·ther [ˋfɑðɚ]

Track 0303

名 父親 反 mother 母親

▶My father is my favorite man. 我爸爸是我最愛的男人。

fear [fɪr]

Track 0304

名 恐怖、害怕 動 害怕、恐懼 同 fright 恐怖

▶名 He has a huge fear of water. 他對水充滿恐懼。

▶動 I fear that he won't arrive in time. 我怕他無法及時趕到。

實用片語用語

in time 及時地

Feb·ru·ar·y/Feb. [ˋfɛbrʊ͵ɛrɪ]

Track 0305

名 二月

▶Would you like to go to Europe with us next February?
明年二月你願意跟我們一起去歐洲嗎？

feed [fid]

Track 0306

動 餵 同 nourish 滋養

▶The cat gets angry when we don't feed her.
我們如果沒餵貓，牠就會生氣。

文法字詞解析

feed 的動詞變化：feed, fed, fed

feel [fil]

Track 0307

動 感覺、覺得 同 experience 經歷、感受

▶I feel tired after the party. 派對之後，我覺得很累。

文法字詞解析

1. feel 的動詞變化：feel, felt, felt
2. feel 是連綴動詞，後面可接形容詞補充說明主詞。

feel·ing [ˋfilɪŋ]

Track 0308

名 感覺、感受 同 sensation 感受

▶I have a feeling that this won't work.
我有種感覺，覺得這不會成功。

feel·ings [ˋfilɪŋz]

Track 0309

名 感情、敏感

▶You have to think more about other people's feelings.
你要多想想別人的感受。

few [fju]

Track 0310

形 少的 名（前面與a連用）少數、幾乎 反 many 許多

▶形 He has very few friends. 他的朋友很少。

▶名 There are a few students in the room. 房間裡有幾個學生。

文法字詞解析

few 是否定用字，後面接可數名詞。

fif·teen [ˋfɪfˋtin]
Track 0311

名 十五

▶Did you order fifteen books from our store?
您從我們書店訂購了十五本書是嗎？

fif·ty [ˋfɪftɪ]
Track 0312

名 五十

▶Fifty dollars is enough for me to live for a month.
五十美元夠我生活一個月了。

fight [faɪt]
Track 0313

名 打仗、爭論 動 打仗、爭論 同 quarrel 爭吵

▶名 The boys got into a fight at school again.
那些男孩們又在學校和人家打架了。

▶動 They fought so hard, but still lost.
他們很努力地戰鬥，但還是敗陣了。

文法字詞解析
fight 的動詞變化：fight, fought, fought

fill [fɪl]
Track 0314

動 填空、填滿 反 empty 倒空

▶I filled the glass with water. 我用水填滿了玻璃杯。

實用片語用語
fill A with B　用 B 填滿 A

fi·nal [ˋfaɪnl̩]
Track 0315

形 最後的、最終的 反 initial 最初的

▶Is this your final decision（決定）？
這是你最終的決定嗎？

find [faɪnd]
Track 0316

動 找到、發現

▶I can't find my glasses. 我找不到我的眼鏡。

fine [faɪn]
Track 0317

形 美好的 副 很好地 名 罰款 動 處以罰金 同 nice 好的

▶形 It's such a fine day today, isn't it? Let's go out for a walk!
今天天氣真好，對不對？我們出去散步吧！

▶副 The kids are doing fine in school.
孩子們在學校表現得不錯。

▶名 You have to pay the fine before this weekend.
這週末前，你必須繳罰款。

▶動 I heard that the judge（法官）fined him heavily.
我聽說法官重罰了他。

文法字詞解析
「such a (an) + 形容詞 + 單數可數名詞」用來表示「這樣的、這等的」，有加強語氣的功能。

fin·ger [ˋfɪŋgɚ]
Track 0318

名 手指 反 toe 腳趾

▶The man gave us the middle finger. 那個男人對我們比了中指。

fin·ish [ˋfɪnɪʃ]
Track 0319

名 完成、結束 動 完成、結束 同 complete 完成

▶名 He was lazy from start to finish.
從開始到結束他都是個懶人。

▶動 About how long will it take you to finish all your summer homework? 你大概要多久才能完成你所有的暑假作業？

文法字詞解析
from start to finish 從頭到尾

fire [faɪr] Track 0320

名 火 動 射擊、解雇、燃燒 同 dismiss 解雇

▶名 If your kid gets too close to the fire, he will get burnt（燃燒）easily.
如果你的孩子離火太近的話，他很容易會被燒傷的。

▶動 If you don't work hard, you may get fired by your boss（老闆）. 如果你工作不夠努力，你就可能被老闆炒魷魚。

first [fɝst] Track 0321

名 第一、最初 形 第一的 副 首先、最初、第一 反 last 最後的

▶名 I'd never met a firefighter before; he's the first.
我之前都沒遇過消防員，他是第一個。

▶形 He's the first person to arrive every day.
他每天都第一個抵達。

▶副 Let's finish our homework first, shall we?
我們先來把功課做完好嗎？

fish [fɪʃ] Track 0322

名 魚、魚類 動 捕魚、釣魚

▶名 The fish are swimming around happily.
魚兒們快樂地游來游去。

▶動 Would you like to go fishing with us next Saturday or Sunday? 你想不想下週六或週日跟我們一起去釣魚呢？

文法字詞解析
這裡的介系詞 around 有四處、到處的意思。

five [faɪv] Track 0323

名 五

▶There are five members in her family. 她家有五個人。

floor [flor] Track 0324

名 地板、樓層 反 ceiling 天花板

▶Would you like me to sweep（打掃）the floor again? It's still very dirty. 你要我再掃一遍地板嗎？它看起來還是很髒。

flow·er [ˋflaʊɚ] Track 0325

名 花

▶I brought my mom some flowers. 我帶了一些花給我媽媽。

fly [flaɪ] Track 0326

名 蒼蠅、飛行 動 飛行、飛翔

▶名 The whole office is trying to kill the fly.
整間辦公室的人都在試著殺蒼蠅。

▶動 Birds are born to fly. 鳥兒們生來就是要飛行。

文法字詞解析
fly 的動詞變化：fly, flew, flown

fog [fɑg] Track 0327

名 霧

▶The fog is so heavy today. 今天的霧好濃。

fol·low [ˋfɑlo] Track 0328

動 跟隨、遵循、聽得懂 同 trace 跟蹤

▶My dog follows my mom everywhere.
我的狗去哪都跟著我媽。

實用片語用語
as follows 如下
例如：The names of candidates are as follows: John, Mary, Andy and Claire.
候選人的名字如下：約翰、瑪莉、安迪與克萊兒。

food [fud]

Track 0329

名 食物

▶Would you like some food? You haven't had anything for the whole day. 你要吃點東西嗎？你已經一整天都沒吃東西了。

foot [fʊt]

Track 0330

名 腳

▶There is a small temple（廟宇）at the foot of that big mountain. 在那座大山的山腳下有一個小寺廟。

文法字詞解析

foot 的複數是 feet。

實用片語用語

athlete's foot 香港腳。

例如：Dad suffers from athlete's foot. 爸爸為香港腳所苦。

for [fɔr]

Track 0331

介 為、因為、對於 連 因為 同 as 因為

▶介 An apology is not enough for the hurt you made me feel. 你對我造成的傷害，僅僅道歉是不夠的。

▶連 She was sad, for her husband had left her. 她很傷心，因為她丈夫離開她了。

實用片語用語

be for + N. 同意、贊成。

例如：Are you for his opinion? 你贊成他的意見嗎？

force [fors]

Track 0332

名 力量、武力 動 強迫、施壓 同 compel 強迫

▶名 May the force always be with you. 願力量永與你同在。

▶動 I forced my brother to come with me. 我逼我弟弟跟我一起來。

實用片語用語

be with sb. 和……在一起

for·eign [ˋfɔrɪn]

Track 0333

形 外國的 反 native 本土的

▶I would love to visit a foreign country someday. 我總有一天想要去國外。

for·est [ˋfɔrɪst]

Track 0334

名 森林 同 wood 森林

▶There are all kinds of animals in the forest. 森林裡有各種動物。

for·get [fɚˋgɛt]

Track 0335

動 忘記 反 remember 記得

▶I forgot to bring my dictionary. 我忘記帶字典了。

文法字詞解析

forget 後若接 to v，表示「忘記做……」，forget 加 V-ing 則表示「忘記已經做過……」。

fork [fɔrk]

Track 0336

名 叉

▶He got so mad he threw a fork at her. 他氣到拿叉子丟她。

實用片語用語

throw A at/to B 把 A 丟向 B

for·ty [ˋfɔrtɪ]

Track 0337

名 四十

▶There are forty students in my class. 我們班上有四十個學生。

four [for]

Track 0338

名 四

▶My four sisters all work in the same company. 我的四個姊妹都在同一家公司工作。

four·teen ['for'tin]

Track 0339

名 十四

▶There are fourteen staff（員工）members in our store now, but I still think we need some more.
我們店裡現在有十四名員工了，但是我覺得我們還需要幾個。

文法字詞解析
some 在這裡做代名詞使用。

free [fri]

Track 0340

形 自由的、免費的 動 釋放、解放 同 release 解放

▶形 Would you like some beer while having your dinner? They are for free tonight. 您要不要在吃晚餐的時候來點啤酒呢？今晚的啤酒是免費的。

▶動 They freed the bird and watched it fly away.
他們釋放了那隻鳥，看著牠飛走。

實用片語用語
for free 免費

萬用延伸句型
Feel free to... 此用法用來告知對方不需要猶豫、有需要就可以盡量請求幫助。
例如：If you have any questions, feel free to send an email to this address.
如果你有任何問題，歡迎寫電子郵件到這個信箱。

fresh [frɛʃ]

Track 0341

形 新鮮的、無經驗的、淡（水）的 反 stale 不新鮮的

▶Those vegetables aren't fresh.
那些蔬菜不新鮮。

實用片語用語
fresh from 新的、剛到的
例如：These apples are fresh from farms.
這些蘋果是剛從農場送來的。

Fri·day/Fri. ['fraɪˌde]

Track 0342

名 星期五

▶Let's go to visit the Browns on Friday night. They have moved to a new house.
這週五晚上我們去拜訪布朗一家吧，他們已經搬到新房子了。

文法字詞解析
姓氏前加 the、後面再加上 s 可以表示一個家族。

friend [frɛnd]

Track 0343

名 朋友 反 enemy 敵人

▶My friends are all really easily excited people.
我的朋友們都是非常容易興奮的人。

frog [frɑg]

Track 0344

名 蛙

▶The small frog is my brother's pet.
那隻小青蛙是我弟弟的寵物。

from [frɑm]

Track 0345

介 從、由於

▶I come from the south.
我從南部來的。

實用片語用語
from now on 從現在開始
例如：From now on, you must call me every two hours.
從現在開始，你必須每兩小時打一次電話給我。

front [frʌnt]

Track 0346

名 前面 形 前面的 反 rear 後面、背後

▶名 He always sits in the front of the classroom.
他總是坐在教室最前面。

▶形 The people who sit in the front row are all short.
坐前排的人都很矮。

文法字詞解析
第二個例句中，who 所引導的形容詞子句用來修飾先行詞 the people。

fruit [frut]

Track 0347

名 水果

▶Watermelon is my favorite fruit.
西瓜是我最喜歡的水果。

full [fʊl]

Track 0348

形 滿的、充滿的 反 empty 空的

▶The room is full of people. 房間裡滿滿都是人。

實用片語用語

be full of 充滿

fun [fʌn]

Track 0349

名 樂趣、玩笑 同 amusement 樂趣

▶The zoo is such a fun place to visit.
動物園真是個有趣的地方。

實用片語用語

make fun of 取笑

例如：Stop making fun of your sister! She's about to cry.
別在取笑你妹妹了！她都快哭了。

fun·ny [`fʌnɪ]

Track 0350

形 滑稽的、有趣的 同 humorous 滑稽的

▶My uncle thinks himself very funny. 我舅舅覺得自己很有趣。

game [gem]

Track 0351

名 遊戲、比賽 同 contest 比賽

▶I'm sad because my favorite team lost the game.
我難過，因為我最喜歡的球隊輸了比賽。

gar·den [`gɑrdn̩]

Track 0352

名 花園

▶It takes a lot of time to keep a garden.
要管理好花園很花時間。

文法字詞解析

這裡的 keep 有整理的意思。

gas [gæs]

Track 0353

名 汽油、瓦斯

▶I'll wait for you at the gas station by my house.
我在我家旁邊的加油站等你。

gen·er·al [`dʒɛnərəl]

Track 0354

形 大體的、一般的 名 將軍
反 specific 特定的

▶形 The general idea of this story is quite simple.
這故事大概的意思還蠻簡單的。

▶名 The old general is always talking about his dead friends.
那位老將軍總是在講他已死的朋友們的事。

實用片語用語

talk about sb. 講關於某人的事

get [gɛt]

Track 0355

動 獲得、成為、到達 同 obtain 獲得

▶How about getting some advice（建議）from our teachers?
我們從老師那裡請教一些建議怎麼樣？

文法字詞解析

get 的動詞變化：get, got, gotten 或 get, got, got

ghost [gost]

Track 0356

名 鬼、靈魂 同 soul 靈魂

▶Have you ever seen a ghost before?
你見過鬼嗎？

gift [gɪft]

Track 0357

名 禮物、天賦 同 present 禮物

▶What gift did you get her for her birthday?
你買了什麼生日禮物給她？

girl [gɜl]

Track 0358

名 女孩 反 boy 男孩

▶The girls in my class are always talking about clothes.
我們班的女生總是在討論衣服的事。

give [gɪv]

Track 0359

動 給、提供、捐助 反 receive 接受

▶Did you give her anything for Christmas?
你聖誕節有買什麼送她嗎？

文法字詞解析

give 的動詞變化：give, gave, given

實用片語用語

give away sth. 送、分發

例如：Be good or I'll give away all your toys. 你要乖乖的，不然我就把你的玩具都送走。

glad [glæd]

Track 0360

形 高興的 同 joyous 高興的

▶I'm so glad to see you today. 很高興今天見到你。

glass [`glæs]

Track 0361

名 玻璃、玻璃杯 同 pane 窗戶玻璃片

▶Would you like a large glass of beer（啤酒）?
你要不要來一大杯啤酒呢？

glass·es [`glæsɪz]

Track 0362

名 眼鏡

▶Did you notice her new glasses? 你有注意到她的新眼鏡嗎？

go [go]

Track 0363

動 去、走 反 stay 留下

▶I'm sorry, but I can't go to your party.
我很抱歉，但我不能去你的派對。

文法字詞解析

go 動詞變化：go, went, gone

實用片語用語

go ahead 繼續前進

例如：Just go ahead! I'll catch up with you in a few minutes.
你先走吧！我幾分鐘後會跟上。

god/god·dess [gɑd]/[`gɑdɪs]

Track 0364

名 神 / 女神

▶There are lots of gods and goddesses in ancient（古代的）tales. 古代故事中有很多神和女神。

gold [gold]

Track 0365

形 金的 名 金子

▶形 These gold coins（硬幣）are not enough for him to buy a house. 這幾枚金幣還不夠他買棟房子。

▶名 In the past, people used gold to buy food and other things from the market.
在過去，人們用金子從市場裡購買食物和其他物品。

good [gʊd]

Track 0366

形 好的、優良的 名 善、善行 同 fine 好的

▶形 The book I bought was really good.
我買的那本書真是寫得很好。

▶名 His only dream is to do good. 他唯一的夢想就是做善事。

文法字詞解析

第一句中的 The book (that) I bought 是作為整句的主詞。

萬用延伸句型

so far so good 目前為止一切良好。

例　如：A: How's your work going ? B: Well, so far so good.
甲：你的工作進展如何？乙：嗯，目前為止都還好。

good-bye/good·bye/good-by/good·by/bye·bye/bye

Track 0367

[gʊd`baɪ]/[gʊd`baɪ]/[gʊd`baɪ]/[`baɪˌbaɪ]/[baɪ]

名 再見

▶We said goodbye to our friends at the airport.
我們在機場和朋友們道別。

實用片語用語
say goodbye to sb. 和某人道別

goose [gus]

Track 0368

名 鵝

▶The goose on my aunt's farm is bigger than a dog.
我阿姨農場上的鵝比狗還大隻。

grand [grænd]

Track 0369

形 宏偉的、大的、豪華的 同 large 大的

▶Those buildings are really grand. 那些建築很宏偉。

grand·child [`grændˌtʃaɪld]

Track 0370

名 孫子

▶How often do you take your grandchild to the park?
您多常帶您的孫子去公園啊？

實用片語用語
take sb. to... 帶某人去……

grand·daugh·ter [`grændˌdɔtɚ]

Track 0371

名 孫女、外孫女

▶His granddaughter is not old enough to find the way to the kindergarten（幼稚園）.
他的孫女不夠大，還找不到去幼稚園的路。

grand·fath·er/grand·pa

Track 0372

[`grændˌfɑðɚ]/[`grændpɑ]

名 祖父、外祖父

▶My grandfather died a happy man.
我祖父直到過世都很快樂。

grand·moth·er/grand·ma [`grændˌmʌðɚ]/[`grændˌmʌ]

Track 0373

名 祖母、外祖母

▶My grandmother is always angry about something or another.
我祖母總是為某些大小事生氣。

實用片語用語
something or another，某些微不足道的事，也可以說「something or other」。

grand·son [`grændˌsʌn]

Track 0374

名 孫子、外孫

▶He is fond of his little grandson and always gives him whatever（無論什麼）he wants.
他十分喜愛他的小孫子，總是他要什麼就給他什麼。

實用片語用語
be fond of 喜歡

grass [græs]

Track 0375

名 草 同 lawn 草坪

▶Don't step on the grass; they're sleeping.
別踩草地，小草在睡覺呢。

文法字詞解析
祈使句是用來表示請求、命令、禁止或勸告的句型。句中主詞會被省略，直接以動詞開頭。

gray/grey [gre]/[gre]

Track 0376

名 灰色 形 灰色的、陰沉的

▶名 The color grey has become popular because of a movie.
因為一部電影的關係，灰色變得受歡迎了。

▶形 I have so many grey hairs, it's sad.
我有好多根灰髮，真是悲慘。

great [gret]

Track 0377

形 大量的、很好的、偉大的、重要的 同 outstanding 突出的、傑出的

▶I think your idea is great. 我覺得你的點子很棒啊。

實用片語用語
be great on / at 對……很拿手。
例如：John is really great at doing houseworks. 約翰很會做家事。

green [grin]

Track 0378

形 綠色的 名 綠色

▶形 Follow the green sign and you'll get there.
跟著綠色的牌子走就會到了。

▶名 I always wear green on Thursdays. 我星期四都穿綠色。

ground [graʊnd]

Track 0379

名 地面、土地 同 surface 表面

▶The little boy likes sitting on the ground more than on a chair.
比起坐椅子，那個小男孩更愛坐地上。

group [grup]

Track 0380

名 團體、組、群 動 聚合、成群 同 gather 收集

▶名 This game is supposed to be played in groups.
這個遊戲應該要分組玩。

▶動 She grouped all the flowers of the same color together.
她把同樣顏色的花聚集在一起。

文法字詞解析
be supposed to 和 should 有同樣的意思，都是「應該」，後面要加原形動詞。

實用片語用語
a group of 一群，可以作為單位詞使用，
例如：There is a group of people waiting at the traffic light. 有一群人在等紅綠燈。

grow [gro]

Track 0381

動 種植、生長 同 mature 變成熟、長成

▶The puppy had grown into a giant dog.
那隻小狗已經長成了一隻大狗。

文法字詞解析
grow 的動詞變化：grow, grew, grown

實用片語用語
grow into 長大成為……

guess [gɛs]

Track 0382

名 猜測、猜想 動 猜測、猜想 同 suppose 猜測、認為

▶名 I'll give you three guesses as to what my dog's name is.
我讓你猜三次我的狗叫什麼名字。

▶動 I guess the answer is probably B. 我猜答案大概是B。

萬用延伸句型
Guess what? 你知道嗎？ 這個句子可以用在開頭，吸引他人的注意。
例如：Guess what? He just proposed to me! 你知道嗎？他剛剛跟我求婚了！

guest [gɛst]

Track 0383

名 客人 反 host 主人、東道主

▶There are not enough chairs for our guests.
椅子不夠我們的客人坐。

guide [gaɪd]

Track 0384

名 引導者、指南 動 引導、引領 同 lead 引導

▶名 He is the most famous（有名的）guide here, so you won't get lost in the forest.
他是這兒最有名的嚮導，所以你是不會在森林裡迷路的。

▶動 I am familiar with this place, so I'll guide you around.
我對這個地方很熟悉，讓我來帶你到處玩。

實用片語用語
get lost 迷路

gun [gʌn]

Track 0385

名 槍、砲

▶I've never fired a gun before. 我從來沒開過槍。

實用片語用語
fire a gun 開火、開槍

hair [hɛr]

Track 0386

名 頭髮

▶My mom cut my hair yesterday. 我媽媽昨天幫我剪了頭髮。

hair·cut [ˋhɛr,kʌt]

Track 0387

名 理髮

▶You really should get a haircut. 你真的該剪頭髮了。

文法字詞解析
「get a haircut」也可以說成「get sb.'s hair cut」，這個用法使用到「get + 主詞 + 主詞補語」的形式，如果是主動語態的話，主詞補語就用 to + V.，如果是被動語態就用 V. p.p.。

half [hæf]

Track 0388

形 一半的 副 一半地 名 半、一半

▶形 I'll have half an apple, thanks. 我吃半個蘋果好了，謝謝。

▶副 The little boy is almost half dead from hunger.
那小男孩幾乎餓得半死了。

▶名 The team did badly in the second half.
球隊下半場打得很爛。

ham [hæm]

Track 0389

名 火腿

▶Would you like a slice of ham? It's so yummy（美味的）!
要不要來一片火腿？它太美味了！

hand [hænd]

Track 0390

名 手 動 遞交 反 foot 腳

▶名 Could you give me a hand with the baggage（行李）?
你能幫我拿一下行李嗎？

▶動 I handed my dad a glass of beer. 我遞給我爸一杯啤酒。

實用片語用語
give sb. a hand 幫某人一個忙

hap·pen [ˋhæpən]

Track 0391

動 發生、碰巧 同 occur 發生

▶What happened? Why do you look so mad?
發生什麼事了？你怎麼看起來這麼火大？

萬用延伸句型
What happened? 怎麼了？
因為是已經發生的事情，所以 happen 用過去式。

hap·py [ˋhæpɪ]

Track 0392

形 快樂的、幸福的 反 sad 悲傷的

▶I'm so happy to see that my brother has won the race.
看到我弟弟贏了賽跑，我真是高興。

實用片語用語
as happy as a clam
是固定用法，形容非常高興。
例如：She has been as happy as a clam since she got the diploma.
自從她拿到文憑後，她就一直十分雀躍。

hard [hɑrd]

Track 0393

形 硬的、難的 副 努力地 同 stiff 硬的

▶形 The test was very hard. 那場考試好難。

▶副 My grandparents worked hard every day.
我的祖父母每天都努力工作。

hat [hæt] *Track 0394*

名 帽子 同 cap 帽子

▶Would you like to go shopping with me? I want to buy a hat.
你想跟我去逛街嗎？我想去買頂帽子。

hate [het] *Track 0395*

名 憎恨、厭惡 動 憎恨、不喜歡 反 love 愛、愛情

▶名 He felt hate toward his enemies（敵人）.
他對他的敵人感到憎恨。

▶動 This restaurant is terrible（糟糕的）. I hate their service attitude（態度）.
這家餐廳很糟糕，我討厭他們的服務態度。

have [hæv] *Track 0396*

助動 已經 動 吃、有

▶助動 Have you tried their famous burger（漢堡）yet?
你已經試過了他們家超有名的漢堡了嗎？

▶動 I had the cake but still felt hungry.
我吃了蛋糕，可是還是很餓。

文法字詞解析
1. have 的動詞變化：have, had, had
2. 第一個例句中，是詢問對方「從以前到現在這整段時間內」有沒有吃過那家店的漢堡，所以是用現在完成式。

he [hi] *Track 0397*

代 他

▶How often does he come to see you? Once a week or twice a month?
他多久來看你一次？一週一次還是一個月兩次？

head [hɛd] *Track 0398*

名 頭、領袖 動 率領、朝某方向行進 同 lead 引導

▶名 The head of our group is a strong woman.
我們組織的領袖是個強壯的女人。

▶動 Where are you headed? We'll be going to Kaohsiung.
你們要往哪去？我們會去高雄。

實用片語用語
to be heading/ headed somewhere 去某個地方

health [hɛlθ] *Track 0399*

名 健康

▶He had to take a day off because of health reasons.
他因為健康理由必須請一天假。

hear [hɪr] *Track 0400*

動 聽到、聽說 同 listen 聽

▶I heard that he's a really nice guy. 我聽說他是個超級好人。

文法字詞解析
hear 的動詞變化：hear, heard, heard

萬用延伸句型
I heard that... 我聽說……

heart [hɑrt] *Track 0401*

名 心、中心、核心 同 nucleus 核心

▶I gave you my heart, but you just didn't care.
我把心都給你了，你卻不在乎。

heat [hit] *Track 0402*

名 熱、熱度 動 加熱 反 chill 寒氣

▶名 I hate the summer heat. 我很討厭夏天的酷熱。

▶動 Sit down and I'll heat the soup. 你坐下來，我來把湯加熱。

實用片語用語
heat sth up. 把……加熱。
例如：I heated the milk up before I drank it. 我在喝牛奶前先把它拿去加熱。

heav·y [ˋhɛvɪ]
Track 0403

形 重的、猛烈的、厚的 反 light 輕的

▶Could you help me carry this heavy case to my bedroom?
您可不可以幫我把這個重重的箱子搬到我的臥室裡去？

hel·lo [həˋlo]
Track 0404

感 哈囉（問候語）、喂（電話應答語）

▶How about saying hello to our new neighbors?
去向我們的新鄰居打個招呼怎麼樣？

help [hɛlp]
Track 0405

名 幫助 動 幫助 同 aid 幫助

▶名 Don't worry, you've already been of great help.
別擔心，你已經幫了大忙了。

▶動 Not every person likes to help others.
並不是每個人都樂於助人。

實用片語用語
be of great help 大有幫助，或者也可以說「very helpful」。

her [hɝ]
Track 0406

代 她的

▶Her kids are always very polite. 她的孩子總是很有禮貌。

hers [hɝz]
Track 0407

代 她的東西

▶This book is mine, and that book is hers.
這本書是我的，那本書是她的。

文法字詞解析
hers 作為所有格代名詞使用，代替所有格和所有格所修飾的名詞。

here [hɪr]
Track 0408

名 這裡 副 在這裡、到這裡 反 there 那裡

▶名 There is a mall 100 miles away from here.
離這裡一百英里處有一家購物中心。

▶副 There are a few mistakes（錯誤）here and there, but it's still a good essay（文章）.
雖然這裡那裡有一些錯誤，但這還是篇很好的文章。

實用片語用語
here and there 這裡那裡、到處

high [haɪ]
Track 0409

形 高的 副 高度地 反 low 低的

▶形 My hat is too high for me to reach.
我的帽子放太高了，我拿不到。

▶副 There's a plane flying high up there.
有架飛機飛得很高。

實用片語用語
1. up there 在那裡、在上面的
2. high and low 到處
例如：The wolf has been hunting high and low for its prey for a while.
那匹狼已經四處尋找獵物好一段時間了。

hill [hɪl]
Track 0410

名 小山 同 mound 小丘

▶How about going to the hill for a walk next Sunday?
下週日我們去山丘散散步怎麼樣？

him [hɪm]
Track 0411

代 他

▶Have you ever talked to him before?
你有跟他講過話嗎？

萬用延伸句型
Have you ever...?
你是否曾經……？

his [hɪz]
Track 0412

代 他的、他的東西

▶He is very tall and fat but his wife is small and short.
他又高又胖，但他的妻子很矮小。

his·to·ry [ˋhɪstərɪ]
Track 0413

名 歷史

▶History is my least favorite class. 歷史是我最不喜歡的課。

hit [hɪt]
Track 0414

名 打、打擊 動 打、打擊 同 strike 打、打擊

▶名 The website（網站）tracks（追蹤）how many hits it gets each day. 這個網站會記錄每天的點閱數。

▶動 The man is always hitting his dog.
那個男人老是在打自己的狗。

文法字詞解析
1. hit 的動詞變化：hit, hit, hit
2. hit 也有風行、賣座的意思，例如：Have you listened to the greatest hits album of that band? 你有聽過那個樂團的精選輯嗎？

hold [hold]
Track 0415

動 握住、拿著、持有 名 把握、控制 同 grasp 抓緊、緊握

▶動 Would you like me to hold your baby while you pay for the tickets? 你買票時要不要我幫你抱小孩？

▶名 I can never get a steady（穩定）hold on the heavy camera.
我總是無法把這個重重的相機握穩。

文法字詞解析
hold 的動詞變化：hold, held, held

萬用延伸句型
Hold on.（電話用語）請稍等。

hole [hol]
Track 0416

名 孔、洞 同 gap 裂口

▶There are so many holes in my jeans. 我的牛仔褲破了好多洞。

hol·i·day [ˋhɑlə͵de]
Track 0417

名 假期、假日 反 weekday 工作日、平常日

▶How about we spend our wonderful（美妙的）holiday in London? 我們去倫敦度過一個美妙的假期如何？

home [hom]
Track 0418

名 家、家鄉 形 家的、家鄉的 副 在家、回家 同 dwelling 住處

▶名 This is a beautiful place, but it's not my home.
這地方好美，但畢竟不是我的家鄉。

▶形 Don't give strangers your home phone number.
別把你家電話給陌生人。

▶副 I don't think he's home now. 我覺得他現在應該不在家。

萬用延伸句型
Make yourself at home. 請別拘束。
此句用在招呼客人時，告訴對方不用客氣。

home·work [ˋhom͵wɝk]
Track 0419

名 家庭作業 同 task 工作、作業

▶There is so much homework to do today; I have to start right now. 今天有好多功課要做，我得馬上開始做了。

hope [hop]
Track 0420

名 希望、期望 動 希望、期望 反 despair 絕望

▶名 He has no hope of being accepted（接受）.
他絕對沒希望被接受的。

▶動 I hope that the money I earn（賺取）is enough for me to support my family. 希望我賺的錢能足夠我養家。

文法字詞解析
第二句I hope後面的that也可以省略不寫。

horse [hɔrs] Track 0421

名 馬

▶My favorite horse is the brown one over there.
我最喜歡的馬是那邊棕色那匹。

實用片語用語
over there 在那裡

hot [hɑt] Track 0422

形 熱的、熱情的、辣的 反 icy 冰冷的

▶Do you like to wash your face with hot water or cold water?
你喜歡用熱水還是冷水洗臉？

hour [aʊr] Track 0423

名 小時

▶It took her ten hours to finish reading the book.
她花了十個小時讀完這本書。

文法字詞解析
finish 後面的動詞必須是 V-ing 的形式。

house [haʊs] Track 0424

名 房子、住宅 同 residence 房子、住宅

▶Your house is a lot bigger than mine. 你的房子比我的大好多。

how [haʊ] Track 0425

副 怎樣、如何

▶How do I open this bottle? 我要怎麼開這個瓶子啊？

文法字詞解析
疑問副詞 how 用來詢問某事如何進行、對某事的意見等。

萬用延伸句型
How do you do? 你過得怎麼樣？
用於和對方第一次見面時，較正式的問候。

huge [hjudʒ] Track 0426

形 龐大的、巨大的 反 tiny 微小的

▶That dog is really huge! It's bigger than me!
那狗也太巨大了吧！比我還要大欸！

hu·man [ˋhjumən] Track 0427

形 人的、人類的 名 人 同 man 人

▶形 He rarely（很少）smiles, and when he does he finally seems human.
他很少微笑，當他一笑，看起來終於比較像個人了。

▶名 Sometimes I really don't think my grandma is human.
有時候我真覺得我奶奶不是人。

實用片語用語
rarely 很少、幾乎不，有否定的含義。

hun·dred [ˋhʌndrəd] Track 0428

名 百、許多 形 百的、許多的

▶名 She has hundreds of dresses. 她有數百件洋裝。

▶形 I've got a hundred things to do. 我有好多事情要做。

hun·gry [ˋhʌŋgrɪ] Track 0429

形 饑餓的

▶You must be hungry. Would you like something to eat?
你一定覺得餓了。想要吃點東西嗎？

hurt [hɝt] Track 0430

形 受傷的 動 疼痛 名 傷害

▶形 There is a hurt look on her face; let's ask her what happened.
她的表情看起來很受傷，我們去問問她出什麼事了。

▶動 Does your head still hurt? 你的頭還痛嗎？

文法字詞解析
hurt 的動詞變化：hurt, hurt, hurt

▶名 I can't bear to see the hurt in her eyes.
我真不忍看她那受傷的眼神。

hus·band [ˋhʌzbənd] Track 0431

名 丈夫 反 wife 妻子

▶My husband is always trying out new ways to cook.
我丈夫總是在嘗試新的烹飪技巧。

實用片語用語
try out + V-ing 嘗試、試驗

I [aɪ] Track 0432

代 我

▶I don't like insects at all. 我一點都不喜歡昆蟲。

ice [aɪs] Track 0433

名 冰 動 結冰 同 freeze 結冰

▶名 Do you want ice in your drink? 你的飲料裡要加冰嗎？

▶動 Is the beer iced? You know your uncle likes it best that way.
這啤酒有加冰嗎？你知道你舅舅最喜歡冰的。

實用片語用語
ice over / up 結冰
例如：Every car on the road was iced over because of the storm. 由於暴風雪的緣故，路上所有的車都結冰了。

i·de·a [aɪˋdiə] Track 0434

名 主意、想法、觀念 同 notion 主意

▶Your idea sounds great.
你的主意聽起來很棒。

if [ɪf] Track 0435

連 如果、是否

▶If you talk to him more, you'll see that he's not that bad.
如果你多跟他講點話，你就會發現他也沒那麼糟。

文法字詞解析
此句型用於表達未來可能發生的事情，if 所引導的子句用現在式，主要子句則用未來式。

im·por·tant [ɪmˋpɔrtn̩t] Track 0436

形 重要的 同 principal 重要的

▶He's the most important person on the team.
他是隊上最重要的人。

in [ɪn] Track 0437

介 在……裡面、在……之內 反 out 在……外面

▶Are you looking for mom? She's in the house.
你在找我媽喔？她在房子裡。

文法字詞解析
look for 尋找

inch [ɪntʃ] Track 0438

名 英吋

▶How many inches have you grown since last summer?
你去年夏天以來長了幾吋？

in·side [ˋɪn͵saɪd] Track 0439

介 在……裡面 名 裡面、內部 形 裡面的 副 在裡面

反 outside 在……外面

▶介 Can we eat inside the car?
我們可以在車裡吃東西嗎？

▶名 There was a label（標籤）on the inside of the box.
盒子內側有個標籤。

▶形 He told me some inside news about the meeting（會議）.
他告訴我一些會議的內幕新聞。

▶副 He knows the city inside out.
他徹底瞭解這座城市。

in·ter·est [ˋɪntərɪst]

Track 0440

名 興趣、嗜好 動 使……感興趣 同 hobby 嗜好

▶名 The man has some really strange interests.
這男人有一些很奇怪的興趣。

▶動 You never talk, so I still don't know what interests you.
你都不講話，所以我還是不知道什麼事會讓你感興趣。

文法字詞解析
interest 除了興趣、嗜好之外，在商業用語上還有「利息」的意思，是不可數名詞。

in·to [ˋɪntu]

Track 0441

介 到……裡面

▶Let's go into the house before it starts raining.
我們在開始下雨前進房子裡去吧。

i·ron [ˋaɪən]

Track 0442

名 鐵、熨斗 形 鐵的、剛強的 動 熨、燙平 同 steel 鋼鐵

▶名 Would you like me to go to my aunt's and borrow an iron?
你要我去我姑姑家借個熨斗來嗎？

▶形 He has an iron will and is a strong fighter.
他擁有剛強的意志，是個有力的戰士。

▶動 Your clothes look terrible. Go iron them, okay?
你的衣服看起來超糟的，去燙一下好不好？

萬用延伸句型
Would you like me to...? 你要我去做……嗎？用在詢問他人是否需要協助。

is [ɪz]

Track 0443

動 是

▶This is an apple. 這是一個蘋果。

it [ɪt]

Track 0444

代 它

▶It is hot today. 今天好熱。

its [ɪts]

Track 0445

代 它的

▶Do you know its price? 你知道它的價格嗎？

jam [dʒæm]

Track 0446

名 果醬、堵塞

▶I like strawberry jam the best.
我最喜歡草莓果醬了。

實用片語用語
traffic jam 塞車
例如：The car accident caused a traffic jam. 車禍造成了交通堵塞。

Jan·u·ar·y/Jan. [ˋdʒænjʊˌɛrɪ] Track 0447

名 一月

▶I really wonder（想知道）what Australia looks like in January.
我真的很想知道澳洲在一月份的時候看起來是什麼樣子。

job [dʒɑb] Track 0448

名 工作 同 work 工作

▶Because of the financial crisis（金融危機）, it's too hard for people to find a job. 由於金融危機，人們很難找到工作。

join [dʒɔɪn] Track 0449

動 參加、加入 同 attend 參加

▶Would you like to join in our discussion（討論）?
你願意參與我們的討論嗎？

萬用延伸句型
Would you like to join us?
你要加入我們嗎？

joke [dʒok] Track 0450

名 笑話、玩笑 動 開玩笑 同 kid 開玩笑

▶名 His joke was not funny at all but we still pretended to laugh.
他的笑話不好笑，但我們還是假裝笑一下。

▶動 My friends are always joking around.
我的朋友們總是在開玩笑。

實用片語用語
joke around 開玩笑

joy [dʒɔɪ] Track 0451

名 歡樂、喜悅 反 sorrow 悲傷

▶It is too difficult for me to describe（描述）my joy in words.
我的喜悅難以用語言來形容。

juice [dʒus] Track 0452

名 果汁

▶Would you like to have some orange juice or a cup of coffee?
你是想喝點柳橙汁，還是來杯咖啡呢？

July/Jul. [dʒuˋlaɪ] Track 0453

名 七月

▶The summer holiday starts in early July.
暑假是從七月初開始放的。

jump [dʒʌmp] Track 0454

名 跳躍、跳動 動 跳越、躍過

▶名 I took a small jump over the dog poop（大便）.
我小小跳躍了一下以越過狗屎。

▶動 He kept jumping from one topic（話題）to the next so that it's too hard for me to follow.
他總是從一個話題跳到另一個話題，以致於我很難聽懂。

文法字詞解析
第二個例句中的 keep + V-ing 有一直、持續不斷的意思。

實用片語用語
jump into action 馬上行動
例如：After knowing what to do, he jumped into action.
他一知道要做什麼以後就立刻著手。

June/Jun. [dʒun] Track 0455

名 六月、瓊（女子名） 同 spring 跳、躍

▶It's always so hot in June. 六月總是很熱。

just [dʒʌst] *Track 0456*

形 公正的、公平的 副 正好、恰好、剛才 同 fair 公平的

▶形 The principal（校長）is a just, wise（有智慧的） man.
校長是個公正、有智慧的男人。

▶副 I'm just a little older than you are. 我只比你大一點點。

實用片語用語
just because 只因為
例如：You lent him 1 million dollars just because he is your classmate?
你只因為他是你同學就借他一百萬？

keep [kip] *Track 0457*

名 保持、維持 動 保持、維持 同 maintain 維持

▶名 You'd better get a job and start earning your keep.
你最好現在就去找份工作，負擔自己的生活費吧。

▶動 I want to keep jogging, but I have a class to go to.
我想要繼續慢跑，但我還得去上課。

文法字詞解析
1. keep 的動詞變化：keep, kept, kept
2. 第一句的 you'd better 是 you had better 的縮寫，表示「最好」，有命令的語氣。

keep·er [ˋkipɚ] *Track 0458*

名 看守人

▶The inn keeper is always drinking beer.
那個旅店主人總是在喝啤酒。

key [ki] *Track 0459*

形 主要的、關鍵的 名 鑰匙 動 鍵入

▶形 Which key word should I search with?
我該用哪個關鍵字搜尋？

▶名 I left my keys inside the house. 我把鑰匙留在房子裡了。

▶動 Can you key in these numbers for me?
可以幫我把數字打進去嗎？

實用片語用語
key in 鍵入

kick [kɪk] *Track 0460*

名 踢 動 踢

▶名 The horse's kick made him fall to the ground.
那匹馬一踢他就倒地了。

▶動 Stop kicking your brother! That's not funny!
不要一直踢你哥哥，這一點都不有趣！

kid [kɪd] *Track 0461*

名 小孩 動 開玩笑、嘲弄 同 tease 嘲弄

▶名 The kid won't stop making noise.
那個孩子一直不肯停止製造噪音。

▶動 You're a vampire（吸血鬼）? Are you kidding?
你是吸血鬼？你在開玩笑吧？

文法字詞解析
kid 的動詞變化：kid, kidded, kidded

kill [kɪl] *Track 0462*

名 殺、獵物 動 殺、破壞 同 slay 殺

▶名 The lion looks proud as he sits beside his kill.
那頭獅子看起來很驕傲地坐在牠的獵物旁。

▶動 Did you kill your sister or did you not?
你到底有沒有殺你姐姐？

kind [kaɪnd]
Track 0463

形 仁慈的 名 種類 反 cruel 殘酷的

▶形 It's so kind of you to invite（邀請）us to dinner.
感謝您邀請我們吃晚餐。

▶名 They sell all kinds of fruit here. 他們這裡各種水果都有賣。

實用片語用語
kind of 有點
例如：It's kind of embarrassing to let her know that I love her.
讓她知道我喜歡她有點丟人。

king [kɪŋ]
Track 0464

名 國王 同 ruler 統治者

▶The king treated（對待）his people badly all the time.
這個國王一直對百姓很不好。

文法字詞解析
all the time 和 always 的意思相同。

kiss [kɪs]
Track 0465

名 吻 動 吻

▶名 He gave her a kiss on the lips. 他親吻了她的嘴唇。

▶動 The woman says she has never been kissed.
那位女子說她從來沒被親過。

kitch·en [ˋkɪtʃɪn]
Track 0466

名 廚房

▶Where's your dad? Is he in the kitchen? 你爸呢？在廚房嗎？

kite [kaɪt]
Track 0467

名 風箏

▶There are a few people flying kites on the beach.
有一些人在海灘放風箏。

實用片語用語
fly a kite 放風箏

kit·ten/kit·ty [ˋkɪtn̩]/[ˋkɪtɪ]
Track 0468

名 小貓

▶The kitten often scratches people who touch it.
那隻貓常常抓那些摸牠的人。

knee [ni]
Track 0469

名 膝、膝蓋

▶My sister fell over and hurt her knee. 我妹妹跌倒摔傷了膝蓋。

實用片語用語
fall over 跌倒、坍塌

knife [naɪf]
Track 0470

名 刀 同 blade 刀片

▶Would you like to use chopsticks or a fork and knife?
您想用筷子還是刀叉？

文法字詞解析
know 的動詞變化：know, knew, known

know [no]
Track 0471

動 知道、瞭解、認識 同 understand 瞭解

▶I don't know the answer to this question.
我不知道這題的答案。

萬用延伸句型
Trust me, you don't want to know.
此句用於告知對方可能會被接下來要說的內容嚇到或不高興。

lack [læk]

Track 0472

名 缺乏 動 缺乏 同 absence 缺乏

▶名 I can't do much because of the lack of money.
因為缺錢，所以我沒辦法做什麼事。

▶動 If you lack confidence, it'd be hard to do anything well.
如果你缺乏信心，那什麼事情都會很難做好。

文法字詞解析
注意 lack 在名詞和動詞裡的用法，許多人會在 lack 是動詞時加上 of，這種用法是錯誤的。

實用片語用語
lacking in 缺乏
例如：The town has been lacking in water for two days. 那個小鎮已經兩天沒有水了。

la·dy [ˋledɪ]

Track 0473

名 女士、淑女 反 gentleman 紳士

▶Would you like to know that young lady? I can introduce you to her. 你想不想認識那位年輕的小姐？我可以把你介紹給她。

實用片語用語
introduce A to B 把 A 介紹給 B

lake [lek]

Track 0474

名 湖 同 pond 池塘

▶There are lots of white swans（天鵝）in the middle of the lake in the park. 公園的湖中央有很多隻白天鵝。

lamb [læm]

Track 0475

名 羔羊、小羊

▶My grandma loves eating lamb, but I really don't.
我奶奶喜歡吃羊，但我真的不喜歡。

lamp [læmp]

Track 0476

名 燈 同 lantern 燈籠、提燈

▶The street lamp is not bright enough for me to see clearly beyond（超出）3 meters.
路燈不夠亮，所以我看不清楚三公尺以外的東西。

land [lænd]

Track 0477

名 陸地、土地 動 登陸、登岸 反 sea 海

▶名 Would you like to send your goods（貨物）by sea or by land? 您的貨物要透過海路運輸還是陸路運輸？

▶動 We landed in Hawaii two hours ago.
我們兩個小時前在夏威夷降落了。

實用片語用語
1. by sea 海運、by land 陸運、by air 空運

large [lɑrdʒ]

Track 0478

形 大的、大量的 反 little 小的

▶The large cat is my mom's. 那隻大貓是我媽的貓。

last [læst]

Track 0479

形 最後的 副 最後 名 最後 動 持續 同 final 最後的

▶形 The last train has already gone.
最後一班火車已經開走了。

▶副 I saw him last in New York.
我最後一次見到他是在紐約。

▶名 He's the last to arrive, as always.
他一如往常最後一個到。

▶動 How long does the show last? 這個節目持續多久？

文法字詞解析
「have been to + 地方」和「have gone to + 地方」都是現在完成式表達「去某地」的意思，但前者意指旅程已經結束、已經從某地回來了，後者則表示去了某個地方但還沒回來。

late [let]　　Track 0480

形 遲的、晚的 副 很遲、很晚 反 early 早的

▶形 Why are you late again? 你怎麼又遲到了？

▶副 He always comes to work late. 他每次上班都遲到。

laugh [læf]　　Track 0481

動 笑 名 笑、笑聲 反 weep 哭泣

▶動 He is laughing so hard he's on the floor.
他笑得太厲害，都摔到地上了。

▶名 She has a very cute laugh. 她的笑很可愛。

law [lɔ]　　Track 0482

名 法律 同 rule 規定、章程

▶My sister studies law in school. 我姐姐在學校讀法律。

lay [le]　　Track 0483

動 放置、產卵 同 put 放置

▶That's a rooster（公雞）; it's not going to lay eggs.
那是隻公雞，牠不會生蛋的。

文法字詞解析
lay 的動詞變化：lay, laid, laid

la·zy [ˋlezɪ]　　Track 0484

形 懶惰的 反 diligent 勤奮的

▶My daughter is too lazy to help me with the housework（家事）.
我的女兒太懶了，不願意幫我做家事。

實用片語用語
help sb. with sth. 幫某人做某事

lead [lid]　　Track 0485

名 領導、榜樣 動 領導、引領 反 follow 跟隨

▶名 Let's follow his lead and we will definitely（肯定地）do better. 我們以他為榜樣，就肯定能做得更好。

▶動 He leads his team well. 他把他的團隊領導得很好。

文法字詞解析
lead 的動詞變化：lead, led, led

實用片語用語
lead to 導致、通往
例如：Using cell phones while driving could lead to a car accident.
開車時使用手機可能會導致車禍發生。

lead·er [ˋlidɚ]　　Track 0486

名 領袖、領導者 同 chief 首領

▶The leader of the group is an old man.
那個團隊的領袖是個老男人。

leaf [lif]　　Track 0487

名 葉

▶Help me clean up those leaves. 幫我清一下這些葉子。

learn [lɝn]　　Track 0488

動 學習、知悉、瞭解 反 teach 教導

▶How long have you learned Spanish（西班牙語）?
你學西班牙文多久了？

文法字詞解析
learn 的動詞變化：learn, learned, learned

萬用延伸句型
I learned from sb. that...
我從某人那裡聽說……
例如：I learned from his brother that he's going to study abroad.
我從他哥哥那裡聽說他要去留學了。

least [list]　　Track 0489

名 最少、最小 形 最少的、最小的 副 最少、最小
同 minimum 最少、最小

▶名 Would you like to give him some food? It's the least we can do. 要不要給他一些東西吃？這是我們最起碼能做的事了。

▶形 He has the least money out of all of us.
我們之中他的錢最少。

萬用延伸句型
Last but not least,... 最後，但同樣重要的。通常放在文章最後一段的開頭。

▶副 She's the least tall in her family. 她是全家個子最小的。

leave [liv]

Track 0490

動 離開 名 准假 同 depart 離開

▶動 Please don't leave us here. 請別把我們丟在這裡。

▶名 If you ask for leave, you will not be given the bonus（獎金）this month. 一旦你請假，你就得不到這個月的獎金了。

文法字詞解析

leave 的動詞變化：leave, left, left

left [lɛft]

Track 0491

形 左邊的 名 左邊 反 right 右邊

▶形 The left wheel（輪胎）of the car has burst（爆開）. 車子左邊輪胎爆了。

▶名 Let's count from left to right. 我們從左到右數吧。

leg [lɛg]

Track 0492

名 腿 反 arm 手臂

▶I'd love to have her long legs. 真想擁有像她那麼長的腿。

萬用延伸句型

I'd love to. 我很樂意。當對方邀請你或是請你幫忙的時候，就可以說「I'd love to.」來表示自己的強烈意願，或是自己並不覺得麻煩、很願意幫忙。除此之外，「My pleasure.」也有同樣的意思。

less [lɛs]

Track 0493

形 更少的、更小的 副 更少、更小 反 more 更多

▶形 I have less money than you. 我的錢比你更少。

▶副 My book is less expensive than yours. 我的書比你的更便宜。

實用片語用語

more or less 多多少少

例如：His advice is more or less helpful to me. 他的建議對我來說多少有點幫助。

less·on [ˋlɛsn̩]

Track 0494

名 課

▶I have too many lessons to spare（抽出）some time to play. 我有太多的課要上，根本沒時間玩。

let [lɛt]

Track 0495

動 讓 同 allow 准許

▶She lets her children eat fast food every day. 她每天都讓小孩吃速食。

文法字詞解析

let 的動詞變化： let, let, let

let·ter [ˋlɛtɚ]

Track 0496

名 字母、信

▶I got a letter from a fan! 我收到粉絲寄來的信了！

lev·el [ˋlɛvl̩]

Track 0497

名 水準、標準 形 水平的 同 horizontal 水準的

▶名 Her level of speaking is very high. 她的口說程度很高。

▶形 You need to keep a level head in this situation（狀況）. 面對這種狀況，你必須保持平穩冷靜的心態。

實用片語用語

keep a level head 保持冷靜

lie [laɪ]

Track 0498

名 謊言 動 說謊、位於、躺著 反 truth 實話

▶名 There are lots of lies in the newspapers. 報紙上充滿了謊言。

▶動 He lies better than I ever can. 他比我更會撒謊。

文法字詞解析

lie 的動詞變化：

lie, lay, lain（當作「躺下」意思的時候）

lie, lied, lied（當作「說謊」意思的時候）

life [laɪf]
Track 0499

名 生活、生命 同 existence 生命

▶I have never met this man in my life.
我這一生還沒見過這男人。

lift [lɪft]
Track 0500

名 舉起 動 升高、舉起 同 raise 舉起

▶名 Could you give me a lift to the train station?
能讓我搭個便車去火車站嗎？

▶動 Would you like me to lift the box for you?
你要我幫你舉起這個箱子嗎？

實用片語用語
give sb. a lift 讓某人搭便車

light [laɪt]
Track 0501

名 光、燈 形 輕的、光亮的 動 點燃、變亮 反 dark 黑暗

▶名 Turn on the lights, please.
請開個燈吧，謝謝。

▶形 She's very light so I can carry her easily.
她很輕，所以我可以很容易地背起她。

▶動 Her face lights up when she hears the good news.
她聽到這個好消息，整張臉都亮了起來。

實用片語用語
light up 容光煥發

like [laɪk]
Track 0502

動 喜歡 介 像、如 反 dislike 不喜歡

▶動 You know I'll always like you the best.
你知道我永遠最喜歡你了。

▶介 He's like my little brother. 他就像我弟弟似的。

萬用延伸句型
How do you like...? 你覺得……如何？
例如：How do you like your English class? 你覺得英文課如何？

like·ly [ˋlaɪklɪ]
Track 0503

形 可能的 副 可能地 同 probable 可能的

▶形 John is likely to be late again.
約翰很可能又要遲到了。

▶副 He may be at home as likely as not.
他說不定在家呢。

文法字詞解析
likely 前面可以加 most、more 等副詞來加強程度。

lil·y [ˋlɪlɪ]
Track 0504

名 百合花

▶The lady is as beautiful as a lily. 這個女子像百合一樣漂亮。

line [laɪn]
Track 0505

名 線、線條 動 排隊、排成 同 string 繩、線

▶名 The line is too long. 這個隊伍太長了。

▶動 The streets were lined on both sides with people.
街道兩旁都站著人。

實用片語用語
line up sb. / sth. 使某人／某物排隊。
例如：The girl lined up all her dolls and pushed them over.
小女孩把她的洋娃娃全都排成一排然後推倒它們。

li·on [ˋlaɪən]
Track 0506

名 獅子

▶The captain is as brave as a lion.
這位上尉有如獅子一般地勇敢。

lip [lɪp]
Track 0507

名 嘴唇

▶She has really thick lips. 她的嘴唇很厚。

list [lɪst]

Track 0508

名 清單、目錄、列表 動 列表、編目

▶名 Did you see the list of the people I'm going to invite?
你有看到我要邀的人的名單嗎？

▶動 Is your name listed here? 你的名字有列在這裡嗎？

lis·ten [ˋlɪsn̩]

Track 0509

動 聽 同 hear 聽

▶Are you even listening to me?
你到底有沒有在聽我講話？

文法字詞解析

listen 和 hear 雖然都是聽，但用法不太一樣。llisten 是專注的聽，hear 則是不經意的聽到。

lit·tle [ˋlɪtl̩]

Track 0510

形 小的 名 少許、一點 副 很少地 反 large 大的

▶形 I feel tired; let's rest a little while, shall we?
我覺得累了，我們稍微休息一下好嗎？

▶名 He had little to tell us. Let's go ask another person.
他沒有什麼可以告訴我們，我們去問另一個人吧。

▶副 His health is improving（改善）little by little.
你的健康狀況正逐漸好轉。

實用片語用語

little by little 漸漸地

live [laɪv]/[lɪv]

Track 0511

形 有生命的、活的 動 活、生存、居住 反 die 死

▶形 Don't touch the live wire（電線）!
不要碰那個帶電的電線！

▶動 It's too expensive for me to rent（租）a house alone, so I have to live with others.
我獨自一人租房子太貴了，我只能和別人合住。

實用片語用語

live with... 和……一起住

long [lɔŋ]

Track 0512

形 長（久）的 副 長期地 名 長時間 動 渴望 反 short 短的

▶形 The report is too long; what about we shorten（縮短）it to one page? 這個報告太長了，我們把它縮減成一頁怎麼樣？

▶副 They have worked hard all day long.
他們工作了一整天了。

▶名 Before long, all the children had left the room.
過不了多久，孩子們全都離開房間了。

▶動 He longs for a chance to visit Shanghai.
他渴望有機會去上海。

實用片語用語

1. all day long 一整天
2. as long as 只要

例如：I'll buy you your favorite cake as long as you help me do the dishes.
只要你幫我洗碗，我就買你最喜歡的蛋糕給你。

look [lʊk]

Track 0513

名 看、樣子、臉色 動 看、注視 同 watch 看

▶名 The look on his face after he heard the news was heartbreaking（令人心碎的）.
他聽到新聞之後臉上的表情令人心碎。

▶動 Stop looking at me, it makes me uncomfortable.
不要一直看我啦，很不舒服耶。

文法字詞解析

make + 受詞 + adj. / V. / V. p.p. / N.
使……變得……

lot [lɑt]

Track 0514

名 很多 同 plenty 很多

▶A lot of kids in my class love the zoo.
我們班上很多小朋友都很喜歡動物園。

loud [laʊd]

Track 0515

形 大聲的、響亮的 反 silent 安靜的

▶Don't be so loud; you'll wake the neighbors.
不要這麼大聲，你會把鄰居吵醒。

love [lʌv]

Track 0516

動 愛、熱愛 名 愛 同 adore 熱愛

▶動 She loves rock music. 她很喜愛搖滾樂。

▶名 I fell in love with him at first sight.
我第一眼看到他就墜入情網了。

實用片語用語
fall in love with 墜入情網、戀愛

low [lo]

Track 0517

形 低聲的、低的 副 向下、在下面 同 inferior 下方的

▶形 My low grades made my parents mad.
我很低的成績讓我的父母很生氣。

▶副 The apple is hanging（懸掛）low and is easy to pick.
那個蘋果掛得很低，很容易採到。

luck·y [ˋlʌkɪ]

Track 0518

形 有好運的

▶Not everyone can be lucky enough to win the big prize（獎）.
並不是每個人都能幸運地抽中這個大獎。

lunch/lunch·eon [lʌntʃ]/[ˋlʌntʃən]

Track 0519

名 午餐

▶How about going out for lunch? I don't want to cook today.
我們去外面吃午餐好不好？我今天不想煮飯了。

實用片語用語
There's no such thing as a free lunch.
天下沒有白吃的午餐。

ma·chine [məˋʃin]

Track 0520

名 機器、機械

▶We know nothing about the machine, so it's too difficult for us to operate（操作） it.
我們一點都不瞭解這台機器，因此我們很難操縱它。

mad [mæd]

Track 0521

形 神經錯亂的、發瘋的 同 crazy 瘋狂的

▶You're eating that? Are you mad? 你連那個也吃？你瘋了喔？

實用片語用語
be mad about... 對……狂熱
例如：All of the people in the bar are mad about soccer.
在酒吧裡的所有人都對足球充滿狂熱。

mail [mel]

Track 0522

名 郵件 動 郵寄 同 send 發送、寄

▶名 We've got so much mail today.
我們今天收到好多郵件喔。

▶動 Can you mail this letter for me?
可以幫我寄一下這封信嗎？

make [mek]　Track 0523

動 做、製造 同 manufacture 製造

▶I've made a cake just for you. 我專為你做了一個蛋糕。

實用片語用語

make up for 補償

例如：How will you make up for all my losses? 你要怎麼補償我的損失？

man [mæn]　Track 0524

名 成年男人 名 人類（不分男女）

反 woman 女人

▶名 There are lots of men but few women in our company（公司）. 我們公司男多女少。

▶名 Climate has changed a lot during the history of man. 氣候在人類歷史上產生了很大的變化。

man·y [ˋmɛnɪ]　Track 0525

形 許多 同 numerous 很多

▶I still have many things to do later. 我待會還有很多事要做。

map [mæp]　Track 0526

名 地圖 動 用地圖表示、繪製地圖

▶名 I can't read maps, which is kind of a problem. 我看不懂地圖，這可真是個問題。

▶動 This newly discovered island hasn't been mapped yet. 這座新發現的島嶼還沒有被繪製在地圖上。

文法字詞解析

map 的動詞變化：map, mapped, mapped

實用片語用語

map out 安排

例如：I asked a travel agency to help us map out our honeymoon. 我請旅行社幫我們安排蜜月行程。

March/Mar. [mɑrtʃ]　Track 0527

名 三月

▶The weather is still a little bit cold in early March. 三月初的天氣還是有點冷。

mar·ket [ˋmɑrkɪt]　Track 0528

名 市場

▶Are you going to the market today? If yes, get me a fish or two. 你今天有要去市場嗎？要的話就幫我帶個一兩條魚。

mar·ry [ˋmærɪ]　Track 0529

動 使結為夫妻、結婚 反 divorce 離婚

▶They were married twenty years ago. 他們是二十年前結婚的。

實用片語用語

marry sb. 和某人結婚

例如：Would you marry me? 妳願意嫁給我嗎？

mas·ter [ˋmæstɚ]　Track 0530

名 主人、大師、碩士 動 精通

▶名 The dog likes sleeping on his master. 那隻狗喜歡睡在主人身上。

▶動 I practiced and practiced but still couldn't master the art of playing the piano. 我一直練習，但還是沒辦法精通彈鋼琴的藝術。

實用片語用語

master at + N. 精通（某領域），例如：He is a master at cooking. 他精通廚藝。

match [mætʃ]　Track 0531

名 比賽 動 相配 同 contest 比賽

▶名 Who won the match anyway? 結果到底是誰贏了比賽？

▶動 The color of the shirt does not match that of the tie. 那件襯衫的顏色和領帶不配。

mat·ter [ˋmætɚ] Track 0532

名 事情、問題 動 要緊 同 affair 事情、事件

▶名 What's the matter? Are you all right?
發生什麼事了？你還好嗎？

▶動 It doesn't matter whether she is here or not.
她是否在這裡一點都不要緊。

萬用延伸句型
No matter S1 + V1, S2 + V2… 不管……
例如：No matter where you are, I will try my best to find you.
不管你在哪，我都會盡全力找到你。

May [me] Track 0533

名 五月

▶I was born in late May, which means that I'm a Gemini（雙子座）. 我是五月底出生的，所以我是雙子座。

may [me] Track 0534

助 可以、可能

▶It may rain in the afternoon, so let's just stay at home.
下午可能要下雨了吧，因此我們就待在家裡好了。

文法字詞解析
may 的時態變化：may, might

may·be [ˋmebɪ] Track 0535

副 或許、大概

▶He will be here at maybe ten.
他大概十點的時候會在這裡。

me [mi] Track 0536

代 我

▶Could you tell me how long I can keep these books and when I have to return them?
您能告訴我這些書我可以保留多久還有何時該歸還嗎？

mean [min] Track 0537

動 意指、意謂 形 惡劣的 同 indicate 指出、顯示

▶動 Huh? I don't know what you mean.
啊？我不懂你的意思耶。

▶形 The boy is really mean to his sister.
那個男孩對他妹妹超壞的。

文法字詞解析
mean 的動詞變化：mean, meant, meant

萬用延伸句型
I didn't mean to... 我不是故意要……。
例如：Sorry, I didn't mean to break your glasses.
抱歉，我不是故意弄壞你的眼鏡的。

meat [mit] Track 0538

名（食用）肉 反 vegetable 蔬菜

▶More vegetables and less meat is good for your health.
多吃蔬菜、少吃肉有益於我們的身體健康。

meet [mit] Track 0539

動 碰見、遇到、舉行集會、開會 同 encounter 碰見

▶Would you like to meet my family?
你想見見我家人嗎？

文法字詞解析
meet 的動詞變化：meet, met, met

實用片語用語
make ends meet 使收支平衡
例如：She loves to go shopping so it's hard for her to make ends meet.
她很喜歡購物，所以她很難平衡收入與支出。

mid·dle [ˋmɪdḷ] Track 0540

名 中部、中間、在……中間 形 居中的

▶名 Don't stand in the middle of the street. It's dangerous.
不要站在街道中間，很危險的。

▶形 Let's sit in the middle row; it's the best place to watch a movie. 我們就坐在中間排吧，那是看電影的最佳地點。

文法字詞解析
center 是指在一個空間的中心點，middle 則是大略在一個空間的中間位置。

A B C D E F G H I J K L **M** N O P Q R S T U V W X Y Z

mile [maɪl]

Track 0541

名 英里（＝1.6 公里）

▶There are still a few miles before we get to Taichung.
要到台中還有幾英里。

milk [mɪlk]

Track 0542

名 牛奶

▶Not everyone likes to drink milk.
並非每個人都喜歡喝牛奶。

mind [maɪnd]

Track 0543

名 頭腦、思想 動 介意 反 body 身體

▶名 You look troubled（煩惱的）. What's on your mind?
你看起來很煩惱，在想什麼呢？

▶動 If you don't mind, would you like to go for a walk with me after supper?
如果你不介意的話，晚飯後可不可以陪我去散散步呢？

實用片語用語

keep sb's mind on sth. 專心於……。
例如：Leave your brother alone, he is keeping his mind on his homework.
別打擾你弟弟，他正在專心做功課。

萬用延伸句型

if you don't mind... 如果你不介意的話……。用在禮貌的請示他人。

min·ute [ˋmɪnɪt]

Track 0544

名 分、片刻 同 moment 片刻

▶He can hold his breath for three minutes. 他可以憋氣三分鐘。

Miss/miss [mɪs]

Track 0545

名 小姐 反 Mr./Mister 先生

▶Miss Smith is a tall young lady.
史密斯小姐是個高挑的年輕女性。

miss [mɪs]

Track 0546

動 想念、懷念 名 失誤、未擊中 反 hit 擊中

▶動 They are bound（必定的）to miss the train.
他們一定會錯過這班火車。

▶名 It is too hard to hit the target（目標）without（沒有）a single（單一的）miss. 打靶要百發百中很難。

mis·take [mɪˋstek]

Track 0547

名 錯誤、過失 同 error 錯誤

▶I made a mistake on the math test.
我在數學考試上犯了錯。

實用片語用語

make a mistake 犯錯

mo·ment [ˋmomənt]

Track 0548

名 一會兒、片刻 同 instant 頃刻、一剎那

▶At the moment, only three people are in the room.
這一刻只有三個人在房間裡。

實用片語用語

at the moment 現在、這一刻

mom·my/mom·ma/mom/ma·ma/ma/mum·my

Track 0549

[ˋmamɪ]/[mamɑ]/[mam]/[ˋmamə]/[ma]/[ˋmʌmɪ]

名 媽咪

▶What did my mom look like when she was a little girl?
媽媽還是個小女孩的時候長什麼樣子呢？

Mon·day/Mon. [ˋmʌnde]　Track 0550

名 星期一

▶I was planning to visit him on Monday.
我本來打算週一去拜訪他的。

實用片語用語
visit / make a visit to... 拜訪

mon·ey [ˋmʌnɪ]　Track 0551

名 錢、貨幣 同 cash 現金

▶Money doesn't mean happiness（幸福）.
金錢並不代表幸福。

實用片語用語
make money 賺錢
例如：He hopes to make lots of money when he grows up.
他希望長大後可以賺大錢。

mon·key [ˋmʌŋkɪ]　Track 0552

名 猴、猿

▶This monkey is six years old. 這猴子六歲了。

month [mʌnθ]　Track 0553

名 月

▶I have to pay rent（租金）every month.
我每個月都要繳房租。

moon [mun]　Track 0554

名 月亮 反 sun 太陽

▶A full moon could cause a big flood tide.
滿月會造成漲潮。

more [mor]　Track 0555

形 更多的、更大的 反 less 更少的、更小的

▶There are more chairs in this room than in that one.
這間房間裡的椅子比那間的多。

實用片語用語
more and more 越來越多
例如：More and more women stand up and fight for their rights.
越來越多的女性站出來捍衛她們的權益。

morn·ing [ˋmɔrnɪŋ]　Track 0556

名 早上、上午

反 evening 傍晚、晚上

▶I go jogging every morning. 我每天早上都去慢跑。

most [most]　Track 0557

形 最多的、大部分的 名 最大多數、大部分 反 least 最少的

▶形 Most students in my class are really nice.
我們班大部分的學生人都很好。

▶名 I don't know about everyone else, but I think most would agree. 我是不知道其他人怎樣啦，但我覺得大部分的人都會同意吧。

文法字詞解析
most 的後面不能跟定冠詞、指示代名詞或所有格代名詞，若遇到這些情況，需改寫成 most of。

moth·er [ˋmʌðɚ]　Track 0558

名 母親、媽媽 反 father 爸爸

▶My mother is always singing in the garden.
我媽媽總是在花園裡唱歌。

moun·tain [ˋmaʊntn̩]　Track 0559

名 高山

▶There is a tall mountain behind our house.
我們家房子的後面有座高山。

mouse [maʊs]

Track 0560

名 老鼠 同 rat 鼠

▶Guess what? I caught a mouse yesterday!
猜猜發生了什麼事？我昨天抓到一隻老鼠耶！

mouth [maʊθ]

Track 0561

名 嘴、口、口腔

▶Shut your big mouth. This has nothing to do with you.
閉上你的大嘴。這和你無關。

實用片語用語
shut one's mouth 閉上……的嘴

move [muv]

Track 0562

動 移動、行動 反 stop 停

▶The family next door is moving away. 隔壁的家庭要搬走了。

實用片語用語
1. move (away) 搬走
2. move on 前進
例如：Could you please move on? I can't see anything.
你可以前進一點嗎？我什麼都看不到。

move·ment [ˋmuvmənt]

Track 0563

名 運動、活動、移動 同 motion 運動、活動

▶This machine（機器）can pick up small movements and catch thieves（小偷）.
這台機器能夠感應很小的動作以逮住小偷。

mov·ie/mo·tion pic·ture/film/cin·e·ma

Track 0564

[ˋmuvɪ]/[ˋmoʃən ˏpɪktʃɚ]/[fɪlm]/[ˋsɪnəmə]

名（一部）電影

▶Would you like to go see a movie with me?
你願意陪我去看場電影嗎？

Mr./Mis·ter [ˋmɪstɚ]

Track 0565

名 對男士的稱呼、先生

▶Mr. Lee is our English teacher. 李先生是我們的英文老師。

Mrs. [ˋmɪsɪz]

Track 0566

名 夫人

▶What does Mrs. Smith look like? We haven't met yet.
史密斯夫人長什麼樣子呢？我們還沒有見過面。

Ms. [mɪz]

Track 0567

名 女士（代替Miss或Mrs.的字，不指明對方的婚姻狀況）

▶Ms. White, would you like to wait a moment? Our manager（經理）is having a meeting now.
懷特小姐，您可以稍等片刻嗎？我們經理正在開會。

文法字詞解析
「開會中」也可以用「at a meeting」來表示。

much [mʌtʃ]

Track 0568

名 許多 副 很、十分 形 許多的（修飾不可數名詞）
反 little 少、不多的

▶名 Stop drinking all the wine; we don't have much left.
不要一直喝酒，我們沒剩多少了。

▶副 I don't like it much. I think it's ugly.
我不太喜歡，我覺得好醜。

▶形 You've eaten too much again! 你又吃太多了。

實用片語用語
pretty much 幾乎
例如：These dogs look pretty much the same. 這些狗長得幾乎一模一樣。

mud [mʌd] Track 0569

名 爛泥、稀泥 同 dirt 爛泥

▶It's too hard for us to walk in the mud, so let's take another road. 在淤泥中走路太難了，我們換條路走吧！

mug [mʌg] Track 0570

名 帶柄的大杯子、馬克杯

▶A mug of hot chocolate（巧克力）is just what I need now. 我現在正需要喝一大杯的熱巧克力。

文法字詞解析
hot chocolate 不可數，所以用 a mug of 來修飾。

mu·sic [ˋmjuzɪk] Track 0571

名 音樂

▶Let's put on some music. It's too quiet in the room. 讓我們放聽點音樂吧，房間裡太安靜了。

實用片語用語
put on some music 放音樂

must [mʌst] Track 0572

助動 必須、必定

▶You must be here at seven or we'll leave without you. 你一定要七點前到，不然我們會丟下你先離開喔。

my [maɪ] Track 0573

代 我的

▶Don't worry; he is my good friend as well as my doctor. 別擔心，他既是我的醫生也是我的好朋友。

name [nem] Track 0574

名 名字、姓名、名稱、名義 同 label 名字、稱號

▶What's your dog's name? 你的狗叫什麼名字？

文法字詞解析
name 做動詞使用有「替……命名」的意思。

na·tion [ˋneʃən] Track 0575

名 國家 同 country 國家

▶Would you like to take part in the nation-wide singing competition（比賽）? 你想參加這個全國性的歌唱比賽嗎？

文法字詞解析
形容詞字尾「-wide」表示「擴及某個領域的」。

na·ture [ˋnetʃɚ] Track 0576

名 自然界、大自然

▶In my view, not all criminals（罪犯）are bad in nature. 在我看來，並不是所有的罪犯本質都是壞的。

實用片語用語
in nature 在本質上

near [nɪr] Track 0577

形 近的、接近的、近親的、親密的 反 far 遠的

▶His house is near mine. 他家離我家很近。

neck [nɛk]

Track 0578

名 頸、脖子

▶The cute little baby has no neck.
那個可愛的小寶寶沒脖子。

---

need [nid]

Track 0579

名 需要、必要 動 需要 同 demand 需要、需求

▶名 Not everyone will give you a hand when you are in need of help. 在需要幫助的時候，不是每個人都會出手幫你。

▶動 I don't need your help. 我不需要你幫忙。

實用片語用語
in need of sth. 需要……

---

nev·er [ˋnɛvɚ]

Track 0580

副 從來沒有、決不、永不 反 ever 始終、曾經

▶I'll never make such a mistake again.
我再也不會犯同樣的錯誤了。

---

new [nju]

Track 0581

形 新的 反 old 老舊的

▶Would you like to try something new?
您要不要嘗試新鮮的東西？

實用片語用語
new to... 對……不熟悉、新手
例如：May I ask for your help? I'm new to this job. 請問你可以幫我嗎？我對這份工作還不熟。

---

news [njuz]

Track 0582

名 新聞、消息（不可數名詞） 同 information 消息、報導

▶Have you heard the news yet? 你有聽到那個消息了嗎？

---

news·pa·per [ˋnjuz͵pepɚ]

Track 0583

名 報紙

▶He sells newspapers at the subway. 他在捷運賣報紙。

---

next [nɛkst]

Track 0584

副 其次、然後 形 其次的 同 subsequent 後來的

▶副 I like this blue dress best and that white one next. What about you?
我最喜歡這條藍色的裙子，再來是那條白色的，你呢？

▶形 The bus has already gone; we'll have to wait for the next one. 公車已經走了，我們得等下一班。

實用片語用語
next to 在旁邊
例如：There's a library next to my house. 我家旁邊有座圖書館。

---

nice [naɪs]

Track 0585

形 和藹的、善良的、好的 反 nasty 惡意的

▶If you are nice to the kid, he will also be friendly（友好的）to you. 只要你對那個孩子親切一點，他也同樣會對你很友好的。

---

night [naɪt]

Track 0586

名 晚上 反 day 白天

▶What do you usually do at night? 你平常晚上都做什麼？

---

nine [naɪn]

Track 0587

名 九個

▶You have nine brothers? You've got to be kidding!
你有九個兄弟喔？開玩笑的吧？

nine·teen [ˋnaɪnˏtin]

Track 0588

名 十九

▶There are nineteen students in her class, including（包括）ten boys and nine girls.
她的班上有十九個學生，包括十個男生和九個女生。

文法字詞解析
including 和 included 都有包括的意思，但 including 是介係詞，要用在名詞或代名詞前，而 included 則是形容詞，用在名詞或代名詞的後方。

nine·ty [ˋnaɪntɪ]

Track 0589

名 九十

▶My grandma is ninety and still so healthy.
我奶奶都九十了依然非常健康。

no/nope [no]/[nop]

Track 0590

形 沒有、不、無

▶Why did you say no to his proposal（求婚）?
妳為什麼對他的求婚說不啊？

noise [nɔɪz]

Track 0591

名 喧鬧聲、噪音、聲音 反 silence 安靜

▶The baby is making a strange noise.
那個寶寶一直發出奇怪的聲音。

nois·y [ˋnɔɪzɪ]

Track 0592

形 嘈雜的、喧鬧的、熙熙攘攘的 反 silent 安靜的

▶It's too noisy for me to concentrate（專心）on my studying.
太吵了，害得我都不能專心唸書。

實用片語用語
concentrate on sth. 專心在……上

noon [nun]

Track 0593

名 正午、中午

▶We'll have lunch together at noon. 我們中午會一起吃午餐。

nor [nɔr]

Track 0594

連 既不……也不、（兩者）都不 反 or 或是

▶He can neither（兩者都不）read nor write.
他既不會讀也不會寫。

文法字詞解析
使用「neithor... nor...」的句型時，兩個子句的主詞和動詞要倒裝，變成「Neither V. + S. , nor V. + S.」。
例如：Neither could I hear what he said, nor could I tell where he is. 我既不能聽到他說的話，也找不到他在哪。

north [nɔrθ]

Track 0595

名 北、北方 形 北方的 反 south 南方、南方的

▶名 How long does it take for you to drive from the north to the south of the city? 你開車從城北到城南要花多久時間？

▶形 The north branch（分支）of the shop is bigger.
這家店的北區分店比較大間。

nose [noz]

Track 0596

名 鼻子

▶There is something wrong with my nose.
我的鼻子有點怪怪的。

萬用延伸句型
There's something wrong with...（某人/事/物）有點問題。

not [nɑt]

Track 0597

副 不（表示否定）

▶You should not talk to your sister like that.
你不應該這樣對你妹妹講話。

note [not]

Track 0598

名 筆記、便條 動 記錄、注釋 同 write 寫下

▶名 Don't pass notes in class. 上課不要傳紙條。

▶動 Please note down every word that the teacher said in class.
請把老師在課堂上所說的每一個字都記下來。

實用片語用語
note / write down 記下來

noth·ing [ˋnʌθɪŋ]

Track 0599

副 決不、毫不 名 無關緊要的人、事、物

▶副 Don't be stupid, it was nothing like that.
別蠢了，根本就不是那樣。

▶名 Nothing can make me change my mind.
沒有任何事物可以讓我改變主意。

no·tice [ˋnotɪs]

Track 0600

動 注意 名 佈告、公告、啓事 反 ignore 忽略

▶動 She didn't notice that I had entered the room.
她沒有看到我走進房間裡。

▶名 There was a notice on the board. 公布板上有張公告。

文法字詞解析
在第一個例句裡，「enter the room（進入房間）」是先發生的動作，「notice（注意）」則在它之後發生，但兩者都是過去發生的事，所以後者用過去式，前者則用過去完成式。

No·vem·ber/Nov. [noˋvɛmbɚ]

Track 0601

名 十一月

▶The next meeting（會議）will be in November.
下次會議將於十一月份舉行。

now [naʊ]

Track 0602

副 現在、此刻 名 如今、目前 反 then 那時、當時

▶副 Let's leave for the meeting now, or we will be late.
我們得馬上前往會議，不然就要遲到了。

▶名 From now on, I promise（保證）I'll never be late again.
從現在起，我保證不會再遲到了。

實用片語用語
from now on 從現在開始

num·ber [ˋnʌmbɚ]

Track 0603

名 數、數字

▶I am afraid you have dialed（撥）the wrong number.
恐怕您打錯號碼了。

萬用延伸句型
I am afraid (that)... 恐怕……

nurse [nɝs]

Track 0604

名 護士

▶The nurse is always very kind even to the most annoying（煩人的）patients（患者）.
這名護士總是很和善，就算是對付很煩人的患者也一樣。

O.K./OK/okay [ˋoˋke]

Track 0605

名 好、沒問題

▶Are you sure you're okay? Do you need to sit down?
你確定你還好嗎？要不要坐下來？

o·cean [`oʃən]
Track 0606

名 海洋 同 sea 海洋

▶We can see the ocean from the top of that mountain.
我們可以從那座山頂看到海洋。

實用片語用語
from the top of... 從……的頂端

o'clock [ə`klɑk]
Track 0607

副 ……點鐘

▶Would you like to come to the party at 8 o'clock tonight?
您願意來參加今晚八點的派對嗎？

Oc·to·ber/Oct. [ɑk`tobɚ]
Track 0608

名 十月

▶Would you like to take your holiday in October? You can choose（選擇）any time you want.
你願意在十月份休假嗎？你可以選擇任何你想要的時間來休。

實用片語用語
take a holiday 休假、放假

of [əv]
Track 0609

介 含有、由……製成、關於、從、來自

▶I'm afraid of snakes. 我很怕蛇。

off [ɔf]
Track 0610

介 從……下來、離開……、不在……之上 副 脫開、去掉

▶介 Could you cut another slice（片）off the loaf（一條麵包）of bread for me? 你能再切一片麵包給我嗎？

▶副 Would you like me to take your coat off, sir?
先生，要我幫你把外套脫下來嗎？

實用片語用語
take off sth. / take sth. off 脫掉、移去

of·fice [`ɔfɪs]
Track 0611

名 辦公室

▶There are few people in the office today.
今天辦公室裡人很少。

實用片語用語
office hour 上班時間
例如：What are the office hours of the nearest bank? 離這裡最近的銀行的營業時間是什麼時候？

of·fi·cer [`ɔfəsɚ]
Track 0612

名 官員 同 official 官員

▶He is a good military（軍事的）officer. 他是名優秀的軍官。

of·ten [`ɔfən]
Track 0613

副 常常、經常

▶This man often goes back on his promise（承諾）.
這個人總是說話不算話。

實用片語用語
every so often 不時
例如：Although I live alone, I still meet my family every so often.
雖然我一個人住，我還是時不時的會和我家人見面。

oil [ɔɪl]
Track 0614

名 油 同 petroleum 石油

▶All those countries are fighting over oil.
這些國家都在爭著搶油。

old [old]
Track 0615

形 年老的、舊的 反 young 年輕的

▶You are never too old to learn. 活到老，學到老。

on [ɑn]

Track 0616

介 （表示地點）在……上、在……的時候、在……狀態中
副 在上

▶介 There's a puppy on the car.
車上有一隻小狗。

▶副 Put your coat on, now.
現在把大衣穿上吧。

實用片語用語
1. once upon a time 從前從前，常用在故事的開頭。
2. at once 立刻、馬上
例如：The police appeared at once when the boy cried for help.
當小男孩求救時，警察立刻出現。

once [wʌns]

Track 0617

副 一次、曾經 連 一旦 名 一次 反 again 再一次

▶副 Once upon a time, there was a clever mouse.
從前，有隻聰明的老鼠。

▶連 Call me once you arrive.
你一旦到了，就打給我。

▶名 Don't say it so many times; once is enough.
別說那麼多次了，一次就夠了。

實用片語用語
one is... and the other is... 一個是……，另一個則是……

one [wʌn]

Track 0618

形 一的、一個的 名 一、一個

▶形 There is only space（空間）for one person in the bathroom.
廁所裡的空間只容得下一個人。

▶名 I have two daughters; one is a teacher and the other is still a student.
我有兩個女兒，一個是老師，一個還是學生。

實用片語用語
only child 獨生子

on·ly [ˋonlɪ]

Track 0619

形 唯一的、僅有的 副 只、僅僅 同 simply 僅僅、只不過

▶形 It is too hard for an only child to support（供養）his parents alone now.
對一個獨生子來說，現在獨自供養父母很難。

▶副 I can finish only one part before next week.
下週前我只能完成其中一部分。

o·pen [ˋopən]

Track 0620

形 開的、公開的 動 打開 反 close 關

▶形 Can you keep the door open? It's a little hot in the office.
要不要讓門一直開著？辦公室有點熱。

▶動 Open the gift! I got you something you'd like.
打開禮物啊！我幫你買了個你會喜歡的東西。

文法字詞解析
or 作為「否則」時，可以這樣使用：You'd better get up right now, or you will be late for school. 你最好現在起床，否則你上學會遲到。

or [ɔr]

Track 0621

連 或者、否則

▶Would you like some ice cream（冰淇淋）or a Coke?
你會想要冰淇淋還是一杯可樂嗎？

or·ange [ˋɔrɪndʒ]

Track 0622

名 柳丁、柑橘 形 橘色的

▶名 Jenny is always eating oranges.
珍妮老是在吃橘子。

▶形 This little girl usually wears orange clothes.
這個小女孩總是穿橘色的衣服。

or·der [ˋɔrdɚ]

Track 0623

名 次序、順序、命令 動 命令、訂購 同 command 指揮、命令

▶名 Let's list the items（項目）in order of importance（重要性）. 我們把這些項目按其重要性的順序列出吧。

▶動 We have no time to go to the train station, so let's just order the tickets by telephone（電話）.
我們沒時間去火車站，那麼就讓我們打電話訂票吧。

文法字詞解析
注意不要把「in order」跟表目的的用法「in order to...（為了……）」搞混了。in order to 可以擺在句首或句中，後面加原型動詞
例如：In order to lose weight, she does exercise every day.
為了減重，她每天都運動。

oth·er [ˋʌðɚ]

Track 0624

形 其他的、另外的 同 additional 其他的

▶If you have any other questions, please let us know as soon as possible. 如果你有任何其他的問題，請儘快通知我們。

文法字詞解析
one..., another..., and the other表示「一個……，一個……，另一個」；
one,... another..., and others則表示「一個……，另一個……，其他剩下的」

our(s) [ˋaʊr(z)]

Track 0625

代 我們的（東西）

▶Do you know where our friends are waiting?
你知道我們的朋友們在哪裡等嗎？

文法字詞解析
請注意 our 和 ours 的用法，our 是所有格，ours 則是所有格代名詞。

out [aʊt]

Track 0626

副 離開、向外 形 外面的、在外的 反 in 在裡面的

▶副 We told her to go out for a moment so that we can prepare（準備）her surprise party.
我們叫她出去一下，好讓我們可以準備她的驚喜派對。

▶形 The baseball player is already out, so he went to sit at the side. 那個棒球選手已經出局了，所以他就去旁邊坐著。

out·side [ˋaʊtˏsaɪd]

Track 0627

介 在……外面 形 外面的 名 外部、外面 反 inside 裡面的

▶介 Who's that outside the door? 門外那個是誰？

▶形 When the outside walls of the house is painted white, it looks like a palace（宮殿）.
當房子外部的牆壁都被漆成白色時，它看起來就像座宮殿。

▶名 The outside of the car looks old but inside it's brand new.
這部車的外部看起來舊舊的，但裡面很新。

實用片語用語
brand new 嶄新的

o·ver [ˋovɚ]

Track 0628

介 在……上方、遍及、超過 副 翻轉過來 形 結束的、過度的

▶介 My aunt lives just over the hill.
我阿姨就住在山坡上方。

▶副 I knocked the vase over last night.
昨晚我把花瓶撞倒了。

▶形 Leaves will turn red when summer is over.
夏天結束後，樹葉就會變紅了。

own [on]

Track 0629

形 自己的 代 屬於某人之物 動 擁有 同 possess 擁有

▶形 Look after your own kids; I'm not going to take care of them for you. 自己的孩子自己顧，我不會幫你照顧他們。

▶代 Why are you eating my ice cream? Why don't you get your own? 你為什麼吃我的冰淇淋？幹嘛不自己去買一支？

▶動 Let's find out who owns the old house in the country.
我們把這棟鄉村老房子的主人查出來吧。

實用片語用語
find out 找出

page [pedʒ]
Track 0630

名（書上的）頁

▶There are 670 pages in total; I need at least a week to finish reading it all.
一共有 670 頁，我至少需要一週的時間才能讀完。

paint [pent]
Track 0631

名 顏料、油漆 動 粉刷、油漆、（用顏料）繪畫
同 draw 畫、描繪

▶名 How long will it take for the paint on the chair to dry?
椅子上的油漆多久才會乾啊？

▶動 How long did it take you to paint all the walls in the room?
你花了多久時間才把房間裡所有的牆粉刷完？

pair [pɛr]
Track 0632

名 一雙、一對 動 配成對 同 couple 一對、一雙

▶名 Would you like to go to the mall（購物中心）with me? I want to buy a pair of shoes.
跟我去一趟那個購物中心好嗎？我想買雙鞋。

▶動 The students are all paired up two by two.
學生們都分組成一對一對的。

實用片語用語
1. a pair of 一雙、一對，可以這樣使用：a pair of jeans 一件牛仔褲、a pair of high heels 一雙高跟鞋、a pair of glasses 一副眼鏡
2. pair up with sb. 和某人搭擋

pants/trou·sers
[pænts]/[ˋtraʊzɚz]
Track 0633

名 褲子

▶Don't take your pants off in front of the children, man!
這位先生，別在孩子面前脫褲子啊！

pa·pa/pop [ˋpɑpə]/[pɑp]
Track 0634

名 爸爸

▶What does her papa look like? 她爸爸長什麼樣子呢？

pa·per [ˋpepɚ]
Track 0635

名 紙、報紙

▶I'm so good at making paper airplanes. 我超會摺紙飛機。

實用片語用語
be good at 善於……

par·ent(s) [ˋpɛrənt(s)]
Track 0636

名 雙親、家長 反 child 小孩

▶My parents are always busy going to meetings.
我的父母總是忙著開會。

park [pɑrk]
Track 0637

名 公園 動 停放（汽車等）

▶名 How often do you go to the park with your kids?
你多久帶你的孩子去一次公園？

▶動 I parked the car in front of your house.
我把車停在你家前面了。

part [pɑrt]
Track 0638

名 部分 動 分離、使分開

▶名 How about taking a part-time job to make some more money?
做份兼職工作賺點外快如何？

▶動 I can't bear to part with you. 我真的不想跟你分開。

實用片語用語
for someone's part 對某人來説
例如：For my part, I prefer drinking tea. 對我來説，我比較想喝茶。

par·ty [ˋpɑrtɪ]
Track 0639

名 聚會、黨派

▶There will be hundreds of guests coming to our party.
將有上百位客人參加我們的派對。

pass [pæs]
Track 0640

名（考試）及格、通行證 動 經過、消逝、通過 反 fail 不及格

▶名 I forgot my bus pass at home.
我把公車月票丟在家了。

▶動 Did you pass the exam?
你考試有通過嗎？

實用片語用語
pass sth. to sb. 把某物傳給某人
例如：Could you pass the tablewares to me? 你可以把餐具傳給我嗎？

past [pæst]
Track 0641

形 過去的、從前的 名 過去、從前 介 在……之後
反 future 未來的

▶形 The danger is past; we can sleep now.
危險已經過去了，我們可以睡了。

▶名 In the past, he used to be a really quiet dog.
過去牠曾是一隻很安靜的狗。

▶介 The boys walked past our house just now.
男孩們剛剛經過我們的房子。

pay [pe]
Track 0642

名 工資、薪水 動 付錢

▶名 Not every college（大學）student can get a good job with high pay now.
現在不是每個大學生都能找到一份薪水高的好工作。

▶動 Not all people with high education（教育）levels are paid well now.
如今並不是所有學歷高的人薪水都很高。

文法字詞解析
pay 的動詞變化：pay, paid, paid

實用片語用語
pay off 得到回報
例如：All her efforts finally paid off. 她的努力終於有了回報。

pay·ment [ˋpemənt]
Track 0643

名 支付、付款

▶There was a long dispute（糾紛）between them over the payment. 他們在付款問題上陷入長期糾紛。

文法字詞解析
over 在這裡有「關於、在……方面」的意思。

pen [pɛn]
Track 0644

名 鋼筆、原子筆

▶My pen won't write. It makes me so mad.
我的筆都寫不出來，讓我很火大。

文法字詞解析
won't 是 will 的否定，在這裡有表達「不能」的意思。

pen·cil [ˋpɛnsl̩]
Track 0645

名 鉛筆

▶How about buying our daughter a beautiful pencil box as her gift? 給我們的女兒買一個漂亮的鉛筆盒作為禮物如何？

peo·ple [ˋpipḷ] Track 0646

名 人、人們、人民、民族

▶How many people are there on the plane?
飛機上有幾個人？

per·haps [pɚˋhæps] Track 0647

副 也許、可能 同 maybe 也許

▶Perhaps you should think about it more before you decide.
你在下決定前，可能應該再多想想。

文法字詞解析
perhaps 比 maybe 要來得更正式，用於講述一個動作在未來有可能會發生。

per·son [ˋpɝsṇ] Track 0648

名 人

▶Who's that person standing at the back?
站在後面那個人是誰？

pet [pɛt] Track 0649

名 寵物、令人愛慕之物 形 寵愛的、得意的

▶名 How about going to the pet shop to look at the cats? 要不要去一下寵物店看看貓？

▶形 This store sells pet food.
這間店有賣寵物食品。

pi·an·o [pɪˋæno] Track 0650

名 鋼琴

▶The little girl plays the piano all day, so her parents can't sleep.
那個小女孩整天在彈鋼琴，所以她父母都沒辦法睡覺。

pic·ture [ˋpɪktʃɚ] Track 0651

名 圖片、相片 動 畫 同 image 圖像

▶名 Would you like me to take a picture of you?
要不要我幫你們拍張照片？

▶動 I picture him with long hair and realize（發覺）it would look great.
我想像他留長髮會是什麼樣子，發覺會超好看的。

文法字詞解析
take a picture of sb. / sth. 拍下某人／某物的照片；
take a picture for sb. 替某人（做）拍照（的動作）

pie [paɪ] Track 0652

名 派、餡餅

▶The apple pies she bakes are the best.
她烤的蘋果派最棒了。

piece [pis] Track 0653

名 一塊、一片 同 fragment 碎片

▶The vase is on the floor in pieces.
花瓶在地上碎成一片片了。

實用片語用語
in one piece 未受損的
例如：After looking for the cell phone for a week, he finally got it back in one piece.
他找手機找了一個禮拜後，終於將它毫無受損地找到了。

pig [pɪg] Track 0654

名 豬

▶Stop the car! A pig is crossing the street.
停車一下！有豬在過馬路。

place [ples]

Track 0655

名 地方、地區、地位 動 放置 反 displace 移開

▶名 My bedroom is my favorite place.
我的臥室是我最喜歡的地方。

▶動 I placed all the cups on the table.
我把杯子都放到桌上了。

plan [plæn]

Track 0656

動 計畫、規劃 名 計畫、安排 同 project 計劃

▶動 I plan to visit her next weekend.
我計畫下週末去拜訪她。

▶名 What are plans for if you don't follow them?
不跟著計畫走的話，那要計畫幹嘛？

文法字詞解析
plan 的動詞變化：plan, planned, planned

plant [plænt]

Track 0657

名 植物、工廠 動 栽種 反 animal 動物

▶名 Tropical plants are really beautiful. 熱帶植物真的很漂亮。

▶動 How about planting some trees in our garden in spring?
春天的時候，我們在花園裡種幾棵樹如何？

play [ple]

Track 0658

名 遊戲、玩耍 動 玩、做遊戲、扮演、演奏 同 game 遊戲

▶名 All work and no play is no fun. 只工作不玩很無趣耶。

▶動 The children are playing with the dog. 孩子們正在跟狗玩。

play·er [`pleə]

Track 0659

名 運動員、演奏者、玩家 同 sportsman 運動員

▶The tennis player has won several gold medals（獎牌）.
那名網球員獲得了不少金牌。

play·ground [`ple͵graʊnd]

Track 0660

名 運動場、遊戲場

▶Lots of kids are playing at the playground.
很多孩子在遊樂場玩。

please [pliz]

Track 0661

動 請、使高興、取悅 反 displease 得罪、觸怒

▶I heard that your dad is hard to please.
我聽說你爸爸很難被取悅。

實用片語用語
as you please 隨你的意
例如：You can use all my things as you please. 你可以隨意使用我的所有的東西。

pock·et [`pɑkɪt]

Track 0662

名 口袋 形 小型的、袖珍的

▶名 I can't find my pen. I thought it was in my pocket.
我找不到我的筆。我還以為在口袋。

▶形 A pocket edition（版本）of the book will come out soon.
那本書的袖珍版即將問世。

po·et·ry [`po•ɪtrɪ]

Track 0663

名 詩、詩集 同 verse 詩

▶He enjoys reading poetry while drinking coffee.
他喜歡邊喝咖啡邊讀詩。

A B C D E F G H I J K L M N O **P** Q R S T U V W X Y Z

point [pɔɪnt]

Track 0664

名 尖端、點、要點、（比賽中所得的）分數 動 瞄準、指向 同 dot 點

▶名 There are many points I don't understand.
我有很多地方不懂。

▶動 Let me point you to the teacher's office.
我來指給你看去老師辦公室的路。

實用片語用語
point sb. to / point sb. in the direction of 替某人指路

po·lice [pəˋlis]

Track 0665

名 警察

▶Could you tell me the way to the nearest police station?
您能告訴我最近的警察局怎麼走嗎？

po·lice·man/cop [pəˋlismən]/[kɑp]

Track 0666

名 警察

▶The policeman over there is very handsome.
那邊那個警察好帥。

pond [pɑnd]

Track 0667

名 池塘

▶There are a great many ducks（鴨子）in the pond.
池塘裡有很多鴨子。

pool [pul]

Track 0668

名 水池

▶Do you know how to get to the swimming pool?
你知道怎麼去游泳池嗎？

萬用延伸句型
Do you know how to get to...? 你知道如何去（某地）嗎？

poor [pʊr]

Track 0669

形 貧窮的、可憐的、差的、壞的 名 窮人 反 rich 富有的

▶形 The poor boy was sick for a whole month.
那個可憐的男孩病了一個月。

▶名 He gave his money to the poor.
他把錢給了窮人。

pop·corn [ˋpɑpˏkɔrn]

Track 0670

名 爆米花

▶What's a movie without popcorn?
看電影沒有爆米花怎麼行？

po·si·tion [pəˋzɪʃən]

Track 0671

名 位置、工作職位、形勢 同 location 位置

▶Can you put the chair back in position?
你能不能把椅子放回原來的位置呢？

實用片語用語
put...back in position 將……放回原位

pos·si·ble [ˋpɑsəbl̩]

Track 0672

形 可能的 同 likely 可能的

▶I don't think what you said is possible.
我覺得你講的事是不可能的。

實用片語用語
possible / likely to... 有可能……
例如：George is likely to come with us tonight. 喬治今晚可能會跟我們一起走。

pow·er [ˋpauɚ]
Track 0673

名 力量、權力、動力 同 strength 力量

▶I don't have any power over my children.
我完全沒辦法管得動我的孩子。

prac·tice [ˋpræktɪs]
Track 0674

名 實踐、練習、熟練 動 練習 同 exercise 練習

▶名 It's such a perfect（完美的）plan; how about putting it into practice?
這個計劃這麼完美，把它付諸實行如何？

▶動 My daughter practices the violin（小提琴）every day.
我女兒每天都練習拉小提琴。

實用片語用語
put sth. into practice 將……付諸實踐

pre·pare [priˋpɛr]
Track 0675

動 預備、準備

▶How long have you prepared for the exam?
你為了考試已經準備多久了？

實用片語用語
prepare for sth. 準備某事物

pret·ty [ˋprɪtɪ]
Track 0676

形 漂亮的、美好的 同 lovely 可愛的

▶My mom is a very pretty lady.
我媽媽是個非常漂亮的女子。

price [praɪs]
Track 0677

名 價格、代價 同 value 價格、價值

▶I love this dress but the price is too high.
我真喜歡這件洋裝，但價格太高了。

實用片語用語
high price 價格高昂 ； low price 價格低廉

print [prɪnt]
Track 0678

名 印跡、印刷字體、版 動 印刷

▶名 The book is already out of print.
這本書已經絕版了。

▶動 Can you print these documents（文件）for me?
可以幫我把這些文件印出來嗎？

實用片語用語
1. out of print 絕版
2. print out/off sth. 列印
例如：Let's print the file out and check it one more time.
我們把文件印出來然後再檢查一次吧。

prob·lem [ˋprɑbləm]
Track 0679

名 問題 反 solution 解答

▶He never tells other people his problems.
他從來不把自己的問題告訴別人。

prove [pruv]
Track 0680

動 證明、證實 同 confirm 證實

▶The evidence（證據）you have is not enough to prove that he is guilty（有罪的）.
你持有的證據還不足以證明他是有罪的。

文法字詞解析
prove 的動詞變化：prove, proved, proven

pub·lic [ˋpʌblɪk]
Track 0681

形 公眾的 名 民眾 反 private 私人的

▶形 The public phone is not working. 那台公共電話壞了。

▶名 I hate speaking in public. 我不喜歡當眾演講。

實用片語用語
in public 當眾、在大眾面前

pull [pʊl]

Track 0682

動 拉、拖 反 push 推

▶Don't pull your classmate's hair! 不要拔你同學的頭髮！

pur·ple [ˋpɝpḷ]

Track 0683

形 紫色的 名 紫色

▶形 This purple bag is mine. 這個紫色的袋子是我的。

▶名 I can't wear purple; it makes me look old.
我不能穿紫色，會讓我看起來很老。

pur·pose [ˋpɝpəs]

Track 0684

名 目的、意圖 同 aim 目的

▶What's the purpose of writing this book?
寫這本書的目的是什麼？

實用片語用語
on purpose 有意地、故意地
例如：You did it on purpose, didn't you?
你是故意的這麼做的，對不對？

push [pʊʃ]

Track 0685

動 推、壓、按、促進 名 推、推動 反 pull 拉、拖

▶動 He pushed his sister off the bed.
他把妹妹推下床了。

▶名 We opened the door with one push.
我們一推就把門打開了。

put [pʊt]

Track 0686

動 放置 同 place 放置

▶Please put the book back after reading it.
看完書以後請把它放回書架上。

文法字詞解析
put 的動詞變化：put, put, put

實用片語用語
put sth. away 把某物收好
例如：Don't forget to put your toys away before you go to bed.
上床前別忘了把你的玩具收好。

queen [ˋkwin]

Track 0687

名 女王、皇后 反 king 國王

▶The queen told the soldiers（士兵）to cut his head off.
皇后命令士兵們把他的頭砍掉。

ques·tion [ˋkwɛstʃən]

Track 0688

名 疑問、詢問 動 質疑、懷疑 反 answer 答案

▶名 To eat or not to eat, that is the question.
到底要吃還是不吃呢？這就是問題所在。

▶動 Are you questioning my sincerity（誠意）?
你是在懷疑我的誠意嗎？

實用片語用語
beyond question 無庸置疑
例如：Her intelligence and assiduity（勤勞）are beyond question. 她的聰穎和勤勞是無庸置疑的。

quick [kwɪk]

Track 0689

形 快的 副 快 同 fast 快

▶形 He has a quick mind, so it's easy for him to solve this problem.
他思維敏捷，因此他來解決這個問題可說是輕而易舉。

▶副 Come quick! Your favorite song is on.
快來啊！在播你最喜歡的歌喔。

qui·et [ˋkwaɪət]

Track 0690

形 安靜的 名 安靜 動 使平靜 同 still 寂靜的

▶形 Be quiet, for someone is sleeping in the room.
安靜點，因為有人在房間裡睡覺呢。

▶名 It's like the quiet before a storm.
感覺好像暴風雨前的寧靜一樣。

▶動 The teacher doesn't know how to quiet the students in the class. 這老師不知道如何讓班上的學生安靜下來。

quite [kwaɪt]

Track 0691

副 完全地、相當、頗

▶There are quite a few people in the hall（大廳）; they are all here for the lecture. 大廳裡有很多人，都是來聽演講的。

實用片語用語
quite a few 非常多

race [res]

Track 0692

動 賽跑 名 種族、比賽 同 folk（某一民族的）廣大成員

▶動 I'll race you to the restaurant. 我跟你比賽誰先跑到餐廳。

▶名 My class won the relay（接力）race.
我們班贏了接力賽。

ra·di·o [ˋredɪˏo]

Track 0693

名 收音機

▶Would you like me to turn down the radio?
你要我把收音機的聲音調小一點嗎？

實用片語用語
turn up / down the music 把音樂的聲音調高／低

rail·road [ˋrelˏrod]

Track 0694

名 鐵路

▶How long does it take for you to get to the railroad station by taxi? 你坐計程車到火車站要花多久時間？

rain [ren]

Track 0695

名 雨、雨水 動 下雨 同 shower 雨、降雨

▶名 We need to get out of the rain or we'll catch a cold.
我們快去躲雨吧，不然就要感冒了。

▶動 I think it's going to rain. Do you have an umbrella?
我想快要下雨了，你有傘嗎？

實用片語用語
get out of 離開、逃避

rain·bow [ˋrenˏbo]

Track 0696

名 彩虹

▶Did you see the rainbow this morning?
你有看到今天早上的彩虹嗎？

raise [rez]

Track 0697

動 舉起、抬起、提高、養育 反 lower 下降

▶My parents raised us to be honest（誠實的）people.
我的父母養育我們成為誠實的人。

rat [ræt]

Track 0698

名 老鼠 同 mouse 老鼠

▶The rat we caught was really fat.
我們抓到的那隻老鼠超胖的。

reach [ritʃ]

Track 0699

動 伸手拿東西、到達 同 approach 接近

▶I can't reach the book on the shelf（架子）. I'm too short.
我拿不到書架上的書。我太矮了。

萬用延伸句型
這裡也可以套用「too...to...（太……以至於不能……）」的句型，寫成：I'm too short to reach the book on the shelf.

read [rid]

Track 0700

動 讀、看（書、報等）、朗讀

▶She learned to read at the age of three.
她三歲就學會閱讀了。

文法字詞解析
read 的動詞變化：read, read, read

實用片語用語
read out 念出
例如：Their names were read out by the teacher. 他們的名字被老師念出來。

read·y [ˋrɛdɪ]

Track 0701

形 作好準備的

▶Are you ready to leave yet? 你準備好要走了嗎？

實用片語用語
ready to V. / ready for N. 準備好（做）某事

re·al [ˋriəl]

Track 0702

形 真的、真實的 副 真正的 同 actual 真的、真正的

▶形 Once you see and touch it, you will believe that it's real.
一旦你看到它並觸摸到它，你就會相信它是真實的。

▶副 My younger brother is real tall. 我弟弟真的很高。

文法字詞解析
once 在這裡是連接詞「一旦……就……」，意同於 as soon as。once 後面接的時間子句要用現在式代替未來式。

rea·son [ˋrizn̩]

Track 0703

名 理由 同 cause 理由、原因

▶Not all people know the reason for her absence（缺席）.
不是所有人都知道她缺席的原因。

實用片語用語
reason for (doing) sth. / to V. / that / why 做……的理由

re·ceive [rɪˋsiv]

Track 0704

動 收到 反 send 發送、寄

▶Have you received my email? 你有收到我的電子郵件嗎？

red [rɛd]

Track 0705

名 紅色 形 紅色的

▶名 The girl in red is his sister. 那個穿紅衣服的女孩是他妹妹。

▶形 My brother believes that wearing red underwear（內衣褲）means good luck. 我哥哥相信穿紅內衣會帶來好運。

re·mem·ber [rɪˋmɛmbɚ]

Track 0706

動 記得 同 remind 使記起

▶Do you remember me? No? I'm so sad!
你記得我嗎？不記得喔？我好傷心！

re·port [rɪˋport]

Track 0707

動 報告、報導 名 報導、報告

▶動 Would you like me to report on the whole event to you?
你要我把整件事向你報告嗎？

▶名 He finished his report late last night.
他昨晚到很晚終於把他的報告寫完了。

實用片語用語
report on 就……提出報告

rest [rɛst]

Track 0708

動 休息 名 睡眠、休息 同 relaxation 休息

▶動 Let's go home and rest. 我們回家休息一下吧。

▶名 Do you want to take a rest? 要不要休息一下？

re·turn [rɪˋtɝn]

Track 0709

動 歸還、送回 名 返回、復發 形 返回的 反 depart 出發

▶動 Could you help me return the book to the library?
你願意幫我把書還給圖書館嗎？

▶名 I ran into my old friend on my return to my hometown（家鄉）. 我回到我家鄉時，遇到了我的老朋友。

▶形 Did you get a return trip ticket? 你有買回程的票嗎？

實用片語用語
return to 回到（某地）

rice [raɪs]

Track 0710

名 稻米、米飯

▶Not all people of the country live on rice.
那個國家的人並非都以米為主食。

rich [rɪtʃ]

Track 0711

形 富裕的 同 wealthy 富裕的

▶Once you see the big villa（別墅）and expensive car, you will understand how rich he is. 一旦你看到他的大別墅和昂貴的車子，你就會明白他有多有錢了。

ride [raɪd]

Track 0712

動 騎、乘 名 騎馬、騎車或乘車旅行

▶動 What about going riding with me?
要不要和我一起去騎馬？

▶名 We're going for a ride. Do you want to come?
我們要搭車去晃晃，你要一起來嗎？

文法字詞解析
ride 的動詞變化：ride, rode, ridden

實用片語用語
go for a ride 兜風

right [raɪt]

Track 0713

形 正確的、右邊的 名 正確、右方、權利 同 correct 正確的

▶形 He is the right person for the position（職位）.
他是那個職位的合適人選。

▶名 I have every right to vote（投票）.
我完全有投票的權利。

ring [rɪŋ]

Track 0714

動 按鈴、打電話 名 戒指、鈴聲

▶動 Your phone is ringing. Do you want me to get it for you?
你的電話在響耶，要我幫你接嗎？

▶名 My boyfriend gave me this expensive ring.
我男朋友給了我這個昂貴的戒指。

文法字詞解析
ring 的動詞變化：ring, rang, rung

rise [raɪz]

Track 0715

動 上升、增長 名 上升 同 ascend 升起

▶動 The sun has not risen yet.
太陽還沒升起。

▶名 He was more surprised at his rise to fame than we were.
對於他的名氣竄升，他比我們還驚訝。

文法字詞解析
rise 的動詞變化：rise, rose, risen

riv·er [ˋrɪvɚ] Track 0716

名 江、河 同 stream 小河

▶My parents live just across the river.
我父母就住在河對面而已。

road [rod] Track 0717

名 路、道路、街道、路線 同 path 路、道路

▶Would you like to transport（運輸）your goods（貨物）by sea or by road? 您的貨物是要透過水路運輸還是陸路運輸？

ro·bot [ˋrobət] Track 0718

名 機器人

▶Can a robot be smarter than man?
機器人有可能比人類更聰明嗎？

rock [rɑk] Track 0719

動 搖晃 名 岩石 同 stone 石頭

▶動 I rocked the baby until she fell asleep.
我搖晃著寶寶，直到她睡著為止。

▶名 Let's go rock-climbing next week.
我們下禮拜去攀岩吧。

roll [rol] Track 0720

動 滾動、捲 名 名冊、卷 同 wheel 滾動、打滾

▶動 Roll up the poster（海報）and put it here.
把那張海報捲好，放在這裡。

▶名 Would you like me to buy a roll of film（底片）for you?
你要我幫你買一卷底片嗎？

實用片語用語
roll up 捲起

roof [ruf] Track 0721

名 屋頂、車頂 反 floor 地板

▶Not all young people like to live under the same roof with their parents now. 現在不是所有年輕人都喜歡跟父母住在一起。

實用片語用語
under the same roof 同一個屋簷下，即「住在一起」。

room [rum] Track 0722

名 房間、室 同 chamber 房間

▶I can't find my cat. She's not in my room.
我找不到我的貓，牠不在我房間。

roost·er [ˋrustɚ] Track 0723

名 雄雞、好鬥者 同 cock 公雞

▶There are many hens（母雞）but only one rooster living in our coop（雞舍）.
我們雞舍裡有很多隻母雞，但是只有一隻公雞。

root [rut] Track 0724

名 根源、根 動 生根 同 origin 起源

▶名 He pulled the plant up from its roots.
他把那個植物連根拔起。

▶動 She was frightened（害怕的）, rooted to the spot（地點）.
她怕得彷彿紮根在地一動也不動。

實用片語用語
be rooted to the spot 因害怕而僵在原地

rope [rop]

Track 0725

名 繩、索 動 用繩拴住 同 cord 繩索

▶名 I tied（綁）a rope around my waist（腰）.
我把繩子綁在腰上。

▶動 I roped these sticks（木棍）together.
我把這些木棍用繩子拴在一起。

rose [roz]

Track 0726

名 玫瑰花、薔薇花 形 玫瑰色的

▶名 Not all women like roses.
不是所有女人都喜歡玫瑰。

▶形 Her face is a lovely rose color.
她的臉是漂亮的玫瑰色。

萬用延伸句型
「not every...」和「not all...」都有部分否定的含意，只是使用上要注意，如果是前者的話，後面要接單數名詞，後者的後面則要接複數名詞。

round [raʊnd]

Track 0727

形 圓的、球形的 名 圓形物、一回合 動 使旋轉 介 在……四周

▶形 Would you like to buy a round table or a square（正方形的）one?
你想買一張圓桌還是方桌？

▶名 We've all eaten already, but we can still go for a second round.
我們都吃過了，但再來吃一回也行。

▶動 As soon as I rounded the corner I saw the car.
我一轉過轉角，就看到那台車。

▶介 All the kids round the block（街區）are my age.
街區四周的所有孩子們都跟我差不多大。

文法字詞解析
當 round 作介係詞時，表達在……周圍時，可以和 around 互換使用。

row [ro]

Track 0728

名 排、行、列 動 划船 同 paddle 划船

▶名 There are eleven football players standing in a row.
有十一名足球運動員站成一排。

▶動 I'm too tired to row across the lake.
我太累了，無法划船到湖的另一邊。

實用片語用語
stand in a row 站成一排

rub [rʌb]

Track 0729

動 磨擦

▶I rubbed my lipstick（口紅）off. 我把口紅擦掉了。

文法字詞解析
rub 的動詞變化：rub, rubbed, rubbed

實用片語用語
rub off 擦掉、抹掉

rub·ber [ˋrʌbɚ]

Track 0730

名 橡膠、橡皮 形 橡膠做的

▶名 The gloves（手套）are made of rubber.
這些手套是橡膠做的。

▶形 I killed the fly with a rubber band.
我用橡皮筋殺死了那隻蒼蠅。

rule [rul]

Track 0731

名 規則 動 統治 同 govern 統治、管理

▶名 Are there any rules I need to know?
有什麼我一定要知道的規則嗎？

▶動 It's said that Charles I ruled England for 11 years.
據說查理一世統治了英國十一年。

run [rʌn]

Track 0732

動 跑、運轉 名 跑

▶動 Would you like to run your own business（生意）?
你想不想經營自己的生意？

▶名 It's still bright outside; we can go for a run.
外面還很亮，我們可以去跑個步。

文法字詞解析
run 的動詞變化：run, ran, run

sad [sæd]

Track 0733

形 令人難過的、悲傷的 同 sorrowful 悲哀的

▶She must be very sad at this news; let's go and console（安慰）her. 聽到這個消息她一定很傷心，我們去安慰一下她吧！

safe [sef]

Track 0734

形 安全的 反 dangerous 危險的

▶Are you sure this boat is safe? 你確定這船安全嗎？

實用片語用語
safe and sound 安然無恙
例如：I hope the missing people would come back safe and sound.
我希望那些失蹤的人能平安歸來。

sail [sel]

Track 0735

名 帆、篷、航行、船隻 動 航行

▶名 He got hit by the sail and fell into the sea.
他被船帆打中，摔進了海裡。

▶動 My uncle is always out sailing. 我叔叔總是在航海。

sale [sel]

Track 0736

名 賣、出售 反 purchase 購買

▶What's on sale today? 今天有什麼在特價？

salt [sɔlt]

Track 0737

名 鹽 形 鹽的 反 sugar 糖

▶名 You eat too much salt. That's unhealthy.
你吃太多鹽了，不健康喔。

▶形 There is a lot of salt water on earth, but we can't drink it.
地球上有大量的鹽水，可是我們卻不能飲用。

文法字詞解析
salt 是不可數名詞，可用 a pinch of salt（一撮鹽）來修飾。

same [sem]

Track 0738

形 同樣的 副 同樣地 代 同樣的人或事
反 different 不同的

▶形 We work in the same company. Would you like me to introduce（介紹）him to you?
我和他在同一家公司工作，要我幫你介紹一下嗎？

▶副 The two books look the same. I can't see any difference.
這兩本書看起來一樣，我看不出有什麼差。

▶代 Your birthday's on August 31st? Mine's the same.
你的生日是八月三十一日喔？我的也是一樣。

sand [sænd]

Track 0739

名 沙、沙子

▶The children are playing in the sand. 孩子們在玩沙。

Sat·ur·day/Sat. [ˋsætəde]

Track 0740

名 星期六

▶I always sleep late on Saturdays. 我每週六都睡很晚。

save [sev]

Track 0741

動 救、搭救、挽救、儲蓄 反 waste 浪費、消耗

▶The man is angry at himself for not being able to save the little girl. 那個男人因無法救起小女孩而生自己的氣。

saw [sɔ]

Track 0742

名 鋸 動 用鋸子鋸

▶名 The man left his saw by the tree.
那男人把他的鋸子留在樹旁邊了。

▶動 Dad is busy sawing through the tree.
爸爸正忙著鋸那棵大樹。

文法字詞解析
saw 的動詞變化：saw, sawed, sawed 或 saw, sawed, sawn

實用片語用語
saw through 鋸開

say [se]

Track 0743

動 說、講

▶"I think you're really cool," he said.
「我覺得你很酷耶，」他說。

文法字詞解析
say 的動詞變化：say, said, said

scare [skɛr]

Track 0744

動 驚嚇、使害怕 名 害怕 同 frighten 使害怕

▶動 The eagle scared the chicks on the ground away.
這隻老鷹把地上的小雞嚇跑了。

▶名 The sound is loud enough to give me a scare.
那個聲音大得把我嚇了一跳。

文法字詞解析
若要表達自己很害怕，要用形容詞 scared，要說明某個東西很可怕，則是用形容詞 scary。

scene [sin]

Track 0745

名 戲劇的一場、風景 同 view 景色

▶That was a really cute scene. 那真是可愛的一幕。

school [skul]

Track 0746

名 學校

▶Is John home from school yet? 約翰從學校回到家了嗎？

sea [si]

Track 0747

名 海 同 ocean 海洋

▶Let's go to the sea next weekend. 我們下週末去海邊吧。

sea·son [ˋsizn̩]

Track 0748

名 季節

▶Autumn is my favorite（最喜歡的）season, because the weather is always fine.
秋季是我最喜歡的季節，因為天氣總是很好。

文法字詞解析
從屬連接詞 because（因為）用來連接有因果關係的兩個句子。

seat [sit]

Track 0749

名 座位 動 坐下 同 chair 椅子

▶名 There aren't enough seats for the guests. 座位不夠客人坐了。

▶動 The little girl seated on the horse is my sister.
坐在馬上的那個小女孩是我的妹妹。

sec·ond ['sɛkənd]

Track 0750

形 第二的 名 秒

▶形 He was still hungry after one pizza so he ate a second one.
他吃了一個披薩還是很餓，所以又吃了第二個。

▶名 We have thirty seconds before the bomb（炸彈）explodes（爆炸）. 還有三十秒炸彈就要爆炸了。

see [si]

Track 0751

動 看、理解 同 watch 看

▶The thief（小偷）broke into this old man's house last night, but no one saw him.
小偷昨晚闖入了老人的家，但是卻沒有人看見。

文法字詞解析
see 的動詞變化：see, saw, seen

萬用延伸句型
I'll be seeing you. 再見。 這句話和「See you soon.」的意思是一樣的。

seed [sid]

Track 0752

名 種子 動 播種於

▶名 My pet mouse loves eating seeds.
我的寵物老鼠就愛吃種子。

▶動 The lawn（草坪）is newly seeded.
這草坪才剛播過種。

seem [sim]

Track 0753

動 似乎

▶She always seems to be very happy.
她似乎隨時都很開心。

see·saw ['siˏsɔ]

Track 0754

名 蹺蹺板

▶There are many children in the park. They are waiting for playing on the seesaw.
公園裡有很多小孩在等著玩蹺蹺板。

self [sɛlf]

Track 0755

名 自己、自我

▶I'm not my usual self today.
我今天實在太不像自己了。

實用片語用語
sb's usual self 某人平常的樣子或個性

self·ish ['sɛlfɪʃ]

Track 0756

形 自私的、不顧別人的

▶She's the most selfish old lady I've ever met.
她是我遇過最自私的老太太。

sell [sɛl]

Track 0757

動 賣、出售、銷售 反 buy 買

▶Are you sure you want to sell this beautiful car?
你確定你真的要賣掉這台美麗的車？

文法字詞解析
sell 的動詞變化：sell, sold, sold

實用片語用語
sell sb. sth. / sell sth. to sb.
將某物賣給某人
例如：The vendor sells swimsuits to those who are heading to the beach.
那位小販賣泳裝給正在前往海灘的人們。

send [sɛnd]

Track 0758

動 派遣、寄出 同 mail 寄信

▶Let's send him an email and tell him everything.
我們寄封電子郵件給他，把事情通通跟他說吧。

文法字詞解析
send 的動詞變化：send, sent, sent

實用片語用語
send sb. sth. 寄某物給某人

sense [sɛns]
Track 0759

名 感覺、意義

▶He has a terrible sense of direction（方向）and always gets lost. 他的方向感超差，每次都迷路。

萬用延伸句型

It doesn't make sense. 這不合理。

「make sense」的意思是「有道理、合理的」，如果覺得某事不可能發生但是卻發生了，就可以用這句話表達自己的訝異。

sen·tence [ˋsɛntəns]
Track 0760

名 句子、判決 動 判決 同 judge 判決

▶名 He wrote only three sentences in the letter.
他在信裡面只寫了三個句子。

▶動 Not everyone thinks that sentencing the man to death is a just decision（判決）.
並非人人都認為判這個人死刑是一個公正的判決。

實用片語用語

sentence sb. to sth. 判決某人（刑期）

Sep·tem·ber/Sept.
Track 0761

[sɛpˋtɛmbɚ]

名 九月

▶A new football（足球）season will begin in September.
新的足球賽季將於九月份開始。

serve [sɝv]
Track 0762

動 服務、招待

▶I've been waiting for twenty minutes but no one has come over to serve me. 我等二十分鐘了，都沒人過來服務我。

serv·ice [ˋsɝvɪs]
Track 0763

名 服務

▶The service here is quite terrible（糟糕的）; let's go to another restaurant（餐廳）.
這裡的服務很糟糕，我們還是換一家餐廳吧！

set [sɛt]
Track 0764

名（一）套、（一）副 動 放、擱置 同 place 放置

▶名 I bought a set of lovely teacups（茶杯）from her.
我從她那裡買了一組可愛的茶杯。

▶動 Would you like to help me set the table?
你願意幫我擺好餐桌嗎？

文法字詞解析

set 的動詞變化：set, set, set

萬用延伸句型

On your marks, get set, go! 各就各位，預備，開始！

這句話裡，set 是形容詞，表示「準備好的」。我們常會在比賽開始前聽到裁判說這句話，和「ready, steady, go!」是同樣的意思。

sev·en [ˋsɛvən]
Track 0765

名 七

▶My dog just had seven puppies.
我的狗剛生了七隻小狗。

sev·en·teen [ˏsɛvənˋtin]
Track 0766

名 十七

▶We walked seventeen miles on foot.
我們走了十七英里的路。

sev·en·ty [ˋsɛvəntɪ]
Track 0767

名 七十

▶Seventy dollars? That's too much.
七十美元喔？太貴了。

萬用延伸句型

It costs too much 太貴了。或者也可以說：「It's too expensive.」

sev·er·al [ˋsɛvərəl]

Track 0768

形 幾個的 代 幾個

▶形 I had dinner with her several times this week.
我這週和她一起吃過幾次晚餐。

▶代 Several of the windows were broken, but we don't know who did it.
有幾扇玻璃窗被砸破了，但不知道是誰幹的。

shake [ʃek]

Track 0769

動 搖、發抖 名 搖動、震動

▶動 Why are you shaking? Are you cold?
你幹嘛發抖？很冷嗎？

▶名 I gave the bottle several shakes before I drank the juice.
我搖了瓶子幾下，然後才喝果汁。

文法字詞解析
shake 的動詞變化：shake, shook, shaken

shall [ʃæl]

Track 0770

連 將

▶We shall be there in a few minutes.
我們幾分鐘內將會到。

文法字詞解析
1. shall 的動詞變化：shall, should, should
2. shall 可用在表示未來將發生的事，也可用在徵求他人的意見，例如：Shall we go to the movies tonight?

shape [ʃep]

Track 0771

動 使成形 名 形狀 同 form 使成形

▶動 My parents are the ones who shaped my personality（個性）. 我的父母是塑造我的人格的人。

▶名 There's a cloud in the shape of a cat.
那裡有朵雲，是貓的形狀。

shark [ʃɑrk]

Track 0772

名 鯊魚

▶Everyone screamed when the shark appeared（出現）.
鯊魚一出現，每個人都尖叫了。

sharp [ʃɑrp]

Track 0773

形 鋒利的、刺耳的、尖銳的、嚴厲的 同 blunt 嚴厲的

▶Her eyes are sharp for an old lady.
對一個老太太來說，她的眼睛超銳利的。

實用片語用語
have a sharp tongue 嘴巴很苛刻的
例 如：My brother has a sharp tongue and he always hurts me.
我哥哥的嘴很苛刻，我總是因為他說的話而傷心。

she [ʃi]

Track 0774

代 她

▶She is always talking to her sister and never looks at anyone else. 她總是在跟她姊姊講話，都不理別人。

sheep [ʃip]

Track 0775

名 羊、綿羊

▶I've never seen so many sheep at once before.
我從沒一次見過這麼多羊。

sheet [ʃit]

Track 0776

名 床單

▶This sheet is big enough to cover the bed.
這個床單鋪到這張床上夠大。

shine [ʃaɪn]

Track 0777

動 照耀、發光、發亮 名 光亮 同 glow 發光

▶動 The rain has stopped and the sun is shining; let's open the window and let in some air.
雨停後太陽照耀著，我們也打開窗來透透氣吧。

▶名 The old car has lost its shine.
那台舊車已經失去光亮了。

文法字詞解析
shine 的動詞變化有兩種，
解釋成「擦亮」時：shine, shined, shined
解釋成「發亮」時：shine, shone, shone

ship [ʃɪp]

Track 0778

名 大船、海船 同 boat 船

▶The ship is departing in fifteen minutes.
船十五分鐘之後就要開了。

文法字詞解析
ship 作為動詞則有「用船運送」的意思，例如：I'd like to ship this package to Japan. 我想把這個包裹用船運寄到日本。

shirt [ʃɜt]

Track 0779

名 襯衫

▶Which shirt would you like? This one or that one?
你要哪一件襯衫，這件還是那件？

shoe(s) [ʃu(z)]

Track 0780

名 鞋

▶There are too many shoes in this store; I don't even know which pair to buy.
這家店的鞋子太多了，我都不知道該買哪雙了。

文法字詞解析
除非是特別要講一隻鞋子，否則大部分的情況下是都用複數 shoes。

shop/store [ʃɑp]/[stor]

Track 0781

名 商店、店鋪

▶There's a new shop around the corner. 轉角有一家新開的店。

shore [ʃor]

Track 0782

名 岸、濱 同 bank 岸

▶They were walking along the shore and talking.
他們沿著海岸邊走邊聊。

實用片語用語
along the shore 沿著海岸

short [ʃɔrt]

Track 0783

形 矮的、短的、不足的 副 突然地 反 long 長的；遠的

▶形 This ruler is too short to measure the box; let's find another one. 這把尺太短了，量不了這個箱子的長度，我們再找另一把尺吧！

▶副 He stopped short when he saw that no one was following him. 他發現沒人跟著他時，就突然停了下來。

實用片語用語
stop short 突然停下

shot [ʃɑt]

Track 0784

名 子彈、射擊 同 bullet 子彈

▶He used only two shots to kill the bird.
他只用了兩顆子彈就殺死了那隻鳥。

shoul·der [ˋʃoldɚ]

Track 0785

名 肩、肩膀

▶My right shoulder hurts after work.
下班後我的右肩好痛。

shout [ʃaʊt]

Track 0786

動 呼喊、喊叫 名 叫喊、呼喊 同 yell 叫喊

▶動 I can hear you; there's no need to shout.
我聽得到啦，你沒有必要用喊的。

▶名 I heard a shout for help; someone must be in trouble.
我聽到了呼救聲，肯定有人遇上麻煩了。

實用片語用語
in trouble 陷入困境

show [ʃo]

Track 0787

動 出示、表明 名 展覽、表演 同 display 陳列、展出

▶動 Let me show you some pictures of my boyfriend.
我來給你展示一些我男朋友的照片。

▶名 I'm going to a stage show tomorrow.
我明天要去看劇場表演。

shut [ʃʌt]

Track 0788

動 關上、閉上

▶I wish she would shut her mouth sometimes.
我真希望她偶爾可以閉嘴。

文法字詞解析
shut 的動詞變化：shut, shut, shut

實用片語用語
shut down 結束營業
例如：The convenience store at the corner shut down a week ago. 街角那家便利商店一個禮拜前結束營業了。

shy [ʃaɪ]

Track 0789

形 害羞的、靦腆的 反 bold 大膽的

▶The little boy is too shy to speak in front of the whole class.
這個小男孩太害羞了，都不敢在全班人面前說話。

sick [sɪk]

Track 0790

形 有病的、患病的、想吐的、厭倦的

▶He was very sick all day and didn't wake up.
他整天都在生病，一直沒有起來。

實用片語用語
be sick of doing sth. 對……感到厭惡
例如：I'm sick of cleaning up your messes. 我受夠一直幫你收拾善後了。

side [saɪd]

Track 0791

名 邊、旁邊、側面 形 旁邊的、側面的 同 ill 生病的

▶名 Whose side are you on, mine or Jay's?
你站哪一邊，我這一邊還是阿傑這一邊？

▶形 Let's go through the side door; it's closer.
我們走側門好了，比較近。

sight [saɪt]

Track 0792

名 視力、情景、景象

▶It's almost love at first sight.
這簡直就是一見鍾情。

實用片語用語
fall in love at first sight 一見鍾情

sil·ly [ˋsɪlɪ]

Track 0793

形 傻的、愚蠢的 同 foolish 愚蠢的

▶My uncle gets really silly when he's drunk.
我叔叔一喝醉就變得很蠢。

sil·ver [ˋsɪlvɚ]

Track 0794

名 銀 形 銀色的

▶名 The necklace is made of silver. 這項鍊是銀製的。

▶形 The silver dress is very hard to wash. 這銀色洋裝好難洗。

sim·ple [ˋsɪmpl] Track 0795

形 簡單的、簡易的 反 complex 複雜的

▶This is a very simple story, but not everyone can understand it.
雖然這是一個非常簡單的故事，但是卻並非所有人都能聽懂。

實用片語用語
be simple to use 容易使用
例如：I bought a cell phone for my mom which is really simple to use. 我幫我媽媽買了一支容易操作的手機。

since [sɪns] Track 0796

副 從……以來 介 自從 連 從……以來、因為、既然

▶副 He went to Canada（加拿大）ten years ago and has stayed there ever since.
他十年前去了加拿大，從那時以來就一直待在那裡了。

▶介 I have lived here since September.
自九月份以來我一直住在這裡。

▶連 I can't go to your party since my sister is having a baby.
我無法去參加你的派對，因為我姊姊在生孩子。

實用片語用語
ever since = at all time since 從……以來要搭配現在完成式。

萬用延伸句型
since 用在現在完成式中：S. + have/has V p.p. since S. + Ved.

sing [sɪŋ] Track 0797

動 唱

▶She's always singing this same song.
她每次都唱這同一首歌。

文法字詞解析
sing 的動詞變化 sing, sang, sung

sing·er [ˋsɪŋɚ] Track 0798

名 歌唱家、歌手、唱歌的人

▶I like that popular singer's sweet voice very much.
我很喜歡那位流行歌手甜美的嗓音。

sir [sɝ] Track 0799

名 先生 反 madam 小姐

▶Would you like to order some wine with your meal（餐）, sir?
先生，您要不要叫些酒來配你的餐點呢？

sis·ter [ˋsɪstɚ] Track 0800

名 姐妹、姐、妹 反 brother 兄弟

▶Which one is your sister, the one on the left or the one on the right?
哪個是你姊姊，左邊的那個還是右邊的？

實用片語用語
on the left / right (hand side) 左／右手邊

sit [sɪt] Track 0801

動 坐 反 stand 站

▶Come sit down beside me.
來我旁邊坐嘛。

文法字詞解析
sit 的動詞變化 sit, sat, sat

實用片語用語
sit on / in a chair 坐在椅子上。介係詞用 on 時表示坐的是在硬挺的椅子，用 in 時則表示坐的是像沙發等柔軟、會陷進去的椅子。

six [sɪks] Track 0802

名 六

▶I slept about six hours last night.
我昨天晚上大概睡了六小時。

six·teen [sɪksˋtin] Track 0803

名 十六

▶My cat is already sixteen. Hard to believe, isn't it?
我的貓已經十六歲了呢，真難相信對不對？

six·ty [ˋsɪkstɪ]

Track 0804

名 六十

▶This room is big enough to hold sixty people at least, so please don't worry about it.
這個房間很大，絕對能夠容納下六十個人，因此請不要擔心。

實用片語用語
at least 至少

size [saɪz]

Track 0805

名 大小、尺寸

▶This pair of shoes comes in three different sizes.
這雙鞋有三種不同的尺寸。

skill [skɪl]

Track 0806

名 技能 同 capability 技能

▶His dancing skills are great. 他的舞蹈技巧很好。

skin [skɪn]

Track 0807

名 皮、皮膚

▶Staying under the sun too long is bad for your skin.
曬太陽太久對皮膚不好。

sky [skaɪ]

Track 0808

名 天、天空

▶There are a number of stars shining in the night sky.
夜空中群星閃爍。

sleep [slip]

Track 0809

動 睡 名 睡眠、睡眠期 反 wake 醒來

▶動 How long do you usually sleep every night?
你每晚大概睡多久？

▶名 How much sleep have you had? You look so tired.
你睡了多久啊？你看起來好累。

文法字詞解析
1. sleep 的動詞變化：sleep, slept, slept
2. 在第二個例句中，sleep 是名詞，所以用 How much 來詢問睡眠時間的多寡，如果換作使用動詞的 sleep，就可以說：How long have you slept?
要注意，疑問詞「how long」是問時間長短，要問距離的長短（遠近）則要用「how far」。

slow [slo]

Track 0810

形 慢的、緩慢的 副 慢 動 （使）慢下來 反 fast 快的

▶形 The slower train is cheaper. 比較慢的火車也比較便宜。

▶副 The girl runs slower than her sister.
那個女孩跑得比她妹妹慢。

▶動 Slow down please, the kids can't catch up.
請慢一點，孩子們跟不上了。

實用片語用語
slow down 慢下來、減速

small [smɔl]

Track 0811

形 小的、少的 反 large 大的

▶My sister looks very small by the side of her friend.
我妹妹和她朋友站在一起時顯得很矮小。

實用片語用語
by the side of 和……在一起比較

smart [smɑrt]

Track 0812

形 聰明的 同 intelligent 聰明的

▶His son is smart enough to solve these difficult mathematical （數學的）problems.
他兒子很聰明，能夠解答出這些數學難題。

實用片語用語
solve a problem 解決問題

smell [smɛl]
Track 0813

動 嗅、聞到 名 氣味、香味 同 scent 氣味、香味

▶動 I can't smell anything strange. 我沒聞到什麼奇怪的味道啊。

▶名 The smell of old shoes is horrible. 舊鞋子的氣味超糟糕的。

文法字詞解析
smell的動詞變化：smell, smelled, smelled 或smell, smelt, smeltt

smile [smaɪl]
Track 0814

動 微笑 名 微笑 反 frown 皺眉

▶動 Remember to smile even if you are tired.
就算累了也要記得微笑一下。

▶名 Why is there a smile on your face? Did something funny happen? 你臉上為什麼帶著微笑？有發生什麼好笑的事嗎？

萬用延伸句型
Did something (adj.) happen?
發生了什麼（……的）事嗎？

smoke [smok]
Track 0815

名 煙、煙塵 動 抽菸 同 fume 煙、氣

▶名 I see smoke. Is something on fire?
我看到煙耶，有什麼東西著火了嗎？

▶動 Would you like to tell me how you quit smoking?
你能告訴我你是如何戒菸的嗎？

實用片語用語
on fire 著火

snake [snek]
Track 0816

名 蛇

▶He was taken to the hospital（醫院）because of a snake bite.
他因為遭蛇咬而被送到醫院去了。

snow [sno]
Track 0817

名 雪 動 下雪

▶名 There was heavy snow fall in the afternoon.
今天下午有場大雪。

▶動 It is always snowing here in December.
這裡十二月老是下雪。

文法字詞解析
現在進行式 be 動詞後放頻率副詞 always 用來表示經常發生的事。

實用片語用語
heavy snow/ rain 大雪／雨

so [so]
Track 0818

副 這樣、如此地 連 所以

▶副 I am so glad that you came to see me. 很高興你來看我。

▶連 My colleague（同事）is ill today, so I have to go to the meeting alone.
我的同事今天生病了，所以我要一個人去開會了。

文法字詞解析
so 作為對等連接詞「所以」時，不可和 because 連用。

soap [sop]
Track 0819

名 肥皂

▶Do you wash your dishes with soap? 你用肥皂洗碗嗎？

so·da [ˋsodə]
Track 0820

名 汽水、蘇打

▶After drinking too much soda, I felt kind of sick.
喝了這麼多汽水，我感覺有點想吐。

實用片語用語
feel sick 想吐

so·fa [ˋsofə]
Track 0821

名 沙發 同 couch 沙發

▶The sofa my grandma bought is made of leather.
我奶奶買的沙發是皮製的。

soft [sɔft]

Track 0822

形 軟的、柔和的 反 hard 硬的

▶Her voice is very soft, like a cat walking across a piano.
她的聲音很柔和，有如貓走過鋼琴的聲音一般。

soil [sɔɪl]

Track 0823

名 土壤 動 弄髒、弄汙 同 dirt 泥、土

▶名 Let's rest the soil for a year. 我們讓土地休耕一年吧。

▶動 I soiled my hands repairing（修理）the machine.
我修理機器的時候弄髒了手。

文法字詞解析
for + 一段時間 表達「持續的一段時間裡」，要搭配完成式使用。

some [sʌm]

Track 0824

形 一些的、若干的 代 若干、一些 同 certain 某些、某幾個

▶形 Could you buy some books for me when you go downtown（市區）? 你去城裡的時候能幫我買些書回來嗎？

▶代 Some dogs are friendly, but some are scary.
有些狗很友善，但有些很可怕。

some·one [ˋsʌmˏwʌn]

Track 0825

代 一個人、某一個人 同 somebody 某一個人

▶There is someone sitting in my seat, so I have to find another one.
有人坐在我的座位上了，所以我不得不再找另外一個座位。

some·thing [ˋsʌmθɪŋ]

Track 0826

代 某物、某事

▶Is there something wrong? Your face is pale（蒼白的）
出了什麼事情嗎？你的臉色好蒼白耶。

some·times [ˋsʌmˏtaɪmz]

Track 0827

副 有時

▶I go to school by bus sometimes. 我有時候會搭公車去上學。

文法字詞解析
sometimes 是頻率副詞，表示動作發生的頻率多寡。
頻率副詞還有以下幾個（依頻繁程度由高至低）：usually（常常）, often（通常）, never（從不）。

son [sʌn]

Track 0828

名 兒子 反 daughter 女兒

▶My son is always playing basketball outside.
我的兒子總是在外面打籃球。

song [sɔŋ]

Track 0829

名 歌曲

▶What's this song called? I can't remember.
這首歌叫什麼？我不記得了。

文法字詞解析
此處用到被動語態 be +V p.p.。意思是「這首歌被稱做什麼」，但中文不會這樣使用。

soon [sun]

Track 0830

副 很快地、不久 同 shortly 不久

▶Get ready soon; your aunt will be here to pick you up in five minutes. 快點準備好，你阿姨過五分鐘要來接你了。

sorry [ˋsɔrɪ]

Track 0831

形 難過的、惋惜的、抱歉的 反 glad 開心的

▶I'm sorry for saying those words. 我很抱歉我說了那些話。

實用片語用語
sorry for / about N.；sorry to V.；sorry that + 子句 感到抱歉的、感到惋惜的

soul [sol] Track 0832

名 靈魂、心靈 反 body 身體

▶Food is good for the soul. 食物對心靈很有益處。

sound [saʊnd] Track 0833

名 聲音、聲響 動 發出聲音、聽起來像 同 voice 聲音

▶名 What's the strange sound coming from outside? Is it a ghost? 外面傳來的怪怪的聲音是什麼？是鬼嗎？

▶動 Your idea sounds good. Good job!
你的點子聽起來真不錯。幹得好！

萬用延伸句型
It sounds like + 子句 聽起來似乎……。
例如：It sounds like we have no choice but to do that. 聽起來我們好像不得不做那件事了。

soup [sup] Track 0834

名 湯 同 broth 湯

▶This soup is too bland（淡而無味的）. We should have ordered（點餐）another kind.
這湯喝起來好淡，早知道就點另一種了。

文法字詞解析
should have + p.p.
當時／原本應該……，表示過去應該做卻沒做的事。

sour [ˋsaʊr] Track 0835

形 酸的 動 變酸 名 酸的東西

▶形 This candy tastes really sour.
這糖吃起來好酸啊。

▶動 The milk will sour in warm weather.
牛奶在暖和的天氣會發酸。

▶名 I like the sweeter candies, and he likes the sour.
我喜歡甜的糖果，他喜歡酸的。

實用片語用語
(food) turn / go sour （食物）變酸

south [saʊθ] Track 0836

名 南、南方 形 南的、南方的 副 向南方、在南方 反 north 北方

▶名 There is a tall mountain in the south of Europe.
在歐洲的南部有座高山。

▶形 There is a pet shop on the south side of the street.
這條街的南邊有家寵物店。

▶副 The birds fly south for the winter.
鳥兒們南飛過冬。

space [spes] Track 0837

名 空間、太空 動 隔開、分隔

▶名 Give him some space. Talking to him now might make him angry.
給他一點空間吧，現在跟他講話他說不定會生氣。

▶動 You should space the chairs further from each other.
你應該把那些椅子隔開一點。

speak [spik] Track 0838

動 說話、講話 同 talk 講話

▶I can't speak Japanese at all. 我完全不會講日文。

文法字詞解析
speak 的動詞變化：speak, spoke, spoken

spe·cial [ˋspɛʃəl] Track 0839

形 專門的、特別的 反 usual 平常的

▶His accent is quite special.
他的口音非常特別。

speech [spitʃ] Track 0840

名 言談、說話

▶Not all the students will go to listen to his speech in the hall（大廳）. 並非所有的學生都會去大廳聽他的演講。

spell [spɛl] Track 0841

動 用字母拼、拼寫

▶How do you spell "tongue"（舌頭）?
「tongue」這個單字怎麼拼？

文法字詞解析
spell 的動詞變化：spell, spelled, spelled 或 spell, spelt, spelt

spend [spɛnd] Track 0842

動 花費、付錢 同 consume 花費

▶Where should we spend our holiday? How about Hong Kong（香港）? 我們該去哪裡度假呢？香港怎麼樣？

文法字詞解析
spend 的動詞變化 spend, spent, spent

spoon [spun] Track 0843

名 湯匙、調羹

▶There is a small spoon in the cup; you can use it to eat pudding（布丁）. 杯子裡有個小湯匙，你可以用來吃布丁。

實用片語用語
use sth. to do... 利用某物去做某事

sport [sport] Track 0844

名 運動 同 exercise 運動

▶Tennis is my favorite sport. 網球是我最喜歡的運動。

文法字詞解析
spring 的動詞變化 spring, sprang, sprung

spring [sprɪŋ] Track 0845

名 跳躍、彈回、春天 動 跳、躍、彈跳 同 jump 跳

▶名 Spring is when my allergies（過敏）gets the worst.
春天是我過敏最嚴重的時候。

▶動 The cat sprung onto the sink. 那隻貓跳到了洗手台上。

stair [stɛr] Track 0846

名 樓梯

▶Climbing the stairs is good for your health but not your knees.
爬樓梯對身體好，但對膝蓋不好。

stand [stænd] Track 0847

動 站起、立起 名 立場、觀點 反 sit 坐

▶動 Will Marie please stand up? 瑪麗，可以請妳站起來嗎？

▶名 His stand toward the matter has not changed.
他對這個問題的立場沒有改變。

文法字詞解析
stand 的動詞變化 stand, stood, stood
在第二個例句中，介係詞 toward 用在表達對某事的看法。

star [stɑr] Track 0848

名 星、恆星 形 著名的、卓越的 動 扮演主角

▶名 There are countless stars in the sky, just like many small but bright eyes.
天空中佈滿無數顆星星，就像很多明亮的小眼睛。

▶形 The star player on my team is very handsome.
我們球隊的明星選手很帥。

▶動 Audrey Hepburn starred in this film.
奧黛麗・赫本主演了這部電影。

實用片語用語
star in a film / show 在電影／表演中擔任主角

start [stɑrt]

Track 0849

名 開始、起點 動 開始、著手 同 begin 開始

▶名 We'd better make an early start to avoid（避開）the traffic.
我們最好早點出發以避開塞車。

▶動 Where should we start? Do you have a plan?
我們要從哪裡開始著手？你有計畫嗎？

實用片語用語
make a start on N. 開始著手做……

state [stet]

Track 0850

名 狀態、狀況、情形；州 動 陳述、說明、闡明
同 declare 聲明、表示

▶名 What's the state of affairs（事件）at the front?
前線情勢如何？

▶動 He stated his view at the meeting.
他在會議上陳述了他的觀點。

state·ment [ˋstetmənt]

Track 0851

名 陳述、聲明、宣佈

▶His statement is very confusing.
他的陳述很令人困惑。

sta·tion [ˋsteʃən]

Track 0852

名 車站

▶The train station is always full of people.
火車站總是滿滿多人。

實用片語用語
be full of 充滿

stay [ste]

Track 0853

名 逗留、停留 動 停留 同 remain 留下

▶名 I really enjoyed my stay here.
我真的很享受這次在這裡停留的經驗。

▶動 How long do you plan to stay here?
你打算在此停留多久

文法字詞解析
How long 有「多久、多長時間」的意思，使用時須注意要搭配stay, live 等含有「延續」含意的動詞。

step [stɛp]

Track 0854

名 腳步、步驟 動 踏 同 pace 步

▶名 I'll teach you how to do it step by step.
讓我一步一步教你做吧。

▶動 As soon as she stepped out of the room he walked in.
她一踏出房間，他就走了進來。

實用片語用語
step by step 一步一步、按部就班

萬用延伸句型
As soon as... 一……就……

still [stɪl]

Track 0855

形 無聲的、不動的 副 仍然

▶形 The nights here are so quiet and still.
這裡的夜晚總是安靜無聲。

▶副 I still think we should try again.
我還是覺得我們應該再試一次。

stone [ston]

Track 0856

名 石、石頭 同 rock 石頭

▶The little boy is throwing stones at birds.
那個小男孩一直拿石頭丟鳥。

stop [stɑp]

Track 0857

名 停止 動 停止、結束 同 halt 停止

▶名 I got off at the wrong stop this morning.
我今天早上下錯車站了。

▶動 The rain has already stopped. 雨已經停了。

文法字詞解析
stop 的動詞變化：stop, stopped, stopped

實用片語用語
get on / off + 交通工具 上／下（交通工具）

sto·ry [ˋstorɪ]

Track 0858

名 故事 同 tale 故事

▶The kids are always asking their mom to tell them stories.
那些孩子們總是在求他們的媽媽跟他們講故事。

strange [strendʒ]

Track 0859

形 陌生的、奇怪的、不熟悉的 反 familiar 熟悉的

▶It's strange enough to see a penguin（企鵝）appearing in our city. 居然在我們的城市看到了一隻企鵝，這真夠奇怪的。

street [strit]

Track 0860

名 街、街道

▶There is a very long street in this old town.
這個古鎮有條很長的街道。

strong [strɔŋ]

Track 0861

形 強壯的、強健的 副 健壯地 反 weak 虛弱的

▶形 He is a strong man; you don't need to worry about him.
他是個健壯的男人，不必為他擔心。

▶副 He is now well over sixty, but is still going strong.
他已經六十多歲了，可是還強壯得很。

實用片語用語
1. well over 流出、氾濫，在第二個例句中有「超過」之意。
2. go strong（身體）硬朗、（情況）良好

stu·dent [ˋstjudn̩t]

Track 0862

名 學生 反 teacher 老師

▶Not every student can understand what the teacher said in class. 並非每個學生都能明白老師在課堂上說過的話。

stud·y [ˋstʌdɪ]

Track 0863

名 學習 動 學習、研究

▶名 My dad devotes（奉獻）himself to the study of birds.
我的父親致力於研究鳥類。

▶動 I don't have time to study after work.
我工作完就沒空唸書了。

實用片語用語
devote oneself to... 致力於……
to 在這裡做介係詞使用。

stu·pid [ˋstjupɪd]

Track 0864

形 愚蠢的、笨的 反 wise 聰明的

▶This may sound like a stupid question, but he really doesn't understand it.
這個問題聽起來可能很愚蠢，但是他確實不明白。

文法字詞解析
助動詞 may 後面的動詞要改為原形動詞。

such [sʌtʃ]

Track 0865

形 這樣的、如此的 代 這樣的人或物

▶形 I felt like such a fool when I couldn't answer the question the teacher asked.
當我回答不出老師問的問題時，我感覺自己像個傻子。

實用片語用語
such as 例如、像是
例如：Please give me your contact information, such as your cell phone number and your email address.
請給我你的連絡方式，像是手機號碼跟電子信箱地址之類的。

▶代 He thought I wanted to make him angry, but such was not my intention（意圖）.
他以為我想惹他生氣，但那不是我的本意。

sug·ar [ˋʃugɚ] *Track 0866*

名 糖 反 salt 鹽

▶Why did you put sugar in the soup? It tastes strange now.
你怎麼把糖放到湯裡去了？味道變得好奇怪。

sum·mer [ˋsʌmɚ] *Track 0867*

名 夏天、夏季

▶What's the weather like in summer here? I know nothing about this place.
這裡的夏季天氣如何呢？我一點也不瞭解這個地方。

實用片語用語
know something / nothing about...
對……有所了解／完全不了解

sun [sʌn] *Track 0868*

名 太陽、日 動 曬

▶名 I like it when the sun is up.
我喜歡太陽掛在空中的日子。

▶動 My parents are outside sunning themselves.
我父母在外面曬太陽。

文法字詞解析
sun 的動詞變化 sun, sunned, sunned

Sun·day/Sun. [ˋsʌnde] *Track 0869*

名 星期日

▶Would you like to have a picnic on Sunday?
你想星期天去野餐嗎？

文法字詞解析
「星期」前方的介係詞必須用 on

su·per [ˋsupɚ] *Track 0870*

形 很棒的、超級的

▶Not everyone can be lucky enough to be a super star like her.
並非人人都能像她一樣，很幸運地成為一個超級巨星。

sup·per [ˋsʌpɚ] *Track 0871*

名 晚餐、晚飯 反 breakfast 早餐

▶I had a wonderful（極好的）supper yesterday. What about you? 昨天我吃了一頓很棒的晚飯，你呢？

文法字詞解析
「用餐」的「用」動詞要用 have。

sure [ʃur] *Track 0872*

形 一定的、確信的 副 確定 反 doubtful 懷疑的

▶形 I am sure he lied about this matter.
我確定他在這件事上撒了謊。

▶副 It sure is cold outside. Let's just stay at home today.
外面實在很冷。我們今天就待在家裡吧。

萬用延伸句型
在對話中，"Sure."可以表達「yes（好）」或是「you're welcome（不客氣）」的意思，例如："Do you want me to get you a drink?" "Sure. Please."「要我幫你拿點喝的嗎？」「好啊，麻煩了。」

sur·prise [sɚˋpraɪz] *Track 0873*

名 驚喜、詫異 動 使驚喜、使詫異 同 amaze 使大為驚奇

▶名 The surprise we prepared for her made her so happy.
我們為她準備的驚喜讓她好開心。

▶動 He surprised us all by bringing his wife.
他帶了太太來，把我們都嚇了一跳。

sweet [swit]

Track 0874

形 甜的、甜味的 名 糖果

▶形 The drink is too sweet. 這飲料太甜了。

▶名 I gave the little girl some sweets. 我給了小女孩一些糖果。

swim [swɪm]

Track 0875

動 游、游泳 名 游泳

▶動 Let's go swimming in the river.
我們一起去河裡游泳吧。

▶名 It has been hot for days. Let's go for a swim on Saturday.
天氣炎熱了好幾天了。我們週六去游泳吧。

文法字詞解析
swim 的動詞變化：swim, swam, swum

ta·ble [ˋtebl̩]

Track 0876

名 桌子 同 desk 桌子

▶There are many kinds of dishes and pastries（糕點）on the table. Just enjoy whatever（任何東西）you like.
桌子上有各式菜餚和糕點，喜歡什麼就吃什麼吧。

萬用延伸句型
There is / are... 可放在句首，指出「某地點有某物」。

tail [tel]

Track 0877

名 尾巴、尾部 動 尾隨、追蹤 反 head 率領

▶名 We are at the tail of the bus queue（長隊）.
我們在公車候車隊伍的末尾。

▶動 I tailed him all the way to this little bar（酒吧）.
我一路跟蹤他到這個小酒吧。

實用片語用語
all the way 一路、從頭到尾

take [tek]

Track 0878

動 抓住、拾起、量出、吸引

▶Can you take me to the train station?
你可以帶我去火車站嗎？

文法字詞解析
take 的動詞變化：take, took, taken

實用片語用語
take someone to somewhere 帶某人去某地

tale [tel]

Track 0879

名 故事 同 story 故事

▶All little girls love fairy（仙女）tales.
小女孩們都喜歡童話故事。

talk [tɔk]

Track 0880

名 談話、聊天 動 說話、對人講話 同 converse 談話

▶名 We made small talk as we waited for the bus.
我們邊等公車邊瞎聊。

▶動 I am too shy to talk to her.
我太害羞了，不敢跟她說話。

tall [tɔl]

Track 0881

形 高的 反 short 矮的

▶Not every girl is tall enough to become a stewardess（空姐）.
並不是每個女孩身高都足以成為空姐。

taste [test]
Track 0882

名 味覺 動 品嘗、辨味

▶名 This dish is not to my taste. 這道菜不合我的口味。

▶動 I haven't ever tasted something so strange before.
我從來沒嚐過這麼奇怪的東西。

實用片語用語
to one's taste 符合某人胃口／喜好

tax·i·cab/tax·i/cab
Track 0883

[ˋtæksɪˏkæb]/[ˋtæksɪ]/[kæb]

名 計程車

▶You're drunk. I'll call a taxi for you.
你醉了，我幫你叫台計程車吧。

tea [ti]
Track 0884

名 茶水、茶

▶Would you like a cup of tea, a glass of water or a cup of coffee?
你是想要一杯茶、一杯水還是一杯咖啡呢？

文法字詞解析
tea 是不可數名詞，前方可以加上單位量詞修飾。

teach [titʃ]
Track 0885

動 教、教書、教導

▶She teaches at night and works by day.
她晚上教書、白天工作。

文法字詞解析
teach 的動詞變化：teach, taught, taught

teach·er [ˋtitʃɚ]
Track 0886

名 教師、老師

▶All the teachers are in the office over there.
所有的老師都在那邊的辦公室裡。

tell [tɛl]
Track 0887

動 告訴、說明、分辨 同 inform 告知

▶Did you tell him about what happened?
你跟他講發生了什麼事了嗎？

文法字詞解析
tell 的動詞變化：tell, told, told

ten [tɛn]
Track 0888

名 十

▶There are still ten pictures left in my camera（照相機）after I deleted（刪除）most of the others.
我刪除了很多照片後，相機裡還有十張照片。

than [ðæn]
Track 0889

連 比 介 與……比較

▶連 I'd rather go by bus than by train.
比起搭火車我寧願搭公車。

▶介 She looks younger than I am, but she's actually a lot older.
她看起來比我年輕，但她的年紀其實大我很多。

實用片語用語
would rather...than...
寧願……也不要……

thank [θæŋk]
Track 0890

動 感謝、謝謝 名 表示感激

同 appreciate 感謝

▶動 I can't thank you enough. 我對您真是感激不盡。

▶名 I gave him a present as a token（象徵）of thanks.
我送了他一個禮物以表謝意。

that [ðæt]

Track 0891

形 那、那個 副 那麼、那樣

▶形 Is that book yours or is it Charlie's?
那本書是你的還是查理的？

▶副 She's not that bad! She just talks a lot.
她也沒那麼糟嘛！只是話有點多而已。

the [ðə]

Track 0892

冠 用於知道的人或物之前、指特定的人或物

▶The cake is really good. 這個蛋糕真是好吃。

their(s) [ðɛr(z)]

Track 0893

代 他們的（東西）、她們的（東西）、它們的（東西）

▶My class is generally friendly with each other, but theirs is a mess（混亂）.
我們班大致上都還算互相很友善，但他們班則是一片混亂。

文法字詞解析
each other 是代名詞，可以代表兩兩互相，如果是多人之間的互相，就用 one another。

them [ðɛm]

Track 0894

代 他們

▶Can you tell them about this for me?
你可以幫我跟他們講這件事嗎？

then [ðɛn]

Track 0895

副 當時、那時、然後

▶I walked into the room, then he came in too.
我走進房間，然後他也進來了。

there [ðɛr]

Track 0896

副 在那兒、往那兒 反 here 在這兒

▶The girl there is my sister. Pretty, right?
那裡的那個女孩是我妹妹。她很漂亮吧？

these [ðiz]

Track 0897

代 這些、這些的（this的複數） 反 those 那些

▶Would you like to help me wash up all these bowls and plates（盤子）? 你願意幫我洗洗這些碗和盤子嗎？

實用片語用語
do the washing-up 洗碗盤
例如：It's my turn to do the washing-up tonight. 今天輪到我洗碗盤了。

they [ðe]

Track 0898

代 他們

▶Have you heard that they got married secretly（秘密地）last month? 你聽說了嗎？他們上個月秘密地結婚了。

thing [θɪŋ]

Track 0899

名 東西、物體 同 object 物體

▶I like a lot of things but spiders are not one of them.
我喜歡的東西很多，但不包含蜘蛛在內。

think [θɪŋk]

Track 0900

動 想、思考 同 consider 考慮

▶Do you think she will get mad at me? 你想她會生我的氣嗎？

文法字詞解析
think 的動詞變化 think, thought, thought

third [θɝd] Track 0901

名 第三 形 第三的

▶形 There is an interval（間隔）between the third and fourth acts. 第三和第四幕之間有一次休息。

▶名 She came in third in the contest（競賽）and got a prize of 200 dollars. 她比賽得了第三名，有兩百元美元的獎金。

文法字詞解析
between（用於兩者）之間；among（用於三者以上）之間

thir·teen [ˋθɝtin] Track 0902

名 十三

▶This math problem seems to be too difficult to work out for a thirteen-year-old. 這道數學題對於一個十三歲的人來說太難了。

實用片語用語
work out 解決問題、計算

thir·ty [ˋθɝtɪ] Track 0903

名 三十

▶It's almost seven thirty! Let'a hurry up or we may miss our flight（航班）.
快七點半了，我們趕快吧，否則就可能錯過我們的航班了。

this [ðɪs] Track 0904

形 這、這個 代 這個 反 that 那個

▶形 Which hat do you like better? What about this light blue one?
你比較喜歡哪頂帽子呢？這個淺藍色的怎麼樣？

▶代 How about buying this? I think it's the most beautiful one.
買這個怎麼樣？我覺得這是最漂亮的一個了。

those [ðoz] Track 0905

代 那些、那些的（that的複數）

▶Would you like to help me put aside（在一邊）all those useless（沒用的）things?
你願意幫我把那些沒有用的東西全部放到一旁嗎？

實用片語用語
put aside sth. 將……放到一邊

though [ðo] Track 0906

副 但是、然而 連 雖然、儘管 同 nevertheless 雖然

▶副 It was a hard job; he took it though.
這是份苦差事，但他還是接受了。

▶連 He does not lead a happy life though he is rich.
他的生活並不開心，雖然他很有錢。

文法字詞解析
從屬連接詞 though /although 所引導的子句可以放在主要子句之前或之後，做副詞子句。

thought [θɔt] Track 0907

名 思考、思維

▶My first thought when I saw him was “what big ears”!
我見到他時，第一個想法是「他耳朵好大啊！」

thou·sand [ˋθaʊzn̩d] Track 0908

名 一千、多數、成千

▶There are thousands of people in this shopping center now.
這購物中心現在有上千人。

three [θri] Track 0909

名 三

▶Are you sure you can finish in three days? 你確定三天做得完？

文法字詞解析
這個句子是在詢問未來的情況，因此 in three days 表示「三天後」。

throw [θro]
Track 0910

動 投、擲、扔

▶I threw away all the clothes I don't wear.
我把我不穿的衣服全丟了。

文法字詞解析
throw 的動詞變化：throw, threw, thrown

Thurs·day/Thurs./Thur. [ˋθɝzde]
Track 0911

名 星期四

▶How about having dinner together on Thursday?
我們週四一起吃晚飯怎麼樣？

thus [ðʌs]
Track 0912

副 因此、所以 同 therefore 因此

▶She was not tall enough to be a model, thus she decided to become a fashion（時尚）designer（設計師）.
做模特兒，她個子不夠高，因此她決定成為一名時裝設計師。

tick·et [ˋtɪkɪt]
Track 0913

名 車票、入場券

▶Could you buy a movie ticket for me?
你能幫我買張電影票嗎？

tie [taɪ]
Track 0914

名 領帶、領結 動 打結

▶名 I don't know how to put on a tie.
我不知道怎麼打領帶。

▶動 I tied my shoelaces（鞋帶）just now but they've come apart（分開）again.
我才剛綁好了鞋帶，結果鞋帶又掉了。

文法字詞解析
tie 的動詞變化 tie, tied, tied

ti·ger [ˋtaɪgɚ]
Track 0915

名 老虎

▶The tiger in the zoo has gotten out of the cage（籠子）.
動物園的老虎跑出籠子了。

實用片語用語
get out of 離開

time [taɪm]
Track 0916

名 時間

▶How many times have you been there? 你去過那裡幾次了？

萬用延伸句型
How many times...? 詢問「做某事做了多少次」。

ti·ny [ˋtaɪnɪ]
Track 0917

形 極小的 反 giant 巨大的

▶Her eyes are tiny and cute. 她的眼睛又小又可愛。

tire [taɪr]
Track 0918

動 使疲倦 名 輪胎

▶動 Long walks tire me out easily.
走很長一段路很容易就會讓我很累。

▶名 We have a flat tire. Good thing we have a spare（備用的）.
我們爆胎了，幸好還有備用的。

文法字詞解析
tire 的動詞變化 tire, tired, tired

實用片語用語
It's a good thing that... 幸好……。第二句例句中，原始句子應該這樣寫：It's a good thing that we have a spare. 句中省略了 It's a 和關係代名詞 that。

to [tu] Track 0919

介 到、向、往

▶Are you going to the post office later? 你待會要去郵局嗎？

to·day [tə'de] Track 0920

名 今天 副 在今天、本日 反 tomorrow 明天

▶名 Today is Mother's birthday. 今天是媽媽的生日。

▶副 Let's go to visit the Williams today.
我們今天就去拜訪威廉斯一家吧。

to·geth·er [tə'gɛðɚ] Track 0921

副 在一起、緊密地 同 alone 單獨地

▶We always go to school together. 我們總是一起去上學。

實用片語用語
get together 聚集
例如：Let's get together and have dinner someday. 我們找個時間聚聚、吃個晚餐吧。

to·mor·row [tə'mɔro] Track 0922

名 明天 副 在明天

▶名 Tomorrow is my birthday. 明天是我生日。

▶副 How about going out for dinner tomorrow?
我們明天出去吃晚飯怎麼樣？

tone [ton] Track 0923

名 風格、音調

▶She is pretty much tone deaf（聾的）.
她是個完全的音痴。

實用片語用語
tone deaf 音痴

to·night [tə'naɪt] Track 0924

名 今天晚上 副 今晚

▶名 Tonight is John's birthday party.
今晚是約翰的生日派對。

▶副 Let's go out for a drink tonight.
今晚我們出去喝一杯吧。

too [tu] Track 0925

副 也

▶Where are you going? Can I come too?
你要去哪裡？我可以一起來嗎？

文法字詞解析
「too」和「either」都有「也」的意思，也都放在句尾，但「too」是放在肯定句句尾，「either」則是放在否定句句尾。

tool [tul] Track 0926

名 工具、用具 同 device 設備、儀器

▶I need some tools to fix the lamp with.
我需要一些工具來修這個燈。

top [tɑp] Track 0927

形 頂端的 名 頂端 動 勝過、高於 反 bottom 底部

▶形 There are 26 floors in that apartment（公寓）, and he lives on the top floor.
那座公寓有二十六層，而他住在頂樓。

▶名 There is a national（國家的）flag（旗幟）on top of the building. 在大樓的頂端有一面國旗。

▶動 I've seen a lot of strange things but nothing can top that.
我看過很多怪事，但沒什麼能比這個更怪了。

實用片語用語
on top of / at the top of 在……的頂端

to·tal [ˋtotḷ]

Track 0928

形 全部的 名 總數、全部 動 總計 同 entire 全部

▶形 His project ended in total failure. 他的計劃徹底失敗。

▶名 How long have you worked in that company（公司）in total? 你在那家公司一共工作多長時間了？

▶動 His spending last week totaled 100 dollars.
他上禮拜的花費總計一百美元。

實用片語用語
in total 總計

touch [tʌtʃ]

Track 0929

名 接觸、碰、觸摸 同 contact 接觸

▶Please keep in touch. 請保持聯絡。

to·ward(s) [təˋwɔrd(z)]

Track 0930

介 對……、向……、對於……

▶We walked together towards the department store.
我們一起走向百貨公司。

town [taʊn]

Track 0931

名 城鎮、鎮

▶Would you like to go to the town to do some shopping with your mother? 你想不想陪你媽媽到鎮上買些東西？

toy [tɔɪ]

Track 0932

名 玩具

▶How about giving our daughter a toy dog as her birthday gift?
送我們的女兒一隻玩具狗作為生日禮物怎麼樣？

文法字詞解析
as 介係詞在這裡的有「當作」之意。

train [tren]

Track 0933

名 火車 動 教育、訓練 同 educate 教育

▶名 How long does it take for you to go to London by train?
你坐火車去倫敦要多長時間？

▶動 She is training to become a nurse.
她在經過訓練成為一名護士。

實用片語用語
train to do something 接受……的訓練

tree [tri]

Track 0934

名 樹

▶Would you like me to climb up the tree and get the ball for you?
你要我爬到樹上幫你把球拿回來嗎？

trip [trɪp]

Track 0935

名 旅行 動 絆倒 同 journey 旅行

▶名 I'm taking a trip to Beijing tomorrow.
我明天要去北京旅行一趟。

▶動 I tripped on a tree root（根）and fell.
我被一個樹根絆倒了。

文法字詞解析
trip 的動詞變化：trip, tripped, tripped

trou·ble [ˋtrʌbḷ]

Track 0936

名 憂慮 動 使煩惱、折磨 同 disturb 使心神不寧

▶名 What's the trouble? You look really tired.
有什麼問題嗎？你看起來好累。

▶動 Don't trouble yourself over such stupid things.
別因這種蠢事煩惱了。

文法字詞解析
look 是感官動詞，屬於連綴動詞的一種，因此後方可直接接主詞補語。

true [tru]
Track 0937

形 真的、對的 反 false 假的、錯的

▶Is it true that Joey and Linda broke up?
喬依和琳達分手是真的嗎？

萬用延伸句型
Is it true that...？……是真的嗎？

try [traɪ]
Track 0938

名 試驗、嘗試 動 嘗試 同 attempt 企圖、嘗試

▶名 What's that new flavor? I'll have a try.
那個新口味是什麼？我來試試看吧。

▶動 I tried on ten dresses but none of them fit.
我試了十件洋裝，沒一件合身的。

文法字詞解析
try 的動詞變化：try, tried, tried

實用片語用語
try on + 衣服 試穿

T-shirt [ˋtiʃɝt]
Track 0939

名 T恤

▶I bought a T-shirt for my mother. 我幫我媽買了件T恤。

Tues·day/Tues./Tue. [ˋtjuzde]
Track 0940

名 星期二

▶I will be visiting Mr. Smith on Tuesday; do you want to come with me? 我星期二要去拜訪史密斯先生，跟我一起去怎麼樣？

文法字詞解析
例句中使用未來進行式，暗示「拜訪史密斯先生」是已經安排好要做的事情。

tum·my [ˋtʌmɪ]
Track 0941

名 （口語）肚子

▶Johnny, would you like the doctor to examine your tummy?
強尼，要不要醫生幫你檢查一下你的肚子？

turn [tɝn]
Track 0942

名 旋轉、轉動 動 旋轉、轉動 同 rotate 旋轉

▶名 Take a left turn and you'll reach my house.
左轉就到我家了。

▶動 Could you turn on the TV? It's time for the news.
打開電視好嗎？播新聞的時間到了。

實用片語用語
It's time for N / to V ……的時間到了。

twelve [twɛlv]
Track 0943

名 十二

▶How about buying a dozen（一打）of cups? You know we have twelve guests in all.
買一打茶杯怎麼樣？你知道我們一共有十二位客人。

實用片語用語
in all = in total 總共、總計

twen·ty [ˋtwɛntɪ]
Track 0944

名 二十

▶There are around twenty cows and ten bulls（公牛）on that farm. 那個農場裡大約有二十頭乳牛和十頭公牛。

twice [twaɪs]
Track 0945

副 兩次、兩倍

▶How often do you get a physical（身體的）examination? Twice a year? 你多久做一次身體檢查？一年做兩次嗎？

two [tu]
Track 0946

名 二

▶Two hours is too short for me to clean up the house.
兩個小時讓我打掃整個房子似乎太短了。

un·cle [ˋʌŋkḷ]
Track 0947

名 叔叔、伯伯、舅舅、姑父、姨父

▶When are you going to visit your uncle? How about this Saturday? 你打算什麼時候去看你叔叔啊？這週六如何？

萬用延伸句型
When are you going to...?
你打算什麼時候要……？

un·der [ˋʌndɚ]
Track 0948

介 小於、少於、低於 副 在下、在下面、往下面
反 over 在……上方

▶介 Let's sit under the tree for a while.
我們在樹下坐一下吧。

▶副 The submarine（潛水艇）went under an hour ago.
那艘潛水艇一小時前潛下去了。

un·der·stand [ˏʌndɚˋstænd]
Track 0949

動 瞭解、明白 同 comprehend 理解

▶I don't understand why you're always so angry.
我不懂你為什麼總是在生氣。

萬用延伸句型
I don't understand... 我不明白……
understand 後面可以依情況接 how / why / where 等疑問詞。

u·nit [ˋjunɪt]
Track 0950

名 單位、單元

▶The textbook has twelve units. 這個課本有十二個單元。

un·til/till [ənˋtɪl]/[tɪl]
Track 0951

連 直到……為止 介 直到……為止

▶連 I didn't know how long he had been waiting in the office until he called me.
直到他打電話給我的時候我才知道他在辦公室等了多久。

▶介 I'll wait for you until seven. If you're still not here, I'll leave.
我會等你到七點，如果你還沒來，我可要走了。

萬用延伸句型
Not until..., V + S... 直到……才……。
not until 置於句首時，主要子句要用倒裝句。例如：Not until now did he realize the importance of his wife. 直到現在他才意識到他妻子的重要性。

up [ʌp]
Track 0952

副 向上地 介 在高處、向（在）上面 反 down 向下地

▶副 It's too early for me to get up. Please let me sleep for a few more minutes. 現在起床還太早，請讓我再睡幾分鐘吧。

▶介 There's a little house up the hill.
山丘上有間小房子。

實用片語用語
get up 和 wake up 是同樣的意思，都是「起床」。

up·stairs [ˋʌpˏstɛrz]
Track 0953

副 往（在）樓上 形 樓上的 名 樓上

▶副 Can you go upstairs and get my bag for me?
你到樓上幫我拿包包好不好？

▶形 I like watching birds from the upstairs window.
我喜歡從樓上的窗戶賞鳥。

▶名 The house has no upstairs.
這房子沒有樓上（只有一層）。

us [ʌs] Track 0954

代 我們

▶Let's go and ask her if she could give us some help.
我們去問問她是否能給我們一些幫助。

文法字詞解析
在這個例句中，使用了 if 所引導的名詞子句做為受詞補語。

use [juz] Track 0955

動 使用、消耗 名 使用

▶動 I don't know how to use this machine.
我不知道如何使用這台機器。

▶名 This computer is for personal（個人的）use only.
這台電腦只供個人使用。

文法字詞解析
在第一個例句中，使用了含疑問詞 how 的間接問句。原本的句子應該是：I don't know how I can use this machine. 此句將主詞和情狀助動詞 I can 用 to 代替。

use·ful [ˋjusfəl] Track 0956

形 有用的、有益的、有幫助的

▶These tools are not very useful.
這些工具不是很有用。

veg·e·ta·ble [ˋvɛdʒətəbḷ] Track 0957

名 蔬菜 反 meat 肉類

▶Would you like to go to the market to buy some vegetables with me? 想不想跟我去市場買些蔬菜？

文法字詞解析
vegetable 是可數名詞，因此在泛指蔬菜時要用複數 vegetables。

ver·y [ˋvɛrɪ] Track 0958

副 很、非常

▶She's a very tall girl.
她是個很高的女孩。

view [vju] Track 0959

名 看見、景觀 動 觀看、視察 同 sight 看見、景象

▶名 The view from this window is great.
從這窗戶看出去的景觀超棒的。

▶動 I view him as my friend and enemy（敵人）.
我把他視為我的朋友與敵人。

vis·it [ˋvɪzɪt] Track 0960

動 訪問 名 訪問

▶動 Let's go visit the new neighbor（鄰居）this afternoon.
我們今天下午去拜訪新鄰居吧。

▶名 Let's pay a visit to our former（以前的）English teacher this weekend.
我們這週末去拜訪以前的英語老師吧。

實用片語用語
pay a visit to sb. / pay sb. a visit 拜訪某人

voice [vɔɪs]

Track 0961

名 聲音、發言

▶The singer has a lovely voice.
那名歌手有很甜美的聲音。

wait [wet]

Track 0962

動 等待 名 等待、等待的時間

▶動 I've been waiting for two hours and the bus still won't come.
我等了兩小時公車還不來。

▶名 It'll be a long wait; you can sleep a little.
要等很久，你可以睡一下。

walk [wɔk]

Track 0963

動 走、步行 名 步行、走、散步

▶動 How long will it take for you to walk home?
你走回家要多長時間？

▶名 Let's take a walk after dinner.
我們吃完晚餐來散個步吧。

實用片語用語
take a walk 散步

wall [wɔl]

Track 0964

名 牆壁

▶There are lots of posters（海報）on my wall.
我牆上有很多海報。

want [wɑnt]

Track 0965

動 想要、要 名 需要 同 desire 想要

▶動 I want to go abroad when I grow up.
我長大後想出國。

▶名 Our company（公司）is in want of an engineer（工程師）.
我們公司需要一名工程師。

實用片語用語
be in want of 需要
be in want of 和 need 是同樣的意思。

war [wɔr]

Track 0966

名 戰爭 反 peace 和平

▶His grandfather never stops talking about the war.
他爺爺總是在講戰爭的事。

warm [wɔrm]

Track 0967

形 暖和的、溫暖的 動 使暖和

▶形 This jacket is warmer than it looks. 這外套比看起來更暖。

▶動 They warmed themselves by the fire. 他們在火旁邊取暖。

wash [wɑʃ]

Track 0968

動 洗、洗滌 名 洗、沖洗 同 clean 弄乾淨

▶動 Wash your hands before you eat. 吃東西前請先洗手。

▶名 This car really needs a wash. 這車真的需要洗了。

實用片語用語
wash up 也有洗手的意思。因此第一個例句也可以這樣寫：Wash up before you eat.

waste [west] Track 0969

動 浪費、濫用 名 浪費 形 廢棄的、無用的 反 save 節省

▶動 He wasted too much money when he was young.
他年輕的時候浪費了太多的錢。

▶名 That meeting was a waste of time.
那次開會真是浪費時間啊。

▶形 The waste products（產品）are taken away by the garbage truck. 那些廢棄產品被垃圾車帶走了。

watch [wɑtʃ] Track 0970

動 注視、觀看、注意 名 手錶 反 ignore 忽略

▶動 Do you like watching baseball games?
你喜歡看棒球賽嗎？

▶名 There is a watch on the bench. Who left it here?
長椅上有支錶，會是誰丟在那裡的呢？

萬用延伸句型
watch out! 小心！

wa·ter [ˋwɔtɚ] Track 0971

名 水 動 澆水、灑水

▶名 Drink lots of water to stay healthy. 要多喝點水，才會健康。

▶動 Can you water my flowers for me when I'm gone?
我不在的時候你可以幫我的花澆水嗎？

way [we] Track 0972

名 路、道路

▶Can you show me the way to the zoo?
你可以告訴我走哪條路去動物園嗎？

實用片語用語
on the way 在路上、在途中
例如：I'm on the way to the zoo.
我正在去動物園的路上。

we [wi] Track 0973

代 我們

▶We'll be arriving at around ten. 我們大概十點會到。

weak [wik] Track 0974

形 無力的、虛弱的 同 feeble 虛弱的

▶Is she sick? Why does she sound so weak?
她生病了嗎？怎麼聽起來這麼虛弱？

wear [wɛr] Track 0975

動 穿、戴、耐久

▶She looks very beautiful when she wears this blue skirt（裙子）. 她穿這件藍裙子的時候看起來很漂亮。

文法字詞解析
wear 的動詞變化：wear, wore, worn

weath·er [ˋwɛðɚ] Track 0976

名 天氣

▶If you don't know what to say, you can just talk about the weather. 不知道說什麼的話，那就聊天氣吧。

wed·ding [ˋwɛdɪŋ] Track 0977

名 婚禮、結婚 同 marriage 婚禮、結婚

▶Would you like to come to our wedding?
你願意來參加我們的婚禮嗎？

Wedne·sday/Wed./Weds. [ˋwɛnzde]

Track 0978

名 星期三

▶Can you finish your work by Wednesday?
你星期三前可以完成工作嗎？

文法字詞解析
在這個例句中，by 有「在……之前、不遲於」的意思。

week [wik]

Track 0979

名 星期、工作日

▶How many times do you play tennis（網球）per week?
你一星期打幾次網球啊？

week·end [ˋwikˏɛnd]

Track 0980

名 週末（星期六和星期日）

▶What are you going to do this weekend?
這個週末你打算怎麼過？

weigh [we]

Track 0981

動 稱重

▶He weighs sixty kilos. 他有六十公斤重。

實用片語用語
weigh oneself 量體重
例如：You'd better face the truth. Go weigh yourself. 你還是面對現實吧，去量體重。

weight [wet]

Track 0982

名 重、重量

▶Why do you want to lose weight? You're thin enough as it is.
你為什麼想減重？你已經夠瘦了啊。

實用片語用語
as it is 照現在這樣子

wel·come [ˋwɛlkəm]

Track 0983

動 歡迎 名 親切的接待 形 受歡迎的 感（親切的招呼）歡迎

▶動 Let's welcome the most popular（受歡迎的）movie star in our country. 讓我們一起歡迎全國最受歡迎的電影明星。

▶名 Let's give the professor（教授）a warm welcome.
讓我們熱烈歡迎教授。

▶形 You're always welcome here at our home.
隨時歡迎你來我們家。

▶感 Welcome! I hope you enjoy our party.
歡迎！希望你很享受這次派對。

實用片語用語
give sb. a warm welcome 給予某人熱烈歡迎

well [wɛl]

Track 0984

形 健康的 副 好、令人滿意地 反 badly 壞、拙劣地

▶形 I am not well today, so it's too hard for me to concentrate（專心於）on my work.
我今天不舒服，因此難以集中精神工作。

▶副 I know this city well enough, so it's too easy for me to find the place. 我很瞭解這個城市，因此對我來說要找到這個地方太容易了。

west [wɛst]

Track 0985

名 西方 形 西部的、西方的 副 向西方 反 east 東方

▶名 Do you know which country lies to the west of Egypt?
你知道埃及以西是哪個國家嗎？

▶形 The west wind is too strong for the ship to sail.
西風刮得太猛了，那艘船都沒辦法航行了。

文法字詞解析
whether 也可用 if 代替，若用 if 時，字尾的 or not 可以省略。

實用片語用語
A lies to the（方向）of B A 位於 B 的某個方向

▶副 I can't tell whether I am driving west or not.
我不會判斷我到底是不是在向西行駛。

what [hwɑt]
Track 0986

形 什麼 代（疑問代詞）什麼

▶形 What day is today? 今天星期幾？

▶代 I can't hear what he said. 我聽不到他說什麼。

when [hwɛn]
Track 0987

副 什麼時候、何時 連 當……時 代（關係代詞）那時

▶副 Not all the people know when to work hard and when to have a good rest.
並非所有的人都知道何時該努力工作，何時該好好休息。

▶連 I'll call you when I get there. 當我到那裡時會打給你。

▶代 Since when has he lived here?
他從什麼時候開始住這裡的？

萬用延伸句型
Since when...? 從什麼時候開始……？
使用這個句型的話，後面要接現在完成式。

where [hwɛr]
Track 0988

副 在哪裡 代 在哪裡 名 地點

▶副 Where did you park the car? 你把車停在哪？

▶代 Few people know where the man comes from.
很少有人知道這個男子來自哪裡。

▶名 I've been to where he's talking about.
我去過他在講的那個地方。

文法字詞解析
「few」是「很少、幾乎沒有」的意思，「a few」卻是「有一些、有幾個」的意思，兩者並不一樣，使用時要注意。

wheth·er [ˋhwɛðɚ]
Track 0989

連 是否、無論如何 同 if 是否

▶I don't know whether he's gone yet.
我不知道他走了沒。

which [hwɪtʃ]
Track 0990

形 哪一個 代 哪一個

▶形 Not every student knows which university（大學）he or she should enter.
不是每個學生都知道他（她）要上哪個大學。

▶代 Blue? White? Which color looks better?
藍色？白色？哪個顏色比較好看？

while [hwaɪl]
Track 0991

名 時間 連 當……的時候、另一方面

▶名 I haven't seen him for a long while.
我已經很久沒見到他了。

▶連 I never visited her while she was here.
她在這裡的時候，我都沒去拜訪她。

white [hwaɪt]
Track 0992

形 白色的 名 白色 反 black 黑色

▶形 The white car over there is mine.
那邊那輛白色的車是我的。

▶名 I don't look good when wearing white.
我穿白色不好看。

實用片語用語
wear + 顏色 穿……顏色的衣服

who [hu]
Track 0993

代 誰

▶Who's the lady in red? 穿紅色的那位小姐是誰？

whole [hol]
Track 0994

形 全部的、整個的 名 全體、整體 反 partial 部分的

▶形 I ate the whole bag of potato chips（洋芋片）.
我吃了整包的洋芋片。

▶名 What do you think about the plan as a whole?
你對這個計畫整體而言感覺如何？

實用片語用語
as a whole 整體看起來

whom [hum]
Track 0995

代 誰

▶That is the man whom they were talking about.
這就是他們一直在談論的那個男人。

萬用延伸句型
To whom it may concern,... 敬啟者。常用在書信的開頭，如果收信人是不特定或不確定的人，就可以用這種說法。

whose [huz]
Track 0996

代 誰的

▶Whose cup is this? 這杯子是誰的？

why [hwaɪ]
Track 0997

副 為什麼

▶Why were you late yesterday? 你昨天怎麼遲到了？

wide [waɪd]
Track 0998

形 寬廣的 副 寬廣地 同 broad 寬的、闊的

▶形 The road is wide enough to let four cars run on it at the same time. 這條路夠寬，能允許四輛車同時在上面行駛。

▶副 I've travelled far and wide but there's no place I like as much as home.
我到處旅遊過，但沒有一個地方比家鄉更讓我喜愛。

實用片語用語
far and wide 到處、四面八方

wife [waɪf]
Track 0999

名 妻子 反 husband 丈夫

▶His wife is very pretty and a good cook.
他太太又漂亮又會煮菜。

will [wɪl]
Track 1000

名 意志、意志力 助動 將、會

▶名 You shouldn't force people to do things against their will.
你不該要人家做違背他們意志的事啊。

▶助動 Will you be at the meeting tomorrow?
你明天會去開會嗎？

win [wɪn]
Track 1001

動 獲勝、贏 反 lose 輸

▶Did the team you like win? 你喜歡的那隊有贏嗎？

文法字詞解析
win 的動詞變化：win, won, won

wind [wɪnd]
Track 1002

名 風 同 breeze 微風

▶The wind is so strong today. 今天風好強喔。

win·dow ['wɪndo]
Track 1003

名 窗戶

▶Help me shut the windows before it starts raining.
在下雨前幫我把窗戶關好吧。

文法字詞解析
help sb. (to) do sth. 幫某人做某事

wine [waɪn]
Track 1004

名 葡萄酒

▶I like to have some red wine at supper every day.
我每天晚飯的時候都愛喝點紅酒。

win·ter ['wɪntɚ]
Track 1005

名 冬季 反 summer 夏天

▶I don't like winters because I'm afraid of the cold.
我不喜歡冬天，因為我怕冷。

wish [wɪʃ]
Track 1006

動 願望、希望 名 願望、希望

▶動 I wish I could travel（旅行）to space one day.
我希望有一天我能遨遊太空。

▶名 It's your birthday! Make a wish!
今天是你的生日！許個願吧！

文法字詞解析
I wish(that)... / I hope(that)... 我希望……。雖然「wish」和「hope」在中文都有「希望」的意思，但兩者後面接子句的用法卻不同。wish 多半接的是不太可能成真，無法改變、與事實相反的事情，而「hope」後面則會接可能發生的事，因此 wish 後常接假設語氣，hope 則接現在式、未來式、完成式等一般時態。

with [wɪð]
Track 1007

介 具有、帶有、和……一起、用 反 without 沒有

▶She already went out with her mom.
她已經跟她媽媽一起出去了。

wom·an ['wʊmən]
Track 1008

名 成年女人、婦女 反 man 成年男人

▶The woman is looking for her son. 那個女人在找她的兒子。

wood(s) [wʊd(z)]
Track 1009

名 木材、樹林

▶The boys got lost in the woods. 那些男孩在樹林裡迷路了。

實用片語用語
in the woods 在森林裡

word [wɝd]
Track 1010

名 字、單字、話

▶How many words are there in this article（文章）?
這篇文章有幾個字？

work [wɝk]
Track 1011

名 工作、勞動 動 操作、工作、做 同 labor 工作、勞動

▶名 How long will it take for you to finish this work, Mike?
邁克，你完成這項工作需要多長時間？

▶動 I can't work out this difficult problem. 我解不了這道難題。

文法字詞解析
work 的動詞變化 work, worked, worked

work·er ['wɝkɚ]
Track 1012

名 工作者、工人

▶We don't have enough skilled workers to finish this project（工程）. 我們沒有足夠有經驗的工人來完成這項工程。

world [wɝld]

Track 1013

名 地球、世界

▶Who's your favorite singer in the world?
你全世界最喜歡的歌手是誰？

實用片語用語
in the world 在世界上、全世界。可以用來強調形容詞最高級。

worm [wɝm]

Track 1014

名 蚯蚓或其他類似的小蟲 動 蠕行 同 crawl 蠕行

▶名 The early bird catches the worm. 早起的鳥兒有蟲吃。

▶動 The children wormed their way over to us through the crowd（人群）. 孩子們緩慢地從人群中擠到我們身旁。

實用片語用語
worm (one's way) through something
緩慢的移動、前進

wor·ry [ˋwɝɪ]

Track 1015

名 憂慮、擔心 動 煩惱、擔心、發愁

▶名 The little girl has no worry in her life.
這個小女孩人生中完全無憂無慮。

▶動 I can't help worrying about the old man's health.
我忍不住為這名老人的健康擔憂。

萬用延伸句型
can't help V-ing 忍不住……

worse [wɝs]

Track 1016

形 更壞的、更差的 副 更壞、更糟 名 更壞的事 反 better 更好的

▶形 I'm bad at math, but he's even worse.
我數學很爛，但他還比我更差。

▶副 His illness（病況）keeps getting worse.
他的病況越來越惡化了。

▶名 That's not really bad. I've seen worse.
那不算太糟啦，我還看過更糟的。

worst [wɝst]

Track 1017

形 最壞的、最差的 副 最差地、最壞地
名 最壞的情況（結果、行為） 反 best 最好的

▶形 It was said to be the worst storm（暴風雨）in years.
這場暴風雨據說是幾年來最厲害的一次。

▶副 He did the worst out of us all. 他是我們之中做得最差的。

▶名 Hope for the best, but prepare for the worst.
抱最好的願望，作最壞的準備。

實用片語用語
in years 幾年來

文法字詞解析
1.「in + 時間」代表的是「在（一段時間）內……」可和過去式或未來式連用。
2. out of 從數個之中

write [raɪt]

Track 1018

動 書寫、寫下、寫字

▶Can you write your name here? 你可以把名字寫在這裡嗎？

文法字詞解析
write 的動詞變化：write, wrote, written

實用片語用語
write down 寫下
例如：Please write down your name on your answer sheet.
請在你的答案卷上寫下你的名字。

writ·er [ˋraɪtɚ]

Track 1019

名 作者、作家 同 author 作者

▶Not all people know this writer, though they know his books well.
儘管大家都聽過這位作家的書，卻不一定知道作者本人是誰。

wrong [rɔŋ]

Track 1020

形 壞的、錯的 副 錯誤地、不適當地 名 錯誤、壞事
同 false 錯的

▶形 Something is wrong with my watch. 我的手錶怪怪的。

▶副 He guessed wrong three times in a row.
他一連猜錯了三次。

▶名 Lots of people can't tell right from wrong.
很多人不會分辨善惡。

實用片語用語
分辨善惡 tell right from wrong

yam/sweet po·ta·to
Track 1021

[jæm]/[swit pə`teto]

名 山藥、甘薯

▶My grandma loves eating yam all day. 我奶奶最愛整天吃蕃薯。

文法字詞解析
love、like、hate 後面的動詞可以接 to V. 或是 V-ing。

year [jɪr]
Track 1022

名 年、年歲

▶How many times have you been to the movies this year?
你今年去了電影院幾次？

萬用延伸句型
How many times... ?
用於詢問次數時。

yel·low [`jɛlo]
Track 1023

形 黃色的 名 黃色

▶形 The yellow dress suits you better. 黃色那件洋裝比較適合妳。

▶名 How long will it take for you to paint all the walls yellow?
你把所有的牆壁都粉刷成黃色的話要花多長時間？

yes/yeah [jɛs]/[jɛə]
Track 1024

副 是的 名 是、好

▶副 Yes, not all people I met like to talk about the weather.
是的，不是我遇到的所有人都喜歡談論天氣。

▶名 Can I go with you? Please say yes!
我可以跟你去嗎？說好嘛！

yes·ter·day [`jɛstəde]
Track 1025

名 昨天、昨日

▶Where were you yesterday? I couldn't find you anywhere.
你昨天去哪了？我到哪都找不到你。

yet [jɛt]
Track 1026

副 直到此時、還（沒） 連 但是、而又 反 already 已經

▶副 It's already ten but he hasn't come home yet.
已經十點了，他還沒回家。

▶連 He tried hard, yet he couldn't succeed（成功）.
他努力試過，但沒有成功。

文法字詞解析
yet 作為時間副詞時，通常用在否定句和疑問句的句尾。

you [ju]
Track 1027

代 你、你們

▶Are you all right? 你還好嗎？

young [jʌŋ]
Track 1028

形 年輕的、年幼的 名 青年 反 old 老的

▶形 Those young men are really good at dancing.
那些年輕人很會跳舞。

▶名 The adult animals take good care of their young.
那些成年動物都將幼獸照顧得很好。

實用片語用語
take care of sth. 照顧

---

your(s) [jʊr(z)]

Track 1029

形 你的（東西）、你們的（東西）

▶It's your turn to clean the classroom after school.
放學後輪到你們打掃教室了。

實用片語用語
It's sb.'s turn 輪到某人（的順序）

---

yuck·y [jʌkɪ]

Track 1030

形 令人厭惡的、令人不快的

▶The food in that restaurant is yucky. 那家餐廳的食物很難吃。

---

yum·my [ˋjʌmɪ]

Track 1031

形 舒適的、愉快的、美味的

▶Where did you buy this cake? It's so yummy!
你這蛋糕是在哪裡買的啊？真好吃！

ze·ro [ˋzɪro]

Track 1032

名 零

▶I can count from zero to ten in Japanese.
我會用日文從零數到十。

文法字詞解析
「in + 語言」是固定用法，表示「使用某種語言」。

---

zoo [zu]

Track 1033

名 動物園

▶There are a great many kinds of animals in the zoo.
動物園裡有很多種動物。

NOTE

A B C D E F G H I J K L M N O P Q R S T U V W X Y Z

基礎英文能力——
邁向 2200 單字

學英文從單字開始，
許自己一個不可思議的滿分奇蹟！

Level 2 基礎英文能力——邁向2200單字

a·bil·i·ty [ə`bɪlətɪ]
Track 1034

名 能力 同 capacity 能力

▶His ability to speak in Japanese is not very good.
他的日文口說能力並不是很好。

實用片語用語
ability to do something 做……的能力

a·broad [ə`brɔd]
Track 1035

副 在國外、到國外 同 overseas 在國外

▶It won't be too long before I come back from abroad.
沒多久之後我就會從國外回來的。

ab·sence [`æbsn̩s]
Track 1036

名 缺席、缺乏 反 presence 出席

▶Would you please tell me the real reason of your absence from the meeting? 您能告訴我您沒能參與會議的真正原因嗎？

ab·sent [`æbsn̩t]
Track 1037

形 缺席的

▶He is always absent on Thursdays. 他每星期四都會缺席。

文法字詞解析
星期的前面必須加介係詞 on

ac·cept [ək`sɛpt]
Track 1038

動 接受 反 refuse 拒絕

▶The manager（經理）accepted my suggestion as soon as I proposed（提出）it at the meeting.
在會議上我一提出建議，經理就馬上接受了。

萬用延伸句型
As soon as S + V, S + V. 一……就……。
這個句型用於表達幾乎同時發生的兩個動作，如果是說明過去發生的事，則從屬連接詞片語 As soon as 所引導的副詞子句和主要子句都用過去式，如果是要說明未來發生的事，As soon as 所引導的副詞子句要用現在式，主要子句則要用未來式。

ac·tive [`æktɪv]
Track 1039

形 活躍的 同 dynamic 充滿活力的

▶She is always very active at school. 她在學校總是很活躍。

實用片語用語
at school 在學校、在上課

ad·dition [ə`dɪʃən]
Track 1040

名 加、加法 同 supplement 增補

▶In addition to being strong, he is also handsome.
他不但強壯，而且還很帥。

實用片語用語
in addition to 除此之外

文法字詞解析
副詞 in addition 和介係詞 in addition to 意思相同，但兩者的用法不同。In addition 放句首時，後面必須加上逗號，再接主詞、動詞組成的完整句；in addition to 則是直接加上名詞或動名詞。

ad·vance [əd`væns]
Track 1041

名 前進 動 使前進 同 progress 前進

▶名 It'd be great if you could finish the work in advance.
你能提前完成工作的話就太好了。

▶動 It is no wonder that he has soon advanced to the manager（經理）position. He is born to be a leader.
怪不得不久他就被提升為經理。他有當領導者的天賦。

萬用延伸句型
(It is) no wonder... 難怪……

af·fair [əˋfɛr] Track 1042

名 事件 同 matter 事件

▶What do you think of the love affair between the president（總統）and his secretary（秘書）?
你覺得總統和他秘書之間的戀愛事件如何？

aid [ed] Track 1043

名 援助 動 援助

▶名 It doesn't matter whether he offers aid to me or not.
他要不要幫我的忙，對我來說沒有影響。

▶動 Can you aid me in doing this job?
你可以幫我處理這個工作嗎？

實用片語用語
aid sb. in / with (doing) sth. 幫忙某人做某事

aim [em] Track 1044

名 瞄準、目標 動 企圖、瞄準 同 target 目標

▶名 Our aim is to become the number one company in this field.
我們的目標是成為此領域第一名的公司。

▶動 We aim to become the best team ever.
我們的目標是成為史上最棒的團隊。

實用片語用語
aim to do sth. 旨在……、以……作為目標

air·craft [ˋɛr͵kræft] Track 1045

名 飛機、飛行器 同 jet 噴射飛機

▶I learnt from the newspaper that the aircraft crashed（墜毀）as soon as it took off.
我從報紙上獲悉，那架飛機剛一起飛就墜毀了。

實用片語用語
learn (sth.) from sb./ sth. 從……上知道

air·line [ˋɛr͵laɪn] Track 1046

名（飛機）航線、航空公司

▶Which airline are you booking for your trip next month?
你下個月的旅行要訂哪一家航空公司的班機？

a·larm [əˋlɑrm] Track 1047

名 恐懼、警報器 動 使驚慌

▶名 Why is the alarm ringing? Is there a fire?
警報器怎麼響了呢？火災了嗎？

▶動 I don't want to alarm you, but there's a bee on your head.
我不是要使你驚慌喔，可是你頭上有一隻蜜蜂。

文法字詞解析
fire 若是指具體的「一場」火災時，是可數名詞，如果是講抽象的概念，就是不可數名詞。

al·bum [ˋælbəm] Track 1048

名 相簿、專輯

▶Would you please buy me Mayday's new album?
你能買五月天的新專輯給我嗎？

實用片語用語
buy sb. sth. / buy sth. for sb. 買某物給某人

a·like [əˋlaɪk] Track 1049

形 相似的、相同的 副 相似地、相同地 反 different 不一樣的

▶形 No wonder that they look so alike—they are twins!
怪不得他們長那麼像，原來他們是雙胞胎。

▶副 They talk alike and even think alike.
他們說話很像、連想法都很像。

文法字詞解析
副詞 even（甚至）應放在被修飾語的前方，否則會改變強調的事物，造成語意的不同。

A B C D E F G H I J K L M N O P Q R S T U V W X Y Z

a·live [ə`laɪv] Track 1050

形 活的 反 dead 死的

▶I'm surprised I'm still alive. 我居然還活著，我自己都很驚訝。

al·mond [`ɑmənd] Track 1051

名 杏仁、杏樹

▶Can you make some almond cakes for the guests?
你可以做些杏仁餅來招待客人嗎？

a·loud [ə`laʊd] Track 1052

副 高聲地、大聲地

▶She told the student to read the book aloud.
她要那名學生大聲地把書唸出來。

實用片語用語
read sth. aloud = read sth. out aloud
大聲唸出……

al·pha·bet [`ælfə͵bɛt] Track 1053

名 字母、字母表

▶How long did it take for you to remember the English alphabet?
你花了多長時間背誦英語字母表？

al·though [ɔl`ðo] Track 1054

連 雖然、縱然 同 though 雖然

▶Although she's tall, she actually weighs quite little.
她雖然高，但其實體重很輕。

文法字詞解析
表達「雖然……，但是……」時，不可用「Although S +V, but S + V」的句型，因為 Although 和 but 都屬於連接詞。

al·to·geth·er [͵ɔltə`gɛðɚ] Track 1055

副 完全地、總共 反 partly 部分地

▶I counted; there were a hundred tickets altogether.
我算過了，共有一百張票。

a·mount [ə`maʊnt] Track 1056

名 總數、合計 動 總計 同 sum 總計

▶名 The amount of water has been increasing. 水量一直在增加。

▶動 The total cost of repairs amounts to US$100.
修理費用總計要一百美元。

實用片語用語
amount to sth. 總計為

an·cient [`enʃənt] Track 1057

形 古老的、古代的 同 antique 古老的

▶It took three months for the scientists to finish excavating（挖掘）the ancient tomb（墳墓）.
科學家們花了三個月的時間才挖掘完那個古墓。

文法字詞解析
finish 後面如果要加動詞，必須得用 V-ing 的形式，不能接 to V。

an·kle [`æŋkl̩] Track 1058

名 腳踝

▶What? Have you broken your ankle again?
什麼？你又弄傷腳踝了嗎？

an·y·bod·y/an·y·one Track 1059

[`ɛnɪ͵bɑdɪ]/[`ɛnɪ͵wʌn]

代 任何人

▶It doesn't matter whether you tell anyone else or not.
你要不要告訴別人都沒差。

an·y·how [ˋɛnɪˏhaʊ] Track 1060

副 隨便、無論如何 同 however 無論如何

▶The accident was terrible, right? Anyhow, at least we're all okay now.
那次意外太慘了，對吧？總之，至少我們現在都沒事了。

an·y·time [ˋɛnɪˏtaɪm] Track 1061

副 任何時候 同 whenever 無論何時

▶If you want to order from us, you can call me anytime.
如果您想從我們這裡訂貨，請隨時給我打電話。

萬用延伸句型
例句中用的是「if S + V, S shall / will / can / may + V 」的條件句型，用來描述不變的事實。

an·y·way [ˋɛnɪˏwe] Track 1062

副 無論如何

▶She knows that he doesn't like her but she still tries to talk to him anyway.
她知道他不喜歡她，但她還是試著跟他說話。

文法字詞解析
對等連接詞 but 用來連接前後含意相反的句子。

an·y·where/an·y·place Track 1063

[ˋɛnɪˏhwɛr]/[ˋɛnɪˏples]

副 任何地方

▶Eating anywhere is fine with me. 在哪吃我都沒問題。

萬用延伸句型
That's fine by me/That's fine with me.
我都可以。用來表達自己不介意做某事。

ap·art·ment [əˋpɑrtmənt] Track 1064

名 公寓 同 flat 公寓

▶It will take us an hour to get to his apartment by bus.
我們搭公車要花一個小時才能到他的公寓。

實用片語用語
by + 交通工具 搭乘（交通工具）

ap·pear·ance [əˋpɪrəns] Track 1065

名 出現、露面 同 look 外表

▶We all judge people on their appearance to some degree（程度）. 我們某個程度上都會由外表評判他人。

實用片語用語
judge sb. on sth. 藉由某事來判斷某人

ap·pe·tite [ˋæpəˏtaɪt] Track 1066

名 食慾、胃口

▶I don't have an appetite now. 我現在沒什麼食慾。

ap·ply [əˋplaɪ] Track 1067

動 請求、應用 同 request 請求

▶Why don't you apply for the scholarship（獎學金）?
你何不申請獎學金呢？

實用片語用語
apply for / to 申請

a·pron [ˋeprən] Track 1068

名 圍裙 同 flap 圍裙

▶She is the lady in the pink apron. 她是穿著粉紅圍裙那個小姐。

ar·gue [ˋɑrgjʊ] Track 1069

動 爭辯、辯論

▶If you two want to argue, why don't you do it privately（私下地）? 如果你們倆想要爭論，為什麼不私下解決呢？

ar·gu·ment [ˋargjəmənt]

Track 1070

名 爭論、議論 同 dispute 爭論

▶She's always getting into arguments with people.
她總是在和人發生爭論。

實用片語用語
get into an argument with sb. (about sb. / sth.) 和某人爭論（為某人／某事爭論）

arm [arm]

Track 1071

名 手臂 動 武裝、備戰

▶名 His arms got scratched（抓）when he was washing the cat.
他在幫貓洗澡的時候，手臂被抓了。

▶動 Arm yourselves; the enemy is coming.
做好武裝準備吧，敵人要來了。

arm·chair [ˋarm͵tʃɛr]

Track 1072

名 扶椅

▶I bought an armchair for my grandma.
我買了一張有扶手的椅子給我奶奶。

ar·range [əˋrendʒ]

Track 1073

動 安排、籌備

▶Would you like to arrange for a personal（個人的）interview?
你願意安排一次個別面談嗎？

實用片語用語
arrange for 為……作安排
arrange for sb. to sth. 替某人安排某事

ar·range·ment [əˋrendʒmənt]

Track 1074

名 佈置、準備 反 disturb 擾亂

▶Would you please make arrangements for our accommodations（膳宿）? 您能為我們安排好住宿嗎？

實用片語用語
making arrangements for
為……作安排

ar·rest [əˋrɛst]

Track 1075

動 逮捕、拘捕 名 阻止、扣留 反 release 釋放

▶動 The thief was arrested by the police.
小偷被警察逮捕了。

▶名 The police put the man under arrest.
警察扣押了那個男人。

文法字詞解析
第一個例句中，小偷是被警察逮補，所以 arrest 要以被動語態表示。

實用片語用語
place / put sb. under arrest 逮捕某人
arrest sb. for sth. 以……的罪名逮補

ar·rive [əˋraɪv]

Track 1076

動 到達、來臨 反 leave 離開

▶Have our guests arrived yet? 我們的客人抵達了沒？

ar·row [ˋæro]

Track 1077

名 箭 同 quarrel 箭

▶He fired an arrow at the deer（鹿）. 他對那頭鹿射了一箭。

實用片語用語
fire at 朝向……發射

ar·ti·cle/es·say [ˋartɪkḷ]/[ˋɛse]

Track 1078

名 文章、論文

▶What do you think of that article he wrote?
你覺得他寫的那篇文章怎麼樣？

art·ist [ˋartɪst]

Track 1079

名 藝術家、大師

▶That artist is the greatest in the era（時代）.
那名藝術家是那個時代最偉大的一位。

a·sleep [ə`slip]
Track 1080

形 睡著的 反 awake 醒著的

▶It was almost two hours before I fell asleep last night.
昨晚我差不多躺了兩個小時才睡著。

實用片語用語
fall asleep 睡著、入睡

as·sis·tant [ə`sɪstənt]
Track 1081

名 助手、助理 同 aid 助手

▶He worked as an assistant to the president（總統）.
他當過總統助理。

at·tack [ə`tæk]
Track 1082

動 攻擊 名 攻擊 同 assault 攻擊

▶動 The cat attacked the dog when it was sleeping.
那隻貓趁著那隻狗在睡覺的時候攻擊牠。

▶名 There has been many attacks on the president this past month.
這個月來總統被攻擊了好幾次。

實用片語用語
attack (on) 攻擊（某人／某物）

at·tend [ə`tɛnd]
Track 1083

動 出席

▶It doesn't matter whether he will attend the meeting or not.
他會不會出席會議都不要緊。

at·ten·tion [ə`tɛnʃən]
Track 1084

名 注意、專心 同 concern 注意

▶Would you please pay attention when I'm talking?
我在講話時拜託你專心聽好嗎？

實用片語用語
pay attention (to sb.) 關心、注意（某人）

a·void [ə`vɔɪd]
Track 1085

動 避開、避免 反 face 面對

▶Once you've learned a lesson from a mistake, you will avoid making the same mistake next time.
一旦你從一次錯誤中吸取了教訓，你就會避免再次犯同樣的錯誤。

Bb

ba·by·sit [`bebɪˏsɪt]
Track 1086

動 （臨時）照顧嬰孩

▶I asked my sister to babysit for us.
我請了我妹妹來幫我們照顧小孩。

文法字詞解析
ask sb. to do sth. 要求某人做某事

ba·by·sit·ter [`bebɪsɪtɚ]
Track 1087

名 保姆

▶Why don't you hire a babysitter to look after your baby?
為什麼不請一位保姆來替你照顧寶寶呢？

back·ward [ˋbækwɚd]
Track 1088

形 向後方的、面對後方的 反 forward 向前方的

▶The village is considered（被認為是）backward because of how dirty it is.
那個村莊因為太髒亂了，而被認為是個落後的地方。

文法字詞解析
because of 後面要加名詞或名詞片語

back·wards [ˋbækwɚdz]
Track 1089

副 向後地 反 forwards 向前方地

▶He took a step backwards and almost hit a tree.
他往後退了一步，差點撞到樹。

bake [bek]
Track 1090

動 烘、烤 同 toast 烘、烤

▶We have to bake as much bread as possible, because we have so many guests.
我們必須儘量多烤些麵包，因為我們有很多位客人。

bak·er·y [ˋbekərɪ]
Track 1091

名 麵包坊、麵包店

▶What do you think about opening a bakery near the school?
你覺得在學校附近開一家麵包店怎麼樣？

萬用延伸句型
What do you think of / about sb / sth?
你覺得……怎麼樣？

bal·co·ny [ˋbælkənɪ]
Track 1092

名 陽臺 同 porch 陽臺

▶Please keep the balcony clean; we have guests tonight.
請保持陽臺清潔，我們今晚有客人。

bam·boo [bæmˋbu]
Track 1093

名 竹子

▶The bamboo forest behind our house is home to thousands of fireflies（螢火蟲）.
我們家後面的竹林有很多螢火蟲。

bank·er [ˋbæŋkɚ]
Track 1094

名 銀行家

▶My brother got a job as a banker.
我弟弟得到了銀行家的工作。

實用片語用語
get / find a job (as sth.) 找到（某職位）的工作

bar·be·cue/BBQ [ˋbɑrbɪkju]
Track 1095

名 烤肉 同 roast 烤肉

▶What about inviting the Smiths to have a barbecue with us this weekend?
週末請史密斯一家過來和我們一起烤肉怎麼樣？

bark [bɑrk]
Track 1096

動（狗）吠叫 名 吠聲 同 roar 吼叫（獅子）

▶動 The puppy is barking because he is hungry.
那隻小狗一直在叫，因為牠餓了。

▶名 I heard barks outside all night.
我整晚都聽見外面有狗叫聲。

base·ment [ˋbesmənt]
Track 1097

名 地下室、地窖 同 cellar 地窖

▶He kept all his old clothes in the basement.
他把舊衣服都放在地下室。

basics [ˋbesɪks]
Track 1098

名 基礎、原理 反 trivial 瑣碎的

▶I'm not that good at tennis either, but I can teach you some basics. 我也不怎麼擅長網球，但我可以教你一些基礎原理。

ba·sis [ˋbesɪs]
Track 1099

名 根據、基礎 同 bottom 底部

名詞複數 bases

▶They have arguments on a daily basis. 他們天天都吵架。

實用片語用語

on a daily basis 每天

bat·tle [ˋbætl̩]
Track 1100

名 戰役 動 作戰 同 combat 戰鬥

▶名 What do you think of his inspiring（鼓舞的）speech before the battle?
你覺得他在戰前所做的那場鼓舞人心的演講怎麼樣？

▶動 The two sides battled all night. 兩軍徹夜戰鬥。

bead [bid]
Track 1101

名 珠子、串珠 動 穿成一串 同 pearl 珠子

▶名 Would you please buy some prayer（祈禱）beads when you're there?
你去那邊的時候幫我買些念珠回來好嗎？

▶動 Tears are beaded on her cheeks（臉頰）.
她雙頰掛著成串的淚珠。

bean [bin]
Track 1102

名 豆子、沒有價值的東西 同 straw 沒有價值的東西

▶Would you like me to cook some beans for supper?
你想不想要我晚餐煮點豆子？

bear [bɛr]
Track 1103

名 熊 動 忍受 同 endure 忍受

▶名 I've never seen a real bear before.
我都沒看過真正的熊。

▶動 I can't bear to see her like this.
我受不了看到她這個樣子。

文法字詞解析

bear 的動詞變化：bear, bore, born

實用片語用語

can't bear to do / doing sth. 無法忍受做某事

beard [bɪrd]
Track 1104

名 鬍子

▶I like how your beard looks. 我喜歡你鬍子的樣子。

文法字詞解析

look用複數looks時常表示「容貌、外貌」。

bed·room [ˋbɛd͵rum]
Track 1105

名 臥房

▶I think you should open the window to air your bedroom as soon as you get up.
我覺得你應該每天一起床就把窗子打開給臥室通風。

萬用延伸句型

I think (that)... 我認為……

beef [bif] Track 1106

名 牛肉

名詞複數 beeves, beefs

▶It will take me an hour to cook the beef thoroughly（徹底地）.
把牛肉煮熟要花我一個小時的時間。

beep [bip] Track 1107

名 警笛聲 動 發出嗶嗶聲

▶名 My watch makes a beeping sound.
我的手錶會發出嗶嗶的聲音。

▶動 Will you tell me why the computer keeps beeping?
你能告訴我為什麼電腦會一直發出嗶嗶聲嗎？

beer [bɪr] Track 1108

名 啤酒 同 bitter 苦

▶Would you like some beer or wine for your dinner?
晚餐您要喝啤酒或葡萄酒嗎？

bee·tle [ˋbitl̩] Track 1109

名 甲蟲 動 急走

▶名 I am really afraid of beetles. 我非常害怕甲蟲。

▶動 How about beetling off for a drink at that bar during the break? 趁休息時間，我們趕快去那間酒吧喝幾杯怎麼樣？

實用片語用語
beetle off 離開

beg [bɛg] Track 1110

動 乞討、懇求 同 appeal 懇求

▶The dog is begging to be let in.
那隻狗在懇求我們放牠進來。

實用片語用語
beg to 懇求

be·gin·ner [bɪˋgɪnɚ] Track 1111

名 初學者 同 freshman 新手

▶It will take a beginner quite a long time to learn all this.
一名初學者會需要花費相當長的一段時間來學會這些東西。

be·lief [bɪˋlif] Track 1112

名 相信、信念 同 faith 信念

▶His belief that he's always right will cause huge problems.
他「自己永遠是對的」的信念將會造成很大的問題。

實用片語用語
belief in 相信
例如：Her belief in god makes her brave enough to do anything.
她對上帝的虔誠讓她有勇氣做任何事。

be·liev·a·ble [bɪˋlivəbl̩] Track 1113

形 可信任的 同 credible 可信的

▶I think what he said is believable.
我認為他說的是可信的。

belt [bɛlt] Track 1114

名 皮帶 動 圍繞 同 strap 皮帶

▶名 It doesn't matter whether you give the belt back to me or not. I don't need it anymore.
你還不還我皮帶現在都已經不重要了。我不再需要它了。

▶動 If you don't belt your jeans, they're going to fall down.
你不把牛仔褲繫上皮帶的話，褲子可要掉下來了。

bench [bɛntʃ]

Track 1115

名 長凳 同 settle 長椅

▶Do you know the couple sitting on the bench?
你認識坐在長凳上那對情人嗎？

bend [bɛnd]

Track 1116

動 使彎曲 名 彎曲 反 stretch 伸直

▶動 He bent down to pick up the soap. 他彎下腰來撿肥皂。

▶名 You'd better slow down. There is a sharp bend ahead in the road. 你最好減速，前方路上有急轉彎。

文法字詞解析
bend 的動詞變化 bend, bent, bent

be·sides [bɪˋsaɪdz]

Track 1117

介 除了……之外 副 並且 同 otherwise 除此之外

▶介 Is there any other way for us to go to the airport besides a taxi? 除了坐計程車外，還有別的方式能去機場嗎？

▶副 I don't have enough money to travel. Besides, I haven't time to do it, either.
我沒有足夠的錢去旅行。再說，我也沒時間去旅行。

bet [bɛt]

Track 1118

動 下賭注 名 打賭 同 gamble 打賭

▶動 I bet that they will win this game. 我賭他們會贏得這場比賽。

▶名 I'll treat you to dinner if I lose the bet.
如果我賭輸了，我請你吃晚餐。

文法字詞解析
bet 的動詞變化：bet, bet, bet

be·yond [bɪˋjɑnd]

Track 1119

介 在遠處、超過 副 此外 反 within 不超過

▶介 What do you think of this picture? I think it's beautiful beyond description（形容）.
你覺得這幅畫怎麼樣？我覺得它美得讓人無法形容。

▶副 I can't see anything as far as the house and beyond.
我在這棟房子及更遠處實在看不到什麼東西。

bill [bɪl]

Track 1120

名 帳單 同 check 帳單

▶We have finished our meal. Would you please give me the bill?
我們已經吃完了，請您給我帳單好嗎？

萬用延伸句型
Bill, please. 不好意思，我要結帳。

bind [baɪnd]

Track 1121

動 綁、包紮 反 release 鬆開

▶Women in the Qing Dynasty used to bind their feet.
清朝的女人總是裹著小腳。

文法字詞解析
1. bind 的動詞變化：bind, bound, bound
2. used to 用來表示過去常做的行為、過去的習慣。

bit·ter [ˋbɪtɚ]

Track 1122

形 苦的、嚴厲的 反 sweet 甜的

▶Why does medicine always taste bitter? 為什麼藥總是這麼苦呢？

black·board [ˋblæk͵bord]

Track 1123

名 黑板

▶He wrote down the answer on the blackboard.
他在黑板上寫下答案。

blank [blæŋk] Track 1124

形 空白的 名 空白 同 empty 空的

▶形 He gave me a blank look when I asked him a question.
我問他問題時，他的表情一片空白。

▶名 We have to fill in the blanks for the test.
這次考試有填空題。

實用片語用語
blank look 一片空白、無法看透的表情

blind [blaɪnd] Track 1125

形 瞎的

▶Would you please help the blind man cross the road?
你能幫助這位盲人過馬路嗎？

實用片語用語
blind sb to sth 蒙蔽某人、使某人看不見某物。
例如 :You shouldn't let love blind you to his dishonesty.
你不能因為愛而視而不見他對你的不誠實。

blood·y [ˋblʌdɪ] Track 1126

形 流血的

▶Not everyone knows how the bloody incident（事件）was brought about.
並非人人都知道這起流血事件是如何引起的。

board [bord] Track 1127

名 板、佈告欄 同 wood 木板

▶I can't see the words on the board from here.
我從這邊看不到板子上的字。

boil [bɔɪl] Track 1128

動（水）沸騰、使發怒 名 煮 同 rage 發怒

▶動 I think I hear the water boiling.
我好像聽到水煮開的聲音。

▶名 The fire is not big enough to bring the milk to a boil.
火不夠大，沒辦法把牛奶煮沸。

實用片語用語
bring something to a boil 煮沸某物

bomb [bɑm] Track 1129

名 炸彈 動 轟炸

▶名 After the bomb hit, few houses were left standing.
空襲之後，房子所剩無幾。

▶動 Terrorists（恐怖分子）bombed several police stations.
恐怖分子炸毀了幾所警察局。

bon·y [ˋbonɪ] Track 1130

形 多骨的、骨瘦如柴的 同 skinny 骨瘦如柴的

▶It is more important to be healthy than bony slim.
健康總比只剩皮包骨好。

book·case [ˋbʊkˏkes] Track 1131

名 書櫃、書架

▶Would you help me put all the books on the bookcase in my room?
你能幫我把所有的書都放到我房間裡的那個書架上嗎？

bor·row [ˋbɑro] Track 1132

動 借來、採用 反 loan 借出

▶Can I borrow your pencil? 我可以借一下你的鉛筆嗎？

實用片語用語
borrow sth. from sb 跟某人借某物

boss [bɔs]
Track 1133

名 老闆、主人 動 指揮、監督 同 manager 負責人、經理

▶名 The boss called me to his office and asked about this matter.
老闆叫我去他的辦公室並詢問我這件事情。

▶動 She enjoys bossing her husband around.
她喜歡對她丈夫頤指氣使。

文法字詞解析
enjoy 後面的動詞必須加 ing

實用片語用語
boss sb. around 對某人頤指氣使

both·er [ˋbɑðɚ]
Track 1134

動 打擾 同 annoy 打擾

▶Don't bother to come and see me off.
不必如此勞煩地來送我。

實用片語用語
see sb. off 送別某人

bot·tle [ˋbɑtḷ]
Track 1135

名 瓶 動 用瓶裝 同 container

▶名 The bottle broke into pieces on the floor.
瓶子在地板上摔成了碎片。

▶動 He didn't know when this wine was bottled.
他不知道這酒是何時裝瓶的。

bow [baʊ]
Track 1136

名 彎腰、鞠躬 動 向下彎

▶名 He gave a deep bow and left the stage.
他深深一鞠躬，下台了。

▶動 They all bowed down in front of the emperor（皇帝）.
他們都在皇帝面前跪拜了。

實用片語用語
give / take a bow 鞠躬

bowl·ing [ˋbolɪŋ]
Track 1137

名 保齡球

▶Do you want to go bowling this Saturday?
你這星期六要不要去打保齡球？

文法字詞解析
go 後面要加字尾有 ing 的運動或戶外活動，像是 go bowling, go golfing, go swimming 等。

brain [bren]
Track 1138

名 腦、智力 同 intelligence 智力

▶Use your brain! This isn't such a hard question.
用用腦吧！這不是什麼困難的問題啊。

branch [bræntʃ]
Track 1139

名 枝狀物、分店、分公司 動 分支 反 trunk 樹幹

▶名 The bank has many branches in this area.
這家銀行在這個地區有很多分行。

▶動 The store has branched out all over the city.
這家店在整個城市發展出很多家分支。

實用片語用語
branch out 擴大事業、發展新部門

brand [brænd]
Track 1140

名 品牌 動 打烙印 同 mark 做記號

▶名 Which brand of computer do you prefer?
你喜歡哪個牌子的電腦？

▶動 The terrible scene is branded in my mind.
那個可怕的畫面已經烙印在我的心中。

brick [brɪk]

Track 1141

名 磚頭、磚塊

▶He broke the window with a brick. 他用一個磚塊打碎了窗戶。

brief [brif]

Track 1142

形 短暫的 名 摘要、短文 反 long 長的

▶形 There was a brief pause（停頓）in the conversation between the two leaders.
兩位領導人之間的談話出現了一個短暫的停頓。

▶名 Let me tell you about his message in brief.
我來簡短地跟你說一下他的訊息內容。

實用片語用語
in brief 簡短說明

broad [brɔd]

Track 1143

形 寬闊的 反 narrow 窄的

▶My father is tall, broad and very strong. What about your father?
我爸爸長得身高肩寬，非常強壯。你爸爸呢？

broad·cast [ˋbrɔd͵kæst]

Track 1144

動 廣播、播出 名 廣播節目 同 announce 播報

▶動 Would you broadcast this news as quickly（很快地）as possible? 您能儘快播送這條新聞嗎？

▶名 We listened to the broadcast this morning.
我們今天早上聽了廣播。

實用片語用語
as...as possible 越……越好

brunch [brʌntʃ]

Track 1145

名 早午餐

▶Do you want to meet up for brunch tomorrow?
你明天要不要一起來吃個早午餐？

實用片語用語
meet up 相約

brush [brʌʃ]

Track 1146

名 刷子 動 刷、擦掉 同 wipe 擦去

▶名 I used a brush to clean my shoe.
我使用刷子清了清我的鞋子。

▶動 The cat likes it when I brush her. 我的貓喜歡我用梳子刷牠。

bun/roll [bʌn]/[rol]

Track 1147

名 小圓麵包、麵包捲 同 roll 麵包捲

▶I had a cup of tea and a bun in the afternoon.
我下午的時候喝了一杯茶，吃了個小圓麵包。

bun·dle [ˋbʌndḷ]

Track 1148

名 捆、包裹 同 package 包裹

▶Would you please give this bundle of old clothes to the poor people on the street? 請你拿這包舊衣服給街上的窮人們好嗎？

實用片語用語
on the street 在（某條）街上

burn [bɝn]

Track 1149

動 燃燒 名 烙印 同 fire 燃燒

▶動 You should be careful, or you will burn the toast.
你應該小心點，否則你會把土司烤焦的。

▶名 The burns on his body look terrible.
他身上的燒傷看起來很慘。

文法字詞解析
burn 的動詞變化：burn, burned, burnt

burst [bɝst]

Track 1150

動 破裂、爆炸 名 猝發、爆發 同 explode 爆炸

▶動 She burst into tears and then ran out without saying anything.
她突然大哭，然後什麼也沒說就跑出去了。

▶名 The car disappeared in a sudden burst of speed.
那輛車忽然速度全開，很快地消失了。

實用片語用語
1. burst into tears 突然嚎啕大哭
2. run out / away 跑開

busi·ness [ˋbɪznɪs]

Track 1151

名 商業、買賣 同 commerce 商業

▶How's business going these days?
最近生意如何啊？

萬用延伸句型
How's sb. / sth. going? 某人／某事最近如何？

but·ton [ˋbʌtn̩]

Track 1152

名 扣子 動 用扣子扣住 同 clasp 扣住

▶名 A button has fallen off my shirt.
我襯衫上有個扣子掉了。

▶動 Why don't you button up your coat? It is so cold outside.
你為什麼不扣上大衣的鈕扣呢？外頭很冷耶。

實用片語用語
button up 扣釦子

Cc

cab·bage [ˋkæbɪdʒ]

Track 1153

名 包心菜

▶Would you please get me some cabbages?
你幫我買些包心菜回來好嗎？

ca·ble [ˋkebl̩]

Track 1154

名 纜繩、電纜 同 wire 電線

▶Would you like a room with a cable TV?
您想要個有第四台的房間嗎？

café/cafe [kəˋfe]

Track 1155

名 咖啡館

▶I am a little thirsty; let's go to the café to have some coffee.
我有點口渴了，我們去咖啡館喝杯咖啡吧。

文法字詞解析
a little 和 a bit 可以做為程度副詞，表示「稍微、一點」，用來修飾動詞、形容詞、比較級。

caf·e·te·ri·a [ˌkæfəˋtɪrɪə]

Track 1156

名 自助餐館 同 restaurant 餐廳

▶The cafeteria in my high school is horrible.
我們高中的自助餐廳超糟糕的。

cal·en·dar [ˋkæləndɚ]

Track 1157

名 日曆

▶I got a new calendar for this year.
我為了今年買了一個新的日曆。

calm [kɑm]

Track 1158

形 平靜的 名 平靜 動 使平靜 同 peaceful 平靜的

▶形 He's always calm no matter what happens.
無論發生什麼事，他總是很平靜。

▶名 The boss is quiet after receiving the call. I guess it's the calm before the storm.
老闆接到電話後很安靜，我想是暴風雨前的寧靜吧。

▶動 Would you please try to calm down and tell me where you are? 請冷靜下來，告訴我你在哪裡好嗎？

實用片語用語
the calm before the storm 暴風雨前的寧靜

萬用延伸句型
I guess (that)… 我想……

can·cel [ˋkænsḷ]

Track 1159

動 取消 同 erase 清除

▶We'll have to cancel the picnic because of the rain.
因為下雨，我們不得不取消野餐。

文法字詞解析
cancel 的動詞變化：cancel, canceled, canceled 或 cancel, cancelled, cancelled

can·cer [ˋkænsɚ]

Track 1160

名 癌、腫瘤

▶I hope we find a cure for cancer soon.
希望我們能盡早找到治療癌症的方式。

can·dle [ˋkændḷ]

Track 1161

名 蠟燭、燭光 同 torch 光芒

▶These candles not only look cute but also smell good.
這些蠟燭不但看起來可愛，而且聞起來也很香。

萬用延伸句型
not only...but also... 不只……而且……

cap·tain [ˋkæptɪn]

Track 1162

名 船長、艦長 同 chief 首領、長官

▶Hello. This is the captain speaking.
您好，我是機長。

car·pet [ˋkɑrpɪt]

Track 1163

名 地毯 動 鋪地毯 同 mat 地席

▶名 Which carpet do you like best? 你最喜歡哪條地毯？

▶動 The stairs were carpeted so that the children won't get hurt when they fall down.
樓梯上鋪著地毯，孩子們跌倒時就不會受傷。

萬用延伸句型
Which one do you like best?
哪一個是你最喜歡的？
也可以說：Which one is your favorite?

實用片語用語
get hurt 受傷

car·rot [ˋkærət]

Track 1164

名 胡蘿蔔

▶Would you please get me some carrots on the way?
順便幫我買點胡蘿蔔好嗎？

cart [kɑrt]

Track 1165

名 手拉車

▶I think this little cart is too small to hold so many things.
我覺得這台小推車太小了，裝不下這麼多的東西。

萬用延伸句型
too...to... 太……以至於不能……

car·toon [kɑrˋtun]

Track 1166

名 卡通

▶The kids are in the living room watching a cartoon.
孩子們正在客廳看卡通。

cash [kæʃ] Track 1167

名 現金 動 付現 同 currency 貨幣

▶名 Would you like to pay by credit（信用）card or in cash, sir?
先生，請問您是要刷卡還是現金消費呢？

▶動 Would you please cash this check for me?
請幫我兌現這張支票好嗎？

實用片語用語
pay by credit card / in cash 刷卡付款／付現

cas·sette [kæˋsɛt] Track 1168

名 卡帶、盒子

▶There is a little window in the cassette case so that you can see the tape.
錄音帶上有個小窗，能看見裡面的磁帶。

cast·le [ˋkæsl̩] Track 1169

名 城堡 同 palace 皇宮

▶How long did it take you to finish this sand castle?
你建完這個沙堡花了多長時間啊？

cave [kev] Track 1170

名 洞穴 動 挖掘 同 hole 洞

▶名 His hobby is exploring caves.
他的嗜好是探索洞穴。

▶動 Many cellars caved in during the earthquake.
地震中有很多地窖都塌陷了。

實用片語用語
cave in 塌陷、陷落

ceil·ing [ˋsilɪŋ] Track 1171

名 天花板 反 floor 地板

▶My bedroom is a large room with a high ceiling.
我的臥室是一個天花板很高的大房間。

cell [sɛl] Track 1172

名 細胞

▶You can see the red blood cells with this microscope（顯微鏡）. 你可以用顯微鏡看到這些紅血球細胞。

cen·tral [ˋsɛntrəl] Track 1173

形 中央的

▶I plan to go to Central Park this weekend; would you like to go with me?
我打算這個週末去中央公園，你願意跟我一起去嗎？

cen·tu·ry [ˋsɛntʃərɪ] Track 1174

名 世紀

▶It is no wonder that she was regarded as one of the greatest dancers of the century.
難怪她被視為本世紀最偉大的舞蹈家之一。

實用片語用語
be regarded as... 被視為……

ce·re·al [ˋsɪrɪəl] Track 1175

名 穀類作物

▶Do you want cereal for breakfast?
你要吃營養穀片當早餐嗎？

chalk [tʃɔk]

Track 1176

名 粉筆

▶Would you please bring two boxes of chalk for our teacher?
你能幫我們的老師拿兩盒粉筆來嗎？

萬用延伸句型
Would you please (help me)...?
請你（幫忙我）……好嗎？

change [tʃendʒ]

Track 1177

動 改變、兌換 名 零錢、變化 同 coin 硬幣

▶動 I need several minutes to change; would you like to wait downstairs?
我需要幾分鐘來換衣服，你能在樓下等我嗎？

▶名 I don't have any change right now.
我現在沒有零錢耶。

實用片語用語
get changed 換衣服。
例如：It's time to go to the party. Let's get changed. 該出門去參加派對了，我們去換衣服吧。

char·ac·ter [ˋkærɪktɚ]

Track 1178

名 個性

▶They are the two main characters in the play, Tom and Rose.
該劇中有兩個主角，湯姆和羅斯。

charge [tʃɑrdʒ]

Track 1179

動 索價、命令 名 費用、職責 同 rate 費用

▶動 How much do you charge by the hour?
你每小時怎麼收費？

▶名 Would you please tell me who is in charge here?
您能告訴我這裡是誰負責管理嗎？

實用片語用語
be in charge of 負責、主管

cheap [tʃip]

Track 1180

形 低價的、易取得的 副 低價地 反 expensive 昂貴的

▶形 Your dress is cheaper than mine.
你的洋裝比我的更便宜。

▶副 I got the book for cheap at the bookstore.
我在書局以低價買到這本書。

cheat [tʃit]

Track 1181

動 欺騙 名 詐欺、騙子 同 liar 騙子

▶動 He always cheats on exams.
他考試每次都作弊。

▶名 That young man is such a cheat.
那個年輕男子真是個騙子。

實用片語用語
cheat on sb. 對某人不忠
例如：She didn't know until her friend told her that her husband has been cheating on her for a while.
直到她朋友告訴她她才知道原來自己的丈夫已經外遇好一段時間了。

chem·i·cal [ˋkɛmɪkl]

Track 1182

形 化學的 名 化學

▶形 We are doing a chemical experiment（實驗）right now.
我們現在正在做化學實驗。

▶名 I don't think you should touch those chemicals.
我覺得那些化學製品你還是不要摸吧。

chess [tʃɛs]

Track 1183

名 西洋棋

▶Would you like to play chess with me?
你想不想陪我下西洋棋？

child·ish [ˋtʃaɪdɪʃ]

Track 1184

形 孩子氣的 同 naive 天真的

▶When you see the girl, you will know how childish she is.
一旦你見到那個女孩，你就會知道她多麼孩子氣了。

文法字詞解析
在例句中，how childish she is 是名詞子句當作受詞使用。

child·like [ˋtʃaɪldlaɪk]

Track 1185

形 純真的 反 mature 成熟的

▶She is nearly fifty, yet still retains a childlike innocence（天真無邪）.
她年近半百了，卻還是維持著孩童般的天真無邪。

文法字詞解析
yet 在這裡是對等連接詞，連接兩個意思相反的句子。

chin [tʃɪn]

Track 1186

名 下巴

▶She always complains about having a sharp chin.
她總是抱怨自己下巴太尖。

實用片語用語
complain about sth. 抱怨某事

choc·o·late [ˋtʃɔkəlɪt]

Track 1187

名 巧克力

▶Would you please bring me a box of chocolates?
你能幫我帶一盒巧克力嗎？

choice [tʃɔɪs]

Track 1188

名 選擇 形 精選的 同 selection 選擇

▶名 I think he made a good choice.
我覺得他做了個很好的選擇。

▶形 The shop sells choice apples.
那個商店在賣精選蘋果。

實用片語用語
make a choice 做選擇

choose [tʃuz]

Track 1189

動 選擇 同 select 選擇

▶There are many colors for you to choose from.
我們有非常多種顏色可供您選擇。

文法字詞解析
choose 的動詞變化：choose, chose, chosen

chop·stick(s) [ˋtʃɑpˏstɪk(s)]

Track 1190

名 筷子

▶Not everyone likes using chopsticks to eat.
不是每個人都喜歡用筷子吃飯。

cir·cle [ˋsɝkḷ]

Track 1191

名 圓形 動 圍繞 同 round 環繞

▶名 Would you please sit in a circle on the floor?
你們能不能在地板上坐成一圈啊？

▶動 Can you circle the mistakes for me?
你能幫我把錯誤圈出來嗎？

cit·i·zen [ˋsɪtəzṇ]

Track 1192

名 公民、居民 同 inhabitant 居民

▶The government's purpose is to serve citizens.
政府的存在目的本來就是要服務人民。

claim [klem]

Track 1193

動 主張 名 要求、權利 同 right 權利

▶動 He claims to be the first to arrive.
他堅持說他是第一個抵達的。

▶名 Do you believe his claim? I don't.
你相信他的主張嗎？我可不信。

實用片語用語
claim to do / be sth. 聲稱、主張

clap [klæp]

Track 1194

動 鼓（掌）、拍擊 名 拍擊聲

▶動 We clapped really hard when the famous pianist appeared.
當那位著名的鋼琴家出現時，我們大力地鼓掌。

▶名 A clap of thunder reverberated（迴響）through the house.
一聲雷鳴在屋子裡迴響。

clas·sic [ˋklæsɪk]

Track 1195

形 古典的 名 經典作品 同 ancient 古代的

▶形 Would you like to listen to some classic music or pop music?
你想聽古典音樂還是流行音樂？

▶名 Would you like to read this novel? It's a classic.
你想不想讀這本小說？它可是經典作品哦。

萬用延伸句型
Would you like to... ? 你想不想……？

claw [klɔ]

Track 1196

名 爪 動 抓 同 grip 抓、緊握

▶名 The eagle has sharp claws.
那隻老鷹的腳爪非常鋒利。

▶動 The kitten clawed at me when I touched her.
那隻貓在我摸牠時抓了我一把。

實用片語用語
claw at sb. / sth.（用爪子）抓某人／某物

clay [kle]

Track 1197

名 黏土 同 mud 土

▶The pot is made of clay. 這個壺是黏土做的。

clean·er [klinɚ]

Track 1198

名 清潔工、清潔劑 同 detergent 清潔劑

▶The cleaners usually come in the afternoon.
那些清潔工通常都是下午來。

clerk [klɝk]

Track 1199

名 職員

▶There are only four clerks in our company. What about yours?
我們公司只有四個職員，你們呢？

clev·er [ˋklɛvɚ]

Track 1200

形 聰明的、伶俐的 反 stupid 愚蠢的

▶I don't think my son is clever enough to work out the math problem. 我覺得我的兒子還沒聰明到能解出這道數學難題。

實用片語用語
...enough to do sth. ……到足以做某事

cli·mate [ˋklaɪmɪt]

Track 1201

名 氣候 同 weather 天氣

▶What's the climate like in spring in your country?
在你們國家春天是什麼樣的氣候呢？

文法字詞解析
季節前面的介係詞要加 in。

clos·et [ˋklɑzɪt] Track 1202

[名] 櫥櫃 [同] cabinet 櫥櫃

▶I forgot to clean up the closet last week.
上星期我忘記清理櫥櫃了。

cloth [klɔθ] Track 1203

[名] 布料 [同] textile 紡織品

▶Would you please find another piece of cloth to match this one for me?
麻煩你幫我找到和這塊布相配的布料好嗎？

clothe [kloð] Track 1204

[動] 穿衣、給……穿衣

▶What do you think of the girl that is clothed in a red dress over there?
你覺得那邊穿著紅洋裝的那個女孩怎麼樣？

文法字詞解析
clothe 的動詞變化：clothe, clothed, clothed

clothes [kloz] Track 1205

[名] 衣服 [同] clothing 衣服

▶Would you like to go to the mall（購物中心）with me this Saturday? I want to buy some clothes.
這個週六陪我去逛購物中心好嗎？我想買些衣服。

cloth·ing [ˋkloðɪŋ] Track 1206

[名] 衣服 [同] clothes 衣服

▶My favorite kind of clothing is the kind that's easy to wash.
我最喜歡好洗的那種衣服。

cloud·y [ˋklaʊdɪ] Track 1207

[形] 烏雲密佈的、多雲的 [反] bright 晴朗的

▶It's cloudy outside now. My favorite weather!
現在外面烏雲密佈的，我最喜歡這種天氣了！

clown [klaʊn] Track 1208

[名] 小丑、丑角 [動] 扮丑角 [同] comic 滑稽人物

▶[名] A lot of people are afraid of clowns.
有很多人都怕小丑。

▶[動] He was just clowning. Don't take it seriously.
他只是在搞笑而已，別太正經看待。

實用片語用語
take sb / sth. seriously 嚴肅看待某人／某事

club [klʌb] Track 1209

[名] 俱樂部、社團 [同] association 協會、社團

▶Did you belong to any clubs in high school?
你高中的時候有參加社團嗎？

實用片語用語
belong to 屬於

coach [kotʃ] Track 1210

[名] 教練、顧問 [動] 訓練 [同] counselor 顧問、參事

▶[名] The basketball coach is always really serious.
那個籃球教練總是正經八百的。

▶[動] She'll be coaching the football team kids all summer.
她整個夏天都要輔導足球隊的小朋友。

文法字詞解析
第二個例句中，用未來進行式表達計畫要在將來做的事。

coal [kol]

Track 1211

名 煤 同 fuel 燃料

▶There are a great many coal mines in that part of the town.
那座小鎮那裡有很多煤礦。

文法字詞解析
coal 如果要説明「煤礦」的話，是不可數名詞；如果要説明「一塊煤炭」的話，是可數名詞。

cock [kɑk]

Track 1212

名 公雞 同 rooster 公雞

▶The cocks that live by my house crow very early.
我家旁邊的那些公雞都很早叫。

文法字詞解析
例句中用關係代名詞 that 引導形容詞子句來修飾主詞 the cocks。

cock·roach/roach

Track 1213

[ˋkɑk͵rotʃ]/[rotʃ]

名 蟑螂

▶I hate cockroaches, especially when they fly.
我討厭蟑螂，尤其是會飛的那種。

coin [kɔɪn]

Track 1214

名 硬幣 動 鑄造 同 money 錢幣

▶名 I picked up a coin from the ground.
我從地上撿起了一個錢幣。

▶動 He's always coining new phrases.
他總是在創造新的流行語。

實用片語用語
to coin a phrase 創造新詞

col·lect [kəˋlɛkt]

Track 1215

動 收集 同 gather 收集

▶I've been collecting erasers since I was ten.
我從十歲以來就在收集橡皮擦了。

col·or·ful [ˋkʌlɚfəl]

Track 1216

形 富有色彩的

▶There are many colorful balloons in her baby's room.
她寶寶的房間裡有許多五彩繽紛的氣球。

comb [kom]

Track 1217

名 梳子 動 梳、刷 同 brush 梳子、刷

▶名 I got a new comb because my old one fell into the toilet.
我買了一把新的梳子，因為舊的掉進馬桶裡了。

▶動 My daughter likes to comb her own hair.
我女兒最愛梳自己的頭髮。

實用片語用語
comb one's hair 梳某人的頭髮

com·fort·a·ble [ˋkʌmfɚtəbl̩]

Track 1218

形 舒服的 同 content 滿意的

▶The bed feels so soft and comfortable.
這張床好軟好舒服。

文法字詞解析
feel 是連綴動詞，後面接形容詞説明某人或某物所帶來的感受。

com·pa·ny [ˋkʌmpənɪ]

Track 1219

名 公司、同伴 同 enterprise 公司

▶My company building is right next to the bus stop.
我們公司大樓就在公車站旁邊。

文法字詞解析
right 在這裡是副詞，表示「正好、恰好」。

com·pare [kəm`pɛr] Track 1220

動 比較 同 contrast 對比

▶You can't compare apples with oranges.
你不能拿蘋果和橘子來比較啊。

實用片語用語
compare A with B 把 A 和 B 做比較

com·plain [kəm`plen] Track 1221

動 抱怨 同 grumble 抱怨

▶Would you please stop complaining about the weather?
請不要再抱怨天氣了好嗎？

com·plete [kəm`plit] Track 1222

形 完整的 動 完成 同 conclude 結束

▶形 Would you please give me a complete report by next Friday?
麻煩下週五之前給我一份完整的報告好嗎？

▶動 Do you mind completing this survey（調查）for me?
您介意幫我完成這份調查問卷嗎？

萬用延伸句型
Do you mind...? 你介意……嗎？

com·put·er [kəm`pjutə] Track 1223

名 電腦

▶I got a new computer for my brother.
我為我弟買了一台新電腦。

con·firm [kən`fɝm] Track 1224

動 證實 同 establish 證實

▶Can you confirm that this is your number?
你可以確認一下這是不是你的電話號碼嗎？

萬用延伸句型
confirm that + 子句 確認

con·flict [`kɑnflɪkt] Track 1225

名 衝突、爭鬥 動 衝突 同 clash 衝突

▶名 She always does her best to avoid（避免）conflict.
她總是盡全力避免衝突。

▶動 These two points conflict each other.
這兩點互相衝突了。

Con·fu·cius [kən`fjuʃəs] Track 1226

名 孔子

▶Confucius is considered the greatest of the ancient Chinese sages（聖人）.
孔子被認為是中國古代最偉大的聖賢。

文法字詞解析
在這個例句中，孔子是「被人們認為」，所以 consider 用了被動語態。

實用片語用語
be considered (to be) ... 被認為是

con·grat·u·la·tions [kən͵grætʃə`leʃənz] Track 1227

名 祝賀、恭喜 同 blessing 祝福

▶Congratulations on your graduation（畢業）!
恭喜你畢業了！

文法字詞解析
congratulation 作為祝賀詞詞，常以複數型態表示。

實用片語用語
congratulations on sth. 恭喜（某事）

con·sid·er [kən`sɪdə] Track 1228

動 考慮、把……視為 同 deliberate 仔細考慮

▶Not every student considers him as a good professor（教授）.
不是每個學生都認為他是個好教授。

實用片語用語
consider sb. / sth. to be 把某人／某物視為

con·tact [ˋkɑntækt] Track 1229

名 接觸、親近 動 接觸 同 approach 接近

▶名 I don't have a lot of contacts listed in my phone.
我的手機裡沒有列出很多聯絡人。

▶動 I tried to contact her, but couldn't reach her at all.
我有試著跟她聯絡，但一直找不到她。

con·tain [kənˋten] Track 1230

動 包含、含有 反 exclude 不包括

▶There are other laws that contain provisions（條款）that provide personal protection（保護）to citizens.
還有一些法律包含了對公民人身保護的條款。

con·trol [kənˋtrol] Track 1231

名 管理、控制 動 支配、控制 同 command 控制、指揮

▶名 The weather is out of our control. 天氣不是我們能控制的。

▶動 He's not good at controlling his temper. 他不太會控制脾氣。

文法字詞解析
control 的動詞變化：control, controlled, controlled

con·trol·ler [kənˋtrolɚ] Track 1232

名 管理員 同 administrator 管理人

▶The controller is responsible for many things.
管理者必須對許多事情負責。

實用片語用語
be responsible for 對……負責

con·ve·nient [kənˋvinjənt] Track 1233

形 方便的、合宜的 同 suitable 適當的

▶Let's come up with a convenient excuse for not going.
我們來想一個不去的適當藉口吧。

con·ver·sa·tion [kɑnvɚˋseʃən] Track 1234

名 交談、談話 同 dialogue 交談

▶Holding a conversation with someone like him is really hard.
跟他這種人對話超難的。

實用片語用語
hold a conversation with sb. 和某人對話

cook·er [kʊkɚ] Track 1235

名 炊具

▶I bought a slow cooker today. 我今天買了一個慢炊鍋。

cop·y/Xe·rox/xe·rox Track 1236

[ˋkɑpɪ]/[ˋzɪrɑks]

名 拷貝 同 imitate 仿製

▶I made a copy of the document（文件）. 我拷貝了這份文件。

cor·ner [ˋkɔrnɚ] Track 1237

名 角落 同 angle 角

▶She always sits quietly in the corner. 她總是安靜地坐在角落。

文法字詞解析
the corner 前擺的介係詞會影響到語意的變化。如果是 in the corner 的話，就是在「房屋內」的角落；如果是 at the corner，則是「在屋外」，像街角等的角落。

cost·ly [ˋkɔstlɪ] Track 1238

形 價格高的 同 expensive 昂貴的

▶The apartment is too costly for me to buy.
這個公寓太貴了，我根本買不起。

cot·ton [ˋkɑtn̩]

Track 1239

名 棉花

▶I like clothes that are made of cotton.
我喜歡棉花做的衣服。

cough [kɔf]

Track 1240

動 咳出 名 咳嗽

▶動 He's been coughing all day. 他已經咳了一天。

▶名 You have a bad cough. I think you need to see a doctor.
你咳嗽得很厲害，我覺得你該去看個醫生。

實用片語用語
have a bad cough 咳嗽很嚴重

coun·try·side [ˋkʌntrɪˌsaɪd]

Track 1241

名 鄉間

▶What do you think about moving to the countryside after we both retire? 你覺得我們都退休之後搬到鄉下怎麼樣？

coun·ty [ˋkaʊntɪ]

Track 1242

名 郡、縣

▶It will take you about two hours to reach the county I live in by bus. 你坐公車到我住的郡大概要花兩個小時的時間。

cou·ple [ˋkʌpl̩]

Track 1243

名 配偶、一對 動 結合

▶名 There are a couple of other mistakes in this letter. You are so careless（粗心的）.
這封信裡還有其他一些錯字，你太粗心了。

▶動 The two train cars were coupled together, and then the passengers were allowed to board.
火車的兩節車廂連結在一起後，乘客就可以上車了。

文法字詞解析
a couple of 可以用來修飾「一對」東西，也可以說是「少許、少量」的東西。

cour·age [ˋkɝɪdʒ]

Track 1244

名 勇氣 反 fear 恐懼

▶Not everyone has the courage to speak their mind.
不是每個人都有勇氣實話實說。

court [kort]

Track 1245

名 法院

▶Do you want to take this to court? 你要上法庭解決嗎？

文法字詞解析
take sb. to court 對某人提出告訴

cou·sin [ˋkʌzn̩]

Track 1246

名 堂（表）兄弟姊妹

▶I don't even know how many cousins I have; there're too many.
我自己都不知道我有幾個堂（表）兄弟姊妹了，實在太多了。

crab [kræb]

Track 1247

名 蟹

▶We have two kinds of crabs. Would you like to buy hairy（多毛的）or green crabs?
我們有兩種蟹，您是想買毛蟹還是要買青蟹呢？

crane [kren]

Track 1248

名 起重機、鶴

▶We got a crane to move this machine.
我們弄了一台起重機來移動這個機器。

cray·on [ˋkreən]

Track 1249

名 蠟筆

▶Would you please buy a box of crayons for my son?
你能幫我的兒子買一盒蠟筆嗎？

cra·zy [ˋkrezɪ]

Track 1250

形 發狂的、瘋癲的 同 mad 發狂的

▶The idea sounds crazy, but I like it.
這主意聽起來很瘋狂，但我就喜歡。

萬用延伸句型
(It) Sounds + adj. 聽起來很……。

cream [krim]

Track 1251

名 乳酪、乳製品

▶Can you get me some cream to add into the coffee?
你可以給我一點奶精讓我放在咖啡裡嗎？

cre·ate [krɪˋet]

Track 1252

動 創造 同 design 設計

▶He's always creating new music.
他總是在創作新的音樂。

crime [kraɪm]

Track 1253

名 罪、犯罪行為 同 sin 罪

▶I can't come up with any way to control the rising crime rate（犯罪率）.
我想不出什麼方法來控制不斷上升的犯罪率。

cri·sis [ˋkraɪsɪs]

Track 1254

名 危機 同 emergency 緊急關頭
名詞複數 crises

▶The financial crisis（金融危機）is affecting the whole world.
這次金融危機影響了整個世界。

文法字詞解析
affect 是及物動詞，後面直接接受詞。

crop [krɑp]

Track 1255

名 農作物 同 growth 產物

▶The farmers are excited to see the crops doing well.
看到農作物十分茁壯，這些農夫很興奮。

文法字詞解析
如果是人感到興奮，要用 excited；如果是事物令人感到興奮，則是用 exciting。

cross [krɔs]

Track 1256

名 十字形、交叉 動 使交叉、橫過、反對 同 oppose 反對

▶名 Jane wears a small golden（金色的）cross.
珍戴著一隻小小的金十字架。

▶動 Are you going to cross the street now or are you going to just stand here forever?
你到底要過馬路還是要一輩子站在這裡啊？

crow [kro]

Track 1257

名 烏鴉 動 啼叫

▶名 The little girl is making friends with the crow.
那個小女孩正在和烏鴉交朋友。

▶動 This rooster crows at 3 a.m. every day, so we ended up cooking him. 這隻公雞每天都凌晨三點啼叫，我們後來就乾脆把牠煮來吃了。

實用片語用語
end up 以……告終

crowd [kraʊd]

Track 1258

名 人群、群眾 動 擁擠 同 group 群眾

▶名 There's a crowd of people sitting in front of the town hall. Who are they?
有一群人坐在市政府前。他們是誰啊？

▶動 Stop crowding the street and let us pass.
不要擠在路上，讓我們過嘛。

cru·el [ˋkruəl]

Track 1259

形 殘忍的、無情的 同 mean 殘忍的

▶He is really cruel to his wife. 他對他妻子很殘忍。

cul·ture [ˋkʌltʃɚ]

Track 1260

名 文化

▶If you understand the culture of a country, you will not make silly（愚蠢的）mistakes.
一旦你瞭解了一國的文化，你就不會再犯愚蠢的錯誤了。

cure [kjʊr]

Track 1261

動 治療 名 治療 同 heal 治療

▶動 Doctor, can you cure my child?
醫生，你救得了我的孩子嗎？

▶名 Doctors are searching for a cure that will wipe out cancer.
醫生們正在尋找治療癌症的醫療方法。

實用片語用語
wipe sth. out 將……移除、消滅

cu·ri·ous [ˋkjʊrɪəs]

Track 1262

形 求知的、好奇的

▶I am very curious about what his new girlfriend looks like.
對於他的新女朋友長什麼樣子我非常好奇。

萬用延伸句型
What does sb / sth. look like? 某人／某物長什麼樣子？

cur·tain/drape [ˋkɝtn̩]/[drep]

Track 1263

名 窗簾 動 掩蔽

▶名 Would you please draw the curtains? I can hardly open my eyes.
你把窗簾拉上好嗎？我幾乎睜不開眼睛了。

▶動 Would you please buy some material to curtain the house?
你能不能買一些布料來幫房子裝上窗簾？

cus·tom [ˋkʌstəm]

Track 1264

名 習俗、習慣 同 tradition 習俗、傳統

▶It would be better to follow local customs when arriving at a new place.
到達一個新的地方時，最好遵照當地的風俗習慣。

文法字詞解析
當兩個句子的主詞相同時，會使用分詞構句來讓句子更精煉。

萬用延伸句型
分詞構句句型 When V-ing, S. + V.（也可以前後句對調）。

cus·tom·er [ˋkʌstəmɚ]

Track 1265

名 顧客、客戶 同 client 客戶

▶What do you think about sending some beautiful vases（花瓶）to our customers as Christmas presents?
你覺得送客戶一些漂亮的花瓶作為聖誕禮物怎麼樣？

dai·ly [ˋdelɪ]

Track 1266

形 每日的 名 日報

▶形 It takes him two hours to read the daily newspaper.
他要花上兩小時來閱讀日報。

▶名 Has the new daily arrived in the mail yet?
新的日報寄來了沒有？

dam·age [ˋdæmɪdʒ]

Track 1267

名 損害、損失 動 毀損

▶名 The flood did a lot of damage to the crops.
洪水毀壞了大量的農作物。

▶動 The goods are damaged on the way.
貨品在路上毀損了。

實用片語用語
damage to sth. 損壞

dan·ger·ous [ˋdendʒərəs]

Track 1268

形 危險的 反 secure 安全的

▶Crossing the street without looking both sides is dangerous.
沒有先往兩邊看就直接過馬路是很危險的。

da·ta [ˋdetə]

Track 1269

名 資料、事實、材料 同 information 資料

▶Would you please send me any data you can find? I need more information.
請你把你能找到的資料寄給我好嗎？我需要瞭解更多的資訊。

dawn [dɔn]

Track 1270

名 黎明、破曉 動 開始出現、頓悟 反 dusk 黃昏

▶名 He always sets out for work at dawn.
他每次都一破曉就出門去上班。

▶動 It dawned on him that all his grandma really wanted was attention.
他終於頓悟，原來他的奶奶只是想要人家注意她。

實用片語用語
dawn on sb. 某人領悟到……

deaf [dɛf]

Track 1271

形 耳聾

▶Even though he is deaf, he can still play the piano.
雖然他耳聾，他還是會彈鋼琴。

萬用延伸句型
Even though S1 + V1, S2 + V2
雖然……，……。

de·bate [dɪˋbet]

Track 1272

名 討論、辯論 動 討論、辯論 同 discuss 討論

▶名 It took the students a month to prepare for this debate.
這些學生花了一個月的時間來準備這次的辯論賽。

▶動 They've been debating this for an hour and still haven't arrived at an agreement.
他們花了一個小時來討論這個問題，還沒有達成一致意見。

萬用延伸句型
It takes + (time) + to do sth.
某人花了（多少時間）做某事

---

debt [dɛt] Track 1273

名 債、欠款 同 obligation 債、欠款

▶I have to pay all the debts as soon as possible, or the bank will sue me.
我不得不儘快還清所有的債款，否則銀行會告我。

---

de·ci·sion [dɪˋsɪʒən] Track 1274

名 決定、決斷力 同 determination 決定

▶It's too hard for me to make a decision.
要我做出決定實在太難了。

---

dec·o·rate [ˋdɛkəˏret] Track 1275

動 裝飾、佈置 同 beautify 裝飾

▶He decorated the house with many colored lights.
他用彩燈裝飾房子。

---

de·gree [dɪˋgri] Track 1276

名 學位、程度 同 extent 程度

▶Could you tell me what degree you will receive after your graduation（畢業）?
你能告訴我你畢業後將拿到什麼學位嗎？

---

de·lay [dɪˋle] Track 1277

動 延緩 名 耽擱

▶動 The plane was delayed because of the weather.
因為天氣關係，飛機延遲起飛了。

▶名 There was a delay in the schedule.
時程表有點耽擱。

實用片語用語
delay in sth. 某事受到耽擱

---

de·li·cious [dɪˋlɪʃəs] Track 1278

形 美味的 同 yummy 美味的

▶This dish is very delicious. Would you like some more?
這盤菜味道鮮美，你要不要再吃一些？

---

de·liv·er [dɪˋlɪvɚ] Track 1279

動 傳送、遞送 同 transfer 傳送

▶Would you please deliver these goods to our company within（在……內）a week?
您能否在一週內把貨物送到我的公司？

文法字詞解析
介係詞「within」表示「在某一段時間以內」。

---

den·tist [ˋdɛntɪst] Track 1280

名 牙醫、牙科醫生

▶He went to the dentist last week.
他上禮拜去看了牙醫。

實用片語用語
go to a doctor / see a doctor / visit a doctor 看醫生

de·ny [dɪˋnaɪ]

Track 1281

動 否認、拒絕 同 reject 拒絕

▶He kept denying that he stole the money.
他一直否認有偷錢。

de·part·ment [dɪˋpɑrtmənt]

Track 1282

名 部門、處、局 同 section 部門

▶The accounting（會計）department is just next door.
會計部門就在隔壁而已。

de·pend [dɪˋpɛnd]

Track 1283

動 依賴、依靠 同 rely 依賴

▶I have no one but you to depend on.
我只有你一個人可以依靠了。

實用片語用語
depend on sb. / sth.
依靠、取決於某人／某事

depth [dɛpθ]

Track 1284

名 深度、深淵 同 gravity 深遠

▶She's a shallow（淺的）girl. She has no depth.
她是個膚淺的女孩，毫無深度。

de·scribe [dɪˋskraɪb]

Track 1285

動 敘述、描述 同 define 解釋

▶Would you describe what you have seen and heard there in a detailed（詳細的）way?
您能詳細地跟我們描述一下您在那裡的所見所聞嗎？

實用片語用語
in detail / in a detailed way 詳細地

de·sert [ˋdɛzɚt]/[dɪˋzɝt]

Track 1286

名 沙漠、荒地 動 拋棄、丟開 形 荒蕪的 反 fertile 肥沃的

▶名 It's hard to imagine what living in a desert is like unless you've actually lived there.
除非真的在沙漠住過，很難想像住在那裡是什麼感覺。

▶動 All his friends have deserted him, and no one is willing to help him anymore.
他所有的朋友都拋棄了他，也沒人再願意幫他了。

▶形 I used to live in a desert region. It wasn't that bad.
我以前住在沙漠地區，也沒那麼糟啦。

實用片語用語
be willing to do sth. 樂意做某事

de·sign [dɪˋzaɪn]

Track 1287

名 設計 動 設計 同 sketch 設計、構思

▶名 The car is of bad design and performance（性能）.
這輛車設計和性能都不好。

▶動 The machine is designed by a master.
這機器可是大師設計的。

de·sire [dɪˋzaɪr]

Track 1288

名 渴望、期望 同 fancy 渴望

▶There is no one who doesn't desire happiness（幸福）and health.
沒有人不渴望幸福和健康。

des·sert [dɪˋzɝt]

Track 1289

名 餐後點心、甜點

▶Would you like some ice cream as dessert? If so, I can get some for you.
你想吃冰淇淋作為餐後甜點嗎？想要的話，我就幫你拿一些來。

萬用延伸句型
If so, S. + V. 如果是這樣的話，……。反義句：If not, S. + V. 如果不是這樣的話，……。

---

de·tect [dɪˋtɛkt]

Track 1290

動 查出、探出、發現 同 discover 發現

▶It's easy for the radar（雷達）to detect planes.
雷達很容易偵測到飛機。

---

de·vel·op [dɪˋvɛləp]

Track 1291

動 發展、開發

▶We need to develop a way to finish the job faster.
我們得開發一個方式來快點完成工作。

---

de·vel·op·ment [dɪˋvɛləpmənt]

Track 1292

名 發展、開發

▶Product development is the key to success.
產品研發才是成功的關鍵。

---

dew [dju]

Track 1293

名 露水、露

▶My shoes are wet with dew.
我的鞋子被露水弄濕了。

實用片語用語
wet with sth. 被……弄濕

---

di·al [ˋdaɪəl]

Track 1294

名 刻度盤 動 撥（電話） 同 call 打電話

▶名 I looked at the dial to check my speed.
我看了一下儀表板以確認行駛的速度。

▶動 Can you dial his number for me?
你可以幫我撥打他的電話嗎？

實用片語用語
dial sb. 打給某人
例如：She dialed her mom after her got home.
她回到家之後就撥了電話給她媽媽。

---

dia·mond [ˋdaɪmənd]

Track 1295

名 鑽石

▶It took him a long time to earn enough money to buy a diamond ring for his wife.
他花了很長一段時間才賺到足夠的錢來為他的妻子買一枚鑽石戒指。

---

di·a·ry [ˋdaɪərɪ]

Track 1296

名 日誌、日記本 同 journal 日誌

▶There is a diary on this old man's desk.
這個老人的書桌上放著一本日記。

---

dic·tion·ar·y [ˋdɪkʃənˏɛrɪ]

Track 1297

名 字典、辭典

▶Would you be kind enough to look up this word in the dictionary for me?
你能好心地幫我在字典裡查一下這個單字嗎？

實用片語用語
look up 查閱（字典）

dif·fer·ence [ˋdɪfərəns]

Track 1298

名 差異、差別 反 similarity 相似處

▶There is no great difference between the two objects; they are the same in nature.
這兩樣物體沒有太大的差別，它們本質上都是一樣的。

dif·fi·cul·ty [ˋdɪfə͵kʌltɪ]

Track 1299

名 困難 反 ease 簡單

▶I have difficulty understanding this case by myself; would you please help me?
我獨自瞭解這個案件有困難，你能幫我一下嗎？

實用片語用語
have difficulty (in) doing sth. 在做某事上有困難

di·no·saur [ˋdaɪnə͵sɔr]

Track 1300

名 恐龍

▶The dinosaurs disappeared from the Earth in the ancient times.
恐龍在遠古時代就從地球上消失了。

di·rec·tion [dəˋrɛkʃən]

Track 1301

名 指導、方向 同 way 方向

▶Would you take me to the hotel? I have a poor sense of direction, and I am afraid I will get lost.
您能帶我到那個旅館去嗎？我的方向感很差，我擔心我會迷路。

實用片語用語
get lost 迷路

di·rec·tor [dəˋrɛktɚ]

Track 1302

名 指揮者、導演

▶What's the matter? Why is the director so mad?
怎麼了？為什麼導演這麼生氣？

dis·agree [͵dɪsəˋgri]

Track 1303

動 不符合、不同意 反 agree 同意

▶I take it from your silence that you disagree.
從你的沉默中我知道你不同意。

dis·agree·ment [͵dɪsəˋgrimənt]

Track 1304

名 意見不合、不同意 反 agreement 同意

▶They are in disagreement on this issue（問題）; I hope it can be solved as soon as possible.
他們在這個問題上意見不一致，我希望能儘快解決。

萬用延伸句型
I hope (that) + S.+ V. 我希望……

dis·ap·pear [͵dɪsəˋpɪr]

Track 1305

動 消失、不見 同 appear 出現

▶The magician（魔術師）made the rabbit disappear.
那位魔術師把兔子變不見了。

萬用延伸句型
使役動詞句型：S. + make / have / let + O. + V. 須注意第二個動詞如果表主動的話，必為原型動詞，且前面不加 to。

dis·cuss [dɪˋskʌs]

Track 1306

動 討論、商議 同 consult 商議

▶It took them very little time to discuss this matter.
他們只花了一點點時間來討論這件事情。

dis·cus·sion [dɪˋskʌʃən] Track 1307

名 討論、商議 同 consultation 商議

▶The current discussion topic is Jane's new boyfriend.
現在大家正在討論的主題是珍妮的新男友。

dis·hon·est [dɪsˋɑnɪst] Track 1308

形 不誠實的 反 honest 誠實的

▶It was very dishonest of you to lie to them.
你向他們撒謊是很不老實的。

萬用延伸句型
It is adj. of sb.to do sth.
某人這麼做實在太……了。
這個句型中的 adj. 是用來修飾人的。

dis·play [dɪˋsple] Track 1309

動 展出 名 展示、展覽 同 show 展示

▶動 They displayed their products（產品）in the windows.
他們把產品陳列在櫥窗裡。

▶名 There are many fancy cars on display now.
現在有很多豪華汽車展出。

實用片語用語
on display 展出

dis·tance [ˋdɪstəns] Track 1310

名 距離 同 length 距離、長度

▶He is nearsighted, so it's hard for him to see the mountain in the distance. 他有近視，所以想要看見遠山太難了。

實用片語用語
in the distance 遙遠的

dis·tant [ˋdɪstənt] Track 1311

形 疏遠的、有距離的

▶She's been distant ever since we had the fight last week.
我們上禮拜吵架後她就對我很疏遠。

di·vide [dəˋvaɪd] Track 1312

動 分開 同 separate 分開

▶How about dividing all the people into three groups?
把所有人分成三組如何？

實用片語用語
divide A into B 把 A 分成 B

di·vi·sion [dəˋvɪʒən] Track 1313

名 分割、除去

▶They agreed upon a division of the book into ten units.
他們同意將這本書分成十個單元。

diz·zy [ˋdɪzɪ] Track 1314

形 暈眩的、被弄糊塗的

▶He had too much to drink and felt dizzy at night.
他喝多了，因此晚上頭暈。

dol·phin [ˋdɑlfɪn] Track 1315

名 海豚

▶No wonder people like dolphins. They are so cute.
怪不得大家都喜歡海豚。牠們好可愛。

don·key [ˋdɑnkɪ] Track 1316

名 驢子、傻瓜 同 mule 驢，騾子

▶There is a donkey eating grass on the field over there.
有頭驢子正在那邊的田野上吃草。

dot [dɑt]

Track 1317

名 圓點 動 以點表示

▶名 He likes wearing ties with dots on them.
他喜歡打有點點的領帶。

▶動 The lake is dotted with little boats.
湖面上佈滿了小船。

實用片語用語
be dotted with something 散佈、佈滿
此片語通常使用被動。

dou·ble [ˋdʌbḷ]

Track 1318

形 雙倍的 副 雙倍地 名 二倍 動 加倍 反 single 單一的

▶形 It won't be long before the total output（產量）is double that of last year.
不久之後總產量就會是去年的兩倍了。

▶副 You should be double careful when you cross the street.
你過馬路時要加倍小心。

▶名 Your pay is the double of mine.
你的薪資是我的兩倍。

▶動 The population（人口）of the city has doubled over the past year. 這個城市的人口在前一年內已經倍增了。

萬用延伸句型
It won't be long before... 不久後就會……

doubt [daʊt]

Track 1319

名 疑問 動 懷疑 反 believe 相信

▶名 There is no room for doubt, because the police have found enough evidence（證據）.
沒有懷疑的餘地了，因為警察已經找到了足夠的證據。

▶動 I doubt that he really killed his sister.
我不相信他真殺了他的妹妹。

dough·nut [ˋdo͵nʌt]

Track 1320

名 油炸圈餅、甜甜圈

▶My mother is good at making doughnuts.
我媽媽很會做甜甜圈。

down·town [ˋdaʊnˋtaʊn]

Track 1321

副 鬧區的 名 鬧區、商業區

▶副 We went downtown yesterday, but there was nothing we wanted to buy.
我們昨天到市區去，卻沒有什麼東西要買的。

▶名 Many young people are eager（渴望的）to live in downtown New York.
有很多年輕人都渴望能居住在紐約市區。

實用片語用語
eager to do sth. 渴望做某事

Dr. [ˋdɑktɚ]

Track 1322

名 醫生、博士 同 doctor 醫生

▶Would you please tell me how I can find Dr. Wilson? It's urgent（急迫的）.
能請你告訴我如何才能找到威爾遜醫生嗎？我有急事。

實用片語用語
It's urgent (that)...（某事）很緊急

drag [dræg]

Track 1323

動 拖曳 同 pull 拖、拉

▶We don't need the rug（地毯）; let's drag it out of the room.
我們不需要地毯，我們把它拖出房間吧。

drag·on [ˋdrægən] Track 1324

名 龍

▶The Chinese consider the dragon a lucky animal.
中國人認為龍是一種吉祥的動物。

drag·on·fly [ˋdrægənˏflaɪ] Track 1325

名 蜻蜓

▶It looks like a blue dragonfly, but actually it's just a blue flower.
它看上去像隻藍色蜻蜓，但是事實上它只是一朵藍色的花。

文法字詞解析
in fact 和 actually 都有「事實上」的意思，但 in fact 是用在補充前面所說的話，actually 卻是要修正前面所說的話。

dra·ma [ˋdræmə] Track 1326

名 劇本、戲劇 同 theater 戲劇

▶Are you interested in drama? If so, let's go see a play tonight.
你對戲劇感興趣嗎？如果感興趣的話，我們今晚一起去看一齣戲劇吧。

實用片語用語
be interested in sth. 對某事感到有興趣

draw·er [ˋdrɔɚ] Track 1327

名 抽屜、製圖員

▶Would you please open the drawer and get me the files（文件）? 請你打開抽屜，把文件拿給我好嗎？

實用片語用語
get sb. sth. / get sth. for sb. 幫某人拿某物

draw·ing [ˋdrɔɪŋ] Track 1328

名 繪圖 同 illustration 圖表

▶Not every child in the classroom is good at drawing.
並不是在這個教室裡的每一個孩子都很擅長畫畫。

dress [drɛs] Track 1329

名 洋裝 動 穿衣服 同 clothe 穿衣服

▶名 Let's go shopping together and buy some new dresses.
我們一起去逛逛商店並買些新洋裝吧。

▶動 She dressed her kids very casually（隨性的）.
她替孩子穿上隨性的服裝。

drop [drɑp] Track 1330

動（使）滴下、滴

▶The rain dropped to the ground. 雨滴落在地。

實用片語用語
drop to 滴落在……上

drug [drʌg] Track 1331

名 藥、藥物 同 medicine 藥

▶He peddled（兜售）drugs to people.
他販賣毒品給人們。

drug·store [ˋdrʌgˏstor] Track 1332

名 藥房 同 pharmacy 藥房

▶Would you tell me how I can get to the nearest drugstore?
你能告訴我最近的藥房怎麼去嗎？

drum [drʌm] Track 1333

名 鼓

▶Can you stop playing drums at midnight?
你可以不要半夜打鼓嗎？

文法字詞解析
stop 後面接動名詞表示「停止做某事」，接不定詞表示「停下來去做某事」。

dry·er [draɪɚ]

Track 1334

名 烘乾機、吹風機

▶Would you pass the dryer to me? I just had a shower and my hair is totally（完全地）wet.
你能把吹風機遞給我一下嗎？我剛洗了個澡，頭髮全濕了。

實用片語用語
have / take a shower 淋浴

dull [dʌl]

Track 1335

形 遲鈍的、單調的 同 flat 單調的

▶The work in this office is always dull.
這個辦公室的工作總是很單調。

dumb [dʌm]

Track 1336

形 啞的、笨的 反 smart 聰明的

▶The little boys laughed at the girl and called her dumb.
那些小男孩們嘲笑那個小女孩很笨。

實用片語用語
laugh at sb. / sth. 嘲笑某人／某物

dump·ling [ˋdʌmplɪŋ]

Track 1337

名 麵團、餃子

▶It took my mom thirty minutes to make these dumplings on the table. 媽媽花了半小時做了桌子上的這些餃子。

du·ty [ˋdjutɪ]

Track 1338

名 責任、義務 同 responsibility 責任

▶It's my duty to help you. 幫你的忙是我份內該做的事。

萬用延伸句型
It is sb.'s duty to do sth.
做某事是某人的職責。

earn [ɝn]

Track 1339

動 賺取、得到 同 obtain 得到

▶It's time you start earning a living.
你是時候該自己謀生了。

實用片語用語
start V-ing / to V. 開始做某事

earth·quake [ˋɝθ͵kwek]

Track 1340

名 地震 同 tremor 地震

▶I've never experienced an earthquake in my whole life.
我一輩子還沒經歷過地震。

east·ern [ˋistɚn]

Track 1341

形 東方的、東方人 反 western 西方的

▶This eastern country is quite beautiful.
這個東方的國家非常美麗。

ed·u·ca·tion [͵ɛdʒəˋkeʃən]

Track 1342

名 教育 同 instruction 教育

▶Not every child in the poor area has the opportunity（機會）to receive good education.
不是每個貧困地區的孩子都有機會接受良好的教育。

文法字詞解析
主詞 child 是單數，因此前面的修飾語是用 not every 而非 not all，且搭配的動詞要加 s。

ef·fect [ə`fɛkt] Track 1343

名 影響、效果 動 引起、招致 同 produce 引起

▶名 His words have no effect on her.
他說的話對她完全沒有影響。

▶動 You should try to effect an intermediation（調解）to solve the problem.
你們應該要試著透過調解來解決這個問題。

實用片語用語
have an effect (on sb. / sth.)（對某人／某事）有影響

ef·fec·tive [ə`fɛktɪv] Track 1344

形 有效的 反 vain 無效的

▶Let's take some effective measures to control the current（現在的）situation（形勢）.
我們採取一些有效的措施來控制當下的形勢吧。

ef·fort [`ɛfɚt] Track 1345

名 努力 同 attempt 努力嘗試

▶He barely ever makes an effort in anything.
無論是什麼事情，他幾乎從來不付出一點努力。

實用片語用語
make an effort (to do sth.) 努力做某事

el·der [`ɛldɚ] Track 1346

形 年長的 名 長輩 反 junior 晚輩

▶形 I have never seen your elder brother. What does he look like?
我從來沒見過你的哥哥，他長什麼樣子啊？

▶名 I hear that she is the elder of the two sisters.
我聽說她是兩姐妹之中的姐姐。

e·lect [ɪ`lɛkt] Track 1347

動 挑選、選舉 形 挑選的 同 select 挑選

▶動 Who do you want to elect as the club president?
你們想選誰作為社團社長呢？

▶形 An elect group of specialists（專家）are chosen to carry out the plan.
一群精挑細選的專家將要負責執行這個計畫。

實用片語用語
1. elect sb. (as) president / leader 選某人做領導人
2. carry out 執行（計畫）

el·e·ment [`ɛləmənt] Track 1348

名 基本要素 同 component 構成要素

▶What are the crucial（必要的）elements to a successful company? 一個成功的公司需要哪些元素呢？

el·e·va·tor [`ɛlə͵vetɚ] Track 1349

名 升降機、電梯 同 escalator 電扶梯

▶I don't want to walk all the way up to the twentieth floor. Let's take an elevator.
我可不想一路走到二十樓，我們還是搭電梯吧。

e·mot·ion [ɪ`moʃən] Track 1350

名 情感 同 feeling 情感

▶He smiled, but there was some other emotion just below the surface.
他笑了笑，但在他的微笑中隱藏著一種難以捉摸的情感。

實用片語用語
below the surface 在表面下、外表之下

en·cour·age [ɪnˋkɝɪdʒ]
Track 1351

動 鼓勵 同 inspire 激勵

▶Her parents always encouraged her to do better.
她的父母總是鼓勵她做得更好。

實用片語用語
encourage sb. to do sth. 鼓勵某人做某事

en·cour·age·ment [ɪnˋkɝɪdʒmənt]
Track 1352

名 鼓勵 同 incentive 鼓勵

▶Your encouragement will make her more confident.
你的鼓勵會使她更加有信心的。

end·ing [ˋɛndɪŋ]
Track 1353

名 結局、結束 同 terminal 終點

▶Not all lovers have happy endings like that in the fairy tales（童話故事）.
並不是每對戀人都能像童話故事中一樣有個美好的結局。

文法字詞解析
ending 解釋作「結局」時是可數名詞。

en·e·my [ˋɛnəmɪ]
Track 1354

名 敵人 同 opponent 敵手

▶He's made lots of enemies because of his personality（人格）.
因為個性關係，他樹立了很多敵人。

實用片語用語
make an enemy (of sb.) 樹敵

en·er·gy [ˋɛnɚdʒɪ]
Track 1355

名 能量、精力 同 strength 力量

▶I don't have enough energy to go hiking.
我沒有足夠的經歷去爬山。

en·joy [ɪnˋdʒɔɪ]
Track 1356

動 享受、欣賞 同 appreciate 欣賞

▶We all enjoyed the movie a lot. 我們都非常喜歡那部電影。

en·joy·ment [ɪnˋdʒɔɪmənt]
Track 1357

名 享受、愉快 同 pleasure 愉快

▶He recorded the song for his own enjoyment.
他為了自己的享受而錄了這首歌。

en·tire [ɪnˋtaɪr]
Track 1358

形 全部的 反 partial 部分的

▶The entire office is surprised to hear the news.
整個辦公室的人聽到這個消息都很驚訝。

實用片語用語
surprised to hear / learn sth. 驚訝於聽到／知道某事

en·trance [ˋɛntrəns]
Track 1359

名 入口 同 exit 出口

▶Where's the entrance to the railway（鐵路） station?
火車站的入口在哪裡啊？

實用片語用語
entrance to / of sth. 進入某地方的入口。除此之外「access to sth.」也是常見的說法。

en·ve·lope [ˋɛnvəˌlop]
Track 1360

名 信封

▶Will you please put the photo in the envelope and send it for me? 您能幫我把這張照片放在信封裡，並把它寄出去嗎？

en·vi·ron·ment [ɪn`vaɪrənmənt] Track 1361

名 環境

▶We need to protect our environment for a better future.
我們得為了一個更好的未來而保護環境。

e·ras·er [ɪ`resɚ] Track 1362

名 橡皮擦

▶Would you please lend me your eraser? 你能借我橡皮擦嗎？

實用片語用語
lend sb. sth. / lend sth. to sb. 借某人某物。lend 是出借的意思，那向別人借東西怎麼説呢？是「borrow sth. (from sb.)」。

er·ror [`ɛrɚ] Track 1363

名 錯誤 同 mistake 錯誤

▶She always makes the same error in writing.
她在寫作時總犯一樣的錯誤。

實用片語用語
make / commit an error 犯錯。
commit「有犯罪、做錯事」的意思。或者也可以説「make a mistake」。

es·pe·cial·ly [ə`spɛʃəlɪ] Track 1364

副 特別地 反 mostly 一般地

▶Let's pay more attention to the structure（結構） of the article, especially the latter（後面的） part.
我們要多注意這篇文章的結構，特別是後半部分。

e·vent [ɪ`vɛnt] Track 1365

名 事件 同 episode 事件

▶She spent all night planning the event.
她一整個晚上都在計畫這次活動。

ex·act [ɪg`zækt] Track 1366

形 正確的 同 precise 準確的

▶Will you please let me know the exact time of the meeting?
您能告訴我此次會議的確切時間嗎？

ex·cel·lent [`ɛksḷənt] Track 1367

形 最好的 同 admirable 極好的

▶Would you like to tell me where you picked up your excellent English? 你能告訴我你是在哪裡學會這樣一口流利的英語嗎？

實用片語用語
pick up 除了一般常用的「把東西拿起來」之外，還有「藉由聆聽、觀看來向他人學習某個技巧或習慣」的意思。

ex·cite [ɪk`saɪt] Track 1368

動 刺激、鼓舞 反 calm 使鎮定

▶The night before the wedding, Aaron was too excited to fall asleep. 婚禮的前一晚，艾倫興奮得睡不著。

ex·cite·ment [ɪk`saɪtmənt] Track 1369

名 興奮、激動 同 turmoil 騷動

▶I'm accustomed（習慣的） to working in an environment full of noise and excitement. 我習慣在喧鬧的房間裡工作。

實用片語用語
1. full of 充滿
2. be accustomed to 習慣

ex·cuse [ɪk`skjuz] Track 1370

名 藉口 動 原諒 反 blame 責備

▶名 If you love it, you will find a way; if you dislike it, you will find an excuse. 如果你熱愛它，就能想出辦法；如果你不喜歡它，你就會找藉口。

▶動 There's no way we can excuse this behavior（表現）.
我們絕不能原諒這樣的表現。

萬用延伸句型
There's no way + S. + V. 絕對不可能……。和「It is impossible to...」同義。

A B C D **E** F G H I J K L M N O P Q R S T U V W X Y Z

ex·er·cise [ˋɛksɚ͵saɪz]

Track 1371

名 練習 動 運動 同 practice 練習

▶名 Have you done the exercise in the book yet?
書上的練習題你做了沒？

▶動 We should exercise every day; it's good for our health.
我們每天做運動吧，這對我們的身體健康有好處。

實用片語用語
be good for sth. 對……有益。也可以說「be beneficial for sth.」。

ex·ist [ɪgˋzɪst]

Track 1372

動 存在 同 be 存在

▶This kind of bird no longer exists. 這種鳥現在已經不存在了。

ex·pect [ɪkˋspɛkt]

Track 1373

動 期望 同 suppose 期望

▶How long do you expect to stay here? 你打算在這裡待多久？

實用片語用語
expect to do sth. 預期要做某事。另外，「look forward to do sth.」表示「期待做某事」。

ex·pen·sive [ɪkˋspɛnsɪv]

Track 1374

形 昂貴的 反 cheap 便宜的

▶I think this car is too expensive. 我覺得這部車太貴了。

ex·pe·ri·ence [ɪkˋspɪrɪəns]

Track 1375

名 經驗 動 體驗 同 occurrence 經歷、事件

▶名 My experience is that people don't like it when others point out their mistakes.
我的經驗是，人們不喜歡別人指出他們的錯誤。

▶動 Only after you experience what she suffered（遭受）will you understand her.
如果你體會了她經歷的事情，你就會理解她了。

ex·pert [ˋɛkspɝt]

Track 1376

形 熟練的 名 專家 反 amateur 業餘、外行

▶形 She is an expert language teacher.
她是個熟練的語言教師。

▶名 He is an expert on computers; why don't we go and ask him? 他是電腦方面的專家，為什麼不去問他呢？

實用片語用語
expert on / in 在……上是專家

ex·plain [ɪkˋsplen]

Track 1377

動 解釋

▶Would you please explain the math problem to me again? I still don't understand.
您能再為我解釋一下這道數學題嗎？我還是不明白。

實用片語用語
explain sth. to sb. 向某人解釋某事

ex·press [ɪkˋsprɛs]

Track 1378

動 表達、說明 同 indicate 表明

▶I'm not sure how to express what I really feel.
我不知道如何表達我真正的感覺。

ex·tra [ˋɛkstrə]

Track 1379

形 額外的 副 特別地 同 additional 額外的

▶形 Would you like to give yourself an extra day off?
你願意再給自己一天額外的假期嗎？

▶副 They charge extra for wine. 喝酒要額外收費。

eye·brow/brow [ˋaɪ͵braʊ]/[braʊ] Track 1380

名 眉毛

▶I don't think I'm pretty, but I really like my eyebrows.
我不覺得我漂亮，但我挺喜歡自己的眉毛。

fail [fel] Track 1381

動 失敗、不及格 反 achieve 實現、達到

▶I tried to fix this machine, but I failed.
我試著想修好這台機器，但是卻失敗了。

文法字詞解析
try to 後面加原形動詞時，它有「試著達到某個目的」的意思，當 try 用過去式時，則暗示了嘗試的事情沒有成功。

fail·ure [ˋfeljɚ] Track 1382

名 失敗、失策 同 success 成功

▶There might be a power failure tonight.
今天晚上可能會停電。

fair [fɛr] Track 1383

形 公平的、合理的 副 光明正大地 同 just 公正的

▶形 It's not fair to make him do all the work.
讓他一個人做所有的事情太不公平了。

▶副 Their team never plays fair.
他們那隊從來不堂堂正正地比賽。

fa·mous [ˋfeməs] Track 1384

形 有名的、出名的

▶That place is famous for its hot springs.
那個地方以溫泉而著名。

實用片語用語
be famous for sth. 以……而著名

fault [fɔlt] Track 1385

名 責任、過失 動 犯錯 同 error 過失

▶名 There is a fault in this machine; please find someone to fix it soon.
這台機器故障了。請儘快找人來修一下。

▶動 No one could fault his performance（演出）.
他的演出無懈可擊。

fa·vor [ˋfevɚ] Track 1386

名 喜好 動 贊成

▶名 Would you please do me a favor, Tom?
湯姆，幫我個忙好嗎？

▶動 Can you tell me how many people favor the proposal（提議）? 你能告訴我有多少人贊同這項提議嗎？

實用片語用語
do sb. a favor 幫某人的忙。favor 在這裡有「幫助、恩惠、善意的行為」的意思。

fa·vor·ite [ˋfevərɪt] Track 1387

形 最喜歡的 同 precious 珍愛的

▶This is my favorite song ever.
這是我史上最愛的一首歌。

fear·ful [ˋfɪrfəl]

Track 1388

形 可怕的、嚇人的 同 afraid 害怕的

▶I am fearful that his fever might get worse.
我擔心他的高燒會越來越糟。

實用片語用語
be fearful 害怕（某事），後面可以加 that + 子句，也可以加 of + 名詞。

fee [fi]

Track 1389

名 費用 同 fare 費用

▶Is there anything like a management（管理）fee or parking fee in this place? 在這個地方有沒有管理費和停車費？

fe·male [ˋfimel]

Track 1390

形 女性的 名 女性 同 feminine 女性的

▶形 Is your cat male or female?
你的貓是公的還母的？

▶名 It doesn't matter whether you are a male or female; you can all join the club.
是男是女都沒關係，所有人都可以參加這個俱樂部。

fence [fɛns]

Track 1391

名 籬笆、圍牆 動 防衛、防護

▶名 There is a fence around our garden, so that chicks won't eat our vegetables. 我們的園子周圍圍著籬笆，小雞就不會進來吃裡面的菜了。

▶動 We fenced the house to keep thieves out.
我們把房子圍起來，這樣小偷才不會進來。

實用片語用語
keep (sb. / sth.) out 拒（某人／某物）於外、使〈某人／某物〉不能接近。
同樣的用法還有 keep sb. / sth. away，例如：「An apple a day keeps doctor away.（一天一蘋果，醫生遠離我。）」相信大家都聽過這個說法吧。

fes·ti·val [ˋfɛstəvḷ]

Track 1392

名 節日 同 holiday 節日

▶She's all dressed up for the festival.
她為了這個節慶好好打扮了一番。

fe·ver [ˋfivɚ]

Track 1393

名 發燒、熱、入迷

▶I have a slight（輕微的）fever. 我有點輕微的發燒。

實用片語用語
have a slight fever 有輕微的發燒。那發高燒要怎麼說呢？是「Have a high fever」。

field [fild]

Track 1394

名 田野、領域

▶The children are running around in the field.
孩子們在田野奔跑。

fight·er [ˋfaɪtɚ]

Track 1395

名 戰士

▶He's one of our best fighters.
他是我們最優秀的戰士之一。

實用片語用語
one of... 眾多同類事物的其中之一，需要注意的是，因為是「其中之一」，所以 of 後面的名詞是複數，但整個片語則以單數來看。

fig·ure [ˋfɪgjɚ]

Track 1396

名 人影、畫像、數字 動 演算 同 symbol 數字、符號

▶名 Would you tell me what these figures on the paper mean?
你能告訴我紙上的這些數字是什麼意思嗎？

▶動 Can you please figure the total? I'll pay it with a check.
請你把總價算出來好嗎？我將用支票支付。

film [fɪlm]
Track 1397

名 電影、膠捲 同 cinema 電影

▶My friend told me that a new action film is on.
朋友說有一部新的動作片正在上映。

fire·man/fire·wom·an
Track 1398

[ˋfaɪrmən]/[ˋfaɪrwʊmən]

名 消防員／女消防員

▶The firemen are not able to put out the fire.
這些消防人員無法滅火。

實用片語用語
put out the fire 滅火

firm [fɝm]
Track 1399

形 堅固的 副 牢固地 同 enterprise 公司

▶形 His grip is too firm and I can't run away.
他抓得太緊了，我都逃不了。

▶副 Hold firm, or you might fall off the bike.
抓緊點，不然你可能會從腳踏車上摔下去。

實用片語用語
firm up 確定某事
例如：We are going to firm up the year plan.
我們將會把整的年度計畫確定下來。

fish·er·man [ˋfɪʃɚmən]
Track 1400

名 漁夫

▶The fishermen here are very friendly. 這裡的漁夫們都很友善。

fit [fɪt]
Track 1401

形 適合的 動 適合 名 適合 同 suit 適合

▶形 The manager（經理）thinks he is fit for this job.
經理覺得他很適合這份工作。

▶動 These gloves fit you very well. 這些手套很適合你。

▶名 The shoes are a perfect fit for me.
這雙鞋子對我來說剛剛好。

實用片語用語
fit for sb. / sth. 合適於（某人／某物）

fix [fɪks]
Track 1402

動 使穩固、修理 同 repair 修理

▶Would you help me fix this machine?
你能幫我修一下這台機器嗎？

flag [flæg]
Track 1403

名 旗、旗幟 同 banner 旗、橫幅

▶This country had the national flag designed by its people.
這個國家的國旗是自己的人民設計的。

flash [flæʃ]
Track 1404

動 閃亮 名 一瞬間 同 flame 照亮

▶動 That driver keeps flashing his lights at me.
那個司機一直用車燈閃我。

▶名 He was by my side in a flash. 他一瞬間就來到了我的身旁。

實用片語用語
in a flash 一瞬間
或者也可以說「like a flash」，因為「像閃光一樣」不就是形容非常快速的意思嗎？另外要小心不要把 flash 和 flesh 弄混了，後者是「肉」的意思。

flash·light/flash
Track 1405

[ˋflæʃˌlaɪt]/[flæʃ]

名 手電筒、閃光 同 lantern 燈籠

▶Did you bring a flashlight? It's dark down here.
你有帶手電筒嗎？這下面好暗喔。

flat [flæt]
Track 1406

名 平的東西、公寓 形 平坦的

▶名 He decided to move to a new flat because his house was too old. 他決定搬到新公寓去住，因為他的家太老舊了。

▶形 Our ancestors（祖先）thought the earth was flat, not round. 我們的祖先認為地球是平的，而不是圓的。

實用片語用語
decide to do sth. 決定做某事。須注意，decide 後面一定是接不定詞喔。

flight [flaɪt]
Track 1407

名 飛行

▶It took human beings（人類）a long time to realize their dream of flight. 人類花了很長一段時間才得以實現飛行的夢想。

flood [flʌd]
Track 1408

名 洪水、水災 動 淹沒 反 drought 旱災

▶名 No wonder they said that this is the most terrible flood in this country. All crops were destroyed. 難怪他們說這是該國最嚴重的一次水災。所有作物都死光了。

▶動 The rice fields were flooded. 稻田被淹沒了。

flour [flaʊr]
Track 1409

名 麵粉 動 撒粉於

▶名 The flour in the kitchen is not enough to make bread.
廚房的麵粉不夠用來做麵包。

▶動 The board is not dry enough to make pastry（糕餅）; please flour it first.
砧板不夠乾，做不成糕餅。請先在上面撒上麵粉。

flow [flo]
Track 1410

動 流出、流動 名 流程、流量 同 stream 流動

▶動 Most rivers on the earth flow into the sea.
地球上的河流大部分都流入了海洋。

▶名 They have to watch the flow of the river day and night.
他們得日夜監視河水的流動。

實用片語用語
day and night 一整天，有「日日夜夜持續不斷地」的意思，也可以寫成 around the clock。

flu [flu]
Track 1411

名 流行性感冒

▶I have the flu, so I won't be able to make it to class today.
我得了流感，所以今天沒辦法去上課了。

實用片語用語
make it to class 上課

flute [flut]
Track 1412

名 橫笛、用笛吹奏

▶It doesn't matter if you don't play the flute well.
你長笛吹不好不要緊。

fo·cus [`fokəs]
Track 1413

名 焦點、焦距 動 使集中在焦點、集中 同 concentrate 集中

▶名 Her beauty makes her the focus of attention; many men come to invite her to dance.
她的美貌成為眾人的焦點，很多男士都來邀請她跳舞。

▶動 It makes me so sad that no one focuses on the serious problem. 沒有一個人關注這個嚴重的問題，這讓我很傷心。

實用片語用語
focus on sth. 聚焦於
同樣的用法還有「concentrate on sth.」：全神貫注於某事上」；以及「devote one's attention to sth.」：將某人的注意力集中於某事上。

fog·gy [ˋfɑgɪ]

Track 1414

形 多霧的、朦朧的

▶It's very foggy today; would you please drive the car as slowly（緩慢地）as possible?
今天霧很大，能請你儘量把車開慢一點嗎？

文法字詞解析
foggy 除了可以是說霧多、視線不清以外，也可以用「foggy memory」來形容記憶模糊。

fol·low·ing [ˋfɑloɪŋ]

Track 1415

名 下一個 形 接著的 同 next 下一個

▶名 Will the following please come to the front as soon as possible?
能請下列人員儘快到前面來嗎？

▶形 We'll read three chapters this week and three more in the following week.
我們這禮拜會讀三章，下個禮拜再讀三章。

fool [ful]

Track 1416

名 傻子 動 愚弄、欺騙 同 trick 戲弄

▶名 You made me look like a fool.
你害我出醜。

▶動 When I knew he has been fooling me all the time, I was very sad.
當我知道了他一直都在欺騙我時，我感到很傷心。

fool·ish [ˋfulɪʃ]

Track 1417

形 愚笨的、愚蠢的 反 wise 聰明的

▶That's the most foolish thing I've ever heard.
這是我聽過最蠢的事。

foot·ball [ˋfʊt͵bɔl]

Track 1418

名 足球、橄欖球

▶My son is bored because no one wants to play football with him.
沒人想跟我兒子踢足球，所以他覺得很無聊。

文法字詞解析
表示某人感受如何的形容詞字尾常常以「-ed」表示，表示某物令人覺得如何的形容詞得用「-ing」表示。所以如果說某人 boring 的話，就代表那個人很無趣、沒有意思。

for·eign·er [ˋfɔrɪnɚ]

Track 1419

名 外國人

▶What do you think of those foreigners in our company? Do you like them?
你覺得我們公司裡的那些外國人如何？你喜歡他們嗎？

for·give [fɚˋgɪv]

Track 1420

動 原諒、寬恕 反 punish 處罰

▶I can't forgive what you did to my mom.
我無法原諒你對我媽做的事。

文法字詞解析
forgive 的動詞變化：forgive, forgave, forgiven

form [fɔrm]

Track 1421

名 形式、表格 動 形成 同 construct 構成

▶名 Would you please fill out the form on the desk first?
請您先填寫一下桌子上的那張表格好嗎？

▶動 We formed a group quickly to discuss the problem.
我們很快地組成了小組以討論這個問題。

實用片語用語
fill sth. out / fill out sth. 填寫（文件、表格上的）資訊

A B C D E F G H I J K L M N O P Q R S T U V W X Y Z

for·mal [ˋfɔrml̩]
Track 1422

形 正式的、有禮的

▶The letter is too formal in its wording（措辭）; let's rewrite（重寫）it.
這封信在措辭上太正式了，我們重寫一封吧。

for·mer [ˋfɔrmɚ]
Track 1423

形 以前的、先前的 反 present 現在的

▶He always speaks ill of his former friends. He hates them.
他老是說他之前朋友的壞話。他很討厭他們。

for·ward [ˋfɔrwɚd]
Track 1424

形 向前的 名 前鋒 動 發送 同 send 發送

▶形 She's a really forward kind of girl.
她是很前衛大膽的那種女孩。

▶名 Can you tell me who the best forward of the football team is? 你能告訴我這個球隊最好的前鋒是誰嗎？

▶動 Would you please forward the email to your boss?
請你把電子郵件轉寄給你老闆好嗎？

實用片語用語
forward sth. to sb. 將（信件、資訊等）寄給某人

for·wards [ˋfɔrwɚdz]
Track 1425

副 今後、將來、向前

▶Susan leaned（倚靠）forwards against the table without saying anything.
蘇珊欠身向前靠著桌子，一言不發。

fox [fɑks]
Track 1426

名 狐狸、狡猾的人

▶It took the hunter a long time to find the fox and its cubs（幼獸）.
獵人花了很長時間才找到狐狸和牠的小孩。

frank [fræŋk]
Track 1427

形 率直的、坦白的 同 sincere 真誠的

▶To be frank, it doesn't matter whether he joins us or not.
坦白說，他加不加入我們沒什麼關係。

實用片語用語
to be frank 坦白說。常用在句首，用來引導自己認為是事實的事。也可以說「Frankly speaking」。

free·dom [ˋfridəm]
Track 1428

名 自由、解放、解脫 同 liberty 自由

▶There are many people in this country fighting for freedom.
在這個國家有很多人正在為自由而戰。

free·zer [ˋfrizɚ]
Track 1429

名 冰庫、冷凍庫 同 refrigerator 冰箱

▶There is always food in the freezer. Take whatever you want.
冰箱裡總是有食物。你想吃什麼就拿什麼。

friend·ly [ˋfrɛndlɪ]
Track 1430

形 友善的、親切的 同 kind 親切的

▶We are taught to be friendly to strangers.
我們被教導要對陌生人友善。

fright [fraɪt]

Track 1431

名 驚駭、恐怖、驚嚇 同 panic 驚恐

▶The cat gave me quite a fright. 那隻貓嚇了我一跳。

實用片語用語

give sb. a fright 讓某人受到驚嚇。如果要說「某人嚇到的話」則是「sb. get / have a fright」。

fright·en [ˋfraɪtn̩]

Track 1432

動 震驚、使害怕 同 scare 使恐懼

▶The ghost frightened the kids away from the house.
那隻鬼把孩子們從房子嚇走了。

func·tion [ˋfʌŋkʃən]

Track 1433

名 功能、作用

▶I have no idea what the function of this machine is.
我不知道這機器的功能是幹嘛的。

萬用延伸句型

I have no idea. 我不知道。須注意，「have no idea」是固定用法，後面不再加介係詞，而是直接加疑問詞引導的子句。

fur·ther [ˋfɝðɚ]

Track 1434

副 更進一步地 形 較遠的 動 助長

▶副 She refused to further talk about what happened.
她拒絕進一步說出到底發生了什麼事。

▶形 If you want further information（資訊）, please contact us as soon as possible.
想知道更多資訊，請儘快聯繫我們。

▶動 We'll do all we can to further your plans.
我們將盡力促成你們的計畫。

fu·ture [ˋfjutʃɚ]

Track 1435

名 未來、將來 反 past 過往

▶The boy wants to be an astronaut（太空人）in the future and travel in space.
男孩想將來成為一名太空人，在太空中旅行。

文法字詞解析

future 如果要表示「將來」時，前面一定要加定冠詞，如果寫成「in future」的話，意思就不一樣了，會變成「從今以後、日後」的意思。

gain [gen]

Track 1436

動 得到、獲得 名 得到、獲得 同 obtain 得到

▶名 "No pain, no gain" is quite a famous saying.
「一分耕耘，一分收穫」是句很有名的諺語。

▶動 He is still trying to gain her trust.
他仍然在試著得到她的信任。

ga·rage [gəˋrɑdʒ]

Track 1437

名 車庫

▶Would you please drive my car to the garage?
你能幫我把車開到車庫去嗎？

gar·bage [ˋgɑrbɪdʒ]

Track 1438

名 垃圾

▶Clean up the garbage before you leave, please.
請你離開前先把垃圾清一下吧。

gar·den·er [ˋgɑrdn̩ɚ]

Track 1439

名 園丁、花匠

▶There is a gardener trimming（修剪）up the trees in the garden now.
花園裡有個園丁正在修剪花園裡的樹木。

gate [get]

Track 1440

名 門、閘門

▶Could you wait for me at the gate of the park?
你能在那個公園的門口等我嗎？

實用片語用語
wait for sb. 等待某人

gath·er [ˋgæðɚ]

Track 1441

動 集合、聚集 同 collect 收集

▶The children are gathering wood for the campfire（營火）.
孩子們正為了營火收集木材。

gen·er·al [ˋdʒɛnərəl]

Track 1442

名 將領、將軍 形 普遍的、一般的

▶名 The general is an old but good-looking man.
那名將軍雖老但非常帥氣。

▶形 There is a general feeling of anxiety in the room tonight.
今晚這房裡的人普遍都很焦慮。

實用片語用語
in general 一般來說。用來闡述一個普遍或常見的事情。也可以替換成「generally speaking」。
例如：In general, people get nervous before trying new things.
一般來說，人們再嘗試新事物前都會感到緊張。

gen·er·ous [ˋdʒɛnərəs]

Track 1443

形 慷慨的、大方的、寬厚的 反 harsh 嚴厲的

▶Not all people are able to be so generous to their enemies.
不是所有的人都能對他們的敵人如此寬容。

gen·tle [ˋdʒɛntl̩]

Track 1444

形 溫和的、上流的 同 soft 柔和的

▶He is a generous and gentle guy（傢伙）; would you like me to introduce him to you?
他是一個大方而溫和的人，想不想讓我把他介紹給你呢？

實用片語用語
introduce A to B 將 A 介紹給 B

萬用延伸句型
Would you like me to...? 你希望我做……嗎？ 用於禮貌的請示他人的意願。或者也可以說：Do you want me to...?

gen·tle·man [ˋdʒɛntl̩mən]

Track 1445

名 紳士、家世好的男人

▶Would you please bring this gentleman a glass of beer?
請給這位先生來杯啤酒好嗎？

ge·og·ra·phy [dʒiˋɑgrəfɪ]

Track 1446

名 地理（學）

▶Not all students are good at learning geography.
不是所有的學生都擅長學習地理。

gi·ant [ˋdʒaɪənt]

Track 1447

名 巨人 形 巨大的、龐大的 同 huge 巨大的

▶名 Shakespeare is a giant among playwrights（劇作家）.
莎士比亞可是劇作家中的巨擘。

▶形 The giant poster（海報）of the actor hangs in the theater.
那位演員的大型海報掛在劇場裡。

gi·raffe [dʒəˋræf]

Track 1448

名 長頸鹿

▶You'll never believe this. There's a giraffe in our yard!
你絕對無法相信，我們院子裡有一隻長頸鹿耶！

萬用延伸句型
You will never (won't) believe that... 你絕對不會相信……。never 在這裡用來強調語氣。

glove(s) [glʌv(z)]

Track 1449

名 手套

▶It's getting cold; let's take out the woolen（羊毛的）gloves.
天氣變冷了，我們把羊毛手套拿出來吧。

實用片語用語
go / get / become cold 變冷

glue [glu]

Track 1450

名 膠水、黏膠 動 黏、固著

▶名 Would you please buy a bottle of glue for me on the way?
你能不能順便幫我買瓶膠水回來？

▶動 Could you help me glue up the broken mirror?
你能幫我把這個破掉的鏡子黏起來嗎？

goal [gol]

Track 1451

名 目標、終點 同 destination 終點

▶Once you establish a goal in your heart, you have to try your best to reach it.
一旦你心中確立了一個目標，就要竭盡全力去達到它。

goat [got]

Track 1452

名 山羊

▶Would you please tell me the difference between a goat and a sheep? 你能告訴我山羊和綿羊之間的區別嗎？

gold·en [ˋgoldn̩]

Track 1453

形 金色的、黃金的

▶Speech is silver（銀）, silence is golden. At least that's what some people think.
雄辯是銀，沉默是金。至少有些人是這樣想啦。

實用片語用語
at least 至少

golf [gɔlf]

Track 1454

名 高爾夫球 動 打高爾夫球

▶名 I heard that you like playing golf very much.
我聽說你非常喜歡打高爾夫球。

▶動 Do you have time this weekend? Let's go golfing, shall we?
你這個週末有空嗎？我們去打高爾夫球好嗎？

gov·ern [ˋgʌvən]

Track 1455

動 統治、治理 同 regulate 管理

▶This president is not good at governing a country.
這位總統不怎麼懂得治國。

gov·ern·ment [ˋgʌvənmənt]

Track 1456

名 政府 同 administration 政府

▶Don't you think the government isn't doing enough for us?
你不覺得政府為我們做的還不夠多嗎？

grade [gred]
Track 1457

名 年級、等級

▶He skipped（跳過）fourth grade and went straight to the fifth grade. 他跳過四年級不上，直接升上五年級。

實用片語用語
straight to 直接、沒有延遲地

grape [grep]
Track 1458

名 葡萄、葡萄樹

▶Will you please buy some fruit such as apples or grapes and bring them back to me?
你能買些水果回來嗎？例如蘋果或者葡萄。

grass·y [græsɪ]
Track 1459

形 多草的

▶Let's slide down this grassy slope（斜坡）. It looks fun.
我們順著這草坡滑下去吧，看起來好像很好玩。

實用片語用語
slide down 滑下去。slide 接上不同的介系詞就會衍生出不同的意思，像是 slide along 就有「沿著……滑」的意思。

greed·y [`gridɪ]
Track 1460

形 貪婪的

▶Don't be so greedy. Leave some food for the rest of us.
別那麼貪心，留一點食物給我們其他人吃嘛。

greet [grit]
Track 1461

動 迎接、問候 同 hail 招呼

▶She's over there greeting our new neighbors.
她在那裡問候我們的新鄰居。

growth [groθ]
Track 1462

名 成長、發育 同 progress 進步

▶He had a growth spurt（衝刺）when he was fifteen.
他十五歲的時候忽然長高了很多。

guard [gɑrd]
Track 1463

名 警衛 動 防護、守衛

▶名 The guard looks mean, but he's actually a nice man.
那個警衛看起來很兇，但他其實人很好。

▶動 There is a dog guarding his house.
有一隻狗守衛著他的房子。

gua·va [`gwɑvə]
Track 1464

名 芭樂

▶Do you like guava juice or grapefruit（葡萄柚）juice better?
你比較喜歡芭樂汁還是葡萄柚汁？

萬用延伸句型
除了例句中的問法外，也可以換個說法，例如：Which one do you like better, guava juice or grapefruit juice?

gui·tar [gɪ`tɑr]
Track 1465

名 吉他

▶He is really great at playing the guitar. 他吉他彈得好極了。

guy [gaɪ]
Track 1466

名 傢伙

▶What do you think of that guy wearing a blue T-shirt over there?
你覺得那邊那個穿著藍色T恤的傢伙怎麼樣？

hab·it [ˋhæbɪt]

Track 1467

名 習慣

▶Why don't you get rid（擺脫）of this bad habit?
為什麼不戒掉這個壞習慣呢？

實用片語用語
get rid of sb./sth. 擺脫

hall [hɔl]

Track 1468

名 廳、堂

▶There will be a celebration（慶祝）in the hall. Will you attend it? 大廳裡將有個慶祝活動，你會參加嗎？

ham·burg·er/burg·er

Track 1469

[ˋhæmbɝgɚ]/[ˋbɝgɚ]

名 漢堡

▶Not every person likes to eat hamburgers.
並不是每個人都喜歡吃漢堡。

ham·mer [ˋhæmɚ]

Track 1470

名 鐵鎚 動 鎚打

▶名 Would you please find me some nails and a hammer?
請你幫我找一些釘子和一把鎚子來好嗎？

▶動 My heart hammered hard as I ran.
我一邊跑，心臟一邊像被槌子敲一樣猛跳。

hand·ker·chief [ˋhæŋkɚtʃɪf]

Track 1471

名 手帕

▶Would you please lend me a handkerchief? I forgot mine at home. 請你借給我一塊手帕好嗎？我把自己的放在家裡了。

文法字詞解析
如果要說「忘記做某事」時要注意，因為忘記是在想起來之前就發生的事，所以要用過去式。如果使用現在式「Don't forget to ...」的話，是用來提醒、告知「不要忘記做某事」。

han·dle [ˋhændl̩]

Track 1472

名 把手 動 觸、手執、管理、對付 同 manage 管理

▶名 I turned the handle and opened the door, then it took me ten minutes to carry that big box in.
我轉了轉把手，把門打開。然後我花了十分鐘才把那個大箱子搬進屋裡。

▶動 It will take us a week to handle your order; is that OK for you? 我們需要一週來處理你的訂單，這個時間可以嗎？

hand·some [ˋhænsəm]

Track 1473

形 英俊的 同 attractive 吸引人的

▶Everyone who sees him says he is very handsome. What do you think? 每個見過他的人都說他很帥，你覺得呢？

文法字詞解析
雖然 everyone 給人有種「所有人、大家」的錯覺，但要記得 everyone 是單數名詞，動詞現在式要加 s 喔。

hang [hæŋ]

Track 1474

動 吊、掛 同 suspend 吊、掛

▶There is a big picture hanging on the wall of the hall.
大廳裡的牆上掛著一幅很大的畫。

實用片語用語
hang out with sb. 和某人一起打發時間
例如：I'm going to hang out with my best friend this weekend.
我這個周末將和最要好的朋友在一起。

hard·ly [ˋhɑrdlɪ] Track 1475

副 勉強地、僅僅 同 barely 僅僅

▸He could hardly see anything clearly（清楚地）in this room. It is too dark. 他在這個房間裡幾乎什麼也看不清楚。太暗了。

hate·ful [ˋhetfəl] Track 1476

形 可恨的、很討厭的 同 hostile 不友善的

▸He is such a hateful person; it's no wonder that people around him dislike（厭惡）him so much.
他是如此可惡的一個人，難怪他周圍的人都很厭惡他。

heal·thy [ˋhɛlθɪ] Track 1477

形 健康的

▸He is very old yet much healthier than me.
他年紀很大了，卻比我健康多了。

heat·er [ˋhitɚ] Track 1478

名 加熱器

▸There is no gas heater in the house, so we can't cook meals here. 房子裡沒有瓦斯爐，因此我們無法在這裡煮飯。

文法字詞解析
heater 也可以是電暖爐的意思，而一般嵌在牆壁上的壁爐則叫做 fireplace。

height [haɪt] Track 1479

名 高度

▸Do you know what the height of the mountain is?
你知道這座山有多高嗎？

help·ful [ˋhɛlpfəl] Track 1480

形 有用的 同 useful 有用的

▸Why don't we bring them some books? They might（也許）be helpful to them.
為什麼不帶些書給他們呢？也許對他們會有點用。

hen [hɛn] Track 1481

名 母雞

▸How often does the hen lay（生蛋）eggs a month?
這隻母雞一個月生幾次蛋？

文法字詞解析
lay「生蛋」這個字可能會和躺下的動詞「lie」的過去式搞混，而 lie 做為「說謊」時的過去式則是「lied」，閱讀和使用的時候要特別注意。

he·ro/her·o·ine [ˋhɪro]/[ˋhɛroˏɪn] Track 1482

名 英雄、勇士／女傑、女英雄

▸I don't want to be a hero. All I want is to live my life in peace.
我不想成為英雄，只想要過著平靜的生活。

hide [haɪd] Track 1483

動 隱藏 同 conceal 隱藏

▸The cat is hiding under the sofa. 貓正躲在沙發下。

文法字詞解析
hide 的動詞變化：hide, hid, hidden

high·way [ˋhaɪˏwe] Track 1484

名 公路、大路 同 road 路

▸Should we take the highway? It might be faster.
我們要不要走公路？可能會快一點

文法字詞解析
take 後面加上交通工具、道路、路線可以用來表示「利用某交通工具、某條路到達某個地方」。

hip [hɪp] Track 1485

名 臀部、屁股

▶I couldn't help crying out as soon as the needle went into my hip. 針一插進我的臀部，我就忍不住叫了出來。

hip·po·pot·a·mus/ hip·po [͵hɪpəˋpɑtəməs]/[ˋhɪpo] Track 1486

名 河馬

▶There are a lot of hippopotamuses in this river. Have you seen them? 這條河裡有很多河馬，你有看過嗎？

hire [haɪr] Track 1487

動 雇用、租用 名 雇用、租金 同 employ 雇用

▶動 How about hiring a guide to take us on a tour of the city? 雇一個導遊帶我們遊覽這個城市怎麼樣？

▶名 We have several bicycles for hire. 我們這裡有一些腳踏車供出租。

文法字詞解析

hire 和 rent 在某些情況下可以替換使用，像是在租用汽車、腳踏車、電器用品時。

實用片語用語

1. for hire 出租

hob·by [ˋhɑbɪ] Track 1488

名 興趣、嗜好 同 pastime 娛樂

▶My hobby is collecting（收集）stamps; what about yours? 我的嗜好是集郵，你呢？

hold·er [ˋholdɚ] Track 1489

名 持有者、所有人

▶He is the holder of the world record of eating the most hotdogs in a minute. 他是「一分鐘吃最多熱狗」世界紀錄的保持人。

home·sick [ˋhom͵sɪk] Track 1490

形 想家的、思鄉的

▶When I am far away from my home, I often feel homesick. 當遠在他鄉的時候，我總是很想家。

實用片語用語

far away (from somewhere) 和（某地）相距很遠

hon·est [ˋɑnɪst] Track 1491

形 誠實的、耿直的 同 truthful 誠實的

▶You need to be honest with your feelings and tell him what you really think. 你應該誠實面對自己的感受，告訴他你真正的想法。

hon·ey [ˋhʌnɪ] Track 1492

名 蜂蜜、花蜜

▶She drinks honey lemon tea every day. 她每天都喝蜂蜜檸檬茶。

hop [hɑp] Track 1493

動 跳過、單腳跳 名 單腳跳、跳舞 同 jump 跳

▶動 The bunny hopped out of the cage. 那隻兔子從籠子裡跳了出來。

▶名 The bird crossed the lawn（草坪）in a series（系列）of hops. 那隻鳥兒一蹦一跳地穿過草坪。

文法字詞解析

hop 用作名詞時是可數的，要特別注意。

hos·pi·tal [ˋhɑspɪtḷ]

Track 1494

名 醫院 同 clinic 診所

▶Would you please take him to hospital?
請你帶他去醫院好嗎？

文法字詞解析
「去醫院」是一個概念，並沒有特定去哪一家醫院，所以 hospital 的前面不用加定冠詞。

host/host·ess [host]/[ˋhostɪs]

Track 1495

名 主人、女主人

▶His father is away, so he has to play host.
他爸爸不在家，只好由他擔任主人了。

ho·tel [hoˋtɛl]

Track 1496

名 旅館 同 hostel 青年旅舍

▶It took me almost half an hour to get to the hotel.
我花了差不多快半小時才到達那間旅館。

how·ev·er [haʊˋɛvɚ]

Track 1497

副 無論如何 連 然而

▶副 However tired you may be, you must finish the work as soon as possible.
不管你有多累，你都必須儘快完成這份工作。

▶連 She's a lovely girl. However, her brother has no manners.
她是個可愛的女孩，然而她哥哥卻一點禮貌都沒有。

hum [hʌm]

Track 1498

名 嗡嗡聲 動 作嗡嗡聲

▶名 I can hear the hum of bees as I walk out of my room.
我走出房間的時候聽見了蜜蜂的嗡嗡聲。

▶動 The boy hummed so much his mother got mad.
那個男孩太愛哼歌，他媽都生氣了。

hum·ble [ˋhʌmbḷ]

Track 1499

形 身份卑微的、謙虛的 同 modest 謙虛的

▶You can't look down upon a man just because of his humble background（背景）.
你不能因為一個人出身貧寒就瞧不起他。

實用片語用語
1. look down on sb. / sth. 看扁某人／某事、瞧不起
2. humble background 出身寒微

hu·mid [ˋhjumɪd]

Track 1500

形 潮濕的 同 moist 潮濕的

▶It won't be long before the air here becomes humid.
過不了多久這邊的空氣就會變得潮濕起來。

hu·mor [ˋhjumɚ]

Track 1501

名 詼諧、幽默 同 comedy 喜劇

▶There's a lot of humor in the works he writes.
他寫的作品都非常幽默。

實用片語用語
sense of humor 幽默感
例如：He needs to enhance his sense of humor, or he won't be able to stand his colleagues' jokes. 他必須加強他的幽默感，不然他沒辦法忍受同事開的玩笑。

hun·ger [ˋhʌŋgɚ]

Track 1502

名 餓、饑餓

▶The poor boy is half dead from hunger.
那個可憐的男孩已經餓得半死了。

hunt [hʌnt]
Track 1503

動 獵取 名 打獵 同 chase 追捕

▶動 In ancient times, both men and women used to hunt.
在古代，男人與女人都曾狩獵。

▶名 The villagers（村民）asked him to take part in the tiger hunt. 村民們叫他去參加獵虎行動。

hunt·er [ˋhʌntɚ]
Track 1504

名 獵人

▶They made a law to forbid（禁止）the hunters to enter this area. 他們立法禁止獵人們進入這個區域。

hur·ry [ˋhɝɪ]
Track 1505

動（使）趕緊 名 倉促 同 rush 倉促

▶動 Let's hurry a bit, or else we can't catch the bus and get to school on time. 我們得快點吧，要不然我們就沒辦法趕上公車準時到學校了。

▶名 You can drive a little bit slower; there's no hurry.
你可以開慢點，不用趕。

萬用延伸句型

S. + V. , or else S. + V.
……，要不然……。

or else 和 otherwise 同義，但從用法上來看，otherwise 除了可以放在句中之外，也可以放在句首，如果放在句首的話，前後句的中間要有分號隔開。

ig·nore [ɪgˋnor]
Track 1506

動 忽視、不理睬 同 neglect 忽視

▶Stop ignoring me and answer my questions!
不要一直忽視我，回答我的問題啊！

ill [ɪl]
Track 1507

名 疾病、壞事 形 生病的 副 壞地 同 sick 生病的

▶名 It's a doctor's job to cure the ill. 醫生的工作就是治好病人。

▶形 I've felt ill all day. 我整天都覺得病懨懨的。

▶副 He always speaks ill of others behind their backs.
他總是在別人背後說他們壞話。

實用片語用語

speak ill of sb 說某人的壞話

i·mag·ine [ɪˋmædʒɪn]
Track 1508

動 想像、設想 同 suppose 設想

▶I imagine him to be a tall, angry-looking man.
我想像他是一個高高的、看起來很不爽的男人。

實用片語用語

imagine sth. / sb. to be sth. 想像某物／某人是……

im·por·tance [ɪmˋpɔrtn̩s]
Track 1509

名 重要性

▶Not everyone knows the importance of being honest.
並不是每個人都懂得誠實的重要性。

im·prove [ɪmˋpruv]
Track 1510

動 改善、促進

▶His grades improved a lot in the past year.
他這一年來成績進步了很多。

im·prove·ment [ɪm`pruvmənt] Track 1511

名 改善

▶The house feels much bigger after we redecorated（重新裝潢）. What an improvement!
房子在重新裝潢後感覺大多了。真是一大進步啊！

萬用延伸句型
用來表達強烈情緒的感嘆句有兩種寫法，一種是「What a + N. ！」，另一種則是「How + adj. + S. + V. ！」。

in·clude [ɪn`klud] Track 1512

動 包含、包括、含有 同 contain 包含

▶There are 29 students in our class, including 7 boys and 22 girls.
我們班有二十九個學生，其中包括七個男生和二十二個女生。

in·come [`ɪn͵kʌm] Track 1513

名 所得、收入 同 earnings 收入

▶Most of his income went into his wife's pockets.
他大部分的所得都被他太太拿走了。

in·crease [`ɪnkris]/[ɪn`kris] Track 1514

名 增加 動 增加 反 reduce 減少

▶名 His weight showed an increase of 30 pounds in a month.
他的體重在一個月內增加了三十磅。

▶動 I can't believe that the number of people who agree actually increased.
真難相信，同意的人數居然增加了。

in·de·pen·dence [͵ɪndɪ`pɛndəns] Track 1515

名 自立、獨立

▶Today, let us celebrate our Independence Day!
今天讓我們來慶祝獨立紀念日吧！

in·de·pend·ent [͵ɪndɪ`pɛndənt] Track 1516

形 獨立的

▶Not all children are able to be independent of their parents.
不是所有的孩子都能夠離開父母獨立生活。

實用片語用語
be independent of 獨立於……

in·di·cate [`ɪndə͵ket] Track 1517

動 指出、指示 同 imply 暗示

▶Will you please indicate your expected salary（薪水）in your resume（履歷）? 請你在履歷中註明你所期望的薪水好嗎？

in·dus·try [`ɪndəstrɪ] Track 1518

名 工業

▶I really love the hotel industry and I want to dedicate my life to it. 我真的很熱愛飯店服務業，並且我想為之奉獻一生。

實用片語用語
dedicate oneself / one's life to sth. 將某人的生命奉獻給……
也可以說：devote oneself to do sth. 致力於……

in·flu·ence [`ɪnflʊəns] Track 1519

名 影響 動 影響

▶名 Her advice has no influence on Peter.
她的勸告對彼得毫無影響。

▶動 I don't want to influence your decision.
我不想影響你做決定。

實用片語用語
influence on / over sb. / sth. 對某人／某事產生影響

ink [ɪŋk]
Track 1520

名 墨水、墨汁 動 塗上墨水

▶名 Will you please mark the mistakes in the article in red ink?
你能把文章中的錯誤用紅筆標記出來嗎？

▶動 Would you please ink my pen for me?
你能不能幫我把筆多加些墨水？

in·sect [ˋɪnsɛkt]
Track 1521

名 昆蟲 同 bug 蟲子

▶Not all insects in nature are harmful（有害的）to human beings. 自然界中不是所有的昆蟲都對人類有害。

實用片語用語
1. in nature 大自然中、自然界中
2. human beings 人類

in·sist [ɪnˋsɪst]
Track 1522

動 堅持、強調

▶I insist that you stay for dinner.
我堅持要你留下來吃晚餐。

in·stance [ˋɪnstəns]
Track 1523

名 實例 動 舉證 同 example 例子

▶名 There are jobs more dangerous than truck driving; for instance, training lions.
有些工作比開卡車還要危險，例如馴獅就是。

▶動 There are many dirty insects you can instance, such as flies. 你可以列舉出很多骯髒的昆蟲，比如蒼蠅。

in·stant [ˋɪnstənt]
Track 1524

形 立即的、瞬間的 名 立即 同 immediate 立即的

▶形 Would you like to have a cup of instant coffee?
想不想喝杯即溶咖啡？

▶名 He was back from the restroom in an instant.
他一瞬間就從廁所回來了。

實用片語用語
in an instant 頃刻間。通常 instant 會用單數。

in·stru·ment [ˋɪnstrəmənt]
Track 1525

名 樂器、器具

▶The only instrument I can play is the guitar.
我唯一會彈的一種樂器就是吉他。

in·ter·nat·ion·al [ˏɪntɚˋnæʃənḷ]
Track 1526

形 國際的 同 universal 全世界的

▶There are neither international rules nor any international standards here.
這裡不存在任何國際規章或國際準則。

in·ter·view [ˋɪntɚˏvju]
Track 1527

名 面談 動 面談、會面

▶名 Would you please give me a chance? I really hope to have an interview with you.
您能給我一次機會嗎？我真的非常希望有機會與你面談。

▶動 I'm excited to be interviewing the Minister（部長）of Education.
能夠採訪教育部長讓我非常興奮。

實用片語用語
give sb. / sth. a chance 給某人／某物一個機會

in·tro·duce [ˌɪntrəˋdjus]

Track 1528

動 介紹、引進

▶Would you like to introduce him to me?
你能不能把他介紹給我認識呢？

in·vent [ɪnˋvɛnt]

Track 1529

動 發明、創造

▶Not everyone has the ability to invent something new.
不是每個人都有能力發明一些新的東西。

in·vi·ta·tion [ˌɪnvəˋteʃən]

Track 1530

名 請帖、邀請

▶I did send you an invitation. It might have got blocked by your mailbox.
我有送出邀請函給你啊，可能被你的電子郵件信箱擋掉了。

文法字詞解析
在例句中，如果只用「I sent you an invitation」就會比較像在陳述「我寄邀請函給你了」這件事，但寫成「did send」就會變成強調「我『確實』有寄邀請函給你」。

in·vite [ɪnˋvaɪt]

Track 1531

動 邀請、招待

▶Who do you want to invite to your wedding?
你要請誰參加你的婚禮？

is·land [ˋaɪlənd]

Track 1532

名 島、安全島

▶He used to live on a small island off the shore（海岸）.
他過去住在離海邊不遠的一個小島上。

實用片語用語
off shore 不在岸上，也可以說是「away from the coast（遠離海岸）」。

i·tem [ˋaɪtəm]

Track 1533

名 項目、條款 同 segment 項目

▶Are there any interesting（有趣的）news items in the paper this morning? 今天早報上有什麼有趣的項目嗎？

jack·et [ˋdʒækɪt]

Track 1534

名 夾克 同 coat 外套

▶Would you please get me my jacket? My wallet is in it.
請你幫我把外套拿過來一下好嗎？我的錢包在裡面。

jam [dʒæm]

Track 1535

動 阻塞 名 果醬

▶動 The door jammed and I can't get it to open however I try.
門卡住了，我怎麼嘗試都沒辦法把它弄開。

▶名 Strawberry jam is my favorite kind of jam.
草莓果醬是我最喜歡的一種果醬。

文法字詞解析
however 在這裡不用做「然而」解，而是「no matter how」的意思。

實用片語用語
traffic jam 塞車

jazz [dʒæz]

Track 1536

名 爵士樂

▶It doesn't matter whether you like jazz or not.
你喜不喜歡爵士樂都不要緊。

jeans [dʒinz]

Track 1537

名 牛仔褲 同 pants 褲子

▶Mom, would you buy me a pair of jeans? My old pair is torn.
媽媽，妳能買條牛仔褲給我嗎？我舊的那條破了。

文法字詞解析
因為 jeans 通常都用複數，如果以 pair 來修飾可以更清楚表示牛仔褲的數量。

jeep [dʒip]

Track 1538

名 吉普車

▶What's the matter with my jeep? I can't get it to start.
我的吉普車出了什麼毛病？我都發動不了。

jog [dʒɑg]

Track 1539

動 慢跑

▶I like to jog in cool weather to keep fit; what about you?
我喜歡在涼爽的天氣裡跑步以保持身體健康。你呢？

joint [dʒɔɪnt]

Track 1540

名 接合處 形 共同的

▶名 He suffered（遭受）from arthritis（關節炎）in his leg joints.
他的腿得了關節炎。

▶形 It was not long before they completed the project by their joint efforts. 沒過多久他們就透過共同努力完成了這個專案。

實用片語用語
suffer from 遭受（病痛），介係詞 from 後面要加上負面的名詞。

judge [dʒʌdʒ]

Track 1541

名 法官、裁判 動 裁決 同 umpire 裁判

▶名 The judge sentenced him to death in court.
法官在法庭上判他死刑。

▶動 I don't think I can judge this singing contest（比賽）since I know nothing about music. 我應該不能為這個歌唱比賽擔任裁判吧，因為我根本不懂音樂啊。

實用片語用語
1. sentence sb. to sth. 判決某人（刑期）
2. know nothing about sb. / sth. 完全不了解某人／某物

judge·ment/judg·ment

Track 1542

[ˋdʒʌdʒmənt]

名 判斷力

▶It's too early to make a judgment on what the result will be.
現在就對結果下判斷還為時過早。

juic·y [ˋdʒusɪ]

Track 1543

形 多汁的

▶There are some fresh juicy oranges in this store.
這家店裡有些新鮮多汁的柳丁。

ketch·up [ˋkɛtʃəp]

Track 1544

名 番茄醬

▶Would you please pass me a bottle of ketchup?
你能遞給我一罐番茄醬嗎？

kin·der·gar·ten [ˋkɪndɚ͵gartn̩]　Track 1545

名 幼稚園

▶Could you tell me why there are so many children in that kindergarten?
你能告訴我為什麼那個幼稚園有那麼多的孩子嗎？

king·dom [ˋkɪŋdəm]　Track 1546

名 王國

▶Would you please lead me to the kingdom of yours?
你能帶我去你的王國嗎？

文法字詞解析
字尾「-dom」在這裡的意思是「某個特別受到管轄的區域」；另外，用在freedom、boredom等字裡時，則表示「某種狀態」。

實用片語用語
lead sb. to somewhere 帶某人去某地

knock [nak]　Track 1547

動 敲、擊 名 敲打聲 同 hit 打擊

▶動 You should knock on the door before you come in.
你進來之前應該要敲門啊。

▶名 Was there a knock on the door just now, or was it my imagination?
剛剛有敲門聲嗎？還是我自己想像的？

knowl·edge [ˋnalɪdʒ]　Track 1548

名 知識 同 scholarship 學問

▶We should put all this knowledge about the enemy to use.
我們應該好好利用這些關於敵軍的知識。

ko·a·la [kəˋalə]　Track 1549

名 無尾熊

▶Have you ever hugged a koala?
你抱過無尾熊嗎？

實用片語用語
Have you ever...(before)？你有沒有做過……？

la·dy·bug/la·dy·bird　Track 1550

[ˋledɪ͵bʌg]/[ˋledɪ͵bɝd]

名 瓢蟲

▶What does a ladybug look like? I have never seen one.
瓢蟲長什麼樣子呢？我從來沒看過。

lane [len]　Track 1551

名 小路、巷 同 path 小路

▶There are many small lanes in the village.
在這個村莊裡有很多小巷。

lan·guage [ˋlæŋgwɪdʒ]　Track 1552

名 語言

▶He is able to learn languages very quickly.
他學語言非常快速。

lan·tern [ˋlæntən]　Track 1553

名 燈籠 同 lamp 燈

▶The lantern festival is an important Chinese holiday.
元宵燈籠節是一個重要的中國節日。

lap [læp]　Track 1554

名 膝部 動 舐、輕拍

▶名 She sat with her hands on her lap.
她把雙手放在膝上坐著。

▶動 The puppy is lapping up the milk. 那隻小狗在舔牛奶。

文法字詞解析
laptop 就是從 lap 這個字衍生而來，lap 有「膝部」的意思，top 則是「上面」的意思，「放在在膝上的電腦」就成了單字「筆記型電腦」的由來了。

實用片語用語
lap up sth. 舔某物

lat·est [ˋletɪst]　Track 1555

形 最後的

▶I don't want to be the latest person to arrive for the meeting.
我可不想成為最後一個到場開會的人。

law·yer [ˋlɔjɚ]　Track 1556

名 律師

▶I want to study law and become a lawyer in the future.
我想學法律，將來當一名律師。

lead·er·ship [ˋlidɚʃɪp]　Track 1557

名 領導力 同 guidance 領導

▶The people in the company owe（歸功於）the success to his leadership.
對於這次的成功，公司的人必須感謝他的領導能力。

實用片語用語
owe sth. to sb / sth. 將……歸功於……。

le·gal [ˋlig!]　Track 1558

形 合法的 同 lawful 合法的

▶He is the only legal heir（繼承人）of the old man.
他是這名老人唯一的法定繼承人。

lem·on [ˋlɛmən]　Track 1559

名 檸檬

▶I like oranges more than lemons. What about you?
比起檸檬我更喜歡橘子。你呢？

lem·on·ade [ˌlɛmənˋed]　Track 1560

名 檸檬水

▶The kids are selling lemonade by the street.
孩子們在路邊賣檸檬汁。

實用片語用語
by the street 在路旁

lend [lɛnd]　Track 1561

動 借出 反 borrow 借來

▶Can you lend me your eraser? I lost mine.
可以借我你的橡擦嗎？我的不見了。

文法字詞解析
lend 的動詞變化：lend, lent, lent

length [lɛŋkθ]　Track 1562

名 長度

▶The movie at its full length is three hours long.
這部電影完整的長度是三小時。

leop·ard [ˋlɛpɚd]

Track 1563

名 豹

▶The snow leopard is a beautiful but rare animal.
雪豹是一種美麗但不常見的動物。

let·tuce [ˋlɛtɪs]

Track 1564

名 萵苣

▶The rabbit eats only lettuce and nothing else.
這隻兔子除了萵苣什麼也不吃。

實用片語用語
only...and nothing else 除了……之外就沒了
同樣意思的片語還有「nothing but」所以這句也可以寫成：The rabbit eats nothing but lettuce.
順帶一提，「除了……之外都」的說法是「except」。例如：The rabbit eats everything except lettuce. 這隻兔子除了萵苣之外什麼都吃。

li·bra·ry [ˋlaɪˌbrɛrɪ]

Track 1565

名 圖書館

▶Would you please take him to the library?
請你帶他到圖書館去好嗎？

lick [lɪk]

Track 1566

名 / 動 舔食、舔

▶名 The dog gave me a huge lick.
這隻狗狠狠舔了我一下。

▶動 My cat licks herself all day.
我的貓整天在舔自己。

lid [lɪd]

Track 1567

名 蓋子

▶Why don't you lift the lid of the box and have a look at what's inside?
為什麼不打開箱蓋，看看裡面是什麼呢？

實用片語用語
have / take a look (at sb. / sth.) 看一眼某人／某物

light·ning [ˋlaɪtnɪŋ]

Track 1568

名 閃電

▶There were many flashes of lightning during the storm last night. 昨晚下暴雨的時候出現了好多次閃電。

lim·it [ˋlɪmɪt]

Track 1569

名 限度、極限 動 限制 同 extreme 極限

▶名 I am a very patient person, but there's a limit to everything.
我算是很有耐心的人，可是凡事都有個限度吧。

▶動 We must limit ourselves to one cake each.
我們必須限定每人只吃一塊蛋糕。

實用片語用語
limit A to B 限制、限定

link [lɪŋk]

Track 1570

名 關聯 動 連結 同 connect 連結

▶名 There might be a link between the two murders（謀殺案）.
這兩起謀殺案可能有關聯。

▶動 Can you link me to your blog（部落格）？
你可以給我你部落格的連結嗎？

實用片語用語
a link between sth. (and sth.) 某物與某物有關聯

liq·uid [ˋlɪkwɪd]

Track 1571

名 液體

▶What's this strange green liquid on the bathroom floor?
廁所地上這綠綠的奇怪液體是什麼？

lis·ten·er [ˈlɪsn̩ɚ]

Track 1572

名 聽眾、聽者

▶She rarely speaks, but is a good listener.
她不太講話，但是個很好的聆聽者。

loaf [lof]

Track 1573

名 一塊

名詞複數 loaves

▶Would you please give me a loaf of bread? I feel a little bit hungry now.
請你給我一條麵包好嗎？我現在感覺有點餓了。

文法字詞解析
bread 是不可數名詞，可以接上 a loaf of（一條）、a slice of（一片）、a piece of（一小塊）來描述得更精確。

lo·cal [ˈlokl̩]

Track 1574

形 當地的 名 當地居民 同 regional 地區的

▶形 It doesn't matter if you don't know the local customs, because people here are very friendly to tourists. 你不瞭解當地風俗習慣不要緊，因為當地人對遊客都很友善。

▶名 The locals here are always very kind to strangers.
這裡的居民對於陌生人都很親切。

lo·cate [ˈloket]

Track 1575

動 設置、居住

▶The building you're looking for is located at the edge of the town.
你在找的那棟大樓位於城鎮邊緣。

實用片語用語
at the edge of 在……的邊緣

lock [lɑk]

Track 1576

名 鎖 動 鎖上

▶名 We need a new lock for the bike.
我們得為腳踏車買個新鎖了。

▶動 Why didn't you lock the door? No wonder your stuff got stolen.
你怎麼沒鎖門呢？難怪你的東西會被偷。

log [lɔg]

Track 1577

名 圓木 動 伐木、把……記入航海日誌 同 wood 木頭

▶名 He got hit by a log when working in the forest.
他在森林裡工作時被一根圓木打到。

▶動 The captain logged the happenings of the day in his journal.
這名船長把當天發生的事記在日誌裡。

lone [lon]

Track 1578

形 孤單的

▶He is a lone wolf kind of person; he'll never join us.
他是喜歡單打獨鬥的那種人，他不會加入我們的。

文法字詞解析
lone wolf 在這裡變成了形容詞修飾 kind，表示「喜歡孤獨的那種人」。

實用片語用語
a lone wolf 喜歡獨處的人。

lone·ly [ˈlonlɪ]

Track 1579

形 孤單的、寂寞的 同 solitary 寂寞的

▶I often feel lonely at night.
我晚上常常覺得很寂寞。

lose [luz] Track 1580

動 遺失、失去、輸 同 fail 失敗、失去

▶It doesn't matter if you lose the game, you'll still be champion（冠軍）. 就算你輸了這次比賽也沒差，你一樣會是冠軍。

los·er [ˋluzɚ] Track 1581

名 失敗者 反 winner 勝利者

▶I feel like such a loser when I see my friends being rich and famous. 看到我的朋友們又有錢又有名，我就覺得自己很失敗。

文法字詞解析

feel like 接名詞的時候，解釋成「感覺像某東西」。

feel like 也可以接V-ing，表示「想要……」

loss [lɔs] Track 1582

名 損失

▶Who cares if he dumped me? It's his loss.
他甩了我又怎樣？是他自己的損失。

萬用延伸句型

Who cares? 那又怎樣？誰在乎？

用來表達某事或某人一點都不重要、用不著擔心。

love·ly [ˋlʌvlɪ] Track 1583

形 美麗的、可愛的

▶What a lovely little daughter you have! 你的小女兒多可愛啊！

lov·er [ˋlʌvɚ] Track 1584

名 愛人

▶Have you seen his lover? What does she look like?
你見過他的情人嗎？她長什麼樣子呢？

low·er [ˋloɚ] Track 1585

動 降低

▶It doesn't matter if they are unwilling（不願意的）to lower the price. We can always buy from someone else.
他們不願降價也不要緊，我們跟別人買就好啦。

luck [lʌk] Track 1586

名 幸運 同 fortune 幸運

▶Let's go to the casino（賭場）to try our luck.
我們去賭場碰碰運氣吧。

實用片語用語

try/chance one's luck 碰碰某人的運氣

Mm

mag·a·zine [ˌmægəˋzin] Track 1587

名 雜誌

▶Would you please allow me to bring this magazine home?
您允許我把這本雜誌帶回家嗎？

實用片語用語

allow sb. to do sth. 允許某人做某事

ma·gic [ˋmædʒɪk] Track 1588

名 魔術 形 魔術的

▶名 He is going to perform（表演）magic at the party.
他將在晚會上表演魔術。

▶形 The magic show we saw last night was great.
我們昨天晚上看的魔術表演真棒。

ma·gi·cian [mə`dʒɪʃən] Track 1589

名 魔術師

▶I don't think I could ever become a magician.
我覺得我應該永遠不可能當得了魔術師。

---

main [men] Track 1590

形 主要的 名 要點 同 principal 主要的

▶形 What do you think of the main idea of the article（文章）?
你覺得這篇文章的中心思想怎麼樣？

▶名 His ideas are impractical（不切實際的）but very exciting.
他的概念很不實際，但很刺激。

---

main·tain [men`ten] Track 1591

動 維持 同 keep 維持

▶It's too hard for him alone to maintain the whole family.
要他一個人養活全家人太難了。

文法字詞解析
字根「main」的意思是「手」，「tain」是「握著」的意思，兩者合在一起「手一直握著」就成了「維持某個水平、狀態」；如果要表達「維持生命、生活」的話，則要用 sustain，字首「sus-」表示「下面、向下」。

---

male [mel] Track 1592

形 男性的 名 男性 反 female 女性的

▶形 The male nurse standing at the door looks really bored.
站在門口那個男護士看起來覺得很無聊的樣子。

▶名 Males are usually physically（身體上地）stronger than females.
男性在身體上通常要比女性強壯。

文法字詞解析
「physic」是身體的意思，加上形容詞字尾「-al」就變成「身體上的」，在加上附詞字尾「-ly」就成了「身體上地」。

---

man·da·rin [`mændərɪn] Track 1593

名 國語、中文

▶I speak English, French and Mandarin; what about you?
我會講英語、法語和國語，你呢？

---

man·go [`mæŋgo] Track 1594

名 芒果

▶Not all people like eating mangoes.
不是所有的人都喜歡吃芒果。

文法字詞解析
要注意 mango 的複數是加 es 而不是 s，同樣的情況還有「hero(es) 英雄」、「potato(es) 馬鈴薯」。

---

man·ner [`mænɚ] Track 1595

名 方法、禮貌 同 form 方法

▶Her kids have really good manners.
她的孩子們非常禮貌。

---

mark [mɑrk] Track 1596

動 標記 名 記號 同 sign 記號

▶動 Let me mark the correct answers for you.
讓我幫你標出正確答案吧。

▶名 Why is there a mark on the sheep's back? What does it mean? 為什麼那隻綿羊背上有記號？是什麼意思？

---

mar·riage [`mærɪdʒ] Track 1597

名 婚姻

▶Is your marriage a happy one?
你的婚姻愉快嗎？

mask [mæsk]

Track 1598

名 面具 動 遮蓋

▶名 We are supposed to wear masks to the ball（舞會）.
我們應該要戴面具去舞會。

▶動 She always masks her sadness（悲傷）with a smile.
她總是用微笑掩飾自己的悲傷。

> **文法字詞解析**
> be supposed to 如果用現在式，指的是預定要做的計劃；如果用過去式，指的是「預期會發生、實際卻沒發生的事」，也可以用 should have + Vp.p. 表示。
> 另外，「should」在中文也譯做「應該」，只是和 be supposed to 的意思並不一樣，它指的是「做某件事情是正確的、是對的」。例如：You should dry your hair before you go to bed. 你睡前應該把頭髮吹乾。

mass [mæs]

Track 1599

名 大量 同 quantity 大量

▶Do you think this new phone would appeal（受喜愛）to the masses? 你覺得這種新的手機會受大衆歡迎嗎？

> **實用片語用語**
> appeal to sb. 受某人喜愛。另外，appeal to sb. 也很常用做「向某人求助」。
> 例如：My sister appeals to me for help. 我妹妹跟我請求協助。

mat [mæt]

Track 1600

名 墊子、蓆子 同 rug 毯子

▶It is no wonder that she asked for a mat to sit on; the floor is too cold. 怪不得她要墊子來坐，這地板太冷了。

match [mætʃ]

Track 1601

名 火柴、比賽 動 相配

▶名 Will you wear that gray（灰色的）tie? It's a good match with your blue shirt.
你要戴那條灰色的領帶嗎？它跟你的藍襯衫很相配哦。

▶動 Can you recommend（推薦）a blouse（短上衣）to match my new trousers? 您能推薦一款短上衣來配我的新褲子嗎？

> **實用片語用語**
> match A with B 使 A 和 B 成對、相配

mate [met]

Track 1602

名 配偶 動 配對

▶名 The wolf is looking for its mate. 那匹狼正在找牠的配偶。

▶動 It's mating season and the dogs in my house are all getting anxious（焦慮的）.
現在是交配的季節，所以我家的狗都很焦慮。

ma·te·ri·al [məˋtɪrɪəl]

Track 1603

名 物質 同 composition 物質

▶Could you tell me what material this is made of?
你能不能告訴我這是用什麼材料做成的？

> **實用片語用語**
> be made of 用……製成。
> 不要跟 be made up of 搞混了，後者的意思是「由……組成」。
> 例如：The class is made of 15 students from different countries. 這個班級是由十五個從不同國家來的學生所組成。

meal [mil]

Track 1604

名 一餐、餐

▶We had a quick meal and hurried to the meeting.
我們迅速吃了一餐，然後趕去開會了。

mean·ing [ˋminɪŋ]

Track 1605

名 意義 同 implication 含意

▶Will you explain the meanings of these foreign words?
你能解釋這些外文單字的意思嗎？

means [minz]

Track 1606

名 方法

▶I'll make sure we succeed, no matter by what means.
我會確保我們能成功，無論用什麼手段。

> **實用片語用語**
> 1. make sure 確保，後面可以接「that + 子句」或「of (doing) sth.」。
> 2. by what means 無論如何、不管用什麼手段。或者也可以說：in what manner。

mea·sur·a·ble [ˋmɛʒərəbl̩] Track 1607

形 可測量的

▶There has been a measurable improvement in his work.
他的工作已經有了很大的改進。

mea·sure [ˋmɛʒɚ] Track 1608

動 測量

▶I measured the distance between the kitchen and the front door. 我量了一下廚房到大門之間的距離。

mea·sur·ement [ˋmɛʒɚmənt] Track 1609

名 測量 同 estimate 估計

▶It's not polite to ask someone about their measurements.
問人家三圍數字是不禮貌的。

med·i·cine [ˋmɛdəsn̩] Track 1610

名 醫學、藥物 同 drug 藥物

▶You have a cold. You should take some medicine.
你感冒了，該吃點藥了。

實用片語用語
take some medicine 吃藥。要注意這裡的動詞不是用「eat」，而是用take。另外medicine不可數，而pill(s)（藥丸）則是可數名詞。
例如：My doctor told me to take two pills a day. 醫生叫我一天吃兩顆藥。

meet·ing [ˋmitɪŋ] Track 1611

名 會議

▶If we're late for the meeting, we'll be in huge trouble.
如果我們開會遲到，我們就慘了。

mel·o·dy [ˋmɛlədɪ] Track 1612

名 旋律 同 tune 旋律

▶The melody of this song is nice, but the lyrics（歌詞）are really terrible.
這首歌的旋律還不錯，但歌詞超爛的。

mel·on [ˋmɛlən] Track 1613

名 瓜、甜瓜

▶I bought some melons from the market just now.
我剛剛從市場買了一些瓜。

實用片語用語
just now 就在剛剛

mem·ber [ˋmɛmbɚ] Track 1614

名 成員

▶Are you a member of the club?
你是那個社團的社員嗎？

文法字詞解析
去超市買東西時，常常會被問要不要加入會員，這裡的「會員」就是叫做 member。而「會員卡」的說法是「loyalty card」。

mem·o·ry [ˋmɛmərɪ] Track 1615

名 記憶、回憶

▶That was a terrible memory that I'd rather forget.
那個回憶超糟糕的，我還寧可忘記。

me·nu [ˋmɛnju] Track 1616

名 菜單

▶Let's have a look at the menu first and then decide what to eat.
我們先看看菜單吧，然後再決定吃什麼。

mes·sage [ˋmɛsɪdʒ]

Track 1617

名 訊息

▶Since he is not in, would you like to leave a message for him?
既然他不在，您要不要留個訊息給他？

文法字詞解析

in 在例句中是形容詞，表示「在某個空間內」。

met·al [ˋmɛtl̩]

Track 1618

名 金屬 形 金屬的

▶名 The door is made of metal and is cold to the touch.
這扇門是金屬做的，摸起來冰冰的。

▶形 There are lots of metal cooking utensils（器具）in our kitchen.
我們的廚房裡有很多金屬的廚具。

me·ter [ˋmitɚ]

Track 1619

名 公尺

▶The parking meter isn't working.
停車收費器壞了。

文法字詞解析

isn't working 和 doesn't work 雖然都有「壞掉、不能運作」的意思，但 isn't working 表示「在這個當下是壞的，但之前可能還可以運作」，doesn't work 表示「完全不能用」。

meth·od [ˋmɛθəd]

Track 1620

名 方法 同 style 方式

▶How about using a simple method to solve this problem?
用一個簡單的方法解決這個問題怎麼樣？

mil·i·tar·y [ˋmɪlə͵tɛrɪ]

Track 1621

形 軍事的 名 軍事 同 army 軍隊

▶形 I heard that he did a year's military service.
我聽說他服過一年兵役。

▶名 The military has taken over the government.
軍方已經接管政府了。

實用片語用語

1. do military service 服兵役
2. take over 接管

mil·lion [ˋmɪljən]

Track 1622

名 百萬

▶There are millions of American veterans（老兵）from the Second World War.
參加過第二次世界大戰的美國退伍軍人有數百萬人。

mine [maɪn]

Track 1623

名 礦、礦坑 代 我的東西

▶名 The children went to explore the old mine.
孩子們跑去探索那個老礦坑了。

▶代 She is a great friend of mine.
她是我很要好的朋友。

mi·nus [ˋmaɪnəs]

Track 1624

介 減、減去 形 減的 名 負數 反 plus 加的

▶介 Ten minus three is seven. 十減三是七。

▶形 The temperature will be minus 10 degrees tomorrow. 明天氣溫為零下十度。

▶名 Let's discuss the pluses and minuses of moving to the suburbs.
我們討論一下搬到郊區的利弊吧。

mir·ror [ˋmɪrɚ]
Track 1625

名 鏡子 動 反映

▶名 Look in the mirror and you'll see why everyone is staring at you. 照個鏡子吧，你就會知道大家為什麼一直盯著你看了。

▶動 His confused（疑惑的）expression（表情）mirrors mine. 他臉上露出和我一模一樣的困惑神情。

萬用延伸句型
1. you'll see (that) … 你會瞭解到……
2. stare at sb. 盯著某人看

mix [mɪks]
Track 1626

動 混合 名 混合物 同 combine 結合

▶動 Mix it with some milk and it will taste better. 把它跟牛奶混合一下，味道就會比較好了。

▶名 It's a mix of guava juice and orange juice. 那是芭樂汁和柳橙汁的混合物。

mod·el [ˋmɑdḷ]
Track 1627

名 模型、模特兒 動 模仿

▶名 Not every girl is tall enough to be a model. 不是每個女孩都有足夠的身高能去當模特兒。

▶動 The kids model themselves after their mother. 那些孩子們以媽媽為榜樣。

實用片語用語
model oneself after sb. 以……為榜樣

mo·dern [ˋmɑdɚn]
Track 1628

形 現代的 反 ancient 古代的

▶Would you like to go to see an exhibition（展覽）of modern art this afternoon with me? 你想不想今天下午跟我一起去參觀現代藝術展？

mon·ster [ˋmɑnstɚ]
Track 1629

名 怪物

▶When I was a child, I was worried that there were monsters under my bed. 我還是個孩子時，總擔心床下有怪物。

mos·qui·to [məˋskito]
Track 1630

名 蚊子

▶There are so many annoying（討厭的）mosquitoes in summer, especially in the wet areas. 夏天總是有那麼多討厭的蚊子，尤其是在潮濕的地方。

文法字詞解析
especially 用做「尤其、特別是」時，後面接名詞、介系詞片語、副詞片語等。要注意的是，especially 絕對不能用在句首。

moth [mɔθ]
Track 1631

名 蛾、蛀蟲

▶Is that a butterfly or a moth? 那是隻蝴蝶還是飛蛾？

mo·tion [ˋmoʃən]
Track 1632

名 運動、動作 同 movement 運動

▶It's too difficult for me to learn the laws of motion. 學習運動定律對我來說簡直是太難了。

實用片語用語
the law of sth. （某事物的）定律、鐵則
這裡的 law 不是「法律」，而是某件存在於自然中或社會上的不變的規則。
例如：the law of gravity 萬有引力定律

mo·tor·cy·cle [ˋmotɚ͵saɪkḷ]
Track 1633

名 摩托車

▶Will you please let me use your motorcycle tomorrow? 你明天可以借我用你的摩托車嗎？

mov·a·ble [ˋmuvəbl̩] Track 1634

形 可移動的 同 mobile 移動式的

▶This dresser（化妝台）is movable.
這個梳妝檯是可移動的。

MRT/mass rapid transit/sub·way/un·der·ground/me·tro Track 1635

[mæsˋræpɪdˋtrænsɪt]/[ˋsʌbˏwe]/[ˋʌndɚˏgraund]/[ˋmɛtro]

名 地下道、地下鐵

▶How long does it take for you to go to work by MRT?
你搭乘捷運去上班要多久時間？

mule [mjul] Track 1636

名 騾

▶A mule is a cross between a horse and an ass（驢）.
騾是馬和驢交配而生的混種。

實用片語用語
a cross between A and B
A 和 B 的混種、混合物

mul·ti·ply [ˋmʌltəplaɪ] Track 1637

動 增加、繁殖、相乘

▶Let's multiply the height by the width to determine（確定）the area. 我們用寬乘以高來確定面積。

mu·se·um [mjuˋziəm] Track 1638

名 博物館

▶Would you please help me find the Palace Museum on the map? 你能幫我在地圖上找到故宮博物院嗎？

mu·si·cian [mjuˋzɪʃən] Track 1639

名 音樂家

▶He's a talented musician, but he gave up music to work as a lawyer.
他是個天才音樂家，但他卻放棄了音樂，跑去當律師。

萬用延伸句型
要表達某人很有天分，可以說：He / She has talent. 或是 He / She is talented.

nail [nel] Track 1640

名 指甲、釘子 動 敲

▶名 She's painting my nails right now so can't come to the phone. 她現在不能接電話，因為她正在幫我擦指甲油。

▶動 We should nail these boards together.
我們應該要把這些木板釘在一起。

實用片語用語
come to the phone 接電話

na·ked [ˋnekɪd] Track 1641

形 裸露的、赤裸的

▶Don't come in! I'm naked!
不要進來啦！我裸體耶！

nap·kin [ˋnæpkɪn]
Track 1642

名 餐巾紙 同 towel 紙巾

▶Would you please pass me some napkins? I need to wipe（擦）my mouth.
請你遞給我一些餐巾紙好嗎？我要擦一下嘴巴。

nar·row [ˋnæro]
Track 1643

形 窄的、狹長的 動 變窄 同 tight 緊的

▶形 The bridge is too narrow for two trucks to pass.
這座橋太窄，兩輛卡車無法並排通過。

▶動 The road narrows here, so you need to drive carefully.
路在這裡變窄了，你要小心點開車。

文法字詞解析
第二個例句也可以用 because 來寫，變成：You need to drive carefully because the road narrows here.
要注意 because、so 不能同時出現。

na·tion·al [ˋnæʃənl̩]
Track 1644

形 國家的

▶The statue is a national landmark（地標）.
那座雕像是個國家的地標。

nat·u·ral [ˋnætʃərəl]
Track 1645

形 天然生成的

▶Many natural disasters（自然災害）happened this year.
今年發生了不少自然災害。

naugh·ty [ˋnɔtɪ]
Track 1646

形 不服從的、淘氣的

▶The boy is quite naughty both at home and at school.
這個小男孩在家或在學校都很頑皮。

near·by [ˋnɪrˋbaɪ]
Track 1647

形 短距離內的 副 不遠地 同 around 附近

▶形 I can hear a baby crying at a nearby table.
我聽到附近有一桌有個寶寶在哭。

▶副 Will you stop nearby for lunch with us, Bob?
鮑伯，你願意在附近停下來跟我們吃頓飯嗎？

萬用延伸句型
Will you / Would you...?
你是否願意……？

near·ly [ˋnɪrlɪ]
Track 1648

副 幾乎 同 almost 幾乎

▶He is nearly as tall as my brother. 他幾乎和我的哥哥一樣高。

neat [nit]
Track 1649

形 整潔的 反 dirty 髒的

▶Not everyone has the habit of keeping his / her room tidy（整齊的）and neat.
並不是每個人都有讓房間保持整齊清潔的習慣。

文法字詞解析
寫作的時候要注意，中文裡面非特定的性別時可以用「他」來一以代之，但英文則要將「his / her」都寫出來才行。

nec·es·sa·ry [ˋnɛsə͵sɛrɪ]
Track 1650

形 必要的、不可缺少的

▶It took me a whole month to prepare all the necessary materials.
我花了整整一個月的時間才準備好所有必需的資料。

neck·lace [ˋnɛklɪs]　Track 1651

名 項圈、項鍊

▶She doesn't like wearing necklaces. 她不喜歡戴項鍊。

nee·dle [ˋnid!]　Track 1652

名 針、縫衣針 動 用針縫

▶名 What should we do? The cat just ate a needle!
怎麼辦？貓剛剛吃了一根針耶！

▶動 She needled the blisters（水泡） on his feet.
她刺破了他腳上的水泡。

萬用延伸句型
what should sb. do？（某人）該怎麼辦？ 不知道該怎麼做時，就可以用這句來表達。如果説「What should I do with you?」就變成「我該拿你怎麼辦？」了。

neg·a·tive [ˋnɛgətɪv]　Track 1653

形 否定的、消極的 名 反駁、否認 、陰性

▶形 It is no wonder that he has a negative opinion on this matter. 難怪他對這件事持反對意見。

▶名 I ran a test on his blood, but the result was negative.
我驗了一下他的血，不過結果是陰性的。

實用片語用語
進行某件事情時可以用「run」這個字，例如： run a test（進行檢驗），run a business（經營事業）。

neigh·bor [ˋnebɚ]　Track 1654

動 靠近於⋯⋯ 名 鄰居

▶動 Our school neighbors a giant park.
我們學校靠近一個很大的公園。

▶名 I don't like leaving our child in the care of a neighbor.
我不喜歡把孩子留給鄰居照顧。

nei·ther [ˋniðɚ]　Track 1655

副 兩者都不 代 也非、也不 連 兩者都不 反 both 兩者都

▶副 If you're not going, then neither am I.
如果你不去的話，那我也不去。

▶代 Would you like this red coat or that blue coat or neither?
你想要這件紅外套，還是這件藍外套？還是兩件都不喜歡？

▶連 Neither Mike nor I have seen this film.
麥克和我都沒有看過這部電影。

文法字詞解析
either 和 neither 都有否定的意思，但 either 表示「也」，neither 則表示「也不」。所以兩者用法並不相同。
例如：I'm not clever. My brother is not, either.
如果要用 neither 説明同一件事的話，則必須這樣寫：I'm not clever. Neither is my brother.

neph·ew [ˋnɛfju]　Track 1656

名 姪子、外甥

▶My nephew is a member of the school basketball team.
我姪子是籃球校隊的一名隊員。

nest [nɛst]　Track 1657

名 鳥巢 動 築巢

▶名 There were several swallows living in the nest under the roof of our house. 我們家屋簷下的鳥窩中住著幾隻燕子。

▶動 There are several birds nesting in the oak（橡樹） tree.
有幾隻鳥在橡樹上築巢。

net [nɛt]　Track 1658

名 網 動 用網捕捉、結網

▶名 It took the fisherman forty minutes to mend the net.
漁夫花了四十分鐘才將這張漁網補好。

▶動 The little boy netted a butterfly easily.
小男孩輕易地就用網子捕捉到蝴蝶。

實用片語用語
mend a net / clothes / shoes etc. 修理、修補。雖然 mend 和 fix 都有「修理」的意思，但 mend 比較用來表示「補破洞」，fix 比較用來修理「機器」。

niece [nis]
Track 1659

名 姪女、外甥女

▶My niece is a beautiful young lady.
我的姪女是個美麗的年輕女性。

no·bod·y [ˋno͵bɑdɪ]
Track 1660

代 無人 名 無名小卒

▶代 Nobody cares where you're going. 沒人管你要去哪裡啦。

▶名 He's just a nobody in the industry（業界）.
他在業界只不過是個無名小卒。

nod [nɑd]
Track 1661

動 點、彎曲 名 點頭

▶動 He didn't answer my question and merely（只是）nodded.
他沒有回答我的問題，只是點點頭。

▶名 He gave me a nod as he walked by.
他走過的時候對我點了個頭。

實用片語用語
walk by 路過，同樣意思的片語還有「walk past」。
例如：The students lowered their voice when the teacher walked past.
當老師經過那群學生身邊時，他們全都壓低了聲音。

none [nʌn]
Track 1662

代 沒有人

▶If you want a tutor（家庭教師）, there is none better than my sister.
如果你想找一個家教的話，那我妹妹再適合不過了。

文法字詞解析
當 none 做為一個句子的主詞，並且牽涉到一個群體裡的人時，動詞可以用單數或複數的形態表示。
例如：None of them are interested in this film.
他們之中沒有一個人對這部電影有興趣。

noo·dle [ˋnudl̩]
Track 1663

名 麵條

▶He had noodles for breakfast, lunch and dinner.
他早餐、午餐和晚餐都吃麵。

north·ern [ˋnɔrðɚn]
Track 1664

形 北方的

▶It took me fifteen minutes to reach the park in the northern part of the city.
我花了十五分鐘才到達了城市北部的那個公園。

note·book [ˋnot͵bʊk]
Track 1665

名 筆記本

▶I need a new notebook; my current one isn't big enough.
我需要一本新的筆記本，我現在這本不夠大。

nov·el [ˋnɑvl̩]
Track 1666

形 新穎的、新奇的 名 長篇小說 同 original 新穎的

▶形 Everyone thinks that the design is very novel.
大家都認為這個設計很新穎。

▶名 He likes to sit in bed and read novels.
他喜歡坐在床上看小說。

文法字詞解析
在第二個例句中，因為床是軟的，坐在床上時會陷進床墊中，所以介係詞用 sit「in」 bed。

nut [nʌt]
Track 1667

名 堅果、螺帽

▶Experts say that nuts are good for our health.
專家們都說堅果有益於身體健康。

o·bey [ə`be]
Track 1668

動 遵行、服從 同 submit 服從

▶If you do not obey your boss, you might（可能）be fired.
如果你不服從你的上司，你就可能被解雇。

ob·ject [əb`dʒɛkt]
Track 1669

名 物體 動 抗議、反對 同 thing 物、東西 反 agree 同意

▶名 No one knows the names of the objects in this lab（實驗室）.沒人知道這個實驗室裡這些物體的名稱。

▶動 I object to his suggestion.
我反對他的提議。

實用片語用語
object to (doing) something 反對做……

oc·cur [ə`kɝ]
Track 1670

動 發生、存在、出現 同 happen 發生

▶Did anything strange occur when I was gone?
我不在的時候有發生什麼奇怪的事嗎？

of·fer [`ɔfɚ]
Track 1671

名 提供 動 建議、提供

▶名 Would you please give me a special offer?
請你給我一個特別優惠價好嗎？

▶動 He offered me a glass of wine.
他問我要不要一杯葡萄酒。

of·fi·cial [ə`fɪʃəl]
Track 1672

形 官方的、法定的 名 官員、公務員 同 authorize 公認

▶形 This is the group's official website.
這是個團體的官方網站。

▶名 In my opinion, he is a pompous（傲慢自大的）official.
在我看來，他是個傲慢自大的官員。

萬用延伸句型
In my opinion,... 依我看來，……。這個句型可以用來闡述自己的看法、意見。其他類似的開頭語還有 To me, In my (point of) view, As for me 等。

o·mit [o`mɪt]
Track 1673

動 遺漏、省略、忽略 同 neglect 忽略

▶You need to tell me everything without omitting anything.
你必須一字不漏地把一切都告訴我。

on·ion [`ʌnjən]
Track 1674

名 洋蔥

▶My son hates eating onions.
我兒子討厭吃洋蔥。

op·er·ate [`ɑpə,ret]
Track 1675

動 運轉、操作

▶Would you please instruct（指導）me how to operate this computer?
請你教教我如何操作這台電腦好嗎？

o·pin·ion [əˋpɪnjən] Track 1676

名 觀點、意見 同 view 觀點

▶In my opinion, he is not capable（有能力的）enough to cope（對付）with such a difficult affair.
在我看來，他處理這件如此棘手的事情能力還不夠。

實用片語用語
cope with sth. 處理某事，通常後面所接的是非常難應付的事情。
另外deal with也有「應付、對付」的意思；如果是 deal with sb. 就是「應付某人」，deal with + problem 就是「採取措施解決問題」的意思。

---

or·di·nar·y [ˋɔrdṇ͵ɛrɪ] Track 1677

形 普通的 同 usual 平常的

▶I'm just an ordinary girl with ordinary dreams.
我只是個普通的女孩，有著普通的夢想。

文法字詞解析
在 ordinary 前面加上字首 extra-（特別地、超乎一般地）就變成了 extraordinary「異常的、非凡的」。

---

or·gan [ˋɔrgən] Track 1678

名 器官

▶There are concerns（憂慮）that organ recipients（接受者）may be infected（感染）.
器官接受者可能有被感染的疑慮。

---

or·gan·i·za·tion [͵ɔrgənəˋzeʃən] Track 1679

名 組織、機構 同 institution 機構

▶I'm not clever enough to be the brains of the organization.
我不夠聰明，沒有資格成為這個組織的軍師。

文法字詞解析
brain 如果用複數時，代表某個非常有智慧、有能力的人

---

or·gan·ize [ˋɔrgən͵aɪz] Track 1680

動 組織、系統化

▶You should organize the activity（活動）in a more flexible（靈活的）way.
你們應該以更靈活的方式組織這次活動。

實用片語用語
in a... way 用……的方式

---

ov·en [ˋʌvən] Track 1681

名 爐子、烤箱 同 stove 爐子

▶I hope I didn't leave the oven on.
希望我沒忘記關烤箱。

---

o·ver·pass [͵ovəˋpæs] Track 1682

名 天橋、高架橋

▶Traffic has become smoother after they constructed（建造）the overpass.
他們建了那個高架橋後交通就變得比較順暢了。

實用片語用語
smooth traffic 交通順暢

---

over·seas [͵ovəˋsiz] Track 1683

形 國外的、在國外的 副 在海外、在國外 同 abroad 在國外

▶形 Over the years, hundreds of overseas students have studied at that university（大學）.
幾年來，有幾百個留學生在那所大學裡唸過書。

▶副 Many employees（員工）were sent overseas by their employers（雇主）.
有很多員工被雇主派到海外了。

---

owl [aʊl] Track 1684

名 貓頭鷹

▶My pet owl is always sleeping. 我的寵物貓頭鷹總是在睡覺。

own·er [ˋonɚ]
Track 1685

名 物主、所有者 同 holder 持有者

▶Do you know who the owner of this dog is?
你知道這隻狗的主人是誰嗎？

文法字詞解析
這句也可以改寫成：Do you know to whom the dog belongs? 在這個句子中，使用到片語「belongs to sb.」，其中 sb. 是受詞，所以句子裡的代名詞要用 whom 而不是 who。

ox [ɑks]
Track 1686

名 公牛

名詞複數 oxen

▶The ox was mad and started chasing after us.
那頭公牛生氣了，在我們後面跑。

pack [pæk]
Track 1687

名 一包 動 打包

▶名 Will you buy three packs of gum（口香糖）for my kid on your way home?
你能在回家的路上幫我家小孩買三盒口香糖回來嗎？

▶動 How will you pack the goods we ordered?
你們將如何包裝我們訂購的貨物？

pac·kage [ˋpækɪdʒ]
Track 1688

名 包裹 動 包裝

▶名 He brought me a large package this morning.
他今天早上送了一個好大的包裹來給我。

▶動 Products（產品）packaged in beautiful wrappers（包裝紙）sell well. 包著漂亮包裝紙的產品銷量很好。

pain [pen]
Track 1689

名 疼痛 動 傷害

▶名 The pain was too much and he fainted（昏倒）.
實在太疼痛了，於是他昏了過去。

▶動 It pains me to hear you cry. 聽到你哭，我就覺得心痛。

文法字詞解析
第一個例句中，pain 是名詞，所以要用限定詞 much 來修飾；如果說：「It was so painful that he fainted.」的話，painful 是形容詞，所以可以直接用副詞 so 來修飾。

pain·ful [ˋpenfəl]
Track 1690

形 痛苦的

▶Would you please not discuss this painful subject anymore?
請不要再談論這件痛苦的事情了，好嗎？

paint·er [ˋpentɚ]
Track 1691

名 畫家

▶I saw the painter being interviewed on TV last night.
我昨晚在電視上看到這名畫家在受訪。

paint·ing [ˋpentɪŋ]
Track 1692

名 繪畫

▶There are three paintings on the wall; which one do you like best? 牆上有三幅畫，你最喜歡哪一幅呢？

pa·ja·mas [pəˋdʒæməz] Track 1693

名 睡衣
名詞複數 pajamas
▶Would you please show me the pink pajamas over there?
麻煩你把那邊的那套粉紅色睡衣拿給我看一下好嗎？

palm [pɑm] Track 1694

名 手掌
▶Do you believe in palm reading? 你相信掌紋算命嗎？

實用片語用語
palm reading 看手相

pan [pæn] Track 1695

名 平底鍋
▶She hit the thief with a frying pan. 她用平底鍋打了那個小偷。

pan·da [ˋpændə] Track 1696

名 貓熊
▶Pandas are very rare animals. 貓熊是很稀有的動物。

pa·pa·ya [pəˋpaɪə] Track 1697

名 木瓜
▶I can't stand the smell of papaya.
我受不了木瓜聞起來的味道。

par·don [ˋpɑrdn̩] Track 1698

名 原諒 動 寬恕 同 forgive 原諒
▶名 I beg your pardon; It is too noisy for me to hear clearly（清楚地）.
麻煩再說一次好嗎？這裡太吵了，我聽不太清楚。
▶動 We can't pardon this kind of rudeness（無禮）.
我們不能原諒這種無禮行為。

萬用延伸句型
I beg your pardon. 麻煩再說一次。或者也可以很簡潔地說「Pardon?」。

par·rot [ˋpærət] Track 1699

名 鸚鵡
▶Why do parrots like to repeat what people say?
為什麼鸚鵡喜歡學人說話？

par·tic·u·lar [pəˋtɪkjələ] Track 1700

形 特別的 同 special 特別的
▶This is a particular case that should be looked at carefully.
這是一種特殊情況，必須仔細研究。

實用片語用語
looked at (sb. / sth.) adv. ……地看某物／某人。look at 是一般動詞，後面接副詞；look 是連綴動詞，後面接形容詞，表示「看起來……的」。

part·ner [ˋpartnə] Track 1701

名 夥伴
▶Who's going to be your partner at the ball?
你這次舞會的舞伴是誰？

pas·sen·ger [ˋpæsn̩dʒə] Track 1702

名 旅客
▶There are plenty of passengers on the plane flying to New York. 飛往紐約的飛機上有相當多的乘客。

實用片語用語
plenty of 很多的

paste [pest] ◀ Track 1703

名 漿糊 動 黏貼 同 glue 黏著劑、膠水

▶名 The boy glued the paper together with paste.
那個男孩用漿糊把紙黏在一起。

▶動 Paste this note on the board, please.
請把這張紙條貼在板子上。

pat [pæt] ◀ Track 1704

動 輕拍 名 拍 同 tap 輕拍

▶動 He patted my head and said nothing.
他輕拍我的頭，什麼也沒說。

▶名 He gave me a pat on the back as he left the room.
他離開房間時輕拍了一下我的背。

path [pæθ] ◀ Track 1705

名 路徑 同 route 路程

▶Would you tell me which path leads to the village?
你能告訴我哪條路通往那個小村莊嗎？

pa·tient [ˋpeʃənt] ◀ Track 1706

形 忍耐的 名 病人

▶形 He was not patient enough to listen to what I said.
他沒有耐心來聽完我的話。

▶名 The doctor must make sure that the patient has enough time to rest.
醫生必須保證病人有足夠的時間休息。

實用片語用語
listen to sb. / sth. （專注地）聽

pat·tern [ˋpætɚn] ◀ Track 1707

名 模型、圖樣 動 仿照

▶名 The pattern on your tie looks nice.
你領帶上的圖樣看起來不錯。

▶動 We patterned the plan after his old one.
我們這次的計畫是仿照他之前的那個訂的。

實用片語用語
be patterned on / after sth. 仿照某物所做

peace [pis] ◀ Track 1708

名 和平 反 war 戰爭

▶He likes his peace and quiet. 他喜歡過著和平安靜的生活。

實用片語用語
peace and quiet 安詳寧靜

peace·ful [ˋpisfəl] ◀ Track 1709

形 和平的 同 quiet 平靜的

▶The village has always been very peaceful.
那個村莊一直都很和平。

peach [pitʃ] ◀ Track 1710

名 桃子

▶Wash the peach before you eat it.
吃桃子前要先洗一下。

pea·nut [ˋpiˏnʌt] ◀ Track 1711

名 花生

▶I'm allergic to peanuts. 我對花生過敏。

實用片語用語
be allergic to 對……過敏
此外，不喜歡、看不順眼某人也可以說 allergic to sb. 對某人很感冒。

pear [pɛr]

Track 1712

名 梨子

▶The pears he gave us were very juicy.
他給我們的梨子很多汁。

pen·guin [ˋpɛngwɪn]

Track 1713

名 企鵝

▶Penguins like cold environments.
企鵝喜歡寒冷的環境。

文法字詞解析
environment 既是可數也是不可數名詞，不可數的時候代表「自然環境」，可數的時候表示特定地區、有特定的氣溫和特定動植物生存的地方。

pep·per [ˋpɛpɚ]

Track 1714

名 胡椒

▶Add some pepper to the soup and it will taste better.
在湯裡面加點胡椒粉會比較好喝。

per [pɚ]

Track 1715

介 每、經由 同 through 經由

▶Would you like to send these goods per rail, or per plane?
你是想通過鐵路來送這些貨物，還是飛機呢？

per·fect [ˋpɝfɪkt]

Track 1716

形 完美的 同 ideal 完美的、理想的

▶She's perfect in my eyes.
在我的眼中她是最完美的。

實用片語用語
in sb's eyes 在某人眼中，對某人來說

pe·ri·od [ˋpɪrɪəd]

Track 1717

名 期間、時代 同 era 時代

▶During the period, most people in our town were poor.
在那個時期，我們城裡的人幾乎都很窮。

per·son·al [ˋpɝsn̩l]

Track 1718

形 個人的 同 private 私人的

▶Would you like to open a personal account in our bank?
你想在我們銀行開一個個人帳戶嗎？

pho·to·graph/pho·to

Track 1719

[ˋfotəˏgræf]/[ˋfoto]

名 照片 動 照相

▶名 Look at this cute photo of my baby!
快看看我寶寶這張可愛的照片！

▶動 He's trying to photograph the foxes but they keep moving around.
他正在試著拍下那些狐狸，可是牠們一直動來動去的。

實用片語用語
keep doing sth. / keep on doing sth. 繼續做某事。

pho·tog·ra·pher [fəˋtɑgrəfɚ]

Track 1720

名 攝影師

▶It will take some time before the man becomes an excellent photographer.
這個人還需要一段時間才能成為一名優秀的攝影師。

phrase [frez]
Track 1721

名 片語 動 表意

▶名 Try to learn as many English words and phrases as possible. 試著儘可能多學些英文字彙和片語。

▶動 I'm not sure how to phrase it, so let me just show you in a picture.
我不知道怎麼講才能表達我的意思，所以讓我直接用圖解的跟你說明好了。

pick [pɪk]
Track 1722

動 摘、選擇 名 選擇

▶動 Would you please pick up the yellow wallet for me?
請你幫我把那個黃色錢包撿起來好嗎？

▶名 Here are twenty books. Take your pick!
這裡有二十本書，你隨意挑吧！

實用片語用語
have / take your pick 隨意挑選

pic·nic [ˋpɪknɪk]
Track 1723

名 野餐 動 去野餐

▶名 We always have picnics when the weather is fine.
天氣好的時候我們總是會去野餐。

▶動 This is a nice park to picnic in.
這個公園很適合野餐。

pi·geon [ˋpɪdʒən]
Track 1724

名 鴿子 同 dove 鴿子

▶It is no wonder that people like pigeons. They are a symbol of peace. 難怪人們喜愛鴿子。牠們是和平的象徵。

pile [paɪl]
Track 1725

名 堆 動 堆積 同 heap 堆積

▶名 Please collect the books as soon as possible and put them in a pile on my desk.
請儘快把書收起來在我桌上堆成一疊。

▶動 Can you pile the files（文件）over there?
你可以把文件在那邊堆成一疊嗎？

實用片語用語
pile up 將……堆成一堆
例如：He made all his books piled up on the table.
他把他所有的書都放在桌上堆成一堆。

pil·low [ˋpɪlo]
Track 1726

名 枕頭 動 以……為枕 同 cushion 靠墊

▶名 Not everyone likes to sleep on a pillow, but some can't sleep without it.
不是每個人都喜歡枕著枕頭睡覺，但是有些人沒有枕頭睡不著覺。

▶動 The child pillowed his head on his mother's lap.
那個孩子把頭枕在媽媽的大腿上。

pin [pɪn]
Track 1727

名 針 動 釘住 同 clip 夾住

▶名 I have to hold the cloth together with a pin.
我得用針把這塊布別起來。

▶動 She pinned a rose in her hair.
她在頭上別了一朵玫瑰。

實用片語用語
hold together 將……連接在一起
另外，hold together 也有「團結」的意思。
例如：Let's hold together and overcome the difficulties. 讓我們團結起來克服困難吧。

pine·ap·ple [ˋpaɪn͵æpḷ] Track 1728

名 鳳梨

▶I like to eat pineapples very much. 我很喜歡吃鳳梨。

ping-pong/ta·ble ten·nis Track 1729

[ˋpɪŋ͵pɑŋ]/[ˋtebḷˋtɛnɪs]

名 乒乓球

▶Ping-pong is the one sport I can play.
乒乓球是我唯一會的運動。

pink [pɪŋk] Track 1730

形 粉紅的 名 粉紅色

▶形 Do you like this pink skirt? I think it looks great on you.
你喜歡這件粉紅色的裙子嗎？我覺得它很適合你。

▶名 Why do so many girls like pink?
為什麼這麼多女生喜歡粉紅色？

文法字詞解析

衣服穿在某人身上的時候，介係詞要用 on，人穿著某件衣服時，介係詞要用 in。例如：the T-shirt on her 她身上的 T 恤；the girl in the blue T-shirt 穿著藍色 T 恤的女孩。

pipe [paɪp] Track 1731

名 管子 動 以管傳送 同 tube 管子

▶名 It won't be long before the village gets water through pipes.
過不了多久那個村子就能透過水管獲得供水了。

▶動 The music is piped into the restaurant.
音樂透過纜線在餐廳內播送。

實用片語用語

pipe into 以管傳送

pitch [pɪtʃ] Track 1732

動 投擲、間距 同 throw 投、擲

▶The teacher asked us to pitch the ball as far as possible.
老師要求我們儘量把球投得更遠。

piz·za [ˋpitsə] Track 1733

名 比薩

▶There was a traffic jam so my pizza was late.
因為塞車的關係，我的比薩很晚才送到。

plain [plen] Track 1734

形 平坦的 名 平原

▶形 It is quite plain that there are some mistakes in his test.
顯然他的試卷中有一些錯誤。

▶名 There is a road that goes straight across the plain.
有一條路筆直地穿過平原。

萬用延伸句型

It's quite plain that... 很顯然地。也可以用 obviously 來表示。使用時，obviously 可以放在句首，或是放在動詞後面。

plan·et [ˋplænɪt] Track 1735

名 行星

▶It is no wonder that Earth is different from other planets in many aspects（方面）.
怪不得地球在很多方面都與其他的行星都不同。

plate [plet] Track 1736

名 盤子 同 dish 盤子

▶My mom asked me to finish the food on the plate as soon as possible. 媽媽叫我快點把盤子裡的食物吃完。

plat·form [ˋplætˏfɔrm]
Track 1737

名 平臺、月臺 同 stage 平臺

▶Would you please meet me on the third platform?
請你到第三月臺來找我好嗎？

play·ful [ˋplefəl]
Track 1738

形 愛玩的

▶Is he always this playful? 他平常一直都這麼愛玩嗎？

文法字詞解析
形容詞字尾「-ful」表示「充滿……的」。

pleas·ant [ˋplɛzn̩t]
Track 1739

形 愉快的

▶The weather is really pleasant. 天氣很舒服。

pleas·ure [ˋplɛʒɚ]
Track 1740

名 愉悅 反 misery 悲慘

▶It's been a pleasure meeting you. 很高興認識你。

plus [plʌs]
Track 1741

介 加 名 加號 形 加的 同 additional 附加的

▶介 I want a burger plus large fries. 我要一個漢堡加大薯。

▶名 Good looks are always a plus.
長得好看一點總有加分效果嘛。

▶形 It's plus five degrees outside, not minus.
外面溫度是正五度，不是負五度。

po·em [ˋpoɪm]
Track 1742

名 詩

▶I don't really care for poems. 我實在對詩沒興趣。

實用片語用語
not care for sb. / sth. 不喜歡某人／某事

po·et [ˋpoɪt]
Track 1743

名 詩人

▶It is no wonder that so many people like this poet and his poems a lot. He is good at describing people's mood. 難怪這麼多人都很喜歡這位詩人和他的詩。他很擅長描寫人的心情。

poi·son [ˋpɔɪzn̩]
Track 1744

名 毒藥 動 下毒

▶名 He put poison in his mother's tea.
他在他媽媽的茶裡放了毒藥。

▶動 He tried to poison the rats but the rats were too smart for him. 他試著毒死老鼠，但老鼠都太聰明了。

實用片語用語
too... for sth. / sb. 對某人 / 某物來說太……

pol·i·cy [ˋpɑləsɪ]
Track 1745

名 政策

▶The citizens hope the government can enforce（施行）the new policy as soon as possible.
市民們希望政府能儘快施行這個新政策。

po·lite [pəˋlaɪt]
Track 1746

形 有禮貌的

▶Not every clerk in this bank is polite enough to the customers.
不是銀行的每位員工都對顧客夠禮貌。

pop·u·lar [ˋpɑpjələ] Track 1747

形 流行的

▶This song is popular among young people.
這首歌在年輕人當中大受歡迎。

pop·u·la·tion [͵pɑpjəˋleʃən] Track 1748

名 人口

▶Would you tell me what the population of the city is?
你能告訴我這個城市有多少人口嗎？

pork [pork] Track 1749

名 豬肉

▶She doesn't eat pork. 她不吃豬肉。

文法字詞解析
肉類通常都是不可數名詞，例如：beef（牛肉）、pork（豬肉）、lamb（羊肉）。

port [port] Track 1750

名 港口 同 harbor 海港

▶The port is not far from my home. 港口離我家不遠。

pose [poz] Track 1751

動 擺出 名 姿勢 同 posture 姿勢

▶動 You should really pose this issue at the meeting.
你真的應該在會議上提出這個問題。

▶名 Why do you always make such strange poses in pictures?
你為什麼每次拍照都擺很奇怪的姿勢？

實用片語用語
pose a question 提出問題，使用這個片語時，提出的問題通常是需要審慎思考或是充分討論的。

pos·i·tive [ˋpɑzətɪv] Track 1752

形 確信的、積極的、正的 同 certain 確信的

▶There is positive proof（證據）that the man next to me did it.
有確切的證據證明是我身旁的那個男人幹的。

pos·si·bil·i·ty [͵pɑsəˋbɪlətɪ] Track 1753

名 可能性

▶Is there any possibility that you got it wrong?
有沒有可能是你搞錯了？

實用片語用語
get something wrong 弄錯某事、犯錯

post [post] Track 1754

名 郵件 動 郵寄、公佈、快速地

▶名 Would you please tell me where the nearest post office is?
請告訴我最近的郵局在哪好嗎？

▶動 Will you help me post this notice on the wall?
請你幫我把這個通知貼在牆上好嗎？

文法字詞解析
post 也可以用在「在網路上發表文章」，例如；She posted an article on Facebook. 她在臉書上發表了一篇文章。

post·card [ˋpost͵kɑrd] Track 1755

名 明信片

▶No wonder he didn't receive the postcard from his sister. She wrote the wrong address.
難怪他沒收到他妹妹寄來的明信片。她寫錯地址了。

pot [pɑt] Track 1756

名 鍋、壺 同 vessel 器皿

▶Will you help me wash up those pots and plates in the kitchen?
幫忙我洗洗廚房裡的那些鍋碗瓢盆好嗎？

po·ta·to [pə`teto]

Track 1757

名 馬鈴薯

▶Would you like a salad or a baked potato? Both of them are delicious.
你想要一份沙拉還是烤馬鈴薯？它們都很美味。

萬用延伸句型
Would you like A or B？你比較想要 A 還是 B ？也可以說：Do you prefer A or B?

pound [paʊnd]

Track 1758

名 磅、英磅 動 重擊

▶名 Not all the people are willing to buy potatoes at the price of five dollars per pound.
不是所有人都願意買五美元一磅的馬鈴薯。

▶動 Stop pounding on the wall; the neighbors are sleeping.
不要一直打牆壁，鄰居都睡覺了。

文法字詞解析
第二個例句使用了省略主詞的祈使句句型，祈使句的否定形式是在動詞的前面加上 don't 或 never。此外因為使用祈使句時，說話的對象通常都在說話者的身邊，主詞不是「你」就是「我們」，所以不會有「doesn't」的情況出現。

pow·er·ful [`paʊɚfəl]

Track 1759

形 有力的

▶The bomb is powerful enough to destroy this whole village.
這枚炸彈威力很大，足以毀滅整個村莊。

praise [prez]

Track 1760

動 稱讚 名 榮耀 同 compliment 稱讚

▶動 He praised his children a lot.
他經常稱讚自己的孩子。

▶名 Don't be so humble! You deserve（值得）the praise.
不用這麼謙虛，你本來就很值得被稱讚啊。

pray [pre]

Track 1761

動 祈禱 同 beg 祈求

▶Not many people often go to church to pray now.
現在沒有那麼多人常去教堂祈禱了。

pre·fer [prɪ`fɝ]

Track 1762

動 偏愛、較喜歡 同 favor 偏愛

▶Would you tell me which flavor（口味）you prefer?
你能告訴我你比較喜歡哪一種口味嗎？

pres·ence [`prɛzn̩s]

Track 1763

名 出席 同 attendance 出席

▶Will you grace（給某人以榮耀）our banquet（宴會）with your presence?
您願意來參加宴會，讓我們不勝榮幸嗎？

實用片語用語
grace sth. / sb. with one's presence
以某人的出席來讓某場合／某人感到光榮

pres·ent [`prɛzn̩t]

Track 1764

形 目前的 名 片刻、禮物 動 呈現 同 gift 禮物

▶形 How many of the group are present today?
今天這組有多少人出席？

▶名 Are you sure you want to get her a chicken for present?
你確定你真的要送她一隻雞當禮物嗎？

▶動 The situation（情勢）presents a serious problem.
這個事態引起了嚴重的問題。

pres·i·dent [ˋprɛzədənt]

Track 1765

名 總統

▶The president is a serious, calm old man.
這個總統是個正經的、平靜的老人。

press [prɛs]

Track 1766

名 印刷機、新聞界 動 壓下、強迫 同 force 強迫

▶名 The press got really excited over this scandal（醜聞）.
新聞界因為這件醜聞非常興奮。

▶動 If you press the button, terrible things will happen.
如果按下這個按鈕會發生很可怕的事喔。

pride [praɪd]

Track 1767

名 自豪 動 使自豪

▶名 I take pride in being your friend.
能和你作朋友，我很自豪。

▶動 She prided herself on her cooking.
她因自己善於烹飪而自豪。

實用片語用語

1. take pride in sth. 為某事感到驕傲，也可以說：feel proud of sth.
2. pride oneself on (doing) sth. 某人為某事感到自豪

prince [prɪns]

Track 1768

名 王子

▶Have you ever seen Prince William? What does he look like?
你見過威廉王子嗎？他長什麼樣子呢？

prin·cess [ˋprɪnsɪs]

Track 1769

名 公主

▶Not all people know well of the princess and her family.
不是所有人都很瞭解這位公主和她的家庭。

prin·ci·pal [ˋprɪnsəpḷ]

Track 1770

形 首要的 名 校長、首長

▶形 Our principal problem is that we lack money.
我們的主要問題是缺錢。

▶名 It doesn't matter whether you talk with the principal about this or not.
無論你要不要找校長談論這件事，都沒關係。

文法字詞解析

要注意 lack 的詞性，才能確定後面要不要放介係詞。如果是動詞的話，後面要直接接受詞，如果是名詞的話，後面則要加上介係詞 of 才能再接受詞。

prin·ci·ple [ˋprɪnsəpḷ]

Track 1771

名 原則 同 standard 規範

▶He's a man with no principles.
他是個沒原則的男人。

print·er [ˋprɪntɚ]

Track 1772

名 印刷工、印表機

▶What's the matter with this printer? 這台印表機怎麼了？

pris·on [ˋprɪzṇ]

Track 1773

名 監獄 同 jail 監獄

▶He was put into prison for robbing the bank.
他因為搶了銀行而被關進監獄了。

實用片語用語

put sb. in to prison：把……關進監獄。除了 prison 之外，jail 也有監獄的意思，但主要用於表示像拘留所等比較小型的監獄，裡面所關的犯人罪刑也比較輕微；prison 則表示大型監獄。

A B C D E F G H I J K L M N O **P** Q R S T U V W X Y Z

pris·on·er [ˋprɪzn̩ɚ]

Track 1774

名 囚犯

▶The prisoners are hungry and mad.
這些囚犯又餓又生氣。

pri·vate [ˋpraɪvɪt]

Track 1775

形 私密的

▶Did you have a private talk with the man who came to your office yesterday?
你有跟昨天到你辦公室來的那個人私下談談嗎？

prize [praɪz]

Track 1776

名 獎品 動 獎賞、撬開 同 reward 獎品

▶名 He hurt his foot and didn't get the first prize in this race（賽跑）.他的腳受傷了，所以在這次賽跑中沒能獲得第一名。

▶動 He prized the box open with an iron bar.
他用一根鐵棒把那箱子撬開。

文法字詞解析
prize 解釋做「撬開」時是及物動詞，但受詞的後方一定要加上副詞或介係詞。

pro·duce [prəˋdjus]/[ˋprɑdjus]

Track 1777

動 生產 名 產品 同 make 生產

▶動 His factory is too small to produce so many products（產品）. 他的工廠太小，生產不了如此多的產品。

▶名 The place is known for its dairy（乳製品的）produce.
這地方因生產乳製品而出名。

文法字詞解析
be known 後面加上不同的介系詞會產生不同的用法，因此常常會讓人混淆。除了 be known for（因……而著名）之外，還有「be known as（以做為……而著名」，以及「be known to（為……所知）」。

pro·duc·er [prəˋdjusɚ]

Track 1778

名 製造者

▶This company is the best car producer in this area.
這家公司是該地區最好的汽車製造者。

pro·gress [ˋprɑgrɛs]/[prəˋgrɛs]

Track 1779

名 進展 動 進行 同 proceed 進行

▶名 It took us a month to make some progress.
我們花了一個月的時間才取得了一點進展。

▶動 They had to revise（修改）the plan so as to progress their project smoothly（順利地）.
為了使工程能順利進行，他們必須修改方案。

proj·ect [ˋprɑdʒɛkt]/[prəˋdʒɛkt]

Track 1780

名 計畫 動 推出、投射

▶名 We are determined（堅決的）to finish the project.
我們決心完成這項計畫。

▶動 Don't project your own evil thoughts onto other people.
別把自己邪惡的想法投射在其他人身上。

實用片語用語
be determined to do sth. 下定決心要做某事

prom·ise [ˋprɑmɪs]

Track 1781

名 諾言 動 約定 同 swear 承諾

▶名 He never keeps his promises. 他從來不信守諾言。

▶動 I am sorry that I can't promise anything.
很抱歉我無法承諾什麼。

pro·nounce [prə`naʊns]

Track 1782

動 發音

▶Would you tell me how to pronounce this word correctly（正確地）?
你能告訴我這個單字怎樣發音才正確嗎？

pro·pose [prə`poz]

Track 1783

動 提議、求婚 同 offer 提議

▶Why don't you propose to her? 你為什麼不向她求婚呢？

實用片語用語
propose to sb. 向某人求婚

pro·tect [prə`tɛkt]

Track 1784

動 保護

▶He is always working on protecting endangered（瀕臨絕種的）animals. 他總是致力於保護瀕臨絕種的動物。

proud [praʊd]

Track 1785

形 驕傲的 同 arrogant 傲慢的

▶The mother is so proud of her son.
這位母親對兒子非常引以為傲。

pro·vide [prə`vaɪd]

Track 1786

動 提供 同 supply 提供

▶Do you provide towels here at the pool?
你們泳池有提供毛巾嗎？

實用片語用語
provided (that)... 倘若……。這個片語可以用在句首或句中，
例如：You can go to the movies with your friends provided that you clean up your room.
或是：Provided that you clean up your room, you can go to the movies with your friends.
只要你把房間整理好，你就可以跟朋友去看電影。

pud·ding [`pʊdɪŋ]

Track 1787

名 布丁

▶He ate up all the pudding. 他把所有的布丁都吃光了。

pump [pʌmp]

Track 1788

名 抽水機 動 抽水、汲取

▶名 We need a new pump but I don't know where to get one.
我們需要新的抽水機，但我不知道去哪裡買。

▶動 He's helping us pump water out of the flooded house.
他正在幫我們將水從被淹沒的房子裡抽出去。

pump·kin [`pʌmpkɪn]

Track 1789

名 南瓜

▶Would you like some pumpkin pie for a snack?
你要不要來點南瓜派當點心吃？

文法字詞解析
some 可以用來修飾可數或不可數名詞

pun·ish [`pʌnɪʃ]

Track 1790

動 處罰

▶She doesn't like to punish her children.
她不喜歡處罰自己的小孩。

pun·ish·ment [`pʌnɪʃmənt]

Track 1791

名 處罰

▶Not all people believe that punishment is the only way to solve a problem.
不是所有人都認為懲罰是解決問題的唯一方法。

pu·pil [ˋpjup!] 🔈 *Track 1792*

名 學生、瞳孔 同 student 學生

▶Would you tell me how many pupils there are in this class?
你能告訴我這個班有多少學生嗎？

文法字詞解析
pupil 通常指的是中小學的學生，student 則可以是小學生、中學生、大學生。另外，如果要說某學生「就讀於某學校」的話，要說 a student at + (school)。

pup·pet [ˋpʌpɪt] 🔈 *Track 1793*

名 木偶、傀儡 同 doll 玩偶

▶Would you like to take your little son to see a puppet show?
你要不要帶你的小兒子去看場木偶戲呢？

pup·py [ˋpʌpɪ] 🔈 *Track 1794*

名 小狗

▶Why don't we buy a cute little puppy as her birthday present?
為什麼我們不買隻可愛的小狗給她當生日禮物呢？

purse [pɝs] 🔈 *Track 1795*

名 錢包 同 wallet 錢包

▶Is this black purse yours?
這個黑色的錢包是你的嗎？

puz·zle [ˋpʌz!] 🔈 *Track 1796*

名 難題、謎 動 迷惑 同 mystery 謎

▶名 The puzzle is too hard for me.
這謎題對我來說太難了。

▶動 We puzzled over the question for the whole afternoon.
我們整個下午都在苦思這個問題。

文法字詞解析
puzzle over sth. 花長時間苦思

qual·i·ty [ˋkwɑlətɪ] 🔈 *Track 1797*

名 品質

▶The quality of service in this restaurant has improved a lot.
那個飯店的服務品質已經有了很大的改善。

quan·ti·ty [ˋkwɑntətɪ] 🔈 *Track 1798*

名 數量

▶There might be large quantities of crude（天然的）oil beneath（在……之下）the surface.
在地表下可能有大量的原油。

quar·ter [ˋkwɔrtɚ] 🔈 *Track 1799*

名 四分之一 動 分為四等分

▶名 We pay our rent（租金）at the end of each quarter.
我們是在每個季末付房租的。

▶動 There are four people here; how about quartering the pizza?
這裡有四個人，我們把披薩餅分成四等份怎麼樣？

文法字詞解析
quarter 可以用來講時間和金錢，例如：a quarter to nine 表示「還有四分之一個小時就到九點」，也就是八點四十五分；a quarter past eight 表示「過了八點鐘之後的四分之一個鐘頭」，也就是八點十五分。用在金錢上，a quarter dollar 就是25分錢。

quit [kwɪt]

Track 1800

動 離去、解除

▶If you're sick of your job, why don't you just quit?
如果你已經厭煩了現在的工作，那為什麼不乾脆辭職呢？

文法字詞解析
quit 的動詞變化：quit, quit, quit

quiz [kwɪz]

Track 1801

名 測驗 動 對……進行測驗 同 test 測驗

名詞複數 quizzes

▶名 We will have a quiz tomorrow morning.
我們明天早晨有一個小測驗。

▶動 The teacher quizzed us on the last chapter.
老師考了我們上一章的內容。

Rr

rab·bit [ˋræbɪt]

Track 1802

名 兔子

▶My pet rabbit smells really bad. 我的寵物兔子真的很臭。

rain·y [ˋrenɪ]

Track 1803

形 多雨的

▶It's rainy today so we should just stay at home.
今天下雨，我們就待在家裡好了。

range [rendʒ]

Track 1804

名 範圍 動 排列 同 limit 範圍

▶名 Will you provide us with products（產品）within the price range? 你能提供我們這種價格範圍內的產品嗎？

▶動 The price ranges from two thousand to five thousand.
價格的範圍在兩千到五千之間。

實用片語用語
range from sth. to sth. 範圍從……到……之間

rap·id [ˋræpɪd]

Track 1805

形 迅速的 同 quick 迅速的

▶The city's rapid growth surprised all the experts.
這個城市迅速的發展讓所有專家都嚇了一跳。

rare [rɛr]

Track 1806

形 稀有的

▶This is a very rare kind of insect. 這是很稀有的一種昆蟲。

rath·er [ˋræðɚ]

Track 1807

副 寧願

▶I would rather you choose this expensive one.
我寧願你選這個貴的。

real·i·ty [rɪˋælətɪ]

Track 1808

名 真實 同 truth 真實

▶He says he's being honest, but in reality he is lying.
他說他很誠實，但實際上他在說謊。

實用片語用語
in reality 實際上、事實上。有推翻、反駁前述事件的涵義。

real·ize [ˋriə,laɪz] Track 1809

動 實現、瞭解

▶It took him a long time to realize his great dream.
他花了很長的時間來實現他那個偉大的夢想。

re·cent [risn̩t] Track 1810

形 最近的

▶Would you tell me what you have been busy doing in recent years? 你能告訴我你近幾年都在忙些什麼嗎？

re·cord [ˋrɛkɚd]/[rɪˋkɔrd] Track 1811

名 紀錄、唱片 動 記錄

▶名 She broke the world record set by herself.
她打破了自己所創的世界紀錄。

▶動 The song was recorded in our studio（工作室）.
這首歌是我們工作室裡錄的。

實用片語用語
break / beat a record 打破紀錄

rec·tan·gle [ˋrɛktæŋg!] Track 1812

名 長方形

▶The garden is shaped like a rectangle.
這個院子是長方形的。

re·frig·er·a·tor/ fridge/ice·box [rɪˋfrɪdʒə,retɚ]/[frɪdʒ]/[ˋaɪs,bɑks] Track 1813

名 冰箱

▶Why don't you put the soup in the refrigerator?
你為什麼不把湯放到冰箱裡呢？。

re·fuse [rɪˋfjuz] Track 1814

動 拒絕 同 reject 拒絕

▶He refused to do anything I told him to.
他拒絕做任何我要他做的事。

實用片語用語
refuse to do sth. 拒絕做某事

re·gard [rɪˋgɑrd] Track 1815

動 注視、認為 名 注視 同 judge 認為

▶動 It is no wonder that people in China regard pandas as their national treasure.
怪不得中國人把熊貓視為國寶。

▶名 She said you had no regard for her feelings.
她說你沒有考慮到她的心情。

re·gion [ˋridʒən] Track 1816

名 區域 同 zone 區域

▶There aren't many houses in this region.
這個區域的房子不多

reg·u·lar [ˋrɛgjəlɚ] Track 1817

形 平常的、定期的、規律的 同 usual 平常的

▶He's a regular customer（顧客）here.
他是這裡的常客。

實用片語用語
regular customer / visitor 常客

re·ject [rɪ`dʒɛkt]

Track 1818

動 拒絕

▶He asked her to be his girlfriend but was rejected.
他請她做他的女朋友，但被拒絕了。

re·la·tion [rɪ`leʃən]

Track 1819

名 關係

▶There is no relation between the two things.
這兩件事之間沒有聯繫。

re·la·tion·ship [rɪ`leʃən͵ʃɪp]

Track 1820

名 關係

▶We're all interested in the two actors' relationship.
我們都對那兩位演員的關係很感興趣。

re·peat [rɪ`pit]

Track 1821

動 重複 名 重複

▶動 Would you repeat what I just told you?
你能複述一下剛才我說的話嗎？

▶名 I'm tired of seeing all these repeats on TV.
電視上那些重複的節目我都看膩了。

實用片語用語
tired of (doing) sth. 對於做某事感到厭煩

re·ply [rɪ`plaɪ]

Track 1822

名 回答、答覆 同 respond 回答

▶Please reply as soon as possible.
請儘快回覆。

re·port·er [rɪ`portɚ]

Track 1823

名 記者 同 journalist 記者

▶The reporter is very tired after a long night at the scene of the accident.
那名記者在意外現場待了漫長的一晚後非常疲累。

實用片語用語
at the scene 在現場
另外，on the scene 也有「出現在現場」的意思。例如：Ten minutes after the accident, the ambulance arrived on the scene. 意外發生後十分鐘，救護車就抵達現場了。

re·quire [rɪ`kwaɪr]

Track 1824

動 需要 同 need 需要

▶We require food to live. 我們需要食物才能生存。

re·quire·ment [rɪ`kwaɪrmənt]

Track 1825

名 需要

▶Would you tell us what your company's requirements are?
能告訴我們你們公司有哪些要求嗎？

re·spect [rɪ`spɛkt]

Track 1826

名 尊重 動 尊重、尊敬 同 adore 尊敬

▶名 The new teacher earned the respect of students very soon.
這位新老師很快就贏得了學生們的尊敬。

▶動 You need to respect yourself before others can respect you.
在得到別人尊重前，你必須先尊重自己。

實用片語用語
win / earn / gain the respect of sb. 贏得、獲得某人的尊重

re·spon·si·ble [rɪˋspɑnsəbl̩] Track 1827

形 負責任的

▶It took the police a week to find out who was responsible for this accident（事故）.
警察花了一週的時間才查出誰該對這個事故負責任。

res·tau·rant [ˋrɛstərənt] Track 1828

名 餐廳

▶How about we find a restaurant and sit down?
我們找家餐廳坐下來好嗎？

rest·room [ˋrɛst͵rum] Track 1829

名 洗手間、廁所

▶Could you tell me where the restroom is? I can't find it in this building.
能告訴我洗手間在哪嗎？我在這棟樓裡找不到洗手間。

re·sult [rɪˋzʌlt] Track 1830

名 結果 動 導致 同 consequence 結果

▶名 Would you tell me the final result of the poll（投票）?
能告訴我這次投票最後的結果嗎？

▶動 The accident resulted in many deaths.
這次意外造成不少人死亡。

萬用延伸句型
As a result, S. +V. 結果……
例如：She did exercise every morning since last winter. As a result, she has lost twenty pounds. 她從去年冬天就每天早上都做運動，結果她減了二十磅。

re·view [rɪˋvju] Track 1831

名 複習 動 回顧、檢查 同 recall 回憶

▶名 It took us several weeks to have a review of the term's work. 我們花了幾週的時間來複習一學期的功課。

▶動 It will take me an hour to review my English lessons.
我將要花一個小時的時間來複習我的英語課程。

rich·es [ˋrɪtʃɪz] Track 1832

名 財產 同 wealth 財產

▶Riches do not always bring contentment. 財富並不總使人滿足。

rock [rɑk] Track 1833

動 搖動 名 岩石

▶動 She rocked the baby until he fell asleep.
她搖晃著寶寶直到他睡著為止。

▶名 You shouldn't let the kids climb those huge rocks.
你不應該讓孩子在那些大岩石上面爬。

rock·y [ˋrɑkɪ] Track 1834

形 岩石的、搖擺的

▶The landscape（地表）is really rocky there.
那裡的地形充滿了岩石。

文法字詞解析
形容詞字尾「-y」表示「某物有……的質地」。

role [rol] Track 1835

名 角色

▶What's your role in the school drama?
你在學校的戲劇中扮演什麼角色？

實用片語用語
play a role of... 扮演……的角色

roy·al [ˋrɔɪəl]　Track 1836

形 皇家的 同 noble 貴族的

▶Have you met any member of the royal family?
你有遇過任何皇室成員嗎？

rude [rud]　Track 1837

形 野蠻的、粗魯的

▶The boy is always so rude to his parents.
那個男孩總是對自己的父母很沒禮貌。

rul·er [ˋrulɚ]　Track 1838

名 統治者 同 sovereign 統治者

▶The ruler of the country is quite stupid.
這個國家的統治者挺笨的。

文法字詞解析
字尾「-er」表示「做……的人」，因此ruler就是「負責統治的人」，employer就是「雇用他人的人」，也就是「雇主」。不過「-er」還有「用來做……的物品」之意，「rule」則有「畫線」的意思，所以「ruler」也可以是「用來畫線的工具」，也就是「尺」。

run·ner [ˋrʌnɚ]　Track 1839

名 跑者

▶Would you tell me which runner won the first place in this race? 你能告訴我哪位跑者在這次的比賽中獲得了第一嗎？

rush [rʌʃ]　Track 1840

動 突擊 名 急忙、突進

▶動 Many students rushed out to watch the fight.
很多學生衝出去看他們打架。

▶名 It's a bit of a rush, but we'll still try to be there on time.
是有點趕啦，但我們會盡量準時到。

實用片語用語
do something in a rush 趕著做完某事
例如：I got up late so I had to do my work in a rush.
我太晚起了，所以我必須趕工完成我的工作。

Ss

safe·ty [ˋseftɪ]　Track 1841

名 安全 同 security 安全

▶He did his best to ensure（確保）the safety of the children.
他盡力確保孩子們的安全。

sail·or [ˋselɚ]　Track 1842

名 船員、海員

▶He has always dreamed of being a sailor.
他一直夢想著當一名船員。

實用片語用語
dream of / about (doing) sth. 夢想做……

sal·ad [ˋsæləd]　Track 1843

名 生菜食品、沙拉

▶What do you want to eat? How about some fruit salad?
你想吃什麼？來點蘋果沙拉怎麼樣？

salt·y [ˋsɔltɪ]　Track 1844

形 鹹的

▶The dish is too salty; will you please bring me a glass of water? 這菜太鹹了，請你幫我拿杯水好嗎？

sam·ple [ˋsæmpḷ]

Track 1845

名 樣本

▶Thousands have written in to us for a free sample.
現在已有數千人來信向我們索取免費樣品。

sand·wich [ˋsændwɪtʃ]

Track 1846

名 三明治

▶The sandwich I got today tasted terrible.
我今天買的那個三明治超難吃的。

sat·is·fy [ˋsætɪs͵faɪ]

Track 1847

動 使滿足 同 please 使滿意

▶I guess not all people are satisfied with their jobs.
我猜並不是所有的人都對他們的工作感到滿意。

實用片語用語
be satisfied with 對……感到滿意

sauce [sɔs]

Track 1848

名 調味醬 動 加調味醬於……

▶名 Would you please to tell me what sauces go best with fish?
你能不能告訴我吃魚用什麼調味醬最好？

▶動 Would you like me to sauce the beef with pepper?
你想不想要我用胡椒粉給牛肉調味？

sci·ence [ˋsɔsɚ]

Track 1849

名 科學

▶50 students graduated from the science department last year.
去年有五十名理科畢業生。

實用片語用語
graduate from... 畢業、得到文憑

sci·en·tist [ˋsaɪəntɪst]

Track 1850

名 科學家

▶Both his parents are distinguished scientists.
他的父母都是卓越的科學家。

scis·sors [ˋsɪzɚz]

Track 1851

名 剪刀

名詞複數 scissors

▶Will you please pass me the scissors?
請遞給我剪刀好嗎？

score [skor]

Track 1852

名 分數 動 得分、評分

▶名 I can never get a high score in math examinations.
我總是無法在數學考試中獲得高分。

▶動 He scored a zero on the test.
他在這次考試得了零分。

screen [skrin]

Track 1853

名 螢幕

▶There's something off with my computer screen. It's all green.
我的電腦螢幕怪怪的，整個變成綠色了。

萬用延伸句型
There's something off with sth. / sb. 某物／某人有點不對勁。
也可以說：There's something unusual about sth. / sb.

search [sɜtʃ] Track 1854

動 搜索、搜尋 名 調查、檢索 同 seek 尋找

▶動 We're searching for mom's lost glasses.
我們在找媽媽消失的眼鏡。

▶名 The police are off on a search for the lost child.
警察們正在尋找那個失蹤的孩子。

文法字詞解析
第二個例句中，副詞 off 的意思是「離開某地」。

se·cret [ˋsikrɪt] Track 1855

名 秘密

▶What do you think about arranging（安排）to let them meet in secret?
你覺得安排他們秘密會面怎麼樣？

sec·re·ta·ry [ˋsɛkrə͵tɛrɪ] Track 1856

名 秘書

▶Not everyone can be an efficient（效率高的）secretary.
不是每個人都能成為一個高效率的秘書。

sec·tion [ˋsɛkʃən] Track 1857

名 部分

▶Please don't smoke here. Go to the smoking section instead.
請不要在這裡吸菸，去吸菸區吧。

文法字詞解析
副詞「instead」的意思是「反而」，除了放在句尾之外也可以放句首引導子句；「instead of 」是「作為……的替換」，後面要加動名詞或名詞。

萬用延伸句型
1. S. not V.. Instead, S. + V..沒有……，反而……
例如：She didn't drink alcohol. Instead, she drank soft drinks. 她沒喝酒，反而喝了軟性飲料。
2. Instead of + N, S + V ... .
例如：Instead of drinking alcohol, she drank soft drinks. 她沒喝酒，反而喝了軟性飲料。

se·lect [səˋlɛkt] Track 1858

動 挑選 同 pick 挑選

▶Would you please help me select a tie for my boss?
您能幫我挑一條給我老闆的領帶嗎？

se·lec·tion [səˋlɛkʃən] Track 1859

名 選擇、選定

▶We have a selection of new and cheap skirts.
我們這裡有精選新且便宜的裙子。

se·mes·ter [səˋmɛstɚ] Track 1860

名 半學年、一學期

▶George failed history last semester.
喬治上學期歷史被當了。

sep·a·rate [ˋsɛpə͵ret] Track 1861

形 分開的 動 分開

▶形 Would you please give us separate bedrooms?
請你為我們各自安排一個臥室好嗎？

▶動 Can you separate the apples from the peaches for me?
你可以幫我把蘋果和桃子分開放嗎？

實用片語用語
separate A from B 將 A 和 B 分開

se·ri·ous [ˋsɪrɪəs] Track 1862

形 嚴肅的

▶It is no wonder that the company was in serious financial（金融的）difficulties.
難怪這家公司陷入嚴重的財政困難。

ser·vant [ˋsɝvənt]

Track 1863

名 僕人、傭人

▶The cat thinks we're all her servants.
這隻貓覺得我們都是牠的僕人。

set·tle [ˋsɛtḷ]

Track 1864

動 安排、解決

▶Let's settle down and start studying. 讓我們定下心來讀書吧。

實用片語用語

settle down 安定下來、安頓下來。除了字面上的意思之外，settle down (with someone) 也有結婚、成家的意思。
例如：My boyfriend said to me that he's ready to settle down. 我男朋友告訴我說他已經準備好要定下來了。

set·tle·ment [ˋsɛtḷmənt]

Track 1865

名 解決、安排

▶I think there is no chance of a settlement for the dispute（糾紛）. 我認為這場糾紛根本無法解決。

share [ʃɛr]

Track 1866

名 份、佔有 動 共用

▶名 He gave his son a minor（較小的）share of his wealth（財產）. 他把小部分的財產分給了兒子。

▶動 Would you like to share your experience with us?
你願意跟我們分享你的經驗嗎？

shelf [ʃɛlf]

Track 1867

名 棚架、架子

▶There are many Russian（俄國的）romance（浪漫）novels on her shelves. 她的書架上有很多俄國愛情小說。

shell [ʃɛl]

Track 1868

名 貝殼 動 剝

▶名 The building was an empty（空的）shell after the fire.
這場大火過後，這座建築剩下的只是一個空殼。

▶動 It is no wonder that she shells peas（豌豆）so fast.
怪不得她剝豌豆剝得那麼快。

實用片語用語

come out of one's shell「從貝殼裡出來」，意思就是「不再羞怯」。
例如：After getting along with her roommates for three months, she finally came out of her shell. 經過三個月和室友的相處，她終於不再感到害羞了。

shock [ʃɑk]

Track 1869

名 衝擊 動 震撼、震驚 同 frighten 驚恐

▶名 The news of his death was a shock to me.
他去世的消息令我震驚。

▶動 I was shocked to hear that she was actually forty. She looks eighteen!
聽到她居然四十歲，真是嚇死我了。她看起來像十八耶！

shoot [ʃut]

Track 1870

動 射傷、射擊 名 射擊、嫩芽

▶動 There was a man with a gun shooting at the crowds.
有一名持槍男子向人群射擊。

▶名 There are several deer eating the young shoots on the trees. 有幾頭鹿正在吃樹上的嫩枝。

文法字詞解析

shoot 的動詞變化：shoot, shot, shot

實用片語用語

shoot at 向……射擊

shorts [ʃɔrts]

Track 1871

名 短褲

▶I want to buy a pair of shorts. Would you like to go with me?
我想去買條短褲。你能陪我去嗎？

show·er [ˋʃauɚ]

Track 1872

名 陣雨、淋浴 動 淋浴、澆水

▶名 You should really go take a shower.
你真的該去沖個澡了。

▶動 I already showered. It's your turn now.
我已經淋浴過了，換你了。

shrimp [ʃrɪmp]

Track 1873

名 蝦子

▶I don't like shrimp because they give me hives（疹子）.
我不喜歡蝦子，牠們會害我起疹子。

實用片語用語
give sb. hives 讓某人起疹子

side·walk [ˋsaɪd͵wɔk]

Track 1874

名 人行道 同 pavement 人行道

▶There is a big crack（裂縫）in the sidewalk, so be careful.
人行道上有一條大裂縫，所以你要小心。

sign [saɪn]

Track 1875

名 記號、標誌 動 簽署

▶名 What does this sign mean?
這個標誌是什麼意思？

▶動 Would you please allow me to sign up for this course in advance?
您能允許我提前報名這一個課程嗎？

si·lence [ˋsaɪləns]

Track 1876

名 沉默 動 使……靜下來

▶名 She needs complete silence to sleep.
她需要完全的安靜才能睡覺。

▶動 The teacher tried to silence the pupils.
那個老師試著要讓學生們安靜下來。

實用片語用語
break silence 打破沉默
例如：Because nobody knows the answer, the teacher breaks silence and tells them the solution. 因為沒有人知道答案，所以老師打破沉默並公布解答。

si·lent [ˋsaɪlənt]

Track 1877

形 沉默的

▶Would you please be silent? My baby is sleeping now.
請您保持安靜好嗎？我的寶寶正在睡覺呢。

silk [sɪlk]

Track 1878

名 絲、綢

▶Not every woman's skin is as smooth as silk.
不是每個女人的皮膚都像絲綢一樣光滑。

sim·i·lar [ˋsɪmələ]

Track 1879

形 相似的、類似的 同 alike 相似的

▶The boys look really similar to each other.
那些男孩彼此間實在長得很像。

實用片語用語
be similar to... 和……很相像

sim·ply [ˋsɪmplɪ]

Track 1880

副 簡單地、樸實地、僅僅

▶Would you please explain it more simply?
請您解釋得再簡單一點好嗎？

sin·gle [ˋsɪŋgḷ]

Track 1881

形 單一的 名 單一

▶形 She remained（保持）single for the rest of her life.
她終其一身都維持單身。

▶名 Have you listened to her new single yet?
你聽了她的新單曲了沒？

實用片語用語
for the rest of one's life（某人）的餘生

sink [sɪŋk]

Track 1882

動 沉沒、沉 名 水槽

▶動 My feet sank into the mud. 我的雙腳陷到泥裡去了。

▶名 The housewife（家庭主婦）always keeps the sink as clean as possible.
那個主婦總是儘量保持洗手台的清潔。

文法字詞解析
sink的動詞變化：sink, sank, sunk (sunken)

skill·ful/skilled [ˋskɪlfəl]/[skɪld]

Track 1883

形 熟練的、靈巧的

▶She is very skilled in music. 她非常擅長音樂。

skin·ny [ˋskɪnɪ]

Track 1884

形 皮包骨的

▶He looks much too skinny to be a weightlifter（舉重運動員）.
他看起來太瘦了，不可能是舉重運動員。

文法字詞解析
much too 後面要接形容詞，比 too + adj. 要來得強度更強。

skirt [skɝt]

Track 1885

名 裙子

▶What do you think of my new skirt? It cost me two hundred dollars. 你覺得我的新裙子怎麼樣？它可花了我兩百美元。

sleep·y [ˋslipɪ]

Track 1886

形 想睡的、睏的

▶You look so sleepy. Are you sure you don't need a rest?
你看起來昏昏欲睡的，你確定你不用休息一下嗎？

slen·der [ˋslɛndɚ]

Track 1887

形 苗條的 同 slim 苗條的

▶She was slender and had beautiful long hair.
她身材苗條，而且有一頭美麗的長髮。

slide [slaɪd]

Track 1888

動 滑動 名 滑梯

▶動 The boys like sliding down the hill.
那些男孩們喜歡滑下山坡。

▶名 I bought a slide for your little daughter.
我為你的小女兒買了一個滑梯。

slim [slɪm]

Track 1889

形 苗條的 動 變細

▶形 She looks slim, but she's actually surprisingly heavy.
她看起來很苗條，但體重意外地重。

▶動 She hopes to slim down in a few months.
她希望幾個月內可以變苗條。

實用片語用語
slim down 瘦下來、變苗條

slip [slɪp]
Track 1890

動 滑倒

▶She slipped on a banana peel（皮）. 她踩到香蕉皮滑倒了。

slip·per(s) [ˋslɪpɚ(z)]
Track 1891

名 拖鞋

▶Your slippers are all worn out. 你的拖鞋都已經穿壞了。

實用片語用語
be worn out 壞掉，太過老舊或破損太嚴重以至於不能再使用。

snack [snæk]
Track 1892

名 小吃、點心 動 吃點心

▶名 Would you like to have some snacks? 你想不想吃些點心？

▶動 The little boy is snacking on donuts.
那個男孩正在吃甜甜圈當點心。

實用片語用語
snack on sth 吃某物當點心

snail [snel]
Track 1893

名 蝸牛

▶I picked up the snail and put it down at the side of the street.
我把那隻蝸牛撿起來，放在街道的旁邊。

snow·y [snoɪ]
Track 1894

形 多雪的、積雪的

▶The snowy forest was beautiful. 那座積雪的森林非常美麗。

soc·cer [ˋsɑkɚ]
Track 1895

名 足球

▶Would you like to play soccer with us next weekend?
下個週末你願意跟我們一起踢足球嗎？

so·cial [ˋsoʃəl]
Track 1896

形 社會的

▶There are many social groups providing voluntary（自願的）service in our city.
在我們的城市有許多提供自願服務的社會團體。

文法字詞解析
字根「volunt」有「意願、希望」的意思；加上形容詞字尾「-ry」變成「自願的」，如果加上表「從事特別活動的人」的名詞字尾「-eer」，就變成「volunteer 志願者、志工」。

實用片語用語
voluntary work / service 志願服務

so·ci·e·ty [səˋsaɪətɪ]
Track 1897

名 社會 同 community 社區、社會

▶It is no wonder that this event had a bad influence on society.
難怪這件事情對社會造成了壞影響。

sock(s) [sɑk(s)]
Track 1898

名 短襪

▶There is a hole in one of my socks. 我有隻襪子上有個洞。

sol·dier [ˋsoldʒɚ]
Track 1899

名 軍人

▶Do you know how long your brother has been a soldier for?
你知道你兄弟當了多久的兵了嗎？

so·lu·tion [səˋluʃən]
Track 1900

名 溶解、解決、解釋 同 explanation 解釋

▶I think the solution to this problem is acceptable（可接受的）.
這個問題的解決方案是可接受的。

實用片語用語
solution to / for sth. 某事的解決方法

solve [sɑlv]

Track 1901

動 解決

▶Would you please help us find a method to solve this problem?
請您幫我們想個辦法來解決這個難題好嗎？

some·bod·y [ˋsʌm͵bɑdɪ]

Track 1902

代 某人、有人 名 重要人物 同 someone 某人

▶代 Why don't you ask somebody else to help you?
為什麼不請別人幫助你呢？

▶名 He thinks he's somebody, but he actually isn't that famous.
他覺得自己是重要人物，但他其實也沒那麼有名。

some·where [ˋsʌm͵hwɛr]

Track 1903

副 在某處

▶Your phone must be somewhere in this room.
你的手機應該在這房間裡某處。

文法字詞解析

要注意的是，somewhere 不能用於否定，所以如果已經預期答案是肯定的話，疑問句才能用 somewhere，否則的話要用 anywhere。
例如：Are you going somewhere next weekend?
你下個周末有要去哪嗎？
Is there a spare seat anywhere for my little girl?
哪裡有座位可以讓我的小女兒坐？

sort [sɔrt]

Track 1904

名 種 動 一致、調和

▶名 What sort of person is he? 他是哪種人？

▶動 They sort apples by their quality before selling them.
他們在賣蘋果之前先把它們按品質分類。

source [sors]

Track 1905

名 來源、水源地 同 origin 起源

▶My wages（薪水）are the principal source of my income.
薪資是我收入的主要來源。

south·ern [ˋsʌðɚn]

Track 1906

形 南方的

▶Not all students in this school are from the southern part of the country.
這個學校不是所有的學生都是來自那個國家的南部。

soy·bean/soy·a/soy [ˋsɔɪˋbin]/[ˋsɔɪə]/[sɔɪ]

Track 1907

名 大豆、黃豆

▶This drink is made from soybeans.
這個飲料是黃豆做的。

文法字詞解析

「be made from」和「be made of」都是「用……製成」的意思。但用法卻截然不同。be made of 表示物質在製作過程中的本質不會改變，為物理變化；而 be made from 則是物質的本質在製作過程中會經過徹底的改變，為化學變化。

speak·er [ˋspikɚ]

Track 1908

名 演說者

▶There are a crowd of people gathered around the speaker.
有一大群人在演說者周圍聚集起來。

speed [spid]

Track 1909

名 速度、急速 動 加速 同 haste 急速

▶名 She drives at a high speed.
她開車的速度很快。

▶動 Would you please speed up? We want to get there in time.
您能加快速度嗎？我們想準時到達那裡。

文法字詞解析

speed 的動詞變化：speed, sped, sped

spell·ing [ˋspɛlɪŋ]
Track 1910

名 拼讀、拼法

▶There are many spelling mistakes; however, it's still quite a good article.
這篇文章有許多拼寫錯誤，然而仍不失為一篇好文章。

spi·der [ˋspaɪdɚ]
Track 1911

名 蜘蛛

▶I can't stand spiders. 我完全受不了蜘蛛。

spin·ach [ˋspɪnɪtʃ]
Track 1912

名 菠菜

▶Would you like cabbage or spinach? 你要甘藍菜還是菠菜？

spir·it [ˋspɪrɪt]
Track 1913

名 精神 同 soul 精神、靈魂

▶This necklace will protect you from evil spirits.
這條項鍊會保護你免受惡靈傷害。

實用片語用語
protect sb. from sth. 保護某人免受某物傷害

spot [spɑt]
Track 1914

動 弄髒、認出 名 點 同 stain 弄髒

▶動 I spot my sister over there. 我認出我妹妹在那裡。

▶名 Why not find a shady（陰涼的）spot where we can sit down and have a rest?
我們為什麼不找個陰涼的地方坐下來休息一下呢？

spread [sprɛd]
Track 1915

動 展開、傳佈 名 寬度、桌布 同 extend 擴展

▶動 The news spread like wild fire.
這消息像野火般迅速傳播開來。

▶名 The spread of pests（害蟲）damaged countless（無數的）fruit trees. 蟲害的蔓延損害了無數的果樹。

spring [sprɪŋ]
Track 1916

動 彈開、突然提出 名 泉水、春天

▶動 They sprung a surprise attack on the enemy.
我們對敵人發動了一次突擊。

▶名 I will graduate next spring. What about you?
我明年春天畢業，你呢？

文法字詞解析
spning 的動詞變化：spring, sprang, sprung

square [skwɛr]
Track 1917

形 公正的、方正的 名 正方形、廣場

▶形 Do you prefer a square table or a round one?
你比較想要方形的桌子還是圓的？

▶名 There is a big fountain（噴泉）in the center of the square.
廣場中央有一個大噴泉。

實用片語用語
in the center of 在……的中心

squir·rel [ˋskwɝəl]
Track 1918

名 松鼠

名詞複數 squirrels

▶Have you ever touched a squirrel? 你摸過松鼠嗎？

stage [stedʒ]

Track 1919

名 舞臺、階段 動 上演

▶名 The disease is still in its primary（初期的）stage.
這個疾病仍然在初發階段。

▶動 They're staging a play in this theater next month.
他們下個月將在這座戲院上演一齣戲。

stamp [stæmp]

Track 1920

動 壓印 名 郵票、印章

▶動 He stamped her card passport quickly.
他很快地在她的護照上蓋了印章。

▶名 How much are these stamps? 這些郵票多少錢？

stan·dard [ˋstændɚd]

Track 1921

名 標準 形 標準的 同 model 標準

▶名 She is still single because she has high standards.
她的標準很高，所以還是單身。

▶形 This is a standard process, nothing to worry about.
這是標準程序，沒什麼好擔心的。

實用片語用語

meet / reach / attain a standard 達到某個標準。

例如：She studied hard in order to reach the standard, yet she still failed. 為了要達到標準，她認真讀書，但她還是沒有通過考試。

steak [stek]

Track 1922

名 牛排

▶Can you give me some steak and bread?
您能給我一些牛排和麵包嗎？

steal [stil]

Track 1923

動 偷、騙取

▶He stole her purse when she wasn't paying attention.
他在她不注意的時候偷了她的錢包。

文法字詞解析

steal 的動詞變化：steal, stole, stolen

steam [stim]

Track 1924

名 蒸汽 動 蒸、使蒸發、以蒸汽開動

▶名 That ship runs on steam. 那艘船是靠著蒸汽行駛的。

▶動 Lots of ships are steaming into the harbor（港口）.
有很多輪船正駛抵港口。

steel [stil]

Track 1925

名 鋼、鋼鐵

▶How about installing（安裝）a steel door?
我們裝一扇鋼製的門怎麼樣？

stick [stɪk]

Track 1926

名 棍、棒 動 黏 同 attach 貼上

▶名 It doesn't matter whether the stick is strong or not.
這條木棍結不結實都沒什麼關係。

▶動 The note won't stick to the wall.
這字條都沒辦法好好黏在牆上。

文法字詞解析

stick 的動詞變化：stick, stuck, stuck

實用片語用語

stick A to B 把 A 黏在 B 上

stom·ach [ˋstʌmək]

Track 1927

名 胃 同 belly 胃

▶My stomach is making a strange noise.
我的肚子發出好奇怪的聲音。

storm [stɔrm]

Track 1928

名 風暴 動 襲擊

▶名 The weather man says there will be a storm soon. 天氣預報員說很快會有暴風雨。

▶動 It stormed all day yesterday so many trees were blown down. 昨天整日颳風下雨，以致有很多樹被吹倒了。

stove [stov]

Track 1929

名 火爐、爐子 同 oven 爐子

▶The room is as hot as a stove. 這屋子熱得像火爐一樣。

straight [stret]

Track 1930

形 筆直的、正直的

▶She walked straight up to him and slapped（打巴掌）him. 她筆直地走向他，賞了他一巴掌。

實用片語用語
up to sb. / sth. 距離某人或某物非常近

strang·er [ˋstrendʒɚ]

Track 1931

名 陌生人

▶It doesn't matter if you feel nervous among strangers. 你在陌生人面前覺得緊張也不要緊的。

straw [strɔ]

Track 1932

名 稻草

▶Her hair looks like straw. 她的頭髮像稻草似的。

straw·ber·ry [ˋstrɔˏbɛrɪ]

Track 1933

名 草莓

▶Why don't you try some strawberry jam? 為什麼不試試看草莓果醬呢？

萬用延伸句型
Why don't you ...? 你為什麼不……呢？這個句型可以用來提供他人建議。

stream [strim]

Track 1934

名 小溪 動 流動

▶名 The stream behind my house flows（流動）quite fast. 我家後面的小溪流得很快。

▶動 Tears are streaming down her face. 淚水沿著她的臉流下。

stress [strɛs]

Track 1935

名 壓力 動 強調、著重 同 emphasis 強調

▶名 Would you please tell me how you handle your stress? 請您告訴我您是如何處理壓力的嗎？

▶動 You need to stress the second syllable（音節）of this word. 這個單字第二個音節應該要念重音。

stretch [strɛtʃ]

Track 1936

動/名 伸展

▶動 I stretched in my seat because I felt so tired. 我在位子上伸展了一下，因為我覺得好累。

▶名 Let's have a stretch before we start playing basketball. 我們打籃球前先伸展一下吧。

strict [strɪkt]

Track 1937

形 嚴格的 同 harsh 嚴厲的

▶Mr. Green is very strict with his students.
格林先生對他的學生非常嚴格。

實用片語用語
strict with sb. 對某人很嚴格

strike [straɪk]

Track 1938

動 打擊、達成(協議) 名 罷工

▶動 It took them half a month to strike a bargain（交易）.
經過了半個月的時間，他們雙方才達成了交易。

▶名 It was three months before the strike ended.
過了三個月的時間，罷工才結束。

文法字詞解析
strike 的動詞變化：
strike, struck, stricken

string [strɪŋ]

Track 1939

名 弦、繩子、一串

▶The kitten loves playing with string. 那隻小貓最愛玩繩子。

strug·gle [ˋstrʌgḷ]

Track 1940

動 努力、奮鬥 名 掙扎、奮鬥

▶動 Not all people have to struggle every day for their survival（生存）. 不是所有的人都必須為了生存而每天奮鬥。

▶名 He got wounded in the struggle. 他在搏鬥中受了傷。

實用片語用語
struggle for sth. / to V. 為……而努力、掙扎

sub·ject [ˋsʌbdʒɪkt]

Track 1941

名 主題、科目 形 服從的、易受……的 同 topic 主題

▶名 What's your favorite subject at school?
你在學校最喜歡哪個科目？

▶形 If there is a heavy snow, the trains are subject to delay.
如果下大雪，火車往往就會延誤。

sub·tract [səbˋtrækt]

Track 1942

動 扣除、移走

▶Not every child is able to add and subtract at the age of two.
不是每個兩歲的孩子都會加減法。

實用片語用語
order of operation 四則運算
其中，加、減、乘、除分別是：addition, subtraction, multiplication, division

sub·way [ˋsʌb͵we]

Track 1943

名 地下鐵

▶How long will it take for you to get there by subway?
你搭乘地鐵去那裡要花多長時間啊？

suc·ceed [səkˋsid]

Track 1944

動 成功

▶If you put all your heart into your work, you will succeed.
如果你把心思全部放在工作上，你就會成功的。

suc·cess [səkˋsɛs]

Track 1945

名 成功

▶It is no wonder that his new book was a great success.
難怪他的新書十分成功。

suc·cess·ful [səkˋsɛsfəl]

Track 1946

形 成功的

▶He is a successful businessman. 他是個成功的商人。

sud·den [ˋsʌdn̩]

Track 1947

形 突然的 名 意外、突然

▶形 What do you think about that movie star's sudden death?
對於那個電影明星突然過世，你怎麼看？

▶名 All of a sudden, everything went quiet.
突然一切都安靜了下來。

實用片語用語
all of a sudden 突然之間

suit [sut]

Track 1948

名 套 動 適合 同 fit 適合

▶名 Can you help me pick out a black suit?
你可以幫我挑一套黑色西裝嗎？

▶動 Would you like to make an appointment in advance? Would Friday morning suit you?
您想不想提前預約呢？星期五早上對你來說合適嗎？

實用片語用語
in advance 預先

sun·ny [ˋsʌnɪ]

Track 1949

形 充滿陽光的 同 bright 晴朗的

▶It's such a sunny day. Why don't we go out for a walk?
今天的天氣真好，為什麼我們不出去散散步呢？

su·per·mar·ket [ˋsupɚ͵mɑrkɪt]

Track 1950

名 超級市場

▶Let's head to the supermarket to buy some groceries.
我們到超級市場買些東西吧。

sup·ply [səˋplaɪ]

Track 1951

動 供給 名 供應品 同 furnish 供給

▶動 Plenty of food was supplied from the other states.
從其他各州來了不少充足的食品供給。

▶名 Who's responsible for the supplies? 是誰負責供貨？

sup·port [səˋport]

Track 1952

動 支持 名 支持者、支撐物 同 uphold 支持

▶動 Can you give some examples to support your argument（論點）? 你能舉幾個例子來證實你的論點嗎？

▶名 Would you like to cite（引用）any evidence（證據）in support of your opinion?
你願意引用證據來支持自己的意見嗎？

實用片語用語
in support of + N. 支持某人、事、物

sur·face [ˋsɝfɪs]

Track 1953

名 表面 動 使形成表面 同 exterior 表面

▶名 On the surface everything looks fine, but actually there are a lot of problems.
表面上看起來一切安好，但其實有很多的問題。

▶動 The boy surfaced from underneath the water.
男孩從水底浮上水面。

sur·vive [sɚˋvaɪv]

Track 1954

動 倖存、殘存

▶The little boy survived the earthquake.
那個小男孩從地震中倖存下來。

swal·low [ˋswɑlo]

Track 1955

名 燕子 動 吞咽

▶名 There are swallows flying in the sky.
有一群燕子在天空中飛。

▶動 He couldn't swallow because there was a lump（腫塊）in his throat（喉嚨）. 他因喉嚨上有一個腫塊而不能吞嚥。

實用片語用語

swallow up sth. / sb. 把某物／某人吞噬、併吞。

例如：The company was swallowed up by its competitor. 這間公司被它的競爭者併購了。

swan [swɑn]

Track 1956

名 天鵝

▶Do you see the swans? They're so beautiful!
你有看到天鵝嗎？牠們很漂亮吧！

sweat·er [ˋswɛtɚ]

Track 1957

名 毛衣、厚運動衫

▶It is cold outside. Why don't you put on a sweater?
外面很冷，你為什麼不套上一件毛衣呢？

sweep [swip]

Track 1958

動 掃、打掃 名 掃除、掠過

▶動 Grandma is always sweeping the house.
奶奶總是在打掃房子。

▶名 Let's give our room a good sweep.
讓我們把房間好好掃一下吧。

文法字詞解析

sweep 的動詞變化：
swept, swept, swept

swing [swɪŋ]

Track 1959

動 搖動

▶The monkey is swinging from branch to branch.
那隻猴子從這根樹枝晃到另一根樹枝。

文法字詞解析

swing 的動詞變化：
swing, swung, swung

sym·bol [ˋsɪmbḷ]

Track 1960

名 象徵、標誌 同 sign 標誌

▶The lion is the symbol of courage. 獅子是勇氣的象徵。

tal·ent [ˋtælənt]

Track 1961

名 天分、天賦

▶He has a lot of talent in acting. 他很有演戲天分。

talk·a·tive [ˋtɔkətɪv]

Track 1962

形 健談的 反 mute 沉默的

▶She is too talkative to keep secrets.
她太多嘴，保守不了秘密的。

文法字詞解析

形容詞字尾「-ative」表示「喜歡做某事的、傾向於做某事的、有某種特質的」，所以 talkative 就是「喜歡講話的、健談的」；competitive 就是「競爭性的、好競爭的」。

tan·ge·rine [ˋtændʒə͵rɪn]

Track 1963

名 柑、桔

▶Would you like some tangerines? I got some from my granny（奶奶）. 你要不要吃些橘子？是我從我奶奶那拿來的。

tank [tæŋk] Track 1964

名 水槽、坦克

▶Is there any water left in the tank? If not, please fill it up.
水箱裡還有水嗎？沒有的話，請將它灌滿水。

tape [tep] Track 1965

名 帶、捲尺、磁帶 動 用捲尺測量 同 record 磁帶、唱片

▶名 Would you lend me your tape? I want to do some listening practice on the weekends.
能借用你的錄音帶嗎？我想在週末做些聽力練習。

▶動 Would you please help me tape up the envelope?
能請你幫我把信封用膠帶貼起來嗎？

tar·get [ˋtɑrgɪt] Track 1966

名 目標、靶子 同 goal 目標

▶The company didn't meet its target this year.
這個公司今年沒有實現目標。

實用片語用語
meet / achieve / reach a target 達到目標

task [tæsk] Track 1967

名 任務 同 work 任務

▶We need someone to perform（執行）this task.
我們需要人來執行這項任務。

tast·y [ˋtestɪ] Track 1968

形 好吃的 同 delicious 好吃的

▶The food here is very tasty. 這裡的食物很美味。

team [tim] Track 1969

名 隊 同 group 組、隊

▶Would you tell me which team won this game in the end?
你能告訴我最後是哪一隊贏了這場比賽嗎？

實用片語用語
in the end 最後、終於

tear [tɪr]/[tɛr] Track 1970

名 眼淚 動 撕、撕破

▶名 His sad story moved me to tears.
他那悲傷的故事讓我感動得流下了眼淚。

▶動 She tore his letter up and walked away.
她把他的信撕了，然後揚長而去。

文法字詞解析
tear 的動詞變化：tear, tore, torn

實用片語用語
moved sb. to tears 感動某人、使某人流下眼淚

teen(s) [tin(z)] Track 1971

名 十多歲

▶What did he look like when he was in his teens?
當他還是十幾歲的時候，他長什麼樣子呢？

teen·age [ˋtinˏedʒ] Track 1972

形 十幾歲的

▶My teenage daughter wants to learn dancing.
我那十幾歲的女兒想去學跳舞。

teen·ag·er [ˋtinˏedʒɚ] Track 1973

名 青少年

▶His family is really poor, so he has been earning money since he was a teenager.
他的家很窮，所以他十幾歲的時候就開始賺錢了。

tel·e·phone/phone [ˋtɛləˏfon]/[fon] Track 1974

名 電話 動 打電話

▶名 There is a telephone on my desk, but I seldom（很少）use it. 我的書桌上有台電話，但是我卻很少用它。

▶動 More people are willing to telephone than to write.
比起寫信來，有更多人願意打電話。

實用片語用語
telephone sb. = give sb. a (phone) call 打電話給某人
例如：I telephoned her to ask for her help. 我打給她以尋求她的幫忙。

tel·e·vi·sion/TV [ˋtɛləˏvɪʒən] Track 1975

名 電視

▶How often do you watch television at home every week?
你每週在家看幾次電視？

tem·ple [ˋtɛmpḷ] Track 1976

名 寺院、神殿

▶I've never been to this famous temple before.
我從未去過這個著名的寺院。

ten·nis [ˋtɛnɪs] Track 1977

名 網球

▶Would you like to play tennis with us tomorrow?
你願意明天和我們一起去打網球嗎？

tent [tɛnt] Track 1978

名 帳篷

▶There are several tents at the foot of the mountain.
山腳下有幾個帳篷。

實用片語用語
the foot of the mountain 山腳，或者也可以說 foothill；另外，山頂的說法是 hilltop；山腰則是 hillside。

term [tɝm] Track 1979

名 條件、期限、術語 動 稱呼

▶名 Why not agree to these terms? They are beneficial（有利的）for us at least.
為什麼不同意這些條件呢？它們至少對我們是有利的啊。

▶動 They termed the play a tragedy.
他們把這齣戲稱為一齣悲劇。

ter·ri·ble [ˋtɛrəbḷ] Track 1980

形 可怕的、駭人的 同 horrible 可怕的

▶It will be a terrible blow to him. 這對他將是一個可怕的打擊。

實用片語用語
blow 作為名詞可以解釋做「身體上的毆打」和「精神上的打擊」。如果要說某人受到打擊的話，可以說「(sb.) suffer / receive a blow」。

ter·rif·ic [təˋrɪfɪk] Track 1981

形 驚人的

▶The thief drove the car away at a terrific speed.
那個小偷以驚人的速度駕車飛奔而去。

test [tɛst]

Track 1982

名 考試 動 試驗、檢驗

▶名 Can you tell me what I should bring for this test?
你可以告訴我這次考試我要帶什麼東西嗎？

▶動 Let's test this theory（理論）and see if it works.
我們來試驗看看這個理論是不是真的有用。

text·book [ˋtɛkst͵bʊk]

Track 1983

名 教科書

▶John got mad and burned all his textbooks.
約翰一怒之下就把他的課本全燒了。

the·a·ter [ˋθiətɚ]

Track 1984

名 戲院、劇場 反 stadium 劇場

▶Would you tell me what play is on at your theater now?
你能告訴我你們戲院現在正在上演什麼戲嗎？

there·fore [ˋðɛr͵for]

Track 1985

副 因此、所以 同 hence 因此

▶She got sick and therefore didn't got to school.
她生病了，所以就沒去學校。

文法字詞解析
除了 therefore 之外，so、thus、as a result 等也都是表達因果關係的詞語。

thick [θɪk]

Track 1986

形 厚的、密的

▶He put on a thick coat and went out.
他穿上了一件厚外套才出門。

thief [θif]

Track 1987

名 小偷、盜賊

名詞複數 thieves

▶The thief couldn't find anything valuable（有價值的）in the man's house. 這個小偷在那個人家中找不到任何有價值的東西。

文法字詞解析
形容詞字尾「-able」有「具備某種特質或條件」的意思，所以像是 valuable 就是「有價值的」、comfortable 就是「舒服的」。

thin [θɪn]

Track 1988

形 瘦的、薄的、稀疏的 同 slender 薄的

▶Why don't you wear a thinner shirt today? It is so hot outside.
今天你為什麼不穿件較薄的襯衫呢？外面很熱哦。

thirs·ty [ˋθɝstɪ]

Track 1989

形 口渴的

▶I'm thirsty. Can we get a drink please?
我很渴，拜託我們去喝個飲料好不好？

throat [θrot]

Track 1990

名 喉嚨

▶I have this strange feeling in my throat.
我的喉嚨裡有種怪怪的感覺。

through [θru]

Track 1991

介 經過、通過 副 全部、到最後

▶介 There is a path that runs through the woods.
有條小路穿過樹林。

▶副 There was an awful（可怕的）storm last night but the baby slept right through it.
昨夜風雨很大，但這個寶寶卻一直睡著沒醒。

實用片語用語
right through 整段時間裡、從頭到尾

through·out [θru`aʊt]
Track 1992

介 遍佈、遍及 副 徹頭徹尾

▶介 You can find this plant throughout this region.
你能在這個地區到處發現這種植物的存在。

▶副 The material was flawed（使有缺陷）throughout.
那個材料處處有瑕疵。

thumb [θʌm]
Track 1993

名 拇指 動 用拇指翻

▶名 The baby enjoys sucking（吸）his thumb.
那個寶寶喜歡吸大拇指。

▶動 He thumbed through the book and decided that it was boring. 他迅速翻過這本書，然後判斷這本書應該很無聊。

實用片語用語
thumb through sth. 快速瀏覽

thun·der [`θʌndɚ]
Track 1994

名 雷、打雷 動 打雷

▶名 The sound of the thunder last night was loud enough to wake me up. 昨晚的雷聲很大，把我吵醒了。

▶動 It thundered all night and the cat was horrified.
整晚一直在打雷，那隻貓嚇死了。

tip [tɪp]
Track 1995

名 小費、暗示 動 付小費

▶名 How much should I give the porter as a tip?
我該給行李搬運工多少小費？

▶動 Will you tip the waiter later? 你等一下會給服務生小費嗎？

ti·tle [`taɪtl̩]
Track 1996

名 稱號、標題 動 加標題 同 headline 標題

▶名 In my opinion, the title of this book is very beautiful.
在我看來，這本書的書名真是取得漂亮。

▶動 I haven't yet titled my novel. Any suggestions?
我還沒有給我的小說定標題，你有什麼建議嗎？

toast [tost]
Track 1997

名 土司麵包 動 烤、烤麵包

▶名 Toast for breakfast again? Come on, let's get something else! 早餐又吃土司喔？唉唷，我們吃點別的嘛！

▶動 He toasted the bread quickly for his sister.
他為他妹妹很快地烤好了麵包。

實用片語用語
toast for sb. 舉杯敬某人
例如：Let's toast for the sixtieth birthday of our grandmother with wine. 我們用紅酒來敬祖母的六十大壽吧。

toe [to]
Track 1998

名 腳趾

▶She is dressed in white from head to toe.
她從頭到腳穿得一身白。

實用片語用語
from head to toe 從頭到腳

tofu/bean curd [ˋtofu]/[bin kɝd] Track 1999

名 豆腐

▶Tofu is very popular in this area. 在這個地區豆腐很受歡迎。

toi·let [ˋtɔɪlɪt] Track 2000

名 洗手間

▶Will you please flush the toilet after you use it?
麻煩上完洗手間請沖水好嗎？

to·ma·to [təˋmeto] Track 2001

名 番茄

▶Is a tomato a kind of vegetable or a kind of fruit?
番茄到底是蔬菜還是水果？

tongue [tʌŋ] Track 2002

名 舌、舌頭

▶I bit my tongue and it hurt a lot. 我咬到自己的舌頭，好痛喔。

實用片語用語

bite one's tongue 閉口不語。如果知道某個話題或某句話可能會引發他人的不快時，閉上嘴巴而不說出事實，就可以用這個說法。

例如：Your words hurt her feelings. You should have bitten your tongue. 你的話傷了她的心，你應該選擇避口不談的。

tooth [tuθ] Track 2003

名 牙齒、齒

名詞複數 teeth

▶Remember to brush your teeth before you go to bed.
睡前請記得刷牙。

top·ic [ˋtɑpɪk] Track 2004

名 主題、談論 同 theme 主題

▶He often jumps from one topic to another.
他常從一個主題跳到另一個主題。

tour [tʊr] Track 2005

名 旅行 動 遊覽 同 travel 旅行

▶名 Are you coming on this tour too? 你也要參加這次旅行嗎？

▶動 The two brothers plan to tour the world.
這兄弟倆計畫環遊世界。

tow·el [taʊl] Track 2006

名 毛巾

▶Would you pass me a towel? I had a shower just now and my hair is still wet.
能遞給我一條毛巾嗎？我剛洗了個澡，頭髮還是濕的。

tow·er [ˋtaʊɚ] Track 2007

名 塔 動 高聳

▶名 There is a tower on the top of the hill. Can you see it?
山丘上有座塔，你看見了嗎？

▶動 An old castle towers over the bustling（熙攘的）city.
有座古老的城堡高聳於這個繁華的城市之上。

實用片語用語

tower above / over 聳立

track [træk] Track 2008

名 路線 動 追蹤

▶名 What do you think of the fresh bear tracks in the forest?
你怎麼看待森林裡那些新的熊腳印呢？

▶動 The hunter tracked the wolf late into the night.
獵人追蹤狼直到深夜。

實用片語用語
late into the night 直到深夜。late into the night 是從某個時間點開始持續到深夜，但是「late at night」只是靠近午夜的某個時刻。

trade [tred]
Track 2009

名 商業、貿易 動 交易

▶名 Women's clothing has become a trade of its own.
女性服飾業已經成了自成一格的行業了。

▶動 This company trades with many foreign companies.
這個公司跟多個外國公司有貿易往來。

tra·di·tion [trəˋdɪʃən]
Track 2010

名 傳統 同 custom 習俗

▶Not all people like to follow traditions; some like new things.
不是所有人都喜歡遵循傳統，有些人喜歡新事物。

tra·di·tion·al [trəˋdɪʃənḷ]
Track 2011

形 傳統的

▶This is a really traditional kind of wedding.
這是很傳統的那種婚禮。

traf·fic [ˋtræfɪk]
Track 2012

名 交通

▶What do you think of the heavy traffic in the city?
你怎麼看待城市交通雍塞這一現象呢？

實用片語用語
heavy traffic 交通壅塞

trap [træp]
Track 2013

名 圈套、陷阱 動 誘捕 同 snare 誘捕

▶名 The mouse trap didn't catch any mice.
這個捕鼠器沒抓到半隻老鼠。

▶動 The cat trapped the mouse in the corner.
那隻貓把老鼠擋在角落不讓牠離開。

trav·el [ˋtrævḷ]
Track 2014

動 旅行 名 旅行

▶動 He has traveled to a lot of places. 他到過很多地方旅行。

▶名 More and more people are going abroad for travel.
有越來越多的人出國旅遊。

trea·sure [ˋtrɛʒɚ]
Track 2015

名 寶物、財寶 動 收藏、珍藏

▶名 He found a chest（箱子）full of treasures.
他找到了一個滿是寶藏的箱子。

▶動 You should treasure your friendships all your life.
你應該一生都珍惜友誼。

實用片語用語
treasure chest 藏寶箱
chest除了解釋作「箱子」之外，還有「胸部、胸腔」的意思。
例如：If there's something bothering you, just get it off your chest. 如果有什麼煩惱的話，就說出來吧。

treat [trit]
Track 2016

動 處理、對待

▶You should just treat this matter lightly; it's not a big deal.
你應該將這件事輕輕帶過就好，這不是什麼大不了的事。

萬用延伸句型
it's not a big deal. 這沒什麼大不了的。

treat·ment [ˋtritmənt] Track 2017

名 款待

▶His unfair treatment of his students made us quite unhappy.
他對於學生不公平的對待讓我們不怎麼開心。

tri·al [ˋtraɪəl] Track 2018

名 審問、試驗 同 experiment 實驗

▶The case is still under trial. I will let you know as soon as I get the news. 案子還在審訊當中。我一得到消息就會讓你知道。

tri·an·gle [ˋtraɪ,æŋg!] Track 2019

名 三角形

▶What does this triangle sign mean?
這個三角形牌子是什麼意思？

trick [trɪk] Track 2020

名 詭計 動 欺騙、欺詐

▶名 He pulled a magic trick in front of everyone.
他在所有人面前表演了個魔術詭計。

▶動 I was tricked into handing him my money.
我被他騙了，把我的錢給了他。

實用片語用語
pull a trick 用詭計騙過某人

trou·sers [ˋtraʊzɚz] Track 2021

名 褲、褲子 同 pants 褲子

▶How do you like this pair of trousers? It looks terrific on you.
你喜歡這條褲子嗎？穿在你身上好看極了。

truck [trʌk] Track 2022

名 卡車 同 van 貨車

▶Would you lend me your truck? I have some goods to transport（運送）. 能把你的卡車借給我用嗎？我有一些貨要運。

trum·pet [ˋtrʌmpɪt] Track 2023

名 喇叭、小號 動 吹喇叭

▶名 My dad plays the trumpet and I play the guitar.
我爸爸會吹小號，而我會彈吉他。

▶動 Will you teach me how to trumpet? I would like to learn.
你能教我吹喇叭嗎？我想學。

trust [trʌst] Track 2024

名 信任 動 信任 同 believe 相信

▶名 A good marriage is based on trust.
美滿的婚姻建立在互相信任的基礎上。

▶動 You shouldn't trust him. He's a good liar.
你不該相信他，他非常擅長說謊。

實用片語用語
based on 以……為基礎、根據……

truth [truθ] Track 2025

名 真相、真理 同 reality 事實

▶I have every right to know the truth.
我有權利知道真相。

文法字詞解析
every 在這裡修飾名詞 right，強調「一切可能的，充分的」權力。

tube [tjub] Track 2026

名 管、管子 同 pipe 管子

▶Let's heat the glass tube before we start our experiment（實驗）. 開始實驗之前，我們先把玻璃管熱一下。

tun·nel [ˋtʌn!] Track 2027

名 隧道、地道

▶The tunnel is so long. 這隧道好長喔。

tur·key [ˋtɝkɪ] Track 2028

名 火雞

▶They roasted（烤）a turkey for dinner.
他們烤了一隻火雞當晚餐。

tur·tle [ˋtɝt!] Track 2029

名 龜、海龜

▶The turtles' eggs on the beach are eaten up by many large birds. 海龜在沙灘上的蛋被很多大鳥們吃光了。

type [taɪp] Track 2030

名 類型 動 打字

▶名 I don't like this type of skirt. 我不喜歡這種裙子。

▶動 Would you type up this form for me?
幫我打一下這份表格好嗎？

ty·phoon [taɪˋfun] Track 2031

名 颱風

▶It was said that there were many people injured（受傷的）in this typhoon. 據說這次颱風導致很多人受傷。

ug·ly [ˋʌglɪ] Track 2032

形 醜的、難看的

▶Even though she is pretty, she considers herself ugly.
雖然她很漂亮，但她還是覺得自己很醜。

um·brel·la [ʌmˋbrɛlə] Track 2033

名 雨傘

▶It's going to rain outside; let's bring an umbrella with us.
外面要下雨了，我們帶把雨傘吧。

un·der·wear [ˋʌndɚ͵wɛr] Track 2034

名 內衣

▶When nobody is home I don't bother dressing up and walk around in my underwear.
沒人在家的時候，我就懶得穿衣服，直接穿著內衣走來走去。

文法字詞解析

tube 在英國還有「underground（地鐵）」的意思，所以如果有人問你「Where's the nearest tube station?」就是在問「最近的地鐵站在哪裡？」

實用片語用語

type sth. up 打字

實用片語用語

not bother doing sth. 懶得做某事、不努力去做某事

u·ni·form [ˋjunə͵fɔrm]

Track 2035

名 制服、校服、使一致 同 outfit 全套服裝

▶Not all staff（員工）in that company are required to wear uniforms. 那個公司不是所有的員工都需要穿制服。

up·on [əˋpɑn]

Track 2036

介 在……上面

▶The cat is sitting upon the chair. 那隻貓坐在椅子上。

文法字詞解析

upon 的意思等同於 on 或 onto，不過是比較正式的用法。

up·per [ˋʌpɚ]

Track 2037

副 在上位 同 superior 上級的

▶What rooms are there on the upper level?
上面那層有哪些房間？

used [juzd]

Track 2038

形 用過的、二手的

▶Would you like to buy a used car? It's a real bargain（便宜貨）! 你想不想買輛二手車呢？它是個便宜貨哦！

used to [just tu]

Track 2039

副 習慣的

▶I'm used to having a bath in the morning when I get up.
我習慣每天早上起來洗澡。

us·er [ˋjuzɚ]

Track 2040

名 使用者 同 consumer 消費者

▶Some users have complained that the website（網站）is too confusing（令人困惑的）. 有些使用者抱怨這個網站太難懂了。

u·su·al [ˋjuʒuəl]

Track 2041

副 通常的、平常的 同 ordinary 平常的

▶Would you like to meet me at the usual place?
我們在老地方見面好嗎？

實用片語用語

as usual 就跟平常一樣

例如：As usual, I drank a cup of coffee after I woke up. 一如往常，我起床後喝了一杯咖啡。

Vv

va·ca·tion [veˋkeʃən]

Track 2042

名 假期 動 度假 同 holiday 假期

▶名 Do you have any plans for this winter vacation?
這個寒假你有什麼打算？

▶動 They will vacation in Switzerland during Christmas.
他們耶誕節期間將到瑞士度假。

val·ley [ˋvælɪ]

Track 2043

名 溪谷、山谷

▶They have a farm down in the valley.
他們在山谷有一間農場。

val·ue [ˋvælju]

Track 2044

名 價值 動 重視、評價

▶名 These old coins are now of no value.
這些舊硬幣現在已沒有什麼價值了。

▶動 I value our friendship a lot. 我非常重視我們之間的友誼。

實用片語用語
value 前面加上形容詞可以表示「某方面的價值」，例如「market value（市值）」、「historical value（歷史價值）」。

vic·to·ry [ˋvɪktərɪ]

Track 2045

名 勝利 同 success 勝利、成功

▶Let's hold a party to celebrate（慶祝）the victory.
我們辦個派對來慶祝一下這次勝利吧。

vid·e·o [ˋvɪdɪ͵o]

Track 2046

名 電視、錄影

▶Video games are good for the brain. 電動玩具對腦部有幫助喔。

vil·lage [ˋvɪlɪdʒ]

Track 2047

名 村莊

▶It is no wonder that many people living in the cities want to move to villages. 難怪很多在城市居住的人想搬到村莊裡去住。

vi·o·lin [͵vaɪəˋlɪn]

Track 2048

名 小提琴 同 fiddle 小提琴

▶I think you play the violin quite well.
我覺得你的小提琴拉得很好。

文法字詞解析
play 後面加球類運動的話，兩者之間不用加定冠詞，如果後面加樂器的話，中間就要加上定冠詞來限定後面的名詞。

vis·i·tor [ˋvɪzɪtɚ]

Track 2049

名 訪客、觀光客

▶There is a strange old lady standing in front of your house.
你的房子前面站著一個怪怪的老太太。

vo·cab·u·lar·y [vəˋkæbjə͵lɛrɪ]

Track 2050

名 單字、字彙

▶He has a wide vocabulary. It's no wonder that he can read very difficult articles.
他的辭彙量很大，難怪連很難的文章都能讀懂。

vol·ley·ball [ˋvɑlɪ͵bɔl]

Track 2051

名 排球

▶I am fond（喜歡）of playing volleyball. 我很喜歡打排球。

vote [vot]

Track 2052

名 選票 動 投票 同 ballot 選票

▶名 He got less votes than last time. 他這次獲得的選票比上次少。

▶動 Most women voted for this candidate（候選人）.
大部分婦女都投票給這名候選人。

實用片語用語
vote for sb. 投票給某個人；vote on sth. 為某事投票
例如：I voted for her to be our class leader.
我投她作我們的班長。
Most of the members agreed to vote on this issue. 大部分的成員同意將這件事交付表決。

vot·er [votɚ]

Track 2053

名 投票者

▶Not all the voters think this new policy will be in their favor in the future.
不是所有的投票者都認為新政策在將來會對他們有利。

實用片語用語
in sb's favor 支持、贊同、有利於某人

Ww

waist [west] Track 2054

名 腰部

▶The skirt is too big. You should choose a smaller one with a tighter waist.
這條裙子太大了，你應該選一條小一點、腰部收緊一點的。

wait·er/wait·ress Track 2055
[ˋwetɚ]/[ˋwetrɪs]

名 服務生／女服務生

▶There are ten waiters and fifteen waitresses in that restaurant.
那個餐廳有十個男服務生和十五個女服務生。

wake [wek] Track 2056

動 喚醒、醒

▶Will you please wake me up at five a.m. tomorrow morning?
請你明天早上五點鐘叫我起床好嗎？

wal·let [ˋwɑlɪt] Track 2057

名 錢包、錢袋

▶Since you said the wallet is yours, can you tell me what's in it? 既然你說這個錢包是你的，你能告訴我裡面有些什麼嗎？

文法字詞解析
since 在這個句子裡是連接詞，表示因果關係。

wa·ter·fall [ˋwɔtɚ͵fɔl] Track 2058

名 瀑布

▶I heard that you took many pictures of the waterfall yesterday.
我聽說昨天你拍了許多瀑布的照片。

wa·ter·mel·on [ˋwɔtɚ͵mɛlən] Track 2059

名 西瓜

▶Which flavor do you want, watermelon or mango?
你要哪種口味，西瓜還是芒果？

wave [wev] Track 2060

名 浪、波 動 搖動、波動 同 sway 搖動

▶名 Be careful of the bigger waves. 要小心比較大的浪。

▶動 He waved goodbye and got on the bus.
他揮手告別，上了公車。

實用片語用語
上／下公車、計程車、火車、飛機都有各種不同的說法。
首先，get on / off 是最普遍的說法，用在有地板、空間很大的交通工具，像是 bus、train、plane 等；如果要上／下計程車、汽車，就要說「get into / out of a taxi / car」。
board 也有上車的意思，在 bus、taxi、train、plane 都可以使用；alight 有「從……走下來」的意思，所以只能用在有地板可以走的 bus、train、plane 上。

weap·on [ˋwɛpən] Track 2061

名 武器、兵器

▶What's your favorite weapon? Mine is nunchucks（雙節棍）.
你最喜歡哪種武器？我最喜歡雙節棍了。

wed [wɛd] Track 2062

動 嫁、娶、結婚 同 marry 結婚

▶He thinks that I am too poor to wed his sister.
他認為我太窮，不配娶他的妹妹。

week·day [ˋwikˏde] Track 2063

名 平日、工作日

▶Not all the offices are open from 9:00 a.m. to 5:00 p.m. on weekdays.
不是所有的辦公室在工作日都是從上午九點到下午五點辦公。

萬用延伸句型
Not all S. + V. 不是所有的……都……。

west·ern [ˋwɛstɚn] Track 2064

形 西方的、西方國家的

▶Do you know anything about western table manners?
你瞭解西方的餐桌禮儀嗎？

wet [wɛt] Track 2065

形 潮濕的 動 弄濕

▶形 Your socks are totally wet. 你的襪子都濕透了。

▶動 The dog has wet the floor. 那隻狗把地板都弄濕了。

whale [hwel] Track 2066

名 鯨魚

▶A whale is no less a mammal（哺乳動物）than a horse is.
鯨魚和馬一樣都是哺乳動物。

實用片語用語
No less...than 像……一樣

what·ev·er [hwɑtˋɛvɚ] Track 2067

形 任何的 代 任何

▶形 Whatever flavor ice cream is fine with me.
任何一種冰淇淋口味對我來說都很好。

▶代 Would you like to have something to eat? You can take whatever you want.
你想不想吃點東西呢？你想要什麼就拿什麼。

wheel [hwil] Track 2068

名 輪子、輪 動 滾動

▶名 Generally（一般地）speaking, a car has four wheels, but some cars have more. 一般來講，一輛汽車有四個輪子，但是有的車會多一些輪子。

▶動 He wheeled round and ran away. 他一轉身便跑掉了。

實用片語用語
wheel around 突然轉身

when·ev·er [hwɛnˋɛvɚ] Track 2069

副 無論何時 連 無論何時 同 anytime 任何時候

▶副 Can you come see me whenever it's convenient for you?
你方便的時候可以來看看我嗎？

▶連 You can visit us whenever you want to.
你無論何時想拜訪我們都可以。

wher·ev·er [hwɛrˋɛvɚ] Track 2070

副 無論何處 連 無論何處

▶副 Would you please tell me wherever you found this book?
你能告訴我到底是在什麼地方找到這本書的嗎？

▶連 Would you please leave me alone? You can go wherever you like. 別來吵我好嗎？你愛去哪就去哪吧。

whis·per [ˋhwɪspɚ]
Track 2071

動 耳語 名 輕聲細語 同 murmur 低語聲

▶動 There are some girls whispering in the corner of the room.
房間的角落處有幾個女孩子在竊竊私語。

▶名 Some students are debating the problem in whispers.
有幾個學生在低聲辯論這個問題。

實用片語用語
in a whisper 輕聲地

who·ev·er [huˋɛvɚ]
Track 2072

代 任何人、無論誰

▶I feel sorry for whoever marries her.
無論誰娶她我都會替那個人感到同情。

wid·en [ˋwaɪdn̩]
Track 2073

動 使……變寬、增廣

▶Her eyes widened when she heard the news.
聽到那個消息，她的雙眼睜得老大。

width [wɪdθ]
Track 2074

名 寬、廣 同 breadth 寬度

▶I don't know the width of the road.
我不知道這條路有多寬。

wild [waɪld]
Track 2075

形 野生的、野性的

▶I would love to see some wild animas up close.
我希望能近距離看到一些野生動物。

萬用延伸句型
I would love to ... 我想要／希望……。
用於委婉地表達自己的意願或渴望。

will·ing [ˋwɪlɪŋ]
Track 2076

形 心甘情願的

▶Not everyone is willing to share the sorrows（悲傷）of others.
不是每個人都樂於分擔別人的悲傷。

wind·y [ˋwɪndɪ]
Track 2077

形 多風的

▶It's so windy outside. My umbrella got blown away.
外面風那麼大，我的傘都被吹走了。

wing [wɪŋ]
Track 2078

名 翅膀、翼 動 飛

▶名 The little bird's wing was injured（受傷的）.
這隻小鳥的翅膀受傷了。

▶動 The plane winged over the Alps.
這架飛機飛越了阿爾卑斯山。

win·ner [ˋwɪnɚ]
Track 2079

名 勝利者、優勝者 同 victor 勝利者

▶The winner in the contest（比賽）was Joey.
這場比賽的優勝者是喬伊。

實用片語用語
英文裡表達「比賽」的詞有很多，根據不同種類有不同的說法：
首先，contest 是指需要技巧的比賽，像是「a speech contest（演講比賽）」；match 是有兩個隊伍或兩個人對立的比賽，像是「a boxing match（拳擊比賽）」；race 是有起點跟終點、競速型的比賽，像是「a marathon race（馬拉松比賽）」。

wire [waɪr]

Track 2080

名 金屬絲、電線

▶The rope is not strong enough. Let's use a wire instead.
這根繩子不夠結實，我們改用金屬線吧。

wise [waɪz]

Track 2081

形 智慧的、睿智的 同 smart 聰明的

▶The wise old man always gives us good advice.
這位睿智的老人總是給我們很好的建議。

with·in [wɪð`ɪn]

Track 2082

介 在……之內 同 inside 在……之內

▶We'll arrive within two hours.
我們兩個小時內就會到了。

文法字詞解析
within 和 in 在用法上很容易弄混，in 搭配上未來式時，它的意思是「經過某一段時間以後」，而 within 則是「在那段時間以內」。所以，如果把例句改成「We'll arrive in two hours.」的話，這句話的意思就會變成：「我們過兩小時後回來。」

with·out [wɪð͵aʊt]

Track 2083

介 沒有、不

▶You guys have to go without me.
你們去吧，我不一起去了。

wolf [wʊlf]

Track 2084

名 狼

▶The wolf looks a lot like a dog.
這隻狼看起來真像狗啊。

wond·er [`wʌndɚ]

Track 2085

名 奇蹟、驚奇 動 對……感到疑惑

▶名 No wonder he ended up marrying her.
難怪他最後娶了她。

▶動 He wondered why she was always so unhappy.
他實在不懂她為什麼總是這麼不開心。

文法字詞解析
wonder 後面可以加 wh 開頭的疑問詞作為間接問句，表示「想知道……」。

won·der·ful [`wʌndɚfəl]

Track 2086

形 令人驚奇的、奇妙的 同 marvelous 令人驚奇的

▶The weather has been wonderful. 近來天氣好極了。

wood·en [`wʊdn̩]

Track 2087

形 木製的

▶The cat is sitting in the wooden box.
那隻貓正坐在那個木箱子裡。

文法字詞解析
有字尾「-en」的字可以是形容詞也可以是動詞，如果作為形容詞，意思是「由某種材質所製成」，像是「wooden box（木箱）」、「golden ring（金戒指）」。

wool [wʊl]

Track 2088

名 羊毛

▶This wool suit is too expensive for me to buy.
這套毛料套裝太貴了，我買不起。

worth [wɝθ]

Track 2089

名 價值

▶Whatever is worth doing at all is worth doing well.
凡是值得做的事就值得把它做好。

wound [wund]

Track 2090

名 傷口 動 傷害 同 harm 傷害

▶名 There is a bullet（子彈）wound in his chest（胸部）.
他的胸部有一處槍傷。

▶動 There were many soldiers wounded in the Second World War. 有很多士兵在第二次世界大戰中負傷。

實用片語用語
wound / injure / hurt sb. 傷害某人

yard [jɑrd]

Track 2091

名 庭院、院子

▶There are three apple trees and two pear trees in our yard.
我們家院子有三棵蘋果樹和兩棵梨樹。

youth [juθ]

Track 2092

名 青年

▶The youth who lives next door always seems very curious.
住隔壁的那個青年總是很好奇的樣子。

ze·bra [ˋzibrə]

Track 2093

名 斑馬

名詞複數 zebras, zebra

▶There are several species（種類）of zebras in that zoo.
那個動物園裡有好幾種斑馬。

進階英文能力——邁向 3200 單字

學英文從單字開始，
許自己一個不可思議的滿分奇蹟！

Level 3

進階英文能力——邁向3200單字

a·board [ə`bord] Track 2094

副/介 在船（飛機、火車）上

▶副 All passengers aboard fell into the river.
船上所有的乘客都落入了河中。

▶介 We are the last two to go aboard the ship.
我們是最後上船的兩個人。

文法字詞解析

「aboard」（在船、飛機、火車上）這個單字和「abroad」（在國外）長得實在很像，又常在旅行時用到，因此很容易搞混。那該怎麼分辨呢？很簡單，我們「登機」、「上火車」的動作叫做「board」，上飛機前需要的「登機證」叫「boarding pass」。因此，後面是「board」的「aboard」就是兩者之中表示「在船、飛機、火車上」的單字了。

ac·cept·a·ble [ək`sɛptəbl̩] Track 2095

形 可接受的

▶I don't think your price terms are acceptable, so we won't consider your company. 我們覺得你們的價格條件不可接受，因此不打算考慮貴公司了。

ac·ci·dent [`æksədənt] Track 2096

名 事故、偶發事件 同 casualty 事故

▶He had a terrible accident and almost died.
他遭遇了一場可怕的事故，差點就死了。

ac·count [ə`kaʊnt] Track 2097

名 帳目、記錄 動 視為、負責

▶名 Don't give others the password to your bank account.
別把你銀行帳戶的密碼給別人。

▶動 Can you account for his actions? 你能為他的行為負責嗎？

實用片語用語

account for 為……負責、說明解釋

ac·cu·rate [`ækjərɪt] Track 2098

形 正確的、準確的 同 correct 正確的

▶Would you mind sending the accurate data to our company this afternoon?
您介意今天下午把準確資料送到我們公司來嗎？

萬用延伸句型

Would you mind V-ing... 您介意……嗎？

ache [ek] Track 2099

名 疼痛 同 pain 疼痛

▶My grandparents both feel aches in their backs.
我的祖父母都覺得背在隱隱作痛。

a·chieve·(ment) [ə`tʃiv(mənt)] Track 2100

動 實現、完成 名 成績、成就

▶動 It's time for you to achieve your goal.
該是時候達成你的目標了。

▶名 He made a great achievement in the field of business.
他在商業領域做出了一番成就。

ac·tiv·i·ty [æk`tɪvətɪ]
Track 2101

名 活動、活躍

▶Do you mind if we invite a foreign guest to take part in this activity? 您介意我們邀請一位外賓參加這次活動嗎？

ac·tu·al [`æktʃʊəl]
Track 2102

形 實際的、真實的

▶It's not difficult for you to inform all the parties about the actual situation. 你們要想通知各方實際情形其實並不難。

文法字詞解析
這裡的「parties」指的不是我們平常「開趴」的「派對」，而是指「各方相關人士」。

ad·di·tion·al [ə`dɪʃənl̩]
Track 2103

形 額外的、附加的 同 extra 額外的

▶We might have to ask an additional charge for your items.
我們可能要向您的物品進行額外收費。

ad·mire [əd`maɪr]
Track 2104

動 欽佩、讚賞

▶How do I know whether she admires you or not? You'll have to ask her yourself.
我怎麼會知道她欣不欣賞你啊？你應該自己去問她啊。

ad·mit [əd`mɪt]
Track 2105

動 容許……進入、承認 反 forbid 禁止

▶It's the first time that he has admitted the task is quite difficult.
這是他第一次承認這個任務很艱鉅。

adopt [ə`dɑpt]
Track 2106

動 收養

▶Why don't you adopt a child if you are so fond of kids?
既然你很喜歡小孩子，那為什麼不去領養一個呢？

實用片語用語
be fond of... 喜歡、喜愛（後面接名詞片語或動名詞）

ad·vanced [əd`vænst]
Track 2107

形 在前面的、先進的 同 forward 前面的

▶I don't think this poor country can catch up with the advanced countries（先進國家）.
我覺得這個貧窮的國家趕不上先進的國家。

ad·van·tage [əd`væntɪdʒ]
Track 2108

名 利益、優勢 同 benefit 利益

▶We should take advantage of this chance.
我們應該要好好利用這次機會。

實用片語用語
take advantage of... 利用、佔……便宜。

ad·ven·ture [əd`vɛntʃɚ]
Track 2109

名 冒險

▶I love listening to stories about her adventures.
我喜歡聽關於她各種冒險的故事。

ad·ver·tise(ment)/ ad [ˌædvɚ`taɪz(mənt)]/[æd]
Track 2110

動 登廣告 名 廣告、宣傳

萬用延伸句型
Do you mind if I... 你介意我……
這個句型和「Do you mind V-ing」雖然長得很像，但兩個句型的主角是不同人喔！舉例來說，如果你問：「Do you mind opening the door?」，那麼你是要請對方去關門。如果你問：「Do you mind if I open the door?」，那麼要去關門的人是你自己，對方不用移動。

▶動 Do you mind if I advertise our goods（商品）on television?
你介意我在電視上幫我們的商品做廣告嗎？

▶名 I suggest putting an advertisement in the newspaper.
我建議在報紙上登廣告。

ad·vice [əd`vaɪs]

Track 2111

名 忠告

▶Would you mind if I ask the workers in the factory for advice?
您介意我向工廠的工人徵求意見嗎？

ad·vise [əd`vaɪz]

Track 2112

動 勸告

▶It was the second time that she had advised me to take part in this plan. 這是她第二次來勸我參與這次計畫了。

ad·vi·ser/ad·vi·sor [əd`vaɪzɚ]

Track 2113

名 顧問

▶By the time you find the adviser, we will have solved all the problems. 等你找到顧問，我們都已經解決完所有問題了。

萬用延伸句型
By the time... 到了……的時候（後面可接各種時態的動詞）

af·fect [ə`fɛkt]

Track 2114

動 影響 同 influence 影響

▶I don't believe that this disease will affect people all around the world. 我不相信這種疾病會影響到全世界的人。

af·ford [ə`ford]

Track 2115

動 給予、供給、能負擔

▶Can you really afford to buy a car? 你真的買得起車嗎？

af·ter·ward(s) [`æftɚwɚd(z)]

Track 2116

副 以後

▶Paul has an appointment with his boss, so he ate dinner and went out soon afterwards.
保羅跟他的老闆有約，所以他吃過晚飯不久以後就出去了。

ag·ri·cul·ture [`ægrɪ͵kʌltʃɚ]

Track 2117

名 農業、農藝、農學

▶My sister studies agriculture in university. 我姊姊在大學念農業。

文法字詞解析
要說「某人在大學念的是……」的時候，可以用「study + 某科目」這個說法。如果要說「主修是……」，則可以說「major in + 科目」。例如，若這位姊姊主修的就是農業學，就可以說她「majors in agriculture」。

air-con·di·tion·er [`ɛr͵kən`dɪʃənɚ]

Track 2118

名 空調

▶Do you mind if I turn off the air-conditioner?
你介意我關掉空調嗎？

文法字詞解析
把冷氣打開則是說「turn on」。雖然「open」也是「打開」的意思，但一般不說「open the air conditioner」，可能會讓人誤會你是真的要把冷氣拆開來看。

al·ley [`ælɪ]

Track 2119

名 巷、小徑

▶There is a long narrow alley behind the house.
這房子後面有條狹長的小徑。

a·maze·(ment) [ə`mez(mənt)] Track 2120

動 使……吃驚 名 吃驚

▶動 It amazed me that he was actually younger than me.
他居然比我還年輕，真是太讓我震驚了。

▶名 The students all looked at me in amazement when I told them the test was cancelled.
我跟學生們說考試取消時，他們都很驚愕地看著我。

am·bas·sa·dor [æm`bæsədɚ] Track 2121

名 大使、使節

同 diplomat 外交官

▶It's time for the ambassador to sign the treaty（協議）.
大使該簽訂協議了。

am·bi·tion [æm`bɪʃən] Track 2122

名 雄心壯志、志向

▶His daughter wants to be an astronaut（太空人）in the future; what a great ambition!
他女兒長大後想成為一名太空人，多麼遠大的抱負啊！

實用片語用語

in the future 未來

此外，也可以在這個片語中加上形容詞修飾。例如「in the near future」（不久的將來）、「in the distant future」（比較遠一點的將來）等。

an·gel [`endʒəl] Track 2123

名 天使

▶She's such a sweet angel of a girl.
這甜美的女孩簡直是天使。

an·gle [`æŋgḷ] Track 2124

名 角度、立場

▶You should look at this problem from a different angle.
你應該從另外一個角度來看待這件事情。

an·nounce·(ment) [ə`naʊns(mənt)] Track 2125

動 宣告、公佈、通知 名 宣佈、宣告 同 declare 宣佈

▶動 It would be so kind of you to announce the guests when they come in.
你能在客人來的時候通報一聲的話就太好了。

▶名 Have you heard the boss's announcement?
你聽到老闆宣布的事了沒？

文法字詞解析

hear 的動詞變化：hear, heard, heard

a·part [ə`pɑrt] Track 2126

副 分散地、遠離地 反 together 一起地

▶The two towns are miles apart.
兩個城鎮之間相隔好幾英里。

文法字詞解析

apart 的意思是「分散地、遠離地」，它和「a part」（一部分）兩字長得很像，因此連母語人士都常會不小心寫錯。但它們的意思和用法可是大不同，要小心喔！

ap·par·ent [ə`pærənt] Track 2127

形 明顯的、外表的 同 obvious 明顯的

▶It's apparent that she is unwilling（不願意的）to go with us.
很明顯，她不願意跟我們出去。

ap·peal [ə`pil] Track 2128

名 吸引力、懇求 動 引起……的興趣

▶名 I really don't see the appeal of this product.
我真看不出這個產品的吸引力在哪。

▶動 This new design really appeals to me.
這個新的設計真的很吸引我。

ap·pre·ci·ate [ə`priʃɪ‚et] Track 2129

動 欣賞、鑒賞、感激

▶We can't fully（完全地）appreciate foreign works unless we can understand their cultures.
除非我們能了解其他文化，要不然我們無法完全欣賞到外國作品的精髓。

文法字詞解析
在這一句中的「works」不是我們常見的「工作、職業」的意思喔！它代表的是「作品」，例如藝術作品、音樂作品、文學作品等，都包含在這個範圍內。

ap·proach [ə`protʃ] Track 2130

動 接近

▶I don't think the driver slowed down when the car approached the intersection（十字路口）.
我認為車子向十字口靠近的時候，司機沒有減速。

ap·prove [ə`pruv] Track 2131

動 批准、認可

▶I approve of your idea, but I don't think the others do.
我認可你的點子，但其他人好像不怎麼同意的樣子。

實用片語用語
approve of 贊同、認可

a·quar·i·um [ə`kwɛrɪəm] Track 2132

名 水族館

▶Would you like to go to the aquarium with me?
你要不要和我一起去水族館？

a·rith·me·tic [ə`rɪθmə‚tɪk] Track 2133

名 算術 形 算術的

▶名 My little brother is not good at arithmetic.
我弟弟數學不好。

▶形 Maybe you should get your brother to help you work out the arithmetic problem.
你或許應該叫哥哥來幫你解答這道算術題。

ar·riv·al [ə`raɪvḷ] Track 2134

名 到達

▶He rushed off to the restroom upon his arrival.
他才一到達就跑去廁所了。

實用片語用語
rush off to 趕去（某處）
直接使用「rush off」（後面不加 to 以及地點）也可以喔！
例如：He finished the coffee in a hurry then rushed off.
他很快地喝完咖啡，然後就趕去別的地方了。

ash [æʃ] Track 2135

名 灰燼、灰

▶His ashes were placed in a pot. 他的骨灰被放進一個壺裡。

a·side [ə`saɪd] Track 2136

副 在旁邊

▶Tom took me aside and talked to me about this matter.
湯姆把我拉到一邊來談這件事。

as·sist [ə`sɪst]
Track 2137

動 說明、援助 同 help 說明

▶Would you assist me in moving out these boxes in my room?
你能幫我把屋裡的這些箱子搬出來嗎？

ath·lete [`æθlit]
Track 2138

名 運動員

▶I don't think he is the most experienced athlete in the team.
我認為他並不是隊上最有經驗的運動員。

at·tempt [ə`tɛmpt]
Track 2139

動 / 名 嘗試、企圖

▶動 It was the first time that he had attempted to get in touch with his mom after the quarrel.
這還是他吵架後第一次試圖聯繫母親。

▶名 It is the first time that the shy boy has made an attempt at a joke in front of us.
這是這個害羞的男孩子第一次試圖在我們面前開玩笑。

實用片語用語
attempt to V. 試著

at·ti·tude [`ætəˏtjud]
Track 2140

名 態度、心態、看法

▶Will you tell me what your attitude towards this plan is?
能告訴我你對這個計畫的看法是怎麼樣的嗎？

at·tract [ə`trækt]
Track 2141

動 吸引

▶The park in that city is very famous and attracts many people.
這公園在這個城市非常有名，吸引了很多人。

at·trac·tive [ə`træktɪv]
Track 2142

形 吸引人的、動人的

▶It is the first time we've seen her look so attractive.
我們還是第一次看到她如此光鮮亮麗。

文法字詞解析
attractive 經常用來形容人的「長相」或其他事物的「外型」吸引人，不過也可以用在說一個點子聽起來很吸引人喔！

au·di·ence [`ɔdɪəns]
Track 2143

名 聽眾 同 spectator 觀眾

▶I feel nervous speaking in front of such a large audience.
在這麼多觀眾面前說話，讓我感覺很緊張。

au·thor [`ɔθɚ]
Track 2144

名 作家、作者 同 writer 作者

▶He is my favorite author. I've read every single one of his books.
他是我最喜愛的作家，他的每本書我都讀過了。

實用片語用語
every single one of... 每一個都
其實說「every one of...」就足以表達「每一個都」的意思，加上 single 含有強調的意思。

au·to·mat·ic [ˏɔtə`mætɪk]
Track 2145

形 自動的

▶Would you like to buy a fully automatic washing machine or a semi-automatic（半自動）one?
你是想買一台全自動的洗衣機呢？還是一台半自動的洗衣機？

au·to·mo·bile/au·to

Track 2146

[ˋɔtəmə͵bil]/[ˋɔto]

名 汽車 同 car 汽車

▶There is no one who can design an automobile which pleases every driver.
沒有人能設計出能讓每個司機都滿意的車。

文法字詞解析
大家常常用的「please」（請）也可以當作動詞喔！在這句中的 please 就是動詞，它是「討好」、「使開心」的意思。

a·vail·a·ble [əˋveləbḷ]

Track 2147

形 可利用的、可取得的

▶Would you tell me when you will be available this week?
能告訴我你這星期什麼時候有空嗎？

文法字詞解析
雖然英文中大部分的形容詞都是放在名詞前面，但也有一些會放在後面，這些形容詞就叫做「後置形容詞」，像 available 這種以「able」結尾的形容詞就幾乎都是如此。

av·e·nue [ˋævə͵nju]

Track 2148

名 大道、大街

▶Can you tell me where Second Avenue is?
你能告訴我第二大街在哪裡嗎？

av·er·age [ˋævərɪdʒ]

Track 2149

名 平均數

▶It's not easy for him to spend one hour a day on average on English.
每天平均花一個小時來唸英語對他來說並不容易。

實用片語用語
on average 平均

a·wake [əˋwek]

Track 2150

動 喚醒、提醒

▶The sound of the drums awoke him from his sleep.
鼓聲把他從睡夢中喚醒了。

a·wak·en [əˋwekən]

Track 2151

動 使……覺悟

▶There must be something which can awaken him to a sense of duty.
肯定有什麼事情能夠喚起他的責任感。

a·ward [əˋwɔrd]

Track 2152

名 獎品、獎賞 動 授與、頒獎

▶名 The novel earned the writer a literary（文學的）award.
這部長篇小說為作家贏得了文學獎。

▶動 He was awarded the top prize by the committee.
他被委員會授予了頭獎。

a·ware [əˋwɛr]

Track 2153

形 注意到的、覺察的

▶It will be a long time before people are aware of this consequence（後果）.
人們要過很久才會意識到這個後果。

萬用延伸句型
It will be a long time before...
要很久以後才會……

aw·ful [ˋɔfʊl]

Track 2154

形 可怕的、嚇人的 同 horrible 可怕的

▶The awful earthquake killed many people.
那個糟糕的地震造成許多人身亡。

ax/axe [æks] Track 2155

名 斧 動 劈、砍

▶名 People in the ancient times used stone axes.
以前古人使用石斧。

▶動 The man felt very tired after axing the tree.
那個男人在砍了那棵樹後覺得很累。

Bb

back·ground [ˋbæk͵graʊnd] Track 2156

名 背景

▶I don't mind his impoverished（貧困的）background, but my parents might.
我不介意他貧困的背景，但我父母可能會介意。

文法字詞解析

這一句的 might 後面其實省略了「mind his impoverished back-ground」，也就是說整個句子的完整意思是「我不介意他貧困的背景，但我父母可能會介意他貧困的背景」。同樣的事情重複兩次不是很奇怪嗎？在英文中也很討厭重複，因此才把 might 後面的內容都乾脆省略了。

ba·con [ˋbekən] Track 2157

名 培根、燻肉

▶I love having bacon for breakfast.
我最愛早餐吃培根。

bac·te·ri·a [bækˋtɪrɪə] Track 2158

名 細菌

▶It is possible for lab（實驗室）assistants（助手）to multiply bacteria in the laboratory（實驗室）.
實驗助手能夠在實驗室繁殖細菌。

文法字詞解析

這一句中出現了 lab 和 laboratory，但其實它們的意思根本是一樣的，lab 是 laboratory 的縮寫。此外，lab 還可以當作拉布拉多狗（labrador retriever）的縮寫。所以當有人告訴你他有 lab 時，不見得代表他很有錢、擁有一座實驗室。

bad·ly [ˋbædlɪ] Track 2159

副 非常地、惡劣地

▶I don't believe that Tom would speak badly of Bill.
我不相信湯姆會說比爾的壞話。

bad·min·ton [ˋbædmɪntən] Track 2160

名 羽毛球

▶Would you like to play badminton with us this afternoon?
你今天下午想不想跟我們一起打羽毛球？

bag·gage [ˋbægɪdʒ] Track 2161

名 行李

同 lugguge 行李

▶Jane, hurry up! It's time for us to check in our baggage.
珍妮，快點啦！我們該去托運行李了。

文法字詞解析

baggage 和 luggage 同樣都能當作「行李」的意思，不過 baggage 能夠拿來暗示人「心理上的」包袱，例如「emotional baggage」指的就是「情緒上的負擔」，luggage 則沒有這層意思。

bait [bet] Track 2162

名 誘餌 動 誘惑

▶名 The fish took the bait and we caught it easily.
那隻魚咬了誘餌，我們很快就逮到牠了。

▶動 He baited me into giving him my password.
他引誘我給他我的密碼。

ba·lance [ˋbæləns]

Track 2163

名 平衡 動 使平衡

▶名 Not every woman is able to keep balance between her family and career.
不是每個女人都能在自己的家庭和事業上維持平衡。

▶動 Not everyone can balance the advantages of living in a big city against the disadvantages（不利）.
不是每個人都能權衡住在大城市的利與弊。

實用片語用語
keep balance between A and B
將 A 和 B 保持平衡

ban·dage [ˋbændɪdʒ]

Track 2164

名 繃帶

▶He just had a car accident and therefore had bandages around his injured arm.
他剛出了車禍，所以受傷的手臂纏上了繃帶。

bang [bæŋ]

Track 2165

動 重擊、雷擊

▶He banged the door in anger.
他怒得大聲甩上門。

文法字詞解析
這裡說 bang 是「雷擊」的意思，那大聲甩上門為什麼也可以用 bang 呢？因為大聲甩上門不是也會發出如雷聲般大的聲音嗎？因此，像是用力捶門、槍響等等這類如雷貫耳的聲音，也可以用 bang 來表示。

bare [bɛr]

Track 2166

形 暴露的、僅有的 同 naked 暴露的

▶He is bare to the waist because it's so hot.
他光著上身，因為實在太熱了。

bare·ly [ˋbɛrlɪ]

Track 2167

副 簡直沒有、幾乎不能

▶I barely know him at all, so can't tell you what he's like.
我幾乎不太認識他，所以無法跟你說他到底是怎樣的人。

barn [bɑrn]

Track 2168

名 穀倉

▶The soldiers bedded down in a barn.
那些士兵們在穀倉裡打地鋪過夜。

實用片語用語
bed down 睡覺
我們都知道「bed」是床的意思，那麼在床上躺下來當然就是「睡覺」的意思啦！不過這個片語不見得一定要用來指在「床上」睡覺，像例句中的士兵們打地鋪也可以用 bed down。

bar·rel [ˋbærəl]

Track 2169

名 大桶

▶Would you please draw me a glass of beer from the barrel?
請你從大桶子裡裝一杯啤酒給我好嗎？

bay [be]

Track 2170

名 海灣

▶Let's go to the bay later and have a swim.
我們待會去海灣游泳吧。

beam [bim]

Track 2171

動 放射、發光

▶He beamed with joy upon hearing the news.
他一聽到這個消息就眉開眼笑。

beast [bist]

Track 2172

名 野獸

▶Long long ago, there was war between the birds and the beasts.
很久很久以前，鳥類與獸類之間發生了一場戰爭。

文法字詞解析
beast 指的是「野獸」的意思，聽起來很可怕。但大家想到野獸，常會想到牠們擁有強大的蠻力，也就是說野獸多半都「很強」。因此近年來口語中可以用 beast 來描述某人「很強」，例如若你朋友籃球打得很好，就可以說「My friend is a beast at basketball」。

beg·gar [ˋbɛgɚ]

Track 2173

名 乞丐

▶What do you think about the story of that beggar's misfortunes（不幸）?
你覺得那位乞丐不幸的故事怎樣？

be·have [bɪˋhev]

Track 2174

動 行動、舉止 同 act 行動

▶It's very hard for parents to train their children to behave well at the table.
父母要訓練自己的孩子用餐時舉止得體是很困難的。

be·ing [ˋbiɪŋ]

Track 2175

名 生命、存在

▶I don't believe that there are strange beings from outer space.
我不相信有來自外太空的奇特生物。

萬用延伸句型
I don't believe that... 我不相信……

bel·ly/stom·ach/tum·my [ˋbɛlɪ]/[ˋstʌmək]/[ˋtʌmɪ]

Track 2176

名 腹、胃

▶His belly is huge, probably because he eats so much.
他的肚子超大的，大概是因為他吃很多吧。

be·neath [bɪˋniθ]

Track 2177

介 在……下

▶My sister lives on the floor beneath ours.
我姊姊住在我們樓下那一層。

文法字詞解析
有些自認高高在上的人，會覺得一些其他的人、事、物都在自己「之下」，這時就可以用 beneath 這個字。例如若叫一位自認高高在上的人去掃地，他可能會 說：「Things like that are beneath me!」（這種事在我「之下」，我怎麼可能去做呢！）

ben·e·fit [ˋbɛnəfɪt]

Track 2178

名 益處、利益 同 advantage 利益

▶名 This project is of great benefit to everyone.
這項工程對每個人都大有好處。

ber·ry [ˋbɛrɪ]

Track 2179

名 漿果、莓

▶The girls have gone picking berries. 女孩子們採莓果去了。

bi·ble [ˋbaɪbl]

Track 2180

名 聖經

▶She reads the bible every day before going to sleep.
她每天睡覺前都會讀聖經。

bil·lion [ˋbɪljən]

Track 2181

名 十億、一兆、無數

▶There are billions of stars in the sky. 天上有無數的星星。

實用片語用語
billions of（+ 複數名詞）無數的

bin·go [ˋbɪŋgo]
Track 2182

名 賓果遊戲

▶They play bingo to kill time before their mom comes home.
他們玩賓果以消磨時間、等媽媽回家。

bis·cuit [ˋbɪskɪt]
Track 2183

名 餅乾、小甜麵包

▶Put the biscuits in the box over there.
請把餅乾放到那邊的盒子裡。

blame [blem]
Track 2184

動 責備 同 accuse

▶Both you and I were to blame for the mistake.
你我都應該承擔這個錯誤的責任。

文法字詞解析
blame 這個單字的用法常會有人搞錯，認為只要是「罵人」（例如吵架的時候互相謾罵）都可以用這個字。其實 blame 並不是「罵」的意思，它含有「責怪」的意思，而人們在責怪別人時常會順口罵出來，才會因此讓許多人誤以為 blame 就是「罵」。事實上，如果你在罵人的時候並沒有要責怪對方，純粹只是想罵他而已，那是不能用 blame 這個字來表示的。

blan·ket [ˋblæŋkɪt]
Track 2185

名 氈、毛毯

▶It's a little cold tonight. Would you like me to bring you a blanket?
今晚有點冷，我幫您拿條毯子好嗎？

bleed [blid]
Track 2186

動 流血、放血

▶You're bleeding! What happened?
你在流血耶！怎麼了？

文法字詞解析
bleed 的動詞變化：bleed、bled、bled

bless [blɛs]
Track 2187

動 祝福

▶He was blessed with great talent.
他天資非常聰穎。

blouse [blaʊs]
Track 2188

名 短衫

▶I don't think this blouse matches your skirt well.
我覺得這個短衫和你的裙子不相配。

bold [bold]
Track 2189

形 大膽的 同 brave 勇敢的

▶He is a very bold man. 他是個非常大膽的男子。

boot [but]
Track 2190

名 長靴

▶My boots are too small. They're giving me blisters（水泡）.
我的靴子太小了，我都長水泡了。

實用片語用語
give sb. the boot 炒（某人）魷魚、開除某人
例如：If you keep playing videogames at work, I bet the boss will give you the boot.
如果你再這樣上班打電動，我看老闆會開除你的。

bor·der [ˋbɔrdɚ]
Track 2191

名 邊 同 edge 邊

▶My white handkerchief with blue borders got lost on my way to school.
我那條藍色花邊的白手帕丟在我去學校的路上了。

bore [bor]　Track 2192

動 鑽孔 名 無聊的人 同 drill 鑽孔

▶動 I don't think that they need to bore for water.
我認為他們不需要鑿井取水。

▶名 My grandma is a dreadful（可怕的）bore.
我奶奶是個超級無趣的人。

文法字詞解析
bore是現在式，但它同時也是「bear」（忍受、承擔）的過去式，我們來大致整理一下：
bear的動詞變化：bear, bore, born
或bear, bore, borne
bore的動詞變化：bore, bored, bored
另外也要注意，不要把bored的過去式跟形容詞bored（感到厭倦的）搞混了喔。

brake [brek]　Track 2193

名 / 動 煞車

▶名 The brakes on this bike aren't working.
這腳踏車上的煞車壞了。

▶動 Why did the driver brake suddenly?
為什麼司機突然煞車了？

brass [bræs]　Track 2194

名 黃銅、銅器

▶Not everyone knows that brass is an alloy（合金）of copper（銅）and zinc（鋅）.
不是每個人都知道黃銅是銅和鋅的合金。

brav·er·y [ˋbrevərɪ]　Track 2195

名 大膽、勇敢 同 courage 勇氣

▶It's hard to show bravery in the face of danger.
面臨危險時，很難表現出大無畏的精神。

breast [brɛst]　Track 2196

名 胸膛、胸部

▶How about having chicken breast today for dinner?
今天我們晚餐吃雞胸肉怎麼樣？

breath [brɛθ]　Track 2197

名 呼吸、氣息

▶It took us a few minutes to catch our breath after the race.
賽跑後我們花了好幾分鐘才恢復了正常呼吸。

實用片語用語
catch one's breath 喘過氣來、恢復正常呼吸

breathe [brið]　Track 2198

動 呼吸、生存

▶You're hugging me too tightly. I can't breathe!
你抱太緊了，我都不能呼吸了！

breeze [briz]　Track 2199

名 微風 動 微風輕吹、經鬆通過

▶名 We sit here enjoying the cool breeze from the lake.
我們坐在這裡享受湖面上吹來的涼爽微風。

▶動 He breezed through the test without even trying.
他毫無努力就輕輕鬆鬆地通過了這次考試。

bride [braɪd]　Track 2200

名 新娘

▶Let's drink a toast to the bride and bridegroom（新郎）!
讓我們舉杯向新娘和新郎祝賀！

實用片語用語
drink a toast to（某人） 敬某人、為某人乾杯
drink a toast to、cheers 和 bottoms up 在中文裡都叫做「乾杯」，但其實英文裡的用法是不同的。drink a toast 是用在舉杯前所說的「敬（某人）」，cheers 則時在杯子碰撞時所說的用語，類似中文的「喝吧」；而bottoms up則是真正「杯子見底」的「乾杯」。

bril·liant [ˋbrɪljənt] Track 2201

形 有才氣的、出色的

▶He is a brilliant scholar（學者）in physics.
他是個出色的物理學者。

brook [brʊk] Track 2202

名 川、小河、溪流

▶There is a brook winding through the woods.
有一條小河蜿蜒地流過樹林。

broom [brum] Track 2203

名 掃帚、長柄刷

▶Witches ride brooms. 女巫都騎掃帚。

brow(s) [braʊ(z)] Track 2204

名 眉毛

▶Her brow is wrinkled in outrage（憤怒）. 她憤怒得皺起了眉頭。

文法字詞解析
句中的 outrage（憤怒）還有一個伙伴叫「outrageous」，是形容詞。既然 outrage 是「憤怒」，outrageous 就是「令人憤怒的」囉！同時，outrageous 還能用來表示「很難以置信的」，例如若你的鄰居把他家的汽車停進了你家的游泳池，你不但憤怒，同時又覺得這難以置信，就可以說：That's outrageous!

bub·ble [ˋbʌbl̩] Track 2205

名 泡沫、氣泡

▶The children were playing with bubbles in the bath.
孩子們在澡盆裡玩泡泡。

buck·et/pail [ˋbʌkɪt]/[pel] Track 2206

名 水桶、提桶

▶Would you please go and fill this bucket with water for me?
請你去替我裝滿一桶水來好嗎？

bud [bʌd] Track 2207

名 芽 動 萌芽 同 flourish 茂盛

▶名 The branches in the garden are in full bud.
花園裡的枝頭都長滿了花蕾。

▶動 Unless you water the seeds regularly（定期地）, they will not bud in spring. 如果你不定期給那些種子澆水，它們在春天是不會發芽的。

文法字詞解析
和 bud 相關的形容詞 budding 即「萌芽的」、「新崛起的」的意思。像是剛出道的歌手如同剛冒出來的嫩芽一般還有很大的成長空間以及無限可能性，就可以稱為 budding singer。

budg·et [ˋbʌdʒɪt] Track 2208

名 預算

▶Our company didn't make much money last year, so next year's budget will have to be drastically（激烈地）reduced. 我們公司去年沒賺到什麼錢，所以下一年度的預算要大幅度削減。

buf·fa·lo [ˋbʌfl̩o] Track 2209

名 水牛、野牛

▶There were lots of buffaloes in North America 100 years ago.
一百年前，北美有大量的野牛。

buf·fet [ˋbʌfɪt] Track 2210

名 自助餐

▶The buffet on the first floor is always crowded.
一樓的自助餐每次都很多人。

bulb [bʌlb] Track 2211

名 電燈泡

▶The bulb has burned out. Can we get someone to replace（取代）it? 燈泡燒壞了，我們可不可以找人來換一個啊？

實用片語用語
light bulb 燈泡
例如：We've got some light bulbs in the drawer.
抽屜裡面有一些燈泡。

---

bull [bʊl] Track 2212

名 公牛

▶The bull rushed at the man in a fit of madness.
那頭公牛憤怒地朝著那個男子奔去。

---

bul·let [ˋbʊlɪt] Track 2213

名 子彈、彈頭

▶He got hit by a bullet, but luckily didn't die.
他被子彈射中了，但幸好沒死。

---

bump [bʌmp] Track 2214

動 碰、撞

▶The bus was driving too fast and bumped into another bus.
那台巴士開得太快了，撞到了另一台巴士。

實用片語用語
bump into sth. / sb. 撞到
除了「撞到」以外，bump into sb. 也有「和某人不期而遇」的意思。

---

bunch [bʌntʃ] Track 2215

名 束、串、捆

▶Miss White received a bunch of flowers from her admirer（愛慕者）.
懷特小姐收到愛慕者所送的一束花。

實用片語用語
a bunch of 一捆、一串、一束
例如：They had a bunch of grapes after lunch.
他們午餐後吃了一串葡萄。

---

bur·den [ˋbɝdn̩] Track 2216

名 負荷、負擔

▶I'll never see you as a burden.
我才不會把你看做是負擔呢。

---

bur·glar [ˋbɝglɚ] Track 2217

名 夜盜、竊賊

▶As soon as I came downstairs, the burglar ran away.
我一下樓，竊賊便狂奔而逃。

---

bur·y [ˋbɛrɪ] Track 2218

動 埋

▶The dog buried the bone in the yard.
那隻狗把骨頭埋在院子裡。

---

bush [bʊʃ] Track 2219

名 灌木叢

▶Who is there hiding behind the bush?
灌木叢後面躲著的那個人是誰？

---

buzz [bʌz] Track 2220

名 嗡嗡聲

▶I can hear a buzz of conversation going on.
我聽到竊竊私語的聲音。

實用片語用語
buzz of excitement 興奮
當一群人聚在一起，發生令人興奮的事時，大家開始熱烈討論起來，總會發出一片嗡嗡聲，因此才有這個片語的誕生。
例如：The good news caused a buzz of excitement in the room.
這好消息讓房間裡的大家都興奮地討論起來。

cabin [ˋkæbɪn]
Track 2221

名 小屋、茅屋

▶There is a small cabin in the woods, but no one lives in it.
樹林裡有個小屋，但是沒人住。

cam·pus [ˋkæmpəs]
Track 2222

名 校區、校園

▶Would you tell me something about your campus life?
能告訴我有關你校園生活的一些事嗎？

文法字詞解析
說「校園裡」時，我們比較少說「inside the campus」，而是說「on campus」。而「校外」則可以說「off campus」。

cane [ken]
Track 2223

名 手杖、棒

▶Grandpa likes hitting people with his cane.
爺爺喜歡拿枴杖打人。

ca·noe [kəˋnu]
Track 2224

名 獨木舟 動 划獨木舟

▶名 Do you know the man in the canoe?
你認識在獨木舟裡的那個男人嗎？

▶動 I don't think they can canoe across the river in such weather.
我不認為他們能在這樣的天氣划著小舟過河。

can·yon [ˋkænjən]
Track 2225

名 峽谷 同 valley 山谷

▶I've never been to the Grand Canyon.
我從來沒去過大峽谷。

ca·pa·ble [ˋkepəbl̩]
Track 2226

形 有能力的 同 able 有能力的

▶He is capable of many things, but not including playing the erhu. 他能夠做很多事，但不包含演奏二胡。

實用片語用語
be capable of... 能夠……

cap·i·tal [ˋkæpətl̩]
Track 2227

名 首都、資本 形 主要的

▶名 There is no doubt that this city should be the capital of our nation.
毫無疑問，這個城市應該成為我們國家的首都。

▶形 What you suggested was quite a capital idea.
你的建議是個非常好的主意。

萬用延伸句型
There is no doubt that...毫無疑問地，……

cap·ture [ˋkæptʃɚ]
Track 2228

動 捉住、吸引 名 擄獲、戰利品

▶動 The villagers（村民）hope they can capture the tiger as soon as possible.
村民們希望他們能儘快抓住那隻老虎。

▶名 He had to play dead to avoid（避免） capture by the enemy.
他不得不裝死，以免被敵人俘虜。

car·pen·ter [ˋkɑrpəntɚ]
Track 2229

名 木匠

▶How long have you been a carpenter here?
你在這個地方做了幾年木匠了啊？

car·riage [ˋkærɪdʒ]
Track 2230

名 車輛、車、馬車

▶I don't believe that people nowadays（現在）are willing to take a carriage anywhere.
我相信現在人們再也不會願意乘馬車到處去了。

實用片語用語
be willing to 願意

cast [kæst]
Track 2231

動 用力擲、選角 名 投、演員班底 同 throw 投、擲

▶動 I won't cast a glance at her unless she apologizes（道歉）to me.
除非她向我道歉，否則我看都不會看她一眼。

▶名 No one will know who is in the cast until Friday.
週五前沒人知道演員陣容裡會有誰。

實用片語用語
cast a glance 瞄一眼

ca·su·al [ˋkæʒuəl]
Track 2232

形 偶然的、臨時的

▶It doesn't matter if you wear casual clothes here.
你在這裡穿便服也沒什麼關係。

cat·er·pil·lar [ˋkætɚˏpɪlɚ]
Track 2233

名 毛毛蟲

▶The caterpillar has turned into a butterfly.
那隻毛毛蟲長成了一隻蝴蝶。

cat·tle [ˋkætl̩]
Track 2234

名 小牛

▶It doesn't matter whether the cattle are in the shed or not.
牛在不在圍欄裡都不要緊。

萬用延伸句型
It doesn't matter whether...
無論是否……都沒有關係

cel·e·brate [ˋsɛləˏbret]
Track 2235

動 慶祝、慶賀

▶I heard that you won the first place in the contest（比賽）. Let's go celebrate!
聽說你比賽得了第一名，我們去慶祝吧！

cen·ti·me·ter [ˋsɛntəˏmitɚ]
Track 2236

名 公分、釐米

▶My brother is six centimeters taller than me.
我弟弟比我高六公分。

文法字詞解析
centimeter 是美式的用法，在英式英文中則是拼成 centimetre。

ce·ram·ic [səˋræmɪk]
Track 2237

形 陶瓷的 名 陶瓷品

▶形 It's so kind of you to exhibit（展覽）these ceramic works.
你真是太好了，展出了這些陶瓷作品。

▶名 I'm good at designing ceramics.
我很擅長設計陶瓷品。

chain [tʃen] Track 2238

名 鏈子 動 鏈住

▶名 Why is there a chain on the door? 你的門上為什麼裝鏈子？

▶動 Do you mind if I chain the dog to a post?
你介意我把狗拴在柱子上嗎？

chal·lenge [ˋtʃælɪndʒ] Track 2239

名 挑戰 動 向……挑戰

▶名 I don't think the company is ready to meet the challenges of the latter half of the year.
我覺得公司還沒有準備好迎接下半年的挑戰。

▶動 I don't think he will challenge us anytime soon.
我不覺得他最近會向我們發出挑戰。

實用片語用語
accept the challenge 接受挑戰
例句：You want me to eat this whole pizza? All right, I'll accept the challenge.
你要我吃掉這整個披薩嗎？好啊，我接受挑戰。

cham·pi·on [ˋtʃæmpɪən] Track 2240

名 冠軍 同 victor 勝利者

▶He is the world champion of swimming this year.
他是今年的游泳世界冠軍。

change·a·ble [ˋtʃendʒəbl̩] Track 2241

形 可變的

▶I think these terms are changeable.
我認為這些條件是可變的。

chan·nel [ˋtʃænl̩] Track 2242

名 通道、頻道 動 傳輸

▶名 A good marketing channel is more important than the quality of a product itself.
良好的銷售管道比產品品質本身更重要。

▶動 I don't believe that he will channel the information（消息）to me. 我不相信他會傳遞消息給我。

實用片語用語
channel surfing 漫無目的地隨手轉台
channel 有「頻道」的意思，而如果在看電視時漫不經心地一台一台切換，也沒有很認真在看電視上演什麼，這個動作就叫做「channel surfing」。

chap·ter [ˋtʃæptɚ] Track 2243

名 章、章節

▶It took me two and a half hours to finish one chapter of this novel. 看完這本小說的一章花了我兩個半小時。

charm [tʃɑrm] Track 2244

名 魅力

▶I think she is a woman of great charm.
我覺得她是一個很迷人的女人。

chat [tʃæt] Track 2245

動 聊天、閒談

▶Do you mind if I chat with him for a couple of minutes?
你介意我跟他聊幾分鐘嗎？

實用片語用語
chat room 聊天室
網路聊天室也可以稱作 Internet chat room。不過因為聊天室本來就幾乎都在網路上才存在，通常沒有必要特別說出 Internet 這個字。

cheek [tʃik] Track 2246

名 臉頰

▶He kissed her on the cheek last night.
他昨晚親吻了她的臉頰。

cheer [tʃɪr]
Track 2247

名 歡呼 動 喝采、振奮

▶名 You can hear the cheers of the crowd.
你可以聽到群眾們的歡呼聲。

▶動 People standing on both sides cheered as soon as he crossed the finish line.
他一越過終點線，站在兩邊的人群就歡呼起來。

cheer·ful [`tʃɪrfəl]
Track 2248

形 愉快的、興高采烈的

▶He is a cheerful old man in his nineties.
他是個九十幾歲的樂觀老人。

cheese [tʃiz]
Track 2249

名 乾酪、乳酪

▶Try this cheese! My mom made it herself.
試試看這個乳酪吧！這可是我媽媽親手做的哦。

cher·ry [`tʃɛrɪ]
Track 2250

名 櫻桃、櫻木

▶Who's the one who cut down the cherry tree?
砍櫻桃樹的人是誰？

文法字詞解析
這裡出現了一個連母語人士都常用錯的字：Who's。Who's 是 Who is 的縮寫，它念起來和 whose（誰的）一模一樣，所以常有人把它們兩個搞混。我們來看看例句：
Who's the owner of this cat? = Who is the owner of this cat? 誰是這貓的主人？
Whose cat is this? 這貓是誰的？

chest [tʃɛst]
Track 2251

名 胸、箱子 同 box 箱子

▶It wasn't long before he died from a chest wound.
他不久後就因胸部受傷而過世。

chew [tʃu]
Track 2252

動 咀嚼

▶You must chew your food well so that you can digest（消化）it easier.
你必須把食物嚼碎，這樣你才能很容易就消化它。

child·hood [`tʃaɪld,hʊd]
Track 2253

名 童年、幼年時代

▶Whether happy or sad, childhood memories can follow you throughout your whole life.
不管是喜是悲，童年的記憶可能會跟著你一輩子。

chill [tʃɪl]
Track 2254

動 使變冷、名 寒冷

▶動 It's easy for us to catch a chill in such weather.
我們在這種天氣裡很容易著涼。

▶名 Don't stand outside in the chill.
別站在外面的冷天中。

實用片語用語
1. catch a chill 著涼
2. 美國年輕人說話時，常常會用到「chill out」這個用語，這是什麼意思呢？就是「稍微放下壓力、平靜一下」。另外，在舞曲中，也有一種曲風叫「chill out」，中文就叫做「弛放音樂」。

chill·y [`tʃɪlɪ]
Track 2255

形 寒冷的

▶It's a little bit chilly out here. Did you bring a coat?
外面這裡有點冷，你有帶外套嗎？

chim·ney [ˋtʃɪmnɪ]

Track 2256

名 煙囪

▶The little boy is cleaning the chimney for his family because he's the only one who fits.
那個小男孩在掃他家的煙囪，因為只有他的身材進得去煙囪裡。

chip [tʃɪp]

Track 2257

名 碎片 動 切

▶名 The ground is littered with chips of wood.
地上滿是木屑。

▶動 Put in some water after chipping the potatoes.
把馬鈴薯切成片後往裡面多加點水吧。

實用片語用語

chip in 提供微薄的金額
「chip」有「一小片」、「碎片」的意思，如果每個人都提供「一小片」，聚沙成塔還是蠻可觀的，因此當你為了某事貢獻出「一點點微薄的金額」時，這個動作就可以叫做 chip in。

choke [tʃok]

Track 2258

動 使窒息

▶The old lady choked on some water.
那位老太太被水嗆到了。

chop [tʃɑp]

Track 2259

動 砍、劈

▶We don't have much wood in the house; let's go chop some more.
屋裡柴火不多了，我們再去砍些柴吧。

文法字詞解析

chop 多半用於「砍樹」、「劈柴」、「切菜」等方面，一般不會用在人身上，因為感覺很危險。但空手道中不是也會有「劈」的動作嗎？這個動作就可以稱做 karate chop。

cig·a·rette [ˋsɪgəˏrɛt]

Track 2260

名 香菸 同 smoke 香菸

▶He only smokes the most expensive cigarettes.
他只抽最貴的香菸。

cir·cus [ˋsɝkəs]

Track 2261

名 馬戲團

▶Would you like to go to the circus with me?
你要不要跟我一起去看馬戲表演啊？

civ·il [ˋsɪvḷ]

Track 2262

形 國家的、公民的

▶You can't deprive（剝奪）us of our basic civil rights.
你不能剝奪我們基本的公民權利。

clas·si·cal [ˋklæsɪkḷ]

Track 2263

形 古典的

▶Do you mind if I play some classical music in the office?
你介意我在辦公室放些古典音樂嗎？

click [klɪk]

Track 2264

名 滴答聲

▶I heard not only the click of the lock but also the sound of footsteps（腳步）.
我不但聽見了門鎖的喀嚓聲，而且還聽見了腳步聲。

文法字詞解析

我們在按滑鼠的時候也會發出類似時鐘在走的那種「滴答聲」，因此按滑鼠的這個動作也叫做 click。在這個人手一電腦的時代，這可是個很重要的單字喔！

cli·ent [ˋklaɪənt] Track 2265

名 委託人、客戶 同 customer 客戶

▶Would you like me to introduce some clients to you?
要不要我為你介紹幾個客戶？

clin·ic [ˋklɪnɪk] Track 2266

名 診所

▶By the time he arrived at the clinic, he found that it was closed.
等到了診所，他才發現診所關門了。

clip [klɪp] Track 2267

名 夾子、紙夾

▶Would you fasten these forms with a paper clip?
你能用迴紋針把這些表格夾起來嗎？

實用片語用語
hair clip 髮夾
例如：Her hair clips are scattered all over the floor.
她的髮夾掉得滿地都是。

clue [klu] Track 2268

名 線索

▶We have no clue as to where he has gone.
我們對他的去向毫無線索。

cock·tail [ˋkɑkˏtel] Track 2269

名 雞尾酒

▶Would you like to come to our cocktail party tomorrow?
你願意來參加我們明天的雞尾酒會嗎？

co·co·nut [ˋkokəˏnət] Track 2270

名 椰子

▶I like to drink coconut juice when I feel thirsty.
我口渴的時候喜歡喝椰子汁。

col·lar [ˋkɑlɚ] Track 2271

名 衣領

▶He seized the man by the collar and yelled some words unfit for children's ears.
他抓住那個男人的衣領，嚷嚷一些兒童不宜的字眼。

實用片語用語
white-collar worker 白領階級
例如：Both his parents are white-collar workers.
他父母兩人都是白領階級。
如果white-collar worker是白領階級，那blue-collar worker就是藍領階級了！

col·le·ction [kəˋlɛkʃən] Track 2272

名 聚集、收集 同 analects 選集

▶He has a large collection of CDs of this singer.
他收集了很多這個歌手的唱片。

col·lege [ˋkɑlɪdʒ] Track 2273

名 學院、大學

▶My son is going to college in September.
我的兒子九月份就要上大學了。

col·o·ny [ˋkɑlənɪ] Track 2274

名 殖民地

▶Not every person knows that this nation used to be a British colony. 不是人人都知道這個國家曾是英國的一個殖民地。

col·umn [ˋkɑləm] Track 2275

名 圓柱、專欄、欄

▶There are hundreds of white marble columns in the temple.
神廟裡有上百根白色的大理石柱。

文法字詞解析
是否有時會覺得「行」跟「列」誰是直的、誰是橫的很難分呢？英文的「column」跟「row」就比較不會有這種煩惱。「column」既然有「柱子」的意思，那它當然是直的，剩下的「row」就是橫的了。

---

com·bine [kəmˋbaɪn] Track 2276

動 聯合、結合 同 join 連結

▶He is heavier than all three of us combined.
我們三個人加起來都沒他一個人重。

---

com·fort [ˋkʌmfət] Track 2277

名 舒適 動 安慰

▶名 I prefer a life of safety and comfort.
我比較想要一個充滿安全感與舒適感的人生。

▶動 It's really hard to comfort crying girls. 安慰在哭的女生超難的。

實用片語用語
comfort food 安慰食物
什麼叫做「安慰食物」？其實就是當你心情不好、或覺得一整天工作很累需要被慰藉一番時，拿來自我安慰的食物。有些人的 comfort food 是冰淇淋，有些人的是洋芋片，這就看大家個人的喜好決定了。

---

com·ma [ˋkɑmə] Track 2278

名 逗號

▶You should put a comma here instead of a period.
你應該在這裡放個逗號，而不是句號。

---

com·mand [kəˋmænd] Track 2279

動 命令、指揮 名 命令、指令

▶動 He commanded several troops（軍隊）when he was young. 他年輕的時候指揮了好幾個軍隊。

▶名 We all listened to our boss's comand.
我們都聽從老闆的指令。

---

com·mer·cial [kəˋmɝʃəl] Track 2280

形 商業的 名 商業廣告 同 business 商業

▶形 Would you tell me how I can get to the commercial bank nearby? 你能告訴我如何才能到這附近的商業銀行嗎？

▶名 I've seen this commercial a dozen times and still don't understand it.
我都看這廣告好多次了，還是不懂它要表達什麼。

---

com·mit·tee [kəˋmɪtɪ] Track 2281

名 委員會、會議

▶What do you think of the committee's decision? Do you agree with it? 你是怎麼看待委員會的決定的？你同意這個決定嗎？

萬用延伸句型
What do you think of...? 你對……有什麼想法？

---

com·mu·ni·cate [kəˋmjunəˏket] Track 2282

動 溝通、交流

▶Not all people know how to communicate with their boss and colleagues（同事）.
不是所有人都知道如何與他們的上司和同事溝通。

---

com·par·i·son [kəmˋpærəsn̩] Track 2283

名 對照、比較 同 contrast 對照

▶It is hard for us to make a comparison between the two pieces of china. 我們很難比較這兩件瓷器。

實用片語用語
make a comparison between A and B
比較 A 和 B

com·pete [kəm`pit]
Track 2284

動 競爭

▶This contract is very valuable; it is no wonder that several companies are competing for it. 這份合約非常值錢，難怪好幾家公司正在為這一份合約而競爭。

com·plaint [kəm`plent]
Track 2285

名 抱怨、訴苦

▶Would you tell me how you will handle our customers' complaints?
能告訴我你將如何處理顧客的投訴嗎？

萬用延伸句型
Would you tell me...? 你能告訴我……嗎？

com·plex [`kɑmplɛks]
Track 2286

形 複雜的、合成的 名 複合物、綜合設施

▶形 Don't write too many complex sentences unless it's necessary.
除非必要，否則不要寫太多的複雜句。

▶名 The new building complex can't be built here unless the government approves it.
除非政府同意，要不然這棟大樓是不能建在這裡的。

萬用延伸句型
Unless it is necessary,...
除非必要，否則……

con·cern [kən`sɝn]
Track 2287

動 關心、涉及

▶Don't mess with what doesn't concern you; let's just stand aside.
不要插手與自己無關的事，我們還是置身事外的好。

con·cert [`kɑnsɝt]
Track 2288

名 音樂會、演奏會

▶He'll be giving a concert in our city.
他會在我們的城市開演唱會。

實用片語用語
concert hall 演藝廳、音樂廳
例如：The concert hall was crowded with music-lovers.
音樂廳擠滿了音樂愛好者。

con·clude [kən`klud]
Track 2289

動 締結、結束、得到結論 同 end 結束

▶We have to conclude the meeting before 6 o'clock in the afternoon. 我們必須在下午六點之前結束會議。

con·clu·sion [kən`kluʒən]
Track 2290

名 結論、終了

▶I don't think we can draw any conclusion from the evidence（證據）at hand.
我們從手頭上的這些證據還無法得出任何結論。

實用片語用語
1. at hand 手邊有的
2. draw a conclusion 做結論、得出結論

con·di·tion [kən`dɪʃən]
Track 2291

名 條件、情況 動 以……為條件

▶名 My car is in good condition all the time.
我的車狀況一直很好。

▶動 Jessica just got promoted recently; no wonder that they say ability and effort condition success.
潔西卡最近升官了，怪不得他們會說才幹和努力是成功的條件。

cone [kon]

Track 2292

名 圓錐

▶Do you mind if I buy some ice cream cones with my pocket money, Mom? 媽媽，你介意我用零用錢買幾個冰淇淋甜筒嗎？

文法字詞解析
除了大家常吃的冰淇淋甜筒叫做「cone」以外，還有一種常見的 cone，也就是我們在街上可能會看到的那種橘色的交通用圓錐。它可以稱為 traffic cone。

con·fi·dent [ˋkɑnfədənt]

Track 2293

形 有信心的 同 certain 有把握的

▶He will win this game. I am confident enough about that.
我有信心，他肯定會贏得這場比賽的。

con·fuse [kənˋfjuz]

Track 2294

動 使迷惑

▶He confused the meanings of the two words.
他把這兩個字的意思弄混了。

con·nect [kəˋnɛkt]

Track 2295

動 連接、連結 同 link 連接

▶The bridge connects both sides of the river.
這座橋將河的兩岸連結起來。

con·nec·tion [kəˋnɛkʃən]

Track 2296

名 連接、連結

▶It's difficult for me to figure out the connection between these two things. 指出這兩個事物間的關聯對我而言太難了。

實用片語用語
Internet connection 網路連線
在這年代，這個片語實在是太重要了。此外還有一個很重要的片語叫做 wi-fi connection（無線網路連線）。

con·scious [ˋkɑnʃəs]

Track 2297

形 意識到的 同 aware 意識到的

▶He was not conscious of having made a mistake.
他沒有意識到自己犯了錯誤。

con·sid·er·a·ble [kənˋsɪdərəbḷ]

Track 2298

形 應考慮的、相當多的

▶There is a considerable sum of money in the wallet.
錢包裡有一筆可觀的錢。

con·sid·er·a·tion [kən͵sɪdəˋreʃən]

Track 2299

名 考慮

▶What a good plan! We must give it our fullest consideration.
多好的計畫啊！我們必須認真地考慮一下它。

con·stant [ˋkɑnstənt]

Track 2300

形 不變的、不斷的

▶The phone's constant ringing is very bothersome.
電話不斷地響，非常煩人。

文法字詞解析
bother 作為動詞是「打擾」的意思，因此加上形容詞字尾「-some」就變成了「擾人的、煩人的」的意思。

con·ti·nent [ˋkɑntənənt]

Track 2301

名 大陸、陸地

▶There are seven continents in the world.
世界上有七大洲。

con·tract [ˋkɑntrækt]/[kənˋtrækt]
Track 2302

名 契約、合約 動 訂契約 同 pact 契約

▶名 It doesn't matter whether we make the contract or not.
我們是否簽署合約都不重要了。

▶動 I wonder if he will contract an agreement with them.
真好奇他會不會跟他們締結協議。

couch [kaʊtʃ]
Track 2303

名 長沙發、睡椅

▶He just got off work and headed straight to the couch to take a nap.
他才剛下班，馬上就走去長沙發上小睡了。

實用片語用語

couch potato 賴在沙發上看電視的人

例如：I cannot become a couch potato as there is no couch in my apartment.

我沒辦法賴在沙發上，因為套房裡沒有沙發。

count·a·ble [kaʊntəbḷ]
Track 2304

形 可數的

▶Will you tell me what the function of this countable noun（名詞）in this sentence is?
你能告訴我在這個句子中的這個可數名詞作用是什麼嗎？

cow·ard [ˋkaʊəd]
Track 2305

名 懦夫、膽子小的人

▶I don't think he is a coward, though others laugh at him.
儘管別人都嘲笑他，但是我認為他不是一個懦夫。

cra·dle [ˋkredḷ]
Track 2306

名 搖籃 動 放在搖籃裡

▶名 We've known each other from the cradle.
我們從還躺在搖籃裡時就相互認識了。

▶動 I don't think you need to cradle the baby in your arms all day.
我認為你不用整天都把嬰兒抱在懷裡搖晃著。

crash [kræʃ]
Track 2307

名 撞擊 動 摔下、撞毀

▶名 When he heard the news about the plane crash, he couldn't help bursting into tears.
聽到空難消息的時候，他忍不住放聲哭了起來。

▶動 She knocked into a customer and the dishes crashed to the floor.
她撞到一名顧客，盤子都摔到地板上了。

實用片語用語

car crash 車禍、撞車

例如：The reporter headed to the place where the car crash happened to take photos.

記者前往車禍發生的地點照相。

crawl [krɔl]
Track 2308

動 爬

▶You have to crawl before you can walk.
人要學走，先得學爬。

cre·a·tive [krɪˋetɪv]
Track 2309

形 有創造力的 同 imaginative 有創造力的

▶How beautiful this picture it is! The painter is creative indeed.
多美的一幅畫啊！這位畫家確實很有創造力。

cre·a·tor [krɪˋetɚ] Track 2310

名 創造者、創作家

▶Who's the creator of this brilliant music piece?
這首極好的樂曲的創造者是誰？

crea·ture [ˋkritʃɚ] Track 2311

名 生物、動物

▶This creature lives in the depths of the sea.
這種生物生活在海洋深處。

cred·it [ˋkrɛdɪt] Track 2312

名 信用、信託 動 相信、信賴 同 faith 信任

▶名 Can I use a credit card here?
這裡可以用信用卡嗎？

▶動 They credited her for this new invention.
他們把此新發明歸功於她。

實用片語用語

1. credit card 信用卡
2. credit sb. for sth. 將某事物的功勞歸於某人

creep [krip] Track 2313

動 爬、戰慄

▶The tortoise（烏龜）is creeping along quite slowly.
那隻烏龜爬得很慢。

crew [kru] Track 2314

名 夥伴們、全體船員

▶The crew on this ship is mostly from Malaysia（馬來西亞）.
這艘船上的船員幾乎都是馬來西亞來的。

crick·et [ˋkrɪkɪt] Track 2315

名 蟋蟀

▶We can only find this kind of cricket in North America.
我們只能在北美洲找到這種蟋蟀。

crim·i·nal [ˋkrɪmənl̩] Track 2316

形 犯罪的 名 罪犯

▶形 Robbery is a criminal act and should be condemned.
搶劫是犯罪行為，應該要譴責。

▶名 The police should catch the criminal as soon as possible.
警察應該儘快抓到罪犯。

實用片語用語

as soon as possible 盡快
一個很常見的片語，也常縮寫成 A.S.A.P.。此外，soon 可以換入其他的形容詞或副詞，表達「越……越好」的意思，例如「as slowly as possible」（越慢越好）、「as big as possible」（越大越好）等等。

crisp/crisp·y [krɪsp]/[ˋkrɪspɪ] Track 2317

形 脆的、清楚的

▶There are some crisp apples on the table; would you like one? 桌上有些脆蘋果，你要不要來一個？

crown [kraʊn] Track 2318

名 王冠 動 加冕、報酬 同 reward 酬報

▶名 The little girl wears the fake crown proudly.
那個小女孩很驕傲地戴著假皇冠。

▶動 The king crowned his son in 1456.
國王在 1456 年為他的兒子加冕。

crun·chy [ˋkrʌntʃɪ] Track 2319

名 鬆脆的、易裂的

▶How about buying some crunchy fresh vegetables today?
今天去買點又脆又新鮮的蔬菜怎麼樣？

萬用延伸句型
How about...? ……如何？

crutch [krʌtʃ] Track 2320

名 支架、拐杖

▶I don't think he is so badly hurt that he needs a pair of crutches.
我認為他沒有傷得嚴重到需要用拐杖的地步。

cul·tu·ral [ˋkʌltʃərəl] Track 2321

形 文化的

▶It's no wonder that this city has become the cultural center of this country.
難怪這個城市會成為這個國家的文化中心。

萬用延伸句型
It's no wonder that... 難怪……

cup·board [ˋkʌbəd] Track 2322

名 食櫥、餐具櫥

▶Do you need some sugar? I will get some from the cupboard for you.
你要一點些糖嗎？我幫你到櫥櫃裡去拿一些來。

cur·rent [ˋkɝənt] Track 2323

形 流通的、目前的 名 電流、水流 同 present 目前的

▶形 She's our current advisor so you should go talk to her.
她是我們目前的諮詢人，所以你應該去跟她談。

▶名 The current is quite strong in this river, so you need to be careful.
這條河的水流很強，所以你要小心點。

cy·cle [ˋsaɪkl] Track 2324

名 週期、循環 動 循環、騎腳踏車

▶名 That can be a dangerous cycle unless someone can prevent it.
除非有人能阻止，否則這有可能成為一個惡性循環。

▶動 My dad cycles to work every day.
我爸爸每天騎腳踏車去上班。

dair·y [ˋdɛrɪ] Track 2325

名 酪農場 形 酪農的

▶名 Would you like to work in a dairy?
你覺得在一個酪農場工作怎麼樣？

▶形 That place is known for its dairy produce.
那個地方因生產乳品而出名。

文法字詞解析
dairy 這個單字和 diary（日記）長得很像，非常容易搞混。diary 唸起來多一個音節，要注意其中的差別喔！

dam [dæm]

Track 2326

名 水壩 動 堵住、阻塞

▶名 The Egyptians（埃及人）built the Aswan Dam a long time ago.
埃及人在很早以前就建造了阿斯旺大壩。

▶動 The man tried to dam his sadness in front of others.
那名男子試著在別人面前制住自己的悲傷。

dare [dɛr]

Track 2327

動 敢、挑戰 同 brave 勇敢的面對

▶Don't you dare touch me again! I will call the police at once!
你敢再碰我，我會立刻報警！

實用片語用語
at once 立刻

darl·ing [`dɑrlɪŋ]

Track 2328

名 親愛的人 形 可愛的 同 lovely 可愛的

▶名 Good morning, darling! What a beautiful day today!
早安，親愛的！今天天氣多好啊！

▶形 We should hold a party for our darling son.
我們應該幫親愛的兒子開一個派對。

dash [dæʃ]

Track 2329

動 碰撞、投擲

▶Congratulations on winning first place in the 100-meter dash!
恭喜你獲得百米賽跑第一名！

deaf·en [`dɛfən]

Track 2330

動 使耳聾

▶The loud explosion almost deafened her.
那個巨大的爆炸聲幾乎把她弄聾了。

文法字詞解析
動詞字尾「-en」具有「讓……有某種特質」的意思，因此這個單字 deaf 是「耳聾的」，加了字尾 -en 中就變成了「讓……耳聾」。

deal·er [`dilɚ]

Track 2331

名 商人 同 merchant 商人

▶Would you be kind enough to tell me where the nearest motorcycle dealer is?
可以請您告訴我離這最近的摩托車商在哪裡嗎？

文法字詞解析
在玩撲克牌的時候，「發牌」的動作可以稱為 deal。因此，發牌的人也可以稱為 dealer。

dec·ade [`dɛked]

Track 2332

名 十年、十個一組

▶It's the first time I've been back to my college since a decade ago. 這是十年來我第一次回到我的母校。

deck [dɛk]

Track 2333

名 甲板

▶There are some passengers sitting on the deck chatting.
有些旅客正坐在甲板上聊天。

文法字詞解析
說起來，deck 這個字也和撲克牌有關，我們平常玩的「一疊」牌組，也可以稱為 a deck of cards。不只撲克牌，其他的紙牌也適用。

deed [did]

Track 2334

名 行為、行動

▶Her good deeds went unnoticed.
她的善行從來沒有人發現。

de·ep·en [ˋdipən]   Track 2335

動 加深、變深

▶We need to deepen our understanding of the subject before we can make a decision.
我們在下決定前，需要先加深對這個主題的瞭解。

de·fine [dɪˋfaɪn]   Track 2336

動 下定義

▶Would you like to tell me how you define "courage"?
你能告訴我你是如何定義什麼叫勇氣的嗎？

def·i·ni·tion [ˏdɛfəˋnɪʃən]   Track 2337

名 定義

▶It's difficult for me to give a definition of happiness（幸福）.
對我來說為幸福下個定義很難。

實用片語用語
give a definition of sth. 替……下定義

萬用延伸句型
It's difficult for sb. to... 要某人（做某事）很難

de·liv·er·y [dɪˋlɪvərɪ]   Track 2338

名 傳送、傳遞 同 distribution 分配、分發

▶Would you please tell me when you will make a delivery?
能請您告訴我你們什麼時候可以送貨嗎？

de·moc·ra·cy [dəˋmɑkrəsɪ]   Track 2339

名 民主制度

▶It is no wonder that Athens is said to be the cradle of democracy.
難怪雅典被認為是民主的搖籃。

實用片語用語
the cradle of sth. 某事物的搖籃

de·moc·ra·tic [ˏdɛməˋkrætɪk]   Track 2340

形 民主的

▶The laws really reflect the democratic spirit of the country.
這些法律確實反映了這個國家的民主精神。

de·pos·it [dɪˋpɑzɪt]   Track 2341

名 押金、存款 動 存入、放入

▶名 I don't think I need a deposit account.
我覺得我不需要開個定期存款帳戶。

▶動 You'll have to deposit your bags at the counter（櫃檯）.
你必須把皮包寄放在櫃檯。

de·scrip·tion [dɪˋskrɪpʃən]   Track 2342

名 敘述、說明 同 portrait 描寫

▶It's hard for me to give a description of her beauty in words.
她的美我難以用語言來形容。

de·sign·er [dɪˋzaɪnɚ]   Track 2343

名 設計師

▶My dream was to be an interior（內部的）designer when I was young.
我小時候的夢想是做一名室內設計師。

實用片語用語
designer bag 名牌包包
除此之外，還有 designer clothes（名牌服裝）、designer brand（名牌）、designer shoes（名牌鞋子）等等片語。

de·sir·a·ble [dɪˋzaɪrəbḷ]

Track 2344

形 值得的、稱心如意的

▶She is searching high and low for a desirable job.
她正在到處找一份好工作。

de·stroy [dɪˋstrɔɪ]

Track 2345

動 損毀、毀壞 反 create 創造

▶Did you destroy the papers like I told you to?
你有聽我的話，把那些文件銷毀嗎？

de·tail [ˋditel]

Track 2346

名 細節、條款

▶Would you tell me what happened in detail?
您能詳細地告訴我發生了什麼事嗎？

實用片語用語
in detail 詳細地

de·ter·mine [dɪˋtɝmɪn]

Track 2347

動 決定 同 decide 決定

▶The exam results could determine your future.
考試成績可能會決定你的前途。

dev·il [ˋdɛvḷ]

Track 2348

名 魔鬼、惡魔

▶Her husband is such a handsome devil.
她老公真是個帥氣的壞傢伙。

di·a·logue [ˋdaɪəlɔg]

Track 2349

名 對話 同 conversation 對話

▶Not every writer is very good at writing dialogues.
不是每個作家都非常擅長寫對白。

diet [ˋdaɪət]

Track 2350

名 飲食 動 節食

▶名 A healthy diet creates a body resistant（有抵抗力的）to disease.
保健飲食有助於增強體內對疾病的抵抗力。

▶動 Susan is dieting to lose weight, isn't she?
蘇珊正在節食減肥，不是嗎？

實用片語用語
be on a diet 正在節食
例如：Don't offer cookies to Joanna. She's on a diet.
別拿餅乾給喬安娜吃，她正在節食。

dil·i·gent [ˋdɪlədʒənt]

Track 2351

形 勤勉的、勤奮的

▶The little girl is not only clever but also diligent.
那個小女孩不但聰明而且還很勤奮。

dim [dɪm]

Track 2352

形 微暗的 動 變模糊

▶形 The light in the room is too dim for me to read.
這個房間裡的光線太暗了，我沒辦法看書。

▶動 The light dimmed and the movie started.
光線變黯淡了，電影開始了。

實用片語用語
dim the lights 把燈調暗
例 如：Please dim the lights and turn on the projector.
請把燈光調暗、打開投影機。

dime [daɪm]

Track 2353

名 一角的硬幣

▶Can you give me a dime for two nickels（五分硬幣）?
你能不能用兩個五分硬幣換一個一角的硬幣給我？

dine [daɪn]

Track 2354

動 款待、用膳

▶How about dining with us tonight? I'll pay.
今晚和我們一起吃飯怎麼樣？我請客。

dip [dɪp]

Track 2355

動 浸、沾 名 浸泡、(價格)下跌

▶動 He dipped his injured finger in the disinfectant（消毒劑）?
他把受傷的手指浸在消毒劑裡。

▶名 I heard that the price of grain has taken a dip.
我聽說穀物價格下跌了。

dirt [dɝt]

Track 2356

名 泥土、塵埃

▶The dog enjoys digging around in the dirt.
那隻狗喜歡在泥土裡亂挖。

實用片語用語
dirt poor 非常窮
例如：Don't ask him to lend you money. He's already dirt poor.
別叫他借你錢，他都已經那麼窮了。

dis·ap·point [͵dɪsə`pɔɪnt]

Track 2357

動 使失望

▶He doesn't like disappointing his friends.
他不喜歡讓朋友失望。

dis·ap·point·ment [͵dɪsə`pɔɪntmənt]

Track 2358

名 令人失望的舉止

▶The singer won't be performing? What a disappointment!
那個歌手不會來表演嗎？真是令人失望！

disco/dis·co·theque [`dɪsko]/[͵dɪskə`tɛk]

Track 2359

名 迪斯可、酒吧、小舞廳

▶Why don't you come to the disco with me tonight?
你晚上何不和我一起去迪斯可？

萬用延伸句型
Why don't you...? 你何不……？

dis·count [`dɪskaʊnt]

Track 2360

名 折扣 動 減價

▶名 These dresses are on discount right now.
這些洋裝正在打折。

▶動 That store is discounting all its slow-selling goods.
那家商店正在削價出售所有滯銷貨。

文法字詞解析
slow-selling goods 是「賣不好的商品、滯銷品」，那「供不應求的商品」又是什麼呢？就是「hot commodity」囉！而如果要說某個東西賣得很好、炙手可熱，就可以說「sth. sells like hotcakes」。

dis·cov·er·y [dɪ`skʌvərɪ]

Track 2361

名 發現

▶It is no wonder that the discovery caused a big sensation（轟動）in the scientific world.
毫無意外地，那項發現在科學界引起了巨大轟動。

實用片語用語
cause a sensation 造成轟動

dis·ease [dɪˋziz]

Track 2362

名 疾病、病症

▶The disease he has is very rare.
他得的那種疾病非常罕見。

disk/disc [dɪsk]

Track 2363

名 唱片、碟片、圓盤狀的東西

▶Would you please help me save the data on a disc?
請您幫我把那些資料儲存到磁片上好嗎？

dis·like [dɪsˋlaɪk]

Track 2364

動 討厭、不喜歡 名 反感

▶動 I dislike getting up early in the morning.
我不喜歡早上早起，你呢？

▶名 I took an instant dislike to him.
我一見他就不喜歡。

實用片語用語
take an instant dislike to sb. 對某人立刻產生反感

ditch [dɪtʃ]

Track 2365

名 排水溝、水道 動 挖溝、拋棄

同 trench 溝、溝渠

▶名 He nodded off when driving and ended up driving into the ditch.
他邊開車邊打盹，結果把車開進排水溝了。

▶動 She ditched her boyfriend to hang out with her friends.
她丟下她的男朋友，和朋友們出去玩了。

實用片語用語
nod off 睡著、打盹

dive [daɪv]

Track 2366

動 跳水 名 垂直降落

▶動 He dove into the water and disappeared from sight.
他跳進水裡，從視線中消失了。

▶名 What a beautiful dive! Don't you think so?
多麼優美的跳水！你不覺得嗎？

實用片語用語
dive into 跳進……
這個片語除了可以形容實質上的「跳進（水裡）」之外，也可以形容某人一頭栽進一件事物中、不可自拔。

dock [dɑk]

Track 2367

名 船塢、碼頭 動 裁減、停泊 同 anchor 停泊

▶名 Would you please give me a lift? I'm afraid my car is still in dock.
請讓我搭個便車好嗎？我的汽車還在修理中。

▶動 Would you please not dock my wages? I swear this will never happen again.
請您不要扣我的工資好嗎？我發誓這件事再也不會發生了。

dodge [dɑdʒ]

Track 2368

動 閃開、躲開 同 avoid 躲開

▶She is fast enough to dodge the attack.
她的速度夠快，能夠避開別人的攻擊。

文法字詞解析
大家小時候玩的「躲避球」，英文就叫做「dodgeball」。

do·mes·tic [dəˋmɛstɪk]

Track 2369

形 國內的、家務的

▶The meeting concerns both foreign and domestic policies.
這會議關係到國內外的政策。

dose [dos]

Track 2370

名 一劑（藥）、藥量 動 服藥

▶名 How often should I take a dose of this medicine?
這個藥我多久要吃一劑？

▶動 It's time to dose up the children with cough syrup（糖漿）.
該給孩子們喝止咳糖漿了。

實用片語用語
a dose of 一劑
就像我們中文說「打一劑強心針」並不是真的要打針一樣，「a dose of」這個片語不但可以用來表示一劑「藥物」，也可以拿來比喻一些和藥物無關的事情，例如「a dose of happiness」。畢竟「快樂」有時候也像是藥一般有效啊。

doubt·ful [`daʊtfəl]

Track 2371

形 有疑問的、可疑的

▶I'm doubtful that he's really going to come to the meeting.
我懷疑他不會真的來開會。

drain [dren]

Track 2372

動 排出、流出、喝乾 名 排水管 同 dry 乾

▶動 Can you pull out the plug（塞子）and drain the bathtub?
你把塞子拔出來，讓浴缸的水排乾好不好？

▶名 It is no wonder that the drains overflowed（溢出）after the heavy rain.
雨下得很大，難怪下水道會溢出水來。

dra·mat·ic [drə`mætɪk]

Track 2373

形 戲劇性的 同 theatrical 戲劇性的

▶She always speaks in such a dramatic way.
她講話總是很戲劇性的樣子。

文法字詞解析
dramatic 這個單字還有個伙伴「melodramatic」。雖然兩個都是「戲劇化的」的意思，但 melodramatic 帶有貶意，暗示「太過誇張地戲劇化」、「不需要很戲劇化的事還搞得很戲劇化」。

drip [drɪp]

Track 2374

動 滴下 名 滴、水滴 同 drop 水滴

▶動 Why is the ceiling dripping? Should we call a plumber?
天花板怎麼在滴水？我們應該叫水管工人來嗎？

▶名 There is an increasing switch to drip irrigation（灌溉）in all areas.
所有地區轉換成滴灌的趨勢正在增加。

drown [draʊn]

Track 2375

動 淹沒、淹死

▶The boy drowned in the river behind his school.
那個男孩在他學校後面的河裡淹死了。

實用片語用語
drown one's sorrows（利用飲品）澆熄憂愁
雖然說用任何液體都可以達到 drown（淹沒）的效果，但通常這個片語都是用酒，表示借酒澆愁的意思。

drowsy [`draʊzɪ]

Track 2376

形 沉寂的、懶洋洋的、睏的 同 sleepy 睏的

▶I felt drowsy in my philosophy（哲學）and math classes.
哲學課和數學課讓我感到昏昏欲睡。

drunk [drʌŋk]

Track 2377

形 酒醉的、著迷的 名 醉漢

▶形 My dad likes drinking, and he often gets drunk.
我爸爸喜歡喝酒，而且他還經常喝醉。

▶名 The drunk got hurt because he bumped into a pole yesterday.
那個醉漢受傷了，因為昨天他撞到柱子了。

文法字詞解析
除了 drunk 以外還有一個類似的形容詞 drunken，它們有什麼差別呢？原來，drunk 純粹是指喝醉的狀態，喝醉一次不代表就會一直喝醉。而 drunken 則指長期酗酒的、經常喝醉的。

due [dju]

Track 2378

形 預定的 名 應付款、應得的東西

▶形 When is the flight due?
航班是預定在什麼時候？

▶名 She asked no more than her due. 她並沒有提出非分的要求。

dump [dʌmp]

Track 2379

動 拋下 名 垃圾場

▶動 You shouldn't dump your stuff in front of other people's house. 你不該在人家家門口亂倒東西啊。

▶名 There is a very big dump out of the town.
鎮外有個很大的垃圾場。

實用片語用語

down in the dumps 心情極差

中文常說「心情差到谷底」，而這個片語表示「心情差到垃圾場」。既然都到垃圾場去了，可以想像心情肯定是很糟的。

例如：He had been down in the dumps since he broke up with his ex.
他自從分手後就悶悶不樂的。

dust [dʌst]

Track 2380

名 灰塵、灰 動 打掃、拂去灰塵 同 dirt 灰塵

▶名 The bookshelves are coated in dust. 書架上積了一層灰塵。

▶動 Why don't you dust the room every day?
你為什麼不每天都打掃房間呢？

Ee

ea·ger [ˋigɚ]

Track 2381

形 渴望的

▶She is eager to have you meet her friends.
她很渴望你見見她的朋友。

earn·ings [ˋɝnɪŋz]

Track 2382

名 收入 同 salary 薪水

▶It's impolite（不禮貌的）of you to ask people about their earnings. 詢問別人他們的收入情況是不禮貌的。

萬用延伸句型

It's impolite of you to...（+原形動詞）你（做某事）很不禮貌

ech·o [ˋɛko]

Track 2383

名 回音 動 發出回聲

▶名 The room is so large you can hear echoes in it.
這房間大到你在裡面可以聽到回聲。

▶動 His cries echoed through the tunnel.
他的大叫聲在山洞中迴盪。

ed·it [ˋɛdɪt]

Track 2384

動 編輯、發行

▶He had to edit the book before it can be published（出版）.
在這本書能出版前，他得先編輯一下。

e·di·tion [ə`dɪʃən]

Track 2385

名 版本

▶Would you like to buy a pocket edition so that you can take it with you everywhere（到處）?
你要不要買本袖珍版的？那樣你就可以到處帶著它了。

實用片語用語

pocket edition 袖珍版

pocket 是「口袋」的意思，既然是可以放進口袋的版本，也難怪可以用來表示「袖珍版」了。

ed·i·tor [ˋɛdɪtɚ] Track 2386

名 編輯者

▶Will you have a talk with our chief editor in the office?
你能到辦公室去跟我們的總編輯談談嗎？

ed·u·cate [ˋɛdʒə͵ket] Track 2387

動 教育 同 teach 教導

▶He paid a lot of money to have his son educated.
他花了很多錢在他兒子的教育上。

文法字詞解析
have sb. Vp.p. 讓某人（接受）……
這裡用到了使役動詞的被動用法，表示受詞並不是主動去做某事，而是被動的接受某事。

ed·u·ca·tion·al [͵ɛdʒəˋkeʃənḷ] Track 2388

形 教育性的

▶What do you think of the recent educational policy? Does it really work?
你怎麼看待最近的教育政策？它真的有效嗎？

ef·fi·cient [ɪˋfɪʃənt] Track 2389

形 有效率的

▶Isn't she an efficient secretary? I don't think anyone can deny that.
難道她不是一個很有能力的秘書嗎？我想沒人可以否認這一點吧。

el·bow [ˋɛl͵bo] Track 2390

名 手肘

▶Not many people can lick their own elbow.
沒有很多人舔得到自己的手肘。

萬用延伸句型
Not many people can... 很少人可以……

eld·er·ly [ˋɛldɚlɪ] Track 2391

形 上了年紀的 同 old 老的

▶When the elderly get on the bus, the young are expected to give them their seats.
老人上車來的時候，年輕人被認為應該讓座給他們。

election [ɪˋlɛkʃən] Track 2392

名 選舉

▶I don't think he will take part in the election this year.
我覺得他今年不會參加競選。

實用片語用語
take part in 參與

e·lec·tric/e·lec·tri·cal Track 2393

[ɪˋlɛktrɪk]/[ɪˋlɛktrɪkḷ]

形 電的

▶Would you help me turn off the electric power?
能幫我把電源關掉嗎？

e·lec·tric·i·ty [͵ɪlɛkˋtrɪsətɪ] Track 2394

名 電

▶The electricity bill is surprisingly large this month.
這個月的電費驚人地多。

e·lec·tron·ic [ɪ,lɛk`trɑnɪk] Track 2395

形 電子的

▶Nothing will change unless you buy some new electronic instruments.
除非你購買一些新的電子儀器，不然什麼也不會改變。

e·mer·gen·cy [ɪ`mɝdʒənsɪ] Track 2396

名 緊急情況 同 crisis 危機

▶I always look for the emergency exit first when I enter a building. 我每次進入一棟大樓就先找緊急出口。

實用片語用語
emergency exit 緊急出口
此外，還有 emergency stairs（緊急用樓梯）、emergency lad-der（緊急用梯子）、emergency button（緊急按鈕）等片語。

em·per·or [`ɛmpərɚ] Track 2397

名 皇帝 同 sovereign 君主、元首

▶This emperor is considered stupid by most historians.
大部分的歷史學家都認為這個皇帝很蠢。

em·pha·size [`ɛmfə,saɪz] Track 2398

動 強調 同 stress 強調

▶Please emphasize this matter and its importance so that they know what to do next.
請強調一下這件事及其重要性，好讓他們知道下一步該做什麼。

em·ploy [ɪm`plɔɪ] Track 2399

動 從事、雇用 同 hire 雇用

▶They decided to employ the woman after careful consideration.
仔細考慮後，他們決定雇用這名女性。

實用片語用語
decide to（+ 原形動詞）決定（做某事）

em·ploy·ment [ɪm`plɔɪmənt] Track 2400

名 職業

▶He has been out of employment for two years.
他已經失業兩年了。

em·ploy·ee [,ɛmplɔɪ`i] Track 2401

名 從業人員、職員 同 worker 工作人員

▶The loyal（忠實的）employees hang on to their boss's every word. 那些忠誠的員工專注地聽老闆講話。

em·ploy·er [ɪm`plɔɪɚ] Track 2402

名 老闆、雇主 同 boss 老闆

▶What do you think of our new employer? Do you think he is kind enough?
你覺得我們的新老闆怎麼樣？你覺得他是否夠親切呢？

文法字詞解析
從以上幾個單字可以看出字尾的妙用喔！字尾「-er」有「……者」之意，而字尾「-ee」則是「被……者」之意。employ（雇用）加上字尾「-ee」就是「被雇用者」，也就是員工；而加上字尾「-er」就是「雇用者」，也就是老闆。

emp·ty [`ɛmptɪ] Track 2403

形 空的 動 倒空 同 vacant 空的

▶形 Would you find me an empty glass?
能給我找一個空杯子嗎？

▶動 I emptied the box and threw it away.
我把箱子倒空，然後拿去丟。

en·a·ble [ɪn`ebl̩] Track 2404

動 使能夠

▶Computers enable people in different countries to know more about each other.
電腦能使不同國家的人更加瞭解彼此。

實用片語用語
enable sb. to... 讓某人能……

en·er·ge·tic [͵ɛnɚ`dʒɛtɪk] Track 2405

形 有精力的 同 vigrous 精力旺盛的

▶Exercise makes you feel more energetic.
運動會讓你感覺更精力充沛。

en·gage [ɪn`gedʒ] Track 2406

動 僱用、允諾、訂婚

▶My sister is engaged with her boyfriend of ten years.
姊姊和她交往十年的男友訂婚了。

en·gage·ment [ɪn`gedʒmənt] Track 2407

名 預約、訂婚

▶Her engagement ring was not as expensive as her wedding ring.
她的訂婚戒指沒有結婚戒指那麼貴。

en·gine [`ɛndʒən] Track 2408

名 引擎

▶How about getting a new engine for your car? It will run faster.
給你的車換個新的引擎如何？它會跑得更快的。

en·gi·neer [͵ɛndʒə`nɪr] Track 2409

名 工程師

▶I want to be a civil engineer in the future; what about you?
我將來想成為一名土木工程師，你呢？

實用片語用語
civil engineer 土木工程師
前面學過，civil 有「國家的、公民的」的意思，那 civil engineer 又是什麼呢？字面上來說是「替國家實施工程」的人，換句話講就是規劃、營造國家土地的「土木工程師」了。而「土木工程」就是「civil engineering」。

en·joy·a·ble [ɪn`dʒɔɪəbl̩] Track 2410

形 愉快的

同 delighyful 愉快的

▶I think the movie last night was very enjoyable.
我覺得昨晚的電影很有趣。

en·try [`ɛntrɪ] Track 2411

名 入口

▶He was denied（拒絕）entry because he didn't have a ticket.
他因為沒有票，不被允許進入。

en·vi·ron·men·tal [ɪn`vaɪrənmənt!] Track 2412

形 環境的

▶People should pay attention to not only environmental protection but also to animal protection.
人們應該同時關注環境保護和動物保護這兩個方面。

實用片語用語
pay attention to N. / V-ing 注意

en·vy [ˋɛnvɪ]
Track 2413

名 羨慕、嫉妒 動 對……羨慕

▶名 It wasn't long before he admitted that he did this entirely（完全地）out of envy.
不久他就承認他做那件事純粹是出於嫉妒。

▶動 I really envy her for getting to go abroad all the time.
她可以常常出國，我好羨慕啊。

e·rase [ɪˋres]
Track 2414

動 擦掉

▶It is hard for him to erase that painful experience from his mind.
要忘掉那段痛苦的經歷對他來說很難。

es·cape [əˋskep]
Track 2415

動 逃走 名 逃脫 同 flee 逃走

▶動 He had successfully（成功地）escaped from the prison.
他越獄成功了。

▶名 We planned our escape ten days beforehand.
我們十天前就計畫了如何逃脫。

e·vil [ˋivḷ]
Track 2416

形 邪惡的 名 邪惡

▶形 The evil man kills his wives and hides them in a room.
那名邪惡的男人殺掉自己的妻子們，把屍體藏在房間裡。

▶名 Some say that the love of money is the root of all evil.
有人說貪財是萬惡之源。

實用片語用語

be the root of... 是……的根源

root 即是植物的「根」。evil（邪惡）雖然不是一種植物，但句中還是可以用這個片語來表達「錢是一切邪惡的『根源』」的意思。

ex·cel·lence [ˋɛksḷəns]
Track 2417

名 優點、傑出

▶There is no shortcut（捷徑）to excellence.
成功沒有捷徑。

ex·change [ɪksˋtʃendʒ]
Track 2418

名 交換 動 兌換

▶名 The book exchange our department held was a success.
我們系上辦的書籍交換會很成功。

▶動 Can we exchange money in this bank?
可以在這家銀行換錢嗎？

實用片語用語

exchange a glance 交換眼神

例如：I exchanged a glance with John that says “what is she even talking about?”
我與約翰交換了一個「她到底在講什麼啊」的眼神。

ex·hi·bi·tion [ˌɛksəˋbɪʃən]
Track 2419

名 展覽

▶They went to the photo exhibition this afternoon.
他們今天下午去了攝影展。

ex·is·tence [ɪgˋzɪstəns]
Track 2420

名 存在

▶Not all people believe in the existence of ghosts.
不是所有人都相信有鬼存在。

ex·it [ˋɛgzɪt]
Track 2421

名 出口 動 離開 反 entrance 入口

▶名 Will you tell me where the exit is? I can't find it.
你能告訴我出口在哪嗎？我找不到。

▶動 He exited the room in a hurry after picking up the call.
接了那通電話後，他匆匆離開了房間。

ex·pec·ta·tion [ˏɛkspɛkˋteʃən]
Track 2422

名 期望

▶His son exceeded（超越）everyone's expectations by getting into a good school.
他的兒子超越了每個人的期望，進入了一所好學校。

實用片語用語
exceed expectations 超越期望

ex·pense [ɪkˋspɛns]
Track 2423

名 費用 同 payment 付款

▶I'll get back to you after I add up this month's expenses.
我把這個月的費用加一加再回覆你。

ex·per·i·ment [ɪkˋspɛrəmənt]
Track 2424

名 / 動 實驗

▶名 What do you think of this experiment with the foreign experts? 你覺得和外國專家進行的這次實驗如何？

▶動 They plan to experiment on animals.
他們打算在動物身上做實驗。

ex·plode [ɪkˋsplod]
Track 2425

動 爆炸、推翻

▶We have to find the bomb before it explodes.
我們得在炸彈爆炸前找到它。

ex·port [ˋɛksport]
Track 2426

動 輸出 名 出口貨、輸出

▶動 Our company exports a variety of products.
我們公司出口各種商品。

▶名 The country's exports are mostly agriculture products.
那個國家的出口貨大部分是農產品。

文法字詞解析
相反地，「進口」則是「import」。export 與 import 不只可以用在商務的進出口上，也可以拿來表示數位檔案的匯入、匯出等功能。

ex·pres·sion [ɪkˋsprɛʃən]
Track 2427

名 表達

▶The picture was beautiful beyond expression.
這張圖美得無法形容。

ex·pres·sive [ɪkˋsprɛsɪv]
Track 2428

形 表達的

▶I like expressive pieces of music. 我喜歡很有表現力的樂曲。

ex·treme [ɪkˋstrim]
Track 2429

形 極度的 名 極端的事

▶形 Her views on marriage are quite extreme.
她對結婚的觀點蠻極端的。

▶名 I don't think it's the time to resort to（依靠、求助於）extremes yet. 我覺得現在還沒必要一定要用極端的方式來解決。

文法字詞解析
extreme 加上「-ly」後就變成副詞「extremely」（非常）。如果厭倦了在對話中不斷地使用「very」，不妨換成「extremely」試試看吧！更能夠以誇張的方式表達強調之意喔。

fa·ble [ˋfebḷ]

Track 2430

名 寓言 同 legend 傳說

▶I heard that fable when I was little. 我小時候就聽過那個寓言了。

fac·tor [ˋfæktɚ]

Track 2431

名 因素、要素 同 cause 原因

▶We need to consider several factors before proceeding.
我們在繼續前，必須先考慮幾個因素。

fade [fed]

Track 2432

動 凋謝、變淡

▶The jacket faded after the wash.
那件夾克在洗過後顏色就變淡了。

實用片語用語

fade out 淡出

在聽音樂時，有時歌曲的最後沒有一個明確的結尾，而是一點點一點點慢慢變小聲，最後消失。這就可以用 fade out 這個片語來描述。

faint [fent]

Track 2433

名 昏厥 形 暗淡的

▶名 He went into a faint after hearing the news.
他聽到了那個消息後就昏過去了。

▶形 Our chances of victory are very faint now.
現在我們獲勝的機會已經微乎其微了。

fair·ly [ˋfɛrlɪ]

Track 2434

副 相當地、公平地

▶It's a fairly good book. You really should read it.
這是一本相當不錯的書，你真的應該讀一讀。

fair·y [ˋfɛrɪ]

Track 2435

名 仙子 形 神仙的

▶名 When I was little, I wanted to be a fairy. 我小時候想當仙女。

▶形 Her fairy godmother（教母）appeared as soon as she started crying. 她一哭起來，仙女教母就出現了。

faith [feθ]

Track 2436

名 信任 同 trust 信任

▶Have faith, he's stronger than you think.
有信心點吧，他比你想的更堅強。

實用片語用語

have faith in sb. 相信某人

此處的「相信」，並非指「相信某人沒說謊、沒騙人」的那種「相信」，而是「相信某人的能力一定做得到」的那種相信，也就是「對某人有信心」的意思。

fake [fek]

Track 2437

形 冒充的 動 仿造

▶形 He sold fake paintings to earn money. 他賣假畫來賺錢。

▶動 He faked his father's signature（簽字）on the credit card.
他偽造了他父親的信用卡簽名。

fa·mil·iar [fəˋmɪljɚ]

Track 2438

形 熟悉的、親密的

▶Not all people are familiar with the local laws.
不是所有的人都熟悉當地的法律。

fan/fa·nat·ic [fæn]/[fə`nætɪk] Track 2439

名 狂熱者、迷（粉絲） 同 follower 跟隨者

▶The Internet（網路）is a great way to meet fellow fans.
要認識其他的粉絲，網路是個很好的管道。

fan·cy [`fænsɪ] Track 2440

名 想像力、愛好

▶The old lady has taken a fancy to the little girl.
那個老太太非常喜歡這個小女孩。

實用片語用語
take a fancy to 開始喜歡

fare [fɛr] Track 2441

名 費用、運費 同 fee 費用

▶Let us split the taxi fare. 我們來分攤計程車費吧。

far·ther [`fɑrðə] Track 2442

副 更遠地 形 更遠的 同 further 更遠的

▶副 We can't go any farther. Why don't we take a break?
我們走不動了，為什麼不歇一會兒呢？

▶形 The farther hill is five kilometers away.
那座更遠的小山在五公里以外。

fash·ion [`fæʃən] Track 2443

名 時髦、流行 同 style 時髦

▶Would you please tell me what fashion means to you?
能請你告訴我時尚對你來說意味著什麼嗎？

萬用延伸句型
Would you please tell me...
可不可以請你告訴我……

fash·ion·a·ble [`fæʃənəbḷ] Track 2444

形 流行的、時髦的

▶There is a small store selling fashionable dresses in that street. 那條街有一家賣流行服飾的小店。

fas·ten [`fæsṇ‚et] Track 2445

動 緊固、繫緊

▶Fasten your seatbelt（安全帶）or you might get fined.
把安全帶繫好，不然你可能會被罰喔。

fate [fet] Track 2446

名 命運、宿命

▶Who knows what fate has in store for us?
誰知道接下來有什麼樣的命運在等待我們呢？

萬用延伸句型
Who knows... 誰知道……

fau·cet/tap [`fɔsɪt]/[tæp] Track 2447

名 水龍頭

▶Let's leave the faucet open to fill the sink with water.
我們用把水龍頭開著讓水槽注滿水。

fax [fæks] Track 2448

名 傳真

▶Would you like to tell me your telephone number or fax number?
請告訴我你的電話號碼或者傳真號碼好嗎？

實用片語用語
send a fax 發傳真
例如：I sent a fax to his office an hour ago.
我一個小時前發了傳真到他的辦公室。

feath·er [ˋfɛðɚ]

Track 2449

名 羽毛、裝飾

▶Her coat is made of fake feathers.
她的外套是假羽毛做的。

fea·ture [ˋfitʃɚ]

Track 2450

名 特徵、特色

▶I believe this is a key feature of all oil paintings in that period.
我相信這是那個年代油畫的一個關鍵特徵。

文法字詞解析
我們聽音樂、看 MV 的時候，常會看到歌名後面寫著「ft.（某個人的名字）」，其中「ft.」表示「featuring」，也是從「feature」這個字衍生出來的，有「客串、特別出演」的意思。

file [faɪl]

Track 2451

名 檔案 動 存檔、歸檔

▶名 Would you please collect the files for me?
請你幫我把這些檔案收集一下好嗎？

▶動 I filed the letters carefully.
我小心地把這些信件歸檔了。

fire·work [ˋfaɪr͵wɝk]

Track 2452

名 煙火

▶Would you like to see the firework display with us?
你想不想跟我們一起去看煙火秀？

萬用延伸句型
Would you like to...? 你想不想要……？

fist [fɪst]

Track 2453

名 拳頭、拳打、緊握

▶He punched the wall and hurt his fist.
他搥了牆壁一拳，結果傷了拳頭。

文法字詞解析
punch 的意思是「用力一擊」，而「punchline」就是一個笑話中的「笑點、梗」。所以如果有人把某件好笑的事情「破梗」了，就可以說他「screw up the punchline」。

flame [flem]

Track 2454

名 火焰 動 燃燒

▶名 Don't play with the flames, kids.
孩子們，不要玩火。

▶動 Her anger flamed up in an instant.
她的怒火一瞬間就燃燒了起來。

fla·vor [ˋflevɚ]

Track 2455

名 味道、風味 動 添情趣、添風味

▶名 I don't like the flavor of this soup.
我不喜歡這湯的味道。

▶動 How about flavoring the fish with sugar and vinegar（醋）?
我們用糖和醋給魚調味怎麼樣？

文法字詞解析
如果想要說某個東西是「某某口味」，該怎麼說呢？很簡單，用「（口味名稱）-flavored」就可以了。例如草莓口味的冰淇淋就是 strawberry-flavored ice cream。

flea [fli]

Track 2456

名 跳蚤

▶Let's go to the flea market later.
我們待會去個跳蚤市場吧。

flesh [flɛʃ]

Track 2457

名 肉體、軀殼

▶The flesh-colored stockings are on sale now.
肉色絲襪現在在特價。

float [flot]
Track 2458

動 使漂浮

▶There is a log floating in the middle of the river.
河中央漂浮著一根圓木。

flock [flɑk]
Track 2459

名 禽群、人群

▶Crowds of visitors flock to the zoo to see the animals.
大批遊客湧向動物園去看動物。

實用片語用語
flock to / into 大批湧向（某處）

fold [fold]
Track 2460

動 折疊

▶Would you please fold your own clothes neatly（整潔地）?
請你把自己的衣服疊整齊好嗎？

folk [fok]
Track 2461

名 人們 形 民間的

▶名 They are the best folks on earth, for they are not only kind but also diligent.
他們是世上最好的人，因為他們不但善良而且勤勞。

▶形 He is not only a very popular folk singer but also a famous writer. 他不但是一位很受歡迎的民歌手，而且還是一位著名的作家。

fol·low·er [ˋfɑloɚ]
Track 2462

名 跟隨者、屬下

▶Many ancient Greeks were followers of Socrates（蘇格拉底）.
許多古希臘人都是蘇格拉底的追隨者。

文法字詞解析
follower 這個字即是大家都知道的 follow（跟隨）加上字尾「-er」（……者）所組成的，變成「跟隨者」的意思。

fond [fɑnd]
Track 2463

形 喜歡的

▶She is very fond of little children.
她非常喜歡小朋友。

實用片語用語
be fond of 喜歡
例如：I'm fond of kittens.
我喜歡小貓。

fore·head/brow
[ˋfɔr͵hɛd]/[braʊ]
Track 2464

名 前額、額頭

▶I don't like my foreheard very much. It's too wide.
我不怎麼喜歡自己的額頭，太寬了。

for·ev·er [fɚˋɛvɚ]
Track 2465

副 永遠 同 always 永遠

▶Pharaohs（法老）in ancient Egypt believed they could live forever.
古埃及的法老相信自己有個不死之軀。

forth [forθ]
Track 2466

副 向外、向前、在前方

▶Can whoever has a problem come forth and say it?
覺得有問題的人可不可以向前一步把問題提出來呢？

for·tune [ˋfɔrtʃən]

Track 2467

名 運氣、財富 同 luck 幸運

▶If I get rich, I'll be sure to share my fortune with you.
如果我變有錢，我一定會跟你分享我的財富。

實用片語用語
make a fortune 賺大錢
例如：He made a fortune selling handmade soap.
他賣手工香皂賺了大錢。

found [faʊnd]

Track 2468

動 建立、打基礎 同 establish 建立

▶They founded the company together.
他們一起建立了那個公司。

文法字詞解析
found 是動詞原形，意為「建立、打基礎」，但它同時也是動詞 find（找到）的過去式形式，因此很容易搞混。我們來把兩者比較看看：
find 的動詞變化：find, found, found
found 的動詞變化：found, founded, founded

foun·tain [ˋfaʊntn̩]

Track 2469

名 噴泉、噴水池

▶There is a beautiful stone fountain in the middle of the garden.
花園中央有一個漂亮的石頭噴水池。

freeze [friz]

Track 2470

動 凍結

▶All the water in the river was frozen. 河裡的水都結冰了。

fre·quent [ˋfrikwənt]

Track 2471

形 常有的、頻繁的 同 regular 經常的

▶Not everyone in my family enjoys his frequent visits.
我們家不是每個人都喜歡他經常來訪。

friend·ship [ˋfrɛndʃɪp]

Track 2472

名 友誼、友情

▶I always cherish（珍惜）my friendships.
我總是珍惜我的每段友誼。

實用片語用語
friendship bracelet 友誼手環
例如：The girls in my class love making friendship bracelets.
我們班上的女生很喜歡編友誼手環。

frus·trate [ˋfrʌstret]

Track 2473

動 使受挫、擊敗 同 defeat 擊敗

▶The terrible weather frustrated our hopes of going out.
惡劣的天氣使我們外出的願望無法實現了。

fry [ˋfraɪ]

Track 2474

動 油炸、炸

▶What do you think of frying the fish for our dinner?
你覺得炸魚來作為我們的晚飯怎麼樣？

文法字詞解析
fry 的動詞變化：fry、fried、fried

fund [fʌnd]

Track 2475

名 資金、財源 動 投資、儲蓄

▶名 Would you like to raise funds for a new laboratory（實驗室）? 你想不想募款建一個新的實驗室？

▶動 Can you tell me who is funding the project?
您能告訴我是誰為這個計畫提供資金嗎？

fur [fɝ]

Track 2476

名 毛皮、軟皮

▶Would you please let me know for whom you have bought this fur coat? 請問您能告訴我這件皮大衣是買給誰的嗎？

fur·ni·ture [ˋfɝnɪtʃɚ]

Track 2477

名 傢俱、設備

▶Let's go buy some furniture for our new house.
我們去為我們的新房子買些傢俱吧。

gal·lon [ˋgælən]

Track 2478

名 加侖

▶How many miles can you drive with a gallon of gas?
你一加侖汽油能開多少英里？

gam·ble [ˋgæmbḷ]

Track 2479

動 賭博 名 賭博、投機 同 bet 打賭

▶動 It was so foolish of the old man to gamble away all his money.
這個老人賭博輸掉了自己所有的錢，真是太愚蠢了。

▶名 All of us think it is a gamble.
我們都認為這是一場豪賭。

實用片語用語
gamble away 把……賭光

gang [gæŋ]

Track 2480

名 一隊（工人）、一群（囚犯）

▶The gang is planning a robbery.
那幫罪犯正在計畫搶劫。

gap [gæp]

Track 2481

名 差距、缺口

▶There is a generation gap between my father and me.
我和爸爸之間有代溝。

實用片語用語
1. generation gap 世代隔閡
就像例句中說的，如果你和你的上一代或下一代之間的價值觀不同、無法互相理解的話，就可以說你們之間有「generation gap」。
2. 另外，最近台灣大學生很流行畢業後去旅行壯遊、打工度假，但歐美從很久以前就開始有這樣的活動了。他們畢業後會給自己一年的時間去體驗各種事物、充實經歷，一年後再回來找工作，這段時間就稱做「gap year」。

gar·lic [ˋgɑrlɪk]

Track 2482

名 蒜

▶Would you like to try this garlic flavored rice?
你要不要試試這種蒜味的飯？

gas·o·line/gas·o·lene/gas [ˋgæsḷˏin]/[ˏgæsḷˋin]/[gæs]

Track 2483

名 汽油 同 petroleum 石油

▶An automobile can consume a lot of gasoline.
一輛汽車能消耗很多的汽油。

實用片語用語
gas station 加油站
也稱 petrol station 或 filling station。

ges·ture [ˋdʒɛstʃɚ]

Track 2484

名 手勢、姿勢 動 打手勢

▶名 Would you tell me what this gesture means in sign language（手語）?
你能告訴我這個手勢在手語中是什麼意思嗎？

▶動 I gestured to the waiter to come over.
我打手勢要服務生過來。

A B C D E F G H I J K L M N O P Q R S T U V W X Y Z

glance [glæns]
Track 2485

動 瞥視、看一下 名 一瞥 同 glimpse 瞥見

▶動 Will you stop glancing left and right in a meeting? It's not polite. 請不要在會議上左顧右盼好嗎？這不禮貌。

▶名 They exchanged glances and walked out.
他們互使眼色，然後走了出去。

glob·al [ˋglobḷ]
Track 2486

形 球狀的、全球的

▶Our world has become a global village.
我們的世界成為了一個地球村。

實用片語用語

global warming 全球暖化

例如：Global warming has become an issue that needs to be dealt with soon.
全球暖化已經成了一個需要即早對付的問題。

glo·ry [ˋglorɪ]
Track 2487

名 榮耀、光榮 動 洋洋得意

▶名 His good deeds had brought glory to our family.
他的善行為我們家帶來了光榮。

▶動 The team gloried in their eventual（最終的）victory.
這支球隊因最後獲勝而洋洋得意。

glow [glo]
Track 2488

動 熾熱、發光 名 白熱光 同 blaze 光輝

▶動 The wolf's eyes glowed in the darkness（黑暗）.
狼的眼睛在黑暗中發亮。

▶名 Do you see the glow of the sunset over there?
你看到那邊落日的光輝了嗎？

gos·sip [ˋgɑsəp]
Track 2489

名 閒聊 動 說閒話 同 chat 閒聊

▶名 Have you heard the latest gossip? 你有聽到最新的八卦嗎？

▶動 She likes to gossip with her friends.
她喜歡跟朋友們講閒話。

gov·er·nor [ˋgʌvənɚ]
Track 2490

名 統治者 同 president 總統

▶Do you mind if I invite the governor of the state to our banquet（宴會）? 你不介意我請州長來參加宴會吧？

萬用延伸句型

Do you mind if...? 你介意……嗎？

例如：Do you mind if I turn off the music?
你介意我關掉音樂嗎？

gown [gaʊn]
Track 2491

名 長袍、長上衣

▶Would you like this wedding gown or that one?
你是喜歡這件結婚禮服呢，還是那件？

grab [græb]
Track 2492

動 急抓、逮捕 同 snatch 抓住

▶He grabbed her hand before she could walk away.
在她能走遠前，他抓住了她的手。

grad·u·al [ˋgrædʒʊəl]
Track 2493

形 逐漸的、漸進的 反 sudden 突然的

▶I hope there will be a gradual improvement in this patient.
我希望這個病人能逐漸恢復健康。

grad·u·ate [ˋgrædʒʊˏet]

Track 2494

名 畢業生 動 授予學位、畢業

▶名 Isn't he a college graduate?
他不是大學畢業生嗎？

▶動 He has been working in this famous company before he even graduated from university（大學）.
他大學還沒畢業就已經在這家知名企業工作了。

實用片語用語

1. graduate student 研究生
例如：All graduate students in the department work as teaching assistants.
系上所有的研究生都有當助教。
2. 如果研究生是graduate student，那麼「undergraduate student」就泛指「還沒唸研究所的高等教育學生」，也就是大專生。

grain [gren]

Track 2495

名 穀類、穀粒

▶Farmers in this country grow grain for a living.
這個國家的農民靠種穀物為生。

gram [græm]

Track 2496

名 公克

▶Would you tell me how much per gram your silver is?
你能告訴我你的銀製品每克多少錢嗎？

grasp [græsp]

Track 2497

動 掌握、領悟、抓牢 同 grab 抓住

▶It's hard to grasp the meaning of his words.
他講的話的意思實在很難懂。

grass·hop·per [ˋgræsˏhɑpɚ]

Track 2498

名 蚱蜢

▶That grasshopper is as big as my hand!
那隻蚱蜢跟我的手一樣大耶！

green·house [ˋgrinˏhaʊs]

Track 2499

名 溫室

▶He couldn't care less about the greenhouse effect.
他對溫室效應的議題毫無興趣。

萬用延伸句型

can't care less about... 完全不關心

grin [grɪn]

Track 2500

動 / 名 露齒而笑

▶動 Would you tell me why he grins from ear to ear all day long?
你能告訴我他為什麼整天都咧嘴大笑嗎？

▶名 She walks in with a huge grin.
她帶著大大的笑容走進來。

實用片語用語

grin from ear to ear 咧嘴大笑
笑得時候，嘴巴從左耳裂開到右耳，那當然就是笑容非常大、笑得非常開心了。

gro·cer·y [ˋgrosərɪ]

Track 2501

名 雜貨店

▶I don't think you can buy everything you want in this grocery store.
我認為你在這個雜貨店買不到你想要的所有東西。

文法字詞解析

一般而言，會在 grocery store（生鮮雜貨店）或超市買到的東西可以通稱為 groceries，注意要用複數形式喔！不能說「我去超市買了『一個 grocery』」。

guard·i·an [ˋgɑrdɪən]

Track 2502

名 保護者、守護者

▶The police are supposed to be guardians of law and order.
警察應該要是法律和秩序的護衛者才對。

guid·ance [ˋgaɪdn̩s] Track 2503

名 引導、指導

▶The little girl looked to her mother for guidance.
那個小女孩看向她的母親等她指示。

gum [gʌm] Track 2504

名 膠、口香糖

▶What flavor of gum do you like best? 你最喜歡哪種口香糖？

gymnasium [dʒɪmˋnezɪəm] Track 2505

名 體育館、健身房

▶How often do you go to the gymnasium nearby?
你多常去附近的健身房？

文法字詞解析
gymnasium 也可以簡稱 gym，是比較常用的用法。

hair·dres·ser [ˋhɛr͵drɛsɚ] Track 2506

名 理髮師

▶Why don't you ask the hairdresser to trim（修剪）your beard?
為什麼不讓理髮師幫你修剪一下鬍鬚呢？

hall·way [ˋhɔl͵we] Track 2507

名 玄關、門廳

▶Would you please not leave your garbage in the hallway? It's attracting flies here.
請您別把垃圾放在玄關裡好嗎？這樣會引來蒼蠅。

hand·ful [ˋhænd͵fəl] Track 2508

形 少量、少數

▶Why did only a handful of people attend the meeting?
為什麼只有少數的人參加這場會議？

實用片語用語
a handful of 一把、一點點、少數

handy [ˋhændɪ] Track 2509

形 手巧的、手邊的

同 convenient 方便的、隨手可得的

▶You should bring a flashlight. It might come in handy.
你帶個手電筒吧，可能會派上用場。

har·bor [ˋhɑrbɚ] Track 2510

名 港灣 同 port 港口

▶The harbor smells like fish. 港口聞起來有魚的味道。

harm [hɑrm] Track 2511

名 損傷、損害 動 傷害、損害 同 damage 損害

▶名 If we interfere（干涉）, we will cause more harm than good. 倘若我們進行干預，造成的問題會比帶來的好處多。

▶動 There was a traffic accident, but no one was harmed.
發生了交通事故，但沒有人受傷。

harm·ful [ˋharmfəl]

Track 2512

形 引起傷害的、有害的 同 destructive 破壞的

▶It is harmful for you to drink too much wine.
過量喝酒對你的身體有害。

文法字詞解析
是不是覺得「harmful」和「harm」長得很像，似乎有關係呢？確實，harmful 就是 harm 加上形容詞字尾「-ful」，變成表示「有害的」的形容詞。

har·vest [ˋharvɪst]

Track 2513

名 收穫 動 收穫、收割穀物

▶名 The farmers believe that heavy snow promises a good harvest. 那些農夫相信瑞雪兆豐年。

▶動 We will harvest the fruit before first frost（霜）.
我們會在初霜之前採摘這些水果。

hast·y [ˋhestɪ]

Track 2514

形 快速的

▶I don't think that it's right to make such a hasty decision.
我認為如此倉促地做出決定是不正確的。

hatch [hætʃ]

Track 2515

動 計畫、孵化

▶Would you tell me when the eggs will hatch?
您能告訴我蛋什麼時候孵化嗎？

萬用延伸句型
Would you tell me when...
你可不可以告訴我什麼時候……

hawk [hɔk]

Track 2516

名 鷹

▶We watched the hawk with binoculars（望遠鏡）.
我們用望遠鏡觀賞那隻鷹。

文法字詞解析
binoculars 和 telescope 都是望遠鏡的意思，那他們之間有什麼不同呢？從字首可以看出，前者的「bi-」代表有兩個鏡片的「雙筒望遠鏡」，多半是在距離沒有那麼遠的活動中使用，像是賞鳥、看演唱會等；而「tele-」則有「在遠方」的意思，所以後者就是可以看很遠的大型望遠鏡，例如天文望遠鏡。

hay [he]

Track 2517

名 乾草

▶There are several children playing in the hay.
有幾個孩子正在乾草上玩。

head·line [ˋhɛd͵laɪn]

Track 2518

名 標題、寫標題 同 title 標題

▶Would you please give this article a headline?
請您為這篇文章擬一個大標題好嗎？

文法字詞解析
headline 這個單字經常以複數形式出現。例如報紙上的頭條我們常會稱為「the headlines on the newspaper」，而「上頭條」則可以說成「make the headlines」。

head·quar·ters [ˋhɛd͵kwɔrtəz]

Track 2519

名 總部、大本營

▶Where are your company's headquarters? 你公司的總部在哪？

heal [hil]

Track 2520

動 治癒、復原 同 cure 治癒

▶Has your wound healed yet? 你的傷癒合了沒？

heap [hip]

Track 2521

名 積累 動 堆積

▶名 There are a lot of books lying in a heap on the floor.
有很多書堆放在地板上。

▶動 He heaped all his clothes on the ground.
他把衣服堆了一堆在地上。

實用片語用語
heaps of 一大堆的、很多的
例如：She's got heaps of brains; she just doesn't use them.
她的腦筋非常好，她只是不用。

heav·en [ˋhɛvən]
Track 2522

名 天堂

▶They are a match made in heaven.
他們是天造地設的一對。

heel [hil]
Track 2523

名 腳後跟

▶I only wear high heels on special occasions; what about you?
我只在特殊場合穿高跟鞋，妳呢？

文法字詞解析
高跟鞋「high heels」也可以簡稱為「heels」。相對地，平底的鞋則可以簡稱「flats」。

hell [hɛl]
Track 2524

名 地獄、悲慘處境 同 misery 悲慘、苦難

▶They believe that evil people will go to hell.
他們相信邪惡的人會下地獄。

hel·met [ˋhɛlmɪt]
Track 2525

名 頭盔、安全帽

▶If you wear a safety helmet, you won't get hurt.
如果你戴安全帽就不會受傷了。

hes·i·tate [ˋhɛzə͵tet]
Track 2526

動 遲疑、躊躇

▶He hesitated before answering me.
他在回答我前猶豫了一下。

hike [haɪk]
Track 2527

名 徒步旅行、健行

▶I am going hiking next month; would you like to go with me?
下個月我要去健行，你想不想跟我一起去呢？

hint [hɪnt]
Track 2528

名 暗示 同 imply 暗示

▶Didn't you pick up the subtle hints in his letter?
你難道沒有發現他信中的微妙暗示嗎？

實用片語用語
give sb. a hint 給（某人）提示
例如：I can't think of an answer. Could you please give me a hint?
我想不出答案，你可以給我一個提示嗎？

his·to·ri·an [hɪsˋtorɪən]
Track 2529

名 歷史學家

▶Evans is not only a writer but also a historian.
伊文斯不但是個作家，還是位歷史學家。

his·tor·ic [hɪsˋtɔrɪk]
Track 2530

形 歷史性的

▶I have no interest in historic sites.
我對歷史遺跡實在沒興趣。

實用片語用語
1. have no interest in 對（某事物）毫無興趣
2. 如果是要說對一件事「有強烈的興趣」的話，就可以說「have a keen / strong interest in」。

his·tor·i·cal [hɪsˋtɔrɪk]
Track 2531

形 歷史的

▶We should look at all of this from a historical standpoint（觀點）.
我們應該從歷史的觀點來看待這一切。

hive [haɪv]

Track 2532

名 蜂巢、鬧區

▶Can you tell me how many bees there are in the hive?
你能否告訴我這個蜂巢裡有多少蜜蜂？

萬用延伸句型
Can you tell me...? 你可不可以告訴我……？

hol·low [ˋhalo]

Track 2533

形 中空的、空的 同 empty 空的

▶The tree is hollow inside. 這棵樹是中空的。

ho·ly [ˋholɪ]

Track 2534

形 神聖的、聖潔的

▶Saints are holy people. 所謂聖人就是神聖的人。

home·town [ˋhomˋtaʊn]

Track 2535

名 家鄉

▶Would you like to tell me what your hometown is like?
你能告訴我你的家鄉是什麼樣子嗎？

hon·es·ty [ˋanɪstɪ]

Track 2536

名 正直、誠實

▶I value honesty above all else.
我把誠實看得比什麼都重要。

實用片語用語
honesty is the best policy 誠實至上
單字 policy 的意思是「政策」，用在這裡也就是「誠實為上策」的意思。

hon·or [ˋanɚ]

Track 2537

名 榮耀、尊敬 同 respect 尊敬

▶Would you honor me by dining with me tonight?
今晚你能賞光與我共進晚餐嗎？

horn [hɔrn]

Track 2538

名 喇叭

▶He honked（按喇叭）the horn so that the car in front would hurry. 他按喇叭要前面的車快點。

文法字詞解析
除了車子的喇叭，一些像喇叭一樣會發出響聲的樂器也可以稱為 horn。例如法國號 French horn、英國管 English horn 等等。

hor·ri·ble [ˋharəbl̩]

Track 2539

形 可怕的

▶The accident was horrible, as I'm sure all who witnessed（見證）it could tell you.
這次意外超慘的，我相信所有看到它發生的人都會這麼說。

horror [ˋharɚ]

Track 2540

名 恐怖、畏懼 同 panic 恐慌

▶He ran out in horror of the flying cockroaches.
他被這些飛來飛去的蟑螂嚇得跑了出去。

hour·ly [ˋaʊrlɪ]

Track 2541

形 每小時的 副 每小時地

▶形 I'm paid on an hourly basis; what about you?
我的工資是以小時計算的，你呢？

▶副 This medicine is to be taken hourly.
這個藥是每小時服一次。

house·keep·er [ˋhaʊs͵kipɚ] Track 2542

名 主婦、管家

▶Our housekeeper is already very old but still quite efficient.
我們的管家年紀很大了，但做事還是很有效率。

文法字詞解析
我們都知道 house 指的是房子，keep 有維持的意思，再加上意思是「……者」的字尾「-er」，可知 house-keeper 就是「維持房子的人」，也就是管家了。

hug [hʌg] Track 2543

動 抱、緊抱 名 緊抱、擁抱 同 embrace 擁抱

▶動 They hugged each other before saying goodbye.
他們在說再見前擁抱了一下。

▶名 I give my children a hug every day. 我每天都抱抱孩子一下。

hu·mor·ous [ˋhjumərəs] Track 2544

形 幽默的、滑稽的 同 funny 好笑的

▶The story was more humorous than romantic.
那個故事不是很浪漫，但很好笑。

萬用延伸句型
be more... than... 比起……更……

hush [hʌʃ] Track 2545

動 使寂靜 名 寂靜 同 silence 寂靜

▶動 Can you hush the baby for me? 可以幫我讓寶寶安靜一下嗎？

▶名 Why is there such a hush in the room?
為什麼房間裡一片寂靜？

hut [hʌt] Track 2546

名 小屋、茅舍

▶Let's go to visit the old man living in the little wooden hut.
我們去探望一下那個住在一間小木屋裡的老人吧。

Ii

ic·y [ˋaɪsɪ] Track 2547

形 冰的

▶It was stupid of him to walk on the icy road at night.
他晚上在結冰的路上走真是太笨了。

萬用延伸句型
It was stupid of sb. to... （某人）這樣做很笨

i·de·al [aɪˋdiəl] Track 2548

形 理想的、完美的 同 perfect 完美的

▶I don't think today's weather is an ideal one for a picnic in the open air. 我覺得今天的天氣不是到戶外野餐的理想天氣。

i·den·ti·ty [aɪˋdɛntətɪ] Track 2549

名 身分

▶Would you please show me your identity card?
你能出示一下你的身分證嗎？

萬用延伸句型
Would you please...? 可不可以請您……？

ig·no·rance [ˋɪgnərəns] Track 2550

名 無知、不學無術 反 knowledge 學識

▶Some people's ignorance makes me really mad.
有些人的無知讓我實在不太開心。

im·age [ˋɪmɪdʒ] Track 2551

名 影像、形象

▶The program（程式）is used for editing images.
這個程式是用來編輯影像的。

i·mag·i·na·tion [ɪˏmædʒəˋneʃən] Track 2552

名 想像力、創作力

▶The little girl has a really active imagination.
這個小女孩的想像力非常豐富。

im·me·di·ate [ɪˋmidɪɪt] Track 2553

形 直接的、立即的

▶We need your immediate reply.
我們需要你立即回覆。

文法字詞解析
immediate 的副詞形式 immediately 比 immediate 還更常見，尤其在要求別人盡快為你完成某個工作、或馬上跟你聯絡時，經常用到這個字。

im·port [ɪmˋport]/[ˋɪmport] Track 2554

動 進口、輸入 名 輸入品、進口 反 export 出口

▶動 Many countries plan to import more rice from our nation.
許多國家打算從我國進口更多的米。

▶名 The import of tea has gone up sharply（急劇地）these years.
近年來茶葉的進口大大增加了。

im·press [ɪmˋprɛs] Track 2555

動 留下深刻印象、使感動

▶The audience was impressed by her performance.
她的表演給所有的觀眾都留下了深刻的印象。

im·pres·sive [ɪmˋprɛsɪv] Track 2556

形 印象深刻的

▶Don't you think the film was quite impressive?
你不覺得那部電影很令人印象深刻嗎？

萬用延伸句型
Don't you think...? 你不覺得……？
Don't you think 和 Do you think 的意思差不多，但就像中文的「你不覺得……」與「你覺得 ......」之間也有微妙差異一樣，「Don't you think...」多了一點反問的味道。

in·deed [ɪnˋdid] Track 2557

副 實在地、的確

▶After I met him, I realized that he was indeed a very strange man.
見過他後，我發現他的確是個怪人。

in·di·vid·u·al [ˏɪndəˋvɪdʒʊəl] Track 2558

形 個別的 名 個人

▶形 It is difficult for a teacher to give individual attention to his or her students.
老師很難照顧到每一個學生。

▶名 Every individual in this room is a suspect（嫌疑人）.
這房間裡人人都是嫌犯。

in·door [ˋɪnˏdor] Track 2559

形 屋內的、室內的 反 outdoor 戶外的

▶Are you interested in indoor sports?
你對室內運動感興趣嗎？

萬用延伸句型
Are you interested in...? 你對……有興趣嗎？

in·doors [ˌɪnˋdorz]

Track 2560

副 在室內 反 outdoors 在戶外

▶I don't think a patient should stay indoors all day long.
我覺得病人不應該整天待在屋裡。

in·dus·tri·al [ɪnˋdʌstrɪəl]

Track 2561

形 工業的

▶Industrial pollution is becoming a huge problem.
工業污染現在成為了很嚴重的問題。

in·fe·ri·or [ɪnˋfɪrɪɚ]

Track 2562

形 較低的、較劣的 同 worse 較差的

▶The food in this restaurant was inferior to that of the one next to it. 這家餐廳的菜比隔壁那家更難吃。

文法字詞解析
inferior 有「比較差的」的意思，那麼「比較好的」呢？可以說 superior。

in·form [ɪnˋfɔrm]

Track 2563

動 通知、報告

▶Do you mind if I inform him about the bad news now?
你介意我現在就把壞消息告訴他嗎？

in·jure [ˋɪndʒɚ]

Track 2564

動 傷害、使受傷 同 hurt 傷害

▶I heard he got injured in this accident. How is he now?
聽說他在事故中受了傷，那他現在怎麼樣了？

in·ju·ry [ˋɪndʒərɪ]

Track 2565

名 傷害、損害

▶He has suffered serious injuries. 他受了很嚴重的傷。

inn [ɪn]

Track 2566

名 旅社、小酒館

▶How about staying in that inn for tonight?
今晚在那家小旅館住怎麼樣？

in·ner [ˋɪnɚ]

Track 2567

形 內部的、心靈的 同 outer 外部的

▶It is hard for anyone to know what others' inner thoughts might be. 我們很難知道別人內心的想法。

實用片語用語
inner peace 內心平靜
We can achieve inner peace if we learn to like ourselves.
如果學會喜歡自己，就能內心平靜。

in·no·cent [ˋɪnəsn̩t]

Track 2568

形 無辜的、純潔的 反 guilty 罪惡的

▶There is still no hard evidence（證據）to prove that he is innocent.
還沒有確切的證據可以證明他是無辜的。

in·spect [ɪnˋspɛkt]

Track 2569

動 調查、檢查

▶It took them a lot of time to inspect these public buildings in the city.
他們花了很多時間來檢查這座城市裡的公共建築。

萬用延伸句型
It took sb. a lot of time to（+ 原形動詞）
花了某人很多時間（做某事）

in·spec·tor [ɪn`spɛktɚ] Track 2570

名 視察員、檢查者

▶The inspector is asking for details of the missing cars.
視察員正要求提供遺失汽車的細節。

in·stead [ɪn`stɛd] Track 2571

副 替代

▶I think we should go right instead of left.
我覺得我們應該走右邊而不是走左邊。

instruction [ɪn`strʌkʃən] Track 2572

名 指令、教導

▶Why don't you give your staff some detailed instructions about this matter?
為何不給你的下屬有關此事的詳細指令呢？

in·ter·nal [ɪn`tɝnl̩] Track 2573

形 內部的、國內的

▶Linda, can you talk to Mike on the internal telephone now?
琳達，妳可以用內線電話跟邁克交談一下嗎？

實用片語用語
internal telephone 內線電話
另外，講電話時常常會用到的「可以幫我轉接分機……嗎？」的說法是「Could you put me through extension（分機號碼）, please?」

in·ter·rupt [͵ɪntə`rʌpt] Track 2574

動 干擾、打斷 同 intrude 打擾

▶Sorry to interrupt you, but would you please send me the documents（文件）this afternoon?
對不起，打擾了，您能在今天下午就把檔案寄送給我嗎？

萬用延伸句型
Sorry to interrupt you, but...
很抱歉打擾你，但……（可接上需要對方幫忙的事物）

in·tro·duc·tion [͵ɪntrə`dʌkʃən] Track 2575

名 引進、介紹

▶Do you mind if I give a brief introduction about our product first?
你介意我先簡短介紹一些我們的產品嗎？

in·ven·tor [ɪn`vɛntɚ] Track 2576

名 發明家

▶I don't think this inventor is as talented as they say.
我覺得這名發明家不如大家所說的那麼有才華。

萬用延伸句型
as... as they say 如人們所說的一樣……

in·ves·ti·gate [ɪn`vɛstə͵get] Track 2577

動 研究、調查 同 inspect 調查

▶If the police won't investigate this matter, let's just do it ourselves.
如果警察不調查這件事，那我們就自己來調查。

i·vo·ry [`aɪvərɪ] Track 2578

名 象牙 形 象牙製的

▶名 Ivory is costly and hard to obtain（取得）.
象牙很寶貴，很難取得。

▶形 She said we were living in an ivory tower.
她說我們是在象牙塔中生活。

jail [dʒel]

Track 2579

名 監獄 同 prison 監獄

▶Not all neighbors knew that he had been in jail for two years.
不是所有的鄰居都知道他曾在監獄被關了兩年。

實用片語用語
go to jail 坐牢
例如：You'll go to jail if you rob a bank.
如果你搶銀行的話，會坐牢的。

jar [dʒɑr]

Track 2580

名 刺耳的聲音、廣口瓶

▶Would you please help me loosen（鬆開）the lid of this jar?
你能幫我把這個瓶蓋鬆開嗎？

jaw [dʒɔ]

Track 2581

名 顎、下巴

▶Her jaw looks like a man's.
她的下顎看起來像個男人的下巴似的。

jeal·ous [ˋdʒɛləs]

Track 2582

形 嫉妒的 同 envious 嫉妒的、羨慕的

▶I don't think he is jealous of his colleague's success.
我認為他並不是嫉妒他同事的成功。

實用片語用語
be jealous of 嫉妒（某人）

jel·ly [ˋdʒɛlɪ]

Track 2583

名 果凍

▶Would you like to put some jelly on the bread?
你想不想在麵包上塗些果醬呢？

jet [dʒɛt]

Track 2584

名 噴射機、噴嘴 動 噴出

▶名 Did you see the jet in the sky?
你有看到天上的飛機嗎？

▶動 Water is jetting out from the broken pipe.
水正從破裂的水管裡噴出來。

jew·el [ˋdʒuəl]

Track 2585

名 珠寶

▶My mother doesn't really care about jewels.
我媽媽對珠寶沒什麼興趣。

文法字詞解析
jewelry 和前一個 jewel 都是「珠寶」的意思，那麼差別在哪裡呢？原來，jewelry 通常用於表示「珠寶的通稱」，所以你的項鍊手環耳環墜子擺在一起，就可以統稱 jewelry。jewel 的複數 jewels 也可以通稱珠寶，但單數時則可以單個單個的算「一件珠寶」。

jew·el·ry [ˋdʒuəlrɪ]

Track 2586

名 珠寶

▶The jewelry I own is mostly cheap.
我擁有的珠寶大部分很便宜。

jour·nal [ˋdʒɝnḷ]

Track 2587

名 期刊 同 magazine 雜誌

▶How about subscribing（訂購）to a journal this year?
我們今年訂購一份期刊怎麼樣？

jour·ney [ˋdʒɝnɪ] Track 2588

名 旅程 動 旅遊

▶名 He gave a very descriptive（描述的）account of his journey. 他對他這次旅行做出十分生動的敘述。

▶動 He used to journey to that small town a lot.
他常常旅行到那個小鎮。

萬用延伸句型
used to... 以前習慣……
例如：We used to be such good friends, but not anymore.
我們以前是很好的朋友，但現在不是了。

joy·ful [ˋdʒɔɪfəl] Track 2589

形 愉快的、喜悅的 同 glad 高興的

▶Birthdays are such joyful events.
生日真是愉快的事情。

jun·gle [ˋdʒʌŋgl̩] Track 2590

名 叢林

▶Can you tell me what you saw in the jungle?
你能不能告訴我在叢林中你看到了什麼？

junk [dʒʌŋk] Track 2591

名 垃圾 同 trash 垃圾

▶Why did you buy such a piece of junk?
你買這垃圾幹嘛？

文法字詞解析
junk 後面常常會再接一些其他的名詞，例如 junk mail 就是我們電子信箱裡常會收到的垃圾郵件，也可以說是「spam」；junk call 則是推銷電話、廣告電話的意思；或者小時候我們一定學過 junk food 這個字，意指不健康的垃圾食物。

jus·tice [ˋdʒʌstɪs] Track 2592

名 公平、公正

▶I demand justice for the people. 我要求還人民一個公道。

Kk

kan·ga·roo [͵kæŋgəˋru] Track 2593

名 袋鼠

▶Have you ever seen a kangaroo? What does it look like?
你有看過袋鼠嗎？牠長什麼樣子呢？

ket·tle [ˋkɛtl̩] Track 2594

名 水壺

▶Would you like me to boil water in the kettle and make some tea? 你要不要我燒壺水來泡茶？

實用片語用語
pot calling the kettle black 五十步笑百步
pot（鍋子）和 kettle（燒水用的水壺）都燒得黑黑的，因此鍋子嘲笑水壺黑，就帶有「五十步笑百步」的意思，畢竟兩個都一樣黑。注意此處的 kettle 指的是燒水用的水壺喔！平常帶著去郊遊的那種單純裝水的水壺不會叫做 kettle。

key·board [ˋki͵bord] Track 2595

名 鍵盤

▶What's the matter with your keyboard? I can't type with it at all. 你的鍵盤怎麼了？我根本沒辦法用它打字。

萬用延伸句型
What's the matter with...? ……是怎麼了？

kid·ney [ˋkɪdnɪ] Track 2596

名 腎臟

▶Would you like some pig's kidney soup?
你要不要喝豬肝湯？

ki·lo·gram/kg [ˋkɪlə͵græm] Track 2597

名 公斤

▶Will you tell me how much I should pay for the two kilograms of pork?
能告訴我這兩公斤豬肉要多少錢嗎？

ki·lo·me·ter/km [ˋkɪlə͵mitɚ] Track 2598

名 公里

▶How many kilometers can this car go in an hour?
這輛車一個小時可以開多少公里？

kit [kɪt] Track 2599

名 工具箱

▶I hope you remembered to bring your tool kit.
希望你有記得帶工具箱。

kneel [nil] Track 2600

動 下跪

▶He said he wouldn't forgive you even if you kneeled down before him.
他說他不會原諒你的，就算你在他面前下跪也一樣。

文法字詞解析
kneel 的動詞變化：kneel, kneeled, kneeled 或 kneel, knelt, knelt

knight [naɪt] Track 2601

名 騎士、武士 動 封……為爵士

▶名 Have you heard stories about the Knights of the Round Table?
你有聽過圓桌武士的故事嗎？

▶動 He wasn't knighted by the Queen at that time.
他當時沒被女王封為爵士。

knit [nɪt] Track 2602

動 編織 名 編織物

▶動 When I arrived home, I saw my mom knitting a sweater.
我到家的時候，看到母親正在織毛衣。

▶名 My sister bought some winter knits for me.
我姐姐買了幾件冬天穿的針織衫給我。

實用片語用語
knit sb's brows 皺起眉頭
皺起眉頭的動作就像是把眉頭「織」在一起一般，因此這個字才會出現在表達皺眉的片語中。

knob [nɑb] Track 2603

名 圓形把手、球塊

▶Why don't you replace the old knobs on the doors?
為什麼不把門上的舊把手都換掉呢？

knot [nɑt] Track 2604

名 結 動 打結

▶名 There are several knots in your hair.
你的頭髮都打好多結了。

▶動 He knotted the ends of the rope together.
他把繩頭結在一起。

Ll

la·bel [ˋlebḷ] Track 2605

名 標籤 動 標明

▶名 Tom has been given the label of "playboy" by his friends.
湯姆被他的朋友們貼上了「花花公子」的標籤。

▶動 The boy was labeled a troublemaker（鬧事者）.
這男孩被人稱作搗蛋鬼。

lace [les] Track 2606

名 花邊、緞帶 動 用帶子打結

▶名 I like the cushion with the lace better.
我比較喜歡有花邊的那個抱枕。

▶動 Her dress was laced with gold.
她的洋裝鑲有金色飾帶。

lad·der [ˋlædɚ] Track 2607

名 梯子

▶It's considered unlucky（不吉利的）to walk under a ladder.
從梯子下面走過去被認為是不吉利的。

萬用延伸句型
It is considered... 被認為是……
這個句型的原句應該是 It is considered to be (+ adj.)，是用 it 當虛主詞的被動用法，真正的主詞則是後面很長一串的「to walk under a ladder」。

lat·ter [ˋlætɚ] Track 2608

形 後者的

▶I think the latter idea is better. What do you think?
我覺得後面這個主意更好，你覺得呢？

laugh·ter [ˋlæftɚ] Track 2609

名 笑聲

▶There was a burst of laughter in the next room.
隔壁房間裡突然爆發出一陣笑聲。

laun·dry [ˋlɔndrɪ] Track 2610

名 洗衣店、送洗的衣服

▶When does the wash come back from the laundry?
洗衣店的衣服什麼時候能取回來？

實用片語用語
do laundry 洗衣服
例如：I want to go to bed but still need to do laundry.
雖然我想睡了，但還得洗衣服。

lawn [lɔn] Track 2611

名 草地

▶I'd much rather lie down on the lawn than work in the office.
比起在辦公室工作，我更想躺在草坪上。

leak [lik] Track 2612

動 洩漏、滲漏 名 漏洞

▶動 Would you please not leak the news to the press?
請不要把這則消息洩漏給新聞界好嗎？

▶名 Would you please come over to my place and mend a leak in my hot water tank?
你能不能到我家修補一下熱水箱上的洞？

實用片語用語
leak the news 洩漏消息
此外也可以用 leak the secret 來表示洩漏秘密。

leap [lip]

Track 2613

動 使跳過 名 跳躍

▶動 A lot of fish leapt out of water and landed on the shore.
有很多條魚躍出水面落到岸上。

▶名 There has been a great leap in the number of births in these past five years.
這五年來，出生人數大幅的增長。

leath·er [ˋlɛðɚ]

Track 2614

名 皮革

▶This wallet feels to me like leather.
我覺得這錢包像是皮革製的。

lei·sure [ˋliʒɚ]

Track 2615

名 空閒

▶What do you usually do in your leisure time?
你空閒時間通常都在幹嘛？

length·en [ˋlɛŋθən]

Track 2616

動 加長

▶Some people say that to save time is to lengthen life.
有人說節約時間就等於延長壽命。

文法字詞解析

在 lengthen 的後面加上表示「……者」的字尾「-er」，就變成 lengthener，是「加長器」的意思。加長器要用來加長什麼？那就看前面加上什麼字而定了。例如加長睫毛的就是 eyelash lengthener，加長裙子的就是 skirt lengthener，還有鉛筆削一削變得太短、很難拿，也可以靠 pencil lengthener 來解決。

lens [lɛns]

Track 2617

名 透鏡

▶Would you please bring me that pair of glasses with plastic lenses?
你能把那副塑膠鏡片的眼鏡拿給我嗎？

li·ar [ˋlaɪɚ]

Track 2618

名 說謊者

▶Are you simple enough to believe what that liar told you?
你會蠢到相信那騙子說的話嗎？

lib·er·al [ˋlɪbərəl]

Track 2619

形 自由主義的、開明的、慷慨的 同 generous 慷慨的

▶There are many educators（教育家）advocating（提倡）a liberal education.
有很多教育家提倡開明教育。

lib·er·ty [ˋlɪbɚtɪ]

Track 2620

名 自由 同 freedom 自由

▶I don't suppose that protecting individual liberty is the only purpose of law.
我認為保護個人自由並不是法律的唯一目的。

萬用延伸句型

I don't suppose that... 我不認為……

li·brar·i·an [laɪˋbrɛrɪən]

Track 2621

名 圖書館員

▶My father is the librarian of our school.
我父親是我們學校的圖書館館員。

life·boat [ˋlaɪf͵bot]

Track 2622

名 救生艇

▶There were not enough lifeboats to save all the people on the ship. 沒有足夠的救生艇來營救船上所有的人。

life·guard [ˋlaɪf͵gɑrd]

Track 2623

名 救生員

▶It is best for you to swim only in places where there is a lifeguard. 你最好只在有救生員的地方游泳。

萬用延伸句型
It is best for you to... 對你來說……最好

life·time [ˋlaɪf͵taɪm]

Track 2624

名 一生

▶It's the chance of a lifetime. 這是一生中難得再遇到的機會。

light·house [ˋlaɪt͵haʊs]

Track 2625

名 燈塔

▶There is a lighthouse flashing in the distance.
有一座燈塔在遠處發出閃爍的光。

實用片語用語
in the distance 在遠處

limb [lɪm]

Track 2626

名 枝幹

▶The little girl likes sitting on the limb of this tree.
這個小女孩喜歡坐在這棵樹的枝幹上。

lin·en [ˋlɪnɪn]

Track 2627

名 亞麻製品

▶I spent all weekend washing dirty linen.
我花了一個週末洗髒的亞麻床單。

lip·stick [ˋlɪp͵stɪk]

Track 2628

名 口紅、唇膏

▶I don't think that bright red lipstick looks good on you.
我覺得你塗鮮紅色的唇膏不好看。

文法字詞解析
lip 是「嘴唇」的意思，而 stick 則是指棒狀物。其他類似也是棒狀的東西有口紅膠、護唇膏等。前者可以稱為 glue stick，後者可稱為 chapstick。

lit·ter [ˋlɪtɚ]

Track 2629

名 雜物、一窩（小豬或小狗）、廢物 動 散置

同 rubbish 廢物、垃圾

▶名 Don't throw litter about. Put it in the trash can.
不要亂丟紙屑，請把它丟到垃圾桶吧。

▶動 You should not litter in the classroom.
你不應該在教室亂丟垃圾。

live·ly [ˋlaɪvlɪ]

Track 2630

形 有生氣的 同 bright 有生氣的

▶She is usually more lively in front of her friends.
她在朋友面前通常表現得比較活躍。

liv·er [ˋlɪvɚ]

Track 2631

名 肝臟

▶The doctor said there's something wrong with my liver.
醫生說我的肝臟有些毛病。

load [lod]　　Track 2632

名 負載 動 裝載

▶名 Her grief is a heavy load to bear. 她心情沉重得難以承受。

▶動 Let's load these goods（貨物）into the truck together.
我們一起把這些貨物裝到卡車上吧。

實用片語用語
loads of 很多的
例如：Why are you worried about having nothing to wear? You've got loads of dresses.
你何必擔心沒有衣服可穿？你的洋裝那麼多。

lob·by [ˋlɑbɪ]　　Track 2633

名 休息室、大廳 同 entrance 入口

▶Wait for me in the lobby at three p.m. 下午三點在大廳等我。

lob·ster [ˋlɑbstɚ]　　Track 2634

名 龍蝦

▶Would you like to have a lobster for dinner?
你晚餐想不想吃龍蝦？

lol·li·pop [ˋlɑlɪ͵pɑp]　　Track 2635

名 棒棒糖

▶The little boy is eating a purple lollipop.
那個小男孩在吃一根紫色的棒棒糖。

loose [lus]　　Track 2636

形 寬鬆的

▶The shirt is too loose for me. 這襯衫對我來說太寬鬆了。

loos·en [ˋlusn̩]　　Track 2637

動 鬆開、放鬆 同 relax 放鬆

▶You have to loosen up and have some fun.
你應該要放輕鬆好好玩才對啊。

實用片語用語
loosen up 放鬆

lord [lɔrd]　　Track 2638

名 領主 同 owner 物主

▶He used to be a lord, but not anymore.
他以前是個君主，但現在不是了。

loud·speak·er [ˋlaudˋspikɚ]　　Track 2639

名 擴音器

▶They announced the news over the loudspeaker.
他們透過擴音器宣布消息。

lug·gage [ˋlʌgɪdʒ]　　Track 2640

名 行李 同 baggage 行李

▶Can you help me carry my luggage to my room?
可以幫我把我的行李搬到我房間嗎？

萬用延伸句型
Can you help me...? 可以幫我……嗎？
例如：Can you help me open this bottle?
可以幫我打開這個瓶子嗎？

lull·a·by [ˋlʌlə͵baɪ]　　Track 2641

名 搖籃曲

▶名 The baby fell asleep as soon as his mother began singing a lullaby.
小嬰兒的媽媽一哼搖籃曲，這個小嬰兒就很快睡著了。

lung [lʌŋ] Track 2642
名 肺臟
▶There is a close connection between smoking and lung cancer.
吸煙跟肺癌之間有密切的關係。

實用片語用語
a close connection between A and B A 和 B 之間的密切關連

mag·i·cal [ˋmædʒɪkḷ] Track 2643
形 魔術的、神奇的
▶I don't believe that the magician（魔術師）has magical powers.
我不相信那個魔術師擁有魔力。

mag·net [ˋmægnɪt] Track 2644
名 磁鐵
▶New York is a great magnet for many foreigners.
紐約對於外國人來說是一個具有極大吸引力的地方。

maid [med] Track 2645
名 女僕、少女
▶Why don't you ask your house maid to clean your study today?
為什麼不叫你的女傭今天把你的書房打掃一下呢？

萬用延伸句型
Why don't you...? 你何不……？

ma·jor [ˋmedʒɚ] Track 2646
形 較大的、主要的 動 主修
▶形 What's the major industry of your nation?
你們國家的主要行業是什麼？
▶動 I major in English in university.
我在大學主修英語。

ma·jor·i·ty [məˋdʒɔrətɪ] Track 2647
名 多數 反 minority 少數
▶It is hard for the majority of the students to live on the money they earn.
對於大多數學生來說，要靠自己賺的錢來維持生活很難。

mall [mɔl] Track 2648
名 購物中心
▶Would you like to go to the shopping mall with me? I want to buy some clothes there.
你想不想跟我一起去購物中心呢？我想到那裡買些衣服。

實用片語用語
shopping mall 購物中心

man·age [ˋmænɪdʒ] Track 2649
動 管理、處理
▶I don't believe that he can manage this by himself.
我不相信他能一個人處理這件事。

man·age·ment [ˋmænɪdʒmənt] Track 2650

名 處理、管理

▶What do you think of the management of the hotel? Good or bad?
你覺得這間旅館經營得如何？是好還是壞呢？

man·age·a·ble [ˋmænɪdʒəbl̩] Track 2651

形 可管理的、易處理的

▶Why don't we divide the task into several small, manageable sections?
為什麼不把任務分成幾個容易處理的小部分呢？

man·ag·er [ˋmænɪdʒɚ] Track 2652

名 經理

▶What do you think of the new manager?
你覺得新來的經理怎麼樣？

文法字詞解析
從以上四個單字中，可以看出字尾的重要性喔！字根 manage（管理、處理）加上名詞字尾「-ment」變成了名詞形式「management」，加上意為「能夠」的形容詞字尾「-able」變成了意為「可管理的」的「manageable」，加上意為「……者」的名詞字尾「-er」變成了意為「管理者」（也就是經理）的 manager。

man·kind/hum·an·kind [mænˋkaɪnd]/[ˋhjumən͵kaɪnd] Track 2653

名 人類 同 humanity 人類

▶Do you think that mankind has made the world a better place?
你覺得人類有讓世界成為一個更好的地方嗎？

man·ners [ˋmænɚz] Track 2654

名 禮貌、風俗 同 custom 風俗

▶Old people like to lecture kids on their manners.
老人喜歡教訓小孩要有禮貌。

文法字詞解析
manners 當作「禮貌、風俗」時，那個「s」是必要的。如果是單數 manner，意思則是「方式、樣子」，例如「in a friendly manner」就是「以友善的方式……」。

mar·ble [ˋmɑrbl̩] Track 2655

名 大理石

▶There is a huge marble statue at the square.
廣場上有座巨大的大理石雕塑。

march [mɑrtʃ] Track 2656

動 前進、行軍 名 行軍、長途跋涉 同 hike 健行

▶動 Lots of people are marching on the street.
很多人在大街上遊行。

▶名 These shoes are good for long marches.
這雙鞋子很適合長途跋涉時穿著。

mar·vel·ous [ˋmɑrvələs] Track 2657

形 令人驚訝的

▶I think that's a marvelous idea.
我覺得這主意太棒了。

文法字詞解析
「marvel」是「令……感到驚奇」的意思，加上形容詞字尾「-ous（帶有某種特質的）」就變成了「marvelous（令人驚奇的）」。

math·e·mat·i·cal [͵mæθəˋmætɪkl̩] Track 2658

形 數學的

▶Will you tell me how to work out this mathematical problem?
你能告訴我怎樣才能算出這道數學題嗎？

math·e·mat·ics/ math [͵mæθəˋmætɪks]/[mæθ] *Track 2659*

名 數學

▶My brother does well in mathematics at school.
哥哥在學校的數學成績很好。

ma·ture [məˋtjʊr] *Track 2660*

形 成熟的 同 adult 成熟的、成年的

▶He is not mature enough to be given such an important task.
他還不夠成熟，還無法勝任如此重大的任務。

may·or [ˋmeɚ] *Track 2661*

名 市長

▶Would you tell me how I can get in touch with the mayor?
你能告訴我如何才能與市長取得聯繫嗎？

實用片語用語
get in touch with sb. 與某人聯絡、取得聯繫

mead·ow [ˋmɛdo] *Track 2662*

名 草地

▶There are many herds（獸群）of cattle on the meadow.
草地上有許多牛群。

mean·ing·ful [ˋminɪŋfəl] *Track 2663*

形 有意義的 同 significant 有意義的

▶I don't think what the president said is very meaningful.
我認為總統講的這些話意義不大。

mean·while [ˋmin͵hwaɪl] *Track 2664*

副 同時 名 期間 同 meantime 同時

▶副 John is washing dishes. Meanwhile, his sister is eating cake. 約翰在洗盤子。同時，他姊姊正在吃蛋糕。

▶名 We have a one-hour break between the two exams. In the meanwhile, what about getting something to eat?
在兩場考試的中間我們有一個小時可以休息。在這期間吃點東西如何？

med·al [ˋmɛdl̩] *Track 2665*

名 獎章

▶It doesn't matter whether you win the gold medal or not. You are still the best in my heart.
你能不能獲得金牌都不重要，在我心中你是最棒的。

萬用延伸句型
It doesn't matter whether...
無論是否……都無所謂

med·i·cal [ˋmɛdɪkl̩] *Track 2666*

形 醫學的

▶He has lots of medical knowledge. 他擁有非常豐富的醫學知識。

me·di·um/me·di·a *Track 2667*
[ˋmidɪəm]/[ˋmidɪə]

名 媒體

▶Don't believe everything that is reported by the media.
不要相信媒體報導的所有事情。

mem·ber·ship [ˋmɛmbɚ͵ʃɪp]

Track 2668

名 會員

▶The membership of this club is limited to women only.
這間俱樂部的成員僅限於女性。

mem·o·rize [ˋmɛmə͵raɪz]

Track 2669

動 記憶

▶It is hard for him to memorize all the words in the book.
要他記住這本書的所有單字很難。

萬用延伸句型
It is hard for sb. to... 對某人來說，（做某事）很難

mend [mɛnd]

Track 2670

動 修補、修改 同 repair 修理

▶Will you please mend the sleeves of this shirt?
請你把這件襯衫的袖子補一下好嗎？

men·tal [ˋmɛntl̩]

Track 2671

形 心理的、心智的

▶We should take care of not only our physical（身體的）health but also our mental health.
我們不僅要照顧身體健康，還要照顧心理健康。

men·tion [ˋmɛnʃən]

Track 2672

動 提起 名 提及

▶動 Do you mind if I mention this matter at the meeting?
你介意我在會議中提及這件事嗎？

▶名 He made no mention of your request.
他沒有提到你的要求。

文法字詞解析
由於有個片語 talk about（說到關於某事），許多人也會使用「mention about」這個說法。但 mention 這個單字本身就包含了「關於」的意思，所以 about 是多餘的，mention about 的說法是不對的喔！

mer·chant [ˋmɝtʃənt]

Track 2673

名 商人

▶The merchants of their country are able to do business all over the world.
他們國家的商人能在世界各地做生意。

mer·ry [ˋmɛrɪ]

Track 2674

形 快樂的

▶Let's eat, drink, and be merry.
我們來大吃大喝、好好享樂吧！

mess [mɛs]

Track 2675

名 雜亂 動 弄亂

▶名 The dog made a mess in the house.
這隻狗把房子裡弄得一團亂。

▶動 I hope I won't mess up. 希望我不會搞砸。

實用片語用語
make a mess 造成一團混亂

mi·cro·phone/ mike [ˋmaɪkrə͵fon]/[maɪk]

Track 2676

名 麥克風

▶Your microphone isn't working. We can't hear you.
你的麥克風壞了，我們聽不到你的聲音。

mi·cro·wave [ˋmaɪkrə͵wev]

Track 2677

名 微波爐 動 微波

▶名 There is a microwave in the kitchen. You can use it whenever you need to.
廚房裡有一台微波爐。你隨時都可以用它。

▶動 Please don't microwave the eggs. It's not safe.
不要把雞蛋放到微波爐去微波，不安全。

might [maɪt]

Track 2678

名 權力、力氣 同 power 權力

▶I pushed with all my might but still can't get the car to move.
我用全身的力氣推，但車子還是不會動。

實用片語用語
with all sb.'s might 盡全力

might·y [ˋmaɪtɪ]

Track 2679

形 強大的、有力的

▶There is no doubt that this country has become a mighty nation. 毫無疑問，這個國家已經成為了一個強國。

mill [mɪl]

Track 2680

名 磨坊、工廠 動 研磨

▶名 Would you like to work in our small paper mill?
你願意到我們的小型造紙廠工作嗎？

▶動 I need to mill flour today; would you like to help me?
我今天需要研磨麵粉，你願意幫我嗎？

mil·lion·aire [͵mɪljənˋɛr]

Track 2681

名 百萬富翁

▶The millionaire lives a very quiet life.
這個百萬富翁過著非常平靜的生活。

min·er [ˋmaɪnɚ]

Track 2682

名 礦夫

▶Not all of us can understand how hard the coal miners' life is.
並不是所有人都能理解煤礦工人的生活有多艱辛。

文法字詞解析
miner 就是「礦坑」（mine）加上表示「……者」的字尾「-(e)r」。

mi·nor [ˋmaɪnɚ]

Track 2683

形 較小的、次要的 名 未成年者

▶形 She's always making a fuss（大驚小怪）over minor things.
她總是大驚小怪的。

▶名 The pub doesn't allow minors inside.
這個酒吧不允許未成年人進來。

實用片語用語
make a fuss over sth. / sb. 對……大驚小怪
或者也可以直接用動詞：fuss over sth. / sb.

mi·nor·i·ty [maɪˋnɔrətɪ]

Track 2684

名 少數 反 majority 多數

▶The minority opinion is that we should focus more on diversity（多樣性）. 少數意見認為，我們應該更重視多樣性的問題。

mir·a·cle [ˋmɪrək!]

Track 2685

名 奇蹟 同 marvel 令人驚奇的事物

▶Don't you think the computer is a miracle of modern science and technology? 難道你不認為電腦是當代科學技術的奇蹟嗎？

mis·er·y [ˋmɪzərɪ]

Track 2686

名 悲慘 同 distress 悲痛

▶There are still many people living a life of misery.
還有很多人正過著悲慘的生活。

實用片語用語
end sb.'s misery 把某人從悲慘中解救出來
雖說是要從悲慘中解救出來，但使用這個片語時常暗示著用一個也不怎麼愉快的方式來結束此人的悲慘狀況。舉例來說，電影中常會出現角色快死了但還沒死，於是他可能會拿起一把槍遞給別的角色，說：End my misery!（殺了我，讓我解脫吧！）

mis·sile [ˋmɪsḷ]

Track 2687

名 發射物、飛彈

▶Many countries are trying to develop all kinds of missiles.
許多國家都在研發各種導彈。

miss·ing [ˋmɪsɪŋ]

Track 2688

形 失蹤的、缺少的

▶The missing child was finally safely home.
那個失蹤的孩子終於安全到家了。

mis·sion [ˋmɪʃən]

Track 2689

名 任務

▶Our mission is to make sure that children in our country receive good education.
我們的任務是確認我國的孩子們得到好的教育。

mist [mɪst]

Track 2690

名 霧 動 被霧籠罩 同 fog 霧

▶名 It is difficult for us to see anything in the heavy mist.
我們很難在濃霧中看見任何東西。

▶動 The hills mist over in the morning.
早上小山丘籠罩在薄霧之中。

實用片語用語
mist over / up 被霧籠罩
我們喝熱湯的時候，如果不摘下眼鏡，往往一靠近湯碗鏡片就會起霧，這時候也可以用「mist over」。

mix·ture [ˋmɪkstʃɚ]

Track 2691

名 混合物

▶Will you tell me the constituents（成分）of the mixture?
你能告訴我這種混合物的成分是什麼嗎？

mob [mɑb]

Track 2692

名 民眾 動 群集

▶名 Would you tell me why this man is surrounded by the mob?
你能告訴我為什麼這個人被民眾包圍起來了嗎？

▶動 I don't want to be mobbed by reporters tomorrow.
我可不想明天被記者包圍。

mo·bile [ˋmobɪl]

Track 2693

形 可動的 同 movable 可動的

▶It is so nice of you to lend me your mobile phone.
你借手機給我用，你人真好。

moist [mɔɪst]

Track 2694

形 潮濕的 同 damp 潮濕的

▶It took her a year to get used to the moist climate here.
她花了一年的時間才適應這裡的潮濕氣候。

文法字詞解析
雖說「潮濕」聽起來似乎不是很舒服的事，但 moist 很多時候其實是個正面的字喔！像是鎖水保濕的化妝品，功能就是讓你的臉部肌膚變得 moist。

mois·ture [ˋmɔɪstʃɚ] Track 2695

名 溼氣

▶It is cold outside but pretty warm inside. It is no wonder that a faint moisture has appeared upon the window.
外面很冷但裡面很熱。難怪窗戶上蒙上了一層稀薄的溼氣。

文法字詞解析
在這個句子裡面，faint 是「稀薄、微弱的」的意思，如果某人生重病，呼吸變得很淺、很微弱，我們就可以說「his / her breathg becomes faint」；另外，要形容非常渺小的希望，也可以說「a faint hope」。

monk [mʌŋk] Track 2696

名 僧侶、修道士

▶The monks who live in that temple are usually dressed in grey. 那個寺廟裡的僧侶通常都穿著灰色。

mood [mud] Track 2697

名 心情 同 feeling 感覺

▶Will you tell me why you are in no mood to study today?
你能告訴我為什麼你今天沒心情唸書嗎？

mop [mɑp] Track 2698

名 拖把 動 擦拭 同 wipe 擦

▶名 Why don't you buy a new mop? 為什麼不去買支新拖把？

▶動 He mopped the floor quickly and then washed the dishes.
他很快地擦了地板，然後洗了盤子。

實用片語用語
a mop of hair 亂蓬蓬的頭髮
有些人的頭髮亂蓬蓬的，看起來是不是像拖把一樣呢？因此才會有這個片語的出現。

mor·al [ˋmɔrəl] Track 2699

形 道德上的 名 寓意

▶形 Do you think euthanasia（安樂死）is moral?
你覺得安樂死符合道德標準嗎？

▶名 The moral of the story is to never envy others for what you don't have.
這個故事的寓意是，不要嫉妒別人擁有你所沒有的。

mo·tel [moˋtɛl] Track 2700

名 汽車旅館

▶Will you tell me where the nearest motel is?
你能告訴我最近的汽車旅館在哪裡嗎？

mo·tor [ˋmotɚ] Track 2701

名 馬達、發電機

▶I don't think the salesman（銷售員）knows which company produces this kind of electric motor.
我認為那個銷售員並不知道這種電動馬達是哪家公司生產的。

mur·der [ˋmɝdɚ] Track 2702

名 謀殺 動 謀殺、殘害 同 assassinate 暗殺

▶名 The police will investigate the murder as soon as possible.
警察會儘快對這個謀殺案進行調查。

▶動 The man murdered the singer and tried to escape.
那個男人謀殺了那位歌手並試圖逃跑。

實用片語用語
commit murder 犯下謀殺罪
例如：I can't believe he would commit murder.
我真難相信他會做出謀殺這種事。

mus·cle [ˋmʌsl̩] Track 2703

名 肌肉

▶Exercising can not only develop your muscles but also help you keep fit. 運動不僅能鍛練肌肉更有助於保持身體健康。

mush·room [ˋmʌʃrum] Track 2704

名 蘑菇 動 急速生長

▶名 It is hard for us to tell which mushroom is edible（可食用的）and which is poisonous（有毒的）.
我們很難辨別出哪種蘑菇可以食用和哪種是有毒的。

▶動 New flats and offices have mushroomed all over the city.
這座城市到處如雨後春筍般地出現了許多新公寓和辦公大樓。

mu·si·cal [ˋmjuzɪkḷ] Track 2705

形 音樂的 名 音樂劇

▶形 Don't you know that he is from a great musical family?
難道你不知道嗎？他出身於一個偉大的音樂世家。

▶名 He hates watching musicals.
他討厭觀賞音樂劇。

mys·ter·y [ˋmɪstərɪ] Track 2706

名 神秘

▶How they got married is still a mystery to me.
他們到底怎麼會結婚，對我來說還是個謎。

實用片語用語
mystery novel 懸疑小說、推理小說
例如：Mystery novels by Agatha Christie are my favorite.
我最喜歡阿嘉莎•克莉絲蒂的推理小說了。

nan·ny [ˋnænɪ] Track 2707

名 奶媽

▶You should hire a nanny to look after your child.
你應該請個保姆來照顧你們的孩子。

nap [næp] Track 2708

名 小睡、打盹

▶It's my habit to take a nap at noon.
我有睡午覺的習慣。

萬用延伸句型
It's sb.'s habit to... ……是某人的習慣

na·tive [ˋnetɪv] Track 2709

形 本國的、天生的

▶I wish I could go back to my native homeland.
我真希望能回到我生長的故鄉。

na·vy [ˋnevɪ] Track 2710

名 海軍、艦隊

▶My brother is in the navy.
我弟弟是海軍。

文法字詞解析
因為海軍的制服多半都會配有類似寶藍色、深海藍的顏色，所以 navy 也可以作為顏色，用中文說就是「海軍藍」。

ne·ces·si·ty [nəˋsɛsətɪ] Track 2711

名 必需品

▶She felt the necessity of accepting the invitation.
她感到有必要接受這個邀請。

neck·tie [ˋnɛkˌtaɪ]

Track 2712

名 領帶

▶How about buying a necktie for your boyfriend（男朋友）as his birthday（生日）gift?
幫你男朋友買條領帶當作生日禮物怎麼樣？

文法字詞解析
領帶也可以直接說 tie。而蝴蝶結形狀的那種領結，則可以稱為 bow tie。

neigh·bor·hood [ˋnebɚˌhʊd]

Track 2713

名 社區

▶Why don't you move to another neighborhood?
你何不搬到別的社區呢？

nerve [nɝv]

Track 2714

名 神經

▶I am always in a state of nerves before an examination.
考試之前我總是非常緊張。

nerv·ous [ˋnɝvəs]

Track 2715

形 神經質的、膽怯的

▶The merest（微小的）little thing makes him nervous.
連微不足道的小事也會使他緊張。

net·work [ˋnɛtˌwɝk]

Track 2716

名 網路

▶There is a network of caves under the mountain.
這座山裡面有許多相通的洞穴。

實用片語用語
a network of 一系統的、網絡的
例如：He asked his network of friends for help.
他請他朋友圈的朋友們幫忙。

nick·name [ˋnɪkˌnem]

Track 2717

名 綽號 動 取綽號

▶名 What was your nickname in high school?
你高中時的綽號是什麼？

▶動 They nicknamed the boy "shorty".
他們幫那個男孩取了「矮子」的綽號。

no·ble [ˋnobl̩]

Track 2718

形 高貴的 名 貴族

▶形 You can tell from the way she carries herself that she's of noble background.
看她的舉止就知道她出身高貴。

▶名 The nobles in the area are mostly very old now.
這一帶的貴族現在大部分都很老了。

nor·mal [ˋnɔrml̩]

Track 2719

形 標準的、正常的 同 regular 正常的、規律的

▶She doesn't like wearing normal clothes.
她不喜歡穿正常的衣服。

文法字詞解析
normal 意為「正常的」，那麼「不正常的」呢？可以在前面加上字首「ab-」，變成「abnormal」，就是不正常的意思了。

nov·el·ist [ˋnɑvl̩ɪst]

Track 2720

名 小說家

▶She is not only a novelist but also a university lecturer（講師）. 她不但是小說家而且還是位大學講師。

nun [nʌn] Track 2721

名 修女、尼姑

▶I was so surprised at the news that she became a nun in the end. 得知她最終當了修女的消息，我感到很震驚。

oak [ok] Track 2722

名 橡樹、橡葉

▶The oak tree beside my house is home to a family of squirrels.
我家外面的橡樹是松鼠一家人的家。

實用片語用語
A is home to B A 是 B 的家園或棲息地

ob·serve [əbˋzɝv] Track 2723

動 觀察、評論

▶We sit here observing the people who walk by.
我們坐在這裡觀察行人。

文法字詞解析
observe 去掉 e 加上形容詞字尾「-ant」就變成了形容詞 observant，它的意思是「富有觀察力的」。

ob·vi·ous [ˋɑbvɪəs] Track 2724

形 顯然的、明顯的 同 evident 明顯的

▶It's really obvious that they're twins. They look so alike!
他們很顯然是雙胞胎，長那麼像！

oc·ca·sion [əˋkeʒən] Track 2725

名 事件、場合 動 引起

▶名 Tomorrow is your stepfather's birthday. Why not take this occasion to thank him?
明天是你繼父的生日。何不藉此機會感謝一下你的繼父呢？

▶動 His remarks（話語）are going to occasion a quarrel（爭吵）sooner or later.
他講的話遲早有一天會引起爭吵。

odd [ɑd] Track 2726

形 單數的、怪異的

▶She's an odd old lady who doesn't talk to anyone.
她是個怪異的老太太，不和任何人說話。

文法字詞解析
「odd number」指奇數（即 1、3、5……等不能被 2 整除的數字），那偶數呢？則叫做 even number。

on·to [ˋɑntu] Track 2727

介 在……之上

▶I don't think you can jump onto the bus while it's moving.
我認為你不能在公車移動的時候跳上車。

op·er·a·tor [ˋɑpəˏretɚ] Track 2728

名 操作者

▶Our company is in need of computer operators.
我們公司需要電腦操作員。

op·por·tu·ni·ty [ˌapɚˋtjunətɪ] Track 2729

名 機遇、機會

▶It's a great opportunity for us to tell him what we really think.
這是個好機會，讓我們能跟他說出我們的真正想法。

op·po·site [ˋapəsɪt] Track 2730

形 相對的、對立的 同 contrary 對立的

▶He always holds opposite views to hers.
他的意見總是和她相反。

文法字詞解析
此句也可以使用表達「站在對立一方」、「反對」的動詞 oppose，寫成 He always opposes her views.。

op·ti·mis·tic [ˌaptəˋmɪstɪk] Track 2731

形 樂觀（主義）的 反 pessimistic 悲觀的

▶It is hard for him to keep optimistic about the whole thing.
他很難對這整件事情保持樂觀的態度。

or·i·gin [ˋɔrədʒɪn] Track 2732

名 起源

▶Don't you think it's fun to study the origin of life?
難道你不認為研究生命的起源很有趣嗎？

o·rig·i·nal [əˋrɪdʒən!] Track 2733

形 起初的 名 原作

▶形 It doesn't matter whether you give me the original copy or not. 你是不是給我正本都沒關係。

▶名 I don't care whether this is a duplicate（複製品）or the original. 這是複製品還是原作我都無所謂。

or·phan [ˋɔrfən] Track 2734

名 孤兒 動 使（孩童）成為孤兒

▶名 The orphan has finally been adopted. 這個孤兒終於被收養了。

▶動 The orphaned child is sent to an asylum（院）.
那個成為孤兒的孩子被送到孤兒院了。

文法字詞解析
句中的 asylum 是「院」的意思，除了孤兒院以外，老人院、精神病院等等的「院」都可以用這個字。另外，孤兒院也可以稱為「orphanage」。

ought to [ɔt tu] Track 2735

助 應該

▶Don't you think you ought to be more careful?
難道你不覺得你應該要更小心點嗎？

out·door [ˋaʊtˌdor] Track 2736

形 戶外的 反 indoor 室內的

▶I think we should have more outdoor activities like this.
我覺得我們應該有更多像這樣的戶外活動。

out·doors [ˋaʊtˋdorz] Track 2737

副 在戶外、在屋外

▶How about giving a party outdoors? 在戶外舉行一個派對如何？

out·er [ˋaʊtɚ] Track 2738

形 外部的、外面的

▶I've always dreamed of going to outer space.
我總是夢想著要去外太空。

實用片語用語
outer space 外太空

out·line [ˋaʊt͵laɪn] Track 2739

名 外形、輪廓 動 畫出輪廓 同 sketch 畫草圖、草擬

▶名 It is hard to see the outline of these buildings clearly（清楚地）in the heavy fog.
很難在大霧中看清楚建築物的輪廓。

▶動 He outlined the plan for her quickly.
他很快地為她大概草擬出計畫的內容。

o·ver·coat [ˋovɚ͵kot] Track 2740

名 大衣、外套

▶I need to put on my overcoat before I go out.
我得先穿上大衣才能出門。

文法字詞解析
其實從單字中的「over-」就可以知道，overcoat 指的是將所有衣服包住、穿在最外層的大衣，通常會是長度及膝、嚴冬才會穿的厚重大衣；如果只是要說一般的大衣，就可以說「topcoat」。

實用片語用語
put on 穿起（衣服、鞋襪）

owe [o] Track 2741

動 虧欠、欠債

▶The bank asked him to pay back what he owed as soon as possible.
銀行要求他盡快償還所欠的款項。

own·er·ship [ˋonɚʃɪp] Track 2742

名 主權、所有權 同 possession 所有物

▶The coffee shop is under new ownership.
這間咖啡店已經換新主人了。

pad [pæd] Track 2743

名 墊子、印臺 動 填塞 同 cushion 墊子

▶名 The mouse pad is designed very nicely.
這個滑鼠墊設計得很好。

▶動 The cat padded softly into the room.
那隻貓輕輕地走進了房間。

實用片語用語
knee pads 護膝
例如：Put on knee pads before you go roller-skating.
去溜直排輪前先穿上護膝吧。

pail [pel] Track 2744

名 桶

▶I noticed that there was a hole in the bottom of his pail.
我注意到他的桶子底下有一個洞。

pal [pæl] Track 2745

名 夥伴 同 companion 同伴

▶My dog is my best pal.
我的狗是我最好的朋友。

文法字詞解析
pal 的意思是很親密的朋友，例如要說自己見了一位老友就可以說「meet up with an old pal」；或是曾經風行過一段時間的交「筆友」就是「pen pal」。

pal·ace [ˋpælɪs] Track 2746

名 宮殿

▶A lot of tourists are visiting the palace.
有好多遊客在參觀那座宮殿。

pale [pel]
Track 2747

形 蒼白的

▶Why are you so pale? Are you sick?
你怎麼這麼蒼白？你生病了嗎？

實用片語用語
pale blonde 極淡的金髮
pale 是「蒼白的」的意思，拿來描述金髮的話，即表示金髮的顏色淡得幾乎要白了，但同時還是保有金色成分在。

pan·cake [ˋpænˏkek]
Track 2748

名 薄煎餅

▶The pancakes made by my mother are really tasty; would you like to have a try?
我媽媽做的煎餅非常好吃，你想不想吃吃看？

pan·ic [ˋpænɪk]
Track 2749

名 驚恐 動 恐慌 同 scare 驚嚇

▶名 The fire alarm caused a panic in the building.
火災警報響起，造成大樓裡一片恐慌。

▶動 Don't panic, boys. There is no danger here.
不要慌，孩子們，這裡沒有危險。

pa·rade [pəˋred]
Track 2750

名 遊行 動 參加遊行、閱兵

▶名 Let's go sit down and wait for the parade to pass by.
我們去坐下來等著遊行隊伍經過吧。

▶動 The peacock（孔雀）paraded the street showing off its feathers. 那隻孔雀招搖地在街上走，炫耀牠的羽毛。

實用片語用語
show off 炫耀

par·a·dise [ˋpærəˏdaɪs]
Track 2751

名 天堂

▶Bhutan（不丹）is a paradise on earth. 不丹是一個人間天堂。

實用片語用語
paradise on earth 人間天堂

par·cel [ˋpɑrsḷ]
Track 2752

名 包裹 動 捆成

▶名 Would you please tell me what this parcel contains?
能請您告訴我這個包裹裡面有什麼嗎？

▶動 Can you parcel some food for the boys to carry to their picnic? 麻煩你包一些食品讓孩子們帶去野餐好嗎？

par·tic·i·pate [pɑrˋtɪsəˏpet]
Track 2753

動 參與

▶I don't know whether you or I should participate in the important meeting.
我不知道你還是我應該參加這次重要的會議。

pas·sage [ˋpæsɪdʒ]
Track 2754

名 通道

▶There's a secret passage in the house.
這間房子有個秘密通道。

pas·sion [ˋpæʃən]
Track 2755

名 熱情 同 emotion 情感

▶She always speaks with passion when it comes to her favorite subject. 談到她喜歡的主題，她總是很熱情地侃侃而談。

實用片語用語
passion fruit 百香果
例如：I like to make juice from passion fruit.
我喜歡用百香果做果汁。

pass·port [ˋpæs͵port]

Track 2756

名 護照

▶Would you please show me your passport, Miss?
小姐，請出示您的護照好嗎？

pass·word [ˋpæs͵wɝd]

Track 2757

名 口令、密碼

▶Why don't you use a password to prevent strangers from using your computer?
為什麼不用密碼來防止陌生人使用你的電腦呢？

pa·tience [ˋpeʃəns]

Track 2758

名 耐心

▶I can tell that his patience is wearing thin.
我看得出來，他快沒耐心了。

實用片語用語
wear thin 變薄、磨損
wear thin 常用來說衣物、布匹因為長期的使用而被磨掉、變薄，而可以想像我們人的耐性如果被別人一直「磨」，也會慢慢被「磨掉」，因此可以用這個片語表示失去耐性。

pause [pɔz]

Track 2759

名 暫停、中止 同 cease 停止

▶There was a pause before she answered my question.
她停頓了一下才回答我的問題。

pave [pev]

Track 2760

動 鋪築

▶I don't believe this treaty（條約）will pave the way for peace.
我不相信這個條約將為和平鋪路。

pave·ment [ˋpevmənt]

Track 2761

名 人行道

▶Don't ride your bike onto the pavement. You might hit someone.
不要把車騎到人行道上，可能會撞到人。

paw [pɔ]

Track 2762

名 腳掌 動 以掌拍擊

▶名 The dog keeps licking her paws.
那隻狗一直舔自己的腳掌。

▶動 He pawed at the air trying to grab at the rope.
他在空中亂抓，試著抓住繩子。

實用片語用語
paw print 動物的腳印
例如：My dog left paw prints all over the ground.
我的狗留下了滿地的腳印。

pay/sal·a·ry/wage

Track 2763

[pe]/[ˋsælərɪ]/[wedʒ]

名 薪水

▶In my opinion, the pay of this company isn't that bad.
在我看來，這間公司的薪水還不錯。

pea [pi]

Track 2764

名 豌豆

▶What do you want to eat, beans or peas?
你要吃哪個，蠶豆還是豌豆？

peak [pik]

Track 2765

名 山頂 動 聳起 同 top 頂端

▶名 By the time of the end of the month, the sales will have reached a new peak.
到月底的時候，銷售額將會達到新的高峰。

▶動 The unemployment（失業）rate peaked at 7.3% last week.
上禮拜失業率已達到百分之七點三的高峰。

實用片語用語

mountain peak 山的頂峰

例如：I can see the snowy mountain peak from here.
從這裡我可以看到山的頂峰白雪皚皚。

pearl [pɝl]

Track 2766

名 珍珠

▶Not all these necklaces（項鍊）are made of real pearls.
這些項鍊不是全部都用真正的珍珠做成的。

peel [pil]

Track 2767

名 果皮 動 剝皮

▶名 Would you please throw the banana peel into the trash can?
請你把香蕉皮丟進垃圾筒裡好嗎？

▶動 I can't peel all these potatoes by myself.
我沒辦法一個人幫這麼多馬鈴薯削皮。

peep [pip]

Track 2768

動 窺視、偷看

▶He peeped through to keyhole into the room.
他透過鑰匙孔窺視房間。

pen·ny [ˋpɛnɪ]

Track 2769

名 便士、分

▶It has been six years since he arrived in this country without a penny.
從他身無分文地來到這個國家後已經六年了。

實用片語用語

A penny for your thoughts.
你在想什麼呢？
這句口語直翻就是「我用一分錢跟你換你的想法」，用來跟看起來似乎在沉思、令你好奇他到底在想什麼的人說。其實意思就是「你在想什麼呢？可以跟我講嗎？」，並不是真的要拿錢給對方。

per·form [pɚˋfɔrm]

Track 2770

動 執行、表演

▶The students will perform an opera next Friday. Would you like to see it?
這些學生下星期五將表演歌劇。你想不想去看？

per·form·ance [pɚˋʃɔrməns]

Track 2771

名 演出

▶This musical is considered a brilliant（出色的）performance.
這齣音樂劇是公認的出色演出。

per·mis·sion [pɚˋmɪʃən]

Track 2772

名 許可 同 approval 許可

▶It's illegal（非法的）for you to read people's private letters without permission.
你未經許可就看別人的私人信件是不合法的。

per·mit [pɚˋmɪt]/[ˋpɝmɪt]

Track 2773

動 容許、許可 名 批准 同 allow 允許

▶動 We won't discuss both questions unless time permits.
除非時間許可，否則我們不會兩個問題都討論。

▶名 Unless you have a work permit, you cannot work here.
除非你有許可證，否則就不能在這裡工作。

文法字詞解析
「-sion」或類似的「-tion」是將字根轉換成名詞的字尾。因此，permit 加上了字尾「-sion」，變成了 permission，也就是 permit 的名詞形式。

per·son·al·i·ty [ˏpɝsn̩ˋælətɪ]

Track 2774

名 個性、人格

▶I really like her personality, kind but strong at the same time.
我很喜歡她的個性，同時又親切又堅強。

per·suade [pɚˋswed]

Track 2775

動 說服 同 convince 說服

▶Would you please persuade her out of her foolish plans?
請你勸她放棄她那些愚蠢的計畫好嗎？

pest [pɛst]

Track 2776

名 害蟲、令人討厭的人

▶The grains are often attacked by pests.
這些穀物經常受到害蟲的破壞。

文法字詞解析
有個相關的實用單字 pesticide（殺蟲劑），就是用來殺害「害蟲」的。

pick·le [ˋpɪkl̩]

Track 2777

名 醃菜 動 醃製

▶名 She was good at making jams and pickles.
她很擅長做果醬和泡菜。

▶動 By the time I came back, Grandmother had already pickled many cucumbers（小黃瓜）for us.
等到我回來的時候，奶奶已經為我們醃好許多小黃瓜了。

pill [pɪl]

Track 2778

名 藥丸

▶It is not good for you to take sleeping pills every night.
每天晚上都服用安眠藥的話對你是不好的。

pi·lot [ˋpaɪlət]

Track 2779

名 飛行員、領航員

▶Not everyone can meet all the requirements（要求）of being a pilot.
不是每個人都能達到成為一名飛行員的所有要求。

pine [paɪn]

Track 2780

名 松樹

▶There is a pine forest near our house.
我們家附近有片松樹林。

實用片語用語
pine tree 松樹、pine cone 松果
例句：Pine trees yield pine cones.
松樹會長出松果。

pint [paɪnt]

Track 2781

名 品脫

▶Tim loves milk very much. No wonder he drank a pint in one go.
提姆很喜歡牛奶。難怪他一口氣喝了一品脫。

pit [pɪt]

Track 2782

名 坑洞 動 挖坑

▶名 Be careful, or you might fall into the pit.
小心點，不然你可能會掉到洞裡。

▶動 His face is pitted with chicken pox（水痘）.
他的臉上都是水痘疤。

pit·y [ˋpɪtɪ]

Track 2783

名 同情 動 憐憫 同 compassion 同情

▶名 It is a pity that you couldn't come to the party.
你不能來參加派對，真是太可惜了。

▶動 I really pity her for having to live with such a crazy mother-in-law.
我真同情她，要跟一個瘋瘋癲癲的婆婆一起住。

plas·tic [ˋplæstɪk]

Track 2784

名 塑膠 形 塑膠的

▶名 Plastics don't rust like metal.
塑膠不像金屬一樣會生銹。

▶形 Can you leave the trash in a plastic bag?
請你把垃圾放在塑膠袋好不好？

實用片語用語

1. plastic bag 塑膠袋
2. 我們如果要說某個人整形了，其中的「整形手術」就是「plastic surgery」，或者也可以說「cosmetic surgery」。那如果是現在流行的「微整形」又怎麼說呢？答案是「microsurgery」。

plen·ty [ˋplɛntɪ]

Track 2785

名 豐富 形 充足的

▶名 There is plenty of time, so we don't have to rush.
時間還很多呢，所以我們不用急。

▶形 Cars didn't use to be so plenty in this area back then.
以前這一區沒有那麼多車子。

plug [plʌg]

Track 2786

名 插頭 動 接插頭

▶名 The plug of my charger is broken. I can't charge my mobile phone.
我充電器的插頭壞掉了。我沒辦法幫我的手機充電。

▶動 He plugged his ears so he didn't have to hear his sister scream. 他把耳朵塞住，就不用聽他妹妹大吼大叫了。

plum [plʌm]

Track 2787

名 李子

▶I bought some plums to eat after dinner.
我買了一些李子晚餐後吃。

文法字詞解析

plum 在英文中也可以用來表示一種「顏色」。因此你可以說你想要一件 plum-colored dress（李子色的洋裝）。

plumb·er [ˋplʌmɚ]

Track 2788

名 水管工

▶Let's get a plumber in to mend that burst pipe.
我們請個水管工來修理那根爆裂的管子吧。

pole [pol]

Track 2789

名 杆

▶He's the guy standing under the flag pole.
他就是站在旗桿下那個傢伙。

pol·i·ti·cal [pəˋlɪtɪkḷ]

Track 2790

形 政治的

▶I think it is a political matter rather than a social matter.
我覺得這是個政治問題，而不是個社會問題。

萬用延伸句型
rather than... 而不是……

pol·i·ti·cian [ˏpɑləˋtɪʃən]

Track 2791

名 政治家

▶I can't stand politicians. Most of them are liars.
我受不了政治人物，他們幾乎都是騙子。

pol·i·tics [ˋpɑləˏtɪks]

Track 2792

名 政治學

▶He has a serious aspiration（抱負）to a career in politics.
他有從政的雄心壯志。

poll [pol]

Track 2793

名 投票、民調 動 得票、投票 同 vote 投票

▶名 What do you think about conducting（實施）a public opinion poll? 你覺得實施一項民意調查如何？

▶動 What do you think of polling all the members about the change in rules?
你覺得我們就規則的變化請全體成員投票怎麼樣？

pol·lute [pəˋlut]

Track 2794

動 污染

▶I feel like it is our duty not to pollute our environment.
我感覺我們有責任不要污染我們的環境。

文法字詞解析
pollute 加上名詞字尾「-tion」則會變成 pollution，也就是「污染」的名詞說法。

po·ny [ˋponɪ]

Track 2795

名 小馬

▶I want a pony for my birthday. 我想要一匹小馬當生日禮物。

pop/pop·u·lar [pɑp]/[ˋpɑpjələ]

Track 2796

形 流行的 名 流行

▶形 He is very interested in popular songs and wants to become a song writer in the future.
他對流行歌曲很感興趣，將來想當個作曲家。

▶名 I love pop. It's my favorite kind of music.
我最愛流行音樂了，那是我最喜歡的一種音樂。

porce·lain/chi·na

[ˋporslɪn]/[ˋtʃaɪnə]

Track 2797

名 瓷器

▶I don't know enough about porcelain to be able to tell the value of these plates. 我不太懂瓷器，所以估不出這些盤子的價錢。

實用片語用語
porcelain doll 陶瓷娃娃
例如：Her skin is so perfect she looks like a percelain doll.
她的皮膚如此完美，以致於她看起來像個陶瓷娃娃。

por·tion [ˋporʃən]

Track 2798

名 部分 動 分配

▶名 Not every rich man is willing to give a large portion of his money to charity（慈善）.
不是每個富翁都願意將大部分的錢捐給慈善機構。

▶**動** She portioned out the cake so that everyone had a piece.
她把蛋糕切成很多塊，讓每人都有一份。

por·trait [ˋportret]
Track 2799

名 肖像

▶The portrait of her mother was her most prized possession（所有物）.
她母親的這張肖像是她最珍愛的物品。

post·age [ˋpostɪdʒ]
Track 2800

名 郵資

▶Will you refund（退款）the postage fee in a case like this?
若發生這種情況你能退還郵資嗎？

post·er [ˋpostɚ]
Track 2801

名 海報

▶I took all the posters off the wall. 我把牆上的海報都拿下來了。

實用片語用語

poster child 極符合某種形象的人
在海報上經常會出現人物的相片來引起對某個議題或活動的關注（例如救濟難民的海報就常會出現難民小孩的照片）。因此，後來 poster child 便延伸為可以用來形容某個人「非常符合某個形象，把他放到海報上一點都不奇怪」。

post·pone [postˋpon]
Track 2802

動 延緩、延遲 **同** delay 延遲

▶If we postpone the release of the new product, our financial（財政的）situation will be precarious（危險的）.
如果我們延遲發佈新產品的話，我們的財務將岌岌可危。

post·pone·ment [postˋponmənt]
Track 2803

名 延後

▶The postponement of the meeting made several people mad.
會議延後的事情讓許多人很生氣。

pot·ter·y/ce·ram·ics
Track 2804

[ˋpɑtɚɪ]/[səˋræmɪks]

名 陶器

▶There is going to be a pottery exhibition at the art gallery（美術館）. 美術館將舉辦一次陶瓷展。

pour [por]
Track 2805

動 澆、倒

▶Would you please help me pour wine into these glasses?
你能幫我把酒倒進這些杯子裡嗎？

萬用延伸句型

Would you please help...? 可以請你幫忙……嗎？

pov·er·ty [ˋpɑvɚtɪ]
Track 2806

名 貧窮

▶The poor children lived their lives in poverty.
那些可憐的孩子一生過著貧窮的生活。

pow·der [ˋpaudɚ]
Track 2807

名 粉 **動** 灑粉

▶**名** I emptied the powder into the washing machine.
我把這些粉倒進了洗衣機。

▶**動** She spends hours powdering her face.
她花好幾個小時在臉上灑粉。

prac·ti·cal [ˋpræktɪkl̩] Track 2808

形 實用的 同 useful 有用的

▶He is a practical person who organizes everything very well.
他是個能幹的人，把一切都弄得井然有序。

prayer [prɛr] Track 2809

名 禱告

▶Not everyone says his or her prayers every night before going to bed. 不是每個人每晚睡覺前都會禱告。

實用片語用語

say one's prayers 禱告、唸禱告詞

pre·cious [ˋprɛʃəs] Track 2810

形 珍貴的 同 valuable 珍貴的

▶He makes good use of every precious minute to study.
他好好利用寶貴的每一分鐘來唸書。

prep·a·ra·tion [ˏprɛpəˋreʃən] Track 2811

名 準備

▶It's time to make some preparations for the dinner party.
是時候為晚宴做點準備了。

pres·sure [ˋprɛʃɚ] Track 2812

名 壓力 動 施壓

▶名 Not everyone can work under high pressure.
不是每個人都能承受龐大的工作壓力，

▶動 He was pressured into signing the contract.
他被施壓強迫簽這個合約。

實用片語用語

peer presure 同儕壓力
例如：Peer pressure was what made the little girl steal the pencils.
是同儕壓力迫使那個小女孩偷鉛筆。

pre·tend [prɪˋtɛnd] Track 2813

動 假裝

▶The little girls like to pretend to be princesses.
這些小女孩喜歡假裝成公主。

pre·vent [prɪˋvɛnt] Track 2814

動 預防、阻止

▶Vitamin C is supposed to prevent colds.
維生素 C 被認為能預防感冒。

文法字詞解析

字首「pre-」有「在……之前」的意思，而字根「vent」是「來」的意思，所以 prevent 就是「在來之前預防、阻止」。如果後面再加上形容詞字尾「-ive」，就變成「預防的、防止的」。

pre·vi·ous [ˋprivɪəs] Track 2815

形 先前的 同 prior 先前的

▶Would you like to tell me some experiences you have had in your previous job? 你能不能告訴我一些你在前一份工作的經驗？

priest [prist] Track 2816

名 神父

▶The priest in this church is a very old man.
這座教堂的神父是個非常老的男人。

pri·mar·y [ˋpraɪˏmɛrɪ] Track 2817

形 主要的

▶Tom's primary defect（缺點）is laziness.
湯姆最主要的缺點就是懶惰。

prob·a·ble [ˋprɑbəbḷ] Track 2818

形 可能的

▶I don't think the probable outcome（結果）would be in our favor. 我認為最可能的結果大概不會對我們有利。

proc·ess [ˋprɑsɛs] Track 2819

名 過程 動 處理

▶名 A lot of goods were damaged in the shipping（運送）process.
在運送過程中，有許多貨物都損壞了。

▶動 Have these forms been processed yet?
這些表格有經過處理了嗎？

實用片語用語
in the process 在過程中

prod·uct [ˋprɑdəkt] Track 2820

名 產品

▶Their product has become the undisputed（無可置疑的）market leader.
他們的產品在市場上無可匹敵。

prof·it [ˋprɑfɪt] Track 2821

名 利潤 動 獲利

▶名 There is very little profit in selling newspapers at present.
現在賣報紙所能獲得的利潤很少。

▶動 A lot of people profit from the activity.
有很多人在這項活動中獲益。

pro·gram [ˋprogræm] Track 2822

名 節目

▶Would you like to tell me what functions this program has?
您能告訴我這一個程式有哪些功能嗎？

實用片語用語
TV program 電視節目
例如：Some TV programs are not made to be watched with your grandparents.
有些電視節目不宜與爺爺奶奶一同觀看。

pro·mote [prəˋmot] Track 2823

動 提倡

▶What do you think of the government's decision to promote public welfare（福利）?
你如何看待政府發展公共福利的決定？

proof [pruf] Track 2824

名 證據 同 evidence 證據

▶I don't think there is enough proof to support the case.
我認為還沒有足夠的證據來證明這個案件。

prop·er [ˋprɑpɚ] Track 2825

形 適當的

▶Not all the rich are able to make proper use of their money.
不是所有的有錢人都會適度地花錢。

prop·er·ty [ˋprɑpɚtɪ] Track 2826

名 財產

▶This land is my property.
這塊地是我的財產。

實用片語用語
property tax 財產稅
例如：I use this app to help me calculate property taxes.
我利用這個應用程式來計算財產稅。

pro·pos·al [prə`pozḷ] Track 2827

名 提議、求婚

▶His proposal to her was rejected.
他對她求婚，卻被拒絕了。

pro·tec·tion [prə`tɛkʃən] Track 2828

名 保護

▶There will be a seminar（研討會）on environmental protection held in London.
倫敦將要舉行一個關於環境保護問題的討論會。

pro·tec·tive [prə`tɛktɪv] Track 2829

形 保護的

▶A mother naturally（自然地）feels protective towards her children.
母親對自己的孩子自然會很保護。

文法字詞解析
如果這位媽媽對自己的孩子不但保護，還太過保護呢？這樣的人也不是沒有，我們可以加上表示「太過、超過」的字首「over-」，描述這樣的人為「overprotective」（保護過度的、保護慾過強的）。

pub [pʌb] Track 2830

名 酒館

▶How about going down to the pub and drinking some beer?
我們去酒館喝幾杯啤酒怎麼樣？

punch [pʌntʃ] Track 2831

動 以拳頭重擊 名 打、擊

▶動 I want to punch his face every time I see him.
我每次看到他就想揍他的臉。

▶名 He landed a punch in his brother's stomach.
他往他弟弟的肚子打了一拳。

pure [pjʊr] Track 2832

形 純粹的

▶I don't think his theory is pure conjecture（猜測）.
我認為他的理論並不僅僅是純粹的主觀猜測。

實用片語用語
pure bliss 純粹的幸福快樂
例如：They enjoyed their vacation in the Maldives in pure bliss.
他們非常幸福快樂地享受著在馬爾地夫的假期。

pur·sue [pɚ`su] Track 2833

動 追捕、追求

▶It is necessary for us to pursue success with the utmost（最大的）effort.
我們有必要以最大的努力來追求成功。

quar·rel [`kwɔrəl] Track 2834

名 / 動 爭吵

▶名 What's the matter with him? Did he have a quarrel with his girlfriend? 他怎麼了？他和他女朋友吵架了嗎？

▶動 What's wrong with them? Why do they quarrel with each other all the time? 他們怎麼了？為什麼老是吵架啊？

queer [kwɪr]

Track 2835

形 違背常理的、奇怪的

▶What a queer story! I've never heard anything like it.
多麼離奇的一個故事啊！我從來沒聽過像這樣的事。

quote [kwot]

Track 2836

動 引用、引證

▶What do you think of these sentences quoted from this book?
你覺得這些從這本書裡引用的句子如何？

文法字詞解析
大家寫文章時，如果要引用某人的話就會使用到「quotation mark」，也就是「引號」。

ra·cial [ˋreʃəl]

Track 2837

形 種族的

▶Racial prejudice（偏見）is still a problem in the world now.
現在的世界上，種族偏見還是個問題。

ra·dar [ˋredɑr]

Track 2838

名 雷達

▶I see an enemy aircraft（飛機）on the radar screen.
我在雷達螢幕上看到了敵人的飛機。

實用片語用語
off the radar 消失的、看不見的
事物應該是消失得無影無蹤，才有可能不被雷達偵測到，因此這個片語就用來描述「消失」，但通常不是「真的消失」，而是用於「我女朋友生氣了，我最好人間蒸發一陣子」（My girlfriend is mad; I'd better stay off the radar for a bit）之類的情境。

rag [ræg]

Track 2839

名 破布、碎片

▶I used rags to scrub（擦）the floor. 我用破布擦地板。

rai·sin [ˋrezn̩]

Track 2840

名 葡萄乾

▶Would you please bring me some raisins when you return from the supermarket?
你從超級市場回來時能幫我帶一些葡萄乾嗎？

rank [ræŋk]

Track 2841

名 行列、等級、社會地位

▶His rank was third in the contest（比賽）.
他在這個比賽中得了第三名。

rate [ret]

Track 2842

名 比率 動 估價

▶名 At this rate we're going to be late.
照這個速率下去，我們要遲到了。

▶動 I rated the app five stars.
我給了這個應用程式評價五顆星。

文法字詞解析
rate 這個單字在這個重視消費者回饋的年代已經越來越常見了。例如在下載 app 的時候，就常會出現請你「rate」這個 app 之類的文字。而你想找些新的 app 來用用時，也可以參考它的「rating」（也就是 rate + 字尾 ing），即它的「評價」。

raw [rɔ]

Track 2843

形 生的、原始的

▶It doesn't matter whether all the raw materials are imported or not. 所有原料是不是進口的都沒關係。

ray [re] *Track 2844*

名 光線

▶It's very hard for me to see clearly under direct rays of light.
在光線的直射下，我很難看清楚東西。

ra·zor [ˋrezɚ] *Track 2845*

名 剃刀、刮鬍刀

▶I accidentally hurt myself with a razor.
我不小心用刮鬍刀弄傷了自己。

re·act [rɪˋækt] *Track 2846*

動 反應、反抗 同 respond 回應

▶I didn't expect him to react so violently.
我沒想到他會有這麼激烈的反應。

萬用延伸句型
I didn't expect sb. to... 我沒預期到（某人）會……

re·ac·tion [rɪˋækʃən] *Track 2847*

名 反應

▶His reaction to the surprise was really funny to watch.
對於這次驚喜，他的反應超好笑。

rea·son·a·ble [ˋriznəbḷ] *Track 2848*

形 合理的

▶I don't think it's a reasonable thing to do.
我不覺得這是合理的事情。

re·ceipt [rɪˋsit] *Track 2849*

名 收據

▶Would you please give me a receipt for this dress?
請您幫我為這件洋裝開張收據好嗎？

re·ceiv·er [rɪˋsivɚ] *Track 2850*

名 收受者

▶You have to put the receiver back after using the phone.
你打完電話後應該要把話筒放回原位啊。

文法字詞解析
receiver 是「接受者」的意思，那麼為什麼在例句中也可以延伸當作「電話的話筒」的意思呢？因為電話的話筒，本來就是用來接收其他人說的話的「接受者」嘛！

rec·og·nize [ˋrɛkəgˏnaɪz] *Track 2851*

動 認知 同 know 知道

▶Do you recognize the man standing there?
你認得那個站在那裡的男人嗎？

re·cord·er [rɪˋkɔrdɚ] *Track 2852*

名 紀錄員

▶Where did you get the recorder?
你這台錄音機是從哪裡買來的？

re·cov·er [rɪˋkʌvɚ] *Track 2853*

動 恢復、重新獲得

▶He recovered from the cold very quickly.
他很快就從感冒中恢復了。

re·duce [rɪˋdjus] Track 2854

動 減輕

▶The cancer patient was reduced to skin and bones.
那個癌症患者瘦得皮包骨。

實用片語用語
skin and bones 皮包骨

re·gion·al [ˋridʒənl̩] Track 2855

形 區域性的

▶Since our team won the regional matches, why don't we go out and celebrate?
既然我們的球隊贏得了區冠軍，為什麼不出去慶祝一番呢？

re·gret [rɪˋgrɛt] Track 2856

動 後悔、遺憾 名 悔意

▶動 I don't believe that I will regret leaving him.
我相信我不會因為離開他而後悔。

▶名 There's a lot of regret in his voice.
他的聲音充滿了悔意。

re·late [rɪˋlet] Track 2857

動 敘述、有關係

▶It's easy for me to relate to the characters in the story.
我很容易可以體會這個故事中的角色。

re·lax [rɪˋlæks] Track 2858

動 放鬆

▶I think music will help you relax.
我覺得音樂會使你感到輕鬆。

實用片語用語
kick back and relax 放鬆好好休息
例如：Why are you studying? You're in a swimming pool! Kick back and relax!
你怎麼在唸書啊？你人在游泳池裡耶！要好好放鬆才對啊！

re·lease [rɪˋlis] Track 2859

動 解放 名 釋放

▶動 Unless he releases the hostage first, we can't shoot him.
除非他先釋放人質，否則我們是不能向他開槍的。

▶名 The release of the prisoners is impossible until the war comes to an end.
除非戰爭結束，否則戰俘是不可能得到釋放的。

re·li·a·ble [rɪˋlaɪəbl̩] Track 2860

形 可靠的 同 dependable 可靠的

▶I don't think it's a reliable brand of washing machine.
我覺得這不是一個可靠的洗衣機品牌。

re·lief [rɪˋlif] Track 2861

名 解除、減輕

▶He breathed a sigh of relief on hearing that she was back.
他一聽到她回來的消息，就如釋重負地鬆了口氣。

實用片語用語
breathe a sigh of relief 如釋重負地嘆一口氣

re·li·gion [rɪˋlɪdʒən] Track 2862

名 宗教

▶He is an expert in religions.
他是個宗教方面的專家。

re·li·gious [rɪˋlɪdʒəs] *Track 2863*

形 宗教的

▶Many religious believers（信教者）go to Mecca（麥加）. 許多虔誠的教徒都會去麥加。

re·ly [rɪˋlaɪ] *Track 2864*

動 依賴

▶Now that you are a grown-up, you should not rely on your parents. 既然你長大了，就不應該依靠你的父母。

實用片語用語

rely on 依靠

re·main [rɪˋmen] *Track 2865*

動 殘留、仍然、繼續

▶The writer remained poor all his life. 那個作家終生貧窮。

re·mind [rɪˋmaɪnd] *Track 2866*

動 提醒

▶Can you remind me to call my mother tomorrow? 你提醒我明天打電話給我母親好嗎？

re·mote [rɪˋmot] *Track 2867*

形 遙遠的

▶I haven't the remotest idea what she meant. 我一點都不明白她是什麼意思。

實用片語用語

remote control 遙控器

既然是可以從 remote（遙遠的）的地方 control（控制）別的物體，也難怪「remote control」就是指「遙控器」了。簡稱「remote」也是可以的。

re·move [rɪˋmuv] *Track 2868*

動 移動

▶We removed the boxes from the room. 我們把箱子從房間裡移出去。

re·new [rɪˋnju] *Track 2869*

動 更新、恢復、補充

▶I don't think they want to renew the contract with us. 我覺得他們不想和我們續訂合約。

rent [rɛnt] *Track 2870*

名 租金 動 租借

▶名 The rent of the house is too expensive for me to afford. 這個房子的租金太貴了，我負擔不起。

▶動 I rent an apartment downtown. 我在市區租一間公寓。

re·pair [rɪˋpɛr] *Track 2871*

動 修理 名 修理

▶動 My dad is trying to repair the car. 我爸正在試著修車。

▶名 The toilet is out of repair. 這馬桶需要修理了。

實用片語用語

out of repair 壞掉的、需要修理的

re·place [rɪˋples] *Track 2872*

動 代替

▶We'll need to replace the broken lamp with a new one. 我們得用新的燈來取代這個壞掉的燈。

re·place·ment [rɪˋplesmənt]

Track 2873

名 取代

▶We need a replacement for the secretary who left.
我們需要一個人代替已離職的秘書。

rep·re·sent [ˌrɛprɪˋzɛnt]

Track 2874

動 代表、象徵

▶Would you represent us in your country?
請你擔任本公司在貴國的代表好嗎？

實用片語用語

represent oneself 在法庭上自辯
例如：Without lawyer, he decided to represent himself in court.
沒有律師的幫忙，他決定在法庭上為自己辯護。

rep·re·sent·a·tive

[rɛprɪˋzɛntətɪv]

Track 2875

形 典型的、代表的 名 典型、代表人員

▶形 The symbol（符號）is representative of peace.
這個符號代表了和平。

▶名 They sent a representative to take part in the meeting.
他們派了個代表參加會議。

re·pub·lic [rɪˋpʌblɪk]

Track 2876

名 共和國

▶I come from the Republic of China. What about you?
我來自中華民國，你呢？

re·quest [rɪˋkwɛst]

Track 2877

名 要求 動 請求 同 beg 乞求

▶名 Would you please allow me to make a small request?
請您允許我提出一個小小的要求好嗎？

▶動 Can you request him to come before ten a.m. tomorrow?
請你告訴他在明天上午十點以前來好嗎？

re·serve [rɪˋzɝv]

Track 2878

動 保留 名 貯藏、保留

▶動 He reserved a table at the restaurant.
他在那家餐廳預訂了一個位子。

▶名 They keep a large reserve of firewood（木柴）for cold weather. 他們貯存大量的木柴，以備天冷時使用。

文法字詞解析

要描述一個人講話「語帶保留」、或個性上比較不喜歡把很多事說出來，則可以用與 reserve 長得很像的形容詞 reserved 來表示。

re·sist [rɪˋzɪst]

Track 2879

動 抵抗

▶Once you see her beauty, you will know that no man could resist her charm. 一旦你看到她的美貌，你就會知道沒有男人能夠抵擋住她的魅力。

re·source [rɪˋsors]

Track 2880

名 資源

▶Resources management is an important business skill.
資源管理是一項重要的經營技能。

re·spond [rɪˋspɑnd]

Track 2881

動 回答

▶Why didn't you respond when she asked you a question?
她問你問題的時候，為什麼你沒回答？

re·sponse [rɪˋspɑns]

Track 2882

名 回應、答覆

▶I'm still waiting for her response. 我還在等待她的答覆。

re·spon·si·bil·i·ty [rɪˏspɑnsəˋbɪlətɪ]

Track 2883

名 責任

▶The little children are too young to feel much responsibility.
孩子們還太小，還沒有什麼責任感。

re·strict [rɪˋstrɪkt]

Track 2884

動 限制

▶Would you like to tell me why the membership of the club is restricted to men only?
你能不能告訴我為什麼這個俱樂部的成員僅限於男士？

re·veal [rɪˋvil]

Track 2885

動 顯示

▶These plans reveal a complete failure of imagination.
這些計畫顯得毫無想像力。

rib·bon [ˋrɪbən]

Track 2886

名 絲帶、破碎條狀物

▶There was a white ribbon in her black hair.
她的黑髮中繫了一條白色的緞帶。

rid [rɪd]

Track 2887

動 使擺脫、除去

▶Let's get rid of this moldy（發霉的）old furniture.
我們把這件發霉的舊傢俱扔掉吧。

rid·dle [ˋrɪdḷ]

Track 2888

名 謎語

▶The children love solving riddles. 這些孩子們很愛解謎語。

ripe [raɪp]

Track 2889

形 成熟的

▶Are the bananas ripe yet? 香蕉成熟了嗎？

risk [rɪsk]

Track 2890

名 危險 動 冒險

▶名 There's a huge risk, but it's worth it. 風險很大，但很值得。

▶動 I don't think I want to risk losing my job over this.
我不覺得我想冒著失去工作的風險做這件事。

roar [ror]

Track 2891

名 吼叫 動 怒吼

▶名 The little girl was frightened by the lion's roars.
小女孩被這獅子的吼叫聲嚇壞了。

▶動 I can hear the tiger roaring in the cage.
我可以聽到老虎在籠子裡吼叫。

實用片語用語

favorable response 正面的答覆

例如：With their favorable response, we're all set to get to work.
既然他們的答覆是正面的，表示我們可以準備開工了。

文法字詞解析

因為緞帶經常被綁成蝴蝶結的形狀，因此 ribbon 這個字也可以引申用來表示「蝴蝶結」的意思。

實用片語用語

take a risk 冒險

例如：He took a risk in sending the soldiers there, but it worked out in the end.
他派遣軍隊去那邊是很冒險的事，但幸好最後成功了。

roast [rost]

Track 2892

動 烘烤 形 烘烤的 名 烘烤的肉

▶動 The beef is roasting in the oven.
烤箱裡正烤著牛肉呢。

▶形 My favorite dish is roast duck.
我最喜歡吃的菜是烤鴨。

▶名 How about having a hot dog roast next Sunday?
我們下個星期天來烤熱狗怎麼樣？

rob [rɑb]

Track 2893

動 搶劫

▶He robbed a bank back when he was young.
他以前年輕的時候搶過銀行。

實用片語用語
rob a bank 搶銀行

rob·ber [`rɑbə]

Track 2894

名 強盜

▶The robber grabbed the purse and ran.
那名強盜抓了皮包就跑。

rob·ber·y [`rɑbərɪ]

Track 2895

名 搶案

▶Three bank robberies happened lately in the city.
這座城市最近發生了三起銀行搶劫案。

robe [rob]

Track 2896

名 長袍 動 穿長袍

▶名 The wise old wizard（巫師）wears a robe.
那個有智慧的老巫師披著長袍。

▶動 The serious old lady is robed in black.
那個正經的老太太穿著黑色的袍子。

rock·et [`rɑkɪt]

Track 2897

名 火箭 動 發射火箭

▶名 We sent an unmanned（無人操縱的）rocket into earth orbit（軌道）. 我們把一個無人駕駛的火箭送入了地球軌道。

▶動 Our profits rocketed recently. 我們最近的利潤劇增。

實用片語用語
rocket science 火箭科學
「和火箭有關的科學」聽起來一副很困難的樣子，但這個片語通常是反過來用，例如若你的朋友不會綁鞋帶，你就可以跟他說：「It's not rocket science!」，意指「這又不是什麼跟火箭有關的科學，明明就很簡單啊！」

ro·man·tic [ro`mæntɪk]

Track 2898

形 浪漫的 名 浪漫主義者

▶形 It is said that Frenchmen are among the most romantic people in the world.
據說法國人是世界上最浪漫的民族之一。

▶名 I heard that he was a romantic. Do you think so?
我聽說他是個浪漫主義者，你覺得他是嗎？

rot [rɑt]

Track 2899

動 腐敗 名 腐壞

▶動 Some people think that too much television rots your brain.
有些人認為看太多電視會使你的頭腦退化。

▶名 He's always talking rot. I wish he would shut up.
他老是在講一些廢話，真希望他閉嘴。

rot·ten [ˋrɑtn̩]

Track 2900

形 腐化的

▶The tomatoes are rotten.
番茄都腐壞了。

實用片語用語
rotten egg 壞蛋
例句：The family had no idea why their son turned out a rotten egg.
這一家人也不明白為什麼他們的兒子會變成壞蛋。

rough [rʌf]

Track 2901

形 粗糙的 名 粗暴的人、草圖

▶形 Can you give me a rough idea when you'll be back?
你能告訴我你大概什麼時候回來嗎？

▶名 Would you please pass me the pencil near the pile of roughs?
請你把那疊草圖旁的那支鉛筆遞給我好嗎？

rou·tine [ruˋtin]

Track 2902

名 慣例 形 例行的

▶名 As soon as she learns the office routine, she will be an excellent assistant.
她一旦熟悉了辦公室的日常事務，就會成為一名優秀的助手。

▶形 I'm having a routine medical（醫學的）examination next week.
我下禮拜要做例行的健康檢查。

實用片語用語
daily routine 每天的例行事務
例如：Checking my Facebook after I get up is my daily routine.
起床後確認我的臉書是我每天必做的事。

rug [rʌg]

Track 2903

名 地毯 同 carpet 地毯

▶There is a big hole in the rug.
這塊地毯上有一個大洞。

ru·mor [ˋrumɚ]

Track 2904

名 謠言 動 謠傳

▶名 Nobody with common sense（見識）will believe such a rumor.
沒有哪個有常識的人會相信這樣的謠言。

▶動 It is rumored that she has committed（犯）suicide, but not everyone believes it.
據傳聞她已經自殺身亡，但不是每個人都相信這是真的。

萬用延伸句型
It is rumored that... 傳聞說……

rust [rʌst]

Track 2905

名 鐵銹 動 生鏽

▶名 She reads extensively（廣泛地）so that she can keep her mind from rust.
她廣泛閱讀以防止腦筋遲鈍。

▶動 You must practice more so that your skills will not rust.
你必須多多練習以防止技術荒廢。

rust·y [ˋrʌstɪ]

Track 2906

形 生鏽的、生疏的

▶My oral（口語的）English is pretty rusty; would you please help me practice?
我對英文口語非常生疏了，你能幫我練習一下嗎？

Ss

sack [sæk] Track 2907

名 大包、袋子

▶What's in the sack? I see something moving.
袋子裡到底是什麼？我看到有東西在動耶。

sake [sek] Track 2908

名 緣故、理由

▶It doesn't matter whether you do this for your own sake or not.
你做這件事是不是為了自身利益都無關緊要。

實用片語用語
for sb.'s sake 為了某人

sat·is·fac·to·ry [ˌsætɪsˋfæktərɪ] Track 2909

形 令人滿意的

▶I don't think his performance is satisfactory.
我不覺得他的表現令人滿意。

sau·cer [ˋsɔsɚ] Track 2910

名 托盤、茶碟

▶I can't find cups and saucers that match.
我找不到相配的茶杯和茶托。

sau·sage [ˋsɔsɪdʒ] Track 2911

名 臘腸、香腸

▶Would you like another helping of pork sausage?
你要不要再來一份豬肉香腸呢？

sav·ing(s) [ˋsevɪŋ(z)] Track 2912

名 拯救、救助、存款

▶Don't put all your savings into a deposit account.
別把你所有的積蓄都存入帳戶。

實用片語用語
savings account 存款帳戶
例如：I opened a savings account at the bank yesterday.
我昨天在銀行開了存款帳戶。

scale(s) [skel(z)] Track 2913

名 刻度、尺度、天秤

▶Lots of lands have become deserts on a large scale.
許多田地大面積地變成了沙漠。

scarce [skɛrs] Track 2914

形 稀少的 同 rare 稀有的

▶Food was scarce in this area and some people starved to death. 這一個地區的食物短缺，有一些人餓死了。

scare·crow [ˋskɛrˌkro] Track 2915

名 稻草人

▶Scarecrows are supposed to scare away birds.
稻草人的功能應該是幫忙嚇走小鳥。

scarf [skɑrf] Track 2916

名 圍巾、頸巾

▶Would you like this blue scarf? 你想要這條藍色的圍巾嗎？

文法字詞解析
scarf 的複數形式可以說成 scarves 或 scarfs。

scar·y [ˋskɛrɪ] Track 2917

形 駭人的

▸Let's tell scary stories at night. 我們晚上來講可怕的故事吧。

scat·ter [ˋskætɚ] Track 2918

動 散佈

▸It's time for the farmers to scatter the seeds in the fields.
到了農民播種的時節了。

sched·ule [ˋskɛdʒʊl] Track 2919

名 時刻表 動 將……列表 同 list 列表

▸名 It was the first time that they had been behind schedule.
他們還是第一次進度落後。

▸動 My boss told me to schedule a meeting for her.
我老闆要我幫她訂好會議時程。

實用片語用語
behind schedule 進度落後

schol·ar [ˋskɑlɚ] Track 2920

名 有學問的人、學者

▸The scholar is always burying himself in books.
這名學者總是埋首於書堆中。

實用片語用語
bury oneself in sth. 某人埋首於……
bury 有「埋葬」的意思，所以「某人把自己埋進某事中」就表示某人很專心地在做某事。

schol·ar·ship [ˋskɑlɚˏʃɪp] Track 2921

名 獎學金

▸It is difficult for a student to win the scholarship in this university（大學）. 學生要在這所大學裡獲得獎學金很難。

sci·en·tif·ic [ˏsaɪənˋtɪfɪk] Track 2922

形 科學的、有關科學的

▸She dedicated her whole life to scientific research（研究）.
她把一生都獻給了科學研究事業。

scoop [skup] Track 2923

名 舀取的器具 動 挖、掘、舀取

▸名 Do you want another scoop of ice cream?
你要再一球冰淇淋嗎？

▸動 I scooped out a handful of peanuts to eat.
我挖了一把花生出來吃。

文法字詞解析
由於小道消息、獨家新聞都是需要去「挖掘」的，就樣挖冰淇淋一樣要挖得很深才挖得到，因此小道消息、獨家新聞也可以稱為「scoop」（名詞）。

scout [skaʊt] Track 2924

名 斥候、偵查 動 斥候、偵查

▸名 It took him several hours to have a scout around to see what he could find.
他花了好幾個小時四處搜尋，看看能找到些什麼。

▸動 I volunteer to go over and scout the enemy grounds.
我自願過去偵察敵營。

scream [skrim] Track 2925

動 大聲尖叫、作出尖叫聲 名 大聲尖叫

▸動 The child is screaming himself red in the face.
這個孩子尖叫得臉都紅了。

▸名 I heard a terrible scream from the next room.
我聽到隔壁房間傳來可怕的尖叫聲。

screw [skru]　Track 2926

名 螺絲 動 旋緊、轉動

▶名 Where did the screw go? Did it roll under the sofa?
那個螺絲去哪了？是滾到沙發下面了嗎？

▶動 Let's screw the two pipes together so that the water won't leak out.
我們把這兩根管子接起來旋緊，這樣水就不會漏出來了。

scrub [skrʌb]　Track 2927

動 擦拭、擦洗 名 刷子

▶動 It took me two hours to scrub the bathtub clean on Saturday.
我週六花了兩小時才把浴缸刷洗乾淨。

▶名 We should really give the floor a good scrub.
我們真的應該好好擦洗一下地板了。

實用片語用語
give sth. a good scrub 好好擦洗一下某物
將 scrub 換成別的單字也可以，例如 give sth. a good wash（好好洗一下某物）。

seal [sil]　Track 2928

名 海豹、印章 動 獵海豹、蓋章、密封

▶名 The cute seal is good at performing tricks.
這隻可愛的海豹很擅長表演。

▶動 He forgot to seal his letter.
他忘了把信封起來。

sec·ond·a·r·y [ˋsɛkənˏdɛrɪ]　Track 2929

形 第二的

▶Women's careers shouldn't be secondary to men's.
婦女的職業生涯不該次於男人們的職業生涯。

se·cu·ri·ty [sɪˋkjʊrətɪ]　Track 2930

名 安全 同 safety 安全

▶The security guards here are always chatting.
這裡的警衛總是在聊天。

seek [sik]　Track 2931

動 尋找

▶Money does not always bring you the happiness you seek.
金錢不見得能帶給你你在找尋的幸福。

文法字詞解析
seek 的動詞變化：seek, sought, sought

seize [siz]　Track 2932

動 抓、抓住

▶Why don't you seize this rare opportunity? It's now or never.
為什麼不抓住這個難得的機會呢？機不可失啊。

sel·dom [ˋsɛldəm]　Track 2933

副 不常地、難得地

▶He seldom mentions his family. 他很少提及他的家庭背景。

sen·si·ble [ˋsɛnsəbḷ]　Track 2934

形 可感覺的、理性的

▶It is sensible to shut up once in a while.
偶爾不要多嘴也是很聰明的作法。

sen·si·tive [ˋsɛnsətɪv]

Track 2935

形 敏感的

▶Women are sensitive to many things.
女人們對很多事都很敏感。

文法字詞解析

相反地，「不敏感的」可說 insensitive。通常這是個負面用語，用來形容某人很不會看人臉色，說出冒犯的話、不體貼。

sep·a·ra·tion [ˏsɛpəˋreʃən]

Track 2936

名 分離、隔離

▶Don't you feel sad after a long separation from your best friends? 和好友分開很久你不會感到難過嗎？

sew [so]

Track 2937

動 縫、縫上

▶Would you sew the button on for me?
你能幫我把扣子縫上嗎？

sex [sɛks]

Track 2938

名 性、性別

▶Can you tell me what sex your cat is? I can't tell.
你能告訴我你的貓的性別嗎？我分不出來。

實用片語用語

have sex 發生性關係

例如：Don't have sex in the elevator. It's very inconvenient for others.
不要在電梯裡發生性關係，這樣別人很不方便。

sex·u·al [sɛkʃuəl]

Track 2939

形 性的

▶Not all the people know that the disease is passed on by sexual contact.
不是所有人都知道這種病會透過性接觸而傳染。

sex·y [sɛksɪ]

Track 2940

形 性感的

▶What do you think of the heroine（女主角）in this film? Don't you think she is sexy?
你覺得這部影片裡的女主角如何？你不覺得她很性感嗎？

shade [ʃed]

Track 2941

名 陰涼處、樹蔭 動 遮住、使陰暗

▶名 Why don't we have a rest in the shade after walking such a long distance?
走了這麼遠的路之後，為什麼不到陰涼處休息一下呢？

▶動 I shaded my eyes from the sun.
我遮著眼睛擋住陽光。

shad·ow [ˋʃædo]

Track 2942

名 陰暗之處、影子 動 使有陰影

▶名 Our shadows follow us everywhere.
我們的影子到哪裡都跟著我們。

▶動 The mountain is shadowed by clouds.
那座山被雲遮住了。

實用片語用語

in sb.'s shadow 活在某人的陰影下

例如：She has been living in her sister's shadow for her whole life.
她一生都活在她姐姐的陰影之下。

shad·y [ˋʃedɪ]

Track 2943

形 多蔭的、成蔭的

▶Let's take a walk on the shady avenue.
到林蔭大道上去散散步吧。

shal·low [ˋʃælo]
Track 2944

形 淺的、膚淺的

▶The water is quite shallow here.
這裡的水很淺。

shame [ʃem]
Track 2945

名 羞恥、羞愧 動 使羞愧

▶名 Don't you feel any shame after making her cry?
把她弄哭，你一點都不羞愧嗎？

▶動 Their team shamed ours by winning by thirty points.
他們隊大贏我們隊三十分，讓我們羞愧極了。

萬用延伸句型

It's a shame that... 真可惜……

例如：It's a shame that we lost the game because of the absence of the team leader. 真可惜，我們因為隊長的缺席而輸了這場比賽。

sham·poo [ʃæmˋpu]
Track 2946

名 洗髮精 動 清洗

▶名 What brand of shampoo do you like best?
你最喜歡哪種牌子的洗髮精？

▶動 He shampooed his dog every week.
他每個禮拜都會洗他的狗。

shave [ʃev]
Track 2947

動 刮鬍子、剃

▶It will be a long time before he shaves off his beard.
他要過很久才會去刮鬍子。

shep·herd [ˋʃɛpɚd]
Track 2948

名 牧羊人、牧師

▶Several shepherds will leave the farm this week.
這週會有幾個牧羊人離開這個農場。

shin·y [ˋʃaɪnɪ]
Track 2949

形 發光的、晴朗的

▶Why is this coin shinier than the others?
為什麼這個錢幣比其他的更亮？

文法字詞解析

shiny 和另一個長得很像的形容詞 shining 都有「發光」的意思，那麼它們之間有什麼差別呢？原來，shining 用來描述「自己本身就會發光」的東西，例如太陽（the sun is shining）；而 shiny 則是用來描述「反射光線、自己本身不會發光」的東西，例如錢幣、擦得很亮的皮鞋等等。

short·en [ˋʃɔrtn̩]
Track 2950

動 縮短、使變短

▶Daytime shortens in the winter.
冬天時白天會變短。

short·ly [ˋʃɔrtlɪ]
Track 2951

副 不久、馬上 同 soon 不久

▶I'll be with you shortly.
我馬上就過來你這裡。

shov·el [ˋʃʌvl̩]
Track 2952

名 鏟子 動 剷除

▶名 It is difficult for him to remove the snow with such a tiny shovel.
用這麼小的一把鏟子鏟雪對他來說很困難。

▶動 It is not easy for him to shovel all the coal into the truck.
把所有的煤都鏟入卡車對他來說並不容易。

shrink [ʃrɪŋk]

Track 2953

動 收縮、退縮

▶My dress shrunk after I washed it.
我的洋裝洗過後就縮水了。

文法字詞解析
shrink 的動詞變化：shrink, shrunk, shrunk

sigh [saɪn]

Track 2954

動 / 名 嘆息

▶動 Will you tell me why she sighs and looks sad all day?
你能告訴我她為何整天嘆氣，而且看起來很傷心的樣子嗎？

▶名 He heaved a sigh and put down the newspaper.
他嘆了口氣，放下報紙。

sig·nal [ˋsɪgn!]

Track 2955

名 信號、號誌 動 打信號

▶名 Can you get a signal on your phone?
你的手機收得到訊嗎？

▶動 He signaled the message with little flags.
他用幾支小旗子打了信號。

sig·nif·i·cant [sɪgˋnɪfəkənt]

Track 2956

形 有意義的

▶I don't think this proposal they put forward is significant.
我認為他們提出的這個提議沒有什麼意義。

文法字詞解析
significant 的相反詞是 insignificant（不重要的、渺小的、無意義的）。字首「in-」即「不、沒有」的意思。

sim·i·lar·i·ty [ˏsɪməˋlærətɪ]

Track 2957

名 類似、相似 同 resemblance 相似

▶There are points of similarity between the two cases.
這兩個案件之間有某些相似之處。

sin [sɪn]

Track 2958

名 罪、罪惡 動 犯罪

▶名 Lying is not always a sin.
說謊不見得一定是種罪。

▶動 I believe that it's human to sin.
我覺得犯錯是人之常情。

sin·cere [sɪnˋsɪr]

Track 2959

形 真實的、誠摯的 同 genuine 真誠的

▶He sounds sincere, but I'm still not sure if I should believe him.
他聽起來很真誠，但我還是不知道是否要相信他。

sip [sɪp]

Track 2960

動 啜飲、小口地喝 同 drink 喝

▶He sipped the wine slowly.
他慢慢地喝這個葡萄酒。

實用片語用語
take a sip 啜飲一小口
例如：He took a sip of the wine and spat it out.
他啜飲了一小口酒，然後就吐了出來。

sit·u·a·tion [ˏsɪtʃʊˋeʃən]

Track 2961

名 情勢 同 condition 情況

▶Can anyone explain the situation to me?
有沒有人可以跟我解釋一下這是什麼情形？

skate [sket]

Track 2962

動 溜冰、滑冰

▶A large number of people like to skate here.
很多人都喜歡來這個地方溜冰。

ski [ski]

Track 2963

名 滑雪板 動 滑雪

▶名 Can you rent skis for us?
可不可以幫我們租滑雪板？

▶動 What about going skiing with us during winter vacation?
寒假期間跟我們一起去滑雪如何？

skip [skɪp]

Track 2964

動 略過、跳過 名 略過、跳過 同 omit 省略

▶動 It doesn't matter if you skip some descriptions in the novel.
你跳過小說裡的幾個描述不看也沒有關係。

▶名 The cute little girl walked with a skip.
那個小女孩邊走邊跳。

實用片語用語

skip classes 蹺課

例如：I never skip classes, except for that time when the bus broke down.
除了公車拋錨那一次以外，我從來不蹺課的。

sky·scrap·er [ˋskaɪˏskrepɚ]

Track 2965

名 摩天大樓

▶There are lots of skyscrapers in New York.
紐約有許多摩天大樓。

slave [slev]

Track 2966

名 奴隸 動 做苦工

▶名 The government treated the slaves badly.
政府對奴隸們很不好。

▶動 People have to slave away to get their own houses.
人們為了能買到屬於自己的房子而得拚死拚活地工作。

sleeve [sliv]

Track 2967

名 衣袖、袖子

▶Let's roll up our sleeves and get down to work now.
讓我們捲起衣袖，現在開始工作吧。

實用片語用語

get down to work 開始認真工作

slice [slaɪs]

Track 2968

名 片、薄的切片 動 切成薄片

▶名 Would you like more slices of bread? You look rather hungry.
要不要再來幾片麵包？你看起來很餓喔。

▶動 Can you please help me wash these potatoes and then slice them?
請你幫我先把馬鈴薯洗乾淨，然後再把它們切成薄片好嗎？

slip·per·y [ˋslɪpərɪ]

Track 2969

形 滑溜的

▶The wet road is very slippery.
這條濕濕的路很滑。

slope [slop]

Track 2970

名 坡度、斜面

▶Do you know any skiing slopes with a nice view?
你知道哪裡有景色不錯的滑雪斜坡嗎？

smooth [smuð]

Track 2971

形 平滑的 動 使平滑、使平和

▶形 The movie star's skin is as smooth as silk.
這位電影明星的皮膚如絲綢般光滑。

▶動 I'm sure the conflicts will smooth out soon.
我相信這些衝突會很快平息下來的。

snap [snæp]

Track 2972

動 折斷、迅速抓住

▶The branch snapped as soon as the boy stood on it.
這個男孩一站上去，樹枝就折斷了。

文法字詞解析

要「折斷」或「迅速抓住」某個東西，需要非常快速、力道大且乾淨俐落的動作才能辦到。在罵人時常常也需要罵得很快、很凶、很狠才能達到效果，因此 snap 這個字也可以用來描述「突然破口大罵」的動作。
例如：“Mind your own business,” he snapped.
「少多管閒事，」他大罵道。

sol·id [ˋsɑlɪd]

Track 2973

形 固體的

▶Babies can't eat solid food.
嬰兒還不能吃固體的食物。

some·day [ˋsʌm͵de]

Track 2974

副 將來有一天、來日

▶I hope I can go to Mars（火星）someday.
我希望有一天能去火星。

some·how [ˋsʌm͵haʊ]

Track 2975

副 不知何故

▶Somehow, he thinks I hate him.
不知道為什麼，他覺得我討厭他。

some·time [ˋsʌm͵taɪm]

Track 2976

副 某些時候、來日

▶I remembering seeing him sometime last week.
我記得上禮拜某個時候有看到過他。

文法字詞解析

sometime（some 與 time 中間沒有空格）指「某些時候、來日」的意思。而如果 some 與 time 中間有空格（some time）則是「一些時間」的意思。
例如：Give me some time to think it over.
給我一點時間讓我想一下。

some·what [ˋsʌm͵hwɑt]

Track 2977

副 多少、幾分

▶I think his report is somewhat exaggerated（誇張）.
我覺得他的報告有點誇張。

sore [sor]

Track 2978

形 疼痛的 名 痛處 同 painful 疼痛的

▶形 I don't think he will get sore about this matter.
我不認為他會為此事而大動肝火。

▶名 I don't think it's necessary for us to reopen（重新打開、重新開放）those old sores.
我認為我們沒必要再提以前那些傷心事了。

sor·row [ˋsɑro]

Track 2979

名 悲傷、感到哀傷 同 grief 悲傷

▶The poor lady's life is full of sorrow.
那個可憐的太太生活中充滿了悲傷。

spade [sped]

Track 2980

名 鏟子

▶What's that spade for? I didn't know you're into gardening.
那個鏟子是幹嘛的？我還真不知道你對園藝有興趣。

實用片語用語
be into sth. 對……有興趣

spa·ghet·ti [spəˋgɛtɪ]

Track 2981

名 義大利麵

▶Would you like spaghetti for dinner?
你晚餐想吃義大利麵嗎？

文法字詞解析
義大利麵依麵的形狀有好幾種說法，以下就來介紹幾種最常見的：spaghetti 是我們常常在家自己煮的細圓麵；fettuccine 是寬扁麵；而小時候常吃到的、跟三色蔬菜一起煮的螺旋麵就是 rotini；最後，可以放在湯裡也可以加醬料食用的通心粉則是 macaroni。而所有義大利麵的統稱則是 pasta。

spe·cif·ic [spɪˋsɪfɪk]

Track 2982

形 具體的、特殊的、明確的 同 precise 明確的

▶Can you give me some specific details?
你能告訴我一些具體細節嗎？

spice [spaɪs]

Track 2983

名 香料

▶Did you add spice to this cake, Mom? It tastes great.
媽媽，妳有在蛋糕裡加香料嗎？它好吃極了。

spill [spɪl]

Track 2984

動 使溢流 名 溢出

▶動 The coffee is so full that it might spill over.
咖啡太滿了，可能會溢出來。

▶名 The oil spill is really bad for the environment.
溢出的石油對環境很不好。

文法字詞解析
spill 的動詞變化：spill, spilled, spilled 或 spill, spilt, spilt

spin [spɪn]

Track 2985

動 旋轉、紡織 名 旋轉

▶動 The top has been spinning for a long time.
那個陀螺轉很久了。

▶名 The ballet dancer did several spins.
那位芭蕾舞者轉了好幾圈。

spit [spɪt]

Track 2986

動 吐、吐口水 名 唾液

▶動 I don't think you can spit wherever you like.
我覺得你不能隨地吐痰。

▶名 Susan's spit flew as she shouted.
蘇珊大叫時口水濺得到處都是。

spite [spaɪt]

Track 2987

名 惡意

▶He stepped on her out of spite.
他惡意地踩她一腳。

實用片語用語
out of spite 惡意地

A B C D E F G H I J K L M N O P Q R **S** T U V W X Y Z

splash [splæʃ]
Track 2988

動 濺起來 名 飛濺聲

▶動 The kids are splashing around in the pool.
孩子們在池裡潑水。

▶名 The rain is coming down in a splash. 大雨飛濺下來。

spoil [spɔɪl]
Track 2989

動 寵壞、損壞

▶You can ruin your children's lives if you spoil them.
如果你把孩子寵壞，可能會毀掉孩子的一生。

sprain [spren]
Track 2990

動 / 名 扭傷

▶動 No one knows how he sprained his wrist.
沒有人知道他是怎麼扭傷自己手腕的。

▶名 What's the difference between a sprain and a strain（拉傷）? 扭傷和拉傷之間有什麼差別？

spray [spre]
Track 2991

名 噴霧器 動 噴、濺

▶名 Is the water spray system ready for use?
水霧噴射系統是不是已經可以用了？

▶動 They sprayed paint on the wall. 他們在牆上噴上油漆。

實用片語用語

hair spray 髮膠
因為髮膠經常是用「噴」的，所以髮膠才稱為 hair spray。
例如：The boy uses up a can of hair spray each month.
那個男孩每個月用掉一罐髮膠。

sprin·kle [ˋsprɪŋkḷ]
Track 2992

動 灑、噴淋

▶How about sprinkling some sugar on the top of this birthday cake? 在這個生日蛋糕上撒點糖如何？

spy [spaɪ]
Track 2993

名 間諜

▶The country sent a spy to Russia last year.
這個國家去年派了一名間諜前往俄羅斯。

squeeze [skwiz]
Track 2994

動 壓擠、擠壓 名 緊抱、擁擠 同 crush 壓、榨

▶動 I don't think we can squeeze our way through the crowd.
我覺得我們沒辦法從人群裡擠過去。

▶名 He gave my hand a squeeze. 他捏了一下我的手。

萬用延伸句型

squeeze into sth. 擠進……裡面
例如：The lady squeezed into the narrow seat .
那位女士擠進窄小的座位裡。

stab [stæb]
Track 2995

動 刺、戳 名 刺傷

▶動 He stabbed his father in the back.
他從他爸爸背後捅他一刀。

▶名 He killed the woman with a stab to the heart.
他向這個女人的心臟刺了一刀，殺死了她。

sta·ble [ˋstebḷ]
Track 2996

形 穩定的 同 steady 穩定的

▶It won't be long before a stable government is formed in this nation. 不久，這個國家就會形成一個穩定的政府了。

sta·di·um [ˋstedɪəm] Track 2997

名 室外運動場

▶Would you tell me where the largest stadium is in this city?
你能告訴我這個城市最大的運動場在哪嗎？

staff [stæf] Track 2998

名 棒、竿子、全體人員

▶I don't think this welfare（福利）policy is fair to all the staff in the company.
我認為這項福利政策並不是對公司所有員工都公平。

文法字詞解析
如果想要說一家店的「人員不足」，可以加上表示「不足、太少」的字首「under-」以及形容詞字尾「-ed」變成「understaffed」。

stale [stel] Track 2999

形 不新鮮的、陳舊的 同 old 老舊的

▶There was only a piece of stale cake left in the refrigerator.
冰箱裡只剩下一塊不新鮮的蛋糕了。

stare [stɛr] Track 3000

名 / 動 盯、凝視

▶名 He gave us a rude stare and walked away.
他很不禮貌地瞪了我們一眼，走掉了。

▶動 It is not polite of you to stare at strangers on the street.
在街上盯著陌生人看很不禮貌。

starve [stɑrv] Track 3001

動 餓死、饑餓

▶I don't think they will starve to death if they continue to work hard. 我認為如果他們繼續努力工作，他們就不會餓死。

實用片語用語
starve to death 餓死
這個片語有兩種意思，一種只是在形容「非常餓」，還有一種是真的「因缺糧食而死亡」。

stat·ue [ˋstætʃʊ] Track 3002

名 鑄像、雕像

▶Not all people know the Statue of Liberty was a gift given by France.
不是所有人都知道自由女神像是法國贈送的一個禮物。

stead·y [ˋstɛdɪ] Track 3003

形 穩固的 副 穩固地

▶形 Will you hold the ladder steady for me, Mike?
麥克，請幫我把梯子扶穩好嗎？

▶副 The young couple is going steady.
那對年輕情侶正在穩定交往中。

steep [stip] Track 3004

形 險峻的

▶The mountain slope is too steep for the visitors to climb.
這個山坡太陡，遊客們爬不上去。

step·child [ˋstɛp͵tʃaɪld] Track 3005

名 前夫（妻）所生的孩子

▶I don't think every parent will treat a stepchild as his or her own. 我認為不是每個父（母）都會將前夫（妻）生的孩子視如己出。

實用片語用語
treat sb. as... 將某人以……來對待

step·father [ˋstɛp͵fɑðɚ]

Track 3006

名 繼父、後父

▶The stepfather doesn't love this child.
這個繼父不愛這個孩子。

step·mother [ˋstɛp͵mʌðɚ]

Track 3007

名 繼母、後母

▶I've heard that he has a new stepmother. What does she look like? 聽說他有一個新後母了，那她長什麼樣子呢？

文法字詞解析
繼父稱為stepfather，繼母稱為stepmother，那孩子呢？很簡單，我們留下「step-」這個字首，改成stepchild、stepson、stepdaughter就可以指「並非自己親生，再婚後跟著新的老公或老婆過來的孩子」了。而如果是跟著繼父或繼母過來的「非親生兄弟姊妹」則可以稱為stepbrother、stepsister。

ster·e·o [ˋstɛrɪo]

Track 3008

名 立體音響

▶We need a newer and better stereo player.
我們需要一個更新更好的立體音響。

stick·y [stɪkɪ]

Track 3009

形 黏的、棘手的

▶Will you tell me what the sticky stuff in the box is?
你能告訴我這盒子裡黏黏的東西是什麼嗎？

實用片語用語
sticky note 便條紙
因為便條紙也是「黏黏的」，所以可以稱為 stick note。此外也可稱為「post-it note」。

stiff [stɪf]

Track 3010

形 僵硬的

▶The old man's back is very stiff.
那個老男人的背很僵硬。

sting [stɪŋ]

Track 3011

動 刺、叮

▶She was stung by bees. 她被蜜蜂叮了。

stir [stɝ]

Track 3012

動 攪拌

▶Please stir the soup a little.
請把湯攪拌一下。

stitch [stɪtʃ]

Track 3013

名 編織、一針 動 縫、繡

▶名 It's time for the doctor to take the stitches out of his wound.
是時候讓醫生把他傷口上縫的線拆掉了。

▶動 You should stitch the buttons on this shirt by yourself.
你應該自己幫這件襯衫縫上鈕扣了。

萬用延伸句型
stitch A on B 將 A 縫到 B 上

stock·ing(s) [ˋstɑkɪŋ(z)]

Track 3014

名 長襪

▶Won't your children ask who put gifts in their stockings on Christmas（耶誕節）？難道你的孩子不會問耶誕節的時候是誰把禮物放在他們的長襪裡嗎？

stool [stul]

Track 3015

名 凳子

▶The stool was broken. 這張凳子壞了。

storm·y [ˋstɔrmɪ] Track 3016

形 暴風雨的、多風暴的

▶I don't think ships are allowed to go to sea in such stormy weather. 我覺得這種天氣沒有船會被允許出海的。

文法字詞解析

也可以用 stormy 這個字描述一個人的表情、五官像暴風雨一樣乖戾不平靜。

例如：His stormy features made him hard to approach.

他的外表看起來脾氣不太好的樣子，讓他顯得很難親近。

strat·e·gy [ˋstrætədʒɪ] Track 3017

名 戰略、策略

▶I think you should change your marketing strategy. 我覺得你們應該改變你們的行銷策略。

strength [strɛŋθ] Track 3018

名 力量、強度

▶His strength is superior to mine. 他的力氣比我大。

strip [strɪp] Track 3019

名 條、臨時跑道 動 剝、剝除

▶名 He ripped the cloth into strips. 他把布撕成了一條條。

▶動 Can you tell me what stripped the trees of its leaves? 你能告訴我是什麼把樹葉全部颳走了嗎？

實用片語用語

strip down 脫光

例如：You'd better strip down so that the doctor could examine you.

你最好脫光，醫生才能作檢查。

struc·ture [ˋstrʌktʃɚ] Track 3020

名 構造、結構 動 建立組織

▶名 It is hard for me to figure out the structure of the long sentence. 我很難明白這個長句的結構。

▶動 It is not so easy for them to structure a strong defensive（防禦的）line. 他們想要構成一條堅固的防線並不容易。

stub·born [ˋstʌbɚn] Track 3021

形 頑固的 同 obstinate 頑固的

▶My grandpa is quite stubborn. 我的爺爺相當頑固。

stu·di·o [ˋstjudɪo] Track 3022

名 工作室、播音室

▶I take classes in the dance studio. 我在舞蹈工作室上課。

實用片語用語

art studio 藝術工作室

例如：I've always dreamed of having my own art studio.

我一直都夢想著能夠擁有自己的藝術工作室。

stuff [stʌf] Track 3023

名 東西、材料 動 填塞、裝填

▶名 I've got lots of stuff in my drawer. 我抽屜裡有很多東西。

▶動 He stuffed himself with food. 他用食物塞滿肚子。

style [staɪl] Track 3024

名 風格、時尚

▶Not all people like his writing style, though he is a famous writer. 儘管他是一個很有名的作家，但卻不是所有人都喜歡他的寫作風格。

sub·stance [ˋsʌbstəns] Track 3025

名 物質、物體、實質

▶What's this sticky substance in the jar? 罐子裡黏黏的物質是什麼啊？

實用片語用語

without substance 無實質根據

例如：All those rumors about her are without substance.

這些和她有關的傳言都沒有實質的根據。

sub·urb [ˋsʌbɝb]

Track 3026

名 市郊、郊區

▶I don't think my neighbors will move out to the suburbs this year. 我覺得我的鄰居今年不會搬到郊區去住。

suck [sʌk]

Track 3027

動 吸、吸取、吸收

▶動 The mosquitoes live on sucking blood.
蚊子們都靠著吸血維生。

suf·fer [ˋsʌfɚ]

Track 3028

動 受苦、遭受 同 endure 忍受

▶He suffers from lung cancer. 他受肺癌之害。

實用片語用語
suffer from 受……之苦

sufficient [səˋfɪʃənt]

Track 3029

形 充足的 同 enough 充足的

▶I don't believe that they have sufficient food and water on the ship. 我相信他們在船上沒有充足的食物和水。

sug·gest [səˋdʒɛst]

Track 3030

動 提議、建議 同 hint 建議

▶It is wise of you to suggest him to borrow money from the bank. 你建議他應該從銀行借款這很明智。

su·i·cide [ˋsuə͵saɪd]

Track 3031

名 自殺、自滅

▶The number of suicides has increased these years.
最近幾年自殺案件的數量增加了。

實用片語用語
commit suicide 自殺
例句：He would never commit suicide. It must have been murder.
他絕不可能自殺的，一定是謀殺。

suit·a·ble [ˋsutəbḷ]

Track 3032

形 適合的 同 fit 適合的

▶I don't think this man is suitable for this job.
我不覺得這個男人適合這個工作。

sum [sʌm]

Track 3033

名 總數 動 合計

▶名 Not even the manager knows the sum required.
經理也不知道所需要的總額是多少。

▶動 The total costs last month sum up to ten thousand dollars.
上月的總花費高達一萬美元。

sum·ma·ry [ˋsʌmərɪ]

Track 3034

名 摘要

▶Can you give me a summary of the movie?
你可以跟我說一下這部電影的摘要嗎？

實用片語用語
brief summary 簡短摘要
例句：We only have time for a brief summary. Make it short.
我們剩下的時間只夠你做個簡短的摘要，所以不要講太長。

sum·mit [ˋsʌmɪt]

Track 3035

名 頂點、高峰

▶Do you know who will attend this summit meeting this year?
你知道今年有誰會來參加這次的高峰會嗎？

su·pe·ri·or [sə`pɪrɪɚ]

Track 3036

形 上級的 名 長官

▶形 According to the latest report, the enemy forces are superior in numbers. 最新報導說敵軍在數量上佔有優勢。

▶名 John has become our direct superior.
約翰成了我們的頂頭上司。

sup·pose [sə`poz]

Track 3037

動 假定

▶Do you suppose they're going to get divorced（離婚）?
你猜他們會離婚嗎？

萬用延伸句型
Do you suppose...? 你猜……嗎？
這個句型可以用來引導他人說出他們的意見。

sur·round [sə`raʊnd]

Track 3038

動 圍繞

▶Let's listen to the sounds of the summer night that surround us. 讓我們仔細聽一聽環繞我們的夏夜之聲吧。

sur·vey [`sɝve]

Track 3039

動 / 名 考察、測量、實地調查

▶動 He surveyed the room carefully.
他小心地環顧了整個房間。

▶名 Would you like to tell me what findings you have got from the market survey?
你能告訴我你在市場調查中有什麼發現嗎？

sur·viv·al [sɚ`vaɪvḷ]

Track 3040

名 殘存、倖存

▶Survival is our first imperative（必要的事）, don't you think so?
我們的當務之急是設法生存下來，你不這樣認為嗎？

萬用延伸句型
Don't you think so? 你不覺得是如此嗎？

sur·vi·vor [sɚ`vaɪvɚ]

Track 3041

名 生還者

▶There was only one survivor from the plane crash.
這次飛機失事只有一名倖存者。

sus·pect [`sʌspɛkt]

Track 3042

動 懷疑 名 嫌疑犯

▶動 I suspect that he killed his parents.
我懷疑是他殺了他的父母。

▶名 There are seven suspects for this murder.
這起謀殺案有七個嫌疑犯。

sus·pi·cion [sə`spɪʃəs]

Track 3043

名 懷疑

▶I have a strong suspicion that John is the killer.
我強烈懷疑約翰就是殺手。

swear [swɛr]

Track 3044

動 發誓、宣誓

▶I swear I didn't do it. 我發誓我沒做這件事。

文法字詞解析
swear 的動詞變化：swear, swore, sworn

sweat [swɛt]

Track 3045

名 汗水 動 出汗

▶名 I guess he must be very nervous; there is sweat on his forehead. 我猜他一定很緊張，他額頭直冒汗。

▶動 I am sweating all over; is there any place here for me to take a shower?
我渾身上下汗水淋漓，這裡有地方可以洗澡嗎？

萬用延伸句型

Don't sweat it！別擔心！這句話常用在口語中，告訴他人沒什麼好憂心的。
例如：Don't sweat it! You still have two days to finish your thesis.
別擔心！你還有兩天可以完成你的論文。

swell [swɛl]

Track 3046

動 膨脹

▶My ankle（腳踝）is swollen. I wonder why?
我的腳踝腫起來了，不知道為什麼？

swift [swɪft]

Track 3047

形 迅速的

▶I think the river is too swift for you to swim here.
我覺得這河水流得太急了，你不能在這裡游泳。

switch [swɪtʃ]

Track 3048

名 開關 動 轉換

▶名 Will you help me turn off the switch in my room?
請你幫我把我房間裡的開關關掉好嗎？

▶動 He walked in and switched on th light.
他走了進來，把燈打了開來。

實用片語用語

light switch 電燈開關
例如：I can't find the light switch in the dark.
太暗了，我找不到電燈開關。

sword [sord]

Track 3049

名 劍、刀

▶I've always wanted to hold a real sword.
我一直想要拿拿看一把真的劍。

sys·tem [ˋsɪstəm]

Track 3050

名 系統

▶It's not right for you to blame the failure all on the system.
你把這次失敗都歸咎於制度是不對的。

萬用延伸句型

It's not right for you to... 你不應該……

tab·let [ˋtæblɪt]

Track 3051

名 塊、片、碑、牌

▶If you take the tablet, your headache will go away.
吃一顆藥，你的頭就不會痛了。

文法字詞解析

由於 tablet 能夠拿來描述各種「片狀」、「塊狀」等物品，因此使用範圍很廣泛，從小小的片狀藥丸到我們常用的平板電腦都可以稱為 tablet。

tack [tæk]

Track 3052

名 大頭釘 動 釘住

▶名 He got hurt because he stepped on a tack.
他因踩到圖釘而受傷了。

▶動 Let's tack some posters to the wall, shall we?
我們把一些海報釘在牆上好嗎？

tag [tæg]

Track 3053

名 標籤 動 加標籤、尾隨 同 label 標籤

▶名 The dog is wearing a name tag.
這隻狗狗有戴名牌。

▶動 He tagged us in the picture.
他把我們標記在相片上了。

文法字詞解析
在社群網站上經常用到的「標記」功能，就是用 tag 這個字喔！所以我們可以請別人把自己「tag」在相片中。

tai·lor [ˋtelɚ]

Track 3054

名 裁縫師 動 裁製

▶名 This tailor is famous for making good suits.
這位裁縫以做高級西裝而出名。

▶動 The clinic tailors its treatment to individual needs.
那個診所的治療方法適合個別需要。

tame [tem]

Track 3055

形 馴服的、單調的 動 馴服

▶形 The horse is very tame.
這匹馬很乖。

▶動 I wouldn't know how to tame a lion.
我可不知道怎麼馴服獅子。

tap [tæp]

Track 3056

名 輕拍聲 動 輕打

▶名 Did you hear a tap on the window?
你有聽到有人有人輕叩窗戶嗎？

▶動 The girl taps her fingers on the desk impatiently（不耐煩地）. 那個女孩不耐煩地用手指輕扣桌面。

實用片語用語
tap dance 踢踏舞
例如：You need to wear special shoes to tap dance.
要跳踢踏舞必須穿特殊的舞鞋。

tax [tæks]

Track 3057

名 稅

▶Can you tell me how much the airport tax is?
您能不能告訴我機場稅是多少錢？

tease [tiz]

Track 3058

動 嘲弄、揶揄 名 揶揄

▶動 Don't tease the girl! She might cry.
不要逗那個女孩了！她會哭喔！

▶名 She is a big tease and really fun to be with.
她很愛戲弄人，跟她在一起很有趣。

tech·ni·cal [ˋtɛknɪkḷ]

Track 3059

形 技術上的、技能的

▶I don't know anything about technical matters.
我完全不懂技術問題。

萬用延伸句型
I don't know anything about... 我不知道任何和……有關的事。

tech·nique [tɛkˋnik]

Track 3060

名 技術、技巧

▶It's necessary for us to learn modern management techniques.
我們有必要學習現代管理技術。

tech·nol·o·gy [tɛk`nɑlədʒɪ]

Track 3061

名 技術學、工藝學

▶Technology is advancing so fast these days.
最近技術真的進步得好快啊。

tem·per [`tɛmpɚ]

Track 3062

名 脾氣

▶He has a terrible temper and is hard to get along with.
他的脾氣很差，很難相處。

實用片語用語
lose sb.'s temper 發脾氣
例 句：He loses his temper easily when it's hot.
天氣熱的時候他很容易就發脾氣。

tem·per·a·ture [`tɛmprətʃɚ]

Track 3063

名 溫度、氣溫

▶How about asking a nurse to take his temperature?
請一位護士幫他量量體溫怎麼樣？

tem·po·ra·ry [`tɛmpə͵rɛrɪ]

Track 3064

形 暫時的

▶The temporary worker will leave tomorrow.
那名臨時工明天就會離開了。

tend [tɛnd]

Track 3065

動 傾向、照顧 同 incline 傾向

▶British people tend to be rather conservative（保守的）.
英國人一般相當保守。

ten·der [`tɛndɚ]

Track 3066

形 溫柔的、脆弱的、幼稚的 同 soft 輕柔的

▶He gave her a tender kiss before he left.
他在離開之前給了她一個溫柔的吻。

文法字詞解析
雖然 tender 有「溫柔的」的意思，但一般是用來描述「動作、事情」，而不是描述「人」。如果你想說自己「很溫柔」，說「I'm tender」，會令人覺得你在說自己的肉「很柔軟、好好吃」喔。這當然是不行的。

ter·ri·to·ry [`tɛrə͵torɪ]

Track 3067

名 領土、版圖

▶That's unfamiliar（不熟悉的）territory to me.
對我來說那是不熟悉的領域。

text [tɛkst]

Track 3068

名 課文、本文

▶I am reading a text on Chinese philosophy（哲學）.
我正在讀中國哲學的課文。

thank·ful [`θæŋkfəl]

Track 3069

形 欣慰的、感謝的 同 grateful 感謝的

▶I am so thankful that she feels better today.
她今天感覺好多了，我真欣慰。

the·o·ry [`θiərɪ]

Track 3070

名 理論、推論 同 inference 推論

▶Not everyone can understand Einstein's Theory of Relativity（相對論）. 不是每個人都能讀懂愛因斯坦的相對論。

實用片語用語
in theory 理論上
例如：In theory, if you block someone, they won't be able to see your posts.
理論上來說，如果你封鎖了某人，他們就不會看到你貼的文章了。

thirst [θɝst]
Track 3071

名 口渴、渴望

▶Many boys have a thirst for adventure.
有許多男孩子都渴望冒險。

實用片語用語
have a thirst for sth. 渴望做某事

thread [θrɛd]
Track 3072

名 線 動 穿線

▶名 Would you please give me a piece of thread and a needle?
請給我一段線和一根針好嗎？

▶動 I'm not good at threading needles.
我超不會穿針的。

threat [θrɛt]
Track 3073

名 威脅、恐嚇

▶Some foods present（引起）a threat to people's health.
有些食物會威脅人體健康。

threat·en [ˋθrɛtn̩]
Track 3074

動 威脅

▶The strikers were threatened with dismissal（解雇）unless they returned to work.
罷工者受到威脅，說如果他們不復工就會被解雇。

實用片語用語
threaten to... 威脅要做某事
例如：He threatened to hang himself to get his way.
為了讓其他人聽他的，他威脅要上吊。

tick·le [ˋtɪkl̩]
Track 3075

動 搔癢、呵癢

▶He tickled my feet. 他搔了我的腳癢。

tide [taɪd]
Track 3076

名 潮、趨勢

▶The tide is low right now, so we can see the island.
現在退潮，所以我們可以看到那座島。

ti·dy [ˋtaɪdɪ]
Track 3077

形 整潔的 動 整頓

▶形 Would you please make your room tidy and put everything in order? 請把你的房間收拾乾淨，把東西都放整齊好嗎？

▶動 You must tidy up your room before going out.
出門之前一定要收拾一下房間。

tight [taɪt]
Track 3078

形 緊的、緊密的 副 緊緊地、安穩地

▶形 This pair of trousers is too tight for me to wear.
這條褲子太緊了，我穿不下。

▶副 The bandage was tied very tight. 繃帶綁得很緊。

文法字詞解析
除了表示「衣物很緊」等等「空間方面」的「緊」之外，tight 也可以用來說人與人之間的關係很「緊密」。

tight·en [ˋtaɪtn̩]
Track 3079

動 勒緊、使堅固

▶Can you help me tighten this screw? It's very loose.
你能幫我把這個螺絲旋緊嗎？它太鬆了。

tim·ber [ˋtɪmbɚ]

Track 3080

名 木材、樹林 同 wood 木材、樹林

▶A lot of timber was destroyed in the forest fire.
有許多木材在這次森林大火中燒毀了。

tis·sue [ˋtɪʃʊ]

Track 3081

名 面紙

▶Can you get me some tissues? 幫我拿點衛生紙來好不好？

to·bac·co [təˋbæko]

Track 3082

名 煙草

▶It's forbidden to sell tobacco to children under the age of 16.
禁止人們向十六歲以下的兒童出售煙草。

萬用延伸句型
It's forbidden to... ……是被禁止的

ton [tʌn]

Track 3083

名 噸

▶How many tons of water is there in the pool?
這個池子裡有多少噸水？

tor·toise [ˋtɔrtəs]

Track 3084

名 烏龜

▶I can't tell if the tortoise is awake or asleep.
我看不出這隻烏龜到底是睡著還是醒著。

toss [tɔs]

Track 3085

動 投擲 名 投、擲 同 throw 投、丟

▶動 He tossed the ball into the air. 他把球丟向空中。

▶名 A toss of a coin decides who should play first.
丟擲錢幣決定誰先開球。

tour·ism [ˋtʊrɪzəm]

Track 3086

名 觀光、遊覽

▶The nation is famous for its tourism. 那個國家以旅遊業聞名。

萬用延伸句型
be famous for... 因……而出名

tour·ist [ˋtʊrɪst]

Track 3087

名 觀光客

▶The tourist complained that the room was too dirty for him to stay in. 那名遊客抱怨說房間太髒了，沒辦法入住。

tow [to]

Track 3088

動 拖曳 名 拖曳 同 pull 拖、拉

▶動 Would you please help me tow my car to the nearest garage?
請你幫我把我的車拖到最近的汽車修理廠好嗎？

▶名 My car's broken down; would you please give me a tow?
我的車拋錨了，能用您的車幫我拖車嗎？

trace [tres]

Track 3089

動 追溯 名 蹤跡

▶動 The kids are learning to trace the letter. 孩子們在學習描字母。

▶名 There was barely（幾乎）a trace of salt in the soup.
湯裡幾乎一點鹽也沒有。

實用片語用語
a trace of... 一點……的蹤跡

trad·er [ˋtredɚ] Track 3090

名 商人

▶The trader was good at finding bargains.
這個商人很擅長找到好的交易機會。

trail [trel] Track 3091

名 痕跡、小徑 動 拖著、拖著走

▶名 I can't see the trail you told me about.
我沒看到你跟我提過的那條小路。

▶動 The dog trailed after me. 那隻狗尾隨著我。

實用片語用語

trail behind 尾隨……
例如：She trailed behind her friends because of her lack of energy.
她因為沒有體力而落後她的朋友們。

trans·port [ˋtrænsport] Track 3092

動 輸送、運輸 名 輸送

▶動 They transported the goods very quickly.
他們很快地運送了貨物。

▶名 They chose another means of transport because it was cheaper.
他們選擇了另一個運輸方法，因為這樣會便宜很多。

trash [træʃ] Track 3093

名 垃圾

▶Can you take out the trash please?
可以請你把垃圾拿出去丟嗎？

實用片語用語

trash can 垃圾桶
例如：The trash can is already full.
垃圾桶已經滿了。

trav·el·er [ˋtrævlɚ] Track 3094

名 旅行者、旅客

▶She was too timid（害羞的）to talk with other travelers.
她很害羞，不敢和其他旅行者交談。

tray [tre] Track 3095

名 托盤

▶Would you mind putting the tray over there?
你介不介意把托盤放到那邊去呢？

trem·ble [ˋtrɛmbl] Track 3096

名 顫抖、發抖 動 顫慄

▶名 There was a tremble in her voice. 她的嗓音有些顫抖。

▶動 The whole house trembled when the train went by.
火車經過時，整座房子都在震動。

實用片語用語

tremble like a leaf 如同樹葉一般顫抖
例如：The puppy trembled like leaf at the sound of thunder.
小狗被雷聲下得不斷顫抖。

trend [trɛnd] Track 3097

名 趨勢、傾向

▶Being skinny is a trend nowadays（現今）.
保持骨感是現今的時尚。

tribe [traɪb] Track 3098

名 部落、種族

▶There is a barbarian（野蠻的）tribe in this forest.
這個林區裡有一個野蠻的部落。

trick·y [ˋtrɪkɪ]

Track 3099

形 狡猾的、狡詐的

▶I'm in a rather tricky position; could you help me out?
我的處境很棘手，你願意幫幫我嗎？

troop [trup]

Track 3100

名 軍隊

▶It's going to be some time before the troops recover their strength. 部隊要過一段時期才能恢復實力。

萬用延伸句型
It's going to be some time before...
要過一段時間才會……

trop·i·cal [ˋtrɑpɪkḷ]

Track 3101

形 熱帶的

▶There is luxuriant（繁茂的）tropical vegetation（植物）in our country. 我們國家有很多繁茂的熱帶植物。

trunk [trʌŋk]

Track 3102

名 樹幹、大行李箱、象鼻

▶Would you please help me open the trunk?
請你幫我打開這個行李箱好嗎？

實用片語用語
tree trunk 樹幹
例如：You can tell the tree trunk is hollow by tapping on it.
只要敲敲樹幹就知道它是空心的。

truth·ful [ˋtruθfəl]

Track 3103

形 誠實的 同 honest 誠實的

▶Don't believe him, not all the news he told you is truthful.
別信他，他告訴你的所有消息未必都是真實的。

tub [tʌb]

Track 3104

名 桶、盤

▶I bought a tub and put it in the bathroom.
我買了一個盆子，放在浴室。

tug [tʌg]

Track 3105

動 用力拉 名 拖拉 同 pull 拖、拉

▶動 The little girl tugged at her mother's sleeve.
那個小女孩扯扯她媽媽的衣角。

▶名 I felt a tug at my sleeve and turned around.
我感覺到有人拉了一下我的袖子，便轉過身來。

實用片語用語
tug-of-war 拔河
例如：My class won the schoolwide tug-of-war.
我們班贏了全校的拔河比賽。

tulip [ˋtjuləp]

Track 3106

名 鬱金香

▶Would you like to see our tulip fields sometime next week?
下個禮拜你們想不想找時間去看看我們那片鬱金香花田？

tum·ble [ˋtʌmbḷ]

Track 3107

動 摔跤、跌落

▶She tumbled down the hill. 她一路翻滾下山坡。

tune [tjun]

Track 3108

名 調子、曲調 動 調整音調

▶名 What's this tune? It sounds familiar.
這是什麼曲調？聽起來好耳熟。

▶動 Do you mind if I tune the television set to Channel 7?
你介不介意我把電視機調到第七頻道？

tutor [ˋtjutɚ]

Track 3109

名 家庭教師、導師 動 輔導

▶名 My tutor is a learned（有學問的）scholar.
我的家教是一位學識淵博的學者。

▶動 How about tutoring your child by yourself?
你要不要自己來輔導你的孩子？

twig [twɪg]

Track 3110

名 小枝、嫩枝

▶It sounded like someone just stepped on a twig right behind me. 聽起來好像是有人在我背後踩到了一根小樹枝。

twin [twɪn]

Track 3111

名 雙胞胎

▶The twin brothers are alike not only in appearance but also in personality. 那對雙胞兄弟不但外表相似，而且性格也很像。

文法字詞解析
一次提到雙胞胎之中的兩個人時使用複數稱為「twins」，而如果要說雙胞胎中的其中一個則使用單數「a twin」。
例如：I'm a twin. My brother and I are twins.
我是雙胞胎的其中一個。我哥和我是雙胞胎。

twist [twɪst]

Track 3112

動 扭曲

▶He twisted his arm in a fight. 他在打架的時候扭到手臂了。

type·writ·er [ˋtaɪpˏraɪtɚ]

Track 3113

名 打字機

▶I still use my old typewriter. 我還是用我的老式打字機。

typ·i·cal [ˋtɪpɪkl]

Track 3114

形 典型的

▶It is typical of him to be so merciless（無慈悲心的）.
他是個典型的冷酷無情的人。

un·ion [ˋjunjən]

Track 3115

名 聯合、組織

▶He was elected the leader of the union.
他被選為工會的領導人。

u·nite [juˋnaɪt]

Track 3116

動 聯合、合併

▶We should unite to achieve our common goal.
我們應該聯手達到我們的共同目標。

實用片語用語
unite against sb. / sth. 聯合起來對抗某人／某事物
例如：All citizens united against corruption.
所有的國民都聯合起來反貪污。

u·ni·ty [ˋjunətɪ]

Track 3117

名 聯合、統一

▶There is little unity of purpose among the members.
成員之間缺乏共同的目標。

u·ni·verse [`junə,vɝs] Track 3118

名 宇宙、天地萬物

▶The universe is much bigger than we can imagine.
宇宙比我想像中的大多了。

實用片語用語
in the universe 全宇宙、全世界
例如：You're the person I love the most in the universe.
我全世界最愛的人是你。

un·less [ən`lɛs] Track 3119

連 除非

▶I won't go to the party unless I'm invited.
除非我被邀請，否則我不會去參加晚會的。

up·set [ʌp`sɛt] Track 3120

動 顛覆、使心煩 名 顛覆、煩惱 同 overturn 顛覆

▶動 The news upset him emotionally（感情上）.
這個消息使他心煩意亂。

▶名 No one expected two upsets in three games.
大家都沒想到，三場球賽中就有兩場是弱隊獲勝。

文法字詞解析
upset 的動詞變化：upset, upset, upset

va·cant [`vekənt] Track 3121

形 空閒的、空虛的

▶There are some vacant offices on the third floor.
三樓有幾間空著的辦公室。

val·u·a·ble [`væljʊəbḷ] Track 3122

形 貴重的

▶Real friendship（友誼）is more valuable than money; don't you think so? 真正的友誼比金錢更寶貴，你不這樣認為嗎？

文法字詞解析
valuable 指的是「貴重的」，有趣的是，如果在前面加上了代表「不、沒有」的字首「in-」，變成 invaluable，意思依然還是「珍貴的」。為什麼呢？原來「invaluable」的意思是「無法表示價值的、無價的」，而無價的東西當然還是很珍貴啦。如果想說一個東西並不貴重，那麼說 not valuable 就可以了。

van [væn] Track 3123

名 貨車

▶My dad is the man in the van. 貨車裡那個男人就是我爸。

van·ish [`vænɪʃ] Track 3124

動 消失、消逝

▶Many types of animals have vanished from the Earth.
已經有很多種類的動物從地球上絕跡了。

va·ri·e·ty [və`raɪətɪ] Track 3125

名 多樣化

▶I have a variety of books in my study.
在我的書房有各式各樣的書。

var·i·ous [`vɛrɪəs] Track 3126

形 多種的

▶Everyone arrived late at the party for various reasons.
每個人都由於種種原因而在派對上遲到了。

萬用延伸句型
for various reasons 因為諸多理由而……

var·y [ˋvɛrɪ] Track 3127

動 使變化、改變

▶The quality of fruits varies from season to season.
水果的品質隨季節變化而有所不同。

vase [ves] Track 3128

名 花瓶

▶Would you please help me glue the broken vase together?
請你幫我把破碎的花瓶黏合起來好嗎？

ve·hi·cle [ˋviɪkl̩] Track 3129

名 交通工具、車輛

▶Two vehicles had bumped into each other. 有兩輛車撞在一起了。

verse [vɝs] Track 3130

名 詩、詩句

▶She could quote any chapter and verse in this book easily.
她能夠毫不費力地引用這本書的任何章節和句子。

文法字詞解析
除了詩句外，在提到歌曲時也可以用 verse 來表示歌曲的某一段。

vest [vɛst] Track 3131

名 背心、馬甲 動 授給

▶名 The policeman survived because of his bulletproof（防彈的）vest. 那名警察因為有穿防彈背心才倖免於難。

▶動 The executive（行政的）power is usually vested in the president. 行政權通常會被賦予總統。

vice-pres·i·dent [vaɪs ˋprɛzədənt] Track 3132

名 副總統

▶Once the president of the company retired, the vice-president took over. 該公司的總經理一退休，公司就變成副總管理了。

vic·tim [ˋvɪktɪm] Track 3133

名 受害者

▶The victims of the flood still don't have a home.
水災的受害者還是沒有家。

實用片語用語
play the victim 裝可憐、假裝是受害者
例如：He's playing the victim again even though he's the one at fault.
雖然明明是他的錯，他卻又在裝可憐了。

vi·o·lence [ˋvaɪələns] Track 3134

名 暴力 同 force 暴力

▶Nothing good ever comes out of violence.
暴力從來沒有帶來過什麼好東西。

vi·o·lent [ˋvaɪələnt] Track 3135

形 猛烈的

▶The man is violent and often beats his wife.
這個男人很暴力，常打自己的太太。

vi·o·let [ˋvaɪəlɪt] Track 3136

名 紫羅蘭 形 紫羅蘭色的

▶名 I bought a bouquet（花束）of violets. 我買了一束紫羅蘭。

▶形 The dress is violet and extremely beautiful.
那件洋裝是紫色的，非常漂亮。

vis·i·ble [ˋvɪzəbḷ]
Track 3137

形 可看見的

▶Police regulations prescribe（規定）that an officer's number must be clearly visible.
警察條例要求執行職務者的號碼標誌必須清楚易見。

文法字詞解析
加上代表「不、沒有」的字首「in-」，變成「invisible」，就成了 visible 的相反詞「看不見的、隱形的」。

vi·sion [ˋvɪʒən]
Track 3138

名 視力、視覺、洞察力

▶How do you cope（對付、解決）with the problem of poor vision? 你是怎樣解決視力不好的問題？

vi·ta·min [ˋvaɪtəmɪn]
Track 3139

名 維他命

▶Lemons are rich in vitamin C. 檸檬含豐富的維生素 C。

viv·id [ˋvɪvɪd]
Track 3140

形 閃亮的、生動的

▶My daughter is a child with vivid imagination.
我女兒是一個想像力活躍的孩子。

vol·ume [ˋvɑljəm]
Track 3141

名 卷、冊、音量、容積

▶Would you please not play your radio at full volume?
請不要把收音機開到最大的音量好嗎？

實用片語用語
play... at full volume
以最大音量播放……

wag [wæg]
Track 3142

動 搖擺 名 搖擺、搖動

▶動 Dogs wag their tails when they are pleased.
狗一高興就搖尾巴。

▶名 The puppy greeted his master with a wag of his tail.
那隻小狗搖了一下尾巴迎接主人。

wage [wedʒ]
Track 3143

名 週薪、工資

▶The wage I earn is not enough for me to support the whole family. 我賺的薪水還不足以維持全家人的生活。

文法字詞解析
這個字也經常使用複數型態 wages 來代表整體的工資。

wag·on [ˋwægən]
Track 3144

名 四輪馬車、貨車

▶Who's the man on the back of the wagon?
貨車後面那個男人是誰？

wak·en [ˋwekən]
Track 3145

動 喚醒、醒來

▶I feel as if I had wakened from a nightmare（噩夢）.
我覺得好像剛從噩夢中醒來。

wan·der [ˋwandɚ] Track 3146

動 徘徊、漫步

▶Would you please not wander off the point?
請你不要離題好嗎？

warmth [wɔrmθ] Track 3147

名 暖和、溫暖、熱忱 同 zeal 熱忱

▶He was touched by the warmth of his family's welcome.
他被他家人的熱烈歡迎而感動。

實用片語用語
be touched by... 被……感動

warn [wɔrn] Track 3148

動 警告、提醒

▶Let me warn you: he's really hard to please.
我警告你一下：他超難取悅的。

wax [wæks] Track 3149

名 蠟、蜂蠟、月盈

▶The doll is made of wax. 這個娃娃是蠟做的。

weak·en [ˋwikən] Track 3150

動 使變弱、減弱

▶Nothing can weaken his resolve（決心）to become a lawyer.
什麼也動搖不了他要當律師的決心。

wealth [wɛlθ] Track 3151

名 財富、財產

▶Health is better than wealth. 健康勝於財富。

實用片語用語
be better than... 比……更好

wealth·y [ˋwɛlθɪ] Track 3152

形 富裕的、富有的

▶She is not only an attractive woman but also a wealthy one.
她不但是個很有魅力的女人，而且還很富有。

weave [wiv] Track 3153

名 織法、編法

▶This cloth is of a coarse（粗糙的）weave. 這塊布織得很粗糙。

文法字詞解析
weave 的動詞變化：weave, wove, woven

web [wɛb] Track 3154

名 網、蜘蛛網

▶I walked straight into a spider web. 我直接撞上了蜘蛛網。

weed [wid] Track 3155

名 野草、雜草

▶You have to clear up the weed before your plants can grow.
你要先把雜草除掉，你的植物才會生長。

weep [wip] Track 3156

動 哭泣，哭 同 cry 哭

▶The mother wept over her dead child.
那個媽媽因孩子死去而哭泣。

文法字詞解析
weep 的動詞變化：weep, wept, wept

wheat [hwit]

Track 3157

名 小麥、麥子

▶This old man is a leading authority on wheat diseases.
這位老人是小麥病蟲害方面的權威。

實用片語用語
leading authority 權威

whip [hwɪp]

Track 3158

名 鞭子 動 鞭打

▶名 It's cruel of you to use your whip on your horse.
你用鞭子抽你的馬是很殘忍的。

▶動 You really shouldn't whip your kids.
你真的不應該拿鞭子抽你的孩子。

whis·tle [ˋhwɪsl̩]

Track 3159

名 口哨、汽笛 動 吹口哨

▶名 She blew the whistle and jumped into the pool.
她吹了哨子，跳進池裡。

▶動 A man cannot whistle and drink at the same time.
沒人可以邊吹口哨邊喝水吧。

萬用延伸句型
at the same time 同時……

wick·ed [ˋwɪkɪd]

Track 3160

形 邪惡的、壞的

▶People thought him dangerous and wicked.
人們認為他是危險且邪惡的。

wil·low [ˋwɪlo]

Track 3161

名 柳樹

▶They're sitting under the willow tree. 他們坐在柳樹下面。

wink [wɪŋk]

Track 3162

動 眨眼、使眼色 名 眨眼、使眼色

▶動 Why did he wink at me? 他幹嘛對我眨眼睛？

▶名 She turned around and gave me a wink.
她轉過身，對我眨眼。

文法字詞解析
wink 和 blink 兩個字都是「眨眼」的意思，那兩者有什麼差別呢？原來，blink 就是普通的眨眼睛，沒什麼特別意思，而 wink 則是帶有暗示或特殊涵意，不是單純地眨眼睛。因此，若有人 wink at you，表示他想暗示你一些事或對你放電。若有人 blink at you，表示他只是呆滯地在那邊眨眼睛而已，那是人類正常的生理運作。

wipe [waɪp]

Track 3163

動 擦拭 名 擦拭、擦

▶動 Would you please wipe the table with a dry cloth?
請你用乾抹布擦擦桌子好嗎？

▶名 He gave the table mats a quick wipe.
他把桌上的碗盤墊快速擦了一下。

wis·dom [ˋwɪzdəm]

Track 3164

名 智慧

▶The old man is full of wisdom. 這個老男人充滿了智慧。

wrap [ræp]

Track 3165

動 包裝 名 包裝紙

▶動 You need to wrap up the gift before you give it to her.
你把禮物給她前要把它包好。

▶名 Why don't you buy a woolen（羊毛製的）wrap for yourself?
為什麼不為你自己買條羊毛圍巾呢？

實用片語用語
wrapping paper 包裝紙
例如：I got some wrapping paper so I could make the presents look pretty.
我找了一些包裝紙來把禮物包得漂漂亮亮。

wrist [rɪst]

Track 3166

名 腕關節、手腕

▶She broke her wrist when she was playing basketball.
她在打籃球的時候手腕斷了。

Yy

yawn [jɔn]

Track 3167

動 打呵欠 名 打呵欠

▶動 It's impolite of you to yawn in front of our guests.
你在客人面前打呵欠是不禮貌的。

▶名 He stretched hard with a yawn. 他大力伸懶腰、打了個呵欠。

萬用延伸句型
It's impolite of you to... 你（做某事）很不禮貌

yell [jɛl]

Track 3168

動 大叫、呼喊

▶I don't think you should yell at that old man like that.
我認為你不該對那位老人那樣大吼大叫。

yolk [jok]

Track 3169

名 蛋黃、卵黃

▶You have yolk on your chin. Rub it off!
你的下巴沾著蛋黃，擦掉吧！

Zz

zip·per [ˋzɪpɚ]

Track 3170

名 拉鏈

▶Can you help me pull up the zipper on the back of my dress?
可以幫我把我洋裝背後的拉鍊拉起來嗎？

zone [zon]

Track 3171

名 地區、地帶、劃分地區

▶Would you please tell me what time zone you are in?
請您告訴我你在哪個時區好嗎？

實用片語用語
time zone 時區

進階英文能力——邁向 4200 單字

學英文從單字開始，
許自己一個不可思議的滿分奇蹟！

Level 4

進階英文能力——邁向4200單字

a·ban·don [ə`bændən]

Track 3172

動 放棄 同 desert 遺棄

▶She abandoned her children and moved to another city.
她丟棄了自己的孩子，搬到另一個城市。

ab·do·men [`æbdəmən]

Track 3173

名 腹部

▶He felt a great deal of pain in his abdomen.
他感到腹部非常痛。

實用片語用語
a great deal of... 很多的
much 和 a great deal of 是一樣的意思，但是 much 只能修飾不可數名詞。

ab·so·lute [`æbsəˌlut]

Track 3174

形 絕對的 同 complete 絕對的

▶You should know that there is no absolute standard for it.
你應該知道這件事情沒有絕對的標準。

ab·sorb [əb`sɔrb]

Track 3175

動 吸收

▶So many good ideas! It's too much for me to absorb all at once. 實在有太多好主意了！我很難一下子完全吸收。

ab·stract [`æbstrækt]

Track 3176

形 抽象的 反 concrete 具體的

▶I wish I could understand such an abstract concept.
真希望我能理解如此抽象的概念。

萬用延伸句型
I wish I could... 真希望我可以……

ac·a·dem·ic [ˌækə`dɛmɪk]

Track 3177

形 學院的、大學的

▶The academic atmosphere in this university is pretty great.
這個大學的學術氛圍很棒。

ac·cent [`æksɛnt]

Track 3178

名 口音、腔調

▶It is obvious that she is Irish, because she speaks with an Irish accent.
顯然她是個愛爾蘭人，因為她說話帶有愛爾蘭口音。

萬用延伸句型
It's obvious that... 很明顯地……

ac·cep·tance [ək`sɛptəns]

Track 3179

名 接受

▶This kind of view has not received wide acceptance yet.
這種觀點還沒有得到廣泛的認可。

ac·cess [ˋæksɛs]

Track 3180

名 接近、會面 動 接近、會面

▶名 Not everyone has access to the full facts of the case.
不是每個人都能看到有關該案全部事實的資料。

▶動 Not everyone in the company has the right to access the secret file.
不是公司裡的每個人都有權利取出這個秘密檔案。

ac·ci·den·tal [ˏæksəˋdɛntl̩]

Track 3181

形 偶然的、意外的

▶Running into her in that coffee shop was purely（純粹地） accidental. 在那家咖啡店遇到她是純粹出於偶然。

萬用延伸句型
run into... 意外遇上（某人）

ac·com·pa·ny [əˋkʌmpənɪ]

Track 3182

動 隨行、陪伴、伴隨

▶Lightning usually accompanies thunder. 閃電通常伴隨著雷聲。

ac·com·plish [əˋkɑmplɪʃ]

Track 3183

動 達成、完成 同 finish 完成

▶I'm afraid that it's too difficult for me to accomplish the task alone. 要我獨自完成這項任務恐怕很難。

實用片語用語
accomplish sth. alone 獨自完成……

ac·com·plish·ment [əˋkɑmplɪʃmənt]

Track 3184

名 達成、成就

▶Don't you think landing on the moon was quite an accomplishment?
你不認為登陸月球上是一項了不起的成就嗎？

ac·coun·tant [əˋkaʊntənt]

Track 3185

名 會計師

▶Would you please help me find a good accountant?
你能幫我找個好的會計師嗎？

ac·cu·ra·cy [ˋækjərəsɪ]

Track 3186

名 正確、精密

▶It is impossible to say with any accuracy how many people are affected. 不可能準確說出到底有多少人受影響。

ac·cuse [əˋkjuz]

Track 3187

動 控告 同 denounce 控告

▶Once we have gathered enough proof, we can accuse him at the court.
一旦收集到足夠的證據，我們就可以在法庭上控告他了。

ac·id [ˋæsɪd]

Track 3188

名 酸性物質 形 酸的

▶名 The acid has burnt a hole in my jacket.
這種酸把我的夾克燒出一個洞。

▶形 No one likes to hear your acid words.
沒有人喜歡聽你尖酸刻薄的話。

實用片語用語
acid rain 酸雨
例如：Acid rain is a result of industrial pollution.
之所以會有酸雨，都是工業污染害的。

ac·quaint [ə`kwent]　Track 3189

動 使熟悉、告知

▶It will take you some time to acquaint yourself with a new job.
要熟悉一項新的工作是需要一些時間的。

ac·quain·tance [ə`kwentəns]　Track 3190

名 認識的人、熟人 同 companion 同伴

▶I made the acquaintance of my husband at a party.
我是在一次聚會上認識我先生的。

實用片語用語
make sb.'s acquaintance 認識某人

ac·quire [ə`kwaɪr]　Track 3191

動 取得、獲得 同 obtain 獲得

▶Would you please tell me how he acquired his wealth?
請你告訴我他的財富是怎樣得來的?

a·cre [`ekɚ]　Track 3192

名 英畝

▶We own more than 100 acres of farmland. What about you?
我們擁有超過一百英畝的農田，你們呢？

a·dapt [ə`dæpt]　Track 3193

動 使適應

▶I'm afraid that she can't adapt herself quickly to the new climate.
恐怕她無法很快適應這種新氣候。

ad·e·quate [`ædəkwɪt]　Track 3194

形 適當的、足夠的 同 enough 足夠的

▶There must be adequate room for people to gather.
必須要有足夠的空間讓人們集合。

文法字詞解析
這個句子中的「room」指的可不是房間喔！它是「空間」的意思，當作這個意思時是個不可數的名詞。

ad·jec·tive [`ædʒɪktɪv]　Track 3195

名 形容詞

▶An adjective is used to describe or add to the meaning of a noun. 形容詞的功能是用來描述或增加名詞的意思。

ad·just [ə`dʒʌst]　Track 3196

動 調節、對準

▶Not all people can adjust themselves to the busy modern life in big cities.
不是所有人都能適應大都市忙碌的現代生活。

ad·just·ment [ə`dʒʌstmənt]　Track 3197

名 調整、調節

▶The company made an adjustment in my salary.
公司對我的薪資作了調整。

ad·mi·ra·ble [`ædmərəbl]　Track 3198

形 令人欽佩的

▶It is obvious that this essay is admirable in all respects.
顯然這篇文章在各方面都是值得欣賞的。

文法字詞解析
其實 admirable 這個字就是由 admire（欣賞）加上意為「可以、能夠」的字尾「-able」變成的。

ad·mi·ra·tion [ˌædməˋreʃən]

Track 3199

名 欽佩、讚賞

▶He has a lot of admiration for his classmate.
他非常欣賞他的同學。

ad·mis·sion [ədˋmɪʃən]

Track 3200

名 准許進入、入場費

▶Can we gain the admission to the Buckingham Palace（白金漢宮）?
我們能獲准進入白金漢宮嗎？

ad·verb [ˋædvɝb]

Track 3201

名 副詞

▶Don't you know that adverbs are used to modify（修飾）verbs and adjectives?
副詞是用來修飾動詞和形容詞的，難道你不知道嗎？

萬用延伸句型

Don't you know that...? 你不知道……嗎？
這個句型頗有把對方當笨蛋的味道，所以如果你不想惹到人，最好避免使用。

a·gen·cy [ˋedʒənsɪ]

Track 3202

名 代理商

▶My company's got many agencies in major cities of the country.
我的公司在國內主要城市有很多家代理機構。

a·gent [ˋedʒənt]

Track 3203

名 代理人

▶Would you please let us know if you don't wish our agent to call?
您若不希望我們的代理人去造訪的話，請告知我們好嗎？

實用片語用語

secret agent 特務
例句：She had no idea that both her parents were secret agents.
她完全不曉得她父母都是特務。

ag·gres·sive [əˋgrɛsɪv]

Track 3204

形 侵略的、攻擊的

▶A good salesman must be aggressive if he wants to succeed.
要做個好推銷員一定要有衝勁才能成功。

a·gree·a·ble [əˋgriəbḷ]

Track 3205

形 令人愉快的

▶She's a very agreeable girl so people like to talk to her.
她是個很好講話的女孩子，所以大家都喜歡跟她講話。

AIDS/ac·quired im·mune de·fi·ciensy syn·drome

Track 3206

[edz]/[əˋkwaɪrd ɪˋmjun dɪˋfɪʃənsɪ ˋsɪnˌdrom]

名 愛滋病

▶As of now, we still haven't found a cure to AIDS.
直到現在，我們還是沒有發現愛滋病的治療方式。

al·co·hol [ˋælkəˌhɔl]

Track 3207

名 酒精

▶There is too great a consumption（消耗）of alcohol in China.
在中國，酒的消耗量太大了。

實用片語用語

alcohol addiction 酒精成癮
例句：Jack's alcohol addiction was what scared all his girlfriends away.
傑克的酒癮把他的女友們都嚇跑了。

a·lert [ə`lɝt]

Track 3208

名 警報 形 機警的

▶名 The dog sat in front of the house, on alert.
那隻狗機警地坐在房門口。

▶形 You left your door open again? You really need to be more alert. 你又忘記關門？你真的應該更機警一點。

al·low·ance/ pock·et mon·ey [ə`laʊəns]/[`pɑkɪt`mʌnɪ]

Track 3209

名 津貼、補助

▶It is clear that they show great anxiety concerning their retirement allowance.
顯然他們對自己的養老金問題顯得十分焦慮。

a·lu·mi·num [ə`lumɪnəm]

Track 3210

名 鋁

▶There are a great many cooking utensils（器具）made of aluminum now. 現在有相當多的炊具都是鋁製的。

文法字詞解析
這個單字說成 aluminum（美式）和 aluminium（英式）都可以，兩者差一個 i。

a.m. [`e`ɛm]

Track 3211

副 上午

▶How about meeting at ten a.m. next Sunday?
我們下星期日早上十點見面好不好？

am·a·teur [`æmə͵tʃʊr]

Track 3212

名 業餘愛好者 形 業餘的

反 professional 專業的

▶名 Not only professionals but also amateurs can take part in the tournament（錦標賽）.
這次錦標賽不僅職業運動員可以參加，業餘運動員也可以參加。

▶形 The pictures can be taken by not only professional photographers but also amateur photographers.
這些照片不但專業攝影師能拍，業餘攝影師也能拍得出來。

am·bi·tious [æm`bɪʃəs]

Track 3213

形 有野心的

▶Don't you think this is quite an ambitious plan?
你不認為這個計畫野心過大了嗎？

a·mid/a·midst [ə`mɪd]/[ə`mɪdst]

Track 3214

連 在……之中

▶Not all people can stand firm amid temptations（誘惑）.
不是所有人都能夠禁得住各種誘惑。

a·muse [ə`mjuz]

Track 3215

動 娛樂、消遣

▶It was too rainy to play outside, so she amused herself with a book.
雨太大不適合在外面玩，所以她看書消遣。

實用片語用語
amuse oneself 自己找事做、自己消磨時間

a·muse·ment [əˋmjuzmənt] Track 3216

名 娛樂、有趣

▶My chief amusement is reading novels; what about you?
我的主要娛樂是看小說，你呢？

a·nal·y·sis [əˋnæləsɪs] Track 3217

名 分析

▶His analysis of the problem shows great insight（洞察力）.
他對該問題的分析顯示出敏銳的洞察力。

an·a·lyze [ˋænḷˏaɪz] Track 3218

動 分析、解析

▶Would you analyze the structure of the sentence for me?
你能幫我分析一下這個句子的結構嗎？

an·ces·tor [ˋænsɛstɚ] Track 3219

名 祖先、祖宗

▶My ancestors used to live in Kaohsuing.
我的祖先過去住在高雄。

文法字詞解析
ancestor 指的是單一的祖先（例如你的曾曾曾祖父就算是一個 ancestor），而要統稱全體的「家族史」則可以說 ancestry。

an·ni·ver·sa·ry [ˏænəˋvɝsərɪ] Track 3220

名 周年紀念日

▶Don't you remember that next Monday is the anniversary of when we first met?
你還記得嗎？下週一是我們相遇的週年紀念日。

an·noy [əˋnɔɪ] Track 3221

動 煩擾、使惱怒 同 irritate 使惱怒

▶He was annoyed by the mosquitoes（蚊子）.
那些蚊子讓他覺得很煩。

an·nu·al [ˋænjʊəl] Track 3222

形 一年的、年度的

▶I guess it's time for me to write an annual report.
看來我該寫年度報告了。

anx·i·e·ty [æŋˋzaɪətɪ] Track 3223

名 憂慮、不安、渴望

▶She paced around the room in anxiety.
她焦慮地繞著房間走。

實用片語用語
anxiety attack 焦慮症發作
例如：He's having an anxiety attack. Give him some space.
他焦慮症發作了，不要通通擠在他旁邊。

anx·ious [ˋæŋkʃəs] Track 3224

形 憂心的、擔憂的

▶We are anxious to ensure that there is no misunderstanding（誤解）between us. 我們急於確保我們之間沒有誤解。

a·pol·o·gize [əˋpɑləˏdʒaɪz] Track 3225

動 道歉、認錯

▶I won't apologize unless she apologizes first.
除非她先道歉，否則我是不會道歉的。

a·pol·o·gy [əˋpɑlədʒɪ] *Track 3226*

名 謝罪、道歉

▶I owe you an apology for what I did last night; I hope you can forgive me.
我為昨天晚上的事向你道歉，希望你能夠原諒我。

實用片語用語
owe sb. an apology 欠某人一個道歉

ap·pli·ance [əˋplaɪəns] *Track 3227*

名 器具、家電用品

▶There are many household appliances in this shop.
這個商店有賣許多家用品。

ap·pli·cant [ˋæpləkənt] *Track 3228*

名 申請人、應徵者

▶It is no wonder that there were few applicants for the job.
難怪沒有什麼人申請這份工作。

ap·pli·ca·tion [ˌæpləˋkeʃən] *Track 3229*

名 應用、申請

▶His application to the school was rejected.
他申請這所學校被拒。

文法字詞解析
大家常下載的「app」就是「application」的簡單說法，指的是「應用程式」。

ap·point [əˋpɔɪnt] *Track 3230*

動 任命、約定、指派、任用

▶He appointed her as his doctor. 他指名她為他看病。

ap·point·ment [əˋpɔɪntmənt] *Track 3231*

名 指定、約定、指派、任用

▶Would you please schedule an appointment for me to meet with Mr. Liu? 您可以幫我安排個時間跟劉先生會面嗎？

實用片語用語
schedule an appointment 安排會面

ap·pre·ci·a·tion [əˌpriʃɪˋeʃən] *Track 3232*

名 賞識、鑑識

▶I have a lot of appreciation for people who are considerate（體貼）. 我很欣賞待人體貼的人。

ap·pro·pri·ate [əˋproprɪˌet] *Track 3233*

形 適當的、適切的 同 proper 適當的

▶Why don't you get a dress appropriate for the occasion?
為什麼不買一件適合該場合穿的洋裝呢？

文法字詞解析
appropriate 的相反詞是 inappropriate，即「不適當的」。

ap·prov·al [əˋpruvḷ] *Track 3234*

名 承認、同意

▶I hope the arrangements will meet with your approval.
希望這些安排會得到您的同意。

arch [ɑrtʃ] *Track 3235*

名 拱門、拱形 動 變成弓形

▶名 It is a pity that I have never been to the Triumphal（凱旋的）Arch. 我從來沒去過凱旋門，真是遺憾。

▶動 He arched an eyebrow at my question.
他聽到我問的問題，弓起了眉毛。

a·rise [ə`raɪz]

Track 3236

動 出現、發生

▶The problem may not arise, but there's no harm in keeping our powder dry. 問題不一定會發生，但有備無患並無害處。

文法字詞解析

arise 的動詞變化：arise, arose, arisen

實用片語用語

keep one's powder dry 有備無患

arms [ɑrmz]

Track 3237

名 武器、兵器

▶The company is a manufacturer（製造者）of arms.
那個公司是武器製造商。

a·rouse [ə`raʊz]

Track 3238

動 喚醒

▶The notice aroused anger among customers.
那個公告激起了消費者的公憤。

ar·ti·cle [`ɑrtɪkḷ]

Track 3239

名 論文、物件

▶Could you tell me what do you think of the article?
你能不能告訴我，你認為這篇文章怎麼樣？

artificial [ˏɑrtə`fɪʃəl]

Track 3240

形 人工的

▶There are some artificial flowers on the table; do you like them? 桌上放著一些假花，你喜歡它們嗎？

實用片語用語

artificial intelligence (A.I.) 人工智慧

例句：With the development of artificial intelligence, our world has become a very different place.

由於人工智慧的發展，我們的世界已經與從前大不相同。

ar·tis·tic [ɑr`tɪstɪk]

Track 3241

形 藝術的、美術的

▶The interior design of her room is very artistic.
她房間的室內設計非常有藝術水準。

a·shamed [ə`ʃemd]

Track 3242

形 以……為恥

▶I'm too ashamed to tell her that I had failed.
我不好意思告訴她我失敗了。

as·pect [`æspɛkt]

Track 3243

名 方面、外貌、外觀

▶We can look at this problem from several aspects.
我們可以從幾個不同的面向探討這個問題。

實用片語用語

from several aspects 從幾個不同的面向

as·pi·rin [`æspərɪn]

Track 3244

名 （藥）阿斯匹靈

▶If you have a headache, why don't you take an aspirin?
既然你頭疼，為什麼不吃一片阿斯匹靈呢？

as·sem·ble [ə`sɛmbḷ]

Track 3245

動 聚集、集合

▶More than 10,000 people assembled at the airport to welcome their idol.
超過一萬人聚集在機場歡迎他們的偶像。

B C D E F G H I J K L M N O P Q R S T U V W X Y Z

as·sem·bly [əˋsɛmblɪ] Track 3246

名 集會、集合、會議

▶Not all citizens have the rights of assembly and expression in that country.
在那個國家不是所有公民都有集會和發表言論的權利。

as·sign [əˋsaɪn] Track 3247

動 分派、指定

▶It is very difficult for the scientists to assign an exact date to this building.
確定這座建築物的確切年代對科學家來說很難。

as·sign·ment [əˋsaɪnmənt] Track 3248

名 分派、任命

▶Would you like to tell me how you are going to finish the assignment?
能告訴我你將如何完成作業嗎？

文法字詞解析
除了工作上的「任務」之外，assignment也能指學生的「回家作業」。

as·sist·ance [əˋsɪstəns] Track 3249

名 幫助、援助

▶It's too hard for me to move this piano without assistance.
沒有人幫忙的話，我很難挪動這架鋼琴。

as·so·ci·ate [əˋsoʃɪt]/[əˋsoʃɪˌet] Track 3250

名 同事 動 聯合

▶名 Not every associate in our company is friendly to me.
在我們公司，不是每一位同事都對我很友善。

▶動 Not every woman associates happiness with having money.
不是每個女人都把幸福和有錢聯想在一起。

as·so·ci·a·tion [əˌsosɪˋeʃən] Track 3251

名 協會、聯合會

▶Would you tell me what association you have with the color green? 能否告訴我綠色會使你產生什麼聯想？

as·sume [əˋsum] Track 3252

動 假定、擔任

▶The prince assumed power when he was only fifteen.
那個王子在十五歲時就掌權了。

實用片語用語
assume power 掌權

as·sur·ance [əˋʃurəns] Track 3253

名 保證、保險 同 insurance 保險

▶I don't believe his assurance that everything will go well.
我不相信他對於一切都會順利的保證。

as·sure [əˋʃur] Track 3254

動 向……保證、使確信 同 guarantee 向……保證

▶They assured me that all the information is accurate.
他們向我保證，所有的資訊都是正確的。

萬用延伸句型
I assure you... 我向你保證……
例如：I assure you that everything is under control.
我向你保證，一切都在掌握之中。

ath·let·ic [æθ`lɛtɪk]   Track 3255

形 運動的、強健的

▶The boy is very athletic. 那個男孩非常地擅長運動。

ATM/au·to·mat·ic tell·er ma·chine [ˏɔtə`mætɪk `tɛlɚ mə`ʃin]   Track 3256

名 自動櫃員機

▶I'm surprised that you've never used an ATM before.
我很驚訝，你居然沒用過自動提款機。

文法字詞解析
ATM 這個縮寫除了拿來表示「自動櫃員機」，同時在網路用語中也可以當作「at the moment」（現在）的縮寫。通常只用於線上傳訊息、留言時，口語中不會出現。
例如：Give me a sec, I'm all tied up atm.
等一下，我現在超忙的。

at·mos·phere [`ætməsˏfɪr]   Track 3257

名 大氣、氣氛

▶There is an atmosphere of peace and calm in the country.
在鄉間有一種和平寧靜的氣氛。

at·om [`ætəm]   Track 3258

名 原子

▶I read that we're all made of atoms.
我在書上讀到，我們都是原子做的。

a·tom·ic [ə`tɑmɪk]   Track 3259

形 原子的

▶The Second World War was when the atomic bomb was first used. 在第二次世界大戰中，第一次使用了原子彈。

實用片語用語
atomic bomb 原子彈

at·tach [ə`tætʃ]   Track 3260

動 連接、附屬、附加

▶You shouldn't attach all the blame to the taxi-driver.
你不應該把全部責任都歸咎於計程車司機。

實用片語用語
attach the blame to... 把責任歸咎於……

at·tach·ment [ə`tætʃmənt]   Track 3261

名 連接、附著

▶Please see the attachment in the email.
請看一下那個電子郵件的附件。

at·trac·tion [ə`trækʃən]   Track 3262

名 魅力、吸引力

▶Would you like to tell me what the best attraction in New York is? 你能不能告訴我紐約最具吸引力的是什麼？

au·di·o [`ɔdɪˏo]   Track 3263

名 聲音

▶First of all, let's have a look at our audio-visual classroom.
首先，讓我們看一下視聽教室吧。

實用片語用語
audio file 音訊檔案
例如：This computer doesn't come with software to open audio files with.
這台電腦沒有可以開音訊檔案的軟體。

au·thor·i·ty [ə`θɔrətɪ]   Track 3264

名 權威、當局

▶Most of the young people nowadays don't have respect for authority. And to be honest why should they? 現在的年輕人大都不尊重權威。而且說真的，他們為什麼要尊重權威？

au·to·bi·og·ra·phy

[ˌɔtəbaɪˋɑgrəfɪ] Track 3265

名 自傳

▶I enjoyed reading Mark Twain's autobiography.
我喜歡讀馬克・吐溫的自傳。

文法字詞解析
biography（傳記）加上代表了「自動、自己」的字首「auto-」，就變成了「自傳」的意思。

a·wait

[əˋwet] Track 3266

動 等待

▶Do you know what delights（快樂的事） await you there?
你知道那裡有什麼快樂的事在等著你嗎？

awk·ward

[ˋɔkwɚd] Track 3267

形 笨拙的、不熟練的

▶I felt very awkward and out of place at the formal ball.
在那個正式的舞會上，我感到局促不安，很不自在。

實用片語用語
feel out of place 不自在

Bb

back·pack

[ˋbækˌpæk] Track 3268

名 背包 動 背負簡便行李旅行

▶名 The more things you put in the backpack, the heavier it becomes. 你在背包裡放的東西越多，它就越重。

▶動 They backpacked through the countryside.
他們在鄉間當背包客。

文法字詞解析
「背包客（backpacker）」就是「backpack」這個字加上「-er」結尾而組成的。

bald

[bɔld] Track 3269

形 禿頭的、禿的

▶Don't you think the bald eagle looks scary?
你不覺得禿鷹看起來很可怕嗎？

實用片語用語
bald spot 禿髮的區塊
例如：I try to style my hair to cover my bald spot.
我試著幫自己弄一個可以蓋住禿頭處的髮型。

bal·let

[ˋbæle] Track 3270

名 芭蕾

▶Can you tell me how long you have been learning ballet up to now? 你能告訴我你目前為止學了多久的芭蕾嗎？

bank·rupt

[ˋbæŋkrʌpt] Track 3271

名 破產者 形 破產的

▶名 He became a bankrupt after gambling all his money away.
他把錢都賭光了後就破產了。

▶形 The factory in the village went bankrupt last month.
上個月村子裡的那間工廠倒閉了。

bar·gain

[ˋbɑrgɪn] Track 3272

名 協議、成交 動 討價還價

▶名 What a bargain! This beautiful dress cost me only two dollars.
真是太划算了！這件漂亮的洋裝只花了我兩美元。

▶動 We refuse to bargain over the price.
我們拒絕在價格上討價還價。

萬用延伸句型
What a bargain! 真便宜！

bar·ri·er [ˋbærɪɚ]
Track 3273

名 障礙

▶Lack of confidence is the biggest barrier to finding a good job.
缺乏自信是找到好工作的最大障礙。

實用片語用語
language barrier 語言障礙
例如：The language barrier became a problem between us and our Romanian client.
我們與羅馬尼亞客戶之間的語言障礙成了問題。

ba·sin [ˋbes]
Track 3274

名 盆、水盆

▶The baby is sitting in the basin. 那個寶寶正坐在水盆裡。

bat·ter·y [ˋbætərɪ]
Track 3275

名 電池

▶Don't forget to charge the battery at night.
別忘了晚上要幫電池充電。

beak [bik]
Track 3276

名 鳥嘴

▶The bird on the balcony has a worm in its beak.
陽臺上的那隻鳥嘴裡叼著一隻蟲子。

beam [bim]
Track 3277

名 光線、容光煥發、樑 動 照耀、微笑

▶名 I can see a beam of light in the cave.
我能在洞穴裡看見一束光線。

▶動 She beamed with joy when she saw her son.
她看到她兒子時面露喜色。

文法字詞解析
不是所有的「光線」都可以稱為 beam 喔！beam 有「樑柱」的意思，因此當作「光線」時，指的就是像柱子這樣「一束」、「很集中」的光線。所以，在黑暗中用手電筒探照的「一束光」就可以稱 beam；走在無遮蔽的路上，太陽照下來，則不能稱為 beam（如果太陽集中成一束光照在你身上，應該會烤焦的）。

be·hav·ior [bɪˋhevjɚ]
Track 3278

名 舉止、行為 同 action 行為

▶Shouldn't you be ashamed of your foolish behavior?
難道你不該對你自己的愚蠢行為感到羞恥嗎？

bi·og·ra·phy [baɪˋɑgrəfɪ]
Track 3279

名 傳記

▶The biography of Steve Jobs is popular. 賈伯斯的傳記很受歡迎。

bi·ol·o·gy [baɪˋɑlədʒɪ]
Track 3280

名 生物學

▶Bob has been bad at biology in school all these years.
這些年鮑伯在學校生物一直都學得不好。

萬用延伸句型
...all these years 這些年來一直都……

blade [bled]
Track 3281

名 刀鋒

▶The man licked the blood from the blade.
那個男人舔掉了刀刃上的血。

blend [blɛnd]
Track 3282

名 混合 動 使混合、使交融

▶名 I love this blend of strawberry and mango juice.
我喜歡這個草莓和芒果汁的混合飲料。

▶動 Just act natural and try to blend in.
自然點，試著混進人群中吧。

bless·ing [ˋblɛsɪŋ]

Track 3283

名 恩典、祝福

▶We sent her our blessings for her birthday.
我們為她的生日送上了祝福。

blink [blɪŋk]

Track 3284

名 眨眼 動 使眨眼、閃爍

▶名 My brother disappeared in the blink of an eye.
我弟弟一眨眼就不見了。

▶動 She blinked when I opened the curtains.
我打開窗簾時她眨了眨眼睛。

實用片語用語
in the blink of an eye 一眨眼就……

bloom [blum]

Track 3285

名 開花期 動 開花

▶名 The daffodils（黃水仙花）are in full bloom now.
水仙花現在正盛開著。

▶動 Will you tell me when these plants bloom? In spring or summer? 你能告訴我這些植物什麼時候開花嗎？是在春天還是夏天？

blos·som [ˋblɑsəm]

Track 3286

名 花、花簇 動 開花、生長茂盛

▶名 The cherries are in full blossom in the park.
公園裡櫻花正盛開。

▶動 The flowers are blossoming in our garden.
我們花園裡的花都盛開了。

實用片語用語
in full blossom / bloom 盛開

blush [blʌʃ]

Track 3287

名 羞愧、慚愧 動 臉紅

▶名 The topic brought a blush to her cheeks.
這個話題讓她羞得兩頰通紅。

▶動 She blushed when she saw her crush（暗戀的人）.
她看到暗戀的人時臉就紅了。

boast [bost]

Track 3288

名 / 動 自誇

▶名 Just ignore his boasts. 別聽他自誇。

▶動 The man loves to boast about his achievements.
這個男人很愛自誇自己的成就。

實用片語用語
boast about... 吹噓（某事）

bond [bɑnd]

Track 3289

名 契約、束縛、抵押

▶The bond between us is hard to break.
我們之間的羈絆是難以打破的。

bounce [baʊns]

Track 3290

名 彈、跳 動 彈回

▶名 My little son can't catch the ball on its first bounce.
我的小兒子在球第一次反彈時接不住球。

▶動 All the kids are bouncing around.
孩子們都跳來跳去的。

實用片語用語
bounce back （很快地）復原
例如：She had been sick for two weeks but she bounced back really quickly.
她病了兩星期，但很快就康復了。

brace·let [ˋbreslɪt]

Track 3291

名 手鐲

▶This is the bracelet that my husband bought for me as a wedding anniversary gift.
這個手鐲是丈夫在我們結婚紀念日的時候買給我的禮物。

bras·siere/bra [brəˋzɪr]/[brɑ]

Track 3292

名 胸罩、內衣

▶I need to go shopping for a new bra. 我得去買新胸罩了。

breed [brid]

Track 3293

動 生育、繁殖 名 品種

▶動 The couple's job is breeding dogs. 這對夫妻的工作是繁殖狗。

▶名 What breed of dog do you think I'm most like?
你覺得我最像哪種狗？

文法字詞解析
breed 的動詞變化：breed, bred, bred

bride·groom/groom

Track 3294

[ˋbraɪd͵grum]/[grum]

名 新郎

▶Have you seen the bridegroom in the car today? What does he look like? 你今天在車上看見新郎了嗎？他長什麼樣子呢？

broil [brɔɪl]

Track 3295

動 烤、炙

▶I am afraid that we can't broil turkey over the fire tonight.
恐怕今晚我們不能在火上烤火雞吃了。

broke [brok]

Track 3296

形 一無所有的、破產的

▶I can't lend you any money. I'm broke myself.
我沒辦法借你錢，我自己都破產了。

bru·tal [ˋbrutl̩]

Track 3297

形 野蠻的、殘暴的

▶I guess it's time to face the brutal reality.
看來是面對殘酷現實的時候了。

實用片語用語
face the brutal reality / facts 面對殘酷的現實

bul·le·tin [ˋbʊlətɪn]

Track 3298

名 公告、告示

▶Will you tell me what is on the school bulletin board today?
你能告訴我今天學校的佈告欄上都寫了些什麼嗎？

實用片語用語
bulletin board 公告欄

Cc

cab·i·net [ˋkæbənɪt]

Track 3299

名 小櫥櫃、內閣

▶Would you please tell me how many cabinet members there are? 您能告訴我到底有多少內閣成員嗎？

cal·cu·late [ˋkælkjə͵let] Track 3300

動 計算

▶I calculated the time we need to get there.
我計算了一下我們要去那裡需花的時間。

> **文法字詞解析**
> 如果在calculate的前面加上意為「誤……」的字首「mis-」，則會變成表示「誤算、計算錯誤」的單字miscalculate。

cal·cu·la·tion [͵kælkjəˋleʃən] Track 3301

名 計算

▶Why didn't they announce the results at each stage of the calculation?
為什麼他們沒有公佈每個階段的計算結果呢？

cal·cu·la·tor [ˋkælkjə͵letɚ] Track 3302

名 計算機

▶I don't think it's proper for you to give him a calculator as a present.
我覺得你送他一個計算機作為禮物不合適。

cal·o·rie [ˋkælərɪ] Track 3303

名 卡、卡路里

▶She always checks the calories before eating anything.
她每次吃東西前都先看一下有多少卡路里。

cam·paign [kæmˋpen] Track 3304

名 戰役、活動 動 作戰、從事活動

▶名 The campaign for the election ended up successful.
那次競選活動結果很成功。

▶動 We decided to campaign for better working conditions.
我們決定積極爭取改善工作條件。

> **實用片語用語**
> campaign for 爭取……

can·di·date [ˋkændə͵det] Track 3305

名 候選人

▶I don't think that he is the best candidate for the job.
我認為他不是這份工作的最佳人選。

ca·pac·i·ty [kəˋpæsətɪ] Track 3306

名 容積、能力 同 size 容量

▶I believe that the theater has a seating capacity of more than 800.
我相信這個劇場可容納超過八百名觀眾。

> **實用片語用語**
> seat capacity 容納座位數

cape [kep] Track 3307

名 岬、海角

▶Have you been to the cape in Kenting?
你去過墾丁那個海岬嗎？

cap·i·tal·(ism) Track 3308

[ˋkæpətḷ]/[͵kæpətḷɪzəm]

名 資本（資本主義）、首都

▶Not everyone knows that Canberra（坎培拉）is the capital of Australia.
不是每個人都知道坎培拉是澳洲的首都。

cap·i·tal·ist [ˋkæpətḷɪst]　Track 3309

名 資本家

▶There is no such thing as a good capitalist.
所謂善良的資本家是不存在的。

ca·reer [kəˋrɪr]　Track 3310

名（終身的）職業、生涯

▶Her mother was an actress, so she is interested in a stage career too.
她媽媽曾經是個女演員，所以她對演藝事業也很感興趣。

實用片語用語
career counseling 職業諮詢
例　如：He didn't know what kind of job he wanted so he went to career counseling.
他不知道自己到底想要怎樣的工作，於是接受了職業諮詢。

car·go [ˋkɑrgo]　Track 3311

名 貨物、船貨

▶Could you tell me how long it will take for the cargoes to arrive?
你能告訴我貨物抵達要多久嗎？

car·ri·er [ˋkærɪɚ]　Track 3312

名 運送者

▶He works as a mail carrier.
他的工作是郵差。

carve [ˋkɑrv]　Track 3313

動 切、切成薄片

▶Would you please carve me another slice of meat?
請再幫我切一片肉好嗎？

文法字詞解析
carve 不只可以用在「切肉」、「切水果」等等美食方面，也可以在藝術方面用來表示「雕刻」，例如木雕就可以稱為 wood carving。

cat·a·logue/ cat·a·log [ˋkætəlɔg]　Track 3314

名 目錄 動 編輯目錄 同 list 目錄

▶名 Please send me your current catalogue as soon as possible.
請將你現有的目錄盡快寄給我。

▶動 Please ask someone to catalogue the new books as soon as possible.
請盡快請人把新書編成目錄吧。

cease [sis]　Track 3315

名 停息 動 終止、停止

▶名 I don't think that the temporary（暫時的）cease of war means permanent peace.
我認為暫時的停火並不意味著永久的和平。

▶動 The general ordered his troops to cease fire.
那位將軍命令了他的軍隊停火。

cel·e·bra·tion [ˌsɛləˋbreʃən]　Track 3316

名 慶祝、慶祝典禮

▶I suppose we shall be having some sort of celebration for the bride.
我想我們大概會為新娘慶賀一番吧。

實用片語用語
some sort of... 某種的……

ce·ment [sə`mɛnt]

Track 3317

名 水泥 動 用水泥砌合、強固

▶名 It is obvious that you should not walk on wet cement.
很顯然水泥沒乾的時候你不應該在上面行走。

▶動 The broken bowl was cemented with glue.
這個破碗是用膠水黏合起來的。

CD/com·pac disk

Track 3318

[`si`di]/[`kɑmpækt dɪsk]

名 光碟

▶Do you mind if I bring this CD home?
你介不介意我帶著這張 CD 回家？

cham·ber [`tʃembɚ]

Track 3319

名 房間、寢室 同 room 房間

▶The prisoners were kept in a narrow chamber.
囚犯們都被關在一個狹小的房間裡。

文法字詞解析
這個單字的念法要特別注意喔！ cham 這個音節跟 ham、am 等看似押韻，但實際上它是和 came、fame 押韻。注意看看後面的音標吧！

cham·pion·ship [`tʃæmpɪən,ʃɪp]

Track 3320

名 冠軍賽

▶It was Susan who won the spelling championship.
蘇珊在拼字比賽中得了第一名。

char·ac·ter·is·tic

Track 3321

[,kærɪktə`rɪstɪk]

名 特徵 形 有特色的

▶名 The curly hair is a distinguishing（有區別的）characteristic of this type of dog. 捲毛是這種狗與眾不同的一個特徵。

▶形 Indecision is characteristic of him. 優柔寡斷是他的特徵。

char·i·ty [`tʃærətɪ]

Track 3322

名 慈悲、慈善、寬容 同 generosity 寬宏大量

▶There are many people regularly giving money to charity.
有很多人經常為慈善事業捐款。

chem·is·try [`kɛmɪstrɪ]

Track 3323

名 化學

▶I prefer chemistry to physics; what about you?
我喜歡化學甚於物理，你呢？

實用片語用語
have chemistry ……之間很來電
兩人很「來電」的時候，不就像是發生了某種化學效應嗎？因此才會用「have chemistry」來描述兩人的關係。
例如：I hope my sister and your brother get together. They have great chemistry.
希望我姊跟你哥會在一起。他們很來電。

cher·ish [`tʃɛrɪʃ]

Track 3324

動 珍愛、珍惜

▶To save water is to cherish life. 節約用水就是珍惜生命。

chirp [tʃɝp]

Track 3325

名 蟲鳴鳥叫聲 動 蟲鳴鳥叫

▶名 She heard nothing but the chirps of insects.
除了蟲的鳴叫聲外，她什麼也沒聽見。

▶動 Do you hear the birds chirping in the trees?
你有聽到小鳥在樹上鳴叫嗎？

chore [tʃor] Track 3326

名 雜事、打雜

▶I don't think cooking and washing are chores.
我並不把洗衣做飯當作雜事。

cho·rus [ˋkorəs] Track 3327

名 合唱團、合唱

▶Let us take part in the church（教堂）chorus.
讓我們去參加教會的合唱團吧。

文法字詞解析
一首歌曲的「副歌」也叫作 chorus。畢竟副歌就是一首歌中出現最多次、大家也最容易記起來一起合唱的部分不是嗎？

ci·gar [sɪˋgɑr] Track 3328

名 雪茄

▶Would you like to tell me how much a cigar costs in Britain?
你能告訴我在英國一支雪茄多少錢嗎？

ci·ne·ma [ˋsɪnəmə] Track 3329

名 電影院、電影

▶How often do you go to the cinema with your family?
你跟家人多久去看一次電影？

cir·cu·lar [ˋsɝkjələ] Track 3330

形 圓形的

▶We took the circular route to get to the airport.
我們走環形道路去機場。

cir·cu·late [ˋsɝkjə͵let] Track 3331

動 傳佈、循環

▶Why not open a window to allow the air to circulate?
為什麼不打開窗子讓空氣流通呢？

cir·cu·la·tion [͵sɝkjəˋleʃən] Track 3332

名 通貨、循環、發行量

▶The book has had a big circulation since it was published.
此書一經問世，便大量發行。

實用片語用語
blood circulation 血液循環
例如：There are some foods that can actually improve your blood circulation.
有些食物真的對你的血液循環有幫助。

cir·cum·stance [ˋsɝkəm͵stæns] Track 3333

名 情況 同 condition 情況

▶It is obvious that it's not a matter of circumstance but of choice.
顯然那不是環境的問題，而是選擇的問題。

ci·vil·ian [səˋvɪljən] Track 3334

名 平民、一般人 形 平民的

▶名 The government is widely disliked by civilians.
這個政府現在深受平民厭惡。

▶形 He resigned his commission（軍職）to take up a civilian job. 他辭去軍職而從事了平民工作。

civ·i·li·za·tion [͵sɪvḷəˋzeʃən] Track 3335

名 文明、開化 同 culture 文化

▶I'm so glad to return from grandma's Internet-less house to civilization. 能從奶奶沒有網路的家回到文明世界真是太開心了。

文法字詞解析
字尾「-less」是「沒有、缺乏……」的意思，所以「Internet-less」就是「沒有網路的」。

clar·i·fy [ˋklærə͵faɪ]

Track 3336

動 澄清、變得明晰

▶I hope that what I say will clarify the situation.
我希望我說的話能澄清這一個情況。

clash [klæʃ]

Track 3337

名 衝突、猛撞 動 衝突、猛撞

▶名 The demonstration ended in a violent clash with the police.
遊行示威以與警察的激烈衝突而告終。

▶動 It's a pity that the two concerts clash; I wanted to go to both of them.
真可惜兩場音樂會時間上有衝突，我本來想兩場都去的。

萬用延伸句型
It's a pity that... 真可惜……。

clas·si·fi·ca·tion

Track 3338

[͵klæsəfəˋkeʃən]

名 分類

▶It's the job of a biologist to make classifications of animals.
把動物分類是生物學家的工作之一。

clas·si·fy [ˋklæsə͵faɪ]

Track 3339

動 分類

▶Would you classify her novels as literature or something else?
你認為她的小說屬於文學類，還是其他類？

cliff [klɪf]

Track 3340

名 峭壁、斷崖

▶It takes courage and strength to climb these cliffs.
攀登這些懸崖需要勇氣和力量。

實用片語用語
jump off a cliff 跳下懸崖
例如：This is so embarrassing that I want to jump off a cliff.
這實在太丟臉了，我簡直要跳崖自盡。

cli·max [ˋklaɪmæks]

Track 3341

名 頂點、高潮 動 達到頂點

▶名 It is clear that there are two climaxes in this novel.
顯然這部小說有兩個高潮。

▶動 The play climaxed in the third act.
那齣戲在第三幕達到高潮。

clum·sy [ˋklʌmzɪ]

Track 3342

形 笨拙的

▶She's a clumsy person who trips over herself a lot.
她是個笨拙的人，常會不小心絆倒。

coarse [kors]

Track 3343

形 粗糙的 同 rough 粗糙的

▶It doesn't matter if my clothes are made of coarse cloth.
我的衣服是用粗布製成的也沒什麼關係。

code [kod]

Track 3344

名 代號、編碼

▶I can't access the file on your computer because I've forgotten the code.
我無法取出你電腦上的檔案，因為我把密碼忘了。

實用片語用語
access code 權限密碼
例如：If you don't have the access code, you won't be able to open the door.
如果你沒有進入權限的密碼，那是打不開門的。

col·lapse [kə`læps]

Track 3345

動 崩潰、倒塌

▶There is fear of a US collapse.
有人擔心美國的經濟可能會崩潰。

com·bi·na·tion [͵kɑmbə`neʃən]

Track 3346

名 結合

▶We tried every conceivable（想得到的）combination but it still didn't work.
我們把所有能想到的各種組合都試了一遍，結果還是沒有用。

com·e·dy [`kɑmədɪ]

Track 3347

名 喜劇

▶This comedy is written by Shakespeare.
這部喜劇是莎士比亞所作。

com·ic [`kɑmɪk]

Track 3348

形 滑稽的、喜劇的 名 漫畫

▶形 What do you think about the comic characters in this play?
你覺得這部劇中的喜劇人物怎麼樣？

▶名 I love reading comic books after school.
放學後我喜歡看漫畫。

文法字詞解析

我們都知道 comic books 是漫畫書，不過其實要注意的是不是所有的漫畫都可以叫 comic books 喔。對美國人而言，日本出品的漫畫叫作 manga，較不會叫作 comic books。說到 comic books，他們會想到的是像 Marvel 等公司出品的那種漫畫，例如蝙蝠俠、蜘蛛人等等。

com·mand·er [kə`mændɚ]

Track 3349

名 指揮官

▶It's very foolish of the commander to expose his men to unnecessary（不必要的）risks.
這個指揮官讓士兵們冒不必要的危險真是太愚蠢了。

com·ment [`kɑmɛnt]

Track 3350

名 評語、評論 動 做註解、做評論

▶名 Stop making so many pointless comments.
不要下那麼多沒必要的評論。

▶動 Would you please comment on the conclusion?
請您對這一個結論發表一下意見好嗎？

com·merce [`kɑmɝs]

Track 3351

名 商業、貿易 同 trade 貿易

▶How can we maximize（最大化）the benefits of electronic commerce? 我們該如何使電子商務的利益最大化？

com·mit [kə`mɪt]

Track 3352

動 委任、承諾

▶He would not commit himself in any way. 他不願做出任何承諾。

實用片語用語

commit a crime 犯罪
例如：He isn't the kind who would commit a crime for money.
他不是會為了錢去犯罪的那種人。

com·mu·ni·ca·tion [kə͵mjunə`keʃən]

Track 3353

名 通信、溝通、交流

▶Don't you think that the satellite has become an important means of communication?
難道你不認為衛星已成為一個重要的通訊工具了嗎？

文法字詞解析

「means」在這裡不是 mean 的複數，而是「……的方法、工具」的意思，例如：a means of transport（交通工具）、a means of communication（通訊工具）

com·mu·ni·ty [kə`mjunətɪ] Track 3354

名 社區

▶Not everyone is willing to invest some time in community service. 不是每個人都願意在社區服務上花時間。

實用片語用語

community service 社區服務

com·pan·ion [kəm`pænjən] Track 3355

名 同伴

▶The dog is my intimate friend and good companion.
這隻狗是我的好朋友、好夥伴。

com·pe·ti·tion [ˌkɑmpə`tɪʃən] Track 3356

名 競爭、競爭者 同 rival 對手

▶The competition for jobs is fierce now.
現在求職的競爭十分激烈。

com·pet·i·tive [kəm`pɛtətɪv] Track 3357

形 競爭的

▶He is a very competitive person and never backs down from a challenge. 他非常愛競爭，遇到挑戰從不退縮。

文法字詞解析

competitive 的意思很多，可以指「競爭力強的」、「喜歡競爭的」、「擅長競爭的」等等。

com·pet·i·tor [kəm`pɛtətɚ] Track 3358

名 競爭者

▶Which competitor do you think will win?
你覺得哪個競爭者會贏？

com·pli·cate [`kɑmpləˌket] Track 3359

動 使複雜

▶In my opinion, there is no need to complicate the issue.
在我看來，沒有必要使問題複雜化。

com·pose [kəm`poz] Track 3360

動 組成、作曲

▶Do you know how to compose music on the computer?
你知道如何在電腦上作曲嗎？

實用片語用語

compose oneself 某人使自己冷靜下來
例如：She composed herself to focus on her assignments.
她讓自己冷靜下來，專注在她的作業上。

com·pos·er [kəm`pozɚ] Track 3361

名 作曲家、設計者

▶He is not only a composer but also a conductor, which made him very busy. 他不但是名作曲家而且還是位指揮家，雙重身份使他非常繁忙。

com·po·si·tion [ˌkɑmpə`zɪʃən] Track 3362

名 組合、作文、混合物

▶There are a lot of spelling mistakes in your composition.
你的作文中有很多拼字錯誤。

con·cen·trate [`kɑnsˌtret] Track 3363

動 集中

▶I'm afraid that I can't concentrate on my work when I'm tired.
當我累了的時候恐怕就無法集中精神來工作。

實用片語用語

concentrate on 專注於（某事）

con·cen·tra·tion [ˌkɑnsˋtreʃən] Track 3364

名 集中、專心

▶It's very hard for me to keep my concentration with such a loud noise.
吵鬧聲讓我很難保持精神集中。

實用片語用語
keep one's concentration 保持精神集中

con·cept [ˋkɑnsɛpt] Track 3365

名 概念

▶Not all people can understand such an abstract concept easily.
不是所有人都能輕易理解如此抽象的概念。

con·cern·ing [kənˋsɝnɪŋ] Track 3366

連 關於

▶Let us see all the official documents concerning the sale of this land.
讓我們看看買賣這塊土地的所有官方文件吧。

con·crete [ˋkɑnkrit] Track 3367

名 水泥、混凝土 形 具體的、混凝土的 反 abstract 抽象的

▶名 The house is made from concrete.
這房子是混凝土做的。

▶形 Would you like to let me know if you got any concrete proposals?
你能不能告訴我你是否有具體的建議呢？

實用片語用語
concrete evidence 具體的證據
例如：I won't believe it unless you provide concrete evidence.
除非你提供具體的證據，不然我不會相信的。

con·duc·tor [kənˋdʌktɚ] Track 3368

名 指揮、指導者

▶My dream when I was young was to be a bus conductor.
我小時候的夢想是當一名公車售票員。

con·fer·ence [ˋkɑnfərəns] Track 3369

名 招待會、會議 同 meeting 會議

▶There will be an international conference held in London next month.
有一個國際性的會議將於下個月在倫敦舉行。

con·fess [kənˋfɛs] Track 3370

動 承認、供認

▶I think it's time for me to confess the whole thing.
我想現在是坦白整件事情的時候了。

萬用延伸句型
confess to V-ing 承認（做了某事）
例如：She confessed to dying her dog green.
她承認自己把狗染成了綠色。

con·fi·dence [ˋkɑnfədəns] Track 3371

名 信心、信賴

▶Too much confidence can hurt you. Don't you think so?
過分的自信會傷害到你，你不這樣認為嗎？

con·fine [kənˋfaɪn] Track 3372

動 限制、侷限

▶I wish the speaker could confine himself to the subject.
我希望演說者不要離題。

con·fu·sion [kən`fjuʒən] Track 3373

名 迷惑、混亂

▶It is no wonder that there was confusion everywhere.
怪不得到處一片混亂。

con·grat·u·late [kən`grætʃəˏlet] Track 3374

動 恭喜

▶He congratulated himself on his narrow escape.
他慶祝了自己能死裡逃生。

實用片語用語
narrowly escape 千鈞一髮，死裡逃生

con·gress [`kɑŋgrəs] Track 3375

名 國會

▶Would you tell me why the President lost the support of the congress? 你能告訴我為什麼總統失去了國會的支持嗎？

con·junc·tion [kən`dʒʌŋkʃən] Track 3376

名 連接、關聯

▶The novel should be read in conjunction with the author's biography. 這本小說應該和作者傳記一起讀。

實用片語用語
be in conjunction with... 與……搭配

con·quer [ˏkɑŋkɚ] Track 3377

動 征服

▶I don't believe man will conquer the weather in the near future.
我不相信人類在不久的將來會征服天氣。

con·science [`kɑnʃəns] Track 3378

名 良心

▶It's surprising that he killed so many people without having a guilty conscience.
他殺了這麼多人還不會良心不安，真是令人驚訝。

萬用延伸句型
It is surprising that... ……真是令人驚訝

con·se·quence [`kɑnsəˏkwɛns] Track 3379

名 結果、影響

▶Think of the consequences before you do something.
做事情前要先想想後果。

con·se·quent [`kɑnsəˏkwɛnt] Track 3380

形 必然的、隨之引起的

▶I'm afraid the rise in price was consequent of the failure of the crops. 恐怕物價上漲是因為收成不好所引起的。

con·ser·va·tive [kən`sɝvətɪv] Track 3381

名 保守主義者 形 保守的、保守黨的

▶名 The conservatives are opposed to changes.
保守分子反對變革。

▶形 My parents are kind of conservative. 我父母有點保守。

實用片語用語
be opposed to... 反對（某事）
形容詞 opposed 後面一定要搭配介係詞 to。

con·sist [kən`sɪst] Track 3382

動 組成、構成

▶I don't think that all people know that matters consist of atoms.
我覺得不是所有人都知道各種物質是由原子組成的。

con·sis·tent [kən`sɪstənt] Track 3383

形 一致的、調和的

▶The last five years have seen a consistent improvement in the country's economy.
在最近的五年裡，這個國家的經濟狀況一直在好轉。

文法字詞解析
consistent 的相反詞是什麼呢？只要在前面加上表示「不、沒有」的字首「in-」即可組成 inconsistent（不一致的、不符合的）。

con·so·nant [`kɑnsənənt] Track 3384

名 子音 形 和諧的 反 vowel 母音

▶名 What do you think of my pronunciation of this consonant?
你覺得我這個子音的發音怎麼樣？

▶形 Her style was consonant with her personality.
她的衣著風格很符合她的性格。

con·sti·tute [`kɑnstə,tjut] Track 3385

動 構成、制定

▶A slight error in thought may constitute a life-long regret.
一念之差就可能變成終身的悔恨。

con·sti·tu·tion [,kɑnstə`tjuʃən] Track 3386

名 憲法、構造

▶I don't know anything about the constitution of the United Nations Organization.
我完全不清楚聯合國組織的章程。

con·struct [kən`strʌkt] Track 3387

動 建造、構築

▶It took them two years to construct the bridge.
他們用了兩年的時間建這座橋。

con·struc·tion [kən`strʌkʃən] Track 3388

名 建築、結構

▶There was a great outcry（強烈抗議）about the construction of the new airport.
民眾強烈抗議修建新的機場。

實用片語用語
under construction 施工中的
例如：We can't go by that road. It's under construction.
我們不能走那條路，那裡在施工。

con·struc·tive [kən`strʌktɪv] Track 3389

形 有建設性的

▶Don't say anything unless your criticism is constructive.
如果你的批評沒有建設性，就別說出來。

con·sult [kən`sʌlt] Track 3390

動 請教、諮詢 同 confer 協商

▶I don't think it's necessary for you to consult him first.
我覺得你沒必要先跟他商量。

con·sul·tant [kən`sʌltənt] Track 3391

名 諮詢者

▶How often do you see the consultant who is in charge of your head treatment?
你多久去看一次負責處理你頭部傷勢的醫師？

實用片語用語
be in charge of 負責（某事）

con·sume [kən`sum]

Track 3392

動 消耗、耗費 同 waste 耗費

▶The kids soon consumed all the food on the table.
孩子們一下子便把桌上的食物全部吃光了。

con·sum·er [kən`sumɚ]

Track 3393

名 消費者

▶We always ask consumers for their feedback.
我們總是會詢問消費者的回饋。

con·tain·er [kən`tenɚ]

Track 3394

名 容器

▶Would you please help me look for my soap container?
你能幫我找找我的肥皂盒嗎？

實用片語用語
plastic container 塑膠容器
例如：Some plastic containers can't be microwaved.
有些塑膠容器不能拿來微波。

con·tent [`kantɛnt]/[kən`tɛnt]

Track 3395

名 內容、滿足、目錄 形 滿足的、願意的

▶名 The contents of the book can be found on the fourth page.
書的目錄可以在第四頁找到。

▶形 He seemed to be more content with his former job than this one.
與這份工作相比，他似乎對自己以前的那份工作更滿意。

實用片語用語
be content with 對……感到滿足

con·tent·ment [kən`tɛntmənt]

Track 3396

名 滿足

▶The man sighed in contentment as he sipped his beer.
那名男子一邊啜飲啤酒一邊滿足地嘆息。

con·test [`kantɛst]/[kən`tɛst]

Track 3397

名 比賽 動 與……競爭、爭奪

▶名 There will be a composition contest in July; would you like to participate（參加）?
七月份將有一場作文比賽，你想不想參加呢？

▶動 There are three candidates contesting for the presidency（總統職位）.
有三個候選人在爭奪總統的位子。

con·text [`kantɛkst]

Track 3398

名 上下文、文章脈絡

▶You can use context to figure out what an unfamiliar word means. 你可以利用上下文來猜出一個陌生的單字是什麼意思。

實用片語用語
figure out 猜出、搞清楚

con·tin·u·al [kən`tɪnjuəl]

Track 3399

形 連續的

▶I've had enough of her continual chatter; what about you?
我已厭煩了她的喋喋不休，你呢？

con·tin·u·ous [kən`tɪnjuəs]

Track 3400

形 不斷的、連續的

▶It's hard to keep up with continuous changes in our lives.
生活中不斷的變化，讓人很難跟上。

con·trar·y [ˋkɑntrɛrɪ]

Track 3401

名 矛盾 形 反對的

▶名 I will go on with my work unless I get an order to the contrary.
我將繼續工作，除非有人叫我停止。

▶形 You should go with me unless your view is contrary to mine.
如果你的看法不是與我的相反，你就應該跟我去。

萬用延伸句型
On the contrary... 相反地……
例如：No, he doesn't hate you. On the contrary, I'm pretty sure he's in love with you.
他才沒有討厭你呢。相反地，我覺得他肯定喜歡你。

con·trast [ˋkɑn͵træst]/[kənˋtræst]

Track 3402

名 對比 動 對照

▶名 The black furnishings provide an interesting contrast to the white walls. Don't you think so?
黑色傢俱和白色牆壁形成很有趣的對比，你不覺得嗎？

▶動 His actions contrast sharply（銳利地）with his promises, don't they?
他的行動與諾言形成鮮明的對照，難道不是嗎？

con·trib·ute [kənˋtrɪbjʊt]

Track 3403

動 貢獻

▶It was generous of her to contribute such a large sum.
她很大方，捐助了這麼一大筆錢。

con·tri·bu·tion [͵kɑntrəˋbjuʃən]

Track 3404

名 貢獻、捐獻

▶There was no mention of her contribution here. Do you know why?
這裡沒有提到她的貢獻，你知道為什麼嗎？

con·ve·nience [kənˋvinjəns]

Track 3405

名 便利

▶Would you please deliver the goods at your earliest convenience?
請您方便的話盡早送貨好嗎？

實用片語用語
at your earliest convenience 方便的話就盡早

con·ven·tion [kənˋvɛnʃən]

Track 3406

名 會議、條約、傳統

▶It is very silly of them to be slaves to social conventions.
他們盲目地跟隨社會習俗是很愚蠢的。

實用片語用語
social convention 社會風俗

con·ven·tion·al [kənˋvɛnʃən!]

Track 3407

形 會議的、傳統的

▶I wish you weren't so conventional in the clothes you wear.
要是你的穿衣風格不要那麼保守就好了。

con·verse [kənˋvɝs]

Track 3408

動 談話

▶Would you give me half an hour to converse with you?
能跟您談談嗎？半小時就可以了。

con·vey [kənˋve]

Track 3409

動 傳達、運送

▶I found it very hard to convey my feelings in words.
我發現我很難用言語來表達我的感情。

萬用延伸句型
find it hard to... 覺得（要做到某事）很難

con·vince [kən`vɪns]

Track 3410

動 說服、信服

▶It's too hard for me to convince him to go with me.
說服他跟我一起去，對我來說很難。

co·op·er·ate [ko`ɑpə,ret]

Track 3411

名 協力、合作

▶You need to cooperate or you'll never get anything done.
你們不合作點的話，什麼也做不完的。

co·op·er·a·tion [ko,ɑpə`reʃən]

Track 3412

名 合作、協力

▶Thank you very much for your cooperation.
非常謝謝您的合作。

co·op·er·a·tive [ko`ɑpə,retɪv]

Track 3413

名 合作社 形 合作的

▶名 Not every town in that county has an agricultural cooperative.
在那個縣不是每個城鎮都有一個農業合作社。

▶形 Not both sides are willing to take cooperative attitudes on this issue.
在這件事情上，並不是雙方都願意採取合作的態度。

文法字詞解析

cooperative 指的是「合作的」，但帶有一點被動的含意在。也就是說，如果一個人很 cooperative，代表他願意乖乖配合、不會做出什麼反抗的行為。然而，他不見得會主動為目標做出任何貢獻、提供任何幫助，他只是「被動地配合」而已。因此，若你老闆叫你要「cooperative」，他的意思是要你不要亂來，配合公司計畫，而不是叫你「主動為公司某個案子貢獻力量」。

cope [kop]

Track 3414

動 處理、對付

▶I don't know how to cope with the problem of poor vision.
我不知道如何解決視力不好的問題。

cop·per [`kɑpɚ]

Track 3415

名 銅 形 銅製的

▶名 China's copper imports increased by 80% last year.
去年中國銅進口激增了百分之八十。

▶形 The copper kettles have higher quality.
銅製的水壺品質較高。

cord [kɔrd]

Track 3416

名 電線、繩

▶Why don't you tie up the package with a heavy cord?
為什麼不用粗繩將行李捆牢呢？

實用片語用語

power cord 電線
例如：This power cord isn't quite long enough.
這電線不夠長啊。

cork [kɔrk]

Track 3417

名 軟木塞 動 用軟木塞栓緊

▶名 The cork flew off with a pop.
瓶塞砰的一聲飛了出去。

▶動 Would you please cork up the bottle? It might leak.
請你用軟木塞塞住瓶子好嗎？它可能會漏水。

cor·re·spond [,kɔrə`spɑnd]

Track 3418

動 符合、相當

▶The goods that arrived don't correspond with my order.
這些送達的貨物與我的訂單不符。

cos·tume [ˋkɑstjum] Track 3419

名 服裝、服飾、劇裝

▶Why would you wear a costume to work?
你為什麼要穿戲服去上班？

cot·tage [ˋkɑtɪdʒ] Track 3420

名 小屋、別墅

▶As far as I know, there are five people living in that cottage.
據我所知，那間小屋裡住著五個人。

萬用延伸句型
As far as I know... 據我所知……

coun·cil [ˋkaʊnsḷ] Track 3421

名 議會、會議

▶What do you think about discussing the problem in the council?
你覺得在會議上討論這個問題如何？

count·er [ˋkaʊntɚ] Track 3422

名 櫃檯、計算機 動 反對、反抗

▶名 There was an enormous cat crouching（蹲坐）on the counter.
櫃檯上蹲坐著一隻碩大的貓。

▶動 If no one counters the plan, we'll carry it out.
沒人反對這個計畫的話，我們就會執行了。

cou·ra·geous [kəˋredʒəs] Track 3423

形 勇敢的

▶It was courageous of him to stand up to his boss.
他敢反對他的上司，真是勇敢。

實用片語用語
stand up to... 主動反抗（某人）

cour·te·ous [ˋkɝtjəs] Track 3424

形 有禮貌的

▶I don't think you need to be so courteous to her.
我認為你沒有必要對她那麼客氣。

cour·te·sy [ˋkɝtəsɪ] Track 3425

名 禮貌

▶Lack of courtesy is considered as a disease of modern society.
缺乏禮貌被認為是當今社會的一大弊病。

crack [kræk] Track 3426

名 裂縫、瑕疵 動 使爆裂、使破裂

▶名 This house is an old building. It is no wonder that there are so many cracks in the wall.
這間房子是一間很老的建築物了，難怪這面牆上有那麼多裂縫。

▶動 Her voice cracked with grief.
她悲傷得語不成聲。

實用片語用語
crack open 裂開
例如：The ceiling cracked open after the earthquake.
地震過後，天花板都裂開了。

craft [kræft] Track 3427

名 手工藝

▶The hotel lobby has a display of local crafts.
飯店的大廳裡有當地的工藝品展覽。

cram [kræm]

Track 3428

動 把……塞進、狼吞虎嚥地吃東西

▶I'm afraid that I need more time to cram for the test.
為了考試，恐怕我需要更多時間來臨時抱佛腳。

實用片語用語
cram school 補習班
例如：I have to go pick up my daughter from cram school.
我得去補習班接我女兒。

cre·a·tion [krɪ`eʃən]

Track 3429

名 創造、創世

▶I think imagination is the source of creation; what do you think of that? 我認為想像是創作之源，你覺得呢？

cre·a·tiv·i·ty [ˏkrie`tɪvətɪ]

Track 3430

名 創造力

▶As an artist, she has a lot of creativity.
身為藝術家，她很有創意。

crip·ple [`krɪpḷ]

Track 3431

名 瘸子、殘疾人

▶It's disgraceful（可恥的）of you to make fun of a cripple.
你取笑瘸子是很可恥的。

文法字詞解析
和這個單字相關的形容詞是 crippled。這個單字可以指有殘疾的人，但也可以描述某人因為某種原因有劣勢、無法正常發揮。舉例來說，若有個摔角選手戴著眼罩去參加比賽，根本看不到，這個情況下就可以用 crippled 來描述他。

crit·ic [`krɪtɪk]

Track 3432

名 批評家、評論家

▶It is no wonder that the newspaper does not regard him as a good critic. 難怪報紙上說他不是個好的評論家。

crit·i·cal [`krɪtɪkḷ]

Track 3433

形 評論的

▶My boss is always critical of me. 我的老闆總愛挑我的毛病。

crit·i·cism [`krɪtəˏsɪzəm]

Track 3434

名 評論、批評的論文

▶Would you like to read his literary criticism?
你想讀他的文藝評論嗎？

crit·i·cize [`krɪtəˏsaɪz]

Track 3435

動 批評、批判

▶It's hard to criticize one's own work, don't you think so?
評價自己的工作並非容易的事，你不覺得嗎？

cru·el·ty [`kruəltɪ]

Track 3436

名 冷酷、殘忍

▶I don't believe she will willingly（甘願地）put up with his cruelty to her. 我相信她不會甘願忍受他的虐待的。

實用片語用語
put up with 忍受……

crush [krʌʃ]

Track 3437

名 毀壞、壓榨 動 壓碎、壓壞

▶名 There was such a crush of spectators that no one could move. 觀衆多到都擠在一起了，誰也無法動彈。

▶動 Don't crush this box; there are flowers inside.
別壓壞這個盒子，裡面有花。

cube [kjub]
Track 3438

名 立方體、正六面體

▶Would you please get me an ice cube from the fridge?
請幫我從冰箱裡拿塊冰塊來好嗎？

cu·cum·ber [ˋkjukʌmbɚ]
Track 3439

名 小黃瓜、黃瓜

▶The rabbit likes eating cucumbers.
那隻兔子很喜歡吃小黃瓜。

實用片語用語
as cool as a cucumber （如同小黃瓜一樣）冷靜
例如：I was really nervous during the meeting but he was as cool as a cucumber.
開會時我相當緊張，但他卻很冷靜。

cue [kju]
Track 3440

名 暗示

▶The actor missed his cue and came onto the stage late.
那個演員錯過了向他發出的暗示，所以太慢上場了。

cun·ning [ˋkʌnɪŋ]
Track 3441

形 精明的、狡猾的

▶I think your new secretary is too cunning to trust.
我覺得你的新秘書太狡猾了，不能相信。

cu·ri·os·i·ty [ˏkjʊrɪˋɑsətɪ]
Track 3442

名 好奇心

▶Will you indulge（遷就）my curiosity and tell me how much it costs? 你能不能滿足我的好奇心，告訴我那個值多少錢？

curl [kɝl]
Track 3443

名 捲髮、捲曲 動 使捲曲

▶名 I prefer to have my hair in curls.
我比較喜歡保持捲頭髮。

▶動 I like to curl up with a story book.
我喜歡蜷曲而臥地看故事書。

實用片語用語
curling iron 電捲棒
例如：She used the curling iron on her hair before leaving for school.
她去上學前用電棒捲了一下頭髮。

curse [kɝs]
Track 3444

動 詛咒、罵

▶He cursed when he stepped on his own foot.
他踩到自己的腳時大罵了一句。

curve [kɝv]
Track 3445

名 曲線 動 使彎曲

▶名 The population curve of this city has slowed down.
這個城市的人口曲線已趨平緩。

▶動 The seacoast curved beautifully.
這海岸的海岸線彎曲得十分美麗。

cush·ion [ˋkʊʃən]
Track 3446

名 墊子 動 緩和……衝擊

▶名 I don't think the cushion matches the sofa（沙發）.
我覺得這個墊子跟這沙發不配。

▶動 I don't think that the training program helps to cushion the effect of unemployment（失業）.
我認為這項訓練計畫無益於緩衝失業造成的影響。

實用片語用語
cushion the fall 減緩墜落的衝擊
例如：He fell from the second-floor window but was surprisingly fine because the flower bed cushioned the fall.
他從二樓窗戶摔下來，但居然完全沒事，因為花圃減緩了墜落的衝擊。

damn [dæm]
Track 3447

動 指責、輕蔑

▶This play is awful. It is no wonder that it is damned by the reviewers（評論家）.
這部戲糟透了。難怪它被評論家們批評得一無是處。

damp [dæmp]
Track 3448

形 潮濕的 動 使潮濕 同 moist 潮濕的

▶形 I don't like the damp weather in this city; what about you?
我不喜歡這個城市潮濕的天氣，你呢？

▶動 How about damping your cloth before cleaning the windows?
擦窗戶前先把布弄濕怎麼樣？

dead·line [ˋdɛd͵laɪn]
Track 3449

名 限期

▶It is impossible（不可能的）for us to meet the deadline because of the terrible weather.
由於天氣惡劣，因此我們無法如期完成任務。

實用片語用語
meet the deadline 在期限內把事情完成

de·clare [dɪˋklɛr]
Track 3450

動 宣告、公告

▶There is no point in declaring a war on such a weak country.
對一個弱小國家宣戰毫無意義。

萬用延伸句型
There is no point in + V-ing 做……是沒有意義的

dec·o·ra·tion [͵dɛkəˋreʃən]
Track 3451

名 裝飾

▶Will you tell me when you can finish the decoration of the living room? 你能告訴我你們什麼時候才能把客廳裝飾好嗎？

de·crease [dɪˋkris]
Track 3452

動 減少、減小 名 減少、減小 反 increase 增加

▶動 I am afraid the population here will decrease year by year.
我擔心這裡的人口會逐年減少。

▶名 I am afraid that there will be some decrease in exports.
恐怕出口貨物會有所減少。

實用片語用語
year by year 逐年地

de·feat [dɪˋfit]
Track 3453

名 挫敗、擊敗 動 擊敗、戰勝

▶名 He was depressed because of the defeat last week.
因為上禮拜被擊敗的事，他非常憂鬱。

▶動 I wish our basketball team could defeat their team next season. 但願我們的籃球隊能在下個賽季中打敗他們那隊。

de·fend [dɪˋfɛnd]
Track 3454

動 保衛、防禦

▶He tried to defend his friend from the bullies.
他試著保護他被霸凌的朋友。

實用片語用語
defend sb. from sb. / sth. 保護某人不受……的侵害

de·fense [dɪ`fɛns]

Track 3455

名 防禦

▶In a basketball game, attack is the best defense.
籃球比賽中，進攻就是最好的防禦。

萬用延伸句型

In my defense... 不過，為我自己辯護一下……

例如：I thought that stranger was my friend. In my defense, they really looked alike.
我以為那個陌生人是我朋友。但要為我自己辯護一下，他們真的長得很像。

de·fen·si·ble [dɪ`fɛnsəbḷ]

Track 3456

形 可辯護的、可防禦的

▶I don't think the theory he put forward is defensible.
我覺得他提出的理論站不住腳。

de·fen·sive [dɪ`fɛnsɪv]

Track 3457

形 防禦的、保衛的

▶He is always very defensive when others criticize his work.
其他人批評他的作品時，他總是防禦心很重。

def·i·nite [`dɛfənɪt]

Track 3458

形 確定的 同 precise 確切的

▶It is obvious that they are unwilling（不願意的）to give us a definite answer.
顯然他們不願意給我們一個明確的答覆。

del·i·cate [`dɛləkət]

Track 3459

形 精細的、精巧的

▶Do you mind buying some delicate instruments for these scientists?
你介意為這些科學家們買些精密的儀器嗎？

實用片語用語

delicate skin 細緻的肌膚

例如：She has delicate skin so she has to be careful when choosing makeup products.
她的肌膚太細緻了，所以在挑化妝品時要很小心。

de·light [dɪ`laɪt]

Track 3460

名 欣喜 動 使高興

▶名 The play was excellent and the audience roared in delight.
這部戲太棒了，觀眾們都興高采烈地歡呼起來了。

▶動 The circus show delights everyone present.
這馬戲團的表演讓每個在場的人都看得很開心。

de·light·ful [dɪ`laɪtfəl]

Track 3461

形 令人欣喜的

▶It was a delightful party. What a pity you couldn't attend!
這是一次愉快的聚會，你沒來真可惜啊。

de·mand [dɪ`mænd]

Track 3462

名 要求 動 要求

▶名 All of them caved in to the boss's demand.
他們都屈從了老闆的要求。

▶動 She demanded a room all to herself last night.
昨晚她要求自己一個人住一個房間。

實用片語用語

in great demand 非常受歡迎、賣得很好

例如：Products like these are in great demand right now.
像這樣的產品現在賣得很好。

dem·on·strate [`dɛmən͵stret]

Track 3463

動 展現、表明

▶This election demonstrated democracy in action.
這次選舉是以實際行動體現了民主。

dem·on·stra·tion

Track 3464

[ˌdɛmənˋstreʃən]

名 證明、示範

▶Will you give us a demonstration? We don't know how to use the machine.
你願意為我們做個示範嗎？我們都不知道如何使用這台機器。

dense [dɛns]

Track 3465

形 密集的、稠密的

▶There was dense fog, so the traffic slowed down.
因為有濃霧，大家都減速行駛。

文法字詞解析
當某人的腦袋已經「密度太高」、「很稠密」，可想而知若還要往裡面裝東西可是很困難的，因此當你覺得有人怎麼講都聽若罔聞、而且明明是簡單的小事卻無法理解時，也可以說他很 dense。

de·part [dɪˋpɑrt]

Track 3466

動 離開、走開 同 leave 離開

▶He departed early in the morning so that he wouldn't miss the early train.
為了不錯過早班的火車，他一大早就離開了。

de·par·ture [dɪˋpɑrtʃɚ]

Track 3467

名 離去、出發

▶I don't think he knows the exact departure time of the flight.
我認為他不知道飛機起飛的準確時間。

de·pend·a·ble [dɪˋpɛndəbl̩]

Track 3468

形 可靠的

▶Don't you think he is a dependable and hard-working（努力工作的）worker?
難道你不認為他是一個值得信賴並且工作刻苦的人嗎？

de·pend·ent [dɪˋpɛndənt]

Track 3469

名 從屬者 形 從屬的、依賴的

▶名 Please list all your dependents here on the form.
請把你所有的受撫養人列在這個表格上。

▶形 I am afraid that I can't be dependent on my old parents any more. 恐怕我再也不能依靠我那年邁的父母了。

文法字詞解析
dependent 的相反詞即 independent，也就是「獨立的」、「自主的」。

實用片語用語
be dependent on ab. 依賴某人

de·press [dɪˋprɛs]

Track 3470

動 壓下、降低

▶Rainy weather always depresses me.
雨天總使我心情抑鬱。

de·pres·sion [dɪˋprɛʃən]

Track 3471

名 下陷、降低

▶The government must take actions at once, or we will have another Great Depression.
政府必須立刻採取措施，否則我們將遭遇另一個大蕭條。

de·serve [dɪˋzɝv]

Track 3472

動 值得、應得

▶Honors do not always go to those who deserve them.
榮譽並非永遠為應得的人所得。

des·per·ate [ˋdɛspərɪt]

Track 3473

形 絕望的

▶Don't you believe a desperate man will stop at nothing to get what he wants? 難道你不相信一個亡命之徒為了達到自己的目的什麼事都做得出來嗎？

文法字詞解析

其實這個字非常微妙，描述的是「幾乎已經絕望但還沒有完全絕望（還是有一點渺小的希望）」的狀態。也就是說，如果有個人真的已經完全絕望了，每天行屍走肉，我們不能形容他是 desperate。如果有個人狀況悽慘但他至少還有做點動作想改善這個情形（例如快要掉下懸崖了但還是拚命抓住繩子），則可以用 desperate 來描述。

de·spite [dɪˋspaɪt]

Track 3474

介 不管、不顧

▶The plane took off despite the fog.
即使起霧，這架飛機還是起飛了。

de·struc·tion [dɪˋstrʌkʃən]

Track 3475

名 破壞、損壞

▶His desire for money will lead him to his destruction one day; I wish he could understand that soon. 對錢的慾望有一天終將導致他的毀滅，但願他能很快明白這一點。

de·tec·tive [dɪˋtɛktɪv]

Track 3476

名 偵探、探員 形 偵探的

▶名 I don't think the detective can reason out how the murderer has escaped.
我認為這名偵探無法弄明白兇手是如何逃脫的。

▶形 Are there any detective agencies here?
這裡有偵探事務所嗎？

實用片語用語

detective work 偵探工作

例如：We should do some detective work and look for clues before we come up with a conclusion.
我們應該先做點偵探該做的事，找找線索，才能下結論。

de·ter·mi·na·tion

[dɪ͵tɝməˋneʃən]

Track 3477

名 決心

▶I don't think he has the determination to overcome this difficulty.
我覺得他沒有克服這個困難的決心。

de·vice [dɪˋvaɪs]

Track 3478

名 裝置、設計

▶A computer is a device for processing information; the more you use it, the more you know.
電腦是用來處理資訊的。你用得越勤，瞭解的就越多。

de·vise [dɪˋvaɪz]

Track 3479

動 設計、想出

▶He is devising a new plan to get us out of here.
他正在設計一個能幫助我們逃出去的計畫。

實用片語用語

devise a plan 擬定計畫

de·vote [dɪˋvot]

Track 3480

動 貢獻、奉獻

▶He has decided to devote himself to becoming a doctor.
他決定投身於醫生事業。

di·a·per [ˋdaɪəpɚ]

Track 3481

名 尿布

▶Will you change the baby's diaper? I am a bit busy now.
你能幫孩子換一片尿布嗎？我現在有點忙。

dif·fer [ˋdɪfɚ]

Track 3482

動 不同、相異

▶You are not mature enough; it is no wonder that I differ with your opinion on this matter.
你還不夠成熟，怪不得我們在這個問題上意見不一。

萬用延伸句型
I beg to differ. 請容我提出反對意見。
例如：You think that we should go with Plan A? I beg to differ.
你覺得我們應該進行 A 計畫嗎？請容我提出反對意見。

di·gest [daɪˋdʒɛst]/[ˋdaɪdʒɛst]

Track 3483

動 瞭解、消化 名 摘要、分類

▶動 It often takes them quite a long time to digest new ideas.
他們吸收新點子往往需要相當長的一段時間。

▶名 It took her ten minutes to read the digest of the week's news. 她花了十分鐘的時間來讀一週新聞摘要。

di·ges·tion [dəˋdʒɛstʃən]

Track 3484

名 領會、領悟、消化

▶This kind of tea acts as an aid to digestion.
這種茶可幫助消化。

dig·i·tal [ˋdɪdʒɪtl̩]

Track 3485

形 數字的、數位的

▶What do you think of this digital camera? It's the latest model this year.
你覺得這款數位相機如何？它可是今年的最新款哦。

實用片語用語
digital watch 數位手錶
例如：I got this digital watch for my brother.
我替我弟買了這支數位手錶。

dig·ni·ty [ˋdɪgnətɪ]

Track 3486

名 威嚴、尊嚴

▶In my opinion, only a truly（真正地）free person has dignity.
在我看來只有真正自由的人才具有尊嚴。

di·li·gence [ˋdɪlədʒəns]

Track 3487

名 勤勉、勤奮

▶It is quite clear that genius is nothing but labor and diligence.
很顯然，天才也不過是勤奮而已。

萬用延伸句型
It is quite clear that... 很明顯地……

di·plo·ma [dɪˋplomə]

Track 3488

名 文憑、畢業證書

▶I wish he could work hard enough to get his history diploma this year.
我希望他能夠勤奮，才能在今年獲得歷史學學位證書。

dip·lo·mat [ˋdɪpləmæt]

Track 3489

名 外交官

▶I am afraid that I am not tactful（機智的）enough to be a good diplomat.
恐怕我沒有那麼機智，無法成為一名出色的外交官。

dis·ad·van·tage [͵dɪsədˋvæntɪdʒ]

Track 3490

名 缺點、不利 反 advantage 優點

▶You will be put at a disadvantage unless you change your plan immediately（立即）.
除非你馬上改變你的計畫，否則你將處於不利的地位。

實用片語用語
at a disadvantage 處於劣勢

dis·as·ter [dɪz`æstɚ] Track 3491

名 天災、災害

▶We can't help asking ourselves what to do after the earthquake disaster.
我們禁不住要捫心自問震災害過後我們該做些什麼。

dis·ci·pline [`dɪsəplɪn] Track 3492

名 紀律、訓練 動 懲戒

▶名 The children lack discipline, and they are not old enough to understand the rules of the school.
孩子們很散漫，同時年齡也不夠大，還不懂學校的規定。

▶動 I've disciplined myself to do two hours of exercise each day. 我堅持每天運動兩個小時。

dis·con·nect [ˏdɪskə`nɛkt] Track 3493

動 斷絕、打斷

▶We forgot to pay the bill; it is no wonder that the electricity company has disconnected our electricity.
我們忘了付電費了，難怪會被電力公司斷電。

實用片語用語

disconnect from the Internet 網路連接中斷
例如：Are you sure you want to turn off the device? You'll be disconnected from the Internet.
你真的要關掉這個機器嗎？網路會斷掉喔。

dis·cour·age [dɪs`kɝɪdʒ] Track 3494

動 阻止、妨礙

▶I don't think this will discourage him from continuing to have a try. 我不認為這會讓他洩氣而不敢再繼續嘗試。

dis·cour·age·ment [dɪs`kɝɪdʒmənt] Track 3495

名 失望、氣餒

▶It is obvious that the failure was a great discouragement to him.很明顯地，那次失敗很令他失望。

dis·guise [dɪs`gaɪz] Track 3496

名 掩飾 動 喬裝、假扮

▶名 It was a surprise that no one recognized her when she was in disguise.
當她喬裝打扮的時候居然沒人認出她，這真令人吃驚。

▶動 I disguised myself as a tree.
我把自己裝扮成一棵樹。

dis·gust [dɪs`gʌst] Track 3497

名 厭惡 動 使厭惡

▶名 She turned away in disgust.
她厭惡地轉過頭去。

▶動 Some of his ideas really disgust me.
他有些點子讓我很反感。

實用片語用語

in disgust 感到噁心地

dis·miss [dɪs`mɪs] Track 3498

動 摒除、解散

▶Class is dismissed. Time to go home!
可以下課解散了，該回家啦！

dis·or·der [dɪsˋɔrdɚ]

Track 3499

名 無秩序 動 使混亂

▶名 It was she who discovered the room in disorder.
第一個發現房間裡亂糟糟的是她。

▶動 Anxiety may disorder the stomach.
憂慮可能會引起胃部不適。

dis·pute [dɪˋspjut]

Track 3500

名 爭論 動 爭論

▶名 His honesty is beyond dispute.
他的誠實是無可爭議的。

▶動 They disputed over the decision.
他們就這個決策吵了起來。

實用片語用語
beyond dispute 無可爭議的

dis·tinct [dɪˋstɪŋkt]

Track 3501

形 個別的、獨特的

▶Don't you think these two ideas are quite distinct from each other? 難道你不覺得這兩種觀念截然不同嗎？

dis·tin·guish [dɪˋstɪŋgwɪʃ]

Track 3502

動 辨別、分辨

▶It is hard for me to distinguish him from his brother.
我很難區分他和他的哥哥。

實用片語用語
distinguish A from B 區分 A 和 B

dis·tin·guished [dɪˋstɪŋgwɪʃt]

Track 3503

形 卓越的

▶It won't be long before you find that he is distinguished in many different areas. 很快你就會發現他在眾多領域中都很出眾。

dis·trib·ute [dɪˋstrɪbjʊt]

Track 3504

動 分配、分發

▶He distributed the flyers（傳單）to the people coming out of the subway station.
他在地下鐵門口發傳單給走出來的人群。

dis·tri·bu·tion [ˏdɪstrəˋbjuʃən]

Track 3505

名 分配、配給

▶It is obvious that they don't agree with his opinion about the distribution of income and wealth.
顯然他們不同意他關於收入和財富分配問題的看法。

dis·trict [ˋdɪstrɪkt]

Track 3506

名 區域 同 region 區域

▶The longer you live here with your family, the more familiar you will get with the district.
你和你的家人在這住得越長，你們就會越熟悉這個區。

dis·turb [dɪˋstɝb]

Track 3507

動 使騷動、使不安 同 annoy 惹惱、打擾

▶It is quite clear that he didn't want to disturb his father at night.
顯然他不想在晚上打擾他的父親。

文法字詞解析
想好好做事卻一直被親友傳的訊息打擾嗎？這時 disturb 這個單字就派上用場了。找找看，你的手機或許有一個「請勿打擾」模式，開啟它後各式各樣的麻煩訊息就不會一直跳出來吵你了。這個東西在英文就叫作「Don't disturb mode」。

di·vine [də`vaɪn]

Track 3508

形 神的、神聖的

▶Jesus is believed by Christians（基督教徒）to have been divine.
基督教徒們都相信耶穌是神。

di·vorce [də`vors]

Track 3509

名 離婚、解除婚約 動 使離婚、離婚

▶名 It took their daughter several years to understand the true cause of their divorce.
他們的女兒花了好幾年的時間才明白他們離婚的真正原因。

▶動 It took my aunt a long time to decide to divorce her husband.
嬸嬸花了很長時間才決定跟她的丈夫離婚。

實用片語用語
the true cause of sth. 導致某事發生的真正原因

dom·i·nant [`dɑmənənt]

Track 3510

形 支配的

▶They built the castle in the dominant position above the town.
他們把這座城堡建在市鎮中的一個高處。

dom·i·nate [`dɑmə͵net]

Track 3511

動 支配、統治

▶A great man can dominate others by force of character.
偉人能以人格的力量支配他人。

文法字詞解析
除了真正支配、統治外，在比賽中佔有極大優勢、把對方壓著打，也可以說是「dominate」。

dor·mi·to·ry/dorm

Track 3512

[`dɔrmə͵torɪ]/[dɔrm]

名 宿舍

▶It takes me half an hour to get to my dormitory from the library.
從圖書館到我的宿舍要花半個小時。

down·load [`daʊn͵lod]

Track 3513

動 下載、往下傳送

▶From the Internet, you can download not only e-books（電子書）but also movies.
你不但能從網際網路上下載電子書，而且還能從那上面下載電影。

doze [doz]

Track 3514

名 打瞌睡 動 打瞌睡

▶名 I has a quick doze on the train, so that I could continue working after the journey.
我在火車上小睡了一會，這樣旅程結束後我就能繼續工作。

▶動 Don't doze off in the middle of the class, or the teacher will get angry with you.
不要在課堂上打瞌睡，否則老師會對你生氣的。

實用片語用語
doze off 打瞌睡
另外，「drop off」、「nod off」也都有打盹的意思。

draft [dræft]

Track 3515

名 草稿 動 撰寫、草擬 同 sketch 草稿、草擬

▶名 There is no point in going over the draft when it hasn't been finished yet.
草稿還未完成時就拿來研讀，沒多大意義。

▶動 There is no point in drafting the contract now, because they haven't agreed to all the terms yet.
現在草擬合約毫無意義，因為他們還未同意全部的條件。

實用片語用語
first draft 第一份草稿
例如：Many writers believe that a good first draft is what makes a good novel.
許多作家相信，第一份草稿要擬得好，小說才能成功。

dread [drɛd]

Track 3516

名 非常害怕 動 敬畏、恐怖 同 fear 恐怖

▶名 It is quite clear that most people have a dread of snakes.
很顯然，大部分人都怕蛇。

▶動 We all dread to think what will happen next.
我們都不敢想下一步會發生什麼事情。

drift [drɪft]

Track 3517

名 漂流物 動 漂移

▶名 A drift of logs just went past us on the river.
河上剛剛有一大堆的木頭漂了過去。

▶動 No one noticed a tiny fishing boat drifting slowly（緩慢地）along.沒有注意到有一隻小小的漁船正在緩緩地漂去。

drill [drɪl]

Track 3518

名 鑽、錐、操練 動 鑽孔

▶名 We will hold a fire drill this morning.
今天上午我們將進行一次消防演習。

▶動 Would you like me to ask some workmen（工人）to drill in the wall?
要不要我叫些工人在牆上鑽孔呢？

實用片語用語
practice drill 演習
例如：This is just a practice drill. There's nothing to worry about.
只不過是演習而已，沒什麼好擔心的。

du·ra·ble [ˋdjʊrəbl̩]

Track 3519

形 耐穿的、耐磨的

▶You'd better buy some canvas（帆布）bags which are durable.
你最好買一些耐用的帆布袋子。

dust·y [ˋdʌstɪ]

Track 3520

形 覆著灰塵的

▶It's windy and dusty here in spring; I wish I could move to another city next year.
這裡的春天有風沙，但願我明年能搬到另外一個城市去住。

DVD/dig·it·al vid·e·o disk/dig·it·al ver·sa·tile disk

Track 3521

[ˋdɪdʒɪtl̩ ˋvɪdɪ͵o dɪsk]/[ˋdɪdʒɪtl̩ ˋvɝsətɪl dɪsk]

名 影音光碟機

▶Can you recommend the best DVD player in the store?
你能推薦一下這家店裡最好的 DVD 機嗎？

實用片語用語
除了 DVD 之外，現在還有新一代的光碟格式，可以儲存更多容量和更高品質的檔案，就是藍光光碟「blue-ray disk」，也可以簡稱為 BD。

dye [daɪ] Track 3522

名 染料 動 染、著色

▶名 What dye did you use to get such lovely golden-red hair?
你到底是用什麼染料弄得這一頭金紅色的亮麗頭髮？

▶動 He dyed his hair blue again.
他又把頭髮染成藍色了。

實用片語用語
hair dye 染髮劑
例 如：The hair dye she used wasn't very effective.
她用的染髮劑不怎麼有效。

dy·nam·ic [ˋdaɪnəˏmaɪt] Track 3523

形 動能的、動力的 同 energetic 有力的

▶It is the economic recession（衰退）that caused the dynamic market disappeared.
由於經濟衰退導致了活躍市場的消失。

實用片語用語
economic recession 經濟蕭條

dyn·as·ty [ˋdaɪnəstɪ] Track 3524

名 王朝、朝代

▶No one knows that why this dynasty disappeared suddenly a thousand years ago.
沒人知道這個王朝為何會在一千年前突然消失。

ear·nest [ˋɝnɪst] Track 3525

名 認真 形 認真的

▶名 I don't think he was apologizing in earnest.
我覺得他並不是真誠地道歉。

▶形 I don't think he was earnest when he said he would come.
我認為他說他會來並不是認真的。

ear·phone [ˋɪrˏfon] Track 3526

名 耳機

▶Why not put on your earphones and try the equipment?
為什麼不戴上耳機試一下設備呢？

ec·o·nom·ic [ˏikəˋnɑmɪk] Track 3527

形 經濟上的

▶The economic situation in our country is pretty sad.
我國的經濟狀況還蠻慘的。

文法字詞解析
sad 不只有難過的意思，還有「糟透了、難以接受」的意思，使用時要注意。

ec·o·nom·i·cal [ˏikəˋnɑmɪkl] Track 3528

形 節儉的

▶This car is economical to run because it doesn't use much fuel.開這輛車蠻省錢的，因為它耗油不多。

文法字詞解析
economic 和 economical 雖然長得很像、都是形容詞、又都和經濟有關，但意思不完全一樣喔！ economic 指的是「和經濟學有關的、和經濟有關的」，而 economical 則有「經濟實惠的」、「節省的」的意思。

ec·o·nom·ics [ˏikəˋnɑmɪks] Track 3529

名 經濟學

▶I majored in economics in college; what about you?
我大學主修經濟學，你呢？

A B C D E F G H I J K L M N O P Q R S T U V W X Y Z

e·con·o·mist [ɪˋkɑnəmɪst]

Track 3530

名 經濟學家

▶What do you think of inviting the famous economist to give us a speech? 你覺得我們邀請那位著名的經濟學家來為我們做一次演講怎麼樣？

e·con·o·my [ɪˋkɑnəmɪ]

Track 3531

名 經濟

▶I'm afraid that the economy has yet to improve.
恐怕經濟狀況還沒改善，你覺得呢？

efficiency [əˋfɪʃənsɪ]

Track 3532

名 效率

▶Their working efficiency is quite high.
他們的工作效率很高。

實用片語用語

efficiency level 效率等級

例如：The efficiency level of these products are quite high.
這些產品的效率等級很高。

e·las·tic [ɪˋlæstɪk]

Track 3533

名 橡皮筋 形 有彈性的

▶名 I used the elastic to shoot a mosquito.
我用橡皮筋射了蚊子。

▶形 The elastic suit is really stretchy.
這件有彈性的衣服超能伸展的。

e·lec·tri·cian [ˌɪlɛkˋtrɪʃən]

Track 3534

名 電機工程師

▶Would you please send an electrician? There is something wrong with my electric meter.
請給我派一位電工好嗎？我的電錶出毛病了。

e·lec·tron·ics [ɪˌlɛktˋtrɑnɪks]

Track 3535

名 電機工程學

▶I work for a small electronics firm; what about you?
我在一家小型的電子公司工作，你呢？

實用片語用語

electronics department 電子產品部門

例如：You might be able to find the kind of TV you want in the electronics department.
您有可能在電子產品部門找到您想要的那種電視。

el·e·gant [ˋɛləgənt]

Track 3536

形 優雅的

▶It is obvious that his elegant clothes contrasted with his rough speech. 顯然他優雅的服飾與粗俗的語言形成鮮明的對比。

el·e·men·ta·ry [ˌɛləˋmɛntərɪ]

Track 3537

形 基本的

▶Not everyone knows that the elementary school is affiliated（隸屬於）to that university.
不是每個人都知道這所小學附屬於那所大學。

e·lim·i·nate [ɪˋlɪməˌnet]

Track 3538

動 消除

▶These two contestants（參賽者）were eliminated from the show last week.
這兩個參賽者上週被從節目上淘汰了。

else·where [ˋɛls,hwɛr]

Track 3539

副 在別處

▶Do you know if there is intelligent life elsewhere in the universe?
你知道宇宙中是否有其他地方有智慧生命嗎？

e-mail/email [ˋimel]

Track 3540

名 電子郵件 動 發電子郵件

▶名 I got an email yesterday that wasn't meant for me.
我昨天收到寄錯的電子郵件。

▶動 I think it's better for you to email us instead of sending a letter.
我認為相對於寄信來說，你們最好是寄電子郵件給我們。

實用片語用語
be meant for sb. 指定（給某人）、本來就是（某人的）

em·bar·rass [ɪmˋbærəs]

Track 3541

動 使困窘

▶It is obvious that Arthur was embarrassed by the question.
顯然亞瑟被這個問題弄得有些窘迫。

em·bar·rass·ment [ɪmˋbærəsmənt]

Track 3542

名 困窘

▶The embarrassment on his face was obvious when he realized that he had a hole in his pants.
他發現褲子上有破洞時，表情顯然超窘的。

實用片語用語
second-hand embarrassment 因為別人丟臉而自己也覺得丟臉
你或許學過「second-hand」是「二手的」的意思，而這「二手丟臉」指的就是因為別人做了丟臉的事，你在旁邊看著都不知不覺地跟著感到羞恥起來的一種心情。

em·bas·sy [ˋɛmbəsɪ]

Track 3543

名 大使館

▶The embassy has become an obvious target for terrorist（恐怖分子）attacks.
大使館已經成為恐怖分子攻擊的明顯目標。

e·merge [ɪˋmɝdʒ]

Track 3544

動 浮現

▶It's still hard for me to tell who will emerge victorious（勝利的）. 我覺得到底鹿死誰手還很難說。

e·mo·tion·al [ɪˋmoʃən!]

Track 3545

形 情感的

▶Her mother is sick; it is no wonder that she had a major emotional breakdown.
她的母親生病了，怪不得她情緒上崩潰得很厲害。

文法字詞解析
emotional 不只可以表示「情感上的」，也可以表示「情感豐富的」。例如當你的朋友看電影哭了四次、一直到出了電影院還停不下來，就可以勸他不要那麼emotional。

em·pha·sis [ˋɛmfəsɪs]

Track 3546

名 重點、強調

▶There is an acknowledged（承認）emphasis on equality for all. 重視人人平等得到社會的普遍認可。

em·pire [ˋɛmpaɪr]

Track 3547

名 帝國

▶The Roman Empire existed for several centuries.
羅馬帝國存在了幾百年。

en·close [ɪnˋkloz]
Track 3548

動 包圍

▶Would you please enclose an address proof dated within the latest three months?
請附上最近三個月內的地址證明書好嗎？

en·coun·ter [ɪnˋkaʊntɚ]
Track 3549

名 遭遇 動 遭遇

▶名 It was a strange encounter that brought us together.
是一次奇妙的邂逅使我們在一起的。

▶動 I'm afraid that you will encounter such problems in the future.
恐怕你將來會遇到這類問題。

實用片語用語
a chance encounter 一次偶遇
例如：A chance encounter was how she met her husband.
她是在一起偶遇中認識了她的丈夫。

en·dan·ger [ɪnˋdendʒɚ]
Track 3550

動 使陷入危險

▶You will endanger your health if you work too hard.
你太賣力工作的話會危害自己的健康。

en·dure [ɪnˋdjʊr]
Track 3551

動 忍受

▶They are deeply in love with each other and endured a lot together.
他們深愛彼此，一起經過許多考驗。

en·force [ɪnˋfors]
Track 3552

動 實施、強迫

▶It is necessary for soldiers to enforce discipline in the army.
士兵在部隊裡執行紀律是必要的。

萬用延伸句型
It is necessary for... 對……來說是必要的。

en·force·ment [ɪnˋforsmənt]
Track 3553

名 施行

▶I don't think that weak law enforcement is the main problem.
我認為執法不力不是問題的關鍵。

en·gi·neer·ing [͵ɛndʒəˋnɪrɪŋ]
Track 3554

名 工程學

▶He gave up engineering and took to medicine.
他放棄了工程學，開始從事醫學。

en·large [ɪnˋlɑrdʒ]
Track 3555

動 擴大

▶You can enlarge the picture by clicking here.
按這裡就可以把圖片放大了。

en·large·ment [ɪnˋlɑrdʒmənt]
Track 3556

名 擴張

▶What do you think of sending my mother an enlargement of our baby's photo?
你覺得給我母親寄張我們小寶寶的放大照片怎麼樣？

萬用延伸句型
What do you think of...? 你覺得……怎樣？

e·nor·mous [ɪˋnɔrməs] Track 3557

形 巨大的 同 vast 巨大的

▶Have you seen the new hotel? It's enormous!
你有看到那家新飯店嗎？超大的耶！

en·ter·tain [ˏɛntɚˋten] Track 3558

動 招待、娛樂

▶He is performing magic tricks to entertain the guests.
他正在表演魔術以娛樂客人們。

en·ter·tain·ment [ˏɛntɚˋtenmənt] Track 3559

名 款待、娛樂

▶Would you like to play the piano for our entertainment?
你願意為我們彈鋼琴助興嗎？

實用片語用語

entertainment business 娛樂業
例如：Being in the entertainment business can be very tiring.
從事娛樂行業可能會相當地疲勞。

en·thu·si·asm [ɪnˋθjuzɪˏæzəm] Track 3560

名 熱衷、熱情 同 zeal 熱心

▶The proposal was greeted with great enthusiasm.
這個建議得到了熱情的回應。

en·vi·ous [ˋɛnvɪəs] Track 3561

形 羨慕的、妒忌的 同 jealous 妒忌的

▶She is envious of Mary's slim figure.
她嫉妒瑪麗的苗條身材。

e·qual·i·ty [ɪˋkwɑlətɪ] Track 3562

名 平等

▶I believe in equality of opportunity. 我相信機會均等。

e·quip [ɪˋkwɪp] Track 3563

動 裝備

▶You need to equip yourself with a sharp pencil and an eraser for the exam.
你必須準備一枝尖銳的鉛筆和一塊橡皮擦去參加考試。

實用片語用語

equip sb. with.... 為（某人）裝上（裝備）、具備……的能力。

e·quip·ment [ɪˋkwɪpmənt] Track 3564

名 裝備、設備

▶The government has an interest in importing scientific equipment. 政府對引進科學設備很感興趣。

e·ra [ˋɪrə] Track 3565

名 時代

▶He was a great emperor. It is no wonder that his death marked the end of an era.
他是個偉大的皇帝。難怪他的死標誌著一個時代的結束。

er·rand [ˋɛrənd] Track 3566

名 任務

▶Can you run an errand for me later in the afternoon?
你待會下午幫我跑個腿好嗎？

es·ca·la·tor [ˋɛskə͵letɚ] Track 3567

名 手扶梯

▶I don't want to walk anymore; let's take the escalator.
我不想再走路了，我們搭手扶梯吧。

實用片語用語
take the escalator 搭電扶梯

es·say [ˋɛse] Track 3568

名 短文、隨筆

▶Would you like to help me write an essay in English?
你能幫我用英文寫一篇論文嗎？

es·tab·lish [əˋstæblɪʃ] Track 3569

動 建立 同 found 建立

▶How do we establish a good credit policy? That's a problem.
如何才能建立好的信貸政策？這是個難題。

es·tab·lish·ment [əˋstæblɪʃmənt] Track 3570

名 組織、建立

▶It took us six years to finish the establishment of that school.
我們花了六年的時間才完成了那所學校的興建。

es·sen·tial [ɪˋsɛnʃəl] Track 3571

名 基本要素 形 本質的、必要的、基本的 同 basic 基本的

▶名 The course only deals with the essentials of management.
這門課程講述的只是管理的基本要點。

▶形 The most essential thing you need to know about this course is that we won't have any exams.
這堂課你最需要知道的重點就是不會有考試。

es·ti·mate [ˋɛstə͵met] Track 3572

名 評估 動 評估

▶名 His estimate of the situation is not so optimistic.
他對形勢的估計不那麼樂觀。

▶動 He is highly estimated among his colleagues.
他在同事之間獲得很高的評價。

e·val·u·ate [ɪˋvælju͵et] Track 3573

動 估計、評價

▶Would you let me know how you evaluate success?
您能否告訴我您是如何評價成功的嗎？

e·val·u·a·tion [ɪ͵væljuˋeʃən] Track 3574

名 評價

▶Would you like to do a quick evaluation for me?
你能幫我迅速地估個價嗎？

e·ve [iv] Track 3575

名 前夕

▶How about holding a party on Christmas（耶誕節）Eve?
在耶誕節前夕舉行一個派對怎麼樣？

實用片語用語
New Year's Eve 新年前夕、除夕
例如：My family celebrated with a big dinner on New Year's Eve.
新年前夕，我們一家人吃大餐慶祝。

e·ven·tu·al [ɪ`vɛntʃuəl]

Track 3576

形 最後的 同 final 最後的

▶It was his foolish behavior that led to his eventual failure.
正是他的愚蠢行為導致了他最後的失敗。

ev·i·dence [`ɛvədəns]

Track 3577

名 證據 動 證明

▶名 There wasn't enough evidence to prove his guilt.
沒有充分的證據能證明他有罪。

▶動 I don't think he has enough to evidence his innocence.
我認為他並不足以證明自己的無辜。

ev·i·dent [`ɛvədənt]

Track 3578

形 明顯的

▶This truth seems to be self-evident, don't you think so?
這個真理似乎是不言而喻的，你不這樣認為嗎？

萬用延伸句型

It is self-evident that… ……是不言而喻的。
例如：It is self-evident that parents affect their children's behavior.
家長對孩子的行為有所影響是不言而喻的。

ex·ag·ger·ate [ɪg`zædʒə͵ret]

Track 3579

動 誇大

▶If you always exaggerate, people will no longer believe you.
一旦你老是誇大事情，人們便不會相信你了。

實用片語用語

no longer... 再也不……

ex·am·i·nee [ɪg͵zæmə`ni]

Track 3580

名 應試者

▶Ten of the examinees failed in the examination.
這次考試中有十名應考者不及格。

ex·am·in·er [ɪg`zæmɪnɚ]

Track 3581

名 主考官、審查員

▶It is my first time as an examiner.
這是我第一次擔任主考官。

ex·cep·tion [ɪk`sɛpʃən]

Track 3582

名 反對、例外

▶There is always an exception to any rule.
任何規律總有例外。

ex·haust [ɪg`zɔst]

Track 3583

名 排氣管 動 耗盡

▶名 They have taken measures to prevent exhaust pollution.
他們已經採取措施防止廢氣污染。

▶動 I really exhausted myself running marathons over the weekend.
我週末跑馬拉松整個耗盡力氣了。

實用片語用語

take measures to... 採取措施

ex·hib·it [ɪg`zɪbɪt]

Track 3584

名 展示品、展覽 動 展示

▶名 There's a painting exhibit at the art gallery this week.
這星期美術館有個畫展。

▶動 Why don't you exhibit your paintings? They are wonderful!
你為什麼不展出你的畫呢？它們太棒了！

ex·pand [ɪk`spænd]

Track 3585

動 擴大、延長

▶Would you like to expand your business in China?
您想將業務擴展到中國市場嗎？

ex·pan·sion [ɪk`spænʃən]

Track 3586

名 擴張

▶It's time for the company to consolidate（整頓）after several years of rapid expansion.
公司經過幾年的迅速發展之後，該整頓一下了。

ex·per·i·men·tal [ɪk͵spɛrə`mɛntl̩]

Track 3587

形 實驗性的

▶The medicine is still in the experimental stage.
這種藥還在實驗階段。

實用片語用語

experimental design 實驗性的設計
例如：We're hoping that customers will like this experimental design.
我們希望顧客會喜歡這實驗性的設計。

ex·pla·na·tion [͵ɛksplə`neʃən]

Track 3588

名 說明、解釋

▶For all your explanation, I understand no better than before.
儘管你做了詳細解釋，我還是不懂。

ex·plore [ɪk`splor]

Track 3589

動 探查、探險

▶Would you explore the market possibility for us?
您能為我們探究一下市場的前景嗎？

ex·plo·sion [ɪk`sploʒən]

Track 3590

名 爆炸

▶More than 40 people were wounded in the explosion.
超過四十人在爆炸事件中受傷。

ex·plo·sive [ɪk`splosɪv]

Track 3591

名 炸藥 形 爆炸的、(性情)暴躁的

▶名 Dynamite is a powerful explosive.
炸藥是一種強有力的爆炸物。

▶形 His explosive personality makes people either hate him or fear him.
他暴躁的個性令人不是討厭他就是怕他。

文法字詞解析

當作名詞時，explosive 經常以複數形式 explosives 出現，統稱「炸藥」。

ex·pose [ɪk`spoz]

Track 3592

動 暴露、揭發

▶You really shouldn't expose certain body parts in public.
在公眾場合不要暴露出某些身體部位比較好吧。

ex·po·sure [ɪk`spoʒɚ]

Track 3593

名 顯露

▶Exposure to strong sunlight（陽光）for long periods of time can be harmful.
長時間受到烈日曝曬會造成傷害的。

ex·tend [ɪkˋstɛnd]

Track 3594

動 延長

▶Can you please extend your visit for a few days?
你們訪問的時間能不能延長幾天？

實用片語用語
extend the deadline 將截止日期延後
例如：Could you please extend the deadline for two days?
可不可以拜託您將截止日期延後兩天？

ex·tent [ɪkˋstɛnt]

Track 3595

名 範圍

▶I was surprised at the extent of his knowledge.
我對他的知識淵博感到驚奇。

Ff

fa·cial [ˋfeʃəl]

Track 3596

形 面部的、表面的

▶I can't really see his facial expression from here.
我從這裡看不清楚他的臉部表情。

文法字詞解析
facial是形容詞，但隨著美容風潮的興起，也可以當作名詞直接稱呼「面部保養」（即 facial treatment 的簡單說法）。
例如：I'm going to get a facial this weekend.
我這週末要去做臉。

fa·cil·i·ty [fəˋsɪlətɪ]

Track 3597

名 容易、靈巧

▶She has great facility in learning languages.
她很有學習語言的才能。

faith·ful [ˋfeθfəl]

Track 3598

形 忠實的、耿直的、可靠的 同 loyal 忠實的

▶Don't you think husbands and wives should be faithful to each other?
難道你不覺得夫妻之間要忠於彼此嗎？

fame [fem]

Track 3599

名 名聲、聲譽

▶He gained fame from posting videos of himself online.
他因為在網路上發佈自己的影片而出了名。

fan·tas·tic [fænˋtæstɪk]

Track 3600

形 想像中的、奇異古怪的

▶He often has lots of fantastic ideas.
他常常異想天開。

文法字詞解析
fantastic 在口語中也可以表示「很棒的」、「極好的」，和 great、wonderful、excellent 同義。

fan·ta·sy [ˋfæntəsɪ]

Track 3601

名 空想、異想

▶That's not a fantasy novel. It's sci-fi.
那本不是奇幻小說啦，是科幻才對。

fare·well [ˋfɛrˋwɛl]

Track 3602

名 告別、歡送會

▶Let's hold a farewell party for her, shall we?
我們為她舉辦一場歡送會，可以嗎？

fa·tal [ˋfetl̩]

Track 3603

形 致命的、決定性的 同 mortal 致命的

▶Don't you think even a very small mistake would be fatal to our plan? 難道你不覺得即使是一個很小的錯誤，對我們的計畫都將是致命的嗎？

實用片語用語

fatal flaw 致命的缺點

例如：He would have been a perfect boyfriend if not for one fatal flaw: he's an alien.
要不是他有個致命的缺點，他肯定會是個完美的男友。他是外星人。

fa·vor·a·ble [ˋfevərəbl̩]

Track 3604

形 有利的、討人喜歡的

▶Your company's price is not the most favorable.
你們公司的價格不是最優惠的。

feast [fist]

Track 3605

名 宴會、節日 動 宴請、使高興

▶名 Why don't we invite him to the feast?
我們為何不邀請他來參加宴會呢？

▶動 You'll have all the time in the world to feast your eyes on the beautiful scenery.
你會有很多時間可以享受這裡的美景。

fer·ry [ˋfɛrɪ]

Track 3606

名 渡口、渡船 動 以船運輸

▶名 They took a ferry to the island. 他們搭乘渡船到島上去。

▶動 Do you ferry people across the river every day?
你每天都會用渡船送人們過這條河嗎？

實用片語用語

take a ferry 搭乘渡船

fer·tile [ˋfɝtl̩]

Track 3607

形 肥沃的、豐富的

▶It is hard for the farmers to get a harvest on these less fertile fields. 農民們很難在這些貧瘠的土地上獲得豐收。

fetch [fɛtʃ]

Track 3608

動 取得、接來

▶My dad asked me to fetch his coat.
爸爸叫我去幫他把外套拿過來。

fic·tion [ˋfɪkʃən]

Track 3609

名 小說、虛構

▶I am fond of reading all kinds of fiction; what about you?
我很喜歡讀各種小說，你呢？

fierce [fɪrs]

Track 3610

形 猛烈的、粗暴的、兇猛的 同 violent 猛烈的

▶The lion is really fierce when hungry.
這獅子餓的時候都很兇暴。

實用片語用語

fierce opposition 激烈的反對

例如：His suggestion that we have sushi for lunch was met with fierce opposition. Everyone wanted pizza.
他建議我們午餐吃壽司，結果遭到激烈的反對。大家都想吃披薩。

fi·nance [faɪˋnæns]

Track 3611

名 財務 動 融資

▶名 Do you mind if I ask you a question about finance?
您介意我向您請教一個有關財務方面的問題嗎？

▶動 Can you tell me who financed this organization?
你可以告訴我是誰在為這個組織提供資金嗎？

fi·nan·cial [faɪˋnænʃəl]

Track 3612

形 金融的、財政的

▶What do you think of the financial crisis? Did it affect your country?
你如何看待這次的金融危機呢？它影響到你們的國家了嗎？

fire·crack·er [ˋfaɪr͵krækɚ]

Track 3613

名 鞭炮

▶Jack ran away immediately（立即）as soon as the firecracker was lit up. 鞭炮一被點燃，傑克就立刻跑開了。

文法字詞解析
firecrackers 通常是在地上點燃的那種鞭炮，而煙火則通常說 fireworks。兩者都常以複數出現，可能是因為像鞭炮、煙火這類東西通常都是大量大量地放，很少會有人去數有幾個。

fire·place [ˋfaɪr͵ples]

Track 3614

名 壁爐、火爐

▶We won't move the portrait hung above the fireplace unless we move into a new house.
除非搬新家，否則我們不會移動掛在壁爐上方的那幅肖像。

flat·ter [ˋflætɚ]

Track 3615

動 諂媚、奉承

▶It is quite obvious that he is flattering you.
顯然他是在奉承你。

flee [fli]

Track 3616

動 逃走、逃避

▶The robber fled the scene really quickly.
這個強盜很快速地從現場逃掉了。

文法字詞解析
flee 的動詞變化：flee, fled, fled

flex·i·ble [ˋflɛksəbl̩]

Track 3617

形 有彈性的、易曲的

▶What's your schedule tomorrow afternoon? I'm pretty flexible.
你明天下午的行程如何？我的時間很有彈性的。

flu·ent [ˋfluənt]

Track 3618

形 流暢的、流利的

▶Tom can speak fluent English.
湯姆能講一口流利的英語。

flunk [flʌŋk]

Track 3619

名 失敗、不及格 動 失敗、放棄 同 fail 失敗

▶名 His flunk in the exam made his parents so mad.
他考試不及格的事讓他父母很生氣。

▶動 Did he flunk in the final exam again this year?
他今年期末考試又不及格了嗎？

flush [flʌʃ]

Track 3620

名 紅光、繁茂 動 水淹、使興奮、用水沖洗

▶名 Susan told us the exciting news with a flush on her face.
蘇珊滿面紅光地跟我們說這個令人興奮的消息。

▶動 Did you forget to flush the toilet again?
你又忘記沖馬桶了喔？

實用片語用語
flush the toilet 沖馬桶

foam [fom]

Track 3621

名 泡沫 動 起泡沫

▶名 Why is the toilet full of foam? 馬桶裡怎麼一堆泡沫？

▶動 The sick dog is foaming at the mouth.
那隻病犬口吐白沫。

for·bid [fɚ`bɪd]

Track 3622

動 禁止、禁止入內

▶She forbids me to call her late at night.
她禁止我深夜給她打電話。

fore·cast [for`kæst]

Track 3623

動 預測、預報

▶No one is able to forecast how long the war will last.
沒有人能預測出這場戰爭會持續多久。

實用片語用語

weather forecast 天氣預報
例句：Sometimes the weather forecast can be wrong too.
有時候天氣預報也是有可能出錯。

for·ma·tion [fɔr`meʃən]

Track 3624

名 形成、成立

▶What do you think of the formation of the new government?
你怎麼看待新政府的組成呢？

for·mu·la [`fɔrmjələ]

Track 3625

名 公式、法則

▶It is difficult for me to remember so many formulas in math.
我很難記住數學中的衆多公式。

fort [fort]

Track 3626

名 堡壘、炮台

▶I don't think the enemy can occupy this fort within a week.
我認為敵軍一週內佔領不了這個要塞。

for·tu·nate [`fɔrtʃənɪt]

Track 3627

形 幸運的、僥倖的 同 lucky 幸運的

▶My sister is fortunate enough to win the first prize in the speech contest. 我妹妹在演講比賽中很幸運地獲得了一等獎。

文法字詞解析

fortunate 的相反詞則是加上表示「不、沒有」的字首「un-」，變成 unfortunate（不幸的）。

fos·sil [`fɑsl̩]

Track 3628

名 化石、舊事物 形 陳腐的

▶名 I wish scientists could find more dinosaur fossils so that we could know more about dinosaurs.
我希望科學家們能找到更多的恐龍化石，以便我們瞭解更多關於恐龍的事情。

▶形 I wanted to find a fossil leaf on the mountain, but in the end I find nothing.
我本來想在山上找到一塊葉子化石，可是最後我什麼也沒找到。

foun·da·tion [faʊn`deʃən]

Track 3629

名 基礎、根基 同 base 基礎

▶Will you tell me how you laid the foundation for your success?
你能告訴我你是如何為你的成功打下基礎的嗎？

文法字詞解析

化妝的時候，在臉上打下「基礎」用的粉底也可以稱為 foundation。

found·er [ˋfaʊndɚ]
Track 3630

名 創立者、捐出基金者

▶Why don't they build a statue in memory of the great founder?
為什麼他們不為這位偉大的創立者建一座雕像呢？

fra·grance [ˋfregrəns]
Track 3631

名 芬香、芬芳

▶Beauty without virtue is a rose without fragrance.
無德之美猶如沒有香味的玫瑰，徒有其表。

fra·grant [ˋfregrənt]
Track 3632

形 芳香的、愉快的

▶The air in the park is warm and fragrant in spring.
春天的時候，公園裡的空氣既溫暖又芬芳。

frame [frem]
Track 3633

名 骨架、體制 動 構築、框架

▶名 He is a tall man with a skinny frame.
他是個高且骨架窄的男子。

▶動 Will you frame the picture for me? It was painted by my daughter studying abroad.
請你為這幅畫加個框好嗎？它是我在國外留學的女兒畫的。

實用片語用語

picture frame 畫框
例如：The picture itself wasn't worth much, but the picture frame was expensive.
這幅畫本身並不值多少，倒是畫框蠻貴的。

free·way [ˋfri͵we]
Track 3634

名 高速公路

▶I didn't know what to do when my car broke down on the freeway yesterday.
昨天我的車在高速公路上拋錨的時候，我都不知道怎麼辦才好。

fre·quen·cy [ˋfrikwənsɪ]
Track 3635

名 時常發生、頻率

▶Don't you think accidents have been happening with increasing frequency these years?
難道你不覺得近幾年來事故的發生越來越頻繁了嗎？

fresh·man [ˋfrɛʃmən]
Track 3636

名 新生、大一生

▶I am afraid I have to live in the dormitory in my freshman year at college.
恐怕我大學一年級得住宿舍了。

frost [frɔst]
Track 3637

名 霜、冷淡 動 結霜

▶名 It was the frost that damaged all the crops in the fields and plants by the road.
是這次的霜凍壞了田地裡的所有穀物和路邊的植物。

▶動 The cold frosted all the windows in the morning.
清晨，低溫使得所有的窗子都結了霜。

萬用延伸句型

It was ... that... 是……（造成……）
此句型被稱做分裂句，可以用來強調主詞、受詞、地點、時間等。

A B C D E F G H I J K L M N O P Q R S T U V W X Y Z

frown [fraʊn]

Track 3638

名 不悅之色 動 皺眉、表示不滿

▶名 He looked at her with a frown, and shook his head.
他皺著眉頭望著她，搖搖頭。

▶動 She is always frowning for some reason.
她不知道為什麼總是皺著眉頭。

frus·tra·tion [ˌfrʌsˋtreʃən]

Track 3639

名 挫折、失敗

▶It is hard for the young man to understand the old man who has met so many frustrations in his life.
這個年輕人很難理解這位曾在生活中歷經無數挫折的老人。

fu·el [ˋfjuəl]

Track 3640

名 燃料 動 燃料補給

▶名 Let's find out what sort of fuel these new machines need.
我們一起來找出這些新機器需要哪種燃料吧。

▶動 I want to fuel my car later. 我待會想幫我的車加油。

實用片語用語

add fuel to the fire 火上加油

例如：They already hate each other's guts. Don't add fuel to the fire.

他們本來就已經很討厭對方了，別在那邊火上加油。

ful·fill [fʊlˋfɪl]

Track 3641

動 實踐、實現、履行 同 finish 完成

▶Once you promise someone, you must fulfill your promise by all means.
一旦你許諾他人了，你就必須盡一切辦法履行你的諾言。

ful·fill·ment [fʊlˋfɪlmənt]

Track 3642

名 實現、符合條件

▶Don't you think work can give you a sense of fulfillment?
你難道不覺得工作能給人一種成就感嗎？

func·tion·al [ˋfʌŋkʃənḷ]

Track 3643

形 作用的、機能的

▶Is the machine fully functional?
這個機器有完全地在運作嗎？

fun·da·men·tal [ˌfʌndəˋmɛntḷ]

Track 3644

名 基礎、原則 形 基礎的、根本的

▶名 They know nothing about these fundamentals.
他們一點都不瞭解這些基本原理。

▶形 Fresh air is fundamental to good health.
新鮮空氣對健康是不可缺少的。

實用片語用語

be fundamental to... 對……來說是不可或缺的

fu·ner·al [ˋfjunərəl]

Track 3645

名 葬禮、告別式

▶It is said that there were hardly any dry eyes at the funeral.
據說在那場葬禮上很少有人不落淚的。

fu·ri·ous [ˋfjʊrɪəs]

Track 3646

形 狂怒的、狂鬧的 同 angry 發怒的

▶His wife was furious with him.
他妻子對他大發雷霆。

實用片語用語

be furious with sb. 對某人感到非常憤怒

fur·nish [ˋfɝnɪʃ] Track 3647

動 供給、裝備

▶Why don't you furnish your own house according to your own taste? 為何不按自己的愛好來佈置自己的房子呢？

fur·ther·more [ˋfɝðɚ͵mor] Track 3648

副 再者、而且

▶I don't think I will go to the cinema with him; furthermore, I have no time to do so.
我想我不會跟他去看電影的，而且我也沒時間去。

gal·ler·y [ˋgælərɪ] Track 3649

名 畫廊、美術館

▶I hope you enjoyed the pictures in the gallery.
我希望你喜歡美術館裡的畫。

gang·ster [ˋgæŋstɚ] Track 3650

名 歹徒、匪徒

▶There are quite a few people interested in movies about American police and gangsters.
有不少人都對看美國警匪片很感興趣。

gaze [gez] Track 3651

名 注視、凝視 動 注視、凝視

▶名 His gaze made me feel uneasy so I turned away.
他的目光讓我很不自在，所以我便轉頭了。

▶動 She gazed lovingly at her cat.
她充滿愛意地凝視著她的貓。

gear [gɪr] Track 3652

名 齒輪、裝具 動 開動、使適應

▶名 Most cars have four forward gears.
大多數汽車有四個前進檔。

▶動 Education should be geared to the children's needs and abilities. 教育應該適合孩子的需要與能力。

gene [dʒin] Track 3653

名 基因、遺傳因子

▶She eats a lot but never gets fat. It must be the genes.
她吃得很多，但都不會胖。大概是基因的關係吧。

gen·er·a·tion [͵dʒɛnəˋreʃən] Track 3654

名 世代

▶There are bound to be generation gaps no matter how hard people try to understand each other.
無論大家如何試著瞭解彼此，世代代溝還是免不了的。

文法字詞解析

與 furnish 相關的一個形容詞是 furnished（有家具的）。這可是相當重要的一個單字，尤其在租房子之前一定要看好是 furnished（有家具的）還是 unfurnished（沒有附家具的），差一點點就差很多。

文法字詞解析

gaze 和 stare 都有「一直盯著看」的意思，那麼兩者的差別在哪裡呢？原來，stare 通常不是很禮貌、甚至帶有比較兇的感覺，例如覺得路人長得很奇怪一直盯著看、或覺得你朋友講了很蠢的話讓你目瞪口呆，這種就是 stare。而 gaze 則通常帶有專注或喜愛的感情成分在其中，例如情侶之間含情脈脈地凝視著就可以用 gaze。

gen·er·os·i·ty [ˌdʒɛnəˋrɑsətɪ]

Track 3655

名 慷慨、寬宏大量 同 charity 寬容

▶I appreciate her generosity in this matter.
我很欣賞她在這件事上表現出來的寬大胸懷。

萬用延伸句型

I appreciate... 我很欣賞（某人）
這個句子還有另一個意思是「我很感激（某事）」。
例如：Thanks for your help. I really appreciate it. 謝謝你的幫忙，我真的很感激。

gen·ius [ˋdʒinjəs]

Track 3656

名 天才、英才

▶I don't think that he is a math genius.
我認為他並不是個數學天才。

gen·u·ine [ˋdʒɛnjʊɪn]

Track 3657

形 真正的、非假冒的 同 real 真的

▶It is not easy for me to distinguish cultured pearls from genuine pearls.
辨別真正的珍珠和養殖珍珠對我來說真不容易。

germ [dʒɝm]

Track 3658

名 細菌、微生物、病菌

▶Wash your hands to get rid of the germs.
要洗手，才能把病菌洗掉。

實用片語用語

get rid of... 除掉、甩掉

gift·ed [ˋgɪftɪd]

Track 3659

形 有天賦的、有才能的

▶That scientist is very gifted and made many discoveries.
那位科學家非常有才華，有了許多大發現。

gi·gan·tic [dʒaɪˋgæntɪk]

Track 3660

形 巨人般的

▶The gigantic monument stands in the center of the park.
這個巨大的紀念碑立在公園的中心。

gig·gle [ˋgɪgḷ]

Track 3661

名 咯咯笑 動 咯咯地笑

▶名 She let out a giggle when he tickled her.
他一搔她癢，她便咯咯笑。

▶動 Jenny giggled when she saw the handsome man.
珍妮看到那個帥哥時，咯咯地笑了起來。

gin·ger [ˋdʒɪndʒɚ]

Track 3662

名 薑 動 使有活力

▶名 I like having ginger milk tea during breakfast.
我喜歡在早餐時間喝薑母奶茶。

▶動 What do you think about gingering up the party by playing a song? 你覺得表演一首歌來活絡宴會的氣氛怎麼樣？

實用片語用語

ginger tea 薑茶
例如：Have some hot ginger tea and you'll feel warm in no time.
喝點熱薑茶，很快你就會覺得暖烘烘了。

glide [glaɪd]

Track 3663

名 滑動、滑走 動 滑行

▶名 The skater went by with a series of glides.
那位溜冰選手以一連串的滑步從旁邊經過。

▶動 An eagle glided past the window.
一隻老鷹從窗邊滑翔而過。

glimpse [glɪmps]

Track 3664

名 瞥見、一瞥 動 瞥見、隱約看見 同 glance 瞥見

▶名 It is the first time you ever gave me a glimpse of your true feelings.
這是你第一次讓我瞥見你內心的真實感情。

▶動 I glimpsed him at the other side of the room but he was soon gone.
我有在房間另一邊瞥見他，但他很快就不見了。

globe [glob]

Track 3665

名 地球、球

▶My dream is to visit every corner of the globe; what about you? 我的夢想是遊遍世界各地，你呢？

實用片語用語

globe-trotting 環遊世界
trot 是「走、踏」的意思（尤其常用來描述馬走路）。「踏遍整個地球」可想而知就是「環遊世界」的意思了。

glo·ri·ous [ˋglorɪəs]

Track 3666

形 著名的、榮耀的

▶The glorious victory was earned after much hard work.
這次輝煌的勝利是靠著許多努力累積而贏得的。

goods [gʊdz]

Track 3667

名 商品、貨物

▶The goods are now in transit（運輸）. You'll need to wait for a few more days.
這批貨物正在運輸途中，你還得再等幾天。

grace [gres]

Track 3668

名 優美、優雅

▶She always handles social situations with grace.
她總是優雅地處理所有社交場合。

grace·ful [ˋgresfəl]

Track 3669

形 優雅的、雅致的

▶She used to be a dancer; it is no wonder that all her motions are quite graceful.
她曾經當過舞者，難怪她的一舉一動都很優美。

文法字詞解析

名詞 grace（優雅）加上意為「充滿」的形容詞字尾「-ful」，就會變成 graceful（優美的、優雅的）。

gra·cious [ˋgreʃəs]

Track 3670

形 親切的、溫和有禮的

▶The gracious lady was well-liked by everyone in the neighborhood.
這名親切的太太很受全社區的人歡迎。

grad·u·a·tion [ˏgrædʒʊˋeʃən]

Track 3671

名 畢業

▶I wish I could get a good job after graduation.
但願我畢業後能找到一份好工作。

gram·mar [ˋgræmɚ]

Track 3672

名 文法

▶It's not necessary for you to worry about your grammar.
你沒有必要擔心你的文法。

gram·mat·i·cal [grə`mætɪk!] *Track 3673*

形 文法上的

▶There are several grammatical mistakes in the composition.
這份作文中有幾處文法上的錯誤。

文法字詞解析
相反地，「不符合文法的」則可以說「ungrammatical」。

grape·fruit [`grep,frut] *Track 3674*

名 葡萄柚

▶It is a kind of very delicious grapefruit. Would you like to try?
這是一種非常好吃的葡萄柚。你想試試看嗎？

grate·ful [`gretfəl] *Track 3675*

形 感激的、感謝的

▶Trust me! No one is more grateful than I am.
相信我！沒有人比我更感激您。

grat·i·tude [`grætə,tjud] *Track 3676*

名 感激、感謝

▶I don't know how to properly express my gratitude.
我真不知道如何適切地表現出我的感激。

grave [grev] *Track 3677*

形 嚴重的、重大的 名 墓穴、墳墓

▶形 The situation is very grave at the moment.
目前的情況非常嚴重。

▶名 She put down flowers on his grave. 她在他的墳墓上放了花。

實用片語用語
dig one's own grave 自掘墳墓
例如：Admitting to committing the crime is like digging your own grave.
承認犯罪就像是自掘墳墓一樣。

greas·y [`grizɪ] *Track 3678*

形 塗有油脂的、油膩的

▶Too much greasy food isn't good for you.
太油膩的食物對你的身體不好。

greet·ing(s) [`gritɪŋ(z)] *Track 3679*

名 問候、問候語

▶He's in a good mood and gave us a cheery greeting this morning. 他今天的心情很好，早上愉快地跟我們打招呼。

grief [grif] *Track 3680*

名 悲傷、感傷

▶It is obvious that the poor woman was buried in grief after her son's death.
顯然這個可憐的婦人在兒子死後一直沉浸在悲痛之中。

實用片語用語
bury in grief 沉浸在悲傷之中

grieve [griv] *Track 3681*

動 悲傷、使悲傷

▶There is no use grieving about past errors.
為過去的錯誤懊悔不已是無濟於事的。

grind [graɪnd] *Track 3682*

動 研磨、碾

▶It took about four or five years for me to grind and polish it.
把它磨平擦亮就花了我四五年的工夫。

文法字詞解析
grind 的動詞變化 grind, ground, ground

guar·an·tee [ˏgærən`ti] Track 3683

名 擔保品、保證人 動 擔保、作保 同 promise 保證

▶名 Can to offer us a life-time guarantee?
您願意為我們提供永久保固嗎？

▶動 Can you guarantee the quality of this product?
您能為我們保證這個產品的品質嗎？

guilt [gɪlt] Track 3684

名 罪、內疚

▶He felt no guilt for stealing his mother's money.
他偷自己母親的錢，卻一點都不覺得內疚。

guilt·y [gɪltɪ] Track 3685

形 有罪的、內疚的

▶Are you guilty of robbing the bank or no?
你到底有沒有犯下搶銀行的罪？

實用片語用語
be guilty of... 有……的罪

gulf [gʌlf] Track 3686

名 灣、海灣

▶I don't think there is a gulf between my daughter and me.
我認為我和我女兒之間沒有隔閡。

ha·bit·u·al [hə`bɪtʃʊəl] Track 3687

形 習慣性的

▶She's a habitual liar so I don't think you should believe her that easily.
她有說謊的習慣，所以我覺得你不該那麼輕易相信她。

halt [hɔlt] Track 3688

名 休止 動 停止、使停止

▶名 You've been working all day; why not call a halt?
你已經工作了一整天，為什麼不歇一歇呢？

▶動 Inputting this command will halt the computer.
輸入這個命令可以使這台電腦停止運行。

實用片語用語
call a halt（命令）停止

hand·writ·ing [`hændˏraɪtɪŋ] Track 3689

名 手寫

▶It is hard for the police to tell who the murderer is from the handwriting.
警察很難從字跡中辨認出兇手來。

萬用延伸句型
It is hard for... to... 對……來說要……很難

hard·en [`hɑrdn̩] Track 3690

動 使硬化

▶The water hardened and ice was formed.
水變硬結成了冰。

hard·ship [ˋhardʃɪp]
Track 3691

名 艱難、辛苦

▶It is obvious that your mom suffered too many hardships in the past. 顯然你媽媽在過去經歷了太多的辛酸。

hard·ware [ˋhardˏwɛr]
Track 3692

名 五金用品

▶I don't think they are very interested in your hardware. 我覺得他們對你的五金用品不是很感興趣。

實用片語用語

hardware store 五金行

例如：You might be able to find it in a hardware store.

這個可能可以在五金行找到。

har·mon·i·ca [harˋmanɪkə]
Track 3693

名 口琴

▶How about buying our daughter a harmonica as her birthday（生日）gift?

買個口琴給我們的女兒當生日禮物怎麼樣？

har·mo·ny [ˋharmənɪ]
Track 3694

名 一致、和諧 同 accord 一致

▶There is perfect harmony between the husband and the wife. 這對夫妻之間的感情非常融洽。

harsh [harʃ]
Track 3695

形 粗魯的、令人不快的

▶It is too difficult for them to accept those harsh facts you just said. 他們無法接受你剛才說的那些嚴酷事實。

haste [hest]
Track 3696

名 急忙、急速

▶She forgot her glasses in her haste to leave. 她在匆忙離開時忘記拿眼鏡了。

實用片語用語

in a haste 在匆忙之中

例如：I made some mistakes because I wrote the article in a haste.

因為文章是匆忙中寫成的，所以犯了一些錯。

has·ten [ˋhesn̩]
Track 3697

動 趕忙

▶We have to hasten to make a decision because there simply isn't time. 我們得趕緊下決定，因為真的沒時間了。

ha·tred [ˋhetrɪd]
Track 3698

名 怨恨、憎惡

▶Many people are full of hatred for the man. 很多人都很憎惡這個人。

head·phone(s) [ˋhɛdˏfon(z)]
Track 3699

名 頭戴式耳機、聽筒

▶What's the matter with the headphones? I can't hear anything at all. 這個耳機怎麼了？我什麼也聽不到啊。

文法字詞解析

earphones 也是「耳機」的意思，差別在於，headphones 通常是頭戴式的耳機，而非插在耳朵裡的那種耳機。

health·ful [ˋhɛlθfəl]
Track 3700

形 有益健康的

▶Not all vegetables in the world are healthful foods. 並非世界上的各種蔬菜都是有益於健康的食物。

hel·i·cop·ter [ˋhɛlɪ͵kɑptɚ]

Track 3701

名 直升機

▶I've never been on a helicopter before.
我都沒搭過直昇機呢。

herd [hɝd]

Track 3702

名 獸群、成群 動 放牧、使成群

▶名 It is hard for the boy to drive the herds of cattle out of the road. 男孩很難把牛群趕出馬路。

▶動 They herded the prisoners onto the train.
他們把這群囚犯驅趕上火車。

hes·i·ta·tion [͵hɛzəˋteʃən]

Track 3703

名 遲疑、躊躇 反 determination 決心

▶I hope our manager could agree to this plan without any hesitation. 但願我們的經理能毫不猶豫地同意這項計畫。

實用片語用語
without a moment's hesitation 一刻也不遲疑
例如：I told her everything without a moment's hesitation.
我一刻也不遲疑地把一切都告訴她了。

high·ly [ˋhaɪlɪ]

Track 3704

副 大大地、高高地

▶The master spoke highly of his works in the exhibition.
在展覽會上大師對他的作品評價很高。

home·land [ˋhom͵lænd]

Track 3705

名 祖國、本國

▶Why don't you go back to your homeland if you miss it so much?
既然你這麼想念你的祖國，那為什麼不回國去呢？

hon·ey·moon [ˋhʌnɪ͵mun]

Track 3706

名 蜜月 動 度蜜月

▶名 Where did you go for your honeymoon?
你們蜜月去了哪裡啊？

▶動 We will honeymoon in Spain.
我們將去西班牙度蜜月。

文法字詞解析
要說兩人「在蜜月中」時，可以說on honeymoon 或 on sb.'s honeymoon。
例如：We will be visiting Germany on our honeymoon.
我們蜜月時會去德國。

hon·or·a·ble [ˋɑnərəbl̩]

Track 3707

形 體面的、可敬的

▶I wish my son could become an honorable man.
我希望我兒子能當個正直的人。

hook [hʊk]

Track 3708

名 鉤、鉤子 動 鉤、用鉤子鉤住

▶名 Will you help me hang my coat on the hook, Susan?
蘇珊，你能幫我把外套掛在鉤上嗎？

▶動 Can you hook the window when you come in?
你能在進屋的時候把窗戶扣好嗎？

文法字詞解析
流行音樂中常常會有一段旋律非常讓人印象深刻、讓人會不自覺跟著哼唱，那一段旋律就叫做歌曲裡的「hook」。

hope·ful [ˋhopfəl]

Track 3709

形 有希望的

▶That sounds very hopeful if you can advance to the second round. 如果你能進入第二輪比賽，那聽起來就很有希望了。

ho·ri·zon [hə`raɪz]　Track 3710

名 地平線、水平線

▶The sun is rising above the horizon.
太陽升到地平線上了。

hor·ri·fy [`hɔrə͵faɪ]　Track 3711

動 使害怕、使恐怖

▶I was horrified by what I saw.
我被我看到的事物嚇壞了。

hose [hoz]　Track 3712

名 水管 動 用水管澆洗

▶名 We need enough hoses to put the big fire out.
我們需要足夠的水管以撲滅大火。

▶動 He hosed the bubbles off the car.
他用水管把車上的泡泡沖掉。

host [host]　Track 3713

動 主辦 名 主人、主持人、一大群 反 guest 客人

▶動 I don't think this country will host the Games this year.
我認為該國今年將不會主辦這屆運動會。

▶名 I don't think he will be the host for tonight's program.
我覺得他不會是今晚的節目主持人。

hos·tel [`hɑstḷ]　Track 3714

名 青年旅社

▶Do you mind if I fix you up for the night at a hostel, sir?
先生，您介意我安頓您到青年旅社過夜嗎？

house·hold [`haʊs͵hold]　Track 3715

形 家庭

▶This young girl often helps her mother with household chores.
這個年輕女孩常常幫她的媽媽做家事。

house·wife [`haʊs͵waɪf]　Track 3716

名 家庭主婦

▶Not every woman wants to be a housewife.
不是每個女人都想成為家庭主婦。

house·work [`haʊs͵wɝk]　Track 3717

名 家事

▶Lots of men are unwilling（願意的）to help their wives with housework at home.
許多男人都不願意在家幫他們的妻子做家事。

hu·man·i·ty [hju`mænətɪ]　Track 3718

名 人類、人道

▶We should treat animals with humanity.
我們應該以仁慈之心對待動物。

文法字詞解析

和 horizon 相關的一個形容詞是 horizontal，指的是「水平的」的意思。horizontal 經常和另一個字 vertical（垂直的）一起出現，一個是橫的一個是直的，依瞬間可能有點難判斷，但只要記得 horizon 是地平線，地平線是橫的，就能馬上知道誰是誰啦。

實用片語用語

fix up 安排

實用片語用語

do housework 做家事
例如：He rarely ever does housework. Instead, he expects his wife to do everything.
他幾乎不做家事，卻要他太太包辦一切。

hur·ri·cane [ˋhɝɪken]

Track 3719

名 颶風

▶The hurricane destroyed several houses in the district.
颶風在該區毀掉了不少房子。

hy·dro·gen [ˋhaɪdrədʒən]

Track 3720

名 氫、氫氣

▶The scientists found that water is made up of oxygen and hydrogen.
科學家們發現水是由氫和氧構成的。

ice·berg [ˋaɪs͵bɝg]

Track 3721

名 冰山

▶The Titanic sank after hitting an iceberg.
鐵達尼號在撞上冰山後就沉了。

實用片語用語

tip of the iceberg 冰山一角
例　如：The problems we see now are only the tip of the iceberg.
我們現在看到的問題還只是冰山的一角。

i·den·ti·cal [aɪˋdɛntɪkl]

Track 3722

形 相同的 同 same 相同的

▶The two little girls are identical twins.
這兩個小女孩是一模一樣的雙胞胎。

i·den·ti·fi·ca·tion/ ID [aɪ͵dɛntəfəˋkeʃən]

Track 3723

名 身分證

▶Will you please give me some forms of identification to prove yourself?
您能給我一些證明身份的文件來證明你自己嗎？

i·den·ti·fy [aɪˋdɛntə͵faɪ]

Track 3724

動 認出、鑑定

▶It took the police some time to identify the accident victims.
警察費了不少時間來驗明事故遇難者的身份。

id·i·om [ˋɪdɪəm]

Track 3725

名 成語、慣用語

▶Some Chinese idioms are kind of funny.
有些中文諺語其實還蠻好笑的。

id·le [ˋaɪdl]

Track 3726

形 閒置的 動 閒混

▶形 I want to just spend all day sitting there being idle.
我真想整天坐在那裡虛度時光。

▶動 They idled the day away on the sofa.
他們坐在沙發上虛度了一天。

實用片語用語

idle sth. away 虛度（時光）

i·dol [ˋaɪdḷ] Track 3727

名 偶像

▶The pop singer is the idol of young people.
這位流行歌手是年輕人崇拜的偶像。

文法字詞解析
idol 可以指平常在電視可以看到、唱唱跳跳的「偶像」（一種職業）、任何你景仰的人、也可以拿來指神明或神像等「被人崇拜的對象」。

ig·no·rant [ˋɪgnərənt] Track 3728

形 缺乏教育的、無知的

▶It is obvious that he is ignorant of what happened.
顯然他不知道發生了什麼事。

il·lus·trate [ˋɪləstret] Track 3729

動 舉例說明

▶Why don't you use a simple example to illustrate the point?
你為什麼不用一個簡單的例子去說明這一點呢？

il·lus·tra·tion [ɪˏlʌsˋtreʃən] Track 3730

名 說明、插圖

▶I like magazines full of illustrations.
我喜歡看插圖多的雜誌。

i·mag·in·able [ɪˋmædʒɪnəbḷ] Track 3731

形 可想像的

▶I don't think that he is the most suitable person imaginable.
我覺得他不是想得到的人選中最合適的一位。

i·mag·i·nar·y [ɪˋmædʒəˏnɛrɪ] Track 3732

形 想像的、不實在的

▶I had an imaginary friend when I was young.
我小時候有個虛構的朋友。

文法字詞解析
imaginary 與下面的單字 imaginative 都是和想像力有關的形容詞，兩者的差別是 imaginary 是「想像出來的、虛構的、並不是真實存在的」，而 imaginative 則是「有想像力的」。所以我們可以稱讚小孩子 imaginative（有想像力），但不能說他們 imaginary，那樣就變成不存在的孩子了。

i·mag·i·na·tive [ɪˋmædʒəˏnetɪv] Track 3733

形 有想像力的

▶She is not only hardworking but also imaginative.
她不但勤奮而且富有想像力。

im·i·tate [ˋɪməˏtet] Track 3734

動 仿效、效法

▶He liked to imitate his brother and annoy him.
他喜歡模仿他哥哥，讓他哥哥很不高興。

im·i·ta·tion [ˏɪməˋteʃən] Track 3735

名 模仿、仿造品

▶That painting is not authentic（真實的）; it's just an imitation.
那幅畫不是真的，是仿造品。

im·mi·grant [ˋɪməgrənt] Track 3736

名 移民者

▶I think there will be more and more immigrants in China.
我認為中國會有越來越多的移民者。

實用片語用語
immigrant policy 移民政策
例如：With the current state of affairs in Europe, countries are reconsidering（重新思考） their immigrant policies.
由於歐洲目前的狀況，許多國家開始重新思考移民政策的問題。

im·mi·grate [ˋɪmə͵gret] Track 3737

動 遷移、移入

▶It doesn't matter to him whether his daughter shall immigrate to Italy or not.
他的女兒是否將移居義大利對他來說都不要緊。

im·mi·gra·tion [͵ɪməˋgreʃən] Track 3738

名（從外地）移居入境

▶Would you like to tell me how to enquire about the immigration state?
你能告訴我如何查詢有關移居的情況嗎？

im·pact [ˋɪmpækt]/[ɪmˋpækt] Track 3739

名 碰撞、撞擊 動 衝擊、影響

▶名 The impact of the stone against the window shattered（打碎）the glass.
石頭撞擊窗戶，打碎了玻璃。

▶動 I don't think my suggestion would impact their decision.
我想我的建議大概不會影響他們做的決定吧。

實用片語用語
make an impact 造成影響
例如：List some inventions that made an impact on our lives.
請列出一些對我們的生活造成影響的發明。

im·ply [ɪmˋplaɪ] Track 3740

動 暗示、含有 同 hint 暗示

▶He didn't outright say that he hated me, but he implied it.
他沒有直接說他討厭我，但他有暗示他討厭我。

im·pres·sion [ɪmˋprɛʃən] Track 3741

名 印象

▶He tried very hard to make a good impression when meeting her for the first time.
他在第一次和她見面時，非常努力留下一個好印象。

in·ci·dent [ˋɪnsədənt] Track 3742

名 事件

▶He resolved never to tell anyone about this incident.
他決定永遠不跟任何人談這件事。

實用片語用語
resolve to... 下決心要……

in·clud·ing [ɪnˋkludɪŋ] Track 3743

介 包含、包括

▶Three others, including the gunman（槍手）, were killed.
另有三人死亡，包括那名槍手。

in·di·ca·tion [͵ɪndəˋkeʃən] Track 3744

名 指示、表示

▶He never gave any indication that he wanted to support us.
他從來沒表示要支持我們。

in·dus·tri·al·ize [ɪnˋdʌstrɪəl͵aɪz] Track 3745

動（使）工業、產業化

▶Many towns in the coastal（沿海的）area have begun to industrialize.
沿海地區的許多鄉鎮已開始工業化。

in·fant [ˋɪnfənt]

Track 3746

名 嬰兒、未成年人

▶This design is suitable for infants.
這種設計很適合嬰兒。

實用片語用語
in its infant stage 還在初期階段
一件事的發展若還在「嬰兒」的階段，可想而知就是才剛開始了。
例如：My novel is still in its infant stage and I'd be embarrassed if you were to read it.
我的小說還在剛開始的階段，如果你讀了它，我會覺得很不好意思的。

in·fect [ɪnˋfɛkt]

Track 3747

動 使感染

▶The wound must be kept clean so that germs do not infect it.
傷口須保持清潔，才不會細菌感染。

in·fec·tion [ɪnˋfɛkʃən]

Track 3748

名 感染、傳染病

▶You need to keep the wound clean, or you might get an infection.
你應該要保持傷口乾淨，否則可能會感染的。

in·fla·tion [ɪnˋfleʃən]

Track 3749

名 膨脹、脹大

▶I don't think that the increase of wages can keep up with inflation.
我認為薪水漲幅跟不上通貨膨脹。

文法字詞解析
inflation 是通貨膨脹，而「通貨緊縮」只要將字首換成「de-」，變成「deflation」即是。

in·flu·en·tial [ˏɪnflʊˋɛnʃəl]

Track 3750

形 有影響力的

▶He used to be a good leader; everything he said was influential.
他曾經是一位很棒的領導者，他說的話都很有影響力。

in·for·ma·tion [ˏɪnfɚˋmeʃən]

Track 3751

名 知識、見聞

▶Would you like to give me any information on this matter?
關於此事，你能提供什麼消息給我嗎？

in·for·ma·tive [ɪnˋfɔrmətɪv]

Track 3752

形 提供情報的

▶We need to design attractive and informative brochures（小冊子）.
我們必須設計吸引人又資訊豐富的小冊子。

文法字詞解析
相反地，要抱怨說明書、課程提供的資訊根本毫無用途、或提供的資訊實在太少，可以說「uninformative」（沒有提供資訊的、提供太少資訊的）。

in·gre·di·ent [ɪnˋgridɪənt]

Track 3753

名 成份、原料

▶Would you like to tell me what the ingredients of the cake are?
您能告訴我這個蛋糕是用什麼原料做成的嗎？

in·i·tial [ɪˋnɪʃəl]

Track 3754

形 開始的 名 姓名的首字母

▶形 My initial reaction when hearing the news was to smile.
我剛聽到這消息時，一開始的反應是微笑。

▶名 He carved his initials on the wall in the classroom.
他把他的姓名字首刻在教室的牆上。

in·no·cence [ˋɪnəsn̩s]

Track 3755

名 清白、天真無邪

▶I don't believe in his innocence; what about you?
我不相信他是清白的，你相信嗎？

in·put [ˋɪn͵pʊt]

Track 3756

名 輸入 動 輸入

▶名 I really need your input. I can't figure this out by myself.
我真的需要你的意見，我沒辦法自己一個人搞清楚這個。

▶動 Would you please input the data into the computer for me?
請你幫我把資料登錄到電腦中好嗎？

實用片語用語
figure sth. out 搞清楚某事、弄懂某事。

in·sert [ˋɪnsɝt]/[ɪnˋsɝt]

Track 3757

名 插入物 動 插入

▶名 What do you think about the special insert in the magazine?
你覺得這本雜誌的那個特別插頁怎麼樣？

▶動 The book would be improved by inserting another chapter.
這本書如果再插入一個章節就更好了。

in·spec·tion [ɪnˋspɛkʃən]

Track 3758

名 檢查、調查

▶Would you please tell me where the customs inspection is?
您能告訴我海關檢查站在哪裡嗎？

in·spi·ra·tion [ɪnspəˋreʃən]

Track 3759

名 鼓舞、激勵

▶Her music was great inspiration to many.
她的音樂激勵了許多人。

文法字詞解析
句中的 many 代稱 many people，在這裡是當作名詞的功能使用。

in·spire [ɪnˋspaɪr]

Track 3760

動 啓發、鼓舞

▶His works inspired many other artists.
他的作品啓發了許多其他的藝術家。

in·stall [ɪnˋstɔl]

Track 3761

動 安裝、裝置 同 establish 建立、安置

▶How long will it take to install a telephone and connect it to the exchange?
安裝電話機並與總機接通要多久？

in·stinct [ˋɪnstɪŋkt]

Track 3762

名 本能、直覺

▶Why don't you trust your instinct and do what you think is right?
為什麼不相信你的直覺，並按你認為對的去做呢？

實用片語用語
by instinct 本能地、直覺地
例如：She was able to choose the correct answer by instinct.
她能夠直覺地選出正確的答案。

in·struct [ɪnˋstrʌkt]

Track 3763

動 教導、指令

▶He instructed the students to finish the assignment.
他教導學生們完成這項作業。

in·struc·tor [ɪnˋstrʌktɚ]

Track 3764

名 教練、指導者

▶The English instructor is very patient.
這位英語講師很有耐心。

in·sult [ɪnˋsʌlt]/[ˋɪnsʌlt]

Track 3765

動 侮辱 名 冒犯

▶動 I never meant to insult you; would you please forgive me?
我不是有意要侮辱你的，請原諒我好嗎？

▶名 When he praises people, somehow it always sounds like an insult.
他稱讚人的時候，不知道為什麼聽起來卻像是在罵人。

萬用延伸句型
I never meant to V. 我不是有意要（做某事）

in·sur·ance [ɪnˋʃurəns]

Track 3766

名 保險

▶Once you join our company, we will make sure that you will get insurance.
一旦你加入我們公司，我們一定會幫你加保。

in·tel·lec·tu·al [ˌɪntl̩ˋɛktʃuəl]

Track 3767

名 知識份子 形 智力的

▶名 The intellectuals always have a huge influence.
知識份子一般都有很大的影響力。

▶形 Both his parents are extremely smart; it is no wonder that he is an intellectual person.
他的父母親都非常聰明，難怪他是個智力超高的人。

in·tel·li·gence [ɪnˋtɛlədʒəns]

Track 3768

名 智能

▶It is obvious that he is a man of very high intelligence.
顯然他是個非常聰明的人。

文法字詞解析
因為知道了很多情報就能夠做出比較聰明的反應，所以間諜們工作上用到的「情報」也可以稱為 intelligence。

in·tel·li·gent [ɪnˋtɛlədʒəjnt]

Track 3769

形 有智慧（才智）的

▶She is not only very intelligent but also very modest.
她不但很聰明，而且非常謙虛。

in·tend [ɪnˋtɛnd]

Track 3770

動 計畫、打算

▶Let's ask her what she intends to do.
我們問問她打算做什麼吧。

in·tense [ɪnˋtɛns]

Track 3771

形 極度的、緊張的

▶The basketball game last night was really intense.
昨晚的籃球賽超緊張的。

文法字詞解析
除了指「情勢」很緊張外，intense 也能拿來描述人的眼神非常有力、專注。

in·ten·si·fy [ɪnˋtɛnsəˌfaɪ]

Track 3772

動 加強、增強

▶The conflict between the two groups is intensifying day by day. 兩個組織間的衝突一天比一天增強了。

in·ten·si·ty [ɪnˋtɛnsətɪ]

Track 3773

名 強度、強烈

▶The poem showed great intensity of feeling.
這首詩表現出強烈的激情。

in·ten·sive [ɪnˋtɛnsɪv]

Track 3774

形 強烈的、密集的

▶It took him four nights to finish the intensive course.
他花了四個晚上完成密集課程。

in·ten·tion [ɪnˋtɛnʃən]

Track 3775

名 意向、意圖

▶I have no intention of coming to this terrible place again!
我再也不想到這個糟糕的地方來了！

萬用延伸句型
have no intention of V-ing 完全沒有意願（做某事）

in·ter·act [ˏɪntəˋrækt]

Track 3776

動 交互作用、互動

▶Why don't we encourage the students to interact in class in English?
我們為什麼不鼓勵學生在課堂上用英語互動呢？

in·ter·ac·tion [ˏɪntəˋækʃən]

Track 3777

名 交互影響、互動

▶There should be more interaction between the social services and local doctors.
社會公益服務機構和當地醫生應該加強互動。

實用片語用語
interaction between A and B A 和 B 之間的互動

in·ter·fere [ˏɪntəˋfɪr]

Track 3778

動 妨礙 同 interrupt 打斷

▶I hope you won't interfere with my plans.
我希望你不要干擾我的計畫。

in·ter·me·di·ate [ˏɪntəˋmidɪɪt]

Track 3779

名 調解 形 中間的

▶名 Not every intermediate is able to solve the dispute perfectly（完美地）each time.
不是每個調解人每次都能夠完美地解決爭端。

▶形 Not every student in our class passed the intermediate level exam of Japanese.
我們班不是每個學生都通過了日語的中級考試。

實用片語用語
intermediate level 中級

Internet [ˋɪntəˏnɛt]

Track 3780

名 網際網路

▶Let us search for the answers on the Internet, shall we?
我們上網找答案好嗎？

in·ter·pret [ɪnˋtɝprɪt]

Track 3781

動 說明、解讀、翻譯

▶Would you please interpret for me? I don't understand what she is talking about.
請你為我翻譯一下好嗎？我聽不懂她在說什麼。

in·ter·rup·tion
[ˌɪntəˋrʌpʃən] Track 3782

名 中斷、妨礙

▶Please go ahead with your story; there won't be any more interruptions.
請繼續講你的故事，不會再有人打岔了。

實用片語用語
go ahead with... 動手做某事

in·ti·mate [ˋɪntəmɪt] Track 3783

名 知己 形 親密的

▶名 He is not only my teacher but also my intimate.
他不但是我的老師，還是我的密友。

▶形 They are not only business associates but also intimate friends.
他們不但是生意上的夥伴，而且還是親密的朋友。

in·to·na·tion [ˌɪntoˋneʃən] Track 3784

名 語調、吟詠

▶Would you be careful about your pronunciation and intonation?
請注意一下你的發音和語調好嗎？

in·vade [ɪnˋved] Track 3785

動 侵略、入侵

▶If the enemies dare to invade us, we won't go easy on them either.
如果敵人膽敢入侵，我們也會還以迎頭痛擊。

實用片語用語
go easy on... 放水、（在比賽中）不使出真正的實力

in·va·sion [ɪnˋveʒən] Track 3786

名 侵犯、侵害

▶The alien invasion in 2528 was predicted in ancient books.
古書中預測了2528年外星人侵襲地球的事。

in·ven·tion [ɪnˋvɛnʃən] Track 3787

名 發明、創造

▶The flying skateboard is my newest invention.
那個飛行滑板是我的最新發明。

in·vest [ɪnˋvɛst] Track 3788

動 投資

▶He invested a lot of time in trying to help poor children.
他把大量時間用在設法幫助貧窮兒童上。

實用片語用語
invest in... 投資於……

in·vest·ment [ɪnˋvɛstmənt] Track 3789

名 投資額、投資

▶Education is a good investment.
教育是很好的投資。

in·ves·ti·ga·tion [ɪnˌvɛstəˋgeʃən] Track 3790

名 調查

▶Would you please take over my investigation?
你們願意接手我的調查嗎？

in·volve [ɪn`vɑlv]

Track 3791

動 牽涉、包括

▶You should involve yourself in school life more.
你應該更融入學校生活。

in·volve·ment [ɪn`vɑlvmənt]

Track 3792

名 捲入、連累

▶He is convinced that Shirley's involvement will ruin their relationship.
他確信雪莉的捲入會毀掉他們的關係。

實用片語用語
be convinced that... 確信（某事）

i·so·late [`aɪsl̩ˌet]

Track 3793

動 孤立、隔離 同 separate 分開

▶He has been isolated by his peers.
他被同儕孤立了。

i·so·la·tion [ˌaɪsl̩`eʃən]

Track 3794

名 分離、孤獨

▶It is difficult for any country to develop in isolation.
任何國家都難以在封閉的狀態下得到發展。

itch [ɪtʃ]

Track 3795

名 癢 動 發癢

▶名 I had an itch on my back all of a sudden.
我的後背突然很癢。

▶動 I'm itching all over. Must be the lobsters I ate for dinner!
我全身癢耶，一定是我晚餐吃的龍蝦害的。

文法字詞解析
itch 是名詞，表示「癢」；也可以當作動詞，表示「發癢」。那如果要用形容詞表示「癢的」呢？可以說「itchy」。
例如：My back has been itchy all week.
我的背已經一整個禮拜都癢癢的了。

Jj

jeal·ous·y [`dʒɛləsɪ]

Track 3796

名 嫉妒

▶A man driven by jealousy is capable of anything.
嫉妒心可使人什麼都做得出來。

ju·nior [`dʒunjɚ]

Track 3797

名 年少者 形 年少的

▶名 She is three years his junior. I hope they can become good friends.
她比他小三歲，我希望他們能成為好朋友。

▶形 I hope I can meet my junior high school classmates as soon as possible.
我希望我能盡快見到我的國中同學們。

實用片語用語
be two / three / five etc. years somebody's junior
比某人小二／三／五……歲

keen [kin]

Track 3798

形 熱衷的、敏銳的

▶She is keen on growing flowers in the garden.
她對在花園種花特別著迷。

實用片語用語
be keen on... 對某事著迷、很熱切地做某事

knuck·le [ˋnʌkḷ]

Track 3799

名 關節 動 將指關節觸地

▶名 The man who's cracking his knuckles looks mean.
那個把關節弄得喀喀作響的男人看起來很兇的樣子。

▶動 Let's stop chatting and knuckle down to work.
別再聊了，我們開始認真工作吧。

實用片語用語
knuckle down to 開始做……

la·bor [ˋlebɚ]

Track 3800

名 勞力 動 勞動

▶名 There is a clear division of labor in ants.
螞蟻間有明確的分工。

▶動 She labored five years on that book.
她寫那本書足足寫了五年。

lab·o·ra·to·ry/lab [ˋlæbrəˏtorɪ]/[læb]

Track 3801

名 實驗室

▶The white rat is frequently（常常）used as a laboratory animal.
白鼠常被用來做為實驗用動物。

lag [læg]

Track 3802

名 落後 動 延緩

▶名 It is obvious that you will get jet lag after traveling overseas.
顯然在出國旅遊之後你會出現時差反應。

▶動 Our son lags behind others in the class because of playing video games.
我們兒子因為玩電動玩具而導致學習落後於班上其他同學。

實用片語用語
jet lag 時差造成的不適反應

land·mark [ˋlændˏmɑrk]

Track 3803

名 路標

▶The Eiffel Tower is regarded as Paris's landmark.
艾菲爾鐵塔被認為是巴黎的地標。

land·scape [ˋlænskep]　Track 3804

名 風景 動 進行造景工程

▶名 He is good at painting not only landscapes but also portraits.
他不但擅長畫風景畫，而且還很擅長畫肖像畫。

▶動 We're having both places landscaped.
我們要在兩處地方都建造園林。

land·slide/mud·slide　Track 3805

[ˋlændˌslaɪd]/[ˋmʌdˌslaɪd]

名 山崩

▶Not all the people think about the causes of landslides when they suffer from it. 不是所有人都會在遭遇土石流的同時，去思考土石流發生的原由。

實用片語用語
win by a landslide 獲得壓倒性的勝利
這個片語不是「靠著山崩獲勝」的意思喔！像是山崩、土石流這類的事情力量強大，能夠將事物完全摧毀，因此若在選舉或其他投票比賽中一方獲得「壓倒性」的勝利，即可用這個片語來表示完全擊垮了對手。

large·ly [ˋlɑrdʒlɪ]　Track 3806

副 大部分地

▶His success is largely due to his hard work.
他的成功主要是靠自己的努力得來的。

實用片語用語
... be 動詞 + due to + N. ……因為……

late·ly [ˋletlɪ]　Track 3807

副 最近

▶He left for Hong Kong last month; it is no wonder that I haven't seen him lately.
他上週去了香港，難怪我最近都沒看到他。

launch [lɔntʃ]　Track 3808

名 開始 動 發射

▶名 I don't think the launch of the new ship will start on time.
我覺得新船下水儀式不會按時進行了。

▶動 This country has already launched a spaceship（太空船）successfully.
這個國家已經成功地發射了太空船。

law·ful [ˋlɔfəl]　Track 3809

形 合法的 同 legal 合法的

▶I don't think he has reached the lawful age to drink in the bar.
我認為他還未達到法定年齡，不能進酒吧喝酒。

lead [lid]　Track 3810

名 / 動 領導

▶名 It doesn't matter whether their team will be in the lead or not at half time.
他們隊在前半場領先與否都沒什麼大不了的。

▶動 He led his team to victory.
他帶領著他的隊伍獲得勝利。

文法字詞解析
lead 的動詞變化：lead, led, led

lean [lin]　Track 3811

動 傾斜、倚靠

▶Be careful! It's very dangerous lean out of the window.
小心！把身子探出窗外是很危險的。

learn·ed [ˋlɝnd]

Track 3812

形 學術性的、博學的

▶Many learned men are arguing with him on the Internet .
有很多學者在網路上跟他爭論。

learn·ing [ˋlɝnɪŋ]

Track 3813

名 學問

▶Not all the students know exactly what their purposes of learning are.
不是所有學生都很清楚自己學習的目的是什麼。

lec·ture [ˋlɛktʃɚ]

Track 3814

名 演講 動 對……演講

▶名 Will you attend the lecture given by Professor Wang tomorrow?
明天你會參加王教授的講座嗎？

▶動 Will you come to lecture to the class on chemistry, Mr. Wright?
萊特老師，你會來為這個班講授化學嗎？

文法字詞解析
由於父母「唸」孩子時有時也彎像是老師在諄諄教誨、講大道理，因此父母「唸」孩子這件事也可以用 give a lecture 來描述。

lec·tur·er [ˋlɛktʃərɚ]

Track 3815

名 演講者

▶Will you tell me what the lecturer's topic is?
你能告訴我這位演講者的題目是什麼嗎？

leg·end [ˋlɛdʒənd]

Track 3816

名 傳奇

▶According to the old legends, it was Romulus who became the founder of Rome.
按照古老的傳說，羅穆盧斯成為了古羅馬的建國者。

lei·sure·ly [ˋliʒɚlɪ]

Track 3817

形 悠閒的 副 悠閒地

▶形 They took a leisurely walk around the small town.
他們在小城中悠閒地散步。

▶副 Latin Americans stroll（漫步）leisurely through life.
拉丁美洲人的生活節奏很從容不迫。

li·cense/li·cence [ˋlaɪsn̩s]

Track 3818

名 執照 動 許可

▶名 It is easy for him to obtain a driver's license in this country.
他很容易就在這個國家考取了駕照。

▶動 It is impossible（不可能的）for the restaurant to sell spirits for it is not licensed for it.
這家飯店不可能賣烈酒，因為它沒有賣烈酒的許可證。

實用片語用語
driver's license 駕照

light·en [ˋlaɪtn̩]

Track 3819

動 變亮、減輕

▶The sky begins to lighten after the storm.
暴風雨後天空開始放晴。

實用片語用語
lighten up 使變輕鬆
例如：He tried to lighten up the mood by making a joke.
他試著講笑話讓氣氛變輕鬆。

lim·i·ta·tion [ˌlɪmə`teʃən] Track 3820

名 限制

▶It is hard for me to accept some limitations on my freedom.
我很難接受對我自由的某些限制。

liq·uor [`lɪkɚ] Track 3821

名 烈酒

▶You must keep away from liquor and tobacco, or your illness will get worse.
你必須不沾菸酒，否則你的病情將會加重。

lit·er·ar·y [`lɪtəˌrɛrɪ] Track 3822

形 文學的

▶I don't like to read this man's literary criticism.
我不喜歡讀這個人的文學評論。

lit·er·a·ture [`lɪtərətʃɚ] Track 3823

名 文學

▶I major in English literature in university; what about you?
我大學主修英國文學，你呢？

實用片語用語

classical literature 經典文學
例如：They are arguing over what books can be classified as classical literature.
他們在爭執到底哪些書才算是經典文學。

loan [lon] Track 3824

名 借貸 動 借、貸

▶名 Will you tell me what it requires to get a loan in the bank?
能告訴我到這個銀行貸款需要辦理什麼手續嗎？

▶動 Will you loan me some money? I need to buy a pair of shoes for a job interview.
你能借我一些錢嗎？我需要買一雙面試穿的鞋。

lo·ca·tion [lo`keʃən] Track 3825

名 位置

▶It is obvious that he doesn't know the location of the World Trade Center.
他顯然不知道世貿中心在哪裡。

lock·er [`lɑkɚ] Track 3826

名 有鎖的收納櫃、寄物櫃

▶I stuffed my backpack into the locker.
我把我的背包塞進了寄物櫃中。

實用片語用語

locker room （有很多置物櫃的）更衣室
例如：The football team is changing in the locker room right now.
足球隊的人現在都在更衣室換衣服。

log·ic [`lɑdʒɪk] Track 3827

名 邏輯

▶There is no logic in spending money on clothes you don't wear.把錢花在你不穿的衣服上是沒有道理的。

log·i·cal [`lɑdʒɪkḷ] Track 3828

形 邏輯上的

▶I must admit his argument is logical.
我必須承認他的論點富有邏輯。

lo·tion [ˋloʃən] Track 3829

名 洗潔劑

▶Her lotion smells like candy and apples.
她的乳液聞起來像是糖果和蘋果的味道。

lousy [ˋlaʊzɪ] Track 3830

形 卑鄙的

▶What lousy weather! I can't go out with my friends and play tennis. 好討厭的天氣啊！我不能跟朋友們出門去打網球。

文法字詞解析

lousy 可以拿來形容卑鄙的、差勁的，除了可以罵人、罵物品品質不好、罵某人表現很差外，也能拿來描述自己的心情或狀態。

loy·al [ˋlɔɪəl] Track 3831

形 忠實的

▶I don't think that there is any necessity to be loyal to a cruel ruler. 我覺得沒有必要為一個殘暴的國君效忠。

loy·al·ty [ˋlɔɪəltɪ] Track 3832

名 忠誠

▶It is a surprise that you should doubt his loyalty to the company and the work.
你居然會懷疑他對公司和工作的忠誠，真令人驚訝。

lu·nar [ˋlunɚ] Track 3833

形 月亮的、陰曆的

▶The stones on the lunar surface are different from each other.
在月球表面的石頭都各有不同。

實用片語用語

Lunar New Year 農曆新年
例如：How does your family celebrate the Lunar New Year?
你們家的人都怎麼慶祝農曆新年的？

lux·u·ri·ous [lʌgˋʒurɪəs] Track 3834

形 奢侈的

▶Don't you think the furniture in the villa is too luxurious?
難道你不覺得這個別墅裡的傢俱都太奢華了嗎？

lux·u·ry [ˋlʌkʃərɪ] Track 3835

名 奢侈品、奢侈

▶Clean water is a luxury for people in some regions.
對一些地區的人來說，乾淨的水是種奢侈品。

ma·chin·er·y [məˋʃinərɪ] Track 3836

名 機械

▶There was a very large sum of expense on new machinery.
添置新機器的開支非常龐大。

實用片語用語

a large sum of … 大量的……

mad·am/ma'am Track 3837

[ˋmædəm]/[mæm]

名 夫人、女士

▶Would you like to see some other dresses, madam?
夫人，您想不想看看其他的洋裝呢？

mag·net·ic [mæg`nɛtɪk]   Track 3838

形 磁性的

▶Once the switch is closed, the magnetic path has a lower reluctance（磁阻）.
一旦開關關閉，磁路就具有較低的磁阻。

文法字詞解析
當我們想說一個人的個性非常有吸引力、能夠像磁鐵一般把大家都吸過去時，就可以說他擁有「a magnetic personality」。

mag·nif·i·cent [mæg`nɪfəsənt]   Track 3839

形 壯觀的、華麗的

▶What a magnificent day! How about going out for a walk?
多棒的天氣啊！出去散散步怎麼樣？

make·up [`mek͵ʌp]   Track 3840

名 結構、化妝

▶She put on so much makeup for her wedding her mom didn't recognize her.
她在婚禮上化的妝太濃，以致連她媽都認不出她。

man·u·al [`mænjʊəl]   Track 3841

名 手冊 形 手工的

▶名 There are a lot of useful tips in this manual.
這本小冊子裡有很多實用的小建議。

▶形 There are a manual control system and an automatic one in this factory.
這間工廠有手控與自動控制系統。

實用片語用語
user's manual 使用手冊
例如：The user's manual must be somewhere in the box.
使用手冊應該在箱子裡的某處可以找到。

man·u·fac·ture [͵mænjə`fæktʃɚ]   Track 3842

名 製造業 動 大量製造

▶名 How about importing some foreign manufactures? Maybe we can learn from them.
進口一些外國製品怎麼樣？或許我們可以從這些產品學到什麼。

▶動 Our firm manufactures cars; what about yours?
我們公司生產汽車，你們公司生產什麼？

man·u·fac·turer [͵mænjə`fæktʃərɚ]   Track 3843

名 製造者

▶The manufacturer has gotten several complaints from customers.
這家製造商從顧客那裡接到不少抱怨電話。

mar·a·thon [`mærə͵θɑn]   Track 3844

名 馬拉松

▶There are thousands of people taking part in this marathon.
參加此次馬拉松比賽的人有幾千人。

文法字詞解析
想要來場 marathon，但又覺得懶惰嗎？沒關係，懶人也有懶人的馬拉松方式。在英文中如果很長很長一段時間都坐在原地，連看好幾部電影或影集，也可以稱為 marathon。畢竟要一次從頭到晚看完每一季的《冰與火之歌》也是很令人疲憊的事。

mar·gin [`mɑrdʒɪn]   Track 3845

名 邊緣 同 edge 邊

▶Would you please write your comments in the margin?
請您在把評論寫在頁緣好嗎？

ma·tu·ri·ty [mə`tjʊrətɪ] Track 3846

名 成熟期

▶This job calls for a person with a great deal of maturity.
這個工作需由成熟老練的人去做。

max·i·mum [`mæksəməm] Track 3847

名 最大量 形 最大的

▶名 I can swim a maximum of two miles; what about you?
我游泳最遠能游兩英里，你呢？

▶形 The maximum speed of this car is 100 miles per hour.
這輛車的最高時速為一百英里。

文法字詞解析

知道了 maximum（最大值），當然就會想要知道「最小值」怎麼說。答案是 minimum，這個字同樣地也可以當作形容詞「最小的」。

mea·sure(s) [`mɛʒɚ(z)] Track 3848

動 度量單位、尺寸

▶Have you gotten your waist measured yet?
你量腰圍了沒？

me·chan·ic [mə`kænɪk] Track 3849

名 機械工

▶There is not a mechanic who hasn't had such problems.
沒有一個技工不會碰到此類問題的。

me·chan·i·cal [mə`kænɪkḷ] Track 3850

形 機械工、技工

▶They were using a mechanical shovel to clear up the streets.
他們在用機械鏟土機清理街道。

mem·o·ra·ble [`mɛmərəbḷ] Track 3851

形 值得紀念的

▶I think graduation is a memorable event.
我認為畢業是一件難忘的事。

文法字詞解析

大家可能學過 memory 是「記憶、回憶」的意思，而大家可能也學過 able 是「能夠」的意思。既然 memorable 是由「能夠回憶」所組成，也難怪它的意思是「值得紀念的」了。

me·mo·ri·al [mə`morɪəl] Track 3852

名 紀念品 形 紀念的

▶名 They erected（豎立） a memorial for those killed in the war.他們為戰爭中犧牲的人豎立了紀念碑。

▶形 He made an entry of the memorial events in his diary.
他把值得紀念的大事記入日記中。

mer·cy [`mɝsɪ] Track 3853

名 慈悲

▶Don't you think that there is no use asking for his mercy?
你不覺得祈求他的同情是沒用的嗎？

mere [mɪr] Track 3854

形 僅僅、不過

▶I don't believe that you want to meet him for the mere purpose of talking.
我不相信你僅僅是為了談話才想見他的。

mer·it [ˋmɛrɪt]
Track 3855

名 價值

▶She has many merits, but being punctual（準時的）is not one of them.
她有很多優點，但準時偏偏不是其中一項。

mes·sen·ger [ˋmɛsn̩dʒɚ]
Track 3856

名 使者、信差

▶Can you act as a messenger for me?
你可以幫我帶個訊息嗎？

mess·y [ˋmɛsɪ]
Track 3857

形 髒亂的 同 dirty 髒的

▶Your bedroom is always so messy.
你的臥室老是這麼亂。

mi·cro·scope [ˋmaɪkrəˏskop]
Track 3858

名 顯微鏡

▶Germs can only be seen with the aid of a microscope because they are too small.
只有借助顯微鏡才能看得見細菌，因為它們太微小了。

實用片語用語
with the aid of... 經由（某物）的幫助

mild [maɪld]
Track 3859

形 溫和的

▶John is a mild-mannered man who never raises his voice.
約翰是一個溫和的人，他從不抬高嗓門說話。

min·er·al [ˋmɪnərəl]
Track 3860

名 礦物

▶Would you please give me a bottle of mineral water? I am thirsty.
請給我一瓶礦泉水好嗎？我渴了。

min·i·mum [ˋmɪnəməm]
Track 3861

名 最小量 形 最小的

▶名 Would you let me know if there is a minimum for the first deposit?
您能不能告訴我第一次儲蓄有沒有最低限額？

▶形 What's the minimum wage per hour if I work here?
如果我在這裡工作的話，最低薪水是每小時多少錢？

萬用延伸句型
Would you let me know if...?
你可以告訴我是否……嗎？

min·is·ter [ˋmɪnɪstɚ]
Track 3862

名 神職人員、部長

▶The minister has indicated that he may resign next year.
該部長已暗示他明年可能辭職。

min·is·try [ˋmɪnɪstrɪ]
Track 3863

名 牧師、部長、部

▶Not everyone knows that the university is under the direct control of Ministry of Education.
不是每個人都知道這所大學直屬教育部管理。

mis·chief [ˋmɪstʃɪf]

Track 3864

名 胡鬧、危害

▶The children love making mischief.
這些孩子最愛惡作劇了。

實用片語用語
make mischief 惡作劇

mis·er·a·ble [ˋmɪzərəbl̩]

Track 3865

形 不幸的

▶There are still many people whose living conditions are miserable.
仍有許多人的生活條件是很艱苦的。

mis·for·tune [mɪsˋfɔrtʃən]

Track 3866

名 不幸

▶I'm really sorry for the poor girl who has the misfortune to get married to him.
我真同情那個不幸和他結婚的可憐女孩啊。

實用片語用語
get married to sb. 和某人結婚

mis·lead [mɪsˋlid]

Track 3867

動 誤導

▶The advice of the aged will not mislead you.
不聽老人言，吃虧在眼前。

文法字詞解析
mislead 的動詞變化：mislead, misled, misled

mis·un·der·stand [ˌmɪsʌndɚˋstænd]

Track 3868

動 誤解

▶He is not good at talking; it is no wonder that his intentions were misunderstood.
他很不擅長說話，難怪他的意圖被誤解了。

文法字詞解析
misunderstand 的動詞變化：misunderstand, misunderstood, misunderstood

mod·er·ate [ˋmadərɪt]

Track 3869

形 適度的、溫和的

▶Do you mind if the position requires moderate travel?
本職缺需要適度的出差，你介意嗎？

mod·est [ˋmadɪst]

Track 3870

形 謙虛的

▶He isn't very modest but sometimes geniuses are like that.
他不怎麼謙虛，不過天才有時候就是這樣嘛。

mod·es·ty [ˋmadəstɪ]

Track 3871

名 謙虛、有禮

▶Her fake modesty bugs her classmates a lot.
她假裝謙虛的態度讓她的同學們覺得有點煩。

mon·i·tor [ˋmanətɚ]

Track 3872

名 監視器 動 監視

▶名 Why don't we install a monitor in the meeting room?
何不在會議室安裝一個監視器呢？

▶動 They monitored his phone calls during this period of time.
他們在這段時間監聽他的電話。

實用片語用語
computer monitor 電腦螢幕
例如：My computer monitor isn't quite wide enough.
我的電腦螢幕不夠寬。

month·ly [ˋmʌnθlɪ] Track 3873

名 月刊 形 每月一次的

▶名 It is clear that the monthly has been popular since it came out.顯然這個月刊自從出版以來就一直很受歡迎。

▶形 The rent for his apartment is his biggest monthly expense.
公寓的租金是他每月最大的一筆開支。

mon·u·ment [ˋmɑnjəmənt] Track 3874

名 紀念碑

▶Would you please take a photo of me in front of the Washington Monument?
請您幫我在華盛頓紀念碑前照張相好嗎？

more·o·ver [morˋovɚ] Track 3875

副 並且、此外

▶The composition is not well written, and moreover, there are many spelling mistakes in it.
這篇作文寫得不好，而且，還有許多拼字錯誤。

文法字詞解析
moreover 是個比較正式的字，用來補充說明前面的資訊或是加強論點，多半用在書寫而非口語中。

most·ly [ˋmostlɪ] Track 3876

副 多半、主要地

▶The audience consists mostly of women.
觀眾多數都是婦女。

實用片語用語
consist of 由……組成

mo·ti·vate [ˋmotəˏvet] Track 3877

動 刺激、激發

▶Do you know how to motivate a team to succeed?
你知道如何激勵團隊以達到成功嗎？

mo·ti·va·tion [ˏmotəˋveʃən] Track 3878

名 動機

▶You can do anything if you've got the motivation.
只要有了動力，什麼都可以做到。

moun·tain·ous [ˋmaʊntənəs] Track 3879

形 多山的

▶He used to live in a mountainous district.
他過去住在山區。

mow [mo] Track 3880

動 收割

▶Can you mow the lawn later when it's less hot?
待會比較不熱的時候你去割個草坪好不好？

文法字詞解析
「割草機」則可以稱為「lawn mower」。

MTV/mu·sic tel·e·vi·sion Track 3881

[ˋmjuzɪk ˋtɛləˏvɪʒən]

名 音樂電視頻道

▶The MTV channels aren't as popular as they used to be.
這些音樂電視頻道沒有像以前那麼受歡迎了。

mud·dy [ˋmʌdɪ] Track 3882

形 泥濘的

▶Would you please help me take off these muddy boots?
請幫我脫掉這滿是泥漿的靴子好嗎？

mul·ti·ple [ˋmʌltəpl̩] Track 3883

形 複數的、多數的

▶He is a man of multiple achievements. 他是個有許多成就的人。

實用片語用語

multiple-personality 多重人格

例如：He has multiple-personality disorder but at least two of his personalities seem quite fine with that.

他是多重人格症患者，不過其中至少有兩個人格似乎覺得這樣挺好的。

mur·der·er [ˋmɝdərɚ] Track 3884

名 兇手

▶It's too hard for him to find the murderer without any help.
沒有任何協助的話，他一個人很難找到兇手。

mur·mur [ˋmɝmɚ] Track 3885

名 低語 動 細語、抱怨

▶名 I heard a low murmur of conversation in the hall.
我聽到大廳裡有竊竊私語聲。

▶動 He murmured something, but I didn't catch what he said.
他嘀咕了一句什麼話，可是我沒聽清楚。

mus·tache [ˋmʌstæʃ] Track 3886

名 髭

▶Why don't you shave off your mustache? It grows so fast.
為什麼不刮掉你的鬍子呢？它長得太快了。

實用片語用語

milk mustache 牛奶鬍鬚

用來描述喝完牛奶時上嘴唇沾上牛奶，有如白白的鬍鬚一般的狀況。

例如：You have a milk mustache. Go wipe it off.

你有一片牛奶鬍鬚，去擦掉吧。

mu·tu·al [ˋmjutʃʊəl] Track 3887

形 相互的、共同的

▶We found that we had a mutual friend.
我們發現我們有一個共同的朋友。

文法字詞解析

在社群網站正夯的這個年代，mutual 這個單字還多了一個含意，就是「我有關注你，你也有關注我」，這種兩邊互相有關注、互相有加好友（而不是一方單方面追蹤）的狀況達成時，兩人的關係就可以稱為「mutuals」，當名詞使用。

mys·te·ri·ous [mɪsˋtɪrɪəs] Track 3888

形 神祕的

▶There are many mysterious stories about the Egyptian（埃及的）pyramids（金字塔）. 關於埃及金字塔有許多神祕的故事。

name·ly [ˋnemlɪ] Track 3889

副 即、就是

▶I think there is only one person good enough to do this job, namely you. 我覺得只有一個人足夠優秀能肩負此任，那就是你。

na·tion·al·i·ty [ˌnæʃənˋælətɪ] Track 3890

名 國籍、國民

▶Not all the people think that people of different nationalities can live together harmoniously（和睦地）.
不是所有人都認為不同國籍的人能和睦地生活在一起。

near·sight·ed [ˋnɪrˋsaɪtɪd]
Track 3891

形 近視的

▶It is hard for a nearsighted person to see distant objects clearly.
一個近視的人很難看清楚遠處的物體。

文法字詞解析
相反地，「遠視的」就可以說成farsighted。此外，farsighted還有「有遠見的」的意思，畢竟「遠視」也可以說成是「看得比較遠」吧。

need·y [ˋnidɪ]
Track 3892

形 貧窮的、貧困的 同 poor 貧窮的

▶There are plenty of needy families in our village.
我們村裡有很多貧困家庭。

ne·glect [nɪˋglɛkt]
Track 3893

名 不注意、不顧 動 疏忽

▶名 His neglect of his children caused them to drift away from him. 他對自己孩子不關心的態度，讓他們逐漸離他而去。

▶動 It is bad for us to pay attention to one side and neglect the other. 只顧一方面，不顧另一方面，對我們是不好的。

實用片語用語
neglect to...（因疏忽而）沒有做到某事
例如：I neglected to lock the door when I left.
我離開的時候疏忽了，忘記鎖門。

ne·go·ti·ate [nɪˋgoʃɪˏet]
Track 3894

動 商議、談判

▶He successfully negotiated a new contract with her company.
他成功地跟她的公司商定了一個新合約。

nev·er·the·less/ none·the·less [ˏnɛvəðəˋlɛs]/[ˏnʌnðəˋlɛs]
Track 3895

副 儘管如此、然而

▶She said she didn't want to go. Nevertheless, her parents still forced her to.
她說她不想去，儘管如此，她的父母還是強迫她去了。

night·mare [ˋnaɪtˏmɛr]
Track 3896

名 惡夢、夢魘

▶I had a nightmare about being knifed by a five-legged man last night.
我昨天晚上做了一個惡夢，夢到被一個五隻腳的男人拿刀砍。

non·sense [ˋnɑnsɛns]
Track 3897

名 廢話、無意義的話

▶In fact, I don't think what he said was total nonsense.
事實上，我覺得他說的話不全是一派胡言。

實用片語用語
talk nonsense 胡言亂語
例如：That man does nothing but talk nonsense all day.
那個男人每天除了胡言亂語外什麼都不做。

noun [naʊn]
Track 3898

名 名詞

▶There is no point in using so many nouns of the same meaning in an article.
在文章中使用太多同義名詞沒有多大意義。

now·a·days [ˋnaʊəˏdez]
Track 3899

副 當今、現在

▶Nowadays more and more people like to travel abroad.
現在越來越多的人喜歡出國旅遊了。

nu·cle·ar [ˋnjuklɪɚ]

Track 3900

形 核子的

▶The nuclear bomb is powerful enough to damage all these villages. 核彈威力無比，能摧毀所有這些村莊。

實用片語用語

nuclear war 核子戰爭

例如：Nuclear war is something I hope never happens.

希望核戰永遠不要發生。

nu·mer·ous [ˋnjumərəs]

Track 3901

形 為數眾多的

▶There are numerous stars shining in the sky.

天空中群星閃爍。

nurs·er·y [ˋnɝsərɪ]

Track 3902

名 托兒所

▶I am afraid that I have to resign my child to the care of the nursery. 恐怕我得把孩子交給托兒所照顧了。

ny·lon [ˋnaɪlɑn]

Track 3903

名 尼龍

▶Don't you think nylon really changed people's life at that time?

難道你不覺得尼龍確實改變了當時人們的生活嗎？

實用片語用語

nylon pants 尼龍做的長褲

例如：I look ridiculous in these nylon pants.

我穿這尼龍長褲看起來超滑稽的。

o·be·di·ence [əˋbidjəns]

Track 3904

名 服從、遵從

▶Some people believe that children should be taught obedience.

有些人相信孩子必須被教導要服從。

萬用延伸句型

Some people believe that... 有些人相信……

o·be·di·ent [əˋbidɪənt]

Track 3905

形 服從的

▶The obedient students listened to their teacher's every word.

那些乖巧的學生非常聽老師的話。

ob·jec·tion [əbˋdʒɛkʃən]

Track 3906

名 反對

▶There is no objection to your opening the window.

你開窗並沒有什麼不可以的。

ob·jec·tive [əbˋdʒɛktɪv]

Track 3907

形 實體的、客觀的 名 目標 同 neutral 中立的 同 goal 目標

▶形 You should try to be more objective about it.

你應該儘量客觀地對待此事。

▶名 The objective of every game is to win.

任何遊戲的目標都是要贏。

文法字詞解析

objective 是「客觀的」，相反地「主觀的」則是 subjective。

ob·ser·va·tion [ˌɑbzɝˋveʃən]

Track 3908

名 觀察力

▶Observation is the best teacher. 觀察是最好的老師。

ob·sta·cle [ˋabstəkḷ]

Track 3909

名 障礙物、妨礙

▶He came in first place in the obstacle race.
他在障礙賽中獲得第一名。

實用片語用語
come in first place 得第一名

ob·tain [əbˋten]

Track 3910

動 獲得

▶She failed to obtain a scholarship.
她沒有獲得獎學金。

oc·ca·sion·al [əˋkeʒənḷ]

Track 3911

形 應景的、偶爾的

▶I enjoy an occasional night out at the theater; what about you?
我偶爾晚上會出去看戲，你呢？

oc·cu·pa·tion [ˏakjəˋpeʃən]

Track 3912

名 職業

▶Would you please state your name, age and occupation?
請說明您的姓名、年齡和職業好嗎？

oc·cu·py [ˋakjəˏpaɪ]

Track 3913

動 佔有、花費（時間）

▶The aliens have occupied earth.
外星人佔據了地球。

of·fend [əˋfɛnd]

Track 3914

動 使不愉快、使憤怒、冒犯

▶A wise man tries not to offend people.
明智的人會盡量不得罪人。

萬用延伸句型
try not to... 試著盡量不做某事

of·fense [əˋfɛns]

Track 3915

名 冒犯、進攻

▶Offense is the best defense when playing sports.
在運動場上，進攻是最好的防禦。

of·fen·sive [əˋfɛnsɪv]

Track 3916

形 令人不快的

▶He likes using offensive language with his brothers.
他喜歡和他的兄弟使用一些無禮的語言。

實用片語用語
offensive language 冒犯人的話語

op·er·a [ˋapərə]

Track 3917

名 歌劇

▶We are planning to go to the opera this Sunday; would you like to go with us? 我們計畫這個星期天去看歌劇表演，你想不想跟我們一起去呢？

op·er·a·tion [ˏapəˋreʃən]

Track 3918

名 作用、操作

▶Was the operation successful, doctor?
醫生，手術成功嗎？

實用片語用語
eye laser operation 眼睛雷射手術
例如：How much does an eye laser operation cost?
眼睛雷射手術要多少錢呢？

op·pose [ə`poz]

Track 3919

動 和……起衝突、反對 反 agree 同意

▶It is no wonder that he is strongly（強烈地）opposed to the plan.難怪他強烈反對這一項計畫。

o·ral [`orəl]

Track 3920

名 口試 形 口述的

▶名 Not everyone is able to pass the orals easily.
不是每個人都能毫不費力地通過口試。

▶形 Not every student has good written and oral English skills.
不是每個學生都有良好的英語寫作及口語能力。

文法字詞解析
因為口試是可以一場一場數出來的考試，所以它是可數名詞。

or·bit [`ɔrbɪt]

Track 3921

名 軌道 動 把……放入軌道

▶名 In recent years a number of communication satellites were put into orbit.
近年來，有很多通訊衛星被送上軌道。

▶動 The earth orbits the sun.
地球沿軌道繞著太陽運行。

or·ches·tra [`ɔrkɪstrə]

Track 3922

名 樂隊、樂團

▶Not all people know that the orchestra was established under the patronage（贊助）of the government.
不是所有人都知道這個交響樂團是在政府贊助下成立的。

文法字詞解析
patron 是贊助者、資助者的意思，所以 patronage 就是「（金錢上的）贊助」。

or·gan·ic [ɔr`gænɪk]

Track 3923

形 器官的、有機的

▶The rich old lady eats organic food only.
那位有錢的老太太只吃有機食品。

oth·er·wise [`ʌðɚ͵waɪz]

Track 3924

副 否則、要不然

▶I've been sick these days; otherwise I would do it myself.
我最近不太舒服，否則這件事我就親自去做了。

out·come [`aʊt͵kʌm]

Track 3925

名 結果、成果 同 result 結果

▶I think there can be but one outcome to this affair.
我認為這件事只可能有一種結局。

out·stand·ing [`aʊt`stændɪŋ]

Track 3926

形 傲人的、傑出的

▶He has become one of the most outstanding writers at that time. 他成為當時最傑出的作家之一。

文法字詞解析
與 outstanding 長得有點像的一個片語是「stand out」。它也有「特別的」的意思，但不見得一定是「特別傑出的」，也有可能純粹只是特別。
例　如：He stands out in the crowd because of his green hair.
因為他的頭髮是綠色的，所以在人群中特別顯眼。

o·val [`ovl̩]

Track 3927

名 橢圓形 形 橢圓形的

▶名 The mirror is an oval shape. 那個鏡子是橢圓形的。

▶形 She has a lovely oval face. 她長著一張可愛的鵝蛋臉。

o·ver·come [ˏovɚˋkʌm]　Track 3928

動 擊敗、克服

▶There is no difficulty in the world that they cannot overcome.
世界上沒有任何困難是他們無法克服的。

文法字詞解析
overcome 的動詞變化：
overcome, overcame, overcome

o·ver·look [ˏovɚˋlʊk]　Track 3929

動 俯瞰、忽略

▶I'll overlook your mistake this time.
我這次就容忍你的錯誤吧。

o·ver·night [ˋovɚˋnaɪt]　Track 3930

形 徹夜的、過夜的 副 整夜地

▶形 Not every actress can win overnight fame with her first film.不是每個女演員都能第一部電影就一舉成名。

▶副 Not every person is lucky enough to became rich overnight.
不是每個人都能幸運地一夜致富。

o·ver·take [ˏovɚˋtek]　Track 3931

動 趕上、突擊

▶He had to drive very fast to overtake the opponent.
他必須開得很快，才能超過敵手。

文法字詞解析
overtake 的動詞變化：
overtake, overtook, overtaken

o·ver·throw [ˏovɚˋθro]　Track 3932

動 推翻、瓦解

▶Their attempt to overthrow the government ended in nothing.
他們推翻政府的企圖終成泡影。

文法字詞解析
overthrow 的動詞變化：
overthrow, overthrew,overthrown

ox·y·gen [ˋɑksədʒən]　Track 3933

名 氧（氧氣）

▶It is quite clear that she died from lack of oxygen.
很顯然她是因為缺氧而死的。

pa·ce [pes]　Track 3934

名 一步、步調 動 踱步

▶名 It is hard for their country to keep pace with other developed countries.
他們國家很難趕上其他已開發國家。

▶動 Why is he pacing around in the living room?
他在客廳裡走來走去幹嘛。

pan·el [ˋpænl]　Track 3935

名 方格、平板

▶They invented a panel which can make full use of the sunshine.
他們發明了一種能充分利用太陽光的平板。

實用片語用語
control panel 控制台
例如：Open up the control panel and I'll show you how to change the settings.
把控制台打開來，我教你怎麼改變設定。

par·a·chute [ˋpærə͵ʃut]

Track 3936

名 降落傘 動 空投

▶名 I don't think anyone dares to jump out of the plane without a parachute.
我覺得沒人敢不用降落傘就跳出飛機。

▶動 I don't think he will parachute the supplies to them.
認為他不會空投補給品給他們。

實用片語用語

parachute jump = parachuting 跳傘
例如：Parachuting is a kind of adventurous sports.
跳傘是一項極限運動。

par·a·graph [ˋpærə͵græf]

Track 3937

名 段落

▶It is hard for us to understand the whole paragraph given by our teacher.
我們很難讀懂老師給的那一整段文章。

par·tial [ˋparʃəl]

Track 3938

形 部分的

▶Do you mind if I only make a partial payment for these goods?
你介意我對這些貨物先付部分的錢嗎？

par·tic·i·pa·tion [par͵tɪsəˋpeʃən]

Track 3939

名 參加

▶His participation is not welcomed by the rest of us.
他的參與不受我們其他人的歡迎。

實用片語用語

be welcomed by... 受……的歡迎

par·ti·ci·ple [ˋpartəsəpḷ]

Track 3940

名 分詞

▶Past participles can get really confusing.
過去分詞有時候真是超難懂的。

part·ner·ship [ˋpartnɚ͵ʃɪp]

Track 3941

名 合夥

▶I wish Mike could take me into partnership in his firm.
真希望麥克能讓我成為他公司的合夥人。

pas·sive [ˋpæsɪv]

Track 3942

形 被動的

▶He is a very passive person, never talking unless talked to.
他很被動，別人不跟他講話，他就不講話。

實用片語用語

passive-aggressive 被動攻擊
passive 是「消極、被動的」，而 aggressive 則是「攻擊的」。要怎麼樣才能夠又被動卻又能攻擊人呢？其實這類的情況在我們的生活中很常見到。舉例來說，像是「好吧，好啦，我想這樣做應該也是可以啦……」這類的句子，看似像是同意，實際上對方聽得出來你根本不同意，就是「被動攻擊」的表現。對付討厭的人時，表面上顯得很和平，背地裡做一些對方討厭的小事（例如打字時大聲地敲鍵盤），也是「被動攻擊」的表現。

pas·ta [ˋpastə]

Track 3943

名 麵團、義大利麵

▶What do you want to eat for lunch? How about pasta?
你午餐想吃什麼呢？義大利麵怎麼樣？

peb·ble [ˋpɛbḷ]

Track 3944

名 小圓石

▶I picked up a pebble and threw it into the water.
我撿起了一個石子，把它扔進了水裡。

pe·cu·liar [pɪˋkjuljɚ] Track 3945

形 獨特的 同 special 特別的

▶The wine on the table has a peculiar taste.
桌上的酒有種怪怪的味道。

ped·al [ˋpɛdḷ] Track 3946

名 踏板 動 踩踏板

▶名 He didn't have enough time to put his foot down on the brake pedal. 他沒有足夠的時間把腳放到煞車踏板上。

▶動 You must pedal rapidly（迅速地）enough to make the machine run smoothly（平穩地）.
你必須快速地踩踏板，才能使機器運轉平穩。

實用片語用語
bike pedal 腳踏車踏板
例如：I'd love to ride your bike but I can't reach the bike pedals.
我很樂意騎你的腳踏車，但我踩不到踏板。

peer [pɪr] Track 3947

名 同輩 動 凝視

▶名 As peers, there are many interesting（有趣的）things we can talk about.
身為同輩，我們有很多有趣的事情可以談論。

▶動 There is no need to peer at them from behind the curtain.
沒必要從簾子後面偷看他們。

pen·al·ty [ˋpɛnḷtɪ] Track 3948

名 懲罰

▶I think a small penalty is quite enough.
我覺得一個小小的懲罰就足夠了。

per·cent [pɚˋsɛnt] Track 3949

名 百分比

▶I am afraid that we can give you only a five percent discount.
恐怕我們只能給你九五折優惠。

文法字詞解析
要說「某物的百分之多少」可以用「（數字）percent of……」來表示。
例如：Forty percent of the students take the bus to school.
40% 的學生搭乘公車上學。

per·cent·age [pɚˋsɛntɪdʒ] Track 3950

名 百分率

▶It is a surprise that the film should attract a large percentage of the people.
這部電影竟然吸引了大部分的觀衆，真令人驚訝。

per·fec·tion [pɚˋfɛkʃən] Track 3951

名 完美

▶His performance was sheer（十足的）perfection, wasn't it?
他的表演十分完美，不是嗎？

per·fume [ˋpɝfjum] Track 3952

名 香水、賦予香味

▶Will you tell me what kind of perfume you like best?
你能告訴我你最喜歡哪種香水嗎？

per·ma·nent [ˋpɝmənənt] Track 3953

形 永久的

▶Don't you want to get a permanent job?
難道你不想得到一份固定的工作嗎？

per·sua·sion [pə`sweʒən] Track 3954

名 說服

▶He still doesn't want to leave his job even after a lot of persuasion.
多次勸說後，他仍然不想離開自己的工作。

per·sua·sive [pə`swesɪv] Track 3955

形 有說服力的

▶I don't think his argument is persuasive enough to convince everyone.
我認為他的論點說服力不強，無法說服大家。

文法字詞解析
persuasive 是從 persuade 這個字延伸而來的。要注意的是，persuade 和 convince 的意思並不一樣，前者是「說服、勸服某人去做某事」，後者則是「使某人相信某種說法是真的」。

pes·si·mis·tic [͵pɛsə`mɪstɪk] Track 3956

形 悲觀的 反 optimistic 樂觀的

▶There is no reason to be pessimistic about your future.
沒有理由對你的未來感到悲觀。

pet·al [`pɛtl̩] Track 3957

名 花瓣

▶She enjoys taking pictures of fallen petals.
她喜歡拍掉在地上的花瓣的照片。

phe·nom·e·non [fə`namə͵nan] Track 3958

名 現象

▶Don't you think it's a common phenomenon? It happens almost everywhere（到處）.
難道你不認為這是一個普遍的現象嗎？它幾乎到處都在發生。

實用片語用語
common phenomenon 普遍現象

phi·los·o·pher [fə`lasəfə] Track 3959

名 哲學家

▶In my opinion, Plato is not only a good philosopher, but also an outstanding thinker（思想家）.
在我看來，柏拉圖不但是一位優秀的哲學家，而且還是一位出色的思想家。

phil·o·soph·i·cal [͵fɪlə`safɪkl̩] Track 3960

形 哲學的

▶It is difficult for the students to answer this philosophical problem.
對於學生而言這個哲學問題們很難回答。

phi·los·o·phy [fə`lasəfɪ] Track 3961

名 哲學

▶Will you tell me what your philosophy on life is?
能告訴我你的生活哲學是什麼嗎？

pho·tog·ra·phy [fə`tagrəfɪ] Track 3962

名 攝影學

▶It is not easy for you to learn photography by yourself.
要自學攝影並不是很容易。

實用片語用語
photography club 攝影社
例如：The students in the photography club meet in this classroom every week.
攝影社的學生們每週在這間教室見面。

phys·i·cal [ˋfɪzɪkḷ] Track 3963

形 身體的

▶It's five o'clock now, time for us to do some physical training (訓練). 現在五點了，我們該進行體育訓練了。

phy·si·cian/doc·tor Track 3964

[fəˋzɪʃən]/[ˋdɑktɚ]

名 （內科）醫師

▶I hope the physician can save his life.
我希望醫生能挽救他的生命。

phys·i·cist [ˋfɪzɪsɪst] Track 3965

名 物理學家

▶It is quite clear that what the physicist thinks about the world differs from others.
很明顯，這位物理學家對世界的看法與其他人不同。

phys·ics [ˋfɪzɪks] Track 3966

名 物理學

▶I wish I could do well in physics.
我希望能把物理學得很好。

實用片語用語
physics test 物理測驗
例如：I failed the physics test again.
我物理又考砸了。

pi·an·ist [pɪˋænɪst] Track 3967

名 鋼琴師

▶His dream was to become a pianist. 他的夢想是成為鋼琴師。

pick·poc·ket [ˋpɪk͵pɑkɪt] Track 3968

名 扒手

▶When the pickpocket was about to leave, he was caught by the police. 扒手正要離開的時候被警察抓住了。

pi·o·neer [͵paɪəˋnɪr] Track 3969

名 先鋒、開拓者 動 開拓

▶名 The old man was the pioneer in modern medicine study.
這位老人正是現代醫學研究的先驅。

▶動 It was this lady who pioneered the use of the drug.
正是這名女士最先使用這種藥品。

pi·rate [ˋpaɪrət] Track 3970

名 海盜 動 掠奪

▶名 The children enjoy hearing stories about pirates.
這些孩子們很喜歡聽海盜的故事。

▶動 It's illegal to pirate files that are not yours.
盜版別人的檔案是不合法的。

文法字詞解析
由於「盜版」版權不屬於自己的東西這樣的行為和海盜似乎也沒什麼兩樣，因此 pirate 這個字也可以拿來表示「盜版」的意思。

plen·ti·ful [ˋplɛntɪfəl] Track 3971

形 豐富的

▶The weather has been very nice; it is no wonder that the farmers had a plentiful harvest this year.
天氣狀況一直都很好，難怪今年農民們獲得了大豐收。

plot [plɑt]

Track 3972

名 陰謀、情節 動 圖謀、分成小塊

▶名 What do you think of the plot of the latest film, Susan?
蘇珊，妳覺得這部最新影片的情節怎麼樣？

▶動 The new factory's district is all plotted out.
新廠區的範圍都已劃定。

plu·ral [ˋplʊrəl]

Track 3973

名 複數 形 複數的

▶名 Does the student know the plural of this word?
這個學生知道這個單字的複數嗎？

▶形 Plural marriage still exists in the area.
這個地區還存在著一夫多妻制。

實用片語用語
plural marriage 一夫多妻或一妻多夫的婚姻
除此之外，名詞「polygamy」也有同樣的意思。字首「poly-」表示「多」的意思，而「gamy」則是「婚姻」的意思。

p.m./P.M. [ˋpiˏɛm]

Track 3974

副 下午

▶I am afraid that he is out of the office in the morning. How about meeting him at 3 p.m.?
恐怕他上午不在辦公室。下午三點見他怎麼樣？

poi·son·ous [ˋpɔɪzəs]

Track 3975

形 有毒的

▶He was bitten by a poisonous snake.
他被毒蛇咬到了。

pol·ish [ˋpəlʃən]

Track 3976

名 磨光 動 擦亮

▶名 Will you give your shoes a polish? We will be going to a party tonight.
你能把你的鞋子擦一擦嗎？今晚我們要出席一場宴會。

▶動 Could you help me polish my article tonight, Professor Li?
李教授，請您今晚幫我潤飾一下文章好嗎？

文法字詞解析
就像第二個例句裡的用法，「polish」不只表示具體的「擦亮」，還可以解釋成「修飾、潤飾」文章。

pol·lu·tion [ˋpɑlɪʃ]

Track 3977

名 污染

▶The air pollution can't be reduced unless the government can pass a new law.
除非國家能頒佈新法，否則空氣污染無法減輕。

pop·u·lar·i·ty [ˏpɑpjəˋlærətɪ]

Track 3978

名 名望、流行

▶Famous people have to pay a high price for popularity, but not all the people know that.
為了出名，名人要付出很高的代價，但不是所有人都知道這一點。

實用片語用語
pay a high price for... 為……付出很高的代價

port·a·ble [ˋportəbl̩]

Track 3979

形 可攜帶的

▶Why not buy a portable radio? I think it's more convenient.
為什麼不買台手提音響呢？我覺得它更方便。

por·ter [ˋportɚ]

Track 3980

名 搬運工

▶Will you tell me how much I should give the porter as a tip?
你能告訴我應該給行李搬運工多少小費嗎？

por·tray [porˋtre]

Track 3981

動 描繪 同 depict 描繪

▶The book portrays his personal experiences.
這本書描繪了他的個人經歷。

pos·sess [pəˋzɛs]

Track 3982

動 擁有

▶The country possesses rich mineral deposits.
這個國家擁有豐富的礦藏。

文法字詞解析
被鬼「附身」時，身體等於是被對方所「擁有」了，因此「附身」也可以用 possess 這個字來表示。

pos·ses·sion [pəˋzɛʃən]

Track 3983

名 擁有物

▶A true friend is the best possession.
真誠的朋友是最寶貴的財富。

pre·cise [prɪˋsaɪs]

Track 3984

形 明確的 同 exact 確切的

▶It is difficult for the police to get precise information about this man. 警察很難獲得有關此人的準確資訊。

pre·dict [prɪˋdɪkt]

Track 3985

動 預測

▶I can't predict when I'll meet her again.
我無法預測什麼時候會再見到她。

文法字詞解析
在後面加上表示「能夠」的字尾「-able」，就能變成形容詞 predictable（能夠預測的）。再在前面加上表示「不、沒有」的字首「un-」，就能變成形容詞 unpredictable（無法預測的）。

pref·er·a·ble [ˋprɛfərəl̩]

Track 3986

形 較好的

▶Health without riches is preferable to riches without health.
有健康而無財富比有財富而無健康更好。

preg·nan·cy [ˋprɛgnənsɪ]

Track 3987

名 懷孕

▶Do you mind telling me what you ate during this pregnancy?
你能告訴我你這次懷孕期間都吃了些什麼嗎？

preg·nant [ˋprɛgnənt]

Track 3988

形 懷孕的

▶What? She's six months pregnant? I didn't even notice that.
什麼？她懷孕六個月了？我竟然都沒注意到。

文法字詞解析
要說「懷了……」可以用「pregnant with...」來表示。例如「懷了雙胞胎」，就是「pregnant with twins」，「懷了兒子」可以說「pregnant with a boy」。

prep·o·si·tion [ˌprɛpəˋzɪʃən]

Track 3989

名 介系詞

▶You must put a preposition between the two words so that they can state a precise meaning together. 你必須在兩個字之間放入一個介詞，這樣它們才能一起表達出確切的意思。

pre·sen·ta·tion [ˌprɛznˋteʃən] Track 3990

名 贈送、呈現

▶He gave a presentation today in class.
他今天在課堂上做了報告。

pres·er·va·tion [ˌprɛzɚˋveʃən] Track 3991

名 保存

▶The china is in an excellent state of preservation.
這個瓷器被保存得極為完好。

實用片語用語
in a state of... 呈現……的狀態

pre·serve [prɪˋzɝv] Track 3992

動 保存、維護

▶Let's preserve our natural resources from now on, shall we?
讓我們從現在開始保護我們的自然資源好嗎？

pre·ven·tion [prɪˋvɛnʃən] Track 3993

名 預防

▶I am greatly convinced that prevention is better than a cure.
我深信預防重於治療。

prime [praɪm] Track 3994

名 初期 形 首要的 同 principal 首要的

▶名 The man could run 100 meters in 11 seconds in his prime.
這個男人在全盛時期一百公尺可以十一秒跑完。

▶形 This problem is a matter of prime importance.
這個問題是一個首要的問題。

實用片語用語
Prime Minister 首相、總理、專案經理
例如：The Prime Minister has declared that he will be resigning.
首相宣布要請辭了。

prim·i·tive [ˋprɪmətɪv] Track 3995

形 原始的 同 original 原始的

▶Our modern society is more advanced than the primitive society.現代社會比原始社會先進多了。

pri·va·cy [ˋpraɪvəsɪ] Track 3996

名 隱私

▶Don't you think it's a violation of your privacy?
難道你不覺得這是對你隱私的一種侵犯嗎？

priv·i·lege [ˋprɪvḷɪdʒ] Track 3997

名 特權 動 優待

▶名 No one has the right to grant（賦予）him such privilege.
沒人擁有賦予他這種特權的權利。

▶動 I'm privileged to enter this room.
我被給予了進入這間房間的特權。

實用片語用語
have the right to V. 有……的權力

pro·ce·dure [prəˋsidʒɚ] Track 3998

名 手續、程序

▶There is some confusion for me about the correct procedure for obtaining a visa（簽證）.
對取得簽證的正確手續我還有點不太明白。

pro·ceed [prə`sid] Track 3999

動 進行

▶Would you tell me how to proceed with the negotiation（談判）?
你能告訴我如何繼續進行這次的談判嗎？

pro·duc·tion [prə`dʌkʃən] Track 4000

名 製造

▶We must reduce the production cost, or we won't be getting any profits.
我們必須降低生產成本，不然我們根本沒辦法獲利啊。

文法字詞解析
除了「製造過程」、「製造」外，production 有時也可以拿來說「製造的成果」，也就是「成品」。例如電影公司製造出來的「電影」，就可以說是 production。

pro·duc·tive [prə`dʌktɪv] Track 4001

形 生產的、多產的

▶I don't think it was a productive meeting.
我覺得這不是一次富有成效的會議。

pro·fes·sion [prə`fɛʃən] Track 4002

名 專業

▶My father is a high school teacher by profession; what about your father?
我爸爸是一名高中老師，你爸爸呢？

pro·fes·sion·al [prə`fɛʃənl] Track 4003

名 專家 形 專業的

▶名 He is a real professional. Why don't we ask him for some advice?
他是個真正的專家，為什麼不問問他的意見呢？

▶形 Why not get some professional advice from the expert before you make the decision?
為何不在你做這個決定之前聽聽專家的意見呢？

pro·fes·sor [prə`fɛsɚ] Track 4004

名 教授

▶When he came to this university, he was the youngest professor there.
他來到這所大學的時候，就成為了那所大學裡最年輕的教授。

實用片語用語
assistant professor 助理教授
例如：The assistant professor isn't in his office right now.
那個助理教授現在不在辦公室。

prof·it·a·ble [`prɑfɪtəbl] Track 4005

形 有利的 同 beneficial 有利的

▶I don't think it's a deal that is profitable to all of the partners.
我認為這並不是一宗對所有合夥人都有利的買賣。

prom·i·nent [`prɑmənənt] Track 4006

形 突出的

▶He has a really prominent chin. 他的下巴很突出。

prom·is·ing [`prɑmɪsɪŋ] Track 4007

形 有可能的、有希望的

▶It is obvious that the result of the experiment is very promising.
顯然這次實驗的結果是很有希望的。

pro·mo·tion [prə`moʃən]

Track 4008

名 增進、促銷、升遷

▶It is great to hear about your promotion. Let's celebrate tonight.
聽到你升遷了真是太好了，我們今晚去慶祝一下吧。

實用片語用語
get a promotion 獲得升遷
例如：I'm just as surprised that I got a promotion as you are.
我能獲得升遷，我跟你一樣驚訝。

prompt [prɑmpt]

Track 4009

形 即時的 名 提詞

▶形 He was very prompt in dealing with the issue.
他非常即時地出面對應這項議題。

▶名 I think she needs to be given a prompt.
我覺得她需要人提詞。

pro·noun [`pronaʊn]

Track 4010

名 代名詞

▶"I", "you" and "he" are all personal pronouns.
I、you 和 he 都是人稱代名詞。

pro·nun·ci·a·tion [prə͵nʌnsɪ`eʃən]

Track 4011

名 發音

▶It is hard for us to imitate the pronunciation of native speakers.
我們很難模仿母語人士的發音。

實用片語用語
native speaker 母語人士

pros·per [`prɑspɚ]

Track 4012

動 興盛

▶The country is prospering because of its strong government.
這個國家正逐漸繁榮起來，是因為有了一個強而有力的政府。

pros·per·i·ty [prɑs`pɛrətɪ]

Track 4013

名 繁盛

▶I wish all of your family happiness and prosperity.
祝福您全家過得快樂、事業繁盛。

pros·per·ous [`prɑspərəs]

Track 4014

形 繁榮的

▶The town used to be a very prosperous one.
這個城鎮過去很繁榮。

pro·tein [`protiɪn]

Track 4015

名 蛋白質

▶Food that is rich in protein helps you build your strength.
富含蛋白質的食物有助於增強你的體質。

實用片語用語
be rich in... 含有豐富的……

pro·test [prə`tɛst]

Track 4016

名 抗議 動 反對、抗議

▶名 It is wrong for the government to turn a deaf ear to people's protests.
政府對人們的抗議充耳不聞，這是不對的。

▶動 He protested that he didn't do it, but they still punished him. 雖然他抗議說自己明明沒做，但他們還是處罰了他。

實用片語用語
turn a deaf ear to... 對……充耳不聞

prov·erb [ˋprɑvɝb] Track 4017

名 諺語

▶It's very difficult for us to trsanslate this proverb into English.
我們很難將這句諺語翻譯成英文。

psy·cho·log·i·cal [ˏsaɪkəˋlɑdʒɪkḷ] Track 4018

形 心理學的

▶The doctor said he had some psychological problems.
醫生說他有心理問題。

psy·chol·o·gist [saɪˋkɑlədʒɪst] Track 4019

名 心理學家

▶It was the psychologist, Sigmund Freud, who put forward a theory and shocked the entire world.
心理學家西格蒙德．佛洛伊德提出了一個震驚全世界的理論。

實用片語用語
put forward 提出（計畫、學說、想法）

psy·chol·o·gy [saɪˋkɑlədʒɪ] Track 4020

名 心理學

▶He obtained a degree in psychology this year; what about you?
他今年獲得了心理學學位，你呢？

pub·li·ca·tion [ˏpʌblɪˋkeʃən] Track 4021

名 發表、出版

▶As an editor, I don't think this article is suitable for publication.
作為一名編輯，我認為這篇文章不宜發表。

pub·lic·i·ty [pʌbˋlɪsətɪ] Track 4022

名 宣傳、出風頭

▶This incident was very famous at that time and got a lot of publicity.
這件事情在當時非常轟動，引起了公眾的極大關注。

pub·lish [ˋpʌblɪʃ] Track 4023

動 出版

▶I hope the writer can publish another book.
我希望作者能再出版一本書。

實用片語用語
get published 獲得出版
例如：His dream is to get published but so far he hasn't succeeded yet.
他的夢想就是能出書，但目前還沒有成功。

pub·lish·er [ˋpʌblɪʃɚ] Track 4024

名 出版者、出版社

▶Will you tell me why the publisher refused to publish this book?
你能告訴我出版社為什麼拒絕出版這本書嗎？

pur·suit [pɚˋsut] Track 4025

名 追求

▶There might be a lot of setbacks（挫折）and failures in his pursuit of success.
在他追求成功的路上也許會充滿挫折和失敗。

quake [kwek]

Track 4026

名 地震、震動 動 搖動、震動

▶名 Many people were killed in the biggest quake ever.
這次最嚴重的地震中死了很多人。

▶動 He stood there quaking with fear when the teacher scolded him. 老師責罵他的時候，他站在那兒嚇得直打哆嗦。

實用片語用語
quake with fear 驚恐地顫抖

quilt [kwɪlt]

Track 4027

名 棉被 動 把……製成被褥

▶名 I don't think the quilt is thick enough to protect him from the cold. 我覺得這條被子的厚度不足以為他禦寒。

▶動 Quilting the secret letters in his belt is still not safe enough.
把密信縫入他的腰帶還是不夠可靠。

quo·ta·tion [kwoˋteʃən]

Track 4028

名 引用

▶I'm afraid that I can't give you our quotation right now. Sorry for the inconvenience.
恐怕現在不能給您我們的報價，帶來不便敬請諒解。

rage [redʒ]

Track 4029

名 狂怒 動 暴怒 同 anger 憤怒

▶名 I wish he wouldn't always fly into a rage over nothing.
我希望他不要每次都沒事就勃然大怒。

▶動 She always rages against her husband over some household affairs.
她總是為一些家庭瑣事而對她的丈夫大發雷霆。

實用片語用語
1. fly into a rage 突然暴怒
2. rage against... 因……而發怒

rain·fall [ˋrenˏfɔl]

Track 4030

名 降雨量

▶There is too much rainfall in this area, isn't there?
這個地區的雨水太多了，不是嗎？

re·al·is·tic [rɪəˋlɪstɪk]

Track 4031

形 現實的

▶I don't think this plan you put forward is realistic enough.
我覺得你提出的計畫還不夠切合實際。

re·bel(1) [ˋrɛbl̩]

Track 4032

名 造反者、叛亂、謀反 同 revolt 叛亂

▶By the time the rebels appeared, most people didn't know what to do. 造反的人出現時，大多數人都不知道怎麼辦。

萬用延伸句型
by the time S1 + V1, S2 + V2
到……的時候，……。

re·bel(2) [rɪˋbɛl]

Track 4033

動 叛亂、謀反

▶It is a surprise that these people should choose to rebel against their government.
這些人竟然會選擇反叛政府，真令人驚訝。

re·call [ˋrɪkɔl]/[rɪˋkɔl]

Track 4034

名 取消、收回 動 回憶起、恢復

▶名 I believe that he has something to do with the temporary recall of embassy staff.
我想他跟這次大使館人員的臨時召回有關係。

▶動 I am afraid that we have to recall our diplomat in Russia.
恐怕我們得召回在俄羅斯的大使。

re·cep·tion [rɪˋsɛpʃən]

Track 4035

名 接受

▶They gave the ambassador a cool reception.
他們很冷淡地接待了這位大使。

文法字詞解析
因為飯店的櫃臺就是「接待、接受」顧客的地方，因此飯店的接待櫃臺也可稱為 reception。

rec·i·pe [ˋrɛsəpɪ]

Track 4036

名 食譜、秘訣

▶Why don't we try this new recipe introduced by the gourmet（美食家）?
為什麼不嘗試一下那位美食家所介紹的新食譜呢？

re·cite [rɪˋsaɪt]

Track 4037

動 背誦

▶Can you recite the poem written by the famous poet, Williams Blake? 你背得出著名詩人威廉．布雷克寫的詩嗎？

rec·og·ni·tion [ˏrɛkəgˋnɪʃən]

Track 4038

名 認知

▶I wish I could avoid recognition by wearing dark glasses.
真希望我戴上墨鏡就不會有人認出我來。

萬用延伸句型
I wish I could... 真希望我可以……（用於事實上做不到的事）

re·cov·er·y [rɪˋkʌvərɪ]

Track 4039

名 恢復

▶He won't make a quick recovery unless he agrees to receive an operation.
除非他能同意接受做手術，否則他無法很快康復。

rec·re·a·tion [ˏrɛkrɪˋeʃən]

Track 4040

名 娛樂

▶Will you tell me what kind of recreation you like best?
你能告訴我你最喜歡的娛樂是什麼嗎？

re·cy·cle [riˋsaɪkḷ]

Track 4041

動 循環利用

▶It is obvious that few people are aware of the importance of recycling at present.
很明顯，現在意識到資源回收的重要性的人並不多。

實用片語用語
be aware of... 注意到……

re·duc·tion [rɪ`dʌkʃən]

Track 4042

名 減少 同 decrease 減少

▸I am afraid that I have to ask you for a 10% reduction in price.
恐怕我必須要求你們在價格上降價百分之十。

re·fer [rɪ`fɝ]

Track 4043

動 參考、提及

▸Don't you think his remark refers to all of us in the company?
難道你不覺得他的話是針對公司所有人的嗎？

ref·er·ence [`rɛfərəns]

Track 4044

名 參考

▸I don't think the reference book is of any use to us.
我覺得這本參考書對我們沒什麼用處。

re·flect [rɪ`flɛkt]

Track 4045

動 反射

▸I think you must reflect upon how to answer the question.
我認為你必須思考一下如何回答那個問題。

實用片語用語

reflect upon 反思

re·flec·tion [rɪ`flɛkʃən]

Track 4046

名 反射、反省

▸Your clothes are a reflection of your personality.
一個人的衣著可以反映出其個性。

re·form [rɪ`fɔrm]

Track 4047

動 改進

▸The unfair systems must be reformed as soon as possible.
這些不合理的制度必須盡快改革。

re·fresh [rɪ`frɛʃ]

Track 4048

動 使恢復精神

▸How about refreshing yourself with a cup of tea before you go out? 在你出門前，喝杯茶提提神怎麼樣？

文法字詞解析

電腦網頁跑不動，等得不耐煩時，不是都會按下「重新整理」嗎？這個動作就叫作 refresh the page。

re·fresh·ment [rɪ`frɛʃmənt]

Track 4049

名 清爽、茶點

▸Would you like some refreshments while waiting?
在等待的時候，您要不要來點提神小點心呢？

ref·u·gee [ˏrɛfjʊ`dʒi]

Track 4050

名 難民

▸It is hard for us to handle the refugee problem properly.
我們很難適當地處理難民問題。

re·fus·al [rɪ`fjuzḷ]

Track 4051

名 拒絕 同 denial 拒絕、否認

▸Will you tell me what your reason for the refusal of payment is?你能告訴我你拒絕付款的理由是什麼嗎？

re·gard·ing [rɪˋgɑrdɪŋ]

Track 4052

介 關於

▶Do you mind telling me what you know regarding the case?
你介意告訴我關於這個案子你都知道些什麼嗎？

文法字詞解析
regarding 主要是用在比較正式的文章或演說中，來引導出相關的主題。另外還有一個很像的片語是「with regard to…」，不要搞混了。

reg·is·ter [ˋrɛdʒɪstɚ]

Track 4053

名 名單、註冊 動 登記、註冊

▶名 Have you filled out the hotel register? Can you tell me how to do it?
你已經填寫過了旅館登記簿嗎？你能告訴我如何填寫它嗎？

▶動 I don't know how to register for the website.
我不知道如何在這個網站上註冊。

reg·is·tra·tion [ˏrɛdʒɪˋstreʃən]

Track 4054

名 註冊

▶Would you mind telling me your registration fee?
請告知我你們的註冊費用是多少好嗎?

reg·u·late [ˋrɛgjəˏlet]

Track 4055

動 調節、管理

▶This equipment helps to regulate the temperature of the room.
這種設備有助於調節室內溫度。

reg·u·la·tion [ˏrɛgjəˋleʃən]

Track 4056

名 調整、法規

▶You must know well of the traffic regulations, or you can't get a driver's license.
你必須熟知這些交通規則，否則你就無法拿到駕照。

實用片語用語
know well of... 熟知（某事）

re·jec·tion [rɪˋdʒɛkʃən]

Track 4057

名 廢棄、拒絕

▶I was annoyed at her rejection of my proposal.
我為她拒絕我的提議而感到不快。

rel·a·tive [ˋrɛlətɪv]

Track 4058

形 相對的、有關係的 名 親戚

▶形 It's time for us to discuss some facts relative to the problem.
我們該討論一下與這個問題相關的一些事實了。

▶名 I have too many relatives to count.
我的親戚太多了，都數不清了。

re·lax·a·tion [ˏrilæksˋeʃən]

Track 4059

名 放鬆

▶It is hard for us to accept this routine that leaves no time for relaxation. 我們很難接受這種不留休息時間的規定。

re·lieve [rɪˋliv]

Track 4060

動 減緩

▶Not even the doctor knows how to relieve his pain.
連醫生都不知道如何減輕他的痛苦。

萬用延伸句型
Not even... 連（某人）都不能……

re·luc·tant [rɪˋlʌktənt]

Track 4061

形 不情願的

▶He is reluctant to visit his aunt.
他很不想拜訪他阿姨。

re·mark [rɪˋmɑrk]

Track 4062

名 注意 動 注意、評論

▶名 This is nothing worthy（值得的）of remark, and not everyone will take it to heart.
這不是什麼值得注意的事，而且也不是每個人都會把它放在心上。

▶動 "Wow, you sure are dressed well today." he remarked.
「哇，你今天穿得真好看啊。」他評論道。

實用片語用語
take sth. to heart 將……放在心上、認真看待……

re·mark·a·ble [rɪˋmɑrkəbl̩]

Track 4063

形 值得注意的

▶He made remarkable progress in his studies very quickly.
他在學習上很快取得顯著進步。

rem·e·dy [ˋrɛmədɪ]

Track 4064

名 醫療 動 治療、補救

▶名 Is there any remedy to heartache?
有什麼方式能夠治療心痛呢？

▶動 Don't you think these tablets will do nothing to remedy my headache（頭痛）?
你不覺得這些藥片一點也治不了我的頭痛嗎？

實用片語用語
find a remedy to... 找到……的解藥
例如：They searched high and low to find a remedy to their Emperor's illness.
他們上山下海地找皇帝的病的解藥。

rep·e·ti·tion [ˏrɛpɪˋtɪʃən]

Track 4065

名 重複

▶Repetition is a good way to learn a language.
重複是學習語言一個不錯的方式。

rep·re·sen·ta·tion [ˏrɛprɪzɛnˋteʃən]

Track 4066

名 代表、表示、表現

▶I don't think this painting is a representation of peace.
我認為這幅畫描繪的並不是和平。

rep·u·ta·tion [ˏrɛpjəˋteʃən]

Track 4067

名 名譽、聲望

▶He has a reputation for being a huge partygoer.
他以愛開趴而出名。

實用片語用語
have a reputation for being... 以……而出名

res·cue [ˋrɛskju]

Track 4068

名 搭救 動 援救

▶名 It is quite clear that all of them were there at the rescue.
很顯然所有人都有去參與救援。

▶動 The police don't know how to rescue the hostage（人質）yet.
警察目前還不知道如何營救人質。

re·search [ˋrisɝtʃ]

Track 4069

名 研究 動 調查

▶名 How will you carry out the research? How long will it last?
你將如何展開這項研究？研究要持續多久呢？

▶動 How long have you been researching into the cause of cancer?
你研究癌症的起因多久了？

實用片語用語
research into... 研究……

re·search·er [riˋsɝtʃɚ]

Track 4070

名 調查員

▶It is difficult for the researchers to prove how this happened.
研究員們很難證明為何此事會發生。

re·sem·ble [rɪˋzɛmbḷ]

Track 4071

動 類似

▶His brother resembles him in looks.
他弟弟和他長得很像。

實用片語用語
resemble sb. in looks 長相神似某人

res·er·va·tion [ˏrɛzɚˋveʃən]

Track 4072

名 保留

▶Would you make the reservations for our holiday this time?
這次能請你為我們度假做一下預訂安排嗎？

re·sign [rɪˋzaɪn]

Track 4073

動 辭職、使順從

▶He resigned last week, and doubtlessly it was a great loss to us.他上星期辭職了，這對我們來說無疑是一個巨大的損失。

res·ig·na·tion [ˏrɛzɪgˋneʃən]

Track 4074

名 辭職、讓位

▶His resignation is accepted by the Board.
董事會接受了他的辭職。

實用片語用語
be accepted by... 被……所接受

re·sis·tance [rɪˋzɪstəns]

Track 4075

名 抵抗

▶There is a lot of resistance to this new law.
反對這項新法律的人很多。

res·o·lu·tion [ˏrɛzəˋluʃən]

Track 4076

名 果斷、決心 同 determination 決心

▶He had a strong resolution to find his father's killer.
他有強烈的決心，要找到他的殺父仇人。

re·solve [rɪˋzɑlv]

Track 4077

名 決心 動 解決、分解

▶名 He has made a resolve to give up smoking.
他已經決定不吸菸了。

▶動 She resolves never to see him again.
她下定決心不再見他了。

re·spect·a·ble [rɪˋspɛktəbl̩]

Track 4078

形 可尊敬的

▶I don't think it is respectable to be drunk in front of your in-laws.
我認為在岳父母面前喝醉實在不太體面。

文法字詞解析
岳父稱 father-in-law，岳母稱 mother-in-law，兩者合在一起就是你的 in-laws。

re·spect·ful [rɪˋspɛktfəl]

Track 4079

形 有禮的

▶Not all the people think it is necessary to listen in respectful silence.
不是所有人都認為有必要畢恭畢敬地靜聽著。

re·store [rɪˋstor]

Track 4080

動 恢復

▶The doctors restored his eyesight.
醫生們恢復了他的視力。

re·stric·tion [rɪˋstrɪkʃən]

Track 4081

名 限制

▶It is a surprise that they should say there is no restriction to how many apples we can take.
他們竟然說沒限制我們可以拿走幾顆蘋果，真是令人驚訝。

re·tain [rɪˋten]

Track 4082

動 保持

▶She still retains a clear memory of the matter.
她仍很清晰地記得這件事。

文法字詞解析
矯正牙齒後，為了不讓牙齒又跑回去原來的地方，有時會使用「維持器」。這個東西就叫作 retainer。

re·tire [rɪˋtaɪr]

Track 4083

動 隱退

▶Everyone thinks that it's time for the man to retire.
大家都覺得這個人該退休了。

re·tire·ment [rɪˋtaɪrmənt]

Track 4084

名 退休

▶He found it difficult to establish a new routine after retirement.
他發覺自己退休後很難建立起新的生活規律。

re·treat [rɪˋtrit]

Track 4085

名 撤退 動 撤退

▶名 They made a hasty retreat when they realized that they were under-equipped.
他們發覺自己的武器帶太少時，就趕緊撤退了。

▶動 A good general knows when to attack and when to retreat.
一名優秀的將軍知道何時進攻，何時撤退。

文法字詞解析
除了從戰爭中撤退外，retreat 也可以表示從現實生活中「撤退」，也就是去找個地方躲起來度假啦！因此像是山中小屋、海邊度假村等，都是理想的 holiday retreat。

re·un·ion [riˋjunjən]

Track 4086

名 重聚、團圓

▶How often do you have a family reunion every year?
你們每年有幾次家庭聚會？

re·venge [rɪ`vɛndʒ]
Track 4087

名 報復 動 報復 同 retaliate 報復

▶名 It is quite clear that he did this all out of revenge.
很顯然，他這樣做完全是出於報復。

▶動 He will come back one day and revenge.
總有一天他會回來報復的。

re·vise [rɪ`vaɪz]
Track 4088

動 修正、校訂

▶It took him two hours to help her revise the article at night.
晚上他花了兩小時才幫她改好了文章。

re·vi·sion [rɪ`vɪʒən]
Track 4089

名 修訂

▶I don't think the law is in need of revision.
我覺得這項法律無需修訂。

實用片語用語
in need of... 需要……

rev·o·lu·tion [ˏrɛvə`luʃən]
Track 4090

名 革命、改革

▶What do you think of the Industrial Revolution that took place in England?
你怎麼看待在英國發生的那場工業革命呢？

實用片語用語
take place 發生

rev·o·lu·tion·ar·y [ˏrɛvə`luʃənˏɛrɪ]
Track 4091

形 革命的

▶Don't you think it is a revolutionary new way of growing wheat?
難道你不認為這是一種全新的種植小麥的方法嗎？

re·ward [rɪ`wɔrd]
Track 4092

名 報酬 動 酬賞

▶名 They offered a reward for anyone who found their lost puppy.
他們提供報酬給找到他們走失小狗的人。

▶動 These villagers（村民）don't know how to reward him for all his help.
這些村民不知道如何報答他的種種幫助。

實用片語用語
offer a reward 提供報酬

rhyme [raɪm]
Track 4093

名 韻、韻文 動 押韻

▶名 He knows nothing about rhyme and meter（格律）.
他對韻律一無所知，真是遺憾。

▶動 It is a pity that the last two lines of this poem don't rhyme properly.
真遺憾，這首詩的最後兩行沒有押好韻。

rhythm [`rɪðəm]
Track 4094

名 節奏、韻律

▶I am fond of the exciting rhythm of African drum music.
我很喜歡非洲鼓樂那令人興奮的節奏。

ro·mance [ro`mæns]

Track 4095

動 羅曼史

▶Don't you think the life of the writer and his wife is full of romance?
難道你不覺得這位作家和他妻子的生活充滿了浪漫色彩嗎？

實用片語用語
romance novel 羅曼史小說
例如：She likes to read romance novels on the train.
她喜歡在火車上讀羅曼史小說。

rough·ly [`rʌflɪ]

Track 4096

副 粗暴地、粗略地

▶The young man roughly pushed the old woman aside.
這個年輕人把這位老婦人粗暴地推到了一邊。

route [rut]

Track 4097

名 路線

▶Don't you think it's the quickest route to America?
難道你不認為這是去美國的最快路線嗎？

ru·in [`rʊɪn]

Track 4098

名 破壞 動 毀滅 同 destroy 破壞

▶名 I can't tell what led to the hero's ruin in the book.
我看不出是什麼導致了書中男主角的毀滅。

▶動 He ruined our surprise party for Susan by accidentally telling Susan about it.
他一不小心跟蘇珊講了要為她開驚喜派對的事，完全毀了這場驚喜。

文法字詞解析
ruin 使用複數形式 ruins 時，常可以用來表示（已經有點毀壞掉的）「遺跡」。例如古希臘、古羅馬等地留下來的一些不怎麼完好的古蹟，就可以稱為 ruins。

ru·ral [`rʊrəl]

Track 4099

形 農村的

▶There are lots of people still living in poverty in rural areas.
在廣大的農村地區，仍有很多人生活在貧困之中。

sac·ri·fice [`sækrə͵faɪs]

Track 4100

名 獻祭 動 供奉、犧牲

▶名 His children had no idea of the sacrifices he made for them.
他的孩子們完全不曉得他為了他們犧牲多少。

▶動 He is willing to sacrifice a great deal for her.
他能夠為她做出巨大的犧牲。

sal·a·ry [`sælərɪ]

Track 4101

名 薪水、薪俸、付薪水 同 wage 薪水

▶It's very difficult for a graduate to get a job with a good salary nowadays.
現在對於畢業生來說找一份薪水高的工作很難。

實用片語用語
salary worker 領固定薪水的上班族
例如：Both my parents are salary workers.
我父母都是領固定薪水的上班族。

sales·per·son/ sales·man/sales·wom·an

Track 4102

[ˋselz͵pɝsn]/[ˋselzmən]/[ˋselz͵wʊmən]

名 售貨員、推銷員

▶Should we ask a salesperson to demonstrate this new washing machine? 我們要不要請一位推銷員來示範一下如何使用這台新式洗衣機呢？

sat·el·lite [ˋsætḷ͵aɪt]

Track 4103

名 衛星

▶There are thirty-two known satellites in the solar system.
太陽系裡已知的衛星數量有三十二個。

sat·is·fac·tion [͵sætɪsˋfækʃən]

Track 4104

名 滿足

▶It is obvious that the success brought him great satisfaction.
顯然成功為他帶來了極大的滿足。

實用片語用語

satisfaction rate 滿意度
例如：Customer satisfaction rates are important for every restaurant.
顧客滿意度對每家餐廳來說都是很重要的。

scarce·ly [ˋskɛrslɪ]

Track 4105

副 勉強地、幾乎不 同 hardly 幾乎不

▶She scarcely earns enough money to make ends meet.
她幾乎沒有賺足夠的錢來平衡收支。

scen·ery [ˋsinərɪ]

Track 4106

名 風景、景色

▶The scenery was beautiful beyond description. Don't you think so? 那風景美麗得難以形容，你不這樣認為嗎？

scold [skold]

Track 4107

名 好罵人的人、潑婦 動 責罵

▶名 His father gave him a bad scold this morning.
他父親今天早上狠狠地罵了他一頓。

▶動 She has a bad temper and is always scolding her children.
她脾氣很壞，老是責備自己的子女。

文法字詞解析

scold 是「罵」的意思，但僅止於上對下的「責罵」，如果吵架時罵對方髒話之類的情境是不能稱為 scold 的。

scratch [skrætʃ]

Track 4108

動 抓

▶The cat is scratching herself again. 這貓又在抓自己了。

screw·driv·er [ˋskru͵draɪvɚ]

Track 4109

名 螺絲刀

▶Will you go and fetch me a screwdriver, please?
請你去幫我拿把螺絲起子來好嗎？

sculp·ture [ˋskʌlptʃɚ]

Track 4110

名 雕刻、雕塑 動 以雕刻裝飾

▶名 There is a sculpture of an ancient Roman God standing in the center of the square.
廣場中央矗立著一尊古代羅馬神的塑像。

▶動 There are two horses sculptured in bronze（青銅）at the gate. 在大門口有兩匹用青銅雕塑的馬。

sea·gull/gull [ˋsigʌl]/[gʌl]

Track 4111

名 海鷗

▶The sound of seagulls crying brings her back to her childhood holidays by the sea.
她聽到海鷗的叫聲就回憶起童年時在海邊度假的情景。

萬用延伸句型
bring sb. back to... 將某人帶回……

sen·ior [ˋsinjɚ]

Track 4112

名 年長者 形 年長的 同 elder 年紀較大的

▶名 You need to talk to some seniors about the problem.
你應該要去和一些年長者討論一下這個問題。

▶形 Not everyone is qualified to be a senior member of the committee.
不是每個人都有資格成為委員會中的資深委員。

set·tler [ˋsɛtḷɚ]

Track 4113

名 殖民者、居留者

▶The first settlers of this country were prisoners.
第一批到達這個國家的移民是囚犯。

se·vere [səˋvɪr]

Track 4114

形 嚴厲的

▶He is a severe critic when it comes to his own work.
對於自己的作品，他是個很嚴厲的批評者。

shame·ful [ˋʃemfəl]

Track 4115

形 恥辱的

▶There is nothing shameful about losing a game.
比賽輸了沒什麼好可恥的。

萬用延伸句型
There is nothing shameful about（+V-ing）
（某事）沒什麼好丟臉的

shav·er [ˋʃevɚ]

Track 4116

名 理髮師

▶I don't think that you should use the shaver while taking a bath.
我覺得你在洗澡的時候不應該使用電動刮鬍刀。

shel·ter [ˋʃɛltɚ]

Track 4117

名 避難所、庇護所 動 保護、掩護 同 protect 保護

▶名 Let's offer what they really need, such as food, clothing and shelter.
我們為他們提供真正需要的東西吧，例如吃的、穿的和住的。

▶動 The hen sheltered her chicks from the rain.
那隻母雞保護她的小雞免受雨淋。

shift [ʃɪft]

Track 4118

名 變換 動 變換

▶名 If you really like the job, would you like to work on the night shift?
如果你真的喜歡這份工作，你願不願意上夜班呢？

▶動 Would you please tell me if I should shift gears before making a turn? 你能告訴我在轉彎之前該不該換檔嗎？

實用片語用語
night shift 晚班、夜班
因為 shift 有變換、轉換的意思，所以就延伸出了「輪班」的字義。相對地，白天班、早班就是「day shift」。

short·sight·ed [ˋʃɔrtˋsaɪtɪd] Track 4119

形 近視的

▶He was too shortsighted to focus on what's really important.
他太短視近利了，無法專注於真正重要的事上。

shrug [ʃrʌg] Track 4120

動 聳肩

▶He never speaks, and mostly just shrugs.
他都不講話，通常只會聳聳肩而已。

shut·tle [ˋʃʌtl] Track 4121

名 縫紉機的滑梭 動 往返

▶名 There is a shuttle service between the city center and the airport. 在市中心和飛機場之間有往返的接駁班車。

▶動 I usually shuttle between these two cities for work.
我常會為了工作在這兩個城市間穿梭。

實用片語用語

shuttle bus 接駁車
例如：We took the shuttle bus to the department store.
我們搭接駁車到百貨公司。

sight·see·ing [ˋsaɪtˏsiɪŋ] Track 4122

名 觀光、遊覽

▶I spent most of my time on sightseeing. What about you?
我大部分時間都用在觀光遊覽上了。你呢？

sig·na·ture [ˋsɪgnətʃɚ] Track 4123

名 簽名

▶It is quite obvious that he faked my signature to get money from the bank.
很顯然他是冒充了我的簽名而從銀行裡取到錢的。

sig·nif·i·cance [sɪgˋnɪfəkəns] Track 4124

名 重要性

▶Nobody can achieve anything of real significance unless he works very hard. 一個人要是不努力，他就將一事無成。

sin·cer·i·ty [sɪnˋsɛrətɪ] Track 4125

名 誠懇、真摯

▶He finds it hard to speak with sincerity.
他覺得要誠懇地講話是很困難的事。

萬用延伸句型

find it hard to（+ 原形動詞）覺得（做到某事）很難

sin·gu·lar [ˋsɪŋgjəlɚ] Track 4126

名 單數 形 單一的、個別的

▶名 The singular of "mice" is "mouse".
「mice」的單數形是「mouse」。

▶形 I had a singular experience in Africa.
我在非洲時有過一次奇特的經歷。

site [saɪt] Track 4127

名 地基、位置 動 設置 同 location 位置

▶名 It is very difficult for us to decide the site of the new factory.
選定新廠的位址對我們來說很難。

▶動 Do you think it is safe to site the power station here?
你覺得在這裡建造發電廠安全嗎？

sketch [skɛtʃ] Track 4128

名 素描、草圖 動 描述、素描

▶名 Will you please give me a sketch of your plan?
請你跟我談談你的計畫概略好嗎？

▶動 He sketched his dog very quickly.
他很快地畫下了他的狗。

實用片語用語
sketch book / sketchbook 素描本
例如：She wouldn't let anyone see her sketch book.
她不讓任何人看她的素描本。

sledge/sled [slɛdʒ]/[slɛd] Track 4129

名 雪橇 動 用雪橇搬運

▶名 The kids are outside playing on the sledge.
孩子們在外面玩雪橇。

▶動 Do you want to go sledging with us later?
待會要不要跟我們一起去玩雪橇？

sleigh [sle] Track 4130

名 有座雪橇、雪橇、乘坐雪橇

▶My feet were as cold as stone when I got out of the sleigh.
我從雪橇上下來時兩隻腳凍得像石頭一樣。

slight [slaɪt] Track 4131

形 輕微的 動 輕視

▶形 It is clear that he was born with a slight deformity（畸形）of the feet which made him limp（跛行）.
顯然他的腳稍微有先天畸形，走起路來一拐一拐的。

▶動 Mr. Paul is highly respected because he never slights anyone.
保羅先生非常受人尊敬，因為他從不輕視任何人。

實用片語用語
be born with 生來就具有……

slo·gan [ˋslogən] Track 4132

名 標語、口號

▶Our slogan is “Time is money, efficiency is life”.
我們的口號是「時間就是金錢，效率就是生命」。

smog [smɑg] Track 4133

名 煙霧、煙

▶There are still some big cities with smog problems.
仍有些大城市有著煙霧排放的問題。

sneeze [sniz] Track 4134

名 噴嚏 動 輕視、打噴嚏

▶名 I counted seven sneezes coming from the neighboring room. 我聽到隔壁房間有人打了七個噴嚏。

▶動 You've been sneezing a lot today.
你今天老是打噴嚏。

sob [sɑb] Track 4135

名 啜泣 動 哭訴、啜泣 同 cry 哭

▶名 A sob welled up in his throat when he saw his mother.
他看到媽媽時，喉嚨裡發出一聲嗚咽。

▶動 The poor little boy sobbed himself to sleep.
那個可憐的小男孩啜泣著入睡了。

實用片語用語
sob story 賺人熱淚的故事
例如：He won the pity of the judges with a sob story.
他講了一個賺人熱淚的故事，贏得了評審們的同情。

sock·et [ˋsɑkɪt]

Track 4136

名 凹處、插座

▶I'm afraid that you forgot to put the electric plug into the socket.
恐怕你忘了將插頭插到插座上了。

soft·ware [ˋsɔftˏwɛr]

Track 4137

名 軟體

▶There are many kinds of software in my computer.
我的電腦裡有很多軟體。

so·lar [ˋsolɚ]

Track 4138

形 太陽的 反 lunar 月球的

▶Don't you think that we can use solar energy to do many things today? 你不覺得如今我們可以利用太陽能做很多事情嗎？

實用片語用語
solar power 太陽能
例如：This boat runs on solar power.
這艘船是靠著太陽能行駛的。

soph·o·more [ˋsɑfmˏor]

Track 4139

名 二年級學生

▶As a sophomore, I really feel that time flies.
作為一名大二學生，我真的感覺時光飛逝。

sor·row·ful [ˋsɑrəfəl]

Track 4140

形 哀痛的、悲傷的

▶Why does the whole family look so sorrowful?
為什麼那一家人全都看起來很悲傷？

sou·ve·nir [ˏsuvəˋnɪr]

Track 4141

名 紀念品、特產

▶Would you please accept this as a souvenir for our friendship?
請接受這個作為我們友誼的紀念好嗎？

spare [spɛr]

Track 4142

形 剩餘的 動 節省、騰出

▶形 It is obvious that he has nothing to do in his spare time.
顯然他在休閒時間裡無事可做。

▶動 Take a chair, I have lots to spare anyway.
拿一張椅子去吧，反正我還有很多張可以騰出來。

實用片語用語
spare tire 備胎
例如：Don't worry, I've got a spare tire in the trunk.
不用擔心，後車廂裡面有備胎。

spark [spɑrk]

Track 4143

名 火花、火星 動 冒火花、鼓舞

▶名 There is a wild spark in his eyes.
他的眼裡有著野性的火花。

▶動 It was this incident that sparked her interest in politics.
是這個事件激起了她對政治的興趣。

文法字詞解析
除了真的火花外，兩人相當來電擦出的「火花」也可稱為 spark。

spar·kle [ˋspɑrkḷ]

Track 4144

名 閃爍 動 使閃耀

▶名 His eyes always have sparkles in them when he's excited.
他在興奮時眼睛總是閃閃發亮。

▶動 The diamonds sparkle under the sun.
那些鑽石在太陽下閃閃發亮。

spar·row [ˋspæro] Track 4145

名 麻雀

▶There is a worm in the sparrow's beak.
那隻麻雀的嘴裡叼著一隻蟲子。

spear [spɪr] Track 4146

名 矛、魚叉 動 用矛刺

▶名 Could you teach me how to catch fish with a spear?
您能教我如何利用魚叉來捕魚嗎？

▶動 Do you know how to spear fish?
你知道怎樣叉魚嗎？

spe·cies [ˋspiʃɪz] Track 4147

名 物種

▶There are millions of species of animals and plants on the earth. 地球上動物和植物種類有幾百萬種。

實用片語用語
endangered species 瀕危物種
例如：The panda is an endangered species.
熊貓是一種瀕危物種。

spic·y [ˋspaɪsɪ] Track 4148

形 辛辣的、加香料的

▶What about having some spicy food for a change?
嚐嚐辛辣的菜換一下口味如何？

spir·i·tu·al [ˋspɪrɪtʃʊəl] Track 4149

形 精神的、崇高的 反 material 物質的

▶She strikes me as a very spiritual lady.
我覺得她是個很重精神層面的太太。

splen·did [ˋsplɛndɪd] Track 4150

形 輝煌的、閃耀的

▶Have you seen her wedding dress? It's just splendid!
妳有看到她的結婚禮服嗎？超級美的！

split [splɪt] Track 4151

名 裂口 動 劈開、分化

▶名 The little girl did a split out of nowhere just to show off.
那個小女孩沒事就劈個腿以示炫耀。

▶動 I think it's better for us to split up so that the enemy can't track us.
我覺得我們還是分開走比較好，敵人就追蹤不到我們。

文法字詞解析
split 的動詞變化：split, split, split

實用片語用語
split up 分開、兵分兩路

sports·man/ sports·wom·an [ˋsportsmən]/[ˋsports͵wʊmən] Track 4152

名 男運動員／女運動員

▶I'm not a great sportsman, but I enjoy watching football matches. 我不是一名偉大的運動員，但我喜歡看足球比賽。

sports·man·ship [ˋsportsmən͵ʃɪp] Track 4153

名 運動員精神

▶Shaking hands with the losing team shows good sportsmanship.
和輸球的隊伍握手展現了良好的運動精神。

sta·tus ['stetəs]　Track 4154

名 地位、身分

▸I'm afraid that women's social status hasn't changed much over the years.
恐怕這些年來婦女的社會地位沒有多大改變。

文法字詞解析
在社群網站上也常會需要「update status」，也就是分享你的最新狀態讓朋友們知道。

stem [stɛm]　Track 4155

名 杆柄、莖幹 動 起源、阻止

▸名 It is clear that the stem of the rose was broken by someone.
顯然這支玫瑰的莖是被人折斷的。

▸動 His error stemmed from carelessness.
顯然他的錯誤是由於粗心大意而造成的。

sting·y ['stɪndʒɪ]　Track 4156

形 有刺的、會刺的

▸It is no wonder that nobody is willing to talk to such a stingy man.
這樣小氣的人，難怪誰也不願意和他說話。

strength·en ['strɛŋθən]　Track 4157

動 加強、增強

▸Exercise will strengthen your body.
運動會使你身體強健。

strive [straɪv]　Track 4158

動 苦幹、努力

▸Just wishing for peace is not enough. We must strive for it.
只希望和平是不夠的。我們一定要去爭取它。

文法字詞解析
strive 的動詞變化：strive, strove, striven

stroke [strok]　Track 4159

名 打擊、一擊 動 撫摸

▸名 I felt so bad when I heard that he had a stroke yesterday.
聽說他昨天中風了，我感到非常遺憾。

▸動 She stroked her child's hair as he slept.
她在孩子睡覺時輕撫他的頭髮。

sub·ma·rine ['sʌbmə͵rin]　Track 4160

名 潛水艇 形 海底的

▸名 Would you please tell me why a submarine can float and sink?
你能告訴我為什麼潛水艇既能浮在水面，又能潛入水底嗎？

▸形 When were the submarine cables laid across the Atlantic?
橫越大西洋的海底電纜是什麼時候鋪設的？

sug·ges·tion [səg'dʒɛstʃən]　Track 4161

名 建議

▸What an interesting suggestion! Don't you think so?
多麼有趣的建議啊！你不覺得嗎？

實用片語用語
take sb.'s suggestion 接受某人的建議
例如：She took her mom's suggestion and went to the party in the blue dress.
她聽從媽媽的建議，穿藍色的洋裝去參加派對。

sum·ma·rize [ˋsʌməˏraɪz] Track 4162

動 總結、概述

▶I think it is worthwhile（值得的）for us to try to summarize our Engilsh learning experiences.
我認為我們總結一下學習英語的經驗是值得的。

萬用延伸句型
It is worthwhile to... 做……是值得的

surf [sɝf] Track 4163

名 湧上來的波 動 衝浪、乘浪

▶名 They took off their clothes and ran into the surf.
他們脫掉衣服，奔向海浪。

▶動 How about going surfing with us next weekend?
下週末跟我們去衝浪怎麼樣？

sur·geon [ˋsɝdʒən] Track 4164

名 外科醫生

▶I'm afraid that you should go to see the surgeon first.
恐怕你應該先去看看外科醫生。

sur·ger·y [ˋsɝdʒərɪ] Track 4165

名 外科醫學、外科手術

▶Would you tell her that the surgery is scheduled within two weeks? 請告訴她手術將在兩週內進行好嗎？

實用片語用語
undergo surgery 接受手術
例如：Don't disturb him. He has just undergone surgery.
別打擾他，他才剛接受完手術。

sur·ren·der [səˋrɛndɚ] Track 4166

名 投降 動 屈服、投降

▶名 The enemy were forced to make an unconditional（無條件的）surrender. 敵軍被迫無條件投降。

▶動 He would rather die than surrender. 他寧死也不投降。

sur·round·ings [səˋraʊndɪŋz] Track 4167

名 環境、周圍

▶It took him a long time to adapt himself to new surroundings.
他花了好長一段時間才適應了新環境。

sus·pi·cious [səˋspɪʃən] Track 4168

形 可疑的

▶There were suspicious circumstances about his death.
關於他的死，有一些值得懷疑的情況。

sway [swe] Track 4169

名 搖擺、支配 動 支配、搖擺

▶名 It is clear that he is under the sway of his parents.
顯然他是受他父母控制的。

▶動 Did you manage to sway him after talking to him yesterday?
昨天跟他聊過以後，你有成功勸他改變主意嗎？

實用片語用語
be swayed by... 因……而動搖
例如：His opinion is easily swayed by his friends.
他的想法很容易就會因為朋友們而動搖了。

syl·la·ble [ˋsɪləbḷ] Track 4170

名 音節

▶Would you please tell me which syllable the stress of this word falls on?
請你告訴我這個字的重音是在哪個音節上好嗎？

sym·pa·thet·ic [ˌsɪmpəˋθɛtɪk]

Track 4171

形 表示同情的

▶My uncle is a very sympathetic person.
我叔叔是一個富有同情心的人。

sym·pa·thy [ˋsɪmpəθɪ]

Track 4172

名 同情

▶Not everyone feels much sympathy for the disabled（殘疾人士）.不是每個人都對殘疾人士深感同情。

實用片語用語

have sympathy for... 同情（某人）
例如：He has a lot of sympathy for stray animals.
他對流浪動物充滿了同情。

sym·pho·ny [ˋsɪmfənɪ]

Track 4173

名 交響樂、交響曲

▶I don't think that the first movement of the symphony is beautiful.
我覺得這部交響樂的第一樂章沒有那麼優美。

文法字詞解析

movement 一般的意思是「運動」，但用在音樂術語中就表示一個「樂章」。

syr·up [ˋsɪrəp]

Track 4174

名 糖漿

▶Would you like to have some bread with syrup?
你想不想吃一些配糖漿的麵包？

sys·tem·at·ic [ˌsɪstəˋmætɪk]

Track 4175

形 有系統的、有組織的

▶We explained the problem in a systematic way.
我們以有系統的方式解釋了這個問題。

Tt

tap [tæp]

Track 4176

名 輕拍聲 動 輕打

▶名 He gave the microphone a tap before speaking to make sure it works.
他在講話前先輕叩一下擴音器，以確定它能用。

▶動 She tapped her fingers on the table.
她用手指輕輕敲著桌面。

實用片語用語

tap sb. on the shoulder 拍某人的肩膀
例如：Was it you who tapped me on the shoulder?
剛剛是你拍我肩膀嗎？

tech·ni·cian [tɛkˋnɪʃən]

Track 4177

名 技師、技術員

▶The company sent two technicians there to fix the machine.
公司派兩個技術員去那裡修理機器。

tech·no·log·i·cal [tɛknəˋlɑdʒɪkḷ]

Track 4178

形 工業技術的

▶We must further strengthen collaboration in technological fields so that we won't lag behind others.
我們必須進一步加強技術領域的合作，才不致於落後於他人。

tel·e·gram [ˋtɛlə͵græm]

Track 4179

名 電報

▶People rarely send telegrams anymore today.
現在的人幾乎不發電報了。

實用片語用語
send a telegram 發電報

tel·e·graph [ˋtɛlə͵græf]

Track 4180

名 電報機 動 打電報

▶名 The news came by telegraph.
消息以電報傳來。

▶動 Would you telegraph us if you are interested in our products?
如果你對我們的產品感興趣的話，能否以電報回覆？

tel·e·scope [ˋtɛlə͵skop]

Track 4181

名 望遠鏡

▶I wish we could find another planet like Earth with the Hubble Space Telescope（哈伯太空望遠鏡）.
我希望我們能透過哈伯太空望遠鏡找到另外一個跟地球類似的星球。

ten·den·cy [ˋtɛndənsɪ]

Track 4182

名 傾向、趨向

▶By the time you reach the age of forty, you will have had a tendency to forget things.
等你到了四十歲的時候，你就會有健忘的傾向了。

實用片語用語
have a tendency to.V.有……的傾向
另外還有一個有點關連的片語是「tend to…」，意思是「傾向於……」。
例如：She tend to use cell phone while taking the MRT.
她往往會在坐捷運的時候使用手機。

tense [tɛns]

Track 4183

動 緊張 形 拉緊的

▶動 She tensed when she noticed that there was a stranger outside.
當她發現外頭有個陌生人的時候她就緊張起來了。

▶形 There was a tense silence in the waiting crowd.
在等候的人群中有一種緊張的寂靜感。

ten·sion [ˋtɛnʃən]

Track 4184

名 拉緊

▶Didn't you feel the air of tension at the meeting?
你沒感覺到會議上的氣氛有點緊張嗎？

ter·ri·fy [ˋtɛrə͵faɪ]

Track 4185

動 使恐懼、使驚嚇

▶Not all people are terrified by spiders. 不是所有人都怕蜘蛛。

ter·ror [ˋtɛrɚ]

Track 4186

名 駭懼、恐怖 同 fear 恐懼

▶He fled in terror when he saw the murder happen.
他看到謀殺案發生時，害怕地逃開了。

theme [θim]

Track 4187

名 主題、題目

▶Do you mind telling me what the theme of your paper is?
你介意告訴我你的論文主題是什麼嗎？

實用片語用語
theme park 主題樂園
例如：Disneyland is one of my favorite theme parks.
迪士尼樂園是我最喜歡的主題樂園之一。

thor·ough [ˋθɝo] Track 4188

形 徹底的

▶It is quite clear that our planes are in need of a thorough overhaul（大修）.
很顯然我們的飛機需要徹底檢修一次了。

thought·ful [ˋθɔtfəl] Track 4189

形 深思的、思考的

▶He has a thoughtful look on his face all the time.
他臉上總是帶著沉思的表情。

tim·id [ˋtɪmɪd] Track 4190

形 羞怯的

▶He is too timid to talk to strangers.
他太膽小了，不敢跟陌生人講話。

tire·some [ˋtaɪrsəm] Track 4191

形 無聊的、可厭的

▶Her nagging is so tiresome. 她一直念個不停，煩死了。

實用片語用語
nag sb. about sth. 對某人嘮叨某事
例如：Mom keeps nagging me about my assignment.
媽媽一直碎念，叫我去做功課。

tol·er·a·ble [ˋtɑlərəbl̩] Track 4192

形 可容忍的、可忍受的

▶The noise is loud, but tolerable.
那個雜音很吵，但還可忍受。

tol·er·ance [ˋtɑlərəns] Track 4193

名 包容力

▶A wise man cannot only put forward his opinions but must also develop tolerance for others' opinions. 一個聰明的人不僅要能提出自己的意見，還要能包容他人的意見。

tol·er·ant [ˋtɑlərənt] Track 4194

形 忍耐的

▶If you are tolerant of others, they will be tolerant in turn.
你對別人容忍，別人也會對你容忍。

實用片語用語
be tolerant of 能夠容忍（某人或事物）

tol·er·ate [ˋtɑlə͵ret] Track 4195

動 寬容、容忍

▶Not many people would tolerate lateness.
沒有多少人能夠容忍別人遲到。

tomb [tum] Track 4196

名 墳墓、塚 同 grave 墳墓

▶It is too far for me to see clearly（清楚地）what is said on the tomb stone. 離得太遠，所以我看不清楚墓碑上的字。

tough [tʌf] Track 4197

形 困難的

▶The questions on the test were really tough.
考試題目超難的。

實用片語用語
tough luck 運氣不好
例如：You lost the bet again? Well, tough luck!
你又賭輸了？運氣真差啊！

trag·e·dy [ˋtrædʒədɪ] Track 4198

名 悲劇

▶I prefer comedy to tragedy. What about you, Bob?
我喜歡喜劇甚於悲劇。鮑勃，你呢？

trag·ic [ˋtrædʒɪk] Track 4199

形 悲劇的

▶She fainted as soon as she heard the tragic news.
她一聽到這個悲慘的消息就暈過去了。

trans·fer [trænsˋfɝ] Track 4200

名 遷移、調職 動 轉移

▶名 I don't think I can get there without a transfer.
我不認為我到那裡不用轉車。

▶動 I don't believe he will transfer all his property to his daughter.
我不相信他會把他所有的財產都轉移給他的女兒。

實用片語用語

transfer student 轉學生
例如：Everyone was curious about the transfer student.
大家都對這位轉學生很好奇。

trans·form [trænsˋfɔrm] Track 4201

動 改變

▶How about transforming the garage into a guest house?
把車庫改成客房怎麼樣？

trans·late [trænsˋlet] Track 4202

動 翻譯

▶Can you translate the article from English into Japanese?
你能把這篇文章由英文翻譯成日文嗎？

trans·la·tion [trænsˋleʃən] Track 4203

名 譯文

▶I haven't read the translation of the article yet.
我還沒讀過那篇文章的翻譯。

trans·la·tor [trænsˋletɚ] Track 4204

名 翻譯者、翻譯家

▶It is difficult for one to become an excellent translator.
要想成為一名出色的譯者很難。

文法字詞解析

translator 指的是筆譯的譯者，如果要說「口譯員」的話則是 interpreter。

trans·por·ta·tion [ˌtrænspɚˋteʃən] Track 4205

名 輸送、運輸工具

▶Will you tell me how much the transportation of these goods by train costs?
如果用火車裝運這批貨物的話要花多少錢呢？

tre·men·dous [trɪˋmɛndəs] Track 4206

形 非常、巨大的 同 enormous 巨大的

▶There is a tremendous difference between this plan and that one. 這個計畫和那個計畫之間有著極大的區別。

trib·al [ˋtraɪbḷ]

Track 4207

形 宗族的、部落的

▶Does anyone know this rare tribal language?
這裡有人懂這種罕見的部落語言嗎？

實用片語用語
tribal language 部落語言

tri·umph [ˋtraɪəmf]

Track 4208

名 勝利 動 獲得勝利

▶名 She shouted in triumph when she won the game.
贏得遊戲時，她發出勝利的喊叫。

▶動 Justice will triumph over evil, at least that's what people say.
正義必將戰勝不義，至少大家都是這樣說的。

trou·ble·some [ˋtrʌbḷsəm]

Track 4209

形 麻煩的、困難的

▶It is a troublesome problem. Let's discuss it together.
這是一個棘手的問題。我們一起討論一下吧。

文法字詞解析
字根「-some」的意思是「有……性質的」，前面常常接名詞。

tug-of-war [tʌg əv wɔr]

Track 4210

名 拔河

▶It doesn't matter which team will win the tug-of-war.
哪個隊贏得拔河比賽都不重要。

twin·kle [ˋtwɪŋkḷ]

Track 4211

名 閃爍 動 閃爍、發光

▶名 The fog has vanished, and we can see the distant twinkle of the harbor light.
霧散了，我們能看見港灣的燈光在遠處閃爍。

▶動 There are few stars twinkling tonight.
今晚閃爍的星星寥寥無幾。

typ·ist [ˋtaɪpɪst]

Track 4212

名 打字員

▶It is quite clear that the new typist in our company is incompetent（無法勝任的）.
很顯然我們公司新來的打字員不能勝任工作。

un·der·pass [ˋʌndɚˏpæs]

Track 4213

名 地下道

▶It's safer for us to take the underpass. Don't you think so?
我們走地下通道吧，這樣比較安全。你不這樣認為嗎？

文法字詞解析
相對於 underpass，從地上架空過去的「天橋」或「高架道路」則可以稱為 overpass。

u·nique [juˋnik]

Track 4214

形 唯一的、獨特的

▶Her ideas are always strange and unique.
她的點子總是又奇怪又獨特。

u·ni·ver·sal [ˌjunəˋvɝsḷ] Track 4215

形 普遍的、世界性的、宇宙的

▶English is widely used all over the world. It is no wonder that it is referred to as a universal language.
英語在世界上被廣泛運用。難怪它被稱為世界語言。

u·ni·ver·si·ty [ˌjunəˋvɝsətɪ] Track 4216

名 大學

▶How long will it take for us to get to that university by bus?
我們搭公車到那所大學要花多長時間？

up·load [ʌpˋlod] Track 4217

動 上傳（檔案）

▶What do you think about uploading these pictures onto the Internet? 你覺得把這些照片上傳到網路上怎麼樣？

文法字詞解析
相反地，要「下載」東西則是稱為download。

ur·ban [ˋɝbən] Track 4218

形 都市的

▶It is obvious that this play depicts urban life at that time.
顯然這個劇本是當時城市生活的寫照。

實用片語用語
at that time 在當時

urge [ɝdʒ] Track 4219

動 驅策、勸告

▶He strongly urged us to leave.
他強烈勸告我們趕快離開。

ur·gent [ˋɝdʒənt] Track 4220

形 急迫的、緊急的

▶I'm afraid something urgent has come up. Perhaps I won't be able to see you tonight. 我有些急事，恐怕今晚不能見你了。

us·age [ˋjusɪdʒ] Track 4221

名 習慣、習俗、使用

▶In writing, one has to conform to usage as well as to the rules of grammar. 寫作時既要遵守文法規則，又要符合習慣用法。

vain [ven] Track 4222

形 無意義的、徒然的

▶All his efforts were in vain.
他所有的努力都是徒然。

實用片語用語
in vain 徒然

vast [væst] Track 4223

形 巨大的、廣大的 同 enormous 巨大的

▶There is a vast expanse（廣闊的區域）of desert in this poor country. 在這個貧窮的國家裡有著大片的沙漠。

veg·e·tar·ian [ˌvɛdʒəˋtɛrɪən]   Track 4224

名 素食主義者

▶Tina likes to eat meat very much, so it is impossible（不可能的）for her to be a vegetarian.
蒂娜很喜歡吃肉，因此她不可能當一個素食主義者。

實用片語用語
vegetarian meal 素食餐
例如：Do you serve vegetarian meals in your restaurant?
你們餐廳有賣素食餐點嗎？

verb [vɝb]   Track 4225

名 動詞

▶Will you tell me how to use the verb in this sentence?
你能告訴我如何在句中運用這個動詞嗎？

ver·y [ˋvɛrɪ]   Track 4226

副 很、完全地

▶Don't you think they are very eager to go there with us?
難道你不覺得他們很想跟我們一起去那裡嗎？

ves·sel [ˋvesl̩]   Track 4227

名 容器、碗

▶What about putting some water into the vessel to see what will happen next?
要不要往容器裡倒入一些水，看看下一步會發生什麼樣的事情？

文法字詞解析
vessel 這個單字也常拿來表示「船」的意思，畢竟船也能容得下很多東西。

vin·eg·ar [ˋvɪnɪgɚ]   Track 4228

名 醋

▶The soup tasted strange because I added too much vinegar.
這湯喝起來怪怪的，因為我加太多醋了。

vi·o·late [ˋvaɪəˌlet]   Track 4229

動 妨害、違反

▶Didn't he violate the traffic regulations?
他不是違反交通規則了嗎？

vi·o·la·tion [ˌvaɪəˋleʃən]   Track 4230

名 違反、侵害

▶It is obvious that this rule is a violation of the right of free speech. 這一規定很顯然是對言論自由權的一種侵犯。

實用片語用語
the right of free speech 言論自由權

vir·gin [ˋvɝdʒɪn]   Track 4231

名 處女 形 純淨的

▶名 There are some stories about the Virgin Mary. Have you heard them?
有一些關於聖母瑪利亞的故事。你有聽過嗎？

▶形 There are large stretches（連綿）of virgin forests in the northern part of the country.
在這個國家北部有大片的原始森林。

vir·tue [ˋvɝtʃu]   Track 4232

名 貞操、美德

▶People say honesty is the best virtue.
人們說誠實是最好的美德。

vir·us ['vaɪrəs]

Track 4233

名 病毒

▶I wish we human beings could find ways to destroy all the viruses soon.
我希望我們人類能很快找到方法消滅所有的病毒。

vis·u·al ['vɪʒuəl]

Track 4234

形 視覺的

▶The design is quite novel. It is no wonder that it has such a strong visual appeal.
這個設計相當新穎。怪不得它會在視覺上如此具有感染力。

實用片語用語

visual effects 視覺效果

例如：The visual effects in this movie were spectacular.
這部電影的視覺效果實在太壯觀了。

vi·tal ['vaɪtl̩]

Track 4235

形 生命的、不可或缺的

▶We consider this discovery of vital importance.
我們認為這個發現非常重要。

vol·ca·no [vɑl'keno]

Track 4236

名 火山

▶The volcano has become a popular tourist spot.
這座火山已成為一個受歡迎的觀光景點了。

實用片語用語

tourist spot 觀光景點

vol·un·tar·y ['vɑlən͵tɛrɪ]

Track 4237

形 自願的、自發的

▶His decision to leave was voluntary.
他離開的決定是自願的。

vol·un·teer [͵vɑlən'tɪr]

Track 4238

名 自願者、義工 動 自願做……

▶名 How long have you been working in this community as a volunteer?
你在這個社區當義工多久了？

▶動 She volunteered to teach in the school, but I don't know how long she will stay there.
她自願到那個學校教書，但我不知道她會在那待多久。

實用片語用語

volunteer work 志工工作

例如：Volunteer work is much harder than you think.
志工的工作比你想的難多了。

vow·el ['vaʊəl]

Track 4239

名 母音 反 consonant 子音

▶Will you tell me the differences between vowels and consonants（子音）in English?
你能告訴我英語中母音和子音之間的區別嗎？

voy·age ['vɔɪɪdʒ]

Track 4240

名 旅行、航海 動 航行

▶名 Life is compared to a voyage, and it takes everyone a lifetime to finish it.
人生好比是一趟旅行，每個人都要用上一生的時間來完成它。

▶動 It took the captain and his sailors five years to finish voyaging the world. 船長和他的船員們花了五年的時間才完成了航行世界的任務。

wal·nut [ˋwɔlnət]
Track 4241

名 胡桃樹

▶How about we use walnuts to make a cake?
我們用胡桃來做蛋糕怎麼樣？

web·site [ˋwɛb͵saɪt]
Track 4242

名 網站

▶I'm afraid that we don't have enough money to improve the website.
恐怕我們沒有足夠的經費來改良網站。

文法字詞解析
website 也可以簡稱 site。此外，還有一個相關的單字 webpage，指的是「網頁」的意思。

week·ly [ˋwiklɪ]
Track 4243

名 週刊 形 每週的 副 每週地

▶名 I wish I could publish an article in this weekly one day.
要是有一天我能在這本週刊上發表文章就好了。

▶形 Her boyfriend writes weekly love letters to her.
她的男朋友每個星期都寫一封情書給她。

▶副 My parents and I go to the park weekly.
每個星期爸爸媽媽跟我都一起去公園。

wel·fare [ˋwɛl͵fɛr]
Track 4244

名 健康、幸福、福利 同 benefit 利益

▶The welfare of the individual is bound up with the welfare of the community. Don't you think so?
個人的福利與社會的福利有著密切的關係。你不這樣認為嗎？

實用片語用語
be bound up with 和……有緊密關係

wit [wɪt]
Track 4245

名 機智、賢人

▶Her articles are full of wit.
她的文章充滿了機智。

witch/wiz·ard [wɪtʃ]/[ˋwɪzɚd]
Track 4246

名 女巫師／男巫師

▶The wedding was in full swing when the witch came in.
當女巫進來時婚禮正進行得熱鬧。

實用片語用語
in full swing （活動）正順利進行、如火如荼

with·draw [wɪðˋdrɔ]
Track 4247

動 收回、撤出

▶The motion was withdrawn in the end.
那項動議最終被撤銷了。

文法字詞解析
withdraw 的動詞變化：
withdraw, withdrew, withdrawn

wit·ness [ˋwɪtnɪs]
Track 4248

名 目擊者 動 目擊

▶名 I'm afraid that the witness needs to be investigated.
恐怕那名證人還需要調查一下。

▶動 Several people witnessed the car crash.
許多人目擊了車禍。

wreck [rɛk]

Track 4249

名（船隻）失事、殘骸 動 遇險、摧毀、毀壞

▶名 Why not try to save what you can from the wreck now?
現在為什麼不盡量設法收拾殘局呢？

▶動 They were looking for the person who set the fire and wrecked the hotel.
他們在調查到底是誰放火把飯店燒毀了。

wrin·kle [ˋrɪŋkḷ]

Track 4250

名 皺紋 動 皺起

▶名 It is obvious that she is beginning to get wrinkles round her eyes.
顯然她的眼角開始有皺紋了。

▶動 The quality of this shirt is very good; it will not wrinkle.
這件襯衫的品質非常好，不會皺。

實用片語用語

wrinkle-free 不會起皺紋的

例如：Because of its fabric, this dress is wrinkle-free.
因為布料的關係，這件洋裝不會起皺紋。

year·ly [ˋjɪrlɪ]

Track 4251

形 每年的 副 每年、年年

▶形 The rainfall this year exceeded the yearly average.
今年的雨量超過了年平均降雨量。

▶副 She can only go home yearly.
她每年只能回家一次。

yo·gurt [ˋjogɚt]

Track 4252

名 優酪乳

▶Would you like to have some low fat yogurt? It tastes very good.
你想不想喝點低脂的優酪乳？它味道很好哦。

文法字詞解析

yogurt 也可以拼成 yoghurt，唸起來一樣。

youth·ful [ˋjuθfəl]

Track 4253

形 年輕的

▶It is obvious that no one can remain youthful forever.
顯然沒有人能夠永保青春。

NOTE

A
B
C
D
E
F
G
H
I
J
K
L
M
N
O
P
Q
R
S
T
U
V
W
X
Y
Z

挑戰英文能力——邁向 5400 單字

學英文從單字開始，
許自己一個不可思議的滿分奇蹟！

Level 5 挑戰英文能力——邁向5400單

a·bide [ə`baɪd] Track 4254

動 容忍、忍耐 同 tolerate 容忍

▶Both his father and mother have to abide his bad temper.
他的父親和母親都得容忍他的壞脾氣。

文法字詞解析
abide 的動詞變化：abide, abode, abode 或是 abide, abided, abided

實用片語用語
abide by 遵守

a·bol·ish [ə`bɑlɪʃ] Track 4255

動 廢止、革除 反 establish 建立

▶People would continue to fight to abolish slavery（奴隸制度）.
人們會繼續為廢除奴隸制度而奮鬥。

a·bor·tion [ə`bɔrʃən] Track 4256

名 流產、墮胎

▶The reason why abortion is illegal（違法的）in some countries is that it is not allowed by their religions. 墮胎在一些國家屬於違法行為，原因是它不被他們的宗教信仰所允許。

a·brupt [ə`brʌpt] Track 4257

形 突然的 同 sudden 突然的

▶He drove his car quickly even if the road is full of abrupt turns.
儘管那條路有很多急轉彎，他卻還是開得很快。

萬用延伸句型
even if... 即使……

ab·surd [əb`sɝd] Track 4258

形 不合理的、荒謬的

▶What an absurd suggestion! 多麼荒唐的建議！

a·bun·dant [ə`bʌndənt] Track 4259

形 豐富的 反 scarce 稀少的

▶It is said that the area is abundant with mineral resources.
據說這個地區礦藏資源豐富。

a·cad·e·my [ə`kædəmɪ] Track 4260

名 學院、專科院校

▶This academy of music is so famous that many students are eager to enter it.
這所音樂學院非常有名，所以有很多學生都想進去就讀。

實用片語用語
be eager to... 極期待做某事、很想要做某事

ac·cus·tom [ə`kʌstəm] Track 4261

動 使習慣於

▶I have gradually become accustomed to the work.
我越來越習慣這份工作了。

ace [es] Track 4262

名 傑出人才 形 一流的、熟練的

▶名 He is regarded the ace of his team.
他被認為是他們隊上的王牌。

▶形 He is the ace mechanic here.
他是這裡第一流的機械師。

ac·knowl·edge [əkˋnɑlɪdʒ] Track 4263

動 承認、供認 反 deny 否認

▶People used to not acknowledge that the earth is round.
以前的人們不承認地球是圓的事實。

ac·knowl·edge·ment [əkˋnɑlɪdʒmənt] Track 4264

名 承認、坦白、自白 反 denial 否認

▶Why don't you send him a small sum of money in acknowledgement of his help?
為何不寄一小筆錢給他以感謝他的幫助呢？

實用片語用語
in acknowledgement of... 以表示對……的感謝、以表示對……的認知

ac·ne [ˋæknɪ] Track 4265

名 粉刺、面皰

▶The reason why many young people suffer from acne is that they pay no attention to their skin care.
很多年輕人患有粉刺的原因是他們不注意皮膚的護理。

ad·mi·ral [ˋædmərəl] Track 4266

名 海軍上將

▶My son wants to be an admiral when he grows up. What about yours?
我兒子長大後想當海軍上將。你兒子呢？

ad·o·les·cence [ˏædḷˋɛsṇs] Track 4267

名 青春期

▶The period of adolescence is very important in forming one's character. 青春期對人格的形成是非常重要的。

實用片語用語
be important in... 對……來說很重要

ad·o·les·cent [ˏædḷˋɛsṇt] Track 4268

形 青春期的、青少年的 同 teenage 青少年的

▶The adolescent life will influence the young people a lot in their later life.
青春期的生活會對年輕人之後的生活產生很大的影響。

a·dore [əˋdor] Track 4269

動 崇拜、敬愛、崇敬

▶I adore my boss very much and so do other people who know him. 我很喜愛我的老闆，認識他的人也都很喜愛他。

adult·hood [əˋdʌltˏhʊd] Track 4270

名 成年期

▶It is a characteristic of adolescence or early adulthood.
據說這是青春期或成年期初期所特有的現象。

A B C D E F G H I J K L M N O P Q R S T U V W X Y Z

ad·ver·tis·er [ˋædvɚˏtaɪzɚ] Track 4271

名 廣告客戶

▶The job of advertisers is to capture our attention.
廣告商的工作就是要吸引我們的注意。

實用片語用語
capture sb.'s attention 吸引某人的注意
也可以說成 catch sb's attention 或 attract sb.'s attention。

af·fec·tion [əˋfɛkʃən] Track 4272

名 親情、情愛、愛慕 反 hate 仇恨

▶She has a deep affection for this old friend.
她對這位老朋友感情很深。

a·gen·da [əˋdʒɛndə] Track 4273

名 議程、節目單

▶Let's work out the agendas for the next two meetings.
我們把下兩次會議的議程制定出來吧。

ag·o·ny [ˋægənɪ] Track 4274

名 痛苦、折磨 同 torment 痛苦

▶The patient is writhing（翻滾）on the bed in agony.
病人痛得在床上打滾。

實用片語用語
agony aunt 聆聽並解決煩惱的人
什麼叫作「疼痛阿姨」呢？就是聆聽讓你痛苦的事、並提供你建議的人。以前的報紙上常會有 agony aunt 的專欄，刊登讀者的來信並針對信中內容提供建議。通常這類專欄的作者都是阿姨級的人物，讓讀者倍感親切，因此才有 agony aunt 這個說法。

ag·ri·cul·tur·al [ˏægrɪˋkʌltʃərəl] Track 4275

名 農業的

▶The country is facing a food shortage even though it once was an agricultural country.
雖然這個國家曾經是一個農業國，但現在也面臨著糧食短缺。

AI/ar·ti·fi·cial in·tel·li·gence [ˏɑrtəˋfɪʃəl ɪnˋtɛlədʒəns] Track 4276

名 人工智慧

▶I wish one day we could produce lots of AI robots to work for us.
我希望有一天我們能製造出許多智慧型機器人來為我們工作。

air·tight [ˋɛrˏtaɪt] Track 4277

形 密閉的、氣密的

▶You'd better send the goods in an airtight package. That would be better.
你最好把這批貨物密封包裝運送。這樣會更好些。

實用片語用語
airtight container 密閉容器
例如：Put those cookies in an airtight container so cockroaches can't touch them.
把那些餅乾放到密閉容器中，這樣蟑螂才不會碰到它們。

air·way [ˋɛrˏwe] Track 4278

名 空中航線

▶It is said that a royal airway will be built at this airport.
據說這個機場將建造一條皇家專用的飛機跑道。

aisle [aɪl] Track 4279

名 教堂的側廊、通道

▶Would you like an aisle seat or a window seat, madam?
夫人，您想要走道旁的座位還是靠窗的座位呢？

al·ge·bra [ˋældʒəbrə]

Track 4280

名 代數

▶I was not good at algebra in middle school.
我中學時不怎麼擅長代數。

a·li·en [ˋelɪən]

Track 4281

形 外國的、外星球的 名 外國人、外星人 同 foreign 外國人

▶形 It doesn't matter whether they are alien workers or not.
他們是不是外國工作人員都不要緊的。

▶名 I've never seen an alien before but I sure hope to one day.
我沒見過外星人，不過我真希望有一天能見到。

實用片語用語

be alien to sb. 對某人來說很陌生

例如：That concept is completely alien to me. I've never heard of it in my life.
這個概念對我來說完全是陌生的，我一生從來沒聽過這樣的事情。

al·ler·gic [əˋlɜdʒɪk]

Track 4282

形 過敏的、厭惡的

▶Will you tell me why some people are allergic to dust but some are not?
你能告訴我為何有些人會對粉塵過敏，而有些人卻不會嗎？

al·ler·gy [ˋælədʒɪ]

Track 4283

名 反感、食物過敏

▶The doctor diagnosed（診斷）him as having a pollen（花粉）allergy. 醫生診斷出他有花粉過敏症。

al·li·ga·tor [ˋæləˏgetə]

Track 4284

名 鱷魚

▶It is said that alligators usually（通常）live in the rivers and lakes in the hot wet parts.
據說鱷魚一般生活在濕熱地帶的河流和湖泊中。

萬用延伸句型

It is said that... 據說……

al·ly [əˋlaɪ]

Track 4285

名 同盟者 動 使結盟 反 enemy 敵人

▶名 The reason why you failed this campaign was that you didn't find an ally to support you.
你們在這場戰役中失敗的原因是你們沒有找到一個能支持你們的盟友。

▶動 The reason why the small country allied itself to the stronger power was that it could save itself from being destroyed.
小國和強國聯盟的原因是為了使自己免於滅亡。

al·ter [ˋɔltə]

Track 4286

動 更改、改變 同 vary 變更

▶I don't think there is any necessity to alter our plan at present.
我認為目前還沒有必要修改我們的計畫。

al·ter·nate [ˋɔltəˏnet]/[ˋɔltəˏnɪt]

Track 4287

動 輪流、交替 形 交替的、間隔的

▶動 Don't you know the rule? The players must alternate serving until the end of the game. 難道你不知道比賽規則嗎？雙方必須輪流發球，直到比賽結束。

▶形 There will be a week of alternate rain and sunshine（陽光）. 下禮拜將會有時雨天有時晴天。

al·ti·tude [ˋæltə͵tjud]

Track 4288

名 高度、海拔 同 height 高度

▶I don't know the altitude of the mountain.
我不知道這座山的海拔高度。

am·ple [ˋæmpḷ]

Track 4289

形 充分的、廣闊的 同 enough 充足的

▶I wish I could find a room that provides ample sunlight（陽光）through windows.
我希望能找到一個有充足陽光透進窗戶來的房間。

實用片語用語
ample evidence 足夠的證據
例如：There is ample evidence that he stole the money.
有足夠的證據證明錢是他偷的。

an·chor [ˋæŋkɚ]

Track 4290

名 錨狀物 動 停泊、使穩固

▶名 I am afraid that we have to lie at anchor outside the harbor. There is no room for us in it.
恐怕我們得在港外拋錨停泊了。裡面沒有空位了。

▶動 We have to anchor the tent with pegs, or the wind will blow it away.
我們得用樁子來固定帳篷，要不然風會把它吹走的。

an·them [ˋænθəm]

Track 4291

名 讚美詩、聖歌

▶Do you mind telling me which song is the American national anthem?
麻煩你告訴我哪一首才是美國的國歌？

實用片語用語
national anthem 國歌

an·tique [ænˋtik]

Track 4292

名 古玩、古董 形 古舊的、古董的 同 ancient 古代的

▶名 The King is fond of collecting curiosities. It is no wonder that the palace is full of priceless antiques.
國王熱愛收藏珍品。難怪宮殿裡到處都是無價的古玩。

▶形 This is an antique chair, so all those salespeople want to buy it.
這是一把古董椅，所以那些商人都想把它買下來。

文法字詞解析
curiosity 除了解釋成「好奇心」以外，在這個句子中的意思則是「珍玩、珍品」。

ap·plaud [əˋplɔd]

Track 4293

動 鼓掌、喝采、誇讚

▶It is a surprise that they all applauded him for his decision.
他們居然一致贊成他的決定，這真令人驚訝。

ap·plause [əˋplɔz]

Track 4294

名 喝采 同 praise 稱讚

▶There was a shower of applause after the performance.
表演結束後，響起一片熱烈的掌聲。

apt [æpt]

Track 4295

形 貼切的、恰當的 同 suitable 適當的

▶A man apt to promise is apt to forget.
輕易承諾的人容易忘記承諾。

實用片語用語
be apt to 容易；傾向於……
例如：She is very apt to faint.
她很容易昏倒。

ar·chi·tect [ˋɑrkə͵tɛkt] Track 4296

名 建築師

▶Not every man is the architect of his or her own fortune.
並非每一個人都是自己命運的建築師。

ar·chi·tec·ture [ˋɑrkə͵tɛktʃɚ] Track 4297

名 建築、建築學、建築物 同 building 建築物

▶My sister studies architecture at the university. What about your sister?
我妹妹在大學裡學建築。你妹妹呢？

a·re·na [əˋrinə] Track 4298

名 競技場 同 stadium 競技場

▶It is said that it is the remains of an arena from ancient Roman（古羅馬的）times.
據說這就是古羅馬時期的競技場遺跡。

ar·mor [ˋɑrmɚ] Track 4299

名 盔甲 動 裝甲

▶名 The knight（騎士）was busy polishing his armor.
那名騎士正忙著擦洗自己的盔甲。

▶動 It was useful to armor the troops in ancient wars.
在古代戰爭中給軍隊裝備盔甲很有用。

實用片語用語
be busy in（V-ing） 忙著做某事

as·cend [əˋsɛnd] Track 4300

動 上升、登

▶We spent too much time ascending the mountain.
我們爬上山實在花太久了。

ass [æs] Track 4301

名 驢子、笨蛋、傻瓜

▶The ass on our farm is always very quiet.
我們農場上的驢子總是很安靜。

as·sault [əˋsɔlt] Track 4302

名 攻擊 動 攻擊 同 attack 攻擊

▶名 The soldiers made a strong assault on the town.
士兵們猛烈攻擊這座城。

▶動 It is impossible（不可能的）for us to assault the castle on all sides.
我們是不可能從四面八方向城堡發起突擊的。

文法字詞解析
除了戰爭方面的「攻擊」外，assault 也能指生活中可能遇到的侵犯、侵害事件。例如「性侵害」就可稱為 sexual assault。

as·set [ˋæsɛt] Track 4303

名 財產、資產 同 property 財產

▶Her greatest asset is her speed.
她最重要的強項就是速度很快。

as·ton·ish [əˋstɑnɪʃ] Track 4304

動 使……吃驚

▶He astonished us with wine he brewed（釀造）himself.
他拿出自己親手釀的酒，讓我們大吃一驚。

A B C D E F G H I J K L M N O P Q R S T U V W X Y Z

as·ton·ish·ment [əˋstɑnɪʃmənt] Track 4305

名 吃驚

▶I look around in astonishment, wondering how I woke up in someone else's room.
我驚愕地環視四周，想知道我怎麼會在別人房間裡醒來。

實用片語用語
in astonishment 驚訝地

a·stray [əˋstre] Track 4306

副 迷途地、墮落地 形 迷途的、墮落的

▶副 If it weren't for the guide, they would have gone astray.
如果不是那個領隊的話，他們就迷路了。

▶形 The letter is astray; we didn't get it in the mail.
那封信遺失了，我們沒有收到。

as·tro·naut [ˋæstrə͵nɔt] Track 4307

名 太空人

▶Up to now, there are only four astronauts in the spacecraft.
到目前為止，這艘太空船只有四名太空人。

萬用延伸句型
Up to now... 直到現在……

as·tron·o·my [əsˋtrɑnəmɪ] Track 4308

名 天文學

▶Will you tell me the differences between astrology（占星術）and astronomy?
你能告訴我占星術和天文學之間的區別嗎？

at·ten·dance [əˋtɛndəns] Track 4309

名 出席、參加 反 absence 缺席

▶The teacher takes attendance before classes.
這位老師在上課前都會記錄出席人數。

實用片語用語
take attendance 點名

au·di·to·ri·um [͵ɔdəˋtorɪəm] Track 4310

名 禮堂、演講廳 同 hall 會堂

▶There are so many students in the auditorium that I can't find my friends.
禮堂裡人山人海，以致於我找不到我的朋友們。

aux·il·ia·ry [ɔgˋzɪljərɪ] Track 4311

形 輔助的

▶You'd better bring auxiliary light in case of certain emergencies.
你最好隨身帶上輔助的照明設備，以防突發事件。

awe [ɔ] Track 4312

名 敬畏 動 使敬畏 同 respect 尊敬

▶名 His paintings filled people with awe and joy.
他的畫使人們心中充滿喜樂與敬畏。

▶動 She was awed by his amazing piano skills.
他驚人的鋼琴技巧讓她完全著迷了。

實用片語用語
in awe of 充滿了對……的敬畏、景仰之意
例如：I'm in awe of your artistic talent.
我對你的藝術天分充滿了景仰。

a·while [əˋhwaɪl] Track 4313

副 暫時、片刻 反 forever 永遠

▶Please stay awhile and have a rest.
請待在這裡休息一下吧。

bach·e·lor [ˋbætʃələ˞] Track 4314

名 單身漢、學士 同 single 單身男女

▶I prefer remaining a bachelor to marrying someone I don't care about. 我寧願保持單身，也不想跟我不喜歡的人結婚。

back·bone [ˋbæk͵bon] Track 4315

名 脊骨、脊柱 同 spine 脊柱

▶It is obvious that he is an Englishman to the backbone. 顯然他是一個道道地地的英國人。

badge [bædʒ] Track 4316

名 徽章

▶The boy always forgets to wear the school badge. 這男孩總是忘記佩戴校徽。

bal·lot [ˋbælət] Track 4317

名 選票 動 投票 同 vote 投票

▶名 It is reported that the chairman of the committee was elected by ballot. 據報導該委員會的主席是投票選舉出來的。

▶動 They balloted for a new chairman. 他們投票選出了新主席。

ban [bæn] Track 4318

動 禁止 名 禁令、查禁

▶動 Swimming in this lake is banned. 規定禁止人們在這個湖裡游泳。

▶名 There is a ban on smoking in the theatre. 這個劇院裡禁止吸煙。

ban·dit [ˋbændɪt] Track 4319

名 強盜、劫匪 同 robber 強盜

▶Most people hate bandits very much. 大部分人們都非常痛恨強盜。

ban·ner [ˋbænə˞] Track 4320

名 旗幟、橫幅 同 flag 旗幟

▶I'm afraid that banner ads and photographs attract more attention than artwork. 恐怕旗幟廣告和照片比藝術品更能吸引注意力。

ban·quet [ˋbæŋkwɪt] Track 4321

名 宴會 動 宴客 同 feast 宴會

▶名 We held a banquet in their honor. 我們設宴招待他們。

▶動 They banqueted all day and night. 他們沒日沒夜地在開宴會。

實用片語用語

have no backbone 懦弱

「have no backbone」的人想當然一定「無法為自己站起來爭取權益」，因為他沒有背脊，軟綿綿的根本站不起來，所以才會用來描述懦弱的人。

例如：That man has no backbone and listens to everything his mom says.

那個男人非常懦弱，媽媽叫他往東他就不敢往西。

文法字詞解析

bandit 和同義詞 robber 都有強盜、搶匪的意思，那麼它們之間有沒有差別呢？硬要說的話，bandit 比較可能是集團犯案，也就是屬於一個強盜集團；而 robber 則不一定，就算只有一個人也可以當 robber。無論你的本業是什麼，如果一時興起想去搶劫，就可以稱為 robber，而 bandit 既然是集團的一部分就比較有系統一點，不是隨隨便便一個人就可以變成 bandit 的。

bar·bar·i·an [bɑrˋbɛrɪən]
Track 4322

名 野蠻人 形 野蠻的

▶名 The barbarians used to cut off people's heads.
那些野蠻人以前都會砍人頭。

▶形 It's said that there is a barbarian tribe living in this forest.
據說有一個原始部落居住在這個林區。

實用片語用語
barbarian tribe 原始部落

bar·ber·shop [ˋbɑrbɚ͵ʃɑp]
Track 4323

名 理髮店

▶The barbershop is an immense success.
那間理髮店的生意興隆。

bare·foot [ˋbɛr͵fʊt]
Track 4324

形 赤足的 副 赤足地

▶形 The barefoot boy began to cry because he stepped on glass.
那個赤腳的男孩因為踩到了玻璃而大哭。

▶副 You'd better not walk barefoot on the damp hard sand.
你最好不要赤著腳在既潮濕又硬梆梆的沙灘上行走。

bar·ren [ˋbærən]
Track 4325

形 不毛的、土地貧瘠的 反 fertile 肥沃的

▶The land is barren, not a single plant in sight.
那是片不毛之地，完全看不到半顆植物。

實用片語用語
in sight 在視野內

bass [bes]
Track 4326

名 低音樂器、男低音歌手 形 低音的

▶名 It is obvious that the opera star is a fine bass.
這位歌劇明星顯然是位優秀的男低音歌手。

▶形 The bass soloist（獨唱者）had an excellent voice.
這位男低音獨唱者的聲音非常棒。

batch [bætʃ]
Track 4327

名 一批、一群、一組 同 cluster 群、組

▶My grandma baked a batch of cookies.
我奶奶烤了一堆餅乾。

bat·ter [ˋbætɚ]
Track 4328

動 連擊、重擊 同 beat 打擊

▶It is the second time that I heard someone battering at the door.
這是我第二次聽到有人在使勁敲門。

文法字詞解析
在 batter 後面加上字尾「-ed」即能變成形容詞 battered，意思是「受到打擊的、被打得狼狽不堪的」。

ba·zaar [bəˋzɑr]
Track 4329

名 市場、義賣會

▶There are many pretty tablecloths for sale at the bazaar.
市場上出售許多漂亮的桌布。

beau·ti·fy [ˋbjutə͵faɪ]
Track 4330

動 美化

▶We should spare no effort to beautify our environment.
我們應該不遺餘力地美化我們的環境。

before·hand [bɪˋfor͵hænd]
Track 4331

副 事前、預先 反 afterward 之後、後來

▶I'm afraid that we should arrive at the meeting place beforehand.
我們恐怕應該提前到達碰面的地點。

be·half [bɪˋhæf]
Track 4332

名 代表

▶It is obvious that the lawyer should speak on behalf of his client.
律師顯然應該代表他的當事人發言。

實用片語用語
on sb's behalf 代表某人
例如：Could you go to the meeting on my behalf?
你可以代表我去參加會議嗎？

be·long·ings [bəˋlɔŋɪŋz]
Track 4333

名 所有物、財產 同 possession 財產

▶We came home to find our belongings scattered about the room.
我們回到家裡，看到東西被扔得滿屋都是。

be·lov·ed [bɪˋlʌvd]
Track 4334

形 鍾愛的、心愛的 同 darling 親愛的

▶He bought his beloved daughter a pony.
他買了一匹小馬給他心愛的女兒。

ben·e·fi·cial [͵bɛnəˋfɪʃəl]
Track 4335

形 有益的、有利的 反 harmful 有害的

▶It's beneficial for us to exercise in the morning every day.
每天早晨做運動對我們是有益的。

be·ware [bɪˋwɛr]
Track 4336

動 當心、小心提防

▶Please beware of snakes.
請小心有蛇。

文法字詞解析
不是所有的事情都可以用「beware」這個字來提醒人家小心。beware 通常是用來警告人家要小心「還沒發生但有可能會發生」的事，例如若某處可能會有蛇出沒，就可以提醒人「beware of snakes」；若朋友已經快被蛇咬到了，要叫他小心，用「beware」就嫌太遲了。

bid [bɪd]
Track 4337

名 投標價 動 投標、出價

▶名 That small obscure（無名的）firm won the bid finally.
那個不起眼的小公司最終得了標。

▶動 He bid $30000 on the oil painting.
他出價三萬美元來買下那幅油畫。

文法字詞解析
bid 的動詞變化：bid, bidded , bidded
或是 bide, bade, bidden

black·smith [ˋblæk͵smɪθ]
Track 4338

名 鐵匠、鍛工

▶A blacksmith's job is not an easy one. What do you think?
鐵匠的工作很不容易。你覺得呢？

blast [blæst]
Track 4339

名 強風、風力 動 損害 反 breeze 微風

▶名 It is reported that the bomb blast killed 5 harmless（無惡意的）passers-by（路人）.
據報導，炸彈的爆炸使五名無辜的行人受傷。

▶動 If he doesn't open the door, we'll have to blast it open.
他還是不開門的話，我們只好把門炸開了。

blaze [blez]
Track 4340

動 火焰、爆發

▶Lights were blazing in every room yesterday.
昨天每個房間都燈火通明。

bleach [blitʃ]
Track 4341

名 漂白劑 動 漂白、脫色 反 dye 染色

▶名 You'd better put the dirty clothes in household bleach overnight. 你最好把髒衣服用家用漂白劑泡一夜。

▶動 You should really bleach your white shirt.
你最好用漂白粉漂洗你的白襯衫。

萬用延伸句型
You'd better... 你最好……

bliz·zard [ˋblɪzɚd]
Track 4342

名 暴風雪

▶It is very dangerous for you to attempt to drive during a blizzard.
你試圖在暴風雪中開車是很危險的。

實用片語用語
a blizzard of 一大堆的、雪片般的
例如：I got a blizzard of mails after coming back from my vacation.
我從假期回來後收到了一大堆的郵件。

blond/blonde [blɑnd]
Track 4343

名 金髮的人 形 金髮的

▶名 We would like a blond to appear in this advertisement.
我們想找一個金髮的人來拍這支廣告。

▶形 Would you tell me who that blond girl standing at the corner of the room is?
你能告訴我站在牆角的那個金髮女郎是誰嗎？

blot/stain [blɑt]/[sten]
Track 4344

名 污痕、污漬 動 弄髒、使蒙羞

▶名 Is there any way to remove the ink blot on my dress?
有什麼辦法能去掉我洋裝上的墨漬嗎？

▶動 Many names were blotted out from the list.
有很多人的名字從名單上被刪掉了。

blues [bluz]
Track 4345

名 憂鬱、藍調

▶I listen to the blues on rainy days.
我在下雨天聽藍調。

文法字詞解析
大家熟知的 R&B 其實就是 Rhythm & Blues（節奏藍調）的縮寫。

blur [blɝ]
Track 4346

名 模糊、朦朧 動 變得模糊

▶名 We're traveling so fast that everything outside passed by in a blur.
我們前進得很快，外面的一切景物都看不清楚了。

▶動 My sight was blurred because of tears.
我的視線因淚水變得模糊。

bod·i·ly [ˋbɑdɪlɪ]
Track 4347

形 身體上的 副 親自、親身 反 spiritual 精神的

▶形 He cares too much about his bodily comforts.
他太過注重物質上的舒適了。

▶副 He carried the baby bodily into the car.
他把寶寶整個抱進車子裡。

body·guard [ˋbadɪ͵gard] Track 4348

名 護衛隊、保鑣

▶The big guy standing at his side may be his bodyguard.
站在他身旁的那個大個子可能是他的保鑣。

bog [bag] Track 4349

名 濕地、沼澤 動 陷於泥沼

▶名 Don't try to walk across that bog.
別試著去穿越那個沼澤。

▶動 I'm afraid that the important negotiations are likely to bog down.
這些重要的談判恐怕很可能會停滯不前。

實用片語用語

bog down 被……限制住、被……壓住，以致於停滯不前

例如：He couldn't swim far because he was bogged down by his heavy clothes.
因為厚重的衣服限制，他沒辦法游得很遠。

bolt [bolt] Track 4350

名 門閂 動 閂上、吞嚥

▶名 You can slide the bolt back and open the door.
你可以推開門閂，把門打開。

▶動 You'd better bolt all the doors and windows before you leave.
你出去前最好把所有門窗都閂上。

bo·nus [ˋbonəs] Track 4351

名 分紅、紅利

▶It is clear that the workers are expecting a large Christmas bonus. 顯然工人們正期待著在耶誕節得到一大筆獎金。

boom [bum] Track 4352

名 隆隆聲、繁榮 動 發出低沉的隆隆聲、急速發展

同 thunder 隆隆聲

▶名 It is said that he made a lot of money during the property boom.
據說他在房地產業繁榮的期間發了大財。

▶動 The economy boomed during the past two years.
前兩年，經濟快速地發展。

booth [buθ] Track 4353

名 棚子、攤子

▶Would you please watch over my booth? I have to do something urgent at once. 請您幫忙留意一下我的攤位好嗎？我必須馬上去辦一些緊急的事。

實用片語用語

telephone booth 電話亭

例如：They had to hide in the telephone booth to wait for the rain to stop.
他們得躲在電話亭裡等雨停。

bore·dom [ˋbordəm] Track 4354

名 乏味、無聊

▶I don't think boredom is a ground for divorce.
我認為乏味不能成為離婚的理由。

bos·om [ˋbʊzəm] Track 4355

名 胸懷、懷中 同 breast 胸部

▶She hugged the baby at her bosom.
她把孩子抱在胸口。

bot·a·ny [ˋbɑtənɪ]

Track 4356

名 植物學

▶Not everyone knows that zoology（動物學）and botany are the two main branches of biology.
不是每個人都知道動物學和植物學是生物學的兩大分支。

實用片語用語
branch of... ……的分支

bou·le·vard [ˋbuləˏvɑrd]

Track 4357

名 林蔭大道 同 avenue （林蔭）大道

▶Do you know how long Jones Boulevard is?
你知道瓊斯大街有多長嗎？

bound [baʊnd]

Track 4358

名 彈跳 動 跳躍

▶名 His ability to sing improved in leaps and bounds.
他的歌唱能力簡直是大躍進了。

▶動 The children bounded all the way to the ice cream stand.
孩子們一路跳躍著到冰淇淋攤。

實用片語用語
in leaps and bounds 突飛猛進

bound·a·ry [ˋbaʊndərɪ]

Track 4359

名 邊界 同 border 邊界

▶It is obvious that the river is the boundary between the two countries. 顯然這條河就是兩國的分界線。

實用片語用語
boundary between A and B
A 和 B 之間的分界線

bow·el [ˋbaʊəl]

Track 4360

名 腸子、惻隱之心

▶He has noticed some blood in his bowel movements.
他發現大便裡有點血。

box·er [ˋbɑksɚ]

Track 4361

名 拳擊手

▶It is said that the boxer has fought many opponents.
據說那個拳擊手已經和許多對手交手過。

box·ing [bɑksɪŋ]

Track 4362

名 拳擊

▶I enjoy all the sports with the exception of boxing. What about you? 我喜歡拳擊之外的所有運動。你呢？

萬用延伸句型
with the exception of... 除了……，和 except 同義。

boy·hood [ˋbɔɪhʊd]

Track 4363

名 少年期、童年

▶Not everyone has a happy boyhood.
不是每個人都擁有一個幸福的童年。

brace [bres]

Track 4364

名 支架、鉗子 動 支撐、鼓起勇氣 同 prop 支撐物

▶名 The little girl has been wearing braces since two years ago.那個小女孩從兩年前就在戴牙套了。

▶動 Brace yourself, the boss is going to come in and yell at us.
你要做好心理準備喔，老闆要進來大罵我們了。

braid [bred]

Track 4365

名 髮辮、辮子 動 編結辮帶或辮子

▶名 He likes pulling his classmates' braids.
他喜歡拉他同學的辮子。

▶動 It takes me about ten minutes in the morning to braid my hair. 每天早上我都要花大概十分鐘的時間綁我的辮子。

實用片語用語
French braid 法式辮子
此外還有 fishtail braids（像魚尾巴造型的辮子）、Dutch braid（荷蘭式辮子）、waterfall braid（瀑布造型的辮子）等等，長頭髮的人可以研究看看有沒有適合自己的造型變化。

breadth [brɛdθ]

Track 4366

名 寬度、幅度 反 length 長度

▶She is admired for the great breadth of her learning.
她由於學識極其淵博而受到尊敬。

bribe [braɪb]

Track 4367

名 賄賂 動 行賄

▶名 He is honest enough to reject bribe.
他夠忠誠老實，不會收受賄賂。

▶動 It is said that they tried to bribe the reporter into silence.
據說他們曾試圖收買該記者好堵住他的嘴。

brief·case [ˋbrifˏkes]

Track 4368

名 公事包、公文袋

▶Would you please open your briefcase? It's routine inspection.
請你打開公事包好嗎？這是例行檢查。

實用片語用語
routine inspection 例行檢查

broad·en [ˋbrɔdn̩]

Track 4369

動 加寬 同 widen 加寬

▶Education and experience had broadened his vision and understanding.
教育和經歷使他的眼界開闊。

bronze [brɑnz]

Track 4370

名 青銅 形 青銅製的

▶名 There will be a display of bronze works in this museum next week.
據說下星期這個博物館將舉辦一個青銅雕塑作品的展覽。

▶形 It is said that this bronze bell dates from the 16th century.
據說這座青銅鐘是在十六世紀時製造的。

實用片語用語
date from... 始於……、可以追溯到……

brooch [brotʃ]

Track 4371

名 別針、胸針

▶What do you think about buying a beautiful brooch as her present?
你覺得買一個漂亮的胸針當作送她的禮物怎麼樣？

brood [brud]

Track 4372

名 同一窩孵出的幼鳥 動 孵蛋、擔憂

▶名 I found a brood of little birds in my garden.
我在我家花園找到了一窩幼鳥。

▶動 There is no use brooding over one's failure.
老是擔憂失敗是沒有用的。

實用片語用語
brood over sth. 為某事心煩、憂鬱

A B C D E F G H I J K L M N O P Q R S T U V W X Y Z

broth [brɔθ]

Track 4373

名 湯、清湯 同 soup 湯

▶I wonder what you put in this broth? It tastes amazing.
你到底放了什麼到這湯裡面？喝起來超棒的。

broth·er·hood [ˋbrʌðɚhʊd]

Track 4374

名 兄弟關係、手足之情

▶Soldiers who fight together often have a strong feeling of brotherhood.
一起作戰的士兵之間常懷有深厚的兄弟情誼。

browse [braʊz]

Track 4375

名 瀏覽 動 瀏覽、翻閱

▶名 Are these books yours? Can I have a browse?
這些書是你的嗎？我可以瀏覽一下嗎？

▶動 You shouldn't browse other people's files.
你不應該瀏覽其他人的檔案。

文法字詞解析
大家上網常用的「瀏覽器」叫作 browser，就是從這個單字來的。

bruise [bruz]

Track 4376

名 青腫、瘀傷 動 使……青腫、使……瘀傷

▶名 I have a few cuts and bruises, would you please buy some band-aid（OK繃）for me?
我身上有幾處割傷和瘀傷，麻煩您幫我買幾個OK繃好嗎？

▶動 Would you tell me how you bruised your arm?
你能告訴我你是怎麼把手臂弄瘀青的嗎？

文法字詞解析
bruise 不只是身體上的受傷、瘀傷，也用來講讓某人在感情、心靈上受到傷害。

bulge [bʌldʒ]

Track 4377

名 腫脹 動 鼓脹、凸出 同 swell 腫脹

▶名 The bag of candy made a bulge in the child's pocket.
那袋糖果使得這孩子的口袋凸出一塊。

▶動 Can you see those muscles bulging under his shirt?
你有沒有看到他衣服下面凸出的肌肉？

bulk [bʌlk]

Track 4378

形 容量、龐然大物

▶Would you let me know if there is a discount on bulk purchases?
請告訴我如果我大量購買的話是否能有些折扣呢？

bul·ly [ˋbʊlɪ]

Track 4379

名 暴徒 動 脅迫

▶名 The little boy kicked his bullies.
那個小男孩踢了霸凌他的人一腳。

▶動 You really shouldn't bully your classmates.
你真的不應該欺負同學。

實用片語用語
bully victim 霸凌對象
例如：The bully victim finally couldn't take it anymore and found a way to revenge.
這個被霸凌的人終於受不了了，找了一個方法來報復。

bu·reau [ˋbjʊro]

Track 4380

名 政府機關、辦公處 同 agency 行政機關

▶We should maintain a good relationship with the local tax bureau.
我們應該要跟當地稅務局保持良好的關係。

butch·er [ˋbʊtʃɚ] Track 4381

名 屠夫 動 屠殺、殘害 同 slaughter 屠殺

▶名 The butcher handed me the meat I bought happily.
那名屠夫開心地把我買的肉遞給我。

▶動 He butchered the pig with a small sharp knife.
他用一把鋒利的小刀殺豬。

cac·tus [ˋkæktəs] Track 4382

名 仙人掌

▶How often do you have to water this cactus a month?
你每個月給仙人掌澆幾次水？

文法字詞解析
cactus 的複數可以說成 cactuses 或 cacti。

calf [kæf] Track 4383

名 小牛

▶What happened to the cute little calf on your farm?
你們農場那頭可愛的小牛怎麼了？

cal·lig·ra·phy [kəˋlɪgrəfɪ] Track 4384

名 筆跡、書法

▶Will you tell me whom you learned Chinese calligraphy from?
你能告訴我你是跟誰學書法的嗎？

ca·nal [kəˋnæl] Track 4385

名 運河、人工渠道 同 ditch 管道

▶It took the poor men more than ten years to finish building the canal. 這些可憐的人們花了十幾年的時間才修築完這條運河。

can·non [ˋkænən] Track 4386

名 大砲

▶It was hard for them to win the fight without enough cannons.
沒有足夠的大炮，他們很難打贏這場仗。

文法字詞解析
從大砲裡面射出來的砲彈則稱為 cannonball。

car·bon [ˋkɑrbən] Track 4387

名 碳、碳棒

▶The reason the temperature is rising is the large amount of carbon dioxide（二氧化碳）.
氣溫之所以會升高是因為大量的二氧化碳。

card·board [ˋkɑrd͵bord] Track 4388

名 卡紙、薄紙板

▶How about taking all these things home in a cardboard box?
把所有的東西放在紙箱裡帶回家去怎麼樣？

實用片語用語
cardboard box 紙箱

care·free [ˋkɛr͵fri] Track 4389

形 無憂無慮的 反 anxious 憂慮的

▶Once you graduate, there will be no carefree vacation anymore.
一旦你畢業了，就不會再有無憂無慮的假期了。

care·tak·er [ˋkɛr͵tekɚ]

Track 4390

名 看管人、照顧者

▶I'm afraid that I have to tell this matter to our school caretaker at once.
恐怕我得立刻把這件事報告給學校管理員。

car·na·tion [kɑrˋneʃən]

Track 4391

名 康乃馨

▶She bought a bouquet of carnations for her mother.
她為媽媽買了一束康乃馨。

實用片語用語
a bouquet of 一束

car·ni·val [ˋkɑrnəvl̩]

Track 4392

名 狂歡節慶 同 festival 節日

▶Will you tell me what you plan to do at the carnival?
你能告訴我你去參加狂歡節的時候打算做什麼嗎？

carp [kɑrp]

Track 4393

名 鯉魚 動 吹毛求疵

▶名 He caught a lot of carps in the lake.
他在湖中抓到了不少鯉魚。

▶動 She's always carping about prices when shopping.
她購物的時候總是對於價格吹毛求疵。

car·ton [ˋkɑrtn̩]

Track 4394

名 紙板盒、紙板

▶The empty carton is big enough to store all the eggs you bought. 這空紙盒夠大，可以裝得下你買的所有雞蛋。

實用片語用語
milk carton 牛奶盒
例如：Milk cartons can be recycled. Put it in the bin over there.
牛奶盒可以回收，把它放到那邊的垃圾桶裡吧。

cat·e·go·ry [ˋkætə͵gorɪ]

Track 4395

名 分類、種類 同 classification 分類

▶Which category should I put this book in? Maybe sci-fi?
我該把這本書放在哪個分類？科幻嗎？

ca·the·dral [kəˋθidrəl]

Track 4396

名 主教的教堂 同 church 教堂

▶There is no other building older than this cathedral in the city.
這座教堂是城裡最古老的建築。

cau·tion [ˋkɔʃən]

Track 4397

名 謹慎 動 小心 同 warn 小心、警告

▶名 It is wise for you to exercise caution in crossing the street.
你過馬路時採取小心的態度是明智的。

▶動 I must caution you against the danger because it's difficult for you to fulfill this task. 我必須告誡你應該慎防危險，因為這次任務完成起來會很艱難。

實用片語用語
with caution 小心地
例如：Please proceed with caution on this path; it's not very safe.
走這條小路時要小心，這裡不是很安全。

cau·tious [ˋkɔʃəs]

Track 4398

形 謹慎的、小心的 同 wary 小心的

▶You'd better be cautious in the use of words when you meet such a sensitive person.
你去見這樣一個敏感的人時，最好用詞謹慎些。

ce·leb·ri·ty [sə`lɛbrətɪ]　Track 4399

名 名聲、名人

▶How are you getting along with the celebrity next door to you?
你和住在你隔壁的那個名人相處得怎麼樣？

cel·er·y [`sɛlərɪ]　Track 4400

名 芹菜

▶Would you like some water celery soup and beef cutlet（炸肉排）? 你要不要來點水芹菜湯和牛排？

cel·lar [`sɛlɚ]　Track 4401

名 地窖、地下室 動 貯存於 同 basement 地下室

▶名 It is said that wine shall be stored in a cool cellar.
據說葡萄酒應該儲存在涼快的地下室裡。

▶動 It is said that the wine has been cellared for twenty years.
據說酒已經在地窖裡存了有二十年之久。

文法字詞解析
用來儲藏東西的地下室可以稱為 cellar 或 basement；相反地用來儲藏東西的閣樓則可以稱為 attic。

cel·lo [`tʃɛlo]　Track 4402

名 大提琴

▶My elder sister plays the cello in an orchestra.
我姐姐在管弦樂隊中演奏大提琴。

cell-phone/cell·phone/cel·lu·lar phone/mo·bile phone　Track 4403

[sɛl fon]/[sɛl fon]/[`sɛljʊlɚ fon]/[`mobɪl fon]

名 行動電話

▶You'd better buy a new cell-phone so that we can contact you.
你最好買個新手機，好讓我們能聯繫上你。

Cel·si·us/Cen·ti·grade/cen·ti·grade　Track 4404

[`sɛlsɪəs]/[`sɛntə͵gred]/[`sɛntə͵gred]

形 攝氏的

▶The normal temperature of the human body is 37 degrees Celsius.
人體的正常溫度是攝氏三十七度。

文法字詞解析
雖然台灣是用攝氏做為衡量溫度的標準，但在美國則是用華氏作為溫標，而華式的英文是「Fahrenheit」。

cer·e·mo·ny [`sɛrə͵monɪ]　Track 4405

名 慶典、儀式 同 celebration 慶祝

▶Would you like to attend the opening ceremony held in five days?
你願意來參加五天後即將舉行的開幕式嗎？

實用片語用語
graduation ceremony 畢業典禮
例如：He didn't show up on his own graduation ceremony.
他沒去參加自己的畢業典禮。

cer·tif·i·cate [sɚ`tɪfəkɪt]　Track 4406

名 證書、憑證 動 發證書

▶名 Will you please show me all the certificates you brought, sir?
先生，請把你帶來的所有證明書都給我一下看好嗎？

▶動 Since you say his abilities are certificated, will you show it to me?
既然你說他的能力有文件為證，那你願意給我看一下嗎？

chair·per·son/chair/ chair·man [ˋtʃɛr͵pɝsn̩]/[tʃɛr]/[ˋtʃɛrmən] Track 4407

名 主席

▶It won't be long before we know who the chairman of Senate（參議院）is.
很快我們就會知道誰是參議院的主席了。

chair·wom·an [ˋtʃɛr͵wʊmən] Track 4408

名 女主席

▶Don't you think the new chairwoman is very well-spoken?
你不覺得新上任的女主席很會說話嗎？

chant [tʃænt] Track 4409

名 讚美詩、歌 動 吟唱 同 hymn 讚美詩

▶名 There are several beautiful chants I want to teach you today.
今天我要教你們唱幾首十分美妙的歌。

▶動 There are many people chanting a Christmas carol（頌歌）in the church.
有很多人正在教堂裡唱聖誕頌歌。

文法字詞解析
由於讚美詩歌經常都是一群人齊聲唱的，因此即使不是歌曲，只要一群人一起唸誦重複的文字（例如遊行抗議時喊的口號）也可以稱為 chant。

chat·ter [ˋtʃætɚ] Track 4410

動 喋喋不休

▶The teacher asked the children to stop chattering in class.
老師叫孩子們在課堂上不要一直嘰嘰喳喳地講話。

check·book [ˋtʃɛk͵bʊk] Track 4411

名 支票簿

▶It's not possible for you to retrieve（找回）the lost checkbook.
指望你找回遺失的支票本是不可能的。

check-in [tʃɛk͵ɪn] Track 4412

名 報到、登記

▶Would you please tell me where the check-in desk is?
請你告訴我旅客登記櫃檯在哪？

check-out [ˋtʃɛk͵aʊt] Track 4413

名 檢查、結帳離開

▶I am afraid that this check-out time is not so convenient for me.
恐怕這個退房時間對我來說不是很方便。

文法字詞解析
check out 中間沒有連在一起，分開來當作片語用時，意思是「看看、檢查」某物。例如：Come check this out! It's a purple ladybug!
快過來看看這個！是紫色的瓢蟲耶！

check·up [ˋtʃɛk͵ʌp] Track 4414

名 核對

▶What's the matter with her? I think she should have a general checkup.
她怎麼了？我覺得她應該去做一下全面檢查。

chef [ʃɛf] Track 4415

名 廚師 同 cook 廚師

▶Isn't he one of the top chefs in America?
他不是美國最好的廚師之一嗎？

chem·ist [ˋkɛmɪst] Track 4416

名 化學家、藥商

▶I don't think you can get this kind of medicine at the chemist's shop. 我覺得你在藥房買不到這種藥。

chest·nut [ˋtʃɛsnət] Track 4417

名 栗子 形 紅棕栗色的

▶名 A man in the street is selling bags of hot chestnuts. 街上有個男人在賣一包包的熱栗子。

▶形 She got her long chestnut hair cut. 她把她栗色的長頭髮剪掉了。

實用片語用語

chestnut tree 栗樹

例如：The squirrel disappeared up the chestnut tree.
那隻松鼠躲到栗樹上去了。

chill [tʃɪl] Track 4418

動 使變冷 名 寒冷 形 冷的 同 cold 冷

▶動 The night air chilled my bones. 夜間的氣候使我寒冷徹骨。

▶名 There is a chill in the air this morning. 今天早上有點寒氣襲人。

▶形 There was no one walking on the streets on that chill morning. 在那個寒冷的早晨，沒有人走在街道上。

chim·pan·zee [ˏtʃɪmpænˋzi] Track 4419

名 黑猩猩

▶The chimpanzee loved eating bananas. 那隻猩猩很愛吃香蕉。

choir [kwaɪr] Track 4420

名 唱詩班 同 chorus 合唱隊

▶Do you know that the church choir is to sing tonight? 你知道今晚教堂唱詩班要唱詩嗎？

文法字詞解析

注意這個字的發音，「ch」是發「k」的音喔。

chord [kɔrd] Track 4421

名 琴弦

▶His speech struck a deep chord in the audience's hearts. 他的一席話深深地撥動了觀眾們的心弦。

文法字詞解析

彈吉他、鋼琴等都常會用到的「和弦」就是稱為 chord。因此當你要彈奏某首歌，抓不到和弦時，可以上網搜尋「歌名 + chords」，說不定會有好心人為你詳細地列出來。

chub·by [ˋtʃʌbɪ] Track 4422

形 圓胖的、豐滿的

▶What a naughty chubby kid! Does anyone here know him? 好頑皮的一個胖小孩啊！這裡有人認識他嗎？

cir·cuit [ˋsɝkɪt] Track 4423

名 電路、線路

▶He knows well of not only the circuit device itself but also its design principle. 他不僅很瞭解電路設備本身，還很瞭解它的設計原理。

cite [saɪt] Track 4424

動 例證、引用 同 quote 引用

▶Will you cite another case like this one? If not, you can't convince me. 你能舉出另一個像這樣的例子嗎？如果不能的話，你就無法讓我信服了。

civ·ic [ˋsɪvɪk]
Track 4425

形 城市的、公民的 同 urban 城市的

▶It is a civic duty for us to not throw garbage on the street.
不隨地丟垃圾是公民的義務。

文法字詞解析
在外國也有一些學校會上的「公民課」可以稱為 civics。

clam [klæm]
Track 4426

名 蛤、蚌

▶The restaurant's specialties are clams.
這間餐廳的特色菜是蛤蠣。

clan [klæn]
Track 4427

名 宗族、部落 同 tribe 部落

▶Will you tell me what the clan system is?
你能告訴我族譜系統是什麼嗎？

clasp [klæsp]
Track 4428

名 釦子、鉤子 動 緊抱、扣緊 同 buckle 釦子、扣緊

▶名 I think you'd better fasten it with a clasp, or it will come loose again.
我覺得你最好用鉤子把它扣住，要不然它又會變鬆的。

▶動 You'd better clasp the bracelet your mother gave you around your wrist. 你最好把你媽媽送給你的手鐲戴在手腕上。

實用片語用語
come loose 鬆掉

clause [klɔz]
Track 4429

名 子句、條款

▶It is obvious that you misunderstood what the main clause was. 很顯然你誤解了主要子句應該是哪一個。

cling [klɪŋ]
Track 4430

動 抓牢、附著 同 grasp 抓牢

▶He clings to the hope that she is still alive.
他始終對於她仍活著還抱持著一絲希望。

文法字詞解析
cling 的動詞變化 cling, clung, clung

clock·wise [ˋklɑk͵waɪz]
Track 4431

形 順時針方向的 副 順時針方向地

▶形 The P.E. teacher（體育老師）had his students running in a clockwise direction on the playground.
體育老師讓他的學生們在操場上按順時針方向跑步。

▶副 You must twist the knob clockwise, or you can't open it.
你必須按順時針方向轉動門把，否則你開不了門。

clo·ver [ˋklovɚ]
Track 4432

名 苜蓿、三葉草

▶Have you ever seen a four-leaf clover?
你有看過四葉草（幸運草）嗎？

clus·ter [ˋklʌstɚ]
Track 4433

名 簇、串 動 使生長、使成串 同 batch 組、群

▶名 I wish the patient could see the cluster of flowers as soon as he opened his eyes.
我希望病人一睜開眼就能看到這束花。

萬用延伸句型
I wish sb. could... 真希望某人能……

▶動 There are roses clustering round my window and I can see them in bloom every day.
有很多玫瑰花繞著我的窗戶生長，而且我能每天看到它們盛開。

實用片語用語
cluster around 叢生、聚集在一起

---

clutch [klʌtʃ]
Track 4434

名 抓握 動 緊握、緊抓 同 hold 抓握

▶名 He made a clutch at the branch but still fell.
他伸手要抓那根樹枝，但還是摔下來了。

▶動 The mother clutched her baby in her arms.
媽媽緊緊地把嬰兒抱在手臂裡。

---

coast·line [ˋkost͵laɪn]
Track 4435

名 海岸線

▶Believe it or not, there is only one port along this long coastline.
信不信由你，在這麼長的一條海岸線上竟然只有一個海港。

---

co·coon [kəˋkun]
Track 4436

名 繭 動 用防水布遮蓋

▶名 You can find many cocoons in the forest now.
你現在能在森林裡找到很多繭。

▶動 He cocooned the machine to keep it dry.
他把機器遮蓋起來，它才不會濕掉。

---

coil [kɔɪl]
Track 4437

名 線圈、捲 動 捲、盤繞 同 curl 捲

▶名 Would you please pass me a coil of thread, Tom? I need to sew these clothes.
湯姆，請你遞給我一捲線好嗎？我需要縫一下這些衣服。

▶動 Can you help me coil the rope on the deck?
請幫我把甲板上的繩子繞好好嗎？

實用片語用語
a coil of rope 一捲繩子
例如：If we had a coil of rope we could get over the wall.
如果我們有一捲繩子就能爬過這堵牆了。

---

col·league [ˋkɑlig]
Track 4438

名 同僚、同事

▶What do you think of the new colleague in the marketing department?
你覺得行銷部門新來的那個同事怎麼樣？

---

colo·nel [ˋkɝnl]
Track 4439

名 陸軍上校

▶The white-haired colonel is always eating fried chicken.
那個白髮的上校總是在吃炸雞。

---

co·lo·ni·al [kəˋlonɪəl]
Track 4440

名 殖民地的居民 形 殖民地的

▶名 It is obvious that these men are colonials and have lived here for a long time. 顯然這些人都是殖民地的居民，並且已經在這生活了很久。

▶形 The empire has to give up many of its colonial territories.
這個帝國現在不得不放棄很多它的殖民領地。

實用片語用語
colonial territory 殖民地
或者也可以直接用colony這個字來表示。

com·bat [ˋkɑmbæt]
Track 4441

名 戰鬥、格鬥 動 戰鬥、抵抗 同 battle 戰鬥

▶名 There were plenty of people killed in the combat zone.
有很多人死在戰場上。

▶動 He has decided to combat with his bad habits.
他決定和自己的壞習慣戰鬥了。

實用片語用語
combat boots 軍用靴
例如：She looks amazing in those combat boots.
她穿那雙軍用靴超好看的。

co·me·di·an [kəˋmidɪən]
Track 4442

名 喜劇演員

▶The comedian's performance was very amusing（有趣的）.
這名喜劇演員的表演很有趣。

com·et [ˋkɑmɪt]
Track 4443

名 彗星

▶Will you tell me why the ancients regarded the comet as an evil omen?
你能告訴我為什麼古人認為彗星是一種不祥的預兆嗎？

com·men·ta·tor [ˋkɑmən͵tetɚ]
Track 4444

名 時事評論家 同 critic 評論家

▶I don't think they will invite him to be the commentator.
我覺得他們不會請他當評論家。

com·mis·sion [kəˋmɪʃən]
Track 4445

名 委任狀、委託 動 委託做某事

▶名 Do you mind if we approve of the commission of authority to him?
如果我們都贊成把職權委任於他，你介意嗎？

▶動 Do you mind telling me who you will commission to sell your house?
你介意告訴我你會委託誰來賣你的房子嗎？

文法字詞解析
在這個網路發達的時代，要在網路上「委託」事情也越來越容易。例如若你忽然很想要掛一張犀牛在滑雪的圖在牆上，但自己畫不出來，就可以上網「委託」會畫畫的人幫忙。這類的情形越來越普遍，也稱為 commission。

com·mod·i·ty [kəˋmɑdətɪ]
Track 4446

名 商品、物產 同 product 產品

▶On one hand, the prices of commodities are stable this year, but on the other hand, the wages are relatively（相對地）low.
一方面，今年的物價穩定，但是另一方面工資卻相對偏低。

com·mon·place [ˋkɑmən͵ples]
Track 4447

名 平凡的事 形 平凡的 同 general 一般的

▶名 Jet travel is now a commonplace.
搭乘噴射機旅行已經是平凡不過的事了。

▶形 Such agents will be commonplace in the next decades even if it's not so popular now.
儘管這樣的代理商現在不是很流行，但是未來幾十年裡就會很普遍了。

com·mu·nism [ˋkɑmjʊ͵nɪzəm]
Track 4448

名 共產主義

▶He's very familiar with the idea of communism.
他對共產主義相當熟悉。

實用片語用語
be familiar with... 對（某人事物）相當熟悉

com·mu·nist [ˋkɑmjʊ͵nɪst]

Track 4449

名 共產黨員 形 共產黨的

▶名 Many communists gave their lives for the revolutionary cause in the past.
過去眾多的共產黨人為革命事業獻出了自己的生命。

▶形 There are several books about communist theory on my desk. 我的書桌上有幾本關於共產主義理論的書。

實用片語用語
give one's life for... 將某人的一生奉獻給……

com·mute [kəˋmjut]

Track 4450

動 變換、折合、通勤 同 shuttle 往返

▶He has to commute five miles to work every day.
他每天都要通勤五英里路去工作。

com·mut·er [kəˋmjutɚ]

Track 4451

名 通勤者

▶The commuters all look very tired at night.
這些通勤的人晚上看起來都很累。

com·pact [ˋkɑmpækt]/[kəmˋpækt]

Track 4452

名 契約 形 緊密的、堅實的

▶名 We agreed to make a compact with your country so that we can maintain the peace between us.
我們同意和貴國訂約，以此來保持彼此之間的和平。

▶形 Please help me stamp the soil down so that it's compact.
請幫我把泥土踩結實。

實用片語用語
compact car 小型車
例如：Only a compact car can fit in this tiny garage.
只有小型車能塞入這小小的車庫。

com·pass [ˋkʌmpəs]

Track 4453

名 羅盤 動 包圍

▶名 It is easy for you to find the place you want to go with a compass.
有了羅盤，你可以很容易就找到你想要去的那個地方。

▶動 Suddenly enemies compassed them on all sides, and it was difficult for them to break through.
敵人突然從四面八方將他們包圍，使得他們很難突圍。

com·pas·sion [kəmˋpæʃən]

Track 4454

名 同情、憐憫 同 sympathy 同情

▶It is quite clear that he showed no compassion for the patient.
很顯然他對病人毫無同情心。

com·pas·sion·ate [kəmˋpæʃənɪt]

Track 4455

形 憐憫的 反 cruel 殘忍的

▶I wish the compassionate judge could give him a light sentence.
我希望仁慈的法官能從輕判決他。

com·pel [kəmˋpɛl]

Track 4456

動 驅使、迫使、逼迫 同 force 迫使

▶I don't feel compelled to support this cause.
我不覺得有什麼動力要支持這個行動。

實用片語用語
feel compelled to... 覺得有動力要（做某事）

com·pli·ment [ˋkαmpləmənt] Track 4457

名 恭維 反 insult 侮辱

▶Doesn't the man deserve the compliment?
難道這個人不應當受到這樣的讚揚嗎？

com·pound Track 4458

[ˋkαmpaʊnd]/[kαmˋpaʊnd]

名 合成物、混合物 動 使混合、達成協定 同 mix 混合

▶名 Let's start our new lesson: air is a mixture, not a compound of gases.
我們開始新的課程：空氣是混合物，不是氣體的化合物。

▶動 People can compound water, sand and soil and form bricks.
人們能夠把水、沙和土混合在一起做成磚頭。

com·pre·hend [ˏkαmprɪˋhɛnd] Track 4459

動 領悟、理解

▶Not all people around her can comprehend what she said.
不是她身邊的每個人都能理解她說過的話。

com·pre·hen·sion Track 4460

[ˏkαmprɪˋhɛnʃən]

名 理解

▶How about giving the class a comprehension test today?
今天給全班進行一次理解力測驗如何？

實用片語用語

beyond sb.'s comprehension （某人）無法理解的

例如：What he said was way beyond my comprehension.

他講的事情已經是我完全無法理解的境界了。

com·pro·mise [ˋkαmprəˏmaɪz] Track 4461

名 和解 動 妥協 同 concession 讓步

▶名 A good negotiator（談判者）knows when to make a compromise.
一個好的談判者知道何時該妥協。

▶動 Do you know what to do now? You must refuse to compromise your principles.
你知道你現在應該做些什麼嗎？你必須堅守你的原則，寸步不讓。

com·pute [kəmˋpjut] Track 4462

動 計算 同 calculate 計算

▶Can you compute the distance from the moon to the earth?
你能計算出從地球到月球的距離嗎？

com·pu·ter·ize [kəmˋpjutəˏraɪz] Track 4463

動 用電腦處理

▶Let's work out a scheme to computerize the library service.
我們來制定一個使圖書館服務電腦化的方案吧。

com·rade [ˋkαmræd] Track 4464

名 同伴、夥伴 同 partner 夥伴

▶He is outgoing and responsible. It is no wonder that they all think he is a good comrade to work with. 他既開朗又有責任感。難怪他們都認為他是一個能共事的好夥伴。

萬用延伸句型

It is no wonder that... 難怪……

con·ceal [kən`sil] Track 4465

動 隱藏、隱匿 同 hide 隱藏

▶I think you should conceal your feelings before these serious people. 我覺得你應該在這些嚴肅的人面前隱藏你的感情。

con·ceive [kən`siv] Track 4466

動 構想、構思

▶To tell you the truth, I cannot conceive of anything funnier than this.
說實話，我還真想不出比這更好笑的事情。

延伸萬用句型
To tell you the truth,... 說實話……

con·demn [kən`dɛm] Track 4467

動 譴責、非難、判刑 同 denounce 譴責

▶There is no doubt that the prisoner will be condemned.
毫無疑問這名罪犯將會被判刑。

con·duct [`kɑndʌkt]/[kən`dʌkt] Track 4468

名 行為、舉止 動 指揮、處理

▶名 He is famous for his good conduct.
他因善行而遠近聞名。

▶動 Many actors hire agents to conduct their affairs.
很多演員雇用經紀人掌管他們的事務。

實用片語用語
conduct 除了「指揮別人做事情」外，在交響樂團中，站在最前面引導整個樂團演奏音樂的動作也是「conduct」，而做這個動作的人就叫作「conductor」。

con·fes·sion [kən`fɛʃən] Track 4469

名 承認、招供

▶The little boy made a confession that he broke the window.
小男孩承認他打破了窗戶。

con·front [kən`frʌnt] Track 4470

動 面對、面臨 同 encounter 遭遇

▶I wish I could confront my accuser（原告）in a court of law.
我希望我能和控告我的人當庭對質。

con·sent [kən`sɛnt] Track 4471

名 贊同 動 同意、應允 同 agree 同意

▶名 There is but a faint hope that my father will give his consent to our marriage.
父親同意我們結婚的希望渺茫。

▶動 There is a possibility that he will consent to your plan.
他有可能會同意你的計畫。

實用片語用語
without sb.'s consent 沒有經過（某人的）同意
例如：How could you wear my shoes without my consent?
你怎麼可以沒有經過我的同意就穿我的鞋呢？

con·serve [kən`sɝv] Track 4472

動 保存、保護 同 preserve 保護

▶Not every man will do his best to conserve water.
不是每個人都會盡自己的所能去節約用水。

con·sid·er·ate [kən`sɪdərɪt] Track 4473

形 體貼的

▶I think that he is more considerate than any others I have met.
我認為他比我碰到的其他人更能體諒人。

con·sole [ˋkɑnsol]/[kənˋsol]

Track 4474

名 操作控制台 動 安慰、慰問 同 comfort 安慰

▶名 Neither of us know how to exit the console.
我們都搞不清楚怎麼退出控制台。

▶動 I don't know how to console him after his dog died.
他的狗死後，我都不知道該怎麼安慰他才好。

文法字詞解析
玩電動遊戲用的操作機台就可以稱為 gaming console， 像 PlayStation、Xbox、Wii 這類的都是。

con·sti·tu·tion·al [ˏkɑnstəˋtjuʃən!]

Track 4475

名 保健運動 形 有益健康的、憲法的 同 healthful 有益健康的

▶名 She's out on her daily constitutional.
她在外頭進行她每天的健身運動。

▶形 Will you tell me what happened at the Constitutional Convention?
你能告訴我制憲會議上發生什麼事了嗎？

con·ta·gious [kənˋtedʒəs]

Track 4476

形 傳染的 同 infectious 傳染的

▶Chicken pox（水痘）is a contagious disease.
水痘是一種透過接觸而傳染的疾病。

con·tam·i·nate [kənˋtæməˏnet]

Track 4477

動 污染 同 pollute 污染

▶Don't drink the water. It's contaminated.
不要喝那個水，那是污染過的。

文法字詞解析
這個字加上「-d」就變形容詞「contaminated（受到汙染的）」；還有加上「-tion」的 contamination（汙染、致汙物）也是語出同源。

con·tem·plate [ˋkɑntɛmˏplet]

Track 4478

動 凝視、苦思

▶He contemplated the problem all day but still couldn't solve it.
他苦思了一整天依然解決不了那個問題。

實用片語用語
contemplate V-ing 思考要不要做某事
例如：I contemplated going to the library but decided not to in the end.
我本來思考了一下要不要去圖書館，但最後決定不去。

con·tem·po·rar·y [kənˋtɛmpəˏrɛrɪ]

Track 4479

名 同時代的人 形 同時期的、當代的

▶名 Not all people know that the writer once was looked down upon by his contemporaries.
不是所有人都知道這位作家曾被他同時代的人瞧不起。

▶形 Contemporary artists don't interest me.
我對當代藝術家沒有興趣。

con·tempt [kənˋtɛmpt]

Track 4480

名 輕蔑、鄙視 同 scorn 輕蔑

▶There is no reply as sharp as silent contempt.
無言的輕蔑是最強而有力的回擊。

con·tend [kənˋtɛnd]

Track 4481

動 抗爭、奮鬥

▶The company is too small to contend against large companies.
這家公司太小，無法與大公司競爭。

con·ti·nen·tal [ˏkɑntəˋnɛntḷ] Track 4482

形 大陸的、洲的

▶The continental weather here is not what I'm used to.
這個地方是大陸性氣候，我不是很習慣。

實用片語用語
continental breakfast 歐洲大陸式的早餐
例如：Guests staying at this hotel can enjoy a free continental breakfast.
這家旅館的住客可以免費想用歐陸式的早餐。

con·ti·nu·i·ty [ˏkɑntəˋnjuətɪ] Track 4483

名 連續的狀態

▶Don't you think the three parts of the book lack continuity?
你不覺得這本書裡的這三個部分缺乏連貫性嗎？

con·vert [kənˋvɝt] Track 4484

動 變換、轉換 同 change 改變

▶Will you tell me at what rate the dollar converts into pounds?
你能告訴我美元兌換成英鎊的匯率嗎？

con·vict [ˋkɑnvɪkt]/[kənˋvɪkt] Track 4485

名 被判罪的人 動 判定有罪

▶名 The lawyer says he has enough evidence to prove that the convict is innocent.
律師說他有足夠的證據可以證明犯人是無辜的。

▶動 We have enough evidence to convict this young man now.
我們現在有足夠的證據來給這個年輕人定罪。

cop·y·right [ˋkɑpɪˏraɪt] Track 4486

名 版權、著作權 動 為……取得版權

▶名 It is obvious that the book is protected by copyright.
顯然該書受版權的保護。

▶動 This book is copyrighted in your father's name.
這本書的版權歸屬於你父親的名下。

實用片語用語
copyright notice 版權聲明
例如：Read the copyright notice before downloading it.
下載之前先看一下版權聲明。

cor·al [ˋkorəl] Track 4487

名 珊瑚 形 珊瑚製的

▶名 Coral is often used for making jewelry.
珊瑚常被用來製作首飾。

▶形 The largest coral reef system of the world is in Australia.
世界上最大的珊瑚礁系在澳洲。

實用片語用語
coral reef 珊瑚礁

cor·po·ra·tion [ˏkɔrpəˋreʃən] Track 4488

名 公司、企業 同 company 公司

▶What do you think of working at a nonprofit（非營利的）corporation? 你覺得到一家非營利公司工作怎麼樣？

cor·re·spon·dence [ˏkɔrəˋspɑndəns] Track 4489

名 符合、相似之處 同 accordance 符合

▶There are many correspondences between the two books.
這兩本書有很多相似之處。

cor·ri·dor [ˋkɔrədɚ] Track 4490

名 走廊、通道

▶Will you tell me why he is walking back and forth along the corridor? 你能告訴我他為什麼要在走廊上走來走去嗎？

實用片語用語
back and forth 前後反覆地

cor·rupt [kəˋrʌpt]

Track 4491

動 使墮落 形 腐敗的 同 rotten 腐敗的

▶動 Her mind was corrupted by her older brothers and sisters.
她的心靈在她兄姊的影響下變得墮落了。

▶形 The file is corrupt; I can't get it to open.
文件已損壞，我打不開了。

coun·sel [ˋkaʊnsḷ]

Track 4492

名 忠告、法律顧問 動 勸告、建議 同 advise 勸告

▶名 Listen to the counsel of your elders, or you might regret later on.
聽從長輩們的勸告吧，否則你以後會後悔的。

▶動 I would counsel you to say nothing about the affair.
關於這件事情我勸你什麼也別說了。

coun·sel·or [ˋkaʊnsḷɚ]

Track 4493

名 顧問、參事

▶I think you'd better go to the marriage counselor. Maybe things will change for the better.
我覺得你們最好去諮詢一下婚姻顧問。也許事情還會有轉機。

實用片語用語
marriage counselor 婚姻諮詢師、婚姻顧問

coun·ter·clock·wise
[ˋkaʊntɚ ˋklɑkˏwaɪz]

Track 4494

形 反時針方向的 副 反時針方向地

▶形 Can you count these numbers for me in a counterclockwise direction?
你能按照逆時針的方向來數這些數字嗎？

▶副 Should I turn the knob counterclockwise?
我應該用逆時針方向旋轉這個門把嗎？

文法字詞解析
還有另外一個字也是「逆時針」的意思，就是「anticlockwise」。從字首「counter-」和「anti-」都可以看到「對抗」、「反」的含義。

cou·pon [ˋkupɑn]

Track 4495

名 優待券

▶Would you like to have a coffee coupon? You can get a cup of coffee for free at that counter. 你想要一張咖啡券嗎？你可以憑券到那邊櫃臺免費換取一杯咖啡。

court·yard [ˋkortˏjɑrd]

Track 4496

名 庭院、天井

▶How often does your mother sweep the courtyard?
你媽媽多久打掃一次庭院？

cow·ard·ly [ˋkaʊɚdlɪ]

Track 4497

形 怯懦的 反 heroic 英勇的

▶He is a cowardly boy who runs away as soon as there is trouble. 他是個怯懦的孩子，一有了麻煩就會馬上跑掉。

萬用延伸句型
as soon as... 一……就立刻……

co·zy [ˋkozɪ]

Track 4498

形 溫暖而舒適的

▶I really love the cozy atmosphere in your house.
我真的很喜歡你家溫馨的氣氛。

crack·er [ˋkrækɚ] Track 4499

名 薄脆餅乾

▶Would you like some crackers? If so, I will buy some for you on my way home. 你要不要吃脆餅呢？如果要的話，我回來的時候就給你買一些。

cra·ter [ˋkretɚ] Track 4500

名 火山口 動 噴火、使成坑

▶名 It is too dangerous for any animal or man to approach the crater.
任何人和動物接近火山口都太過危險。

▶動 Artillery（大炮）cratered the road, making it hard to walk on. 大炮把路面轟得凹凸不平，變得很難走。

creak [krik] Track 4501

名 輾軋聲 動 發出輾軋聲

▶名 The door opened with a creak as soon as he knocked at the door.
他一敲門，門就「呀」地一聲開了。

▶動 The bridge creaked when I walked on it.
我過橋時，橋嘎吱嘎吱地響。

文法字詞解析
如果要用形容詞描述某物「會發出輾軋聲」呢？可以用 creaky 這個形容詞。例如會發出輾軋聲的樓梯就可以說是 creaky staircase。

creek [krik] Track 4502

名 小灣、小溪

▶We often swim in the creek behind the house.
我們常在房子後面的小溪裡面游泳。

crib [krɪb] Track 4503

名 糧倉、木屋 動 放進糧倉、作弊

▶名 Why is the baby not in his crib?
寶寶怎麼沒有在嬰兒床上？

▶動 He cribbed from Mike in the exam.
他在考試的時候抄了麥克的答案。

實用片語用語
crib sth. from sb. 抄襲（某人的答案等）

croc·o·dile [ˋkrɑkə͵daɪl] Track 4504

名 鱷魚

▶The big crocodile lives down there in the river.
那隻大鱷魚住在下面的河中。

cross·ing [ˋkrɔsɪŋ] Track 4505

名 橫越、橫渡

▶They had a rough crossing from Japan to China.
它們頂著險風惡浪從日本橫渡到了中國。

實用片語用語
zebra crossing 斑馬線
例如：There's a zebra crossing over there in front of the McDonald's.
那家麥當勞前面有斑馬線。

crouch [krautʃ] Track 4506

名 蹲伏、屈膝姿勢 動 蹲踞 同 squat 蹲

▶名 He waited there in a crouch.
他以蹲姿在那邊等著。

▶動 There is a cat crouching in the corner. Do you see it?
角落裡蜷縮著一隻貓。你看見了嗎？

crunch [krʌntʃ]

Track 4507

名 嘎吱的聲音、危機、關鍵時刻、踩碎、咬碎

動 嘎吱嘎吱地碾或踩、壓過、喀嚓喀嚓地咬嚼

▶名 I don't think they will support us even when it comes to the crunch.
我認為即使是到了緊要關頭，他們也不會支持我們的。

▶動 The shells crunched under our feet.
那些貝殼在我們腳下發出脆脆的聲音。

crys·tal [ˋkrɪstḷ]

Track 4508

名 結晶、水晶 形 清澈的、透明的

▶名 These fine wine glasses are made of crystal.
這些漂亮的酒杯是用水晶做的。

▶形 The cabin stands by a crystal stream.
那個小木屋坐落在清澈的小溪旁邊。

實用片語用語
crystal clear 非常清楚的
例如：I made it crystal clear that I don't want to marry him.
我已經說得非常清楚了，我不要跟他結婚。

cui·sine [kwɪˋzin]

Track 4509

名 烹調、烹飪、菜餚

▶Would you like to try some real Sichuan cuisine in this restaurant? 你想不想到這間餐廳吃點真正的四川菜呢？

curb [kɝb]

Track 4510

名 抑制器 動 遏止、抑制 同 restraint 抑制

▶名 The reason why they place a curb on expenditures（經費）is that they are in want of funds.
他們限制經費的原因是他們現在資金匱乏。

▶動 He could not curb his anger and shouted at her.
他按捺不住自己的憤怒朝著她大吼大叫。

cur·ren·cy [ˋkɝənsɪ]

Track 4511

名 貨幣、流通的紙幣

▶Will you tell me what a commodity currency is?
你能告訴我什麼是商品貨幣嗎？

實用片語用語
commodity currency 商品貨幣

cur·ric·u·lum [kəˋrɪkjələm]

Track 4512

名 課程

▶Life itself is a classroom, and the curriculum is patience.
生活本身就是教室，而耐心便是課程。

cur·ry [ˋkɝɪ]

Track 4513

名 咖哩粉 動 用咖哩粉調味

▶名 How much chilli（辣椒）did you put in the curry?
你在咖哩裡放了多少辣椒啊？

▶動 Do you know how to cook curried chicken?
你知道如何煮咖哩雞嗎？

cus·toms [ˋkʌstəmz]

Track 4514

名 海關

▶Do you mind telling me where I should go through the customs?
能麻煩您告訴我應該在哪裡過海關嗎？

實用片語用語
go through customs 過海關

dart [dɑrt] Track 4515

名 鏢、鏢槍 動 投擲、發射、猛衝 同 throw 投、丟

▶名 I'm terrible at throwing darts.
我超不會射飛鏢的。

▶動 She screamed and darted out of the room.
她尖叫一聲，衝出房間。

daz·zle [ˋdæzḷ] Track 4516

名 恾然耀眼的光 動 眩目、眼花撩亂

▶名 It is clear that the dazzle of the spotlights made him ill at ease. 顯然聚光燈的耀眼強光使他侷促不安。

▶動 The splendid room dazzled the young girl.
這個富麗堂皇的房間使小女孩眼花了。

文法字詞解析
想要說「被弄得眼花繚亂」，可以用「bedazzled」這個相關形容詞。

de·cay [dɪˋke] Track 4517

名 腐爛的物質 動 腐壞、腐爛 同 rot 腐爛

▶名 It is reported that they are trying to stop the decay of the ancient building.
據報導他們正想辦法試圖阻止這個古老建築朽壞。

▶動 It is said that the Turkish Empire decayed in the nineteenth century. 據說土耳其帝國是在十九世紀時衰落的。

de·ceive [dɪˋsiv] Track 4518

動 欺詐、詐騙 同 cheat 欺騙

▶It's not honorable of you to deceive them in such a mean way.
你以如此卑鄙的手段去欺騙他們是不光彩的。

dec·la·ra·tion [͵dɛkləˋreʃən] Track 4519

名 正式宣告

▶These events led to the declaration of war.
是這些事件導致了宣戰。

文法字詞解析
這個字也可以表示寫在紙本上的「宣言」
例如：Declaration of Independence（美國獨立宣言）；還有向海關申報物品也叫作declaration，而「申報」的動作則是用動詞declare。

del·e·gate [ˋdɛləgɪt]/[ˋdɛləget] Track 4520

名 代表、使節 動 派遣 同 assign 指派

▶名 What do you think about recommending Bill as an official delegate? 你們覺得推薦比爾作為一名正式代表怎麼樣？

▶動 I think a boss must know how to delegate.
我認為當老闆的要知人善任。

del·e·ga·tion [͵dɛləˋgeʃən] Track 4521

名 委派、派遣、代表團

▶Our cultural delegation met with a hearty welcome.
我們的文化代表團受到了熱烈歡迎。

dem·o·crat [ˋdɛmə͵kræt] Track 4522

名 民主主義者

▶My grandfather is a democrat. 我爺爺是民主主義者。

de·ni·al [dɪ`naɪəl]

Track 4523

名 否定、否認

▶He's still in denial and won't believe that his girlfriend is dead. 他還是拒絕承認、面對他女友已死的事實。

實用片語用語
be in denial 不願意承認（某事）、拒絕面對（某事）

de·scrip·tive [dɪ`skrɪptɪv]

Track 4524

形 描寫的、說明的

▶The report was so descriptive that I understood everything clearly. 這個報導寫得非常生動，我清楚瞭解了。

de·spair [dɪ`spɛr]

Track 4525

名 絕望 動 絕望 反 hope 希望

▶名 The boss rejected his project ten times and he finally gave up in despair.
老闆駁回他的計畫十次了，他在絕望之下就放棄了。

▶動 I despaired of them ever arriving.
我已經放棄他們會過來的希望了。

de·spise [dɪ`spaɪz]

Track 4526

動 鄙視、輕視 同 scorn 輕視

▶I don't think that you should despise a man because he is poor. 我覺得你不應該因為一個人貧窮而輕視他。

des·ti·na·tion [ˏdɛstə`neʃən]

Track 4527

名 目的地、終點 反 threshold 起點

▶How long will it take for my mail to reach its destination?
我的信件到達目的地要多久？

文法字詞解析
在搭飛機的時候，飛機上可能會貼心地為你列出「time to destination」（還有多久到目的地）、或「local time at destination」（目的地當地時間）等等。

des·ti·ny [`dɛstənɪ]

Track 4528

名 命運、宿命 同 fate 命運

▶It is a pity that it was his destiny never to see her again.
命運註定他再也見不到她，真是遺憾。

de·struc·tive [dɪ`strʌktɪv]

Track 4529

形 有害的 反 constructive 有建設性的、有益的

▶Does the country own any destructive weapons?
那個國家擁有哪些毀滅性的武器嗎？

de·ter·gent [dɪ`tɝdʒənt]

Track 4530

名 清潔劑

▶I got a new brand of detergent to use in my bathroom.
我買了一種新品牌的清潔劑在浴室使用。

實用片語用語
laundry detergent 洗衣精
例如：We ran out of laundry detergent so I couldn't do the laundry.
我們沒有洗衣精了，所以我沒辦法洗衣服。

de·vo·tion [dɪ`voʃən]

Track 4531

名 摯愛、熱愛、奉獻

▶His devotion to company was what got him promoted.
他對公司的奉獻是他升官的主因。

de·vour [dɪ`vaʊr]

Track 4532

動 吞食、吃光 同 swallow 吞嚥

▶It was only minutes before the big fire devoured the entire building. 僅僅幾分鐘的時間大火就吞沒了整棟大樓。

di·a·lect [ˋdaɪəlɛkt] Track 4533

名 方言

▶He is able to pick up different dialects easily.
他很容易能夠學起各地的方言。

dis·be·lief [ˏdɪsbəˋlif] Track 4534

名 不信、懷疑 反 belief 相信

▶A look of disbelief replaced the smile on his face.
他原本微笑的臉上出現了一種不信任的表情。

實用片語用語
in disbelief 不相信地
例如：He could only stare in disbelief at the huge robot his grandma built.
他只能目瞪口呆地看著他奶奶建造的巨大機器人。

dis·card [dɪsˋkɑrd] Track 4535

名 被拋棄的人 動 拋棄、丟掉

▶名 Collect all the discards in a pile and shuffle them.
把拋棄掉的牌收集成一疊洗一洗牌。

▶動 It's not wise for us to discard the present system entirely（完全地）. 我們完全拋棄現行制度是不明智的。

dis·ci·ple [dɪˋsaɪpl] Track 4536

名 信徒、門徒 同 follower 跟隨者

▶Judas was one of the twelve disciples of Jesus.
猶大是耶穌的十二門徒之一。

dis·crim·i·nate [dɪˋskrɪməˏnet] Track 4537

動 辨別、差別對待 同 distinguish 區別

▶It is important for parents to teach their children to discriminate between right and wrong.
對於父母來說教育他們的小孩分辨是非很重要。

dis·pense [dɪˋspɛns] Track 4538

動 分送、分配、免除 同 distribute 分配

▶Press this button and hand sanitizer（清潔劑）will be dispensed.
按這個按鈕，手部清潔劑就會跑出來。

文法字詞解析
能夠「分送」某物的東西就可以稱為 dispenser。例如按它一下就會跑出肥皂泡泡沫的機器，就可以稱為 soap dispenser。

dis·pose [dɪˋspoz] Track 4539

動 佈置、處理 同 arrange 安排、佈置

▶Can you get those old clothes disposed of?
你可不可以把這些舊衣服處理掉？

dis·tinc·tion [dɪˋstɪŋkʃən] Track 4540

名 區別、辨別 同 discrimination 區別

▶I don't see the distinction between this book cover and that one.
我看不出這兩本書的封面有什麼差別。

dis·tinc·tive [dɪˋstɪŋktɪv] Track 4541

形 區別的

▶I think she has a very distinctive way of dressing.
我覺得她穿衣服很有特色。

dis·tress [dɪˋstrɛs] Track 4542

名 憂傷、苦惱 動 使悲痛

▶名 Her death was a great distress to all the family.
她的去世使全家人感到萬分悲痛。

▶動 Mary's illness distressed her greatly.
瑪莉生病的事使她非常憂傷。

實用片語用語

distress signal 緊急求救訊號
又稱 distress call，和我們比較常聽到的「Mayday」是差不多的意思，像是船快沉或是飛機遇到狀況時就會發出這樣的信號。

doc·u·ment [ˋdɑkjəmənt] Track 4543

名 文件、公文 動 提供文件

▶名 Would you please give me a copy of this document?
請您給我一份這個文件的副本好嗎？

▶動 Will you please document the case for me?
可以請你幫我把這個案件建檔嗎？

door·step [ˋdor͵stɛp] Track 4544

名 門階

▶There is a puppy sitting on our doorstep.
有隻小狗坐在我們家門口。

door·way [ˋdor͵we] Track 4545

名 門口、出入口

▶Don't stand in the doorway. Other people can't get out.
不要站在門口，這樣別人都不能出去了。

dor·mi·to·ry [ˋdɔrmə͵torɪ] Track 4546

名 學校宿舍

▶Could you tell me where the dormitory is?
你能告訴我宿舍在哪裡嗎？

文法字詞解析

dormitory 也可以簡稱 dorm。

dough [do] Track 4547

名 生麵團

▶Could you tell me how to make dough from wheat powder?
你能告訴我如何用麵粉做麵團嗎？

down·ward [ˋdaʊnwɚd] Track 4548

副 下降地、向下地 反 upward 上升地

▶He looked downward to avoid my eyes.
他低著頭看以避開我的目光。

down·wards [ˋdaʊnwɚdz] Track 4549

副 下降地、向下地

▶There are several monkeys hanging head downwards from the branch.
有幾隻猴子頭朝下倒掛在樹枝上。

drape [drep] Track 4550

名 幔、窗簾 動 覆蓋、裝飾 同 curtain 窗簾

▶名 It's getting dark. Let's draw the drapes, shall we?
天快黑了。我們拉上窗簾好嗎？

▶動 The little girl draped herself all over her daddy.
那個小女孩整個人攤在她爸爸身上。

延伸萬用句型

Let's ..., shall we?（我們）這樣做好嗎？
這裡用到祈使句的附加問句，用來提議做某件事情。

dread·ful [ˋdrɛdfəl] Track 4551

形 可怕的、恐怖的 同 fearful 可怕的

▶What a dreadful movie! I give it one star out of five.
多麼糟糕的電影啊！五顆星的話我只給它一顆星。

dress·er [ˋdrɛsɚ] Track 4552

名 梳妝臺、鏡臺

▶Did you leave the watch on your dresser?
你是把手錶放在梳妝台上了嗎？

dress·ing [ˋdrɛsɪŋ] Track 4553

名 藥膏、服飾、裝飾

▶You'd better put the dressing table on the left.
你最好把梳粧台放在左邊。

文法字詞解析
沙拉上面灑的沙拉「醬」也可以稱為dressing，畢竟對沙拉來說沙拉醬就有如穿在身上的衣服一樣有覆蓋、增添色彩的效果吧。

drive·way [ˋdraɪv͵we] Track 4554

名 私用車道、車道

▶The truck entered the driveway and drove up towards that house. 那輛卡車進入車道後向那間房屋開過去了。

du·ra·tion [djʊˋreʃən] Track 4555

名 持久、持續

▶I don't think that the duration of their marriage will be very long. 我認為他們的婚姻不會持續太久。

dusk [dʌsk] Track 4556

名 黃昏、幽暗 同 twilight 微光、朦朧

▶It's already dusk; I don't think you should let the children play outside.
都黃昏了，我覺得你不應該讓小孩在外面玩。

實用片語用語
from dawn to dusk 從白晝到黑夜
例如：The farmers worked from dawn to dusk on the crops.
農夫們從白晝到黑夜努力耕種。

dwarf [dwɔrf] Track 4557

名 矮子、矮小動物 動 萎縮、使矮小 反 giant 巨人

▶名 The seven dwarves live in the forest.
七個小矮人住在森林裡。

▶動 The new building dwarves all the other buildings in the town.
有一棟新大樓使城裡所有其他建築物都顯得矮小了。

dwell [dwɛl] Track 4558

動 住、居住、詳述

▶Not all his friends know that he'd dwelled in London for two years. 不是他的所有朋友都知道他曾在倫敦住了兩年。

dwell·ing [ˋdwɛlɪŋ] Track 4559

名 住宅、住處 同 residence 住宅

▶He changed his dwelling recently because the original place is too noisy.
他最近搬了家，因為他原來住的地方太吵了。

e·clipse [ɪ`klɪps] *Track 4560*

名 蝕（月蝕等） 動 遮蔽 同 cover 遮蓋

▶名 Have you ever seen an eclipse before?
你有看過日蝕嗎？

▶動 The moon eclipsed the sun so we can only see half of it.
月亮遮住了太陽，我們只看得到半個太陽。

eel [il] *Track 4561*

名 鰻魚

▶How about asking Mom to buy some eels for dinner today?
叫媽媽今天買些鰻魚做晚餐怎麼樣？

e·go [`igo] *Track 4562*

名 自我、我 同 self 自我

▶He has the hugest ego I've ever seen.
他是我見過最自戀的人。

文法字詞解析
「ego」可以當作字首使用，因此從 ego 延伸出來的字有很多，例如要說一個人非常地「自我」可以稱他為 egoistic（自我的），要說一個人「自我到非常誇張、簡直有病的程度」，可以稱他為 egomaniac。

e·lab·o·rate [ɪ`læbəˌrɪt]/[ɪ`læbəˌret] *Track 4563*

形 精心的 動 精心製作、詳述 反 simple 簡樸的

▶形 I hear that you have made an elaborate plan of attack.
聽說你制定了一個精心的攻擊計畫。

▶動 Do you mind elaborating your ideas before these leaders?
你介意在這些領導人面前詳述你的想法嗎？

el·e·vate [`ɛləˌvet] *Track 4564*

動 舉起 同 lift 舉起

▶I can't elevate the bucket full of water unless someone helps me. 除非有人幫我，要不然我吊不起這個裝滿了水的水桶。

實用片語用語
elevated railroad 高架鐵路
例如：Look! There's someone walking on the elevated railroad!
看！有人走在高架鐵道上！

em·brace [ɪm`bres] *Track 4565*

動 包圍、擁抱 名 擁抱

▶動 She embraced her little daughter.
她擁抱了她的小女兒。

▶名 They gave each other an awkward embrace.
他們尷尬地擁抱了對方。

en·deav·or [ɪn`dɛvɚ] *Track 4566*

名 努力 動 盡力 同 strive 努力

▶名 It is obvious that they have made every endeavor to satisfy their customers. 顯然他們已經盡全力來使顧客滿意。

▶動 His father endeavored to persuade him to work hard.
他的父親在努力設法去說服他努力工作。

實用片語用語
make every endeavor tor... 盡全力地……

en·roll [ɪn`rol] *Track 4567*

動 登記、註冊 同 register 註冊

▶Can you tell me when to enroll in this cooking class?
你能告訴我什麼時候要報名參加這門烹飪課嗎？

en·roll·ment [ɪn`rolmənt] Track 4568

名 登記、註冊

▶It is a pity that the enrollment period has already passed.
很遺憾註冊時間已經截止了。

en·sure/in·sure [ɪn`ʃʊr]/[ɪn`ʃʊr] Track 4569

動 確保、保證

▶I don't believe that a letter of introduction will ensure you an interview. 我不相信一封介紹信就能保證他們會跟你面試。

en·ter·prise [`ɛntəˏpraɪz] Track 4570

名 企業

▶The enterprise must make profits soon, or it will go bankrupt sooner or later.
這個企業必須很快獲利，否則它遲早會破產的。

實用片語用語
sooner or later 遲早

en·thu·si·as·tic [ɪnˏθjuzɪ`æstɪk] Track 4571

形 熱心的

▶My brother is very enthusiastic about singing.
我弟弟很喜歡唱歌。

en·ti·tle [ɪn`taɪtḷ] Track 4572

動 定名、賦予權力 反 deprive 剝奪

▶He feels entitled to enter the office any time.
他覺得自己有權利可以隨時進入這個辦公室。

e·quate [ɪ`kwet] Track 4573

動 使相等

▶You can't equate being rich to being happy.
你不能說有錢和快樂是相等的。

實用片語用語
equate to sth. 等於……

e·rect [ɪ`rɛkt] Track 4574

動 豎立 形 直立的 同 upright 直立的

▶動 He plans to erect a monument in the town.
他計畫在鎮上建一座紀念碑。

▶形 There is an erect pine on the hill in front of our yard.
我們家院子前面的山上有一棵挺拔的松樹。

實用片語用語
stand erect 直立
例如：The tree stood erect despite the thunderstorm.
這棵樹屹立不搖，毫不畏懼暴風雨的侵襲。

e·rupt [ɪ`rʌpt] Track 4575

動 爆發

▶Don't you believe the volcano may erupt at any time?
你不相信這座火山隨時可能會爆發嗎？

es·cort [ɛs`kɔrt]/[`ɛskɔrt] Track 4576

動 護衛、護送 名 護衛者

▶動 Will you tell me who will escort this young lady home?
你能告訴我誰將護送這位小姐回家嗎？

▶名 He offered to be her escort, but she declined.
他主動說要護送她，但她謝絕了。

es·tate [ə`stet]

Track 4577

名 財產 同 property 財產

▶Real estate is really expensive these days.
最近房地產真的很貴。

實用片語用語
real estate 房地產

es·teem [əs`tim]

Track 4578

名 尊重 動 尊敬

▶名 All of them have a great esteem for the old man.
他們全都非常尊敬這位老人。

▶動 The lady was greatly loved and esteemed there.
這位太太在那裡備受愛戴和尊敬。

e·ter·nal [ɪ`tɝnl̩]

Track 4579

形 永恆的 同 permanent 永恆的

▶Isn't a wedding ring a symbol of eternal love between them?
結婚戒指難道不是他們之間永恆的愛的一種象徵嗎？

eth·ics [`ɛθɪks]

Track 4580

名 倫理（學）

▶Ethics deals with moral conduct.
倫理學研討的是道德行為。

文法字詞解析
這個字加上形容詞字尾「-al」就變成「ethical」，意思是「論理的、道德的」，例如：ethical issues 倫理議題。

ev·er·green [`ɛvɚ͵grin]

Track 4581

名 常綠樹 形 常綠的

▶名 There are many evergreens on both sides of the road.
道路兩旁有很多萬年青。

▶形 There is a small evergreen shrub（灌木）in the park.
公園裡有一小塊常綠灌木叢。

實用片語用語
evergreen tree 長青樹
例如：Several evergreen trees stand in our garden.
我們的院子裡有好幾棵長青樹。

ex·ag·ger·a·tion [ɪg͵zædʒə`reʃən]

Track 4582

名 誇張、誇大

▶What I said was just an exaggeration.
我剛剛說的只是誇張說法而已。

ex·ceed [ɪk`sid]

Track 4583

動 超過 同 surpass 勝過

▶The demand for vegetables exceeds the supply.
蔬菜供不應求。

ex·cel [ɪk`sɛl]

Track 4584

動 勝過 同 outdo 勝過

▶He excels in many different things.
他擅長許多事情。

實用片語用語
excel in 擅長、做得很好

ex·cep·tion·al [ɪk`sɛpʃənl̩]

Track 4585

形 優秀的

▶I don't think he is a man of exceptional talent.
我不認為他是一個具有非凡才能的人。

ex·cess [ɪk`sɛs]

Track 4586

名 超過 形 過量的

▶名 Anything in excess is a bad thing.
任何事一旦過了頭就不太好了。

▶形 They said we should boil the excess liquid away.
他們說我們應該把多餘的液體煮掉。

ex·claim [ɪk`sklem]

Track 4587

動 驚叫

▶"John, why are you naked?" she exclaimed.
「約翰，你怎麼裸體呢？」她驚叫。

ex·clude [ɪk`sklud]

Track 4588

動 拒絕、不包含 反 include 包含

▶All of us are here excluding Jenny.
除了珍妮以外，我們大家都在這邊。

文法字詞解析
字首「ex-」常有「外、除外」的意思，而相反的字首「in-」則常有「裡、內」的意思。因此 exclude 是「不包含、排除」的意思，而字根相同字首不同的「include」則是「包含」的意思。

ex·e·cute [`ɛksɪ͵kjut]

Track 4589

動 實行 同 perform 實行

▶I don't agree with how he executes decisions.
我不喜歡他實施決策的方式。

ex·ec·u·tive [ɪg`zɛkjʊtɪv]

Track 4590

名 執行者、管理者 形 執行的

▶名 How are you getting on with your new executive, Michael?
麥克，你和你們那個新來的管理人員相處得怎麼樣啊？

▶形 He is a man of executive ability. 他是一個有執行能力的人。

ex·ile [`ɛksaɪl]

Track 4591

名 流亡 動 放逐

▶名 Will you tell me why they sent Napoleon into exile?
你能告訴我他們為什麼要把拿破崙流放嗎？

▶動 Why was the famous writer exiled from his country?
這個著名的作家為何被流放到國外去了呢？

ex·ten·sion [ɪk`stɛnʃən]

Track 4592

名 擴大、延長 同 expansion 擴張

▶It is obvious that the students dislike the extension of the term.
顯然學生們不願延長學期。

文法字詞解析
extension 有「在原本的東西上再『附加』東西」的意思，因此我們常用的網頁瀏覽器添加的附加功能（例如擋廣告的功能等）就可以稱為 extension。

ex·ten·sive [ɪk`stɛnsɪv]

Track 4593

形 廣泛的、廣大的 同 spacious 廣闊的

▶He benefited a lot from extensive reading.
他從廣泛的閱讀中受益匪淺。

ex·te·ri·or [ɪk`stɪrɪɚ]

Track 4594

名 外面 形 外部的 反 interior 內部的

▶名 It is very difficult for us to judge a person by his exterior.
依據外表我們很難評判一個人。

▶形 We are painting the exterior wall of the house.
我們正在給房子的外牆上漆。

ex·ter·nal [ɪkˋstɝnl̩]

Track 4595

名 外表 形 外在的 反 internal 內在的

▶名 It is unwise（不明智的）to judge people by externals.
以貌取人是不明智的。

▶形 Don't you think the external features of the building are very attractive?
難道你不認為這棟建築物的外觀很吸引人嗎？

ex·tinct [ɪkˋstɪŋkt]

Track 4596

形 滅絕的 同 dead 死的

▶Do you know how long dinosaurs have been extinct?
你知道恐龍滅絕多久了嗎？

實用片語用語

go extinct 滅絕
例如：That kind of bird went extinct years ago.
那種鳥很多年前就已經滅絕了。

ex·tra·or·di·nar·y [ɪkˋstrɔrdn̩ˏɛrɪ]

Track 4597

形 特別的 反 normal 正規的

▶What an extraordinary hat! How much does it cost?
多麼奇特的帽子呀！它多少錢？

eye·lash/lash [ˋaɪˏlæʃ]/[læʃ]

Track 4598

名 睫毛

▶He has very long eyelashes that keep getting stuck in his eyes.
他的睫毛很長，常倒插在眼睛裡。

實用片語用語

eyelash curler 捲睫毛夾
例如：She uses the eyelash curler every morning before going to school.
她每天早上去上學之前都會用睫毛夾捲一下睫毛。

eye·lid [ˋaɪˏlɪd]

Track 4599

名 眼皮

▶My eyelids feel heavy after a long day.
在漫長的一天過後，我的眼皮非常沉重。

fab·ric [ˋfæbrɪk]

Track 4600

名 紡織品、布料 同 cloth 布料

▶Would you please help me find a piece of cloth to match this fabric?
你能幫我找一塊和這塊布料相配的布嗎？

fad [fæd]

Track 4601

名 一時的流行 同 fashion 流行

▶Learning English is much more than a fad, it is really a must!
學英文不僅只是一個流行而已，而是一件必須要做的事！

萬用延伸句型

be more thanr... 不只是……

Fahr·en·heit [ˋfærənˏhaɪt]

Track 4602

名 華氏、華氏溫度計

▶Water freezes at 32 degrees Fahrenheit (32˚F).
水在華氏三十二度時結冰。

fal·ter [ˋfɔltɚ]
Track 4603

動 支吾、結巴地說、猶豫 同 stutter 結巴地說

▶He faltered for a while and was still unable to make a decision.
他猶豫了一陣子還是無法做決定。

fas·ci·nate [ˋfæsn̩,et]
Track 4604

動 迷惑、使迷惑

▶It is obvious that the students were fascinated by his ideas.
顯然學生們都被他的思想吸引住了。

實用片語用語
be fascinated byr... 被……迷住、被……吸引住

fa·tigue [fəˋtig]
Track 4605

名 疲勞、破碎 動 衰弱、疲勞

▶名 It is a treat to have a drink after the fatigue of the day.
累了一天之後喝杯酒可說是其樂無窮。

▶動 Sarah often complains she fatigues easily. Don't you think there's something wrong with her?
薩拉常訴說自己容易疲勞。難道你不覺得她身體有問題嗎？

fed·er·al [ˋfɛdərəl]
Track 4606

形 同盟的、聯邦（制）的

▶It is the federal government that decides U.S. foreign policy.
美國的外交政策是由聯邦政府來決定的。

fee·ble [fibl̩]
Track 4607

形 虛弱的、無力的 同 weak 虛弱的

▶He is a man with a feeble personality in my opinion.
在我看來他是個個性軟弱的人。

fem·i·nine [ˋfɛmənɪn]
Track 4608

名 女性 形 婦女的、溫柔的 反 masculine 男性、男子氣概的

▶名 The masculine nouns are used differently from the feminine in German.
在德文中，陽性名詞和陰性用法不同。

▶形 He is very feminine and gentle.
他是個女性化、溫柔的人。

實用片語用語
feminine products 女性用品（衛生棉等）
例如：Which aisle are the feminine products on?
女性用品是放在哪一條走道呢？

fer·ti·liz·er [ˋfɝtl̩,aɪzɚ]
Track 4609

名 肥料、化學肥料

▶It is obvious that fertilizer will accelerate（加快）the growth of these tomato plants. 顯然肥料將促進這些番茄樹的生長。

fi·an·ce/fi·an·cee [,fiənˋse]
Track 4610

名 未婚夫 / 未婚妻

▶His fiancee is a young dancer with a bright future.
他的未婚妻是個有前途的年輕舞蹈家。

fi·ber [ˋfaɪbɚ]
Track 4611

名 纖維、纖維質

▶It is no wonder that the doctor recommended more fiber in his diet. 難怪醫生建議他多吃一些纖維性的食物。

fid·dle [ˋfɪdḷ]

Track 4612

名 小提琴 動 拉提琴、遊蕩 同 violin 小提琴

▶名 Why don’t you let your daughter learn to play the fiddle?
為什麼不讓你的女兒學拉小提琴呢？

▶動 Stop fiddling around and go do something useful.
別再到處閒晃了，去做點有用的事。

實用片語用語
fiddle around 到處閒晃

fil·ter [ˋfɪltɚ]

Track 4613

名 過濾器 動 過濾、滲透

▶名 I'm afraid that we have to buy a coffee filter.
恐怕我們得去買一個咖啡過濾器了。

▶動 I think we need to filter the drinking water first.
我們需要把飲用水先過濾一下。

文法字詞解析
現代人常用手機拍照，而手機的相機中都會內建濾鏡功能，這個功能在英文就叫做「filter」。

fin [fɪn]

Track 4614

名 鰭、手、魚翅

▶I see a shark’s fin in the distance. 我看到遠方有個鯊魚鰭。

fish·er·y [ˋfɪʃərɪ]

Track 4615

名 漁業、水產業、養魚場

▶It is clear that the fishery is confronted with a financial crisis now. 顯然這個養魚場正面臨財務危機。

flake [flek]

Track 4616

名 雪花、薄片 動 剝、片片降落、使成薄片 同 peel 剝

▶名 Have some flakes! It’s my favorite kind of breakfast.
吃點穀片吧！這是我最喜歡的早餐。

▶動 I'm afraid that the paint is going to flake off the walls.
恐怕油漆要從牆上剝落下來了。

實用片語用語
snow flake 雪花
例如：Snow flakes are beautiful if you look at them up close.
仔細近看雪花，會發現它們非常地漂亮。

flap [flæp]

Track 4617

名 興奮狀態、鼓翼 動 拍打、拍動、空談

▶名 Even though they apologized to the hosts, it did cause a bit of flap.
儘管他們向主人道了歉，但還是引起了一點兒小騷動。

▶動 The bird flapped its wings and flew away.
那隻鳥拍拍翅膀飛走了。

flaw [flɔ]

Track 4618

名 瑕疵、缺陷 動 弄破、破裂、糟蹋 同 defect 缺陷

▶名 Can you spot the flaw in their argument?
你能指出他們論點中的瑕疵嗎？

▶動 I am afraid the story is a bit flawed because its ending is so weak. 恐怕這故事有點缺陷，結尾寫得太沒力了。

flick [flɪk]

Track 4619

名 輕打聲、彈開 動 輕打、輕拍 同 pat 輕拍

▶名 He gave a flick of the whip his father gave him.
他輕抽他父親送給他的鞭子。

▶動 The snake's tongue was flicking from side to side.
那條蛇忽左忽右地吐著舌頭。

文法字詞解析
近年來 flick 在口語中也能夠引申為「電影」的意思。

flip [flɪp]

Track 4620

名 跳動、拍打 動 輕拍、翻轉

▶名 The boat is too small. It is no wonder that a flip of the whale's tail upset it.
那條船太小了。難怪鯨魚的尾巴輕輕一拍就把它打翻了。

▶動 The dolphin flipped in the air.
那隻海豚在空中翻轉。

文法字詞解析
夏天在海灘常穿的「flip-flops（夾腳拖鞋）」就是從這個字延伸而來。

flour·ish [ˈflɝɪʃ]

Track 4621

名 繁榮、炫耀、華麗的詞藻 動 誇耀、繁盛 反 decline 衰退

▶名 She finished her speech with flourish.
她華麗地結束了演講。

▶動 There were two palm trees flourishing in the central garden.
中心花園裡有兩棵枝葉茂盛的棕櫚樹。

flu·en·cy [ˈfluənsɪ]

Track 4622

名 流暢、流利

▶Fluency in English will be an added advantage.
流利的英語將是另一個優勢。

foe [fo]

Track 4623

名 敵人、仇人、敵軍 同 enemy 敵人

▶I'm afraid that this is the most serious challenge from his political foe. 恐怕這是來自他政敵的最嚴重挑戰。

實用片語用語
friend or foe 朋友或敵人
例如：He doesn't let anyone get in his way, no matter friend or foe.
無論是朋友或敵人，他都不讓任何人阻擋他做他要做的事。

foil [fɔɪl]

Track 4624

名 箔片、箔、薄金屬片

▶Can you wrap this in foil for me? 幫我用鋁箔包好好不好？

folk·lore [ˈfokˌlor]

Track 4625

名 沒有隔閡、平民作風、民間傳說、民俗

▶Would you please tell us some tales from folklore?
請您為我們講一些民間故事好嗎？

for·get·ful [fɚˈgɛtfəl]

Track 4626

形 忘掉的、易忘的、忽略的、健忘的

▶Old people are sometimes forgetful. 老人有時很健忘。

for·mat [ˈfɔrmæt]

Track 4627

名 格式、版式 動 格式化

▶名 It's the same book, but a new format.
這是同一本書，但版型是新的。

▶動 Are you trying to format this floppy disc?
你是打算要將這張軟碟格式化嗎？

實用片語用語
paper format 論文格式
例如：Paper formats are something that always confuses him even though he's a professor.
雖然他是個教授，但他對於論文格式還是霧煞煞。

foul [faʊl]

Track 4628

動 使污穢、弄髒、使堵塞 形 險惡的、污濁的 反 clean 清潔的

▶動 Grease has fouled this drain.
油污使這條下水道塞住了。

▶形 Why don't you open the window to let out the foul air?
為什麼不打開窗戶以排放出汙濁的空氣呢？

fowl [faʊl]

Track 4629

名 鳥、野禽 同 bird 鳥

▶What do you think of having roast fowl for dinner?
你們覺得我們晚餐吃烤雞怎麼樣？

frac·tion [ˋfrækʃən]

Track 4630

名 分數、片斷、小部份 同 segment 部分

▶He has done only a fraction of his homework.
他只做了作業的一小部分。

實用片語用語
a fraction of r...⋯的一小部分

frame·work [ˋfremˏwɝk]

Track 4631

名 架構、骨架、體制 同 structure 結構

▶You'd better adhere（堅持）to a basic framework when writing the paper.
你最好照一個基本的結構來寫這篇論文。

fran·tic [ˋfræntɪk]

Track 4632

形 狂暴的、發狂的

▶That noise is driving me frantic. Would you mind turning off the music?
那種噪音真要把我弄瘋了。你介意關掉音樂嗎？

實用片語用語
drive sb. frantic 使某人抓狂

freight [fret]

Track 4633

名 貨物運輸 動 運輸

▶名 It's more expensive to mail the box by express than by freight.
用快遞運送這個箱子比普通貨運要貴很多。

▶動 It is less costly to freight these products than to mail it.
貨運這些產品比郵寄更省錢。

fron·tier [frʌnˋtɪr]

Track 4634

名 邊境、國境、新領域 同 border 邊境

▶I'm afraid that we have not had any more news from the frontier.
恐怕我們還沒有得到來自邊境的進一步消息。

萬用延伸句型
I'm afraid that... 恐怕⋯⋯

fume [fjum]

Track 4635

名 蒸汽、香氣、煙 動 激怒、冒出（煙、蒸汽等）
同 vapor 蒸汽

▶名 Tobacco fumes filled the air in the room.
室內的空氣中充滿了香菸的煙霧。

▶動 He was fuming when he stepped into the room.
他走進房間時火冒三丈的。

fu·ry [ˋfjʊrɪ]

Track 4636

名 憤怒、狂怒 同 rage 狂怒

▶Would you like to tell me why he is white with fury? What happened?
你能告訴我他為什麼會氣得臉色發白嗎？發生什麼事了？

fuse [fjuz]

Track 4637

名 引信、保險絲 動 熔合、裝引信

▶名 I don't know how to mend a fuse. 我不會修保險絲。

▶動 Could you instruct us how to fuse the pipes?
您能指導我們怎樣焊接管子嗎？

實用片語用語

have a short fuse 很容易生氣

「保險絲很短」，可想而知就會很容易燒壞，而燒壞的話事情就大條了，因此「have a short fuse」就可以拿來描述很容易發脾氣的人。

例如：Don't let your children disturb him. He has a short fuse.

別讓你的孩子打擾他，他很容易發脾氣。

fuss [fʌs]

Track 4638

名 大驚小怪 動 焦急、使焦急、小題大作、過分講究

▶名 There's nothing to make a fuss over. 沒什麼好大驚小怪的。

▶動 She fussed over her children a lot.
她總是對孩子的事情小題大作的。

gal·lop [ˋgæləp]

Track 4639

名 疾馳、飛奔 動 使疾馳、飛奔 同 run 跑

▶名 He rode off at a gallop as soon as he got the news.
他一聽到消息就騎馬疾馳而去。

▶動 The horse galloped away into the sunset.
那匹馬朝著夕陽奔去。

gar·ment [ˋgɑrmənt]

Track 4640

名 衣服

▶There are many shops selling all kinds of garments in the mall. 購物中心有很多商店出售各種衣服。

gasp [gæsp]

Track 4641

名 喘息、喘 動 喘氣說、喘著氣息

▶名 The patient is nearly at his last gasp.
那位病人幾乎是奄奄一息了。

▶動 The man sits there gasping desperately for breath.
那個男人坐在那裡拚命喘氣。

實用片語用語

gasp for air 喘氣

例如：The dying fish were gasping for air on the ground.

瀕死的魚兒們在地上喘氣。

gath·er·ing [ˋgæðərɪŋ]

Track 4642

名 集會、聚集

▶Will you invite him to our small social gathering this time?
你這次會邀請他來參加我們的小型社交聚會嗎？

gay [ge]

Track 4643

名 同性戀的 形 快樂的、快活的 反 sad 悲傷的

▶名 I didn't realize that Joey was a gay.
我沒發覺喬伊是同性戀。

▶形 I have lots of gay friends. 我有很多同性戀朋友。

gen·der [ˋdʒɛndɚ]

Track 4644

名 性別 同 sex 性別

▶Don't you think some majors have a gender bias（偏見）?
難道你不覺得某些主修科目存在性別偏見嗎？

實用片語用語

gender discrimination 性別歧視

例如：Gender discrimination in workplaces is no longer tolerable.

職場上的性別歧視不再是可接受的事了。

ge·o·graph·i·cal [ˌdʒiəˋgræfɪkḷ] Track 4645

形 地理學的、地理的
▶People can know each other quickly（很快地）even if they are in different geographical regions.
儘管人們處在不同的地理區域，但是他們也能很快的知道彼此的事情。

ge·om·e·try [dʒɪˋɑmətrɪ] Track 4646

名 幾何學
▶Unlike you, I am really fond of geometry.
跟你不一樣，我真的很喜歡幾何學。

gla·cier [ˋgleʃɚ] Track 4647

名 冰河
▶A glacier is a moving mass of snow and ice.
冰河是一大片會移動的雪和冰。

glare [glɛr] Track 4648

名 怒視、瞪眼 動 怒視瞪眼
▶名 Susan looked at him with an angry glare.
蘇珊生氣地瞪著他。
▶動 I saw my sister glaring at my father.
我看見妹妹正瞪著爸爸。

實用片語用語
glare at 瞪著（某人）看

gleam [glim] Track 4649

名 一絲光線 動 閃現、閃爍
▶名 Don't you see the gleam of a lamp ahead? Maybe we can find someone there. 難道你沒看到前面的燈光嗎？也許我們可以在那裡找到人。
▶動 The lights of the little town are gleaming in the distance.
遠處小鎮有燈光在閃爍。

文法字詞解析
gleam 和 glitter 雖然都有「光」的意思，但用法卻不太相同，gleam 通常是平滑表面上發光的樣子（例如：gleaming white teeth），glitter 則是大量小光點構成閃閃發光的樣子（the glittering frost）。

glee [gli] Track 4650

名 喜悅、高興 同 joy 高興
▶The little girl clapped her hands in glee. 小女孩喜悅地拍著手。

glit·ter [ˋglɪtɚ] Track 4651

名 光輝、閃光、華麗 動 閃爍、閃亮 同 sparkle 閃爍
▶名 It won't be long before she sees through the gloss（虛假的表面）and glitter of Hollywood.
不久她就會看透好萊塢的虛榮與繁華。
▶動 The diamond ring is glittering on her finger.
鑽戒在她的手指上閃閃發亮。

文法字詞解析
小朋友做美勞很喜歡用的那種很難洗掉的「亮粉」也稱為 glitter。

gloom [glum] Track 4652

名 陰暗、昏暗 動 幽暗、憂鬱 同 shadow 陰暗處
▶名 It was difficult for me to see anything distinctly（清楚地）in the gloom. 我在昏暗之中什麼東西都看不清。
▶動 Dark clouds are glooming the streets. I think it is necessary for me to take an umbrella.
烏雲使大街上陰沉沉的。我覺得我有必要帶一把傘。

gnaw [nɔ] Track 4653

動 咬、嚙 同 bite 咬

▶The cheese has been gnawed by a mouse.
這乳酪已被老鼠咬過了。

gob·ble [ˋgɑbḷ] Track 4654

動 大口猛吃、狼吞虎嚥 同 devour 狼吞虎嚥

▶By the time he was gobbling up the food, his brother had gone to bed.
他狼吞虎嚥地吃那些食物的時候，他弟弟就已經去睡覺了。

實用片語用語

gobble down 狼吞虎嚥地吃下

例如：The children gobbled down all the food and went out to play.

孩子們狼吞虎嚥地把食物吃光，然後就出去玩了。

gorge [gɔrdʒ] Track 4655

名 岩崖、山峽、隘道 動 狼吞虎嚥

▶名 There is a deep gorge separating the two halves of the city.
有一道深谷把這座城市分成了兩部分。

▶動 The hungry boy gorged on turkey.
那個餓壞了的男孩大吃火雞。

gor·geous [ˋgɔrdʒəs] Track 4656

形 炫麗的、華麗的、極好的 同 splendid 壯麗的

▶What a gorgeous day it is today! Why don't we have a picnic?
今天天氣多好啊！為什麼不去野餐呢？

go·ril·la [gəˋrɪlə] Track 4657

名 大猩猩

▶How can a monkey be more powerful than a gorilla?
猴子怎麼可能比猩猩更強大呢？

gos·pel [ˋgɑspḷ] Track 4658

名 福音、信條

▶I don't think you should take his words as gospel.
我認為你不該把他的話當作信條。

實用片語用語

gospel truth 事實

對於虔誠的信徒而言，寫在福音中的事情本來就是不可動搖的事實，因此 gospel truth 就成了「事實」的意思。

例如：He believes that everything his boss says is the gospel truth.

他覺得他老闆說的每句話都是不可動搖的事實。

grant [grænt] Track 4659

名 許可、授與 動 答應、允許、轉讓（財產） 同 permit 允許

▶名 Will you tell me when we can get the grant from the government?
請你告訴我我們何時可以得到政府的許可？

▶動 Will you grant this technical license to our company?
你們願意轉讓這項技術的許可證給我們公司嗎？

grav·i·ty [ˋgrævətɪ] Track 4660

名 重力、嚴重性

▶The reason why you can't walk on the moon is that it lacks gravity. 你無法在月球行走的原因是它的引力不夠。

graze [grez] Track 4661

動 吃草、畜牧

▶I am afraid that your cattle are grazing in others' fields, not yours.
恐怕你的牛群不是在你自己家，而是別人家的田裡吃草呢。

grease [gris]

Track 4662

名 油脂、獸脂 動 討好、塗脂、用油脂潤滑

▶名 You won't get the grease off the plates even if you use this soap. 即使你用這個肥皂，你也洗不掉盤子上的油膩。

▶動 He greases the machine very carefully（仔細地）every day even though they don't ask him to.
即使他們沒叫他做，他也會每天都很仔細地為機器加潤滑油。

greed [grid]

Track 4663

名 貪心、貪婪

▶Is it simple greed that made you steal the bike from others' house?
你偷別人家的自行車完全是因為貪心作祟嗎？

grim [grɪm]

Track 4664

形 嚴格的、糟糕的 同 stern 嚴格的

▶It is obvious that the climate here can be pretty grim in winter.
顯然這裡的冬天相當寒冷。

grip [grɪp]

Track 4665

名 緊握、抓住 動 緊握、扣住 反 release 鬆開

▶名 He never loosened his grip on the rope.
他一直緊握著繩子沒有放開。

▶動 She gripped his hand when she heard the strange sound.
她聽到那奇怪的聲音時緊緊抓住了他的手。

groan [gron]

Track 4666

名 哼著說、呻吟 動 呻吟、哼聲 同 moan 呻吟

▶名 You can hear the man's groans from here.
你從這裡都能聽到那個男人的呻吟聲。

▶動 The sick woman groaned all day long.
那個生病的女子呻吟了一整天。

gross [gros]

Track 4667

名 總體 動 獲得……總收入 形 粗略的、臃腫的 同 total 總數

▶名 The manager says that the goods are to be sold only by the gross.
經理說這些貨物只能成批出售。

▶動 The firm grossed $5 million last year.
該公司去年獲得五百萬美元毛利。

▶形 I make a gross judgment of the distance between the two cities.
我粗略地判斷了一下這兩個城市之間的距離。

growl [graʊl]

Track 4668

名 咆哮聲、吠聲 動 咆哮著說、咆哮 同 snarl 咆哮

▶名 Didn't you hear the growl? You'd better leave the dog alone.
你沒聽見狗吠聲嗎？你最好別惹這條狗。

▶動 The man growled at his wife.
那個男人對他太太咆哮。

文法字詞解析

兩句例句分別用了 even if 與 even though 兩個句型。兩者都是「即使」的意思，但它們之間還是有差別喔！ even if 帶有假設的含意，even though 則沒有假設的含意。舉例來說，如果說「I wouldn't say yes even if he cried」，就表示「就算他哭，我也不會同意」（他其實沒哭，說話者只是假設這個情境）；「I didn't say yes even though he cried」則是「雖然他哭了，我還是沒同意」（他真的有哭）。

實用片語用語

grim reaper 死神
例如：The old man shouted that he saw the grim reaper.
那個老男人大喊說他看到了死神。

文法字詞解析

此外，gross 也有「噁心的」的意思。如果你朋友忽然沒事放了一個很多汁的屁，就可以跟他說一句「gross!」。

grum·ble [ˋgrʌmbḷ]

Track 4669

名 牢騷、不高興 動 抱怨、發牢騷 同 complain 抱怨

▶名 Tell me all your grumbles. I'm a good listener.
把你的滿腹牢騷都跟我說吧，我是個很好的傾聽者。

▶動 There is no point in grumbling at them after it happened.
事情都發生了，再向他們抱怨也沒多大意義。

guide·line [ˋgaɪd͵laɪn]

Track 4670

名 指導方針、指標

▶Nothing is more effective than this guideline.
沒有東西比這個指導方針更有效的了。

gulp [gʌlp]

Track 4671

名 滿滿一口 動 牛飲、吞飲

▶名 I took a gulp of the milk.
我喝了滿滿一口牛奶。

▶動 The boy was gulping for air after holding his breath for two minutes. 那個男孩在憋氣兩分鐘後大口地吸著氣。

實用片語用語
gulp down 大口吃掉、喝掉
例如：I gulped down the whole glass of orange juice.
我大口喝掉整杯柳橙汁。

gust [gʌst]

Track 4672

名 一陣狂風 動 吹狂風 同 blast 疾風

▶名 A gust of wind blew the door shut just now.
剛才一陣大風吹來，把門給關上了。

▶動 The wind will gust up to 35 miles an hour.
風速即將達每小時三十五英里。

gut(s) [gʌt(s)]

Track 4673

名 內臟、腸

▶He vomited his guts out after riding the roller coaster.
他在坐雲霄飛車後，吐得快把腸子都吐出來了。

實用片語用語
have the guts (to do sth.) 有膽量（去做某事）
例如：He has no guts to tell the girl that he loves her.
他沒有膽量去告訴那個女孩說他愛她。

gyp·sy [ˋdʒɪpsɪ]

Track 4674

名 吉普賽人 形 吉普賽人的

▶名 I had a gypsy predict my future.
我請一個吉普賽人幫我算命。

▶形 He'd always wanted to live a gypsy life.
他總是夢想著過著吉普賽式的生活。

hail [hel]

Track 4675

名 歡呼、雹 動 歡呼 同 cheer 歡呼

▶名 The hail damaged several houses.
那陣冰雹毀損了不少房子。

▶動 There is an old friend hailing me from the other side of the street. 有一個老朋友在街道的對面喊我。

實用片語用語
hail a cab / taxi 招計程車
例如：We don't have time. Let's hail a cab. 我們沒時間了，招計程車吧。

hair·style/hair·do
['hɛr͵staɪl]/['hɛr͵du] Track 4676

名 髮型

▶What do you think of my new hairstyle?
你覺得我的新髮型怎麼樣？

hand·i·cap ['hændɪ͵kæp] Track 4677

名 障礙、吃虧 動 妨礙、吃虧、使不利

▶名 Being short is a handicap in a crowd like this.
在這樣一群人中，個子小很吃虧。

▶動 He was handicapped by lack of education.
他因知識水準低而吃了虧。

hand·i·craft ['hændɪ͵kræft] Track 4678

名 手工藝品 同 craft 工藝

▶It's hard for me to pick between the two handicraft articles.
我很難從這兩件工藝品中挑選一個。

har·dy ['hardɪ] Track 4679

形 強健的、能吃苦耐勞的 同 sturdy 強健的

▶Both their children are quite hardy.
他們的兩個孩子都非常能吃苦耐勞。

har·ness ['harnɪs] Track 4680

名 馬具 動 裝上馬具、利用、治理

▶名 A bridle is a kind of harness.
馬勒是一種馬具。

▶動 I am afraid it will take several years to harness that river.
恐怕治理那條河流要花幾年的時間。

haul [hɔl] Track 4681

名 用力拖拉、一次獲得的量 動 拖、使勁拉 同 drag 拖、拉

▶名 We brought back a big haul of fish.
我們捕了一大網魚回來。

▶動 Fine, let's just haul out our swords and start fighting.
好，讓我們都拔出劍來開始戰鬥吧！

haunt [hɔnt] Track 4682

名 常到的場所 動 出現、常到（某地）

▶名 This coffee shop is one of his haunts.
這家咖啡館是他經常出入的地方。

▶動 It is said that the building was haunted by the ghost of a mad woman.
據說這棟大樓有一個瘋女人的鬼魂出沒。

heart·y ['hartɪ] Track 4683

形 親切的、熱心的 反 cold 冷淡的

▶Would you please accept my hearty congratulations on your wedding?
請接受我對你們婚禮的最熱烈祝賀好嗎？

文法字詞解析

hairstyle 和 hairdo 的不同點在於，就算你什麼都不做也可以稱為 hairstyle（畢竟把長髮放下來不綁也是一種「髮型」）；而需要在頭髮上動手腳（綁起來、夾起來、噴髮膠等）才能稱為 hairdo。

萬用延伸句型

take several years to... 花好幾年（做某事）

實用片語用語

hearty breakfast 很大份的早餐
例如：We had a hearty breakfast before hitting the road.
我們吃了很豐盛的早餐，然後才動身出發。

heav·en·ly [ˋhɛvənlɪ]

Track 4684

形 天空的、天國的

▶It is definitely a heavenly place of rest and tranquility（寧靜）.
那的確是一個寧靜的天堂，是個休息的好地方。

hedge [hɛdʒ]

Track 4685

名 樹籬、籬笆 動 制定界線、圍住

▶名 There is an opening in the hedge.
那個籬笆上有個洞。

▶動 There are low hills hedging the town.
這座城鎮的四周圍有低山環繞。

heed [hid]

Track 4686

名 留心、注意 動 留心、注意 同 notice 注意

▶名 It is obvious that a good leader should always pay heed to the voice of the masses.
顯然一位好領導應該經常注意傾聽群眾的聲音。

▶動 It is clear that she does not want to heed my advice.
顯然她不想聽從我的勸告。

實用片語用語
heed sb.'s advice 聽從某人的勸告

height·en [ˋhaɪtn̩]

Track 4687

動 增高、加高 反 lower 放低

▶As she waited, her excitement heightened. 她越等就越興奮。

heir [ɛr]

Track 4688

名 繼承人

▶It is said that he is the only legal heir of the rich man.
據說他是這位富翁的唯一法定繼承人。

hence [hɛns]

Track 4689

副 因此 同 therefore 因此

▶She is a musician, hence her interest in the details of the concert.
她是個音樂家，所以她才會對那場音樂會的細節這麼有興趣。

文法字詞解析
除了 hence 之外，在寫作中也可以用「therefore」、「thus」等字來表達因果關係。

her·ald [ˋhɛrəld]

Track 4690

名 通報者、使者 動 宣示、公告 同 messenger 使者

▶名 In England the cuckoo（杜鵑鳥）is the herald of spring.
在英國，杜鵑鳥預示春天的來臨。

▶動 In any event, they will herald the final result.
在任何情況下，他們都將公告最終結果。

萬用延伸句型
in any event... 無論如何……

herb [ɝb]

Track 4691

名 草本植物

▶There are many herbs that are used in traditional Chinese medicine. 傳統中醫裡會使用很多種草藥。

her·mit [ˋhɝmɪt]

Track 4692

名 隱士、隱居者

▶It is no wonder that the old hermit didn't want to mention his past life. 難怪那位老隱士不願提起自己過去的生活。

he·ro·ic [hɪˋroɪk] Track 4693

名 史詩 形 英雄的、勇士的 反 cowardly 懦弱的

▶名 The heroics he wrote became very popular after his death.
他過世後，他寫的史詩變得很受歡迎。

▶形 The newspapers glorified（頌揚）his heroic deeds.
報紙上頌揚了他的英雄事蹟。

het·er·o·sex·u·al [ˌhɛtərəˋsɛkʃʊəl] Track 4694

名 異性戀者 形 異性戀的 反 homosexual 同性戀

▶名 I don't think that the heterosexuals should discriminate against the homosexuals.
我認為異性戀者不應該歧視同性戀者。

▶形 The heterosexual girl was sad because she fell in love with a gay boy.
那個異性戀的女孩因為愛上了同性戀的男孩而傷心。

實用片語用語
discriminate against... 歧視……

hi-fi/high fi·del·i·ty [ˋhaɪˋfaɪ]/[ˋhaɪ fɪˋdɛlətɪ] Track 4695

名 高傳真（靈敏度）音響

▶I' m thinking of buying a hi-fi unit. Any recommendations?
我正在考慮買一套高靈敏度的音響設備。你有推薦的嗎？

文法字詞解析
unit 在這裡不是「單位」的意思，而是指「一套設備」。

hi·jack [ˋhaɪˌdʒæk] Track 4696

名 搶劫、劫機 動 劫奪

▶名 I'm afraid that the hijack might be organized by a group of terrorists. 這次劫持事件恐怕是由恐怖組織規劃的。

▶動 They are planning to hijack an airliner.
他們正在計畫劫持班機。

hiss [hɪs] Track 4697

名 嘘聲 動 發嘘聲

▶名 He rushed in and turned the gas off as soon as he heard the hiss. 一聽到瓦斯外洩的嘘嘘聲，他就衝進來把它關掉了。

▶動 The snake hissed at the rat. 那條蛇向那隻老鼠發出嘘嘘聲。

hoarse [hors] Track 4698

形 （嗓音）刺耳的、沙啞的

▶She has coughed herself hoarse. 她咳得連嗓子都沙啞了。

文法字詞解析
cough oneself hoarse 是「咳到自己都沙啞了」的意思；以此類推，「yell oneself hoarse」、「shout oneself hoarse」是「喊到自己都沙啞了」的意思。

hock·ey [ˋhɑkɪ] Track 4699

名 曲棍球

▶They got the silver medal in women's field hockey.
她們奪得了一面女子曲棍球銀牌。

ho·mo·sex·u·al [ˌhoməˋsɛkʃʊəl] Track 4700

名 同性戀者 形 同性戀的

▶名 Two out of three of my cousins are homosexuals.
我的三個堂哥中有兩個是同性戀。

▶形 What do you think about the discrimination against homosexual people? 你如何看待對同性戀者的歧視？

honk [hɔŋk]

Track 4701

名 雁鳴、汽車喇叭聲 動 雁鳴叫、發出汽車喇叭聲

▶名 He woke us with a honk of his car horn.
他按一下汽車的喇叭把我們叫醒。

▶動 She honked the horn of the car so that her friend would hurry up.
她按汽車喇叭，要她的朋友動作快一點。

hood [hʊd]

Track 4702

名 罩、蓋 動 掩蔽、覆蓋 反 uncover 揭露

▶名 Let's lift the engine hood and take a look.
我們把引擎蓋打開來檢查一下吧。

▶動 The man was hooded and therefore I couldn't see his face.
那個男人遮著臉，我看不到他的臉。

實用片語用語
hooded T-shirt 連帽的 T 恤
例如：I bought my son a hooded T-shirt and now my daughter wants one too.
我買了一件連帽 T 給我兒子，現在我女兒也嚷著想要了。

hoof [huf]

Track 4703

名 蹄 動 用蹄踢、步行

▶名 I'm afraid that there's something wrong with the horse's hooves. 恐怕這匹馬的蹄出了什麼毛病。

▶動 I'm afraid that the last bus had gone so we had to hoof it home.
末班公車恐怕已經開走了，我們只好走路回家了。

hor·i·zon·tal [͵harəˋzantḷ]

Track 4704

名 水平線 形 水準線、水平面、地平線的 反 vertical 垂直的

▶名 I drew a vertical line and he drew a horizontal.
我畫了一條垂直的線，他畫了一條水平線。

▶形 Do you see the horizontal line on your book? Now draw another one above it.
你有看到書上這條水平的線嗎？現在請你在它上方再畫一條線。

hos·tage [ˋhastɪdʒ]

Track 4705

名 人質 同 captive 俘虜

▶More than 60 foreigners have been taken hostage in recent months in Iraq.
最近幾個月來，超過六十名外國人在伊拉克遭到挾持成為人質。

實用片語用語
hostage situation 人質挾持事件
例如：There's a hostage situation here on this bus.
這輛公車上發生了人質挾持事件。

hos·tile [ˋhastɪl]

Track 4706

形 敵方的、不友善的

▶I don't know why she is hostile to me.
我不知道她為什麼對我懷有敵意。

hound [haʊnd]

Track 4707

名 獵犬、有癮的人 動 追逐、追獵 同 hunt 打獵

▶名 My sister is a crazy movie hound.
我妹妹是個瘋狂的影迷。

▶動 He has been hounded by his creditors（債主）in the past few months. 近幾個月來，他一直被債主追債。

hous·ing [ˋhaʊzɪŋ]

Track 4708

名 住宅的供給、住宅

▶There are hundreds of people who need new housing.
有許多人需要新的住宅。

hov·er [ˋhʌvɚ]

Track 4709

名 徘徊、翱翔 動 翱翔、盤旋

▶名 A helicopter is in hover above the house. No wonder there's so much noise!
有一架直昇機在房子上方盤旋。難怪那麼吵！

▶動 There is a hawk hovering overhead. Can't you see it?
有一隻老鷹在頂上盤旋。你看不到嗎？

實用片語用語

hover above 在上方盤旋

howl [haʊl]

Track 4710

名 吠聲、怒號 動 吼叫、怒號 同 shout 喊叫

▶名 The little girl let out a howl all of a sudden.
那個小女孩突然嚎啕大哭。

▶動 The dog was howling over its master's dead body.
那隻狗對著主人的屍體哀嚎。

hurl [hɝl]

Track 4711

名 投 動 投擲 同 fling 丟、擲

▶名 It is said that his perfect hurl got him the championship.
據說是他完美的投擲使他得了冠軍。

▶動 It is said that the best way to forget your sadness is to hurl yourself into your work.
據說忘掉悲傷最好的方法是讓自己投入工作之中。

實用片語用語

hurl insults at... 不斷謾罵某人

例如：The crazy old man is hurling insults at another crazy old man.
那個發瘋的老人不斷謾罵另一個發瘋的老人。

hymn [hɪm]

Track 4712

名 讚美詩 動 唱讚美詩讚美 同 carol 讚美詩

▶名 I can hear the hymn from the nearby church.
我能聽到從附近的教堂傳來的聖歌。

▶動 The old ladies are hymning together.
那些老太太正在一起唱聖歌。

id·i·ot [ˋɪdɪət]

Track 4713

名 傻瓜、笨蛋 同 fool 傻瓜

▶Are you an idiot? Cats don't grow on trees!
你是白癡嗎？貓才不是長在樹上！

文法字詞解析

如果說某個東西是「idiot-proof」的，就表示那個東西操作起來非常簡單，不管再怎麼傻的人都會。

例如：This cell phone comes with idiot-proof instructions, so it's very easy to use.
這支手機附有讓傻瓜也能懂的指示，所以使用起來非常簡單。

im·mense [ɪˋmɛns]

Track 4714

形 巨大的、極大的 反 tiny 極小的

▶The students in the class had an immense improvement in English.
班上的學生在英語方面有了極大的進步。

im·pe·ri·al [ɪm`pɪrɪəl] Track 4715

形 帝國的、至高的 同 supreme 至高的

▶There are many ways for you to get to the Imperial Theater.
到帝國戲院有很多條路。

im·pose [ɪm`poz] Track 4716

動 徵收、佔便宜、欺騙

▶He always wants to impose on those who help him, so let's keep at a distance. 他總是想佔幫助他的那些人的便宜，所以我們還是跟他保持距離吧。

實用片語用語
impose A on B 將 A 加諸於 B

im·pulse [`ɪmpʌls] Track 4717

名 衝動

▶Don't you think my uncle bought the house on an impulse?
難道你不覺得我叔叔是一時衝動才買下了那間房子嗎？

in·cense [`ɪnsɛns] Track 4718

名 芳香、香 動 激怒、焚香 同 provoke 激怒

▶名 Do you mind if I light some candles or incense in the room?
你介意我在這個房間裡點一些蠟燭或是薰香嗎？

▶動 Why was she incensed at his behavior yesterday?
她昨天為什麼對他的行為感到很憤怒？

in·dex [`ɪndɛks] Track 4719

名 指數、索引 動 編索引

▶名 I am afraid that the new colleague knows nothing about the Dow Jones Index.
新來的那個同事恐怕對道瓊指數一點都不瞭解。

▶動 I don't think the places mentioned are carefully indexed.
我覺得被提到的地名並沒有被仔細地編入索引中。

實用片語用語
index finger 食指
因為我們「指引」方向時通常都是用「食指」，所以食指才會稱為 index finger。
例如：He wore a ring on his index finger.
他在食指上戴了戒指。

in·dif·fer·ence [ɪn`dɪfərəns] Track 4720

名 不關心、不在乎

反 concern 關心

▶Not everyone present can feel his indifference at the party.
不是每個在場的人都能感覺到他在宴會上的冷淡。

in·dif·fer·ent [ɪn`dɪfərənt] Track 4721

形 中立的、不關心的

▶I am so excited to see snow that I am indifferent to the cold.
我看到雪激動得連寒冷都不在乎了。

in·dig·nant [ɪn`dɪgnənt] Track 4722

形 憤怒的

▶He was indignant when his mom accused him of lying.
他媽媽說他說謊時，他非常惱怒。

in·dis·pen·sa·ble [ˌɪndɪ`spɛnsəbl̩] Track 4723

形 不可缺少的 同 essential 不可缺少的

▶Both fruits and vegetables are indispensable to life.
水果和蔬菜對生命來說都是不可或缺的。

文法字詞解析
相反地，拿掉表示「不、無」的字首「in-」，變成 dispensable，意思就變成「可以丟棄的」、「不重要的」。

A B C D E F G H I J K L M N O P Q R S T U V W X Y Z

in·duce [ˋɪnˋdjus]

Track 4724

動 引誘、引起

▶Nothing in the world will induce me to do that.
什麼都不能引誘我做那種事。

實用片語用語
induce sb. to do sth. 引誘某人做某事

in·dulge [ɪnˋdʌldʒ]

Track 4725

動 沉溺、放縱、遷就

▶Do not indulge your child, or he will be spoiled.
絕不能放縱你的小孩，否則他會被寵壞的。

in·fi·nite [ˋɪnfənɪt]

Track 4726

形 無限的

▶It was the war that brought infinite harm to the nation.
正是這場戰爭給這個國家帶來了無窮的災難。

in·her·it [ɪnˋhɛrɪt]

Track 4727

動 繼承、接受

▶It doesn't matter if you can't inherit a fortune from your parents. You can earn a lot by yourself. 你無法從父母那繼承到財產也沒什麼大不了。你可以靠自己賺很多錢。

萬用延伸句型
It doesn't matter if... 就算……也沒關係

i·ni·ti·ate [ɪˋnɪʃɪɪt]/[ɪˋnɪʃɪet]

Track 4728

名 初學者 動 開始、創始 形 新加入的 同 begin 開始

▶名 He's an initiate into the world of politics.
他是個剛進入世界政壇的人。

▶動 Why don't we initiate a direct talk with the trade union? That will help solve the problem sooner. 為什麼不和貿易工會開始直接談判呢？這將有助於快點解決問題。

▶形 The initiate member of the team is still young.
隊伍新加入的成員還很年輕。

實用片語用語
initiate sb. into sth. 使某人初步了解某事
例如：He initiates his brother into the techniques of magic.
他教導他的弟弟魔術的技巧。

in·land [ˋɪnlənd]

Track 4729

名 內陸 副 在內陸 形 內陸的

▶名 The population of the inland is growing faster than we imagined. 內陸人口增長得比我們想像中的快。

▶副 Will you travel inland with me? 你願意和我一起去內地旅行嗎？

▶形 The economy of the inland areas has developed faster than that of coastal（沿海的）areas these years.
近幾年內地經濟發展得比沿海要快。

in·nu·mer·a·ble [ɪnˋnjumərəbl̩]

Track 4730

形 數不盡的

▶I hope this technological innovation（創新）would bring innumerable benefits to us.
我希望這項技術創新能給我們帶來無窮的好處。

in·quire [ɪnˋkwaɪr]

Track 4731

動 詢問、調查

▶I don't know whether it is necessary for me to send this by registered mail. Let's inquire at the post office.
我不知道有沒有必要寄掛號信。咱們到郵局去問一下吧。

萬用延伸句型
I don't know whether it is necessary for...
我不知道有沒有必要……

in·sti·tute [ˋɪnstətjut] Track 4732

名 協會、機構 動 設立、授職 同 organization 機構

▶名 There is an exhibition held in our city by the Institute of Modern Art.
現代藝術協會正在我們的城市舉辦一個展覽。

▶動 There is a necessity for us to institute a rational（合理的）welfare system.
我們有必要設立一個合理的福利制度。

in·sure [ɪnˋʃʊr] Track 4733

動 投保、確保

▶I prefer to insure with this company instead of putting my money in the bank.
我寧願向這家公司投保，也不願意把錢放在銀行。

in·tent [ɪnˋtɛnt] Track 4734

名 意圖、意思 形 熱心的、急切的、專心致志的

▶名 He sold the house with the intent to cheat her.
他出售那棟房子是因為企圖去詐騙她。

▶形 The merchant was intent on making money.
那名商人非常專注於賺錢。

實用片語用語
hostile intent 敵意
例如：Obviously the missiles were sent with hostile intent.
這些飛彈當然是因為對方抱有敵意才會發射的。

in·ter·fer·ence [ˏɪntɚˋfɪrəns] Track 4735

名 妨礙、干擾

▶There is so much interference that I can't listen to the radio.
干擾太大以致於我無法聽收音機。

in·te·ri·or [ɪnˋtɪrɪɚ] Track 4736

名 內部、內務 形 內部的 反 exterior 外部

▶名 It is the first time that we have found water in the interior of the cave.
我們還是第一次發現山洞的內部有水。

▶形 We have arrived at the interior town.
我們到達了這個內地城鎮。

文法字詞解析
Interior 還有一個延伸出來的字義，就是跟國家內部有關的事務。所以 Department of the Interior 就是一個國家的「內政部」。

in·ter·pre·ta·tion [ɪnˏtɝprɪˋteʃən] Track 4737

名 解釋、說明 同 explanation 解釋

▶What do you think about his interpretation of this passage?
對於他對這段文章的解釋，你認為如何呢？

in·ter·pret·er [ɪnˋtɝprɪtɚ] Track 4738

名 解釋者、翻譯員

▶Would you like me to arrange for an interpreter to be present, sir?先生，要不要我幫你安排一位口譯員在場呢？

實用片語用語
be present 在現場

in·tu·i·tion [ˏɪntjuˋɪʃən] Track 4739

名 直覺 同 hunch 直覺

▶She had an intuition that she would find you.
她有一種直覺能找到你。

in·ward [ˋɪnwɚd]

Track 4740

形 裡面的 副 向內、內心裡 反 outward 向外

▶形 She never talked about her inward fears with others.
她從來不會把自己內心的恐懼拿出來跟別人討論。

▶副 The door opens inward into the room. 門是朝房間裡面開的。

in·wards [ˋɪnwɚdz]

Track 4741

副 向內

▶Will you tell me whether the windows in our new house open inwards or outwards?
你能告訴我我們新房子裡的窗戶是朝裡開還是朝外開的嗎？

實用片語用語
open inwards 往內開

isle [aɪl]

Track 4742

名 島 同 island 島

▶It doesn't matter if you don't know the locations of the British Isles. 你不知道不列顛群島的位置也沒關係。

is·sue [ˋɪʃjʊ]

Track 4743

名 議題 動 發出、發行

▶名 Do you accept the professor's views on the environmental issues? 你接受教授在環境議題上的那些觀點嗎？

▶動 Will you tell me when the post office will issue the stamps?
你能告訴我郵局何時將發行這些郵票嗎？

實用片語用語
view on / about 對……的觀點、對……的看法

i·vy [ˋaɪvɪ]

Track 4744

名 常春藤

▶The front of the building was covered with ivy.
建築物的前面爬滿了常春藤。

實用片語用語
Ivy league 長春藤（學校）
例 如：His parents wanted him to go to an Ivy league school.
他父母想要他去念長春藤名校。

jack [dʒæk]

Track 4745

名 起重機、千斤頂 動 用起重機舉起

▶名 I'm afraid that you need an automobile jack to lift the car before repairing it.
恐怕在修汽車前你得用千斤頂把汽車抬起來。

▶動 Help me jack up this huge machine.
幫我把這個大型機器用起重機吊起來。

jade [dʒed]

Track 4746

名 玉、玉石

▶The bracelet is made of jade. 這個手環是玉做的。

jan·i·tor [ˋdʒænɪtɚ]

Track 4747

名 管門者、看門者

▶It is obvious that the janitor knows all the ins and outs of the big school building.
顯然管理員瞭解學校大樓的詳細情況。

實用片語用語
ins and outs 詳細情況、內行人才知道的情況

jas·mine [ˋdʒæsmɪn]

Track 4748

名 茉莉

▶Would you like to try the jasmine tea? It tastes good.
你想試試茉莉花茶嗎？它味道還不錯。

jay·walk [ˋdʒe͵wɔk]

Track 4749

動 不守交通規則穿越街道

▶I don't think that jaywalking is allowed.
我認為隨意橫穿馬路是不被允許的。

jeer [dʒɪr]

Track 4750

動 戲弄、嘲笑 同 mock 嘲笑

▶It's very unkind of you to jeer at the person who came last in the race. 你嘲笑賽跑中跑在最後的人是很不友善的。

實用片語用語
jeer at sb. 嘲笑某人

jin·gle [ˋdʒɪŋg!]

Track 4751

名 叮鈴聲、節拍十分規則的簡單詩歌 動 使發出鈴聲

▶名 The bells made a jingle when I opened the door.
開門時，鈴鐺發出了叮噹聲。

▶動 Would you please stop jingling your keys like that?
請你不要把鑰匙弄得叮噹亂響好嗎？

萬用延伸句型
Would you please stop + V-ing? 可以請你不要……嗎？

jol·ly [ˋdʒɑlɪ]

Track 4752

動 開玩笑、慫恿 形 幽默的、快活的、興高采烈的 副 非常地 反 melancholy 憂鬱的

▶動 Let's jolly her into going with us, shall we?
我們慫恿她跟我們一起去吧，怎麼樣？

▶形 What a jolly morning it is! Let's go out for a walk.
多麼令人陶醉的早晨啊！我們出去散散步吧。

▶副 He's going to be a jolly tough candidate to beat.
他會是個很難擊敗的選手。

jour·nal·ism [ˋdʒɝn!͵ɪzəm]

Track 4753

名 新聞學、新聞業

▶After he left school, he took up journalism.
他畢業離校後從事了新聞業。

jour·nal·ist [ˋdʒɝn!ɪst]

Track 4754

名 新聞工作者

▶He feels a prior obligation（責任）to his job as a journalist.
他覺得要優先為他作為新聞記者的工作盡職。

jug [dʒʌg]

Track 4755

名 帶柄的水壺

▶He poured the milk into a jug.
他把牛奶灌進了壺裡。

文法字詞解析
jug 通常是指大小比較大的水壺，可以用來裝水、牛奶、果汁等。一般喝熱茶用的比較小的茶壺則不會稱為 jug。

ju·ry [ˋdʒurɪ]

Track 4756

名 陪審團

▶It is a surprise that the jury found the prisoner not guilty.
陪審團判定囚犯無罪，這真令人驚訝。

jus·ti·fy [ˋdʒʌstə͵faɪ]

Track 4757

動 證明……有理

▶Nothing can justify your cheating on an exam.
任何事情都不能成為你考試作弊的理由。

ju·ve·nile [ˋdʒuvən!]

Track 4758

名 青少年、孩子 形 青少年的、孩子氣的

▶名 How to sentence juveniles has always been a controversial topic in law.
如何判決青少年一直是法律上一個有爭議的問題。

▶形 I'm afraid that he'll ultimately（最終）become a juvenile delinquent（行為不良的人）.
恐怕他最終會成為一名青少年罪犯。

實用片語用語
juvenile delinquent 不良少年

joy·ous [ˋdʒɔɪəs]

Track 4759

形 歡喜的、高興的

▶Why don't we convey the joyous news to her as soon as possible?
為什麼不儘快告訴她這一個令人歡喜的消息呢？

kin [kɪn]

Track 4760

名 親族、親戚 形 有親戚關係的 同 relative 親戚

▶名 He gave all his money to his next of kin.
他把所有的錢都給了最近的親屬。

▶形 He is kin to me, so we cannot marry.
他是我的親戚，所以我們無法結婚。

實用片語用語
next of kin 最親近的親屬

kin·dle [ˋkɪnd!]

Track 4761

動 生火、起火

▶Do you know how to kindle a fire? 你知道怎麼點火嗎？

knowl·edge·a·ble [ˋnɑlɪdʒəb!]

Track 4762

形 博學的

▶My teacher majored in music at college. It is no wonder that he is very knowledgeable about music. 我的老師大學時學的是音樂。怪不得他在音樂方面的知識很豐富。

實用片語用語
major in 主修（科目）

lad [læd]

Track 4763

名 少年、老友

▶The young lad over there is my nephew.
那邊的年輕小伙子是我的姪子。

lame [lem]　Track 4764

形 跛的、站不住腳的

▶That is a lame excuse. You could do better.
那不是一個充分的藉口，你還可以想一個更好的藉口。

land·la·dy [ˋlændˏledɪ]　Track 4765

名 女房東

▶I'm afraid my landlady wouldn't allow us to do that.
恐怕我的房東太太不會允許我們那麼做的。

實用片語用語
allow sb. to... 允許某人做某事

land·lord [ˋlændˏlɔrd]　Track 4766

名 房東、主人、老闆

▶The landlord wouldn't let me keep a cat.
房東不讓我養貓。

la·ser [ˋlezɚ]　Track 4767

名 雷射

▶He pulled out a laser gun and shot the monsters.
他拿出一把雷射槍射了怪物。

實用片語用語
pull out 拔出……

lat·i·tude [ˋlætəˏtjud]　Track 4768

名 緯度 反 longitude 經度

▶It is obvious that the two cities are at approximately（大約）the same latitude.
顯然這兩個城市差不多位於同一緯度上。

law·mak·er [lɔˋmekɚ]　Track 4769

名 立法者

▶We need to bring this issue to the lawmakers' attention.
我們得讓立法者注意到這件事。

實用片語用語
bring sth. to sb.'s attention
讓（某人）注意到（某事）

lay·er [ˋleɚ]　Track 4770

名 層 動 分層

▶名 The pollution had affected the ozone layer.
污染影響了臭氧層。

▶動 He layered cement to build the wall.
他一層一層地疊上水泥以蓋起牆壁。

league [lig]　Track 4771

名 聯盟 動 同盟 同 union 聯盟

▶名 Those nations formed a defense league to fight against their common enemy.
那些國家結成了防禦聯盟，要對付共同的敵人。

▶動 Those four countries leagued together for this battle.
那四個國家在這場戰爭中結成同盟。

實用片語用語
Major League Baseball 棒球大聯盟
例如：It has always been his dream to pitch for a Major League baseball team.
他一直以來的夢想是到大聯盟當投手。

leg·is·la·tion [ˏlɛdʒɪsˋleʃən]　Track 4772

名 立法

▶It is obvious that legislation will be difficult and takes time.
顯然立法將會困難又費時。

less·en [ˋlɛsn̩]
Track 4773

動 減少 同 decrease 減少

▶Would you tell me what we can do to lessen your vexation（煩惱）？你能告訴我們做些什麼才能減輕你的煩惱嗎？

lest [lɛst]
Track 4774

連 以免

▶You need to take off your hat, lest it gets blown away.
你應該要把帽子拿下來，以免它被吹走。

lieu·ten·ant [luˋtɛnənt]
Track 4775

名 海軍上尉、陸軍中尉

▶It is a surprise that he was promoted to lieutenant so soon.
他那麼快就被提升為海軍上尉，這真令人驚訝。

萬用延伸句型
It is a surprise that... 令人驚訝地……

life·long [ˋlaɪfˋlɔŋ]
Track 4776

形 終身的

▶They've become lifelong friends.
他們成了終身的朋友。

like·li·hood [ˋlaɪklɪ͵hʊd]
Track 4777

名 可能性、可能的事物 同 possibility 可能性

▶There is a strong likelihood that the matter will soon be settled.
事情極可能不久就會獲得解決。

萬用延伸句型
There is a strong likelihood that...
有很大的可能性……

lime [laɪm]
Track 4778

名 萊姆（樹）、石灰 動 灑石灰

▶名 This drink is made of lime.
這飲料是萊姆做的。

▶動 Is it that careless worker who limed our backyard?
就是那個粗心的工人把石灰灑在我們的後院嗎？

limp [lɪmp]
Track 4779

動 跛行

▶He limped all the way home.
他一路跛著腳走回家。

實用片語用語
walk with a limp 跛腳走路
例如：Why are you walking with a limp? What happened?
你為什麼跛著腳走路？怎麼了？

lin·ger [ˋlɪŋgɚ]
Track 4780

動 留戀、徘徊 同 stay 停留、逗留

▶He lingered outside the school after everybody else had gone home.
其他人都回家後，他仍在學校外面徘徊。

live·stock [ˋlaɪv͵stɑk]
Track 4781

名 家畜

▶It is reported that the heavy rain and flood killed scores of livestock.
據報導大雨和洪水淹死了很多家畜。

liz·ard [ˋlɪzɚd]
Track 4782

名 蜥蜴

▶No matter what he did, somehow the lizard always got into his room.
無論他怎樣做，那隻蜥蜴總是有辦法跑進他的房間。

萬用延伸句型
No matter whatr... 無論什麼……

lo·co·mo·tive [ˌlokəˋmotɪv]
Track 4783

名 火車頭 形 推動的、運動的

▶名 Can you tell me how many coaches that locomotive can pull?
你能告訴我那個火車頭能拉多少節車廂嗎？

▶形 What other locomotive organs do we have besides arms and legs?
除了手和腳，我們還有哪些其他的運動器官？

文法字詞解析
coach 在這裡是「車廂」的意思，或者也可以說「car」；另外，在國外旅行的時候免不了選擇搭長途巴士移動以節省開支，而長途巴士的講法也是「coach」。

lo·cust [ˋlokəst]
Track 4784

名 蝗蟲

▶It is a pity that the locusts have destroyed all the crops and vegetables. 真遺憾蝗蟲群已經毀壞了所有的穀物和蔬菜。

lodge [lɑdʒ]
Track 4785

名 小屋 動 寄宿

▶名 Would you please find a lodge for us to stay in for some days? 你能幫我們找一間小屋暫住幾天嗎？

▶動 Would you please lodge us for the night in your house?
您能讓我們在您家暫住一晚嗎？

萬用延伸句型
Would you please...? 您可不可以……？

實用片語用語
lodge sb. in / at sth. 讓某人暫時居住於……

loft·y [ˋlɔftɪ]
Track 4786

形 非常高的、高聳的

▶I don't like her lofty treatment of her visitors.
我不喜歡她對來訪者的高傲態度。

log·o [ˋlɔgo]
Track 4787

名 商標、標誌

▶I don't know what the Olympics logo means.
我不知道奧運會的標誌代表什麼。

lone·some [ˋlonsəm]
Track 4788

形 孤獨的 同 lonely 孤獨的

▶I felt lonesome at home alone last night.
我昨天獨自在家裡度過了一個寂寞的夜晚。

lon·gi·tude [ˋlɑndʒəˌtjud]
Track 4789

名 經度 反 latitude 緯度

▶Each point on earth is specified by latitude and longitude.
地球上的每個點都可以用緯度和經度來定位。

實用片語用語
be specified by... 用……來判定

lo·tus [ˋlotəs]
Track 4790

名 睡蓮

▶Chinese people regard lotus as an emblem（象徵）of purity.
中國人把蓮花看作是純潔的象徵。

A B C D E F G H I J K **L** M N O P Q R S T U V W X Y Z

lot·ter·y [ˋlɑtərɪ]

Track 4791

名 彩券、樂透

▶Dave, let's go buy some lottery tickets.
大衛，我們去買彩券吧。

lum·ber [ˋlʌmbɚ]

Track 4792

名 木材 動 採伐 同 timber 木材

▶名 There are piles of lumber stacked in front of his house.
他家門前堆放著大量的木材。

▶動 This valley was lumbered hard during the past decade.
在過去十年裡，這個山谷的林木被大肆採伐。

lump [lʌmp]

Track 4793

名 塊 動 結塊、笨重地移動 同 chunk 大塊

▶名 There is a lump on his head where he was beaten.
他頭上被別人毆打的地方有個腫塊。

▶動 We lumped all the dirty clothes in a pile.
我們把髒衣服都成團疊成一疊。

實用片語用語
lump sth. together 把（某物）堆在一起
例如：We lumped the old newspapers and used notebooks together.
我們把舊報紙和用過的筆記本堆在一起。

mag·ni·fy [ˋmægnə͵faɪ]

Track 4794

動 擴大 同 enlarge 擴大

▶Will you tell me how I can magnify my pictures?
你能告訴我要怎麼放大我的照片嗎？

實用片語用語
magnifying glass 放大鏡，和megascope同義。
例如：He liked to look at ants through a magnifying glass.
他喜歡透過放大鏡看螞蟻。

maid·en [ˋmedn̩]

Track 4795

名 處女、少女 形 少女的、未婚的、處女的

▶名 The fair young maiden is the envy of many.
那位年輕美麗的少女是許多人嫉妒的對象。

▶形 When will the ship's maiden voyage start?
這艘船的處女航何時要開始？

main·land [ˋmen͵lænd]

Track 4796

名 大陸

▶The company's investment in mainland China has increased.
這家企業在中國大陸的投資增加了。

main·stream [ˋmen͵strim]

Track 4797

名 思潮、主流

▶He never listens to mainstream music.
他從來不聽主流音樂。

main·te·nance [ˋmentənəns]

Track 4798

名 保持

▶The machine requires constant maintenance, otherwise it won't work well.
這台機器需要經常保養維修，要不然它就會無法正常運作。

實用片語用語
high-maintenance 要求很高的、麻煩的、吹毛求疵的
例如：He thinks his girlfriend is high-maintenance.
他覺得他的女朋友要求很多。

ma·jes·tic [mə'dʒɛstɪk]

Track 4799

形 莊嚴的 同 grand 雄偉的

▶The king looks really majestic when he isn't smiling.
那個國王在不笑的時候看起來非常莊嚴。

maj·es·ty [ˋmædʒɪstɪ]

Track 4800

名 威嚴

▶Both the king and the queen were seated on the throne（王座）in all their majesty.
國王和王后威嚴地坐在王座上。

文法字詞解析
身為市井小民，面對皇帝、國王這類的人當然是不能用「you」來稱呼的，因此在英文中我們可以尊稱它們為「Your Majesty」。

mam·mal [ˋmæml̩]

Track 4801

名 哺乳動物

▶Not everyone knows that whales are mammals that live in the sea. 不是每個人都知道鯨魚是生活在海洋中的哺乳動物。

man·i·fest [ˋmænə͵fɛst]

Track 4802

動 顯示 形 明顯的 同 apparent 明顯的

▶動 He was the kind of person who always manifested a lot of emotion.
他是那種總是表現出很多情緒的人。

▶形 Fear was manifest on his face when he ran into the bear.
他遇到那頭熊時，臉上明顯地表現出恐懼。

文法字詞解析
這個字加上字尾「-tion」就變成名詞「manifestation」，除了有「顯示」的意思之外，還有「示威運動」的意思，畢竟示威就是要讓自己的彰顯自己的想法和不滿嘛。

man·sion [ˋmænʃən]

Track 4803

名 宅邸、大廈

▶Will you tell me when the old mansion was built?
你能告訴我這座古宅是什麼時候建造的嗎？

ma·ple [ˋmepl̩]

Track 4804

名 楓樹、槭樹

▶There are many maples in the park you mentioned yesterday.
你昨天提到的那個公園裡有好多楓樹。

實用片語用語
maple leaf 楓葉
例如：There is a maple leaf on Canada's national flag.
加拿大的國旗上有一片楓葉。

mar·gin·al [ˋmɑrdʒɪnl̩]

Track 4805

形 邊緣的

▶It's just a marginal issue that won't affect our decision.
那只是個不重要的小議題，不會影響我們做出決定。

ma·rine [məˋrin]

Track 4806

名 海軍 形 海洋的

▶名 He is a U.S. marine, and therefore rarely at home.
他是一名美國海軍陸戰隊士兵，因此不常在家裡。

▶形 There are lots of marine mammals such as seals in the sea.
海洋裡有許多諸如海豹的海生哺乳動物。

mar·shal [ˋmɑrʃəl]

Track 4807

名 元帥、司儀

▶I don't think the general will be appointed（任命）marshal of the armies. 我覺得這名將軍不會被任命為軍隊的元帥。

mar·tial [ˋmɑrʃəl]

Track 4808

形 軍事的 同 military 軍事的

▶The war criminal will be tried by the martial court.
這名戰犯將被軍事法庭審判。

實用片語用語
martial arts 武術
例如：These children have been taking martial arts classes since they were four. 這些孩子四歲就開始上武術課了。

mar·vel [ˋmɑrvḷ]

Track 4809

名 令人驚奇的事物、奇蹟 動 驚異 同 miracle 奇蹟

▶名 Acupuncture（針灸）can work marvels. 針灸能創造奇蹟。

▶動 I marveled at her singing skills.
我對於她的歌唱技巧感到驚奇。

mas·cu·line [ˋmæskjəlɪn]

Track 4810

名 男性 形 男性的 反 feminine 女性

▶名 "Host" is the masculine noun for "hostess".
host 是與 hostess 相對應的陽性名詞。

▶形 The lady has a very masculine voice.
這名太太有個很陽剛的聲音。

mash [mæʃ]

Track 4811

名 麥芽漿 動 搗碎

▶名 Would you please put the mash in the bottle?
請你把麥芽漿放在這個瓶子裡好嗎？

▶動 I love eating mashed potatoes. 我好喜歡吃馬鈴薯泥。

文法字詞解析
mashed 是「被搗碎成泥的」的意思，後面可以加上不同的食物。例如：mashed potatoes（馬鈴薯泥）、mashed apples（蘋果泥）、mashed pumpkin（南瓜泥）。

mas·sage [məˋsɑʒ]

Track 4812

名 按摩 動 按摩

▶名 I wish someone would give me a massage when I'm tired.
我希望在我疲憊的時候，能有人幫我按摩。

▶動 He walked over and massaged my shoulders.
他走了過來，幫我按摩了一下肩膀。

文法字詞解析
massage（按摩） 和 message（訊息）長得很像，但除了意思不一樣之外，唸法也完全不一樣喔。massage 的重音是在第二個音節。

mas·sive [ˋmæsɪv]

Track 4813

形 笨重的、大量的、巨大的 同 heavy 重的

▶There is a massive monument in the square.
廣場上有一座巨大的紀念碑。

mas·ter·piece [ˋmæstɚ͵pis]

Track 4814

名 傑作、名著

▶It took the artist ten years to finish this great masterpiece.
這名藝術家花了十年的時間才完成了這個偉大的傑作。

may·on·naise [͵meəˋnez]

Track 4815

名 橄欖油、蛋黃醬、美乃滋

▶I don't like mayonnaise in my sandwiches.
我不喜歡三明治裡面有美乃滋。

mean·time [ˋmin͵taɪm]

Track 4816

名 期間、同時 副 同時

▶名 The waiters will serve food in five minutes. Is there anything else you need in the meantime, madam? 五分鐘之後服務生將上菜。夫人，在此期間您還需要什麼嗎？

實用片語用語
in the meantime 在這同時……

▶副 There are some students playing football. Meantime, some are playing games.
有些學生在踢足球。同時，有些學生在玩遊戲。

me·chan·ics [mə`kænɪks] Track 4817

名 機械學、力學

▶Can you explain the mechanics of this to me?
你可以跟我解釋一下這個東西的運作方式嗎？

me·di·ate [`midɪˏet] Track 4818

動 調解

▶Do you think the government will offer to mediate the dispute（爭端）? 你覺得政府會主動提出調解爭端嗎？

實用片語用語
mediate between A and B 在A和B之間斡旋
例如：It's hard to be the person who mediates between Dad and Mom.
要當爸和媽之間的調停者真的很難。

men·ace [`mɛnɪs] Track 4819

名 威脅 動 脅迫 同 threat 威脅

▶名 In dry weather, forest fires are a great menace to people.
在乾燥的天氣裡，森林起火對人們構成了很大的威脅。

▶動 The poor country is menaced by war.
這個可憐的國家受到了戰爭威脅。

mer·maid [`mɝˏmed] Track 4820

名 美人魚

▶Have you read the story about the little mermaid?
你讀過小美人魚的故事嗎？

實用片語用語
mermaid tail 美人魚的尾巴
例如：Many little girls often wished that they had a mermaid tail.
很多小女孩都夢想能夠擁有美人魚的尾巴。

midst [mɪdst] Track 4821

名 中央、中間 介 在……之中

▶名 Don't you believe there is a thief in our midst?
你不相信我們當中有小偷嗎？

▶介 The summit（峰頂）of the mountain can be seen midst the clouds. 可以在雲朵間看到山頂。

mi·grant [`maɪgrənt] Track 4822

名 候鳥、移民 形 遷移的

▶名 I don't believe they will treat these migrants well and give them a good wages.
我不相信他們會好好對待這些移民並給他們不錯的工資。

▶形 A lot of factory work is done by migrant workers.
大量的工廠工作是由外藉勞工們來做的。

mile·age [`maɪlɪdʒ] Track 4823

名 里數

▶Will you tell me your car's mileage?
你能告訴我你的汽車已經跑了多少英里嗎？

實用片語用語
your mileage may vary 你可能有不同的見解
開的里程數不一樣，見過的風景也不一樣，所以當然見解可能就不一樣。這句常用於要表達個人意見時，先強調「這是我的看法，你可能有不同的意見或經驗」。

mile·stone [`maɪlˏston] Track 4824

名 里程碑

▶The year 2008 marked an important milestone in the diplomatic（外交上的）history of the two countries.
2008 年是兩國外交史上的一個重要里程碑。

min·gle [ˋmɪŋg!]
Track 4825

動 混合 同 blend 混合

▶I like to go to parties to mingle with people.
我喜歡去派對跟不同的人混在一起。

min·i·mal [ˋmɪnɪm!]
Track 4826

形 最小的

▶There is a minimal quantity of imperfection（瑕疵）in these goods.
這批貨物的瑕疵品極少。

mint [mɪnt]
Track 4827

名 薄荷

▶These candies he bought taste of mint.
他買的這些糖果有薄荷味。

實用片語用語
mint chocolate chip 薄荷巧克力
例如：Mint chocolate chip is my favorite ice cream flavor.
我最喜歡的冰淇淋口味是薄荷巧克力。

mi·ser [ˋmaɪzɚ]
Track 4828

名 小氣鬼

▶The miser doesn't like to part with his money.
那個小氣鬼不喜歡與他的錢分開。

mis·tress [ˋmɪstrɪs]
Track 4829

名 女主人

▶The mistress of the family doesn't like to give parties.
這個家庭的女主人不喜歡開辦宴會。

moan [mon]
Track 4830

名 呻吟聲、悲嘆 動 呻吟 同 groan 呻吟

▶名 I can hear his moans from over here.
我在這裡都能聽到他在呻吟。

▶動 My colleague always moans about all the work he has to do. 我同事總是抱怨他有很多的工作要做。

實用片語用語
moan about 抱怨、發牢騷

mock [mɑk]
Track 4831

名 嘲弄、笑柄 動 嘲笑 形 模仿的

▶名 The boy has become the mock of the class.
那個男孩成了班上的笑柄。

▶動 She mocked him for having a giant belly.
她嘲笑他肚子很大。

▶形 I didn't do that well in the mock test.
我模擬考考得不好。

實用片語用語
mock test 模擬考

mode [mod]
Track 4832

名 款式、方法 同 manner 方法

▶They should have told us the mode of payment first.
他們本來應該先告訴我們支付方式的。

mod·ern·ize [ˋmɑdɚn͵aɪz]
Track 4833

動 現代化

▶They lack funds to modernize their factory.
他們資金匱乏，沒辦法使自己的工廠現代化。

mod·i·fy [ˋmɑdə͵faɪ] Track 4834

動 修改

▶We need to modify the rules to make the game more playable.
我們應該修改一下規則，這遊戲才會更好玩。

mold [mold] Track 4835

名 模型 動 塑造、磨練

▶名 Can you lend me a pastry（糕點）mold?
你可以借我一個糕點模子嗎？

▶動 He's teaching these children to mold figures out of clay.
你在教這些孩子們用黏土來製造人像。

實用片語用語

cast in the same mold 一個模子刻出來的
例如：These triplets look like they were cast in the same mold.
這三胞胎看起來好像一個模子刻出來的。

mol·e·cule [ˋmɑlə͵kjul] Track 4836

名 分子

▶We're all formed by countless molecules.
我們都是無數分子組成的。

mon·arch [ˋmɑnɚk] Track 4837

名 君主、大王 同 king 君主

▶They attempted to overthrow the monarch.
他們企圖要推翻這個國王。

mon·strous [ˋmɑnstrəs] Track 4838

形 奇怪的、巨大的 同 bulky 龐大的

▶Did you see that horse? It's monstrous!
你有看到那匹馬嗎？牠超大一隻的啊！

mor·tal [ˋmɔrtl̩] Track 4839

名 凡人 形 死亡的、致命的 同 deadly 致命的

▶名 We're all mortals, with our human faults and weaknesses（弱點）.
我們都是凡人，自然都有過錯和弱點。

▶形 All things that live are mortal.
所有生物都會死。

文法字詞解析

相反地，不是凡人、可以永遠活在世上的神仙則稱為 immortal。

moss [mɔs] Track 4840

名 苔蘚、用苔覆蓋

▶Be careful not to slip on the moss.
小心別在青苔上滑倒了。

moth·er·hood [ˋmʌðɚhʊd] Track 4841

名 母性

▶Not every mother has time to appreciate every moment of motherhood.
不是每個母親都能有時間細細品味當母親的點滴時刻。

文法字詞解析

名詞字尾「-hood」是用來表示一段時期或是某個狀態，例如：childhood（孩童時期）、fatherhood（父親的身分）。

mo·tive [ˋmotɪv] Track 4842

名 動機 同 cause 動機

▶The police haven't found the motive for the murder.
警察還未能找到謀殺的動機。

mound [maʊnd]

Track 4843

名 丘陵、堆積、築堤

▶There is a mound of papers on my father's desk every day.
我爸爸的辦公桌上每天都有一大堆文件。

實用片語用語
pitching mound 投手丘
例如：The ball flew in the direction of the pitching mound.
球朝著投手丘的方向飛去。

mount [maʊnt]

Track 4844

名 山 動 攀登 同 climb 攀爬

▶名 Have you been to Mount Everest? 你去過聖母峰嗎？

▶動 The higher the climbers（登山者）mount, the more views they can enjoy.
登山者爬得越高，他們欣賞到的景色就越多。

mow·er [ˋmoɚ]

Track 4845

名 割草者（機）

▶I have to borrow a lawn mower for my father.
我得幫父親借一台割草機來。

mum·ble [ˋmʌmbḷ]

Track 4846

名 含糊不清的話 動 含糊地說 同 mutter 含糊地說

▶名 I heard a mumble from someone in the crowd.
我聽到人群中有人含糊不清地說話。

▶動 Stop mumbling and speak up!
不要講得這麼含糊，講大聲點！

實用片語用語
speak up 講大聲點、說出自己的意見

mus·cu·lar [ˋmʌskjələ]

Track 4847

形 肌肉的

▶The player is tall and muscular. 那名運動員身高力大。

muse [mjuz]

Track 4848

名 靈感來源

▶The beautiful lady is the artist's muse.
那位美麗的太太是那個藝術家的謬思女神。

實用片語用語
muse on 深思
例如：She muses on what happened yesterday.
她思考著昨天發生了什麼事。

mus·tard [ˋmʌstɚd]

Track 4849

名 芥末

▶This meat should be seasoned with salt and mustard.
這肉裡面應該加點鹽和芥末。

mut·ter [ˋmʌtɚ]

Track 4850

名 抱怨 動 低語、含糊地說 同 complain 抱怨

▶名 I heard a mutter of discontent（不滿）, but I have no idea who from.
我聽到有人竊竊私語表示不滿，但不知道是誰。

▶動 She is so lonely that she keeps on muttering to herself every day.
她是如此孤獨，以致於她每天老是一個人喃喃咕咕的。

實用片語用語
keep on（V-ing）一直持續做某事

mut·ton [ˋmʌtṇ]

Track 4851

名 羊肉

▶Not all people like to have mutton in the winter.
不是所有人都喜歡在冬天吃羊肉。

myth [mɪθ] Track 4852

名 神話、傳說 同 tale 傳說

▶I enjoy reading Greek myths.
我喜歡讀希臘神話。

nag [næg] Track 4853

名 嘮叨的人 動 使煩惱、嘮叨 同 annoy 使煩惱

▶名 I don't want to be a nag, but you really should start getting dressed.
我不想做一個嘮叨的人，但你真的應該開始穿衣服了。

▶動 Would you please stop nagging, grandma?
奶奶，不要嘮叨了行不行？

文法字詞解析
nagging 是 nag 的形容詞，表示「嘮叨的、挑剔的」，而名詞 nagger 則是「愛嘮叨的人」，書寫時要注意字尾必須重複。

na·ive [nɑ`iv] Track 4854

形 天真、幼稚 反 sophisticated 世故的

▶She's a naïve little girl that believes everything others tell her.
她是個天真的小女孩，別人跟她說什麼她都信。

文法字詞解析
naive 這個字是從法文來的，所以它的唸法比較特別，重音在第二個音節。

nas·ty [`næstɪ] Track 4855

形 汙穢的、惡意的

▶Did you just eat a booger（鼻屎）? That's just nasty!
你剛吃鼻屎喔？有夠髒的！

nav·i·gate [`nævə͵get] Track 4856

動 控制航向 同 steer 掌舵

▶Not all people know who first navigated the Atlantic Ocean.
不是所有人都知道是誰首先橫渡大西洋的。

news·cast [`njuz͵kæst] Track 4857

名 新聞報導

▶Did you see her on the evening newscast?
你有看到她主持晚間新聞嗎？

nib·ble [`nɪbl̩] Track 4858

名 小撮食物 動 連續地輕咬

▶名 This chocolate is great. Would you like a nibble?
這巧克力好好吃，你想吃一點嗎？

▶動 I could feel a fish nibbling at the bait.
我能感覺到有條魚在輕咬魚餌。

文法字詞解析
nibble 指的是「小口咬」，而且限定是用門牙咬，想當然就不可能咬太大口（因為門牙會痛）。老鼠、兔子一類愛用門牙啃東西的小動物就常搭配這個字出現。

nick·el [`nɪkl̩] Track 4859

名 鎳 動 覆以鎳……

▶名 Would you allow me to put in two nickels instead of a dime?
您允許我放兩個五美分鎳幣來代替一個十美分硬幣嗎？

▶動 Can you help me nickel the wire?
您能不能幫我在這條金屬線上鍍鎳？

night·in·gale [ˋnaɪtn̩ɡel]

Track 4860

名 夜鶯、歌聲美妙的歌手

▶I've never actually heard a nightingale sing.
我從來沒真的聽過夜鶯唱歌。

nom·i·nate [ˋnɑmə͵net]

Track 4861

動 提名、指定 同 propose 提名

▶I wish to nominate Jane Morrison as a president of the club.
我想提名珍・莫莉森為俱樂部主席。

萬用延伸句型
I wish tor... 我想要（做某事）

none·the·less [͵nʌnðəˋlɛs]

Track 4862

副 儘管如此、然而

▶He is young, but I respect him nonetheless.
儘管他年輕，我並不因此而減少對他的尊重。

non·vi·o·lent [nɑnˋvaɪələnt]

Track 4863

形 非暴力的 反 violent 暴力的

▶It is obvious that Martin Luther King made many enemies in his nonviolent quest for equality at that time.
顯然當時馬丁・路德・金在以非暴力手段尋求平等的過程中，樹立了許多敵人。

nos·tril [ˋnɑstrəl]

Track 4864

名 鼻孔

▶He would be good-looking if his nostrils weren't so big.
如果他的鼻孔沒那麼大，那他一定很帥。

no·ta·ble [ˋnotəbl̩]

Track 4865

名 名人、出衆的人 形 出色的、著名的 同 famous 著名的

▶名 There are many notables attending the reception.
有許多著名人士參加了那個招待會。

▶形 It is obvious that she played a notable role in compiling（編纂）the series.
顯然在編纂這系列書的過程中，她起了顯著的作用。

實用片語用語
play a role in... 在……扮演了……的角色

no·tice·a·ble [ˋnotɪsəbl̩]

Track 4866

形 顯著的、顯眼的

▶There was a noticeable transformation in her appearance.
她的容貌有了明顯的變化。

no·ti·fy [ˋnotə͵faɪ]

Track 4867

動 通知、報告 同 inform 通知

▶Would you please notify us if there is any change of the address?
地址如有變動，請通知我們好嗎？

no·tion [ˋnoʃən]

Track 4868

名 觀念、意見 同 opinion 意見

▶I haven't the faintest（模糊的）notion what they mean. Do you?
我一點也不知道他們是什麼意思。你呢？

實用片語用語
be a novice in... 是……的新手
例如：I'm a novice in photography.
我是攝影的新手。

nov·ice [ˋnɑvɪs]

Track 4869

名 初學者

▶Whether novice or master, they should be treated equally.
我認為不管是新手還是達人都應該一視同仁。

實用片語用語
novice at 在……方面是新手
例如：I'm a compete novice at golfing.
我在打高爾夫球方面完全是新手。

no·where [ˋno͵hwɛr]

Track 4870

副 無處地 名 不為人知的地方

▶副 The young girl would go nowhere without her bodyguards.
難怪那個年輕女孩去任何地方都有保鏢跟著。

▶名 He says that nowhere is more beautiful than his hometown.
他說他的家鄉是最美麗的地方。

nu·cle·us [ˋnjuklɪəs]

Track 4871

名 核心、中心、原子核 同 core 核心

▶It took a long time for humans to learn how to separate the electrons（電子）from their nucleus.
人們花費很長時間才學會怎樣把電子和原子核分開。

nude [njud]

Track 4872

名 裸體、裸體畫 形 裸的 同 naked 裸的

▶名 What do you think of that nude he painted?
你覺得他畫的那幅裸體畫怎麼樣呢？

▶形 The nude lady walked right past us.
那個裸體的小姐就這樣從我們身邊走了過去。

實用片語用語
in the nude 裸體的
例如：He likes to sleep in the nude.
他喜歡裸體睡覺。

oar [or]

Track 4873

名 槳、櫓

▶He lost the oars so had nothing to row the boat with.
他把槳弄丟了，沒有東西可以用來划船。

o·a·sis [oˋesɪs]

Track 4874

名 綠洲

▶It took us half a day to reach the oasis at sunset（日落）.
我們花了半天時間才在日落時到達了這片綠洲。

oath [oθ]

Track 4875

名 誓約、盟誓 同 vow 誓約

▶They swore an oath of loyalty to the country.
他們宣誓要報效祖國。

oat·meal [ˋot͵mil]

Track 4876

名 燕麥片

▶Would you like to have oatmeal and toast for breakfast?
你想吃麥片和吐司當早餐嗎？

萬用延伸句型
Would you like tor...? 你想要……嗎？

ob·long [ˋɑblɔŋ]

Track 4877

名 長方形 形 長方形的

▶名 I told him to draw a circle but he drew an oblong.
我叫他畫圓，他卻畫了一個長方形。

▶形 I bought an oblong table, not a square one.
我買了一張長方形的桌子，而不是正方形的。

ob·serv·er [əbˋzɝvɚ]

Track 4878

名 觀察者、觀察員 反 performer 表演者、執行者

▶Any casual observer could see that he was nervous.
任何人只要隨便觀察一下就能發現他很緊張。

實用片語用語
casual observer 無心注意的人、漫不經心的人

ob·sti·nate [ˋɑbstənɪt]

Track 4879

形 執拗的、頑固的 反 obedient 順從的

▶My elder sister is too obstinate to let anyone help her.
我姐姐太倔強了，她是不會讓任何人幫她的。

oc·cur·rence [əˋkɝəns]

Track 4880

名 出現、發生

▶I am afraid that the occurrence of storms will delay our trip.
我擔心暴風雨會延誤我們的旅行。

oc·to·pus [ˋɑktəpəs]

Track 4881

名 章魚

▶We saw a giant octopus in the sea.
我們在海裡看到了一隻巨大的章魚。

文法字詞解析
字首「oct-」是「八」的意思，所以「octopus」是「八爪魚」，也就是「章魚」；「octagon」是「八邊形」。
不過「October」卻不是「八月」而是「十月」，是因為羅馬的統治者凱薩和奧古斯都分別都以自己的名字為七月和八月命名，而原本的八月就被順延兩個月成為十月了。

odds [ɑds]

Track 4882

名 勝算、差別

▶The odds that he will win this game are really low.
他會贏得這場比賽的機率很低。

o·dor [ˋodɚ]

Track 4883

名 氣味 同 smell 氣味

▶What's that strange odor coming from outside?
外面飄來那個奇怪的氣味是什麼？

ol·ive [ˋɑlɪv]

Track 4884

名 橄欖 形 橄欖的、橄欖色的

▶名 Have you ever eaten olives before? What do they taste like?你吃過橄欖嗎？吃起來如何呢？

▶形 She has rich lips and olive eyes.
她有著豐厚的嘴唇和橄欖色的雙眼。

實用片語用語
olive oil 橄欖油
例如：We're all out of olive oil. Pick some up at the supermarket on your way home.
我們沒有橄欖油了，回家路上去超市買一點吧。

op·po·nent [əˋponənt]

Track 4885

名 對手、反對者 反 alliance 同盟

▶You must beat your opponent in the election.
你必須在選舉中擊敗你的對手。

op·ti·mism [ˋɑptəmɪzəm]
Track 4886

名 樂觀主義 反 pessimism 悲觀主義

▶Her eternal optimism can get kind of annoying.
她永遠都這麼樂觀，有時候真的有點討厭。

or·chard [ˋɔrtʃɚd]
Track 4887

名 果園

▶My family decided to expand the orchard.
我們家決定要擴大果園。

or·gan·i·zer [ˋɔrgən͵aɪzɚ]
Track 4888

名 組織者

▶There is no doubt that he is a wonderful event organizer.
毫無疑問，他是一名出色的活動組織者。

文法字詞解析
organizer 除了指組織某事的「人」以外，也可以指幫助你組織行程的工具，例如行程表、筆記本、APP 等。

o·ri·ent [ˋorɪənt]
Track 4889

名 東方、東方諸國 動 使適應、定位 同 adapt 使適應

▶名 They import perfumes and spices from the Orient.
他們從東方進口香水和香料。

▶動 I oriented myself by looking at the road signs.
我藉由看路牌找到自己的位置。

o·ri·en·tal [͵orɪˋɛntḷ]
Track 4890

名 東方人 形 東方諸國的

▶名 There are a great many Orientals living in this city.
在這個城市中住有很多的東方人。

▶形 There are more than 300 kinds of oriental cherries in all in our world. 世界上一共有三百多種東方櫻花。

or·na·ment [ˋɔrnəmənt]
Track 4891

名 裝飾（品） 動 以裝飾品點綴 同 decoration 裝飾品

▶名 The ornaments in the living room fell down when the earthquake happened.
地震發生時，在客廳裡的裝飾都掉下來了。

▶動 She ornamented the room with flowers.
她用花來裝飾房間。

實用片語用語
Christmas ornaments 聖誕裝飾
例如：Who wants to help me put up Christmas ornaments?
誰要幫我把聖誕裝飾掛上去？

or·phan·age [ˋɔrfənɪdʒ]
Track 4892

名 孤兒、孤兒院

▶The boy used to live in an orphanage before he was adopted.
那個男孩在被收養前住在孤兒院裡。

os·trich [ˋɔstrɪtʃ]
Track 4893

名 鴕鳥

▶The ostrich is the fastest animal on two legs in the world.
鴕鳥是世界上跑得最快的兩條腿動物。

ounce [aʊns]
Track 4894

名 盎司

▶I put too many ounces of sugar in the juice.
我在果汁裡加太多盎司的糖了。

out·do [ˌaʊtˋdu]　Track 4895

動 勝過、淩駕 同 surpass 勝過

▶He totally outdid himself today.
他今天的表現完全超越了自己平常的水準。

文法字詞解析
outdo 的動詞變化：outdo, outdid, outdone

out·go·ing [ˋaʊtˌgoɪŋ]　Track 4896

形 擅於社交的、外向的

▶Not all people in the office think he is an outgoing person.
不是辦公室所有的人都認為他是一個外向的人。

out·put [ˋaʊtˌpʊt]　Track 4897

名 生產、輸出 動 生產、大量製造、輸出 同 input 輸入

▶名 The country ranks last in industrial output.
這個國家的工業生產排名最後。

▶動 This program can output the file into another file.
這個程式能將一個文件輸出成為另一個文件。

out·sid·er [ˌaʊtˋsaɪdɚ]　Track 4898

名 門外漢、局外人

▶It is not easy for an outsider to understand his logic.
要瞭解一個門外漢的邏輯是很難的。

萬用延伸句型
It is not easy for sb. tor... 對（某人）來說，（做到某事）很不容易

out·skirts [ˋaʊtˌskɝts]　Track 4899

名 郊區 同 suburb 郊區

▶It has been a week since I got back to the outskirts of London.
我回到倫敦郊區已經一週了。

out·ward(s) [ˋaʊtwɚd(z)]　Track 4900

形 向外的、外面的 副 向外 反 inward 向內

▶形 Her outward appearance is calm but she is seething（生氣的）inside.
她外表很鎮定，但她內心可是火大無比。

▶副 Don't you know that this window opens outwards?
難道你不知道那個窗戶是向外開的嗎？

o·ver·all [ˋovɚˌɔl]　Track 4901

名 罩衫、吊帶褲 形 全部的 副 整體而言 同 whole 全部的

▶名 These overalls are too big for me.
這吊帶褲對我來說太大了。

▶形 How long will it take for you to finish the overall renovating（重新裝潢）?
你完成所有的重新裝潢要多久？

▶副 Prices are still rising overall at this moment.
現在總體來看物價仍在上漲。

o·ver·do [ˌovɚˋdu]　Track 4902

動 做得過火 同 exaggerate 誇張

▶You should work hard, but don't overdo it, or you will make yourself ill.
你應該努力工作，但也不能過頭，否則你會把自己累出病來的。

文法字詞解析
overdo 的動詞變化：overdo, overdid, overdone

over·eat [ˋovɚˋit]

Track 4903

動 吃得過多

▶The reason why you are fat is that you often overeat.
造成你肥胖的原因是你常常吃太多。

o·ver·flow [ˏovɚˋflo]

Track 4904

名 滿溢 動 氾濫、溢出、淹沒 同 flood 淹沒

▶名 We can't stop the overflow from the toilet.
我們都無法止住馬桶裡的水溢出。

▶動 The water in the bathtub is overflowing.
澡盆裡的水都溢出來了。

o·ver·hear [ˏovɚˋhɪr]

Track 4905

動 無意中聽到

▶I overheard someone crying when I was going upstairs.
我上樓的時候無意中聽見有人在哭。

文法字詞解析
overhear 的動詞變化：overhear, overheard, overheard

over·sleep [ˋovɚˋslip]

Track 4906

動 睡過頭

▶I'm afraid he overslept this morning and has already missed his usual bus.
恐怕他今天早上睡過頭了，而且錯過了他平常坐的那班公車。

o·ver·whelm [ˏovɚˋhwɛlm]

Track 4907

動 淹沒、征服、壓倒

▶A great wave overwhelmed the boat.
一個巨浪吞沒了那艘小船。

文法字詞解析
如果加上「-ing」就會變成形容詞「overwhelming（壓倒性的）」。
例如：An overwhelming majority 壓倒性的大多數。

o·ver·work [ˋovɚˋwɝk]

Track 4908

名 過度工作 動 過度工作

▶名 My uncle got ill because of overwork. I wish he could recover soon.
我叔叔因為工作過度而病倒了。我希望他能很快恢復健康。

▶動 I hope the boss did not overwork that poor boy.
我希望老闆沒有使那個可憐的男孩過度工作。

oys·ter [ˋɔɪstɚ]

Track 4909

名 牡蠣、蠔

▶I enjoy eating these oysters; they're really delicious.
我喜歡吃這些牡蠣，它們真美味。

o·zone [ˋozon]

Track 4910

名 臭氧

▶Scientists are concerned over the current state of our ozone layer.
科學家對於我們的臭氧層目前的狀況很擔憂。

實用片語用語
current state 現狀

pa·cif·ic [pə`sɪfɪk]
Track 4911

名 太平洋（首字大寫） 形 平靜的

▶名 The Pacific Ocean is much larger than the Atlantic Ocean.
太平洋比大西洋大得多。

▶形 It is obvious that the number of pacific people is much larger than that of those who love war.
顯然愛好和平的人比喜歡戰爭的人多得多。

pack·et [`pækɪt]
Track 4912

名 小包 同 package 包裹

▶Would you please deliver the packet to my hometown for me?
請您幫我把這個包裹寄送到我的家鄉好嗎？

pad·dle [`pædḷ]
Track 4913

名 槳、踏板 動 以槳划動、戲水 同 oar 槳

▶名 Can you hand me a paddle? I'll row us to the shore.
拿根槳給我好嗎？我來把我們的船划上岸。

▶動 The children were paddling in the water. 孩子們在水裡玩。

實用片語用語

doggie paddle 狗爬式
例如：The little boy can't swim, but he can do the doggie paddle.
那個小男孩不會游泳，但他會狗爬式。

pane [pen]
Track 4914

名 方框

▶Someone broke the window pane. 有人打破了窗框。

par·a·dox [`pærəˏdɑks]
Track 4915

名 似是而非的言論、矛盾的事

▶It is a paradox that in such a rich country there should be so many poor people.
在這麼一個富有的國家中竟有這麼多窮人，真是矛盾。

文法字詞解析

字首「para-」有「超越」的意思，而「-dox」表示「意見、信仰」；兩者合在一起就成了「paradox」。另外，還可以在加上「-ical」變成形容詞「paradoxical（似是而非的、自相矛盾的）」。

par·al·lel [`pærəˏlɛl]
Track 4916

名 平行線 動 平行 形 平行的、類似的

▶名 She is an excellent singer, without parallel in the country.
她是個非常厲害的歌手，國內沒有人能達到她的水準。

▶動 Her story closely parallels what he told me.
她的說法跟他告訴我的情況極為相似。

▶形 Linda and her friends have parallel likes and dislikes.
琳達和她的朋友喜好相同。

par·lor [`pɑrlɚ]
Track 4917

名 客廳、起居室

▶I'm afraid that you have no chioce but to invite him into the parlor. 恐怕你除了邀請他進客廳外別無選擇。

萬用延伸句型

have no choice but to... 別無選擇，只好⋯⋯

par·tic·i·pant [pɑr`tɪsəpənt]
Track 4918

名 參與者

▶The participants in the contest all look very excited.
參賽者們看起來都很興奮。

par·ti·cle [ˋpɑrtɪkl]　Track 4919

名 微粒、極少量

▶There wasn't a particle of truth in what he said.
他說的沒有半點真話。

part·ly [ˋpɑrtlɪ]　Track 4920

副 部分地

▶It is obvious that his ideas were shaped partly by his early experiences.
顯然他的一些想法在一定程度上是由他早期的經歷所形成的。

pas·sion·ate [ˋpæʃənɪt]　Track 4921

形 熱情的

▶She's very passionate about the things she likes.
她對喜歡的事情充滿了熱情。

實用片語用語
be passionate aboutr... 對……充滿熱情

pas·time [ˋpæs͵taɪm]　Track 4922

名 消遣 同 recreation 消遣

▶Gardening is a very rewarding pastime. Don't you think so?
園藝是非常有益的消遣。你不這樣認為嗎？

pas·try [ˋpestrɪ]　Track 4923

名 糕餅

▶What's your favorite kind of pastry? 你最喜歡哪種糕餅？

patch [pætʃ]　Track 4924

名 補丁 動 補綴、修補 同 mend 縫補

▶名 I am afraid that it will take me some time to remove all the patches on the child's jeans.
恐怕我得花些時間拆掉這孩子的牛仔褲上所有的補丁。

▶動 Is there any way to patch things up between us?
我們之間的關係還有得挽救嗎？

實用片語用語
patch up 修補、挽救

pat·ent [ˋpetn̩t]　Track 4925

名 專利權 形 公開、專利的 同 copyright 著作權

▶名 She handles cases of patent and trademark infringement（侵權）. 她負責受理專利和商標侵權的案件。

▶形 Would you like to try some of this new patent medicine?
你想不想試試這種新的專利藥物？

pa·tri·ot [ˋpetrɪət]　Track 4926

名 愛國者

▶Not every citizen can be a fervent（狂熱的）patriot.
不是每個公民都能成為一名狂熱的愛國者。

文法字詞解析
字首「patri-」是「父親、組國」的意思，「-ot」是名詞字尾，表示「人」，合在一起就變成「patriot」。

pa·trol [pəˋtrol]　Track 4927

名 巡邏者 動 巡邏

▶名 I'm afraid that we will have to chance meeting an enemy patrol. 恐怕我們不得不去冒可能遇上敵人巡邏兵的危險了。

▶動 There will be many police patrolling the streets.
會有很多警察在街上巡邏。

pa·tron [ˋpetrən] Track 4928

名 保護者、贊助人

▶It is said that modern artists have difficulty in finding patrons.
據說現代藝術家們很難找到贊助人。

萬用延伸句型
have difficulty in... 在（某領域）上有困難

pea·cock [ˋpiˏkɑk] Track 4929

名 孔雀

▶These children have never seen a peacock before.
這些孩子從來都沒看過孔雀長什麼樣子。

peas·ant [ˋpɛzn̩t] Track 4930

名 佃農 同 farmer 農夫

▶The peasants all bowed down to the king.
那些佃農都在國王面前跪下了。

peck [pɛk] Track 4931

名 啄、啄痕、輕吻 動 啄食

▶名 She gave him a peck on the cheek.
她在他臉頰上輕輕地吻了一下。

▶動 The pigeons（鴿子）are pecking around on the ground.
那些鴿子在地上到處啄食。

實用片語用語
give sb. a peck on the cheek 輕輕吻一下某人的臉頰

ped·dler [ˋpɛdlɚ] Track 4932

名 小販

▶The peddler tried to sell me some small articles.
那個小販試圖賣給我一些小東西。

文法字詞解析
去掉字尾的「(e)r」後，就變成動詞peddle，意思是叫賣、兜售，但這個字長得跟 paddle（船槳）很像，寫的時候要注意。

peek [pik] Track 4933

名 偷看 動 窺視

▶名 Let's just take a peek at the list, shall we?
我們很快地看一下名單吧，好嗎？

▶動 It looks like there is someone peeking in through the keyhole（鑰匙孔）.
好像有個人從鑰匙孔往裡面偷看。

peg [pɛg] Track 4934

名 釘子 動 釘牢

▶名 Would you please help me hang the coat on the peg?
請你幫我把把這件上衣掛在釘子上好嗎？

▶動 The boss pegged the photo to the board.
老闆把那張照片釘在板子上。

實用片語用語
peg sb. as... 認定某人是……
例如：She pegged him as a dishonest person before she even knew him.
她還不認識他，就已經認定他是會說謊的那種人。

pen·e·trate [ˋpɛnəˏtret] Track 4935

動 刺入 同 pierce 刺穿

▶The eyes of owls can penetrate the dark.
貓頭鷹的眼睛可透視黑暗。

per·ceive [pɚˋsiv] Track 4936

動 察覺 同 detect 察覺

▶His movements were so subtle that they were hard to perceive.
他的動作非常微小，難以察覺。

perch [pɜtʃ] Track 4937

名 鱸魚 動 棲息

▶名 I like fishing for perch. 我喜歡釣鱸魚。

▶動 The stone buildings perch on a hill crest（頂部）.
那些石頭房子坐落在山頂上。

per·form·er [pɚ`fɔrmɚ] Track 4938

名 執行者、演出者

▶The performer received only pitying（同情的、憐憫的）looks from his audience.
觀眾只對那位表演者投以同情和憐憫的眼神。

文法字詞解析
performer 是動詞「perform（表演）」加上名詞字尾「-er」形成的，perform 後面還可以加上另一個名詞字尾「-ance」變成「performance」來表示「演出」。

per·il [`pɛrəl] Track 4939

名 危險 動 冒險 同 danger 危險

▶名 The hero saved the old man in peril.
那名英雄救了那個有危險的老人。

▶動 He periled himself by heading into the haunted house.
他冒險走進鬼屋。

實用片語用語
in peril 處於危險之中

per·ish [`pɛrɪʃ] Track 4940

動 滅亡 同 die 死亡

▶Almost a hundred people perished in the hotel fire last night.
昨夜有近百人在旅館的大火中喪生。

per·mis·si·ble [pɚ`mɪsəbḷ] Track 4941

形 可允許的

▶Hearsay（謠傳）is not permissible evidence in court.
謠傳在法庭上是不能作為證據的。

per·sist [pɚ`sɪst] Track 4942

動 堅持 同 insist 堅持

▶It is reported that the cold weather will persist for the rest of the week.
根據報導，這樣寒冷的天氣將會持續到本週末。

實用片語用語
persist in 堅持做某事
例如：He persisted in yelling at the birds even though we told him to stop.
雖然我們叫他不要吵了，他還是一直對小鳥大吼大叫的。

per·son·nel [ˌpɜsṇ`ɛl] Track 4943

名 人員、人事部門 同 staff 工作人員

▶Could you let me know how to contact the related personnel in this case?
你能告訴我該如何連繫這件案子的相關人員嗎？

pes·si·mism [`pɛsəmɪzəm] Track 4944

名 悲觀、悲觀主義

▶I'm afraid that he has a tendency towards pessimism.
我擔心他有悲觀主義的傾向。

pier [pɪr] Track 4945

名 碼頭 同 wharf 碼頭

▶It took him ten minutes to walk along the pier and climb down into the boat.
他花了十分鐘的時間沿著碼頭走過去，並爬進了小船。

pil·grim [ˋpɪlgrɪm]

Track 4946

名 朝聖者

▶It is obvious that the story of pilgrims is well known among Americans. 顯然朝聖者的故事已經廣為美國人民所知。

實用片語用語

be well-known among... 在……之中廣為人知

pil·lar [ˋpɪlɚ]

Track 4947

名 樑柱

▶The young people will be the pillar of society.
年輕一代將會成為社會的棟樑。

pim·ple [ˋpɪmp!]

Track 4948

名 面皰

▶Jane doesn't want anyone to see the pimple on her nose.
珍妮不想要別人看到她鼻子上的痘子。

pinch [pɪntʃ]

Track 4949

名 捏、少量 動 捏痛、捏 同 squeeze 擠、擰

▶名 He gave the little girl an affectionate（親暱的）pinch on the face. 他親暱地擰了那個小女孩的臉一下。

▶動 This pair of shoes pinched my toes.
這雙鞋夾得我的腳趾很痛。

實用片語用語

take sth. with a pinch of salt 不必太在意某事，聽聽就好

例如：Take his words with a pinch of salt. He knows nothing about the subject.
不用太在意他的意見，他根本就不懂這主題。

piss [pɪs]

Track 4950

名 小便 動 尿液、激怒

▶名 He took a piss by the street. 他在路邊尿尿了。

▶動 I'm afraid that your secretary has pissed my boss off on the meeting yesterday.
恐怕你的秘書在昨天的會議上激怒了我的老闆。

pis·tol [ˋpɪstl̩]

Track 4951

名 手槍 動 以槍擊傷 同 gun 槍

▶名 It sounded like a small pistol going off.
那聲音聽起來像一支小手槍的槍響。

▶動 It sounded like he was threatening to pistol her at that time.
聽起來像是那時他在威脅她要用手槍射擊她。

plague [pleg]

Track 4952

名 瘟疫

▶He's been avoiding me like the plague since our quarrel.
我們吵架以後，他一直像瘟疫似的躲著我。

實用片語用語

avoid sb. like the plague 像避開瘟疫一樣地躲著某人

plan·ta·tion [plænˋteʃən]

Track 4953

名 農場 同 farm 農場

▶There were hundreds of slaves in the plantation.
這個農場裡有數百名的奴隸。

play·wright [ˋple͵raɪt]

Track 4954

名 劇作家

▶It is obvious that Bernard Shaw was the foremost（首要的）playwright of his time.
蕭伯納顯然是他那個時代最重要的戲劇作家。

plea [pli]

Track 4955

名 藉口、懇求 同 excuse 藉口

▶名 He ignored his children's pleas and still went out.
他不聽孩子們的懇求，還是走出去了。

plead [plid]

Track 4956

動 懇求、為……辯護 同 appeal 懇求

▶The girl who was charged with murder was mad and unable to plead for herself in the court.
那個被指控謀殺的女孩是瘋子，無法在法庭上為自己辯護。

文法字詞解析
此句中的「mad」並非「生氣的」的意思，而是「瘋的」，意同 crazy。

pledge [plɛdʒ]

Track 4957

名 誓約 動 立誓 同 vow 誓約

▶名 Please take this ring as a pledge of our friendship.
請收下這個戒指作為我們友誼的信物。

▶動 He pledged to be faithful to her forever.
他發誓對她永遠忠誠。

實用片語用語
pledge to do sth. 發誓做……

plow [plaʊ]

Track 4958

名 犁 動 耕作 同 cultivate 耕作

▶名 You had better not put the plow before the oxen（牛）.
你最好不要把犁放到牛面前（本末倒置）。

▶動 He plowed his way through the crowd to look for his friends.
他用力從人群中擠過去，找尋他的朋友。

pluck [plʌk]

Track 4959

名 勇氣 動 摘、拔、扯

▶名 She showed a lot of pluck in dealing with the intruders（闖入者）.她對付那些闖入的歹徒時表現得十分勇敢。

▶動 He plucked the letter from her hands angrily.
他生氣地從她手裡把信抓了過來。

plunge [plʌndʒ]

Track 4960

名 陷入、急降 動 插入

▶名 The price of cooking oil has started to go on a downward plunge.
食用油的價格開始狂跌了。

▶動 You had better not plunge your hand into hot water directly.
你最好不要直接將手伸進熱水裡。

實用片語用語
plunge into 跳入、落入
例如：He jumped and plunged into the deep end of the pool.
他跳入游泳池比較深的那一端。

poc·ket·book [ˋpɑkɪt͵bʊk]

Track 4961

名 錢包、口袋書

▶Would you please hand me my pocketbook, Evan?
伊凡，麻煩你把我的錢包拿給我好嗎？

po·et·ic [poˋɛtɪk]

Track 4962

形 詩意的

▶The dancer moved with poetic grace.
這位舞者的舞姿如詩一般優美。

poke [pok]

Track 4963

名 戳 動 戳、刺、刺探

▶名 He gave the sleeping dog a poke.
他戳了那隻在睡覺的狗一下。

▶動 He poked his head into the room to say hi.
他探頭進房間打個招呼。

po·lar [ˋpolɚ]

Track 4964

形 極地的 同 arctic 北極的

▶Are there any animals living in the polar circles?
南極圈和北極圈內有動物居住嗎？

實用片語用語
polar bear 北極熊
例如：Protect the earth or polar bears will go extinct.
保護地球，不然北極熊就要絕種了。

porch [portʃ]

Track 4965

名 玄關

▶Let's wait on the porch until it stops raining.
我們在玄關處等到雨停吧。

po·ten·tial [pəˋtɛnʃəl]

Track 4966

名 潛力 形 潛在的

▶名 I don't think she has any performing potential.
我覺得她完全沒有表演潛力。

▶形 Would you tell us about the potential problems that can arise?
你能告訴我們有哪些潛在問題可能發生嗎？

poul·try [ˋpoltrɪ]

Track 4967

名 家禽 同 fowl 家禽

▶Poultry is rather cheap now. Don't you think so?
現在的家禽肉類相當便宜。你不覺得嗎？

prai·rie [ˋprɛrɪ]

Track 4968

名 牧場、大草原

▶On the one hand, the vast Kansas prairie is beautiful; on the other hand, it holds hidden dangers.
廣大無垠的堪薩斯草原一方面很美麗；另一方面也隱藏著無法預知的危險。

萬用延伸句型
On the one hand... on the other hand...
一方面……，一方面……

preach [pritʃ]

Track 4969

動 傳教、說教、鼓吹

▶It is said that the man devoted all his life to preaching peace.
據說這個男人將一生奉獻於鼓吹和平。

pre·cau·tion [prɪˋkɔʃən]

Track 4970

名 警惕、預防

▶I think we need to take precautions against fire.
我認為我們有必要採取防火措施。

pref·er·ence [ˋprɛfərəns]

Track 4971

名 偏好 同 favor 偏愛

▶Would you tell me which your preference is, tea or coffee?
請您告訴我您是喜歡喝茶還是喝咖啡呢？

實用片語用語
No preference 沒有特別的偏好
例如："Chicken or beef?" "No preference."
「雞肉還是牛肉？」「我隨便。」

pre·hi·stor·ic [ˌprihɪsˋtɔrɪk]

Track 4972

形 史前的

▶How about visiting the prehistoric burial grounds discovered last year?
我們去參觀去年發現的史前墓地怎麼樣？

pre·vail [prɪˋvel]

Track 4973

動 戰勝、普及 同 win 贏

▶Virtue will prevail against evil.
美德必將戰勝邪惡。

pre·view [ˋpriˌvju]

Track 4974

名 預演、預習 動 預演、預習、預視

▶名 Have you seen the preview of the movie yet?
你有看那部電影的預告嗎？

▶動 Could you tell me how to preview and publish my online article?
能請您告訴我如何預覽和發佈我的網路文章嗎？

文法字詞解析
就像我們學過的，「-view」是「觀看」的意思，所以加上「pre-（預先）」就會變「預習」，如果加上「re-（重複）」就是「review（複習）」。

prey [pre]

Track 4975

名 犧牲品 動 捕食 同 hunt 獵食

▶名 The lion on TV is hunting for its prey.
電視裡的那頭獅子正在覓食。

▶動 Don't you know that strong animals prey upon weaker ones?
弱肉強食的道理你不懂嗎？

實用片語用語
prey on... 捕食

price·less [ˋpraɪslɪs]

Track 4976

形 貴重的、無價的 同 invaluable 無價的

▶I believe that knowledge is priceless.
我認為知識是無價的。

prick [prɪk]

Track 4977

名 刺痛 動 紮、刺、豎起 同 sting 刺

▶名 He felt a sharp prick when he stepped on an upturned（朝上的）nail.
他一腳踩在一枚尖頭朝上的釘子，感到一陣劇痛。

▶動 She pricked her finger with a needle.
她不小心用針紮到了手指。

pri·or [ˋpraɪɚ]

Track 4978

形 在前的、優先的 副 居先、先前

▶形 I was unable to attend the meeting because of a prior engagement.
我因有約在先所以未能參加這個會議。

▶副 Would you tell me what happened prior to her departure?
您能不能告訴我在她走之前發生了什麼事？

實用片語用語
prior to sth. 在……之前

pri·or·i·ty [praɪˋɔrətɪ]

Track 4979

名 優先權

▶You should really learn to manage your priorities.
你真的應該學著搞清楚事情的輕重緩急。

實用片語用語
priority seat 博愛座
例如：Let the pregnant lady have the priority seat.
把博愛座讓給這個懷孕的太太吧。

pro·ces·sion [prə`sɛʃən]

Track 4980

名 進行、行列

▶Thousands of people joined the funeral procession.
有上千人參加了送葬的行列。

pro·file [`profaɪl]

Track 4981

名 側面 動 畫側面像、顯出輪廓

▶名 She is prettier in profile than from the front in my opinion.
在我看來，她的側面比正面好看。

▶動 The trees are profiled larger against the night sky than they are in the day.
這些樹的輪廓在夜空的映襯下顯得比在白天更大。

實用片語用語

profile picture 大頭照
我們用社群網站時，都會需要放上「profile picture」讓大家知道自己的長相，這裡的profile picture就是「大頭照」。
例如：You can use this app to edit your profile picture.
你可以用這個應用軟體來編輯你的大頭照。

pro·long [prə`lɔŋ]

Track 4982

動 延長 反 shorten 縮短

▶Scientists are working on prolonging human life.
科學家們在努力設法延長人類的生命。

prop [prɑp]

Track 4983

名 支撐 動 支持

▶名 The worker put a prop against the wall of the tunnel to keep it from falling down.
那名工人用東西支撐住隧道的牆壁，以使它不會倒塌。

▶動 She propped the ladder against the wall.
她把梯子靠在牆邊。

文法字詞解析

或許是因為道具是「支撐」著整場表演的幕後功臣，演戲或表演魔術用的道具也稱做「props」。

proph·et [`prɑfɪt]

Track 4984

名 先知

▶It was said that the prophet foretold a glorious future for the young ruler.
據說那位先知預言這位年輕的統治者會有輝煌的前程。

pro·por·tion [prə`porʃən]

Track 4985

名 比例 動 使成比例 同 ratio 比例

▶名 It is obvious that her head is out of proportion to the size of her body. 顯然她的頭部與身體的大小不成比例。

▶動 It is clear that the punishment should be proportioned to the crime. 顯然應當罪罰應該相當。

pros·pect [`prɑspɛkt]

Track 4986

名 期望、前景 動 探勘 同 anticipation 期望

▶名 The prospects of this venture（投資）aren't looking good.
這次投資的前景似乎不是很好。

▶動 They are prospecting the region for oil.
他們正在該區勘察油礦。

prov·ince [`prɑvɪns]

Track 4987

名 省（行政單位）

▶Will you please name a province on the Pacific coast of Canada?
請你舉出一個位於加拿大太平洋沿岸的省份來好嗎？

文法字詞解析

此句的「name」意思並非「為……命名」，而是「舉出……的名字」。

prune [prun]

Track 4988

名 乾梅子 動 修剪

▶名 The little girl was eating prunes as she read a book.
那個小女孩一邊看書一邊吃梅乾。

▶動 I'm trying to prune the bushes.
我正試著修剪樹叢。

pub·li·cize [ˋpʌblɪˏsaɪz]

Track 4989

動 公佈、宣傳、廣告

▶She did not make efforts to publicize her works.
她沒有花力氣去宣傳自己的作品。

puff [pʌf]

Track 4990

名 噴煙、吹 動 噴出、吹熄

▶名 Not everyone is able to blow out all candles with a single puff. 不是每個人都能一口氣吹滅所有的蠟燭。

▶動 He is not willing to go outside and puff out the kerosene（煤油）lamp. 他不願意出去吹滅那盞煤油燈。

實用片語用語

huff and puff 氣喘吁吁

例如：He huffed and puffed but still couldn't blow out the candle.

他氣喘吁吁的卻還是無法把蠟燭吹熄。

pulse [pʌls]

Track 4991

名 脈搏 動 脈搏、跳動

▶名 He asked a doctor to take her pulse at once.
他請醫生立刻幫她量脈搏。

▶動 I can literally feel blood pulsing through my veins（血管）because of how mad I was.
我氣到都可以感覺到熱血在血管中搏動了。

pur·chase [ˋpɝtʃəs]

Track 4992

名 購買 動 購買

同 buy 買

▶名 How about making several purchases in the dress shop?
我們去服裝店裡買幾件衣服怎麼樣？

▶動 He purchased cheap fruniture at an auction.
他在拍賣會買了便宜的傢俱。

文法字詞解析

這個字加上名詞字尾「-(e)r」就變成了「purchaser」，purchaser 不只有「買家、買主」的意思，也可以是一個工作的職位，例如：I work as a purchaser in my company. 我在公司擔任採購的職務。

pyr·a·mid [ˋpɪrəmɪd]

Track 4993

名 金字塔、角錐

▶I've always wanted to go to Egypt to see pyramids.
我一直很想去埃及看金字塔。

quack [kwæk]

Track 4994

名 嘎嘎的叫聲 動 嘎嘎叫

▶名 Not everyone noticed the duck's peculiar quack.
不是每個人都注意到了這隻鴨子的獨特叫聲。

▶動 Can you hear wild ducks quacking on the river?
你有聽到野鴨子在河上呱呱叫嗎？

qual·i·fy [ˋkwɑləˏfaɪ] Track 4995

動 使合格

▶It took his brother seven years to be qualified as a doctor.
他弟弟花了七年時間才獲得醫師資格。

實用片語用語
qualifying exams 資格考
例如：You need to pass the qualifying exams before graduating.
畢業前必須先考過資格考才行。

quart [kwɔrt] Track 4996

名 夸脫（容量單位）

▶There is a quart of milk left in the pail.
桶子裡還剩下一夸脫牛奶。

quest [kwɛst] Track 4997

名 探索、探求

▶Man will suffer many disappointments in his quest for truth.
人類在探索真理的過程中必然會遭受挫折。

quiver [ˋkwɪvɚ] Track 4998

名 / 動 顫抖

▶名 There is a slight quiver in his voice as he speaks.
他說話時聲音有些顫抖。

▶動 He quivered all over with rage.
他氣得渾身發抖。

實用片語用語
quiver with rage 氣得發抖

rack [ræk] Track 4999

名 架子、折磨 動 折磨、盡力使用 同 shelf 架子

▶名 Would you please put my bag on the luggage rack?
請把我的包放在行李架上好嗎？

▶動 I couldn't think of a single example after racking my brain. Would you please help me?就算絞盡腦汁我還是連一個例子也想不出來。你能幫幫我嗎？

實用片語用語
dish rack碗盤架
例如：Don’t leave the dishes lying around. Put them onto the dish rack.
別把碗盤到處亂放，放到碗盤架上吧。

rad·ish [ˋrædɪʃ] Track 5000

名 蘿蔔

▶These radishes are so fresh that people rushed to buy them.
這些蘿蔔如此新鮮，以致於人們爭著要買。

ra·di·us [ˋredɪəs] Track 5001

名 半徑

▶We can calculate the circular area if we know the radius.
如果我們知道半徑多少，就能計算出圓的面積。

rag·ged [ˋrægɪd] Track 5002

形 破爛的 同 shabby 破爛的

▶I don't think that anyone should be ashamed of his or her ragged clothes.
我認為任何人都不需要因為穿破爛的衣服而感到羞恥。

rail [rel]

Track 5003

名 橫杆、鐵軌

▶I think it's cheaper to ship goods by road than by rail.
我覺得公路運輸比鐵路運輸更便宜。

文法字詞解析
「欄杆」的另一個說法是 railings，例如若你在陽台上靠著欄杆，可能就會有人叫你不要 lean on the railings，那是很危險的。

ral·ly [ˋrælɪ]

Track 5004

名 集合、集會 動 召集 同 gathering 聚集

▶名 It is time for us to hold a rally in support of the civil-rights movement.
我們該舉行集會來支持民權運動了。

▶動 It is time for us to rally our own defense force.
我們是時候組織自己的防衛隊了。

ranch [ræntʃ]

Track 5005

名 大農場 動 經營大農場 同 plantation 大農場

▶名 It takes me about 10 minutes from here to my ranch on foot. 從這兒到我的農場步行約十分鐘就到了。

▶動 He spent almost all his life ranching the large farm.
他幾乎花了他一生的時間經營那個大農場。

ras·cal [ˋræskḷ]

Track 5006

名 流氓

▶It is said that the rascal who beat the little boy was arrested this morning.
據說那個毆打小男孩的流氓今天上午被抓起來了。

文法字詞解析
這裡用形容詞子句「who beat the little boy」來修飾前面的名詞「the rascal」。

ra·tio [ˋreʃo]

Track 5007

名 比率、比例 同 proportion 比率、比例

▶Would you please tell me what the ratio of boys to girls in your class is?
請告訴我你們班上男女生的比例是多少好嗎？

rat·tle [ˋrætḷ]

Track 5008

名 嘎嘎聲 動 發出嘎嘎聲、喋喋不休地講話

▶名 It is obvious that it's the rattle of the windows.
顯然那是窗戶嘎嘎作響的聲音。

▶動 He rattled on about his job, not noticing how bored she was. 他只顧喋喋不休地說自己工作上的事，沒注意到她有多無聊。

realm [rɛlm]

Track 5009

名 王國、領域

▶He made outstanding contributions in the realm of foreign affairs.
他在外交領域中有卓越的成績。

reap [rip]

Track 5010

動 收割

▶The peasants reap the corn from what they planted in spring.
農民們在收割他們春季播種的玉米。

實用片語用語
因為死神是來「收割」生命的，所以常被稱為 the grim reaper。

rear [rɪr]

Track 5011

名 後面 形 後面的 同 front 前面

▶名 There's something stuck at the rear of the car.
車子後面有東西黏住了。

▶形 We had to get out by the rear door because the front ones didn't work.
由於前面的門都打不開，我們只得從後門出來。

reck·less [ˋrɛklɪs]

Track 5012

形 魯莽的 同 rash 魯莽的

▶The reckless boy was playing in the river even though he was told not to.
雖然那個魯莽的男孩不被允許在河裡玩，他還是去河裡玩了。

reck·on [ˋrɛkən]

Track 5013

動 計算、依賴 同 count 計算

▶Do you reckon we can climb this hill in one hour?
依你的計算，我們有可能一個小時爬完這座小山丘嗎？

rec·om·mend [͵rɛkəˋmɛnd]

Track 5014

動 推薦、託付

▶Would you please recommend a good dictionary to me?
你能為我推薦一本好字典嗎？

reef [rif]

Track 5015

名 暗礁

▶It is reported that the ship struck a hidden reef and went down.
據報導，那艘船撞上暗礁沉沒了。

reel [ril]

Track 5016

名 捲軸 動 捲線、搖擺

▶名 A reel of the movie is missing. Would you help me look for it?
那部電影的一捲片子不見了。請幫我找找好嗎？

▶動 The man quickly reeled the fish in.
那個男人很快地把魚捲上岸。

ref·e·ree/um·pire

Track 5017

[͵rɛfəˋri]/[ˋʌmpaɪr]

名 裁判者 動 裁判、調停

▶名 The referee was so unfair.
這裁判真的很不公正。

▶動 My dad's job is to referee matches.
我爸爸的工作是當球賽的裁判。

ref·uge/san·ctu·ar·y

Track 5018

[ˋrɛfjudʒ]/[ˋsæŋktʃʊ͵ɛrɪ]

名 避難（所）

▶The thunderstorm forced him to take refuge at a hut.
那場雷雨迫使他躲在草屋裡。

實用片語用語

rear mirror 後照鏡

例如：Remember to check your rear mirror when you drive in reverse.
倒車時記得注意一下你的後照鏡。

萬用延伸句型

Do you reckon...? 你認為……嗎？

文法字詞解析

「reel...in」這個片語除了用在魚身上，表示釣魚時把魚拉上岸以外，也可以拿在人身上，表示把某人捲入某個計畫、活動中。

re·fute [rɪ`fjut] Track 5019

動 反駁 同 oppose 反對

▶"You can't tell me not to watch TV when you yourself watch it all day," she refuted. 「你不能叫我不要看電視啊，你自己還不是整天看，」她反駁道。

reign [ren] Track 5020

名 主權 動 統治 同 rule 統治

▶名 The reign of Queen Victoria lasted more than sixty years. 維多利亞女王的統治持續了六十多年。

▶動 He reigned over the country for ten years. 他統治這個國家長達十年。

實用片語用語

reign over 統治（某地）
除了表示統治某個國家之外，這個片語也能表示某人在某個地方（例如公司、團隊、球場等）佔有主導地位。

re·joice [rɪ`dʒɔɪs] Track 5021

動 歡喜 反 lament 悲痛

▶Let us rejoice together on your success. 讓我們一起歡慶你的成功吧。

rel·ic [`rɛlɪk] Track 5022

名 遺物

▶Not everybody knows that this custom is a relic of ancient times. 不是每個人都知道這個習俗是古代的遺風。

re·mind·er [rɪ`maɪndɚ] Track 5023

名 提醒者

▶Send me a reminder to buy milk on my way home. 請提醒我回家路上要買牛奶。

re·pay [rɪ`pe] Track 5024

動 償還、報答 同 reward 報答

▶I wish I could repay you somehow for your kindness. 但願對你的好意我能有所報答。

實用片語用語

repay sb.'s kindness 報答某人的善意

re·pro·duce [ˌriprə`djus] Track 5025

動 複製、再生

▶Most fish reproduce by laying eggs. 大多數的魚透過產卵來繁殖。

rep·tile [`rɛptaɪl] Track 5026

名 爬蟲類 形 爬行的

▶名 I can't stand most reptiles but iguanas are really cute. 我受不了大部分爬蟲類，但美洲鬣蜥超可愛的。

▶形 The land is teeming（充滿）with reptile life. 這片土地上有很多爬行動物。

re·pub·li·can [rɪ`pʌblɪkən] Track 5027

名 共和主義者 形 共和主義的 反 democratic 民主主義的

▶名 Richard is a dyed-in-the-wool（徹頭徹尾的）Republican. Don't you think so? 理查是個徹頭徹尾的共和主義者。難道不是嗎？

▶形 This is a very difficult moment for the Republican Party. 這對共和黨來說是非常艱難的時刻。

文法字詞解析

dyed-in-the-wool 直接翻譯就是「染在羊毛中的」，可想而知，染在羊毛上的顏色非常難洗掉，就如同理查的共和主義色彩很難洗掉一樣，因此才會說他是「徹頭徹尾的」共和主義者。

re·sent [rɪˋzɛnt]

Track 5028

動 憤恨

▶I resent having to get his permission for everything I do.
我討厭做每件事都要得到他的許可。

re·sent·ment [rɪˋzɛntmənt]

Track 5029

名 憤慨 同 irritation 惱怒

▶They did not dare to show their resentment.
他們不敢表現出憤慨的樣子。

實用片語用語
dare (to) do sth. 敢於做某事

re·side [rɪˋzaɪd]

Track 5030

動 居住 同 dwell 居住

▶This family has resided in this city for more than 60 years.
這個家族住在這座城已有六十多年了。

res·i·dence [ˋrɛzədəns]

Track 5031

名 住家

▶It was said that he married an English woman and took up his residence in London.
據說他與一名英國女子結婚並且定居在倫敦。

實用片語用語
take up sb.'s residence（某人）在（某處）定居

res·i·dent [ˋrɛzədənt]

Track 5032

名 居民 形 居留的、住校的

▶名 Many local residents took part in that activity.
很多當地居民參加了那個活動。

▶形 There are many resident students in my class.
我們班上有很多住宿生。

re·sort [rɪˋzɔrt]

Track 5033

名 休閒勝地 動 依靠、訴諸

▶名 The place has become a famous summer resort.
這個地方已經成為一個避暑勝地。

▶動 He resorted to force after repeated failures.
多次失敗之後，他就訴諸於暴力解決了。

re·strain [rɪˋstren]

Track 5034

動 抑制

▶The child was unable to restrain her tears.
那孩子無法抑制住她的眼淚。

re·sume [ˋrɛzə͵me]/[rɪˋzjum]

Track 5035

名 摘要、履歷表 動 再開始

▶名 Would you please send a detailed resume to our company?
請寄給我們公司一份詳細的履歷表好嗎？

▶動 Would you please resume your job as a general manager?
您能重新做總經理的工作嗎？

文法字詞解析
要注意喔！這個單字有兩個唸法，一個指「履歷表」，重音在第一個音節；另一個意指「再開始」，重音在第二個音節。

re·tort [rɪˋtɔrt]

Track 5036

名 反駁 動 反駁、回嘴

▶名 Luckily the boss didn't hear his retort.
幸好他老闆沒聽到他反駁的話。

▶動 "You're no better than I am," he retorted.
「你也沒有比我好啊，」他反駁道。

re·verse [rɪˋvɝs]　Track 5037

名 顛倒 動 反轉 形 相反的

▶名 I am afraid that the truth is just the reverse.
恐怕真實情況恰好相反吧。

▶動 Can you help me reverse my car into the garage?
你能幫我倒車入庫嗎？

▶形 The man drove in the reverse direction.
這個男人朝著相反的方向開車。

實用片語用語
reverse into a garage / parking place 倒車入庫

re·vive [rɪˋvaɪv]　Track 5038

動 復甦、復原 同 restore 復原

▶They were unable to revive the drowned boy.
他們無法讓那個溺水的男孩復甦。

re·volt [rɪˋvolt]　Track 5039

名 叛亂 動 叛變、嫌惡 同 rebel 叛亂

▶名 It was the revolt of the British North American colonies that resulted in the establishment of the US. 是英國的北美殖民地人民的反抗鬥爭，導致了美國的建國。

▶動 The violence in the movie revolted me.
電影中的暴力情節使我反感。

文法字詞解析
第一個例句用了分裂句句型「It was... that...」來強調「revolt」。

re·volve [rɪˋvɑlv]　Track 5040

動 旋轉、循環

▶It is obvious that their troubles revolve around money management.
顯然他們的麻煩圍繞在對金錢的處理上。

rhi·noce·r·os/rhi·no　Track 5041

[raɪˋnɑsərəs]/[ˋraɪno]

名 犀牛

▶Have you ever seen a rhinoceros? What does it look like?
你見過犀牛嗎？牠長什麼樣子？

rib [rɪb]　Track 5042

名 肋骨 動 支撐、嘲弄

▶名 I don't know how many ribs a person has.
我不知道人有多少根肋骨。

▶動 They ribbed him for wearing mismatching（不成對的）socks. 他們嘲笑他穿了不成對的襪子。

實用片語用語
pork ribs 豬肋排
例如：We had pork ribs for dinner. The dog was excited.
我們晚餐吃豬肋排，家裡的狗好興奮。

ridge [rɪdʒ]　Track 5043

名 背脊、山脊 動（使）成脊狀

▶名 There were beautiful flowers growing all about this ridge.
山脊上到處都是美麗的花朵。

▶動 The ocean floor of the Atlantic ridges in the middle from north to south.
大西洋海底在中部形成一道由北向南的海脊。

ri·dic·u·lous [rɪˋdɪkjələs] Track 5044

形 荒謬的

▶What a ridiculous suggestion! Don't you think so?
多麼荒唐的建議！你不這樣認為嗎？

ri·fle [ˋraɪfl̩] Track 5045

名 來福槍、步兵 動 掠奪

▶名 It is said that he has been appointed captain of a company of rifles. 據說他已經被任命為步兵連連長了。

▶動 The thief rifled every drawer in the room.
竊賊洗劫了房內所有抽屜裡的東西。

實用片語用語
be appointed 被任命為……

rig·id [ˋrɪdʒɪd] Track 5046

形 嚴格的

▶It is obvious that the new recruits are not used to the rigid disciplines of the army.
顯然新兵不習慣於軍隊的嚴格紀律。

rim [rɪm] Track 5047

名 邊緣 動 加邊於

▶名 There is a red flower on the rim of the girl's hat.
那個女孩的帽子邊上有一朵紅花。

▶動 Lots of trees rimmed the cemetery（公墓）.
有很多樹木環繞在公墓四周。

rip [rɪp] Track 5048

名 裂口 動 扯裂

▶名 She sewed up the rip in his sleeve very fast.
她很快就縫好了他衣袖上的裂口。

▶動 The poster was ripped to pieces. 那張海報被撕得粉碎。

實用片語用語
rip-off 騙錢生意
例如：What? This banana costs 100 USD? What a rip-off!
什麼？這根香蕉要一百美金嗎？你坑錢啊！

rip·ple [ˋrɪpl̩] Track 5049

名 波動 動 起漣漪

▶名 I wish I could lie on the bank and listen to the ripple of the stream. 我希望能躺在河岸上傾聽小河的潺潺流水聲。

▶動 My grandmother's laughter rippled through my heart.
奶奶的笑聲在我的內心蕩漾。

ri·val [ˋraɪvl̩] Track 5050

名 對手 動 競爭 同 compete 競爭

▶名 I don't believe that they are rivals for the same position.
我不相信他們是爭奪同一個職位的敵手。

▶動 I don't think that anyone could rival him in this respect.
我認為在這方面沒有人能勝過他。

roam [rom] Track 5051

名 漫步 動 徘徊、流浪 同 wander 徘徊

▶名 Let's take a roam in the beautiful park.
我們在這個美麗的公園漫步吧。

▶動 He has roamed the city for years.
他在這個城市流浪了很多年。

文法字詞解析
出國可能會用到的「手機國際漫遊」也和「roam」這個字相關。

rob·in [ˋrɑbɪn]

Track 5052

名 知更鳥

▶If you see a robin, it means that spring is coming soon.
一旦你看見了一隻知更鳥，就表示春天就要到了。

ro·bust [roˋbʌst]

Track 5053

形 強健的 反 weak 虛弱的

▶The old man is ninety but very robust.
那個老男人九十歲了，但身體還是很強健。

rod [rɑd]

Track 5054

名 竿、棒、教鞭 同 stick 棒

▶Can you grab that fishing rod for me?
幫我拿一下那根釣竿好不好？

rub·bish [ˋrʌbɪʃ]

Track 5055

名 垃圾 同 garbage 垃圾

▶How to get rid of rubbish is a big problem.
如何處理垃圾是個大問題。

實用片語用語
rubbish heap 垃圾堆
例如：Why is John out there searching through the rubbish heap?
為什麼約翰會在外面的垃圾堆裡面翻來找去的？

rug·ged [ˋrʌgɪd]

Track 5056

形 粗糙的 反 smooth 柔順的

▶Would you please forgive my husband's rugged manners?
請原諒我丈夫粗魯的態度好嗎？

rum·ble [ˋrʌmbl]

Track 5057

名 隆隆聲 動 發出隆隆聲

▶名 We heard the occasional rumble of a passing truck.
我們偶爾聽到卡車駛過的隆隆聲。

▶動 His stomach rumbled from hunger.
他的肚子餓得咕咕叫。

rus·tle [ˋrʌsl̩]

Track 5058

名 沙沙響 動 沙沙作響

▶名 I heard a rustle from a snake in the bushes.
我聽到了灌木叢中的蛇所發出的聲響。

▶動 Did you hear something rustling in the trees?
你有聽到有東西在樹上沙沙作響嗎？

實用片語用語
rustle up sth. 快速地作一份餐點
例如：I rustled up some fries for dinner.
我弄了些薯條當晚餐。

sa·cred [ˋsekrɪd]

Track 5059

形 神聖的 同 holy 神聖的

▶It's our duty and responsibility to protect this sacred Earth.
我們有責任保護這神聖的地球。

sad·dle [ˋsædl̩]

Track 5060

名 鞍 動 套以馬鞍

▶名 Will you please give me a lift onto the saddle, Tom?
湯姆，請你扶我上馬鞍好嗎？

▶動 Can you tell me how I should saddle up a horse?
你能告訴我該如何為馬套上鞍嗎？

saint [sent]

Track 5061

名 聖、聖人 動 列為聖徒

▶名 You would need to be a saint to put up with her husband.
只有聖人才有辦法容忍她的老公。

▶動 Do you think he will be sainted one day?
你認為他有一天會被列為聖徒嗎？

實用片語用語
put up with sb. 忍受某人

salm·on [ˋsæmən]

Track 5062

名 鮭 形 鮭肉色的、淺橙色的

▶名 I am afraid the smoked salmon is sold out in the early morning.
恐怕燻鮭魚一大早就賣完了。

▶形 What you described is not the salmon pink which we want.
你描述的並不是我們所需要的淺橙色。

文法字詞解析
在第二個例句中，「what you described」做為整句的主詞，其中的「what」用來代替不確定的事物。

sa·lute [səˋlut]

Track 5063

名 招呼、敬禮 動 致意、致敬 同 greeting 招呼

▶名 The soldiers exchange salutes as soon as they meet each other.士兵們一遇到彼此就會互相敬禮。

▶動 The teacher asked his students to salute the flag.
那位老師要求他的學生們向國旗致敬。

san·dal [ˋsændl̩]

Track 5064

名 涼鞋、便鞋

▶The girls are all wearing cute sandals.
女孩們都穿了可愛的涼鞋。

文法字詞解析
此外，有一種木材也和 sandal 有關，叫作 sandalwood，是「檀香」的意思。

sav·age [ˋsævɪdʒ]

Track 5065

名 野蠻人 形 荒野的、野性的 同 fierce 兇猛的

▶名 There is an island on the sea over there inhabited（居住）by savages.
在那邊的海上有個野蠻人居住的島嶼。

▶形 It is said that there is a savage lion in the forest.
據說森林裡有頭猛獅。

scan [skæn]

Track 5066

名 掃描 動 掃描、審視

▶名 Why didn't he ask the doctors to give him an ultrasonic（超音波的）brain scan?
他為什麼不叫醫生給他做個腦部超音波掃描檢查呢？

▶動 Use this machine to scan the materials. It'll be quicker.
用這台機器掃描一下這些檔案，會更快一點。

scan·dal [ˋskændl̩]
Track 5067

名 醜聞、恥辱 同 disgrace 恥辱

▶By the time he was taken away by the police, all people knew about the scandal.
到他被警察抓走的時候，所有人就都知道了這件醜事。

scar [skɑr]
Track 5068

名 傷痕、疤痕 動 使留下疤痕

▶名 Would you tell me whether the cut will leave a scar on my face?
你能告訴我這個傷口會不會在我的臉上留下疤痕嗎？

▶動 Can you tell me when and how he scarred his face?
能請你告訴我他是何時、如何在臉上弄出傷疤嗎？

文法字詞解析
除了「真正的」疤痕外，scar 也可以拿來表示心理上的創傷、疤痕。例如若有人給你看了一個讓你一輩子難忘的恐怖影片，你就可以說：「It scarred me for life.」（這讓我留下一輩子的創傷。）

scent [sɛnt]
Track 5069

名 氣味、痕跡 動 聞、嗅 同 smell 氣味

▶名 The scents of flowers fill the grove（樹林）now.
現在花香充滿了小樹林。

▶動 I scent a whiff（些微的氣味）of fragrance in the house.
我在房子裡聞到了一股香味。

scheme [skim]
Track 5070

名 計畫、陰謀 動 計畫、密謀、擬訂

▶名 Why don't you ask about the outcome of his scheme directly（直接地）?
為什麼不直接詢問他計畫的結果呢？

▶動 Why don't we scheme out a new method?
為什麼不擬訂一種新的辦法？

scorn [skɔrn]
Track 5071

名 輕蔑、蔑視 動 不屑做、鄙視 同 contempt 輕蔑

▶名 They all look at the boy with scorn.
他們都以蔑視的眼光看著這個男孩。

▶動 No one has the right to scorn this poor girl.
這裡的每一個人都無權鄙視這個貧窮的女孩。

實用片語用語
with scorn 帶著鄙視的

scram·ble [ˋskræmbl̩]
Track 5072

名 攀爬、爭奪 動 爭奪、湊合

▶名 It was a long scramble to the top of the hill.
我們爬了一段長路到山頂。

▶動 It took him half a day to scramble some data for his company.
他花了半天時間才為公司收集到了一些資料。

實用片語用語
scrambled egg 炒蛋
例如：Would you want some scrambled egg for brunch?
你想來點炒蛋當早午餐嗎？

scrap [skræp]
Track 5073

名 小片、少許 動 丟棄、爭吵 同 quarrel 爭吵

▶名 I don't think there's a scrap of truth in the claim.
我認為這種說法毫無真實性。

▶動 We have to scrap our plans because there is no hope of realizing them.
我們不得不放棄我們的計畫，因為它們根本無法實現。

scrape [skrep]

Track 5074

名 磨擦聲、擦掉 動 磨擦、擦刮 同 rub 磨擦

▶名 She fell off the bike and got a scrape on her knee.
她從自行車上摔下來，擦破了膝蓋。

▶動 Can you help me scrape the ashes from the furnace（火爐）, Bill?
比爾，請你幫我把爐灰刮乾淨好嗎？

scroll [skrol]

Track 5075

名 卷軸 動 把……寫在捲軸上、（電腦術語）捲頁

▶名 The professor was presented with a scroll.
這名教授被授予了一幅卷軸。

▶動 My mouse was broken and I couldn't scroll down.
我的滑鼠壞掉了，我都沒辦法往下捲頁了。

實用片語用語
scroll down （把電腦網頁）往下拉
相反地，往上拉就是 scroll up。

sculp·tor [ˋskʌlptɚ]

Track 5076

名 雕刻家、雕刻師

▶In my opinion, the sculptor is greater than anyone else in his time.
在我看來，這名雕刻家比他同時代的任何其他人都要偉大。

se·cure [sɪˋkjʊr]

Track 5077

動 保護 形 安心的、安全的 同 safe 安全的

▶動 This national hero secured the nation against attack.
這個民族英雄使得國家免於受到攻擊。

▶形 The contract shall be kept in a secure place.
這份合約要保管在安全的地方。

實用片語用語
secure sth. against sb. /sth. 保護……免於受到……（的侵害）

seg·ment [ˋsɛgmənt]

Track 5078

名 部分、段 動 分割、劃分 同 section 部分

▶名 Will you tell me how our company can dominate this segment of the market?
你能告訴我我們公司如何才能控制這一部分市場嗎？

▶動 The show was segmented so that it wouldn't be too long and boring. 這個節目分了好幾段，才不會又長又無聊。

sen·sa·tion [sɛnˋseʃən]

Track 5079

名 感覺、知覺 同 feeling 感覺

▶Don't you just love the sensation of warmth when you slip into a hot bath? 你不覺得滑進熱水澡中的感覺很棒嗎？

實用片語用語
pop sensation 流行界紅人
例如：Janet, the newest pop sensation, will be performing here next month.
最新流行界紅人珍妮下個月將在此表演。

sen·si·tiv·i·ty [ˏsɛnsəˋtɪvətɪ]

Track 5080

名 敏感度、靈敏度

▶It is her sensitivity that enabled her to create so many touching stories.
正是她的多愁善感使她能寫出這麼多感人的故事。

sen·ti·ment [ˋsɛntəmənt]

Track 5081

名 情緒

▶I don't think sentiment should be controlled by reason.
我覺得感情不應該受理智的控制。

ser·geant [ˋsɑrdʒənt] Track 5082

名 士官

▶It has been two years since my elder brother became a sergeant. 我哥哥當士官已經兩年了。

se·ries [ˋsɪriz] Track 5083

名 連續 同 succession 連續

▶It was reported that a series of deadly attacks happened in India. 據報導，在印度發生了一系列的致命襲擊。

實用片語用語

TV series 電視連續劇

例如：There are several TV series that I could watch all day.

有好幾部電視連續劇我就算看一整天也不會累。

ser·mon [ˋsɝmən] Track 5084

名 佈道、講道 同 detect 察覺

▶It is not easy to deliver a sermon. 佈道並不是容易的事。

serv·er [ˋsɝvɚ] Track 5085

名 侍者、服役者 同 waiter 侍者

▶Will you let a server here introduce the pub to us?

你能讓這裡的一名服務生為給我們介紹一下這家酒店嗎？

set·ting [ˋsɛtɪŋ] Track 5086

名 安置的地點、背景

▶It was said that the setting of the story is a hotel in London.

據說故事的背景在倫敦的一家旅館裡。

shab·by [ˋʃæbɪ] Track 5087

形 衣衫襤褸的 反 decent 體面的

▶The tramp（流浪漢） looked rather shabby in those clothes on the busy street.

這個流浪漢在繁華的街道上顯得衣著相當寒酸。

文法字詞解析

除了表達衣衫破舊之外，shabby 也可以拿來描述衣物以外的東西「不體面」。相反地，如果你覺得某物還算體面，也可以反過來説：「Not too shabby, isn't it?」（還算夠體面吧？）

sharp·en [ˋʃɑrpn̩] Track 5088

動 使銳利、使尖銳

▶My pencil is blunt（鈍的）. Will you lend me a knife to sharpen it, Mike? 我的鉛筆鈍了。麥克，你能借我把刀子削一削嗎？

shat·ter [ˋʃætɚ] Track 5089

動 粉碎、砸破 同 break 砸破

▶Nothing can shatter the old man's faith.

任何事都不能動搖老人的信念。

sher·iff [ˋʃɛrɪf] Track 5090

名 警長

▶There is a sheriff in town that none of the kids and adults like.

鎮上有個大人小孩們都討厭的警長。

shield [ʃild] Track 5091

名 盾 動 遮蔽

▶名 The shield was solid enough to protect him from the blows of his enemy. 這盾牌很堅固，足以保護他免受敵人的打擊。

▶動 These trees are not big enough to shield us from strong winds. 這些樹還不夠大，所以還不能替我們擋住強風。

實用片語用語

shield sb. from... 保護（某人）免受（某事物）的傷害

shiv·er [ˋʃɪvɚ]

Track 5092

名 顫抖 動 冷得發抖 同 quake 顫抖

▶名 She gave a tiny shiver.
她輕輕顫抖了一下。

▶動 You're shivering! Don't stand outside, come in the house.
你在發抖耶！不要站在外面，快點進房子裡來。

short·age [ˋʃɔrtɪdʒ]

Track 5093

名 不足、短缺 同 deficiency 不足

▶The bad harvest led to severe food shortage.
欠收引起食物嚴重短缺。

short·com·ing [ˋʃɔrt͵kʌmɪŋ]

Track 5094

名 短處、缺點 同 deficiency 不足

▶She likes telling people about her husband's shortcomings.
她喜歡到處跟人家說她丈夫的缺點。

shove [ʃʌv]

Track 5095

名 推 動 推、推動

▶名 He gave her a shove when she was standing by the lake.
她站在湖邊的時候，他推了她一把。

▶動 It's impolite for you to shove old people like that.
你那樣推老人很不禮貌哦。

實用片語用語
shove sb. into 把某人推進……
例如：The boy shoved his sister into the pool.
這個男孩把姐姐推進游泳池裡了。

shred [ʃrɛd]

Track 5096

名 細長的片段 動 撕成碎布

▶名 Susan, will you peel the carrots and cut them into shreds?
蘇珊，妳能將紅蘿蔔削皮切成絲嗎？

▶動 This machine can shred all kinds of vegetables easily.
這個機器可將各種蔬菜切絲切條。

shriek [ʃrik]

Track 5097

名 尖叫 動 尖叫、叫喊 同 scream 尖叫

▶名 All of a sudden he let out a piercing（尖銳的）shriek.
他突然發出一聲尖叫。

▶動 She shrieked, but not all people on the street heard it.
她尖叫了一聲，但卻不是街上所有的人都聽了。

shrine [ʃraɪn]

Track 5098

名 廟、祠

▶How often does your grandma go to pray at the shrine every month?
你奶奶每月去廟裡拜拜幾次啊？

萬用延伸句型
How often...? 多常……？

shrub [ʃrʌb]

Track 5099

名 灌木 同 bush 灌木

▶Shrubs are much like trees, but they are much smaller than trees.灌木很像樹，但又比樹小得多。

shud·der [ˋʃʌdɚ] Track 5100

名 發抖、顫抖 動 顫抖、戰慄 同 tremble 顫抖

▶名 A shudder of fear ran through him when the police came.
警察到的時候他被嚇得渾身直發抖。

▶動 The man's harsh words made her shudder with fear.
那個男人兇狠的話使她害怕得顫抖起來了。

shut·ter [ˋʃʌtɚ] Track 5101

名 百葉窗 動 關上窗

▶名 Will you open the shutter and let some fresh air in?
你能把百葉窗打開，好讓一些新鮮空氣流進來嗎？

▶動 Will you make sure all the windows are shuttered before you leave?
能請你離開前確保所有窗戶都關上了嗎？

silk·worm [ˋsɪlkwɝm] Track 5102

名 蠶

▶There are not enough people to raise silkworms in the village.
村裡養蠶的人不是很夠。

萬用延伸句型
not enough... to...
沒有足夠的……能夠做……

sim·mer [ˋsɪmɚ] Track 5103

名 沸騰的狀態 動 煲、怒氣爆發 同 stew 燉、燜

▶名 I don't think you can bring water to a simmer in such a way.
我覺得你用這樣的方法是無法將水慢慢燒開的。

▶動 I don't think the soup will be delicious if we simmer it too long. 我覺得這湯如果燉太久會不好喝。

skel·e·ton [ˋskɛlətn̩] Track 5104

名 骨骼、骨架 同 bone 骨骼

▶The sick kid was reduced almost to a skeleton.
那個生病的孩子現在幾乎是皮包骨了。

skull [skʌl] Track 5105

名 頭蓋骨

▶I hope the scientists can find the lost crystal skull as soon as possible.
我希望科學家們能盡快找到遺失的那個水晶頭蓋骨。

slam [slæm] Track 5106

名 砰然聲 動 砰地關上

▶名 He threw his books down with a slam angrily.
他生氣地砰然一聲把書摔在桌上。

▶動 You'd better not slam the door. It might scare someone.
你最好不要使勁關門。那可能會嚇到人。

實用片語用語
grand slam 滿壘全壘打
例如：The grand slam won the team four points and helped them win the game.
他們藉由滿壘全壘打獲得四分，最後贏得比賽。

slap [slæp] Track 5107

名 掌擊 動 用掌拍擊

▶名 It hit him like a cold slap in the face.
這件事對他來說簡直就是晴天霹靂。

▶動 He slapped her across the face and made her cry.
他摑了她一記耳光，讓她哭了。

slaugh·ter [ˋslɔtɚ]

Track 5108

名 屠宰 動 屠宰

▶名 I am to send the cattle to the city for slaughter tomorrow.
我打算明天把牛送到城市裡去屠宰。

▶動 Millions of cattle are slaughtered every day in this country.
這個國家每天都有數百萬頭牛被屠宰。

slay [sle]

Track 5109

名 殺害、殺 同 kill 殺

▶It is illegal（違法的）for people to slay the cattle in most of India. 殺牛在印度大部分地區都是違法的。

文法字詞解析
就像我們中文也可能會以「很殺」當作稱讚來描述某人很厲害、氣勢很強一樣，英文也可以用「slay」來表達稱讚之意，說某人或某事物非常厲害、令人折服。

slop·py [ˋslɑpɪ]

Track 5110

形 不整潔的、邋遢的 同 neat 整潔的

▶Why is your handwriting so sloppy?
為什麼你寫的字這麼不整齊？

slump [slʌmp]

Track 5111

名 下跌 動 暴跌

▶名 There was a serious slump in the rice market.
稻米市場呈現出嚴重衰退的趨勢。

▶動 Sales have slumped badly recently, and many companies went bankrupt.
最近銷售量銳減，很多企業正面臨倒閉。

sly [slaɪ]

Track 5112

形 狡猾的、陰險的 反 frank 坦白的

▶The sly fox tricked the rabbit. 那隻狡猾的狐狸騙了兔子。

smash [smæʃ]

Track 5113

名 激烈的碰撞 動 粉碎、碰撞 同 shatter 粉碎

▶名 The dog ran into the door with a smash.
那隻狗狠狠地撞上了門。

▶動 They not only robbed him but also smashed all the furniture in the house.
他們不僅搶劫他，而且還砸壞了家裡所有的傢俱。

實用片語用語
smash hit 大轟動
例如：The singer's new album was a smash hit.
這位歌手的新專輯造成了大轟動。

snarl [snɑrl̩]

Track 5114

名 漫罵、爭吵 動 吼叫著說、糾結

▶名 I don't think the snarls we heard last night were from their home. 我覺得昨天晚上我們聽到的咆哮聲不是從他們家傳出來的。

▶動 I don't think you can fall asleep when the dog is snarling all night. 我覺得狗整夜吠著你是睡不著的。

snatch [snætʃ]

Track 5115

名 片段 動 奪取、抓住 同 grab 抓取

▶名 He had a snatch of sleep sitting in this chair.
他坐在這張椅子上小睡了一會。

▶動 He snatched the notebook away from her.
他從她手中搶走了筆記本。

sneak [snik]

Track 5116

動 潛行、偷偷地走

▶No one noticed him sneaking up behind Mike.
沒有人注意到他從麥克的後面偷偷溜了上來。

實用片語用語
sneak out 溜出……
例如：The children sneaked out the room when their parents were playing cards.
父母在打牌的時候，孩子們偷偷溜出了房間。

sneak·er(s) [ˋsnikɚ(s)]

Track 5117

名 慢跑鞋

▶It is hard for us to find a pair of comfortable and durable（耐用的）sneakers. 我們很難找到既舒服又耐穿的運動鞋。

sniff [snɪf]

Track 5118

名 吸氣 動 用鼻吸、嗅、聞 同 scent 嗅、聞

▶名 One sniff of this is enough to kill you. Don't you believe that? 聞一聞這個東西就足以致命。你不信嗎？

▶動 Sniffing flowers is enough to make me happy.
聞一聞花香就足以使我開心。

snore [snor]

Track 5119

名 鼾聲 動 打鼾

▶名 Her husband's snores are so loud that she often has to take some sleeping pills before sleeping.
她老公的鼾聲很大以致於她睡前得吃些安眠藥才行。

▶動 When her husband snored, she threw a pillow at him.
她丈夫一打鼾，她就拿枕頭丟他。

實用片語用語
sleeping pills 安眠藥

snort [snɔrt]

Track 5120

名 鼻息、哼氣 動 哼著鼻子說

▶名 He gave a snort when he heard her comment.
他聽到她的評語，就哼了一聲。

▶動 She snorted when she heard him boasting about himself.
她聽到他自吹自擂時，哼了一聲。

soak [sok]

Track 5121

名 浸泡 動 浸、滲入

▶名 Let's give these clothes a long soak before washing.
洗衣服之前我們先將這些衣服多泡久一點。

▶動 You have to use paper towels to soak up the cooking oil.
你應該用紙巾把油吸乾。

so·ber [ˋsobɚ]

Track 5122

動 使清醒 形 節制的、清醒的

▶動 A cup of strong tea can sober up a drunk person.
一杯濃茶可以讓酒醉的人清醒過來。

▶形 No man in his sober senses would act like this.
任何一個頭腦清醒的人都不會這樣行事。

實用片語用語
sober up 使清醒、變清醒

soft·en [ˋsɔfən]

Track 5123

動 使柔軟 反 harden 使變硬

▶Why don't you buy this special cream? It will help to soften up your skin. 為什麼不買這種特殊的護膚霜呢？它有助於使你的皮膚變得柔軟。

sole [sol]

Track 5124

形 唯一的、單一的

▶Farming is not their sole livelihood（謀生）.
務農是他們的唯一謀生之道。

sol·emn [ˋsaləm]

Track 5125

形 鄭重的、莊嚴的 同 serious 莊嚴的

▶Our headmaster（校長）looked very solemn when he announced the news.
宣佈這一消息時，校長顯得非常嚴肅。

sol·i·tar·y [ˋsaləˏtɛrɪ]

Track 5126

名 隱士、獨居者 形 單獨的 同 single 單獨的

▶名 This solitary lives far away from people.
那位隱士與人們住的很遠。

▶形 Emily led a very solitary life most of the time.
艾蜜莉大部分時間都一直過著非常孤獨的生活。

實用片語用語
solitary life 獨居生活

so·lo [ˋsolo]

Track 5127

名 獨唱、獨奏、單獨表演 形 單獨的

▶名 In this concert, there will be two piano solos. I am sure you will like them very much.
在這次的音樂會上，有兩首鋼琴獨奏曲。我保證你會很喜歡聽的。

▶形 He made his first solo flight in 1988.
他在 1988 年第一次做了單人飛行。

sov·er·eign [ˋsavrɪn]

Track 5128

名 最高統治、獨立國家 形 自決的、獨立的

▶名 No sovereign can do what he pleases, or he will be overthrown by his people. 沒有哪個君主可以為所欲為，否則他就會被他的人民推翻。

▶形 Don't look down on our sovereign nation.
別鄙視我們這個主權國家。

實用片語用語
sovereign nation 主權國家

sow [so]

Track 5129

動 播、播種

▶It is too early for the farmers of this country to sow yet.
現在還不到該國農民們播種的時候。

space·craft/space·ship

Track 5130

[ˋspesˏkræft]/[ˋspesˏʃɪp]

名 太空船

▶The spaceship makes it possible to travel to the moon.
太空船的出現使得去月球旅行成為可能。

萬用延伸句型
make it possible to...
使……成為可能的事

spe·cial·ist [ˋspɛʃəlɪst]

Track 5131

名 專家 同 expert 專家

▶They said that your elder brother is a specialist in cell phone chips（晶片）.
他們說你哥哥是一位手機晶片的專家。

spec·i·men [ˋspɛsəmən] Track 5132

名 樣本、樣品 同 sample 樣本

▶I am afraid that this specimen of the new fabric is of inferior quality.
恐怕這新布料的樣品品質很差。

spec·ta·cle [ˋspɛktək!] Track 5133

名 奇觀

▶What a spectacle! I will suggest my friends to visit here one day.
多麼壯麗的景色呀！我要建議我的朋友們有時間也來這看看。

spec·ta·tor [ˋspɛktetɚ] Track 5134

名 觀衆、旁觀者

▶There are a great many spectators watching the football game.
很多觀衆都在觀看這場足球比賽。

實用片語用語
a great many 很多

spine [spaɪn] Track 5135

名 脊柱、脊骨

▶It is so cold outside that I feel a chill go down my spine.
外面太冷了，以致我覺得有一股寒氣順著我的脊骨往下竄。

splen·dor [ˋsplɛndɚ] Track 5136

名 燦爛、光輝

▶All the splendor in the world is not worth a good friend.
人世間所有的榮華富貴都不如有一個好朋友。

sponge [spʌndʒ] Track 5137

名 海綿 動 依賴、（用海綿）擦拭

▶名 Why don't you use a clean sponge to wipe the surface?
為何不用乾淨的海綿來擦拭表面呢？

▶動 He sponged the wound quickly.
他很快地用棉球擦洗了一下傷口。

實用片語用語
sponge sth. off (sth.) 用海綿將某物（從某物上面）吸掉
例如：Wait a sec. I have to sponge the sauce off my shirt.
稍等一下，我得把這醬汁從我的襯衫上吸掉。

spot·light [ˋspɑt͵laɪt] Track 5138

名 聚光燈 動 用聚光燈照明

▶名 The stage was lit by several spotlights.
舞臺被幾盞聚光燈照亮。

▶動 I don't think that the pictures should be spotlighted from below.
我認為這些畫不該用下面的聚光燈來照明。

實用片語用語
be in the spotlight 成為焦點、受到眾人注目
例如：The boy was shy and hated being in the spotlight.
那個害羞的男孩不喜歡受到眾人的注目。

sprint [sprɪnt] Track 5139

名 短距離賽跑 動 衝刺、全力奔跑 同 speed 迅速前進

▶名 He made a sprint for shelter so that he wouldn't be wounded by the bomb.
為了不被炸彈傷到，他全速奔向躲避處。

▶動 I think you have to sprint so that you can catch the early bus.
我覺得你得用盡全力來奔跑才能趕上早班車。

spur [spɝ]

Track 5140

名 馬刺 動 策馬、飛奔

▶名 The man dug in his spurs. 那個男人用馬刺策馬前進。

▶動 You shouldn't spur this poor horse on.
你不該驅策這匹可憐的馬。

squash [skwɑʃ]

Track 5141

名 擠壓的聲音 動 壓扁、壓爛

▶名 Many people heard the squash.
很多人都聽到了那個擠壓的聲音。

▶動 He sat on the cake and squashed it.
他坐在蛋糕上，把它壓扁了。

squat [skwɑt]

Track 5142

名 蹲下的姿勢 動 蹲下、蹲 形 蹲著的

▶名 The boy is under the table in a squat.
那個男孩蹲在桌下。

▶動 Come over here and squat down, or you'll be seen.
過來這裡，蹲下來，不然你會被看到喔。

▶形 You've been working in a squat position for a long time.
你已經蹲著工作很久了。

實用片語用語
in a squat 呈蹲下的姿勢

stack [stæk]

Track 5143

名 堆、堆疊 動 堆疊 同 heap 堆

▶名 It took him twenty minutes to find his document from a stack of papers.
他花了二十分鐘才從一堆紙中找到了自己的檔案。

▶動 It took me just five minutes to stack up the plates and bowls. 我才花五分鐘就把碟子和碗疊起來了。

實用片語用語
stack up sth. / stack sth. up 整齊地堆疊某物

stag·ger [ˋstægɚ]

Track 5144

名 搖晃、蹣跚 動 蹣跚 同 sway 搖動

▶名 He was so shocked on hearing the news that he gave a stagger.
他聽到這消息時很震驚，所以連步伐都變得搖晃了。

▶動 My father was tired but he still staggered to his feet.
我父親很累，但他還是搖搖晃晃地站了起來。

stain [sten]

Track 5145

動 弄髒、汙染 名 汙點 同 spot 汙點

▶動 I am afraid that you have stained your tie with coffee.
恐怕你的領帶沾到咖啡了。

▶名 You can't remove the stain on the table cloth if you don't use this liquid. 不用這種液體的話，你無法去掉桌布上的汙漬。

實用片語用語
blood stain 血漬
例如：Why is there a blood stain on your shirt?
你的襯衫上為什麼有血漬呢？

stake [stek]

Track 5146

名 樁 動 把……綁在樁上、以……作為賭注

▶名 Will you put up a stake to support the newly planted tree?
你能豎一根樁來支撐新種的樹嗎？

▶動 Would you please not stake all your money on the risky business?
能不能請你別把所有的錢都賭在這充滿風險的生意上？

stalk [stɔk] Track 5147

名 莖 同 stem 莖

▶Let's put some stalks of wheat into the vase as decoration.
我們放些麥稈到花瓶裡當裝飾吧。

stall [stɔl] Track 5148

名 商品陳列台、攤位

▶How about buying some food from the market stall over there?
到那邊的小攤上買些吃的怎麼樣？

實用片語用語

bathroom stall （眾多）公用廁所（的其中一間）

例如：Mom, which bathroom stall are you in?
媽媽，妳是在哪一間廁所裡啊？

stan·za [ˋstænzə] Track 5149

名 節、段

▶What do you think of the first stanza in the poem, Bob?
鮑勃，你覺得這首詩的第一節怎麼樣？

star·tle [ˋstɑrtḷ] Track 5150

動 使驚跳 同 surprise 使吃驚

▶I was startled when the cat suddenly jumped onto the table.
那隻貓突然跳到桌上，嚇了我一跳。

states·man [ˋstetsmən] Track 5151

名 政治家

▶This man is not only an excellent statesman, but also a famous poet.
這個人不僅是一位出色的政治家，還是一位著名的詩人。

sta·tis·tic(s) [stəˋtɪstɪk(s)] Track 5152

名 統計值、統計量

▶It is a pity that they didn't add an explanatory（說明的）note to the list of statistics.
他們沒有在統計表前加上一段說明文字真可惜。

萬用延伸句型

It is a pity that... 很可惜……

sta·tis·ti·cal [stəˋtɪstɪkḷ] Track 5153

形 統計的、統計學的

▶The statistical data we have at hand isn't quite enough.
我們手邊的統計資料實在不太夠。

steam·er [ˋstimɚ] Track 5154

名 汽船、輪船

▶Who was the first man who built a steamer?
誰是建造汽船的第一個人？

steer [stɪr] Track 5155

名 忠告、建議 動 駕駛、掌舵

▶名 He gave me a bum steer before I got into the car.
在我上車前，他給了我一些忠告。

▶動 Can you steer the boat towards the island for me?
你能幫我把船開往那座島嗎？

文法字詞解析

除了用於開船時的「掌舵」以外，steer也可以用在掌控話題的方向，例如說「steer the topic into another direction」即「巧妙地把話題轉到另一個方向」。畢竟改變話題和掌舵都和「轉向」有關啊。

ster·e·o·type [ˋstɛrɪə͵taɪp] Track 5156

名 鉛版、刻板印象 動 把……澆成鉛版、定型

▶名 He doesn't conform（符合）to the usual businessman stereotype.
你很容易就會發現他不像典型的商人。

▶動 It's wrong to stereotype people, I know, but I still do it.
我知道用刻板印象看人是不對的，可是我還是會這樣做。

stern [stɝn] Track 5157

形 嚴格的 同 severe 嚴格的

▶She received a stern rebuke（責難）from her superior yesterday.
她昨天受到上司的嚴厲斥責。

stew [stju] Track 5158

名 燉菜 動 燉煮、燉

▶名 Why don't you have some more stew? It is the specialty（特色菜）here.
為什麼不再吃點燉菜呢？它可是這裡的特色菜哦。

▶動 You should stew the pears in red wine for several hours.
你應該要把梨放在紅葡萄酒中燉上幾小時。

實用片語用語

beef stew 燉牛肉
例如：The beef stew we had in this bar was unforgettable.
我們在這家酒吧吃的燉牛肉真是太難忘了。

stew·ard/stew·ard·ess/at·tend·ant [ˋstjuwɚd]/[ˋstjuwɚdɪs]/[əˋtɛndənt] Track 5159

名 服務生、空服員

▶A steward will arrive instantly（馬上）as soon as you press the buzzer（呼叫器）in the room.
你一按房間裡的呼叫器，服務生就會馬上過來。

stink [stɪŋk] Track 5160

名 惡臭、臭 動 弄臭 反 perfume 弄香

▶名 What a stink! I think you should clean your house as soon as possible.
真臭！我想你該盡快打掃你的房子了。

▶動 What did you just eat? It stinks!
你剛剛吃了什麼？很臭耶！

文法字詞解析

stink 可以加上不同的形容詞字尾來表達不同的含義，例如：加上「-ing」變成「stinking」就是「散發惡臭的」；加上「-y」變成「stinky」就是「臭的」。另外，stinky 也可以用 smelly 來表示，是一樣的意思。

stock [stɑk] Track 5161

名 庫存、紫羅蘭、股票

▶This store keeps a large stock of toys.
這家商店備有大量玩具。

stoop [stup] Track 5162

名 駝背 動 自貶、使屈服

▶名 I don't believe that he is the man walking with a slight stoop in the movie.
我不相信他就是電影裡頭那個弓著背行走的人。

▶動 I don't think my neighbor would stoop to such behavior.
我相信我的鄰居不會墮落到做出如此惡劣的行為。

實用片語用語

stoop down 彎下腰
例如：He stooped down to pick up the coin.
他彎下腰來撿錢幣。

stor·age [ˋstorɪdʒ]
Track 5163

名 儲存、倉庫 同 warehouse 倉庫

▶Don't you think these fish should be kept in cold storage?
你不覺得這些魚應該冷藏起來嗎？

stout [staʊt]
Track 5164

形 強壯的、堅固的 反 feeble 虛弱的

▶He bought a pair of stout boots from the store nearby.
他從附近的商店買了雙結實的靴子。

straight·en [ˋstretn̩]
Track 5165

動 弄直、整頓

▶This big room is a mess. Let's straighten it up.
這個大屋子一團亂。我們來整理一下吧。

實用片語用語
hair straightener 拉直頭髮的機器、電棒
例如：She used a hair straightener to look her best before the dance.
她在舞會前使用拉直頭髮的機器讓自己看起來完美無瑕。

straight·for·ward [ˋstretˌfɔrwəd]
Track 5166

形 直接的、正直的 同 straight 正直的

▶Why don't you just give me a straightforward answer?
你為什麼不給我一個直截了當的回答？

strain [stren]
Track 5167

名 緊張 動 拉緊、強逼、盡全力 反 relax 放鬆

▶名 Don't take this job, or you will have to work under a lot of strain.
不要接受這份工作，否則你會在沉重的壓力下工作。

▶動 Don't strain the rope too hard, or it may break.
不要把繩子拉得太緊，要不然會斷的。

strait [stret]
Track 5168

名 海峽

▶It is quite dangerous to cross the strait in such terrible weather.
在這樣糟糕的天氣渡過海峽是非常危險的。

strand [strænd]
Track 5169

名 濱 動 擱淺、處於困境

▶名 There are many people walking along the strand.
有很多人沿著海灘散步。

▶動 He said that he was stranded in a strange town.
他說他被困在一個陌生的城市。

實用片語用語
stranded in... 被困在（某處）

strap [stræp]
Track 5170

名 皮帶 動 約束、用帶子捆 同 bind 捆、綁

▶名 Will you buy a new strap for me? This one is broken.
能給我買條新皮帶嗎？這條破了。

▶動 Will you help me strap up the luggage?
你能幫我把行李捆紮好嗎？

stray [stre]
Track 5171

名 漂泊者 動 迷路、漂泊 形 迷途的

▶名 The cat used to be a stray.
這隻貓以前是流浪貓。

▶動 It has been five days since the boy strayed away from home.
男孩離家走失已經五天了。

▶形 I like to feed stray dogs.
我喜歡餵流浪狗。

streak [strik] Track 5172

動 加條紋 名 條紋 同 stripe 條紋

▶動 His hand was streaked with blood.
他的手上有血痕。

▶名 The man ran away like a streak of lightning.
那個男人快如閃電般地跑掉了。

stride [straɪd] Track 5173

名 跨步、大步 動 邁過、跨過 同 step 步伐

▶名 Everyone does things with their own stride and pace.
每個人做事都有自己的步伐和節奏。

▶動 He strode into the boss' office angrily.
他生氣地大步走進了老闆的辦公室。

文法字詞解析
stride 的動詞變化：stride, strode, stridden

stripe [straɪp] Track 5174

名 斑紋、條紋

▶Do you want stripes on your skirt?
你想要有條紋的裙子嗎？

stroll [strol] Track 5175

名 漫步、閒逛 動 漫步

▶名 How about taking a stroll in the garden with your father?
和你的父親一起到花園散步怎麼樣？

▶動 I notice a man strolling on the street.
我注意到有個人在街上閒逛。

實用片語用語
take a stroll 散步

struc·tur·al [ˋstrʌktʃərəl] Track 5176

形 構造的、結構上的

▶It is a surprise that the earthquake should cause no structural damage.
地震居然沒有對建築結構造成破壞，這真令人驚訝。

stum·ble [ˋstʌmbl̩] Track 5177

名 絆倒 動 跌倒、偶然發現

▶名 It was just a stumble; no big deal.
稍微絆倒一下而已，沒什麼大不了的。

▶動 You'd better buy this rare book if you stumble upon it one day.
如果某天你偶然找到了這本珍貴的書，你最好把它買下來。

實用片語用語
stumble upon 偶然發現（某物或某地）

stump [stʌmp] Track 5178

名（樹的）殘株、殘餘部分 動 遊說、難倒
同 remainder 殘餘物

▶名 It is very clever of you to use the stump as a table.
把樹樁當桌子來用，你真聰明。

▶動 The question got me stumped; it was too complicated for me to understand.
這問題難倒我了。它太過複雜，所以我無法理解。

stun [stʌn] Track 5179

動 嚇呆

▶The film indeed stunned the whole world.
這部電影確實震驚了整個世界。

sturd·y [ˋstɝdɪ] Track 5180

形 強健的、穩固的 同 strong 強壯的

▶The chair in my study is not sturdy enough to hold an adult.
我書房裡的椅子不夠堅固，承受不了一個大人的重量。

實用片語用語
sturdy shoes 穩固的鞋子
例如：Please wear a pair of sturdy shoes on the hike.
去健行的時候，請穿穩固的鞋子。

stut·ter [ˋstʌtɚ] Track 5181

名 結巴 動 結結巴巴地說 同 stammer 結結巴巴地說

▶名 He has a slight stutter, but it doesn't affect him much.
他有點口吃，但對他來說沒什麼影響。

▶動 He stutters a lot in front of the boss.
他常在老闆面前結結巴巴。

styl·ish [ˋstaɪlɪʃ] Track 5182

形 時髦的、漂亮的 同 fashionable 時髦的

▶You had better wear stylish clothes to the party.
你最好穿上時髦的衣服去派對。

sub·mit [səbˋmɪt] Track 5183

動 屈服、提交

▶Let's not submit our proposal to the manager today.
我們今天還是先別把提案交給經理吧。

sub·stan·tial [səbˋstænʃəl] Track 5184

形 實際的、重大的 同 actual 實際的

▶We have no need to buy a substantial number of weapons unless we're facing a war.
除非戰爭來臨，否則我們沒有必要購買大量武器。

萬用延伸句型
have no need to... 不需要……

sub·sti·tute [ˋsʌbstəˏtjut] Track 5185

名 代替者 動 代替 同 replace 代替

▶名 There's no substitute for experience.
沒有什麼能夠取代經驗。

▶動 Up to now, we haven't found anything that could substitute for petrol（汽油）.
到目前為止，我們還找不到可代替汽油的東西。

實用片語用語
substitute teacher 代課老師
例如：The class will be given by a substitute teacher today because your math teacher is ill.
今天的課會由代課老師來上，因為你們的數學老師生病了。

suit·case [ˋsutˏkes] Track 5186

名 手提箱

▶Don't worry. He will have your suitcases sent forward to the hotel. 別擔心。他會叫人先把你的行李箱送到旅館去的。

sul·fur [ˋsʌlfɚ]

Track 5187

名 硫磺

▶Sulfur can be used to make gunpowder（火藥）.
硫磺可以被人們用來製造火藥。

sum·mon [ˋsʌmən]

Track 5188

動 召集

▶The man summoned us for a meeting.
那個男人召集我們來開會。

文法字詞解析
除了用在召集「人」以外，文學作品中 summon 這個字也常用於召喚怪物、惡魔、動物、鬼魂等。

su·per·fi·cial [ˋsupɚˋfɪʃəl]

Track 5189

形 表面的、外表的 反 essential 本質的

▶Maybe we are too superficial to appreciate great literature like this. 也許我們都太膚淺，無法欣賞這類文學巨著。

su·per·sti·tion [ˏsupɚˋstɪʃən]

Track 5190

名 迷信

▶The more you know, the less likely you are to believe in superstitions.
你知道的越多，你就越不會相信迷信。

su·per·vise [ˋsupɚvaɪz]

Track 5191

動 監督、管理 同 administer 管理

▶Do you mind if I ask him to supervise the workers loading the lorry（卡車）?
你介意我叫他去監督工人把貨物裝上卡車嗎？

萬用延伸句型
Do you mind if...? 你介意……嗎？

su·per·vi·sor [ˏsupɚˋvaɪzɚ]

Track 5192

名 監督者、管理人 同 administrator 管理人

▶I don't believe that such a devious（不坦誠的）man can become a good supervisor.
我不相信這樣一個不坦誠的人能成為一個好主管。

sup·press [səˋprɛs]

Track 5193

動 壓抑、制止 同 restrain 抑制

▶It is quite clear that they are trying in every way to suppress the truth. 他們很明顯是在千方百計地掩蓋事實的真相。

su·preme [səˋprim]

Track 5194

形 至高無上的

▶Isn't the Pope（教皇）the supreme leader of the Roman Catholic Church（羅馬天主教會）?
教皇難道不是羅馬天主教的最高領袖嗎？

surge [sɝdʒ]

Track 5195

名 大浪 動 洶湧

▶名 A surge of shoppers（顧客）poured into the store.
有一批顧客湧入商店中。

▶動 A great wave surged over the ship.
巨浪沖打著船。

實用片語用語
pour into 湧入

sus·pend [sə`spɛnd] Track 5196

動 懸掛、暫停 同 hang 懸掛

▶The boy has been suspended from school many times.
那個男孩已經被勒令停學很多次了。

實用片語用語
be suspended from school 被勒令停學

sus·tain [sə`sten] Track 5197

動 支持、支撐 同 support 支持

▶It is hard for us to sustain our development without investment.
沒有投資我們難以維繫發展。

swamp [swɑmp] Track 5198

名 沼澤 動 陷入泥沼 同 bog 沼澤

▶名 The heavy rain has turned not only my garden but also my neighbor's into swamps.
大雨把我和鄰居的花園都變成了沼澤地。

▶動 Not only the horse but also the carriage were swamped in the mud.
馬和馬車都陷在泥沼中了。

swarm [swɔrm] Track 5199

名 群、群集 動 聚集、一塊 同 cluster 群、組

▶名 There is a swarm of bees in the tree at the back of our house.
我家屋後的樹上有一窩蜜蜂。

▶動 Lots of people swarmed into the cinema tonight because of this new film.
因為這部新片的緣故，今晚有很多人湧進電影院。

實用片語用語
a swarm of 一群（常用於蜜蜂）

sym·pa·thize [`sɪmpə͵θaɪz] Track 5200

動 同情、有同感 同 pity 同情

▶It's hard for us to sympathize with his political opinions.
我們難以贊同他的政治觀點。

tack·le [`tækḷ] Track 5201

動 著手處理、捉住 同 undertake 著手處理

▶Can you suggest us how to tackle this big problem?
我們該如何處理這個大難題呢？你能給個建議嗎？

tan [tæn] Track 5202

名 日曬後的顏色 形 棕褐色的

▶名 His arms and legs had a dark tan from working outside all day long.
他的手臂和腿曬得黑黑的，因為他整天都在室外工作。

▶形 He is a tan, healthy man.
他是個皮膚黝黑、健康的男人。

實用片語用語
tanning machine 日光浴機
例如：Death by being locked in a tanning machine sounds like a horrible way to die.
被關在日光浴機裡曬死聽起來似乎是個很慘的死法。

tan·gle [ˋtæŋgḷ]

Track 5203

名 混亂、糾結 動 使混亂、使糾結

▶名 The dog's fur is in tangles.
她那隻狗的毛都糾結起來了。

▶動 My shoelaces are tangled up.
我的鞋帶都纏在一起了。

tar [tɑr]

Track 5204

名 焦油、柏油 動 塗焦油於

▶名 This road is uneven. Why not cover it with tar?
這條路很不平。何不在上面鋪柏油呢？

▶動 The street has already been tarred.
那條街道已經鋪上了柏油。

tart [ˋtɑrt]

Track 5205

形 酸的、尖酸的 同 sour 酸的

▶I wish you hadn't given him such a tart answer.
我真希望你沒給過他如此尖酸的回答。

萬用延伸句型
I wish you hadn't... 我真希望你沒有（做某事）（用於對方已經做了某事，無法改變此情形時）

taunt [tɔnt]

Track 5206

名 辱罵 動 嘲弄

▶名 The little girl had to endure the taunts from her classmates.
那個小女孩不得不忍受同學們的奚落。

▶動 We shouldn't taunt others for their shortcomings.
我們不該嘲笑其他人的缺點。

tav·ern [ˋtævɚn]

Track 5207

名 酒店、酒館

▶How about finding a tavern to have a drink?
我們去找間酒館喝一杯怎麼樣？

tell·er [ˋtɛlɚ]

Track 5208

名 講話者、敘述者、出納員

▶As soon as I complete my training, I am going to become a bank teller.
一旦我結束訓練，我就將成為一名銀行出納員。

tem·po [ˋtɛmpo]

Track 5209

名 速度、拍子 同 rhythm 節拍

▶The tempo of this song is too slow.
這首歌的節奏太慢了。

實用片語用語
tempo of life 生活的步調
例如：The tempo of life of the people in this city is very different from what I'm used to.
這個城市的人們生活步調和我所習慣的大不相同。

tempt [tɛmpt]

Track 5210

動 誘惑、慫恿

▶Nothing could tempt him to do such a terrible thing.
什麼都不能誘使他做出這麼糟的事。

temp·ta·tion [tɛmpˋteʃən]

Track 5211

名 誘惑

▶It is a pity that he couldn't resist the temptation of drugs in the end. 很遺憾他最終還是沒能抵擋住毒品的誘惑。

ten·ant [ˋtɛnənt] Track 5212

名 承租人 動 租賃 同 landlord 房東

▶名 I am afraid that it's difficult for you to sell a house with a tenant still living in it.
恐怕你很難賣出還住著房客的房子。

▶動 That old house has not been tenanted for many years.
那幢老房子已經多年無人居住了。

ten·ta·tive [ˋtɛntətɪv] Track 5213

形 暫時的

▶I think we can draw up a tentative plan now.
我認為現在可以先草擬一個臨時方案。

實用片語用語
draw up 擬出

ter·mi·nal [ˋtɝmənl] Track 5214

名 終點、終站 形 終點的

▶名 Let's put the data into the computer terminal.
我們把這些資料輸入電腦終端吧。

▶形 The terminal disease will kill him very soon.
這個末期的疾病很快就會致他於死了。

ter·race [ˋtɛrəs] Track 5215

名 房屋的平頂、陽臺 動 使成梯形地

▶名 This open-air terrace is really spacious. Don't you think so?這個陽臺很寬敞，你不覺得嗎？

▶動 Terraced fields can be seen everywhere in this area.
這一地區梯田到處可見。

thigh [θaɪ] Track 5216

名 大腿

▶The water is already up to my thighs.
水已經淹到了我的大腿。

實用片語用語
up to 有……之多、在……的高度

thorn [θɔrn] Track 5217

名 刺、荊棘

▶Be careful not to be pricked by thorns when picking the flowers.
採花的時候請小心不要被荊棘刺到。

thrill [θrɪl] Track 5218

名 戰慄 動 使激動 同 excite 使激動

▶名 He felt a thrill when he went upon the stage.
他一上了台就覺得很激動。

▶動 He was thrilled to hear the good news.
他聽到這個好消息非常興奮。

thrill·er [ˋθrɪlɚ] Track 5219

名 恐怖小說、令人震顫的人事物

▶There's a new American thriller on. Would you like to go to see it?
有一部新的美國驚悚片正在上映。你想不想去看呢？

throne [θron] Track 5220

名 王位、寶座

▶The prince ascended to his throne. 王子登上了王位。

throng [θrɔn] Track 5221

名 群眾 動 擠入

▶名 She pushed through the throng of people on the street.
她從街上的人群中推擠著過去。

▶動 There are many passengers thronging the station waiting for their trains. 火車站擠滿了等車的乘客。

thrust [θrʌst] Track 5222

名 用力推 動 猛推 同 shove 推

▶名 They finally opened the door with a thrust.
他們用力地一推，終於推開了門。

▶動 He thrust the key into the keyhole. 他把鑰匙用力推進鑰匙孔。

tick [tɪk] Track 5223

名 滴答聲 動 發出滴答聲、標上記號

▶名 Even the ticks of the clock are too noisy for me.
就連時鐘的滴答聲都太吵了。

▶動 The clock ticked too loudly for me to sleep.
時鐘發出的滴答聲太大，以致於我睡不著。

tile [taɪl] Track 5224

名 瓷磚 動 用瓦蓋 同 slope 傾斜

▶名 Would you please help me collect some tiles?
你能幫我收集一些瓷磚嗎？

▶動 Would you please tile a little house for our pet dog?
你能不能用磚瓦為我們的寵物狗蓋個小房子呢？

tilt [tɪlt] Track 5225

動 傾斜、刺擊 同 pierce 刺穿

▶I felt like the ground is tilting. 我感覺地板好像要歪斜了一樣。

tin [tɪn] Track 5226

名 錫 動 鍍錫

▶名 I fed the cat with food from a tin can.
我從錫罐拿出貓食餵了貓。

▶動 He brought some tinned meat for the camping trip.
他帶了一些罐頭肉類去露營。

tip·toe [ˋtɪp͵to] Track 5227

名 腳尖 動 用腳尖走路 副 以腳尖著地

▶名 I'm afraid that I can only reach the shelf if I stand on tiptoe.
我恐怕得踮著腳才剛能碰得到架子。

▶動 You have to tiptoe quietly up the stairs, for everyone has fallen asleep.
你得踮著腳輕輕走上樓梯，因為大家都已經睡了。

▶副 He stood tiptoe on a chair to see the stage.
他踮著腳站在一把椅子上，才能看到舞台。

文法字詞解析

除了用於真的有皇室身分的人坐的「王座」之外，throne 也可以單純指在某領域、某比賽第一名的人所擁有的「冠軍寶座」。

實用片語用語

floor tile 地板磁磚

例如：As the floor tiles of the room are black, it is hard to see if there is dirt on them. 因為這房間的地板磁磚是黑色的，很難看清楚上面有沒有灰塵。

toad [tod]

Track 5228

名 癩蛤蟆

▶Even though toads have an ugly appearance, they are useful.
儘管蟾蜍外表醜陋，但牠們很有用。

toil [tɔɪl]

Track 5229

名 辛勞 動 辛勞 反 leisure 悠閒

▶名 It is obvious that he is quite exhausted with the toil.
顯然他因那件辛苦的工作而感到十分疲憊。

▶動 The workers toiled all day and night.
工作人員們辛苦工作了整天整夜。

實用片語用語
day and night 一整天、整天整夜

to·ken [ˋtokən]

Track 5230

名 表徵、代幣 同 sign 象徵

▶Would you please accept this token of our appreciation?
請接受這一禮物好嗎？這象徵著我們對您的謝意。

torch [tɔrtʃ]

Track 5231

名 火炬、引火燃燒、手電筒

▶Why don't you light the torch? I can't see the path.
為什麼不打開手電筒呢？我看不見路了。

文法字詞解析
torch 後來也延伸成能夠當作動詞，表示「用火炬放火燒某處」的行為。例如「torch a store」就是「放火去燒一家店」。

tor·ment [ˋtɔrˏmɛnt]

Track 5232

名 苦惱 動 使受苦、煩擾 同 comfort 安慰

▶名 What a little torment that child is!
這孩子真煩人！

▶動 She always torments everyone with silly questions.
她總是用很多無聊的問題來煩擾大家。

tor·rent [ˋtɔrənt]

Track 5233

名 洪流、急流

▶The torrent of water turned our little boat over.
急流將我們的小船掀翻了。

tor·ture [ˋtɔrtʃɚ]

Track 5234

名 折磨、拷打 動 使……受折磨

▶名 There are a lot of scenes of torture in the movie.
那個電影裡有很多折磨人的畫面。

▶動 They tortured him by burning his legs.
他們燒了他的腿來折磨他。

tour·na·ment [ˋtɝnəmənt]

Track 5235

名 競賽、比賽 同 contest 競賽

▶The tournament is open to not only the professionals but also the amateurs. 這次比賽不僅職業運動員可以參加，而且業餘運動員也可以參加。

實用片語用語
tennis tournament 網球比賽
例如：We're off to Wimbledon to watch a tennis tournament.
我們要去溫布頓看網球比賽。

tox·ic [ˋtɑksɪk]

Track 5236

形 有毒的 同 poisonous 有毒的

▶You'd better be careful when you handle the toxic chemicals.
你最好小心處理有毒的化學藥品。

trade·mark [ˋtred͵mɑrk] Track 5237

名 標記、商標 同 brand 商標

▶The trademark license contract shall be submitted to the Trademark Office for record.
商標使用許可合約應當呈報商標局備案。

trai·tor [ˋtretɚ] Track 5238

名 叛徒

▶He was denounced as a traitor to his country.
他被指責為賣國賊。

tramp [træmp] Track 5239

名 不定期貨船、長途跋涉、徒步旅行 動 踐踏、長途跋涉

▶名 I want to go for a tramp in the country. Would you like to go with me?
我想在鄉下徒步旅行。你想不想跟我一起去呢？

▶動 We have already tramped through the wood.
我們已經吃力地走過樹林了。

實用片語用語
tramp through 跋涉越過（某地）

tram·ple [ˋtræmpl̩] Track 5240

動 踐踏 名 踐踏、踐踏聲

▶動 You'd better not trample on the grass.
你最好不要踐踏草地。

▶名 I heard the trample of many feet.
我聽到許多人的腳步聲。

實用片語用語
trample on sth. 踐踏
這個片語除了可以用在踐踏草地等實際的物質，也可以用在踐踏某人的感受，例如：trample on sb's feelings

trans·par·ent [trænsˋpɛrənt] Track 5241

形 透明的

▶Not all glass is transparent.
並非所有玻璃都是透明的。

trea·sur·y [ˋtrɛʒərɪ] Track 5242

名 寶庫、金庫、財政部

▶The authorities believe that there is a mole in the Treasury Department.
當局認為財政部裡有內奸。

實用片語用語
Treasury Department 財政部

trea·ty [ˋtritɪ] Track 5243

名 協議、條約 同 contract 合約

▶The treaty gave fresh impetus（推動）to trade.
這條約使貿易又前進了一步。

trench [trɛntʃ] Track 5244

名 溝、渠 動 挖溝渠 同 ditch 渠

▶名 The farmer dug several trenches so that he can irrigate the rice fields.
這個農民挖了好幾條溝以便灌溉稻田。

▶動 They were busy trenching the fields so that they can drain the water.
他們正忙著在田裡挖溝渠以便能夠排水。

trib·ute [ˋtrɪbjut]

Track 5245

名 致敬、進貢

▶It was said that many conquered nations had to pay tribute to the rulers of ancient Rome.
據說許多被征服的國家要向古羅馬的統治者納貢。

實用片語用語
pay tribute to 致敬、進貢

tri·fle [ˋtraɪfl]

Track 5246

名 瑣事 動 疏忽、輕忽、戲弄

▶名 I think it's not wise of you to trouble yourself with such a trifle.
我覺得你因為這樣的小事而煩惱是不明智的。

▶動 It's immoral（不道德的）of you to just trifle with her affections. 你只是在玩弄她的感情，這是不道德的。

trim [trɪm]

Track 5247

名 齊備狀態、整齊、整潔 動 整理、修剪、削減
形 整齊的、整潔的、苗條的 同 shave 修剪

▶名 Your hair needs a good trim.
你的頭髮需要好好修剪一下了。

▶動 I hope the school budgets won't be trimmed back.
我希望學校預算不會被削減。

▶形 I wish I could have a trim figure.
我希望能有勻稱漂亮的身材。

tri·ple [ˋtrɪpl]

Track 5248

名 三倍的數量 動 變成三倍 形 三倍的

▶名 It is obvious that fifteen is the triple of five.
顯然十五是五的三倍數。

▶動 In the past five years, the company has tripled its sales.
在過去五年中，該公司銷售量增加至三倍。

▶形 He received triple pay because of his extra work.
他得到三倍的報酬，是因為超額工作。

文法字詞解析
和這個字長得很像的一個單字是「triplets」，是「三胞胎」的意思。

trot [trɑt]

Track 5249

動 使小跑步 名 小跑步

▶動 The horses trotted down the road happily.
馬兒們開心地沿著路小跑步。

▶名 The horses broke into a trot when it started raining.
開始下雨時，馬兒們都開始小跑步。

trout [traʊt]

Track 5250

名 鱒魚

▶I caught seven trout in fifteen minutes.
我十五分鐘內捉到七條鱒魚。

tuck [tʌk]

Track 5251

名 縫褶 動 打褶

▶名 Mom put a tuck in the dress because it was too big.
由於衣服太大了，所以媽媽在裡面打了褶。

▶動 The lady tucked her son into bed.
那個太太幫她兒子把毯子蓋好。

實用片語用語
tuck away 收好、藏好
例如：All the old clothes were safely tucked away under the bed.
舊衣服都已經好好地收到床下了。

tu·i·tion [tju`ɪʃən]　Track 5252

名 教學、講授、學費 同 instruction 教學

▶She works very hard so that she can earn enough money to pay for her son's tuition.
她非常努力地工作，以便賺到足夠的錢來支付兒子的學費。

實用片語用語
tuition fees 學費
例　如：Do you know how much the tuition fees of this university costs?
你知道這所大學的學費是多少嗎？

tu·na [`tunə]　Track 5253

名 鮪魚

▶My cat loves tinned tuna fish.
我的貓很愛鮪魚罐頭。

ty·rant [`taɪrənt]　Track 5254

名 暴君、獨裁者

▶Mr. Smith is a tyrant in his office.
史密斯先生在他辦公室裡是個獨裁者。

um·pire [`ʌmpaɪr]　Track 5255

名 仲裁者、裁判員 動 擔任裁判 同 judge 裁判員

▶名 Will you tell me why they refuse to accept the umpire's decision?
你能告訴我他們為什麼拒絕接受裁判的判決嗎？

▶動 Can you umpire the cricket match for us next week?
請你下週來擔任我們板球比賽的裁判好嗎？

un·der·grad·u·ate [ˏʌndɚ`grædʒʊɪt]　Track 5256

名 大學生

▶Not all undergraduates want to enter a gradute school.
不是所有大學生都想唸研究所。

un·der·line [ˏʌndɚ`laɪn]　Track 5257

名 底線 動 畫底線

▶名 Please highlight（使突出）the underlines in the article so that I can notice them.
請突出文中的底線，以便我能注意到它們。

▶動 Please underline those important sentences so that you can easily find them later.
請在重要的句子下面畫線，以便你以後能輕易地找到它們。

文法字詞解析
句子中的 highlight 為「使突出」的意思。要讓文字中的底線突出該怎麼做呢？用螢光筆就會很明顯了。螢光筆的用途就是讓文字變得突出，因此英文中螢光筆叫作 highlighter。

un·der·neath [ˏʌndɚ`niθ]　Track 5258

介 在下面 同 below 在下面

▶The ball has rolled underneath the desk. Will you help me pick it up?
球滾到了桌下。你能幫我把它撿起來嗎？

un·der·stand·a·ble [ˏʌndɚˋstændəbḷ]

Track 5259

形 可理解的

▶Her reluctance（不願意）to agree is understandable to me.
她不願同意，我可以理解。

un·doubt·ed·ly [ʌnˋdaʊtɪdlɪ]

Track 5260

副 無庸置疑地

▶Undoubtedly, the point you made does hold water.
毫無疑問地，你提的論點確實是站得住腳的。

文法字詞解析
和 undoubtedly 意思差不多的一個字是 doubtlessly（毫無疑問的），兩個都有 doubt 這個字根，一個在前面加上表示「不、無」的字首「un-」，一個在後面加上表示「沒有」的字尾「-less」。

up·date [ʌpˋdet]

Track 5261

名 最新資訊 動 更新

▶名 It is time for us to explain the fake news update to our audience. 我們該向觀眾們解釋這條造假的新聞了。

▶動 It's time for us to update the old computer systems in our company. 我們該更新公司的舊電腦系統了。

up·right [ˋʌpˏraɪt]

Track 5262

名 直立的姿勢 形 直立的 副 直立地 同 erect 直立的

▶名 If I put it upright, would it look better?
我把它直著放會不會比較好看？

▶形 What do you think of moving the upright post there?
把這根直立的柱子移到那去怎麼樣？

▶副 The sack is empty, and therefore cannot stand upright.
那個袋子是空的，所以站不直。

up·ward(s) [ˋʌpwɚd(z)]

Track 5263

形 向上的 副 向上地 反 downward 向下

▶形 It doesn't matter if you encounter an upward current at high altitudes.
你要是在高空中遇到了上升氣流也沒什麼關係。

▶副 It doesn't matter what they do, sales won't move upwards any more. 不管他們怎麼做，銷售額都不會再好轉了。

萬用延伸句型
It doesn't matter... ……都沒關係

ut·ter [ˋʌtɚ]

Track 5264

形 完全的 動 發言、發出 同 complete 完全的

▶形 I was so shocked that I was at an utter loss what to do.
我震驚到完全不知道該怎樣做才好。

▶動 He was so astonished that he couldn't utter a word.
他驚訝到連一個字都說不出來。

va·can·cy [ˋvekənsɪ]

Track 5265

名 空缺、空白

▶George is the best person to fill this vacancy.
喬治是填補這一個空缺的最佳人選。

vac·u·um [ˋvækjʊəm]

Track 5266

名 真空、空虛 動 以真空吸塵器打掃

▶名 It is obvious that his wife's death left a vacuum in his life.
顯然他妻子的去世使他的生活變得空虛。

▶動 It is clear that it was Mom who vacuumed my room yesterday. 顯然昨天是媽媽用吸塵器清掃了我的房間。

實用片語用語
vacuum cleaner 吸塵器
例如：The cat is scared of the vacuum cleaner.
這貓怕吸塵器。

vague [veg]

Track 5267

名 不明確的、模糊的 反 explicit 明確的

▶If you want me to go, why not say so in plain English instead of making vague hints?
如果你想叫我走，為什麼要拐彎抹角而不直說？

van·i·ty [ˋvænətɪ]

Track 5268

名 虛榮心、自負 同 conceit 自負

▶Would you please not buy things just to gratify your vanity?
能不能請你別為了滿足自己的虛榮心而買東西？

va·por [ˋvepɚ]

Track 5269

名 蒸發的氣體 同 mist 水氣

▶A cloud is a mass of vapor. 雲是天空中的水氣形成的團塊。

veg·e·ta·tion [ˏvɛdʒəˋteʃən]

Track 5270

名 草木、植物 同 plant 植物

▶There is luxuriant tropical vegetation in our country.
我們國家有很多繁茂的熱帶植物。

實用片語用語
tropical vegetation 熱帶植被

veil [vel]

Track 5271

名 面紗 動 掩蓋、遮蓋 同 cover 遮蓋

▶名 It is obvious that she likes the veil very much; she wears it almost every day.
顯然她很喜歡這個面紗。她幾乎每天都戴著它。

▶動 He tried to veil his contempt at my ignorance.
他試圖掩飾對我的無知的蔑視。

vein [ven]

Track 5272

名 靜脈 反 artery 動脈

▶She is so skinny you can practically see veins under her skin.
她瘦到你都能看見她皮膚之下的靜脈了。

vel·vet [ˋvɛlvɪt]

Track 5273

名 天鵝絨 形 柔軟的、平滑的、天鵝絨製的 同 soft 柔軟的

▶名 The lawn looks like green velvet.
那草坪看上去就像綠色的天鵝絨。

▶形 What do you think about buying that velvet dress?
你覺得買那件天鵝絨製的洋裝怎麼樣？

實用片語用語
velvet gown 天鵝絨袍
例如：The rich old man wears a velvet gown to bed every night.
這個有錢的老人每晚都穿著天鵝絨袍去睡覺。

ven·ture [ˋvɛntʃɚ]

Track 5274

名 冒險 動 以……為賭注、冒險

▶名 Not everyone can take a costly venture like this.
不是每個人都能夠冒代價如此高的風險。

▶動 He ventured into the burning house to look for his pet.
他冒險進入燃燒著的房子裡找尋他的寵物。

ver·bal [ˋvɝbḷ] Track 5275

形 言詞上的、口頭的 同 oral 口頭的

▶How about writing a memorandum（備忘錄）to confirm our verbal agreement?
何不寫份備忘錄以確認我們口頭上的協議呢？

ver·sus [ˋvɝsəs] Track 5276

介 ……對……（縮寫為vs.）

▶I'm afraid that this election is about the new generation versus the old generation.
恐怕這個選舉是新世代和舊世代之間的鬥爭。

ver·ti·cal [ˋvɝtɪkḷ] Track 5277

名 垂直線、垂直面 形 垂直的、豎的

▶名 The so-called vertical has inclined.
那條所謂的垂直線已經傾斜了。

▶形 It is obvious that the northern side of the mountain is almost vertical.
顯然這座山的北側幾乎是垂直的。

文法字詞解析
相對地，「水平的」則是 horizontal，而「斜的」則是 diagonal。

ve·to [ˋvito] Track 5278

名 否決 動 否決 同 deny 否定

▶名 It is said that the president threatened to use his veto over the bill. 據說總統威脅要對這個議案行使否決權。

▶動 It is reported that the plan was vetoed by the government in the end. 據報導這個計畫最終被政府否決了。

vi·a [ˋvaɪə] Track 5279

介 經由 同 through 經由

▶Let's keep in contact via email, shall we?
讓我們以後透過電子郵件來保持聯繫，好嗎？

vi·brate [ˋvaɪbret] Track 5280

動 震動

▶Your phone is vibrating. 你的手機在震動喔。

文法字詞解析
vibrate 多半用於機械方面或地殼震動等比較固定形式的震動，人類或動物發抖時不會用這個字來表示。

video·tape [ˋvɪdɪoˏtep] Track 5281

名 錄影帶 動 錄影

▶名 People don't use videotapes anymore.
人們現在不使用錄影帶了。

▶動 Would you like to videotape this program for us?
你能幫我們把這個節目錄到帶子裡嗎？

view·er [ˋvjuɚ] Track 5282

名 觀看者、電視觀眾 同 spectator 旁觀者

▶Letters from viewers express their dissatisfaction（不滿）with the current program.
電視觀眾來信表示對此節目的不滿。

vig·or [ˋvɪgɚ]

Track 5283

名 精力、活力 同 energy 精力

▶It is obvious that the leader of the expedition must be a man of great vigor.
顯然探險隊的負責人必須是個精力充沛的人。

萬用延伸句型
It is obvious that... 顯然地……

vig·or·ous [ˋvɪgərəs]

Track 5284

形 有活力的 同 energetic 有活力的

▶There are three vigorous young birds in the nest.
這鳥巢裡有三隻活潑的小鳥。

vil·lain [ˋvɪlən]

Track 5285

名 惡棍 同 rascal 惡棍

▶I don't think the guy is a villain.
我認為這個傢伙不是個壞人。

vine [vaɪn]

Track 5286

名 葡萄樹、藤蔓

▶It's very hard for them to pass through a jungle woven with vines. 他們非常艱難地穿過一個被藤蔓植物纏繞的叢林。

文法字詞解析
句中的 woven 是 weave（織）的完成式形態，weave 的動詞三態是 weave, wove, woven。

vi·o·lin·ist [ˌvaɪəˋlɪnɪst]

Track 5287

名 小提琴手

▶I wish I could become a famous violinist one day.
我希望有朝一日能成為一位著名的小提琴家。

vi·sa [ˋvizə]

Track 5288

名 簽證

▶I'm afraid that we have to cut a few corners to get your visa ready in time. 恐怕我們得簡化手續才能把你的簽證及時辦妥。

vow [vaʊ]

Track 5289

名 誓約、誓言 動 立誓、發誓 同 swear 發誓

▶名 Once he took the vow, his loyalty never wavered（動搖）.
他一旦宣了誓，就會一直忠貞不渝。

▶動 Once she vowed that she would take the matter to court, it will be more difficult for us to handle this.
一旦她誓要把這件事訴諸法律，那麼我們就更難處理了。

實用片語用語
take a vow 發誓

Ww

wade [wed]

Track 5290

名 涉水、跋涉 動 艱辛地進行、跋涉

▶名 They went for a wade in the shallows.
他們由水淺的地方涉水過去。

▶動 He waded to the opposite side of the creek.
他涉水過溪到對岸去。

wail [wel]
Track 5291

名 哀泣 動 哭泣

▶名 The child burst into loud wails.
那個小孩突然大哭起來。

▶動 The girl wailed when the dog barked at her.
那隻狗對那個小女孩吠時，她大哭起來。

ward [wɔrd]
Track 5292

名 行政區、守護、病房 動 守護、避開 同 avoid 避開

▶名 His illness is so serious that he is put in an isolation ward.
他病得重到被送進了隔離病房。

▶動 He reacted quickly and warded off the blow.
他反應很快，避開了這一擊。

實用片語用語
psychic ward 精神病房
例如：Working at a psychic ward can get scary at nights.
晚上在精神病房工作可能會變恐怖的。

ware [wɛr]
Track 5293

名 製品、貨品

▶The shop sells a great variety of porcelain（瓷器）ware.
這家店鋪出售種類繁多的瓷器。

實用片語用語
a great variety of 種類繁多的

ware·house [ˋwɛr͵haʊs]
Track 5294

名 倉庫、貨棧 動 將貨物存放於倉庫中

▶名 Don't you think the warehouse full of paper is a fire hazard（危險）?
你不覺得裝滿紙張的倉庫有引發火災的危險嗎？

▶動 We should warehouse these goods as quickly as we can.
我們應該儘快把這批貨物存放到倉庫中。

war·rior [ˋwɔrɪɚ]
Track 5295

名 武士、戰士 同 fighter 戰士

▶I am fond of reading the stories of ancient warriors. What about you?
我很喜歡讀有關古代武士的故事。你呢？

war·y [ˋwɛrɪ]
Track 5296

形 注意的、小心的 同 cautious 小心的

▶You'd better keep a wary eye on the weather before you go out for a long journey.
你出門長途旅行前最好密切注意一下天氣。

實用片語用語
keep a wary eye on... 密切注意……

wea·ry [ˋwɪrɪ]
Track 5297

形 疲倦的 動 使疲倦

▶形 Why not sit on the bench in the park and rest your weary limbs? 為什麼不到公園的長凳上坐坐，讓你疲倦的腿休息一下呢？

▶動 The long journey has wearied us.
長途旅行使我們疲憊不堪。

weird [wɪrd]
Track 5298

形 怪異的、不可思議的 同 strange 奇怪的

▶My brother likes to wear really weird clothes.
我弟弟喜歡穿很奇怪的衣服。

wharf [hwɔrf]
Track 5299

名 碼頭 同 pier 碼頭

▶Let's wait for others on the small wharf, shall we?
我們到那個小碼頭上等其他人吧，可以嗎？

where·a·bouts [ˋhwɛrəˋbaʊts]
Track 5300

名 所在的地方 副 在何處 同 location 位置、所在地

▶名 In fact, no one knows his whereabouts.
事實上，沒有人知道他的行蹤。

▶副 Whereabouts on earth did you leave your bag?
你到底把包包放在哪了啊？

文法字詞解析

句中的「on earth」並非真的想問「在地球上的哪裡」，純粹是一個強調用的慣用語。也可以問「where on earth...」、「why on earth...」、「what on earth...」等等變化形式。

where·as [hwɛrˋæz]
Track 5301

連 雖然、卻、然而

▶Some people like the cold weather, whereas some hate it.
有些人喜歡冷天氣，然而有些人卻很討厭。

whine [hwaɪn]
Track 5302

名 哀泣聲、嘎嘎聲 動 發牢騷、怨聲載道

▶名 Do you hear the whines of the dog?
你聽見了那隻狗的哀鳴聲嗎？

▶動 The dog was whining outside the door last night.
昨晚那隻狗在門外哀叫。

whirl [hwɝl]
Track 5303

名 迴轉 動 旋轉 同 turn 旋轉

▶名 Put the fruits into the blender and give them a whirl.
把水果放到果汁機裡面讓它轉一下吧。

▶動 The leaves whirled beautifully as they fell.
樹葉美麗地旋轉飄落。

whisk [hwɪsk]
Track 5304

名 小掃帚 動 掃、揮 同 sweep 掃

▶名 Will you borrow a whisk from the neighbors?
你能從鄰居那借把掃帚來嗎？

▶動 The lady whisked the kids out of the room.
那個女士迅速把孩子們掃出門外。

實用片語用語

whisk away 被迅速帶走、掃走
例如：The kids were whisked away before they could see anything exciting.
還沒看到什麼刺激的畫面，孩子們就被帶走了。

whis·key/whis·ky [ˋhwɪskɪ]
Track 5305

名 威士忌

▶Whisky is stronger than beer. 威士忌比啤酒還要烈。

whole·sale [ˋholˌsel]
Track 5306

名 批發 動 批發賣出 形 批發的

▶名 Would you like to tell me how we can buy these goods at wholesale? 你能告訴我我們如何才能整批買進這批貨嗎？

▶動 They wholesale these shirts at $6 each.
他們以每件六美元的價格批發出售這些襯衫。

▶形 Do you know this wholesale merchant? Can you introduce me to him?
你認識這個批發商人嗎？你願意把我介紹給他嗎？

whole·some [ˋholsəm]
Track 5307

形 有益健康的 反 harmful 有害的

▶The food we cook is really wholesome.
我們煮的菜都很有益健康。

實用片語用語
wholesome milk 營養豐富的牛奶
例如：Having wholesome milk really does help you grow taller.
喝營養豐富的牛奶真的可以幫助長高。

wide·spread [ˋwaɪdˏsprɛd]
Track 5308

形 流傳很廣的、廣泛的 同 extensive 廣泛的

▶The news has caused widespread panic.
這則消息引起了廣泛的恐慌。

wid·ow/wid·ow·er
Track 5309

[ˋwɪdo]/[ˋwɪdəwɚ]

名 寡婦 / 鰥夫

▶It was the widow who brought him up.
正是這個寡婦把他扶養長大。

wig [wɪg]
Track 5310

名 假髮

▶His wig was blown away by the strong wind.
他的假髮被強風吹走了。

wil·der·ness [ˋwɪldɚnɪs]
Track 5311

名 荒野

▶The man got lost in the Canadian wilderness.
那個男人在加拿大的荒野迷路了。

實用片語用語
get lost in... 在（某處）迷路

wild·life [ˋwaɪldˏlaɪf]
Track 5312

名 野生生物

▶We must protect wildlife and their habitats（棲息地）by all means.
我們該盡一切辦法來保護野生生物以及它們的棲息地。

with·er [ˋwɪðɚ]
Track 5313

動 枯萎、凋謝 同 fade 枯萎、凋謝

▶The reason why the flower withered was that there was no water. 這朵花枯萎的原因是缺水。

woe [wo]
Track 5314

名 悲哀、悲痛 同 sorrow 悲痛

▶She told her friend all her woes.
她把所有傷心事都跟朋友說了。

萬用延伸句型
Woe is me! 我真是悲慘！（用於自我怨嘆的時候）
例如：Woe is me! All the plants I keep are dead!
我真是太慘了！我種的植物都死光了！

wood·peck·er [ˋwʊdˏpɛkɚ]
Track 5315

名 啄木鳥

▶How long will it take for a woodpecker to peck a hole in a tree? 啄木鳥在樹上啄個洞要花多久的時間？

work·shop [ˋwɝkˏʃɑp]
Track 5316

名 小工廠、研討會

▶There are more than sixty workers in a workshop here.
這裡的一間小工廠裡有六十多個工人。

wor·ship [ˋwɝʃɪp]

Track 5317

名 禮拜 動 做禮拜

▶名 My father asked us to attend worship by ourselves this morning.
爸爸早上叫我們自己去做禮拜。

▶動 People are busy with their work now. It is no wonder that they have little time to worship.
人們現在都忙於工作。難怪他們很少有時間去做禮拜了。

worth·while [ˋwɝθˋhwaɪl]

Track 5318

形 值得的 同 worthy 值得的

▶Not all people think it worthwhile to take classes.
不是所有人都認為去上課很值得。

實用片語用語
be worthwhile to... （做某事）是值得的

wor·thy [ˋwɝðɪ]

Track 5319

形 有價值的、值得的

▶This book is worthy of reading.
這本書很值得一讀。

wreath [riθ]

Track 5320

名 花環、花圈

▶They hung a wreath above the door.
他們在門上掛了一個花圈。

wring [rɪŋ]

Track 5321

名 絞、絞扭 動 握緊、絞 同 twist 絞、扭

▶名 Give those clothes a wring, so that they'll dry faster.
把那些衣服擰一擰，這樣比較快乾。

▶動 The girl was wringing her hands as she cried.
那個小女孩邊哭邊絞著手。

實用片語用語
wring one's hand （因擔心而）扭絞著手

yacht [jɑt]

Track 5322

名 遊艇 動 駕駛遊艇、乘遊艇

▶名 The new yacht is big enough to hold all the people here.
這艘新遊艇夠大，能容納這裡所有的人。

▶動 I have time to go yachting with you this weekend.
我這週末有時間來陪你去坐遊艇。

yarn [jɑrn]

Track 5323

名 冒險故事、紗 動 講故事

▶名 How long will it take for you to wind the yarn into a ball?
你把毛線纏成一個球要多久？

▶動 How long did the old mariner（水手）yarn about his sea adventures?
老水手講他的海上奇遇講了多久？

實用片語用語
spin a yarn 講一個故事
例如：I'm bored. Can you spin a yarn and make me less bored?
我好無聊，你講個故事讓我比較不無聊一點好嗎？

yeast [jist]

Track 5324

名 酵母、發酵粉

▶Don't you know yeast can be used in making beer and bread?
你不知道嗎？酵母可用於釀啤酒和發酵麵包。

yield [jild]

Track 5325

名 產出 動 生產、讓出 同 produce 生產

▶名 The weather was favorable this year. It is no wonder that these trees give a high yield of fruit.
今年風調雨順。怪不得這些果樹獲得了大豐收。

▶動 The farmers have taken good care of these apple trees, so they yield plenty of fruit. 農民們仔細地照顧了這些蘋果樹，所以它們結了許多果實。

yo·ga [ˋjogə]

Track 5326

名 瑜伽

▶I am so busy everyday that I have no time to go to yoga lessons. 我每天都很忙，以致於我都沒時間去上瑜伽課。

實用片語用語

yoga mat 瑜伽墊
例如：The students bring their own yoga mats to class.
學生們都自己帶瑜伽墊來上課。

zinc [zɪŋk]

Track 5327

名 鋅 動 鍍鋅

▶名 Zinc can be used to cover other metals to keep them from rusting. 鋅可塗在其他金屬表面上用來防銹。

▶動 I heard that he can zinc on the container.
我聽說他能在那個容器上鍍鋅。

zip [zɪp]

Track 5328

名 尖嘯聲、拉鍊 動 呼嘯而過、拉開或拉上拉鍊

▶名 The car passed by in a zip.
那台車呼嘯而過。

▶動 My zipper won't zip. Can you help me?
我的拉鏈拉不上去了。你能幫我一下嗎？

實用片語用語

zip up 拉上（拉鍊）
例如：Zip up your jacket. It's getting cold.
把外套拉鍊拉上吧，開始冷了。

ZIP [zɪp]

Track 5329

名 郵遞區號

▶Would you please tell me your complete address and ZIP code, Mr. Kelly?
凱利先生，您能告訴我您的完整地址及郵遞區號嗎？

zoom [zum]

Track 5330

動 調整焦距使物體放大或縮小

▶Do you know how to use the "zoom in" function of the copier（影印機）?
你知道怎麼把影印機設定成放大模式嗎？

挑戰英文能力——邁向 7000 單字

學英文從單字開始，
許自己一個不可思議的滿分奇蹟！

Level
6
挑戰英文能力
——邁向7000單字

ab·bre·vi·ate [əˋbrivɪ͵et]
Track 5331

動 將……縮寫成 同 shorten 縮短

▶"Cardiopulmonary resuscitation" can be abbreviated to "CPR".
「心肺復甦術」可以縮寫成「CPR」。

實用片語用語
be abbreviated to... 縮寫為……

ab·bre·vi·a·tion [ə͵brivɪˋeʃən]
Track 5332

名 縮寫

▶Not everyone knows that "Mr." is the abbreviation of "Mister".
不是每個人都知道「Mr.」是「Mister」的縮寫。

ab·nor·mal [æbˋnɔrm!]
Track 5333

形 反常的

▶I'm afraid that it's abnormal for the boy to eat so much.
這個男孩吃這麼多恐怕不太正常吧。

萬用延伸句型
It's abnormal for sb. to... 對某人來說做某事很不正常

ab·o·rig·i·nal [͵æbəˋrɪdʒən!]
Track 5334

名 土著、原住民 形 土著的、原始的

▶名 It seems that all the aboriginals there are very good at singing and dancing.
那裡的土著似乎都非常擅長唱歌和跳舞。

▶形 It seems that more and more people are beginning to appreciate the beauty of aboriginal works of art.
似乎越來越多的人開始欣賞當地土著居民的工藝之美。

ab·o·rig·i·ne [æbəˋrɪdʒəni]
Track 5335

名 原住民

▶There are many aborigines living in this mountain.
有很多原住民住在這座山裡。

a·bound [əˋbaʊnd]
Track 5336

動 充滿 同 overflow 充滿

▶Both animals and plants abound in the forest.
森林裡充滿了許多動物和植物。

ab·sent·mind·ed [ˋæbsəntˋmaɪndɪd]
Track 5337

形 茫然的

▶It is no wonder that the absent-minded boy always loses his books.
難怪這個心不在焉的男孩總是把書弄丟。

萬用延伸句型
It is no wonder that... 難怪……

ab·strac·tion [æb`strækʃən] Track 5338

名 抽象、出神

▶It's hard to describe this idea to you in abstraction.
用抽象的方式解釋這個概念給你聽是很困難的。

a·bun·dance [ə`bʌndəns] Track 5339

名 充裕、富足

▶There are sheep in abundance on the meadow.
草地上有許多綿羊。

a·buse [ə`bjuz] Track 5340

名 濫用、虐待 動 濫用、虐待、傷害 同 injure 傷害

▶名 There are many child abuse cases in that country.
那個國家有很多孩童受虐的案例。

▶動 The man abused his children when he got drunk.
這個男人喝醉時就會虐待小孩。

實用片語用語
domestic violence 家庭暴力
例如：She has suffered from domestic violence since she was a child.
她從還是小孩的時候開始就承受著家庭暴力。

ac·cel·er·ate [æk`sɛlə,ret] Track 5341

動 促進、加速進行

▶Let's accelerate the speed of our community construction.
讓我們加快我們社區建設的速度吧。

ac·cel·er·a·tion [æk,sɛlə`reʃən] Track 5342

名 加速、促進

▶It is said that this type of car has good acceleration.
據說這種車的加速性能很好。

ac·ces·si·ble [æk`sɛsəbl̩] Track 5343

形 可親的、容易接近的

▶I'm afraid that this database is only accessible for the authorized manager.
恐怕只有授權的管理員才可以使用此資料庫。

ac·ces·so·ry [æk`sɛsərɪ] Track 5344

名 附件、零件 形 附屬的

▶名 Would you please ask him to buy some car accessories for me? 請你叫他幫我買些汽車零件好嗎？

▶形 The watch is a valuable accessory item.
這支手錶是很有價值的配件。

實用片語用語
hair accessory 髮飾
例如：My daughter wants all the hair accessories she can see.
我女兒只要是她看得到的髮飾她都想要。

ac·com·mo·date [ə`kɑmə,det] Track 5345

動 使……適應、提供 同 conform 適應

▶The bank is accommodating its customers more than it used to. 這家銀行現在給客戶貸款比以前多。

ac·com·mo·da·tion [ə,kɑmə`deʃən] Track 5346

名 便利、適應

▶I'm afraid that the accommodation is rather rough and ready.
恐怕這個住處還算差強人意。

實用片語用語
rough and ready 差強人意的、簡單但還能用的

ac·cord [ə`kɔrd]

Track 5347

名 一致、和諧 動 和……一致

▶名 His words are in accord with his actions.
他做的跟說的如出一轍。

▶動 I'll try to accord the controversy over the housing scheme.
我會試著調解在住房建築規劃方面的爭議。

實用片語用語
in accord with 與……一致

ac·cor·dance [ə`kɔrdn̩s]

Track 5348

名 給予、根據、依照

▶I am in accordance with him in this matter. What about you?
在這件事情上我和他是一致的。你呢？

ac·cord·ing·ly [ə`kɔrdɪŋlɪ]

Track 5349

副 因此、於是、相應地

▶I have told you the circumstances, and you are supposed to act accordingly.
我已將情況告訴你了，你應該酌情處理。

ac·count·a·ble [ə`kaʊntəbl̩]

Track 5350

形 應負責的、有責任的、可說明的 同 responsible 有責任的

▶We should both be accountable for this.
我們兩人都該為這件事負責。

ac·count·ing [ə`kaʊntɪŋ]

Track 5351

名 會計、會計學

▶I don't think he is quite fit for accounting work.
我覺得他不是很適合這份會計工作。

實用片語用語
fit for 適合

ac·cu·mu·late [ə`kjumjə͵let]

Track 5352

動 累積、積蓄 同 gather 聚集

▶Rubbish has been accumulating in the front yard.
垃圾在前院裡堆積。

ac·cu·mu·la·tion

Track 5353

[ə͵kjumjə`leʃən]

名 累積

▶Would you please be quick? An accumulation of work is waiting to be done.
請你快點好嗎？一堆工作等著要做呢。

ac·cu·sa·tion [͵ækjə`zeʃən]

Track 5354

名 控告、罪名

▶No one believed his accusation because he was prone to lying.
因為他太愛說謊，沒人相信他的指控。

實用片語用語
be prone to N. / V-ing 有……傾向的

ac·qui·si·tion [͵ækwə`zɪʃən]

Track 5355

名 獲得

▶The man devoted his life to the acquisition of knowledge.
那個男人把一生的時間都用在獲取知識上。

實用片語用語
devote sb.'s life to...
將某人的人生都奉獻給……

ac·tiv·ist [ˋæktɪvɪst] Track 5356

名 行動者

▶What if all these activists complain about the decision?
如果把這些積極分子都抗議這個決策呢？

a·cute [əˋkjut] Track 5357

形 敏銳的、激烈的 同 keen 敏銳的

▶This area has an acute shortage of water. 這個地方缺水嚴重。

ad·ap·ta·tion [ˏædəpˋteʃən] Track 5358

名 適應、順應

▶It is said that this play is an adaptation of a novel.
據說這一個劇本是由小說改編而成的。

ad·dict [ˋædɪkt]/[əˋdɪkt] Track 5359

名 有毒癮的人 動 對……有癮、使入迷

▶名 There are no lengths to which an addict will not go to obtain his drugs. 癮君子為了得到毒品什麼事都做得出來。

▶動 It is no wonder that she is addicted to television.
難怪她對電視入了迷。

實用片語用語
drug addict 藥物成癮者
例如：She had no idea that her boyfriend was a drug addict.
她完全不曉得她的男友是藥物成癮者。

ad·dic·tion [əˋdɪkʃən] Track 5360

名 熱衷、上癮

▶It was his addiction to drugs that propelled him towards a life of crime. 吸毒成癮使他走上了犯罪的道路。

實用片語用語
propel sb. into / to / towards sth. 促使某人做某事

ad·min·is·ter/ ad·min·is·trate [ədˋmɪnəstɚ]/[ədˋmɪnəˏstret] Track 5361

動 管理、照料

▶It takes brains to administer a large corporation.
管理大公司要有頭腦。

ad·min·is·tra·tion [ədˏmɪnəˋstreʃən] Track 5362

名 經營、管理、政府 同 government 管理

▶Her work involved more than administration of first aid to the wounded. She also has to assist other doctors.
她的工作不僅僅是對傷者的急救，她還得協助其他的醫生。

ad·min·is·tra·tive [ədˋmɪnəˏstretɪv] Track 5363

形 行政上的、管理上的

▶It is obvious that he regarded all these administrative details as beneath his notice.
顯然他認為行政上的這些瑣事都不值得一顧。

實用片語用語
regard sb. / sth. as beneath one's notice
對某人／某物不屑一顧

ad·min·is·tra·tor [ədˋmɪnəˏstretɚ] Track 5364

名 管理者

▶You had better not underestimate（低估）an administrator's resolutions! 你最好不要低估管理者的決心！

A B C D E F G H I J K L M N O P Q R S T U V W X Y Z

ad·vo·cate [ˋædvəkɪt]/[ˋædvə͵ket] Track 5365

名 提倡者 動 提倡、主張 同 support 擁護

▶名 I don't think that they are advocates of free trade.
我不認他們是自由貿易的宣導者。

▶動 I don't believe that he really advocates reforming the prison system. 我不相信他是真的主張改良監獄制度。

af·fec·tion·ate [əˋfɛkʃənɪt] Track 5366

形 摯愛的

▶She was always affectionate with her children.
她總是和孩子們很親暱。

af·firm [əˋfɝm] Track 5367

動 斷言、證實 同 declare 斷言

▶I can affirm that the girl did quite a bit of reading.
我能證實這個女孩子讀了不少書。

實用片語用語

do quite a bit of... 經常做某事、做了很多次某事

ag·gres·sion [əˋgrɛʃən] Track 5368

名 進攻、侵略

▶It is obvious that such an action constitutes an aggression upon women's rights.
顯然這種行為是對婦女權利的侵犯。

al·co·hol·ic [͵ælkəˋhɔlɪk] Track 5369

名 酗酒者 形 含酒精的

▶名 She has had enough of her alcoholic husband.
她對酒鬼丈夫再也無法容忍了。

▶形 She never has alcoholic beverages because she is allergic.
她從來不喝含酒精的飲料，因為她對酒精過敏。

a·li·en·ate [ˋeljən͵et] Track 5370

動 使感情疏遠 同 separate 使疏遠

▶You'd better not alienate yourself from your colleagues.
你最好還是不要與同事們疏遠。

文法字詞解析

alien 有「外星人」的意思，加上帶有「使變成……」意思的動詞字尾，alienate 就成了「使變成外星人」的意思。讓某人「變成外星人」，大家當然就不敢親近他，也難怪這個單字的意思會是「使感情疏遠」了。

al·li·ance [əˋlaɪəns] Track 5371

名 聯盟、同盟

▶They formed an alliance against the common enemy.
他們聯合起來抵禦共同的敵人。

al·lo·cate [ˋælə͵ket] Track 5372

動 分配 同 distribute 分配

▶It seems that I can never allocate my time properly.
我似乎總是無法適當地分配我的時間。

a·long·side [əˋlɔŋsaɪd] Track 5373

副 沿著、並排地 介 在……旁邊

▶副 The police car pulled up alongside all of a sudden.
那輛警車突然在旁邊停下了。

▶介 The boat stopped alongside the dock so that the passenger can get off. 那條船停靠在碼頭旁，好讓那名乘客可以下船。

al·ter·na·tive [ɔlˋtɝnətɪv] Track 5374

名 二選一、供選擇的東西 形 二選一的 同 substitute 代替

▶名 It seems that there is no alternative.
似乎沒有別的選擇了。

▶形 Can we take an alternative route instead?
我們改走別條路好不好？

實用片語用語
alternative energy 替代性能源
例如：We can use alternative energy such as solar power.
我們可以使用替代性能源，例如太陽能。

am·bi·gu·i·ty [͵æmbɪˋgjuətɪ] Track 5375

名 曖昧、模稜兩可

▶I'm afraid that the dispute resulted from ambiguities in the contract.
恐怕爭議是由合約中模稜兩可的詞句引起的。

am·big·u·ous [æmˋbɪgjuəs] Track 5376

形 曖昧的 同 doubtful 含糊的

▶It is obvious that his ambiguous reply made her all the more irritated. 顯然他模稜兩可的回答讓她更加惱怒。

am·bu·lance [ˋæmbjələns] Track 5377

名 救護車

▶He's in a pretty bad way. You'd better get an ambulance.
他的狀況很不好。你最好叫輛救護車。

實用片語用語
in a pretty bad way 狀況相當不好

am·bush [ˋæmbʊʃ] Track 5378

名 埋伏、伏兵 動 埋伏並突擊 同 trap 陷阱

▶名 We fell into the enemy's ambush.
我們中了敵人的埋伏。

▶動 They ambushed the enemy the very next day.
他們第二天就突襲了敵軍。

a·mi·a·ble [ˋemɪəbl̩] Track 5379

形 友善的、可親的

▶The next-door neighbors are amiable people.
隔壁鄰居們都是和藹可親的人。

am·pli·fy [ˋæmplə͵faɪ] Track 5380

動 擴大、放大

▶Would you please amplify your remarks by giving us some examples?
請舉例詳述你的話好嗎？

文法字詞解析
能夠把聲音「放大」的揚聲器就稱為amplifier。

an·a·lects [ˋænə͵lɛkts] Track 5381

名 語錄、選集 同 collection 收集品

▶There are some errors in the annotation（注解）of the Analects.
這本《論語》中有不少釋義不當的地方。

文法字詞解析
Analects 大寫時專門指《論語》。

a·nal·o·gy [əˋnælədʒɪ] Track 5382

名 類似

▶I don't think that it is always reliable to argue by analogy.
我認為用類推法論證並不總是可靠的。

an·a·lyst [ˋænəlɪst] Track 5383

名 分解者、分析者

▶I hope I could become a highly trained and practiced（熟練的）system analyst.
我希望我能成為一位受過嚴格訓練、經驗豐富的系統分析員。

an·a·lyt·i·cal [ˏænəˋlɪtɪkḷ] Track 5384

形 分析的

▶What if the analytical result and experiment results are different?
如果分析結果與實驗結果是不同的呢？

文法字詞解析
analytical 也能用來描述一個人的個性，說這個人「擅長分析」、「喜歡分析」。

an·ec·dote [ˋænɪkˏdot] Track 5385

名 趣聞

▶Would you tell me some anecdotes about that famous actor?
你能為我講幾個關於那位名演員的趣聞嗎？

an·i·mate [ˋænəˏmet] Track 5386

動 賦予……生命 形 活的 同 encourage 激發、助長

▶動 It is obvious that Jim's arrival served to animate the whole party.
顯然吉姆的到來使聚會的整個氣氛活躍了起來。

▶形 There are so many beautiful things in animate nature.
充滿生命力的大自然中有許多美麗的事物。

文法字詞解析
這個字後面加上名詞字尾「-tion」就變成了「animation」，而這個字不僅有「生氣、活潑」的意思，還可以表示「動畫片」，因為動畫片賦予了所有的卡通人物生命嘛。

an·noy·ance [əˋnɔɪəns] Track 5387

名 煩惱、困擾

▶The man slammed the door in annoyance.
那個男人不高興地甩上了門。

a·non·y·mous [əˋnɑnəməs] Track 5388

形 匿名的

▶I keep receiving anonymous letters.
我一直收到匿名信。

實用片語用語
anonymous letter 匿名信

Ant·arc·tic/ant·arc·tic Track 5389

[ænˋtɑrktɪk]

名 南極洲 形 南極的

▶名 It is reported that the scientist has spent three months in the solitude of the Antarctic.
據報導這位科學家已經在人跡罕至的南極待了三個月了。

▶形 It is said that the Antarctic Peninsula hasn't been polluted yet.
據說南極半島尚未受到污染。

an·ten·na [ænˋtɛnə] Track 5390

名 觸角、觸鬚、天線

▶There is a TV antenna upon the roof.
屋頂上有一根電視天線。

an·ti·bi·ot·ic [ˌæntɪbaɪˋɑtɪk] Track 5391

名 抗生素、盤尼西林 形 抗生的、抗菌的 同 medicine 藥物

▶名 Antibiotics can be used against infection.
抗生素可以用來防止感染。

▶形 It is said that earthworms（蚯蚓）can produce antibiotic substances.
據說蚯蚓可以產生抗菌物質。

文法字詞解析
antibiotic 這個字當作名詞時，較常以複數形式（antibiotics）出現。

an·ti·bod·y [ˋæntɪˌbɑdɪ] Track 5392

名 抗體

▶It seems that the antibody to hepatitis（肝炎）hasn't been produced in my body.
我的體內似乎還沒有產生肝炎的抗體。

an·tic·i·pate [ænˋtɪsəˌpet] Track 5393

動 預期、提前支用 同 expect 預期

▶He didn't anticipate being chosen for the show.
他沒預期到他會被選上去上節目。

an·tic·i·pa·tion [ænˌtɪsəˋpeʃən] Track 5394

名 預期、預料

▶The girl paced around the room in anticipation.
女孩期待地在房間裡走來走去。

an·to·nym [ˋæntəˌnɪm] Track 5395

名 反義字

▶It is quite clear that "long" is the antonym of "short".
很顯然「長」是「短」的反義詞。

文法字詞解析
字首「ant-」是「anti-」的變形，也就是「相反」的意思，字尾「-nym」的意思則是「字、名字」，所以兩者合在一起就是「相反的字」，也就變成「反義字」了。那「同義字」又要怎麼說呢？就是「synonym」。「syn-」有「將分開的東西結合在一起」的意思。

ap·pli·ca·ble [ˋæplɪkəbl̩] Track 5396

形 適用的、適當的 同 appropriate 適當的

▶I don't think that the regulation is applicable to this case.
我認為那條規定不適用於這一情況。

ap·pren·tice [əˋprɛntɪs] Track 5397

名 學徒 動 使……做學徒 同 beginner 新手

▶名 Not all people know that the painting was actually finished by his apprentice.
不是所有人都知道這幅畫實際上是由他的徒弟完成的。

▶動 Not all parents in that village want to apprentice their children to a carpenter.
那個村子裡不是所有的家長都想讓他們的孩子去當木匠的學徒。

實用片語用語
be apprentice to... 在……底下見習
例如：I have been apprentice to a sculptor for 5 years.
我在一位雕刻家手下見習五年了。

ap·prox·i·mate [əˋprɑksəmɪt] Track 5398

動 相近 形 近似的、大致準確的

▶動 The distance was approximated as three kilometers.
估計這段距離大約為三公里。

▶形 Would you please give me an approximate figure of the budget?
您能不能給我一個關於預算的大概數據呢？

ap·ti·tude [ˋæptə͵tjud]

Track 5399

名 才能、資質 同 ability 才能

▶It is obvious that the little girl has an aptitude for languages.
顯然這個小女孩具有學習語言的才能。

實用片語用語
have an aptitude for... 有……的才能

Arc·tic/arc·tic [ˋɑrktɪk]

Track 5400

名 北極地區 形 北極的

▶名 The Arctic is much colder than the place we live.
北極地區比我們住的地方冷多了。

▶形 I guess there are much less people in the Arctic regions than here. 我想北極地區的人要比這裡的少得多。

ar·ro·gant [ˋærəgənt]

Track 5401

形 自大的、傲慢的 反 humble 謙虛的

▶One should never be arrogant unless he has every right to be. 做人不應傲慢，除非你的能力強到可以傲慢。

ar·ter·y [ˋɑrtərɪ]

Track 5402

名 動脈、主要道路

▶Now, how am I supposed to get around that artery?
現在，我要如何繞過那條主要道路？

ar·tic·u·late [ɑrˋtɪkjə͵let]/[ɑrˋtɪkjəlɪt]

Track 5403

動 清晰地發音 形 清晰的

▶動 Would you please articulate your words carefully? I don't quite follow you.
請把話仔細地說清楚好嗎？我聽不太明白。

▶形 He can't come up with an articulate argument.
他想不出一個清楚有力的論點。

延伸萬用句型
I don't quite follow you. 我聽不太懂你的意思。

ar·ti·fact [ˋɑrtɪ͵fækt]

Track 5404

名 加工品

▶I feel that the ancient Egypt artifacts in the exhibition are gorgeous. 我覺得展覽中的古埃及手工藝品真是美極了。

as·sas·si·nate [əˋsæsṇ͵et]

Track 5405

動 行刺 同 kill 殺死

▶It is reported that the police has uncovered a plot to assassinate the president.
據說警察已破獲一起暗殺總統的陰謀。

as·sert [əˋsɜt]

Track 5406

動 斷言、主張

▶He asserted that we should agree to sign the contract.
他主張我們應該要同意簽合約。

as·sess [əˋsɛs]

Track 5407

動 估計價值、課稅

▶It is too early to assess the effects of the new legislation.
現在來評價新法規的效果還為時過早。

萬用延伸句型
It is too early to... 要（做某事）還太早

as·sess·ment [ə`sɛsmənt] Track 5408

名 評估、稅額

▶It is obvious that his assessment of the situation was quite right. 顯然他對形勢的判斷非常正確。

as·sump·tion [ə`sʌmpʃən] Track 5409

名 前提、假設、假定 反 conclusion 結論

▶My assumption is that the man and the girl are probably father and daughter.
我猜測這個男人和那個女孩大概是父女。

asth·ma [`æzmə] Track 5410

名 【醫】氣喘

▶Secondhand smoke has been proven over and over again to be a major trigger of asthma attacks.
二手菸一再被證實是引發氣喘的主要原因之一。

實用片語用語
over and over again 一再地

a·sy·lum [ə`saɪləm] Track 5411

名 收容所

▶He was soon committed to an insane asylum.
不久他就被送進了精神病院。

實用片語用語
orphan asylum 孤兒院
例如：Both of them grew up in the same orphan asylum.
他們兩個是在同一家孤兒院長大的。

at·tain [ə`ten] Track 5412

動 達成 反 fail 失敗

▶I finally attained a diploma at the university.
我終於在大學取得了文憑。

at·tain·ment [ə`tenmənt] Track 5413

名 到達

▶He's a man of great attainments in several fields.
他在幾個領域中都有很高造詣，這真令人驚訝。

at·ten·dant [ə`tɛndənt] Track 5414

名 侍者、隨從 形 陪從的

▶名 Being a good flight attendant means making your passengers feel relaxed.
當一個好的空服員就是要讓乘客們感到旅途輕鬆愉快。

▶形 What do you think about hiring an attendant nurse to take care of her? 你覺得請一位隨行護士來照顧她怎麼樣？

實用片語用語
flight attendant 空服員

at·tic [`ætɪk] Track 5415

名 閣樓、頂樓

▶Would you pack these books together and put them in the attic?
你把這些書包裝在一起，然後放在閣樓裡好嗎？

auc·tion [`ɔkʃən] Track 5416

名 拍賣 動 拍賣 同 sale 拍賣

▶名 They sold the villa by auction.
他們拍賣了那棟別墅。

▶動 It is said that they are going to auction the pictures at the end of the month. 據說他們將在月底拍賣這些畫。

au·then·tic [ɔˋθɛntɪk]

Track 5417

形 真實的、可靠的

▶Not until last century did they find this authentic manuscript of the book.
直到上個世紀，他們才發現了該書的真正手稿。

萬用延伸句型
Not until... did + S... 直到……才……
須注意，當 not until 放在句首時，主要子句必須倒裝。

au·thor·ize [ˋɔθə͵raɪz]

Track 5418

動 委託、授權、委任

▶It is really a joy that I've been authorized by the court to repossess（重新擁有）this property.
我得到法庭認可重新擁有這筆財產，這真是件樂事。

au·to·graph/ sig·na·ture [ˋɔtə͵græf]/[ˋsɪgnətʃɚ]

Track 5419

名 親筆簽名 動 親筆寫於…… 同 sign 簽名

▶名 Would you please give me your autograph? You are my idol! 您能幫我簽個名嗎？您是我的偶像！

▶動 Would you please autograph my T-shirt?
您能把名字簽在我的 T 恤上嗎？

au·ton·o·my [ɔˋtɑnəmɪ]

Track 5420

名 自治、自治權

▶Not everyone in this city think that it's necessary to strive for autonomy.
這城市裡不是每個人都認為有必要爭取自治權。

實用片語用語
strive for 爭取、為……奮鬥

a·vi·a·tion [͵evɪˋeʃən]

Track 5421

名 航空、飛行 同 flight 飛行

▶Both his father and he devoted all their lives to aviation.
他和他的父親都把自己的一生奉獻給了航空事業。

awe·some [ˋɔsəm]

Track 5422

形 有威嚴的

▶I think that movie was totally awesome.
我覺得那部電影真是太棒了。

文法字詞解析
awesome 這個單字一開始是「有威嚴的」的意思，後來在口語中逐漸轉化成了「很棒」的稱讚意味，而這個新的意思已經逐漸取代了這個單字的原意，因此如果聽到有人稱讚你做的某事很 awesome，他有很大的機率不是在說你有威嚴，純粹覺得你很棒而已。

ba·rom·e·ter [bəˋrɑmətɚ]

Track 5423

名 氣壓計、晴雨錶

▶The stock market is a barometer for business, isn't it?
股票市場是商業的晴雨錶，不是嗎？

beck·on [ˋbɛkn̩]

Track 5424

動 點頭示意、招手

▶Do you mind telling me why he beckoned me to come nearer?
麻煩你告訴我他為什麼招手叫我過去？

be·siege [bɪˋsidʒ] Track 5425

動 包圍、圍攻 **反** release 釋放

▶The enemy has been besieged by us since last month.
自從上個月起，敵軍就被我們包圍了。

be·tray [bɪˋtre] Track 5426

動 出賣、背叛 **同** deceive 欺騙

▶I am afraid that these people will betray us soon.
我擔心這些人很快就會背叛我們。

bev·er·age [ˋbɛvrəɪdʒ] Track 5427

名 飲料

▶This beverage is in a new flavor. Would you like to have a drink?
這種飲料是新口味的。你要不要喝喝看？

bi·as [ˋbaɪəs] Track 5428

名 偏心、偏袒 **動** 使存偏見

▶**名** You must deal with the matter without bias.
你必須無偏見地解決這件事情。

▶**動** Don't you know that he is biased against the plan from the beginning?
難道你不知道他從一開始就對這個計畫心存偏見嗎？

實用片語用語
be biased towards... 偏袒（某人、事、物）
例如：These judges are biased towards female students.
這些評審偏袒女學生。

bin·oc·u·lars [baɪˋnɑkjələ·z] Track 5429

名 雙筒望遠鏡

▶How about buying a pair of binoculars for your son as his birthday present?
買一副雙筒望遠鏡給你兒子作為他的生日禮物怎麼樣？

bi·o·chem·i·stry [ˏbaɪoˋkɛmɪstrɪ] Track 5430

名 生物化學

▶He does better in biochemistry than anyone else in his class.
他的生化學得比班上的任何其他人都要好。

bi·o·log·i·cal [ˏbaɪoˋlɑdʒɪkl] Track 5431

形 生物學的、有關生物學的

▶The advice has a solid biological basis; don't you think so?
這個建議具有堅固的生物學基礎，你不覺得嗎？

實用片語用語
biological clock 生理時鐘
例如：Going to sleep in the morning can mess up your biological clock.
早上才去睡覺可能會擾亂你的生理時鐘。

bi·zarre [bɪˋzɑr] Track 5432

形 古怪的、奇異的

▶The story sounds too bizarre to believe.
這個故事聽起來太奇怪了，我很難相信。

bleak [blik] Track 5433

形 淒涼的、暗淡的

▶I am afraid that our company's prospects will look rather bleak because of the financial crisis.
恐怕我們公司將會因為這次的金融危機而顯得前景異常暗淡。

blun·der [ˋblʌndɚ]

Track 5434

名 大錯 動 犯錯

▶名 Even if you make a terrible blunder, I believe she will forgive you.
即使你犯了天大的錯誤，我相信她也會原諒你的。

▶動 Even the best workman（工匠）sometimes blunders, so there is no need to blame yourself.
即使是最厲害的工匠也難免出錯，因此你沒必要自責。

實用片語用語
make a blunder 犯錯

blunt [blʌnt]

Track 5435

動 使遲鈍 形 遲鈍的 反 sharp 敏銳的

▶動 The drug blunted his senses, so it is too hard for him to keep awake.
藥使得他的感覺遲鈍了，因此他很難保持清醒。

▶形 The axe you gave me is too blunt to cut down the tree.
你給我的那把斧頭太鈍，砍不倒這棵樹。

bom·bard [bɑmˋbɑrd]

Track 5436

動 砲轟、轟擊

▶The man bombarded us with questions.
那個男人連珠砲似地問了我們一大堆問題。

bond·age [ˋbɑndɪdʒ]

Track 5437

名 奴役、囚禁

▶It is easy for a man to fall under the bondage of gold.
人很容易被金錢所奴役。

boost [bust]

Track 5438

名 幫助、促進 動 推動、增強、提高 同 increase 增加

▶名 They really need a boost to their morale.
他們非常需要激勵一下士氣。

▶動 This method should help boost sales.
這個策略應該能夠幫助促進銷售。

實用片語用語
give sb. a boost 將某人舉起
例如：Can you give me a boost? I can't get over the wall by myself.
可以幫忙把我推上去嗎？我自己翻不過這道牆。

bout [baʊt]

Track 5439

名 競賽的一回合

▶Will you tell me how many rounds there are in a bout?
你能告訴我一場比賽有幾局嗎？

boy·cott [ˋbɔɪˏkɑt]

Track 5440

名 杯葛、排斥 動 杯葛、聯合抵制

▶名 The law has harmed their interests. It is no wonder that they want to put it under a boycott. 該法律已侵害到了他們的利益。怪不得他們想聯合抵制它。

▶動 The delegates（代表） boycotted the meeting.
代表們都拒絕參加會議。

break·down [ˋbrekˏdaʊn]

Track 5441

名 故障、崩潰

▶The man had a nervous breakdown at the hospital.
那名男子在醫院情緒崩潰了。

實用片語用語
mental breakdown 崩潰
例如：He had a mental breakdown at work today.
他今天在工作時崩潰了。

break·through [ˋbrek͵θru]

Track 5442

名 突破

▶I hope the scientists could make a breakthrough in the treatment of that disease.
我希望科學家們能在治療那種疾病方面獲得突破。

break·up [ˋbrek͵ʌp]

Track 5443

名 分散、瓦解

▶It was a sequence of incidents that led to the couple's breakup. 正是這一連串的事件導致了這對情侶的分手。

brew [bru]

Track 5444

名 釀製物 動 釀製

▶名 I know what his favorite brew of beer is.
我知道他愛喝什麼樣的啤酒。

▶動 This wine brewed from rice tastes good.
這種酒是用米釀造的，味道不錯哦。

brink [brɪŋk]

Track 5445

名 陡峭邊緣

▶The company is on the brink of bankruptcy（破產）because of poor management.
這家公司已瀕臨破產的邊緣，因為它的管理不善。

實用片語用語
on the brink of... 在……的邊緣

brisk [brɪsk]

Track 5446

形 活潑的、輕快的

▶The old lady is a brisk walker. 這名老太太走路很快。

bro·chure [broˋʃʊr]

Track 5447

名 小冊子 同 pamphlet 小冊子

▶Would you please send me a brochure about your company?
請寄給我你們公司的簡介手冊好嗎？

brute [brut]

Track 5448

名 殘暴的人 形 粗暴的

▶名 He is an unfeeling（無情的）brute. You'd better stay away from him. 他是個無情的畜生。你最好離他遠一點。

▶形 He opened the door by brute force.
他以暴力將門打開。

buck·le [ˋbʌkḷ]

Track 5449

名 皮帶扣環 動 用扣環扣住 同 fasten 扣緊

▶名 The seatbelt buckle seems to be broken.
這安全帶扣環好像壞掉了。

▶動 Buckle up, or you might get fined.
要繫安全帶，不然你可能會被罰錢喔。

實用片語用語
buckle sb. in 幫某人綁好安全帶
例如：You'd better buckle your kids in.
你最好幫孩子們綁好安全帶。

bulk·y [ˋbʌlkɪ]

Track 5450

形 龐大的

▶It's so bulky and heavy that I can't manage to carry it alone.
它是如此龐大而沉重，以致我一個人搬不動它。

bu·reau·cra·cy [bjʊˋrɑkrəsɪ] Track 5451

名 官僚政治

▶It is impossible（不可能的）for us to understand the workings（運轉）of such a huge bureaucracy. 想瞭解這樣龐大的官僚體系的運作情況，對我們而言是不可能的。

bur·i·al [ˋbɛrɪəl] Track 5452

名 埋葬、下葬 同 funeral 葬儀、出殯

▶Her burial will take place next Monday. Will you go? If yes, I will go with you.
她的葬禮下星期一舉行，你會去嗎？你要去的話，我就跟你一起去。

實用片語用語
take place 舉行，發生

byte [baɪt] Track 5453

名【電算】位元組

▶How many megabytes can this computer hold?
這台電腦可以裝得下幾百萬位元的東西？

caf·feine [ˋkæfiɪn] Track 5454

名 咖啡因

▶There is a large amount of caffeine in this kind of coffee.
在這種咖啡裡有大量的咖啡因。

文法字詞解析
沒有咖啡因的咖啡可以稱為「decaf」，在這裡字首「de-」有「去除、沒有」的意思。

cal·ci·um [ˋkælsɪəm] Track 5455

名 鈣

▶It is obvious that calcium is beneficial to our bones.
顯然鈣對我們的骨骼有益。

can·vass [ˋkænvəs] Track 5456

名 審視、討論 動 詳細調查

▶名 There will be a canvass in the neighborhood next month.
下個月在鄰近地區有一次募捐活動。

▶動 It seems that the city council has canvassed the plan thoroughly.
市議會似乎已經詳細討論了那個計畫。

ca·pa·bil·i·ty [͵kepəˋbɪlətɪ] Track 5457

名 能力

▶As a scientist, he must have the capability of doing important research.
作為一名科學家，他必須具有從事重要科學研究的能力。

cap·sule [ˋkæpsḷ] Track 5458

名 膠囊

▶Would you please tell me how many capsules I should take per day? 可以請你告訴我每天該吃幾顆膠囊嗎？

實用片語用語
time capsule 時空膠囊
例如：The students buried a time capsule under the tree.
學生們在樹下埋了一個時空膠囊。

cap·tion [ˋkæpʃən]
Track 5459

名 標題、簡短說明 動 加標題

▶名 I am sure you can understand the meaning of this picture, because there is a caption under it.
我保證你能了瞭這幅圖片的意思，因為圖片下面附有說明。

▶動 I forgot to caption this article.
我忘了幫這篇文章加標題了。

cap·tive [ˋkæptɪv]
Track 5460

名 俘虜 形 被俘的 同 hostage 人質

▶名 He became a captive to her charms since the first time they met.
從他們第一次相見起，他就成了她美色的俘虜。

▶形 John was taken captive for almost 10 days by the enemy.
約翰被敵軍俘虜了將近十天。

cap·tiv·i·ty [kæpˋtɪvətɪ]
Track 5461

名 監禁、囚禁

▶It is said that he has been released from his long captivity.
據說他已經從長期被囚禁的生活中被釋放了。

實用片語用語
be released from sth.
從……當中釋放

car·b·o·hy·drate [ˏkɑrboˋhaɪdret]
Track 5462

名 碳水化合物、醣

▶You'd better not have too much carbohydrates in your diet.
在日常飲食中你最好不要吃過多的碳水化合物。

文法字詞解析
單字裡的「carbo-」就是從「carbon（碳）」而來，「hydrate-」則是「水合物」的意思，兩者合併一起看，是不是就能猜到「碳水化合物」了呢？

ca·ress [kəˋrɛs]
Track 5463

名 愛撫 動 撫觸 同 touch 碰觸

▶名 The lonely child is longing for the caress of his mother.
這個孤獨的孩子渴望母親的擁抱。

▶動 The young lady caressed that baby lovingly.
那位年輕的小姐疼愛地撫摸那個嬰兒。

car·ol [ˋkærəl]
Track 5464

名 頌歌、讚美詞

▶Children go caroling during the week before Christmas in lots of western countries.
在西方許多國家，耶誕節前一周孩子們會到各家各戶去報佳音。

cash·ier [kæˋʃɪr]
Track 5465

名 出納員

▶I wish I could find a position as a cashier after graduation.
我希望畢業後能得到一個出納員的職位。

cas·u·al·ty [ˋkæʒʊəltɪ]
Track 5466

名 意外事故、橫禍 同 accident 事故、災禍

▶There were dozens of casualties in the train crash.
在那次火車撞擊事故中有數十人傷亡。

實用片語用語
dozens of 非常多的、數十的

ca·tas·tro·phe [kəˋtæstrəfɪ]

Track 5467

名 大災難

▶This catastrophe killed over 16000 people, injuring more than 20000 people.
這場災難導致超過 16000 人死亡，以及 20000 人以上受傷。

ca·ter [ˋketɚ]

Track 5468

動 提供食物、提供娛樂

▶Some newspapers cater to people's love of scandal.
似乎有些報紙滿足了人們愛看醜聞的需要。

文法字詞解析
如果 cater 加上了字尾「-ing」就變成了名詞「提供食物」，也就是「外燴、承辦酒席」的意思。

cav·al·ry [ˋkævḷrɪ]

Track 5469

名 騎兵隊、騎兵

▶Not all his neighbors know that he was an officer in the cavalry when he was young.
不是他所有的鄰居都知道他年輕時曾是騎兵軍官。

cav·i·ty [ˋkævətɪ]

Track 5470

名 洞、穴

▶I am afraid that the cavity is not wide enough for me to get in.
洞口太窄了，我怕我會進不去。

文法字詞解析
因為蛀牙也是在牙齒中蛀出一個「洞穴」來，因此蛀牙也可以稱為 cavity。

cem·e·ter·y [ˋsɛməˏtɛrɪ]

Track 5471

名 公墓

▶It is said that his remains were shipped back and laid down in a cemetery. 據說他的遺體被運回並埋葬在一個公墓裡。

cer·tain·ty [ˋsɝtṇtɪ]

Track 5472

名 事實、確定的情況

▶I'm afraid that I have no certainty of success.
我恐怕沒有成功的把握。

cer·ti·fy [ˋsɝtəˏfaɪ]

Track 5473

動 證明

▶You should ask the bank manager to certify this check.
你應該請銀行經理來簽署證明這張支票。

cham·pagne [ʃæmˋpen]

Track 5474

名 白葡萄酒、香檳

▶Let's open a bottle of champagne to celebrate, shall we?
我們開瓶香檳酒來慶祝一下，好嗎？

文法字詞解析
champagne 這個單字是從法國來的，因此它的發音也比較特別。注意一下開頭的 ch 和我們常說的 chair 的 ch 發音方法不一樣喔！

cha·os [ˋkeɑs]

Track 5475

名 無秩序、大混亂 同 confusion 混亂

▶There was chaos in the town after the hurricane had struck.
颶風過後，城裡一片混亂。

char·ac·ter·ize [ˋkærɪktəˏraɪz]

Track 5476

動 描述……的性質、具有……特徵

▶This kind of dog is characterized by its curly fur.
這種狗的特徵是捲捲的毛。

char·coal [ˋtʃɑr͵kol]

Track 5477

名 炭、木炭

▶Would you please help me move the charcoal to the trunk?
可以請你幫我把木炭搬到後車廂裡嗎？

文法字詞解析
charcoal 也可以當作一種「顏色」（即指木炭的顏色）。

char·i·ot [ˋtʃærɪət]

Track 5478

名 戰車、駕駛戰車

▶There is a picture of a fighter standing on a chariot on the wall. 牆上有一幅武士站在戰車上的畫。

char·i·ta·ble [ˋtʃærətəbl̩]

Track 5479

形 溫和的、仁慈的

▶He enjoys doing charitable work.
他是個樂善好施的人。

cho·les·ter·ol [kəˋlɛstə͵rol]

Track 5480

名 膽固醇

▶His high cholesterol levels are a huge worry for his family.
他的高膽固醇對於他的家人造成很大的煩惱。

chron·ic [ˋkrɑnɪk]

Track 5481

形 長期的、持續的 同 constant 持續的

▶There is a chronic unemployment problem in America.
美國存在著長期失業的問題。

實用片語用語
chronic disease 慢性疾病
例如：This kind of chronic disease runs in his family.
他們家裡都有遺傳這個慢性疾病。

chuck·le [ˋtʃʌkl̩]

Track 5482

名 滿足的輕笑 動 輕輕地笑

▶名 She let out a small chuckle when she saw the picture in the magazine.
她看到雜誌裡那張圖時輕輕笑了一下。

▶動 The boys were chuckling over the photograph.
那些男孩們看著照片咯咯地笑了起來。

chunk [tʃʌŋk]

Track 5483

名 厚塊、厚片

▶A good chunk of my time was spent on correcting your mistakes.
我大部分的時間都花在修正你的錯誤上。

實用片語用語
a good chunk of time 很大一部份的時間

civ·i·lize [ˋsɪvə͵laɪz]

Track 5484

動 啓發、使開化 同 educate 教育

▶The people in that area have not been civilized yet.
那一區的人還沒有開化。

clamp [klæmp]

Track 5485

名 夾子、鉗子 動 以鉗子轉緊

▶名 He had to hold the hooks together with a clamp.
他得用一個夾子把那些勾子夾在一起。

▶動 Why don't you clamp these two pieces of wood together?
為什麼不把兩根木頭鉗緊呢？

實用片語用語
clamp together 夾緊

cla·r·ity [ˋklærətɪ] Track 5486

名 清澈透明

▶He speaks with clarity and grace.
他說話的方式清楚而優雅。

cleanse [klɛnz] Track 5487

動 淨化、弄清潔

▶You had better cleanse the wound before stitching it.
在縫合之前你最好先把傷口清洗乾淨。

clear·ance [ˋklɪrəns] Track 5488

名 清潔、清掃

▶All these clothes are labeled for clearance.
這些衣服都標示要出清。

clench [klɛntʃ] Track 5489

名 緊握 動 握緊、咬緊

▶名 I felt the clench of someone's hand on my arm.
我感覺到有個人的手牢牢地抓住我的手臂。

▶動 He clenched his teeth and refused to tell anything.
他咬緊牙關什麼也不肯說。

實用片語用語

clench sb.'s fist 握緊拳頭
例如：He clenched his fists in nervousness before the match.
比賽前他緊張地握緊拳頭。

clin·i·cal [ˋklɪnɪkl̩] Track 5490

形 門診的

▶It seemed that this new therapy hasn't passed the clinical trial（試驗）yet.
這個新療法似乎尚未通過臨床試驗。

clone [klon] Track 5491

名 無性繁殖、複製 同 copy 複製

▶I don't know why this new laptop is so popular; it is obvious that it's nothing but an IBM clone.
我不知道這台筆記型電腦為什麼這麼受歡迎，很顯然地它不過是台IBM的複製品罷了。

clo·sure [ˋkloʒɚ] Track 5492

名 封閉、結尾 同 conclusion 結尾

▶The closure of the large factory sent many workers into unemployment.
那家大工廠倒閉使許多工人失業。

coffin [ˋkɔfɪn] Track 5493

名 棺材

▶He is so tall that he can't fit in the coffin.
他高到棺材都裝不下了。

實用片語用語

coffin lid 棺材蓋
例如：This coffin lid doesn't fit the coffin.
這棺材蓋和棺材不合啊。

co·her·ent [koˋhɪrənt] Track 5494

形 連貫的、有條理的

▶The lyrics he wrote were all over the place and not coherent at all.
他寫的歌詞毫無重點，完全沒有條理。

co·in·cide [koɪn`saɪd] Track 5495

動 一致、同意 同 accord 一致

▶It is obvious that the demonstration had been carefully stage-managed to coincide with the Prime Minister's visit.
顯然這次示威活動事先作了精心的安排，正好在首相訪問時進行。

co·in·ci·dence [ko`ɪnsdəns] Track 5496

名 巧合

▶I'm afraid that that's the most incredible coincidence I've ever heard of!
恐怕那是我聽說過的最難以置信的巧合！

實用片語用語
by coincidence 巧合地
例如：We ran into each other by coincidence yesterday.
我們昨天很巧地遇到對方。

col·lec·tive [kə`lɛktɪv] Track 5497

名 集體 形 共同的、集體的

▶名 Only with organization can the wisdom of the collective be given full play.
集體智慧唯有組織後才能充份被發揮。

▶形 The collective consensus is that we really should not accept these terms.
大家的共識是我們真的不應該接受這些條件。

實用片語用語
give sth. full play 充分發揮……

col·lec·tor [kə`lɛktɚ] Track 5498

名 收集的器具

▶The stamp collector had hundreds of volumes containing valuable stamps.
那位集郵迷有上百本裝著高價郵票的冊子。

col·lide [kə`laɪd] Track 5499

動 碰撞 同 bump 碰撞

▶It is reported that the bus collided with a van when turning the corner.
根據報導這台公車在轉過街角時與小貨車相撞。

萬用延伸句型
It is reported that... 據報導……

col·li·sion [kə`lɪʒən] Track 5500

名 相撞、碰撞、猛撞

▶The car was completely wrecked by the force of the collision.
這輛汽車由於受到很大的撞擊力而全部損毀。

col·lo·qui·al [kə`lokwɪəl] Track 5501

形 白話的、通俗的

▶It's much more useful to learn colloquial English than super formal English.
學口語英文比學超級正式的英文來得有用多了。

col·um·nist [`kɑləmɪst] Track 5502

名 專欄作家

▶There is a very popular columnist commenting on current affairs for that newspaper.
有一位深受歡迎的專欄作家為那家報紙評論時事。

文法字詞解析
是不是覺得這個字很眼熟呢？我們先前學過的「column」有「樑柱」和「專欄」的意思，因為報紙中的專欄都是長長一條、像柱子一樣的；而 columnist 就是在後面加上代表「專精某個領域的人」的名詞字尾「-ist」。

com·mem·o·rate [kə`mɛmə,ret]

Track 5503

動 祝賀、慶祝 同 celebrate 慶祝

▶It is said that Christmas commemorates the birth of Christ.
據說耶誕節是為了紀念耶穌的誕生。

萬用延伸句型
It is said that... 據說……

com·mence [kə`mɛns]

Track 5504

動 開始

▶The performances will commence from 6：30 p.m. It's time for us to set out.
演出將於晚上 6 點 30 分開始，我們該出發了。

com·men·tar·y [`kɑmən,tɛrɪ]

Track 5505

名 注釋、說明

▶I don't think that his commentary on this issue is correct.
我不認為他對這個問題的評論是正確的。

com·mit·ment [kə`mɪtmənt]

Track 5506

名 承諾、拘禁、託付

▶Your commitment towards your work is highly appreciated.
我們很欣賞你對工作的投入奉獻。

實用片語用語
commitment towards sth.
對某事的投入奉獻

com·mu·ni·ca·tive [kə`mjunə,ketɪv]

Track 5507

形 愛說話的、口無遮攔的

▶Both Sara and her sister are very communicative people with positive personalities.
莎拉和她的姐姐都非常暢談，且擁有積極的個性。

com·pan·ion·ship [kəm`pænjən,ʃɪp]

Track 5508

名 友誼、交往

▶The reason why I trust her so much is that we have a companionship of many years.
我之所以能如此信任她，是因為我們有多年的交情。

com·pa·ra·ble [`kɑmpərəbl̩]

Track 5509

形 可對照的、可比較的

▶It is obvious that their achievements are not comparable.
顯然他們的成就不能相提並論。

com·par·a·tive [kəm`pærətɪv]

Track 5510

形 比較上的、相對的

▶I majored in comparative literature in college. What about you?
我大學的主修是比較文學。你呢？

實用片語用語
comparative literature 比較文學

com·pat·i·ble [kəm`pætəbl̩]

Track 5511

形 一致的、和諧的

▶Even though Susan and I have very different backgrounds, we are very compatible.
雖說我和蘇珊的背景很不相同，但我們非常合得來。

com·pen·sate [ˋkɑmpən͵set] Track 5512

動 抵銷、彌補

▶I'm afraid that nothing can compensate for the loss of one's health. 恐怕什麼都不能補償健康的受損。

com·pen·sa·tion [͵kəmpənˋseʃən] Track 5513

名 報酬、賠償

▶The reason why he didn't get any compensation was that his insurance policy had lapsed（失效）. 他因保險單失效而未能獲得任何補償。

實用片語用語

as compensation 以作為補償

例如：We would send you a thousand dollars as compensation.

我們會送給您一千美元作為補償。

com·pe·tence [ˋkɑmpətəns] Track 5514

名 能力、才能

▶He has shown a lot of competence in the week he has been here. 他在這裡的一週來表現出來相當大的才幹。

com·pe·tent [ˋkɑmpətənt] Track 5515

形 能幹的、有能力的

▶He is competent enough to fill that position in my view. 在我看來，他足以勝任那個職位。

com·pile [kəmˋpaɪl] Track 5516

動 收集、資料彙編 同 collect 收集

▶It takes years of hard work to compile a good dictionary. 編一本好字典需要多年的艱苦工作。

com·ple·ment [ˋkɑmpləmənt] Track 5517

名 補足物 動 補充、補足

▶名 It is obvious that homework is a necessary complement to classroom study. 顯然功課是課堂教學的必要補充。

▶動 This wine complements the food perfectly. 顯然用這種酒配這些菜餚是相得益彰。

實用片語用語

complement to sth. ……的補充

com·plex·ion [kəmˋplɛkʃən] Track 5518

名 氣色、血色

▶I'm afraid that that color doesn't suit your complexion. 恐怕那個顏色不適合你的膚色。

com·plex·i·ty [kəmˋplɛksətɪ] Track 5519

名 複雜

▶I am afraid that this is a political problem of great complexity. 恐怕這是一個複雜的政治問題。

com·pli·ca·tion [͵kəmpləˋkeʃən] Track 5520

名 複製、混亂

▶We're trying to solve all the complications that have arisen in the past two weeks. 我們正在試著解決前兩週出現的一堆新問題。

com·po·nent [kəm`ponənt]

Track 5521

名 成分、部件 形 合成的、構成的 同 part 部分

▶名 A computer consists of thousands of components.
電腦是由上千萬的零件所組成。

▶形 Yoga is an important component part in her life.
瑜伽是她生活中重要的組成部分。

實用片語用語
be an important component in...
在……之中是很重要的一部分

com·pre·hen·sive [ˌkɑmprɪ`hɛnsɪv]

Track 5522

形 廣泛的、包羅萬象的

▶I read the comprehensive guide to game designing, but there are still lots of things I don't understand.
我讀了遊戲設計的綜合指南，但還是有很多點我不太懂。

com·prise [kəm`praɪz]

Track 5523

動 由……構成

▶The medical team comprises of three doctors and six nurses.
這個醫療團隊是由三位醫師和六個護士所組成的。

con·cede [kən`sid]

Track 5524

動 承認、讓步 同 confess 承認

▶I am afraid that you have no choice but to concede in this matter.
恐怕在這件事情上你只能讓步了。

萬用延伸句型
have no choice but to...
無可選擇，只能……

con·ceit [kən`sit]

Track 5525

名 自負、自大

▶His conceit makes him hard to approach.
他的自負讓他很難以接近。

con·cep·tion [kən`sɛpʃən]

Track 5526

名 概念、計畫 同 idea 計畫、概念

▶He has absolutely no conception of how to run a business.
他對於經營生意完全一點概念都沒有。

con·ces·sion [kən`sɛʃən]

Track 5527

名 讓步、妥協

▶I wish you could make some concession. Can you?
我希望你能做一些讓步。可以嗎？

實用片語用語
make concession 讓步、妥協

con·cise [kən`saɪs]

Track 5528

形 簡潔的、簡明的

▶Would you please give me a clear and concise summary?
請你給我一個簡潔扼要的總結好嗎？

con·dense [kən`dɛns]

Track 5529

動 縮小、濃縮

▶I'm afraid that you are supposed to condense your report; it's too long.
恐怕你應該濃縮一下你的報告，它太冗長了。

con·fer [kən'fɝ] *Track 5530*

動 商議、商討

▶Why don't we confer with the advisers before making a decision? 為什麼不先請教顧問然後再來做決定呢？

con·fi·den·tial [ˌkɑnfə'dɛnʃəl] *Track 5531*

形 可信任的、機密的 同 secret 機密的

▶This meeting and the entire arrangement are supposed to be confidential. 這次會議以及所有安排應該都是保密的。

實用片語用語

confidential files 機密文件

Do not let anyone see those confidential files.
不要讓任何人看見這些機密文件。

con·form [kən'fɔrm] *Track 5532*

動 使符合、類似

▶I am afraid that if you don't start conforming to the rules, you may be kicked out of the school.
如果你不遵守校規的話，恐怕就有可能被退學。

con·fron·ta·tion *Track 5533*

[ˌkɑnfrʌn'teʃən]

名 對抗、對峙

▶The confrontation with him yesterday was still fresh in my mind. 昨天和他起衝突的事，我現在依然記得很清楚。

con·gress·man/
con·gress·wom·an *Track 5534*

['kɑŋgrəsˌmæn]/['kɑŋgrəsˌwʊmən]

名 眾議員／女眾議員

▶It is reported that the congressman was murdered.
據報導那位眾議員是被謀殺的。

con·quest ['kɑŋkwɛst] *Track 5535*

名 征服、獲勝 同 submit 使屈服

▶The handsome and rich man made a conquest of Mary's heart. 這個又帥又有錢的男人擄獲了瑪莉的芳心。

實用片語用語

make a conquest of 征服

con·sci·en·tious [ˌkɑnʃɪ'ɛnʃəs] *Track 5536*

形 本著良心的、有原則的 同 faithful 忠誠的

▶She is the most conscientious staff member in our office.
她是我們辦公室裡最盡責的員工。

con·sen·sus [kən'sɛnsəs] *Track 5537*

名 一致、全體意見

▶The consensus of the whole team is that we should practice on Saturdays only.
我們全隊的共識是我們只要在每週六練習。

con·ser·va·tion [ˌkɑnsə'veʃən] *Track 5538*

名 保存、維護

▶People need to understand the need for conservation of natural resources.
人們必須認識到保護自然資源的必要性。

文法字詞解析

這個字和 conversation（會話）很像，只是把 s 和 v 調換過來而已，但意思卻大不相同，要注意不要寫錯了。

con·so·la·tion [ˌkɑnsəˋleʃən] Track 5539

名 撫恤、安慰、慰藉 反 pain 使痛苦

▶It is obvious that her child is her only consolation.
顯然她的孩子是她唯一的安慰。

萬用延伸句型
If it's any consolation... 如果這樣能安慰到你的話……
例如：If it's any consolation, I'm just about as clueless as you are.
如果這樣能安慰到你的話，那就是「我也跟你一樣完全不懂呢」。

con·spir·a·cy [kənˋspɪrəsɪ] Track 5540

名 陰謀

▶You had better be cautious about their conspiracy.
你最好要小心他們的陰謀。

con·stit·u·ent [kənˋstɪtʃuənt] Track 5541

名 成分、組成要素 形 組成的、成分的 同 component 成分

▶名 It is obvious that political harmony is the important constituent of a harmonious society.
顯然政治和諧是和諧社會的重要組成要素。

▶形 Not everyone knows what the constituent parts of happiness are.
不是每個人都知道幸福的組成要素是什麼。

con·sul·ta·tion [ˌkɑnsḷˋteʃən] Track 5542

名 討教、諮詢

▶The couple resolved their differences with consultation.
那對夫妻透過諮商來解決他們之間的不愉快。

con·sump·tion [kənˋsʌmpʃən] Track 5543

名 消費、消費量 同 waste 消耗

▶I think there is too great a consumption of alcohol in China.
我覺得酒在中國的消耗量太大了。

實用片語用語
alcohol consumption 酒精消耗量

con·tem·pla·tion [ˌkɑntɛmˋpleʃən] Track 5544

名 注視、凝視

▶He reached a decision after a good deal of contemplation.
他在經過深思熟慮後才做出決定。

con·test·ant [kənˋtɛstənt] Track 5545

名 競爭者

▶The contestants are asked to get to know each other.
參賽者們被要求先彼此熟悉。

con·trac·tor [ˋkɑntræktɚ] Track 5546

名 立契約者

▶Would you let me know who the contractor of the new motorway（高速公路）is?
麻煩您告訴我誰是這條新公路的承包商？

con·tra·dict [ˌkɑntrəˋdɪkt] Track 5547

動 反駁、矛盾、否認

▶It is obvious that the report contradicts what we heard yesterday.
顯然這個報導與我們昨天聽到的有所出入。

實用片語用語
contradict oneself 自相矛盾
例如：The muddled girl often contradicts herself when telling a story.
這個腦筋不太清楚的女孩在說故事時總是自相矛盾。

con·tra·dic·tion [ˌkɑntrəˋdɪkʃən] Track 5548

名 否定、矛盾 同 denial 否認

▶There is a contradiction between his statement and hers.
他和她的聲明之間有矛盾之處。

con·tro·ver·sial [ˌkɑntrəˋvɝʃəl] Track 5549

形 爭論的、議論的

▶The lawyer loves challenges and was glad to take up this controversial case.
那位律師很喜歡挑戰，所以很樂意處理這件有爭議的案件。

con·tro·ver·sy [ˋkɑntrəˌvɝsɪ] Track 5550

名 辯論、爭論

▶There was a huge controversy over the plans for the new school.
眾人對建造新學校的計畫存有極大爭議。

文法字詞解析
上面幾個字都可以感覺到「相反、牴觸」的意思存在，因為字首「contra-、contro-」就有「相對」的意思。不過「contractor」是從「contract（合約）」在加上名詞字尾「-or（人）」而來，和其他的字是不一樣的，不要搞混了。

con·vic·tion [kənˋvɪkʃən] Track 5551

名 定罪、說服力

▶There is no conviction in your voice.
你說話的聲音中毫無決心。

實用片語用語
lack conviction 沒有說服力
例如：His arguments lack conviction. He doesn't seem to even believe in them himself.
他的論點缺乏說服力，似乎連他自己都不太相信。

co·or·di·nate Track 5552

[koˋɔrdṇet]/[koˋɔrdṇɪt]

動 調和、使同等 形 同等的 同 equal 同等的

▶動 Once we coordinate our efforts, we will be sure to win this game.
一旦我們同心協力，我們一定能夠打贏這場比賽。

▶形 These are coordinate clauses.
這是兩句並列句。

cor·dial [ˋkɔrdʒəl] Track 5553

形 熱忱的、和善的

▶He received a cordial welcome at Cambridge.
他在劍橋受到了熱誠的歡迎。

core [kor] Track 5554

名 果核、核心

▶Let us get to the core of the matter, okay?
讓我們回到事情的重點好嗎？

cor·po·rate [ˋkɔrpərɪt] Track 5555

形 社團的、公司的

▶The corporate spy got into deep trouble.
這位商業間諜惹了大麻煩。

實用片語用語
corporate spy 商業間諜

corps [korps] Track 5556

名 軍團、兵團

▶It is said that his father served in the medical corps during World War II.
據說在第二次大戰時，他父親在醫務部隊服過役。

corpse [kɔrps]
Track 5557

名 屍體、屍首

▶The girl screamed when she saw the corpse.
那個女孩看到屍體的時候尖叫了起來。

cor·re·spon·dent
Track 5558

[ˌkɔrəˋspɑndənt]

名 通信者 同 journalist 新聞工作者

▶There are many correspondents from *The New York Times* residing in many countries.
在許多國家都有很多《紐約時報》的通訊記者。

cor·rup·tion [kəˋrʌpʃən]
Track 5559

名 敗壞、墮落

▶The corruption in their government isn't something that can be solved in one day.
他們政府的腐敗不是一天兩天就能解決的事情。

萬用延伸句型
...isn't something that can be solved in one day ……不是一天就能解決的事

cos·met·ic [kɑzˋmɛtɪk]
Track 5560

形 化妝用的

▶You had better solve this problem by using cosmetic cream.
你最好透過使用美容霜來解決這個問題。

cos·met·ics [kɑzˋmɛtɪks]
Track 5561

名 化妝品

▶How about buying some cosmetics for her as a Mother's Day present?
買點化妝品給她作為母親節禮物怎麼樣？

cos·mo·pol·i·tan
Track 5562

[ˌkɑzməˋpɑlətn̩]

名 世界主義者 形 世界主義的 同 international 國際的

▶名 Aaron is not only a scholar but also a rootless（無根的）cosmopolitan.
艾倫不但是個學者，還是個四海漂泊的人。

▶形 Beijing is not only the capital of China but also a cosmopolitan city.
北京不僅是中國的首都，而且是一個國際大都市。

coun·ter·part [ˋkaʊntɚˌpɑrt]
Track 5563

名 副本

▶Not everybody knows that the U.S. Congress is the counterpart of the British Parliament.
不是每個人都知道美國的國會相當於英國的議會。

實用片語用語
be the counterpart of... 相當於……

cov·er·age [ˋkʌvərɪdʒ]
Track 5564

名 覆蓋範圍、保險範圍

▶We need more media coverage if we really want the whole country to know about what happened.
如果真要讓全國的人知道發生了什麼事，我們就需要更多媒體報導。

cov·et [ˋkʌvɪt]

Track 5565

動 垂涎、貪圖

▶It is Tom who finally won the prize that all of us coveted.
是湯姆最終贏得了大家都渴望得到的獎品。

cramp [kræmp]

Track 5566

名 抽筋、鉗子 動 用鉗子夾緊、使抽筋

▶名 She got cramps in her leg when she was swimming.
她游泳的時候腿抽筋了。

▶動 The room is so cramped and stuffy. Let's just leave.
這房間太擠了、又悶，我們還是離開吧。

實用片語用語
get cramps 抽筋

cred·i·bil·i·ty [ˏkrɛdəˋbɪlətɪ]

Track 5567

名 可信度、確實性

▶The president has lost all credibility with the people.
那名總統在人民眼中的威信已喪失。

實用片語用語
lost credibility 失去可信度

cred·i·ble [ˋkrɛdəbḷ]

Track 5568

形 可信的、可靠的

▶Is the evidence you found credible?
你找到的證據可靠嗎？

cri·te·ri·on [kraɪˋtɪrɪən]

Track 5569

名 標準、基準 同 standard 標準

▶Would you tell me what criteria you use when judging the quality of a student's work?
您能告訴我您是用什麼標準來衡量學生的課業嗎？

文法字詞解析
這裡要注意，criterion 的複數形是 criteria。

crook [krʊk]

Track 5570

名 彎曲、彎處 動 使彎曲

▶名 Watch out! There's a crook in the road.
小心點！前面的路有個拐彎。

▶動 He crooked his arm around the box.
他把手臂彎著圈住了箱子。

文法字詞解析
因為惡棍的個性多半是「不正直的」，既然不直也就是「彎的」，因此惡棍也可以稱為 crook。

crooked [ˋkrʊkɪd]

Track 5571

形 彎曲的、歪曲的

▶His back is so crooked that he cannot stand upright.
他的背彎得都站不直了。

cru·cial [ˋkruʃəl]

Track 5572

形 關係重大的 同 important 重大的

▶These negotiations are crucial to the future of our firm.
這些談判對我們公司的前途非常重要。

crude [krud]

Track 5573

形 天然的、未加工的

▶It is said that the great man was born in a crude hut.
據說那個偉人生於一個簡陋的小屋裡。

cruise [kruz]

Track 5574

動 航行、巡航

▶The ship cruised lazily on the river.
那艘船在河上緩緩地航行。

實用片語用語
cruise ship 遊輪
例如：I've always wanted to spend a holiday on a cruise ship.
我一直都很想搭遊輪度假。

cruis·er [ˋkruzɚ]

Track 5575

名 遊艇

▶The cruiser fell behind the others because its controls was broken.
那艘遊艇落在其他艦隻的後面，因為它的控制盤壞掉了。

crumb [krʌm]

Track 5576

名 小塊、碎屑、少許

▶The birds are eating crumbs off the ground.
這些小鳥在吃地上的碎屑。

crum·ble [ˋkrʌmbl̩]

Track 5577

名 碎屑、碎片 動 弄成碎屑 同 mash 壓碎

▶名 The puppy is eating the cookie crumbles.
那隻小狗在吃餅乾碎屑。

▶動 She has a tendency to crumble her bread on the table.
她很容易把麵包碎屑弄到桌子上。

crust [krʌst]

Track 5578

名 麵包皮、派皮 動 覆以外皮

▶名 How about putting tomato sauce and cheese on the crust?
我們把番茄醬和起司放在派皮上怎麼樣？

▶動 The snow crusted the lake last night.
昨夜的雪使湖面結了冰。

實用片語用語
pie crust 派皮
例如：The pie crust is my favorite part of the pie.
派皮是在一整個派中我最喜歡的部分。

cul·ti·vate [ˋkʌltəˏvet]

Track 5579

動 耕種

▶My parents work hard to cultivate the plants.
我的父母很努力培育植物。

cu·mu·la·tive [ˋkjumjəˏletɪv]

Track 5580

形 累增的、累加的

▶The process of improvement is a cumulative one.
進步的過程是逐漸積累的。

cus·tom·ar·y [ˋkʌstəmˏɛrɪ]

Track 5581

形 慣例的、平常的

▶It's customary for people to give others gifts on their birthdays.
有人生日時送他生日禮物是很平常的事。

萬用延伸句型
It's customary for... 對……來說是一種慣例

daf·fo·dil [ˋdæfədɪl]　Track 5582

名 黃水仙

▶Have you ever seen a daffodil? What does it look like?
你有看過黃水仙嗎？它長什麼樣子呢？

dan·druff [ˋdændrəf]　Track 5583

名 頭皮屑

▶Would you like some hair tonic（護髮素）? It helps prevent dandruff.
要擦點護髮素嗎？它有助於防止頭皮屑。

萬用延伸句型
sth. helps prevent...（某物）有助於預防……

day·break [ˋde͵brek]　Track 5584

名 破曉、黎明

▶By the time my father came back home, it was daybreak.
父親回來時天已破曉。

dead·ly [ˋdɛdlɪ]　Track 5585

形 致命的 副 極度地

▶形 If only the doctors could cure this deadly disease soon.
要是醫生們能很快治好這種致命的疾病，該有多好啊。

▶副 If only I could stay at home when the air was deadly cold.
在極度寒冷的時候，我要是能待在家裡就好了。

de·cent [ˋdisn̩t]　Track 5586

形 端正的、正當的 同 correct 端正的

▶It is not decent for one to laugh at a funeral, so please keep a straight face.
在葬禮時發笑是失禮的，因此請保持嚴肅。

實用片語用語
keep a straight face 板起臉孔、保持嚴肅的面貌

de·ci·sive [dɪˋsaɪsɪv]　Track 5587

形 有決斷力的

▶She's not a very decisive person.
她這個人相當優柔寡斷。

文法字詞解析
相反地，「沒有決斷力的」、「優柔寡斷的」則可以用 indecisive 這個字來形容。

de·cline [dɪˋklaɪn]　Track 5588

名 衰敗 動 下降、衰敗、婉拒

▶名 Grandpa is on the decline and may die soon.
爺爺的健康每況愈下，可能不久於人世。

▶動 I declined his invitation because I had another appointment.
我婉拒了他的邀請，因為我還有約。

ded·i·cate [ˋdɛdə͵ket]　Track 5589

動 供奉、奉獻 同 devote 奉獻

▶He dedicated his first book to his teacher.
他把自己的第一本書獻給了自己的老師。

ded·i·ca·tion [ˌdɛdəˋkeʃən] Track 5590

名 奉獻、供奉

▶Her talent and dedication will insure her success, won't they?
她的才氣和奉獻將確保她成功，不是嗎？

deem [dim] Track 5591

動 認為、視為 同 consider 認為

▶Not everyone deems it his / her duty to help others.
不是每個人都認為幫助他人是自己的責任。

萬用延伸句型
deem it sb.'s duty to...
認為……是自己的責任

de·fect [dɪˋfɛkt] Track 5592

名 缺陷、缺點 動 脫逃、脫離

▶名 This product has several defects. 這個產品有許多缺陷。

▶動 The young scientist defected to another country.
這名年輕的科學家叛逃到另一國家去了。

de·fi·cien·cy [dɪˋfɪʃənsɪ] Track 5593

名 匱乏、不足 同 shortage 短缺

▶It is obvious that there are many deficiencies in the system.
顯然這一制度存在諸多缺陷。

de·grade [dɪˋgred] Track 5594

動 降級、降等

▶You are not supposed to degrade yourself by telling such a lie. 你不應該說那樣的謊話來降低自己的人格。

實用片語用語
degrade oneself by V-ing 以……來降低自己的人格

de·lib·er·ate [dɪˋlɪbəret]/[dɪˋlɪbərɪt] Track 5595

動 仔細考慮 形 慎重的

▶動 We still need to deliberate how the plan should be carried out. 我們仍需慎重考慮該如何去做那件事。

▶形 He slammed the door in a deliberate manner.
他故意摔上了門。

實用片語用語
in a deliberate manner 故意地

de·lin·quent [dɪˋlɪŋkwənt] Track 5596

名 違法者 形 拖欠的、違法的

▶名 He became a delinquent in the end. 他最後成了罪犯。

▶形 Several years have passed since it happened and still we had not found the delinquent party.
這件事情已經過去好幾年了，但我們還是沒找到違法的當事人。

de·nounce [dɪˋnaʊns] Track 5597

動 公然抨擊

▶She denounced her sister for being unfaithful to her husband.
她抨擊她妹妹對丈夫不忠。

den·si·ty [ˋdɛnsətɪ] Track 5598

名 稠密、濃密

▶I don't like the density of population in the city.
我不喜歡城市這麼高的人口密度。

den·tal [ˋdɛntļ]

Track 5599

形 牙齒的

▶Do you mind telling me what causes dental cavities（蛀牙）?
麻煩你告訴我蛀牙是由什麼引起的？

實用片語用語
dental floss 牙線
例如：I make it a habit to use dental floss after eating.
我習慣吃完東西後用牙線。

de·pict [dɪˋpɪkt]

Track 5600

動 描述、敘述

▶The picture depicts the dark, gloomy scenes of war.
那幅畫描繪的是戰爭黑暗而悲傷的景象。

de·prive [dɪˋpraɪv]

Track 5601

動 剝奪、使……喪失

▶It is clear that the government cannot deprive its people of their basic rights.
顯然政府不能剝奪人民的基本權利。

de·rive [dəˋraɪv]

Track 5602

動 引出、源自

▶Not all people know that many English words are derived from Latin.
不是所有人都知道許多英語單字其實是源於拉丁文。

實用片語用語
be derived from 源於……
除了 be derived from 之外，originate from... 也有「源自……」的意思。

dep·u·ty [ˋdɛpjətɪ]

Track 5603

名 代表、代理人 同 agent 代理人

▶Would you like to be my deputy while I am away, Mike?
麥克，你願意在我不在的時候當我的代理人嗎？

de·scend [dɪˋsɛnd]

Track 5604

動 下降、突襲 同 drop 下降

▶The elevator descended into the basement.
電梯降入地下室。

de·scen·dant [dɪˋsɛndənt]

Track 5605

名 子孫、後裔

▶Suppose you were a descendant of a loyal family. What would you do for the people?
假如你是一位皇族後裔，你會為人民做些什麼呢？

萬用延伸句型
Suppose you were... 假如你是……

de·scent [dɪˋsɛnt]

Track 5606

名 下降

▶The descent of the plane was smooth and without trouble.
飛機下降的過程順利且毫無問題。

des·ig·nate [ˋdɛzɪg͵net]

Track 5607

動 指出 形 選派的

▶動 They designated Boston as the unloading（卸貨）port.
他們選擇波士頓為卸貨港。

▶形 Why don't we talk about this matter with the ambassador designate?
為何不跟大使指定人選探討一下這件事呢？

des·tined [ˋdɛstɪnd]

Track 5608

形 命運註定的

▶They are destined never to see each other again.
他們命中註定再也不能相見了。

de·tach [dɪˋtætʃ]

Track 5609

動 派遣、分開 同 separate 分開

▶You'd better not detach the watch from your wrist, or you might lose it very easily.
你最好不要把錶從手腕上取下來，要不然你會很容易就把它搞丟。

文法字詞解析
要說一個人的態度很「抽離」，可以用相關的形容詞 detached 來描述。

de·tain [dɪˋten]

Track 5610

動 阻止、妨礙

▶The bad weather has detained us for several hours.
這惡劣的天氣耽擱了我們好幾個小時。

de·ter [dɪˋtɝ]

Track 5611

動 使停止做

▶The bad weather deterred us from going out.
壞天氣使得我們不想出門。

de·te·ri·o·rate [dɪˋtɪrɪəˏret]

Track 5612

動 惡化、降低

▶Once the food is in contact with air, it will deteriorate rapidly.
一旦這種食物接觸到空氣，它就會迅速變壞。

實用片語用語
deteriorating health 惡化的健康
例如：Grandpa's deteriorating health has everyone worried.
爺爺逐漸惡化的健康讓大家都很擔心。

de·val·ue [diˋvælju]

Track 5613

動 降低價值

▶The country has decided to devalue the dollar to mitigate（緩和）the economic recession.
該國對美元實行貶值來減緩經濟衰退。

di·a·be·tes [ˏdaɪəˋbitiz]

Track 5614

名 糖尿病

▶It seems that the stranger on the plane knows a lot about diabetes.
聽起來在飛機上的這個陌生人似乎很瞭解糖尿病。

di·ag·nose [ˋdaɪəgnoz]

Track 5615

動 診斷

▶It is rather difficult for the doctor to diagnose the rare disease.
醫生很難診斷出這種罕見的疾病。

di·ag·no·sis [ˏdaɪəgˋnosɪs]

Track 5616

名 診斷（複數）

▶Not until the next day did I know the doctor's diagnosis of my disease.
直到第二天我才獲知醫生對我的病的診斷情況。

實用片語用語
make a diagnosis 做出診斷
例如：The doctor was unable to make a diagnosis right away.
這位醫生無法立即就做出診斷。

di·a·gram [ˋdaɪə͵græm]

Track 5617

名 圖表、圖樣 動 圖解 同 design 圖樣

▶名 Will you help me alter the diagram today, Susan?
蘇珊，你今天能幫我修改一下圖表嗎？

▶動 Will you diagram the floor plan so that we can understand what you said better?
你能把樓面的平面圖畫出來嗎？這樣我們對於你說的話就會更明白些了。

di·am·e·ter [daɪˋæmətɚ]

Track 5618

名 直徑

▶The lake has a diameter of two hundred meters.
這湖的直徑有兩百公尺。

dic·tate [ˋdɪktet]

Track 5619

動 口授、聽寫

▶I don't think they are now in a position to dictate their own demands.
我不認為他們現在有提出自己的要求。

文法字詞解析
現在許多的手機也有好用的 dictate 功能，對著它說話，它就會把你所說的轉換成文字了。當然實際效果視不同手機而定。

dic·ta·tion [dɪkˋteʃən]

Track 5620

名 口述、口授

▶He asked the secretary to take down his dictation at once.
他叫秘書立刻將他口述的寫下來。

dic·ta·tor [ˋdɪk͵tetɚ]

Track 5621

名 獨裁者、發號施令者

▶It won't be long before the people revolt against this dictator.
不久人民就會起來反抗這個獨裁者的。

dif·fer·en·ti·ate [dɪfəˋrɛnʃɪ͵et]

Track 5622

動 辨別、區分

▶I can't differentiate these two pens. They look exactly the same. 我分辨不了這兩枝筆，它們長得完全一樣啊。

di·lem·ma [dəˋlɛmə]

Track 5623

名 左右為難、窘境

▶My elder brother is in a dilemma whether to stay on at school or get a job.
該繼續求學還是找工作，我哥哥感到難以抉擇。

實用片語用語
be in a dilemma 陷入左右為難的狀況

di·men·sion [dəˋmɛnʃən]

Track 5624

名 尺寸、方面 同 size 尺寸

▶We're facing a problem with alarmingly enourmous dimensions.
我們面對的這個問題大得驚人。

di·min·ish [dəˋmɪnɪʃ]

Track 5625

動 縮小、減少

▶If I were you, I would try to diminish the cost of production.
如果我是你的話，我會盡力減少生產成本。

實用片語用語
diminish the cost of sth. 減少……的成本

di·plo·ma·cy [dɪ`plomәsɪ] Track 5626

名 外交、外交手腕 同 politics 手腕

▶I am afraid that this can only be done with diplomacy.
恐怕這只能透過外交手腕才能辦得到吧。

dip·lo·ma·tic [͵dɪplә`mætɪk] Track 5627

形 外交的、外交官的

▶The two countries have broken off diplomatic relations again.
兩國再次終止了外交關係。

實用片語用語
break off 終止（關係）

di·rec·to·ry [dә`rɛktәrɪ] Track 5628

名 姓名地址錄

▶Will you tell me what number I shall dial for directory enquiry?
你能告訴我查號台的電話號碼是多少嗎？

dis·a·bil·i·ty [͵dɪsә`bɪlәtɪ] Track 5629

名 無能、無力

▶He never lets his disability bring him down.
他從來不讓自己行動不便的事影響自己。

dis·a·ble [dɪs`ebḷ] Track 5630

動 使無能力、使無作用

▶That teacher was disabled in the car accident.
那位老師在那次車禍中成了殘廢。

文法字詞解析
「disable」這個單字在這個數位時代也非常重要喔！使用手機等電子產品時，有時會開啟各種有的沒的內建功能，你根本不想要用它們，這時就可以選擇 disable 來把它們關掉。舉例來說，如果你一不小心設了鬧鐘，就可以選擇 disable alarm 讓鬧鐘不要響。

dis·ap·prove [͵dɪsә`pruv] Track 5631

動 反對、不贊成 同 oppose 反對

▶His mother disapproved of his new girlfriend.
他媽媽不喜歡他的新女友。

dis·as·trous [dɪz`æstrәs] Track 5632

形 災害的、悲慘的 同 tragic 悲慘的

▶If you don't work harder the results could be disastrous.
如果你不更努力一點，結果會很悲慘。

dis·charge [dɪs`tʃɑrdʒ] Track 5633

名 排出、卸下 動 卸下

▶名 Can you tell me how long the discharge of the cargo will take? 你能告訴我需要多久才能卸完貨嗎？

▶動 How long will it take if we discharge the cargo at Hong Kong? 如果我們在香港卸貨的話需要多久時間？

dis·ci·pli·nar·y [`dɪsәplɪn͵ɛrɪ] Track 5634

形 訓練上的、訓育的

▶In cases of this kind, it is wrong for you to take disciplinary measures. 在這種情況下，給予紀律處分是不正確的。

實用片語用語
take disciplinary measures 給予紀律處分

dis·close [dɪs`kloz] Track 5635

動 暴露、露出

▶I hope they would disclose the truth to the press one day.
我真希望有天他們能向新聞界透露真相。

dis·clo·sure [dɪsˋkloʒɚ]
Track 5636

名 暴露、揭發

▶The disclosure that he had been in jail made him lose his job.
公開他曾坐牢一事，令他丟了工作。

dis·com·fort [dɪsˋkʌmfɚt]
Track 5637

名 不安、不自在 動 使不安、使不自在

▶名 The weather is so hot that it causes me a lot of discomfort.
天氣熱得令我好難受。

▶動 She is so melancholy that she is often discomforted over trifles.
她是如此地憂鬱，以致她總是會為一些瑣事而苦惱。

dis·creet [dɪˋskrit]
Track 5638

形 謹慎的、慎重的

▶It isn't discreet of you to ring him up at the office when he is busy.
他正在忙的時候，你打電話到他辦公室，真是太魯莽了。

萬用延伸句型
It isn't discreet of you to... 你（做某事）不謹慎

dis·crim·i·na·tion [dɪˏskrɪməˋneʃən]
Track 5639

名 辨別

▶What do you think of racial discrimination in America?
你是如何看待美國種族歧視的現象呢？

實用片語用語
racial discrimination 種族歧視
discrimination 除了指「辨別、區別」以外，還有以「不公平的方式看待、歧視」的意思，所以使用時要特別小心。

dis·grace [dɪsˋgres]
Track 5640

名 不名譽 動 羞辱 同 shame 羞恥

▶名 Don't you think such an act is a disgrace to your family?
你不覺得這種行為會為你全家帶來恥辱嗎？

▶動 The man has disgraced the family name.
那個男人讓他們全家丟臉了。

dis·grace·ful [dɪsˋgresfəl]
Track 5641

形 可恥的、不名譽的

▶You are not supposed to remain silent about this disgraceful affair. 你不應該對這件可恥的事保持緘默。

實用片語用語
remain silent about... 對（某事）保持緘默

dis·man·tle [dɪsˋmæntḷ]
Track 5642

動 拆開、分解、扯下

▶Will you help me dismantle the faulty（有毛病的）machine, Bob?
鮑勃，你能幫我把這台有毛病的機器拆開嗎？

dis·may [dɪsˋme]
Track 5643

名 恐慌、沮喪 動 狼狽、恐慌

▶名 The little boy looked at me in dismay.
那個小男孩驚慌地望著我。

▶動 The man is dismayed to hear that the plane he is supposed to take has already taken off.
那個男人聽到他要搭的飛機已經起飛了，顯得非常困擾。

dis·patch [dɪˋspætʃ]

Track 5644

名 急速、快速處理 動 派遣、發送 同 send 發送

▶名 The commander's hasty dispatch of the messangers won them the battle.
指揮官迅速地派出了信差，讓他們在這次戰役中獲勝了。

▶動 Can't you dispatch the goods by sea instead of by air?
你不能用海運代替空運嗎？

dis·pens·a·ble [dɪˋspɛnsəbḷ]

Track 5645

形 非必要的

▶I don't think it's a good idea to bring so many dispensable things with us.
我覺得帶一堆不必要的東西在我們身邊不是個好點子。

文法字詞解析
相反地，非常必要、絕對要帶著的東西則可以用 indispensable 來描述。

dis·perse [dɪˋspɝs]

Track 5646

動 使散開、驅散

▶A large crowd of protesters（抗議者）has gathered in the square. I am afraid the police will come to disperse them soon. 衆多抗議者已經聚集在廣場上。恐怕警察很快就會來驅散他們了。

dis·place [dɪsˋples]

Track 5647

動 移置、移走

▶The war has displaced thousands of people.
這場戰爭使得成千上萬的人離鄉背井。

dis·please [dɪsˋpliz]

Track 5648

動 得罪、使不快

▶I am afraid that your reply will displease your boss.
恐怕你的回答會令你的老闆不快。

dis·pos·a·ble [dɪˋspozəbḷ]

Track 5649

形 可任意使用的、免洗的

▶Will you buy some disposable diapers for my baby?
你能幫我的小寶貝買些免洗尿布嗎？

實用片語用語
disposable underwear 免洗內褲
例如：She packed a set of disposable underwear in her suitcase.
她在行李箱裡收進了一套免洗內褲。

dis·pos·al [dɪˋspozḷ]

Track 5650

名 分佈、配置

▶You'd better discuss with you wife the disposal of the furniture in advance.
你最好事先和你的妻子討論一下如何佈置這些傢俱。

dis·re·gard [ˌdɪsrɪˋgɑrd]

Track 5651

名 蔑視、忽視 動 不理、蔑視

▶名 He did it in disregard of my advice.
他不顧我的勸告做了這件事。

▶動 It will be very dangerous for you to disregard your father's advice.
你漠視你父親的忠告，這樣是很危險的。

dis·si·dent [ˋdɪsədənt] Track 5652

名 異議者 形 有異議的

▶名 How are you getting along with the political dissident?
你和那個跟你持不同政見的人相處得好嗎？

▶動 I've never talked to the dissident Russian novelist.
我從來沒和那位持不同意見的俄國小說家說過話。

實用片語用語
get along with 與（某人）相處

dis·solve [dɪˋzɑlv] Track 5653

動 使溶解

▶The tablet dissolved in the warm water.
藥片在溫水中溶解了。

dis·suade [dɪˋswed] Track 5654

動 勸阻、勸止 同 discourage 勸阻

▶My teacher dissuaded me from accepting the difficult job.
老師勸我不要接受這份艱難的工作。

dis·tort [dɪsˋtɔrt] Track 5655

動 曲解、扭曲

▶His face was distorted with rage when he heard about their betrayal. 他聽到他們背叛的事情時，怒得臉都扭曲了。

dis·tract [dɪˋstrækt] Track 5656

動 分散

▶It is obvious that the noise outside distracts her from her work. 顯然外面的噪音使她無法專心工作。

實用片語用語
be distracted by 被（某事）分散注意力
例如：I was trying to do my homework, but was distracted by the fire alarm.
我本來想做功課，但被火警警鈴給分散注意力了。

dis·trac·tion [dɪˋstrækʃən] Track 5657

名 分心、精神渙散、心煩不安

▶There are too many distractions here for one to work properly.
這裡讓人分心的事太多，使人無法好好工作。

dis·trust [dɪsˋtrʌst] Track 5658

名 不信任、不信 動 不信

▶名 He looked at the man with distrust.
他用懷疑的眼光打量著那個男人。

▶動 He distrusts even his own father.
他就連自己的爸爸都不相信。

dis·tur·bance [dɪˋstɝbəns] Track 5659

名 擾亂、騷亂

▶There was a violent disturbance in the suburb of Paris last week. 上週巴黎市郊發生了激烈的騷亂。

di·verse [dəˋvɝs] Track 5660

形 互異的、不同的 同 different 不同的

▶It is clear that the opinions of the two factions are widely diverse. 顯然這兩個派系的意見大相逕庭。

實用片語用語
diverse culture 差異很大的文化
例如：The diverse cultures in the country made living there quite interesting.
該國各色各樣的文化使得住在那裡非常有趣。

di·ver·si·fy [daɪ`vɝsə,faɪ]

Track 5661

動 使……多樣化

▶You are supposed to diversify your investments, not to have all your eggs in one basket.
你應該多方面投資，而不該孤注一擲。

di·ver·sion [də`vɝʒən]

Track 5662

名 脫離、轉向、轉換

▶I'll create a diversion and you can use this chance to run away.
我來轉開他們的注意力，你趁機趕快跑。

實用片語用語
use the chance to... 利用機會……

di·ver·si·ty [də`vɝsətɪ]

Track 5663

名 差異處、不同點、多樣性

▶Don't you think that it is important to develop a great diversity of interests?
你不覺得培養多方興趣很重要嗎？

di·vert [də`vɝt]

Track 5664

動 使轉向

▶I'm using iPad games to divert the kids' attention.
我在用iPad遊戲來轉移孩子們的注意力。

實用片語用語
divert sb.'s attention 轉移某人的注意

doc·trine [`dɑktrɪn]

Track 5665

名 教義

▶It is obvious that his doctrine contains nothing novel.
顯然他的學說並未包含新穎的思想。

doc·u·men·ta·ry [,dɑkjə`mɛntərɪ]

Track 5666

名 紀錄 形 文件的

▶名 Would you like to watch the documentary on the Civil War with me? 你願意和我一起去看那部關於內戰的紀錄片嗎？

▶形 Would you like to show us the documentary evidence at the court? 你願意在法庭上向我們出示書面證據嗎？

實用片語用語
Civil War 內戰

dome [dom]

Track 5667

名 拱形圓屋頂、穹窿 動 覆以圓頂、使成圓頂、拱形屋頂上的

▶名 What's wrong with the dome lamp? It doesn't work.
頂燈出了什麼毛病？它不亮了。

▶動 The underlying（潛在的）magma（岩漿）domes the surface. 地下岩漿使地面呈圓頂形。

do·nate [`donet]

Track 5668

動 贈與、捐贈 同 contribute 捐獻

▶He donated a large sum of money to this stranger.
他捐了一大筆錢給這名陌生人。

實用片語用語
a large sum of... 很大一筆……

do·na·tion [`doneʃən]

Track 5669

名 捐贈物、捐款

▶He made a huge donation to the orphanage.
他捐贈了一大筆錢給孤兒院。

do·nor [ˋdonɚ] Track 5670

名 寄贈者、捐贈人

▶It is hard for the doctors to find a blood donor for him at once because of his blood type.
由於他血型的緣故，醫生們很難立刻替他找到一個捐血的人。

doom [dum] Track 5671

名 命運 動 注定

▶名 They can do nothing but await their doom.
他們只能坐以待斃了。

▶動 If you do nothing but wait, then your plan is doomed to fail.
如果你只是等待，那麼計畫注定是要失敗的。

實用片語用語
doom to... 注定要⋯⋯

dos·age [ˋdosɪdʒ] Track 5672

名 藥量、劑量

▶A large dosage of this can cause death.
大劑量的這種藥物能致命。

實用片語用語
daily dosage 每日劑量
例如：You should follow the instruction of daily dosage to take medicine.
你應該遵照每日劑量的指示來服藥。

dras·tic [ˋdræstɪk] Track 5673

形 激烈的、猛烈的 同 rough 劇烈的

▶I am afraid that it will require a drastic revision of the plan.
恐怕這個計畫需要進行大幅度地修改。

draw·back [ˋdrɔ͵bæk] Track 5674

名 缺點、弊端

▶Every one of these plans has its drawbacks.
這些計畫每個皆有不足之處。

drear·y [ˋdrɪərɪ] Track 5675

形 陰鬱的、淒涼的

▶The old lady's life was very dreary.
那個老太太的生活非常陰鬱。

實用片語用語
dreary weather 陰鬱的天氣
例如：The dreary weather makes me not want to do anything.
這陰鬱的天氣讓我什麼也不想做。

driz·zle [ˋdrɪzḷ] Track 5676

名 細雨、毛毛雨 動 下毛毛雨 同 rain 雨

▶名 Why are you walking outside in the drizzle? You'll catch a cold.
你為什麼在細雨中在外面散步？你會感冒的。

▶動 It has been drizzling all day, so I can't go out.
毛毛雨下了一整天，害得我都不能出門。

drought [draʊt] Track 5677

名 乾旱、久旱

▶How long do you think the drought will last this year?
你覺得今年的乾旱會持續多久呢？

du·al [ˋdjuəl] Track 5678

形 成雙的、雙重的 同 double 成雙的

▶I am afraid that US dollar revaluation（升值）has dual effects.
恐怕美元升值有雙重效應。

du·bi·ous [ˋdjubɪəs]

Track 5679

形 曖昧的、含糊的

▶What he said yesterday was dubious. 他昨天說的話很含糊。

文法字詞解析

如果一個東西是「曖昧的、含糊的」，想當然你也不會太信任它，因此 dubious 還包含了「不可信的、可疑的」的意思。

dy·na·mite [ˋdaɪnə͵maɪt]

Track 5680

名 炸藥 動 爆破、炸破 同 explosive 炸藥

▶名 Don't leave the dynamite where the children could touch them. 別把炸藥放在孩子們碰得到的地方。

▶動 A part of the mountain was dynamited.
山有一部份炸毀了。

Ee

ebb [ɛb]

Track 5681

名 退潮 動 衰落

▶名 I'm afraid that the scandal brought his credibility to the lowest ebb. 恐怕那件醜聞使他的信譽跌到最低點。

▶動 Our hope of winning began to ebb in the forth round.
比賽進入第四回合時，我們獲勝的希望就變得渺茫了。

ec·cen·tric [ɪkˋsɛntrɪk]

Track 5682

名 古怪的人 形 異常的

▶名 The old lady is a bit of an eccentric. Can you communicate with her? 這位老太太是個有點古怪的人。你能跟她溝通嗎？

▶形 I wonder how to explain his eccentric behaviors.
我想知道該如何解釋他這種古怪的行為。

實用片語用語

be a bit of a(n)... 有點像是某種人

e·col·o·gy [ɪˋkɑlədʒɪ]

Track 5683

名 生態學

▶I wish I could study ecology in college.
要是我能在大學裡能修生態學就好了。

ec·sta·sy [ˋɛkstəsɪ]

Track 5684

名 狂喜、入迷 同 joy 歡樂

▶He listened to the song in ecstasy. 他聽這首歌聽得入迷。

ed·i·ble [ˋɛdəbḷ]

Track 5685

形 食用的

▶You'd better throw that meat away. It's not edible.
你最好把那塊肉扔了。它不能吃了。

ed·i·to·ri·al [͵ɛdəˋtorɪəl]

Track 5686

名 社論 形 編輯的

▶名 Would you like to tell me which you like better, the news or the editorial?
你能不能告訴我新聞和社論你比較喜歡看哪一個？

▶形 Would you like to expand the editorial staff?
你想不想擴大編輯部呢？

萬用延伸句型

Would you like to...? 你想要……嗎？

e·lec·tron [ɪ`lɛktrɑn] Track 5687

名 電子

▶It is said that the electron microscope can show the object as a million times its original size.
據說那架電子顯微鏡可以把物體放大一百萬倍。

el·i·gi·ble [`ɛlɪdʒəbl̩] Track 5688

形 適當的

▶Men and women of eighteen and above are eligible to vote.
顯然年齡在十八歲以上的男女都有投票表決權。

e·lite [e`lit] Track 5689

名 精英 形 傑出的

▶名 She has become a famous political elite.
她成了政界名人。

▶形 They trained their son from childhood so that he could become an elite pianist. 他們在兒子小的時候就訓練他，要他成為一名傑出的鋼琴家。

實用片語用語
political elite 政治菁英

el·o·quence [`ɛləkwəns] Track 5690

名 雄辯

▶Her eloquence is so impressive that we can't help but be convinced.
她的口才如此之好，我們都不由得被說服了。

萬用延伸句型
can't help but（+ 原形動詞） 不由得……

el·o·quent [`ɛləkwənt] Track 5691

形 辯才無礙的

▶She is not only eloquent but also elegant.
她不但口才好，而且還很高雅。

em·bark [ɪm`bɑrk] Track 5692

動 從事、搭乘

▶I heard that he was about to embark on a new business venture.
我聽說他就要開始一項新的事業。

em·i·grant [`ɛməgrənt] Track 5693

名 移民者、移出者 形 移民的、移居他國的

同 immigrant 外來移民

▶名 It is said that he is a British emigrant to Australia.
據說他是個移居澳洲的英國人。

▶形 It is said that they are emigrant laborers.
據說他們是移民勞工。

em·i·grate [`ɛmə͵gret] Track 5694

動 移居

▶His family emigrated from Italy to America after the war broke out in Italy.
義大利發生戰爭後，他們家從義大利移居到了美國。

實用片語用語
break out（戰爭、疾病等）爆發

em·i·gra·tion [ˌɛməˋgreʃən] Track 5695

名 移民

▶There's a wide diversity of opinions on the issue of the emigration.
關於移民這個議題存在著相當多元的意見。

em·phat·ic [ɪmˋfætɪk] Track 5696

形 強調的

▶He rejected my request with an emphatic shake of his head.
他很堅決地搖頭，拒絕了我的要求。

en·act [ɪnˋækt] Track 5697

動 制定

▶It is time to stop arguing and enact a measure into law.
現在該是停止爭辯並把它制定為法律的時候了。

萬用延伸句型
It is time to... 是時候該……

en·act·ment [ɪnˋæktmənt] Track 5698

名 法規

▶It is obvious that this enactment is useless in preventing people from exceeding the speed limit.
顯然這個法規無助於阻止人們超速。

實用片語用語
exceed the speed limit 超速

en·clo·sure [ɪnˋkloʒɚ] Track 5699

名 圍住

▶There are several enclosures in the envelope. You'd better keep them well.
信封內裝有幾份附件。你最好把它們收好。

en·cy·clo·pe·di·a/ en·cy·clo·pae·di·a [ɪnˌsaɪkləˋpidɪə] Track 5700

名 百科全書

▶Would you please put the encyclopedia back on the shelf?
請把百科全書放回架上好嗎？

en·dur·ance [ɪnˋdjʊrəns] Track 5701

名 耐力

▶She showed great endurance during the climb.
她在攀登過程中表現出極大的耐力。

文法字詞解析
climb 較常當作動詞，有「攀爬」的意思，在此則是當名詞，表示「攀爬的整個過程」。

en·hance [ɪnˋhæns] Track 5702

動 提高、增強 同 improve 提高、增進

▶It is obvious that the knowledge you have will enhance your reputation.
顯然你擁有的知識會為你提高聲譽。

en·hance·ment [inˋhænsmənt] Track 5703

名 增進

▶Nicotine（尼古丁）is what they call a flavor enhancement.
尼古丁是他們所稱的提味劑。

en·light·en [ɪn`laɪtn̩]

Track 5704

動 啓發

▶I don't understand this paragraph that you've written. Would you enlighten me?
我讀不懂你寫的這段話。你能為我講解嗎？

en·light·en·ment [ɪn`laɪtn̩mənt]

Track 5705

名 文明

▶The teacher's attempts at enlightenment failed; I remained as confused as before.
老師雖盡力開導卻徒勞而無功，我還是跟之前一樣疑惑。

實用片語用語
attempt at... 嘗試某事

en·rich [ɪn`rɪtʃ]

Track 5706

動 使富有

▶Putting spices in food can enrich the flavor.
把調味料放進食物中可以使味道更豐富。

en·rich·ment [ɪn`rɪtʃmənt]

Track 5707

名 豐富

▶Good books are an enrichment of life.
好書能使人生變得充實。

ep·i·dem·ic [ˏɛpɪ`dɛmɪk]

Track 5708

名 傳染病 形 流行的

▶名 It is reported that a flu epidemic has raged through the school for weeks.
據報導流感已經在那所學校裡蔓延了幾個星期了。

▶形 Buying in installments has become epidemic in recent years.
近幾年來十分流行用分期付款的方式來購物。

實用片語用語
installment buying 分期付款購物

ep·i·sode [`ɛpəˏsod]

Track 5709

名 插曲

▶There was a rather amusing episode in the pub last night.
昨晚小酒館裡發生了一段相當有趣的插曲。

文法字詞解析
episode 也有「一齣、一集連續劇」的意思，我們常在一系列的影片的標題中看到「ep. XX」，其中「ep.」就是 episode 的縮寫。

EQ/ e·mo·tion·al quo·tient/ e·mo·tion·al in·tel·li·gence

Track 5710

[i kju]/[ɪ`moʃənl̩ `kwoʃənt]/[ɪ`moʃənl̩ ɪn`tɛlədʒəns]

名 情緒智商

▶A good EQ helps you predict how other people feel.
高EQ能幫助你預測他人的感覺。

e·qua·tion [ɪ`kweʃən]

Track 5711

名 相等

▶The equation of wealth and happiness can be dangerous. Don't you think so?
把財富與幸福等同起來是很危險的。你不這樣認為嗎？

e·quiv·a·lent [ɪˋkwɪvələnt] Track 5712

名 相等物 形 相當的

▶名 I'm afraid that some English words have no Chinese equivalents.
恐怕有些英文字在中文裡沒有相對應的詞。

▶形 Moving him to another position like that is equivalent to giving him the sack.
恐怕那樣調換他的工作就等於是解雇了他。

實用片語用語
give sb. the sack 解雇某人

e·rode [ɪˋrod] Track 5713

動 蝕

▶The sea have eroded the cliff over the years.
海水經年累月的沖刷已經侵蝕了峭壁。

e·rup·tion [ɪˋrʌpʃən] Track 5714

名 爆發

▶There have been several volcanic eruptions this year.
今年已經出現了好幾次火山爆發。

es·ca·late [ˋɛskəˏlet] Track 5715

動 擴大、延長

▶The tension between the countries soon escalated into war.
這些國家間的緊張很快地發展成了戰爭。

文法字詞解析
我們常搭的電扶梯（escalator）功能就是將你舉到比較高的地方、將你去到的範圍「延伸」，因此才會和有「擴大、延長」意味的 escalate 語出同源。

es·sence [ˋɛsn̩s] Track 5716

名 本質

▶The essence of this article is pretty interesting, but the article itself isn't written well.
這篇文章的精華內容很有趣，但文章本身卻寫得不太好。

e·ter·ni·ty [ɪˋtɝnətɪ] Track 5717

名 永遠、永恆

▶Time has no meaning in eternity.
在永恆之中時間是沒有意義的。

e·thi·cal [ˋɛθɪkl̩] Track 5718

形 道德的

▶It is obviously it's not ethical to do that.
顯然這麼做並不符合道德。

eth·nic [ˋɛθnɪk] Track 5719

名 少數民族的成員 形 人種的、民族的

▶名 It is an enthusiastic and friendly ethnic.
那是一個充滿熱情和友好的民族。

▶形 China is a united country of many ethnic groups.
中國是一個統一的多民族國家。

實用片語用語
ethnic group 民族

e·vac·u·ate [ɪˋvækjuˏet] Track 5720

動 撤離 同 leave 離開

▶A typhoon is coming; you had better get everything ready to evacuate. 颱風快要來了，你最好做好一切撤離的準備。

ev·o·lu·tion [ˌɛvəˋluʃən] Track 5721

名 發展

▶The picture depicts the process of the evolution of a seed into a plant.
這張圖描繪的是種子發展成為植物的過程。

e·volve [ɪˋvɑlv] Track 5722

動 演化 同 develop 發展

▶The simple plan has evolved into a complicated scheme.
這個簡單的計畫已經發展成了一項複雜的規劃。

ex·cerpt [ˋɛksɝpt]/[ɪkˋsɝpt] Track 5723

名 摘錄 動 引用

▶名 I like to read the excerpt of a book before buying it.
我喜歡先讀書中摘錄的部分，然後才把那本書買下來。

▶動 She excerpted a passage from the magazine.
她從那本雜誌上摘錄了一段。

實用片語用語
book excerpt 書籍的摘錄內容
例如：You can read book excerpts on this website.
在這個網站上可以讀到書籍的摘錄內容。

ex·ces·sive [ɪkˋsɛsɪv] Track 5724

形 過度的

▶The quality of urban living has been damaged by excessive noise. 城市生活的品質已被過度的噪音所破壞。

ex·clu·sive [ɪkˋsklusɪv] Track 5725

形 唯一的、排外的、獨家的

▶This is an exclusive interview on the famous singer.
這是這名知名歌星的獨家專訪。

ex·e·cu·tion [ˌɛksɪˋkjuʃən] Track 5726

名 實行

▶Even though the idea is good, the execution leaves much to be desired.
這個想法雖好，但執行的方式卻不怎麼樣。

實用片語用語
leave much to be desired
還有很大的進步空間

ex·ert [ɪgˋzɝt] Track 5727

動 運用、盡力 同 employ 利用

▶He exerted all his influence to make them accept his plan.
他用盡一切影響力使他們接受他的計畫。

ex·ot·ic [ɛgˋzɑtɪk] Track 5728

形 外來的

▶The film retains much of the book's exotic flavor.
這部電影保存了原著的許多異國情調。

ex·pe·di·tion [ˌɛkspɪˋdɪʃən] Track 5729

名 探險、遠征

▶It is said that they are planning to organize a scientific expedition.
據說他們正計畫組織一次科學探險。

ex·pel [ɪk`spɛl]

Track 5730

動 逐出

▶The headmaster had decided to expel him from the school.
校長決定開除該名學生。

實用片語用語
be expelled 被退學
例如：He was expelled for setting fire to the school.
他因為放火燒學校而被退學了。

ex·per·tise [ˌɛkspɚ`tiz]

Track 5731

名 專門知識

▶His business expertise is of help to all of us.
他的商業知識對我們大家都有助益。

ex·pi·ra·tion [ˌɛkspə`reʃən]

Track 5732

名 終結

▶Would you please tell me the expiration date of your card?
請您告訴我您信用卡的期限好嗎？

實用片語用語
expiration date 有效日期、到期日

ex·pire [ɪk`spaɪr]

Track 5733

動 終止

▶I'm afraid your lease will expire on July 30th of this year.
不好意思，您的租約今年7月30日到期。

ex·plic·it [ɪk`splɪsɪt]

Track 5734

形 明確的

▶It seems that he's avoiding giving us an explicit answer.
他似乎在避免給我們明確的回答。

文法字詞解析
「限制級、兒童不宜」的內容常稱為explicit content，因此當看到CD、電影光碟上有標示「explicit content」時，就知道別拿給小孩子看了。

ex·ploit [ɪk`splɔɪt]

Track 5735

名 功績 動 利用

▶名 His daring exploits are the talk of the company.
他大膽的行為是整個公司閒聊的話題。

▶動 We should exploit our rich resources to develop the economy.
我們應該利用我們豐富的資源來發展經濟。

ex·plo·ra·tion [ˌɛksplə`reʃən]

Track 5736

名 探測

▶It is obvious that the Elizabethan age was a time of exploration and discovery.
顯然英國女王伊莉莎白一世時代是探索和發現的時代。

ex·qui·site [`ɛkskwɪzɪt]

Track 5737

形 精巧的

▶It is said that the hostess had exquisite taste in clothes.
據說那位女主人對衣著十分講究。

萬用延伸句型
have + adj. taste in sth. 對某事物有……的品味

ex·tract [`ɛkstrækt]/[ɪk`strækt]

Track 5738

名 摘錄 動 引出、源出

▶名 Let's just read several extracts from the poem, shall we?
我們就讀從詩中摘錄的幾段吧，如何？

▶動 He tried to extract this pole from the mud.
他試著把竿子從泥中拔出來。

extra·cur·ric·u·lar [ˏɛkstrəkəˋrɪkjələ] Track 5739

形 課外的

▶You should take part in extracurricular activities. That will help you make friends. 你應該要參加課外活動，這會幫助你交朋友。

實用片語用語
extracurricular activity 課外活動

eye·sight [ˋaɪˏsaɪt] Track 5740

名 視力

▶The animal's good sense of smell compensates for its poor eyesight. 這種動物靈敏的嗅覺彌補了其視力之不足。

fa·bu·lous [ˋfæbjələs] Track 5741

形 傳說、神話中的 同 marvelous 不可思議的

▶The little boy's performance was fabulous.
那個小男孩的表演真是精彩。

fa·cil·i·tate [fəˋsɪləˏtet] Track 5742

動 利於、使容易 同 assist 促進

▶Zip codes are used to facilitate mail service.
郵遞區號利於郵遞服務。

實用片語用語
zip code 郵遞區號

fac·tion [ˋfækʃən] Track 5743

名 黨派、當中之派系

▶The party has split into petty factions.
該黨分裂成了若干小派系。

fac·ul·ty [ˋfækl̩tɪ] Track 5744

名 全體教員、系所

▶The faculty at this school is quite excellent.
這所學校的教職員非常傑出。

fa·mil·i·ar·i·ty [fəˏmɪlɪˋærətɪ] Track 5745

名 熟悉、親密、精通

▶His familiarity with the local languages is a great asset to us.
他對當地語言的精通對我們有很大的幫助。

fam·ine [ˋfæmɪn] Track 5746

名 饑荒、饑饉、缺乏 同 starvation 飢餓

▶Both the war and famine have made the country poverty-stricken（被貧苦所困惱的）.
戰爭和饑荒使這個國家變得貧困不堪。

文法字詞解析
stricken 是 strike（打擊）的過去分詞，此處即指這個國家「受到了貧苦的打擊」。

fas·ci·na·tion [ˏfæsəˋneʃən] Track 5747

名 迷惑、魅力、魅惑

▶She has a fascination for all things astrology-related.
她對和占星相關的事情都充滿了興趣。

fea·si·ble [ˋfizəbḷ] Track 5748

形 可實行的、可能的

▶It's quite clear that this is a feasible scheme.
很顯然這是一個切實可行的計畫。

fed·er·a·tion [ˏfɛdəˋreʃən] Track 5749

名 聯合、同盟、聯邦政府

▶Will you tell me which federation will attract most people?
你能告訴我哪個聯盟最有吸引力嗎？

feed·back [ˋfidˏbæk] Track 5750

名 回饋 同 response 反應

▶The more feedback we get from the customers the better.
從顧客那兒得到的回饋越多越好。

萬用延伸句型
The more... the better 越多……越好

fer·til·i·ty [fɝˋtɪlətɪ] Track 5751

名 肥沃、多產、繁殖力

▶She is taking medicine to increase her fertility, isn't she?
她為了增強生育能力而服藥，不是嗎？

fi·del·i·ty [fɪˋdɛlətɪ] Track 5752

名 忠實、精準度、誠實 同 faith 誠實

▶Fidelity towards your spouse is important.
對於配偶忠誠是很重要的。

文法字詞解析
相反地，若對配偶「不忠」則可加上表示「不、無」的字首「in-」稱為 infidelity。

fire·proof [ˋfaɪrˏpruf] Track 5753

形 耐火的、防火的

▶It is impossible for us to make the house completely fireproof.
我們無法使房屋完全防火。

flare [flɛr] Track 5754

名 閃光、燃燒 動 搖曳、閃亮、發怒

▶名 We all saw a match flare in the darkness at that time.
我們大家當時都看到有火柴的光亮在黑暗中閃了一下。

▶動 Her temper flares up very easily.
她總是動不動就發脾氣。

fleet [flit] Track 5755

名 船隊、艦隊、車隊

▶It is said that the company owns a fleet of cars for its employees to use.
據說這家公司擁有一個車隊來供其員工使用。

flick·er [ˋflɪkɚ] Track 5756

名 閃耀 動 飄揚、震動

▶名 I saw a flicker of interest in her eyes.
我看到她的眼中閃過了一絲感興趣的神情。

▶動 A faint hope still flickers in his heart.
一絲微弱的希望仍在他的心中閃動著。

實用片語用語
a flicker of interest 閃過的感興趣的神情

fling [flɪŋ]

Track 5757

名 投、猛衝 動 投擲、踢、跳躍

▶名 He tossed the coat onto the hook with a careless fling.
他隨手一丟就把外套掛上了勾子。

▶動 The children were flinging mud everywhere.
孩子們在到處丟泥巴。

flu·id [ˋfluɪd]

Track 5758

名 流體 形 流質的 反 solid 固體

▶名 The fluids you drank is enough to meet the physical needs.
你喝的流質足夠滿足你身體的各項需要。

▶形 We don't have enough fluid capital to work on this project.
我們沒有足夠的流動資金來做這個計畫。

實用片語用語
fluid capital 流動資金

flut·ter [ˋflʌtɚ]

Track 5759

名 心亂、不安 動 拍翅、飄動

▶名 Did you hear a flutter of wings among the trees?
你有聽到樹林裡響起一陣飛鳥的拍翅聲？

▶動 There is a bird fluttering its wings in the cage.
有隻鳥在籠中拍著翅膀。

fore·see [forˋsi]

Track 5760

動 預知、看穿

▶We can't foresee what will happen in the future.
我們無法預知將來會發生什麼事。

文法字詞解析
foresee 的動詞變化：
foresee, foresaw, foreseen

for·mi·da·ble [ˋfɔrmɪdəbl̩]

Track 5761

形 可怕的、難應付的

▶My grandma is a really formidable old lady.
我奶奶是個很難應付的老太太。

for·mu·late [ˋfɔrmjəˏlet]

Track 5762

動 明確地陳述、用公式表示 同 define 使明確

▶He is able to formulate his thoughts clearly.
他能夠清楚地表達自己的想法。

for·sake [fɚˋsek]

Track 5763

動 拋棄、放棄、捨棄 同 abandon 拋棄

▶It is a surprise that he should forsake his wife and children.
他竟遺棄了他的妻兒，真令人驚訝。

文法字詞解析
若要說「被放棄的、被拋棄的」，則可以用 forsaken 這個形容詞。

forth·com·ing [ˏforθˋkʌmɪŋ]

Track 5764

形 不久就要來的、下一次的

▶Will you give me a list of their forthcoming books now?
你能現在就給我一張他們即將出版的書籍的目錄嗎？

for·ti·fy [ˋfɔrtəˏfaɪ]

Track 5765

動 加固、強化工事

▶It's high time that this country fortified the coastal（沿海的）areas. 這個國家真該好好加強一下沿海地區的防禦了。

fos·ter [ˋfɔstɚ]   Track 5766

動 養育、收養 形 收養的

▶動 He fostered an interest in nature in his children.
他在他的孩子們心中培養起對大自然的興趣。

▶形 She took care of his foster child after he died.
他死後，就由她來照顧他的養子。

實用片語用語
foster child 養子

frac·ture [ˋfræktʃɚ]   Track 5767

名 破碎、骨折 動 挫傷、破碎 同 crack 破裂

▶名 The doctor said that the fracture in his left leg was very serious. 醫生說他的左腿骨折的情況很嚴重。

▶動 It was the fall that fractured his skull.
正是這一跤把他的顱骨給摔裂了。

實用片語用語
fracture one's leg / arm etc. 讓某人的大腿／手臂骨折

frag·ile [ˋfrædʒəl]   Track 5768

形 脆的、易碎的

▶These glasses look very fragile, so please handle them carefully. 這些玻璃杯看起來很容易碎，因此請小心地拿著。

frag·ment [ˋfrægmənt]   Track 5769

名 破片、碎片

▶I saw lots of fragments of the vase on the floor in the morning.
早上的時候我看見地板上有很多花瓶碎片。

frail [frel]   Track 5770

形 脆弱的、虛弱的 同 weak 虛弱的

▶My grandpa is too frail to get out of the bed himself now.
我爺爺現在太虛弱了，都無法自己下床。

fraud [frɔd]   Track 5771

名 欺騙、詐欺

▶It's no less than a fraud; don't you think so?
這簡直是一場騙局，難道你不這樣覺得嗎？

萬用延伸句型
It is no less than... 簡直是……、根本是……

freak [frik]   Track 5772

名 怪胎、異想天開 形 怪異的

▶名 He is such a freak that no one likes to talk to him.
他真的是個怪胎，怪不得沒人喜歡和他講話。

▶形 What we got in the experiment was a freak result.
我們在那次實驗中得到的是異常的結果。

fret [frɛt]   Track 5773

動 煩躁、焦慮

▶I wish she wouldn't fret over something so unimportant.
我真希望她不要為一些小事而焦慮不安。

fric·tion [ˋfrɪkʃən]   Track 5774

名 摩擦、衝突 同 conflict 衝突

▶It is quite clear that family frictions will have a harmful effect on a child. 很顯然家庭中的爭吵會對孩子產生很不好的影響。

文法字詞解析
friction 不但可以用來指人與人之間的衝突、「摩擦」，也可以拿來指真正的「摩擦力」，在學物理時就常會用到這個單字。

gal·ax·y [ˋgæləksɪ] Track 5775

名 星雲、星系

▶How many stars can you name in the galaxy?
整個星系中，你能說出幾個星星的名字？

gen·er·a·lize [ˋdʒɛnərəˏlaɪz] Track 5776

動 一般化

▶I don't think you can generalize about people's intentions.
我認為你不能把人的意圖一概而論。

gen·er·ate [ˋdʒɛnəˏret] Track 5777

動 產生、引起

▶Investments can generate higher income.
投資能帶來更高的收入。

gen·er·a·tor [ˋdʒɛnəˏretɚ] Track 5778

名 創始者、產生者

▶Not all of us know how to use a generator.
我們當中不是所有人都知道如何使用發電機。

文法字詞解析

generator 不但能用來表示「產生電」的發電機，也能拿來表示產生許多其他東西的「產生者」。例如不知道自己生了孩子該取什麼名字時，就可以使用「baby name generator」（寶寶姓名產生器）來隨機為自己的寶寶「產生」一個名字。

ge·net·ic [dʒəˋnɛtɪk] Track 5779

形 遺傳學的

▶He chose genetic engineering to be his lifelong career.
他選擇了遺傳工程學作為終生的事業。

ge·net·ics [dʒəˋnɛtɪks] Track 5780

名 遺傳學

▶It is said that professors at the University of Edinburgh think that genetics play an important role in modern science.
據說愛丁堡大學的教授認為遺傳學在當代科學扮演重要角色。

glam·our [ˋglæmɚ] Track 5781

名 魅力

▶It seems that the palace was full of glamour and romance.
這座宮殿似乎充滿了魅力和浪漫氣息。

萬用延伸句型

It seems that... 看來……、似乎……

glass·ware [ˋglæsˏwɛr] Track 5782

名 玻璃製品、玻璃器皿

▶He felt he had to buy this lovely piece of glassware for his wife.
他覺得他該買下這個可愛的玻璃器皿給他太太。

glis·ten [ˋglɪsn̩] Track 5783

動 閃耀、閃爍

▶Her eyes glistened with tears as she ran out the door.
她跑出門外時，眼中的淚水在閃爍。

gloom·y [ˋglumɪ]

Track 5784

形 幽暗的、暗淡的

▶He looked a little bit gloomy and troubled.
顯然他看起來有些憂愁不安。

GMO/ge·net·i·cal·ly mod·i·fied or·gan·ism

Track 5785

[dʒəˋnɛtɪklɪ ˋmɑdəˏfaɪd ˋɔrgəˏnɪzm̩]

名 基因改造食品

▶You really shouldn't eat GMO food, because it may have a bad impact on your health.
你最好別吃基因改造食品，因為它們有可能對健康有不良影響。

實用片語用語
have a bad impact on...
對……有不好的影響

graph [græf]

Track 5786

名 曲線圖、圖表 動 圖解

▶名 Can you draw this into a graph for me?
你可以幫我把這畫成一個圖表嗎？

▶動 I am afraid it's impossible for me to graph it.
恐怕把這個用圖表表示是不可能的。

graph·ic [ˋgræfɪk]

Track 5787

形 圖解的、生動的

▶The article gave a graphic description of the earthquake.
那篇文章生動地描述了地震的情況。

grill [grɪl]

Track 5788

名 烤架 動 烤 同 broil 烤

▶名 You had better clean the grill first before starting a fire.
在生火前你最好先把烤架清理乾淨。

▶動 You had better confess, or the police will keep grilling you.
你最好坦白承認，否則警察會一直對你嚴加盤問的。

實用片語用語
grill sb. about sth. 盤問某人某事
例如：Mom never grilled me about my school life.
媽媽從來不過問我的學校生活。

gro·cer [ˋgrosɚ]

Track 5789

名 雜貨商

▶There is a grocer's at the corner of the street.
在街道轉彎處有一間食品雜貨店。

grope [grop]

Track 5790

名 摸索 動 摸索找尋

▶名 He found his way upstairs with a quick grope.
他摸索了一下，找到上樓的路。

▶動 I'm afraid that we have to grope our way through the dark hall.恐怕我們得摸黑走過這個走廊了。

guer·ril·la [gəˋrɪlə]

Track 5791

名 非正規的軍隊、游擊隊 同 soldier 軍人

▶The guerrilla force was in trouble and had to go into hiding.
游擊隊陷入了困境，因此只能躲了起來。

hab·it·at [ˋhæbə͵tæt]　Track 5792

名 棲息地

▶It is reported that the place is the habitat for giant pandas.
據報導這個地區是大熊貓的棲息地。

實用片語用語
natural habitat 自然的棲息地
例如：This forest is the natural habitat of many birds.
這樹林是許多鳥兒的自然棲息地。

hack [hæk]　Track 5793

動 劏、劈、砍

▶You'd better hack off the branches of that big tree.
你最好把那棵大樹的枝椏砍掉。

hack·er [ˋhækɚ]　Track 5794

名 駭客

▶The hacker can obtain your passwords easily.
這名駭客很容易就能取得你的密碼。

hail [hel]　Track 5795

名 歡呼、冰雹 動 歡呼 同 cheer 歡呼

▶名 It has hailed the whole afternoon.
整個下午不停地下冰雹。

▶動 People hailed these famous singers as soon as they got out of the car.
這些有名的歌手一下車，人們就開始歡呼。

實用片語用語
hail a taxi 招計程車
例如：I hailed a taxi for my grandma.
我幫我奶奶招了一台計程車。

ha·rass [ˋhærəs]　Track 5796

動 不斷地困擾 同 bother 打擾

▶It is said that the villagers have been harassed by thieves recently.
據說最近村民們常常受到小偷的騷擾。

ha·rass·ment [ˋhærəsmənt]　Track 5797

名 煩惱、侵擾

▶Does what just happened count as sexual harassment?
剛剛發生的事情算是性騷擾嗎？

haz·ard [ˋhæzɚd]　Track 5798

名 偶然、危險 動 冒險、受傷害

▶名 If you leave those chemicals there, they can become a hazard.
如果把這些化學物質放在那裡，可能會造成危險。

▶動 Let me hazard a guess: you're a Virgo（處女座）, right?
我來冒險猜一猜：你是處女座對不對？

文法字詞解析
在這個字的前面加上表示「生物的」的字首「bio-」就成了 biohazard，即「生化危機」的意思。

hem·i·sphere [ˋhɛməs͵fɪr]　Track 5799

名 半球體、半球

▶I don't think this kind of animal is to be found only in the Northern Hemisphere.
我不相信只能在北半球找到這種動物。

here·af·ter [ˌhɪr`æftɚ]

Track 5800

名 來世 副 隨後、從此以後

▶名 We have done our best. I guess now we can do nothing but speculate about the hereafter.
我們已經盡力了。我想我們現在只能預測未來了。

▶副 There's nothing you can do except work harder hereafter.
我猜想你今後只能用功點學習了。

her·i·tage [`hɛrətɪdʒ]

Track 5801

名 遺產

▶These ancient buildings are part of the national heritage.
這些古建築是民族遺產的一部分。

he·ro·in [`hɛroɪn]

Track 5802

名 海洛因

▶It is illegal for one to sell heroin.
販賣海洛因是違法的。

萬用延伸句型
It is illegal for sb. to...
對某人來說（做某事）是犯法的

high·light [`haɪˌlaɪt]

Track 5803

名 精彩場面 動 使顯著、強調 同 emphasize 強調

▶名 Will you please let me show you the highlights of the event?
請允許我為您展示這個活動最精彩的部分好嗎？

▶動 I will highlight the need for educational reform at the meeting. 我會在會議上強調一下教育改革的必要性。

實用片語用語
educational reform 教育改革

hon·or·ar·y [`ɑnəˌrɛrɪ]

Track 5804

形 榮譽的

▶The college is supposed to give the remarkable scholar an honorary degree.
學院應該授予這位出色的學者榮譽學位。

hor·mone [`hɔrmon]

Track 5805

名 荷爾蒙

▶Scientists found that emotional states can affect our hormone levels. 科學家發現，情緒會影響荷爾蒙的濃度。

hos·pi·ta·ble [`hɑspɪtəbḷ]

Track 5806

形 善於待客的 同 generous 慷慨的

▶The islanders are said to be hospitable.
住在島上的居民們很好客。

萬用延伸句型
be said to be... 被說成是……

hos·pi·tal·i·ty [ˌhɑspɪ`tælətɪ]

Track 5807

名 款待、好客

▶The family shows great hospitality to everyone they meet.
這家人對遇到的所有人都熱情款待。

hos·pi·tal·ize [`hɑspɪtəˌlaɪz]

Track 5808

動 使入院治療

▶He is seriously ill and is hospitalized for three weeks.
他的病情嚴重，必須住院三個星期。

hos·til·i·ty [hɑsˋtɪlətɪ] Track 5809

名 敵意

▶It was said that there was open hostility between the two candidates. 據說兩位候選人已表現出公開的敵意。

hu·man·i·tar·i·an [hjuˏmænəˋtɛrɪən] Track 5810

名 人道主義者、博愛 形 人道主義的

▶名 The famous humanitarian passed away yesterday.
那位有名的人道主義者昨天過世了。

▶形 Not until he met this man did he begin to devote himself to humanitarian causes.
直到他遇到了這個人，他才開始投身於人道主義事業。

實用片語用語
pass away 過世

hu·mil·i·ate [hjuˋmɪlɪˏet] Track 5811

動 侮辱、羞辱

▶He felt so humiliated that he left the room immediately.
他感到很屈辱，於是立刻離開了房間。

hunch [hʌntʃ] Track 5812

名 瘤 動 突出、弓起背部 同 bump 凸塊

▶名 I have a hunch that he is lying.
我的直覺告訴我他在撒謊。

▶動 She hunched up her shoulders as she sat at the desk thinking about this problem.
她聳著肩坐在書桌前想這個問題。

萬用延伸句型
sb. has a hunch that... 某人有種預感……

hur·dle [ˋhɝdl] Track 5813

名 障礙物、跨欄 動 跳過障礙

▶名 You should try to overcome the hurdles ahead, no matter how difficult they are.
你應該努力克服前面的困難，不管它們有多艱難。

▶動 He hurdled the fence and jumped into her yard.
他翻過籬笆跳進她家的院子。

實用片語用語
hurdle race 跨欄賽跑
例如：He won first place in the school's hurdle race yesterday.
他在昨天學校的跨欄賽跑得了第一名。

hy·giene [ˋhaɪdʒin] Track 5814

名 衛生學、衛生

▶No matter where we go, we must pay attention to our personal hygiene. 無論我們人在哪裡，都必須注意個人衛生。

hy·poc·ri·sy [hɪˋpɑkrəsɪ] Track 5815

名 偽善、虛偽

▶To tell you the truth, his hypocrisy made us sick all the time.
說實話，我們一直都很討厭他的虛偽。

hyp·o·crite [ˋhɪpəˏkrɪt] Track 5816

名 偽君子

▶The old lady is a hypocrite. She talks about the importance of kindness, yet is mean herself.
這位老太太是個偽君子。她總是在說待人善良很重要，然而她待人卻很不好。

文法字詞解析
與 hypocrite 相關的形容詞（言行不一的）是 hypocritical。

hys·ter·i·cal [hɪsˋtɛrɪkḷ]

Track 5817

形 歇斯底里的 同 upset 心煩的

▶The victims' family members all became quite hysterical after the accident.
事故發生後受害者的家人都變得非常歇斯底里。

文法字詞解析
這個字是從名詞「hysteria」延伸出來的，而hysteria有疾病「歇斯底里症」的意思，但也可以單純用來說明情緒非常激動。

il·lu·mi·nate [ɪˋluməˏnet]

Track 5818

動 照明、點亮、啓發

▶A sudden smile illuminated her face.
突然的微笑使她容光煥發。

il·lu·sion [ɪˋljuʒən]

Track 5819

名 錯覺、幻覺

▶He is under the illusion that his position is secure.
他誤以為他的地位很穩固。

im·mune [ɪˋmjun]

Track 5820

形 免除的

▶It seemed that he was immune to criticism.
他似乎不受批評的影響。

實用片語用語
be immune to... 對（某事物）免疫的

im·per·a·tive [ɪmˋpɛrətɪv]

Track 5821

名 命令 形 絕對必要的

▶名 I'm afraid that job creation has become an imperative for the government.
恐怕創造就業機會已經成為一件政府必須做的事了。

▶形 It is imperative for me to find a food source.
對我來說最首要的問題是取得食物來源。

im·ple·ment [ˋɪmpləmənt]

Track 5822

名 工具 動 施行

▶名 I don't think the store supplies agricultural implements.
我不覺得這商店會供應農具。

▶動 Implementing a policy by force is not a good idea.
強迫推行一項政策不是個好辦法。

im·pli·ca·tion [ˏɪmplɪˋkeʃən]

Track 5823

名 暗示、含意

▶I didn't gather the implications of her remark.
我沒聽出她那番話的含義。

im·plic·it [ɪmˋplɪsɪt]

Track 5824

形 含蓄的、不表明的 反 explicit 明確的

▶It seems that there was implicit consent in her silence.
她的沉默似乎是表示了默許。

實用片語用語
implicit memory 內隱記憶
例如：Implicit memory is a kind of memory you don't remember remembering but exists anyway.
內隱記憶是一種你自己都不曉得自己記得，但就是存在的記憶。

im·pos·ing [ɪm`pozɪŋ]   Track 5825

形 顯眼的

▶What an imposing building it is! Don't you think so?
多麼氣勢宏偉的建築物啊！你不覺得嗎？

im·pris·on [ɪm`prɪzn̩]   Track 5826

動 禁閉

▶It is said that they don't usually imprison first offenders（罪犯）. 據說他們通常不監禁初次犯罪的人。

im·pris·on·ment [ɪm`prɪzn̩mənt]   Track 5827

名 坐牢

▶He was sentenced to life imprisonment.
他被判終身監禁。

in·cen·tive [ɪn`sɛntɪv]   Track 5828

名 刺激、誘因 形 刺激的

▶名 Money is still a major incentive to most people.
對於大多數人來說，金錢仍是主要的誘因。

▶形 I'm afraid that my incentive payments this month will end up in smoke. 恐怕我這個月的獎金要泡湯了。

實用片語用語
have no incentive to... 沒有做某事的誘因
例如：Why would I steal my dad's car? I have no incentive to do that.
我幹嘛要偷我爸的車？我根本沒有做這種事的動機啊。

in·ci·den·tal [ˌɪnsə`dɛntl̩]   Track 5829

形 臨時發生的

▶It is said that this couple fell in love with each other through an incidental meeting on a bus.
據說這對情侶是因公車上的邂逅而愛上彼此的。

in·cline [ɪn`klaɪn]   Track 5830

動 傾向 名 傾斜面

▶動 I'm inclined to believe that he's innocent. How about you?
我傾向於相信他是無辜的。你呢？

▶名 The road has a very steep incline.
這條路有個非常陡的斜坡。

in·clu·sive [ɪn`klusɪv]   Track 5831

形 包含在內的 反 exclusive 排外的

▶I'm afraid that this is not an inclusive tour.
恐怕這不是包括一切費用在內的旅遊。

in·dig·na·tion [ˌɪndɪg`neʃən]   Track 5832

名 憤怒 同 anger 憤怒

▶He could scarcely keep in his indignation when he realized that he was lied to.
他發現自己被騙了時，憤怒得難以自持。

實用片語用語
be lied to 被騙了

in·ev·i·ta·ble [ɪn`ɛvətəbl̩]   Track 5833

形 不可避免的

▶It is inevitable for us to lose because our rival is so strong.
既然我們遇到了如此強大的對手，失敗是不可避免的。

in·fec·tious [ɪnˋfɛkʃəs] Track 5834

形 能傳染的

▶Flu is an infectious disease characterized by fever, aches and pains and exhaustion（疲勞）.
流感是一種傳染病，其特徵是發熱、全身疼痛和疲乏無力。

in·fer [ɪnˋfɝ] Track 5835

動 推斷、推理 同 suppose 假定、猜想

▶It is possible for us to infer two completely opposite conclusions from this set of facts.
從這些事實中我們可能推斷出兩種截然相反的結論。

in·fer·ence [ˋɪnfərəns] Track 5836

名 推理

▶Suppose he is guilty, then by inference so is she.
假設他有罪的話，那麼可以推斷出她也有罪。

實用片語用語
by inference 藉此推斷

in·gen·ious [ɪnˋdʒinjəs] Track 5837

形 巧妙的

▶This book shows that he is an ingenious author.
這本書表明了他是一個有創造力的作家。

in·ge·nu·i·ty [ˌɪndʒəˋnuətɪ] Track 5838

名 發明才能

▶She had the ingenuity to succeed when everyone else had failed. 她發揮了聰明才智而成功辦到了別人辦不到的事。

in·hab·it [ɪnˋhæbɪt] Track 5839

動 居住

▶It is said that there are only a few people inhabiting the island.
據說只有少數人在這個島上居住。

文法字詞解析
inhabit 是及物動詞，所以後面直接接受詞，而不需要再加介係詞。

in·hab·it·ant [ɪnˋhæbətənt] Track 5840

名 居民

▶Most of the inhabitants in the town are rather nice.
這個城裡的居民都是不錯的人。

in·her·ent [ɪnˋhɪrənt] Track 5841

形 天生的 同 internal 固有的、本質的

▶I'm afraid that there is an inherent weakness in the design.
恐怕這設計本身就存在著弱點。

i·ni·ti·a·tive [ɪˋnɪʃətɪv] Track 5842

名 倡導 形 率先的

▶名 It is hoped that the government's initiative will bring the strike to an end.
希望政府採取的主動措施可以結束罷工。

▶形 The new company is hoping to bring about its initiative prosperity.
那間新公司希望能實現初步繁榮。

in·ject [ɪn`dʒɛkt] *Track 5843*

動 注入

▶They injected him with a new drug.
他們給他注射了新的藥。

實用片語用語
inject sb. with... 將（某物）注射入（某人）體內

in·jec·tion [ɪn`dʒɛkʃən] *Track 5844*

名 注射

▶The doctor gave her an injection to alleviate her pain.
醫生替她注射以減輕她的疼痛。

in·jus·tice [ɪn`dʒʌstɪs] *Track 5845*

名 不公平 反 justice 公平

▶They complained bitterly（憤怒地）about the injustice of the system.
他們憤恨地抱怨制度的不公平。

in·no·va·tion [ˌɪnə`veʃən] *Track 5846*

名 革新 同 formation 公平

▶It seems that the innovation of air travel during this century has made the world smaller.
本世紀的空中旅行革新似乎使世界變小了。

in·no·va·tive [`ɪnoˏvetɪv] *Track 5847*

形 創新的

▶She always comes up with innovative ideas.
她總是能想出一些創新的點子。

in·quir·y [ɪn`kwaɪrɪ] *Track 5848*

名 詢問、調查 同 research 調查

▶Would you mind filling out this inquiry form?
請您填一下這張問卷好嗎？

實用片語用語
inquiry form 問卷 除了這種説法外，前面學過的「questionnaire」也是「問卷」的意思。

in·sight [`ɪnˏsaɪt] *Track 5849*

名 洞察

▶The book is filled with remarkable insights.
這本書很有真知灼見。

in·sis·tence [ɪn`sɪstəns] *Track 5850*

名 堅持

▶His insistence that they stay for lunch was not actually genuine.
他堅持要他們留下來吃午餐，但其實這堅持不是真心的。

in·stal·la·tion [ˌɪnstə`leʃən] *Track 5851*

名 就任、裝置

▶The installation of the telephone in our room will take a few hours. 我們房間的電話要花幾個小時才能安裝好。

文法字詞解析
我們在電腦上「安裝」軟體常用到的「安裝」這個動作就稱為「install」。

in·stall·ment [ɪn`stɔlmənt] *Track 5852*

名 分期付款

▶I had to pay for the car in installements.
我得用分期付款的方式付這台車的錢。

in·sti·tu·tion [ˌɪnstəˋtjuʃən] Track 5853

名 團體、機構、制度

▶Marriage is an institution in most societies.
婚姻是大多數社會早已確立的制度。

in·tact [ɪnˋtækt] Track 5854

形 原封不動的

▶It is a surprise that his honor remained intact after the scandal affair. 醜聞事件過後他的名譽竟然完整無損，這真令人吃驚。

實用片語用語
remain intact 保持原樣、保持完整

in·te·grate [ˋɪntəˌgret] Track 5855

動 整合

▶It has been very difficult for central government to integrate all of the local agencies into the national organization. 中央政府將所有的地方機構合併為全國性的機構一直非常困難。

in·te·gra·tion [ˌɪntəˋgreʃən] Track 5856

名 統合、完成

▶The secret of learning lies in the integration of theory and practice. 學習的秘訣在於理論與實踐的統一。

實用片語用語
the integration of theory and practice 理論和實務的整合

in·teg·ri·ty [ɪnˋtɛgrətɪ] Track 5857

名 正直 同 honesty 正直

▶A good man will respect a woman of integrity.
好男人都會尊敬那些正直誠實的女性。

in·tel·lect [ˋɪntḷˌɛkt] Track 5858

名 理解力

▶I'm afraid that you have estimated his intellect too highly.
恐怕你把他的智力評估得太高了。

in·ter·sec·tion [ˌɪntɚˋsɛkʃən] Track 5859

名 橫斷、交叉

▶There was a car accident at the intersection last night.
昨晚在交叉路口發生了一場交通事故。

in·ter·val [ˋɪntɚvḷ] Track 5860

名 間隔、休息時間 同 break 休息

▶The interval between the game lasted for 20 minutes.
比賽中間的休息時間共有20分鐘。

in·ter·vene [ˌɪntɚˋvin] Track 5861

動 介入

▶You had better not intervene in the affairs of others.
你最好不要干涉別人的事務。

實用片語用語
intervene in 介入

in·ter·ven·tion [ˌɪntɚˋvɛnʃən] Track 5862

名 介入、調停

▶It seems that it is necessary to accept a proper degree of state intervention.
似乎接受適當程度的國家干預是必要的。

in·ti·ma·cy [ˋɪntəməsɪ] Track 5863

名 親密

▶He was not surprised at the rapidity（迅速）of their intimacy. 他對他們的一見如故並不覺得奇怪。

in·tim·i·date [ɪnˋtɪmə͵det] Track 5864

動 恐嚇

▶Not everyone knows how to react when he or she is intimidated. 不是每個人都知道當自己被恐嚇時該如何反應。

in·trude [ɪnˋtrud] Track 5865

動 侵入、打擾 同 interrupt 打擾、打斷

▶This isn't your room, these people are not your friends, they're not talking about you, so you really shouldn't intrude. 這不是你的房間，這些人不是你的朋友，他們也沒在討論你，所以你真的不應該打擾。

in·trud·er [ɪnˋtrudɚ] Track 5866

名 侵入者

▶They chased out the intruders with guns. 他們拿槍把入侵者趕出去了。

實用片語用語
chase sb. out 把（某人）趕出去

in·val·u·a·ble [ɪnˋvæljəbl̩] Track 5867

形 無價的

▶A dictionary is an invaluable aid in learning a new language. 在學習一種新語言時，字典是非常貴重的工具。

in·ven·to·ry [ˋɪnvən͵torɪ] Track 5868

名 物品的清單 動 製作目錄

▶名 How often do we need to conduct an inventory check? 我們需要多久做一次庫存清點？

▶動 Could you tell me how often you inventory your store? 您能不能告訴我你多久清點一次你店裡的庫存？

文法字詞解析
在會計學中，inventory 有「存貨」的意思，例如：merchandise inventory（商品存貨）。

in·ves·ti·ga·tor [ɪnˋvɛstə͵getɚ] Track 5869

名 調查者、研究者

▶Investigators are searching the wreckage of the plane so that they can find the cause of the tragedy. 調查人員正在飛機殘骸中搜索，以便找出造成這一悲慘事件的原因。

IQ/in·tel·li·gence qu·o·ti·ent [ɪnˋtɛlədʒəns ˋkwoʃənt] Track 5870

名 智商

▶Even though his IQ is high, he has almost no EQ. 儘管他的智商很高，但他的情緒智商幾乎是零。

文法字詞解析
此處提到的 EQ 則是 Emotional quotient 的意思。

i·ron·ic [aɪˋrɑnɪk] Track 5871

形 譏諷的、愛挖苦人的

▶The boy who laughed at the cripple（殘障人士）ended up losing one leg himself. Ironic, isn't it? 那個嘲笑殘障人士的男孩自己也失去了一條腿。很諷刺，對吧？

i·ro·ny [ˋaɪrənɪ]

Track 5872

名 諷刺、反諷

▶The greatest irony was that he was actually not lying this time, yet no one believed him anymore.
最諷刺的是：他這次其實沒撒謊，但大家都不相信他了。

ir·ri·ta·ble [ˋɪrətəbl̩]

Track 5873

形 暴躁的、易怒的 同 mad 發狂

▶Even though she is irritable, she never loses her temper in front of children.
儘管她脾氣雖然很壞，她從不在孩子們面前發怒。

ir·ri·tate [ˋɪrəˏtet]

Track 5874

動 使生氣

▶You had better not irritate her. She's on a short fuse today.
你最好別惹她。她今天動不動就發火。

實用片語用語
be on a short fuse 容易發火的

ir·ri·ta·tion [ˏɪrəˋteʃən]

Track 5875

名 煩躁

▶He could not hide his irritation at his little sister.
他無法掩飾他的妹妹讓他覺得有多煩。

Jj

joy·ous [ˋdʒɔɪəs]

Track 5876

形 歡喜的、高興的 同 cheerful 高興的

▶This is really a joyous moment.
真是歡喜的時刻。

文法字詞解析
joy（名詞，歡樂的意思）加上形容詞字尾「-ous」即變成了 joyous 這個形容詞。

ker·nel [ˋkɝnl̩]

Track 5877

名 穀粒、籽、核心

▶Heat these kernels and they'll become popcorn.
把這些穀粒加熱，就會變成爆米花囉。

kid·nap [ˋkɪdnæp]

Track 5878

動 綁架、勒索 同 snatch 搶奪、綁架

▶Supposing the boy is kidnapped, what then?
假如那個男孩被綁架了，那怎麼辦？

文法字詞解析
要表示「綁架犯」的話，只要在 kidnap 後面加上表示「……者」的字尾「-er」，並重複尾音的 p，變成 kidnapper 即可。

la·ment [lə`mɛnt]
Track 5879

名 悲痛 動 哀悼 同 sorrow 悲痛

▶名 Her laments were ignored by most people.
大部分的人都忽視了她的哀嘆聲。

▶動 People often lament the passing of the good old days.
人們常常會惋惜美好過往的逝去。

la·va [`lɑvə]
Track 5880

名 熔岩

▶Do you think there is lava on the moon?
你覺得月球上有熔岩嗎？

實用片語用語
lava cake 熔岩蛋糕
例如：We split the lava cake between us after dinner.
吃完晚餐後我們就把熔岩蛋糕分一分吃掉了。

lay·man [`lemən]
Track 5881

名 普通信徒

▶The terms are difficult for a layman to understand.
這些術語對外行人來說很難理解。

lay·out [`le͵aʊt]
Track 5882

名 規劃、佈局

▶Can you tell me what the layout of this house is like?
你能告訴我房子的格局是怎麼樣的嗎？

LCD/liq·uid crys·tal dis·play [`ɛl`si`di]/[`lɪkwɪd `krɪstḷ dɪ`sple]
Track 5883

名 液晶顯示器

▶You'd better get a new LCD screen for your laptop.
你最好為你的手提電腦換一個新的液晶螢幕。

leg·end·ar·y [`lɛdʒənd͵ɛrɪ]
Track 5884

形 傳說的

▶Everyone thinks he is a legendary hero.
大家都認為他是一個傳奇英雄。

leg·is·la·tive [`lɛdʒɪs͵letɪv]
Track 5885

形 立法的

▶It's high time that the country undertook legislative reform.
國家該開始進行立法改革了。

萬用延伸句型
It is high time that S + V（過去式）
是時候做……
要注意這個句型其實用到了與現在事實相反的假設，因為在說話的當下並還沒做那件事，所以動詞要用過去式。

leg·is·la·tor [`lɛdʒɪs͵letɚ]
Track 5886

名 立法者

▶It is said that five legislators will be elected this time.
據說這次將選舉出五名立法委員。

leg·is·la·ture [`lɛdʒɪs͵letʃɚ]
Track 5887

名 立法院

▶He is an outstanding member of the legislature.
他是立法機關中的傑出成員。

le·git·i·mate

Track 5888

[lɪˋdʒɪtə͵met]/[lɪˋdʒɪtəmɪt]

動 使合法 形 合法的

▶動 We're working on legitimating homosexual marriage.
我們正努力將同性戀婚姻合法化。

▶形 You have to give me a legitimate reason for being late.
你得給我一個合理的遲到理由。

實用片語用語
be working on sth. 正努力（做某事）

length·y [ˋlɛŋθɪ]

Track 5889

形 漫長的

▶Her speech was lengthy and boring.
她的演講又冗長又無聊。

li·a·ble [ˋlaɪəbḷ]

Track 5890

形 可能的 同 probable 可能的

▶People are liable to make mistakes when they're tired.
人們疲勞的時候容易出錯。

實用片語用語
be liable to... 容易……的

lib·er·ate [ˋlɪbə͵ret]

Track 5891

動 使自由 同 free 使自由

▶They liberated the gorillas from the zoo.
他們放生了動物園的猩猩。

lib·er·a·tion [͵lɪbəˋreʃən]

Track 5892

名 解放

▶The people in that area are still struggling for liberation?
那一區的人仍然在為解放運動而奮鬥。

實用片語用語
struggle for... 為……而奮鬥

like·wise [ˋlaɪk͵waɪz]

Track 5893

副 同樣地

▶He walked straight through the door, and I did likewise.
他筆直地走進門，我也同樣這麼做。

lim·ou·sine/limo

Track 5894

[lɪmə͵zin]/[ˋlɪmo]

名 小客車

▶Will you tell me where I can take the limousine for the Royal Hotel?
請告訴我在哪裡可以搭乘皇家飯店的接駁巴士？

lin·er [ˋlaɪnɚ]

Track 5895

名 定期輪船（飛機）

▶It is reported that a liner collided with an oil tanker（油輪）last night.
據報導昨晚有一艘客輪與一艘油輪相撞了。

lin·guist [ˋlɪŋgwɪst]

Track 5896

名 語言學家

▶I'm no linguist, so I wouldn't be able to tell you what language this is written in. 我不是語言學家，所以我可沒辦法告訴你這是用什麼語言寫成的。

實用片語用語
be written in... 用（某種語言）寫成

li·ter [ˋlitɚ]
Track 5897

名 公升

▶A liter of gas has less mass than a liter of water.
一公升汽油的質量比一公升水的質量小。

lit·er·a·cy [ˋlɪtərəsɪ]
Track 5898

名 讀寫能力

▶It is a pity that he didn't pass the literacy test again.
很遺憾他這次讀寫測驗又沒過。

lit·er·al [ˋlɪtərəl]
Track 5899

形 文字的

▶Do you mind telling me what the literal meaning of the word is? 麻煩你告訴我這個字的原義是什麼好嗎？

lit·er·ate [ˋlɪtərɪt]
Track 5900

名 有學識的人 形 精通文學的 同 intellectual 知識分子

▶名 The literate read the letter for the illiterate man.
那個識字的人讀了那封信給那名不識字的人聽。

▶形 He's a very literate man and everything he writes is beautiful.
他是個精通文學的男人，寫出來的作品都非常美。

文法字詞解析
在 literate 前面加上含有「不、不是」含意的字首「il-」，就變成了 illiterate（不識字的）的意思。

lon·gev·i·ty [lɑnˋdʒɛvətɪ]
Track 5901

名 長壽

▶Proper rest and enough sleep contribute to longevity. What do you think about it?
適當的休息和足夠的睡眠有益於長壽。你覺得呢？

lounge [laʊndʒ]
Track 5902

名 交誼廳 動 閒逛

▶名 The manager is in a conference, so the secretary asked me to wait in the lounge.
經理正在開會，所以秘書叫我在交誼廳等候。

▶動 The old man enjoys lounging around at home.
那個老人喜歡懶洋洋地在家裡坐著。

lu·na·tic [ˋlunətɪk]
Track 5903

名 瘋子 形 瘋癲的 同 crazy 瘋的

▶名 The lunatic has escaped from the asylum.
那個瘋子從精神病院逃出來了。

▶形 Isn't his lunatic behavior a menace to our society?
他的瘋狂行為對我們的社會不是構成一種威脅了嗎？

lure [lʊr]
Track 5904

名 誘餌 動 誘惑 同 attract 吸引

▶名 I don't believe that your brother can resist the lure of money. 我不相信你哥哥抵擋得住金錢的誘惑。

▶動 This high price will probably not lure plenty of buyers（買家）.
這個高價格大概不能夠吸引多少買家。

實用片語用語
lure sb. to somewhere 把某人引誘到某處
例如：They lured the little boy to the dark alley with candy.
他們用糖果把小男孩引誘到暗巷。

lush [lʌʃ]

Track 5905

形 青翠的

▶The pasture（牧場）is filled with lush grass.
這個牧場滿是茂盛的青草。

lyr·ic [ˋlɪrɪk]

Track 5906

名 抒情詩 形 抒情的

▶名 The lyrics of the song are really terrible.
那首歌的歌詞實在寫得太爛了。

▶形 This is a good example of Wordsworth's lyric poetry.
這首詩是華滋華斯抒情詩的一個好範例。

mag·ni·tude [ˋmægnə͵tjud]

Track 5907

名 重大

▶The earthquake that just happened was magnitude 5.
剛剛發生的地震是震度5級。

實用片語用語
用來測量地震規模大小的「芮氏規模」就叫做 Richter magnitude scale。

ma·lar·i·a [məˋlɛrɪə]

Track 5908

名 瘧疾、瘴氣

▶It is said that malaria is an endemic（地方病）in many hot countries.
據說瘧疾是許多熱帶國家特有的疾病。

ma·nip·u·late [məˋnɪpjə͵let]

Track 5909

動 巧妙操縱

▶He manipulated them to voting for him.
他巧妙操縱他們為他投票。

文法字詞解析
manipulate 除了表示操縱「人心」以外，也能用來表示「操縱、改變」一些其他的東西。舉例來説，我們使用影像編輯功能來將照片修得更漂亮，就可以稱為 photo manipulation。

man·u·script [ˋmænjə͵skrɪpt]

Track 5910

名 手稿、原稿

▶I'm afraid that only an expert would understand the manuscript.
恐怕只有專家才看得懂這份手稿。

mar [mɑr]

Track 5911

動 毀損

▶His reputation is marred by several small scandals.
他的名聲被許多小的緋聞給毀了。

mas·sa·cre [ˋmæsəkɚ]

Track 5912

名 大屠殺 動 屠殺 同 slaughter 屠殺

▶名 Many people witnessed the horrendous（令人驚悚的）massacre.
許多人目擊那次令人不寒而慄的大屠殺。

▶動 The German fascists（法西斯主義者）massacred almost all the Jews in town.
德國法西斯分子幾乎殺光了城裡所有的猶太人。

文法字詞解析
除了用來表示真的大屠殺之外，massacre 在口語中也可以表示在比賽中實在贏太多，對方等於「被屠殺了」一樣。例如籃球比賽以 90 比 50 贏了敵隊，就可以説「We massacred them.」（我們贏他們很多）。

mas·ter·y [ˋmæstərɪ] Track 5913

名 優勢、精通、掌握

▶Her mastery of the violin impressed all the spectators.
她對小提琴的精通給觀眾們留下了深刻的印象。

ma·te·ri·al(ism) Track 5914

[məˋtɪrɪəl]/[məˋtɪrɪəˏlɪzm]

名 材質、材料、唯物論

▶We're in short of this kind of material now.
我們現在缺乏這種材料。

mat·tress [ˋmætrɪs] Track 5915

名 墊子

▶Would you please go and buy a new mattress for my bed with me?
你能陪我去買個新床墊嗎？

實用片語用語
spring mattress 彈簧床墊
例如：This spring mattress is so comfortable to sleep on.
這彈簧床墊真好睡啊。

mech·a·nism [ˋmɛkəˏnɪzəm] Track 5916

名 機械裝置 同 machine 機械

▶An airplane engine is a complex mechanism.
飛機引擎是種複雜的機械裝置。

med·i·ca·tion [ˏmɛdɪˋkeʃən] Track 5917

名 藥物治療

▶You had better not share this medication with others.
你最好不要把這種藥分給其他人使用。

me·di·e·val [ˏmɪdɪˋivəl] Track 5918

形 中世紀的

▶It is said that this church is a classic example of medieval architecture.
據說這座教堂是中世紀建築風格的典型實例。

實用片語用語
be a classic example of...
是……的典型例子

med·i·tate [ˋmɛdəˏtet] Track 5919

動 沉思

▶He is meditating on the meaning of life.
他正在思考人生的意義。

med·i·ta·tion [ˏmɛdəˋteʃən] Track 5920

名 熟慮

▶He reached his decision only after much meditation.
他是在經過一番沉思後才做出了決定。

mel·an·chol·y [ˋmɛlənˏkɑlɪ] Track 5921

名 悲傷、憂鬱 形 悲傷的 同 miserable 悲慘的

▶名 A deep melancholy runs through her poetry.
她的詩中貫穿著悲傷的情調。

▶形 He is a melancholy man who never smiles.
他是一個鬱鬱寡歡的人，從來都不笑。

文法字詞解析
「憂鬱症」的英文說法也和這個字相關，可以說成 melancholia（另一個更常見的說法則是 depression）。

mel·low [ˋmɛlo]

Track 5922

動 成熟 形 成熟的、圓潤的

▶動 Age has mellowed his attitude to some things.
隨著年齡的增加，他對某些事情的看法已日趨成熟。

▶形 Her voice sounded nice and mellow.
她的嗓音聽起來很圓潤好聽。

men·tal·i·ty [mɛnˋtælətɪ]

Track 5923

名 智力

▶I'm afraid that he has a get-rich-quick mentality.
他有一種急於一夜致富的心態。

mer·chan·dise [ˋmɝtʃən͵daɪz]

Track 5924

名 商品 動 買賣 同 product 產品

▶名 It is more expensive to mail merchandise than to freight it.
郵寄商品比貨運更昂貴。

▶動 If this product is properly merchandised, it should sell better than before.
這個產品如果促銷得當，應該會銷售得比以前更好。

merge [mɝdʒ]

Track 5925

動 合併 同 blend 混合

▶Why didn't they merge the two firms into a big one?
他們為什麼沒把兩家公司合併成為一家大公司呢？

實用片語用語
merge together 融合
例 如：The two teams merged together into one.
這兩隊融合起來變成一隊了。

met·a·phor [ˋmɛtəfɚ]

Track 5926

名 隱喻

▶In poetry the rose is often a metaphor for love.
玫瑰在詩中常被作為愛的象徵。

met·ro·pol·i·tan [͵mɛtrəˋpɑlətn̩]

Track 5927

名 都市人 形 大都市的 同 city 城市的

▶名 The metropolitan's behavior is different from us villagers.
那個都市人的行為方式跟我們鄉下人不一樣。

▶形 She left the small island and became famous in metropolitan France.
她離開了小島後在法國的都市地區中成名。

mi·grate [ˋmaɪgret]

Track 5928

動 遷徙、移居

▶Many birds migrate here from the north in winter.
冬天時有許多小鳥從北方遷徙而來。

實用片語用語
migrating birds 候鳥
例如：The migrating birds used to come here to the wetlands but not anymore.
以前候鳥會來這裡的濕地，但牠們現在都不來了。

mi·gra·tion [maɪˋgreʃən]

Track 5929

名 遷移

▶There was a huge migration of people into Europe because of the war.
因為戰爭，大量的移民湧入歐洲。

mil·i·tant [ˋmɪlətənt]

Track 5930

名 好戰份子 形 好戰的 同 hostile 懷敵意的

▶名 He is a militant in my opinion.
在我看來他是個好戰份子。

▶形 It seems that nothing could foil their militant spirit.
似乎沒有什麼能挫傷他們的鬥志。

mill·er [ˋmɪlɚ]

Track 5931

名 磨坊主人

▶This miller is a rich man who never leaves his mill.
這個磨坊主人很有錢，從不離開自己的磨坊。

mim·ic [ˋmɪmɪk]

Track 5932

名 模仿者 動 模仿

▶名 One of his brothers is a wonderful mimic.
他的一個兄弟很善於模仿。

▶動 He can mimic his uncle's voice and gestures perfectly.
他能把他叔叔的聲音和姿態模仿得惟妙惟肖。

文法字詞解析

mimic 在變成進行式的形式時，後面不能只加上 -ing，必須多一個 k 變成 mimicking。

min·i·a·ture [ˋmɪnɪətʃɚ]

Track 5933

名 縮圖、縮印 形 小型的

▶名 She is just like her mother in miniature. Don't you think so?
她簡直是她母親的縮影。你不覺得嗎？

▶形 The little girl has miniature furniture for her dolls.
那個小女孩有供洋娃娃用的迷你型傢俱。

min·i·mize [ˋmɪnəˏmaɪz]

Track 5934

動 減到最小

▶Minimize the window so that I can see your desktop（桌面）.
把視窗縮到最小，我才能看到你的桌面。

mi·rac·u·lous [məˋrækjələs]

Track 5935

形 奇蹟的

▶The army won a miraculous victory over a much stronger enemy.
這支軍隊打敗了比他們強勁的敵人，奇蹟般地贏得了勝利。

實用片語用語

miraculous cure 奇蹟的療藥
例如：They found a miraculous cure that could save the little boy's life.
他們找到了一種奇蹟的藥物能夠拯救小男孩的性命。

mis·chie·vous [ˋmɪstʃɪvəs]

Track 5936

形 淘氣的、有害的

▶What if the mischievous boy keeps behaving like that?
如果這個淘氣的男孩繼續這樣淘氣會怎麼樣？

mis·sion·ar·y [ˋmɪʃənˏɛrɪ]

Track 5937

名 傳教士 形 傳教的

▶名 I wish I could go to India as a missionary one day in the future. 要是將來有一天我能以傳教士的身份去印度就好了。

▶形 The whole group understood the value of missionary work.
整個團體的人都瞭解傳教工作的價值。

mo·bi·lize [ˋmobə͵laɪz] Track 5938

動 動員

▶Our country's in great danger; I'm afraid that we must mobilize the army.
我們國家正處於嚴重危險之中，恐怕我們必須把軍人動員起來。

mod·er·ni·za·tion [͵madənəˋzeʃən] Track 5939

名 現代化

▶Modernization has its pros and cons.
現代化有利也有弊。

實用片語用語
pros and cons 好處與壞處、利弊得失

mold [mold] Track 5940

名 鑄模 動 鑄造 同 shape 塑造

▶名 The two children look like they came out of the same mold.
那兩個孩子看起來像是一個模子刻出來的。

▶動 The children can mold figures out of clay.
孩子們能用黏土塑造人像。

mo·men·tum [moˋmɛntəm] Track 5941

名 動量、動力

▶The struggle for independence is gaining momentum every day.
為獨立而鬥爭的氣勢日益增長。

mo·nop·o·ly [məˋnapḷɪ] Track 5942

名 獨佔、壟斷

▶No one could compete with these steel monopolies.
沒有人能和這些鋼鐵壟斷企業競爭。

mo·not·o·nous [məˋnatənəs] Track 5943

形 單調的

▶Doing the same work each day can get really monotonous.
每天都做同樣的工作真是單調。

實用片語用語
monotonous speech 單調的演講
例如：His monotonous speech bored me to tears.
他單調的演講無聊得我都要哭了。

mo·not·o·ny [məˋnatənɪ] Track 5944

名 單調

▶These activities help people add color to the monotony of everyday life.
這些活動能為人們平日單調的生活增添色彩。

mo·rale [məˋræl] Track 5945

名 士氣

▶Our team needs to boost its morale.
我們的球隊需要恢復士氣。

mo·ral·i·ty [mɔˋrælətɪ] Track 5946

名 道德、德行 同 character 高尚品德

▶Mr. Huang is a man of strict morality.
黃先生是一個品行極為端正的人。

mot·to [ˋmɑto]

Track 5947

名 座右銘 同 proverb 諺語

▶My motto is "Never give up". 我的座右銘是「永不氣餒」。

實用片語用語
give up 放棄

mourn·ful [ˋmornfəl]

Track 5948

形 令人悲痛的

▶The children looked mournful because of their brother's death.
那些孩子因為哥哥過世而看起來很悲痛。

文法字詞解析
because of 後面要接名詞或動名詞，不能接子句。

mouth·piece [ˋmaʊθ͵pis]

Track 5949

名 樂器吹口、代言人

▶I forgot to clean the mouthpiece of the flute.
我忘記清理長笛的吹口了。

mouth·piece/spokes·per·son/spokes·man/spokes·wom·an

Track 5950

[ˋmaʊθ͵pis]/[ˋspoks͵pɝsn̩]/[ˋspoksmən]/[ˋspokswʊmən]

名 發言人、代言人

▶Tom is the mouthpiece of this company.
湯姆是這家公司的代言人。

mu·nic·i·pal [mjuˋnɪsəpl̩]

Track 5951

形 內政的

▶The municipal affairs of this country are very corrupt.
這個國家的內政相當腐敗。

實用片語用語
municipal affairs 內政事務

mute [mjut]

Track 5952

名 啞巴 形 沉默的 同 silent 沉默的

▶名 It was the accident ten years ago that made him a mute.
是十年前的一次事故使他變成了啞巴。

▶形 The child has been mute since birth.
那個孩子生來就是啞巴。

my·thol·o·gy [mɪˋθɑlədʒɪ]

Track 5953

名 神話

▶It is necessary for you to read poetry, novels, mythology and other works if you want to get a PhD in literature.
如果你想成為一位文學博士，就應該閱讀詩歌、小說、神話等其他作品。

文法字詞解析
mythology 也可以簡稱 myth。

nar·rate [næˋret]

Track 5954

動 敘述、講故事 同 report 報告

▶The writer narrated his own experiences in the book.
作家在書中講述的是他自身的經歷。

nar·ra·tive [ˋnærətɪv]

Track 5955

名 敘述、故事 形 敘事的

▶名 The narrative of the book was quite hard to understand.
書中的敘述很難懂。

▶形 Will you explain what this narrative poem means?
請你為我解釋一下這首敘事詩的意思好嗎？

nar·ra·tor [næˋretɚ]

Track 5956

名 敘述者、講述者

▶In fact, I don't think the narrator is the author himself.
事實上，我不認為敘述者是作者本人。

萬用延伸句型
In fact... 事實上……

na·tion·al·ism [ˋnæʃənḷˏɪzəm]

Track 5957

名 民族主義、國家主義

▶It is hard for the students to understand what nationalism means.
學生們很難理解民族主義的含義。

nat·u·ral·ist [ˋnætʃərəlɪst]

Track 5958

名 自然主義者

▶It is a surprise that his theory should be so similar to that of the famous naturalist, Charles Darwin.
他的理論竟然跟著名的博物學家查爾斯・達爾文如此相似，這真令人驚訝啊。

實用片語用語
be similar to... 和……相似

na·val [ˋnevḷ]

Track 5959

形 有關海運的

▶It is said that the old man used to be a great naval officer in World War II.
據說這位老人曾是第二次世界大戰中的偉大海軍軍官。

na·vel [ˋnevḷ]

Track 5960

名 中心點、肚臍

▶I want to get a ring on my navel.
我想在肚臍上穿個環。

nav·i·ga·tion [ˏnævəˋgeʃən]

Track 5961

名 航海、航空

▶We cannot do without a compass in navigation.
在航海中我們不能沒有羅盤。

實用片語用語
do without sth. 沒有（某物）而仍能繼續運作

ne·go·ti·a·tion [nɪˏgoʃɪˋeʃən]

Track 5962

名 協商、協議

▶Do you mind telling me how the negotiation is going?
能麻煩你告訴我協商進行得怎麼樣了嗎？

ne·on [ˋniˏɑn]

Track 5963

名 霓虹燈

▶You will see the colorful neon lights in the city wherever you go. 城市裡霓虹燈隨處可見。

neu·tral [ˋnjutrəl] Track 5964

名 中立國 形 中立的、中立國的 同 independent 無黨派的

▶動 Was Switzerland a neutral during World War II?
瑞士在第二次大戰中是一個中立國嗎？

▶形 Suppose you were him. Would you also remain neutral during the debate?
如果你是他的話，你也會在辯論中保持中立嗎？

new·ly-wed [ˋnjulɪ͵wɛd] Track 5965

名 新婚夫婦

▶How is the newly-wed couple getting on?
這對新婚夫婦最近怎麼樣了？

文法字詞解析
「新婚夫婦」也可以直接稱「newly-weds」，後面不一定需要加上 couple。

news·cast·er/an·chor·man/an·chor·wom·an Track 5966

[ˋnuzkæstə]/[ˋæŋkəmæn]/[ˋæŋkə͵wumən]

名 新聞播報員

▶Do you have a favorite newscaster?
你有最喜歡的新聞播報員嗎？

nom·i·na·tion [͵nɑməˋneʃən] Track 5967

名 提名、任命 同 selection 被挑選出的人或物

▶His nomination of her was rejected.
他提名了她，卻被否決了。

nom·i·nee [͵nɑməˋni] Track 5968

名 被提名的人

▶The presidential nominee was always starting quarrels on TV.
那個總統候選人總是在電視上跟人家吵架。

norm [nɔrm] Track 5969

名 基準、規範 同 criterion 準則

▶Everyone in the nation is supposed to abide by the social norms. 國家裡的每一個人都應該遵守社會行為準則。

實用片語用語
out of the norm 不正常的
例如：I looked around the room but didn't see anything out of the norm.
我環顧房間四周，並沒有看到什麼不正常的事物。

no·to·ri·ous [noˋtorɪəs] Track 5970

形 聲名狼藉的

▶Isn't Hitler a notorious dictator?
希特勒不是一個惡名昭彰的獨裁者嗎？

nour·ish [ˋnɝɪʃ] Track 5971

動 滋養

▶Don't you think that milk is a nourishing drink?
你不覺得牛奶是富含營養的飲料嗎？

nour·ish·ment [ˋnɝɪʃmənt] Track 5972

名 營養

▶You need more nourishment. Come in and let me get you something to eat.
你還需要吃得更營養一些。進來，我弄點東西給你吃。

文法字詞解析
nourishment 指的不一定是身體上的營養喔！事實上「心靈上的養分」也可以稱做 nourishment of the mind。

nui·sance [ˋnjusn̩s] Track 5973

名 討厭的人、麻煩事

▶Did the rats get in the kitchen again? What a nuisance!
老鼠們又跑進廚房了嗎？真是麻煩。

nur·ture [ˋnɝtʃɚ] Track 5974

名 養育、培育 動 培育、養育

▶名 Nurture is more important than nature, according to some philosophers. 有些哲學家認為教養勝過天性。

▶動 It's a mother's duty to nurture her children.
養育子女是一個母親的責任。

nu·tri·ent [ˋnjutrɪənt] Track 5975

名 營養物 形 有養分的、營養的

▶名 The plant drew minerals and other nutrients from the soil.
植物從泥土中吸收礦物質和其他養分。

▶形 Even though she ate so much nutrient food, she is still very slim.
即使她吃了這麼多營養的食物，她還是這麼苗條。

nu·tri·tion [njuˋtrɪʃən] Track 5976

名 營養物、營養 同 nourishment 營養

▶People nowadays eat much more food, yet gain less nutrition.
現代的人吃得更多，卻得到更少的營養。

實用片語用語

nutrition label 營養成分標籤

例如：She always reads the nutrition label before buying things from the supermarket.
她在超市買東西之前，總是先閱讀營養成分標籤。

nu·tri·tious [njuˋtrɪʃəs] Track 5977

形 有養分的、營養的

▶Buying all kinds of nutritious food won't make you healthier if you don't exercise.
你不運動的話，買各種營養食品也不會變得比較健康。

ob·li·ga·tion [ˏɑbləˋgeʃən] Track 5978

名 責任、義務

▶You're under no obligation to pay for goods which you did not order. 如果你沒有訂購貨物就無須付款。

o·blige [əˋblaɪdʒ] Track 5979

動 使不得不、強迫

▶He was finally obliged to abandon that plan.
他終於不得不放棄那個計畫。

實用片語用語

be obliged to 不得不（做某事）

ob·scure [əbˋskjʊr] Track 5980

動 使陰暗 形 陰暗的

▶動 The clouds obscured the moon. 雲朵遮住了月亮。

▶形 The poem is completely obscure to me.
這首詩對我來說完全看不懂。

of·fer·ing [ˋɔfərɪŋ]

Track 5981

名 供給

▶They ended up not only having to apologize but also offering a refund.
他們最後不但同意道歉，而且還會退款。

off·spring [ˋɔfsprɪŋ]

Track 5982

名 子孫、後裔 同 descendant 子孫、後裔

▶The parents are both brilliant people. It is no wonder that their offspring are so intelligent.
父母都是很傑出的人，怪不得他們的後代那麼聰明。

op·er·a·tion·al [͵ɑpəˋreʃənḷ]

Track 5983

形 操作的

▶Do you mind telling me what the operational hours of the restaurant are?
您介意告訴我這家餐廳營業的時間嗎？

實用片語用語
operational hours 營業時間

op·po·si·tion [͵ɑpəˋzɪʃən]

Track 5984

名 反對的態度 同 disagreement 反對

▶There is a fierce opposition to the new tax program.
針對新的徵稅計畫，出現了強烈的反對意見。

op·press [əˋprɛs]

Track 5985

動 壓迫、威迫

▶A tyrannic（暴虐的）government which oppresses people will be overthrown one day.
一個壓迫人民的暴虐政府終究會被推翻的。

文法字詞解析
oppress 加上「-ed」就變成了形容詞「oppressed（受壓迫的）」。

op·pres·sion [əˋprɛʃən]

Track 5986

名 壓迫、壓制

▶It is said that the early sex anxiety and sex oppression will cause the distortion of the personality.
據說早期性焦慮與性壓抑將導致人格扭曲。

op·tion [ˋɑpʃən]

Track 5987

名 選擇、取捨 同 choice 選擇

▶Could you tell me how many options there are open to us?
你能告訴我們有多少種可能的選擇嗎？

op·tion·al [ˋɑpʃənḷ]

Track 5988

形 非強制性的、可選擇的

▶Would you please tell me if the optional course is as hard as everybody says?
你能不能告訴我那門選修課真的像大家所說的那麼難嗎？

實用片語用語
optional course 選修課程

or·deal [ɔrˋdiəl]

Track 5989

名 嚴酷的考驗

▶His courage was severely tried by his ordeal.
他的勇氣在艱難困苦中經受了嚴峻的考驗。

or·der·ly [ˋɔrdəlɪ]

Track 5990

名 勤務兵 形 整潔的、有秩序的

▶名 The orderlies in this hospital are very professional.
這家醫院的護理人員非常專業。

▶形 He gave an orderly answer to that strict teacher.
他條理分明地回答了那個嚴格的老師的問題。

or·gan·ism [ˋɔrgən͵ɪzəm]

Track 5991

名 有機體、生物體 同 organization 有機體

▶Do you know how many single-celled（單細胞的）organisms there are in the world? 你知道世界上有多少單細胞生物體嗎？

o·rig·i·nal·i·ty [ə͵rɪdʒəˋnælətɪ]

Track 5992

名 獨創力、創舉 同 style 風格

▶Tom is distinguished for his originality and for having produced many special products.
湯姆以有創意著稱，且創造出許多特別的產品。

實用片語用語
be distinguished for... 因……而著稱

o·rig·i·nate [əˋrɪdʒə͵net]

Track 5993

動 創造、發源

▶It is said that the style of architecture originated from the ancient Greeks. 據說這種建築風格起源於古希臘。

out·break [ˋaʊt͵brek]

Track 5994

名 爆發、突然發生

▶I'm afraid that the outbreak of the war will paralyze the traffic in the city. 恐怕戰爭的爆發將使城內的交通癱瘓。

out·fit [ˋaʊt͵fɪt]

Track 5995

名 裝備 動 提供必需的裝備

▶名 My dad bought a new outfit for me.
我爸爸幫我買了一套新服裝。

▶動 You need to outfit yourself with the latest equipment.
你得用最新的設備把自己裝備起來。

文法字詞解析
除了「裝備」外，outfit 也可以指平常穿在身上的一整套衣服，例如「春裝」就可以稱為 spring outfit。你現在穿在身上的，從衣帽到鞋襪都是你「outfit」的一部分。

out·ing [ˋaʊtɪŋ]

Track 5996

名 郊遊、遠足

▶It's a pity that the weather isn't better for our outing today.
今天天氣不好所以我們不能去遠足，真遺憾。

out·law [ˋaʊt͵lɔ]

Track 5997

名 逃犯 動 禁止

▶名 I hope the outlaw will be caught as soon as possible.
我希望那個逃犯能夠儘快被抓住。

▶動 I hope the sale of tobacco will be outlawed someday.
要是有朝一日煙草製品被禁止銷售就好了。

out·let [ˋaʊt͵lɛt]

Track 5998

名 逃離的出口

▶There is a huge sales outlet for weight-losing products.
我認為瘦身產品有極大的市場。

out·look [ˋaʊt͵lʊk] Track 5999

名 觀點、態度 同 attitude 態度

▶Optimism is a healthy outlook on life.
樂觀是一種健康的人生觀。

out·num·ber [aʊtˋnʌmbɚ] Track 6000

動 數目勝過 同 exceed 超過

▶Men outnumber women here in the ratio of three to one.
此地的男子數量以三比一的比例超過女子。

文法字詞解析
字首「out-」有「超過、越過」的意思，而既然超過了「number」（數字），也就是「數目比……大」、「數目勝過……」的意思了。

out·rage [ˋaʊt͵redʒ] Track 6001

名 暴行 動 施暴

▶名 What an outrage! How could he do something like that?
真是太過份了吧！他怎麼可以做這樣的事？

▶動 The people were outraged by the government's decision.
大眾對政府的這一決定非常憤怒。

out·ra·geous [aʊtˋredʒəs] Track 6002

形 暴力的

▶The outrageous book created a sensation.
那部聳人聽聞的書曾轟動一時。

out·right [ˋaʊt͵raɪt] Track 6003

形 毫無保留的、全部的 副 無保留地、公然地

▶形 She is the outright winner without question.
毫無疑問她是優勝者。

▶副 Why don't you tell him outright what you thought of him?
為什麼不坦率地向他說出你對他的想法呢？

out·set [ˋaʊt͵sɛt] Track 6004

名 開始、開頭

▶The novel fascinates the reader from the outset.
這本小說一開頭就把讀者迷住了。

文法字詞解析
調換一下順序的話，set out 是一個片語，意思是「出發（去某地、做某事）」的意思。例如：The kids set out to look for the dog.
孩子們出發去找狗。

o·ver·head [ˋovɚ͵hɛd] Track 6005

形 頭頂上的、位於上方的 副 在上方地、在頭頂上地
同 above 在上方

▶形 Would you please help me put the luggage in the overhead compartment（隔間）?
您能幫我把行李放進頭頂上的行李置放櫃嗎？

▶副 The people in the room overhead are very noisy.
樓上那個房間的人很吵。

o·ver·lap [͵ovɚˋlæp] Track 6006

名 重疊的部份 動 重疊

▶名 There is an overlap between the two courses.
這兩門課程之間有衝堂的問題。

▶動 The functions of the new office overlaps the functions of the one already in existence.
新機構的機能與現存機構的機能有部分重疊。

A B C D E F G H I J K L M N **O** P Q R S T U V W X Y Z

o·ver·turn [ˋovɚ͵tɝn]/[͵ovɚˋtɝn] *Track 6007*

名 顛覆 動 顛倒、弄翻

▶名 The overturn of that irresponsible government was something worth celebrating.
那個不負責任的政府垮臺，真是太值得慶祝了。

▶動 The boat overturned because of the huge waves.
那艘船因為大浪而翻覆了。

pact [pækt] *Track 6008*

名 契約

▶I have no idea what the Warsaw Pact stood for.
我不知道華沙條約的意義是什麼。

pam·phlet [ˋpæmflɪt] *Track 6009*

名 小冊子 同 brochure 小冊子

▶I have no time to distribute these pamphlets.
我沒有時間分發這些小冊子了。

實用片語用語
political pamphlet 政治宣傳冊
例如：My grandfather still keeps some of the political pamphlets he helped distribute.
我爺爺還留著一些他以前發過的政治宣傳冊。

par·a·lyze [ˋpærə͵laɪz] *Track 6010*

動 麻痺

▶This kind of poison can quickly paralyze the fish.
這種毒素會讓魚很快麻痺。

par·lia·ment [ˋpɑrləmənt] *Track 6011*

名 議會
同 congress 美國國會

▶Will you tell me when Parliament first came into existence?
你能告訴我議會最初是什麼時候形成的嗎？

pa·thet·ic [pæˋθɛtɪk] *Track 6012*

形 悲慘的

▶What a pathetic performance! I am sure it is the worst I have seen.
好爛的一場表演！我敢確定這是我看過最糟糕的一場表演。

文法字詞解析
和 pathetic 相關的一個形容詞是 apathetic，意思是「無感覺的、冷淡的」。

pa·tri·ot·ic [͵petrɪˋɑtɪk] *Track 6013*

形 愛國的 同 loyal 忠誠的

▶This is a song that can arouse patriotic sentiment.
這首歌能喚起人的愛國情操。

PDA [ˋpiˋdiˋe] *Track 6014*

名 個人數位秘書、掌上型電腦

▶PDA stands for "Personal Digital Assistant".
PDA 是「個人數位助理」的縮寫。

文法字詞解析
除了表示 Personal Digital Assistant 以外，PDA 還可以代表 Public Display of Affection，即在公開場合公然表現親暱行為的意思。也就是說，如果你在圖書館，對面坐了一對情侶在卿卿我我，他們做的事就是一種 PDA。

ped·dle [ˋpɛdl] Track 6015

動 叫賣、兜售 同 sell 銷售

▶His brother has been peddling from house to house for weeks.
他弟弟挨家挨戶地叫賣已經有好幾個星期了。

實用片語用語
from house to house 挨家挨戶

pe·des·tri·an [pəˋdɛstrɪən] Track 6016

名 行人 形 徒步的

▶名 The pedestrians are supposed to cross the road when they see the green light.
行人應該在看見綠燈時穿過馬路。

▶形 They should cross the road at the pedestrian crossing.
他們應該從行人穿越道過馬路。

pen·in·su·la [pəˋnɪnsələ] Track 6017

名 半島

▶There's a lighthouse at the end of the peninsula.
在半島的尾端有一座燈塔。

pen·sion [ˋpɛnʃən] Track 6018

名 退休金 動 給予退休金
同 allowance 津貼、發津貼

▶名 The reason he claimed a pension was that he had been ill for a long time.
他之所以申請救助金是因為他長期生病。

▶動 He is pensioned off because the company wants to replace him with a young man.
他被迫提早退休的原因，是公司想讓一位年輕人來接替他的職務。

實用片語用語
retirement pension 退休金
例如：The old man was cheated out of his retirement pension.
那個老人被騙了，以致於拿不到退休金。

per·cep·tion [pəˋsɛpʃən] Track 6019

名 感覺、察覺 同 sense 感覺

▶He is admired for the depth of his perception.
他因為深具洞察力而受到了賞識。

per·se·ver·ance [ˏpɝsəˋvɪrəns] Track 6020

名 堅忍、堅持

▶I don't think you can make it if you lack perseverance.
如果你缺乏毅力，我覺得你就無法成功。

per·se·vere [ˏpɝsəˋvɪr] Track 6021

動 堅持

▶Even if you persevere, you won't always succeed.
即使你堅持下去，最終也不見得一定會獲得成功。

萬用延伸句型
Even if... 就算……、即使……

per·sis·tence [pəˋsɪstəns] Track 6022

名 固執、堅持 同 maintenance 維持

▶His persistence in the matter is getting a bit annoying.
他一直固執在這件事上面，令人覺得有點煩。

per·sist·ent [pə`sɪstənt] Track 6023

形 固執的

▶His persistent phone calls made her throw her cell phone at the wall. 他堅持不懈地一直打電話給她，讓她受不了地把手機砸向牆壁。

per·spec·tive [pə`spɛktɪv] Track 6024

名 透視、觀點 形 透視的 同 position 立場

▶名 It is from here that you can get a perspective of the whole city. 就是從這裡，你可以看到城市的全景。

▶形 This teacher taught me what perspective drawing is. 這位老師教了我透視畫的畫法。

實用片語用語

from sb.'s perspective 從某人的觀點
例如：From my perspective, it definitely won't work.
從我的觀點來看，絕對不會成功的。

pes·ti·cide [`pɛstɪ͵saɪd] Track 6025

名 農藥

▶It's time for the farmers to spread the pesticide over the rice fields. 該是農民們在稻田裡噴灑農藥的時候了。

pe·tro·le·um [pə`trolɪəm] Track 6026

名 石油

▶There is a shortage of petroleum recently in our nation. 最近我國的石油短缺。

pet·ty [`pɛtɪ] Track 6027

形 瑣碎的、小的 同 small 小的

▶Why are you fighting over such a petty matter? 你們為什麼要因為這麼小的事情而吵架？

phar·ma·cist [`fɑrməsɪst] Track 6028

名 藥劑師

▶I obtained my pharmacist's license last month. 我上個月拿到了藥劑師執照。

實用片語用語

pharmacist's license 藥劑師執照

phar·ma·cy [`fɑrməsɪ] Track 6029

名 藥劑學、藥局

▶Would you like me to get some painkillers（止痛藥）from the pharmacy for you? 要不要我到藥局去幫你買一些止痛藥啊？

phase [fez] Track 6030

名 階段 動 分段實行 同 stage 階段

▶名 It was a very important phase in history. 它是一個非常重要的歷史階段。

▶動 Not all people believe that the U.S. army will complete the phased withdrawal（撤軍）in four months. 不是所有人都相信美軍會在四個月內完成分段撤軍。

pho·to·graph·ic [͵fotə`græfɪk] Track 6031

形 攝影的

▶I have no idea what this photographic equipment is used for. 我對這種攝影器材的用處一無所知。

實用片語用語

photographic equipment 攝影器材

pic·tur·esque [ˌpɪktʃəˋrɛsk]　Track 6032

形 如畫的

▶I took photos of the picturesque shores beside the river.
我用相機照下景色如畫的河岸。

pierce [pɪrs]　Track 6033

動 刺穿

▶She got her ears pierced back in high school.
她以前高中的時候打了耳洞。

pi·e·ty [ˋpaɪətɪ]　Track 6034

名 虔敬

▶They came to the temple not because of curiosity but because of piety.
他們來到這座廟不是因為好奇，而是出於虔誠信仰。

實用片語用語
filial piety 孝道
例如：Filial piety is concept that is taught in schools here.
這裡的學校有教孝道的概念。

pi·ous [ˋpaɪəs]　Track 6035

形 虔誠的　同 faithful 忠誠的

▶He is a pious follower of God, like his parents.
他跟他的父母親一樣也是個虔誠的基督徒。

pipe·line [ˋpaɪpˌlaɪn]　Track 6036

名 管線

▶It took the workers two years to lay these oil pipelines.
工人們花了兩年的時間才把這些輸油管鋪設好。

pitch·er [ˋpɪtʃɚ]　Track 6037

名 投手

▶The handsome pitcher led his team to victory.
這個英俊的投手領導了他的球隊獲得勝利。

plight [plaɪt]　Track 6038

名 誓約、婚約

▶It seemed that the man is in a sad plight.
這個男人的處境似乎非常困難。

實用片語用語
be in a sad plight 處於困境中

pneu·mo·nia [njuˋmonjə]　Track 6039

名 肺炎

▶A lot of people caught pneumonia in a short time.
在很短的時間內，有很多人感染肺炎。

文法字詞解析
要注意 pneumonia 開頭的 p 是不發音的喔！

poach [potʃ]　Track 6040

動 偷獵、水煮

▶Will you teach me how to poach eggs for my breakfast?
你能教我怎麼用煮水波蛋當早餐嗎？

poach·er [ˋpotʃɚ]　Track 6041

名 偷獵者

▶The poacher is fined heavily by the authorities.
偷獵者被管理機構罰了不少錢。

pol·lu·tant [pəˋlutənt]

Track 6042

名 污染物 形 污染物的

▶名 We found a lot of industrial pollutants in the lake.
我們在湖中發現了很多工業污染物。

▶形 Few people pay attention to the Pollutant Standards Index.
很少有人關注空氣污染指數。

實用片語用語
industrial pollutant 工業污染物
pollutant 前面可以加不同的形容詞來講不同方面的汙染物，例如：chemical pollutant 化學污染物。

pon·der [ˋpandɚ]

Track 6043

動 仔細考慮 同 consider 考慮

▶The boy sat there pondering the problem.
男孩坐在那裡思考這個問題。

pop·u·late [ˋpapjəˏlet]

Track 6044

動 居住

▶The city is heavily populated by immigrants.
這個城市居住著很多外來移民。

pos·ture [ˋpastʃɚ]

Track 6045

名 態度、姿勢 動 擺姿勢

▶名 Good posture is very important for health.
良好的姿勢對健康很重要。

▶動 He enjoys posturing in front of people, so nobody likes him. 他很喜歡在人前裝模作樣，所以沒人喜歡他。

實用片語用語
bad posture 姿勢不良
例如：Bad posture may lead to terrible health during old age.
不良的姿勢可能會造成年老時不健康。

pre·cede [priˋsid]

Track 6046

動 在前 同 lead 走在最前方

▶It is obvious that this duty should precede all others.
顯然這項義務應該優先於其他一切義務。

pre·ce·dent [ˋprɛsədənt]

Track 6047

名 前例

▶She is the first queen who broke the precedent by sending her children to a public school.
她是首位破例讓自己的孩子到公立學校就讀的女王。

pre·ci·sion [priˋsɪʒən]

Track 6048

名 精準 同 accuracy 準確

▶You must make sure that all instruments are made with precision.
你必須確保這些儀器製造精密。

實用片語用語
with precision 精準地

pred·e·ces·sor [ˌprɛdɪˋsɛsɚ]

Track 6049

名 祖先、前輩

▶The new worker is better than his predecessor.
這名新的工作人員比他的前任做得更好。

pre·dic·tion [prɪˋdɪkʃən]

Track 6050

名 預言

▶He was as surprised as anyone that his prediction came true.
他的預言成真了，連他自己都跟其他人一樣驚訝。

pref·ace [ˋprɛfɪs] Track 6051

名 序言 同 introduction 序言

▶Will you find someone to translate the preface from French to English?
你能找個人將序言從法文翻譯成英文嗎？

prej·u·dice [ˋprɛdʒədɪs] Track 6052

名 偏見 動 使存有偏見

▶名 Prejudice sometimes hampers（妨礙）a person from doing the right thing.
偏見有時候會妨害人做正確的事情。

▶動 Don't you think these facts will prejudice them in his favor?
你不覺得這些事實會使他們偏袒他嗎？

實用片語用語
without prejudice 沒有偏見的
例如：We need someone without prejudice to decide the winner.
我們需要一個沒有偏見的人來決定誰能贏得比賽。

pre·lim·i·nar·y [prɪˋlɪməˌnɛrɪ] Track 6053

名 初步 形 初步的

▶名 The exciting matches will begin soon now that the preliminaries are almost over.
預賽快比完了，真正刺激的比賽快要開始了。

▶形 The preliminary results are posted on the board.
佈告板上把初步的結果貼出來了。

pre·ma·ture [ˌprimə`tjʊr] Track 6054

形 過早的、未成熟的

▶It's premature to say what will happen for sure now.
現在要確定地說出會發生什麼事還太早了。

pre·mier [ˋprimɪɚ] Track 6055

名 首長 形 首要的 同 prime 首要的

▶名 He requested the premier to meet him in secret.
他要求總理秘密接見他。

▶形 People think this is Europe's premier port.
人們都認為這裡是歐洲第一大港。

實用片語用語
request sb. to... 要求（某人）做某事

pre·scribe [prɪˋskraɪb] Track 6056

動 規定、開藥方

▶All the public officials are supposed to do as the laws prescribe.
所有的政府官員都應該依法辦事。

pre·scrip·tion [prɪˋskrɪpʃən] Track 6057

名 指示、處方

▶Do you mind my leaving this prescription with you?
你介意我把這張處方留在你這兒嗎？

pre·side [prɪˋzaɪd] Track 6058

動 主持

▶Until now, who is to preside over the meeting still hasn't been decided.
直到現在，這個會議要由誰來主持還未決定。

A B C D E F G H I J K L M N O **P** Q R S T U V W X Y Z

pres·i·den·cy [ˋprɛzədənsɪ] Track 6059

名 總統的職位

▶I don't think he is going to run for presidency this year.
我不覺得他今年會競選總統。

實用片語用語
run for presidency 參選總統

pres·i·den·tial [ˋprɛzədɛnʃəl] Track 6060

形 總統的

▶They are the front runners in the presidential elections.
這些人在總統競選中最有可能獲勝。

pres·tige [prɛsˋtiʒ] Track 6061

名 聲望

▶He will probably suffer a loss of prestige because of the scandal.
他大概會因為這件醜聞而威信掃地。

pre·sume [prɪˋzum] Track 6062

動 假設 同 guess 推測

▶You can't just presume that he will approve of the plan.
你不能就這樣假設他一定會支持這個計畫。

pre·ven·tive [prɪˋvɛntɪv] Track 6063

名 預防物 形 預防的

▶名 She took some preventives before the headache started.
她在開始頭痛前就先吃了預防的藥。

▶形 It's about time that we took preventive measures.
我們該採取預防措施了。

實用片語用語
preventive measure 預防措施

pro·duc·tiv·i·ty [ˌprodʌkˋtɪvətɪ] Track 6064

名 生產力

▶It is wrong for us to underestimate or overestimate（高估）our agricultural productivity.
低估和高估我們的農業生產力都是不對的。

pro·fi·cien·cy [prəˋfɪʃənsɪ] Track 6065

名 熟練、精通

▶They were surprised at his English proficiency.
他們對於他精通英語的程度驚訝不已。

pro·found [prəˋfaʊnd] Track 6066

形 極深的、深奧的

▶He has a profound knowledge of history.
他的歷史知識極為淵博。

實用片語用語
profound effect 很深的影響
例如：Parents' behavior has a profound effect on their children.
家長的行為對小孩會有很深的影響。

pro·gres·sive [prəˋgrɛsɪv] Track 6067

形 前進的

▶What do you think of the progressive party in the country? I heard they once carried out many reforms. 你如何看待這個國家的改革派？聽說他們曾經進行過很多改革。

pro·hi·bit [prə`hɪbɪt] Track 6068

動 制止

▶We are prohibited on feeding animals in the zoo.
我們被禁止餵食動物園裡的動物。

pro·hi·bi·tion [ˏproə`bɪʃən] Track 6069

名 禁令、禁止

▶There's a prohibition of smoking in this area.
這一區有吸菸的禁令。

pro·jec·tion [prə`dʒɛkʃən] Track 6070

名 計畫、預估

▶The company has made projections of sales of 2000 aircrafts.
據說該公司已預估將銷售兩千架飛機。

prone [pron] Track 6071

形 俯臥的、易於……的

▶It seems that children of poor health are very prone to colds in winter.
健康不佳的孩子似乎容易在冬天感冒。

實用片語用語
be prone to... 很容易……、易於……

prop·a·gan·da [ˏprɑpə`gændə] Track 6072

名 宣傳活動 同 promotion 促銷活動

▶In recent years, there has been a lot of anti-global warming propaganda.
近年來，一直有許多抗暖化的宣導活動。

pro·pel [prə`pɛl] Track 6073

動 推動

▶He is a man propelled by ambition.
他是一個被野心所驅策的男人。

pro·pel·ler [prə`pɛlɚ] Track 6074

名 推進器

▶His job is to install the propeller of the plane.
他的工作是安裝飛機的螺旋槳。

prose [proz] Track 6075

名 散文

▶Would you like to have a look at his latest prose?
你要不要看一下他最新的散文？

實用片語用語
purple prose 過於華麗的詞藻
例如：I can't tell what the plot of the novel is like because I can't read past the purple prose.
我看不出這本小說的劇情到底如何，因為華麗的詞藻讓我看不下去。

pros·e·cute [`prɑsɪˏkjut] Track 6076

動 檢舉、告發

▶Can you tell me who you want to prosecute? And for what?
您可以告訴我您要投訴誰嗎？還有，為什麼要投訴他？

pros·e·cu·tion [ˏprɑsɪ`kjuʃən] Track 6077

名 告發

▶New evidence has revealed the weakness of the prosecution's case. 新的證據已顯示出原告的理由不充足。

pro·spec·tive [prəˋspɛktɪv] Track 6078

形 將來的 同 future 未來的

▶They are not likely to be our prospective clients.
他們不太可能是我們潛在的顧客。

實用片語用語
prospective husband 將來可能成為老公的人
例 如：This lady spends all her time hunting for prospective husbands for her daughter.
這位太太將時間都花在替女兒找個未來老公上。

pro·vin·cial [prəˋvɪnʃəl] Track 6079

名 省民 形 省的

▶名 Whenever I go to the big city, I feel like a provincial.
我每次到這座大城市都覺得自己像個鄉巴佬。

▶形 Talking to smart and well-dressed people makes me feel so provincial.
和聰明、穿著體面的人講話，會讓我覺得自己很土氣。

pro·voke [prəˋvok] Track 6080

動 激起

▶No matter what you do, please don't provoke the bears.
不管你做什麼，請千萬不要激怒那些熊。

prowl [praʊl] Track 6081

名 徘徊 動 潛行

▶名 The mad man is still on the prowl around the streets at night. 那個瘋子深夜時還在街上徘徊。

▶動 Did you see someone prowling around among the trees?
你有沒有看見有人在樹林裡鬼鬼祟祟地走動？

實用片語用語
prowl around 四處徘徊

punc·tu·al [ˋpʌŋktʃuəl] Track 6082

形 準時的

▶Everyone in the class is supposed to be punctual, including the teachers. 班上的每個人都應該守時，包括老師。

pu·ri·fy [ˋpjʊrə͵faɪ] Track 6083

動 淨化 同 cleanse 淨化

▶You can purify the water by distilling（蒸餾）.
你可以透過蒸餾來淨化水。

pu·ri·ty [ˋpjʊrətɪ] Track 6084

名 純粹

▶The book depicts her as a woman of purity and goodness（善良）. 書中把她描寫成一個純潔善良的婦女。

實用片語用語
depict sb. as sth. 將某人描繪為……

qual·i·fi·ca·tion(s) Track 6085

[͵kwɑləfəˋkeʃən(z)]

名 賦予資格、證照 同 competence 勝任

▶Do you mind telling me what sort of qualifications I need for the job? 能麻煩您告訴我這份工作需要具備什麼樣的資格嗎？

quar·rel·some [ˋkwɔrəlsəm] Track 6086

形 愛爭吵的

▶It seems that his brothers are very greedy and quarrelsome.
他的兄弟們似乎都非常貪婪而且喜歡爭吵。

quench [kwɛntʃ] Track 6087

動 弄熄、解渴

▶Having a can of soda is not enough to quench my thirst.
喝一罐汽水不夠我解渴。

實用片語用語
quench sb.'s thirst 解（某人的）渴

que·ry [ˋkwɪrɪ] Track 6088

名 問題 動 質疑 同 inquire 詢問

▶名 I have forwarded the customer's query to the relevant personnel（人員）.
我已經把那個消費者的疑問轉達給相關人員了。

▶動 "Are you sure you're not mistaken?" John queried.
「你確定你沒搞錯嗎？」約翰懷疑地問。

ques·tion·naire [ˏkwɛstʃənˋɛr] Track 6089

名 問卷、調查表

▶They gave the passers-by some questionnaires.
他們發給路人一些問卷。

文法字詞解析
要說「填」問卷的「填」這個動作，可以用 fill out 這個片語。
例如：I filled out the questionnaire and handed it back to the man.
我填完問卷就把它交回給那個先生了。

rac·ism [ˋresɪzəm] Track 6090

名 種族岐視

▶Would you please tell me how we can bring racism to an end?
你能告訴我我們怎樣才能消除種族歧視嗎？

ra·di·ant [ˋredjənt] Track 6091

名 發光體 形 發光的、輻射的

▶名 I heard that they saw a mysterious radiant that day.
據說他們那天看見了一個神秘的發光體。

▶形 Did something good happen? You look radiant.
發生了什麼好事嗎？你看起來滿面容光。

ra·di·ate [ˋredɪˏet] Track 6092

動 放射 形 放射狀的

▶動 The sun in the sky radiates both light and heat every day. That is why things can grow on the earth. 天空中的太陽每天發出光和熱。這就是萬物能在地球上生長的原因。

▶形 There was a radiate head of the president on the coin.
那枚錢幣上畫著一個光芒四射的總統頭像。

實用片語用語
radiate joy 歡樂四射
例如：That cute puppy seems to radiate joy wherever he goes.
那隻可愛的小狗似乎走到哪就把歡樂帶到哪。

ra·di·a·tion [ˏredɪˋeʃən] Track 6093

名 放射、發光

▶The apparatus（儀器）emits harmful radiation.
這台儀器會放射出有害的輻射物。

A B C D E F G H I J K L M N O P Q R S T U V W X Y Z

ra·di·a·tor [ˋredɪ͵etɚ] Track 6094

名 發光體

▶Would you like me to look over the radiator for you, sir?
先生，要我幫你檢查一下散熱器嗎？

rad·i·cal [ˋrædɪkḷ] Track 6095

名 根本 形 根源的

▶名 Some radicals are seeking to overthrow the social order.
有些激進分子正企圖擾亂社會秩序。

▶形 He decided to make a radical change to the plan.
他決定對計畫做一次徹底的修改。

raft [ræft] Track 6096

名 筏 動 乘筏

▶名 Can you tell me how long the survivors were adrift（漂流的）on the raft?
你能告訴我倖存者們在木筏上漂浮了多久嗎？

▶動 How long will it take for me to raft down the stream?
我搭乘木筏順流而下要花多久的時間呢？

實用片語用語
life raft 救生筏
例如：In order to escape from the sinking ship, the passengers tried to be the first to take the life raft. 為了逃離沈船，乘客們爭先恐後地要搭上救生筏。

raid [red] Track 6097

名 突擊 動 襲擊

▶名 I heard from a source that the police would carry out a dawn raid. 我接獲線報，聽說警方將在清晨展開突擊。

▶動 Their troops will raid the enemy camp by night.
他們的部隊要夜襲敵營。

ran·dom [ˋrændəm] Track 6098

形 隨意的、隨機的 反 deliberate 蓄意的

▶I always listen to music on random.
我聽音樂都是隨機播放。

ran·som [ˋrænsəm] Track 6099

名 贖金 動 贖回

▶名 They have to pay a large ransom for their child.
他們為了救回孩子需要支付一大筆贖金。

▶動 The police promise to ransom the child with 100,000 dollars.
警察保證會用十萬美金來贖回那個孩子。

rash [ræʃ] Track 6100

名 疹子 形 輕率的

▶名 My skin has broken out in a rash for some reason.
我的皮膚不知道為什麼起了疹子。

▶形 I wish my colleague would keep himself from doing anything rash. 我希望我的同事不要做出任何莽撞的事來。

實用片語用語
rash decision 魯莽的決定
例如：His rash decision could cost us the game.
他這魯莽的決定可能會害我們輸掉這場比賽。

ra·tion·al [ˋræʃənḷ] Track 6101

形 理性的 反 absurd 不合理的

▶I know you're worried about your child's safety, but you need to be rational now.
我知道你很擔心孩子的安全，但你現在一定要理性點。

rav·age [ˋrævɪdʒ] Track 6102

名 毀壞 動 破壞

▶名 The ravage of inflation（通貨膨脹）led to the hardship in people's lives. 通貨膨脹的惡果使得人們生活困難。

▶動 The whole area was ravaged by forest fires last week. 上星期整個地區都被森林大火給毀滅了。

re·al·ism [ˋriəl͵ɪzəm] Track 6103

名 現實主義

▶Works of magical realism let readers see the world they're used to from a different point of view.
魔幻現實主義的作品讓讀者從不同的角度看他們已知的世界。

re·al·i·za·tion [͵rɪələˋzeʃən] Track 6104

名 現實、領悟

▶She was suddenly hit with the realization that he had never loved her. 她忽然領悟到，他根本從來沒愛過她。

實用片語用語
sudden realization 突然的領悟、突然瞭解到
例如：I was hit by the sudden realization that this man was probably my cousin.
我突然發覺到這個男人大概是我的表哥。

re·bel·lion [rɪˋbɛljən] Track 6105

名 叛亂

▶No one knows who led or planned the rebellion.
沒有人知道到底是誰領到、計畫了這次叛亂。

re·ces·sion [rɪˋsɛʃən] Track 6106

名 衰退

▶Many countries suffered an economic recession this year.
很多國家今年都遭遇了經濟衰退。

re·cip·i·ent [rɪˋsɪpɪənt] Track 6107

名 接受者、接受的 同 receiver 接受者

▶If the recipient is not found, the mail will be returned to the sender（發送人）.
如果沒能找到收件者，郵件就會被退回給寄信的人。

rec·om·men·da·tion [͵rɛkəmɛnˋdeʃən] Track 6108

名 推薦 同 reference 推薦

▶Will you write a recommendation for me, Professor Wang?
王教授，您能替我寫一封推薦信嗎？

實用片語用語
recommendation letter 推薦信
例如：The professor sealed the recommendation letter in an envelope.
這位教授把推薦信放進信封封好。

rec·on·cile [ˋrɛkən͵saɪl] Track 6109

動 調停、和解

▶You'd better have someone reconcile the disputes among them, or it will affect the whole organization.
你最好請人去調解一下他們之間的糾紛，否則它將會影響到整個組織。

rec·re·a·tion·al [͵rɛkrɪˋeʃənl̩] Track 6110

形 娛樂的

▶It is said that there are running tracks built in the recreational center. 據說休閒中心建有跑道。

re·cruit [rɪˋkrut]

Track 6111

動 徵募 名 新兵 同 draft 徵兵

▶動 Most of the teachers in this school are recruited from abroad. 這所學校大部分的老師都是從國外聘請來的。

▶名 This job presents many difficulties to the new recruits. 這項工作對新手來說困難重重。

re·cur [rɪˋkɝ]

Track 6112

動 重現

▶This kind of problem is likely to recur, so you need to be more careful. 這類問題可能還會再發生，所以你最好更小心。

實用片語用語

recurring headache 重複發作的頭痛

例如：He tried to combat his recurring headache by drinking lots of coffee.

他喝很多咖啡，試圖打擊他不斷發作的頭痛。

re·dun·dant [rɪˋdʌndənt]

Track 6113

形 過剩的、冗長的 反 concise 簡要的

▶The manager promised there would be no question of anyone being made redundant.

經理承諾絕對不會裁掉任何人。

re·fine [rɪˋfaɪn]

Track 6114

動 精練 同 improve 改善

▶Works of taste can refine the soul.

高雅的作品能陶冶心靈。

re·fine·ment [rɪˋfaɪnmənt]

Track 6115

名 精良

▶Both good manners and correct speech are works of refinement.

彬彬有禮和談吐得體都是文雅的象徵。

re·flec·tive [rɪˋflɛktɪv]

Track 6116

形 反射的

▶The reflective glasses raised the temperature of the surrounding air. 顯然反光玻璃使周圍的氣溫提高了。

實用片語用語

reflective surface 反射面

例如：You can use anything with a reflective surface as a mirror.

你可以用任何有反射面的東西當鏡子。

re·fresh·ment(s) [rɪˋfrɛʃmənt(s)]

Track 6117

名 清爽、提神之物

▶In an office where everyone's always mad, his pleasant personality is a refreshment. 在一個大家總是很容易生氣的辦公室中，他好相處的個性令人感到舒爽。

re·fund [rɪˋfʌnd]/[ˋrɪfʌnd]

Track 6118

名 償還、退款 動 償還

▶名 The store won't give me a refund for the product I bought because I have lost my receipt.

這家商店不肯為我購買的產品退款，因為我已經把發票給弄丟了。

▶動 I am afraid that the travel agency won't refund you the full cost of your fare because you didn't inform them of your cancellment immediately.

恐怕這家旅行社不會退還你全部的旅費，因為你沒有及時通知他們要取消。

re·gard·less [rɪˋgɑrdlɪs] Track 6119

形 不關心的 副 不關心地、無論如何 同 despite 儘管

▶形 He climbed the tower regardless of the dangerous weather.
他不顧危險的天氣，爬上了高塔。

▶副 Despite all their efforts to stop him, he still went through with the plan regardless.
雖然他們盡力阻止他，他還是不顧一切進行了計畫。

實用片語用語
regardless of... 不顧……

re·gime [rɪˋʒim] Track 6120

名 政權

▶It seems that many things will change under the new regime.
在新政權下似乎很多事情將會發生變化。

實用片語用語
regime change 政權更迭
例如：Regime change is inevitable in human history.
政權更迭在人類歷史上是不可避免的。

re·hears·al [rɪˋhɝsḷ] Track 6121

名 排演 同 practice 練習

▶Would you like to participate in our rehearsal, Mrs. Wang?
王女士，您願意來參加我們的排練嗎？

re·hearse [rɪˋhɝs] Track 6122

動 預演

▶How about rehearsing the play after the break?
休息之後來排練戲劇怎麼樣？

rein [ren] Track 6123

名 箝制 動 控制

▶名 The boy pulled at the reins nervously.
那個男孩緊張地使勁拉韁繩。

▶動 He was unable to rein in his anger any longer.
他再也按捺不住他的怒氣了。

實用片語用語
rein sth. in 控制住某物

re·in·force [ˌriɪnˋfors] Track 6124

動 增強 同 intensify 增強

▶You'd better reinforce the packing（包裝）with metal straps. It's safer.
你們最好用鐵箍來加強包裝。這樣比較安全。

re·lay [ˋrɪle]/[rɪˋle] Track 6125

名 接力（賽） 動 傳達

▶名 Do you know how many people took part in the torch relay?
你知道有多少人參與了這次的火把傳遞接力嗎？

▶動 Will you please relay the news to his mother in the country?
請你把這個消息轉達給他住在鄉下的母親好嗎？

rel·e·vant [ˋrɛləvənt] Track 6126

形 相關的

▶You'd better send me the relevant papers on the case today.
你最好今天就把跟案件有關的檔案送過來給我。

文法字詞解析
相反地，「不相關的、不重要的」則是 irrelevant。

re·li·ance [rɪ`laɪəns]

Track 6127

名 信賴、依賴

▶Don't place too much reliance on what he said, or you will regret it.
對他所說的話不要過於信賴，要不然你會後悔的。

實用片語用語
place reliance on 依賴……

rel·ish [`rɛlɪʃ]

Track 6128

名 嗜好、美味 動 愛好、品味

▶名 Reading without comprehension is like eating with no relish.
讀書如果不知其義，就有如食髓不知味。

▶動 The dog relished the food we gave him.
那隻狗極享受地吃了我們給牠的食物。

re·main·der [rɪ`mendɚ]

Track 6129

名 剩餘 同 remain 殘留

▶He spent the remainder of his life alone in the country.
他獨自在鄉間度過了餘生。

re·mov·al [rɪ`muvl̩]

Track 6130

名 移動

▶The factory has announced its removal to another town.
這家工廠已經宣佈將遷往另一座城市。

實用片語用語
hair removal 除毛
例如：Does this hair removal product really work?
這除毛產品真的有用嗎？

re·nais·sance [ˌrə`nesn̩s]

Track 6131

名 再生、文藝復興

▶Da Vinci was a very famous painter in the Renaissance period.
達文西是文藝復興時期非常著名的一位畫家。

ren·der [`rɛndɚ]

Track 6132

動 給予、讓與

▶As an organization for public benefit, we are supposed to render them economic assistance.
作為一個公益性組織，我們應該向他們提供經濟援助。

re·nowned [rɪ`naʊnd]

Track 6133

形 著名的 同 famous 著名的

▶He had become a renowned landscape painter.
他後來成為一名著名的風景畫畫家。

rent·al [`rɛntl̩]

Track 6134

名 租用物

▶The yearly rental of her house is 12,000 dollars.
她這棟房子的年租金要一萬兩千美元。

實用片語用語
car rental 租車行
例如：We need to return this car to the car rental with full gas.
我們得把這台車加滿油才能還給租車行。

re·press [rɪ`prɛs]

Track 6135

動 抑制

▶She could not repress a shiver whenever she thought of the cruel criminal.
每當想到這名殘暴的罪犯時，她就會忍不住顫抖。

re·sem·blance [rɪˋzɛmbləns] Track 6136

名 類似 同 similarity 類似

▶There's a strong resemblance between Mike and Bob.
麥克和鮑勃長相非常類似。

res·er·voir [ˋrɛzɚ͵vɔr] Track 6137

名 儲水池、倉庫 同 warehouse 倉庫

▶It is reported that this new reservoir can supply water to the whole city.
根據報導，這座水庫能供應水給整座城市。

res·i·den·tial [͵rɛzəˋdɛnʃəl] Track 6138

形 居住的

▶I wish our residential building would be located next to the park.
我希望我們的住宅大樓可以座落在公園旁。

實用片語用語

residential area 住宅區

例如：The residential area is located close to the business area.
這個住宅區離商業區很近。

re·si·stant [rɪˋzɪstənt] Track 6139

形 抵抗的

▶A healthy diet creates a body resistant to disease.
健康的飲食有助於增強體內對疾病的抵抗力。

res·o·lute [ˋrɛzə͵lut] Track 6140

形 堅決的

▶We tried to persuade him not to do it, but he was resolute.
我們有試著說服他不要做，但他很堅決。

re·spec·tive [rɪˋspɛktɪv] Track 6141

形 個別的 同 individual 個別的

▶These people all excel in their respective fields.
這些人在各自的領域裡都很出類拔萃。

實用片語用語

go respective ways 各走各的路

例如：After we came to an agreement, we all went our respective ways.
我們達成協議後，就各自朝不同的方向離開了。

res·to·ra·tion [͵rɛstəˋreʃən] Track 6142

名 恢復

▶The restoration of the files took a surprisingly long time.
把檔案復原花了異常久的時間。

re·straint [rɪˋstrent] Track 6143

名 抑制

▶He always eats without restraint. 他吃東西總是毫不節制。

re·tail [ˋritel] Track 6144

名 零售 動 零售 形 零售的 副 零售地 反 wholesale 批發

▶名 Will you sell these goods by retail? Is it profitable?
你會零售這些商品嗎？這樣有利可圖嗎？

▶動 If he intends to retail these shoes, will you order some there?
如果他打算零售這些鞋子的話，你會從那訂購一些嗎？

▶形 Can you tell me the retail prices of these slippers?
你能告訴我這些拖鞋的零售價嗎？

▶副 His method of buying wholesale and selling retail helped him gain a lot of profit.
他整批買下來之後拿去零售的作法幫他賺了不少錢。

實用片語用語

retail price 零售價

re·tal·i·ate [rɪˋtælɪ͵et] Track 6145

動 報復

▶The terrorists retaliated by killing the travelers.
恐怖份子以殺害旅客作為報復。

re·trieve [rɪˋtriv] Track 6146

動 取回

▶The dog retrieved the ball for me.
那隻狗幫我把球叼了回來。

rev·e·la·tion [͵rɛvəˋleʃən] Track 6147

名 揭發 同 disclosure 揭發

▶His revelation that he was actually gay wasn't much of a surprise to me.
他揭露了自己其實是同性戀的事實，我一點都不覺得驚訝。

rev·e·nue [ˋrɛvə͵nju] Track 6148

名 收入

▶Let's try our best to minimize the cost and maximize the revenue.
讓我們盡力將成本減到最少、同時將收益增加到最多。

萬用延伸句型
Let's try our best to... 我們盡力來（做某事）

re·viv·al [rɪˋvaɪvḷ] Track 6149

名 復甦

▶There is a visible sign of a revival in the stock market.
有明顯的跡象顯示股市即將復甦。

rhet·o·ric [ˋrɛtərɪk] Track 6150

名 修辭（學）

▶His rhetoric is too profound for us to understand.
他說話的方式深奧無比，我們難以理解。

rhyth·mic [ˋrɪðmɪk] Track 6151

形 有節奏的

▶I can hear the rhythmic beating of the baby's heart.
我可以聽到那個嬰兒富有節奏的心跳。

rid·i·cule [ˋrɪdɪkjul] Track 6152

名 嘲笑 動 嘲笑

▶名 To say something this ignorant is basically like inviting ridicule.
說出這麼無知的話，簡直就是在邀請別人來嘲笑你。

▶動 He ridiculed his sister's unfortunate outfit choices.
他嘲笑了他妹妹選的衣服難看。

實用片語用語
subject of ridicule 嘲笑的對象
例如：The strange way he talks is often a subject of ridicule.
他奇怪的說話方式常成了大家的笑柄。

rig·or·ous [ˋrɪgərəs] Track 6153

形 嚴格的

▶The scientists are making a rigorous study of the rare plants in the area.
科學家們正在對該地的稀有植物進行縝密的研究。

ri·ot [ˋraɪət]

Track 6154

名 暴動 動 騷動、放縱

▶名 The demonstration soon went out of control and became a riot. 根據報導，示威遊行很快失控，變成了一場暴動。

▶動 It is reported that a mob（一群暴民）was rioting against the government yesterday.
根據報導，昨天有一群暴民鬧事並反對政府。

ri·te [raɪt]

Track 6155

名 儀式、典禮

▶Will you tell me how much you know about the religious rite?
能請告訴我你對這一個宗教儀式瞭解多少嗎？

rit·u·al [ˋrɪtʃuəl]

Track 6156

名（宗教）儀式 形 儀式的 同 ceremony 儀式

▶名 Would you like to attend my ritual of inauguration（就職）next week?
你願意來參加我下星期的就職典禮嗎？

▶形 Having some water before going to sleep is a ritual habit for him.
睡前喝點水是他每天必經的儀式。

實用片語用語

make it a ritual to... 讓……變成一種固定的習慣

例如：He makes it a ritual to jog for an hour every morning.
他每天早上都有晨跑一小時的習慣。

ri·val·ry [ˋraɪvəlrɪ]

Track 6157

名 競爭

▶The rivalry among business firms is intense now.
現在公司間的競爭非常激烈。

ro·tate [roˋtet]

Track 6158

動 旋轉

▶How about rotating watches? Then we'll be less tired.
我們輪流看守如何？這樣比較不累。

ro·ta·tion [roˋteʃən]

Track 6159

名 旋轉

▶It is the earth's rotation that enables us to see the sun rise and set.
正是因為有地球的自轉，才會有日出和日落。

roy·al·ty [ˋrɔɪəltɪ]

Track 6160

名 貴族、王權 同 commission 職權

▶He claimed that his ancestors were royalty.
他聲稱他是皇室的後裔。

ru·by [ˋrubɪ]

Track 6161

名 紅寶石 形 紅寶石色的

▶名 Will you tell me which attracts you more, rubies or emeralds（綠寶石）?
你能告訴我紅寶石和綠寶石兩者你比較喜歡哪個嗎？

▶形 Can I have some more ruby wine? It tastes quite good.
我可以再喝一些深紅色葡萄酒好嗎？它的味道相當不錯。

文法字詞解析

第一個例句中用到了「S + V + IO + DO」的句型，會使用這類句型的動詞通常是像 tell 這樣的授與動詞，而句中的名詞子句「which attracts you more」當作直接受詞，me 是間接受詞。

safe·guard [ˋsef͵gɑrd] Track 6162

名 保護者、警衛 動 保護

▶名 It is reported that the new law constitutes a safeguard against the abuse of government power.
根據報導，新法律可以防止濫用政府權力。

▶動 This agreement will safeguard the newspapers from government interference.
這一協議將保護報社不受政府干涉。

實用片語用語
safeguard against sth. 防止……

sa·loon [səˋlun] Track 6163

名 酒店、酒吧

▶He left the saloons of New York for the green glades（林間空地）of the country.
他離開了紐約的歡樂酒店，來到鄉村綠色的林間空地。

sal·va·tion [sælˋveʃən] Track 6164

名 救助、拯救

▶After so much dry weather, the rain became the farmers' salvation. 天氣乾旱了這麼久，這場雨成了農民的救星。

sanc·tion [ˋsæŋkʃən] Track 6165

名 批准、認可 動 批准、認可 同 permit 准許

▶名 It seems that the book was translated without the sanction of the author.
這本書好像未經作者許可就翻譯了。

▶動 His old-fashioned parents did not sanction his second marriage. 他老派的父母不認可他的第二次婚姻。

sanc·tu·ar·y [ˋsæŋktʃʊ͵ɛrɪ] Track 6166

名 聖所、聖堂、庇護所 同 refuge 庇護所

▶The found their sanctuary on the island.
他們在這個島上找到了他們的避難所。

實用片語用語
find sanctuary in / on / at...
在某地找到了庇護

sane [sen] Track 6167

形 神智穩健的

▶After being tortured for months, he was no longer sane.
被凌虐了好幾個月後，他的精神狀態已經不正常了。

san·i·ta·tion [͵sænəˋteʃən] Track 6168

名 公共衛生

▶Public sanitation rules are something everyone really should follow. 公共衛生規定是大家確實都應該遵守的。

sce·nic [ˋsinɪk] Track 6169

形 舞臺的、佈景的

▶It is said that there is a scenic route across the Alps.
據說有一條風景優美的路穿越阿爾卑斯山。

實用片語用語
scenic spot 景點
例如：They had a picnic at the scenic spot.
他們在那個景點野餐。

scope [skop]　Track 6170

名 範圍、領域 同 range 範圍

▶I'm afraid your question is beyond the scope of my understanding.
恐怕你所問的問題已超出了我的理解範圍。

script [skrɪpt]　Track 6171

名 原稿、劇本 動 編寫

▶名 You can't have a good performance without a decent script. 沒有像樣的劇本就不可能有好的表演。

▶動 What do you think about scripting this novel in to a TV show? 你覺得把這部小說改編成電視劇本怎麼樣？

sec·tor [`sɛktɚ]　Track 6172

名 扇形

▶There are several sectors in the building that we are not allowed to enter. 這棟大樓有幾區我們不被允許進入。

文法字詞解析
sector 除了指面積上的「扇形區域」外，也可以指「區域、部門」，例如「政府部門」就可以稱為 government sector。這個部門的形狀不一定要是扇形的。

se·duce [sɪ`djus]　Track 6173

動 引誘、慫恿 同 tempt 引誘

▶She is trying to seduce him to bed. 她試著引誘他到床上。

se·lec·tive [sə`lɛktɪv]　Track 6174

形 有選擇性的

▶She is selective in people she talk to.
她只選擇性地和某些人說話。

sem·i·nar [`sɛmənɑr]　Track 6175

名 研討會、講習會

▶I'm afraid that I will not be able to attend the seminar.
我恐怕將無法參加這次的研討會。

實用片語用語
business seminar 商業研討會
例如：I heard that there will be cookies at the business seminar.
聽說那場商業研討會有餅乾可以吃喔。

sen·a·tor [`sɛnətɚ]　Track 6176

名 參議員、上議員

▶It is said that there are three senators who voted against the bill. 據說有三位參議員投票反對這一個議案。

sen·ti·men·tal [͵sɛntə`mɛntl]　Track 6177

形 受情緒影響的 同 emotional 情緒的

▶She kept all the old photographs for sentimental reasons.
她保存所有這些舊照片是出於情感的緣故。

se·quence [`sikwəns]　Track 6178

名 順序、連續 動 按順序排好 同 succession 連續

▶名 The test asked us to put the mixed historical facts in sequence.
這次考試要我們把混淆的歷史事件按順序排列。

▶動 You had better sequence the names right away. The manager needs the list later on.
你最好馬上按順序排列好名單。經理稍後會用到它。

se·rene [sə`rin]

Track 6179

形 寧靜的、安祥的 反 furious 狂暴的

▶The story took place on a serene summer night.
故事發生在一個寧靜的夏夜。

se·ren·i·ty [sə`rɛnətɪ]

Track 6180

名 晴朗、和煦、平靜 同 peace 平靜

▶I just want to find a place with peace and serenity where I can hide from my troubles.
我只想找到一個和平安靜的地方來躲起來逃避煩惱。

serv·ing [`sɝvɪŋ]

Track 6181

名 服務、服侍、侍候

▶You had better let the hot pie cool off a little before serving.
你最好等熱騰騰的派涼了一些再端上桌。

ses·sion [`sɛʃən]

Track 6182

名 開庭、會議 同 conference 會議

▶Do you mind telling me when the court will be in session?
能麻煩您告訴我法庭何時開庭嗎？

文法字詞解析

除了「會議」、「法庭」等這類比較正式的場合外，其實一些比較沒那麼正式，但也是「一段固定的時間」的事情也可以用上 session 這個字。像是「一堂課的時間」可以稱為「a class session」，「一場遊戲」也可以稱為「a gaming session」。

set·back [`sɛt͵bæk]

Track 6183

名 逆流、逆轉、逆行

▶What happened just now was a huge setback to the plan.
剛剛發生的事情對於這個計畫造成很大的麻煩。

sew·er [`sjuɚ]

Track 6184

名 縫製者

▶She was the best sewer in the factory.
她是這間工廠最好的縫紉工。

shed [ʃɛd]

Track 6185

動 流出、發射出

▶She shed many tears over the loss of her beloved puppy.
她因失去了心愛的小狗而流了不少淚。

文法字詞解析

shed 的動詞變化：shed, shed, shed

sheer [ʃɪr]

Track 6186

形 垂直的、絕對的 副 完全地 動 急轉彎

▶形 His face was twisted in sheer agony.
他因為絕對的痛苦而臉部扭曲。

▶副 The mountain rises sheer from the plain.
那座山陡峭地矗立在平原上。

▶動 The boat came close to the rocks and then sheered away.
據說那艘船靠近了礁石，然後緊接著轉向行駛。

shil·ling [`ʃɪlɪŋ]

Track 6187

名 （英國幣名）先令

▶The beggar was overjoyed（欣喜若狂的）when I gave him a shilling.
當我給這個乞丐一先令時，他喜出望外。

shop·lift [ˋʃɑpˏlɪft]
Track 6188

動 逛商店時行竊 同 pirate 掠奪

▶The boy was caught shoplifting.
那個男孩在商店順手牽羊被逮到了。

shrewd [ʃrud]
Track 6189

形 敏捷的、精明的

▶He is not only an artist but also a shrewd businessman.
他不但是位藝術家，而且還是個精明的商人。

實用片語用語
shrewd smile 精明的笑容
例如：His words sound sincere, but that shrewd smile makes it hard to trust him.
他說的話聽起來很誠懇，但那精明的笑容讓我很難信得過他。

shun [ʃʌn]
Track 6190

動 避開、躲避

▶The children shunned the little girl because of her ugly face.
那些孩子們因為那個小女孩長得很醜而避開她。

siege [sidʒ]
Track 6191

名 包圍、圍攻 同 surround 包圍

▶Close to one million people died as the result of the siege.
此次圍攻造成了近百萬人死亡。

sig·ni·fy [ˋsɪgnəˏfaɪ]
Track 6192

動 表示

▶Would you please tell me what these marks signify?
你能告訴我這些符號代表什麼意思嗎？

sil·i·con [ˋsɪlɪkən]
Track 6193

名 矽

▶The Silicon Valley has become a new economic model because of its advanced science and technology.
矽谷因先進的科技成為了一種新的經濟模式。

實用片語用語
economic model 經濟模式

sim·plic·i·ty [sɪmˋplɪsətɪ]
Track 6194

名 簡單、單純

▶The beauty of the plan lies in its simplicity.
此計畫的妙處正在於它的簡潔明瞭。

sim·pli·fy [ˋsɪmpləˏfaɪ]
Track 6195

動 使……簡易、使……單純 反 complicate 使複雜

▶I think it is too hard to simplify the complex subject.
我覺得這個主題太複雜了，很難簡化。

si·mul·ta·ne·ous [ˏsaɪmḷˋtenɪəs]
Track 6196

形 同時發生的

▶My dream is to become a simultaneous interpreter in the future. What about yours?
我的夢想是將來成為一名同步口譯員。你的夢想呢？

skep·ti·cal [ˋskɛptɪkḷ]
Track 6197

形 懷疑的

▶It is no wonder that many were skeptical about this solution.
難怪許多人對這一個解決辦法表示懷疑。

實用片語用語
be skeptical about... 對……感到懷疑

skim [skɪm] Track 6198

動 掠去、去除 名 脫脂乳品

▶動 It took me a few seconds to skim the book.
我花了幾秒把這本書瀏覽了一遍。

▶名 When I drink milk, I like it skim.
我喝牛奶時喜歡喝脫脂的。

slang [slæŋ] Track 6199

名 俚語 動 謾罵、說俚語

▶名 It seems that this slang is quite widespread in this area.
這句俚語在這個區域似乎相當普遍。

▶動 He slanged his friend with all the dirty words he knew.
他用他所知的所有髒話罵他朋友。

slash [slæʃ] Track 6200

名 刀痕、裂縫 動 亂砍、鞭打 同 cut 砍

▶名 The knife made a slash across his leg.
刀在他的腿上劃出了一道傷口。

▶動 You had better not slash your horse in that cruel way.
你最好不要那麼殘忍地鞭打你的馬。

文法字詞解析
那種常有人拿著刀到處砍人的「殺人魔電影」就可以稱為 slasher film。

slav·er·y [ˋslevərɪ] Track 6201

名 奴隸制度 反 liberty 自由

▶It was Abraham Lincoln who abolished slavery in the United States.
是亞伯拉罕．林肯廢除了美國的奴隸制度。

slot [slɑt] Track 6202

名 狹槽、職位 動 在……開一狹槽

▶名 He replaced me in the game and took my slot.
他在此遊戲中取代我的位置。

▶動 I'll slot you for the nine a.m. appointment.
我會把你的約診安排在九點。

slum [slʌm] Track 6203

名 貧民區 動 進入貧民區

▶名 It was a story about slum life in Chicago.
那是一篇關於芝加哥貧民窟生活情況的故事。

▶動 We were forced to slum it for a few days because our house was flooded.
因為我們家淹水了，我們不得不過幾天苦日子。

文法字詞解析
要說「在貧民窟中」可以直接使用 slum 的複數，說「in the slums」。

smack [smæk] Track 6204

動 拍擊、甩打 同 slap 拍擊

▶You'd better put that down, otherwise I'll smack you.
你最好把它放下來，不然我就會揍你。

small·pox [ˋsmɔl͵pɑks] Track 6205

名 天花

▶Smallpox has been brought under control by the use of vaccines（疫苗）. 透過接種疫苗，使得天花已得到控制。

smoth·er [ˋsmʌðɚ]

Track 6206

動 使窒息、掩飾 名 使窒息之物

▶動 You had better not put that cloth over the baby's face, or you'll smother him! 你最好不要把那塊布蓋在嬰兒的臉上，否則你會害他窒息的！

▶名 The air has been polluted by the smother of industrial smog. 空氣已經被令人窒息的工業煙霧污染了。

smug·gle [ˋsmʌgḷ]

Track 6207

動 走私

▶It's impossible for you to smuggle the prisoners out of the prison camp. 你要從戰俘營裡偷偷帶出戰俘是不可能的。

snare [snɛr]

Track 6208

名 陷阱、羅網 動 誘惑、捕捉

▶名 He has fallen into a snare laid by his enemy. 他已經落入了敵人設的圈套。

▶動 The rabbit was snared by the hunter. 那隻兔子被獵人捕住了。

實用片語用語
fall into a snare 落入圈套

sneak·y [ˋsnikɪ]

Track 6209

形 鬼鬼祟祟的

▶The sneaky girl was disliked by the rest of the class. 全班都不喜歡這個賊頭賊腦的女學生。

sneer [snɪr]

Track 6210

名 冷笑 動 嘲笑地說

▶名 The man let out a sneer and took out a gun. 那個男人冷笑一聲拔出槍。

▶動 "You think you're so smart," sneered the woman. 「你以為你很聰明，」那個女子嘲諷地說道。

soar [sor]

Track 6211

動 上升、往上飛

▶The hot-air balloon soared into the sky. 那個熱汽球飛上了天空。

實用片語用語
hot-air balloon 熱汽球

so·cia·ble [ˋsoʃəbḷ]

Track 6212

形 愛交際的、社交的

▶She is a sociable person who is liked by almost everyone. 她是個愛交際的人，幾乎每個人都喜歡她。

so·cial·ism [ˋsoʃəl͵ɪzəm]

Track 6213

名 社會主義

▶My father doesn't believe in socialism. What about yours? 我爸爸不信奉社會主義，你爸爸呢？

so·cial·ist [ˋsoʃəlɪst]

Track 6214

名 社會主義者

▶It's obvious that most of the people in this country are socialists. 這個國家大多數的人顯然都是社會主義者。

so·cial·ize [ˋsoʃəl͵aɪz]

Track 6215

動 使社會化 同 civilize 使文明、使開化

▶A good salesperson needs to learn how to socialize with his or her customers.
好的業務員要學習如何和客戶交際。

文法字詞解析
除了「使社會化」外，socialize 更含有「與人社交」、「交際」的意思。

so·ci·ol·o·gy [͵soʃɪˋɑlədʒɪ]

Track 6216

名 社會學

▶It is said that sociology was the most popular subject for undergraduates years ago.
據說幾年前，社會學是最受大學生歡迎的課程。

so·di·um [ˋsodɪəm]

Track 6217

名 鈉

▶The reason you should avoid high-sodium foods is that they may raise blood pressure.
你應該避免食用鈉含量高的食物，因為這些食物可能會使血壓升高。

sol·i·dar·i·ty [͵sɑləˋdærətɪ]

Track 6218

名 團結、休戚相關

▶The people showed solidarity for the unfortunate victims that lost their homes in the flood. 那些人們對在水災中失去家園的受害者表現出了一致同情的態度。

sol·i·tude [ˋsɑlə͵tjud]

Track 6219

名 獨處、獨居

▶He is searching for a place where he can live in solitude.
他正在尋找一個可以過隱居生活的地方。

實用片語用語
in solitude 單獨地、獨自地

soothe [suð]

Track 6220

動 安慰、撫慰 同 comfort 安慰

▶Why aren't you soothing the crying child?
為什麼你不去哄哄那個在哭的孩子呢？

so·phis·ti·cat·ed [səˋfɪstɪ͵ketɪd]

Track 6221

形 世故的

▶Not everybody knows that she is actually a sophisticated woman. 不是每個人都知道她其實是個世故的女人。

sov·er·eign·ty [ˋsɑvrɪntɪ]

Track 6222

名 主權

▶The treaty violated and trampled on the sovereignty of the country. 這個條約是對該國主權的侵犯和踐踏。

spa·cious [ˋspeʃəs]

Track 6223

形 寬敞的、寬廣的

▶The hotel is not only spacious but also comfortable.
這間旅館不但寬敞而且還很舒適。

文法字詞解析
這個字加上名詞字尾「-ness」就變成「spaciousness（寬敞、寬廣）」。

span [spæn] Track 6224

名 跨距 動 橫跨、展延

▶名 Over a short span of three years, we've achieved a surprising success.
在短短三年時間裡，我們已經取得了驚人的成就。

▶動 His research in cancer that spanned 5 years has made considerable headway.
他對癌症持續五年的研究取得了重大進展。

spe·cial·ize [ˋspɛʃəl͵aɪz] Track 6225

動 專長於

▶She specializes in business law. 她的專長是商務法律。

spe·cial·ty [ˋspɛʃəltɪ] Track 6226

名 專門職業、本行

▶What's the specialty today? 今天的特餐是什麼？

實用片語用語

specialty dish 拿手菜、今日特餐
例如：My specialty dish is Thai fried rice.
我的拿手菜是泰式炒飯。

spec·i·fy [ˋspɛsə͵faɪ] Track 6227

動 詳述、詳載

▶Would you please specify when you will be at home tomorrow?
請你確切說明你明天什麼時候會在家好嗎？

spec·tac·u·lar [spɛkˋtækjələ] Track 6228

名 大場面 形 可觀的 同 dramatic 引人注目的

▶名 This movie is a real spectacular.
這部電影真是一部很棒的影片。

▶形 The new play was a spectacular success.
這部新劇獲得了巨大的成功。

spec·trum [ˋspɛktrəm] Track 6229

名 光譜

▶There's a wide spectrum of opinions on this problem.
針對這個問題的說法眾說紛紜，莫衷一是。

文法字詞解析

光譜的一端到另一端之間是兩個極端，因此一些其他的事情（不只是「光」）也可以使用 spectrum 來測量。舉例來說，自閉症的程度就有一個 autism spectrum，由在光譜上的位置來判斷一個人的症狀嚴重程度。

spec·u·late [ˋspɛkjə͵let] Track 6230

動 沉思

▶We were speculating on how this might have happened.
我們在思考這事到底是怎麼發生的。

sphere [sfɪr] Track 6231

名 球、天體

▶There are nine spheres in the solar system.
在太陽系裡有九大行星。

spike [spaɪk] Track 6232

名 長釘、釘尖 動 以尖釘刺、把烈酒攙入……

▶名 They forced the prisoner to sit on a chair with spikes.
他們逼迫那名囚犯坐在上有長釘的椅子上。

▶動 The boys spiked the drinks, so everyone at the party got drunk.
男孩們把烈酒攙入飲料，所以宴會中的每個人都喝醉了。

spi·ral [ˋspaɪrəl]

Track 6233

名 螺旋 動 急遽上升或下降 形 螺旋的 同 twist 旋轉

▶名 The bubbles drifted in an upward spiral.
泡泡以螺旋狀向上漂移。

▶動 Their profits have begun to spiral downwards.
他們的利潤開始急遽地下降。

▶形 The snail's shell is spiral in form.
蝸牛的殼是螺旋形的。

實用片語用語
spiral downwards 急速下降

spire [spaɪr]

Track 6234

名 尖塔、尖頂 動 螺旋形上升、發芽

▶名 It's possible for us to see the spire of the church in the distance.
我們可以看到遠處教堂的尖塔。

▶動 It's necessary for us to sow the seeds before they spire.
我們必須在種子發芽前播種。

spokes·per·son/ spokes·man/spokes·wom·an

Track 6235

[ˋspoks͵pɝsn̩]/[ˋspoksmən]/[ˋspoks͵wʊmən]

名 發言人

▶It is reported that the IOC spokesperson will investigate the incident.
根據報導，國際奧委會發言人將對此事展開調查。

實用片語用語
IOC 是 International Olympic Committee 的縮寫，而 committee 就是「委員會」的意思。如果要說「一名委員」可以說 a committee member 或 a commissioner。

spon·sor [ˋspɑnsɚ]

Track 6236

名 贊助者 動 贊助、資助

▶名 I am afraid that if there are not enough sponsors, we have to give up this plan.
恐怕如果沒有足夠的贊助者，我們就得放棄這個計劃。

▶動 It is a pity that he doesn't have enough money to sponsor the project.
遺憾的是，他沒有足夠的錢來支持這項計畫。

spon·ta·ne·ous [spɑnˋtenɪəs]

Track 6237

形 同時發生的

▶The joke was so funny that we burst into spontaneous laughter. 這笑話太有趣了，所以我們忍不住同聲大笑了起來。

spouse [spaʊz]

Track 6238

名 配偶、夫妻 同 mate 配偶

▶I don't think that you should compare your spouse with other people. 我認為你不應該拿你的伴侶與他人做比較。

sprawl [sprɔl]

Track 6239

名 / 動 任意伸展

▶名 He is still lying on the bed in a sprawl.
他還歪歪斜斜地癱在床上。

▶動 The boy sprawled all over the sofa.
那個男孩癱在沙發上。

squad [skwɑd]

Track 6240

名 小隊、班

▶My boyfriend is the squad leader in the army.
我的男朋友在軍中當班長。

文法字詞解析
除了真的有組織的那種小隊、小組外，「一群朋友」在口語中也可以稱為squad。

squash [skwɑʃ]

Track 6241

名 壓擠 動 壓擠

▶名 I think you should get on the bus though it is a bit of a squash, or you'll be late.
雖然擠了點，你但還是應該上這輛公車，否則你會遲到的。

▶動 Don't sit on my hat, or you will squash it!
別坐在我的帽子上，否則你會把它壓扁的！

sta·bil·i·ty [steˋbɪlətɪ]

Track 6242

名 穩定、穩固

▶The government has taken a measure to maintain the stability of prices. 政府已採取措施以確保物價穩定。

sta·bi·lize [ˋstebḷ͵aɪz]

Track 6243

動 保持安定、使穩定

▶Do you know how to stabilize the price of vegetables?
你知道該如何穩定蔬菜的價格嗎？

stalk [stɔk]

Track 6244

名 軸、莖 動 蔓延、追蹤

▶名 He poured wine into the glass with a tall stalk.
他把酒倒到那個高腳玻璃杯裡了。

▶動 He stalked her all the way home.
他一路跟蹤了她回家。

文法字詞解析
在 stalk 後面加上意為「……者」的字尾「-er」，則變成了 stalker，是「跟蹤狂」的意思。

stam·mer [ˋstæmɚ]

Track 6245

名 口吃 動 結結巴巴地說

▶名 The boy is often laughed at by his classmates because of his stammer. 這個小男孩常常因為結巴而被同學嘲笑。

▶動 He stammers when he feels nervous.
他一緊張就結巴。

sta·ple [ˋstep!]

Track 6246

名 釘書針、主要產物 動 用釘書針釘住、分類、選擇

同 attach 貼上

▶名 That song is a staple that's performed in every one of her concerts. 這首歌在她每場演唱會都會表演，已經變成固定的形式了。

▶動 The letter was stapled to the other documents in the file.
那封信與檔案夾裡的其他文件釘在一起了。

sta·pler [ˋsteplɚ]

Track 6247

名 釘書機

▶Would you please lend me your stapler? Mine doesn't work.
能借我用一下你的釘書機嗎？我的壞了。

starch [stɑrtʃ] Track 6248

名 澱粉 動 上漿

▶名 Corn and potatoes contain a lot of starch.
玉米和馬鈴薯含有大量澱粉。

▶動 He wore a starched cap to the party.
他戴了一頂上漿上得筆挺的帽子去派對。

實用片語用語
corn starch 玉米粉
例如：You can use corn starch to make soup thicker.
你可以用玉米粉來把湯變得更濃稠。

star·va·tion [stɑrˋveʃən] Track 6249

名 饑餓、餓死 同 famine 饑餓

▶There are still many people living on the verge（邊緣）of starvation nowadays.
如今仍然有很多人在饑餓的邊緣掙扎。

sta·tion·ar·y [ˋsteʃənˏɛrɪ] Track 6250

形 不動的

▶We were stationary for a while on the street because of the traffic. 我們因為塞車，在路上卡了一會。

sta·tion·er·y [ˋsteʃənˏɛrɪ] Track 6251

名 文具

▶Excuse me, can you tell me where to find a stationery store?
不好意思，能請您告訴我哪裡有文具店嗎？

stat·ure [ˋstætʃɚ] Track 6252

名 身高、身材

▶It is his red hair and short stature that made him easy to recognize.
正是他的一頭紅髮與五短的身材讓人一眼就能認出他來。

實用片語用語
tall stature 高高的身高
例如：His tall stature made him the envy of many others.
他的身高很高，讓許多人都很羨慕。

steam·er [ˋstimɚ] Track 6253

名 汽船、輪船

▶There is a steamer sailing into the harbor.
有一艘汽船正開進港口。

stim·u·late [ˋstɪmjəˏlet] Track 6254

動 刺激、激勵 同 motivate 刺激

▶I hope my advice will stimulate her to work harder.
我希望我的勸告會促使她更努力。

stim·u·la·tion [ˏstɪmjəˋleʃən] Track 6255

名 刺激、興奮

▶No amount of stimulation could make him show any reaction.
無論怎樣刺激他，他還是一點反應也沒有。

萬用延伸句型
No amount of... can...
無論多少……都沒辦法……

stim·u·lus [ˋstɪmjələs] Track 6256

名 刺激、激勵

▶Books with a different worldviews are a stimulus to endless imagination.
有不同世界觀的書能夠刺激無垠的想像力。

stock [stɑk]　Track 6257

名 庫存 動 庫存、進貨

▶名 It is said that the store always takes stock on Monday.
據說那家商店每逢星期一都進行盤點。

▶動 That store stocks all types of fur coats.
那家商店供應各種毛皮大衣。

stran·gle [ˋstræŋgl̩]　Track 6258

動 勒死、絞死

▶The man strangled his boss in a fit of anger.
那個男人一氣之下便勒死了自己的老闆。

stra·te·gic [strəˋtidʒɪk]　Track 6259

形 戰略的

▶We made a strategic withdrawal（撤退）so that we could build up our forces for another attack.
我們做了一次戰略性撤退，以便我們能積蓄力量再次進攻。

實用片語用語
strategic move 策略性的行動
例如：The experienced gamer knows that this strategic move will help him win.
這個有經驗的玩家知道這個策略性的行動能讓他贏得遊戲。

stunt [stʌnt]　Track 6260

名 特技、表演 動 阻礙 同 performance 表演

▶名 The stunt was supposed to draw attention to global warming. 此驚人之舉應是為了引起人們對全球氣候暖化問題的關注。

▶動 Inadequate food could stunt a child's development.
食物不足可能會影響到兒童的發育。

sub·jec·tive [səbˋdʒɛktɪv]　Track 6261

形 主觀的 同 internal 內心的、固有的

▶I found the cover ugly, but that's totally my subjective opinion.
我覺得那個封面很醜，但那也完全是我的主觀意見。

sub·or·di·nate [səˋbɔrdn̩ɪt]　Track 6262

名 附屬物 形 從屬的、下級的 同 secondary 從屬的

▶名 It seems that he treats his subordinates very kindly.
他似乎對待他的屬下非常和藹可親。

▶形 All the other issues are subordinate to this one.
所有其他的問題都沒有這一個問題這麼重要。

sub·scribe [səbˋskraɪb]　Track 6263

動 捐助、訂閱、簽署 同 contribute 捐助

▶He subscribed to an online newsletter. 他訂閱了一份線上的刊物。

實用片語用語
subscribe to 訂閱

sub·scrip·tion [səbˋskrɪpʃən]　Track 6264

名 訂閱、簽署、捐款

▶It is said that the subscription of this magazine is very popular.
據說這本雜誌的訂閱相當受歡迎。

sub·se·quent [ˋsʌbsɪˌkwɛnt]　Track 6265

形 伴隨發生的

▶Subsequent events confirmed his suspicions.
後來發生的事實顯示他的懷疑是有道理的。

A B C D E F G H I J K L M N O P Q R **S** T U V W X Y Z

sub·sti·tu·tion [ˌsʌbstəˋtjuʃən] Track 6266

名 代理、代替 同 relief 接替

▶They are looking for a kind of medicine to be used as its substitution. 他們正在找尋一種能代替該藥的藥品。

sub·tle [ˋsʌtḷ] Track 6267

形 微妙的 同 delicate 微妙的

▶Her hints were all subtle, but I understood them quickly. 她的提示都很隱晦，但我還是很快地懂了。

文法字詞解析
我們中文所說的「微妙的」含有「有點奇怪」的意思，但 subtle 沒有這個層面的意思，單純指事物「很難察覺」、「隱晦」。舉例來說，如果化妝化得很淡就可以說這妝很 subtle。

sub·ur·ban [səˋbɝbən] Track 6268

形 郊外的、市郊的

▶There are a lot of good things about suburban life. 在郊區生活有許多優點。

suc·ces·sion [səkˋsɛʃən] Track 6269

名 連續

▶She has been awarded the first prize four years in succession. 她已連續四年獲得第一名。

suc·ces·sive [səkˋsɛsɪv] Track 6270

形 連續的、繼續的 同 continuous 繼續的

▶It is a pleasure that we have had three successive years of good harvest. 我們已連續三年獲得豐收，這真令人高興。

萬用延伸句型
It is a pleasure that... 很令人高興地……

suc·ces·sor [səkˋsɛsɚ] Track 6271

名 後繼者、繼承人 同 substitute 代替者

▶It is known that his son is his only successor. 大家都知道他兒子是他唯一的繼任人。

suf·fo·cate [ˋsʌfəˌket] Track 6272

動 使窒息 同 choke 使窒息

▶It's suffocating in here. Do you mind if I open a few windows? 我覺得這裡很悶。你介意我打開幾扇窗戶嗎？

suite [swit] Track 6273

名 隨員、套房

▶Would you please book a suite in a Tokyo hotel for me? 請你幫我在東京找家旅館訂一間套房好嗎？

文法字詞解析
特別注意這個單字的唸法，它雖然和常見的 suit 長得很像，但唸法卻比較接近 sweet 喔。聽著音檔唸唸看吧！

su·perb [sʊˋpɝb] Track 6274

形 極好的、超群的 同 excellent 出色的

▶From the summit there is a superb panorama（全景）of the Alps. 從山頂俯瞰，阿爾卑斯山壯麗的景色盡收眼底。

su·pe·ri·or·i·ty [səˌpɪrɪˋɔrətɪ] Track 6275

名 優越、卓越

▶Your army has numerical（數字的）superiority over theirs. 與他們相比你們的軍隊佔有人數的優勢。

su·per·son·ic [ˏsupɚˋsɑnɪk] Track 6276

形 超音波的、超音速的

▶Developing the supersonic jet is quite an accomplishment.
開發超音速噴射機是一項了不起的成就。

su·per·sti·tious [ˏsupɚˋstɪʃəs] Track 6277

形 迷信的

▶He was a very superstitious man, so imagine his horror when he broke a mirror.
他非常迷信，所以可以想像他打破鏡子時有多驚慌。

實用片語用語
superstitious beliefs 迷信的想法
例如：She has a lot of superstitious beliefs, such as that black cats are unlucky.
她有很多迷信的想法，例如黑貓不吉利。

su·per·vi·sion [ˏsupɚˋvɪʒən] Track 6278

名 監督、管理 同 leadership 領導

▶You are not supposed to leave children to play without supervision.
你不應該讓孩子在無人照顧的情況下玩耍。

sup·ple·ment Track 6279

[ˋsʌpləmənt]/[ˋsʌpləˏmɛnt]

名 副刊、補充 動 補充、增加

▶名 You'd better buy some diet supplements for your daughter.
你最好給你女兒買點飲食補品。

▶動 He had to get a part-time job to supplement the family income.
他不得不找個兼差工作以增加家庭收入。

sur·pass [sɚˋpæs] Track 6280

動 超過、超越 同 exceed 超過

▶No matter what difficulties are in front of you, you should find the way to surpass them.
無論你們遇到什麼樣的困難，你們都應該想辦法克服它。

sur·plus [ˋsɝplʌs] Track 6281

名 過剩、盈餘 形 過剩的、過多的 同 extra 額外的

▶名 You'd better sell the surplus of grain as soon as possible.
你最好盡快就把多餘的糧食都賣了。

▶形 We must work off the surplus goods as soon as possible.
我們必須儘快把多餘的貨物處理掉。

實用片語用語
work off 清除、排除

sus·pense [səˋspɛns] Track 6282

名 懸而未決、擔心 同 concern 擔心、掛念

▶Everyone is waiting in great suspense for the doctor's diagnosis.
大家都焦急萬分地等著醫生做出診斷。

sus·pen·sion [səˋspɛnʃən] Track 6283

名 暫停、懸掛

▶It is dangerous for the toddler to cross the suspension bridge alone. 那個小孩子一個人過吊橋會很危險的。

swap [swɑp]
Track 6284

名 交換 動 交換 同 exchange 交換

▶名 Since you have what I want and I have what you like, would you do a swap with me? 既然你有我想要的東西，我有你喜歡的東西。那麼我們來交換好嗎？

▶動 I didn't like my drink so I swapped mine with his. 我不喜歡我的飲料，所以就把我的跟他的飲料交換了。

sym·bol·ic [sɪm`bɑlɪk]
Track 6285

形 象徵的

▶It is said that the Christian（基督教的）ceremony of baptism（洗禮）is only a symbolic act. 據說基督教的洗禮儀式只是一種象徵性的做法。

實用片語用語

symbolic meaning 象徵意義

例如：I'm not sure about the symbolic meaning of the colors on the flag. 我不確定這旗子上的顏色有什麼象徵意義。

sym·bol·ize [`sɪmbə͵laɪz]
Track 6286

動 作為……象徵

▶Not everyone knows what the Olympic（奧運會的）rings symbolize. 不是每個人都明白奧運五環的象徵意義。

sym·me·try [`sɪmɪtrɪ]
Track 6287

名 對稱、相稱 同 harmony 和諧

▶They hold that order and symmetry were important elements of beauty. 他們認為秩序和對稱是美的重要因素。

symp·tom [`sɪmptəm]
Track 6288

名 症狀、徵兆

▶You have to tell me first when the symptoms began to appear. 你得先告訴我這種症狀是什麼時候開始的。

syn·o·nym [`sɪnə͵nɪm]
Track 6289

名 同義字 反 antonym 反義字

▶Please don't mix up this pair of synonyms. 請別把這兩個同義詞混淆了。

文法字詞解析

相反地，「反義字」則是 antonym。

syn·thet·ic [sɪn`θɛtɪk]
Track 6290

名 合成物 形 綜合性的、人造的 同 artificial 人造的

▶名 It is said that the type of synthetic sells very expensively. 據說那種合成纖維賣得非常貴。

▶形 The chemists developed a new synthetic material. 這些化學家們研發出了一種新的複合物質。

tact [tækt]
Track 6291

名 圓滑 同 diplomacy 圓滑

▶Don't you think a minister of foreign affairs has to have tact? 難道你不認為作為一名外交部長，必須夠圓滑嗎？

tac·tic(s) [ˋtæktɪk(s)]

Track 6292

名 戰術、策略

▶You'd better plan the tactics for the next few days' games so that we can prepare in advance.
你最好把今後幾天球賽的戰術都擬定好，以便我們可以提前做準備。

實用片語用語
in advance 提前

tar·iff [ˋtærɪf]

Track 6293

名 關稅、稅率 同 duty 稅

▶Jewelry are luxury goods. It is no wonder that there is a very high tariff on it.
寶石類屬於奢侈品。難怪它的稅很高。

te·di·ous [ˋtidɪəs]

Track 6294

形 沉悶的

▶His story is so tedious that I don't think anyone would like to listen to it again.
他的故事太冗長乏味了，所以我想沒有人會再願意聽了吧。

文法字詞解析
tedious 還可以加上副詞字尾「-ly」來修飾另一個形容詞，例如：tediously long 冗長的。

tem·per·a·ment [ˋtɛmprəmənt]

Track 6295

名 氣質、性情 同 character 性格

▶It is obvious that the two brothers differ markedly（明顯地）in temperament.
顯然這兩兄弟的氣質迥異。

tem·pest [ˋtɛmpɪst]

Track 6296

名 大風暴、暴風雨 同 storm 暴風雨

▶You'd better take in the sail because the tempest is approaching.
暴風雨要來了，你最好先將風帆放下。

ter·mi·nate [ˋtɝməˌnet]

Track 6297

動 終止、中斷 同 conclude 結束

▶They told me the next train terminates here.
他們告訴我這是下一班火車的終點站。

文法字詞解析
坐捷運坐到終點站時是不是常會聽到廣播說「terminal station」呢？
terminal和terminate是相關的字，意思是「終點的」，不過它也可以當作名詞，當名詞時除了「終點」之外，也可以作為機場的「航廈」。

tex·tile [ˋtɛkstaɪl]

Track 6298

名 織布 形 紡織成的 同 material 織物

▶名 It is said that the designer has created a new textile.
據說那名設計人員已經創造出了一種新的織布。

▶形 I heard that til（胡麻）can be used as a textile material.
我聽說胡麻可做為紡織原料。

tex·ture [ˋtɛkstʃɚ]

Track 6299

名 質地、結構 動 使具有某種結構（特徵） 同 structure 結構

▶名 Don't you know that each variety of melon has its individual flavor and texture?
你不知道每一種不同的瓜都有自己獨特的味道和質地嗎？

▶動 They textured the bowl with lines and dots.
他們使用線與點裝飾碗的表面。

實用片語用語
wooden texture 木頭質地
例如：The wooden texture of the floor feels really good.
這地板的木頭質地感覺很舒服。

the·at·ri·cal [θɪ`ætrɪkl]

Track 6300

形 戲劇的

▶His theatrical antics（舉動）are kind of funny.
他戲劇化的表現還蠻好笑的。

theft [θɛft]

Track 6301

名 竊盜 同 steal 偷竊

▶The jury has convicted the accused man of theft.
陪審團已宣判被告犯有偷竊罪。

the·o·ret·i·cal [ˏθiə`rɛtɪkl]

Track 6302

形 理論上的

▶This professor is very theoretical and also very hard to understand. 這個教授很精通理論，而且說的話總是很難懂。

ther·a·pist [`θɛrəpɪst]

Track 6303

名 治療學家、物理治療師

▶You should talk to my friend, who is a therapist.
你應該和我的朋友談談，他是治療師。

文法字詞解析
therapist 除了物理方面的復健治療以外，也可以治療心理上的症狀，因此在美國找 therapist 談談是常見的事。

ther·a·py [`θɛrəpɪ]

Track 6304

名 療法、治療 同 treatment 治療

▶He receives speech therapy for his stutter.
他因為口吃而必須接受語言治療。

there·af·ter [ðɛr`æftɚ]

Track 6305

副 此後、以後 同 afterward 以後

▶The meeting concluded last week, and the president signed the bill shortly thereafter.
會議於上星期結束，總統隨後立即簽署了這項議案。

there·by [ðɛr`baɪ]

Track 6306

副 藉以、因此

▶My brother hoped to travel abroad and thereby improve his English ability. 我哥哥希望藉由到國外旅行來加強英文能力。

ther·mom·e·ter [θə`mɑmətɚ]

Track 6307

名 溫度計

▶He put the thermometer in the patient's mouth.
他把溫度計放入了病人口中。

實用片語用語
electric thermometer 電子溫度計
例如：My electric thermometer is out of battery.
我的電子溫度計沒電了。

thresh·old [`θrɛʃold]

Track 6308

名 門口、入口

▶I hope the treaty would be the threshold of lasting peace.
我希望這個條約將成為長久和平的開端。

thrift [θrɪft]

Track 6309

名 節約、節儉 同 economy 節約

▶It is not right to equate thrift with stinginess（吝嗇）.
把勤儉和吝嗇劃上等號是不對的。

thrift·y [ˋθrɪftɪ] Track 6310

形 節儉的 同 economical 節約的

▶Mom is really a thirfty housekeeper, isn't she?
老媽真是個勤儉持家的人，不是嗎？

thrive [θraɪv] Track 6311

動 繁茂

▶Few plants or animals can thrive in a desert.
很少有植物或動物能在沙漠茁壯成長。

實用片語用語

thriving business 生意興隆

例如：His dream was to have a thriving business and an expensive car.
他的夢想就是店裡生意好、擁有名貴的車。

throb [θrɑb] Track 6312

名 脈搏、抽痛 動 悸動、跳動 同 beat 跳動

▶名 A throb of pain ran through my back.
一陣抽痛貫穿了我的背部。

▶動 His good looks made my heart throb.
他帥得讓我小鹿亂撞。

toll [tol] Track 6313

名 裝貨、費用、通行稅 動 徵收、繳費 同 fare 車費

▶名 It is the only bridge that everyone should pay a toll on when crossing.
這是唯一一座要收過路費的橋。

▶動 The officials decided to toll the road into this city.
這些官員決定要對進城的那條路收費。

top·ple [ˋtɑpl̩] Track 6314

動 推倒、推翻 同 tumble 顛覆

▶It seems that the building is going to topple down.
那棟建築物似乎搖搖欲墜了。

實用片語用語

topple over 倒下

例如：The tower we built with blocks toppled over.
我們用積木蓋的塔倒了。

tor·na·do [tɔrˋnedo] Track 6315

名 龍捲風

▶The entire village was destroyed by the tornado.
整個村莊都被龍捲風摧毀了。

trait [tret] Track 6316

名 特色、特性 同 characteristic 特性

▶It is a surprise that the same genes should control more than one physical trait at a time.
相同的基因竟能同時控制多樣顯著的特徵，真令人驚訝。

tran·quil [ˋtræŋkwɪl] Track 6317

形 安靜的、寧靜的 同 peaceful 寧靜的

▶I wish one day I could live a tranquil life in the countryside.
我希望有天能去鄉下過寧靜的生活。

tran·quil·iz·er [ˋtræŋkwɪlaɪzɚ] Track 6318

名 鎮靜劑

▶Laughter is a tranquilizer with no side effects.
笑聲是一種沒有副作用的鎮靜劑。

trans·ac·tion [træn`sækʃən]

Track 6319

名 處理、辦理、交易 同 deal 交易

▶You are not supposed to lend yourself to such a transaction. It is illegal. 你不應該參與這種交易。它是違法的。

實用片語用語
make a transaction 進行交易
例如：You can make a transaction with the ATM in a convenience store.
你可以用便利商店的自動櫃員機進行交易。

tran·script [`trænˏskrɪpt]

Track 6320

名 抄本、副本

▶I am afraid that I can't vouch（擔保）for the correctness of the transcript of proceeding.
恐怕我不能擔保訴訟的官方記錄是正確的。

trans·for·ma·tion [ˏtrænsfɚ`meʃən]

Track 6321

名 變形、轉變

▶It was not until then that we realized the critical transformation.
直到那時我們才發覺到了這一個關鍵轉變。

tran·sis·tor [træn`zɪstɚ]

Track 6322

名 電晶體

▶Many old men always carry about transistors with themselves.
好多老人家總是會隨身攜帶一台電晶體收音機。

tran·sit [`trænsɪt]

Track 6323

名 通過、過境 動 通過

▶名 It is quite clear that the damage was caused during transit.
很顯然這批貨的損壞是在運輸途中造成的。

▶動 This is an aircraft transiting the United States and Canada.
這是一架飛越美國和加拿大的飛機。

萬用延伸句型
It is quite clear that... 很明顯地……

tran·si·tion [træn`zɪʃən]

Track 6324

名 轉移、變遷

▶The transition of her mood from good to bad went by unnoticed.
沒人注意到她的好心情轉變成壞心情。

trans·mis·sion [træns`mɪʃən]

Track 6325

名 傳達

▶There are many ways for the transmission of diseases to happen. 疾病的傳染有很多種途徑。

trans·mit [træns`mɪt]

Track 6326

動 寄送、傳播 同 forward 發送

▶Will you tell me why wood has a poor ability to transmit heat?
能請你告訴我為什麼木頭的導熱性很差嗎？

trans·plant [`trænsplænt]/[træns`plænt]

Track 6327

名 移植手術 動 移植

▶名 It was the first time that the patient had received a heart transplant. 這是該病人第一次接受心臟移植手術。

▶動 I have transplanted the flowers to the garden.
我把這些花移植到花園裡。

萬用延伸句型
It was the first time that...
是（某人）第一次……

trau·ma [ˋtrɔmə] Track 6328

名 外傷、損傷、心理創傷

▶Don't you think minor accidents may cause a lot of trauma?
你不覺得小小的事故就可能引發很大的創傷嗎？

tread [trɛd] Track 6329

名 腳步 動 踩、踏、走 同 walk 走

▶名 When I stepped into the house, I heard his heavy tread up the stairs.
我走進屋裡的時候，聽到他上樓梯的沉重聲。

▶動 He asked me not to tread on the crops.
他叫我不要踩到穀物。

trea·son [ˋtrizn̩] Track 6330

名 叛逆、謀反 同 betray 背叛

▶It was said that the spy was executed for treason.
據說這名間諜因叛國罪被處死。

實用片語用語
commit treason 背叛、謀反
例如：The soldier, surprisingly enough, committed treason.
令人驚訝的是，這個軍人居然背叛了。

trek [trɛk] Track 6331

名 移居 動 長途跋涉

▶名 No matter what he said, I was determined to set off on this long trek. 不管他說什麼，我都決心開始這次的長途旅行。

▶動 You can trek down to the store and buy whatever you like.
你可以慢慢地走到那家商店，買你喜歡的任何東西。

trem·or [ˋtrɛmɚ] Track 6332

名 震動 同 shake 震動

▶The story my grandpa told was so scary that it sent tremors down my spine.
爺爺講的故事太可怕了，它使我不寒而慄。

tres·pass [ˋtrɛspəs] Track 6333

名 犯罪、非法侵入 動 踰越、侵害

▶名 You should sue the man for his trespass.
你應該控告那個人非法侵入。

▶動 There was a sign saying no trespassing, but people ignored it most of the time. 有張「禁止進入」的牌子，但大家大部分的時候都沒在管它。

trig·ger [ˋtrɪgɚ] Track 6334

名 扳機 動 觸發

▶名 The gun went off as soon as I pulled the trigger.
我一扣扳機，槍就響了。

▶動 His action triggered off a revolution as soon as he escaped from the prison. 他一從監獄逃出來，就觸發了一場革命。

文法字詞解析
如果你一旦聽到某件事就會感覺有如心中某個機關被「觸發」了一樣渾身不舒服，就可以將這件事稱為你的「trigger」。例如有的人不喜歡被說胖，聽到任何人講到胖這個字都會不開心，這時「胖」就是他的「trigger」。

tri·um·phant [traɪˋʌmfənt] Track 6335

形 勝利的、成功的 同 successful 成功的

▶There are some defeats more triumphant than victories.
有些戰敗比勝利更值得慶祝。

triv·i·al [ˋtrɪvɪəl]　Track 6336

形 平凡的、淺薄的 同 superficial 淺薄的

▶Will you tell me why she got angry over such trivial matters?
你能告訴我她為什麼要為這種瑣事生氣嗎？

tro·phy [ˋtrofɪ]　Track 6337

名 戰利品、獎品

▶She won't win a trophy for shooting（射擊）unless she keeps practicing every day.
除非她每天持續訓練，否則她在射擊比賽中將得不到獎。

trop·ic [ˋtrɑpɪk]　Track 6338

名 回歸線 形 熱帶的

▶名 His hometown was located in the south of the Tropic of Cancer.
他的家鄉在北回歸線的南邊。

▶形 He has been to many tropic countries these years.
這幾年他去過很多熱帶國家。

文法字詞解析
Tropic of Cancer 是北回歸線，而相反地南回歸線則是 Tropic of Capricorn。

tru·ant [ˋtruənt]　Track 6339

名 蹺課者 形 曠課的、蹺課的 同 absent 缺席的

▶名 You are not supposed to play truant.
你不應該蹺課的。

▶形 These children are likely to be truant.
這些孩子很可能蹺課。

truce [trus]　Track 6340

名 停戰、休戰、暫停 同 pause 暫停

▶Not all people were in favor of the declaration of a truce at that time. 那時並不是所有人都贊成宣佈停戰。

tu·ber·cu·lo·sis [tjuˌbɝkjəˋlosɪs]　Track 6341

名 肺結核

▶His tuberculosis is so serious that he can't be cured at all.
他的肺病已嚴重到無法治療的地步了。

tu·mor [ˋtjumɚ]　Track 6342

名 腫瘤、瘤

▶At present, it is difficult for the doctors to remove the brain tumor. 目前醫生們還很難摘除這個腦瘤。

實用片語用語
benign tumor 良性腫瘤
例如：Doctors told him that he had a benign tumor in his head.
醫生告訴他，他腦中有顆良性腫瘤。

tur·moil [ˋtɝmɔɪl]　Track 6343

名 騷擾、騷動 同 noise 喧鬧

▶It is reported that the town is in turmoil during this election.
根據報導，該城鎮在選舉期間陷入了混亂。

twi·light [ˋtwaɪˌlaɪt]　Track 6344

名 黎明、黃昏 同 dusk 黃昏

▶It's twilight already, so we'd better go home.
黃昏了，我們還是回家吧。

tyr·an·ny [ˋtɪrənɪ]

Track 6345

名 殘暴、專橫

▶They fight against the tyranny together in order to attain freedom. 為了獲取自由，他們共同一起對抗專政。

實用片語用語
fight against... 反抗……、對抗……

ul·cer [ˋʌlsɚ]

Track 6346

名 潰瘍、弊病

▶There's an ulcer in my mouth.
我的口腔出現了潰瘍。

ul·ti·mate [ˋʌltəmɪt]

Track 6347

名 基本原則 形 最後的、最終的 同 final 最後的

▶名 To me, that song was the ultimate. No other song could ever beat it. 對我來說，那首歌是最終極的好歌，沒有哪首歌能贏得過它。

▶形 Even though we suffered many defeats, we won the ultimate victory in the end.
儘管遭受了多次失敗，我們最終還是取得了勝利。

u·nan·i·mous [jʊˋnænəməs]

Track 6348

形 一致的、和諧的

▶She was elected by a unanimous vote.
她獲得一致同意而當選。

實用片語用語
unanimous vote 一致同意

un·cov·er [ʌnˋkʌvɚ]

Track 6349

動 掀開、揭露 同 expose 揭露

▶It was the two young reporters who uncovered the whole plot.
是這兩名年輕記者揭露了整樁陰謀。

un·der·es·ti·mate

Track 6350

[ˋʌndɚˋɛstəmɪt]/[ˋʌndɚˋɛstəˏmet]

動 低估

▶動 You had better not underestimate the difficulties of the job.
你最好不要低估這項工作的艱鉅性。

un·der·go [ˏʌndɚˋgo]

Track 6351

動 度過、經歷

▶It is said that this city underwent great changes.
據說這座城市經歷了巨大的變化。

文法字詞解析
undergo 的動詞變化：
undergo, underwent, undergone

un·der·mine [ˏʌndɚˋmaɪn]

Track 6352

動 削弱基礎 同 destroy 破壞

▶It is obvious that the bad cold had undermined her health.
顯然重感冒損傷了她的健康。

un·der·take [ˏʌndɚˋtek] Track 6353

動 承擔、擔保、試圖 同 attempt 試圖

▶The work was undertaken by members of the committee.
這項工作由委員會成員承擔。

un·do [ʌnˋdu] Track 6354

動 消除、取消、解開 反 bind 捆綁

▶The knot was fastened too tightly to undo.
這個結繫得太緊了，根本解不開。

文法字詞解析
undo 的動詞變化：undo, undid, undone

un·em·ploy·ment [ˏʌnɪmˋplɔɪmənt] Track 6355

名 失業、失業率

▶As there is so much unemployment, the competition for jobs is fierce.
由於失業嚴重，求職的競爭十分激烈。

un·fold [ʌnˋfold] Track 6356

動 攤開、打開 同 reveal 揭示

▶Why don't we unfold the letter and read it before making a decision?
我們為什麼不拆開信讀一讀然後再做決定呢？

u·ni·fy [ˋjunəˏfaɪ] Track 6357

動 使一致、聯合 同 combine 聯合

▶It's almost impossible for us to be unified against the enemy.
我們幾乎不可能聯合起來對抗敵人。

un·lock [ʌnˋlɑk] Track 6358

動 開鎖、揭開

▶It is obvious that we can't unlock the door because we don't have the key.
很顯然我們無法打開門鎖，因為沒有鑰匙。

un·pack [ʌnˋpæk] Track 6359

動 解開、卸下 同 discharge 卸下

▶Let's unpack before we go into the house, shall we?
我們卸下行李後再進房子去吧，好嗎？

文法字詞解析
上面幾個單字都可以看到字首「-un」，相信看了這麼多例子後都能猜出它的意思了：「-un」的意思就是「相反」，所以前面加上「-un」的字，就是和那個單字原本的意思相反。

up·bring·ing [ˋʌpˏbrɪŋɪŋ] Track 6360

名 養育、教養

▶It is obvious that his success is due to the good upbringing he had.
顯然他的成功應歸功於良好的教養。

up·grade [ˋʌpˏgred]/[ˏʌpˋgred] Track 6361

名 增加、向上、升級 動 改進、提高、升級 同 promote 升級

▶名 I'm afraid that this computer requires an upgrade.
恐怕這台電腦需要升級了。

▶動 I think you have to upgrade your computer software.
我覺得你得幫你的電腦軟體升級了。

up·hold [ʌpˋhold]

Track 6362

動 支持、支撐

▶It is obvious that I cannot uphold such conduct.
我當然不能贊成這種行為。

文法字詞解析
uphold 的動詞變化：
uphold, upheld, upheld

u·ra·ni·um [jʊˋrenɪəm]

Track 6363

名 鈾

▶It is illegal for people to trade uranium in some countries.
在某些國家買賣鈾是非法的。

ur·gen·cy [ˋɝdʒənsɪ]

Track 6364

名 迫切、急迫

▶I am afraid you have not realized the urgency of the matter.
恐怕你還沒有意識到這件事的緊迫性。

u·rine [ˋjʊrɪn]

Track 6365

名 尿、小便

▶Did you have a urine test yet?
你驗尿了沒？

實用片語用語
urine test 驗尿、尿液檢查

ush·er [ˋʌʃɚ]

Track 6366

名 引導員 動 招待、護送

▶名 Why don't you let the usher seat them in the front row?
為什麼不讓帶位的人帶領他們去前排就座呢？

▶動 He quickly ushered us into the room.
他很快地把我們招入進房間裡。

u·ten·sil [juˋtɛnsl̩]

Track 6367

名 用具、器皿 同 implement 用具

▶I'm afraid that I have to buy new cooking utensils, because these are too shabby.
恐怕我得去買些新的器皿了，因為這些太破舊了。

實用片語用語
cooking utensils 炊具、烹調器具
或者「cooker」也有一樣的意思。

u·til·i·ty [juˋtɪlətɪ]

Track 6368

名 效用、有用

▶It looks like their research project has limited practical utility.
看來他們研究的實際效用很有限。

u·ti·lize [ˋjutl̩aɪz]

Track 6369

動 利用、派上用場

▶It is reported that scientists are trying to find more efficient ways of utilizing solar energy.
根據報導，科學家們正在尋找能更有效地利用太陽能的方法。

實用片語用語
solar energy 太陽能

ut·most [ˋʌtˌmost]

Track 6370

名 最大可能、極度 形 極端的 同 extreme 極端的

▶名 They have done their utmost to learn the techniques of production. 他們盡了最大努力去學習生產技術。

▶形 Conservation of natural resources is of the utmost importance.
保護自然資源顯然是至關重要的。

vac·cine ['væksin] Track 6371

名 疫苗

▶Will you tell me how much polio（小兒麻痺症）vaccines cost?
請告訴我小兒痲痺疫苗的費用是多少好嗎？

val·iant ['væljənt] Track 6372

形 勇敢的 同 brave 勇敢的

▶The valiant young man saved the little girl from drowning.
那個勇敢的年輕人救了溺水的小女孩。

val·id ['vælɪd] Track 6373

形 有根據的、有效的

▶Is this contract still valid?
這合約還有效嗎？

文法字詞解析
相反地，「無效的」、「已經沒效的」則可以說 invalid。

va·lid·i·ty [və'lɪdətɪ] Track 6374

名 正當、正確 同 justice 正義

▶What he said had no validity at all.
他說的話毫無可信度。

va·ni·lla [və'nɪlə] Track 6375

名 香草

▶Would you like to add a teaspoon（茶匙）of vanilla extract to the tea?
你要不要在茶裡加一茶匙的香草香精呢？

var·i·a·ble ['vɛrɪəbl] Track 6376

形 不定的、易變的

▶Prices are variable according to the rate of exchange in most countries.
大部分國家的物價都是隨匯率而變動的。

文法字詞解析
做實驗時會用到的「變因」也可以稱為 variable。

var·i·a·tion [ˌvɛrɪ'eʃən] Track 6377

名 變動

▶The dial could record very slight variations in pressure.
刻度盤能顯示出壓力的微小變化。

vend [vɛnd] Track 6378

動 叫賣、販賣

▶Would you please buy me a Coke from that vending machine?
你能幫我到那台販賣機買一罐可樂嗎？

ven·dor ['vɛndɚ] Track 6379

名 攤販、小販

▶Let's buy some newspaper copies from the vendor across the street.
我們到對街的攤販那裡買幾份報紙吧。

verge [vɝdʒ]

Track 6380

名 邊際、邊 動 接近、逼近 同 edge 邊緣

▶名 It is said that the firm is on the verge of bankruptcy.
據說這家公司正瀕臨破產。

▶動 He's verging on a nervous breakdown.
他正瀕臨精神崩潰。

實用片語用語

on the verge of tears 快哭出來了

例如：The little girl seems to be on the verge of tears. What happened to her?
那個小女孩看起來快哭出來了。她怎麼了？

ver·sa·tile [ˋvɝsətḷ]

Track 6381

形 多才的、多用途的 同 competent 能幹的

▶Don't you think he is the most versatile actor among us?
你不覺得他是我們當中最多才多藝的一個演員嗎？

ver·sion [ˋvɝʒən]

Track 6382

名 說法、版本 同 edition 版本

▶You'd better read its English version. It would be more helpful to you.
你最好讀一下它的英文版。這樣對你會更有幫助。

vet·er·an [ˋvɛtərən]

Track 6383

名 老手、老練者 同 specialist 專家

▶You have to consult a veteran doctor about your illness, or it will get worse.
你得找一位經驗老到的醫生幫你看病，要不然你的病情會加重的。

實用片語用語

veteran gamer 老手玩家

例如：As a veteran gamer, he gets impatient when playing with newcomers.
他是老手玩家，所以跟新手玩時很容易不耐煩。

vet·er·i·nar·i·an / vet

Track 6384

[ˏvɛtərəˋnɛrɪən]/[vɛt]

名 獸醫

▶I've tried every treatment the vet suggested.
獸醫建議的每一種治療方法我都試過了。

vi·bra·tion [vaɪˋbreʃən]

Track 6385

名 震動

▶I heard the vibration from my cell phone.
我聽到手機震動的聲音。

vice [vaɪs]

Track 6386

名 不道德的行為 反 virtue 美德

▶Despite all his vices, he's quite a nice person.
雖然他做過一些壞事，他還是個不錯的人。

vi·cious [ˋvɪʃəs]

Track 6387

形 邪惡的、不道德的

▶The vicious animal attacked the children.
那隻兇惡的動物攻擊了孩子們。

文法字詞解析

有個和 vicious 長得很像的形容詞 viscous，是「有黏性的」、「黏滑的」的意思，別搞混了。

vic·tim·ize [ˋvɪktɪmˏaɪz]

Track 6388

動 使受騙、使受苦

▶He victimized me by stealing my money.
他騙了我，偷了我的錢。

vic·tor [ˋvɪktɚ]

Track 6389

名 勝利者、戰勝者 同 winner 勝利者

▶The victor of the match will advance to the next round.
這場比賽的獲勝者會晉級到下一輪。

vic·to·ri·ous [vɪkˋtorɪəs]

Track 6390

形 得勝的、凱旋的

▶She walked home victorious from the contest.
這場比賽是她凱旋而歸。

vil·la [ˋvɪlə]

Track 6391

名 別墅

▶It is said that the villa is famous for its style.
據說這所別墅以其風格而著名。

實用片語用語
holiday villa 度假別墅
例如：His family owns a holiday villa by the beach.
他的家人在海邊擁有一座度假別墅。

vine·yard [ˋvɪnjɚd]

Track 6392

名 葡萄園

▶It seems they are planning to arrange a visit to the local vineyards.
他們似乎正在計畫安排去當地葡萄園參觀的事情。

vir·tu·al [ˋvɝtʃuəl]

Track 6393

形 事實上的、實質上的 同 actual 事實上的

▶It is said that the virtual ruler of this country is the president's wife. 據說這個國家實質上的統治者是總統的妻子。

vi·su·al·ize [ˋvɪʒuəlˏaɪz]

Track 6394

動 使可見、使具形象 同 fancy 想像

▶It is hard for me to visualize how the place might have looked in the past.
我很難想像這個地方過去會是什麼樣子。

vi·tal·i·ty [vaɪˋtælətɪ]

Track 6395

名 生命力、活力

▶There is no doubt that it is a country full of energy and vitality.
毫無疑問，這是一個充滿活力和生機的國家。

萬用延伸句型
There is no doubt that... 毫無疑問的……

vo·cal [ˋvokḷ]

Track 6396

名 母音 形 聲音的

▶名 He not only plays the guitar in his band but also does vocals. 他在他的樂團裡不但彈吉他，也唱歌。

▶形 I wish you weren't so vocal about some things.
我真希望你對於某些事不要這麼急於發表意見。

vo·ca·tion [voˋkeʃən]

Track 6397

名 職業 同 occupation 職業

▶Nursing is a vocation as well as a responsibility.
護理工作既是職業又是責任。

vo·ca·tion·al [vo'keʃənl̩] Track 6398

形 職業上的、業務的 同 professional 專業的、職業上的

▶Not everyone thinks vocational training will help them find a good job.
不是每個人都認為職業培訓能使他們找到一份好的工作。

vogue [vog] Track 6399

名 時尚、流行物 同 fashion 時尚

▶This style has become a vogue in the area.
這種風格在當地已成了一種時尚。

vom·it ['vɑmɪt] Track 6400

名 嘔吐、催嘔藥 動 嘔吐、噴出

▶名 She saw his vomit on the bus and threw up too.
她在公車上看見了他的嘔吐物，結果也吐了。

▶動 She got ill and vomited all the food she ate.
她生病了，把所有她吃的食物都吐出來了。

文法字詞解析
除了 vomit 外，throw up、puke 都可以表達「嘔吐」的意思。

vul·gar ['vʌlgɚ] Track 6401

形 粗糙的、一般的 反 decent 體面的

▶The story was vulgar but very popular.
這故事很不雅，但很受歡迎。

vul·ner·a·ble ['vʌlnərəbl̩] Track 6402

形 易受傷害的、脆弱的 同 sensitive 易受傷害的

▶The child was still young and vulnerable.
那個孩子還很小、很脆弱。

Ww

ward·robe ['wɔrd,rob] Track 6403

名 衣櫃、衣櫥 同 closet 衣櫥

▶I'm afraid that the wardrobe takes up too much space.
恐怕這個衣櫥太佔空間了。

實用片語用語
take up 占據（地方、時間）

war·fare ['wɔr,fɛr] Track 6404

名 戰爭、競爭

▶The gesture was equivalent to a flag of truce（休戰）in civilized warfare.
這個手勢相當於文明戰爭中的停戰旗。

war·ran·ty ['wɔrəntɪ] Track 6405

名 依據、正當的理由

▶Do you mind telling me how long the warranty period is?
能麻煩您告訴我保固期是多久嗎？

實用片語用語
warranty period 保固期

wa·ter·proof/ wa·ter·tight [ˋwɔtɚˋpruf]/[ˋwɔtɚˋtaɪt]

Track 6406

形 防水的 同 resistant 防……的

▶I want to buy a waterproof watch.
我想買一隻防水手錶。

what·so·ev·er [ˌhwɑtsoˋɛvɚ]

Track 6407

形 任何的 代 不論什麼 同 however 無論如何

▶形 You can take whatsoever options you like.
你可以照你的意思，做出任何選擇。

▶代 The police found no suspicious document whatsoever.
警察未發現任何可疑的文件。

wind·shield [ˋwɪndˌʃild]

Track 6408

名 擋風玻璃

▶It is dangerous for you to drive with a dirty windshield.
你開一輛擋風玻璃髒了的車子是很危險的。

實用片語用語
windshield wipers 擋風玻璃雨刷
例如：It's raining. Use the windshield wipers.
下雨了，用一下雨刷吧。

with·stand [wɪθˋstænd]

Track 6409

動 耐得住、經得起 同 resist 忍耐

▶I don't think that I could withstand the heat.
我覺得我受不了那樣的溫度。

wit·ty [ˋwɪtɪ]

Track 6410

形 機智的、詼諧的 同 clever 機敏的

▶I like the witty host in the program very much.
我非常喜歡這個節目中風趣的主持人。

woo [wu]

Track 6411

動 求婚、求愛、爭取……的支持

▶Politicians try to woo the voters before an election.
政治家們在選前力爭選民的支持。

wrench [rɛntʃ]

Track 6412

名 扭轉 動 猛扭 同 wring 擰、扭斷

▶名 I used a wrench to fix the broken door.
我用扳手修好了壞掉的門。

▶動 She wrenched the box out of my hands angrily.
她生氣地把箱子從我手中奪走。

實用片語用語
gut-wrenching 令人極為痛苦的
例如：Watching that documentary was a gut-wrenching experience.
看那部紀錄片真是個超級痛苦的經驗。

wres·tle [ˋrɛsḷ]

Track 6413

動 角力、搏鬥 同 struggle 奮鬥

▶I love watching wrestling matches.
我很愛看摔角比賽。

Xe·rox/xe·rox [ˋziraks] Track 6414

名 全錄影印 動 以全錄影印法影印

▶名 Will you help get a Xerox of the material on the desk for me?
請你幫忙把辦公桌上的那些資料複印給我好嗎？

▶動 Can you please Xerox the two letters for me, Susan?
蘇珊，請妳把這兩封信各複印一份給我好嗎？

文法字詞解析
注意這個字的唸法，它的第一個子音比較接近「z」的發音喔！

yearn [jɜn] Track 6415

動 懷念、想念、渴望

▶Many young people in the country yearn for city life.
許多農村的年輕人都渴望城市生活。

實用片語用語
yearn for... 渴望……

zeal [zil] Track 6416

名 熱誠、熱忱

▶He had great zeal for basketball-related activities.
他對於和籃球相關的活動都超有熱忱。

NOTE

NOTE

NOTE

NOTE

原來如此 系列 E145

100%滿分命中奇蹟：
7000英文單字X文法+句型+片語

想要創造英文奇蹟，靠這本就能搞定！

作　　者　許　豪
顧　　問　曾文旭
社　　長　王毓芳
編輯統籌　耿文國、黃璽宇
主　　編　吳靜宜
執行主編　潘妍潔
執行編輯　吳欣蓉、楊詠琦、李欣怡、葉舒文
美術編輯　王桂芳、張嘉容
法律顧問　北辰著作權事務所　蕭雄淋律師、幸秋妙律師

初　　版　2016年08月初版1刷
　　　　　2024年初版22刷
出　　版　捷徑文化出版事業有限公司
電　　話　（02）2752-5618
傳　　真　（02）2752-5619

定　　價　新台幣420元／港幣140元
產品內容　1書

總 經 銷　采舍國際有限公司
地　　址　235 新北市中和區中山路二段366巷10號3樓
電　　話　（02）8245-8786
傳　　真　（02）8245-8718

港澳地區總經銷　和平圖書有限公司
地　　址　香港柴灣嘉業街12號百樂門大廈17樓
電　　話　（852）2804-6687
傳　　真　（852）2804-6409

＊書中圖片由shutterstock網站提供

國家圖書館出版品預行編目資料

100%滿分命中奇蹟：7000單字X文法＋句型＋片語 / 許豪著. -- 初版. -- 臺北市：捷徑文化, 2016.08
面；　公分（原來如此：E145）

ISBN 978-986-93130-4-9(平裝)

1. 英語　2. 讀本

805.18　　105013047